JUSTIFIABLE EVIL

JUSTIFIABLE EVIL

A NOVEL

MARIO J. PABON

IPBOOKS.net
International Psychoanalytic Books

Edited by NY Book Editors
nybookeditors.com

Book design by Maureen Cutajar
www.gopublished.com

ISBN: 978-0-9965481-5-1

For Cira:
This book could not have happened without you.

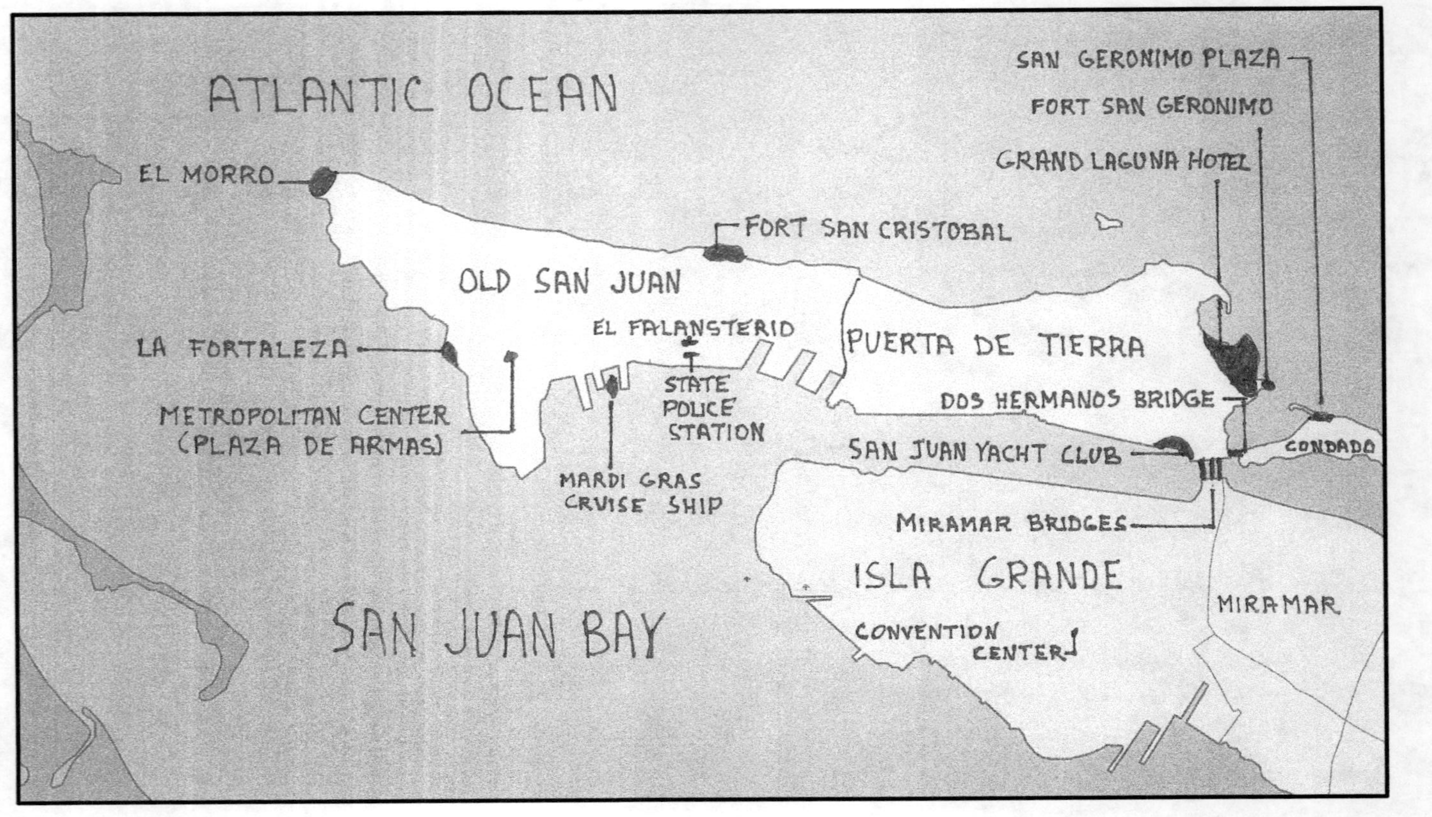

ATLANTIC OCEAN
EL MORRO
SAN GERONIMO PLAZA
FORT SAN GERONIMO
GRAND LAGUNA HOTEL
FORT SAN CRISTOBAL
OLD SAN JUAN
EL FALANSTERID
PUERTA DE TIERRA
LA FORTALEZA
STATE POLICE STATION
DOS HERMANOS BRIDGE
METROPOLITAN CENTER (PLAZA DE ARMAS)
SAN JUAN YACHT CLUB
CONDADO
MARDI GRAS CRUISE SHIP
MIRAMAR BRIDGES
ISLA GRANDE
MIRAMAR
SAN JUAN BAY
CONVENTION CENTER

"Coqui": a brown, very tiny tree frog (about the size of a thimble) with a prodigious voice and lungs of steel (called "coqui" because of the peculiar sound it makes), revered by most—if not all—Puerto Ricans, and adopted as the symbol of their tiny nation, a nation whose voice—like that of their beloved frog—resonates throughout the world.

JUSTIFIABLE EVIL

CHAPTER I

The crowd looked like an overflowing river of heads, bobbing up and down in the torrent of humanity that was San Sebastian Street. The Fiestas de la Calle San Sebastian had nothing to envy New Orleans' Bourbon Street on Mardi Gras. Tens of thousands of night revelers crammed into the narrow cobbled street, barely able to move, framed by an unending row of fantastically colored colonial houses. The tremendous noise of the multitude, a jumble of voices, screams, laughter, curses, whistles, and music mixed with the strong sweet smell of beer and the heavier odor of sweat and urine, overwhelming the senses.

From the second story balcony of his rented house, Angel San Miguel enjoyed an unfettered view of the grand celebration. This was mostly a youthful crowd, sprinkled with older people of young spirits. About fifty feet to his left, a group of celebrants had formed a small ring around two men who danced to the beat of a large conga bass drum, the rattle of a smaller military drum, and the shrill, off-tune notes of two trumpets. *"Al Carnaval de (something or other)"* the people sang, while the two men twisted, jumped, and moved their hands in an improvised, non-sensical, ridiculously funny rhythm, delighting those who watched them, periodically provoking some of the watchers to jump in and out of the circle with their own invented steps.

Almost straight below him, a man too drunk to stand sat on the steps of a house, his head hanging between his knees, his pants darkened by piss, while a teenaged boy surrounded by three giggling girls took pictures of him with his i-phone. Further away, in the opposite direction, several people clad like giant-headed dummies slowly made their way through the sea of partiers, followed by the faint sound of another brassy band. The "Cabezudos" they were called—literally, "the big-headed ones"—and they depicted local characters who had lived, at one time or another, in Old San Juan. One of them seemed to be dressed like a general, his chest brimming with medals. A black woman wearing a red, polka dot bandana around her hair and a slave's long dress of the same material chased him, while the general tried to avoid her.

San Miguel squeezed a last puff out of his cigarette, and absentmindedly flicked its butt into the air. It landed on a man wearing a New York Yankees cap, then bounced onto his shoulder. The man, a curly-haired teenager, hurriedly brushed off the cigarette, and looked up angrily in San Miguel's direction. San Miguel raised his hand apologetically, and mouthed the words "I'm sorry". The youth stared at him for a couple of seconds more, then returned his attention to the massive party around him.

San Miguel smiled. *Old San Juan.*

A soft breeze stirred from the north, bringing with it the sultry smell of the waves that crashed, not more than a hundred yards away, into the massive walls of the city. San Miguel stepped back from the balcony's railing and stretched himself to his full height. In his mid forties, he still retained the lean, athletic frame of his youth, and a full head of mostly black hair. His eyes were dark green, and his mouth carried a crooked, happy-go-lucky grin that instantly endeared him to most strangers, particularly women. He wore a white linen, short-sleeved *guayabera*—a shirt designed for the tropics that was typically worn over the waist—and a pair of khaki slacks. To anyone casting a casual glance at him, he could pass for a high, middle-class local, and that was fine with him.

San Miguel looked at his watch and sighed.

It was time.

He had grown fond of the old city—old by American, not European standards, but old nevertheless. Like in most places where he did business, he had taken it upon himself to learn about its history. Old San Juan had surprised him. He had never thought that such a tiny spot of land in the Caribbean could pack such a rich past.

Founded by Juan Ponce De Leon, the eternal optimist who for a substantial portion of his life had unsuccessfully searched for the Fountain of Youth, San Juan had quickly become a key strategic outpost in the incredibly lucrative trade route that existed between the New World and Spain. Puerto Rico was the first of the large islands—the Antilles—to greet the battered ships that crossed the endless Atlantic Ocean from Europe, and the last port to shelter those returning to their mother country. Like blood in shark-infested waters, the ships laden with treasure that docked in San Juan had attracted the attention of every pirate, privateer, and the navy of every nation hostile to Spain.

To protect its strategic possession, the Spanish government had been forced to build massive defenses, including a sixteen-foot thick wall that enveloped the entire city, and two huge fortresses, El Morro and San Cristobal. El Morro, the larger of the two forts, guarded the entrance to the bay, and had constituted at one time San Juan's last line of defense, should the rest of the city and its fortifications be overrun. San Cristobal, located at the opposite end of the town, defended the northern and eastern approaches to the colonial city, its long rows of cannons pointing both to the sea on the north, and to the land facing the eastern wall.

The defenses had served San Juan well. Like a giant rock standing tall in a turbulent sea, the city had beaten back attack after fierce attack. Sir Francis Drake had attempted to capture it, anchoring a large fleet at the mouth of the bay, but had met an unexpectedly ferocious resistance from the *sanjuaneros*. The *coup de grace* had occurred one night when Sir Francis, anchored far away from El Morro, had invited several officers to dine in his cabin. As they sat at the table, a cannonball fired by the fort's garrison had smashed through the wall of the room, killing several of the diners. Legend says that Drake had escaped unscathed, even though his seat had been shot from under him. A few days later, Sir Francis had sailed away, seeking easier prey.

Scores of other attacks had met a similar fate. The Dutch had once managed to capture San Juan and lay siege to El Morro. However, they had been unable to break through the fort's complex set of defenses, and had been subjected to several damaging counterattacks by the defenders. In the end, decimated by the fighting and malaria, the invaders had been forced to abandon the city, setting it on fire.

It had not been until 1898 that the city finally and permanently fell to a foreign power. It had happened during the Spanish-American War. The American fleet had briefly shelled El Morro, and then invaded Puerto Rico through its soft underbelly, in the southern town of Guanica. Spain had been woefully unprepared for war, sorely neglecting its New World fortifications. El Morro had been a shadow of its former glorious self. Some of the heavy shells fired by the invading battleships had even managed to penetrate the thick walls of the ancient castle, pieces of shrapnel still embedded and visible—even to this day—in the interior walls of the fort.

Like a ripe fruit, the city of San Juan had been plucked by the new emerging world power, and the island of Puerto Rico annexed as a territory of the United States. Since then, the Americans had ruled the island, and eventually made its inhabitants American citizens. A strong bond had been forged between the two countries during the more than one hundred years of American domination.

It was because of that bond that San Miguel was there.

The celebration continued unabated below him. The "Cabezudos" were making progress through the mob, and he could now see the small brass band that heralded their coming. It was being followed by four rows of baton twirlers wearing short, shiny, red-and-gold uniforms and tall white hats. A man in stilts, dressed like a red devil, had also joined the parade, and moved miraculously through the throngs of people as if wading in deep water. Under the balcony, a short, thin man and an obese woman wearing a very tight, undersized halter, argued angrily as the man attempted to pry from the woman's pudgy fingers a small package. The argument had quickly escalated to heavy blows, and the small man would have been seriously hurt if two policemen had not intervened. The scuffle was hardly noticed by the rest of the chaotic crowd.

San Miguel sensed movement behind him but did not stir. "They're here," he stated, more than asked.

"All of them," the new arrival confirmed quietly.

San Miguel nodded into the night, and turned to look at the man standing before him. Daniel Meyer had worked with him for sixteen years. He was shorter than San Miguel, measuring 5'10" to San Miguel's 6'2", and his junior by ten years, but he had the more impressive build of the two, bearing the trim, muscled look of a fighter. He moved with the grace and silence of a cat, and spoke with a certain mocking air of self-assurance that to onlookers sometimes bordered on insolence. That same self-assurance was reflected on his face, which usually wore the amused expression of someone enjoying a private joke.

"How do they look?" San Miguel inquired.

Daniel shrugged, confirming that he did not think much of the visitors.

San Miguel nodded again, suppressing a chuckle. He did not consider Daniel a close friend, and was certain that Daniel felt the same way about him. However, as long-time associates, they had achieved the kind of familiarity that helped them anticipate each other's thoughts, and eliminated the need to communicate by a lot of words, if any. Together, they made a formidable team, and each of them was aware of it.

The two men left the balcony and walked through San Miguel's bedroom, a large chamber heavily decorated in the Spanish colonial fashion, with a huge four-posted bed, an even bigger ornately-carved clothing cabinet, a similarly styled dresser with a mirror, and two high-backed chairs. San Miguel did not particularly care for the décor, but the big, two-story house, rented for a month, constituted a perfect base of operations.

They walked down a long staircase with a wide, wooden handrail and steps decorated with porcelain tiles of exotic flowers and birds, and stopped briefly at the entrance to the dining room. A huge man stood next to the open door that gave access to the chamber, his head nearly touching the upper beam of the doorframe.

"Czecka," San Miguel acknowledged with a smile, placing briefly his hand on the man's wide forearm. It felt as if chiseled out of stone.

The man physically reminded San Miguel of a large oak tree, standing ramrod straight, with arms and legs bulging through his pants and shirt like thick, heavy branches. His hands were enormous, large enough—San Miguel thought—to cover a skull and probably crush it. He stood at 6'6", although he seemed larger. Much larger. Only his head appeared to be disproportionately small. This was an optical illusion, caused by the odd combination of his height and his facial features. His hair was cut so short that it was impossible to tell its color, appearing to the naked eye as a gray gristle. His eyes were light blue and way too small, topped by thin, almost invisible eyebrows. Had it not been for a larger mouth that was partially framed by a dark, wide mustache, his face would have looked like a blank canvas.

His personality also matched that of a tree. He hardly spoke, and when he did, it was mostly in short phrases and grunts. His verbal reticence, however, was not caused by a dull intellect. Czecka was smart in his way, as most mean-spirited men are. More importantly, he had proven time and again to be extremely loyal to San Miguel during the eight years that they had been together. His role in the events to come would be crucial.

"Are we ready?" San Miguel asked softly, not expecting an answer and getting none. He whispered a short prayer, steeling himself for the meeting.

"Gentlemen!" San Miguel walked briskly into the room, but then paused briefly as he became aware that not all of the visitors were men. "And lady," he added, directing a swift, vexed glance at Daniel, who merely smiled, enjoying his associate's surprise and discomfort.

He had entered into a long, ornately decorated dining room with an oval ceiling, where the newly arrived visitors sat. Each of the room's four upper corners was rounded by wide arches and adorned with white stucco showing chubby, child-like angels, while its concave ceiling was covered by a fresco of a semi-naked, slightly hefty goddess, either sitting or emerging from a set of lofty clouds. Several paintings—darkened by time and resin and purportedly depicting Old San Juan during earlier centuries—hung from most of the walls. A tall, black-wood cabinet, housing several blue and white Dutch porcelain plates, cups and teapots, occupied most of the space on the wall at the opposite end of the chamber. Light green, fire-hardened tiles laced with wide white and gold leaf designs—probably the same tiles that had been installed by the original owners of the house a few centuries before—covered the floor. A heavy, ebony-colored table extended through most of the length of the dining room, bordered by high-backed chairs with leather seats. At its head, close to the room's entrance, lay a small laptop and a digital projector. A silver tray in the center of the table held several cold bottles of Evian, sodas, and an ice bucket.

The opulent luxury of the room contrasted markedly with the lack-luster appearance of the group who waited in it. San Miguel beamed at them, examining each of their faces. It was their eyes that interested him the most.

"I am Angel San Miguel," he stated, extending his hand to the man closest to him, one seat away. The man's palm was sweating. "I think you already know Daniel and Czecka," he added, gesturing with his free hand at his two companions, enjoying inwardly how they all stared in awe at his enormous friend.

"I am Johnny Ray," the man with the sweaty palm responded, "President of the FEPI." "FEPI" stood for "Federacion de Estudiantes Pro Independencia"—the Federation of Students Pro Independence—a vehemently anti-American group of students in the University of Puerto Rico who advocated the immediate severing of all ties with the United States, by any means possible.

San Miguel detected fear in Johnny Ray's eyes, even though Johnny attempted to hide it behind a friendly grin. With the exception of another man further down the table, Johnny had been the only one of the visitors to stand up when San Miguel had entered the room. He was very young, not more than twenty years of age, and appeared to be anxious to create a good impression. San Miguel had read his dossier.

Born Jonathan Ray McDonald and raised by a well-to-do family—in his case a retired Army captain who had married locally and decided to stay in Puerto Rico—he had graduated from one of the best private high schools in the island, located in the exclusive area of Miramar. He had attended the University of Puerto Rico, to acquire a degree in psychology. There, he had dated a girl who had brought him to a FEPI activity.

Johnny had been instantly drawn to the dynamic, pro-independence ideals of the group, and by the second school semester was condemning his father as part of the imperialistic war machine that had enslaved his country and prevented it from governing itself, as any free country should. His natural intelligence, good looks, and personal background had catapulted him to the forefront of the movement. He had been arrested twice in student protests that had turned violent. By his junior year, he had been elected FEPI president.

San Miguel had met many men like Johnny Ray before. He instinctively distrusted them.

"This is Felipe Lebron, the Secretary-General of the FEPI." Johnny pointed to a fat, heavily bearded man sitting to his left who reluctantly shifted in his chair. Like San Miguel, he was garbed with a *guayabera*. There, however, all similarities ended. Lebron's shirt bore large, yellowish stains under the armpits, and its color—originally light green—had faded to a sickly, ghoulish tan.

San Miguel stretched his arm just barely enough for Lebron to reach his hand, forcing him to stand up.

"And this," Johnny continued, gesturing with his hand towards an attractive, red-headed female sitting next to Lebron, "is Yajaira Velazquez, my vice-president."

There had been no noticeable change in Johnny's voice as he introduced his colleague, no telltale gestures betraying anything beyond the professional relationship expected between two FEPI leaders. Yet San Miguel immediately concluded that they were sleeping together. He could plainly read it from Lebron's peeved expression when Johnny had referred to her as *"my* vice-president", and from Johnny's expectant, nervous silence after his introduction. The two were even dressed identically, San Miguel observed: fashionable blue, faded jeans and white T-shirts imprinted with a Puerto Rican flag and the phrase "Puerto Rico Libre" ("A Free Puerto Rico") written below it. The printed words on her T-shirt were hardly visible, though, covered almost completely by the bulge of her bra-less breasts.

San Miguel cast a fleeting look at Daniel, who was standing behind Johnny Ray, and confirmed by his mocking expression that his associate had reached a similar conclusion. Czecka's face betrayed no signs of any human thought.

Yajaira greeted San Miguel with an indifference nearing on disdain, extending her long, polished red nails horizontally, as if expecting her hand to be kissed, and not stirring from her seat. *The woman,* San Miguel realized with amused annoyance, *was under the impression that Johnny was running the operation, a belief probably fostered by Johnny himself.*

And she was running Johnny.

San Miguel was not a superstitious man, but he instinctively disliked involving women in any business that he conducted. *And yet...*Johnny Ray's emotional connection to his vice president could under the right circumstances prove useful, depending on the turn that the events took during the next couple of days.

In marked contrast to Lebron, San Miguel made it a point to walk to her chair and lean forward so much that for a moment it seemed as if he would actually kiss her hand. Then, at the last moment, he held it and shook it gently.

"Ms Velazquez," he said with a charming smile, "thank you for help-ing our cause."

"I would be very sorry not to be part of this historic undertaking," she replied in a huskier voice than he expected. "I was telling Johnny yesterday that_"

San Miguel ignored her and turned his attention to the man standing in front of her, at the other side of the table. He would tolerate Yajaira's uninvited presence in the meeting, but he'd be damned if he wasted an-other second listening to her idle chatter. "You must be Colonel Calderon," he said affably. "I am very pleased to meet you, and very grateful for the help that your country is giving us."

The man straightened up and nodded stiffly. "It is an honor to be here. I am Dionisio Calderon, at your service," he responded, as if ad-dressed by a superior military officer. "Venezuela has always kept strong ties with our sister republic of Puerto Rico. Many of your countrymen," he said to the others sitting around the table, "fought alongside our Libertador, Simon Bolivar. I believe that one of them, Antonio Bernabe, even served as a brigadier general in our war of independence."

"Brigadier General Antonio *Valero* Bernabe," Felipe Lebron correct-ed from his chair in a patient tone, beaming beatifically at the Venezuelan officer, as if addressing a small child.

"Of course, please forgive me. Brigadier General Antonio *Valero* Bernabe," Colonel Calderon repeated, taking no evident offense at the FEPI Secretary-General's interruption, emphasizing the *Valero* surname that he had omitted before. "It is time to pay back our debt of honor to our Puerto Rican brothers."

Calderon sported a pair black jeans and a short-sleeved shirt depict-ing a sunset over a palm tree-filled beach, but he still looked like a soldier. His hair, what remained from his receding hairline, appeared as no more than a faint black shadow, somewhat similar to Czecka's nearly invisible hair. His face and arms showed the type of dark tan that could only be acquired by spending endless hours in an open field. He had broad facial features: the flattened, crooked nose of a boxer, large brown eyes with a tinge of yellow, and a clean-shaven, thick-lipped mouth. He stood almost unnaturally straight, as if—one of his subordinates had once described it—somebody had shoved a broom up his ass. He spoke with the easy, self-assured confidence of a man accustomed to give orders, but lacked the arrogance of a man not unaccustomed to receive them.

San Miguel examined him with unfeigned interest. The Venezuelan colonel played a critical part in his plans. Without him and his men, the entire operation could collapse prematurely.

"Welcome. From Chavez down to your present president, your leaders have always been good friends of the oppressed," he expressed to Calderon. "I hope you and your men have not run into any kind of trouble?"

"None whatsoever. We are all here in San Juan, now. My men have been arriving in groups of two's and three's during the last ten days. My two sergeants have kept them busy, off the beach and the bars. Not that I don't trust them, but you can never be too careful, can you?" His eyes rested briefly on Yajaira, and he smiled ruefully, adding as an after-thought, "There are too many beautiful women in this country."

Yajaira stirred uneasily in her seat, unsure if she should take Calderon's statement as a compliment or as a sexist remark.

"Where are they quartered?" San Miguel asked, not referring to the women but to the colonel's men.

"Some are staying at the Courtyard Hotel in Isla Verde, others in the San Juan Sheraton, near the tourist docks," Calderon answered. "I'm lodged in the San Geronimo Plaza."

The colonel commanded a group of twenty-six "volunteers", twenty-nine if he counted his two sergeants and himself. All of them belonged to the "Special Operations Command Generalisimo Francisco de Miranda", an elite unit of Venezuela's "Infanteria Marina" (the "Marine Infantry"). The unit specialized in sabotage and the use of sophisticated weapons.

"The men have walked up and down the streets of Old San Juan for several days now," Calderon continued. "By now, they can find their way around this town with their eyes closed. I suspect that they know the city better than any *sanjuanero*," he boasted proudly, locking his eyes on Lebron as if expecting a new challenge from him. None came.

"Excellent," San Miguel whispered, already focusing his attention on the last and most important of his visitors. All the others followed his gaze, and looked with curiosity at the object of his attention.

The man sat at the opposite end of the long dining table, separated from the rest of the visitors by at least four chairs. He had taken in the introductory chatter without stirring or evincing any kind of interest in the conversation. Although in his late fifties, he seemed much older. A great deal of it had to do with his hair—which cascaded in waves of gray and white streaks down to his shoulders—and to a similarly colored and textured beard that grew several inches straight out of his chin in a Pharaonic fashion. A dark intelligence radiated from his brown eyes like heat reflecting from an asphalt road.

He reminded San Miguel of a lizard, lounging on a rock, taking in the sun, waiting for a fly to wander his way. A frail lizard, at that. Of all those present at the meeting, he was the smallest, looking puny even next to Yajaira. And yet, barring San Miguel's men, he was probably the most dangerous man in the room.

"Aristides Andrade, El Alacran," San Miguel said flatly, earning an almost imperceptible blink of acknowledgement from the man. The distant, merry notes of a horn momentarily managed to pierce through the heavy walls of the house, reminding everyone of the celebrations taking place outside. "We are indeed fortunate to have you here. The presence of the Macheteros increases our chances of success a thousand fold." Because of the distance between them, San Miguel made no attempt to shake his hand.

Andrade's dossier read like a spy novel. Born in 1954 in Bayamon, Puerto Rico from modest middle class parents who taught in the island's public school system. From the outset, he had shown exceptional acumen and aptitude, and had skipped two grades in school. He attended and graduated Magna Cum Laude from the Rio Piedras Campus of the University of Puerto Rico in 1971, as a political science major.

Like Johnny Ray, he had gravitated towards the FEPI, and participated in several acts of violence, including the burning down of the ROTC building in the campus. After graduation, he had traveled to Cuba, where together with other future Machetero members, he had been trained by Castro's G-2 in the art of bomb-making and the use of deadly weapons.

In 1972, he had popped up in New York as part of the "Movimiento Independentista Revolucionario Armado" ("the Armed Revolutionary Movement Pro Independence")—known as "MIRA" by its Spanish initials, and actively participated in placing incendiary devices in several of the city's biggest retail stores, including Gimbels, Bergdof Goodman, and Bonwitt Teller. By 1974 he had returned to Puerto Rico, where together with others like Filiberto Ojeda and his best friend Adalberto Cacho, he had helped found the "Ejercito Popular Boricua" ("the Boricua Popular Army"), better known as the Macheteros.

The Macheteros quickly became the standard bearers for the armed struggle to liberate Puerto Rico from the colonial yoke of the United States. During the second half of the 1970's and through the mid 1980's, they firebombed numerous commercial establishments, robbed several local banks, and even executed U.S. military personnel stationed in Puerto Rico.

Because of his delicate appearance but ruthless and deadly methods of operation he was nicknamed "El Alacran" ("the Scorpion"). And even though the violent methods of the Macheteros were publicly condemned by the official pro-independence faction in Puerto Rico—which supported the attainment of self-government by peaceful means—many independence advocates, or *independentistas*, privately admired their exploits.

Two incidents in particular brought national attention to the Macheteros. In January of 1981, a small band of their group infiltrated the Puerto Rico Air National Guard base, burning or seriously damaging an F-104 Starfighter and ten A-7 Corsair combat jets without sustaining a single casualty. And in 1983, with the help of an insider, the Macheteros conducted a spectacular robbery in a Wells Fargo bank in Connecticut, escaping with a booty of 7.2 million dollars, the second largest bank robbery in the history of the United States at that time. Legend—supported by the Macheteros—has it that in a Robin Hood type gesture, the bank robbers later threw out of a tall building in Puerto Rico part of the money that they had stolen, to "protest the greed of men". San Miguel's dossier indicated otherwise; that most of the money had ended up in the Macheteros' war coffer, and the balance in Cuba.

After the Wells Fargo bank heist, the FBI cracked down hard on the group. Eventually betrayed from within, several of its members were captured, and the rest were forced to run underground. The decimated organization briefly reared its head and managed a few bombings in the 90's, but in 2006 it suffered a devastating blow when its top leader, Filiberto Ojeda, was surrounded and wounded by federal agents in a small town in the interior of the island, and then—popular rumors claim—allowed to bleed to death before medical help was summoned.

Andrade and his friend Adalberto Cacho had been away in Havana when Ojeda had been killed. Upon the news of his friend's death, Cacho had transmitted a voice communiqué assuming command of the Macheteros, and swearing to avenge his fallen comrade. El Alacran became his right-hand man.

Ten years later, however, Cacho himself had been captured in San Juan as he attended in disguise—against El Alacran's counsel—a World Baseball Classic game between Puerto Rico and the Dominican Republic. The captured Machetero leader had been incarcerated under heavy security measures in the federal prison facilities located in the town of Bayamon, a few miles away from San Juan. There, he still awaited trial.

Command of the terrorist group had fallen on El Alacran. In a videotaped message delivered simultaneously to Telemundo and WKPA TV, the two major television networks in Puerto Rico, he appeared clean shaven, wearing a black beret and dark glasses, to warn the FBI and the "lackey government of Puerto Rico" that the Macheteros would not rest until Cacho had been freed and his country liberated from American imperialistic oppression.

His first official act had been to personally execute a Machetero suspected of informing to the FBI about Cacho's whereabouts. The execution had been taped and sent to the television stations, along with instructions on how to locate his body. A few weeks later, the offices of the island's principal gasoline companies had been bombed, and a rash of bank robberies and kidnappings had followed.

The Macheteros had returned with a vengeance.

San Miguel stole a glance at Johnny Ray. As he had expected, the FEPI leader and his companions were staring at El Alacran with absolute awe, as if they had been standing before God. They had reacted exactly as he had hoped, he noted with satisfaction. He had expended a great deal of time, money, and political resources to contact Andrade through his Cuban connections, and suspected that the man would be very difficult to control. But the effort had been worthwhile. The old Machetero would give him trouble, but he would also give tremendous credibility and substance to his very risky and complicated enterprise.

As if reading San Miguel's thoughts, Andrade addressed him for the first time.

"Angel San Miguel...That's a biblical name, isn't it?" he said in a surprisingly cheerful tone, his dark eyes fixed on his folded hands. "The Archangel Saint Michael! Right hand of God, enemy of the devil! Are you here to fight the Great American Lucifer and deliver us from evil?" El Alacran looked up directly at his host and smiled mischievously.

"I've never been compared to an archangel before, but yes, I guess that's an adequate way of putting it," San Miguel responded good-humoredly. Both Johnny Ray and Yajaira laughed, while Lebron managed a weak smile and reached for a bottle of Evian. "Although I believe that you have been far more effective battling the Great Lucifer than I will ever hope to be," San Miguel added graciously. He began to pull away a chair to sit at the table, motioning Daniel to dim the lights of the room. "Now, I would like—"

"How else would you put it?" El Alacran asked mildly, returning his gaze to his hands.

San Miguel stopped moving his chair, and looked with curiosity at the Machetero leader. "What do you mean?" he asked, still in a friendly tone. He felt Czecka stir behind him, as the silence in the room grew thicker.

Andrade shrugged. "I mean, you come highly recommended to me, you know? My friend, the general, Alvaro Lopez from Cuba, my contacts from North Korea, they all vouched for you. Rated you 'A Number One', the best of the best."

San Miguel nodded, apparently pleased by Andrade's references, and opened his mouth to speak.

"But," El Alacran raised his index finger, to let his host know that he had not finished, "I still don't know *you*. I *don't know* who you are, I *don't know* where you came from, and I *especially don't know* why you are here."

Again San Miguel tried to speak, and again Andrade interrupted him.

"I think that the name of San Miguel is cute, I really do. Why, even our friend Daniel here," El Alacran extended his hand in the direction of San

Miguel's companion, who bowed his head in acknowledgement, "whom I've come to know from our several meetings during the last two months, even he has a biblical name, Daniel! The Jew who delivered his people from Babylon's bondage. Is it all a coincidence? A joke? A sign of God, maybe?"

"And Czecka?" Daniel managed to put in before Andrade could continue.

Andrade chuckled, darting an appraising look in the direction of the big man. Czecka's empty features had become animated with the unequivocal promise of violence, his huge hands clenching and unclenching unconsciously by his sides.

"In his case, he can call himself anything he wants," El Alacran answered, prompting a spontaneous burst of laughter from everyone around the table, including Andrade himself. Then his voice hardened. "I can more or less understand why the others are here. Johnny and his people are FEPI. They are here to fight for their country. The colonel from Venezuela was…"convinced" by his President Fanelli to come here with his volunteers, and Fanelli I can understand. Like Chavez and Maduro before him, he is a pimple in the U.S. ass. But *you…You*, I still don't get. Why do you want to fight our fight?"

"I have my own personal reasons," San Miguel responded in a curiously subdued voice.

El Alacran shook his head. "That's not good enough for me, my friend. You are asking all of us here to follow you. To risk our lives and everything we have. To risk the future of our cause. And we don't even get to know who you are? I may be crazy. In fact, I know I am. But I'm not stupid." Andrade leaned forward, his wire-like, wavy beard nearly touching the surface of the table. "So please tell me, Mr. Archangel, what brings you here?"

San Miguel hesitated, and then sighed. He finished pulling back his chair and sat down. For a minute he said nothing, his eyes seeming to focus on another time and place. When he looked up, his expression betrayed anger and pain. It lasted scarcely a second, less than an eye blink, yet his grief became apparent for everyone to see.

"I fight your enemies because they are my enemies as well," he stated calmly. "Fifteen years ago I was an attorney. I practiced real estate law in Kosovo, then part of Bosnia. I believed in the rule of law. I believed that in the normal order of things, justice would punish those who took matters into their own hands. I chose to stay in Bosnia despite the civil war, because I had lived there all my life, even though Yugoslavia was falling apart and I came from a Serbian family."

"The Serbian branch of the San Miguel family?" Andrade expressed with obvious sarcasm, sharing his wit by raising an eyebrow and looking at the others around him. Lebron laughed out loudly. Johnny shifted uncomfortably in his chair, producing a weak smile, while Colonel Calderon stared disapprovingly at the Machetero. Czecka just glared.

"You know that is not my real name," San Miguel replied with no apparent anger. He continued. "Fifteen years ago I had never fired a gun. I had never even held one. When NATO, led by the United States, threatened to intervene in the Kosovo war, I thought, *'These are civilized people. Surely they will avoid killing innocent civilians.'* And even when the bombings started in Kosovo, in March of 1999, I reasoned that they would limit their attacks to military and strategic targets." His last words carried such bitterness that they startled his listeners.

Again, for a fleeting moment, San Miguel fought to keep the anguish out of his voice. Then, in an impressive display of self-control, he continued in a tone devoid of any emotion. "At the time, my wife and children were visiting their grandparents in Belgrade. I urged them to stay where they were until the fighting stopped, but my wife insisted in joining me."

"You have children?" Yajaira asked. Her cool aloofness had melted to sympathetic concern.

San Miguel nodded. "A boy and a girl. Had...a boy and a girl." His expression hardened as he corrected Yajaira's use of the present tense. "At the time he was four, and she was a year older." San Miguel paused, as if gathering the strength to continue. The rest waited in complete silence.

"On April 12, my family left by train for Kosovo. Close to Leskovac, a town near Kosovo, the train began to cross the Grdelica Bridge. A NATO jet attacked it. It hit it with several missiles. The train began to burn, and the passengers tried to escape, but the jet continued to strafe them, even when the emergency vehicles began to arrive to try to get to the wounded. I waited several hours at the Kosovo train station, wondering—" San Miguel stopped for several seconds, unable to speak. "Wondering where the train was," he finished saying, almost in a whisper. "There was a stranger listening to the radio. He was waiting in the station for his brother. The stranger heard about the attack. We got into my car and drove like crazy men to Grdelica."

San Miguel's eyes darted from one place to another, seeming to follow the images that no one but he could see.

"They were still removing bodies from the wreckage when we got there. My wife and children were dead. I could not tell them apart from the other bodies, they were so badly burned. But enough remained of them: my wife's purse and marriage ring, my girl's—" he choked. There were tears in his eyes. "My girl's favorite Cinderella slippers...Other stuff. I knew it was them. I fainted, and spent the next month in a mental hospital. When I got out, I pressed charges against the pilot, a U.S. pilot, in his base. I met with his commander, I demanded that the pilot be punished for his terrible crimes! But he was exonerated. It had all happened because of pilot error, I was told."

"Bastards!" Johnny whispered between his clenched hands. Yajaira was crying into a handkerchief. Andrade looked thoughtful. Daniel averted his gaze to the floor.

"I hate Americans," San Miguel stated with chilling simplicity. "I hate what they stand for, and the suffering and oppression that they bring to the world. I hate their arrogant use of force, which they constantly couch with the words 'freedom' and 'liberty', while in reality sacrificing everybody else's wellbeing to further their own agenda. I hate their cynic disregard for human life. I hate them!"

San Miguel made a visible effort to stop his diatribe, and breathed deeply. Then he looked at the others and managed a faint smile.

"Forgive me," he said. "I did not mean to get carried away."

"I think," Colonel Calderon said out loud, not looking at anyone in particular, "that Mr. San Miguel's reasons to be here have been amply justified."

"Hear! Hear!" Johnny seconded, while El Alacran regressed to his lizard-like silence.

He had convinced them, San Miguel noted with grim satisfaction.

Even though it was all a lie.

Well, not quite everything. Grdelica had occurred as he had told it, and a mother and her two children, aged four and five, had been among those killed in the attack of the train. It could all be easily verified through the internet, as he was certain Andrade would do as soon as he left the meeting. But San Miguel had never married, practiced law, or fathered any children, at least as far as he knew. Daniel had already been working for him for a year when NATO destroyed the train.

He had anticipated El Alacran's question days before the meeting, and manufactured an answer. It never ceased to amaze him how little effort was required to deceive most people. Almost everyone, he had discovered—even the most hardened criminals—rooted for those who had lost loved ones under tragic circumstances. *If children were involved, even better.* His guests proved no exception to the rule. The personal details—the wait for the train that never came, the Cinderella slippers, his temporary internment in an mental hospital—all of them were fake details, designed to lend further credibility to his story. *It had been so easy.*

"Thank you," San Miguel quietly acknowledged the group's support, then said after a pause. "We need to move on and talk about tomorrow's events, if you don't mind. There is much to do and very little time to do it." He turned his head and whispered something to Daniel, who nodded, and with the help of Czecka, began to remove a heavily framed painting of El Morro.

There were powerful reasons to be in San Juan, San Miguel thought as he waited for his associates to finish. *More powerful than the loss of a wife and her children.* It was just that those reasons did not coincide with the particular interests of the FEPIstas or the Macheteros, or even the Venezuelans. In fact, his allies would have been shocked if they found out the real reason why he was there.

So the Grdelica incident would have to do.

CHAPTER II

"This is the island of San Juan." San Miguel used a red laser beam to circle around an area projected on the wall from where the El Morro painting had been removed. The island was shaped like a short, fat, horizontal human thigh bone "It is roughly four miles long by about a mile at its widest. To the west of it," he pointed at the wider end of the thighbone, "is San Juan Bay."

On the highest, westernmost tip of the "bone" were marked the words "El Morro", the massive fortress that for centuries had guarded the narrow entrance into the bay.

"To the northeast," San Miguel continued, moving his laser beam to the opposite side of the island, where the narrower "joint" of the thighbone would be, "is the Grand Laguna Hotel and the small fort of San Geronimo, which are separated from the main island of Puerto Rico by the Condado Lagoon. On the other side of the lagoon, facing the hotel, are the Condado and Miramar areas." San Miguel circled with his laser around the strip of water that separated the islands of San Juan and Puerto Rico.

"Just as a point of interest, did you know that Columbus originally gave the name of 'Puerto Rico' to what is now the island of San Juan, and named 'San Juan' what is now the island of Puerto Rico?" Lebron interrupted, and when no one responded, added mildly, "Just as a point of interest..."

San Miguel resumed his briefing, ignoring him. "To the south of the island of San Juan is Isla Grande, with a small airport and the Convention Center, and the residential area of Miramar. They are separated from San Juan by the San Antonio Channel." San Miguel aimed his laser at the channel, which extended through roughly half of the southern length of the island of San Juan, and ended in the bay. "Four bridges connect San Juan to the rest of Puerto Rico: the Dos Hermanos Bridge, the longest of the bridges, goes to the Condado area. Two new bridges connect San Juan to Miramar. And finally, there is a small, abandoned bridge that also ends in Miramar. We intend to blow up all of them tomorrow night, or rather, in the early hours of Sunday morning."

San Miguel carefully examined the faces of his audience. They were all familiar with his plan. Daniel had discussed it personally with each of them, except with Yajaira and Lebron. Even so, he wanted to see for himself how committed to the operation they were a scant twenty-four hours before it was slated to start.

Most of Johnny's color had drained from his face. He stared at the digital projection on the dining room's wall with an expression of intense concern. *That was not necessarily bad,* San Miguel mused. It showed he had already surmounted the stage of commitment, and was considering the consequences of his actions. Yajaira, on the other hand, seemed fascinated, twirling a lock of her red hair with her fingers. Lebron looked doubtful, while Colonel Calderon seemed lost in his own thoughts, probably gauging how his men would defend their assigned positions. El Alacran looked bored.

"Who will be blowing up the bridges?" Lebron asked.

San Miguel sighed inwardly. That was the type of question that was asked when people were brought at the last moment into a final meeting.

"My men will be in charge of that," Daniel responded, sensing his companion's impatience. He was standing behind the laptop computer and controlling the power point presentation. "They will wear overalls of the Autoridad de Acueductos y Alcantarillados, and will carry a fake work order showing that they are replacing rusted sanitary pipes under the bridges."

"Are there actually sanitary pipes under the bridges?" Lebron interjected. "The police may question what the men are doing there."

"Do you know if there are sanitary pipes under the bridges?" Daniel asked back.

"No."

"Neither does the police."

"We do not anticipate any trouble with the police." San Miguel picked up the briefing where he had been interrupted. "Coordination between the different agencies of the government of Puerto Rico is nearly non-existent. If any police drive by, they will think we're from the Autoridad, and let us do our work."

All of the Puerto Ricans sitting at the table nodded, confirming their host's assessment.

"In any event, Andrade has generously provided Daniel with two of his men, who will dress as policemen, and intervene if the police becomes overly curious. Also, I will be there."

El Alacran's failure to object confirmed the participation of the Macheteros. Lebron opened his mouth to speak again, hesitated, and opted to remain silent. He did not escape San Miguel's attention, however, who motioned his head in the Secretary-General's direction.

"Mr. Lebron, you seem to be concerned about something," he said gently. "If so, please speak up. Now is the time to air doubts that you or any of the rest of us may have."

San Miguel noticed that the sweat stains under Lebron's armpits had expanded since the time that the meeting began. As if to confirm his observation, Lebron fished out from one of his *guayabera's* pockets a white, crumpled handkerchief, and dabbed his forehead with it. "Well...it's just that...Aren't any of you worried about the attention that we will draw by openly working on the bridges in the late hours of the night? Shouldn't we avoid being seen? Maybe if we use rowboats packed with explosives, pretend that the men are fishing, and then set them off..."

San Miguel turned to Daniel, who was leaning on the table, staring at the computer. "You want to answer that one?"

Daniel straightened himself out, and looked at the others. "We have to blow up a total of four bridges in order to cut off San Juan from the rest of the island," he said, not even pausing to acknowledge San Miguel's request. "Fortunately for us, part of the bridge between El Condado and San Juan—a brand new bridge—was recently found to have serious structural defects in a portion close to El Condado. As a result, that part of the bridge was demolished and is currently under repair. While that happens, the Highway Authority has placed a steel structure there, to temporarily bridge the gap. That structure will be easy to destroy. The other bridges..." Daniel shook his head. "That's a different story. Two of those bridges were made with heavily reinforced concrete. We will need a substantial amount of explosives to make a hole in them, certainly more than those we can carry in a rowboat. Don't be fooled by the Hollywood commando movies where you see a frogman placing a gob of silly putty under a bridge and the whole thing goes off in a terrific explosion. That sort of thing at best will blacken the walls under the Miramar bridges, maybe shake loose some of their plaster, perhaps dent a wall, but that's about it. To knock out the bridges, we'll have to drill into their main supports, and use large amounts of heavy explosives."

"That's why doing it as a covert operation will not work," San Miguel picked up where his associate had stopped. "We will need four large vans to move the men, the explosives, and part of the equipment to the bridges. We'll also use three pontoon boats to do the drilling and carry some more of the equipment. There's no way to hide that, so we'll do it openly, to show everyone that we have nothing to hide. And we'd better make certain that the charges are placed properly, or those bridges will not fall."

"I guess it's sort of like, the more visible we are, the less likely we will be seen," Johnny Ray said to Lebron, as if explaining to a slow child. The FEPI president seemed embarrassed by his Secretary-General's constant interruptions. Johnny was rewarded by a full smile from Yajaira, who abhorred Lebron and relished any opportunity to see him humiliated.

"Yes," San Miguel added quickly, trying to make sure that Johnny did not elaborate on his half-witted explanation. He was running out of patience. "Which brings me to the following observation: the success of this entire operation depends on knocking out those bridges. We cannot afford to fail, or to do a half-assed job that allows our enemies to get to San Juan. God knows that we will have our hands full keeping them out of San Juan, even when the bridges are down. Our crew will need a lot of time and effort to do a thorough job. Whatever happens, we need to make certain that they have the best opportunity to do everything that they have to do."

"Do you have enough explosives?" El Alacran asked, grimacing as he scratched his bearded chin.

"We have enough C-4 to blow up half of San Juan," Daniel answered cheerfully. *A bit too cheerfully for San Miguel's liking.* It created the impression that Daniel did not give a fig about what happened to the old city, a feeling not shared by the other people sitting around the table. San Miguel directed a sharp look at his associate, who immediately understood his mistake and shut up.

Trying to lighten the awkward silence that followed, San Miguel shifted his attention to Calderon, and stated in an appreciative tone, "We owe a debt of gratitude to our friends from Venezuela for the explosives."

"How did you get them into Puerto Rico?" Andrade inquired with undisguised interest. San Miguel could almost see the wheels in El Alacran's head turning, already thinking about future, grander Machetero operations.

"We coordinated the shipment of the explosives, and of most of the weapons, I might add, with one of the local drug gangs in Fajardo." Fajardo was a town in the northeast coast of Puerto Rico. "They were integrated to three separate shipments of drugs that were dropped on the beach by small speedboats at night."

San Miguel noted with satisfaction that Andrade's initial cold indifference had thawed to professional curiosity.

"As to the time that we do this..." San Miguel shrugged, showing his lack of concern. "We can't do it during the day, because there's a regular contractor that works on the repairs to the Condado bridge during the day. But emergency crews work at all hours of the night. I don't think that anyone will question our timing, if we explain that we are trying to fix a broken sewage pipe before it fills the entire Condado Lagoon with shit."

San Miguel paused and looked at Lebron.

"Do you still have any doubts?"

"He will always have doubts," Johnny Ray commented. "It's in his nature."

San Miguel continued before Lebron could mouth a response to Johnny's comment. "Once the bridges are down, we will have to neutralize the police in San Juan. There are two police stations. The first one is a small municipal police center, located close to the docks, in the intersection of Covadonga and Corretjer streets." San Miguel shifted his red laser beam to a spot midway between the two ends of the island of San Juan. "There may be from a dozen to fifteen policemen stationed there at the most, maybe less. Andrade's men are prepared to take care of that station."

El Alacran nodded. "That one should be no problem," he said in a dismissive tone that showed the little respect he felt for San Juan's Municipal Guard. "We should capture it easily. It's the other one I worry about more."

"Andrade refers to this station." San Miguel moved his laser beam to a spot located in the southeastern quadrant of San Juan, less than a quarter of a mile from the Miramar bridges.

The image projected on the wall changed to an overhead Google photo, focusing on the area to which San Miguel was referring.

"This is the Puerta de Tierra State Police Station," he said. He nodded to Daniel, who again changed the projection to show an image of two buildings, one much larger than the other, taken from the front at street level. "The more modest of the two, the two-story structure on the right, is the original station." The picture displayed a squat, ugly building, painted in acrylic navy blue, with the horizontal edges between its two floors highlighted in bright, canary yellow. Twin ramps rose from the opposite sides of its front entrance, meeting on a platform at the center that led to a set of open doors. A narrow alley separated the old station from the larger building to its left.

"During the 70's and the 80's, there used to be a high rise building across the street. It was ten or fifteen stories high, I'm not certain. A drug gang used to sell drugs from there. The gang became so brazen in its operation that the police could no longer ignore it and conducted a few raids. The dealers retaliated by taking periodic pot shots at the police from the upper floors of the high rise. The police were forced to cover their windows with steel plates, to avoid getting shot. Some of those plates are still there, even though eventually the government of Puerto Rico vacated the high rise and leveled it to the ground. Presently, the government is constructing a new housing project, but is limiting it to three-story walk-ups."

"Those bureaucrats never learn," Andrade muttered to himself, yawning.

Again, the digital projector changed images. It revealed a more modern, boxlike structure, four times as big as the other one, but in its own way, just as ugly.

"The other building, to the left," San Miguel continued, "is—as you can see from this photo—much larger than the original station, and taller. Three stories high. Most of the administrative offices are in this building."

The walls of the "modern" station had been slapped with the same electric blue and canary yellow paint of its smaller counterpart. Its two upper floors were lined from one end of the building to the other with glass windows that connected waist-high concrete walls to the ceiling. The lower level had narrower windows, added to enhance the floor's interior illumination.

The new station had been constructed further away from the street than its sister structure, and its entire front length, as well as its left flank, were used as an open parking area. The photo showed several police cars parked there. A fence of spiked, vertical steel bars separated the parking space from the sidewalk and the street beyond. Any police vehicles departing the station had to leave through one of two exits, each located at the opposite ends of the fence.

San Miguel paused, and Daniel automatically took over.

"From what we've observed, there are approximately sixty to eighty policemen coming and going from there during the peak hours of the day."

Johnny whistled softly.

"However," Daniel continued, "this weekend they will concentrate most of their manpower in the San Sebastian Street Festival. It means that a lot of the policemen will be working long overtime hours, until the late shift is over. City hall forces the bars to close by two in the morning, and *that* means that by three or four, most of the people in the festival will be gone for the night."

"And so will the police," Johnny observed.

"Exactly. Most of the force will be dispatched home, to rest and to be ready for the next day. At the time that we set off the charges on the bridges, at five o'clock in the morning, the city will be sleeping and nearly deserted, and the police will only keep a skeleton crew in the entire Old San Juan and Puerta de Tierra area of, say...fifty men."

"This is a 'guesstimate'?" Lebron asked.

"A little more than that," Daniel responded. "The drug outfit who smuggled the guns into Puerto Rico has some limited contacts with the police. They did not have access to the exact roster of policemen who will be on duty at the time, but the number is supposed to be pretty reliable."

Colonel Calderon cleared his throat and raised his hand, seeking permission to speak. "I had the opportunity to examine the perimeter of the police station," he said, when San Miguel acknowledged him. "It has a large space for parking where they keep most of their patrol cars. I counted fifteen and twelve cars, the last two times I walked by, although I suspect that some of the cars are 'junkers' that are permanently stationed there. That parking area works very well for our plans. It is the only access to the front of the main building, and it is completely open. Except for the cars, there's no place for the police to take cover or hide. When we attack, they will have to seek refuge inside of the station." The colonel turned to Daniel. "Can you turn to that Google Earth photo we were looking at a few moments ago?"

Daniel clicked twice his remote control, and the aerial photograph of the two buildings returned to the wall. "May I?" he asked San Miguel, pointing at the portable laser. After he received it, Calderon walked closer to the projection. It showed the small, original station surrounded by trees, and the larger, rectangular building, fringed by its parking area on its northern and eastern edges. High walls bounded the eastern border of the parking lot, so that it formed a dead end alley.

"As you can see," the Venezuelan pointed with the laser to the four-lane street in front of the two buildings, "the police facilities are bordered on the north by the Fernandez Juncos Avenue. On the other side of that avenue, facing the smaller of the two police buildings, is the space where the high rise used to be, and where the new public housing project that Mr. San Miguel talked about is—"

"Drop the 'Mr.', please," San Miguel corrected. "Call me Angel or San Miguel."

Calderon nodded. "...That Angel talked about is presently being constructed. Daniel, do you have an aerial photograph that shows more of the area around the two police buildings?"

Daniel flicked through half a dozen projections, until he settled on a photograph of the same buildings but from a slightly higher altitude, displaying more of the neighboring structures and streets that surrounded the Puerta de Tierra Police Station. Calderon waived the pointer, creating a circle of red light around an area opposite to the main police building, on the other side of the Fernandez Juncos Avenue. In it was located what seemed to be a city block-sized fort, its walls made up of small, "H"-shaped, interconnected walk-ups, surrounding an open square.

"I believe this is called El Flan...El Falan..."

"El Falansterio," Johnny prompted.

"Falans?...El Falansterio," Calderon repeated, finally mastering the word. "Thank you. I don't know what it means, but—"

"It means the area occupied by a phalanx, you know, with shields joined and spears overlapping, like in the 300 Spartans," Lebron indicated, in a professorial tone. "It comes from ancient Greece."

"An aptly named place, then," said Calderon with a smile. "Because it is a position of great strength. We will place four of our MAG heavy machine guns on the rooftop of those buildings, and a fifth one on the new construction. Also half a dozen snipers. With that, we will be able to sweep the entire front area of the police buildings with a constant crossfire, and keep anyone from coming in or out of the buildings."

"Aren't there any exits in the back?" Johnny inquired.

"Yes," Calderon replied. "There's a narrow alley in the back of the two buildings. The larger building has two entrances in the back that lead to what seems to be a combination of an indoor garage and a mechanic's shop. The older building also has a small exit in the back. We have prepared something that will permanently seal all of those exits."

"Good," San Miguel said, not bothering to ask what that "something" was, anxious to move on. "You have coordinated the attack on the station with Andrade?"

Calderon and El Alacran exchanged a brief glance, and nodded almost in unison. San Miguel did not sense a good chemistry between them.

"Ten of my men will surround the buildings and supplement Calderon's force," Andrade stated quietly.

San Miguel addressed the colonel. "Your signal to start the attack will be the noise coming from the bridges, when we set off the charges. Under no circumstances should you fire on the police before then."

"Of course," Calderon acknowledged immediately, while El Alacran did not bother to give a response.

"What about the patrol cars that are making their rounds in the city?" Johnny asked.

San Miguel nodded, to show that he had considered the issue. "We will try to draw out of San Juan as many policemen as we can by creating a diversion on the other side of the bridges, in Miramar, about an hour before we blow the bridges up."

"A diversion?" Lebron asked doubtfully.

"Someone will make an anonymous call to the police claiming that the Macheteros have placed explosives in the Convention Center."

El Alacran raised an eyebrow. "Thanks for letting me know," he said in an ironic tone.

"Your people carry a lot of credibility," San Miguel said to him, smiling. "The police will pay attention if the threat comes from you."

"I am very flattered," Andrade said in a bored voice, looking away at one of the paintings.

"Anyway, it will be a false alarm," San Miguel explained. "But hopefully, it will draw away some of the policemen stationed in San Juan."

Calderon cleared his throat again. "No matter what we do, there will always be some patrol cars and police on motorcycles left patrolling Old San Juan. There's no way of really avoiding that," he said. Like Andrade, the colonel considered the state police to be the bigger threat to their operation. He seemed to have given the problem a great deal of thought. "Their initial reaction will probably be one of two: to head towards the bridges—"

"Where my men will deal with them," Daniel interjected.

"Or to go to the police station, when they are informed that it is under attack."

"Where *my* men will ambush them," El Alacran asserted with chilling satisfaction.

To his internal amusement, San Miguel saw Yajaira shudder involuntarily, as the crude details of their undertaking began to sink in. He looked at his watch, and noticed it was nearly midnight. The noise seemed to have abated outside. He had to hurry, before the crowds began to thin out.

"While all of this is taking place, my men will capture the Grand Laguna Hotel," he said in a businesslike tone. "Daniel, can you go back to the map of San Juan?"

Daniel obliged, and San Miguel, retrieving his laser pointer from Calderon, pointed the red dot of light to the upper, easternmost corner of the island of San Juan.

"Thank you. As you all know, the Grand Laguna is the closest point of the island of San Juan to the Puerto Rico mainland. It is separated from the Condado area by the waters of the lagoon, by scarcely the length of a football field. The hotel will be the stage from where we make our demands, in exchange for the release of hostages."

"Hostages?" asked Yajaira in a surprised tone. She looked at Johnny for an explanation, who merely hunched his shoulders in a resigned gesture.

"Yes, hostages," San Miguel answered, with a trace of regret in his voice, as if deploring the need to resort to such an extreme, unsavory tactic. "We do not have enough men or firepower to adequately withstand a determined attack from our enemies, once they figure out what has happened," he explained. "Eventually, the federal government will become involved, and attack us with an overwhelming force. We need to gain time in order to capture the attention of the world. The hostages will give us that time."

Yajaira looked dismayed. Next to her, Lebron furiously wiped his face with his handkerchief. He had refrained from voicing his growing doubts about an operation that Johnny had never fully explained to him, but was becoming increasingly alarmed by what he heard.

"Forgive me for asking, but what will stop the police from flying into San Juan in helicopters before they find out that we have hostages?" he said.

"If, God forbid, anyone tries to fly into San Juan," San Miguel answered, "we have the means to shoot them down."

"How?" Lebron insisted.

San Miguel exchanged a knowing look with Colonel Calderon. "Along with the explosives and arms, Venezuela has provided us a dozen surface-to-air missiles," he stated.

All heads turned towards the colonel, who elaborated on San Miguel's prior statement. "We have fourteen SA-24 Grinch surface-to-air missiles. They are portable, infrared-guided devices that can easily bring down any helicopters—or drones, I may add—that try to invade San Juan's air space. My men will be handling them."

"Calderon's surface-to-air operators will be posted in teams of two, on high spots of the city," San Miguel observed. "Here, at the Metropolitan Building, which is located next to the Plaza de Armas and the old City Hall..." San Miguel flicked his laser beam to the center of Old San Juan. "Here and here, on the highest points of El Morro and San Cristobal; and here, on top of the Grand Laguna Hotel."

San Miguel paused and looked directly at Johnny Ray.

"This, as you know, is where your people come in. There is a lot of real estate to watch over, and Calderon's men cannot cover it all. We do not expect the FEPI to fight, since most of your people have had very little combat training, except for the short shooting lessons that Daniel was able to give to some of you in the past two months. But you will be our eyes."

Johnny nodded emphatically.

"The FEPI will patrol the streets on cars and by foot, and watch the sky from the rooftops," San Miguel told everybody else. "Anything that they see will be reported back to us."

"We will be ready," Johnny asserted, still nodding. "We will not let you down."

"I know you won't," San Miguel replied solemnly, after staring into his eyes.

Standing behind his boss, Daniel tried to suppress a grin. It had been a classic San Miguel performance from the beginning to the end. First he had given them the sappy rendition about the cruel death of his family. Now, he was trying to stiffen the FEPI leader's resolve by exaggerating the importance of his assigned task. And as in the hundred of prior times that he had seen San Miguel perform, it had worked.

"Colonel Calderon also managed to secure for us a dozen portable military radios, which will be just enough to distribute between the field commanders and the Grinch teams. The rest of us will communicate through the satellite phones that we obtained for the operation." San Miguel continued to talk directly to Johnny Ray. "Make certain that your people know how to use them, who to call, and have easy access to their numbers. Be aware of the mundane details, like for example, that the batteries are charged. Our success may hinge on that sort of thing."

A year before, when San Miguel had begun to flesh out with details his then bare-bones plan, he had quickly concluded that it would be impossible to cut off all communications between San Juan and the rest of Puerto Rico. It would constitute a gargantuan task to knock down every cell phone tower, or jam every cell phone call in the old city and its immediacies. Even if that could be managed, they would still have to contend with the regular landlines and the internet. The rebels lacked the time, the manpower and the opportunity to accomplish all, or even a fraction of that. Therefore, San Miguel decided to utilize cell phone technology to his advantage.

There was one factor over which he had no control, however, but which he had to consider. In prior, ground-shaking events such as the attack on the Twin Towers and Katrina, thousands of calls had swamped and rendered useless for hours the local communications systems. San Miguel could not afford for something like that to happen in San Juan. Therefore, during the past four months, he had secured one hundred and fifty satellite phones, each registered under a different, fictitious name. The satellite phones would not be affected by the failure of the local communication systems, since their calls would be received and relayed by satellites orbiting the earth. Therefore, even if the rest of the cell phone companies in Puerto Rico became snarled in the flood of calls that would follow the destruction of the bridges, San Miguel's people would still be able to communicate with each other.

The phones would be distributed to the FEPIstas and the Macheteros within the next twenty-four hours—no use handing them out ahead of time and risking that one of them fell into the wrong hands. They were divided in three categories or "levels". Level 1 phones were assigned to the rank and file. They contained only one telephone number in their memory banks, to be used to report any important or suspicious activity to the Level 2 "supervisors". The Level 2 supervisors, in turn, could contact two types of telephone numbers: those of the Level 1 individuals who were under their direct supervision, and those of the Level 3 "leaders". There were only two Level 3 leaders: for the FEPI, Johnny Ray, and for the Macheteros, Andrade. The latter two could communicate with any of the other key players via their walkie-talkies.

It was a fairly simple system, designed to guarantee effective communications during the coming days. Like every system, it was not foolproof. In order to make or receive a call, the users of the satellite phones had to find an open space to acquire the signal of the orbiting satellites. And if the government forces ever got wind of how they were communicating, they could in theory intercept the calls, or attempt to jam them. But it would take a long time for their adversaries to find out what they were doing, and time was on San Miguel's side.

"You have not mentioned two very important hostages," Andrade said cryptically, earning a puzzled look from San Miguel. "I'm talking about the Governor and Adalberto Cacho."

"Oh, yes!" San Miguel flashed an apologetic smile at the dour Machetero. "Believe me, both form a very important part of my agenda. Which would you like to discuss first?" he asked him, but continued before Andrade could answer. "As soon as the bridges are down, half a dozen of my men and an equal number of Macheteros will move on La Fortaleza."

La Fortaleza, also called the Palace of Santa Catalina, was the Governor's mansion. While studying the history of Puerto Rico, San Miguel had been surprised to find out that La Fortaleza was the oldest residence ever to be used continuously by any head of government in all of the New World. Built by 1540, it had housed uninterruptedly the governor of Puerto Rico for centuries, more than two hundred years before the White House in Washington—or the city of Washington, for that matter—had even been imagined. Like its name implied, La Fortaleza—the "Fortress" in English—still kept as part of its original structure two enormous towers that had been constructed to withstand Indian and pirate attacks. Subsequent governors had continued to add space—sometimes entire structures—to the fortress, transforming it into an elegant, 18th century-style palace.

"Our aim is to capture Governor Pietrantoni alive, and use him in our negotiations," San Miguel indicated.

"And if you can't capture him alive?" Lebron asked pointedly.

San Miguel shrugged indifferently. "Nobody has to know that he died. We will negotiate his release, dead or alive."

El Alacran smiled, a chilling, mirthless smile. "I like that solution better."

"Will he even be in La Fortaleza?" Lebron pressed.

"We know that he is not scheduled to travel outside of Puerto Rico, and we understand that he is presently preparing his State of the Commonwealth address to the Legislature on Tuesday," San Miguel answered. "So we have every reason to believe that he will be there. But if he's not, his son will do as well."

Governor Pietrantoni was a widower. He lived in La Fortaleza with his eight year old son.

"As for Adalberto Cacho, your boss," San Miguel underscored with his voice the word "boss", "it goes without saying that we will demand his release from prison and his immediate transfer to San Juan, to lead our revolution. And I mean lead. Once Cacho gets to San Juan, I will relinquish my command to him."

San Miguel's unexpected announcement was greeted with stunned silence. Behind him, Czecka frowned, as if considering if he could follow orders from anyone but his boss. Even Andrade's reptilian features failed to conceal his surprise.

"You all seem to be shocked." San Miguel looked at the faces that surrounded him, and smiled. "Don't be. I sincerely believe in your cause. I believe that your nation deserves to be freed from American oppression, an oppression to which you have been subjected for more than a century. But I am also a realist. I am an outsider, and I know your countrymen will look at me with suspicion. I have witnessed some of it here already, tonight." San Miguel raised a hand placatingly, as Johnny Ray began to object to his last statement. "Please, I appreciate your confidence in me, but you know I'm right. Once Cacho is released, he will be in charge. A Puerto Rican *should* be in charge. And I will place myself and my men at his disposal."

For more than a minute, nobody spoke. Then El Alacran broke the room's stillness.

"Your generosity overwhelms us," he said with very little emotion and what seemed a tinge of doubt.

Daniel grinned, staring at the floor, and then raised his eyes to meet those of Andrade. The Machetero was momentarily taken aback by the promise of violence that they contained.

"One final matter, before we recess," San Miguel said. "As I mentioned when we were discussing hostages, we have very limited manpower. Our trained combat personnel is made up of twenty-eight volunteers from the Venezuelan special forces, twenty-nine if we count the colonel, twenty of my men, and about...thirty Macheteros?"

"Thirty-seven," Andrade corrected.

"That makes it a total of..." San Miguel did a quick count in his head, "about ninety-six fighting men total? Plus the FEPI volunteers. Not that I am disparaging the FEPI's contribution, which I deem essential, since they will be our eyes in this affair," he added hastily, peering at Johnny. "But the odds that we will be able to hold San Juan for long, and inspire a revolution in the rest of the country, are fifty-fifty at best."

In reality, San Miguel considered the odds of succeeding to be nil. However, he had no real intention of staging a revolution in Puerto Rico.

"Our operation is very complex," he said earnestly. "A hundred unexpected things can, and *will* happen. That has always been my experience, and probably the experience of most of you here. So if worse comes to worse, we may be forced to evacuate. If and when that time comes, we will do it from Terminal B in the dock area. The cruise ship *Mardi Gras* will be docked there. It will have been captured by the Macheteros. In the best scenario, the passengers on board *the Mardi Gras* will be used as another negotiating chip that will help secure our presence in San Juan. At worst, the ship will be our ticket of last resort out of here. We have made arrangements with the Venezuelan government to guarantee us safe passage in exchange for the return of the ship and the passengers. President Fanelli will publicly agree to this deal for humanitarian reasons."

"Are you in effect saying that we are likely to fail?" Lebron asked in a tone that suggested incredulity, not at the notion of failing, but at the notion that San Miguel would admit to it.

"I am saying that it is a real possibility, and as such, we must plan for it," San Miguel acknowledged. "It is essential that if our plan fails, the Macheteros and the Venezuelan volunteers have a means of escape. The FEPIstas, being from here, may be able to mingle with the crowds and walk away without any further consequences. It will be hard for the police to tell who is who in the aftermath. Some may choose to sail in the *Mardi Gras* as well, and fight some other day. I leave that to them."

Lebron sighed nervously, as the enormous import of what they were about to undertake increasingly weighed on his spirit. There was a Spanish saying, San Miguel thought, that went: *"No es lo mismo llamar al Diablo que verlo venir."* ("It's not the same to call the devil than to see him come.") San Miguel had met scores of Lebrons in his career: armchair theoreticians who spouted constant clichés about the oppressed, subjugated masses, and spoke of the armed rebellion by the working classes against their capitalist masters. Now, Lebron had been handed on a silver platter the opportunity to practice what he preached, and had discovered how truly daunting it all was.

The FEPI Secretary-General leaned forward, and took a deep breath, as if to gather strength. He did not have to speak; his body language betrayed his thoughts better than any words ever could. *It was all crazy,* it seemed to say, *pure, unadulterated madness that would lead them to catastrophe.* But before he could open his mouth, Johnny interrupted him.

"I don't believe that we will fail," he expressed with a passion that surprised San Miguel. Johnny, sweaty-palmed Johnny, was reasserting his leadership over the FEPI. "No matter what happens, we *will* win. I mean, look, we are all adults here," he said, not talking to San Miguel, but making his case directly to his followers, Lebron and Yajaira. "No one in this room is under any delusion. Last year, the people of Puerto Rico elected, by almost a sixty percent majority, a governor of the Partido Nuevo Progresista, the pro-statehood party, where a basic part of Governor Pietrantoni's platform was to hold a plebiscite to determine the status of Puerto Rico, and if the statehood option wins, petition the Americans to make us a state."

"The people of Puerto Rico my ass!" Lebron muttered contemptuously. "They're a bunch of American lackeys, dependent on the Americans' money."

Johnny shook his head despairingly. "The pro-independence party got less votes—barely two percent of the total votes cast—than in any other prior election, and it is on the brink of disappearing as a party. Polls suggest that over seventy percent of the population would, at this moment, vote for statehood!"

"Sellouts , all of them!" Lebron raged.

"Lately, there have been statements by President Powell, who is viewed as a sort of Messiah by many Puerto Ricans, that if a majority of them vote for statehood, he will push it in Congress. And you know what? I believe him. It is politically expedient for him to do it, and our people want it. Our culture is threatened by the ceaseless bombardment of the U.S. media, and our language bastardized by English slang. More and more of our people are moving to the States. Our country is on the brink of being absorbed by the American Empire." Johnny spread his hands in a gesture of utter helplessness. "If we don't do anything about it now, we may not be able to do anything later. Oh, sure, we can go back to the United Nations, as we've done on countless of occasions before, and move for a resolution sponsored by Cuba, Venezuela, maybe Iran, condemning the United States for their colonial oppression in Puerto Rico, but what good will that do us? What good has it done us in the past?"

"What good will it do us if we fall flat on our faces now?" the ever-skeptical Lebron countered. "What do we get out of a failed insurrection?"

"What we get, Felipe," Johnny said slowly, as if he was thinking out loud, "is two things. First, an insurrection here will kill statehood even if it lasts a couple of days. Can you imagine the Congress of the United States voting to make Puerto Rico a state after something like what we're planning happens?" Johnny shook his head. "No, Felipe, Congress will not incorporate that kind of trouble into its precious Union, even if the entire population of Puerto Rico went to Washington and petitioned it personally on its knees. They will not swallow us if they face the prospect of a massive indigestion."

Johnny paused, and looked at the others sitting around the table. For the first time in the night, Lebron nodded, even if hesitatingly, as he considered his comrade's argument.

"But there is something else that we will gain out of this, even if our revolution fails," Johnny continued. "And that is the respect of our people. Haven't you noticed how a lot of these pseudo-*statehooders* turn into ultra nationalists any time that a Puerto Rican becomes famous? How they are as anti-American as you and me when our national basketball or baseball teams play an American adversary? Remember when our basketball team defeated their professional Dream Team in the Olympics? The first team ever to do that! Do you remember what happened here? How the entire country went to the streets to celebrate *our* victory? Do you remember what happened when we beat them in baseball, a couple of months ago? And what has happened every time we win the Miss Universe contest? Or one of our actors wins an Academy Award? And how proud we feel any time that some important event takes place in our country? *Our country!* That's how we all referred to Puerto Rico last year, when President Powell announced that the next G-20 meeting of the world economic powers would be held here, in San Juan, *in our country!* Scratch most Puerto Ricans under their skin, and you will find true nationalists. When in the next few days we make our stand, when we make our voices heard, our people *will* remember who they are. They will remember that they are first and foremost Puerto Ricans, not Yankees! That Puerto Rico is their country, not an annex of the United States! We need to stand up to the Americans' might and spit on their faces, and let them know that we will not let them take our country away!"

Johnny stopped, realizing that he was shouting angrily. Nobody else spoke, waiting for him to continue.

"We need to remind our people that they are still Puerto Ricans," he told Lebron in a gentler voice. "And when we do this, we will bring the attention of the international community to our plight, and champion our cause before the entire world, and stop the assimilation of our country..." He stopped again, and then added weakly, "Even if we lose tomorrow."

Several of the people sitting around the table slapped their hands on the table, while Yajaira shouted "Bravo!" with tears shining in her eyes. San Miguel stood up and embraced him.

"I will be very proud to fight at your side," he said enthusiastically, not meaning a single word of it.

CHAPTER III

The meeting ended shortly after Johnny's speech. A handful of logistical problems were discussed, and then the assembled conspirators melted into the receding flow of the San Sebastian revelers.

San Miguel continued to sit at the dining table, marshaling his impressions of the meeting, while Daniel and Czecka remained standing behind him. He stared vacantly at the wall on the other side of the room, where one of the paintings showed some sort of clergyman—probably a bishop, because of his tall, pointed hat—marching in front of hundreds of women who carried torches. San Miguel had heard about the legend that the painting portrayed. If he recalled correctly, the British—or was it the Dutch?—had surrounded the walled city of San Juan with what seemed to be an insurmountable, armed force. The bishop, followed by the women of the city, had led a nighttime torchlight procession to ask God for their city's delivery. The procession of the "eleven thousand virgins", the legend called it, why he had no idea. He doubted that eleven-thousand women lived in San Juan at that time, much less all of them virgins. But their heavenly plea had been answered, as the invaders, watching the glow of the torches from afar, had thought that a mighty army was approaching them. They had fled with such haste that they had abandoned their heavy artillery and ammunition. The city had been spared.

Well, he thought, *there were not enough virgins living in San Juan now to save it from its fate.*

"Is George here?" he asked Daniel, returning his thoughts to the present.

"He's been waiting in the next room for more than two hours," Daniel answered.

"Please get him."

Daniel walked out of the dining room, and returned almost immediately with the object of San Miguel's inquiry.

"Boss!" the man said cheerfully, his wide, toothy grin made more visible by the blackness of his skin. Unlike his prior visitors, George spoke in English, his native tongue. He extended his closed fist, and knocked it gently against San Miguel's, a la Howie Mandel. "How's it all holding up?"

Short of height, with a round face and a perpetual smile, George looked disarmingly harmless. It was a persona that he had carefully cultivated, along with his exaggerated, uncouth speech, and which he used to his advantage with amazing effectiveness. In reality, he was a consummate killer, a sort of deranged, cold-blooded Satchmo, who had raised the art of dispatching human beings with a knife to new and unexplored heights. His weapon of preference was a five-inch double-edged KA-Bar fighting knife made of carbon steel, the type favored by the U.S. Marines, which he had coated several times with a matte gray spray to diminish the blade's reflection. He called it "B.D."—short for "Black Death"—and wore it strapped to his ankle in an old leather harness.

San Miguel had seen George execute several men during the years that they had worked together. He did not know what impressed him the most; the fluid ease with which he could slip a blade into a body, or the puzzled look of his unsuspecting victims, who usually could not believe, even as they were dying, that the beaming man before them had been capable of stabbing them.

"*It* is holding up remarkably well", San Miguel replied. "And by the looks of you, I suspect *it* will keep holding up quite nicely. What do you have for me?"

"Well, boss," George produced his trademark laugh, a deep rumbling chuckle that he usually injected into his speech every two or three sentences, "you know me. I'm just a happy person by nature." Rumbling chuckle. "But yeah, the news are good, they're good. I visited the Institute of Culture with Eduardo, as you asked me to, and they were waiting for us, just like you said. And pretty excited they were to see us too! As if we were a good thing!"

Another chuckle followed, which developed into a full-fledged cough and dwindled into a raspy smile.

"They were very excited that we were going to produce a documentary about the old tunnels of San Juan for the Discovery Channel. Didn't even have to show them my fake Discovery Channel I.D." He shook his head with hidden amusement. "They treated us like British royalty. Took us to Fort San Cristobal, where we met with one of them rangers of the National Park Service."

"Did he give you any trouble?"

"Naw, no trouble at all. The people from the Institute had already spoken with him. The ranger walked us down this steep tunnel, maybe about a hundred yards long, and then we walked out into this open space between the fort's outside and inner walls. On the outside wall there was this old iron gate locked with a padlock."

"I saw it," San Miguel said. He had taken the official tour that the rangers offered to tourists to show some of the tunnels in the fort. "Not much of a padlock. Very easy to pick."

"Yeah," George nodded. "That's the one." He continued. "I was carrying the digital camera that you gave me. And Eduardo carried a spotlight. They gave us construction helmets for our heads, and flashlights, 'cause it was really dark in there. Then they led us down the tunnel until we reached a place where it split in two. The ranger, he told us that the tunnel to the left led to a blind alley. He said that's as far as the rangers take the tourists."

San Miguel prepared for another chuckle and was not disappointed.

"But since I wasn't no tourist, he took me to the right, and we kept walking down it for about five minutes—seemed longer in the dark, let me tell you—until we ended up in a large, round room buried underground. The ranger told us that we were in a smaller fortification outside of San Cristobal, called 'El Abanico'."

"The Fan," San Miguel automatically translated.

"I don't know why they call it "The Fan", 'cause it was hot and stuffy in there. But anyway, there was a door there. A really old, solid metal door, also locked with a padlock. You could tell it was hardly ever used, 'cause after the ranger unlocked the padlock, he really had to pull to get it open, and it was even darker on the other side. And smelly! As if somebody had died and his body had stayed there for a long, long time." George shivered involuntarily. "Man, but there's a beehive of tunnels down there! One drops down to the sea, to where the reefs in front of the fort are. That's the shortest, and it's blocked at the other end by a gate with steel bars." He chuckled. "They're all rusted. They should be easy to break, if we want to go that way."

"You said that was the shortest of the tunnels. The people from the Institute told me over the telephone that there were others. They spoke of at least two other major tunnels, one running under the city's north wall to El Morro, and the second traversing the city diagonally in the direction of La Fortaleza. The Governor's mansion."

"Yeah, that's right, and like you told me to say, I asked them to let me explore that tunnel specifically, you know, the one going to La Fortaleza. They said it wasn't safe, so they only let me go through up to a certain way. They don't know where it ends exactly, there have been some places where it collapsed. But boss, it was fantastic! Like Indiana Jones!" George finished his statement with a rumbling chortle. "After about twenty minutes, the ranger said that we should stop because it wasn't safe any more, but I think he was scared of ghosts, you know what I mean? And I don't blame him, 'cause it sure was dark and spooky in there! Why, even with a flashlight, if I'd taken my clothes off, I would have been invisible!" George laughed at his own joke, prompting a forced smile from San Miguel. "Spooky," he repeated, not entirely in jest.

"How far did you go?" San Miguel asked, trying to stick to the main topic.

"Oh, pretty far, I would say...Hard to tell, under the ground. Probably close to the center of the city, and the tunnel kept going. There were other exits and passages, God knows going where exactly. Some went south, in the direction of the ports, the ranger told me, and one passage going north seemed to have collapsed completely. He also told us that some of the tunnels are connected to the old aqueducts of the city, which means there's all kinds of holes and passages down there. A whole army could move from one place to another without being noticed. God knows what else the Spaniards used them for. Nothing good, I suspect. I think they may have chained some people that they weren't interested in seeing ever again to some of the walls there, and let them rot, you know? It certainly smelled that way, although I didn't see no skeletons there."

San Miguel allowed himself to smile. George's news had been good indeed. Better than he had anticipated.

"Did you bring the video recording?"

George fished a yellow envelope out of his right pants pocket, and handed it to San Miguel.

"I knew you'd be asking for it. If you see any ghosts, let me know!" he said, producing another of his rumbling laughs. San Miguel transferred the envelope to Daniel.

"Thank you, George. As always, your execution is flawless." As in their initial greeting, San Miguel stretched his closed hand and bumped it lightly on his visitor's fist. Then, as George was about to exit the room, he added, almost as an afterthought, "By the way, did you tell the people of the Institute when we would return to begin the official work on the project?"

"Just like you said I should say, boss," he responded, stopping at the opposite end of the table, and tapping it as he continued to speak. "I told them it would be about five or six months before we got our act together and came back to do the actual filming. I gave them one of the cards with our production office's telephone number, 'Los Angeles Enterprises'. I like that name." George snickered as he said "production office", finding the deceit highly amusing.

"Great." In six months, everything would be long over. But just in case any curious caller decided to contact the production crew before that time, the number on the card would connect him with the fictitious "Los Angeles Enterprises", which in turn would reroute the call to him.

Again, the bogus producer turned to exit, and again San Miguel stopped him.

"George!"

"Yes, boss?" he asked patiently.

"On Sunday, I want you to stay by the Governor's side."

"Yes, boss."

"You will personally guard him, and keep him from harm unless I tell you otherwise, is that understood?"

"Yes, boss."

"I'm counting on you."

George chuckled.

"It's okay, boss. You can rely on me. It's not as if I was a half-assed sissy like Daniel."

Daniel made as if to pursue George, but the knifeman rushed out of the door laughing.

CHAPTER IV

Lucas Alfaro started his day with a set of established routines. Most were hard habits that would follow him to his grave, ingrained in him from the days he had trained as an Army Ranger. Like his morning jog. Not the jogging per se; he had jogged since he was seventeen years old—when he wanted to impress teenage girls with an athletic body—but the getting-up-early-in-the-morning-to-jog routine. It had been a pet peeve of his wife, Jeannie, ever since they had started living together: he could not manage a normal, gradual transition from sleep to getting up. When the alarm clock started to beep, usually at 5:15 in the morning, he would swing his legs abruptly out of bed, slip his still half-asleep body into his jogging attire, and scramble downstairs, everything in less than sixty seconds.

Once in the family room below, he would take a minute to stretch—not enough stretching, according to Jeannie, a Pilates expert—and run across the street to the track opposite to his house. He would jog at a fast pace for an hour—lately reduced to forty-five minutes—return home, shave, and take a quick shower.

That morning, as he toweled his head dry and combed himself, he had discovered several more gray hairs, mostly on his sides. It had not alarmed him—he had had a few gray hairs ever since he could remember—but they seemed to have proliferated over the last year, so much so that Jeannie had begun to refer to him as "her silver fox" even though much of his hair retained most of its dark brown color. But it still prompted him to look at himself critically on the mirror every so often.

For a thirty-eight, nearly thirty-nine year old man, he thought, he didn't look that bad. He was not tall—five feet, nine or ten inches, depending on who measured him—but still maintained a lean, athletic body. It was never in the condition it had been when he had served in the Army—and never would be again—but his stomach was still flat, and still kept enough definition to show a six-pack. He had the broad shoulders of a swimmer, strong legs—Jeannie claimed they were better shaped than hers, but that was a lie—and could still manage a hundred push-ups a day. His eyes were hazel and on the small side, his nose surprisingly straight and streamlined for a man who had been in quite a few fights, his lips thin but most of the time framed in a friendly, sometimes humorous smile.

None of his features, by themselves, could be considered to be outstanding, but still, most women found him to be a fairly attractive man. Maybe it had to do something with the fact that he never seemed to take himself very seriously—a trait that many mistook for shyness—that he actually took the time to listen to what others had to say—a very rare commodity in today's tell-all, hear-little, public-media-driven-society—and that ten years into his marriage, he was still madly in love with his wife.

By the time he finished dressing for work and went down for breakfast, it was past six-fifteen in the morning. He found Jeannie feeding Gabriel, two years old and already a mini-clone of his father, and Sofia, four going on twenty and a mixture of both parents that at the same time looked each day more like Lucas' mother. He took over the feeding, allowing Jeannie to have breakfast, and after the children had finished eating, sat on the sofa, one child on each side, to watch cartoons on TV. It was a daily routine, but a temporary one, he was sure, one that would change as the children grew up, and therefore he particularly relished it. "Dora the Explorer" was a definite favorite, and so was "Finding Nemo", a film he had begun watching at least two-hundred times—but seldom finished viewing because he had to leave for work—and one which he found strangely moving and entertaining, mostly because of the wonder-eyed expressions of his children as they watched it.

By a quarter past seven, after sitting with Sofia through her potty time and poring over one of her Disney princess books with her, he was ready to leave for work. He kissed Jeannie hard on the mouth—which invariably made him feel aroused—warned her not to run away with the gardener, and urged her to wait for him naked when he came back from work. Jeannie, a fiery half-Cuban-half-Miamian-with-Cuban-ancestry, answered with a deadpan face that she could not guarantee the former, and then added with a naughty smile that she would consider the latter.

Lucas headed towards Old San Juan still thinking about her. It was not a long drive—less than ten miles, actually—but traffic tended to be heavy, and particularly during school days it could stretch his driving time to nearly an hour. Fortunately, today was Saturday, and the roads at that time of the morning were almost devoid of life. It would all begin to change around noon, when the first of the San Sebastian celebrants would begin to head towards the old city to secure a good parking space.

By six in the afternoon, the Miramar and Condado bridges going into San Juan would be flooded with bumper-to-bumper vehicles, and the traffic jam would extend for several miles.

That morning Lucas got to San Juan by 7:30 AM and, as usual, parked his car—a silver 2001 PT Cruiser—in the municipal parking building located next to the Federal Bankruptcy Court, commonly referred to as "the parking of Doña Fela" in honor of the city's beloved first female mayor. Felicita Gautier, aka Doña Fela, had ruled San Juan in the 1950's and 60's, a time when female mayors were a rarity in Puerto Rico or anywhere else for that matter. Contrary to most politicians, her popularity had increased with time, not only due to her wise administrative skills, but also because of her colorful and unpredictable exploits. Once, for example, she had filled a cargo plane with snow and had it flown to San Juan, so that the poor children of the city could experience how snow felt. Lucas wondered how that stunt would play in modern times. The terms "wasteful spending" and "impeachment" came to mind.

Lucas headed uphill, to have breakfast at "La Bombonera", another of his permanent habits, and one of the few treats he allowed himself every day. The city of San Juan had been founded on a large hill, which rose steeply from what were now the tourist docks in the south, to the Calle San Sebastian in the north, and then dropped back even more abruptly towards El Morro Castle and the Atlantic Ocean. Therefore, each day, Lucas had to climb several blocks in order to eat his breakfast.

He did not mind the walk. Strolling through the narrow streets of the ancient city allowed him to watch as it slowly stirred back to life, and he loved every moment of it.

Just across the parking building, he saw a man step out onto his balcony in his undershirt with a cigarette burning out of his right hand, while below him, a heavyset woman sprayed the steps of her house and the sidewalk with a hose, stopping briefly to let Lucas pass. Half a block away, the already opened doors of a barbershop emitted the muffled voices of a political radio show, mixed with the clean smells of alcohol, talcum, and shaving lotion. Further up, on the corner of Tanca Street, an unlicensed Haitian vendor, dressed in a long robe of bright red and yellow prints, was placing carved wooden figures on a small table, getting ready for the tourists that would soon stream out of the cruise ships. The vendor was flanked by a stray dog that scratched, with intense concentration, its left ear with its hind leg, oblivious of the rest of the world. A few steps further away, two competing, side-to-side souvenir stores were also preparing to open, removing the storm-burglar-proof metal panes that shuttered their windows, placing racks of T-shirts and other wares on small stands on the sidewalk, and brandishing signs of "Sale", "Best

Prices in Town", and other similar lies on their display windows. On the opposite side of the street, three somberly dressed elderly ladies—widows probably—were engaged in an animated conversation as they hurried to the 7:30 morning mass in Santa Ana Church, while above the church's main entrance, several pigeons observed the activity below them with detached curiosity, cooing in an animated conversation of their own, regaling the world under them with some of their droppings.

Lucas continued his upward trek, greeting some of the locals he met along the way. Hardly any cars rolled through the shiny gray, cobblestoned streets, except for the occasional van unloading crates of food or merchandise for the cafes and stores that lined the sidewalks. He turned left on San Francisco Street, the main thoroughfare of the old city, and caught sight of his immediate destination, just a block away.

"La Bombonera, Puig & Abraham", it read overhead in red letters over white glass tiles. A large window, flanked on each side by one of the restaurant's two doors, displayed scores of different pastries, while below it more tiles, made of Moorish-style porcelain, showed ornate drawings of fawns, unicorns, and other mythical figures. Founded in 1902, La Bombonera had been serving hot, frothy lattes long before Starbuck's conquered the world. In 2010 it had abruptly closed, when it had lost its public restrooms, located in a neighboring building that had been put up for sale. It had remained closed for a few years, but then a few enterprising merchants had managed to reopen it, maintaining it—except for the new restrooms—as it had been before, knowing that the residents of San Juan would not have it any other way.

La Bombonera's specialty was *"mallorcas"*, a soft, yellowish bread-like confection larger than a coffee cake, sprinkled with a generous amount of powdered sugar. They were sold everywhere in Puerto Rico, but in La Bombonera they were cut horizontally, slapped with a huge amount of butter, and toasted in a sandwich press. The result had kept Lucas coming to the turn-of-the-century café during every workday that it had been open for the last thirteen years.

The smell of freshly baked bread and strong coffee greeted his senses as he pulled open La Bombonera's door. Even though very early in the day, the morning crowd—mostly locals—already filled the small restaurant to near capacity. He spotted an empty stool at the long counter to his right, and occupied it. Raising a hand, he motioned in the direction of one of the servers, a small man with a pencil-thin mustache, a red vest, and a long paper cap. The man immediately wiped the counter in front of him with a damp cloth and, without saying a word, began to gut a *mallorca*. In less than five minutes, Lucas had been served with the warm pastry, plus a small glass of freshly squeezed orange juice and a latte.

"Been busy with San Sebastian?" Lucas asked casually.

"Busy is not the word," the waiter replied, as he gathered some empty plates and glasses from the counter, and quickly took them away.

Lucas ate slowly, enjoying the food and the dozen or more conversations happening around him. This was a Latin cafeteria, and everyone spoke loudly, dispensing opinions about politics, the *"farandula"* (the entertainment world), baseball, weather, and the latest sex scandals.

The waiter returned and pulled out of his back pocket a small notebook.

"Anything else, my friend?" he asked, as he scribbled a check even before Lucas could answer.

"I'm done," Lucas replied, and after paying the bill, fished in his pocket for some loose change. "Thank you, Javier," he said, placing three quarters and a dime on the counter. "Everything was great, as usual."

"You are such a lousy tipper!" a female voice said behind him. A hand trying to grab the change shot by him, but he slapped it away.

"Watch it, Javier," he warned the waiter, without glancing back at the new arrival, "she steals the tips!"

Javier looked up from the counter, and his businesslike expression melted into a charming smile, which he flashed at the newcomer.

"What? This dream of a woman? This gorgeous television star? This incredibly beautiful...eh...eh...beauty?" Lucas raised his eyebrows in mock despair while Javier continued to rave about the brunette standing behind him. "She can have my tip! No, every tip I get today! Just for the privilege of seeing her." Javier held the woman's hand and kissed it tenderly.

Lucas shook his head with resignation. "If you keep this up," he told the waiter, "I'll take your tip away and report you to the manager."

"Michelle, I love you!" Javier blew a kiss in the newcomer's direction, pocketed the change, and rapidly moved away to take the next order.

Lucas turned and kissed Michelle on the cheek. "Hi, television star."

"Hi, big brother."

"You working this weekend?"

"Today and Sunday. Elba Rosa Pendragon is on vacation, and I'm covering for her in the six and ten o'clock broadcasts. Also in tomorrow's nine o'clock morning news."

Michelle Alfaro was the younger of Lucas' two sisters. During the workweek, she hosted an early morning radio show from six to nine in the morning. Also, in the past two years, she had begun to provide color commentary for WKPA television news, mostly entertaining, inconsequential events that newscasts used as "fillers" on slow news days. Although barely twenty-six, she had shown a special ability to focus on the most appealing details of her assigned stories, and to inject real human interest into them. That, and her stunning good looks, had combined to make her an audience favorite, and had helped her rise in the highly competitive profession she had chosen.

"That's sort of a promotion, isn't it?" Lucas asked, looking at her proudly.

"I don't know how much of a promotion, but the money is good, so I'll take it." Michelle's expression suddenly grew animated, her green eyes lighting up with excitement. "You know what is really great? I'm going to interview President Powell when he comes to Puerto Rico for the G-20 Conference in May! Isn't that awesome?"

Lucas high-fived his kid sister.

"Dad would be very proud of you," he said.

Their father, Mario Alfaro, had been a very famous television actor and director who had helped found Telemundo decades before the station had been acquired by NBC and become the standard bearer for Latin television in North America. His rugged good looks and natural charm had also made him a huge soap opera star in Puerto Rico. He had passed away ten years before, from heart complications.

"Staying or going?" Lucas asked Michelle.

"Actually, I was waiting for you to vacate your seat."

"Javier will be thrilled." He stepped out of the stool.

Michelle smiled. "Are you going to *El Joyero*?" she asked, as she took over Lucas' place.

El Joyero was *"El Joyero de San Juan"*, a jewelry store founded by Jorge Pietri, their maternal grandfather. Don Jorge, as Lucas and Michelle's grandfather had been called by everyone except his family, had been a beloved figure in the community, noted not only for the beauty and superb quality of the jewels that he sold, but also for his generosity and his irreverent sense of humor. The store was now run by his three daughters, including Michelle and Lucas' mother, Fannie.

"Are you working tomorrow?" Michelle asked her brother.

"What do you think?" Lucas responded with a tone of inevitability.

"Those Pietri sisters, they're slave-drivers."

"Yup." Lucas kissed Michelle goodbye, and waved at Javier. "She wants to marry you!" he shouted at him, pointing at his sister, then left hurriedly before Michelle could smack him.

Lucas continued to climb uphill, this time towards Plaza de Armas, located a scant two blocks from La Bombonera along San Francisco Street. The Plaza de Armas had been the principal square of the old walled city during the Spanish rule. It covered a rectangular area approximately the size of half a football field, and was surrounded by colonial style buildings on every side but one.

A round fountain, guarded by four equidistant statues that represented the four seasons, stood close to the western end of the square, along with one of the French-style, dark green, steel booths that served as a café and catered to half a dozen tables scattered about it. A large gazebo, large enough to hold a full band, occupied the eastern end where an ancient laurel tree had grown. Hundreds of pigeons clumsily roamed over a vast portion of the square, hunting for kernels of corn or scraps of bread sold in another of the food booths.

To the north, across San Francisco Street, lay the Casa Alcaldia, or City Hall, an imposing, two story structure with a double-tiered façade of columns connected by arches, crowned on each of its extremities by two tall towers. The mayor of San Juan still kept an office there, although now he spent more time in the multi-story facilities that had been constructed in the business district of Hato Rey, outside of the island of San Juan. The Alcaldia, as it was known, was flanked by other smaller buildings painted in bright yellow, green, and pink that housed a pharmacy, a souvenir shop, and a restaurant.

The Department of State, an imposing edifice built in the Spanish neoclassical style, flanked the entire western side of the square. Its pale blue walls were decorated with false columns and horizontal cornices painted in white, while in the center of its second-of-three floors, a wide, black, iron grilled balcony—backed by three sets of tall cedar doors— provided a bird's eye view of the plaza and its surroundings. Many a times, Lucas had gazed upon the balcony, and considered it the perfect location to film Eva Peron singing "Don't Cry for Me, Argentina". He imagined that in another age, Spanish governors or other officials had used it to read decrees or address the crowds or troops below.

A supermarket and several businesses, including a Subways and a Starbucks, occupied the eastern flank of the square. For several years, these had been the less attractive buildings in the area. Recently, however, they had been restored back to their full splendor, their walls painted in a strikingly deep mustard tone—except for Starbucks, which kept a green façade—with decorative moldings and arches highlighted in white.

Opposite to the Alcaldia, on the southern flank of the square, rose the Metropolitan Center. It was by far the biggest—occupying the entire block—tallest—standing twelve stories high—and most modern structure surrounding the Plaza de Armas. Everything was relative, of course. In a city where the age of most buildings was counted in centuries, the Metropolitan Center was a relative youngster at the paltry age of eighty.

Several floors of the edifice had housed for years one of Puerto Rico's most exclusive department stores, Gonzalez Padin. For several decades, Gonzalez Padin had ruled the retail business in the island. Its yearly Christmas display had attracted throngs of wonder-eyed children, including Lucas, from all over the island. However, by the eighties, the relentless competition of Sears, J.C. Penney's, and Kmart had driven it to insolvency. Recently, Marshall's had moved into the abandoned store.

A large, art deco arch marked the main entrance to the residential apartments in the Metropolitan Center. A thick, ornamental iron-grilled door controlled access into its apartments. A second arch a dozen yards to its left allowed entry into the office floors. Lucas' grandfather had been one of the original tenants of the building, operating from a small office in his fifth floor apartment. Those had been the "good old days", when a select clientele visited him by appointment only. Business had been plentiful. So plentiful, in fact, that in the mid 1960's, Don Jorge had decided to move to a much larger commercial space on the ground floor, next to the residential entrance of the building, where a failed clothing boutique used to be. It was a privileged location, situated in the heart of Old San Juan.

While he had operated from his fifth floor office, Don Jorge had never bothered to give any name to his business. His clients merely referred to it as "Pietri's" or "Pietri's place". But when he opened a full-fledged jewelry store in the tallest, biggest, most prestigious building of San Juan, he decided to give it a name that would set it apart from all of the other jewelry stores in the city. He settled on the name of *"El Joyero de San Juan"*.

It was a play on words. The term *"joyero"* could mean in Spanish both "jeweler" or "jewelry box". Thus, the name of the store could be interpreted to mean *"The Jeweler of San Juan"* or *"The Jewelry Box of San Juan"*. Normally, jewelry stores in Puerto Rico were referred to as "joyerias". But Don Jorge's establishment became known as *"El Joyero"*, the only business in all of Puerto Rico to be known by that name, and that had suited Don Jorge just fine.

During the next quarter of a century, *El Joyero* had prospered and become an institution in its own right, one of the biggest and most prestigious jewelry stores in the city, its name proudly displayed in bold, stylish gold letters over its entrance.

Lucas had been born in 1975, and immediately become his grandfather's favorite person. He still remembered vividly, although barely five at the time, how the old man would take him along during his morning walks, when Don Jorge would deliver or show merchandise to clients, buy supplies for the store, or bring jewels and watches to the repair and engraving shops. His grandfather would invariably introduce the young boy as "his heir", the "next great jeweler" of Old San Juan, and beam proudly as he listened to the compliments showered on his cute grandson. At the end of his rounds, he would stop at La Bombonera, share a gloriously buttered *mallorca* with Lucas, and buy a dozen more for the rest of the *Joyero's* employees. It had been a wonderful time, which Lucas thought would never end.

But change did come, at first slowly and imperceptively, then faster and more drastically. It began during the eighties. A rash of new, big jewelry stores opened in San Juan. Some of them entered into exclusive arrangements with cruise ships and land tour companies to bring their clients directly to their stores. Mega air-conditioned malls thinned out the number of visitors who came to shop to the old city. The age of personal contacts with well-to-do acquaintances slowly gave way to a new era of media advertising and large discounts.

And in 1984, Don Jorge succumbed to cancer.

Lucas' mother, Fannie, and her two younger sisters, Evelyn and Maria, inherited the family business. Although they never managed to return to the golden days of the store, the three sisters managed—with great sacrifice and effort—to maintain *El Joyero de San Juan's* reputation of being one of the top jewelry stores in San Juan. Still, *El Joyero* needed new blood.

Lucas had loved working in the store during his high school summers and learning the ins and outs of the jewelry trade. Under the gentle tutelage of Mr. Romero, an old Cuban gentleman who had been *El Joyero's* top salesman since it had opened in the ground floor of the Metropolitan Center, he had been taught to identify the gamut of precious stones displayed in the store's glass cases, not only by their variations in shades and colors, but by their weight, cut, and even their imperfections. He had learned the vocabulary of a jeweler, and been successful in translating it to those who visited his family's business. He had shown a special talent in identifying what his clients were looking for and—in some instances—convincing them to purchase items they had not sought.

It had therefore been generally assumed by the family that, as his grandfather had so proudly proclaimed, Lucas would assume his mantle, and become the next Don Jorge Pietri. However, when Lucas graduated from high school, he had balked. Even though he loved the small store, and enjoyed the challenges and intricacies of the business, the thought of spending the rest of his life working as a jeweler proved to be a daunting proposition. There were other more glamorous and exciting professions—such as the practice of law or journalism—that appealed to him greatly. He was aware of what the others were expecting of him, and agonized over his decision.

When he graduated from high school, Lucas had just felt confused. Uncertain about what he would do, he enrolled in the University of Puerto Rico as an Arts major. However, he found the experience empty and unfulfilling, and after a couple of months dropped out of school. To everybody's dismay, he decided to take time off to think about his future, and joined the Army.

Lucas enlisted in the infantry, volunteered for airborne training, and then applied to Ranger School. Any expectations of thinking about his future were dashed on his first day of school. During the next three months, he could only focus on how to survive his training. Lucas was submitted to extreme physical and mental stress, designed to weed out those candidates who could not handle the pressure. From long, grueling forced marches in full battle gear through impassable terrain, to the terrifying climbs in the mountains of Georgia, to the exhausting alligator and snake infested treks through the swamps in Florida, his rigorous Ranger training consumed every waking second of his existence, and most of his dreams as well. But he emerged from the ordeal with a mental toughness and self-assurance that set him apart from most people his age.

He graduated from Ranger School in February of 1993, and spent two weeks in San Juan, mostly showing off his uniform to his family and friends. Then, after a brief stint in Jacksonville and Fort Benning, he was flown directly to Mogadishu, Somalia, where he was assigned to Task Force Ranger, a coalition of several Ranger units that attempted to keep the peace in the African nation.

Somalia shocked him. He had never lived in a place where killing another human being basically carried no legal consequences, where no government maintained order of any kind, and where a person's chances of survival were directly related to the firepower that he carried. Clouds of black smoke billowed over the city periodically, and armed thugs, looters, and others belonging to the rogue militia of General Mohammed Farah Aidid roamed the streets with impunity, terrorizing the civilian population. Fifteen thousand United Nations militia had been sent to Mogadishu to reestablish its shattered peace. They had failed miserably, making intermittent incursions from their walled compound into the city, but in reality besieged by the enemy outside.

It was a turbulent time for Somalia. Ambushes were the order of the day. On June of that year, twenty-four Pakistani soldiers had been massacred. A few weeks later, four journalists had been stoned to death. Lucas had participated in several patrols, mostly in missions to protect civilians or to distribute food, and on two occasions briefly exchanged fire with elements of Aidid's militia. He had counted himself fortunate for not being involved in more serious incidents.

And then the ambush had come.

It was October. He and several others of his unit had been assigned as backup to a larger force sent to arrest a prominent member of the Aidid militia. The Somali insurgents had been waiting for them. A Blackhawk helicopter had been shot down, its crew slaughtered. Lucas' unit had been surrounded by hundreds of heavily armed militants crazed by drugs, who sensed an imminent American massacre.

He had never spoken to anyone except Jeannie about what happened that day. He still dreamt about the terrible, frightening moment when the sun had vanished behind the flat roofs of the surrounding houses, and the dark night had swept over him and his unit like an oily tidal wave; about the incessant clatter of the guns, and the screams of the wounded men, and the thud of the incoming bullets as they slammed against the walls; about the frantic running from house to house, and the blind shooting against an invisible, inexhaustible enemy. He had thought that he was going to die that night, in a dusty, God-forsaken corner of a God-forsaken country in Africa, and that he would never meet the people he loved again.

But he had survived, unscathed. And in the glorious, cloudless morning when he and his unit had walked out of the ambush back into the allied compound, he had determined exactly what he would do with the rest of his life.

He had returned to Puerto Rico in 1996, one year after finishing his tour of duty with the Army and after acquiring a degree from the Gemological Institute of America in Los Angeles for the design, repair, and appraisal of jewels and gemstones. A short time later, he established a small workshop in the mostly unused cellar of the jewelry store, where he not only repaired and appraised jewels, but also designed original pieces of jewelry that began to attract a new generation of clients. And so, belatedly, he had fulfilled his grandfather's dream.

Lucas walked diagonally across the Plaza de Armas, and stopped in front of *El Joyero de San Juan*. He unlocked the long, heavy mahogany doors that gave access to the store, switched off the alarm, and closed the doors behind him. He was the first in, as usual, but he preferred it that way. It allowed him to do some of his work without any interruptions, before the rest of the day caught up with him and overwhelmed him. Antonio, their security guard for the last twenty-five years, would be there by eight-thirty, and the rest of the cast would follow gradually. His mother and Maria, who now lived together in an apartment in Miramar, would arrive last—by ten or ten-thirty—after the store had opened.

Lucas left the lights of *El Joyero's* main floor off, and worked his way down a narrow, circular stairway at the back of the store that led to his repair shop. He had to unlock an iron gate to get in. When Lucas had set up his shop, the cellar had looked like a dungeon. He had cleared away a myriad collection of objects, stored there since the days of the clothing store: hairless mannequins, empty clothing racks, seasonal advertising "sales" signs, a broken down, manual cash register. He had installed a green wall-to-wall carpet, his work desk, polishing and soldering tools, a computer, and an espresso coffee machine, as well as a portable air conditioning unit. It had made the place comfortable and a lot less dreary, his refuge from the hustle and bustle upstairs.

Lucas brewed himself an espresso—one of the three he would take during the day—and sat down to work. About three-dozen repair works awaited him, and those were only the ones that needed to be finished for Monday. Sometimes he had stayed until the early hours of the morning getting the work done, but not today. Today was Saturday. If he didn't finish today, he could still do it tomorrow.

He had scarcely slipped his soldering mask over his head and turned on his torch, when his cell phone began to buzz, vibrating over the Formica desktop like an angry, wounded wasp.

Shit, he thought, shutting off the torch. *It was going to be one of those days.*

The cell phone screen flashed the name of "Vanessa", his other sister.

"*Listen,*" she said without any kind of introduction as soon as he took the call, making him smile. It was vintage Vanessa.

"Good morning," he said in a pointedly polite voice, before she could go on.

"*Yeah, yeah, whatever,*" she replied. "*You know what?*" she asked excitedly.

"What?"

"*Al-fre-do,*" she said, exaggerating every syllable for dramatic effect, "*has been invited to spend the night in La Fortaleza with the Governor's son! To-night!*" She screamed. Then in a casual voice she added, "*Isn't that exciting?*"

He chuckled. Alfredo was Vanessa's eight-year-old son, and Lucas' godson. He went to school with the Governor's son...what was the name of the boy? Francisco. Also eight.

"I guess Governor Pietrantoni wants to show that he cares about the lower classes in Puerto Rico. I really wouldn't brag about it."

"*You are such a jerk!*" she shouted, unable to conceal her laughter. "*How many times have you slept in Fortaleza?*" She paused. "*Hummm...Let me see...How about NEVER? Maybe he should invite you, to include people with low IQ's!*"

Lucas smiled. "What is it with my two sisters? First Michelle is going to interview President Powell, now my godson is spending the night in La Fortaleza?"

"Whoa! What Michelle? Our Michelle?"

"What other Michelle do you know? Yes, our Michelle, you dummy!"

"Our Michelle is interviewing Powell?" Vanessa sounded genuinely amazed, not so much because of the Powell interview, Lucas suspected, but because *he* had learned about it before *she* had. She recovered quickly, however, saying, *"I guess you must feel left out, huh?"*

It was his turn to laugh.

"Listen, I feel very proud about Alfredo, but I have to work. Is there anything else I can do for you? If you want, you can drop Alfredo here and I can walk him to Forta—"

"Are you crazy?" she interrupted. *"I'm taking him per-son-al-ly to La Fortaleza. You think I'll miss that? Maybe I'll meet the Governor,"* she added happily.

"Maybe he'll invite you to stay as well. Maybe you should bring Michael with you." Michael was his brother in law. "They have lots of rooms there. Anyway, tell Alfredo to take his camera. He takes good pictures, and I've never been there." Lucas heard Alfredo's voice in the background, warning his mother not to embarrass him. He chortled. The kid had personality. Lucas really liked him. "Well, enjoy yourselves. I love you."

"Love you too," she replied, then said. *"President Powell? Really?"*

"Call her," Lucas suggested.

"I will," she replied, and hung up.

Still smiling, Lucas glanced at his watch; it was 8:30 in the morning. Antonio, the security guard, should be arriving at any moment, and after him, the rest would start to trickle in. He'd better take advantage of the remainder of his quiet time.

Lucas pulled down his mask and relit his torch, a blue flame shooting out of its bent tip. The work could not wait. Not even for President Powell and La Fortaleza.

When he emerged from his repair shop it was 10:30 in the morning and the jewelry store was buzzing. Maria, the youngest of the three Pietri sisters, was sitting at the desk behind the display counters talking animatedly over the phone. She had handled the accounting for the business since Don Jorge passed away, and still made all entries into the *Joyero's* books manually, in very neat handwriting. From her harassed expression, Lucas could tell that she was talking to a bank or a supplier. A large, framed black and white photograph of his grandfather, taken when he was in his forties, lay on the desk, facing the counters, as if overseeing the activity in the store.

Evelyn, the second oldest, stood behind another counter on the opposite side of the floor, close to the entrance. She was showing a necklace made of stringy strips of red coral to a couple of tourists, carefully explaining to them from where and how the coral had been obtained. Of the three sisters, she was the businesswoman, constantly considering new ways of attracting clients. The 75th Anniversary Sale, which started that coming Monday and which had been preceded by a massive mailing, was her brainchild.

Antonio, the security guard, stood by the door wearing a large, covered holster attached to his belt. During the twenty-five years that he had kept watch by the entrance, he had never been forced to use his weapon, which Lucas considered quite fortunate. Measuring barely five feet-six, Antonio was a gentle, soft-spoken, shy man who smiled a lot and diverted his eyes to the floor whenever anyone engaged him in a conversation. Nothing, however, seemed to escape his attention.

Lucas spotted his mother coming out of the small, semicircular office located at the other side of the entrance, opposite to the counter where Evelyn stood. Her face, clouded in deep thought, lit up when she saw him. More than anything else, she had been the main reason why he had returned to *El Joyero,* and even now, many years after his service in the Army, he still felt guilty for the anguish he had caused her by enlisting. She had never reproached him, never seemed anything but proud about his decision to serve, but when he had come back to San Juan, the relief and happiness in her eyes had been engraved in his soul forever.

He had heard her voice about half an hour earlier, while he worked in his shop. There was a hollow, five-inch wide pipe between the two floors. It was part of a system, in disuse for decades, that apparently had used compressed air to move cylindrical tubes with money and invoices from one floor to another. A few years before, Lucas had used it to run some computer wires through it.

However, the empty pipes served as a sound conduit from Fannie's office to Lucas' shop below. Every morning she would sit in her office to sort out the mail and update the inventory. Invariably, she would hum a song in a comically girlish voice, the sound filtering through the open pipe. The song would vary from day to day—usually some old Broadway tune—but every so often a Shakira or Ricky Martin rendition would sneak in. It was one of Lucas' favorite moments in the morning, a spontaneous performance of which Lucas had never spoken, in order not to embarrass her into silence.

She was the smallest of the three Pietri sisters, not taller than 4'10", but she augmented her height with high heels that she wore perennially. Somewhere in her late sixties—she had never revealed her age to anyone—

she still looked beautiful. Like her daughter Michelle, she had emerald colored eyes, and when she smiled, she would crinkle her nose, exuding a contagious joy. She had also inherited her father's wicked sense of humor, which she occasionally used to provoke fights between her two sisters. Lately, she had become hard of hearing, and tended to nod and smile at clients whenever she missed something they had said.

Despite her small size, she was the rock upon which the establishment and its staff rested. All activity in *El Joyero* revolved around her. She dealt with the tough clients, made the difficult decisions, and maintained a steady calm during the days—which seemed to occur more and more often—when the world threatened to collapse around them.

Lucas walked to her and kissed her.

"Good morning, mom. How's the traffic?"

Fannie kissed her son back. "It was still okay when we left our house." She and Maria lived a few blocks away from the bridge that connected Miramar to San Juan. She looked past Lucas at Maria, still engaged in her telephone conversation. "We have to pay the Treasury Department $20,000 to renew our license," she said somberly, nodding in her sister's direction. "I think we'll have the money, but we will be short on cash for the rest of the expenses of *El Joyero*. She's talking to the bank, trying to extend our line of credit."

Lucas looked back at Maria, whom he treated more as an older sister than as an aunt, since she was only eight years his senior, and had been raised in his mother and father's household as another of the children. During the last three years, the fiscal health of *El Joyero* had steadily deteriorated with the rest of the island's economy. As luxury items, jewels were among the first articles to be scratched out from the average household shopping list. The jewelry industry had been hit very hard in San Juan. Of about fifty stores in the old city, eighteen had closed during the past year alone.

Lucas sighed. "If anyone can get the bank to extend our line of credit, it's Maria," he commented. It was true. For some inexplicable reason, Maria had time and again managed to obtain additional financing from the banking entities that serviced *El Joyero*. But there were limits, especially in the present times. "Maybe President Powell will help Governor Pietrantoni to turn things around," he added without really believing it, trying to console his mother.

He could see from Fannie's expression that she had very little faith about what the new president could do for Puerto Rico. Her theory—not an unreasonable one, Lucas thought—was that he would first look after the fifty states, and then think about the territories.

"We need to open our business tomorrow," Evelyn said from the other side of the store, joining their conversation. The tourists had left without purchasing anything. Fannie, blocked from her sister's view by Lucas, closed her eyes in exasperation.

"We *can't* open tomorrow," Maria said from her desk, as she hung up with the bank. "We have to get the store ready for the 75th Anniversary Sale tomorrow. It was *your* idea, remember?" she asked rather sharply, venting her frustration on her sister.

"We can do both!" Evelyn responded defiantly. "We'll just have to work late, that's all."

"We can't do both," Maria replied in an even angrier tone. She was right. They would have to change the display windows, decorate the inside of the store, change hundreds of price tags to show price reductions ranging from thirty-five to sixty percent, and prepare for a small reception, scheduled for Monday night, for the *Joyero's* top clients. But Maria's overly antagonistic tone only served to push Evelyn into a more stubborn position.

"We can—" she began to say, but Fannie gently but firmly cut her short.

"It's not worth it," she stated in a tone that admitted no further discussion. "We'd be here all night and do a poor job, and we need to have a good anniversary sale. Besides, the San Sebastian crowd is not into buying our type of merchandise. We've sold thirty dollars since we opened today. If we get to three hundred, we'll be very lucky. Tomorrow will be even worse. The people who will come to San Juan tomorrow will basically be here to drink beer and have a good time."

"Maybe we should sell beer," Maria suggested sarcastically. Nobody bothered to answer her.

"It's not worth opening," Fannie repeated. Then she turned to Lucas and smiled at him brightly. "But you missed the big show this morning!" she said in a jovial voice, changing the subject without pausing to breathe. Instantly, as if turned off by a light switch, the oppressive mood in the store vanished, and the three sisters began to chat excitedly at the same time, like three young girls. *His mother was good*, thought Lucas with hidden admiration.

"He looked like a...a...Frankenstein!" Evelyn began saying.

"He *was* Frankenstein..." Maria said.

"He was big!" Even Antonio joined in from the entrance.

"He looked like the Hulk!" Evelyn piped in again, laughing.

"What are you talking about?" Lucas asked with a smile.

"The man who was here," Maria explained. "Frankenstein!"

"About half an hour ago. You just missed him!" Evelyn said. It was a typical Pietri conversation, coming at him in bits and pieces from every direction at the same time.

Lucas turned to his mother for guidance. "Frankenstein walked in?"

Fannie grinned. "Maria and I were getting off from Don Moncho's taxicab, in front of the jewelry store..." Don Moncho was the taxi driver who regularly picked up Maria and Fannie at their home, and dropped them off in the evenings. He had become such a good friend with the two sisters, that he would transport them at a lower fare, without turning the meter on. He also often served as Michelle's chauffeur. "And when we walked in, this giant was standing in the middle of the store."

"I was terrified!" Evelyn interjected. She had been the only one behind the counters when the man had made his entrance.

"He was big, Lucas, bigger than you," Maria said.

"I'm not that big."

"You are big," Maria insisted. "You are about what, six feet tall?"

"About five feet nine," Lucas answered. "But I'm handsome," he added with a straight face.

"Five feet nine *is* tall," Maria said stubbornly. "But this man, he was *biiiiig!*" she added, stretching the last word to give it emphasis. "About eight feet tall!"

Everybody laughed except Maria, who glared at the others.

"Holy Blessed Virgin Mary! Some day somebody is going to take you seriously and lock you up with the rest of the lunatics in *Julia!*" Fannie exclaimed, referring to the old clinic for the mentally insane. "He wasn't eight feet tall," she said to Lucas. "But he could have been close to seven."

"How would you know? You're so close to the ground that you can't measure any height adequately," Maria countered with feigned indignation.

Fannie ignored her. "It wasn't so much his height, though. It was...he was...he was..."

"Massive," Maria said, completing her sister's thought.

"Massive," Fannie repeated, nodding. "Big arms, big legs, big shoulders, head like a bowling ball. Big!"

"And he just stood there, in the middle of the store, looking around, not saying anything. Nothing!" Maria stated. "And Evelyn just stood there paralyzed, looking up at him, not saying anything either!"

Lucas tried not to laugh, but could not suppress a smile. Evelyn was a few inches taller than Fannie, but ballerina-thin. He could imagine her staring at the hulking man, like a doe on a road watching an approaching truck.

"I was terrified," Evelyn explained, for the second time.

"Then Maria touched him on the shoulder from behind..."

"You did?"

"I almost couldn't reach him, Lucas!"

"And asked him if there was anything we could do for him, and he turned and just stared at Maria, without saying a word," Fannie said.

"Without saying a word," Maria repeated.

"And you should have seen Maria. You know how her eyes get when she gets nervous." Everybody laughed again. It was a running joke in the family that whenever Maria got nervous, her pupils would twitch uncontrollably.

"You should not mock people with physical disabilities," Maria said in a mortified tone, but could not stop herself from smiling. "At least I talked to the man," she added, directing a withering look in Evelyn's direction.

"And what happened finally? Did he say anything?" Lucas asked.

"Nothing!" his mother replied. "He said nothing! He just looked at Maria for a moment, and left! I was so relieved to see him go, let me tell you!"

"He walked into the entrance to the offices, next door," Antonio volunteered.

"Did he really?" Fannie asked. This was new information to the sisters.

"Yes," Antonio answered, looking very self-conscious because he had become the new focus of attention. "I followed him, to see what he was doing. He looked around in the lobby, just as he did here, and then took the elevator."

A meditative silence followed. Antonio's revelation had dampened the merry mood.

"That's weird," Lucas said.

"What do you make of it?" Fannie asked.

"That was a terrorist," Evelyn stated in a suspicious voice, prompting a groan from Maria.

"Yes," the latter said, raising her eyebrows. "Al Qaeda has decided to wipe out *El Joyero* because it wants to corner the pearl necklace business in Old San Juan."

"Don't be silly!" Evelyn responded indignantly. "The man could have been looking for a way up to the roof of the Metropolitan Center to place a sniper and...and...kill the Governor, or the Mayor, or something like that!"

"Well, whatever he is, I'm glad he's gone." Fannie shuddered involuntarily. "He was really creepy."

"Shouldn't we alert the police?" Evelyn suggested.

"And tell them what? That a tall man walked into the lobby of the commercial offices of the Metropolitan Center? I don't think so," Maria answered.

"Talking about the Governor," Lucas said, trying to avoid a new argument between the two sisters, "do you know that Alfredo is sleeping in La Fortaleza tonight?"

"Alfredo?...What Alfredo?" Evelyn asked, genuinely puzzled.

"How many Alfredos do you know?" Maria said. "Vanessa's Alfredo!"

"Vanessa's Alfredo?" Somehow, Evelyn could not associate her grand-nephew with the Governor's mansion.

"Vanessa just told me," Fannie confirmed. "He's spending the night with Francisco, the Governor's son."

At last, Evelyn comprehended what the conversation was about. "If I was Vanessa, I wouldn't let him hang out with the Governor too much. God knows what strange ideas that man may put into his head," she said, more seriously than joking.

Lucas retreated to his repair shop a few moments later, sorry about the new argument he had unwittingly provoked. It had been inevitable, anyhow. People joked that there were three sports in Puerto Rico: baseball, basketball and politics. And they were right. In any given election, nearly eighty percent of all eligible voters would cast their votes, an unheard of percentage in any democracy where voting was not compulsory. Election campaigns were long and passionate, drawing hundreds of thousands of flag-waving supporters to rallies, marches, and caravans, and generating multiple television debates, commercials, newspaper advertisements, flyer postings, jarring-loudspeaker-jingles, mud-slingings, and even a few fistfights before the votes were counted.

The phenomenon was caused by Puerto Rico's unique status. Since 1952, the island had become a Commonwealth associated to the United States. As such, all Puerto Ricans were American citizens, entitled to travel freely anywhere in the United States without the use of passports, subject to the military draft when it was enforced, bound to the jurisdiction of the federal courts like any state, and qualified to receive limited federal aid for such things as the construction of roads, food coupons, and educational and health programs. Like any of the Union's fifty states, Puerto Rico had its own constitution and system of local courts, a legislative body composed of a Senate and a Chamber of Representatives, and an executive branch led by a governor. Unlike the rest of the American citizens, Puerto Ricans paid no federal taxes—except for Medicare and Social Security—had no votes in Congress, and could not vote for the President of the United States. It was the principle of "No taxation without representation" applied backwards: "No representation without taxation."

The island's exclusive political situation had given rise to three basic parties: the Puerto Rican Pro-Independence Party ("*Partido Independentista Puertorriqueño*" or "*PIP*"), which advocated for Puerto Rico's full-fledged sovereignty as an independent nation, and which had consistently lost ground in every election; the Popular Democratic Party ("*Partido Popular Democratico*" or "*PPD*"), which supported the present status of Commonwealth with enhanced powers; and the New Progressive Party (*"Partido Nuevo Progresista"* or *"PNP"*), which wanted to turn Puerto Rico into America's 51st state, with all of the rights, obligations, and privileges that it entailed.

During the last three decades, the governorship had been won either by the Commonwealth or Statehood parties, much as the presidency of the Unites States had oscillated between the Republican and Democratic parties. But in the last election, an overwhelming majority had elected Roberto Pietrantoni, the pro-statehood candidate. Governor Pietrantoni had promised as part of his platform to hold a referendum, or "plebiscite", to determine if a majority of the people would be in favor of petitioning Congress to make Puerto Rico a state. Recent polls had indicated that for the first time in the island's history, a substantial majority of its four million inhabitants favored becoming a permanent part of the Union. But polls had been wrong before.

The three Pietri sisters, like many other families in Puerto Rico, were as divided in their opinions as most people in their country. Evelyn was a fierce *commonwealther*, Fannie tended to sympathize more with the pro-independence faction, while Maria leaned in the opposite direction. Thus, Evelyn's comment about Alfredo's stay in La Fortaleza had added new fuel to the ongoing debate on status.

Lucas sighed. He tended to avoid political discussions. When he was young and had joined the Army, he had been a firm believer in statehood. He admired the principles upon which the American Republic had been founded, its flawed but constant search for justice and human dignity, its dynamic and inventive drive, and its varied, multifaceted culture. He had formed an unbreakable bond with the men who had trained with him in the fields and mountains of Georgia, and fought next to him in Mogadishu. But in the end, he had concluded that he was first and foremost a Puerto Rican—who thought that his country should be permanently associated to the United States, who fought and would fight again to defend the American ideals, and who infinitely valued his American citizenship—but a Puerto Rican, nevertheless. And so, he had become a Commonwealth supporter, even if a reluctant one.

As he sat down to work, his mind wandered again to the Frankenstein incident. *It was odd*, he agreed. But then again, odd was a normal for *El Joyero*. Just two months before, an old homeless woman had walked into the store and accused his mother of being a "bleached nigger" with "uppity white airs". Just before that, the store's cash entries for the day had mysteriously disappeared, only to reappear intact in the corner supermarket. Both Evelyn and Maria had been there before to buy food, so no accusations were made by either against the other, and Fannie opted to say nothing.

Lucas slipped on his soldering mask and resumed work. Frankenstein had probably been some lost tourist who did not understand Spanish and had been scared away by the shocked faces of the Pietri sisters. God knew they were capable of that, and much more.

El Joyero had sold a grand total of $282 by 5:30 PM—even less than what Fannie had predicted—and nobody had stepped into the store in the last hour. Even Evelyn agreed that staying open any longer would be a waste of time. Sunday would be spent getting ready for the 75th Anniversary Sale. It would be a very busy day, even with the jewelry store's doors closed. Everyone would try to get there by 7:00 in the morning, including Antonio the guard, and work as long as it took to get the sale ready.

Lucas locked his shop and walked up the cellar's circular stairs to the main floor. The Pietri sisters were still busy storing away the trays of merchandise displayed during the day in the glass counters.

"Your sister called," Fannie informed Lucas as he approached her.

"Which one?" he asked, knowing full well she was referring to Vanessa.

"The one whose son hobnobs with the Governor."

Lucas smiled. "Did *she* hobnob with the Governor?"

"Apparently not. She said that the First Nanny and Francisco—"

"The '*First Nanny*'?" Lucas raised an eyebrow. "As in 'First Lady'?"

The Governor had been a widower for four years, after losing his wife in a car accident. Inevitably, rumors about an affair between his son's governess—a very attractive woman—and him had surfaced during the electoral campaign, and followed him to La Fortaleza after he had been elected.

"Those were her words," Fannie confirmed. "She said the First Nanny was very nice, and that Nereida—the nanny's first name—had told her that Francisco considered Alfredo to be his best friend."

"Oh God, no!" Lucas moaned in jest. "From now on, we're going to be dealing with the mother of the best friend of the Governor's son. May the Virgin and all the saints protect us!"

"Your sister said," Fannie stated with a straight face, as if she was referring to *his sister* and not to *her daughter*, "that she will give you a detailed account as soon as you get home."

Lucas shook his head in despair. By purely coincidental reasons, Vanessa lived in the house next to his in Park Side.

"She asked if you could pick up Alfredo tomorrow in Fortaleza around three o'clock in the afternoon, since she is giving tutoring lessons at that time."

He nodded. It would be a nice break from the work in the jewelry store.

"We should be leaving soon, before the San Sebastian traffic gets worse," he told his mother, looking at his watch. He drove them home at night.

"*You* should be leaving now, before traffic gets worse," Fannie responded. Then, answering Lucas' questioning look, she added, "We're staying overnight in Michelle's apartment here in San Juan." Michelle lived in one of the new condominiums built in the renovated area close to the docks.

"Oh? How come?"

"Since we have to be here so early tomorrow, we thought we'd be able to sleep longer if we stayed in San Juan." Fannie explained. Sleep was a sacred commodity for the Pietri sisters, especially Fannie. "Besides," she added with an impish grin, "we're going to the Fiestas de San Sebastian."

"Your mother and Evelyn are hoping to pick a couple of hot dates in Calle San Sebastian," Maria interjected from the back of the store, as she shuffled several trays into the safe.

"How about you?" Lucas asked Maria.

"She's hoping to meet Frankenstein," Evelyn replied before her sister could answer.

"Leave," Fannie urged him. "Before traffic traps you here."

Lucas kissed his mother and his two aunts, who by that time were engaged in another discussion about that morning's visitor.

"Tomorrow at seven?" he asked his mother from the door, knowing that she would probably not make it until eight.

"Seven...ish," she replied with a smile. "Unless I find a rich date."

Night had spread its gentle mantle over the city by the time that Lucas stepped out of the jewelry store. A soft breeze stirred through the trees in the Plaza de Armas, as the first sprinkle of shiny planets and stars ventured into the twilit sky. Sounds dominated this part of the day, not because of their intensity, but because they stood out distinctly in the stillness that otherwise cloaked the streets.

In the distance, the big bronze bells of the cathedral where Ponce De Leon rested, resonated in their deep, baritone voices, announcing the impending celebration of the evening mass. They were almost instantly joined by the peal of the smaller bells from City Hall, which announced that at 6:30 PM, the day had run its course. A block away, the whirring mechanical sound of a garbage truck crushing a load of cans, boxes, and other discharged waste, mixed with the shouts of the garbage men, as they signaled the truck driver to move on.

Groups of mostly young people were already trudging their way up-hill towards San Sebastian Street, some of them dispersing into the various restaurants and bars scattered along the way, hoping to grab a bite or a drink before the real celebrations began. They were mostly quiet, as if affected by the sober mood of the failing day, or maybe saving their energy for the later festivities. The principal roads—San Francisco and Fortaleza streets—had already been closed to vehicular traffic, and teams of state or municipal police were beginning to move to their designated places and patrol the city.

Lucas walked down Fortaleza Street engrossed in his own thoughts, barely paying attention to his surroundings, in what his wife Jeannie called his "automatic pilot mode". He felt uneasy about the financial health of *El Joyero*. The business was going through rough times, weighed down by a drastic reduction in its steady income and a large number of growing debts.

That morning's exchange between Maria and the bank had been just the latest in a series of incidents caused by the recession on the jewelry business. Lately, sales barely provided enough to cover the salaries of the regular employees, and the Pietri sisters had taken a voluntary salary cut in order to pay their suppliers on time. The store's line of credit was stretched to its limit, and a large portion of the business's revenue was being swallowed up by mounting interest payments. *El Joyero* was still a viable business enterprise, but just barely. Lucas wondered if it would weather the economic storm. One thing was for sure, though. If the store survived the present recession, it would survive anything.

The worst part of it all was that he could not find a solution to the problem. He felt less concerned about his own personal situation. His skills were still in high demand. If worse came to worse, he could open his own shop elsewhere. But his mother and his aunts had dedicated a large part of their lives to the continued existence and progress of *El Joyero de San Juan*. To lose it at this stage of their lives would constitute a devastating blow from which they would never recover. It would break their hearts.

Lucas took a deep breath. *It could always be worse.* Mogadishu had taught him that.

He reached the Doña Fela parking station in less than five minutes. A line of eight to ten cars waited to get in. Soon, the situation inside would turn chaotic, as more and more cars crammed into the building, and others attempted to get out. He had to hurry.

His cell phone started buzzing in his pocket, and he flicked it open.

"Hi honey," Jennie said over the voices of her two children, who were half-speaking, half-shouting in the background.

"Hi Jeannie, how was your day?" he answered as he reached his car.

"Oh, the usual. You know that trick that we used with Gabriel when he drank too much chocolate milk? How we would tell him there was no more chocolate milk, and that we had to buy some more in the supermarket?"

"Yes," Lucas replied, as he observed a white pickup truck park in a spot assigned to monthly customers, without having a monthly parking sticker on its windshield.

"It doesn't work any more," Jennie stated, partly frustrated, partly amused. *"When I told him we had to buy more milk, he said, "Store! Go! Now!"*

Lucas laughed.

Three men stepped out of the pickup truck, and opened its rear hatch. They were all dressed in black jeans and shirts, and wore their hair very short, in the military fashion. *Probably some band performing in San Sebastian*, Lucas thought. As if to confirm his impression, the men began to unload several green canvas bags from the back of the truck that, from their size, could only contain musical instruments or electronic equipment.

"Will you be here soon?" Jeannie asked.

"I'm on my way," he answered, staring at the men without realizing it, so much so that the driver noticed him, and after a look of what seemed to Lucas surprised concern, managed to smile at him. The man, almost completely bald, must have been in his late forties, but looked very fit for his age, with the muscled frame of a welterweight boxer. His flat, broken nose seemed to confirm to Lucas his initial impression. "Hold on a second, Jeannie," he said to his wife, and addressed the driver, pointing at a sign that read: "FOR MONTHLY USERS ONLY". "That parking lot is reserved for monthly tenants," he said to the man. "You're going to get a ticket if you leave it there."

"Oh!" The boxer suddenly looked very relieved. Another of the men in the truck had started to walk towards his companion, but the driver waved him away with a slight motion of his hand. "I apologize," he said contritely, in a slightly foreign accent. "I didn't notice the sign. I'll move the truck right away. Thank you!" Again the man smiled, and waved at him.

Lucas nodded, watching the men for a few more seconds. Then he remembered his wife, and put his cell phone back on his ear.

"Are you still there?" he heard Jeannie ask impatiently.

"Sorry. I was talking to some people in the parking area." Lucas climbed into his PT Cruiser and watched through his rear view mirror as the nearly bald driver finished talking to his three companions and reboarded the truck.

"Anyone that I know?" Jeannie asked.

"No, just some people who are going to the San Sebastian festival and parked in the wrong place."

The truck backed out of its space, and quickly headed up the ramp to the building's second floor. The other men grabbed the bags they had unloaded, and began walking towards the parking area's exit. One of them turned his head and cast Lucas a particularly unfriendly look.

"Don't be getting into any arguments," Jeannie warned him, as if she had witnessed what had just happened.

"I never get into arguments," he stated flatly, and with a few notable exceptions, it was true. Another by-product of his Army days, he supposed. In the Rangers, his instructors had taught him to keep his cool in difficult situations, to assess the unfolding events as unemotionally and rationally as possible, and to act accordingly. Because of that, he had survived Mogadishu and many other potentially dangerous situations.

"Good," Jeannie said to him, *"because you remember what we discussed this morning?"*

Lucas paused momentarily. "About not running away with the gardener?"

"The other," Jeannie answered patiently. *"I'm wearing my London Fog raincoat...and nothing else."*

"I'll be there shortly," Lucas stated in his most manly voice.

CHAPTER V

Johnny Ray yawned and stretched his arms. His neck and back hurt because of the stress. After meeting with San Miguel on Friday night, he had dropped off Yajaira at her student dormitory, and headed straightaway to his home. He had taken a shower and gone to bed, but sleep had eluded him completely. By five in the morning, he had given up. He had driven to the FEPI headquarters in Rio Piedras, a squat, concrete-walled structure with aluminum Miami windows that were always closed. A large Puerto Rican flag and a giant closed fist had been stenciled on the wall near its only door. It was located close to the southern boundary of the Rio Piedras campus of the University of Puerto Rico.

He had not expected to run into anyone at that wicked hour of the night, but to his surprise, had found the door unlocked, and Lebron sitting at his desk. He still wore the battered *guayabera* he had worn at the meeting earlier that night.

Lebron had acknowledged Johnny's arrival by looking up and grunting something curt and unintelligible. Then, before Johnny could return the greeting, he had returned his gaze to the large batch of papers spread in front of him.

The two men had never really liked each other. Johnny regarded Lebron as an armchair bureaucrat who mostly mouthed socialist clichés, but never proposed any practical solutions to the serious challenges that his organization faced on a daily basis. Lebron thought of Johnny as shallow, opportunistic, and self-centered, not really interested in promoting any cause except his own.

For the next half hour they had maintained an awkward silence, pretending to be busy even though both felt a desperate urge to talk. Only Lebron's heavy breathing, a trait that normally drove Johnny to irritated distraction, had disturbed the stillness of the room. That night, however, the noise had made Johnny keenly aware of his companion's restlessness, and provoked in him a curious sense of relief.

"You don't have to come," Johnny finally said, breaking the silence.

"What?" Lebron looked at him with the confused silence of someone who had just been shaken awake.

"To San Juan..." Johnny explained. "You don't have to come." He slid his chair closer to the Secretary-General, pushing it with his legs. "Some of us will have to be around, after this is over, if—you know—if it ends badly," he whispered. Even though the room had been swept for electronic hearing devices, he did not trust the walls around him.

Lebron had blinked several times, absorbing Johnny's offer. For a moment his brow creased, as the suspicion that Johnny was attempting to hog all of the glory fleetingly crossed his mind. But just as quickly, his expression softened as he realized that the FEPI president was actually offering him a way out.

"You don't think we will come through this?" he asked in a breathless hiss.

"The thought has crossed my mind," Johnny confessed after a hesitant pause, but then added hurriedly, "Although I stand by what I said in the meeting tonight about what we have to gain."

Lebron nodded slowly. "Thank you," he said. "I really appreciate it."

"So you'll stay?" Johnny insisted.

"Of course not! That is out of the question!" Lebron had answered matter-of-factly, and then sighed resignedly. "Look, you know I don't like Yajaira," he admitted, staring directly at Johnny. "But I agree with what she said a couple of days ago, when you asked *her* to stay behind. What kind of a leader will the FEPI consider me to be if I don't risk my life with the rest of the people?"

Johnny waived his hand urgently, signaling Lebron to lower his voice.

"But thanks anyway," Lebron hissed.

They both smiled and shook hands, content with their newly found peace.

"So by what time are we supposed to be in San Juan?" Johnny asked, knowing fully well the answer to his question.

"At eleven in the morning, sharp, in the Calle San Sebastian house," Lebron answered, reassuming his official Secretary-General demeanor.

"I'll be there earlier," Johnny promised, and left.

He went to Old San Juan, and rambled through its dimly lit, abandoned streets until sunrise. Close to seven in the morning, he wandered into La Bombonera and sat in one of its booths, ordering a full breakfast. He ate it slowly, watching the locals filter in, half-listening to their conversations, enjoying the fact that none of them but he had the slightest inkling of what was about to happen in their city in less than twenty-four hours.

Sometime between seven and eight in the morning, he had noticed Michelle Alfaro—the cute newscaster from WKPA—walk into the restaurant and flirt with a man sitting at the counter. He instantly compared her to Yajaira, as he inevitably did every time he spotted an attractive woman. He thought Michelle might be a shade more beautiful than Yajaira, more feminine looking, perhaps, but Yajaira was by far the more sensuous and well endowed of the two.

He arrived at the San Sebastian house by 8:30 AM. He had hoped to catch San Miguel before he left, but the somber, Arab-looking man who had opened the old, iron-studded door, informed him with a sad shake of his head that his boss, as well as his companions, had departed in the wee hours of the morning and would not be back. He led Johnny to the same dining room with the large paintings and the overhead fresco where they had secretly gathered the night before. Several boxes and crates had been brought there sometime between the moment that the meeting had ended and now, and Emmanuel—as the Arab man called himself—showed him what they contained.

Some of the objects Johnny had seen before. They included three big boxes of satellite cell phones that would be handed out to the FEPI, as well as to most of the others involved in the operation. Another two boxes contained dozens of bullhorns that would be distributed to the FEPI groups patrolling the streets, and that the FEPI would use to impart instructions to the local population.

One large cardboard box was filled with armbands. Since the small army about to liberate San Juan would wear no uniforms, and since many of the rebels did not know each other, the conspirators had decided to use armbands for identification purposes. Johnny and Yajaira—mostly Yajaira—had personally designed them, months before. They were black, showing the Puerto Rican flag, with the phrase "Libre Como el Coqui" ("Free Like the Coqui") imprinted in bold green letters below it. The coqui was a tiny tree frog with lungs of steel, indigenous to Puerto Rico, which boomed at night with a thunderous soprano voice, producing a sound similar to its name, and which had become a beloved symbol of the island. It had been Yajaira's idea to include a reference to the miniscule frog on the armband, as an additional means of gaining the sympathy and support of those who saw it.

Most of the boxes in the dining room—about ten of them—were rectangular wooden crates. Each was stuffed with straw used to protect about a dozen smaller bags made of sturdy cloth. Emmanuel opened one of the bags and pulled out a handgun, three ammunition clips, and a box of ammunition, laying them on the dining room table.

"This is a Glock 19," Emmanuel said, picking up the gun with a gentleness that almost seemed affectionate. "It is a semi-automatic pistol that uses 9 millimeter ammunition." The Arab man tapped with his left index finger the ammunition box. "The Glock is a compact model. Easy to conceal, very light, very reliable." In one smooth movement, he slipped an ammunition clip into its grooved handle, and with a "click-clacking" noise, pulled the gun's slide back, and let it fall back into place. "The pistol holds up to seventeen rounds, sixteen in the clip and one in its chamber. It now has a round in its chamber." He held up the Glock by its barrel, and showed Johnny the right side of the gun. "You see this tiny lever next to the trigger? That's the trigger safety. As long as that lever is in its forward position, the safety is engaged and the gun won't discharge accidentally. Very important point to remember. To fire, you push the lever back, and you're ready to go."

Emmanuel stared at Johnny for a few seconds, pursing his lips into either a thin smile or an expression of doubt. Turning the grip towards the Puerto Rican visitor, he handed the pistol to him. Johnny accepted it reluctantly.

"This one is yours," the Arab man said. "You get these two clips and the one inside it. Use it wisely."

"Hopefully, I won't have to use it at all," Johnny responded, hefting the gun in his hand. He shot a quick glance at Emmanuel, to see how he reacted to his last statement, but could not make anything out of his blank expression.

"I understand that Daniel trained you and some of your men with these guns," the Arab continued saying, more as a statement than a question.

"Yes, we trained for a couple of days, a few months ago, in a farm in Jayuya." Jayuya was a town in the mountains of Puerto Rico. "We mostly fired at tin—"

"Good," Emmanuel weighed in pleasantly, letting Johnny know he had no concern in knowing how the FEPIstas had acquired their limited expertise in firearms. "There are ninety-nine more of these guns here. I will distribute them as you so indicate."

"I will let you know who gets them," Johnny replied, somewhat flustered. "My men will be divided into groups of three. The leader of each group will carry a gun...unless they don't know how to use one, of course."

Emmanuel nodded wordlessly, showing very little interest in the details that Johnny Ray was giving him.

"There is also the matter of the AK-47 assault rifles," the Arab added almost as an afterthought. "We have ten of them left, after we distributed the balance to the Macheteros. Each has ten clips of ammunition. San Miguel instructed me to offer them to you."

"Daniel told me that—" Johnny began to say, but saw Emmanuel's bored expression, and just stated, "Four of my men know how to use them."

Emmanuel's lips pursed into another cryptic smile. "Only four? Very well. The rifles are to be carried out of this house in those bags." He pointed at ten green canvas duffel bags, lying neatly in a row. "The rifles and the ammunition are hidden in the clothes that the bags carry. I will be glad to review with your men how the rifles are used."

"Thank you."

Emmanuel inquired politely if Johnny needed anything else, and upon the latter's negative response, left the room, assuring his guest that he would be within the range of his voice. Alone, Johnny sat at the head of the long dining table, and unsure about what to do next, glimpsed around the room. One of the larger paintings drew his attention. It depicted the bombardment of El Morro Castle by three American battleships during the Spanish-American War. The squadron was headed by the USS Detroit, its cannons spewing fire in unison, clouds of white-gray smoke marking the spots where prior shells had landed. It must have been a spectacular sight, Johnny thought, and wondered if in the future somebody would bother to paint the events in which he was about to participate.

He must have fallen asleep, because it was suddenly ten after ten in the morning, and a very flustered Lebron, fatigued from his long uphill walk from the parking area at the docks, had just burst into the room. Yajaira had joined them later, at about eleven thirty, subjecting her two companions to a barrage of breathless chatter, fussing over the armbands she had designed, and munching on the cold cuts, fruits, and cheeses that Emmanuel had carted into the room a few minutes earlier.

The FEPI recruits began to trickle in by noon. They had been received by Yajaira or Emmanuel, and made to wait in the foyer beyond the main entrance. The groups had been pre-designated a week before, their particular assignments carefully considered. However, to Johnny Ray's dismay, it soon became apparent that not all of the volunteers would show up. Therefore, the FEPI leaders had been forced to consolidate some of the patrols and expand their areas of coverage. By mid-afternoon, with only the last three groups scheduled to be briefed, the total volunteer count had been reduced from one hundred and fifty to one hundred and thirty-two.

Johnny yawned and stretched his arms. The ache to his neck and back had returned, caused by the stress and the hours he had been mostly sitting down. He checked his watch and saw it was four o'clock. It had been a long day.

The dining room door opened and Yajaira popped her head from behind it.

"Ready for the next group?" she asked.

"How many groups are left?"

"Three."

"They are all complete?"

"Yes."

"Bring them all in," he suggested to Lebron, who merely nodded.

He waited, reviewing in his mind the short speech he had already delivered to all of the other volunteers. Having said it close to thirty times, he already knew it by heart.

Nine university students, seven men and two women, slowly filed into the room. Just for the heck of it, Johnny tried to find some common trait, any physical characteristic, that somehow bound them together. But except for their common ideology, he found them as diverse as snowflakes. Three stood much taller than the others, while two—a man and a woman—were very short. Johnny only recognized one of the tall ones that he knew as "Victor", a thin teenager with very long extremities and a bushy head of blond hair that he partially covered with a beret. The two other tall men didn't look anything like him, one seeming—by his heavy muscles—to be a weightlifter, the other slouching and emaciated, and sporting a sparsely haired goatee.

Three of the seven were white, two of them black, and the rest somewhere in between. All nine volunteers used jeans, as the FEPI leadership had required, but there all similarities ended. Some wore expensive-design models, while others favored ripped or more utilitarian versions. One of the women had chosen a set of bright red dungarees.

T-shirts were the order of the day: one of the ever-present face of Che Guevara; two of Albizu Campos, the local revolutionary hero who in the 1950's had fostered an unsuccessful revolt in San Juan, and sent some of his followers to open fire in the House of Representatives in Washington; one of the recently killed Machetero leader, Filiberto Ojeda; two with Taino Indian motifs, the Tainos being the original natives of Puerto Rico at the time that Columbus discovered the island, who were later massacred by the Spaniards. Two wore short-sleeved shirts, and another a Ralph Lauren polo.

Of the two women, one was a natural blonde with beautiful blue eyes and the figure of a thirteen year old boy, the other a tanned brunette with a plain face and a sensational pair of legs. Some were smiling, some were serious.

All looked scared.

"Who are the cell leaders?" Lebron asked without any introduction, looking up from a list he kept in a legal-sized paper pad. He preferred to refer to the groups that would be patrolling the streets as "cells".

The tall, slouching man with the goatee, the plain-looking girl, and a curly-haired youth wearing the Che Guevara T-shirt raised their hands. Lebron handed to each of them a red cell phone.

"These are your special cell phones," he said to them, ignoring the rest. "The rest of you will use the blue satellite phones that Yajaira is distributing now." Lebron waited for his female associate to finish dealing out the cell phones. "You all know how they work, we've been through this drill before. The blue phones can only call the red satellite phones of your cell leaders. There is an additional emergency number, in case you can't reach your cell leader. It is dialed automatically when you hit 'talk', and then the asterisk sign. It will reach an emergency operator who will determine if your information has any value, and if so, pass it on to the appropriate person." In reality, the "emergency operator" would be Johnny, but the FEPI leadership had decided not to reveal his identity, in order to avoid the risk that any of the volunteers would address him by name over the cell phone. "You should dial that emergency number only as a last resort. I repeat, you will only use that number as a last recourse. Is that understood?"

They all nodded, a few voicing their agreement as well.

"As for the cell leaders, your red phones will be able to call back the people in your group. If you need to call us, you will dial # and 1 first, which will automatically connect you to our president." Everybody turned their eyes to Johnny, who was staring vacantly at the table. "If he is not available, you will dial # and 2, which will get me. And if I don't answer, dial # and 3, and Yajaira will take care of you."

Several in the group stared at Lebron with surprise, knowing that if strict protocol had been followed, the #2 call should have been assigned to Yajaira as FEPI vice-president and second-in-command. Some, aware of the active dislike between Lebron and Yajaira, wondered how Lebron had managed to convince Johnny to change the order of the calls.

In fact, it had been the other way around. Johnny had originally intended to exclude Yajaira entirely from the San Juan operation, arguing—as he had with Lebron that morning—that part of the FEPI high command had to remain intact in case the rebellion collapsed. In reality, the only motive behind his decision had been to keep Yajaira safe. When she had prematurely found out about it, she had been outraged, subjecting Johnny to a barrage of insults, and threatening to put into a deep frost their personal relationship. The FEPI president had relented, but since Lebron had already programmed his name into the cell phones as the #2 call option, Yajaira had been forced to settle for #3.

"Did any of you receive any training in the use of handguns?" Lebron asked next. Again, the boy with the goatee and his Che Guevara T-shirted colleague raised their hands. They were joined by the tall weight-lifter and the man wearing the Ralph Lauren polo.

"I did not go to the training," the polo-shirted man acknowledged, "but I am familiar with the use of handguns, so if you need people to carry guns..."

Lebron glanced briefly at Johnny, who nodded.

"After we finish this talk, you four will meet with Emmanuel," Lebron pointed at the Arab man. "He's the one standing by the door. Emmanuel will give you your weapons and ammunition. Any questions?"

The nine FEPIstas maintained an uneasy silence.

"Good. Then I leave you with a final word from our president."

Johnny stood up and looked at the students standing before him. He said something unintelligible, stopped, and cleared his throat.

"Forgive me," he said in a louder voice. "I've been talking all day long to your comrades, and my throat is starting to hurt, so I'll be brief. I want to thank each and every one of you for being here today, and let you know how proud we all are of you. For security reasons, we have been very vague about the details of what we intend to do in the coming days. All that you have been told is that tomorrow we will blockade San Juan and establish our own government. I can now add that in the process, we will arrest the Governor and his staff, dissolve his puppet government, and declare ourselves a free nation. I don't have to tell you about the difficulties that we will be facing during the next few days. You are all very smart people. We are starting a revolution. The Americans will not take our actions sitting down. They will come hard after us. We cannot expect them to give up this profitable colony so easily. Now we have the opportunity to stop them."

Johnny waited, moving his eyes from one face to another, letting them absorb the import of his words. Then he smiled.

"We will not be alone. The Macheteros have joined our cause."

Just as Johnny had expected and already seen in previous groups, the mention of the Macheteros produced a collective gasp and scattered, enthusiastic applause.

"We also have the help of other professional fighters," he added cryptically over the noise. With the corner of his eye, he noticed that Yajaira was beaming at him. It excited him. She was wearing a set of tight, faded jeans that highlighted the curves of her body, and made her the main focus of every male eye in the room. *Maybe*, he thought, *we may have some together time, before this thing starts.*

"Your role in this operation is not to fight, but to be the eyes of our fighters," he informed his tiny audience. "You will be patrolling your assigned zones, and letting us know about any suspicious activities that you spot, especially anything coming from the sea."

"Or the air," Lebron prompted.

"Or the air," Johnny repeated.

"What about our guns?" the thin goateed man asked. "When do we use them?"

"We don't use them," Johnny Ray responded in a tone that admitted no contradiction. "Let me emphasize this. Under no circumstances, I repeat, no circumstances whatsoever are you to use any of your weapons, unless your life or the life of anyone in your group is imminently threatened. Understood?" Again, Johnny looked at the faces surrounding him for emphasis. No one challenged him. "Besides being the lookouts for the revolution," he continued, "you will be the people keeping order in the city. In that sense, the guns you carry will be the symbol of your authority. Before you leave, each group will be handed a bullhorn, which you will use to disperse any crowds gathering in the streets, particularly during the next two or three days, while we secure the city. You will tell the people to return to their homes for their own safety, until further notice."

"And if they refuse to obey?" the tanned girl with the nice legs asked.

"Talk to them firmly, let them know it's for their own good," Johnny responded. The girl began to speak again, but he stilled her with a gentle gesture of his hand. "Look, the chances that somebody will challenge you are very slim. When they see you, when you address them with the bullhorns, when they see your guns, believe me, they will leave. If there is still some asshole out there that refuses to obey, then arrest him. We are setting a provisional detention center at the Tapia Theater for any uncooperative citizens we encounter, but I don't expect any significant number of detainees to be there. In fact, I expect none."

The group silently considered Johnny's instructions.

"Always remember this: we are not here to fight with the local residents. We want to win them to our side. Be firm but gentle. Treat them with respect. If they have an emergency, try to help them. *We* are the face of the revolution. If we antagonize our own people, we will fail. It's as simple as that." Johnny looked at Lebron, who nodded. "Anything else?"

"The armbands," Yajaira reminded him.

Johnny smiled. "I haven't forgotten," he told her. "Yajaira will now give you the armbands that will identify you as members of our army of liberation."

"The Johnny Ray Forces of Liberation," Yajaira suggested for the umpteenth time, and several in the room clapped.

"Nothing of the sort," Johnny corrected her, in a humble, half-hearted fashion. In truth, he would not have minded the designation, but he knew that many Puerto Ricans did not know who he was, and that the liberation movement could not be perceived as somebody's ego trip. In any event, Puerto Rico and the rest of the world would soon find out who he was.

He signaled Yajaira with an imperceptible nod to start distributing the armbands, and was pleased to see his comrades' positive reaction. "These are the badges that will identify you as part of our forces. Don't lose them. Wear them with honor."

"But *don't* wear them yet!" Lebron urged everyone, his words partially lost in the exhilarated chatter of the volunteers.

"Listen up! Listen up, please!" Johnny shouted over the voices of the others, gently rapping the dining table with his knuckles. "Lebron is making a very important point. Listen to him."

"Thank you," Lebron acknowledged with a whisper to Johnny. Then he raised his voice. "What I was trying to say is that the success of our operation depends on its exact timing. We cannot do anything that attracts the attention of the authorities until we successfully block the island of San Juan, and your cell leaders receive a confirmation that you can start your patrols. Otherwise, if the authorities find out prematurely what is happening, they will have the opportunity to send in reinforcements. So no wearing of armbands, no showing of guns, no talking of anything remotely connected to this."

"No drinking!" Yajaira added, provoking several nervous snickers.

"This is no joking matter, comrades," Lebron slapped his stubby hand hard on the table. Johnny noticed that the Secretary-General was regressing to his socialistic jargon, as he did when he got nervous. "Yajaira is right. This is *not* a game! This is a war of liberation! So you will refrain from pursuing any activity that in any way or fashion compromises our operation. You will exhibit model behavior until you are dead certain that the operation has begun! Is that clear?"

Lebron's testy rebuke made the recruits flinch, and instantly quieted them down.

"We expect San Juan to be effectively blocked by five, at the most by six tomorrow morning," Lebron continued in an angry tone, "but to be certain, we will let the cell leaders know, as we said before. And until that happens, you do nothing but wait."

Johnny cast an amused glance at the young volunteers, as if taking them into his confidence. "They all know how important this is, Felipe," he said, addressing Lebron by his first name, trying to lighten the mood suddenly grown somber. "Although...It's not possible to exaggerate how crucial these days will be. At stake is the survival of Puerto Rico as a nation. It is up to us to stop the downward slide that our country is taking into the bowels of the American beast." He raised one of the armbands, showing its emblem "*This* is what we fight for! The star of our flag is too big to fit in the American flag. We *will* be free. Free like the coqui. That will be our motto, and that's what we'll call ourselves. The Coqui Freedom Fighters!"

Lebron raised his left fist into the air.

"To the Coqui Freedom Fighters!"

"To the Coqui Freedom Fighters!" the others shouted enthusiastically, following suit.

Johnny eyed Yajaira, and saw her lips curve into a private smile, just for him. *Perhaps,* he thought, *there might just be enough time...*

CHAPTER VI

The small pontoon boat glided over the dark, glassy water, its twin hulls creating long, smooth ripples that undulated away from it like silent, lazy snakes. Its two brand new outboard motors put-putted placidly at a fraction of their strength, moving the vessel steadily at a speed of four knots.

Daniel leaned against the forward railing of the boat, taking in the gray landscape of the San Antonio Channel that slowly floated past him. He was so close to the water that if he bent over the railing he could touch it. A soft, pleasant breeze ruffled his hair, while the waning rays of the setting sun, sinking in the horizon behind him, stretched and enlarged his shadow and that of his ship more than twenty feet beyond, over the wet, still surface.

Two other boats, identical in size and shape, followed him along the channel, moving as peacefully as his own. To any casual onlooker, the strange twilight procession would have aroused no or little concern. In fact, its uneventful, nearly noiseless progress gave the small convoy an almost mystical aura, as if the three ships were embarked in some sort of religious peregrination. Indeed, had Daniel been a man of faith, he would have thought that God had shielded their tiny party under his protective cloak.

But he did not believe in God. In fact, the concept of a supreme deity in any of its manifestations—Allah, Yahweh, or even Zeus, for that matter—deeply offended his intelligence. They were all human inventions, designed to gloss over the irrefutable fact that death terminated all existence. Permanently. Absolutely.

Organized religions had been humanity's first large corporations, founded by men—very smart men—who had figured out a way of making a living without having to work so much at it. Their roots had become so embedded in the human psyche that even today, in the science-driven 21st century, their bloated bodies continued to suck and feed on mankind's fear of eternal oblivion, their pious representatives promising an everlasting redemption in exchange for a life of "sacrifice". And by "sacrifice", religions meant that their followers should dip into their pockets and contribute to their churches' ample wealth. And that if needs be, they should sacrifice their lives for the continued existence of their spiritual institutions.

That was not for him.

Daniel would live—and die—for himself, and in the meantime, enjoy life to the fullest.

Angel San Miguel, a profoundly religious man, had once asked him why, if he felt that way, he had joined their cause, a cause that—even though secular in nature—was promoted and defended by fundamentally religious men. After considering the question, Daniel had answered, "Because our side has the will to win, and I want to be on the winning side."

To which San Miguel had responded, "Then you chose the wrong profession. You should have been a lawyer, or a professional athlete, or a corporate executive, or something other where you could win without running the risk of getting killed in the process. I believe in everlasting life. I believe in an afterlife where my efforts will be rewarded forever. You, my friend, are convinced that when you die, you will be no more. So why did you join us? Why do you choose to do something that at any moment can terminate your only life prematurely?"

Daniel had flashed his cocky smile. "Ah, but what a life it will have been! Prematurely? Perhaps. But you know as well as me, you pompous ass, that it's not the length of life but its intensity that matters. I chose a profession that makes me relish every second of what you call my *present existence*. Did you ever draw the last smoke out of the spent tip of a reefer, even as it burned the tips of your fingers, even as it turned into cinders, because you enjoyed it so much?" he had asked San Miguel, who had not responded and listened. "That is my aim in life. To draw out of it every last thing I can, and enjoy it to the fullest. Die prematurely? There's no such thing as dying prematurely. There's just people who overextend their stay in this planet without living, that's all."

It was not as simple as that, of course. But Daniel had never been a simple man, and there were times when even he did not know what moved him. He loved shocking San Miguel, and that was certainly part of it. But it went much further than that. He would rather die thinking that he was damning himself to eternal oblivion than join a religious organization that basically told him how to live.

Today, however, he had to admit to himself that even though he did not believe in God, the operation had thus far progressed as if it had been blessed by Him.

It had started at mid-afternoon in Piñones, in the northeastern coast of Puerto Rico. The three boats had been brought by trailer and put afloat from a public ramp, along with dozens of other boats waiting their turn to go out to sea. Each was manned by a crew of four men, most from San Miguel's organization, except for two Macheteros who were familiar with the route they would take, and who would ride on the first and third boats, acting as guides. They were dressed in loose, worn clothing and a faded collection of caps and hats, and brought with them an assortment of fishing rods, bait buckets, beer coolers, and other essential paraphernalia that identified them as Puerto Rican weekend fishermen. And even though the three crafts looked the same, each carrying on its platform, behind its steering wheel, a canvas-covered object that looked suspiciously like a whale-harpooning cannon, nobody bothered to give them a second look.

Except in the case of Czecka. The Kraken-sized man had stilled every conversation around the ramp as he walked mid-calf into the water and climbed on the third pontoon boat, nearly tilting it over. Daniel had laughed and applauded from his boat, and for a brief moment the surrounding crowd had joined in, until Czecka had turned and scoured his audience with a fierce glare, instantly killing any additional merriment.

The tiny flotilla had traveled briefly along the shore, then slipped under the Boca de Cangrejos Bridge and past the yacht club bearing the same name into the murky waters of the Torrecillas Lagoon. Civilization had rapidly vanished, giving way to a mangrove forest that grew directly out of the water and hid the lagoon's shores.

Led by their Machetero guide, a paunchy fisherman with thick sunburned arms and legs and an even bulkier stomach, the three ships had picked their way past scores of small, landless islands. They were formed from the bulky roots of the trees and the stubby tree trunks that exploded into thick, green canopies of leaves, just a few feet from the water's surface. Tall, long-legged egrets, black crow-like "changos", and a myriad of other species of birds perched on the outspread branches or hunted for insects or small fish, while crabs quickly scurried and splashed into the water to escape the approaching intruders.

"Are there any dangerous animals here?" Daniel asked his potbellied guide, named Amador, who everybody called Chago.

"Dangerous? Nah, nothing dangerous here. Except for us." The Machetero grinned at his own joke. He paused, as if thinking a little harder. "Although there have been reports of large boas, boas that people bought as pets, that they bring from other countries and throw away when they get too big to handle. An eighteen footer, somebody saw the other day. And spiders, there's always that."

The ship began to move into open water, and Chago pointed towards a narrow spit of land that jutted like a giant thumb into the lagoon.

"Behind those trees is the Suarez Channel. It connects this lagoon to the San Jose Lagoon," he said.

Daniel nodded. They had chosen to approach San Juan by a series of interconnected canals and lagoons. It was a longer trek than if the boats followed the seacoast to San Juan Bay, but a less visible route. Moreover, it allowed for a much smoother ride, something that Daniel's queasy stomach had appreciated.

The Suarez Channel had continued for about a mile, fringed mostly by dense vegetation. At times, a house or a roof would briefly become visible behind the foliage, and disappear just as quickly. Midway through the waterway, just after a bend, they had come upon a concrete bridge over which a large amount of cars steadily flowed.

"The 65th Infantry Expressway," Chago explained, and even before he had stopped talking, they had left it behind.

The San Jose Lagoon came into view long before they abandoned the canal. By far the largest lagoon in Puerto Rico, it was bisected by the Teodoro Moscoso Bridge. The bridge ran in a long, straight line for one and a half miles, supported by multiple rows of piles. It connected the metropolitan areas of Carolina and San Juan, and its entire span, from one end to the other, was crowned by approximately forty to fifty, evenly distanced flagstaffs that flew alternated, car-sized American and Puerto Rican flags. Daniel had driven over it several times during the two months that he lived in Puerto Rico, and had not grown tired of it.

The three pontoon boats had increased their speed as they left the channel and moved into the calm, open waters of the lagoon. In less than ten minutes they had reached the bridge and glided below its tall underbelly.

Chago had then turned his boat towards the northwest, to a spot where a jumble of wild vegetation spilled into the lagoon. As they approached, Daniel noticed a narrow opening in the otherwise cluttered shoreline.

"Is that where we're going?' he had asked the Machetero.

"No," Chago replied. "Behind it, behind it," he said, waving with his right arm exaggeratedly, not so much to show Daniel where they were going, as for the benefit of the two boats that were following them.

The convoy had passed the protruding strip of coastal forest, and followed the irregular shore.

"There!" Chago shouted, to what seemed to be a very narrow water passageway, covered by trees. He turned to Daniel. "That's the Canal of Martin Peña," he told him. "That will take us to the Bay of San Juan."

Daniel, who was resting on one of the stern's seats while the boat crossed the San Jose Lagoon, stood up and returned to the prow. His heart skipped a beat. When he was a young boy, they had shown one night in the refugee camp where he was interned the classic film "The African Queen". At one point in the movie, Humphrey Bogart had been forced to jump off his boat—a small steamer—and tow it with a rope through snake-infested waters. The Martin Peña Channel barely seemed wider than the water passage that had nearly doomed the African Queen. The wide-beamed pontoon boat on which they were traveling barely seemed to fit in it.

"Does this get any narrower?" he inquired with some concern from Chago.

"A little bit, especially during the first third of the way," the Machetero guide had responded, and casually added in a not very convincing tone, "but we should be able to squeeze through it okay."

Daniel had looked at him with undiluted doubt and sighed. Then he laughed, shaking his head. *What the hell, history had not been written by cowards, San Miguel always used to say, and he was right. The world belonged to those who dared...as long as they knew when to retreat.*

"We better fit," he told Chago sternly, "or you will personally have to drag every one of the boats to the bay," thinking to himself, *and afterwards I will give you to George, so that he can remove your scalp with his knife.*

Chago carefully nudged the boat forward, slowly leading it into the channel. They moved at a crawl speed, followed by the craft's other two siblings.

After a few minutes Daniel began to relax. The waterway wound like one of the large boas that Chago had talked about, narrowing even more in some of the turns, so that branches of the small trees growing out of the water sometimes scraped the boat's railings or dropped so low that the crew had to push them away, and twice the pontoons bumped into protruding roots. But the tiny flotilla managed to forge ahead unhindered by any serious obstacle.

"It's time to change," Daniel had announced to his men about two thirds of the way. He whistled to the boat behind them, took off his T-shirt—which bore a faded 'Corona Beer' logo—and circled it over his head. A man on the prow of the second boat nodded, and spoke to his companions behind him.

One of the men in Daniel's crew, a burly man with greasy, curly hair, called Fangio, pulled up from the deck a burlap duffel bag and unzipped it. He began to distribute to the rest of the crew jeans and dark, navy blue shirts with light blue collars.

"Chago...Daniel...Pedro...me," he said in a loud voice, as he read the names that had been tagged with masking tape to the clothes. "Do you think Czecka will fit in one of these?" he asked, smiling and holding out one of the shirts.

"I heard they borrowed his from the Incredible Hulk," Pedro said, and the others had laughed perhaps a bit harder than the joke merited. *They are nervous,* Daniel realized. Their exaggerated response to the lame remark betrayed the adrenaline coursing through their bodies. He knew the feeling well.

He grabbed his folded shirt by its shoulders and fluttered it open, noting with satisfaction the "Autoridad de Acueductos y Alcantarillados" logo imprinted on the upper left hand side of the shirt. Over it hovered a drawing of three fat drops of water, the Authority's symbol. It was a faithful reproduction of the uniform worn by the Puerto Rico Water and Sewer Authority field employees, the only disguise they would wear when they began to plant in open view the explosive charges in the four Miramar bridges.

Daniel's thoughts were interrupted by the renewed laughter of his men as they mocked Chago, whose shirt stretched tightly over his extended belly, straining the lower three buttons to the point of near bursting, and exposing his hairy navel. Daniel repressed a smile and looked at them reprovingly, quickly extinguishing their merriment. He usually tolerated and even welcomed a little excitement and fun from his men, but the time had come for them to focus on the task at hand. He ordered Fangio to take over the watch at the prow of the ship, and began to put on his jeans.

The lush vegetation of the channel continued to spread out before them, a deep, green scar over the sprawling concrete that covered most of San Juan's metropolitan area. It had never ceased to fascinate Daniel how fragile civilization's hold on nature was. He had seen it time and again, in every country he had visited. You only had to scratch the surface, and plants, weeds, dust or debris would well up from the land, quickly erasing and devouring man's puny efforts to master his immediate surroundings. The San Juan authorities would experience it soon enough. Their tenuous control over that lush corner of the Caribbean would be put shortly under a tremendous strain.

As if to remind the travelers of where they were, the canopy of foliage above them had suddenly opened up and revealed three concrete overpasses of major motorways less than a hundred yards ahead of them. The vegetation bordering the water passageway also thinned out, allowing the men to see some of the nearby houses and, further away, the tall buildings of Hato Rey, San Juan's financial district.

The men's relaxed mood had quickly changed to tense anticipation, as the pontoon boat flotilla glided into the main segment of the Martin Peña Channel. The U.S. Army Corps of Engineers had widened that portion of the canal substantially, in an attempt to connect by ferry the island of San Juan to the Hato Rey financial district. But the ferry had failed after a brief, unsuccessful stint of duty, and now the surrounding vegetation was slowly returning the channel to its natural state. A linear park—a long concrete sidewalk raised over the water on concrete piles— bordered the channel's northern edge. Even though open to the public, Daniel only counted two people over its entire span, one of them, a man, jogging at a quick pace, the second a teenager talking into a cell phone. None of them paid any attention to the passing boats.

Daniel glanced at his watch, noting it was five minutes to five in the afternoon. Ahead, in the distance, loomed San Juan Bay. In order to finish placing the explosive charges on time, they had to reach the bridges by no later than half past six in the afternoon. But he had not been worried. There was still a way to travel, but it was open water from there on.

It had taken them another fifteen minutes to exit the Martin Peña Channel and slowly make their way around the tip of Isla Grande, sailing past the end of its small airport, and skirting an industrial area where thousands of trailers and large metal containers laden with millions of pounds of goods waited either to be towed away into the main island or to be loaded on freight ships to return to the U.S. Then, the three boats had entered the San Antonio Channel, the body of water that separated the southern border of the island of San Juan from the rest of the mainland, their long journey nearly at an end.

As the twin hulls of the ships hovered smoothly over the last stretch of glassy water, and the sun drenched in scarlet sunlight the distant outline of the first of the Miramar bridges, Daniel's spirit soared. *This is what I live for*, he thought. *This is what I relish.* Let other, more cautious men live longer, less dangerous lives. He would not trade one second of his existence for their entire life spans.

The convoy sailed past an enormous cruise ship moored on the only tourist dock located in Isla Grande. It was the huge *Oasis of the Seas*, of the Royal Caribbean Line, a glittering floating city that rose nearly twenty stories high, dwarfing everything else around it. Daniel craned his neck upwards and saw, against the sky's backdrop, the figures of several passengers leaning over the upper deck railings. He waved at them, and a few of them waved back.

A half dozen sailboats, anchored in the middle of the channel, floated placidly a safe distance away from the cruise ship, their aluminum masts clanking as the breeze stirred through their rigging. Some had been taken over by seagulls, a flock of which noisily protested the approach of Daniel's boats, and then lazily flew away.

The long docks of the San Juan Yacht Club—San Juan's foremost marina—sprawled over the water a distance away, near the first of the Miramar bridges. Hundreds of sailboats and luxury yachts lay there berthed next to each other, their white, gleaming hulls tied to the docks by a complex system of crisscrossing lines that made Daniel think of rows of big white moths trapped in a giant spider web. Their names, displayed on their sterns, spoke volumes about their owners. The most conservative ones presumably referred to the proprietors' loved ones, mostly women. Daniel saw a "Serafina", a "Rosa Maria", and a "Roxana", a "Mary Ann", a "Lola" and a "Mizz Ariela". He also noted the name of "La Bilirrubina", which he didn't know corresponded to a lady, a vaccine, or some sort of dance. Other names were intended to convey a message, usually about their owners' status, power, or wealth. Their hulls bore names like "Gold Rush"' "Big Boy"—*usually the sign of a small penis*, Daniel thought—"Market Rally", and "Wuz His". They were San Juan's rich and famous' monuments to themselves.

Daniel despised them all. Not just the rich and famous of San Juan, but anybody else who fitted into that category. There were very few pet peeves within Daniel's universe. The rich and the famous were one of them. With few exceptions, he had found them to be a uniformly arrogant, insensitive, and surprisingly-ignorant-despite-their-wealth bunch, a breed who tended to treat as their equals only those with more power and money. Usually they bored, more than infuriated him, although a few had managed to offend him. Needless to say, those falling in the latter category had not fared well.

The first of the three Miramar bridges loomed straight before him, at the end of the marina. It spanned, with three wide arches, the relatively narrow stretch of water that connected the San Antonio Channel to the Condado Lagoon. The arches rested on narrow concrete abutments that barely cleared the surface of the water.

It was a wide bridge, wide enough to accommodate four vehicular lanes and two sidewalks. A concrete fence bordered its sides to ensure the safety of the vehicles and the pedestrians. Traffic moved in only one direction, from the island of San Juan into the mainland.

Daniel examined the bridge with the deep respect that it deserved. Only a few years old, it had been built with the same rock-like solidity of the fortresses that had guarded for centuries the city of Old San Juan, intended not only to substitute its old counterpart, but to remain there forever, as long as Puerto Rico managed to stay afloat.

It was made of heavily reinforced steel rebars covered by several feet of concrete. Each of the three arches that spanned the water was six feet thick at its narrowest point. It would have taken a professional demolition crew weeks to properly set up the charges needed to knock down the entire structure. The concrete would have been chipped away in certain strategic locations to expose the rebars, in order to be certain that the explosives cut cleanly through them, and all sorts of precautions would have been taken to ensure the public safety. It could not be done in one night.

Fortunately, Daniel's men did not have to collapse the entire structure. It was not in their interest to do so. They just needed to create a gap that would be wide enough to stop any vehicles from crossing into San Juan, and slow down any men foolish enough to attempt to cross it on foot. Eventually—the conspirators realized—their enemies would find the way to bridge the gap. But by then, it would not matter.

Daniel's boat slowed down to a steady crawl to allow him to carefully examine their objective. At less than thirty feet away, the bridge seemed like a formidable obstacle. He could hear the constant hum of tires rolling over the grooved concrete pavement overhead, punctuated sporadically by metallic "clack-clacks" of trucks passing over the three expansion steel joints that crossed the width of the bridge. Occasionally, angry horns, loud booming music, the deep-throated protest of a specialty muffler or the roar of a truck engine would contribute to the din, all of it confirming the incessant flow of traffic mostly invisible to the boaters below. Two boys leaned from the railing—some fifteen feet above—fishing directly from their spools.

The second and third pontoon boats pulled up on each side of the lead boat and waited patiently, their engines generating only enough power to counter the current flowing under the bridge from the Condado Lagoon. Daniel could see Czecka's hulking figure to his right, only his bright eyes betraying the furious activity churning inside his head. He knew immediately, despite the huge man's near blank expression, that something troubled him. As if sensing his eyes, Czecka turned to him and, raising his voice to be heard, shouted, "It's too high!"

"What?" Daniel did not understand him.

"The tide!" Czecka growled. "It's too high!"

Daniel stared uncomprehendingly at his associate, then looked urgently at the bridge as the import of what Czecka was indicating finally struck him.

"Get closer to the bridge," he ordered Chago, who instantly obeyed him, gently nudging the throttle forward.

As they moved towards the bridge, he walked to the canvas-covered object bolted to the ship's deck, and stood behind it. He removed the cover to reveal a piece of equipment that looked like a futuristic laser cannon with a large silencer. It was a diamond-encrusted, state-of-the-art core drill, mounted on a fixed vertical rig that extended six feet up from the pontoon's platform. Each ship carried a similar drill, plus three smaller hand-held drills that could be used to bore holes of a width of up to three inches into the bridge's concrete underbelly.

Daniel urged Chago to keep going, while keeping his eyes fixed on the bridge ahead. The current rushing under the arches pushed against the twin hulls of the boat with surprising strength, as the waters from the lagoon flowed towards the San Antonio Channel and the Bay of San Juan. The tide was dropping. Even so, it soon became apparent that it was too high for the drill's vertical rig to clear the top of the bridge's arch. About two inches too high.

Daniel cursed under his breath. With the present tide, none of the boats would fit under the bridge, where the holes to place the explosive charges were to be drilled. Even worse, none of the ships could cross under the bridge, to begin their work under the other bridges. Without saying a word, he unzipped his duffel bag and pulled out his cell phone. He dialed "talk" and "1", and got an answer on the second ring.

"*Pedro Martinez*," a familiar voice answered. "*Who is this*?"

"Pedro, this is Luis, your mechanic," Daniel replied calmly "I got to your dock, but can't start the repairs. The tide is too high. We can't start until it drops by at least two inches."

"*Hold on a second*," Martinez said matter-of-factly. Had it not been for the short pause after his announcement, Daniel would have thought that Martinez cared little about their predicament. He was forced to smile when he heard his contact humming a song—it sounded like "Strangers in the Night"—probably as he frantically verified in his laptop the time of the tides. "*Yes...*" Martinez said after a pause of about thirty seconds. "*The tide is going down now. It seems you'll have to wait about an hour and a half, 'til seven forty-something. Then you should be all right.*"

"This will mean overtime," Daniel warned. He heard Martinez sigh at the other end of the call.

"*If it must, it must*," he said resignedly. "*I will make the arrangements, and try to help you finish on time.*"

"Okay. I'll go get a beer."

San Miguel snapped his cell phone shut, barely able to contain his anger. *Incredible!* From the outset, when he had first contacted the Macheteros, El Alacran had volunteered—no, demanded—to be in charge of planning the destruction of the bridges. After all, Andrade had argued forcefully, who was better suited to prepare for that stage of the operation than he and his men, some of whom had been born and raised in the area?

"Leave this to us," he had assured Daniel personally, almost a year before. "My men have intimate knowledge of the water passages, the boat traffic, and even the fish that swim in those waters. We will get your people there on time, and make sure that they place those charges with no interruptions." He had personally guaranteed it. Daniel had conveyed El Alacran's message to San Miguel word for word, and San Miguel had grudgingly accepted it.

But Andrade had forgotten about the tides!

And now, his men were forced to wait nearly and hour and a half in the open, within plain view of a busy yacht club, for the tide under the bridges to drop, their entire schedule in jeopardy! *Damn the Macheteros! Damn Andrade! He should never have trusted amateur terrorists to perform such a crucial task.*

Sitting on the passenger's seat of the van next to San Miguel, George watched his boss with alarm. Even though San Miguel did not manifest any emotions, George had learned to read his body language, and could sense how upset he was, even through his seemingly calm demeanor. The clenching of his jaw, the whitening knuckles as his hands squeezed the steering wheel, and his vacant stare into the waning evening light, revealed better than any words San Miguel's present state of mind. It was a dangerous state of mind.

George considered asking if he could be of any help, but thought better of it. His boss would talk when he was ready to do so.

San Miguel breathed in deeply, and considered the unfolding events. *It was his own fault.* He had been accused by his superiors of micromanaging his operations, of not trusting enough his subordinates, but if ever an operation required micromanaging, it was the present one. The most important endeavor of his entire life. A mission that could—*would*—change the course of modern history.

It was his own fault. He should have personally checked the tides, not leave the task to a self-important, overrated local anarchist.

He looked at his digital watch. It was twenty past six, and already dark. There was little that they could do until 7:30 that evening, except wait. *It would be all right,* he told himself. *Daniel was a good man. He would find a way to finish his job.*

"History was never written by cowards," he muttered to himself, slapping gently the steering wheel with his hands, and then turning self-consciously to George, who grinned, showing his full set of teeth.

"No, sir, it hasn't," he agreed, chuckling, "and we ain't no cowards, are we?"

"No," San Miguel responded, smiling ruefully back at his friend. "No, we *ain't.*"

They were parked next to a large abandoned property ringed by a tall concrete wall that had once contained the original Telemundo television studios during the 1950's and 60's. Now, only the surrounding concrete walls remained, the rest of the buildings flattened, its space invaded by wild vegetation.

Three other white vans waited behind the one where George and San Miguel sat. Each of their sides displayed three, large blue drops of water, the logo for the Puerto Rico Water and Sewer Authority, or PRASA, as it was known by the locals. Every van carried a crew of four men, two sitting up front and two hiding in the storage area, plus a full load of four and five-inch wide PVC pipes, several small crates, rolls of wire, and pails of quick-setting epoxy mix.

The vans' engines were turned on, but their headlights were off, and they were parked in a dark spot not covered by the weak fluorescent glow of the street's two distant lampposts.

The street itself did not exceed more than a hundred yards in length from beginning to end and was barely two lanes wide, but it was situated in a key location. To the north, it connected with the Avenida Constitucion, San Juan's widest boulevard with four lanes that headed towards Miramar. Flanked by the Muñoz Rivera Park, the avenue was located less than a quarter of a mile away from the Condado Lagoon. Until the later hours of the night, traffic on the Avenida Constitucion would be relatively light, giving San Miguel and his men easy access—a short drive lasting no more than two or three minutes—to the four bridges.

San Miguel carefully considered the new circumstances forced upon them. The four vans were not supposed to move until 9:00 PM, to avoid getting to the bridges prematurely with the explosives hidden inside the PVC pipes that they carried, and thus lessen the risk of being discovered. By that time, the drilling under the bridges by Daniel's crew would be well under way, and San Miguel's men would be able to begin placing the C-4 charges inside the holes already drilled. But the high tide had changed their schedule. The three pontoon boats loitering about the San Juan Yacht Club were due to attract attention. On the other hand, if the "PRASA" vans got there now and interacted with the men waiting on the boats, they would lend credibility to the latter's presence. They had no choice. They had to move immediately.

"George," San Miguel turned to his companion, "call Andrade, Johnny Ray, and Calderon, and let them know that there has been a delay of about one and a half hours in the setting of the explosives." The code words for the preparation of the bridges was "the surprise party". There-fore, George was to advise the others that "the surprise party" would be delayed. "Tell them that under no circumstances are they to move before the charges are set off. They will hear them, and we will confirm it when it happens. Repeat that to them. Nobody should start before the charges go off. We do not want to alert the mainland prematurely. Got it?"

George nodded emphatically, and when he saw that San Miguel was expecting a verbal confirmation, added, "Yes, boss. No one moves until the surprise party starts."

"We leave for the bridges now," San Miguel announced, opening the door of the van. "As soon as I talk to the others."

He slammed the door and examined the street for other traffic or pe-destrians. There were none.

With measured calmness, he walked across the street to a boarded, abandoned house and entered its gravel driveway, overgrown with weeds. There was another van parked there towards the back, barely visible in the darkness. Unlike the others, it was dirty and covered with rust, its paint too faded to be identified with any particular color, ranging somewhere between a hazy beige and muddy green. Several bumps and dents, includ-ing a warped front bumper, gave the impression that the vehicle had seen much better days. Anybody seeing the van from the sidewalk would prob-ably think that it had been abandoned there for more than a year.

Its outward appearance was deceiving, though. Its hood housed a brand new Ford F-150 SVT V-8 Raptor engine, with more than 400 horsepower. Its windowless cargo space was lined with two-inch thick steel sheets plus a coating of lead. To support its heavy frame, it had been fitted with heavy-duty gas pressure shock absorbers, and it rested on four brand new, puncture resistant, all-terrain tires, dirtied on purpose to match its decrepit exterior.

San Miguel tapped twice on the glass of the driver's door. Its tinted window rolled half way down, and a chubby, bald, thickly bearded man looked out.

"Da'ud," San Miguel said softly, greeting the driver.

"Masaa' al khayr," the man acknowledged in Arabic.

"Spanish or English only, Da'ud," San Miguel warned him sternly.

The man nodded, and then said in English, "Good evening," with a mocking smile.

"Good evening. The plans have changed," San Miguel informed him. "Our party's leaving right away." Da'ud looked at him inquiringly, but San Miguel ignored him and continued. "Your mission remains exactly the same, at least for now. You are to wait here until Czecka arrives. Tell the others in the van. If anything else changes, I will let you know."

"We will wait," Da'ud confirmed.

"Stay alert. Nobody should be looking for you, but sometimes...things happen. So be careful." San Miguel extended his hand to the driver and shook it. "Tomorrow night we celebrate," he said, and started to walk away.

"Inshallah," Da'ud replied and chuckled, as the glass of his window began to scroll up.

San Miguel stopped, irked by Da'ud's joke, but then decided to keep moving. The man was the best driver he had ever known, and he had met many good drivers during his career. But he would have liked him to take matters more seriously than he did, especially during the present mission. Too much was at stake. Fortunately, the three other men assigned to watch the van—two of them hidden among the ruins of the house, the third sitting inside the cargo hold—would be much more careful.

They had to. The entire operation was conceived and based on the successful delivery of the precious cargo stored inside the dilapidated van. Without that, all of San Miguel's plans and hard work, all of the money he had spent and the favors he had called in would be meaningless, even if every other goal of his ambitious agenda was accomplished.

But San Miguel was an optimist, and so, he quickly banished the negative thoughts from his mind, and re-focused on the long list of things that needed to be done.

Everything would be all right. The cargo would be delivered. And they would be triumphant.

Inshallah.

CHAPTER VII

Plaza de Armas was almost deserted by 7:00 PM, most of the action having shifted uphill, to San Sebastian Street. An old lady with several layers of equally dull and oversized clothes sat slumped on one of the square's benches—a shopping cart from the now extinct "Pueblo" supermarket filled with all of her worldly possessions—parked by her side. A few steps away, a couple engaged in an animated conversation pushed a baby stroller towards their home, the ubiquitous pigeons that populated the plaza by day having long flown to the hundreds of ledges, nooks and crannies of the surrounding buildings. All the businesses around the square had closed for the night except for Starbucks, which showed through its large windows a young woman thoroughly engrossed in her laptop computer, and a green-aproned employee cleaning up the counter behind her.

A municipal policeman—a rookie by the neatly-pressed appearance of his uniform and the deep shine of his shoes—was slowly making his round around the block, when he was startled by a tap on his shoulder.

"Please forgive me," a nearly bald man in his late forties or early fifties said with an earnest smile, "I didn't mean to startle you." He was accompanied by two other, younger men carrying green canvas bags, all three of them dressed in black.

"Can I help you?" the policeman asked stiffly, unsuccessfully trying to sound casual.

"Yes, I'm looking for the offices of Jerusalen Alvarez, in the Metropolitan Building." He pulled a business card from his shirt pocket, and brought it closer to his eyes. "It says here 'Office 1221, Metropolitan Center, San Juan'. She is an attorney."

Something about the man struck the policeman as odd. He spoke with a slight accent, definitely not Puerto Rican. And the time to meet an attorney, in the evening of the Fiestas de San Sebastian, did not make any sense. And what was it with the three black outfits?

"You have a case with her?" he asked.

"Oh, no!" The man laughed, and the other two men smiled. "We're from Rodriguez Air Conditioning Service." He fished his wallet out from his back pocket and drew out of it another card, showing the drawing of a grinning man holding a wrench, with the name "Rodriguez Air Conditioning Service" imprinted below it in bold, black letters. The address next to the name placed the business in Vega Baja, a town west of San Juan. "My nephews and I are here to repair her air conditioner. It broke down this afternoon, and she has a trial on Monday, so she needs it repaired now."

The guard looked up at the Metropolitan Center, and confirmed that an office light was on in the twelfth floor.

"She's lucky that she got somebody to work over the weekend. Especially this weekend."

"Oh, she knows us," the man replied. "We installed her central air conditioning unit in her house in Guaynabo just a few months ago. She sure chose a bad time to have the one in her office break down, though!" He shook his head, scratching his baldpate. "San Sebastian weekend! Almost couldn't find any parking!"

The municipal policeman nodded, visibly relaxing. "You got here just in time. An hour more and the traffic congestion wouldn't let you get into San Juan. Your client would have been forced to wait until tomorrow to get her unit fixed." He pointed at the tall building occupying the entire southern boundary of the square. "That's the Metropolitan Center right there. The entrance to the business offices is the one you see on the left."

The officer pointed to a wide, arched entrance four steps higher than the sidewalk, illuminated by two big, elongated lanterns embedded on each side of the entrance, that led to a small lobby. An elegant, wrought-iron staircase rose around the old, ornate, iron-grilled elevator that had originally been used to reach the building's upper levels. The elevator was not operational any more; it stood in the center of the stairwell as part of the decoration of the lobby. Two more modern elevators, hidden in a corridor behind the stairs, had been incorporated into the building in a recent renovation. A glass door barred access to the lobby.

"The entrance is closed now," the policeman informed them. "You'll have to use the intercom to let your client know you're here."

"That's fine. Thank you," the bald man said. "Let's hope this doesn't take all night."

The three repairmen began to walk towards the business entrance.

"Hey!" the policeman called suddenly after them.

The men stopped, and waited for him to catch up.

"Your card," the guard explained, extending his arm to hand it to the bald man.

The repairman chuckled. "Keep it," he said. "You may need us some day," and waved goodbye, renewing his trek towards the Metropolitan Center. The municipal policeman absently deposited the card in his shirt pocket, stared at the men for a few seconds more, and then turned and headed towards the arched corridor of the Casa Alcaldia, across the square.

The three repairmen stopped at the glass door that gave access into the lobby, and one of them buzzed the intercom, while another checked on the patrolman.

"He's gone," the one watching said. The bald man produced a plastic card and swiped it over an electric eye, unlatching the door's lock. The three men strolled into the deserted lobby and entered one of the back elevators, pressing the button to the twelfth floor. Once there, they headed to the stairs going to the roof, passing by office 1221. One of its double glass doors read in gold letters: "Jerusalen Alvarez Law Offices." The reception room was partially illuminated by a light coming from the open door of one of its window offices. Several envelopes lay strewn on the floor, apparently pushed through the gap under the doors.

Colonel Calderon felt relieved. Breaking into the Metropolitan Center had presented a minor but potentially hazardous problem. The break-in into the building could not be attempted until 7:00 PM, after the janitor left. At that time, most pedestrian traffic had stopped, and the sidewalks became desolate strips of concrete. Any attempt to force the lobby door would be clearly observed by any itinerant passerby's and the municipal guard assigned to the Plaza de Armas. And an unknown party of men hefting large duffle bags would arouse the curiosity of anybody with a modest level of intelligence.

Calderon had sent one of his men to case the building one week before the operation. The man had obtained a list of the tenants. They immediately had focused on Jerusalen Alvarez, a sole practitioner of maritime law, who kept her offices on the twelfth floor, assisted by an elderly female secretary. Two days later, Calderon had telephoned her, identifying himself as the captain of a ship docked in Mayaguez, whose cargo had been attached by the federal authorities, and who needed the help of an attorney. He had made an appointment to meet with her that Saturday morning.

On the day of the appointment, Czecka had shown up instead. The human mountain had—as San Miguel put it in a sanitized fashion—"disposed" of the two women, stuffing them in two body bags, and placing them in a closet, not before securing the card to open the electronic lock to the lobby. *It was a pity that two innocent women had had to die,* Calderon thought, *but sometimes, civilian casualties were inevitable.*

Calderon and his men continued to climb the stairs until they reached its end. A steep set of aluminum steps rose from the stairs' final landing to a steel hatch on the roof, locked by a heavy padlock. One of the Venezuelans, a short, stocky man with a heavily pocked-marked face, unzipped one of the duffel bags and brought out a heavy duty bolt cutter that easily snapped open the lock. With a grunt, he pushed the hatch up until it flipped completely open. They quickly climbed to the roof and shut the hatch after them.

Faint strains of music drifted from San Sebastian Street, mingling with the gentle wind flowing from the sea. To the south, the glittering lights of the city sloped towards the docks and stopped at the bay. To the north, the lights rose steadily in the direction of the festivities.

The roof was enclosed by a five-foot wall, and the view of the city by the three men would have been complete if it had not been for a seven foot high partition that divided the top of the building into two, roughly equal rectangles. The Venezuelans had climbed into the eastern portion of the roof, which covered the commercial section of the Metropolitan Center. The Center's residential area lay on the other side. No other structures, except for six large air-conditioning units, cluttered the area where the men stood.

"Get some rest while you can," Calderon instructed his men. "I don't think anyone should bother you, but take turns keeping watch. I'm going to check on the other teams now," he added, shaking hands with both men. "Good luck. Make your country and your president proud."

As Calderon walked out of the Metropolitan Center, he caught sight of the municipal policeman, standing on a distant corner of the Plaza de Armas. He raised his arm and waived heartily, walking away at a steady pace.

Tourist Dock B seemed to have been built out of a LEGO box. Its entrance resembled a large square block supported by vertical rows of LEGO bricks and crowned on each side by white LEGO triangles. Even the two flagpoles in front of the entrance seemed to rise from flat, single LEGO units snapped onto a red LEGO baseboard. The only un-LEGO-like features were the two iron gates that controlled the pedestrian and vehicular access into the dock.

At 8:00 PM of that Saturday night the gates were shut. No cruise ships were moored on either side of the long dock, and except for the night watchman sitting on a metal chair and listening to the radio behind the pedestrian gate, no other activity disturbed the night's peace.

That would soon change. By five AM, a dozen custom agents would make their way to the boarding terminal. They would be followed an hour later by some of the port personnel, dozens of longshoremen, and about twenty representatives from the arriving cruise ship that, along with the ship's crew, would help the passengers disembark. Security would also be enhanced as the day progressed, and the gates controlling the transit of vehicles would be opened to allow the tanker trucks to roll onto the dock more than 1,500 tons of the diesel fuel that the ship need-ed to continue its journey.

The cruise ship *Mardi Gras* was scheduled to arrive by six-thirty AM, and berth on the right side of the pier. The passengers' luggage, already collected during the prior night, would begin to be offloaded immediate-ly, and the first batch of passengers would disembark at seven. At about that same time, and for the next eight hours, a dizzying array of vans and trucks transporting food, liquor, and other supplies would make its way into the loading area, replenishing the ship's dwindling stocks with such items as 20,000 pounds of beef, 9,000 pounds of chicken, 1,700 pounds of lobster, 18,000 pounds of fruit, 4,500 pounds of sugar, 500 gallons of ice cream, 2,000 pounds of coffee, 23,000 pounds of fresh vegetables, and 8,500 dozens of eggs, not to mention some 3,000 bottles of assorted wines, 200 bottles of champagne, and scores of other items.

Each vehicle would be checked for contraband and explosives, and their loads carefully compared to the ship's manifest. By early afternoon, the first cluster of the nearly 2,000 new passengers would begin to check in their luggage and go through customs. And precisely at 10:00 PM, the *Mardi Gras* would cast off from its pier and sail out of San Juan Bay.

But at 8:00 PM of the prior Saturday night, none of those activities had begun. The dock's only security guard sat contentedly listening to the radio, while across the wide open space that separated Dock B from the Fernandez Juncos Avenue, bumper-to-bumper automobiles painfully attempted to make their way to the various public parking areas of the city, blaring their horns non-stop.

A couple of tourists stopped under a neon-lit lamppost close to the pier, and became engaged in an animated conversation over a brochure. The man, dressed in red Bermudas, sandals, and a very flowery shirt, kept pointing towards the west, while his companion, a curvy, short-haired blonde wearing sexy white shorts, flip-flops, and a tight, well-filled tank top, pointed to the north. Their debate continued for several minutes until the man spotted the guard sitting behind the iron gate, showed him to the woman, and they both walked towards him.

"Excuse me, sir," the male tourist said courteously. He made an effort to speak in Spanish, but abandoned it when all he produced sounded like gibberish. "You speak English?" he asked, speaking very slowly, while his female companion kept muttering "Calle Fortaleza, Calle Fortaleza," over and over again.

"Yes," the guard answered tentatively, barely able to take his eyes off the female tourist. He stood up and moved closer to the gate, to take a closer look at the brochure that the man was showing him.

"Can...you...show...me..." the tourist began to say with an exaggerated pronunciation, while prodding his map with his index finger, "where...is...San...Sebastian...Street...Calle...San Sebastian?"

The security guard extended his arm and reached through the gate bars to see the printed map. As he did so, the blond woman leaned forward and gently grabbed his right wrist. Something "clicked" and the guard tried to back away but could not, as his hand was handcuffed to one of the iron bars. Alarmed, he fumbled with his left hand for his gun—which was kept holstered on the right side of his waist—but stopped when he felt a cold, smooth object thrust under his chin.

"This is a Beretta 92," the male tourist calmly informed him in perfect Spanish, his breath smelling of cinnamon gum. "It is loaded with hollow-tipped bullets that will probably blow off the top of your skull and splatter my nice outfit with blood and brains if I pull the trigger. It has a silencer, as you have probably guessed, so nobody in the street will hear it if I kill you."

The tourist prodded the cylindrical barrel further into his captive's chin, forcing the security guard to turn his head up to the night sky. The guard felt a set of hands remove the gun from his holster.

"We can do this one of two ways," the male tourist continued, furiously chewing his gum. "You can carefully reach for your keys, and give them to my girlfriend so that she opens the front gate, or we can kill you and look for them ourselves. Which is it going to be?"

The tourist couple walked into the enclosed area less than a minute later. They led their captive to the booth near the vehicular entrance, and made him show them how to operate the gate controls. As the main gate opened, a dark van, parked at the edge of the entrance, turned on its headlights and quickly sped into the dock, parking about a hundred feet away, next to the pier's two-story building. Its twin back doors opened up even before the vehicle had stopped, spilling eight men that carried AK-47 rifles and several heavy cloth bags. The men rapidly spread along the pier to their pre-assigned positions in the terminal building. Two others, wearing uniforms similar to those of the captured guard, got off the front of the van and walked to the front gate.

The handcuffed captive was removed to a closet in the main terminal, where his ankles were bound tightly by silver duct tape and his wrists similarly tied behind his back.

"We're going to be here, right next to you during the rest of the day," the sexy female tourist huskily whispered in his ear, "so don't make any foolish noises or we'll have to kill you. I'll be back in a couple of hours, to get you something to drink and eat. Try to get some sleep, okay?" she said with a pleasant smile, licking his ear and smoothing a strip of tape over his mouth.

Up at the front of the dock, the male tourist had changed into a guard's uniform, and was busily chewing his gum as he read the schedule attached to a clipboard that he had found in the entrance booth. He was startled as the door to the air-conditioned booth suddenly flew open, and another guard impersonator, a swarthy man with a light goatee, put his head in.

"Everybody is set," he advised, and shut the door.

The tourist-turned-guard nodded. He kept reading the schedule.

Outside, another of the fake guards sat on the metallic chair next to the pedestrian gate, and listened to the radio.

CHAPTER VIII

Lucas moved his knight in front of his white bishop's pawn, causing his brother-in-law to frown and rub his chin.

"Do you give up?" Lucas asked him, not because he was about to win the game—the game had barely started—but because he always asked that question when they played. "It will be less humiliating than check-mating you in a few more moves. More dignified on your part."

Michael continued to stare at the board, considering his next move. "Your braggadocio is only exceeded by your childishness," he replied, "particularly for someone who is about to be pounded into the ground."

Lucas smiled. "Braggadocio? We're using Sunday vocabulary now? Italian Sunday vocabulary?"

"You are so uncouth and ignorant, I won't even grace your braggadocio with a response," Michael said, moving his white queen diagonally halfway across the board, to threaten Lucas' exposed king. "Check!" he said triumphantly.

Lucas leaned forward, and examined his possible options. There was nothing subtle about Michael's attack. One of the benefits of playing chess with someone for a long time—and he had played chess with his brother-in-law since they were both teenagers, even before Michael had married Vanessa—was that you learned what to expect from your opponent. Of course, it worked the other way as well.

Michael favored the General George Patton philosophy of combat; blitzkrieging his adversary into submission, smashing relentlessly through any obstacles that could block his objective. He was quite good at it too, and even bore a remote resemblance to the legendary general, mostly because of his long, crooked nose—broken at least twice during his many high school fights—his frank and fearless gaze, and his quick, outspoken tongue.

He had taught Lucas to play chess, and during their first year of warfare, had overwhelmed him with his sledgehammer offensives. But then Lucas had begun to develop his own style of play, molding his defenses to blunt his attacks, withdrawing at times, feinting a strike from one direction, then pouncing unexpectedly from another, until the ratio of their victories had begun to shift. Now Lucas won seventy percent of their contests, using a technique that Michael called the "chicken shit" approach.

Lucas blocked his king with his queen, daring Michael to take it.

"Oh ho!" his brother-in-law exclaimed, savoring the unexpected challenge, while his two year old godson Gabriel watched him with admiration. "We're getting gutsy all of a sudden!"

"Hi *padrino*!" Gabriel said to Michael, smiling broadly, and moving closer to the board.

"Hi Gabriel," Michael answered, not taking his eyes off the game.

Lucas had met Michael when Michael started dating Vanessa. At that time Lucas, eighteen years old, had returned to San Juan from his training in Ranger School. Lucas' sister Vanessa had come to pick him up at the airport with her new boyfriend, a cocky, then very thin, two-years-his-senior Michael, who had looked at him squarely in the eye and smiled, as if saying, "Yeah, I'm dating your sister, and there's nothing you can do about it."

It had taken them the rest of the day to develop a bond that would bind them to their graves, and that would have even survived a breakup with Vanessa. Inevitably, Lucas had become the godfather—or *padrino*—of Michael and Vanessa's first son, Alfredo, and Michael of Lucas and Jennie's son Gabriel.

Their friendship had led them to many unusual adventures, since Michael had a vivid imagination and usually convinced Lucas, against his better judgment, to come along with him. Once they had been chased by wild dogs in a deserted island that Michael had wanted to explore, and spent half a day in the water waiting for the boat that had dropped them there to return. Another time, they had been caught by a storm as they rowed a mast-less Hobie Cat to an island off the coast, where a friend of Michael was supposed to install a new mast.

"Jennie, don't you think those hamburgers are done?" Lucas asked his wife. Jennie was sitting at the back of their open terrace, talking to Vanessa. Each held a tiny plastic teacup, as well as small plastic plates with plastic pieces of broccoli, tiny plastic chicken legs, and plastic grapes that Sofia had served them from her play-kitchen.

"They must be," Jennie replied matter-of-factly, smiling sweetly at Lucas. "Why don't you stand up and find out?"

Michael laughed softly. "Yeah, Lucas, that's showing her who's boss!"

Lucas smiled back at Jennie, who looked particularly fetching in the short pair of shorts and flip flops that she had put on at the last minute to receive Michael and Vanessa, and walked to the barbecue. Gabriel and Sofia rushed to their father's side, watching with wide-eyed fascination the flames that hissed through the grill, as the meat's grease dripped on the fire.

"Ah-ah, baby Gabriel," Sofia warned in her most motherly tone, raising her hand and carefully wagging her index finger from side to side. "Don't get near, or you'll get burned!"

"These burgers are ready to go, honey. I'm going to need a plate—" Lucas started to say, but stopped when he noticed that Jennie and Vanessa were already exiting the kitchen and bringing with them paper plates, buns, potato chips, cheese, relish and ketchup, which they deposited on the terrace's glass-topped dining table.

Lucas grabbed one of the plates, and withdrew the hamburgers from the grill, closing the barbecue's top and placing the burgers on the table.

"Come and get them," he said.

"Your turn," Michael said, looking very satisfied with the move he had just made. Lucas walked to the board followed by Gabriel, and after a brief pause, took Michael's queen.

Michael groaned. "You *don't* want to do that! I'll take your queen with my pawn!"

Lucas shrugged, and returned to the table, where he placed one of the hamburgers into a bun. "So it's a swap," he said, knowing fully well that his brother-in-law's aggressive game usually sputtered to a halt when he was deprived of his queen.

"Oh man, now it'll take me forever to give you a checkmate!" Michael lamented, leaning over the chessboard, while under the intense scrutiny of his godson.

"Hi *padrino*!" Gabriel repeated happily, his hand constantly straying in the direction of the pieces on the chessboard, then hesitating as he was about to reach one.

"Hi Gabriel," Michael answered absently, desperately trying to look for a way to regain his lost momentum. After a few seconds, he gave up and smiled at his godson, who kept staring at him expectantly. "Let's go eat," he said, sweeping Gabriel off his feet and hanging the giggling toddler upside down over his shoulder.

"It's about time," Vanessa said to his husband, as she squirted a generous portion of ketchup into her bun. "The hamburgers are getting cold."

"What?" Michael asked in shocked disbelief, raising one of his eyebrows *a la* Elvis Presley. "Nobody has prepared my hamburger yet?

What kind of a party is this?" Gabriel stared at him, and even though he did not understand a word of what his uncle had said, laughed at his face, as did Sofia.

They sat around the table and for a while nobody spoke, concentrating on their dinner. It was late, Lucas discovered when he looked at his watch, close to 9:00 PM, way past the bedtime hour of the children. Scheduled to be at the *Joyero* by 7:00 in the morning of the next day, he had envisioned going to bed early. It was not to be.

He had escaped the San Sebastian traffic with surprising ease, and arrived at his home by 6:30 PM. To his extreme delight, he had found Jeannie wearing nothing but a pair of red high heels and a tan raincoat, with which she had flashed him in the garage. With her coat hanging open, she had walked up to him, wrapped her arms around his neck, and given him a long, sensuous kiss that had left him breathless.

"Where are the children?" he had asked, barely able to separate himself from her.

"They are watching TV, already ate, and are ready to go to bed in fifteen minutes," she had answered, looking at him with a naughty smile. He loved her smile, had fallen for it even before they had exchanged a single word the very first time they had met in Jacksonville, while he was on military leave. Well, that and her sensational legs, and her dark brown, almost black eyes, which spoke to him with a language of their own.

"I am overwhelmed," he said, meaning every word.

"Thank the gardener," she had replied, kissing him passionately again. "He wasn't available."

He had savored the moment for just three more minutes, the time that it took them to reach the kitchen and for the telephone to ring. Jeannie had answered. It was Vanessa. She and Michael were going to barbecue some hamburgers, and they would like Lucas and Jennie and the children to join them.

"Tell my brother that that way he can listen about my visit to La Fortaleza, and at least get a notion of how the upper class lives," she had said loud enough for her brother to hear her over the telephone.

Lucas had signaled Jeannie with his hands to tell her no, but after a brief lapse of silence, Jeannie had responded that they would be happy to see them.

"Oh," Vanessa had added, *"and since we don't have a barbecue, could we use yours?"*

"Ask them if they need anything else," Lucas had replied sarcastically, resigning to the fact that his romantic evening was over. "Buns, ketchup...hamburgers..."

"Michael says 'just beer'," Jeannie repeated, after she had asked Vanessa, "and that they will be here in one minute." Vanessa and Michael were Lucas and Jeannie's next-door neighbors. They seemed, however, to have been standing by the door, since doorbell had rung as soon as Vanessa hung up, and Jeannie had been forced to run in her high heels up to their bedroom to put some clothes on.

"So tell us about Alfredo's visit to La Fortaleza," Lucas said to his sister, as they all ate.

Vanessa smiled, her eyes brimming with excitement. "It was sooo incredible!" she said, munching on a potato chip. Vanessa was a great storyteller, and everybody moved in closer to listen better.

"We got there around 3:00 in the afternoon—"

"*We* being?" Lucas asked, interrupting her.

"Alfredo and I, who else?" she answered, and readied to continue.

"You didn't take Michael?" Lucas interrupted again.

"No!"

"Didn't want to be embarrassed, eh?"

"Hush!" Jennie warned Lucas with a severe "stop-interrupting" look, and cut off Michael's response before he could utter a word.

"So anyway," Vanessa continued, ignoring her brother, "we get to the security gates. It was really impressive, you know? You go through this gate, and you identify yourself to this person sitting behind a console watching the security camera screens, just like in the movies. And he asked us if he could help us, and the little brat, before I could say anything, he says: 'Hello, my name is Alfredo Del Valle, and I am visiting Francisco Pietrantoni…The Governor's son…'"

They all smiled, visualizing the moment. For an eight year old, Alfredo acted like an old man, and probably possessed more common sense than most adults. Lucas loved talking to his godson, and listening to his views on politics and sports. Fortunately, Alfredo had not begun to talk about sex yet.

"I had to swallow hard not to laugh, because he was so solemn!" Vanessa said, laughing out loud. "The guard also had trouble keeping his face straight, I could tell, because he looked for a long time at the list he kept on a clipboard, and finally he said, very seriously, he said, 'Oh yes, Mr. Del Valle, I see you in my list…register', he said, 'in my register. We have been expecting you. Would you please give me your luggage and step through the metal detector?'"

Vanessa shook her head with amusement, re-living her son's excitement. "You should have seen his face! He gave me a sideways look, as if saying 'Look how important I am! They have been expecting me!' And he handed his Transformers backpack to the guard, and before he went through the metal detector, he gave me a furtive hand signal, you know, waving his hand from his waist, as if saying 'You can go now'..."

"And you left, of course," Lucas suggested, already knowing the answer.

"Are you crazy?!" she asked indignantly.

"Daddy is crazy!" Sofia repeated, giggling, while Michael circled his index finger around his ear, and pointed it at her father.

"She wanted to be stripped-searched," Michael explained, earning a miffed look from his wife. She continued.

"So after we passed through security, another guard—they were all so young and nice," she added, staring at her husband and stressing the word *nice*, "he took us to the stairway that leads up to La Fortaleza—it's such a grand stairway, like in the palaces in Europe!—and the guard asked us to wait there. And after about two seconds, we heard this shout from the top of the stairs, AAALFREDOOO!" Vanessa changed the pitch of her voice, yelling like Tarzan. "And Francisco—"

"The Governor's son," said Michael and Lucas in unison before she could say it.

"The Governor's son," she repeated as if they had not spoken, "came storming down the stairs like a wild savage, and embraced Alfredo—he completely ignored me—and grabbed his backpack and started leading him up the stairs, and they were almost out of sight when they passed Nereida—"

"Nereida?" Lucas asked, genuinely puzzled.

Jennie nudged him with her elbow. "The nanny," she explained impatiently, wanting to hear the rest of the story.

"The *First Nanny*," Michael said, correcting Jennifer. "The Governor's *special* companion. Don't you don't read *Imagen*?" he asked, viewing Lucas with exaggerated dismay.

"*Imagen*" was a sophisticated social and fashion news magazine that, among other things, followed the activities of Puerto Rico's rich and famous. Something like a mixture of Vogue, People, and Vanity Fair.

Vanessa shot his husband a withering glance. "You have such a filthy mind!"

"He is a sort of pervert," Lucas confirmed with a straight face.

"Those are just rumors that people who have nothing to do invent, and that other *mindless* people" Vanessa said, pointedly turning her face in the direction of her husband, "continue to repeat."

"I don't know..." Michael insisted, disregarding the irritated stare of the two women at the table. "How does that saying go? '*When the river makes noise, it's because it's carrying something with it*'. Or something like that. I've heard some nasty rumors about our stud Governor..."

The rumors about Governor Pietrantoni, a widower, and his son's nanny were in fact, part of the local folklore. Pietrantoni's wife had been killed in a horrible car accident five years before, long before he had been elected as Governor of Puerto Rico, and shortly thereafter Nereida Nieves, a young and beautiful teacher, had become his son's live-in nanny. After the elections, she had followed Governor Pietrantoni into La Fortaleza.

"Well, whatever!" Vanessa said, attempting to resume her story. "But you know what?"

"What?" everyone asked at the same time, laughing.

"She is soooo nice! She came down the stairs, in a very simple blue dress, with hardly any make up on, and she looked beautiful! She is very well endowed, too. She comes to me and she says. 'You must be Alfredo's mother! I'm Nereida Nieves, Francisco's nanny.' I bit my lower lip and stopped myself from laughing like a fool, you know, like I laugh when I'm nervous, and I just smiled, laughing inside. As if I didn't know who she was!"

"You were thinking, 'that's the Governor's hottie'," Michael suggested mischievously.

"Will you shut up!"

Lucas grinned, picturing her sister with Nereida. He knew exactly the type of wide-eyed, open smile Vanessa had flashed on the First Nanny, in order to avoid laughing.

"She invited me to have coffee inside. Alfredo and Francisco were long gone, although we could hear them stomping through the palace. And what a palace it is," Vanessa said in a tone of wonder. "The stairway was even grander than it looked from below, with marble steps and porcelain tiles, and the walls decorated with statues, and arches, and...all sorts of figures. I thought, 'Wow, I could live here'..."

"Maybe you will, when Alfredo becomes Governor," Lucas said, only half in jest. If anybody in the family ever got to be elected to head the country's government, it would probably be his impossibly wise-for-his-age godson.

"We climbed all the way to the third floor, and Nereida took me through all of these beautifully decorated halls. We passed...what's his name, that hateful Secretary of Justice..."

"Rovira Melendez, Walter Rovira Melendez?" Jeannie prompted.

"Rovira Melendez," Vanessa confirmed. "He was sitting with some other politician in one of the rooms, and they both stopped talking when we walked by, but neither of them stood up or said even hi."

Lucas felt tempted to say something about the man, but opted to remain quiet. He considered Rovira Melendez a bully, a snob, and a very dangerous person in the present day political arena, but Michael was a rabid pro-statehood supporter, and to mention anything about the man could potentially convert Vanessa's tale into a bitter political debate.

"And finally, we got to this room that faced the interior courtyard of La Fortaleza. It was a big room that had many doors with louvered windows, you know, like the ones the old houses used to have, and the doors were decorated with square glass panels of many different colors, and the sun shone through them, so that the room glowed, as if it was magic!" Vanessa took a big bite of her hamburger, which she clutched half-eaten as she spoke, but she was so caught up in her story that she continued talking before she had finished swallowing it. "And Nereida told me..." she paused briefly, to continue chewing, "that we were in the 'informal room'! But you know what?"

"What?" they all repeated in unison, making Vanessa laugh.

"There wasn't *anything* informal about it! The floors were made of very polished black and white marble squares, and in the center there were these very plush, padded, armchairs and huge sofas covered with a beautiful mustard-colored fabric, and the rest of the furniture was made of dark mahogany wood, with a large chandelier hanging from the ceiling, and there was even a large statue by Murillo, and a gorgeous Persian rug. I mean, if that is informal, I really don't know what they would call my house!"

"Nereida didn't give you a tour?" Jeannie asked, referring, like Vanessa, to the First Nanny on a first-name basis.

"She apologized to me for not being able to do it, but it seems the Governor is busy meeting with his different Cabinet Members to prepare for a speech he's giving this coming Tuesday."

"That would be the State of the Commonwealth Address," Michael said in an amused tone, as he drew out another bun from its plastic bag, and began to prepare a second hamburger. "It's going to be a biggie. He's talking about the plebiscite."

The plebiscite was a special referendum in which the citizens of Puerto Rico would vote for the status that they preferred: statehood, the continuation of the Commonwealth, or independence. Since the year that the island became a Commonwealth in 1952, three plebiscites had been held. Every time, the Commonwealth status had won by an overwhelming majority. The results of a plebiscite had no binding effect on Congress, and it could opt to ignore them entirely. However, it would prove very difficult for Congress to disregard a petition by the majority of the Puerto Ricans to become a state, particularly when President Powell had pledged his support if such a petition was made.

"I wish him luck," Lucas said, before he could stop himself.

"You don't think Pietrantoni has the votes to win the plebiscite?" Michael inquired in a peeved tone.

Jeannie surreptitiously stepped on Lucas' foot, urging him to drop the subject, but he ignored her.

"I think he has some major problems, don't you? I mean, there's rumors he's going to have to lay off twelve thousand government employees this year. Twelve thousand! And maybe raise taxes. A plebiscite may be the last thing we need right now. And to answer your question, if he holds it, he may not have the votes."

Michael considered his brother-in-law's stark assessment in silence, then shrugged. "Yeah, well, I don't think it's as bad as you paint it, but I agree with you that it's not going to be as easy as the *independentistas* fear it's going to be," he said, choosing not to pursue the matter further, and earning a loving look from his wife Vanessa.

"So anyway, we had coffee, which this butler brings on a small table with wheels, with some butter cookies, Jeannie, that were to die for! I think I ate too many of them. The coffee cups were gorgeous—Limoges porcelain—and the coffee and the milk were served from silver pots."

"Did the butler wear a tuxedo?" asked Lucas, refusing to miss any opportunity to bait her sister. They were what was called Irish twins, siblings born within less than a year from each other, Lucas being the eldest, and he loved her dearly.

"No, dummy, he was not wearing a tuxedo, just a long-sleeved shirt." Then she turned to Sofia, who was listening attentively even though she did not understand most of what was being said, and added, "Your daddy *is* crazy!" She picked her up, and kissed her, and exclaimed enthusiastically, "And you are *so* precious!" Then she continued. "But you know what impressed me the most? Nereida. Because she could have been this stuck-up lady, and instead she was so—" Vanessa groped for the right word.

"Well endowed?" Lucas suggested.

"Hot?" contributed Michael.

"Down-to-earth," Vanessa responded, refusing to engage the men. "Very down-to-earth. I liked her a lot. While we were drinking the coffee, she told us that they were very grateful to Alfredo, because he's been one of the few kids in school who's befriended Francisco, and that the other day he stood up to two fourth graders that were bullying Francisco."

"Really?" Michael asked, surprised, but proud. "I didn't know that."

"Darling, what your son does in school is one of the deep mysteries of the universe. We know he gets good grades, and that the teachers love him, but that's about all we know about him! Have you ever asked him how his day was? If you get a 'Fine' or an 'Okay' out of him you're doing great. He *is* your son, after all."

"Really?" Michael asked again, this time feigning surprise, and then cringed as Vanessa raised her hand to hit him. He was saved by Vanessa's cell phone, which started to play the Macarena song. Vanessa glanced at the fluorescent glow on the phone's screen, and whispered, as if she could be overheard, "Mom," hitting the "Talk" button. "Hell-o!" she answered in a cheery note, automatically increasing the volume of her voice, "How are the Pietri sisters doing on their night out? Have any of you picked up anyone yet?" She paused, and listened, "Mom? I can barely hear you!"

"I mean, I'm not surprised Alfredo could take care of the bullies," Michael interjected, while Vanessa continued to talk over the phone. "He is a brown belt in taekwondo. What surprises me—" He stopped, as his wife signaled him urgently with her hand to be still.

"What?" she asked in an alarmed voice. The exuberance of the group fizzled out instantly. All at the table fixed their eyes on her, and the children, sensing the tension of their elders, searched inquiringly from face to face. Vanessa listened for a long while, trying to ask questions, but could not manage to put in more than a few syllables as her mother continued to interrupt her. "But you're all okay," she managed to ask after a long interlude. She glanced at Lucas and nodded, looking more relieved, silently confirming that Fannie was fine. "I tell you, Mom, I think you should call it a night and go to Michelle's apartment...No, no, forget about the concert...Mom, go to Michelle's apartment now, okay? The three of you. You have work tomorrow...Okay...Okay...I love you."

"What happened?" Lucas asked her with concern. "Is she okay?"

"She's okay," Vanessa answered, still sounding worried. "They're all okay, but it's still scary. Listen to what happened," she said, inclining her head forward and lowering her voice to a conspiratorial tone. "They had just sat at the El Patio del Abuelo Restaurant, in San Sebastian Street, and were ordering some drinks, when Hector Pons—you remember him, right?" she asked her brother.

"Hector? Sure. He sells gold to the *Joyero*. Fat, very nice, talkative. I think he has a secret crush on Maria."

"That's the one. Well, he walks into the restaurant, and he is shaken, looking very, very pale. You know what your mother said?" Vanessa asked, chuckling all of a sudden, and pointing with her hamburger at his brother, "That he looked paler than a nun's behind!"

They were all forced to laugh hard, their brief scare starting to melt away.

"Yes, that does sound like Fannie, God bless her!" Jennie whispered with admiration, grabbing her husband's hand.

"So anyway, the man looks so distressed, that they invite him to sit with them, and they buy him a drink. And his hands are shaking so hard,

Mom says, that he spilled half of his drink on the table, he's so nervous. And guess what he tells them?" she asked, looking theatrically around the table. Nobody answered, so she continued. "*That-there-had-been-a-shoot-out-in-San-Sebastian-Street-just-a-few-minutes-before!*" She announced, crisply pronouncing every syllable for dramatic effect. "And it had happened just *two* houses away from El Patio! Hector said that he was walking down San Sebastian Street, looking at some of the art in the stalls, when somebody close to him started to curse and scream obscenities in English. Apparently, some drunk tourist had started arguing with some drunk *independentista*, and they began to push each other. Then, the *independentista...*"

"How do you know it was an *independentista*?" Lucas asked. "*Independentista*" was the term used to identify sympathizers of the pro-independence movement in Puerto Rico.

Vanessa raised her palm, indicating to his brother to be patient.

"Hector heard him shout, 'Wait until tomorrow, *gringo*! Tomorrow we're going to shove all of your colonial oppression back up your own *hum-hum!*" Vanessa censured the last word, motioning with her head towards the very attentive children. It would have been very funny had she not added, "And then he took out a gun, and fired several shots into the air, and Hector said that there had been panic among those who could see what was happening, and that people started screaming and running and shoving each other, and that some people had been thrown to the ground. Hector himself was pushed against a wall. Can you imagine if Mom and Maria and Evelyn had been there?"

The listeners maintained a sober silence, picturing the melee in their minds. The Fiestas de San Sebastian had always produced their share of mostly drunken street brawls and arrests. But guns had never played a role in the celebrations, and politics had always been set aside in a sort of unspoken truce, to be brandished elsewhere, in less joyous arenas. Now shots had been fired in anger, and partisan rage had reared its ugly head, threatening to shatter the fragile status quo.

"Fortunately, there was a young man close to the gunman who had the presence of mind to tackle him to the ground, and two municipal policemen that were nearby got there in a matter of seconds, and they arrested the man, and took him away. Hector says that as he was locked up in the police van, the drunk man went into a loud rant about a coming revolution, and something about Puerto Rico awakening soon to it's new destiny."

Michael stood up from the table, and walked to the bar, plunking some ice from the ice bucket into a plastic cup, and pouring coke until it boiled over the sides.

"Those assholes!" he said disgustedly. "They're really set on spoiling everything for the rest of us. You know, the U.S. should round them all up and place them all together to live in an island. 'Freeoria', they should call it. See how long they can rule themselves before they seek economic aid from the Americans." Michael finished drinking his coke, and began to chew on the ice.

Vanessa looked scared. She turned to her brother, seeking reassurance. "What do you make about what he said? Isn't it weird?"

It was weird, Lucas thought to himself, but when he saw the concern in the faces of the women, he smiled at them. "People say all sort of things when they get drunk. I wouldn't waste any time trying to find any kind of hidden meaning in what he said, or what Hector thought he heard, anyway. And think about it. If that revolution is being run by clowns like the drunk who just got arrested, then they're in for a very rough time. So don't worry, okay?"

Vanessa nodded, her eyes filled with relief.

"Michelle will probably talk about the incident tonight," Lucas reminded everyone.

"That's right! She'll be in the ten o'clock news tonight!" Vanessa said brightly. "That's less than an hour away. Maybe we should call her so she can talk to mom and Hector Pons."

"Maybe you should," Lucas said with a genial smile. "From your house."

Vanessa looked perplexed, so Michael explained. "They're throwing us out, honey. I think it's time to go home."

"No offense," Lucas confirmed, "but it's way past the kids' bedtime, and I have to get up to work early tomorrow morning, thanks to *your* mother," he said to Vanessa.

"Lucas!" Jennie said while stepping again on his husband's foot. She turned to her visitors. "You can stay as long as you want," she told them, secretly hoping they would leave.

"Oww!" Lucas complained, scowling at her. "Stop crushing my foot!" Then he followed it with another "Oww!" as she stepped harder on him.

"That's okay," Vanessa said cheerfully, enjoying his brother's discomfort. "We just wanted to use your barbecue...And see Jennie and the kids."

"Let's go, Vanessa," said Michael, standing up and, after grabbing the leftover buns and the potato chips, beginning to walk towards the door. "I've heard about fake excuses for not playing chess when you're about to be checkmated," he said with exaggerated indignation, "but this tops them all. Goodbye, and good night!" He walked a couple of paces and swung around abruptly. "Next time, we'll throw you out from *our* house! Only Sofia and Gabriel will be allowed to stay!"

"What about me?" Jennie gasped, "I told you to stay as long as you wanted!"

Michael shook his head sorrowfully. "Sorry, baby, but you made your bed with this man," he said, pointing with an accusatory finger at Lucas, "and now you've got to sleep in it." He knelt on one leg, and opened his arms to the children, who flocked to him immediately. He swept them off the floor, and carried them to the porch.

"Goodnight, everybody!" Vanessa said, kissing Jeannie and Lucas, and hurrying after her husband. There, she rubbed noses with Sofia, and snatched Gabriel from Michael's arms, squeezing him tightly before handing him to his father.

"Bye, *madrina*," Gabriel said, yawning.

"Goodnight, buddy," Michael said, slapping Lucas on the back and handing him Sofia.

"Wait!" Lucas called after them, as they were about to enter their yard. "You didn't finish your Fortaleza story."

Vanessa stopped, pausing to think. "I think I've told you everything...I never got to say goodbye to Alfredo. He disappeared into the palace. I hope they let the Governor work..." She paused again. "Oh, yes, there was something else! As Nereida led me downstairs, and we were saying goodbye, I hear a voice calling 'Vanessa! Vanessa!' And you know who it was?"

"Who?"

"Maria Belen!"

"Who?" The name sounded familiar to Lucas, but he could not place it.

"Maria Belen!" Jeannie repeated, as if the name should have been obvious to him. "You know, Michelle's best friend in high school! She spent so much time in our house during her junior and senior years, that she almost lived there."

"Of course, Maria Belen!" Lucas said, amazed by his wife's incredible memory for details. She would have made an amazing detective had she wanted to pursue that career. "I just didn't associate her with La Fortaleza. What was she doing there?"

"When I tell you, you won't believe it!" Vanessa exclaimed in her typical Vanessa fashion. "She is digging a HOLE in the courtyard of La Fortaleza!"

Everyone remained tight-lipped for a short period of deep thought, and then burst into laughter.

Vanessa grinned. "She's an archeologist! The Governor asked her to investigate—"

"The Governor is into archeology now, as well?" Lucas asked with incredulity.

"It seems that one day, as the Governor's limousine was driving into the courtyard, some people were doing some repair work on some of its cobblestones, and they had uncovered something that looked like a big well." Vanessa explained. "They were about to refill the hole, when the Governor saw it as he got off his car, and stopped them. He called the Institute of Culture to investigate, and they sent Maria Belen."

"And did they find anything in the well?"

"It wasn't a well at all! It was a partially destroyed circular stairway. They have been clearing the rubble away, and examining the area for about two months now, and she told us that they had originally thought it ended in some underground storage room. But yesterday, you know what happened?"

"They found Ponce de Leon's lost fountain of youth!"

"Funny, but no. *They-found-the-entrance-to-a-tunnel!*" she announced, adopting her melodramatic, syllable-by-syllable pronunciation. "Maria Belen told Nereida and I that they had finished digging out most of the rubble, and that the tunnel seemed to be in pretty good shape. We walked to its edge, and the entrance was lit with electric lamps, and even so, it looked spooky. There were two other people there taking buckets of earth out of it and pouring them into a giant strainer, but Maria Belen said that there was not much more rubble to clear. They're going to explore it on Monday! Isn't that exciting?"

It was, Lucas thought. Rumors of tunnels under San Juan surfaced every year at one time or another. For decades, their existence had been denied by the rangers of the National Park Service, who guarded the forts. But then, a year ago, some "unofficial source" within the Service had admitted that a series of tunnels did in fact exist, and that some ran as far as El Morro from the San Cristobal Fort, while others connected to the cisterns under the city that at one time had been used to collect rain water for the houses. It seemed like a beehive of underground passages crisscrossed the ground under San Juan.

The "unofficial source" had stated to his interviewer that the National Park Service was waiting for the assignment of federal funds to undertake a thorough exploration, charting, and partial restoration of the tunnels. However, with the current economic situation, and Congress objecting to the use of funds for all sorts of "unnecessary" projects, the proposed study could be delayed by at least a generation.

It was speculated that the tunnels had been used to move Spanish troops from one defensive position to another without being seen or exposed to enemy fire, which made sense. But others had suggested that the tunnels were also used by the Governor and his officials to travel unobserved to the garrisons, to other government stations, and even to the cathedral to hear mass.

Then there were the government conspiracy theorists, who claimed that the government had known about the tunnels all the time, and had used them for its own sinister purposes. Antonio, the security guard who worked in *El Joyero de San Juan,* had assured Lucas that an acquaintance of "Archie", the *bolitero* friend who sold him his weekly illegal lottery ticket, had visited the tunnels himself, and that they had been sealed by the government, after it was discovered that local drug gangs were using it to move their goods through them.

As a history buff, Lucas had always wondered about the tunnels, and harbored the secret hope of wandering through them with a hard hat and a flashlight or even a torch, *a la* Indiana Jones. Therefore, the news of the courtyard discovery excited his imagination.

"Maybe you should tell Michelle about it," he expressed. "It would attract a lot of interest. It would be right down her alley. That and President Powell in May."

Vanessa assented thoughtfully, his brother's idea already germinating in her fertile imagination. "Yes," she said enthusiastically, "I'm calling her right now," she announced abruptly, and hastened towards her house, dialing her cell phone as she did. "Goodbye!"

Jeannie and Lucas watched as their neighbors disappeared into their house, smiling as Vanessa started her telephone call with her typical "So listen..." Then the door slammed behind her.

"So listen," Jeannie mimicked her sister-in-law's tone, "I really have to run to the bathroom. Do you think you could start putting the kids to bed, and I'll join you in a few minutes?" and she left before Lucas could answer her.

Gabriel had fallen asleep by the time they reached his crib. Lucas placed Sofia on the floor, and whispered, "Shhhh! I'm putting baby Gabriel in his crib, and then I'll take you to bed, okay?"

He had to suppress a chuckle when Sofia raised her index finger to her lips, and squeaked, "Be quiet! You're going to wake up baby Gabriel!" She usually referred to his brother as *baby* Gabriel, emphasizing her two-year seniority.

It took him another fifteen minutes to take Sofia to the potty, oversee her tooth-brushing routine—she insisted on doing it alone, rinsing and gargling from a paper cup—putting on her pajamas, and tucking her in.

"I love you, Sofia," he whispered to her, letting her embrace him and plant a wet kiss on his face.

"I love you too, Daddy," she replied.

He could not find Jennie in their room or their bathroom, so he walked back to the corridor just in time to see her exit quietly from Gabriel's room. She was wearing her tan London Fog raincoat and red high-heeled shoes.

"I changed Gabriel," she said matter-of-factly.

He stared at her in wonder. "That's not all you changed," he mumbled.

"You're leering at me," she protested unconvincingly, as one of her legs slid through the unbuttoned slit of her raincoat all the way up to her thigh.

Lucas approached her, and held her by the waist. He turned his eyes upwards, towards the ceiling, and said, "Thank you, God!"

"For what?" Jeannie asked innocently.

"For the heavy, kinky sex we are about to have."

"You are such a pig!" she said with a wicked smile.

"And you, my love, are a princess," he replied, bringing her closer to him. "And who turned out to have the better deal? The princess who married a pig, or the pig who married a princess?"

It was a rhetorical question.

CHAPTER IX

"That concludes tonight's news," Michelle announced, smiling directly at the camera. "Stay tuned for "Esta Noche," where Lily Garcia will interview Cheyenne, and Marian Pabon will talk about her new movie, 'Casi, casi.' On behalf of Rafael 'Correcaminos' Frontera and Adolfo Martinez, this is Michelle Alfaro, wishing you a great night, and even better dreams."

The camera panned back, showing the three newscasters, as the urgent staccato of a typewriter-like music rose in volume. The three reporters engaged in a friendly, soundless conversation while the credits of the program rolled over them. Had the viewers been able to pan even further back, the tiny set of the newscast would have seemed like an encapsulated bubble of bright light, trapped inside a cavernously dark studio.

As Michelle began to collect her script, Correcaminos slid his hand over the desk and furtively placed it on hers. Michelle darted a look at the studio's monitor, and noticed it had faded to black. Then she deftly slapped Correcamino's hand away.

"Your intransigence bewilders me," Correcaminos lamented in a dignified, soap opera baritone voice. At forty years of age, he was the undisputed king of sportscasters in Puerto Rico, all 5'7" and 150 pounds of him.

He had worked hard to earn that reputation. An impeccable dresser, who wore mostly light colored, tailor-fitted linen suits and scandalously colored silk ties, he was known as much for his slick, combed-back, pitch-black hair, as for his fearless, unrelenting reporting. Those sports figures, local or visiting, who had braved through one of his interviews rated him as tough but fair, the type of reporter who refused to endure any kind of bullshit, who called the facts exactly as he saw them, and who kowtowed to no one, regardless of his or her reputation.

Despite his short stature, he competed in sports with the same ferocity he brought to bear in his work, and was particularly good as a basketball point guard and as a softball shortstop, moving with surprising speed and agility, hence his nickname of "Correcaminos", or "Roadrunner". He also projected the outward aura of an unrepentant ladies' man, but was very happily married, and would never have dared to be unfaithful to his precious Edna.

"Truly, love goddess," Correcaminos insisted, in a whispery, languid voice, "you have no idea of what you're missing."

Michelle stared at him and cracked up, forcing him to grin sheepishly. They had been friends now for six years, and Correcaminos had been a major factor in helping her to break into the business.

"Leave her alone, you creep!" a raspy voice shot out from the darkness, then took the form of another short, middle-aged man. There, however, all similarities with Correcaminos ended.

The best way to describe Doel Reyes would be as an urbanized hippie, a once afro-wearing, drooping-mustached, pure, slogan-spouting idealist who had survived Vietnam unscathed both physically and mentally, and stumbled into a job in the news department of WKPA television. To his everlasting surprise, and that of most of his superiors, he had not only survived but thrived in his position, becoming the improbable driving force behind the award winning news program.

Now at 60, and for the last ten years, he headed the station's news department as its editor in chief. His wild, lofty afro had dwindled to a short, neatly-styled haircut; his Pancho Villa style mustache had been trimmed to a respectable length; his light-brown, curly hair had acquired a certain amount of respectability with small, carefully groomed streaks of gray; and his bell-bottomed pants and wide-collared, polyester shirts had yielded to jeans, pale-colored, buttoned-down Oxford shirts, and—to survive the sub Arctic temperatures of the station—woolen sweaters. Still, his flower-powered soul continued to flourish inside of him, unchanged.

"Great show, Michelle," he said cheerfully. Like Correcaminos, he had become one of the young newscaster's principal patrons in her career, having been a close friend of Michelle's father during the decades they had worked together in television.

"How about me?" Correcaminos asked, but was ignored by his two colleagues.

"That disturbance in the San Sebastian festivities," Doel continued, eyeing Michelle with that half-curious, half-tenacious look she had learned to recognize whenever he latched onto a story that captured his attention, "what do you think of it?"

Correcaminos harrumphed, and lazily stretched his arms over his head, his private way of cautioning her to think carefully before she answered the question. Doel seldom asked an opinion from anybody, and when he did, he usually had formed one himself.

"A random occurrence?" she ventured.

"Maybe," Doel replied with no real conviction.

"Yes, but what about what your mother told us over the telephone?" Correcaminos chimed in, uninvited.

Fifteen minutes before the newscast, Michelle had received a call from her sister Vanessa, telling her about the shootout. The Associated Press report received by the station had made no mention of the words that the drunk man had shouted, merely referring to the shots that he had fired and identifying him as Alejandro Bergara, a student from the University of Puerto Rico. Michelle, Doel, and—even though not within his scope of work—Correcaminos had debated whether a reference to the drunk youth's threat should be mentioned in the telecast. In the end, they had decided against it, unable to verify with Hector Pons the content of what had been shouted, the only direct witness who could attest to the shooter's threat.

"If what your mother said is right," Correcaminos continued unbidden, hijacking the conversation, "and forgive me for being so blunt, my princess, because I do know your mother well, love her, and respect her, but she can come up with some doozies sometimes. But..." he paused, raising his index finger, then placing it on his lower lip, as he attempted to pick up the thread of what he was saying, "but if she is right, then my gut feeling tells me that we need to investigate further. And by the nature of the man's threat, we need to do it fast."

Doel gazed briefly at sportscaster, then shook his head disapprovingly. He knew exactly what Correcaminos was up to. He wanted to give Michelle more time to consider all of the facts before she committed herself to an answer, as well as give her the benefit of his opinion. It upset Doel. Sometimes, Correcaminos tried too hard to help Michelle. Like his colleague, Doel felt that she had a tremendous potential as a newsperson. However, the only way that she would grow professionally was by reaching her own conclusions, and learning from her mistakes.

"I thought Michelle and I were having a private conversation," he said out loud, to nobody in particular.

"Obviously, you were mistaken," Correcaminos answered, with a benign, condescending smile. "But go ahead, Doel, I want to be enlightened by that privileged mind of yours. Although I've been trying to be enlightened for...how many years have we known each other? Twenty? Twenty-two? For twenty-two years...I hear that your mind is a steel trap for details, which probably explains why nothing comes out of it."

"Save your sarcasm for your sports victims," Doel retorted, and turned his attention back to his young reporter. Michelle tried unsuccessfully to keep her face straight, forcing Doel to smile despite himself. He sighed resignedly. He and Correcaminos had been close friends for as long as Michelle could remember, and held a healthy respect of each other's journalistic talents. But Correcaminos could sometimes be over-protective.

"I think it's not so much what the man said," Michelle indicated thoughtfully, "as to what he was carrying...or not carrying, rather. No driver's license or any other personal identification, although he had a previous arrest record and had been fingerprinted before, so the police identified him easily."

Doel nodded, closing his eyes in contented concentration, as he usually did when he picked up the scent of an important story. His competitors had nicknamed him "The Bloodhound", for his uncanny sense of focusing on overlooked details in a news item, and following them to a successful conclusion.

"Go on," he said.

"We don't have any information on the gun yet?" she asked tentatively.

"Not yet. I'm working on it. Think. What else?"

"Well, he said that—"

"No, no, forget about his invectives when he was arrested," interrupted Doel impatiently. "You were on the right track. Continue on the things that we've learned that he carried."

Michelle reviewed in her mind the list of objects the Municipal Police had reported—in a brief videotaped interview—it had found on the arrested man.

"The food! The food in his backpack!" Michelle said suddenly, as the image of the contents of the backpack, strewn over a bare police table, flashed back in her head. "The suspect had several cans of food in his backpack, including corned beef, pork and beans, and Vienna sausages! As if he was going camping, or preparing for a few days in the open."

Correcaminos beamed at Michelle, impressed by her powers of observation, but opted to remain silent. Doel rewarded her with prolonged, emphatic nod.

"Precisely!" said the news director enthusiastically. "Why would somebody bring cans of food to the Fiestas de San Sebastian? I hate to admit it, but what Correcaminos suggested before is right."

"Thank you!"

"There's more to the shootout than meets the eye, and we need to find out about it before anybody else gets the scoop." Doel pulled out of his back pants pocket a small notebook, and reviewed its contents. "Okay," he said after a few seconds. "While you were broadcasting the news, I contacted the Municipal Police station in San Juan. I happen to know someone who works there, Sergeant Brito Morales, who is in charge of the desk where they make the bookings and fingerprint the suspects—"

"What a coincidence!" Correcaminos winked at Michelle. Doel always "happened to have contacts" with most of the police force of Puerto Rico, eighty percent of government employees, and half the population of Puerto Rico.

"Sergeant Morales' shift ends at midnight, and he has agreed to talk to us. And when I told him that it might be you who does the interview, he was so excited that he said he would try to have the policemen who made the arrest with him," Doel said brightly.

"You pimp!" Correcaminos said, sounding shocked.

"What do you say?" Doel asked Michelle straight on, not bothering to acknowledge the presence of his friend. "Can you wing it?"

Michelle glanced at her watch. It was twenty minutes past eleven. If she hurried, and was not caught in a lot traffic, she could probably make it on time.

"Sure!" she responded.

"Excellent!" Doel slapped the desk lightly, finalizing the discussion, and began to walk away towards the studio's control room. "I'll warn Brito that you're coming, so that he waits for you in case you're late!" he added over his shoulder. "Let's meet tomorrow at eight, to discuss what you find out," his disembodied voice called out of the darkness. "Good luck!"

Michelle finished ordering the loose pages of her script, picked up her purse, and stood up to leave.

"See you tomorrow," she said to Correcaminos.

"You want me to go with you?" he asked her gallantly.

"I'll be okay, thanks," she answered. "It's just four blocks from where I live anyway."

"I could always spend the night in your apartment," he said mischievously, throwing out his chest in a manly fashion, and speaking with his masculine, soap-opera voice.

Michelle smiled. "Well, my mother and my aunts will be there, so you'll have to share one of their beds."

"Tempting," Correcaminos said, remaining tight-lipped for several seconds, as if seriously considering the offer, "but I think I'll pass. You, I can handle. Your mother...she's just too wild for me."

"You're working tomorrow, right?" she asked, as she rushed out of the studio, and before he could answer, she blew him a kiss. "See you in a couple hours then!" she shouted.

She couldn't have been more wrong.

CHAPTER X

Governor Roberto Pietrantoni yawned, took off his reading glasses, and rubbed the bridge of his nose. He had been reviewing the speech for six hours now, and the double-spaced, large-lettered words were beginning to blur before his eyes. Except for the tick-tock of the table pendulum clock he had brought with him when he moved into La Fortaleza, and the occasional rustle of a revised page, no noise disturbed the stealth of the office.

It was a cavernous room, set to impress. Its rectangular space extended for more than sixty feet, bounded on each of its two longer sides by four sets of tall, solid oak double doors. The doors were separated by even taller bas reliefs simulating Greek columns that rose about three quarters of the way up into a fifteen-foot high ceiling, and stopped under decorative designs of white stucco and inlaid gold that encircled the entire room. Two crystal chandeliers dropped from the ceiling like twin, giant, gleaming tears, while a huge carpet, with geometrical patterns delineated in red, pink, and yellow, covered most of the tiled floor.

The Governor's desk lay at one end of the office, opposite to its entrance, framed by two sets of glass-paneled doors. Since 1846, when the Executive Mansion—then basically a fortress—had been remodeled and transformed into the Palace of Santa Catalina, any visitor wandering into the enormous hall was forced to amble past a man-sized globe of the world, traverse a sizable expanse of carpet, and pick his way past a big, low table surrounded by four large, lavishly upholstered rocking chairs. It was a long walk, purposely planned to impress and intimidate.

Even the Governor's desk had been designed to display power. Made of solid mahogany, it measured a length of eight feet, slightly more than a third of the width of the room, larger than the desk of the President of the United States in the Oval Office. A smaller table, also of mahogany, extended from the desk's center, ample enough to accommodate two seats. Perched on a cabinet behind the desk, a statue of St. John the Baptist, patron saint of San Juan, held watch over the Governor. Two other tables, located near the back doors, held several photographs of the Governor's family, friends, and acquaintances.

Countless governors, Spaniards appointed by the King of Spain, Americans appointed by the President of the United States, locals appointed by the President of the United States, and finally, Puerto Ricans elected by their own people, had occupied that room throughout more than one and one half centuries. And in total, more than one hundred and seventy men had presided over the island's destiny in an uninterrupted succession since La Fortaleza had been founded by Juan Ponce De Leon, making it the oldest executive mansion in the Western Hemisphere.

Governor Pietrantoni prepared to tackle the content of the next page when his Secretary of State, sitting on one of the two chairs next to the desk's extension, cleared his throat.

"This statement that you make here, on page 12, that..." he took off his glasses and raised the paper closer to his eyes, to see the words better, " *'Under the enlightened guidance of Luis Muñoz Marin, Puerto Rico experienced an unprecedented economic and cultural growth in the decades of the 50's and the 60's, converting an impoverished agrarian society into the showcase of the Americas'...*"

"What about it?" Pietrantoni asked, knowing fully well to what the Secretary objected.

"Must you say it?"

The Governor peered at his friend over his bifocals. He had known Alberto Arizmendi since their law school years in the University of Puerto Rico, where they had become good friends. Upon graduation, both had been hired by the biggest law firm in the island, O'Brian, Freedman, and Sifre. There, the two friends had thrived.

Pietrantoni had quickly built a reputation as an intelligent and fearless litigator, with an uncanny ability to organize complex corporate cases, and a natural talent for cross-examination. His oratorical skills and likable personality endeared him to juries where usually defending large corporations—as he did—was considered to be a tremendous disadvantage. He was regarded by his peers as a tough, no-nonsense adversary, but respected for his honesty. He won very difficult cases, and he won them on the strength of his preparation and the eloquence of his arguments. Not surprisingly, he had been promoted to junior partnership within four years of entering the firm.

So had his friend Alberto. Contrary to Pietrantoni, Arizmendi never set foot in a courtroom. However, he thrived in the rarified atmosphere of the corporate-tax world, spending many twenty-hour workdays over-seeing complicated mergers and acquisitions, and presiding over multi-million dollar closings. Among his clients—pharmaceutical firms, giant retail chains, car manufacturing corporations, and energy wholesalers—he gained almost instant renown for his common sense advice and his sure-footed navigation through the confusing and maze-like provisions of the commercial and income tax laws.

Because of his uncanny knack to instantly get to the gist of problems, and because of his wind-up-toy, accelerated demeanor—an asset in a profession where services were invoiced at $400 per hour—he was dubbed by an unknown admirer as "Double A", and the name stuck. Lat-er, when he became Pietrantoni's campaign manager, and was subsequently appointed to the position of Secretary of State, his detrac-tors would call him other things behind his back.

Only five feet six inches tall, with a cherubic, round face and thinning hair that he combed in long strands over his mostly empty scalp, he served as the perfect foil to his boss, who stood at an athletic six feet and one inch. Thus, he inevitably became Sancho Panza to Pietrantoni's Don Quixote, Robin to Pietrantoni's Batman, or simply Tatoo. Those who crossed swords with him, however, soon learned that Alberto Arizmendi was not a man to be trifled with, and that calling him ridiculous names in no way reduced his prodigious intellectual prowess.

"Why shouldn't I say it?" Pietrantoni answered, baiting his friend. "Isn't it true?"

"With all due respect, truth doesn't have anything to do with it," Double A stated. "You are going to be proposing to the Legislature the enactment of a bill to hold a plebiscite less than a year from now, so why give some free publicity to the Commonwealth formula, and in the pro-cess, mention...What is it..." Arizmendi searched the exact reference on the page he held, " *'the enlightened guidance of Luis Muñoz Marin'*? Every self-respecting Popular in the country will feel duty bound to vote against us!"

Governor Pietrantoni rose from behind his desk, placed his hands in his pockets, and began to pace slowly through the room. It was his litiga-tor's walk, and Double A recognized it immediately. He had witnessed it several times, never in court, but when they argued over issues where his friend had already made up his mind. He would never forget the night, nearly twelve years before, when his then partner had marched into his office, closed the door behind him, and announced he was quitting the firm to take a position as a federal prosecutor.

Arizmendi had argued with him until the wee hours of the morning, questioning his sanity, calling the attention to the hefty, six-digit salary plus five-digit year end bonus that he would be giving up, and accusing him of not thinking of the welfare of his wife or of the firm that had nurtured him for the past six years. Pietrantoni had not flinched, and striding back and forth, had explained to his ex-classmate—and soon to be ex-partner—how his sense of justice would be stifled if he stayed in his present work any longer, and how he would lose his self-respect. *"So what?"* the ever practical Double A had been tempted to answer, but instead, he had tried to convince his friend that he could still seek justice as a partner of the firm. His arguments had not worked, and in retrospect, Arizmendi had known they would not work. He had known it from the moment he saw Pietrantoni walk into his office with his hands tucked into his pockets.

"I don't expect to get any votes for statehood from any self respecting Popular," Pietrantoni said. "Don't you think the *populares* will bring out the work of Muñoz Marin?"

Luis Muñoz Marin had been the first elected governor of Puerto Rico. A pragmatist who originally had favored independence, he founded the Popular Democratic Party, and with the consent of Congress, adopted a Constitution that converted Puerto Rico into a Commonwealth. Like Franklin Roosevelt, he served for four consecutive terms, leading the island into unprecedented prosperity and economic growth. He could have continued to be reelected, but refused to run for a fifth term, retiring from the governorship in 1964. To many Puerto Ricans, he was considered to be the founding father of their modern nation.

"If the *populares* are going to bring out Muñoz Marin, why should you?" Double A protested.

"Read the next sentence of the speech," Pietrantoni indicated to his Secretary of State.

Arizmendi picked up the revised text, and scanned the referenced passage. "Yeah, yeah, I saw it. *'But those days are over,"* he read out loud. *"The tax advantages that once made the Commonwealth status a viable alternative have been eliminated. The Commonwealth has become an albatross around Puerto Rico's neck. We are American citizens, and yet we cannot vote for the President, and are not truly represented in Congress. We gain no economic advantages from our inferior citizenship. On the contrary, every day we lose hundreds of jobs to other states, and we only receive a fraction of the federal funds we would be entitled to receive if we were to become a state. But worse of all, we waste a great portion of our energy and our resources bickering about our status, instead of dealing with the great and varied challenges that our society faces today.'"*

Double A flipped the page and placed it face down on the desk. "That's great, magnificent, even. I like it all. But there's still no need to mention Muñoz Marin."

Pietrantoni stopped moving. He was wearing the same old, rumpled sweater that Double A had seen him use for as long as he could remember, and a pair of faded jeans, which made him look a decade younger than his forty-six years of age. Even so, his first year as Governor had been a rough one, where he had found the government in a substantially worse shape than he had imagined, and been forced to undertake many unpopular measures. A natural athlete, he had nevertheless looked gaunt and, at times, tired during the past few months, and more than a hint of gray had begun to stake its claim over his dark brown hair.

"Like I said before, it's not the diehard *populares* that I worry about," he said. "They will vote for the Commonwealth. If we're going to win this thing, we need to win it on the merits. We need to convince the independent voters, the people who gave me a sixty-five percent majority vote last year, that the Commonwealth served its purpose forty, fifty years ago, but that now it is broken down and cannot be fixed!"

"This is just like a trial for you. You present the evidence to the people, and let the Puerto Rican jury decide," Arizmendi muttered skeptically, more to himself than to his boss.

"You don't believe that's the way to do it?" Pietrantoni asked him.

Double A shrugged. "I suppose," he conceded listlessly, prompting a curious glance from his friend.

"That's not really what's bothering you, is it?" Pietrantoni said, with suspicion.

Double A shrugged again. "Rovira Melendez called me a few hours ago," he confessed.

"Oh?" Pietrantoni asked warily.

"He said he had spoken to you about the elimination of the Commonwealth option from the plebiscite, and that you had been very vague in your position about it. He requested that I talk some sense into you..."

"Requested or demanded?" the Governor cut in quietly, barely able to contain his irritation.

"He used the word 'requested'," Double A responded, stirring in his chair and sounding a bit offended.

"Alberto, you are so good at phrasing careful responses," Pietrantoni said, his blue eyes twinkling with affectionate amusement. "So he used the word 'requested', you say. But did he really request or demand that you speak to me?"

"How should I know?" Double A asked innocently. "I am not paid to interpret the inflections in the voice of the people that talk to me, I'm paid to give you practical advice, especially now that Manuel is in the hospital!" Manuel Mendez was Governor Pietrantoni's chief of staff, another close lawyer friend of his who had worked in another law firm, dealing principally with labor unions, and who was known for his tough negotiating skills. Mendez had suffered a mild heart attack a week before, and had been ordered to stay resting at home, despite his vocal protests.

"And what did you say to Rovira Melendez?" the Governor inquired.

"I told him I would talk to you about the issue," Arizmendi answered.

"Well, I will save you the time and the effort," Pietrantoni said grimly.

"Roberto," Arizmendi implored, using the Governor's first name.

"The answer to him is no. Wait. The answer to him is: no, go fuck yourself and everyone else who happens to be related to you in any fucking way whatsoever!" Pietrantoni said, more loudly than he intended.

Double A sighed, and looked away. For a long time, neither man spoke.

Walter Rovira Melendez had been Pietrantoni's greatest problem since he had become Governor. It was not entirely Pietrantoni's fault. Appointing Rovira as a member of his Cabinet had really been the result of forces set in motion long before Pietrantoni ran for the island's top executive position, during the years when Pietrantoni earned his living as a federal prosecutor. At the time, the island's government was controlled by Oreste Alarcon, a young, energetic, strong-willed *statehooder* who had easily won re-election after his first term.

As governor, Oreste Alarcon had not believed in compromise, preferring to use the sledgehammer approach in order to gain his goals. During his first term, he had shaken up a lethargically bureaucratic government, galvanizing into action a series of bloated agencies that had ceased to function properly. He had also commenced several mega-infrastructure projects that had revived the lagging construction industry, including the Puerto Rico Convention Center and a mass transportation railway system. But his strong-arm tactics, headed by his then Chief of Staff Rovira Melendez, had alienated a large portion of the population, and alarmed some of his most moderate supporters.

After his re-election, a sequence of scandals had rocked his administration. His Secretary of Education was caught red-handed requesting political contributions from would be suppliers, and when arrested, was found to have, hidden in a shoebox, over one million dollars wrapped in tin foil. Several legislators from Alarcon's party had been jailed for extortion and bribery. And various officials from his Cabinet were found to have utilized public funds for glaringly private purposes, such as private family vacations to Europe and Disney World, expensive wardrobe purchases, luxurious restaurant dinners and parties, and even a kitchen remodeling.

To a significant degree, the fiscal abuses of the Alarcon administration had been flushed out into the open by the anti-corruption unit of the federal prosecutors' office, led by then District Attorney Roberto Pietrantoni. In a succession of spectacular cases, a dozen government officials had been indicted, tried and jailed, and half a dozen more had resigned. Pietrantoni's greatest success had come when he proved that the then President of the Senate, Alfonso Oviedo, had been demanding money from prospective contractors in order to help them attain lucrative contracts in ongoing infrastructure projects.

The "Payola Case", as Oviedo's conviction came to be identified by the press, propelled Pietrantoni to the forefront of the news, and made him one of the most admired public figures in Puerto Rico. Trying to salvage his battered image, Governor Alarcon offered him the position of Secretary of Justice to, as he phrased it, "clean the house from within". Pietrantoni accepted, but his cleanup efforts soon struck too close to home. After several attempts to investigate certain shady dealings between the Secretary of State and the government's main contractor, the huge stateside construction firm of Blackwelder & Williams, Pietrantoni found his investigation obstructed by La Fortaleza. Disgusted, he tendered his resignation.

Mostly because of the numerous scandals tied to his administration, Governor Alarcon lost a third bid for reelection, fostering the return of the Pro-Commonwealth Popular Party, led by the House Minority Leader, Ernesto Calderon. Calderon, however, faced the brunt of the recession, and was damaged by certain scandals of his own party. By the next election year, Alarcon, who had retired to live in the United States, returned to Puerto Rico, and attempted to regain the leadership of the Pro-Statehood Party. Like a modern, exiled Caesar, he was received triumphantly by thousands of his diehard supporters, his campaign headed and organized by his right hand man, Walter Rovira Melendez. This time, however, he was challenged by his once Secretary of Justice, Roberto Pietrantoni.

During the last four years, the shattered remnants of the Statehood Party had gravitated to a younger generation of leaders, untainted by the corruption of the prior two administrations. Pietrantoni became the foremost symbol of the new statehood movement, rallying the moderate and the young voters behind him. In the bitterly disputed primaries that followed, Rovira Melendez furtively circulated rumors that Pietrantoni was having an affair with his son's attractive nanny, and overtly accused him of being a rich lawyer who would sell the poor to the interests of his former corporate clients.

Pietrantoni won, but his party did not emerge from its primaries unscathed. In his defeat, Alarcon still managed to garner almost forty percent of the pro-statehood vote, mostly older generation diehards who still viewed the former governor as the Messiah who would lead them to statehood. Without their vote, Pietrantoni risked losing the general elections. In a reconciliatory gesture, which he later dubbed as "the selling of his soul to the Devil", Pietrantoni offered Alarcon and Rovira Melendez cabinet positions in his new government. "Better to keep your enemies close, to know what they are doing," he had justified to his campaign managers, Double A and Mendez. Alarcon had rejected the offer outright, while Rovira Melendez remained silent. However, after a couple of weeks, Alarcon had offered his support if Rovira Melendez was appointed as Pietrantoni's Secretary of Justice. Pietrantoni had accepted.

It had been a tremendous mistake. From the outset, Rovira Melendez had used his position as a pulpit to promote Alarcon's government agenda, and undermine Pietrantoni's position. Under the guise of fiscal economy, he had fired from the Justice Department hundreds of career employees who sympathized with the Commonwealth Party, then filled back most of the positions with Alarcon supporters, involving the government in a costly and prolonged class action. Worst of all, he had begun to hold impromptu press conferences, dispensing his unsolicited opinion on scores of issues that were not related to his office.

One of his pet subjects had been the plebiscite. Echoing Alarcon's philosophy, he had expressed in a televised interview that the Commonwealth was not a real political status, and that it should therefore not be considered as an option in the plebiscite vote. The people's choices should be limited to two: statehood or independence. His statement had made the headlines of all of the island's newspapers the next day. Flooded by press inquiries, La Fortaleza had announced that no decision on the plebiscite or its nature had yet been made, and that the Governor would address the issue in his upcoming State of the Commonwealth Address. It was on that issue that Rovira Melendez had "requested" Double A to talk to Pietrantoni.

"You are aware that Rovira Melendez visited me this afternoon, just before you arrived, to discuss this matter," Pietrantoni stated, more than asked.

Arizmendi dipped his head in acknowledgement.

It had been a very short and unpleasant meeting. Rovira and the present President of the Senate, Carlos Cortes, had sat at the round table in the center of the room and exchanged pleasantries, while one of the maids served them coffee.

"I want to thank you for receiving us on so short notice," Rovira Melendez had said graciously, as she withdrew from the office, "but a subject of grave importance has made it urgent that we speak to you before your speech on Tuesday."

Pietrantoni had nodded, not bothering to reply.

"We are concerned about the plebiscite formula," the Majority Leader had blurted, before his companion could continue. Cortes was the youngest of the three men, and by far the most inexperienced. He had been a stalwart Pietrantoni supporter during the elections, and ridden into power on his coattails. Tall, dark, and handsome, and with an untarnished reputation, he had been elected by his peers to head the pro-statehood majority in the Senate. During the past year, however, he had developed a healthy respect for Rovira Melendez's militant supporters.

Pietrantoni still said nothing, making Cortes squirm. Rovira eyed the Senate leader impatiently, and picked up where his colleague had stopped.

"There are many of us who strongly believe that the Commonwealth status should not be included as an option among the voters' choices in the plebiscite," he had stated in a surprisingly mild tone, at odds with his direct, challenging stare at the Governor.

Like Cortes, Rovira Melendez was a big man. Having grayed prematurely, he proudly displayed a full head of silver hair and a thick, black and white mustache that framed and helped to highlight the fearless, intelligent energy behind his dark eyes.

Pietrantoni had raised his cup, and sipped some of his coffee.

"Go on," he had urged his visitor.

"You know as well as any of us that today's Commonwealth is an artificial contraption, a dead end to all progress, a ruse created to appease the *independentistas* and have them lend to the Popular Party their anti-American votes in every election, so they can stay in power." Rovira Melendez had paused, waiting for the Governor to acknowledge his statement, but had been forced to continue after a prolonged wait. "We are, today, closer to statehood than we have ever been before. However, the *populares* will fight us tooth and nail for the survival of their obsolete form of government. They may muster thirty-five, maybe forty percent of the votes cast in the plebiscite, which will not be a majority, but will not help our cause in Washington, believe me. Such a substantial portion of the voters opposed to statehood may derail the statehood process, even if we win by a considerable majority."

"So I heard you say the other day on television," Pietrantoni had said evenly, barely concealing his disapproval.

"I would be derelict in my duty as Secretary of Justice, Mr. Governor," Rovira had continued arguing enthusiastically, either unaware of his host's hostility, or most likely ignoring it on purpose, "if I failed to point out to you that if the Commonwealth formula is included in the plebiscite, I and an overwhelming majority of our party *may* refrain, in good conscience, from participating in it."

"In other words, you would boycott the plebiscite," Pietrantoni had concluded, more to himself than to the others, showing no surprise.

"Unfortunately, yes, I would," Rovira Melendez had lamented, but his unrelenting dark gray eyes laughed. "I would have no choice."

"Even if it means that the statehood formula fails." The Governor had shifted his gaze to Cortes, who had nodded uncomfortably.

"Yes," Rovira Melendez had confirmed, "even if it means that the statehood formula fails."

Pietrantoni had stood up, and extended his hand to his visitors. "Well, I thank you for your candor," he had said, leading them to the office's exit. The two men had nervously waited for an answer, but had gotten none as the door was shut behind them.

Infuriated, Pietrantoni had walked to the cabinet behind his desk, pulled out a bottle of Black Label, and poured himself a stiff drink. Fifteen minutes later, he had begun to carefully review the section of his speech dealing with the plebiscite.

"Rovira Melendez has a point," Double A finally said. "Without him, we run the risk of not winning the plebiscite."

Pietrantoni walked back to his desk and slumped back in his seat.

"That's a risk we're going to have to take, won't we?" he said, picking up the next page of the revised speech, and trying to concentrate on it. But after a short rumination, he placed the page back on his desk, and addressed his friend.

"If you were a Congressman, and I approached you with the results of a plebiscite where the overwhelming majority of the vote had been cast in favor of statehood, but where roughly forty percent of the voters had boycotted it because the Commonwealth formula had been excluded, would you vote to make us a state?"

Arizmendi shifted in his chair, pondering on the question. Someone knocked softly on the office's door, then it opened slightly. The head of one of the Governor's security men popped out from the other side.

"Your son is asking to see you," the man said, grinning.

Before the Governor could answer, Francisco burst through the door, and ran towards the two men in the office. "Uncle Albert! Dad!" he shouted excitedly. He was chased reluctantly by another boy, who stopped two paces inside the office, and gaped at his surroundings in utter amazement. The boys were followed by a flustered Nereida.

Francisco embraced and kissed his Uncle Albert, then rushed to his father.

"Please forgive the interruption, Mr. Governor, but Francisco wanted to say goodnight," Nereida said, fretting with her hands, as the boy wrapped his arms around his father's neck.

Pietrantoni kissed him, then slogged towards the others with Francisco hanging from one leg.

"You two are up pretty late," the Governor said, looking at his watch. "It's almost 11:30 at night."

"It's my fault, Mr. Governor," said Nereida, blushing.

From his chair, Double A thought she looked very beautiful, more so because she was not aware of it. He had always wondered if some concealed romantic relationship existed between the Governor and her, but had never observed anything—any clandestine stares or words—that hinted to something more than a cordial professional relationship. He was convinced, however, that his friend had a secret crush on her.

"The children have no school tomorrow, and they were having so much fun that—"

"That's okay," Pietrantoni interrupted. "I was missing Francisco, who usually drops by a lot earlier." He cast a quick glance at the other boy, who continued to wait by the entrance. "And you must be the reason why Francisco is not in bed yet," he added, walking closer to him and extending his hand to greet him. "Hi, I'm Roberto Pietrantoni."

"This is my friend Alfredo, Dad!" Francisco said excitedly. "He's my best friend, although," Francisco lowered his voice confidentially, "he's a *popular*. We have to do something about that, Dad."

Alfredo grabbed the Governor's hand, and shook it with as much firmness as he could muster. "It is an honor, Mr. Governor," he said solemnly, looking very embarrassed. Pietrantoni felt tempted to dart a swift glance at Arizmendi, but intuitively knew that the look would not have escaped the boy's sharp eyes.

"There's nothing wrong with being a *popular*," he said, to Alfredo's apparent relief. "Is he a good friend to you?" he asked Francisco, who nodded. "Then that's all that matters. Good friends don't have to agree with everything each thinks. That would be boring. I have a lot of friends who are *populares*. Good friends."

"My dad is a *statehooder*," Alfredo informed the Governor, attempting to smooth over the fact that he wasn't. "My uncle is a *popular*," he then confessed truthfully, "but he likes you. Says that you are a good man, just wrong in your politics," he said, hoping the explanation would satisfy the Governor.

Pietrantoni saw Nereida cover her mouth, and heard Double A chuckle behind him. Even so, he managed to keep a straight face.

"Alfredo... Alfredo Del Valle? You're the boy that helped Francisco fight off the bullies in school?" he asked Alfredo.

Arizmendi never ceased to be amazed by his friend's memory for details. It had been one of his trademarks as a litigator, helping him to remember and make reference to a particular document or piece of evidence from among thousands of other items. And it had become one of his greatest assets as a politician, enabling him to recall the name not only of every *barrio* political leader, but of their families, assistants, and anybody else who happened to wander his way.

Alfredo beamed at him proudly.

"Well, you were very brave," Pietrantoni said to him, and shook his hand again. "We'll have to invite you to come visit us more often."

"Thank you, Mr. Governor," an exulted Alfredo responded.

"It's time to sleep, children," Nereida said from her end of the room, walking towards the door, and summoning the children with her hand to follow her.

"Goodnight," Pietrantoni and Arizmendi said, as the two children scampered behind her.

"Goodnight," she replied, while the children waved briefly, and withdrew in a whirlwind of chatter and laughter.

"Oh, and Nereida!" the Governor called after her, just as she was about to disappear behind the door. "I haven't told Patria that Mr. Arizmendi will stay with us tonight. Could you please ask her to make ready one of the rooms?"

"Of course, sir," she answered, and left, closing softly the door behind her.

"That friend of Francisco's is something else!" Double A said, laughing.

"We could use more independently minded people like him," the Governor responded as he returned to his desk. "Shall we finish this?"

"I take it, then, that it will be useless for me to try to exclude the Commonwealth option from the plebiscite formula?" Double A inquired, manfully pursuing the subject.

Pietrantoni raised his head from the text, and prepared to verbally chastise his friend, but he stopped himself before he uttered any angry words, realizing that Arizmendi was merely doing his job.

"Look," he said, after pondering on his response a bit more, "some time ago, the Chinese warned President Powell that if he received the Dalai Lama, they would consider it as his meddling in their internal affairs, and that it could have serious consequences in the commercial relationship between their countries. China, as you know, has a lot of clout today, as far as the economy of the United States is concerned. Still, Powell went ahead and openly received the Dalai Lama in the White House. You know why?"

"Because the President of the United States cannot allow anyone, particularly another nation, to dictate to him who he can and cannot see," Double A answered, and as the Governor nodded, he added, "See? I'm not so obtuse."

"No, you're not," Pietrantoni confirmed. "When you are the head of the government, you can't let other people tell what you can or cannot do. You can listen to their advice, and consider it, but you can't allow them to push you around, because if you do, well, you're not the head of the government any more."

Arizmendi considered the words of his friend.

"It will be very hard to win, if Rovira Melendez and Alarcon oppose us," Double A warned.

"It will be impossible to become a state if we disenfranchise the *populares*," Pietrantoni responded. "Congress will never accept our half-assed results as a valid manifestation of the will of the Puerto Rican people."

Arizmendi sighed. "So I guess we have less than a year to convince the majority of the people that they should vote in the plebiscite, *and* vote in favor of statehood," he said resignedly.

" '*We*' is too many people, Alberto." The Governor picked up the next page, and began reading it. "*You* need to start the convincing campaign right after Tuesday's speech." The Governor continued to read, without pausing to smile.

"Great!" Double A exclaimed with sarcastic zeal, rubbing his hands with glee, and mumbling to himself, "Shit..."

CHAPTER XI

Michelle exited the municipal police station, and turned left, heading towards the docks and her condominium. A few diehard revelers from the San Sebastian festivities still roamed the cobbled streets, but only sporadically, as the celebrations wound down. In the distance, a dog barked half-heartedly for a few seconds, then quit. The day's heat had dissipated to a "chilly" 67 degrees Fahrenheit, sweater weather in Puerto Rico, and as she treaded over the sidewalk close to the port and the bay, she felt the need to pull over her shoulders the silk shawl she had carried with her.

Her interview with the municipal police had lasted a lot longer than she had anticipated—she glanced at her watch, and saw that it was twenty-five minutes past one in the morning—but it had provided her with a treasure trove of information that she was eager to share with Doel, and which she was certain no other news organization possessed. Interesting information, the type that raised as many questions—maybe more—than it answered. Doel would be pleased.

She had begun by asking if she could interview the prisoner, even though she knew that she would not be allowed to do so. Sergeant Brito, the most senior of the three police officers who met her, had courteously refused, but had allowed the two men who had made the arrest to talk freely.

The man had been drunk out of his mind, they said, the percentage of alcohol in his blood exceeding the .20 level, more than twice the legal limit. As they led him into the police van, he had ranted and raged about an impending revolution, where the "Coqui Fighters" would overthrow the "American imperialists".

"The 'Coqui Fighters'? Who are the 'Coqui Fighters'?" Michelle had asked, wondering if the suspect had referred to some fringe anti-American group she knew nothing about, but the policemen were equally ignorant.

"Did he say anything else?" she had inquired.

They had paid little attention to his words, and he had passed out in the van, shortly after being locked up. They had searched his backpack in the police station, and discovered—in addition to the cans of food—a black armband emblazoned with the words "Free like the Coqui", along with two pairs of jeans, three t-shirts, and half a dozen pairs of socks and underwear.

"It seems," Michelle had commented, "that he intended to stay somewhere for several days."

The policemen had agreed, although with whom or where he could have been planning to stay they could not tell. A friend's house, possibly, they speculated.

"A cheap friend," Michelle had observed, "if Bergara had to bring his own food."

Then there had been the matter of the ski mask that had been found among the items of clothing. Obviously, Brito had said, Bergara was up to no good, since only a madman or a bank robber would use a ski mask in a tropical country.

The news had alarmed Michelle. "Don't you think that the authorities should take some emergency precautions?"

The three municipal officers had looked confused. "Like what?" one of the policemen, called Martinez, had asked. "Call the National Guard? Because of one drunk FEPIsta who disturbed the peace in the Fiestas de San Sebastian?"

"Tomorrow, when he awakes from his alcoholic dreams," Brito had said, prompting some laughs from his two companions, "and we give him two Aspirins and read him his Miranda rights, we'll be able to investigate this matter further. But for now, I'm sorry, Michelle," everybody called Michelle by her first name, "there's just nothing else we can do."

Tomorrow could bring with it the beginning of the "revolution", she had almost answered, concerned by the policemen's apparent indifference to the potentially dangerous situation. Yet even as the thought formed in her mind, she realized the difficulty of taking any preventive measures. Without any further information, what could the municipal police do on such a short-term basis? Call on the police that had worked all day long to return to their posts? And do or protect what? After all, Puerto Rico was a large island with four million inhabitants, full of possible targets for any terrorist act. And what, after all, had Bergara meant by a "revolution"? A full-blast revolt to unseat the present government? During the Fiestas de San Sebastian? It seemed highly unlikely.

"Have you found out anything about the gun?" she queried.

"It's a Glock 19, nine millimeter pistol," Brito replied, while Michelle dutifully wrote down the information, completely meaningless to her, on a small notepad. "The serial number, which this gun carries in a small steel plate on the trigger guard, was blowtorched away, so we can't identify where it came from. The lab may be able to examine the plate more closely tomorrow. We'll see. But he carried a lot of ammunition with him," he added, as an afterthought.

Doesn't that raise further concerns? Shouldn't you be alerting your superiors at the very least, she thought, but kept her misgivings to herself.

"Is that a common type of gun? Is it hard to get?" she asked instead.

"Common enough," Brito answered, while his two partners nodded emphatically. "You can buy it in any gun shop. A lot of people use it for target practice."

"But you need a gun license to carry a gun like that?" she insisted.

"If you want to use it legally in Puerto Rico."

"And Bergara did not have a valid gun license?"

"No."

"Good thing that we're keeping him off the streets, eh?" Martinez added, proud about his timely intervention.

The interview had lasted only a few more minutes after that, as Michelle checked on the suspect's criminal record. One DUI charge on April of last year—which would explain the lack of a driving license—one arrest the previous year for disturbing the peace after blocking the access of theatergoers, along with other FEPIsta demonstrators, to the University Theater, and a misdemeanor charge for spray painting with independence slogans half a dozen cars belonging to Army ROTC students. Certainly the background of an active anti-American, but of a violent revolutionary?

Flipping shut her notepad, Michelle had thanked her three interviewees, and had prepared to leave, when Martinez had taken out his cell phone, and asked if he could be photographed with her. The others, as well as four other policemen in the station, had quickly followed suit.

"I know this is not my business," Michelle had said to Brito as he had escorted her out of the station, "but I believe you should alert your superiors about this matter."

Brito had given her a perfunctory nod, as if considering her advice, but she could tell by his vacant stare that he would do nothing.

Well, she would stir things up tomorrow, she thought, examining once more her watch, and becoming horrified by the lateness of the hour. She hastened her pace towards her apartment, walking briskly past the quiet docks of the port.

There was much to think, and little time to think about it.

But it had been a long day, so any further thinking would have to wait until tomorrow.

Lucas strained his eyes to make out the red luminous numbers on his digital clock—he was not wearing his contact lenses—and saw that it was 3:33 AM. Somebody had once told him that when the numbers on a clock repeated themselves, he should knock on wood three times and make a wish, but he was too tired to reach out to his night table and do it.

The night had lived up fully to all of its promise, and more. However, sleep had eluded him. He felt drained and lethargic, and could not focus his thoughts on any particular subject except the Mickey Mouse Club song, which inexplicably played over and over in his head, and yet he could not fall asleep.

He turned, and in the semidarkness of the room, rested his eyes on the tranquil silhouette of his wife. She lay sideways, and the feminine curves of her body were accentuated in their full splendor by the long shadows of the evening. She was breathing heavily, not quite snoring, but just a tad from doing so, and looked exquisitely beautiful.

He moved closer to her and embraced her, and she stirred and snuggled into his body, making him feel her warmth. He smiled contentedly.

"I love you, Jeannie," he whispered.

CHAPTER XII

Angel San Miguel strode to the edge of the bridge, and stared down at the still, glassy waters of the Condado Lagoon. A chain of expensive high rise condominiums and luxury hotels enveloped most of it, and even at 3:30 in the morning, many of them were peppered with dozens of brightly lit windows that fused to create a man-made constellation on the distant surface of the lagoon.

To his far left extended the temporary two-lane steel bridge that connected the Condado strip of land to the island of San Juan, and which bisected about a third of the waters of the lagoon from its main body. It was called the "Puente de Dos Hermanos", or "The Bridge of the Two Brothers," in honor of the Behn brothers, the two American industrialists who had built the original bridge in 1908, and helped develop the Condado area.

Beyond the Dos Hermanos Bridge, San Miguel could see the proud, giant outline of the Grand Laguna Hotel, rising forty stories high from the easternmost corner of the island of San Juan. Other office and residential buildings clustered about it, but none stood as high as the hotel, a modern glass tower designed to provide the best views of the beautiful Caribbean scenery that surrounded it.

The modern hotel contrasted starkly with the diminutive Spanish fort that lay at its feet, protruding into the waters of the lagoon. Basically a small, thickly walled square, Fort San Geronimo had stood there for several centuries, a lonely sentinel denying access into the waters of the lagoon, and the first line of defense against any invaders that dared to attack San Juan from the land.

In addition to the fort, the open mouth of the lagoon was partially blocked by razor sharp reefs, extending through the water from El Condado to about half of the distance to the island of San Juan. The remaining rift between the two bodies of land was not wide, barely a hundred yards, but on most days large swells from the sea rolled between it, roaring like the jet engines of a landing jumbo jet and spewing torrents of foam over the broken teeth of the reef. At that time of the night, San Miguel could not see the spray of the waves, but he could hear, despite the distance, their angry thunder.

Ever the historian, San Miguel remembered the legend about those reefs, about the lone fisherman who allegedly existed a long, long time ago. Every day, he would launch his boat from a nearby beach, and row into the roiling sea to fish. His dog would see him go, and then swim to one of the rocks on the reefs, sit there, and wait for his master to return. One day, the legend says, the fisherman did not come back. Some claimed that he had been overtaken by a terrible storm, others that he had been swept away by a great wave, and others still that he had been dragged to the depths of the ocean by a terrible sea monster. Whatever the cause, the fisherman was never seen again. But his dog waited, refusing to budge from the spot, and as the days became weeks, and the weeks months, the dog became part of the reef, and turned into stone. And to this day, he looked into the sea, waiting for his master to return.

San Miguel had searched for the rock and found it. It bore an unsettling resemblance to the figure of a large, sitting dog, a Labrador, perhaps, or a German Shepherd, leaning slightly forward and looking attentively in the direction of the sea. "La Peña del Perro," the locals called it, "The Stone of the Dog," and many believed that as long as it kept its eternal watch, no harm would come to San Juan.

They were wrong, unfortunately, San Miguel thought with a certain amount of sincere regret, thinking about the destruction that was about to happen. But sometimes, the greater good required great sacrifices.

He felt tired but elated. It had been a long night of hard work, and the work was far from over. At one time, the rapidly unfolding events had nearly overwhelmed him. But throughout the crisis he had managed to maintain a clear head and remain focused, and he had quickly regained control of the situation. Afterwards, he had walked away from the site of the preparations, and strolled to the bridge closest to the lagoon, where the hectic noise produced by his men could be heard less.

Calmly, he tried to gather his thoughts.

Slightly before 7:00 in the evening, three of the four vans carrying explosives had parked on an open triangle of grass located opposite to the San Juan Yacht Club, at the end of the bridge leading from San Juan to Miramar. The fourth van had squeezed into a smaller space created at the foot of the Dos Hermanos Bridge to accommodate construction equipment. Both sites were empty and unguarded. The crews from the vans, wearing hard hats and the Aqueducts and Sewers Authority uniforms, had immediately cordoned off the areas with wide yellow plastic tape.

San Miguel and George had trudged across the Miramar bridge and leaned over its side, where they had seen the three pontoon boats, still waiting for the tide to drop. One of the boats had been tied to the central arch of the bridge, and Czecka and another man were attempting to drill some 3" wide holes with their hand-held drills, but not much else was going on.

It had not been until 7:40 PM that the tidal flow had fallen sufficiently for the pontoon boats to slide under the bridge. Then the work had started in earnest. Assailing the underside of the structure with heroic intensity, the crews of two of the boats began to use their big drills, attached to fixed stands on the pontoon decks. These were powerful drills, designed to cut through the hardest concrete structures and extract cores three feet long and six inches in diameter. But the pontoon boats did not provide the most stable of platforms, and the drilling had to be interrupted and reset often. Work had progressed slowly.

The third pontoon boat had crossed under the bridge where the drilling was being conducted and continued to the second of the three bridges that connected San Juan to Miramar. This was a much older and smaller structure, which was so deteriorated that if left untouched would have collapsed on its own in a few years. The crew of the boat had bored holes and placed charges at several strategic locations on its narrow support columns. When the moment came, the central portion of the small bridge would collapse as if supported by a deck of cards.

It had taken the large drilling machines four hours to produce thirty holes under the central arch of the first Miramar bridge. They had been drilled in three parallel lines that crossed the span and width of the bridge, each line containing ten evenly spaced holes. A distance of twenty feet separated the rows of holes from each other, so that when the explosives were set off, they would create a forty-foot gap in the structure.

The work had begun long after sunset, and as the darkness increased, the workers had added several bright spotlights. The illuminated underside of the bridge looked from the distance like a bright movie set. Clouds of cement dust wafted out of the sides of the bridge like fog, and slowly dissipated over the slick waters of the lagoon. The large pneumatic drills cut into the concrete with a deafening, shrill intensity that forced the men on the boats to use earplugs and to communicate by signs.

All of the lights and din were clearly noticeable from above, and they had created a traffic jam over the bridge, as the revelers leaving the festivities of San Sebastian slowed down their cars to see what was happening.

San Miguel had been forced to send two of his men with flags, to stand on both sides of the bridge and wave at the cars to hurry along.

About midway through the drilling, the men from the vans had begun to unload and pass on to the pontoon boats the white, six-inch wide PVC pipes that carried inside the C-4 explosive charges, and the large buckets containing the quick drying epoxy that would be used to seal the holes after the charges had been placed. Two demolition experts had begun to extract the shaped charges from inside the tubes, and to pack them tightly into the boreholes.

As soon as each of the charges had been placed, electric blasting caps were connected to them, and their wires allowed to spill out of the holes. The experts then spliced the wires and carefully connected all of them together. In an ideal world, the blasters would have first tested the conductivity of the entire wire circuit, before placing the blasting caps on the charges, to see if everything was properly connected. But in this case they did not have the means or the time to do so. Just in case, they prepared two different circuits, alternating the charges, so that each circuit would fire at least fifteen explosives. That way, if one of the circuits failed, the charges in the other could still be set off.

After the explosives had been prepared, the boreholes were plugged, or "stemmed" with quick drying epoxy. This increased the destructive power of the blast. When the C-4 charges detonated, the explosive materials would violently expand into extremely compressed gas, creating a pressure of such magnitude that it would deform and crumble the concrete around it. Part of the force of the explosions would have escaped through the open ends of the boreholes, had they not been sealed and plugged properly. Usually, sand or clay was used to close or "stem" a hole. However, that would have required the use of several more vans, and additional time and manpower. Instead, the terrorists had decided to use a quick drying epoxy, which would seal the holes as if they had never been opened before. When the time came, the resulting pressure from the explosions inside the boreholes would be devastating.

Nearly half a ton of C-4 had been packed into the first bridge, distributed between the thirty large boreholes and an equal number of smaller perforations done manually with the smaller hand-held three-inch drills. One quarter of a ton of additional explosives had been placed in the second of the three bridges connecting San Juan to Miramar. But it had taken the crews six hours to do all of that, and only within the last hour had the three pontoon boats been able to drift under the third of the Miramar bridges, where San Miguel was now standing. If it took his men that long to conclude the pending work, they would not finish before nine o'clock in the morning.

San Miguel sighed and, leaning over the bridge's railing, looked at the water directly underneath him. A couple of cans and a transparent water bottle floated placidly close to the bridge. Soon, as the tide rose, the water would begin to flow back into the lagoon, and the junk would be pushed away from the bridge by the current. By possibly 7:00 AM, the pontoon boats would no longer fit under the bridges. All the major drilling would have to be finished by then. His men were aware of this, and had redoubled their efforts, performing heroically. It would be close, but they would be ready.

He harbored no concerns about the Dos Hermanos Bridge that crossed from San Juan to El Condado. A separate crew of men, riding two inflatable rafts, had finished setting up the charges there by midnight. Since the bridge was a temporary structure supported by steel beams, the explosives had been set up in slightly more than an hour. Charges of C-4 had been wrapped diagonally around the steel components closest to the Condado area, and were set to demolish a forty-foot length of the road. The hardest part of that job, in fact, had not been placing the charges, but extending the wires under the long structure down to the van parked at the opposite end of the bridge without being seen. Two men had been posted to scare away anybody who, however unlikely, wandered under the bridge by boat to the location where the explosives had been placed.

Despite all the progress, San Miguel worried. A midnight call by Johnny Ray had momentarily shaken his unflappable confidence. The FEPI president had informed him in an unsteady voice that one of his fellow revolutionaries had gotten drunk in the Fiestas de San Sebastian, fired several shots into the air, and been arrested.

Pausing for one second to gather his wits, San Miguel had asked Johnny if he knew the man's name, and where he had been taken. Johnny instead had begun to apologize, but San Miguel had cut him short. Trying to keep the anger out of his voice, he had assured the panicked FEPI president that everything would be fine. Then, reminding him that they should avoid discussing the problem over the telephone, he had repeated his last question.

The name of the arrested student was Alejandro Bergara, Johnny had answered, this time heeding San Miguel's words. He did not know for a fact where he had been taken, since the girl who was with him had run away after the commotion started, but the news media reported that he was being held in the small municipal police station in Old San Juan. Johnny had asked him what else he should do. Stifling the urge to answer sarcastically that the FEPI had already done enough, San Miguel had merely told him to "have faith and pray", and hung up.

With his mind still reeling from the conversation, San Miguel had labored to keep his emotions in check and focus on the problem. He could not help but to think about his long struggle with others in his organization who had opposed his plan for being too ambitious. *"Risky and complicated and doomed to fail"*, one of the elders had called it. The complexity of his operation, they had warned, would only serve to dry up their limited resources, and affect other more plausible projects worldwide.

His rock-hard self-confidence and his enthusiasm had carried the day, however. Their leader had approved the mission, reminding the opposition about San Miguel's prior, spectacular successes. He would not risk that reputation, *and his life*, in an impossible mission, the leader had told the others, casting a sideways glance at San Miguel. It had been a vote of confidence, but also an implied threat. The message between the lines had been clear: if San Miguel failed, not only his reputation would be forfeit.

But he would not fail.

As quickly as the doubts and fears had arisen in his mind, he had brushed them aside and entered into his damage control mode. Taking a deep breath, he had dialed a number so secret and sensitive in nature that he had not recorded it in the phone's caller directory, but committed it to memory.

It belonged to one of the top officers of the Puerto Rico police. He had obtained it on the occasion that he had visited the Ojeda-Santacruz family, one of the most powerful drug cartels of Medellin in Colombia. The purpose of his visit had been to secure the transportation for the weapons he needed to smuggle into Puerto Rico. The Santacruz brothers had been curious about his operation, and had asked how it could affect their business there. San Miguel had assured them that their regular concerns in the island would not be affected. He had apologized for being unable to give them any details about how the weapons would be used, but had promised that the attention of the world would be drawn to Old San Juan, and that it would be an opportune time for them to smuggle as much of their wares as possible into other spots of the island, say Humacao or Guanica.

The Ojeda-Santacruz brothers had checked, through their own sources, the background of their elusive visitor, obtaining mostly the information that San Miguel had allowed to be known, some of which he had made up and circulated. They had been impressed. San Miguel had told them that his operation would greatly damage the standing of the United States in the world, and they believed him. And in the end, when he had innocently asked them, as an afterthought, if they knew of any contact with the local police in Puerto Rico, the two brothers had looked at each other, nodded, and given him the phone number that he was now dialing.

It belonged to one of the highest ranking officers in the Puerto Rico police force, his name being so sensitive that it was known only to the Ojeda-Santacruz brothers, their second in command, and a highly paid go-between. To San Miguel, he would respond under the code name of "Ramon". Ramon was responsible for securing the safe arrival into Puerto Rico of the cartel's major drug shipments. Receiving the schedules of the shipments ahead of time, he would misdirect the police resources, although occasionally—to maintain his credibility—he would be allowed to "score" by capturing smaller shipments of cocaine, or discovering several floating bales of marihuana.

The Ojeda-Santacruz brothers had warned San Miguel that Ramon should be used sparingly and with extreme caution, since he was the cartel's most valuable asset in Puerto Rico. Should anything happen to him, they informed him matter-of-factly, as they relaxed over a drink of scotch and ice by their pool, they would hold San Miguel personally responsible for it. He had thanked them, without acknowledging their threat, and continued talking business.

He had spoken to Ramon only twice. The first time, it had been through a cell phone, to set up the protocol for Ramon's future participation in the operation and for the payment of his services. Ramon had been expecting his call, and had directed him to come alone to an abandoned cement warehouse at night, near the ports. The place would be safe, the police officer had assured him, since it would be watched by his most trusted men. San Miguel had accepted and attended, but not alone, although Ramon's watchmen had never noticed anyone except San Miguel.

Ramon had addressed San Miguel from a dark corner through an electronic voice filter, in order to disguise his voice, and never allowed his client to see him. Before exchanging any information, they had agreed on Ramon's fee, one million dollars, half to be delivered at the same warehouse one week later, the other half to be transferred electronically to a bank in the Grand Caymans, one day after the event occurred. Afterwards, San Miguel had revealed the date of the operation, and delineated Ramon's role in the affair.

He had been particularly sparse in the details of his plan, and had told Ramon that his main function would be to warn him about any unusual activity by the police, and to divert as much of the police resources as he could from the area of the planned activity, which San Miguel had vaguely described as "the island of San Juan". This had provoked a bout of laughter from the man hiding in the shadows, who commended his patron on his ambition. San Miguel had not replied, but instead had briefed Ramon on the only specific action that would be required of him, in addition to his general duties. From his back pocket, San Miguel had pulled out an object and placed it on the floor in front of him.

"What is that?" Ramon had asked with a hint of amusement.

"A satellite phone," San Miguel had replied. "You can pick it up after I leave. Once the operation starts, I expect hundreds of thousands of people to call each other either for help, or to discuss what's happening. The regular communications system may be overwhelmed and stop functioning. I need to have an alternate way to get hold of you. The satellite phone will work, even if there is a logjam in the local communications."

A short silence had followed San Miguel's explanation.

"Smart," Ramon grudgingly conceded.

"Satellite phones don't work in enclosed spaces, so I will need you to periodically check it in the open for my messages. Let's say every two hours."

"Difficult," Ramon had responded, "but I will do my best."

"Please do so," San Miguel had retorted dryly. "Your compensation depends on it. If I need to reach you before the bridges are destroyed, I will reach you through your regular cell phone. Are you with me so far?"

"So far."

"Good. Now even though your role will be mostly passive, there is one thing I need you to do the night before the operation starts."

Ramon had listened, and accepted San Miguel's instructions without further comment, assuring him that he would make the necessary arrangements to be the top officer in control of the metropolitan police forces on the night and early morning hours of the last day of the San Sebastian Festival.

Finally, they had set up a fictitious routine in case they had to communicate with each other in case of any emergency. That routine was about to be put in use.

The number San Miguel had dialed rang twice, and then a gruff, no-nonsense voice answered, "*Hello?*"

"This is Felipe Ortiz, from El Nuevo Dia," San Miguel had said. "I am calling to get your impression about the arrest of Alejandro Bergara, the youth who started shooting a gun in the Fiestas de San Sebastian. What measures is the police taking to avoid any similar incidents?"

San Miguel heard the same voice of the warehouse say to somebody else "*Wait, wait,*" and then ask angrily, "*Who gave you this telephone number?*"

"I really can't reveal the—" San Miguel began to respond, but the man on the other end rudely interrupted him.

"*Listen, you idiot, this is a private number. I don't know who this Bergara is, and I don't really care, but if you waste any more of my very precious time, I will personally look for you and shove your phone up your ass!"* he had said, and cut off the conversation.

Despite his stress, San Miguel had chuckled. During the short exchange, San Miguel had asked Ramon to keep an eye on Alejandro Bergara, and Ramon, by promising to look him up and shove the cell phone up his ass *"if he called again"*, had let him know that there were no news so far, and that if he learned anything important about the arrested man, he would call back San Miguel. The lack of news had reassured San Miguel.

Even so, he had called the service provider for the satellite phone of the arrested student and reported it stolen. He knew that this was a temporary, stopgap measure, and that if their enemies became aware of his plot, they would be able to trace the limited telephone numbers recorded in the phone. But at least, by disabling the phone, the police would be unable to automatically dial any numbers contained in its memory.

Next, San Miguel pressed the number 2 and the pound sign on his cell phone, and made a third call.

"Yes," a voice, totally different from Ramon's, answered in a listless, almost effeminate tone.

"Loubriel?"

"Yes," El Alacran repeated.

"This is Alfredo Bergara. It seems that my son, Alejandro, was arrested for causing a disturbance in the Fiestas de San Sebastian. Apparently he was drunk, and was talking about a revolution."

"Really?" Andrade said, with an apparent lack of interest. San Miguel could picture the Machetero leader yawning, at the opposite end of the line.

"Yes," San Miguel stated. "The news is on the radio. He's been taken to the municipal police station in Old San Juan." It was the police station that El Alacran was supposed to capture immediately after the demolition of the bridges.

"Do you want me to get him out now?" El Alacran had asked, exhibiting the same concern of a television viewer who had been asked to take out the garbage.

"No, just keep a watch on him, will you?" San Miguel had responded. "I think he should stay the night in jail, to learn his lesson. Just call me, if anybody comes to visit him."

"Uhum," Andrade had confirmed good-naturedly, and without saying goodbye, had hung up. It was the second time that San Miguel had been left holding the phone.

Now, more than three hours after his telephone conversations, he felt relatively at peace. No unexpected or urgent calls had disturbed him away from his busy schedule, and he expected that none would.

It seemed as if the arrested student would not cause any problems after all. The municipal police would probably allow him to spend the night in jail, sleeping off his drunken stupor, to bring him in the morning before a magistrate for a preliminary hearing. By that time, anything he could say or do would not hurt their cause. *And what could he say or do, even if he was awake now and decided to cooperate with the authorities?* He did not know about the destruction of the bridges, or the hijacking of the Grand Laguna Hotel, or the capture of the Governor and the cruise ship *Mardi Gras.* Although Johnny Ray knew, and San Miguel would not put it beyond Johnny to have revealed to his followers some of the confidential details of the operation, just to impress them.

The last thought made him feel uneasy. *Even Johnny wouldn't be that foolish,* he told himself without a great deal of conviction.

In any event, in the unlikely case that the arrested student had learned about the inner workings of their scheme, and in the even less likely case that he decided to tell the police about it, who would believe him? Ramon had been warned about the situation, and he would not do anything to jeopardize the half million dollars his bank in the Grand Caymans was about to receive. And anyway, what could they do to prevent the execution of the plan with such short notice? Every passing hour brought him closer to his goal.

Several critical stages of the operation still had to be carried out, but their failure would not cause it to collapse, just make it less successful than expected. Only their failure to disable the bridges could endanger their entire plan. And that was being taken care of at that very moment.

San Miguel glanced at the grassy area where the three "PRASA" vans were parked, and decided it was time to check up on the progress of his men. Making certain that no cars were coming from Miramar, he crossed to the other side of the bridge, and leaned over the railing. By the din of the drills and the bright lights illuminating the underside of the bridge, he was able to confirm even before he looked at the water that all of the crews had finished their work elsewhere and converged on the present structure.

It sounded as if an angry beehive had been disturbed, the concrete under his feet vibrating as the big drills attacked it. Two pontoon boats—really one and a half boats, since one of them was halfway under the bridge—were visible from where he looked. On the prow of the half-concealed one stood Daniel, imparting instructions by hand signals to someone under the bridge.

San Miguel shouted at him several times, but Daniel did not look up, deafened by the noise. Searching the bridge's sidewalk, San Miguel found a small stone and a discarded box of Kentucky Fried Chicken. He threw the small stone at Daniel's helmet, but it missed, plopping unnoticed into the water. The lunch box, however, hit him squarely on the shoulder, showering Daniel and those around him with half consumed pieces of chicken and stale French fries.

Angrily, Daniel shifted his gaze upwards, and for the first time noticed his boss. San Miguel laughed and shrugged apologetically, then shouted at his associate, "Where's Czecka!"

Still Daniel did not understand him, and he motioned with his hands to the men about him to stop the work.

"What?" he asked in the relative silence that followed.

"Czecka," San Miguel answered. "Tell him it's time." Then, as an afterthought, he added, "How's work?"

Daniel nodded absently before answering, as if taking mental stock of what still needed to be done. "It's coming along. It should be ready by seven thirty-ish."

"Make it ready by seven, seven fifteen-ish at the most, and I will be happier," San Miguel replied brightly.

"Maybe if you didn't have to take Czecka away from me..."

"I'll settle for seven thirty-ish," San Miguel said before he could continue.

Daniel laughed, and ordered his men to renew their work.

The intense noise of the drills followed San Miguel back to the parked vans. There, he found George, overseeing the unloading of the PVC pipes, solemnly making notes on a clipboard as several men moved about.

"Do I look official enough?" he asked San Miguel, chuckling.

"You look exactly like a public supervisor should look."

"Why, thank you, boss!" George said, breaking into a broad grin.

"Any problems?"

George shook his head. "Nothing worth mentioning. A police patrol stopped about fifteen minutes ago. Asked if they could be of any service. I said, sure! Get on down there," he pointed towards the underside of the bridge, "and help the rest of our boys!" He chortled, sounding almost as if he was trying to expectorate. "Only one of them spoke *American*, and I could tell they were surprised I didn't speak their lingo, but then I said I had been flown out of Miami, and been workin' for two days on this project, and that I'd never seen such hard workers as his fellow Puerto Ricans, and that set real well with the American speaking officer, real well." George snickered, and shook his head. "It's amazing how far a compliment can take you. The policeman wished us luck and drove away. Didn't even ask what we was doing."

"You were always good with people, George," San Miguel said. "That's why I left you in charge."

A pontoon boat bearing Czecka approached the edge of the lagoon. As the giant stepped off its prow, the boat tilted forward, bouncing back up when he jumped to the shore, and gliding away to return to the bridge. His body and clothes were caked in grayish cement dust and sweat, so that he looked more like a walking marble statue than a man. A cloud of white trailed him as he plodded towards his associates.

"Oh my God!" George shouted in mock horror, throwing up his arms and backing away from the advancing monster. "Save us! Save us! A ghost is coming!" he screamed, hooting with laughter.

Czecka stopped in front of the two men, and stared at George as if he was some strange kind of bug that needed to be squashed.

"Ah, Czecka! There you are." San Miguel said pleasantly. "Are you ready to go?"

"The men need me here," Czecka uttered with a certain degree of irritation in his voice.

"Yes, I know," San Miguel replied. "But it's more important that you handle the black van."

Czecka said nothing, silently acknowledging his superior's last statement.

"Bear in mind that your mission is the most important part of our entire operation," San Miguel reminded the sullen giant. "It is the part of this operation that cannot fail."

"I will not fail," Czecka stated flatly, as a fact that admitted no contradiction.

"I know you won't," San Miguel responded. "That's why I'm placing you in charge. Now go. George will drive you back," he said, slapping his huge associate on the back, and unwittingly lifting a cloud of cement dust. "And for God's sake, wash yourself!"

George guffawed at the sight of it.

"Please don't eat me, Mr. Ghost," he told Czecka as they both walked to one of the vans.

"Keep talking," his surly companion warned him. "You may get to see the afterlife sooner than you think."

CHAPTER XIII

El Falansterio had been an offspring of the Great Depression. Trying to stimulate the collapsed economy, President Franklin Roosevelt had signed into law the "Federal Emergency Relief Act", which assigned millionaire federal funding to projects that promoted the creation of new infrastructure throughout the country. Puerto Rico was no exception. Fueled by the New Deal, the island embarked in a brand new experiment to improve living conditions for indigent families, and in 1937 finished the construction of the first public housing project in its history, El Falansterio.

The Federal Emergency Relief Act failed to jump-start the depressed economy, and in the following decades, scores of other larger public housing projects sprang across Puerto Rico, but from all points of view, El Falansterio from the outset proved to be money well spent, the standard against which all future developments would be measured, and would invariably fail to beat.

The apartment complex spread in the shape of a large rectangle over one city block, composed of a total of eighteen, three story buildings surrounding an enormous interior courtyard. Six buildings lined each of the two longer sides of the rectangle, including the side that faced the Puerta de Tierra Police Station across Fernandez Juncos Avenue. Four units established the length of El Falansterio's two other shorter flanks. Constructed in reinforced concrete, it had endured the devastation of several major hurricanes and the passage of thousands of families without suffering significant structural damage. Its two hundred and sixteen identical apartments contained internal patios and wide balconies that provided ample light and ventilation to its residents, while its wide central courtyard served as a meeting place for the community, and included a small kindergarten and a social activities center.

It was its Art Deco design, however, that set it apart. The housing project contained no sharp corners or angled terminations, the edges of its buildings ending in smooth, clean curves, its long balconies projecting outward with similar lines and adorned with wrought iron railings. Not surprisingly, it had soon become a central landmark of the city of San Juan.

Archie Roman stood nervously at the entrance of the building in the El Falansterio housing complex located closest to the corner of San Juan Street and Fernandez Juncos Avenue, and farthest from the police station. Gazing at his watch, he saw it was already twenty minutes past four o'clock in the morning. He felt miserable. During the past hour, he had guided to the roof of the complex three different groups, each composed by three men, and his bad leg hurt him. He was now waiting for the fourth and final group.

The incoming men spooked him. As a *bolitero*, or illegal lottery vendor, he felt no misgivings in dealing with individuals who skirted the outside boundaries of the law. However, these men were different. They moved differently, acted differently, spoke—if the few words they had uttered could be called "speaking"—differently. They were all very young and very fit, and were garbed in similar black, long-sleeved sweatshirts and dark jeans that could have easily passed as some kind of paramilitary uniforms. Each hefted two long, heavy-looking canvas bags, and interacted with each other with the precision and familiarity that only an intensive military training could produce.

He knew. He had been discharged from the U.S. Army just three years before, after being severely wounded in his right leg by a roadside bomb in Fallujah, Iraq. Known as "El Colorao", or "The Redheaded One", Archie had returned to Puerto Rico, and after a half-hearted attempt at serving at the Puerta de Tierra McDonalds, had decided to supplement his military pension with his commission from the sales of "*la bolita*".

Just two days before, a well-dressed man who identified himself as "Daniel", had approached him as he made his rounds in San Juan, and with a pleasant smile had asked him if he was Archie Roman. Somewhat taken aback by the unknown man's question, Archie had nodded.

"The one who lives in El Falansterio?" the man had insisted, and when Archie had nodded again, had invited the *bolitero* to drink an espresso at the Plaza de Armas' Starbucks, adding, when he saw Archie's hesitation, that it would be worth his while.

"You have been recommended to us," Daniel said cryptically, after the two sat to drink their coffees, "as a man of discretion."

It never occurred to Archie to determine who "us" was, but the slight foreign accent in Daniel's speech gave him a fair idea of the business that he practiced.

"I am also told that even though your business is not exactly within the boundaries of the law," the well-dressed stranger continued, receiving an innocent, blank stare from his redheaded companion, "you are in good standing with the local authorities."

"Some of my best friends are policemen," Archie had responded, not bragging or trying to be facetious. Some of his ex-army buddies had joined the police force when they returned to the island.

Daniel stared at him for several seconds, as if deciding whether he should continue.

"Good," he said eventually, pulling a small, yellow envelope from an expensive-looking "Fossil" messenger bag that Archie would never have used. "I need your services, and I am willing to pay you well for them," Daniel said, handing the envelope to his companion. "There are one thousand dollars in there. If you accept, they are yours, as well as another thousand dollars when the job is finished."

Sensing Archie's unease, Daniel had explained quickly. His "organization" was interested in monitoring the comings and goings of the state police station located in front of El Falansterio, across the Fernandez Juncos Avenue. Archie lived in, and presumably knew well the public project. His job would consist of acting as their guide during one night, and to show some of his organization's employees the way to the roof of the housing complex. Also, he was to allay the suspicions of any nervous neighbors who noticed their movements. To keep their anonymity, the work would be conducted during the very early hours of that coming Sunday, from three-thirty to four-thirty in the morning.

Archie had considered the proposal with a poker face. On the one hand, the job seemed like an easy way to make a considerable amount of money. At 3:30 AM, the buildings' residents would be sleeping, and any restless soul who happened to be awake would know better than to alert the police if he discovered any strangers "visiting" the complex. One of the principal rules that people like him learned was that the best way to stay out of trouble was to mind your own business.

On the other hand, the entire affair smelled wrong. Apart from the occasional reefer that Archie purchased from the neighborhood dealer, he tended to avoid the drug trafficking business altogether. And Daniel's looks and manners, as well as his probably Colombian accent, fitted to a "T" his mental image of what a drug trafficker, an international cartel trafficker, should look and sound like. And that scared him.

Of course, none of this mattered. Archie had already received too much information. If he refused the job, he was certain that he would not be allowed to walk away.

"I will be more than glad to work for you," he had replied with as much enthusiasm as he could muster, to Daniel's apparent pleasure. Of course, the Colombian cartel man had added, the Sunday incursion to El Falansterio had to be kept a secret. If any details of the plan came to be known by anyone but him, serious consequences would follow. Archie had readily agreed, wondering who had recommended him, and cursing that person for doing so.

Now, at 4:40 in the morning, he waited for the last group of Colombians to arrive. Daniel had told him that an undetermined number of men would arrive in four, unevenly spaced time intervals, after they received an "all-is-well-" signal from Archie. The signal would consist of Archie standing on the third step of the short flight of stairs that led into the building's lobby. He had already run through the drill three times, and it had worked without a hitch. Now, he stood on the third step for the fourth and what he hoped would be the final time, and waited.

The darkly clad men did not take long to materialize out of the twilit gloom. Four of them came this time, led by an older man. How much older, Archie could not tell, because like the others, he seemed to be in superb physical condition, and his hair was cut so short that it covered his scalp with a colorless fuzz. As the man climbed the steps, he extended his hand, and his mouth stretched into a broad, mirthless smile that chilled Archie's heart.

"Mr. Roman," he said, encasing the *bolitero's* hand in an iron grip, and examining his face with his yellowish-brown eyes, as if committing it to memory. "They said I would be able to identify you by your red hair, and I see they were not joking."

Archie managed a weak smile, unable to release his hand from the man's vise-like hold. "It's a family curse," he said. "They say that God made us this way so that we could be spotted from far away," he added, attempting to make a joke, and feeling stupid even before he had finished saying it.

The Colombian trafficker continued to smile, releasing Archie's hand, and briefly scanning the lobby. "Shall we go up?" he suggested, pointing to a long, narrow stairway framed by two walls that rose all the way to the next floor.

Archie nodded, and began to limp towards the stairs, but barely two steps up, the Colombian grabbed his right arm, and forced him to turn.

"I almost forgot!" he said, handing to his guide a small yellow envelope. "Daniel asked me to give you this. I believe it's the balance of what we owe you."

Archie stared at the proffered item nervously, then took it and placed in his back pocket.

"Aren't you going to count it?" the drug trafficker asked.

Of course not, Archie thought to himself. *Do you think I'm crazy? That I'm even going to suggest that I question your honesty? No chance, even if the envelope is empty!*

"I trust you," he replied with a conviction that surprised him. Then he turned and resumed his upward climb, followed by the others. At the top of the stairs, they reached a hallway that led to the doors of several apartments. Nothing stirred. The men continued to the next set of steps and up to the third floor, and then took the last flight to the roof.

Before any of the Colombians had begun to filter into the building, Archie had climbed the stairway to the roof, and from the door scanned the area for unwanted visitors. He had always harbored a healthy fear of heights, and it had never occurred to him before to visit the rooftop of the building where he lived. But from his neighbors he had heard stories about addicts sometimes using it to do heroine or cocaine, and of secret lovers, of all genders and ages, meeting to escape the more hectic pace of the floors below them. So in order to avoid any unexpected, potentially dangerous encounters, he had decided to take a look upstairs. Except for a black cat, which had crouched and stared intently at him, and then scampered noiselessly away, the entire area seemed empty.

Just to make sure, he had conducted a brief walk over the central portion of the buildings, as far away from the rim as possible. For the first time since he had moved there two years before, he realized that the rooftops of all of the buildings were interconnected, and that they extended all the way to the end of the block. A one foot parapet fringed the entire edge of the complex, tall enough to delineate the outer boundary of the buildings but too short to stop anyone from tripping and falling to the street below.

If what the South American traffickers had wanted was to keep track of the "comings and goings" of the police during the early hours of the morning, then they had indeed chosen the ideal spot. The uppermost level of El Falansterio offered an unobstructed view of the police station, which rose across the street to about the same height of the residential complex. Concluding his inspection, he had retreated to the relative safety of the stairwell, and had waited there until it was almost time to descend to the lobby and greet the first bunch of his mysterious visitors.

Now, as the last of the Colombians made their way up, he stepped to one side of the stairway, and allowed them to file past him towards the door on the roof, hoping that after the last of the men walked through, he would be allowed to leave. But their leader was bringing up the rear and, placing a hand on his shoulder, he had courteously insisted that Archie precede him onto the rooftop. The redheaded guide had thanked him with a fake smile, inwardly cursing his bad luck, and feeling, in the pit of his stomach, that something was terribly wrong.

After ushering Archie onto the roof, Colonel Calderon stopped to take in the view, innocently blocking the doorframe with his body. A sense of relief washed over him. They had reached their final destination for the night without any incident. During the past week, the Colonel had walked past El Falansterio dozens of times, and twice had strolled into its interior courtyard, eliciting some curious but guarded stares from the few residents in it. Months prior to his arrival in Puerto Rico, he had studied and committed to memory the floor plans of the housing complex, and reviewed dozens of photographs of the project, immediately grasping the strategic importance of its location and admiring, as a non-practicing architect, the simple, beautiful lines of its design. But this was the first time he had been able to take in the view from its rooftop, and to confirm that from that height, he could effectively control the entire street below him.

He saw, with professional pride, that his men had not wasted any time, and were busily unloading their equipment and setting it up in their pre-assigned spots. In total, four machine gun positions would be evenly spread along the side of the rooftop that faced the main police building. Another position was hopefully being established at that very moment by a fifth squad, in a half-constructed building located immediately to the west of El Falansterio, across a narrow side street.

Each team would be equipped with a 7.62 mm FN MAG, a general-purpose machine gun fabricated by the Belgians which was standard issue in the Venezuelan Armed Forces. Each MAG, capable of firing between 650 to 1,000 rounds of ammunition per minute, would rest on a short, three-legged tripod, and would be operated by a two-man team. Scores of metal boxes containing ammunition belts lay in small, orderly piles, next to each of the machine guns.

Those who did not operate the MAGs would act as snipers, picking out any policemen who strayed from the building, and patrolling the roofs behind the machine gun nests, in the improbable case that anyone dared to attack them from behind. They were armed with telescopic sighted, Russian-supplied Dragunov SVD rifles that fired steel jacketed, armor piercing bullets. Calderon had assigned the rifles to his best marksmen, including Sergeant Rodolfo Alfonsin, who held the national title in the 1,300-meter sharpshooting category.

Once the fighting began, the front of the police three-story building and the small station beside it would be hermetically sealed by the withering crossfire from the MAG machine guns and the snipers. And hopefully, El Alacran's men would deal with any stragglers trying to escape from the back. An old warrior who had fought insurgents along Venezuela's borders for years, Calderon disliked violence for violence's sake. Therefore, he prayed to God that the policemen would not resist. Otherwise, the killing could turn into a nightmare.

With the corner of his eye, he observed the shocked reaction in Archie's face as the redhead began to grasp what was taking place around him. As if sensing he was being watched, Archie turned and said to Calderon in a tone that barely held back his rising panic, "I think I can go now." Then his gaze turned to the .45 automatic that the Venezuelan pointed at him.

"I'm sorry, Mr. Roman, but you can't," the Colonel said gently. "Not yet, anyhow."

Archie managed to keep his composure, only a slight increase in the speed of his words betraying his nervousness.

"This is not my concern. You can trust me. I won't say anything to anyone."

"I trust you," Calderon said sincerely, "but too much is at stake if I am wrong."

The Colonel looked at a tall man holding a rifle, who was crouching next to two other men setting up the last of the machine gun positions. "Alfonsin!" he called out softly.

The man immediately crawled away from the edge of the building, and stood up as he neared his superior officer when he could not be seen from the street.

"Colonel!"

The military title provoked a puzzled frown on Archie's face.

"You already know Mr. Roman."

"Yes, sir."

"Bind him up, but don't hurt him," Calderon said to his sergeant. "Place him somewhere where he is safe, but where you can keep an eye on him."

"Yes sir."

"Colonel—" Archie pleaded, addressing Calderon by the rank he had just heard.

"It will be all right," the Venezuelan interrupted, very aware that part of his cover had just been blown. "You will be released tomorrow morning, after we finish our mission here. I give you my word," he promised, as Alfonsin led him away.

"Tomorrow morning," he repeated softly to himself, "after the revolution has started."

CHAPTER XIV

For several centuries, a massive wall had surrounded the city of Old San Juan. Its proportions were epic, averaging forty feet in height, and ranging in width from a mind-boggling twenty feet at the bottom to approximately fifteen feet at the top. Facing the Atlantic, from where most of the attacks were expected, the walls had been connected to the mammoth fortresses of El Morro to the west, at the mouth of San Juan Bay, and San Cristobal to the east. Six large portals had regulated the inflow of supplies and people into the city. One of them provided access from the bay, the other five from the surrounding land. At sundown, the portals were closed shut by sets of huge, wooden doors, and any traveler who had failed to enter the city was forced to spend the night outside.

But not even the walls could contain the growth of the population that they sheltered. By the mid-to-late 19th century, the inhabitants of San Juan had spilled over the fortifications into the unpopulated land that lay beyond them in the east. That growth, coupled with the eradication of pirates and privateers from the neighboring waters, had spelled the partial doom of some of the walls surrounding the city. In 1897, one year before the onset of the Spanish-American War, the portal facing the land to the east, called "Puerta de Tierra" or "Land Gate", as well as its connecting wall, had been demolished, allowing the city to expand unhindered in that direction. The vast new urban area, larger in size than Old San Juan itself, had been called "Puerta de Tierra", as a reminder that once it had served as the antechamber to the city. And with time, even that information had generally been forgotten by the modern *sanjuaneros* who now drove in and out of the ancient town in their modern automobiles.

Towards the north, south, and west, however, the walls still existed almost intact. The Portal to the Bay survived unchanged, although now its giant doors never closed. Being the only portal left, it was now called

"La Puerta de San Juan", or the "Gate to San Juan". In the olden days, the portal had led to a wharf and a modest staging area where the rowboats from the sailing ships anchored in the bay could tie up, meet the customs officers, and unload their freight. Most of the city walls facing the bay, however, had originally risen directly from the water, or had been bordered by jagged rocks that made it nearly impossible for would-be enemies to approach the city from the water.

But that had changed. Now, a wide pedestrian walkway skirted the entire rim of the bay under the city's mighty walls, interspersed with small plazas and rest areas. The walkway went all the way to the very mouth of the bay, and had become a popular spot at night for lovers to watch the cruise ships sail away. To the south, the wide path ushered its strollers to the "Paseo de la Princesa", "The Promenade of the Princess", an even wider boulevard lined with trees, statues, shops, restaurants and, at the very point where it turned to the north, an enormous fountain decorated with the statues of the three races—African, Spanish, and Indian—that had combined to forge the modern Puerto Rican society.

La Fortaleza sat atop a forty foot bluff facing the bay, about midway between the Puerta de San Juan and the beginning of the Paseo de la Princesa. When it had been originally built between 1533 and 1540, La Fortaleza had formed part of the Spanish fortifications that defended the bay; hence its name, "The Fortress". By the 1700's, however, the fortified house of government had evolved into the Governor's Mansion, also known as the Palace of Santa Catalina.

The walls shielding La Fortaleza from any attacks coming from the bay were probably the most formidable in the entire defense system of the city. Crowned with crenellated battlements, the walls rose high above sea level, the governor's abode cradled behind them like a perched eagle.

Not surprisingly, the only serious assault to which the fortress-turned-into-palace had been subjected during the last two centuries had not come from the bay but from the land. It had occurred in the Nationalist Revolt of 1950, when led by Harvard-educated attorney Pedro Albizu Campos, the pro-independence nationalists had attempted a *coup d'état* against the then existing government of Puerto Rico—led by Luis Muñoz Marin—and its "colonial overlord", the United States. In an ill-fated affair, four nationalists had driven a green Plymouth to within twenty-five feet of La Fortaleza's main entrance, and opened fire on the structure with sub machine guns. A fierce, five-hour firefight had ensued, ending in the death of the four men.

As a result, the entire surroundings of La Fortaleza had subsequently been sealed off. In Fortaleza Street, from where the nationalist attack had been launched and where the main entrance to the Governor's Mansion was located, a tall, iron grilled gate topped with golden spikes had been constructed to restrict the access of unauthorized vehicles. Pedestrian traffic had been controlled from a large guardhouse constructed on the sidewalk, and eventually it had been equipped with metal detectors and cameras, and manned by the Governor's personal, civilian-clothed body-guards. Also, at least two state policemen permanently stood guard at the entrance of the gates.

Impregnable from the water, and heavily defended from the land, La Fortaleza had remained at peace for the next six decades. And yet, San Miguel's plans required its capture.

The solution had come almost by accident. Nine months before, San Miguel had taken a leisurely stroll with Daniel down the cobblestone-covered Fortaleza Street, engrossed by the quaint, colonial architecture of its buildings, pausing every so often to photograph some of their most interesting features. They had stopped in front of the main gates of La Fortaleza, where they had observed the palace-like building with the sort of undisguised curiosity displayed by inquisitive, well informed tourists, and where they had taken several pictures through the thick iron bars that blocked the entrance. Then, San Miguel had addressed one of the two policemen guarding the gates, and asked if any tours to view the Governor's Mansion were available.

The guard had pointed with his index finger to an adjacent building, and there San Miguel and Daniel had secured the services of a private guide. They had been informed, to their apparent disappointment, that at that time the Mansion was not being shown, but that they could tour its surrounding grounds and gardens. The tour guide, a short, rather chubby female who seemed to be mildly upset for being interrupted from watch-ing a television soap opera, had led them through the guardhouse and into the open area in front of the main building. As he had stepped through the metal detector and retrieved his camera, San Miguel had noted a security guard sitting behind six small television screens, which displayed the areas surrounding La Fortaleza. To his surprise, none of the images in the screens showed the gardens surrounding the mansion. Instead, the camer-as concentrated on the approaches to the Governor's residence: Fortaleza Street and the gates to the government compound.

The chubby guide had steered San Miguel and Daniel through a wide passage in the main building of the Executive Mansion, walking past a large, elegant stairway—"This is the main entrance to La Fortaleza," the guide had explained—and entering into a wide, interior courtyard, she had guided them to one of its corners, where a narrow set of steps dropped below the ground at the base of a large tower.

"You may go down, if you wish so," she had told them in a bored voice.

The two tourists had complied, descending a claustrophobically narrow, circular stairway that led to the cellar of one of the two round medieval towers that flanked La Fortaleza from the side of the bay. The female guide had stayed above ground, unwilling to climb up and down the steep steps. Their downward trek had taken San Miguel and Daniel to a small, circular room, paved with bricks and containing several old rusted cannonballs, and an ancient, metallic chest, equally rusted. It was a dead end, but the visitors had dutifully taken pictures, hoping that the flashes from their cameras would be noted by their guide.

Exiting the courtyard, the tourists had then followed their chaperone over a wide, paved way that took them to the gardens of La Fortaleza. Extending to the north of the Governor's Mansion, the gardens were comprised of several, multi-tiered levels and terraces, containing immaculately manicured lawns, ornamental flower beds, rows of trimmed shrubs, trees, fountains, iron grilled benches, narrow, winding paths, statues, and stairways that bespoke of the palace's ancient history, and tried to reflect its glory.

The tour had continued along a walkway that was fringed, on its right, by the western boundaries of the gardens, and on its left, by the top ramparts of the walls that cradled La Fortaleza. The two men had stopped to admire and photograph the spectacular view of the bay, and to enjoy the brisk breeze that flowed from the sea. Portions of the battlements that had topped the walls had been removed to improve the view, and had been substituted with a low, spiked fence. Even so, the forty-foot walls still constituted a formidable barrier.

As if on impulse, San Miguel had stepped over a low, trimmed shrub that ran along the entire length of the ramparts, and looked down from the wall. It was a considerable drop to the promenade below. He had withdrawn immediately, even before his flustered guide had finished mouthing her angry reproof, and had apologized profusely, smoothing her ruffled feathers.

The tour had ended thirty minutes later. As they exited through the guard post in Fortaleza Street, San Miguel had cast a casual glance at the six surveillance camera screens, and confirmed that none of them showed the gardens they had just toured.

Abandoning Fortaleza Street, the two men had paused to drink an espresso at the Plaza de Armas, and afterwards walked down to the Gate of San Juan. The old entrance from the bay rose up more than thirty feet, and was wide enough to accommodate a big tour bus. Its long, heavy doors were fastened by chains to the gate's inner walls, destined to never close again.

San Miguel and Daniel had crossed the open portal and turned to their left, following the promenade at the base of the wall. From below, the city wall looked even more forbidding, rising impossibly high, frustrating any would be climbers with its deceptively innocent, smooth façade. A *garita*—a sentry box shaped like a short, thick, baby bottle—extended outwards from the crest of the wall, less than one hundred feet away.

A few yards from the gate, the promenade briefly opened up into a small square or plaza that protruded into the city walls, producing a semi-rectangular indentation in the city defenses. Then, the walls closed up again, and resumed their journey south.

San Miguel and Daniel had exchanged a quizzical look and renewed their pace, reaching the square in seconds, and examining it with curiosity. It was a small, open space, no longer than sixty or seventy feet long and about half that width. In the colonial days, it must have been used as a secondary wharf, to unload cargo destined to San Juan. As such, it was boxed in on three of its sides by the towering defenses of the city, only opening up in the direction of the bay. Thus, any invader attempting to use the tiny wharf as the staging area for an attack, would have faced withering, deadly fire from the square's three, taller flanks.

But with the demise of piracy and the onslaught of tourism, the small landing had been converted into a tiny park, a minute oasis dedicated to Queen Isabella of Spain, Christopher Columbus' main patron in his exploration of the New World. In her honor, a stern looking bust of the queen, resting on an elevated pedestal, had been placed in the center of the square. One large ficus tree grew beside the bronze figure, sheltering the sullen Spanish monarch and much of the rest of the park from the sun. Several benches lined the outer fringes of the square, but except for one lonely reader hidden behind the wide pages of a newspaper, no other human being was at the time taking advantage of the park's peaceful shade.

None of this, however, had mattered to Daniel and San Miguel. Because at that moment, they had both stumbled upon the key to breach the impregnable defenses of La Fortaleza. And it lay in plain view, behind the back of the unsuspecting Queen Isabella.

Now, at 4:30 AM on the Sunday morning of the last day of the Fiestas de San Sebastian, five men clad in dark clothes and carrying green canvas duffel bags, were about to put their boss' theory to the test. Unlike San Miguel and Daniel, they had approached their objective from the south, silently traversing the wide, empty promenade of El Paseo de la Princesa, and then following the contours of the city walls and turning northwards towards the square.

Originally, there had been six men. But as they walked past the Department of Tourism—an elegant, neoclassical building that until scarcely forty years before had served as a jail—its night watchman had committed the mistake of casting a curious, half hostile glance at the group. One of the strollers, a pale, bearded man with curly hair, had detached himself from the others and approached the guard at a half trot, smiling and waving his right hand, as if to call his attention. Less than six feet away, he had pulled a gun from one of his baggy cargo pants pockets, and calmly instructed the surprised watchman to place his hands behind his neck and do as he said.

The terrified night guard had offered no resistance. Following the gunman's instructions, he had opened the entrance door to the Tourism Building, and been led to one of the unlit offices in the facility. There, he had lain on his stomach, and his hands and ankles had been firmly bound with silver duct tape. Afterwards, his captor had used the tape to tie his hands to his feet behind his back, and smoothed another piece of tape over his mouth.

As he abandoned the building, the gunman had locked the main entrance door with the key attached to its lock, and then snapped the key, rendering the lock useless. Afterwards, with an unnerving lack of urgency, he had sauntered to the corner beyond the fountain of the three races that marked the end of the Paseo de la Princesa and the beginning of the promenade by the bay. There, he had chosen a spot under a tree from where he could observe, cloaked by the surrounding darkness, anyone advancing towards the promenade, pulled out his cell phone out from one of his pants pockets, and settled down as comfortably as he could on a bench.

His five other companions had not bothered to wait for him, knowing he would require no help in taking care of the guard. Instead, they had pressed on towards Queen Isabella's park. They did not utter a word, listening intently to the sound of approaching footsteps or the echo of a conversation, but hearing nothing. They need not have worried. At nearly five in the morning, not even the souls of the soldiers who had died there centuries before stirred in the empty walkway.

To their right, the eternal walls of the city loomed massively above them, a constant reminder of what the men were about to do. Large spotlights intermittently illuminated the venerable fortifications, periodically bathing them in a yellowish-orange light, and sometimes projecting large, irregular shadows of the advancing men.

The group reached the small square in less than five minutes. One of the men continued to walk towards the San Juan Gate, to act as a lookout and neutralize any unexpected threat coming from that side. The rest retreated to the back of the square, and in the semidarkness existing between the dim light cast by the park's lampposts, began to unpack the contents of their duffel bags; four AK-47 assault rifles, several gun belts, smaller backpacks with ammunition, food and water, and one other backpack with a limited amount of explosives.

One of the men, a thin, short, wiry man named Hassam, fastened to his waist a webbed, green army belt, to which were attached a nylon holster holding a 9mm Beretta with a black, cylindrical silencer, a pair of long handled-shears to lop off branches, and a KM2000 German combat knife—a wicked-looking contraption with a serrated edge and an angled rather than rounded tip. Then, he pulled out of his duffel bag a set of metallic foot-braces, which he quickly strapped to his boots. From the inner side of each of the braces extended a long, talon-like steel spike, which he would use for climbing. Next, he withdrew from his canvas sack a coiled length of knotted rope with a grappling hook, and a much shorter line, barely three feet in length, with one padded loop at each end.

Ready, Hassam gazed at the wall rising behind Queen Isabella's bust, and shook his head, amazed at how careless the men in charge of the safety of the Governor of Puerto Rico had been. A planting area—a narrow strip of dirt—bordered the entire perimeter of the square. In it, interspersed at irregular intervals, grew four palm trees at a distance of no more than three feet from the face of the walls. The largest, a straight, sturdy royal palm tree, rose over thirty feet in height, not tall enough to reach the wall's top, but sufficient for Hassam to attain his objective.

Saying nothing, the fully geared man approached the palm tree and softly, almost affectionately, slapped its trunk three times. Then he encircled the trunk of the palm tree with the short piece of rope, and threaded one of his hands through each of the loops on the rope's ends. He looked back one last time, making certain that the rest of his men were ready. They were all watching him with nervous fascination.

Nodding at them, he slid the short rope upwards, and raised his right foot up to the height of his left knee. With a low "crunch", he stabbed the trunk of the palm tree with the spike attached to his boot. Then, pushing himself up, he repeated the procedure with his left foot.

He climbed upwards with surprising ease. For more than two months, he had practiced climbing similar palm trees in a private secluded property in another part of the island, until all of the palm trees in the ranch—and a few other types of trees—were riddled with holes from his spikes. He had become an expert doing it.

In less than two minutes, he reached the portion of the palm where its trunk turned green and its leafy fronds branched outwards. Holding on to the base of one of the fronds, he freed his hands from the loops of the short rope, and let it fall.

It took him no time to climb to the crown of the tree. Standing upright on its upper branches, he unhooked the long-handled shears from his belt, and carefully began to cut away some of the fronds, pausing every few seconds to listen for movement from the top of the wall. Finally, after he had cleared enough of the fronds to gain an unobstructed view, he stopped.

The upper battlements of the wall still rose over Hassam by thrice, maybe four times his height. He stared at his digital watch, and saw that eight more minutes would have to pass before the hour turned to 5:00 AM. He squatted, trying to become as less visible as possible, and waited.

At 5:03 AM, three men stumbled noisily towards the Governor's Mansion over the cobblestones of Fortaleza Street, stopping every so often to regain their balance or to exchange a few boisterous words. The policemen standing behind the tall iron grilled doors that barred the entrance to La Fortaleza watched them at first with guarded amusement, and then with mounting concern as they neared the gate and became engaged in a vociferous argument. One of the policemen told them they should leave before they were arrested for disturbing the peace, but the largest of the three, a man with bulging muscles and a very tight, tan shirt, took offense at his words and began to curse him and the mother "who had borne him". Angry, the policeman took out his nightstick and prodded the stomach of the rowdy drunk through the bars.

The muscleman became infuriated, and began to climb the gate, while another of his companions somehow got hold of an empty beer bottle and threw it at the policeman, narrowly missing his head. In the guardhouse, the bodyguard on watch picked up his walkie-talkie and called for help. As three other security men guarding the perimeters of La Fortaleza quickly arrived, the bodyguard in the guardhouse opened the automatic pedestrian gate, and joined them to subdue and arrest the three violent drunks. In the wild melee that ensued, the muscleman was tasered twice, the first time as he was midway up the main gate, and another as he broke the nose of one of the men trying to subdue him. It took nearly twenty-five minutes for the drunken men to be controlled and placed under arrest, and nearly an hour before a state police van arrived and whisked them away.

At 5:05 AM Hassam stretched up to his full height, and slid the length of coiled rope with the grappling hook off his shoulder. By that time, the diversion at the opposite end of La Fortaleza was supposed to have commenced, and would hopefully draw the attention of the guards surrounding La Fortaleza away from what he and his companions were about to do. He knew that they would have a small window of opportunity, of half an hour at the most, and that he would have to hurry.

During the briefing for the mission, Hassam had been warned by Daniel that even though he and San Miguel had detected no surveillance cameras in the gardens, they could still exist. Also, Daniel had no clear idea of the number of men who guarded the perimeter of the Executive Mansion, although "reliable sources" had assured him that the gardens were only periodically checked by random watches. To enhance the chances of success, they had planned to create a noisy, messy diversion that would keep the eyes of the man behind the cameras away from the screens.

"I'm throwing the hook," he hissed to the men below. "Be ready!"

Hassam let the grappling hook slide down to about half the length of his body. The hook had been padded with black, electrical tape, to deaden the noise that it would make when it hit the wall. Still, Hassam hesitated, trying to make certain that no one walked in the gardens beyond the battlements. Only the occasional wind coming from the bay, heavy with the smell of brine and periodically stirring to life the leaves and branches about him, disturbed the night's silence.

Satisfied, he began to swing the grappling hook back and forth like a pendulum, until it gathered momentum and began to rotate in a clockwise manner. Then he released the line, and it floated over the wall, landing with a muted "thunk". He pulled the rope and felt it snag onto something flexible, a bush or a plant of some sort perhaps, but then it broke free. For two heartbeats he pulled on the rope and it slid back freely, giving Hassam the impression that the hook had missed the short spiked iron fence embedded on the wall's crest. Then the rope grew taut and would not budge.

Carefully, Hassam grasped the rope with his hands, and allowed the rest of the coil to stream downwards, towards his companions. In one fluid movement, he jumped from the palm tree's crown, planted his feet on the face of the ancient wall, and began to scale it.

He stopped just after his eyes cleared the edge of the battlements, and strained to see into the area beyond through an opening in the bottom of the iron fence that the grappling hook had snagged.

As his superiors had promised, the garden stretched before him, framed by the dark, distant outline of La Fortaleza. A wide, paved path followed the inner contours of the upper battlements, fringed by low, trimmed bushes. There were lampposts on the other side of the walkway, crowned with large opaque crystal globes, but only one in every three was lit up—*a very serious breach of security,* Hassam thought—since most of the grounds remained submerged in the night's gloom, and even in those places where the lampposts provided illumination, it was tenuous at best. Unknown to him, the lights had been switched off on purpose, as part of the new cost-cutting program adopted by the ever micromanaging Governor Pietrantoni, called "Keeping La Fortaleza Green".

Taking a deep breath, Hassam grabbed hold of the iron fence, and scrambled over it, falling behind the low row of bushes that bordered the garden's walkway. No rushed footsteps or voiced warnings followed his intrusion. He looked at the time, and noticed that barely three minutes had elapsed since he had tossed the grappling hook. Without turning his head, he reached backwards, grabbed the dangling rope, and tugged it three times.

Almost instantly, the rope went taut as the second of the four men began to scale the wall. He gained the summit in no time, and squeezed past Hassam without uttering a word, taking a position fifty feet away, closer to the Governor's quarters. Even before his companion had reached his assigned post, the third intruder poured over the spiked railing, and moved fifty paces in the opposite direction.

So far so good, Hassam told himself, but his reassurance began to falter as the last of his men delayed in making his appearance. Growing impatient, he leaned briefly over the edge of the wall and saw Alexis, the fourth man, making very slow progress, about half of the way up. To his dismay, he noticed that Alexis was carrying three of the AK-47s and the backpack with the explosives, as well as his regular gear, and wondered who had been the genius that had assigned the heaviest load to him.

Hassam ducked back behind the hedges, and tried to allay his frayed nerves by repeatedly breathing deeply through his nose and exhaling through his mouth, as he had been taught in his yoga exercises. Alexis, a beefy Colombian who in different moments had worked for the drug cartels, the CIA, the Direccion General de Inteligencia from Cuba, and only God knew how many other organizations, had been a last minute replacement, after the man originally assigned to the operation had broken his leg, two weeks before. Hassam had objected to the change, arguing that his unit had practiced together for several months, and that the last minute inclusion of the over-muscled stranger would only disrupt their finely coordinated plans. He had been overruled by San Miguel, who had determined that the raiders would need all of the firepower they could muster in order to capture the Governor.

The distant sound of voices, coming from the direction of La Fortaleza, brought Hassam back to the present. He looked inquiringly at the member of his squad closest to the source of the noise, a man nicknamed Faberge because of the exaggerated amount of cologne that he normally splashed on his body, and saw him raise two fingers, indicating that two security guards were approaching. Hassam turned to the man behind him, and repeated the signal. Afterwards, he pulled on the climbing line twice, warning Alexis that he should stop his ascent until further notice.

Two men became visible a scant second later as they walked into the faint glow of one of the few functioning lampposts. They were dressed as civilians, one wearing a long-sleeved *guayabera,* the second a mustard-colored shirt. They displayed no outward signs of carrying any weapons, but Hassam had no trouble detecting the telltale bulge of a holster under the open waist of the *guayabera,* and an even more obvious protuberance on the left ankle of the other man's pant. The *guayaberaed* man also carried a long silver flashlight, but it was turned off and used by his bearer to punctuate some of the words that he was exchanging with his companion. The other man held a small walkie talkie in his right hand, which pulsated intermittently with a small red light.

Amateurs, Hassam thought, as he saw Faberge cringe behind the bushes, just a few feet away from the passing men. He congratulated himself for reminding his subordinate not to wear any cologne that night. Otherwise, his powerful scent would have given him away.

Something moved behind Hassam, and to his dismay, he saw that the climbing rope was shaking. Either Alexis had disobeyed him, or he had forgotten what the two short tugs meant. He stared at the two approaching men, now less than twenty feet away, and jerked again twice on the rope hard, and two more times after that, but Alexis paid no heed to the warnings.

The climber's hand shot out from the edge of the wall, just as the two bodyguards walked by the hanging line. Desperately, Hassam leaned over the short spiked fence, clamping one hand on Alexis' backpack and the other over his mouth. They remained motionless for several minutes, Hassam's heart beating so wildly that he thought it would be overheard. But the two security men never looked back, and eventually they disappeared from sight, descending some invisible steps into a lower courtyard.

Hassam finished pulling the stocky Colombian over the fence, and both men dropped behind the bushes, breathing hard.

"The next time you do something like this," Hassam hissed angrily at his subordinate, "I will cut the rope."

CHAPTER XV

Given that tourism is Puerto Rico's main industry and principal source of revenue, the reopening of Cuba to the U.S. tourist market had constituted for the past two decades a sword dangling over the island's head. Regardless of political affiliation, every administration in power had recognized the threat of an un-blockaded, un-sanctioned Cuba on the local economy, and begun to undertake the necessary measures to prepare for the gathering storm. The Puerto Rico Convention Center had been one of those measures.

At 580,000 square feet, containing enough structural steel to build ninety six Statues of Liberty, and large enough to cover twelve football fields, the behemoth building had been designed to attract and host mega-events with a capacity and state-of-the-art facilities that even an open Cuba would not be able to match for decades. From the outside, its roofline resembled two overlapping waves, rising thirteen stories high, dropping vertically in a shimmering wall of glass.

However, it was still a work in progress. Located in Isla Grande—a large area connected to Miramar and separated from San Juan by the San Antonio Channel—the enormous, cathedral-like edifice could be seen from miles away. It sat at the southern tip of the Convention Center District, one hundred and thirteen acres that had been expropriated and razed to the ground by the government to provide space for the center's massive infrastructure and its satellite facilities.

Its exterior grounds were graced by a grand canal and a great fountain that was illuminated at night and that rose and fell—Bellagio-style—to music. One of the two modern hotels scheduled to be constructed had already been finished, and the second was well on its way. When fully developed, restaurants, shops, nightclubs, and apartment units would line the fountain-strewn canal. The district would contain a museum, movie houses, including the inevitable Imax, and a park, and would connect via the Miramar bridges to the Grand Laguna Hotel entertainment district, also under construction.

Not surprisingly, the Puerto Rico Convention Center had been one of the crown jewels of the prior three government administrations, and continued to be one of the principal projects under the Pietrantoni regime. Therefore, when an anonymous telephone call announced that several bombs had been planted around the building, a massive search followed.

The call had been received at 4:30 AM by the security firm that guarded the convention facilities. Half a dozen explosives, a husky voice whispered, had been left in plain view around the center's perimeter, and were set to go off at 8:30 AM. The caller, who identified himself as "El Alacran", accused the colonial government of Puerto Rico of selling its country to the mega corporations of America, and announced that the Macheteros would blow up the foremost symbol of imperialistic corporate exploitation, the Convention Center Building. The Macheteros, the caller stated, were making an advance warning about the explosives so that the center could be evacuated, and no innocent workers would be hurt. Any attempt to disarm the bombs, "El Alacran" warned, would provoke their instantaneous explosion, since the explosives could be set off remotely, and the center was kept under the Macheteros' constant surveillance.

A quick search by the security guards at the site had uncovered four backpack-sized packages, wedged between the steel beams that angled upwards from the support columns at the entrance of the building. The caller had mentioned six bombs, which meant that two other explosives could be hidden anywhere else in the structure.

Within minutes, the Central Police Headquarters in the financial district of Hato Rey had been alerted, and "Ramon", as the highest-ranking officer in charge, had been briefed on the matter. The Metropolitan Area Bomb Squad had been dispatched to the center, and Ramon had immediately ordered five police patrol cars from Hato Rey, as well as eight other police cars from the Puerta de Tierra Station in San Juan to cordon off a radius of two hundred yards around the building, and to search the outlaying areas for any individuals who could be keeping a watch on the threatened facility. Other policemen from other parts of the city were also recruited to participate in the search.

At twenty minutes past 5:00 AM, Colonel Calderon was alerted by his sergeant that the parking lot of the Puerta de Tierra Police Station had suddenly come to life with men rushing out of the building. Calderon crawled to the edge of El Falansterio's roof in time to see dozens of policemen, many of them carrying shotguns, climbing into several police cars, as well as some motorcycles.

"How many would you say are leaving?" he asked Alfonsin, who in turn made a quick consultation with one of the men crouching beside him.

"Carlos counted thirty-nine," Alfonsin replied.

Calderon rolled on his back, and fished his cell phone out of his shirt pocket, dialing the number 1, followed by the # sign. Then he rolled back on his stomach, and resumed his watch on the parking area. If San Miguel's intelligence about the approximate number of officers in the station proved to be correct, he thought as he waited, that would reduce the number of police officers in the station by more than half.

"*Pedro Martinez*," someone finally answered.

"Dennis Martinez here," Calderon replied. "Seven...no, make that eight police cars and three motorcycles are heading your way."

"Thank you, Dennis," San Miguel replied cheerfully. "Have a great night!"

Two minutes later, the police convoy whizzed past the Aqueduct and Sewer Authority vans in a blur of blue emergency lights and wailing sirens, and continued at full speed towards the Convention Center District. They were followed, within the next ten minutes, by two additional patrol cars that had been making their rounds in Old San Juan.

Ramon had kept his end of the bargain, San Miguel noted with intense satisfaction.

Now everything would be up to them.

CHAPTER XVI

The Ship Security Officer observed with a certain amount of puzzled irritation the two customs men climbing up the crew gangway. *What in the devil were they doing there so early?* The *Mardi Gras* had just docked, and the disembarkation of the passengers was not scheduled to begin until 7:00 AM, almost forty-five minutes from now. Surely they had not come to pick up the passengers and crewmembers' manifests, since that was part of *his* job, and anyway, it did not require the presence of two custom officers. Officers that, by the way, he did not recognize. Even so, Roger Bates clenched his jaws into his best imitation of a courteous smile. He stood up as the two men approached him, and extended his hand.

"Good morning, gentlemen. May I be of any help?"

"I am Gerardo Rodriguez," said the shorter of the two, a thin, sour faced man with a bored expression and cinnamon gum breath. "And this is Michael Rivera," he added, gesturing to his companion, a tall, even thinner man with a black mustache. "U.S. Customs," he explained un-necessarily, as he shook hands with the ship's security officer. "You the SSO?"

"Roger Bates, at your service," the SSO replied. "How may I be of service?"

"We've come to verify that your ship's Security Certificate is in proper order," Rodriguez answered.

Bates hesitated. "Right now?" he asked reluctantly. "I'm in the middle of setting up this position so that the crew can begin to—"

"Right now would be fine," Rodriguez interjected, cutting him short.

"But you verified the certificate three weeks ago!" the security officer protested with spontaneous indignation. "Listen, I have my hands full getting ready to—"

Rodriguez raised his hand, gesturing Bates to stop.

"Then get some help," he replied curtly, and as Bates prepared to speak again, added, "Look, we have no time to argue. We have received anonymous information, from someone in your crew, that the certificate was issued illegally."

"Illegally!" Bates exclaimed with genuine shock. "That's absurd! You gave it to us, for Christ's sake! We passed the inspection in Miami! How can—"

"As I said," Rodriguez interrupted again, in a barely civil tone that admitted no further discussion, "I am not here to argue. We'd like to speak to your captain, please."

Bates' face, naturally ruddy, reddened to a deep crimson. For a long, tense moment, he failed to say anything. Then, taking a deep breath, he nodded curtly.

"Very well," he said resignedly. "The captain is on the bridge. I will call him, and have one of my assistants take you there." Bates unhooked his two-way radio from his belt to communicate with the bridge, but before he could press the "talk" button with his thumb, Rodriguez placed his hand over the transmitting device.

"I'm sorry," the customs officer said, "but this is a surprise inspection. I prefer that the captain not know we are coming until we are there. For that same reason, I must insist that you take us there personally."

"But...but...this is totally unseemly!" Bates stammered angrily, raising his voice, shifting his gaze several times from one man to another. "You don't have the authority to step into this vessel without the captain's authorization!"

It was the wrong thing to say, and Bates knew it even before he had finished saying it. Rodriguez's expression hardened, while Rivera ostensibly braced for action by moving his hand over his holster.

"I have every right to enter this ship pursuant to article twenty one dash two, nine point one of the Convention for the Safety of Life at Sea, and I also have the power to arrest you, which I will do right now if you keep interfering with our inspection of the vessel," Rodriguez retorted in a harsh, staccato-like voice that dangerously verged on violence. Then the moment passed, and he said in a more reasonable tone. "Look, Roger, the accusations were made by this inside man that you have on board, and they are pretty serious. Too serious to believe, in my opinion. But the only way to deal with this is to let us do our work as quickly and discreetly as we can, with as little interference as possible, and if everything pans out as I think it will pan out, we'll be out of here in no time. Okay?"

Bates nodded stiffly, and took a deep breath. He turned his gaze towards Rodriguez's hand, which was still gripping the security officer's two-way radio. "May I use the radio to call one of my people down, so that I may take you to the bridge?"

Rodriguez loosened his hold on the radio, and smiled apologetically. "Of course, go ahead."

As Bates made his call, Rodriguez directed a covert smirk at his partner, who turned his head away, towards the side of the ramp, in order to avoid laughing.

"My substitute should be here in a minute," the security officer stated, in a calmer voice.

"Thank you," Rodriguez said, and he drew out of his shirt pocket a pack of chewing gum. He opened it, and extended it to Bates. "Gum?" he asked, pulling out a piece, unraveling the paper, and popping the gum into his mouth.

"Thank you, no," Bates answered distractedly.

So far so good, the man who called himself Rodriguez thought. It had been a long and tense night, and an even longer, more intense morning. The unsuspecting real customs officers, as well as more than a dozen security men, had started coming into the dock at five in the morning, and one by one had been forced at gunpoint to surrender to his men. They had all been locked up in a conference room, their clothes and badges removed, their feet, hands and mouths securely taped.

A stream of dockworkers, stevedores, and suppliers had begun to flow into the dock about a half hour before the ship arrived. The men were allowed to enter the pier's restricted area through the left vehicular gate—as opposed to the customs and security people, who used the central pedestrian gate—where two of Rodriguez's men "checked" their ID's and documents, and gave them access.

It had taken months of planning and observation to obtain the necessary information to get to that point, information gathered by men "fishing" near the dock, by "tourists" boarding the ship, by "guests" staying at the Sheraton Hotel across the street that were able to tape the daily operations, and even by two employees of one of the ship's suppliers. The fake officers had rehearsed the ship's takeover in a mock "terminal" building, and planned for unexpected contingencies, should anything go wrong. Nothing had so far.

Unlike the other operations taking place in San Juan during that day, the hijacking of the cruise ship did not depend on the demolition of the bridges. Regardless of whatever else happened, Rodriguez's men, all of them Macheteros, would capture the *Mardi Gras*.

In fact, the unexplained delay in the explosions, though troubling, had actually helped the cruise ship hijackers. During the planning of the hijack, a concern had arisen that after news of the destruction of the bridges began to filter out to the general public, the four cruisers docked in the port of San Juan would sail away to another port, in order to protect their passengers. The window of opportunity, the Macheteros thought, would be a small one; no more than an hour after the explosions, while the facts were sorted out and disseminated by the news media. Therefore, the Macheteros had come up with two alternative courses of action, to be implemented at Rodriguez's discretion, as he deemed best at the moment of execution.

Plan A called for half a dozen of the hijackers—dressed as customs agents—to rush aboard the ship after the blasts occurred, in order to "ensure the safety" of the travelers "while the authorities determined what was happening". It seemed like the best plan, instead of surreptitiously climbing the very heavy lines that secured the floating behemoth to the dock—like in the old commando movies—or storming the ship through the gangway in a desperate, all out attack.

A delay in the explosions had been foreseen as a more than real possibility, and therefore the Macheteros had come up with Plan B. Pursuant to that alternative, two of the hijackers would attempt, immediately after the ship docked, to reach the bridge, alleging that they needed to examine the International Ship Security Certificate, a certificate required by the Convention for the Safety of Life at Sea to be carried by all seagoing vessels. Once there, they would wait for the explosions, and force the captain to "request protection from shore", which would be provided immediately.

Hence, their "inspection" that morning. Rodriguez had expected certain resistance from the ship's security officer, and had prepared to argue his way inside. Had that not worked, however, he would have forced Bates to follow his instructions at gunpoint.

A young, harried looking female wearing the ship's white uniform descended the companionway from the deck above.

"Sorry I'm late, sir," she said with a marked British accent.

"Marcy," Bates said drily, not making any reference to her apology, "these are Mr. Rodriguez and Mr..."

"Rivera," Rodriguez prompted.

"Right. Please take over, while I guide these gentlemen to the captain," he ordered, and without further instructions, tramped up the same stairway that Marcy had used. "Please follow me," he called after him, his displeasure apparent, while he bounded up the steps.

As Rodriguez gave chase, he made a mental note to have a chat with the SSO about his manners, after the present business was over.

Lucas woke up with a start. He knew that he had overslept even before he verified the time on his bed table clock. *Six in the morning!* Through the intercom, he heard Gabriel, the earlier riser of the two children, stirring in his crib. Soon, his son would feel hungry and call out for his mom.

"I have to get up," he whispered, and with a grunt, swung out of bed, prompting a muted protest from his wife. He sat back and leaned on one arm towards her, kissing the nape of her neck. She turned, and without opening her eyes, placed her arms over his shoulders.

"What time is it?" she asked huskily, still half asleep.

"Time to get up," he answered, this time kissing her on the lips. She felt warm and soft to his touch, and he was sorely tempted to crawl back into bed. But his mother and his aunts would be expecting him at the *Joyero* by seven, and even though they would not make it by then, Antonio, the guard, would. "I have five minutes. Do you want me to get your raincoat?" he asked mischievously, forcing Jeannie to smile.

She opened her eyes and examined his face lovingly. "Did anyone ever tell you that you are ruggedly handsome?"

"More handsome than rugged, I hope," he answered with a straight face.

"I suppose..." she replied after a pause. "The gardener would be more rugged than handsome," she added with a wicked grin, then squealed with delight as he picked her up with both arms from the bed, her legs flailing in the air.

"Maaaama!" the intercom boomed. Lucas brought Jennie closer to him, kissed her neck, and dropped her back on the bed.

"Your son is calling you," he said, walking towards the bathroom.

"You *are* a pig!" she said laughing.

"Yes, my princess," he answered. "A rugged pig."

Ten minutes later, shaved, bathed, and wearing his faded jeans, an old white shirt, and sneakers, Lucas rushed into the kitchen, where he found Gabriel perched on his high chair and desultorily picking Cheerios from a bowl, while he watched Dora the Explorer on TV. Jeannie sat at the kitchen table, sipping dark coffee with frothy milk from a large cup that read: "Hell of a Woman!" as she scrutinized the morning paper.

Lucas hugged and squeezed his son from behind, blowing on his neck and making loud farting noises that delighted Gabriel.

"Hi, Daddy!" he said between giggles.

"I want some Cheerios!" Lucas said with his "Cookie Monster" voice.

Gabriel very carefully picked up a single cereal "O", and fed it into his father's mouth, laughing nervously and withdrawing his hand quickly before the crazy, grunting "monster" could bite it.

"Sofia still sleeping?" he asked Jeannie.

"Be quiet!" she urged him, shushing him as if the mere mention of their daughter's name would wake her up.

He glanced at his watch, and saw it was 6:30 AM.

"I'm late," he said. "I have to go. Let's have dinner somewhere, okay?"

"You're not eating anything? I don't think you'll have time to eat in La Bombonera."

"I'll send Antonio to buy some food."

"I love you," Jeannie said, pecking his lips lightly. "I'll be waiting for you."

"Will you be wearing your raincoat?" he asked with a straight face.

"Honestly, Lucas!" she replied in an indignant tone, and paused, as if searching for words. "Do you think I would wear anything else?" she finally said innocently.

He was still smiling as he left the house.

Even though very early in the morning, a small crowd had already assembled behind the police barrier to stare at where the bombs had been placed. Some had brought binoculars, and some were trying to take photographs with their cell phones or cameras. Four news vans were stationed close by, broadcasting live, filling in the lack of news by showing live images of the Convention Center or by interviewing anyone they could lay their hands on: policemen, bomb and terrorist experts, and even curious neighbors.

None of them noticed, however, when a black Lexus quietly pulled into the most distant section of the Center's parking lot, and stopped there. A big man stepped out from the front passenger's seat, scowled in the direction of the remote crowd, and cursed under his breath.

"Beto," he said, leaning down to look at his driver through the window of his car, "call Captain Ramirez. Tell him to meet me here, and to be careful that the press doesn't see him."

"Yes, Mr. Superintendent."

Police Superintendent Roberto Maldonado shifted his attention back to the Convention Center, staying behind his car, so that he would be difficult to spot by any newsperson looking in his direction.

It would not have been difficult to spot him. Standing at six feet, three inches, and weighing two hundred and forty pounds, Superintendent Maldonado could have been confused with an upright grizzly bear, had it not been for the navy blue suits and dark ties he wore everywhere, regardless of the temperature, the humidity, or the place. Some members of the police force joked that the suit had been tattooed on his massive body, and that he only changed the ties. Others claimed that he used the suits to hide several flasks of rum, which he allegedly depleted during the course of his sixteen-hour workdays. Still others, mostly disaffected politicians, accused him of wearing them to compensate for his humble origins, to acquire a semblance of respectability.

Regardless of what they said, few questioned his efficiency and dedication. A former policeman, he had risen through the ranks with an unblemished record, reaching the coveted position of police colonel by his early thirties. He had resigned his commission when first appointed as Superintendent—a civilian position—and transformed the then stagnant Police Department into a dynamic, modern force.

Although the position of Superintendent of the Police was a cabinet level post filled by the incoming Governor, Maldonado had served in that capacity for twenty-one of the last twenty-nine years, appointed by governors of both the Commonwealth and Statehood parties. Only during Governor Alarcon's two consecutive terms had his tenure been interrupted, and occupied by five successive, politically savvy appointees who had quickly jeopardized most of his previous work, and demoralized the police force.

Maldonado had been brought back from retirement by Commonwealth Governor Ernesto Calderon to reinvigorate the deteriorating Police Department, and Pietrantoni had kept him there. During the five years after his return, he had whipped the law enforcement agency back into shape and resumed his unrelenting war on criminals. Crime statistics had dropped dramatically during the first four years, only rising in some categories—theft, robbery, and drug-turf killings—particularly in the last, recession-afflicted year.

His men idolized him. They knew that they could rely entirely on him, as long as they performed their duty; that he would stake his life and his reputation for any of them; and that he would take on without hesitation any person that threatened the welfare of the Department, regardless of his prominence or position. At the same time, they knew that he would not tolerate corruption, inefficiency or sloppiness in the execution of their work, and had witnessed his swift and terrible wrath whenever someone betrayed the core values of the police.

He did not look the part of a hero. Many of his critics—and he had many—likened him to a country bumpkin. Dark complexioned, with a big bulbous nose, a walrus mustache, a mop of unruly brown hair, and large, bloodshot eyes, he looked more like an alcoholic panhandler than the chief of the police. His looks, however, were deceiving, since Maldonado possessed one of the keenest and most educated minds in Governor Pietrantoni's Cabinet.

The Superintendent watched as one of the half dozen patrol cars parked close to the news vans detached itself from the others and headed in his direction. Less than a minute later, a tall, distinguished-looking, gray-haired, man wearing a police captain's uniform stepped out of the car, and shook Maldonado's hand briskly.

"Captain Ramirez," the Superintendent said evenly, with no palpable warmth in his voice. "Good morning."

"Good morning," Captain Ramirez repeated in a vibrant, cheery tone, either not sensing his boss's dark mood or choosing to ignore it.

There could have been no greater contrast between the two men: Maldonado, brooding, overweight, and curt, Ramirez, trim, aristocratic, and very self-assured.

"What can you tell me about this...this..." Maldonado made a half-hearted gesture with his hand in the direction of the Convention Center, letting the question to die away unfinished.

"We have spotted a total of six possible explosives, sir. Four have been placed at the base of the support columns. The other two are in the back...they're not visible from here, but I can drive you to a spot from where they can be seen."

Captain Ramirez waited for additional questions, but none came. Instead, the Superintendent stared at him in thoughtful silence. Ramirez's briefing had almost been a word-by-word repetition of the captain's statement to the press that morning, which Maldonado had watched on TV as he shaved.

"Have we heard anything else from the man who called to report the bombs?" he asked at last.

"No, sir," Ramirez replied.

"Has anyone else called to make any further demands?"

"No, sir."

"Have we determined what type of explosives they are?"

"No, sir."

"Do we intend to?"

"Risky, sir," Ramirez answered immediately, raising one of his eyebrows to express his doubts about the obvious. Again, he repeated what he had told a reporter earlier that day in a professional undertone, sounding just as professional now. "The caller said that they could detonate the explosives from very far away. If we go in, anyone watching could set them off."

"Anyone with a cell phone, for example," Maldonado said, returning his gaze to the terrorists' potential target.

Ramirez considered the question, and then nodded, grudgingly. "We swept the area this morning, and found no suspicious-looking persons watching the building from a distance. Still, the risk is great..." he ventured to add.

"How about the people with cell phones right over there?" Maldonado pointed over Ramirez's shoulder at the growing crowd watching the Convention Center. The captain turned around, and for the first time in the conversation, his confidence wavered.

"It seems unlikely that—" he began uncertainly.

"What?" Maldonado said almost mildly. "You don't think someone who had the gumption to place the explosives in the Convention Center would have the nerve to stand there, with the rest of the people, and watch?"

Ramirez shrugged. "Theoretically—"

"How about the television news?" Maldonado said, before Ramirez could continue.

"The television news..." the captain repeated, bewildered.

"The front of the building is being broadcast to the homes of four million Puerto Ricans, give or take a few thousands," the Superintendent said. "Anyone with a cell phone could set off the explosives from the comfort of his own home, while watching TV, don't you agree?"

Ramirez nodded silently, his cheeks reddening slightly.

"Who called the news media?" Maldonado asked.

Ramirez sighed, his self-assurance beginning to crumble. "An anonymous source, the news said," he responded despondently.

"The Macheteros, maybe?" Maldonado suggested. "That way, they could keep a watch from far away?"

The Superintendent's question was followed by an uncomfortable pause.

"I'll clear the area immediately," Ramirez finally said, bleakly.

"No," Maldonado said flatly. He was being hard with the captain on purpose because he deserved it, but in reality, there was very little that Ramirez could have done to avoid the present situation. There were hundreds, if not thousands of places from which the frontal area of the Convention Center could be observed with a good telescope. From Miramar, from the condominiums in the Condado, and even from many of the rooms of the Grand Laguna Hotel, the façade of the gigantic meeting facility would be visible through the use of any normal, self-respecting, distant surveillance gadget. And it would be impossible to search every possible location that could be used as an observation post by a trigger-happy terrorist.

He had deliberately harassed Captain Ramirez because instead of doing his job, and seeking viable solutions, he had spent his limited time playing up to the press. That, and because he was an arrogant son of a bitch, one of Governor's Alarcon's appointees who never should have been appointed to anything.

"No," he repeated, giving the knife lodged into Ramirez's ample self-esteem a further twist. "The damage has been done. But we may gain something out of this yet," he expressed, as if thinking out loud. "You say there are two more unidentified packages in the back of the building?" he asked Ramirez, even though he had known exactly how many unidentified packages had been found, and their exact location, long before he had gotten to the Convention Center.

"Two," Ramirez confirmed, nodding emphatically.

"We'll practice a little of prestidigitation, then," Maldonado said, dead serious. Ramirez stared at him uncomfortably, uncertain of what he meant. "Magic. We'll use magic and misdirection."

Captain Ramirez acknowledged the Superintendent's statement with a bewildered glance. Maldonado sighed.

"There are only about half a dozen structures, mostly abandoned houses, that have any sort of view to the back end of the Convention Center. If we use the suppliers' alley behind the center, we can gain access to that area without being seen from the front." The Superintendent watched with quiet amusement as the captain began to understand what he was after. "We can sneak in the bomb squad people into the back of the building, and see what they can make of those backpacks."

"We'll still have to deal with the explosives in the front of the building," Ramirez indicated lamely, his eyes brimming with resentment.

"Maybe," Maldonado replied, shrugging. "It will depend on what the bomb squad finds in the back. Now, in fifteen minutes, I will be heading to that group of reporters over there, and I will answer their questions. That will be our slight of hand." Ramirez opened his mouth to speak, but Maldonado ignored him. "While I'm doing that, your men will do a sweep of the houses that have any kind view to the rear of the Convention Center, and you'll make certain that the area is clear. Then, the bomb squad will move in to examine the backpacks, and disarm any explosives that are there. Hopefully, we'll learn something that will help us to deal with the other explosives." The Superintendent paused and looked at him directly. "That will be our magic."

Maldonado shifted his gaze to the ground, cleared his throat, and expectorated. Then he looked up again and frowned, as if surprised to see the captain still standing before him. "You can go now," he said mildly, and leaned back into his car's front window, to address his driver. "Beto," he said, "please patch me up with the Governor. I need to give him an update."

As he straightened himself up, he noticed that Ramirez had left.

CHAPTER XVII

For the umpteenth time, Angel San Miguel strode to the edge of the bridge, and leaned over the balustrade. "How much longer?" he inquired coolly of the crew on the boat below. Except for the rapid tapping of his fingers on the flat concrete surface of the railing, he betrayed no concern about the delay in the installation of the explosives.

The noise that had shattered most of the night's peace had stopped two hours before, as the men had finished drilling the last of the bore-holes. It had been grueling, nerve-racking work that had stretched the resistance of his men to near breaking point.

"Twenty, twenty-five more minutes, tops," Daniel pleaded, more than answered, not bothering to look up and shouting something to someone under the bridge. The tide had turned, and a strong current was beginning to run under the bridges towards the lagoon, straining the ropes that anchored the pontoon boats, and rippling around their twin hulls. Dawn was breaking behind the tall buildings of Miramar, casting their long shadows over the gray waters of the lagoon, and washing the sky with a crimson hue that dyed everything below it in pink.

"It is precisely six forty-three AM," San Miguel said. He paused, turning his head briefly to look at the incoming traffic from Miramar. Fortunately, the flow of vehicles was still very light, barely averaging five to six cars a minute. He returned to Daniel. "We go at seven fifteen, sharp!"

Daniel nodded emphatically, still not looking at his boss, and waved an arm in dismissal, concentrating on the work below.

San Miguel marched briskly towards the Miramar end of the bridge, where six men waited. He felt elated, although he kept his emotions to himself. Behind him, San Juan still slept. In a few minutes, years of planning and grueling work would come to fruition. In the span of less than an hour, the eyes of the entire world would turn to San Juan.

"Gentlemen," he said jovially to the men, "we close the bridge in fif-teen minutes."

If only every morning were like this, Lucas thought.

Even though the first yellow beams from the sun were only now pierc-ing the morning gloom, the cloudless sky presaged one of those bright, glorious days that could only happen in a Caribbean winter, when the temperature never rose beyond a balmy seventy-four degrees Fahrenheit, and the rain did not dare to show its misty face. Best of all, Lucas had the road to San Juan all to himself, driving past half a dozen cars at most, in-cluding a 1959 light green Chevrolet Impala that travelled at a regal speed of thirty miles per hour, strutting its wing-like fuselage for all to see.

At 6:45 in the morning, he was running a little late, but it did not bother him. He had already driven through most of the marginal ex-pressway that bypassed Miramar, and with the light traffic he would reach the Doña Fela parking building in another ten minutes.

As he approached the bridge connecting Miramar to San Juan, he saw several employees from the Aqueducts and Sewers Authority talking animatedly among themselves, while they stood next to half a dozen A-frame traffic barricades. He had noticed agency employees working un-der the opposite bridge as he had headed to his home the previous evening, and wondered what type of problem had caused the men to work throughout the weekend night. He concluded that they were prob-ably trying to avoid the massive vehicular flow that would flood the road later that day.

Apparently, they were getting ready to close off the bridge, although they had not begun to carry the barriers onto the road. As he drove by, some of the men briefly stared at him but kept talking. It would have to be a short closure, he thought, since by noon, the San Sebastian crowd would start to funnel through the lagoon overpass from several avenues in alarming numbers.

Fortunately, that would not be his problem. He had cleared the barri-ers just in time, avoiding having to skirt the Condado Lagoon and cross into San Juan over the Dos Hermanos Bridge, which would have delayed him another fifteen minutes.

All in all, it was turning out to be a pretty good day.

"Oh God!" Michelle muttered, as she strapped her watch on her wrist, her auburn hair still partially wet from her morning shower. "It's five past seven!"

She scurried around the dining room table, kissing her mother and her aunts, who were having breakfast, still in their sleeping gowns.

"Gotta go, gotta go, gotta go!" she said, rushing towards the door, and picking up her purse from the telephone table by the entrance.

"Did you call a taxi?" Fannie asked, as she buttered one of her toasts. "I can call Don Moncho, and he can pick you up in ten—"

"I already called him," she interrupted, and blew her a kiss. "I figured you wouldn't need him today."

"You called Don Moncho?" Fannie asked in a surprised tone.

"Do you think you're the only woman in his life?" she asked, causing Maria to nearly choke on her bagel. "He should be downstairs already, waiting for me." She opened the door, and blew some more kisses at the Pietri sisters. "Have a great day!"

"You too!" Evelyn called after her.

"Break a leg!" Maria added, while still chewing her food.

As she closed the door, Michelle heard Evelyn asking Maria not to speak with her mouth full, followed by an instant retort by Maria threatening to stuff Evelyn's mouth with her bagel. Michelle smiled.

It was time.

San Miguel cast a cursory glance at the five lanes of concrete pavement that were about to be shut down. Three major vehicular arteries converged into them, feeding traffic into San Juan through the bridge from three different directions. The Baldorioty De Castro Express bordered the Condado Lagoon, providing a route for cars traveling from the northeastern coastal areas of the main island, including the tourist sector of Isla Verde and the Muñoz Marin International Airport. The Ponce De Leon Avenue handled the flow of vehicles coming from the old commercial district of Santurce, the Hato Rey Financial District, and the residential area of Miramar. And the Luis Muñoz Rivera Expressway skirted Miramar to the south, bringing in travelers from the municipalities of Guaynabo and Bayamon, as well as from other towns in the interior of Puerto Rico.

The clogging of those three arteries would place San Juan on the verge of a major heart attack, reducing the possible inflow of vehicles into the small island to a mere trickle from the El Condado area, along the single-lane Dos Hermanos bridge. And that trickle would be clamped shut as well.

San Miguel turned to the men who waited expectantly by his side. They were Macheteros, not his men, but El Alacran had directed them to follow the tall man's instructions as if they were his own, at least until further notice, and they were anxious to go.

"Close the bridge," San Miguel ordered, flicking his cell phone open and dialing to a similar group of rebels standing by the Condado end of the Dos Hermanos Bridge. "Close the bridge," he repeated as soon as the call was answered, and hung up, and then dialed again, this time to George, who still kept watch with his men by the three parked vans, close to the San Juan Yacht Club. While he waited, he saw one of his Macheteros step up to the middle of the road and raise his hand at two incoming cars, which cautiously decreased their speed, and stopped. Four of the other men began to drag the traffic barricades unto the middle of the street.

"*Yeah, boss?*" George answered.

"Close the bridges," San Miguel repeated into his cell phone, for the third time, and ended the call. Unlike the other crews, George's men would have to cut off the flow of vehicles in two exits: the one accessing the bridge to Miramar, and the one leading to the Dos Hermanos Bridge and El Condado.

In the span of a minute, it was done. No more traffic flowed in or out of the island of San Juan.

San Miguel paused briefly, to see how his men were faring. The mouth of the bridge was shut down completely by the A-frame barricades. Three of the men stood along the barriers, keeping a watchful eye on the accumulating traffic, while two others had unzipped a duffel bag, and were busy extracting AK-47 rifles and attaching their signature curved ammunition clips to them. About half a dozen more cars had rolled to a dead stop, and several others were approaching from the three avenues.

It was time to call Daniel.

"I need five more minutes," Daniel pleaded, his cell phone wedged between his ear and his right shoulder, even before San Miguel could speak. He was hobbling toward the designated firing point, a mound covered by trees, situated about a hundred and fifty yards away from the bridges. A cardboard spool of electrical wire unraveled from his hands like a fishing reel, leaving behind it a black thin line that trailed all the way back to the underbelly of the bridge where San Miguel stood. Two men flanked him, keeping watch. He followed the same route of three other wires that already stretched from the three other bridges to the blasting point.

"*All right,*" San Miguel answered, and ended the conversation.

Daniel was forced to smile, admiring his associate's strenuous effort to sound unconcerned. During the more than a decade they had known each other, they had learned to keep out of each other's way during tense situations, and not to waste any time with unnecessary questions. It was something that required the type of absolute trust that could only develop between men who had risked their lives together on several occasions.

Daniel paused just enough to take his phone off his shoulder and to shove it into one of his pants' back pockets. Then he continued to chase the other three wires through the clump of trees into which they disappeared.

As he cleared the trees, the ground sloped downwards, forming a shallow trench. There, two other men waited for Daniel's arrival, guarding the electric detonators. In reality, the designation of the machines sounded more impressive than their appearance. They were boxes, each about the size of a car battery, with two small posts or poles on top to which the leads of the wires were connected. Like a battery, they would provide a surge of electricity, once a lever on their side was pushed inward, that would energize the blasting caps in each of the charges installed under the bridges and set off the explosives.

There was a total of six detonators, four that would be used, and two brought as spares. Three of the detonators were already connected, each to the circuit of a different bridge.

Daniel staggered down the incline, and handed the spool he was carrying to one of his men, who began to splice the wire and shear the insulation from its edges. Another man crouched behind one of the unused detonators, and after receiving the spliced wire, wrapped one end around each of the posts of the machine.

Daniel began dialing his cell phone even before the man had finished.

"*Speak to me*," San Miguel answered.

"We're ready," Daniel announced excitedly.

"*We go in five minutes, no matter what. Do you understand?*" San Miguel stated with what sounded like indifferent detachment.

"I understand," Daniel replied, in a more subdued tone.

"*Set your watch on my mark*," San Miguel ordered, "*Five...four...three...two...one...Start the countdown*," and he ended the call.

Daniel transferred his attention to the men milling about him. "We go in five minutes. Paco, Aldo, and Figueres, each of you will set off the charges for one of the bridges. I will handle the fourth. Sasha, keep a watch for any curious people. I will count down from minus ten seconds. Be sure to get behind cover."

As the men scrambled to their positions, Daniel wondered if the explosives would actually go off. They had worked with fastidious care, but at a breathtaking speed. Explosives were like women; you could never really tell how they would react when the moment of truth came. But he had never failed with either before.

And he did not intend to fail now.

Don Moncho's taxicab, a white minivan with the words "Rockdale Taxi" printed in blue on its door along with several telephone numbers, was parked in front of the lobby of the condominium, as Michelle had predicted. It had probably been there for several minutes, since its engine was shut off, its driver hidden behind a newspaper.

Don Moncho had been a family tradition for more than a generation, having faithfully provided public transportation for Don Jorge Pietri, Michelle's grandfather, for Fannie, Evelyn and Maria, and now for Michelle. The man, she was convinced, had already bumped into the eighty-year old threshold. He sported an ancient but impeccably kept Panama hat, and wore thick, coke-bottle-bottom-like lenses that made him look permanently confused. Unlike any other taxi driver in the world, he drove at a steady thirty-five miles an hour, constantly humming to himself the same song. There was an ongoing family debate as to what that song could be, since he barely raised the volume of his rendition to a level perceptible to the human ear. Fannie had stopped hearing it for several years.

"Good morning, Don Moncho," Michelle said pleasantly.

Don Moncho neatly folded his newspaper, and placed it on the seat next to him.

"Yes, and good morning to you too, Miss Michelle! Where to?" he asked, not yet turning on the ignition.

"To WKPA," she answered distractedly, while she drew her cell phone out of her purse. She cursed, as she realized that the phone was turned off, and saw, as soon as she switched it on, that there were three "missed calls" from Doel Reyes, plus a voice mail that simply said, *"Where are you? I need you stat!"*

Flustered, she dialed Doel's phone number. His pre-recorded voice, preceded by the Pac Man game music, immediately let her know that he was not available at the moment, but that he would be glad to answer if she left him a short message, which probably meant that he was already in the television studio, and had switched his cell phone off. "Doel," she said, as soon as his message recorder beep-beeped into action, "I know that I'm a little bit late, but I should be there in about twenty minutes. We have many things to talk about. Bye." She paused, then added just in case, "It's Michelle," and finished her call.

As the taxi headed towards Miramar, she noticed that at least four cruise ships were already tied to the docks. San Juan would be crawling with tourists today.

Don Moncho hummed his unrecognizable tune as he steered his taxi through the nearly deserted Fernandez Juncos Avenue, at a heady thirty-five miles per hour. He drove with the calm, practiced ease of a person who for more than half a century had earned his living by transporting other people to other places, slowing down periodically to glimpse at passing pedestrians, particularly of the feminine stripe. Michelle wondered, staring at the back of his immaculately clean Panama hat, if that peaceful, methodical man had always been that way, or if he had refined his outlook of life with the passage of time. She made a mental note to interview him for one of her human-interest reports. She was certain that he would have a lot of fascinating stories to tell.

She felt the taxi slow down, and looked out of her window, to locate Don Moncho's new object of attention. Instead, she saw that he had been forced to reduce his speed by the increasing number of vehicles on the street.

"Looks like something happened up front," Don Moncho told Michelle, craning his long, scrawny neck out of the window to see better. He tried to shift to the left lane as the traffic continued to thicken and slow down, but the car on the left refused to yield him the space, and as the cars slowed to a stop, blocked him.

"An accident?" Michelle ventured.

"Maybe," Don Moncho replied. "I'll try to get to the left lane and turn left on the next street. Avenida Constitucion may be less congested."

That's all I need, Michelle thought grimly, as the taxi approached El Falansterio. *Doel will kill me.*

She retrieved her cell phone from her purse, and redialed her news editor's number. As she waited for an answer, the taxi came to a dead stop.

The three pontoon boats moved smoothly between the rows of yachts tied to the piers of the San Juan Yacht Club. Covered in dust and grime, their ghostly colored crews elicited curious glances from the few early risers—mostly sports fishermen—who were readying their ships to go out.

The pontoon boats continued to travel until they reached a narrow pier adjacent to an elongated, three-story structure lined with rows of large glass windows that faced the water—the marina's main building. Six of their occupants swiftly jumped off the boats and quietly hurried towards the building, even before the boats had been tied up to the dock. Four of the intruders, carrying AK-47s, entered the main lobby of the club, and spread through the building, quickly searching for employees and visitors. The other two continued to walk casually to the parking area's entrance, and disarmed the security guard who sat there.

One of the men, a medium height, broad shouldered, brawny man called Fangio, knocked softly on the club administrator's door, and after receiving no acknowledgement, carefully opened the door. A fat, bald man looked up briefly from his desk as he spoke on the telephone, and gave Fangio a friendly wave, signaling him to walk in. A stuffed blue marlin, about eighth feet long, occupied most of the wall behind the administrator, while a wooden block with large, carved letters announced, at the front of his desk, that he was named "Benitez".

Benitez eyed his visitor as he spoke, not pausing in his rapid-fire instructions to whomever he was addressing at the other end of the line, even after he noticed the semi-automatic assault rifle that the man held in his right hand. While he talked, Fangio looked out of the office's left window, and noticed to his satisfaction that the pontoon boats had already been secured to the dock, and that his men were unloading the last of the boxes containing AK-47 ammunition. Patiently, he waited for Benitez's conversation to end.

"What are you planning to fish with that? Tuna? Marlin? A whale, maybe?" the administrator asked in a friendly tone, pointing at the AK-47 after he hung up the phone.

"I need to borrow your club," Fangio answered wearily.

Benitez picked a brochure from the top of his desk, and handed it to his visitor, who took it wordlessly. "These are our rates for the three halls that we rent, and the alternatives that we offer...Food-wise, that is. How large is your party?"

Fangio was forced to smile. "We're twelve," he replied.

The administrator raised one of his eyebrows, bewildered by the man's response.

"And I need to borrow the club now," Fangio added, placing the unopened brochure back on the desk. "The whole club," he said, dead serious, and pointed the AK-47 at Benitez. "So if you would be so kind as to show me around."

"We leave now," San Miguel quietly indicated to his men.

They started to walk to an Autoridad de Acueductos y Alcantarillados van parked on the curb of the bridge closest to Miramar. Calmly, San Miguel began dialing the same numbers he had dialed before, each time repeating the same instructions to the men blocking the entryways to the other bridges.

As he did so, he sauntered casually to the middle of the street, where traffic had been blocked by the portable barricades, and looked distractedly towards Miramar while he spoke into his phone. More than fifty vehicles—mostly cars, but also a Metropolitan Authority bus and two eighteen wheelers—had crawled to a stop, and now clogged the three avenues that led to bridge, with nowhere to go. Two pesky motorcyclists had zigzagged their way between the bumpers of the stalled vehicles until they had reached the barricades, and stared with curiosity at the men blocking their way, revving their engines every so often, as if to prompt the blockers to hurry up and finish whatever it was they were doing and open the road. Several of the drivers closest to the barriers had turned off their engines, and a couple had gotten off their automobiles to make out what was happening. Further back, some of the cars had begun to blare their horns, impatient to move on.

The impending departure of the men who had closed the bridge, as they clambered into the van while leaving the barricades standing, triggered the simmering anger of the trapped motorists. A tremendous blare of horns, shouts, and even a siren erupted from the stalled vehicles. The two bikers shouted abuse at San Miguel, while half a dozen drivers began to exit from their cars to get to the barriers.

A man dressed in a white shirt and a pink striped tie—one of the first to be stopped by the blockade—began to edge his white Camry towards the standing A frames, threatening to tip one of them over. Almost distractedly, San Miguel motioned him to stop while he flapped his cell phone shut. But the man, red-faced with anger, stuck an arm through the window and flicked his finger at him, to the vocal approval of the people closest to him. Then he continued to inch his car forward until the tilted barricade toppled on its side, the clatter of its fall drowned by the appreciative cheers of those who watched it tumble.

San Miguel walked towards the white Camry until he stood in front of its bumper. He calmly put away his cell phone, and pulled out a gun from one of his pants pockets. The driver in the Camry never saw it until San Miguel leveled it at him and fired twice through the windshield, punching two small, white-rimmed holes through the glass. One of the bullets struck the irate driver on the right side of his chest, perforating his lung, while the second hit him on the chin, shattering most of his lower teeth and jaw, and exiting through his right cheek.

As San Miguel walked away, the stunned driver, still uncertain of what had happened, raised his right hand to his face and withdrew it almost immediately in revulsion, as his fingers probed into the jumble of bone and skin that had been his mouth, and became drenched in a torrent of red, warm fluid. Gagging on his own blood, he pushed the door of his car open, and stumbled out, staggering blindly towards a blue Yaris behind him, the front of his white shirt soaked in his deep crimson. He toppled after a few paces onto the car's hood, oblivious of the screams of the young female behind the wheel. As he raised his head to plead for help, more blood spurted from his mouth. The woman recoiled in horror and—in a fit of panic—backed up her car onto the one behind her. Other nearby drivers abandoned their vehicles and began to run away from the wounded man and his assailant, their horrified shouts drowned by the increasing din of the vehicles stopped further back in the road. The two motorcyclists clumsily turned their bikes around and fled in the opposite direction.

San Miguel signaled to the Autoridad van to approach him, and looked at his watch. Slightly less than three minutes before the explosions. He surveyed for the last time the tumultuous agglomeration of vehicles and people sprawled before him. Then, as the van screeched to a halt next to him, he climbed into the front passenger seat, and shut the door.

"Go!" he ordered. "Don't stop until you reach the Grand Laguna Hotel."

The men guarding the other checkpoints where traffic had been blocked withdrew, mounted their vehicles, and drove away, leaving behind a seething mass of angry and perplexed motorists who could neither advance nor back out of the bottlenecked bridges. Tired but elated, the former "Acueductos" workers headed towards their next objective, the Grand Laguna Hotel. As the small force—comprised by about a dozen of San Miguel's men and about the same number of Macheteros—drove over the empty Ponce de Leon Avenue, they all slipped on their left arms their black "Libre como el Coqui" armbands, and armed themselves with the AK-47 assault rifles, Glock pistols, and a sundry collection of other weapons they had brought along with them.

The men were ready, and anxious to go.

The conquest of San Juan had begun.

CHAPTER XVIII

"Two minutes," Daniel warned his men. He spoke louder than usual, since they were all wearing earplugs. They were lying with their bellies flat on the ground, behind the mound that blocked their view of the bridges, all except one, who sat with his back towards the others, scanning the surrounding area for unexpected intruders, using a pair of binoculars whenever his unaided eyes perceived any movement that he could not identify.

During the last minute, a total of five vans had zoomed past them heading towards the hotel area, less than a quarter of a mile away.

A fly landed on Daniel's ear, and he automatically swatted it away. He was sweating, even though the new morning had still not shed most of the cool night air. It bothered him. He was not supposed to be nervous.

He looked at the other three men lying next to him—one to his left, the other two to his right—and tried to read their body language. He could tell that Paco and Aldo were barely keeping their excitement in check, although each manifested it in a different way. Paco had adopted an unnaturally stiff position behind the electric detonator, his hand poised on the lever that would trigger the explosion. Aldo kept shifting his body, like an impatient toddler trying to avoid going to the bathroom. Figueres, the man lying on Daniel's left, seemed bored to the point of unconsciousness. His eyes were shut, and his chin rested on his folded hands.

"Stay with us, Figueres," Daniel said to him, half-jokingly.

Figueres kept his eyes closed, but the upper corner of his mouth twitched into a lazy smile.

"Bored, are you?" Daniel asked, but just then, Sasha, the lookout, stirred.

"We've got a visitor," he said in an amused tone.

"Where?" Daniel turned his head to look at Sasha, who for several seconds said nothing, staring through his binoculars, and then pointed with his hand to his right.

Daniel searched for the intruder, and finally found him, a man about a hundred yards away, dressed in shorts, a T-shirt, and tennis shoes, jogging towards the lagoon along the sidewalk that fringed the Grand Laguna Hotel's walled boundary.

"Do you think he'll make it to the bridge before the explosion?" Sasha asked, fascinated by the running man. "Poor devil."

"No. Not unless he runs very, very fast," Daniel replied, glancing at his watch. "Get ready," he ordered to the men lying next to him, and began in his mind the regressive countdown from the last thirty seconds. When he reached ten, he began to count out loud. He could see the tension in his men increase with each passing second, their hands reaching for the firing levers.

And then, it was time.

"Fire!" he ordered, and thrust forwards the firing lever of his detonator.

Mark Sampson had led a charmed life in politics. Young, handsome, articulate, and charismatic, he had risen fast in the rough and tumble world of Florida politics, attaining the position of State Speaker of the House by the age thirty-eight. Opposing wasteful spending, higher taxes, and the socialist type of government fomented by the present Washington administration, and favoring the incorporation of Christian values into public schools and government, he had built a solid foundation in Miami-Dade County among Cuban and upper middle class voters, and was being considered as a front runner for the Senatorial elections of November of that year. He was his state's Golden Boy of politics, poised to stake his claim on the U.S. Senate, and if the chips continued to fall in the right place—*God knows*—on the Presidency, later down the road.

His almost religious belief in fiscal oversight and the reduction in spending did not extend, however, to his private life. Mark liked to live well, and discerned no contradiction in lavishly spending money on himself, his family, and his girlfriend. Nor was his conscience concerned about using his party's credit card to pay for a substantial portion of his personal expenses, including luncheons in expensive restaurants, travels to exotic resorts, and stays in five star resorts, such as the Grand Laguna Hotel.

He had flown to Puerto Rico on a "fact-finding-mission", to explore the tourist trade in the island, and to determine new ways of attracting tourism to Florida. It had been a three-day blitzkrieg tour, so he had not brought his wife and two children with him, and had traveled instead with his girlfriend, a busty, long-legged model (listed in the expense report as his public relations aide). After a brief, token meeting with Governor Pietrantoni in La Fortaleza, he had visited the Convention Center, the El Yunque rainforest, and the Fiestas of San Sebastian, and would dedicate Sunday, and a portion of Monday, to "summarize and review" all of his findings and observations with his public relations aide.

He was very proud of his athletic looks and worked hard to keep them, waking up early every morning to do a five-mile run, and then hitting the gym for an hour of weights. He took his physical appearance seriously, knowing what a valuable asset for a politician it could be. During his visit to San Juan, he had enjoyed jogging out of the Grand Laguna Hotel, and trekking over the Dos Hermanos Bridge and around the Condado Lagoon, re-crossing into the island of San Juan over one of the Miramar bridges. It was not quite five miles, but close to it, and the route he followed was quite pleasant, allowing him to plan the rest of his day.

The pink dawn he had witnessed, along with his assistant, from his twenty-second story suite, had blossomed into a beautiful morning, and promised to become an even more spectacular day. He intended to enjoy it to the fullest, before he returned on Monday to the tough hustle and bustle of Florida's politics.

As he jogged towards the lagoon, Mark concentrated so much on his upcoming activities, that he failed to notice the near total absence of vehicles on the avenue next to him, or the group of men, across that avenue, lying on the grass and staring at him with binoculars. It was not until he rounded the entire perimeter of the Grand Laguna Hotel and gained a clear view of the closest Miramar bridge, about fifty yards away, that he became aware of the massed traffic trapped by the Acueductos barriers, heard the echo of their frantic protests, and realized that something was askew.

And by then, it was too late, because the world exploded in front of his eyes.

The ground shuddered, as two tons of plastic charges that were tightly packed and plugged into the bridges instantly vaporized and turned into impossibly powerful gases that had nowhere to go. Inevitably, the vaporized gases pushed outwards, easily buckling and busting through the structural elements that restrained them. Fragments of reinforced concrete flew and scattered in every direction, followed by giant plumes of dark gray dust that fanned out, like the petals of giant flowers, from each exploding charge.

It was the noise, however, which overwhelmed Mark, erupting out of the bridges with the ferocity of a thousand thunderclaps in not one but scores of consecutive, overlapping blasts, producing a succession of powerful shockwaves that knocked him off his feet.

All about the lagoon, dozens of windows from the adjacent buildings shattered, startling residents and tourists out of their sleep. Flying debris rained upon the stalled motorists in the Miramar, Condado, and San Juan streets, with the same deadly effect of artillery shells. Chunks of cement, ranging from pebble-sized, bullet-like projectiles to blocks weighing hundreds of pounds, demolished car windshields, and crashed into the stranded vehicles, injuring many of its occupants.

The blasts had a particularly devastating effect on the people waiting in the Condado end of the Dos Hermanos Bridge. There, the explosives—which had been placed on the metal structure supporting the temporary bridge at a distance of no more than fifty feet away from the stranded traffic—hurled shredded scraps of metal onto the unsuspecting crowd, causing hundreds of injuries. A woman who was walking her dog on the sidewalk next to the Autoridad barriers was killed instantly by a fragment of concrete about the size of a basketball that struck her on the chest, crushing her ribcage. Her dog, a nervous, immaculately groomed Maltese, took turns at barking at the unseen assailant and licking his dead mistress' face, its leash still held by the corpse's hand. Another man, who had gotten off his car to get a better look at what the workers on the bridge were doing, was decapitated by a jagged shard of steel that tore off most of his neck.

Everywhere men and women who had been stopped by the street blockades abandoned their vehicles and fled in panic through the narrow corridors created by the stalled traffic, pushing those that blocked their way, trampling over the fallen wounded, crouching as debris hurled into the air by the explosions continued to pound them from the sky. Some drivers added to the mayhem by repeatedly ramming their cars into other vehicles, trying to open a breach through which they could escape.

Those trees and palms closest to the explosions were torn to bits of wood or splinters, and shorn of their leaves and branches. One large almond tree was impaled by a four foot long piece of rebar, only about a foot of its length sticking out of the trunk. Hundreds of frightened birds took to the air, squawking and shrieking in alarm, scampering in every direction, while others thrashed and flailed in agony on the ground, wounded by the shrapnel-like discharge of the explosions.

Jets of water sprang over most of the lagoon, as bits and pieces of the bridges pelted its surface while they fell back out of the sky. Most of the third floor of the San Juan Yacht Club, the building closest to any of the bridges, was demolished, about half of its roof collapsing. The panoramic windows on both floors of the club were blown inwards, showering everything inside with thousands of glass shards. Some of the boats moored closest to the bridge caught fire, and the wind coming from the lagoon fanned and spread the flames quickly, engulfing in a massive blaze most of the marina. Boats exploded as the fire reached their gas tanks, adding to the general conflagration. The entire width of the San Antonio Channel was covered by a huge, swirling cloud of black smoke that rose high into the air, broken periodically by the flickering orange tongues of the fire that greedily consumed the boats below.

Even the men who had taken over the San Juan Yacht Club were surprised by the violence of explosions. Bits of glass, plaster, and stone covered them. One of the intruders lost a finger, as he sought refuge behind a low wall, but inadvertently left his hand exposed on the wall's upper edge. Another man was nicked on a shoulder by a piece of stone that flew over his cover and ricocheted from the wall behind him. Two men who had established a machine gun position on the third floor barely escaped with their lives, after the heavy concrete slab of the club's roof collapsed and thudded heavily onto the ground, less than two feet from where they crouched for protection.

As the explosions subsided, the dust clouds expanded rapidly, rising and coalescing into a gigantic grayish brown haze that shrouded the bridges, the lagoon, and all of the surrounding streets in a thick fog. Mark—the jogger—stood up uncertainly, still unable to comprehend what had just happened. His legs shook so fiercely that he could barely stay upright, but miraculously, he had survived the destruction unscathed. A large segment of an iron lamppost that had apparently decorated one of the bridges, still attached to its lamp, had landed next to him, but he did not notice it until he nearly tripped over it. His ears hummed, masking the sound of the scores of car and store alarms that had been set off by the shock waves of the detonations.

Picking himself off the sidewalk, Sampson noticed a group of men, no more than a hundred yards away, standing up from behind a small hill and chatting with each other. His first instinct was to run towards them and ask them if they knew what had happened, but something in their relaxed, almost careless attitude warned him to stay away. It seemed, as they casually began to climb the hill, that they had not been surprised by catastrophic events that had just knocked him on his ass.

As unobtrusively as possible, he turned in the direction from where he had come, and began to half walk, half trot towards the Grand Laguna Hotel, trying to put as much distance between him and the strangers as his wobbly legs would allow.

The Grand Laguna Hotel rose forty floors into the sky, a glorious, ultra modern spiral of glass and steel. It was crowned by a fifty-foot nickel and chrome needle containing a rotating laser beacon that at night could be seen from the Cordillera Central mountain range in the center of the island. A second structure to the south of the tower fringed the Condado Lagoon, climbing like a huge tidal swell from a two-story grand hall to half the height of its sister building. The two structures contained a combined one thousand one hundred and seventy six rooms and suites, including three two-level penthouses with private pools and solariums.

Erected barely a year and a half before, in what used to be the old Caribe Hilton Hotel, it had been hailed as a great national achievement by its proponents, and as a cultural abomination by its foes. A group calling itself the "Committee to Save our Patrimony" had stopped its construction for several weeks by invading the building site and climbing onto its cranes, threatening to jump if the authorities attempted to remove them. Two law school professors had filed an injunction, challenging the legality of the project, claiming that the land upon which the hotel was being constructed was public land that could never be deeded to a private entity. The spiral tower had been dubbed "The Screw" by local wits, and the name—as well as hundreds of jokes based on it—had stuck. In the end, private enterprise had prevailed, and the Grand Laguna Hotel had become, along with the Convention Center, a symbol of the new, modern San Juan.

The hotel had been aptly named. Everything about it had been designed to impress, to convey unparalleled luxury, to make it *grand*. Its cavernous, white marble-floored lobby extended from its northern boundary facing the Atlantic Ocean to its southern, crescent-shaped entrance, which could fit the length of twelve cars. A glass wall without any visible supports covered the ground floor's entire façade to the north, so that any visitor arriving at the hotel would have an unfettered view of the roiling sea.

A large dome, sixty feet across, established the lobby's center. From it hung a massive, intricately beautiful Chihuly glass chandelier that filled the dome with hundreds of whimsically shaped, multicolored crystals. It was a stunning display of art, one that competed for attention with the blue, mighty waters of the ocean outside. Half a dozen sitting areas, each differently shaped and sized, were spread over the lobby's vast floor, each delineated by plush, colorful carpets depicting geographical scenes of the island, and illuminated by smaller but not less striking Chihuly chandeliers. Between them, modern, airy furniture provided ample cushioned space for a hundred *derrières*, while ferns, elephant ears, banana trees and other tropical plants softened and warmed the metal and glass surroundings.

Towards the Atlantic, the lobby dropped twenty steps to a swanky, secluded bar designed for those who sought refuge from the sun. An elongated pond inhabited by water lilies and large, golden koi fish bordered it. Beyond that lay the open recreation area; three large pools connected at different levels by waterfalls and slides, and to their left a small private beach, the only private beach in all of Puerto Rico, and one of the original bones of contention of the opponents of the hotel. The beach had been artificially created, wrested in the 1950s from the rough Atlantic Ocean by placing a string of reefs that served as a crash barrier to the waves rolling from the sea, and awarded to the Caribe Hilton, the Grand Laguna's predecessor.

Gardens with more tropical shrubbery and plants covered an area about half the size of a city block at the point closest to the Condado Lagoon. Several pathways laced the gardens, leading to ponds, fountains, and secluded benched spots for reading and meditation.

One particular path led down to the lagoon and to a stone bridge that connected the small Spanish fort of San Geronimo to the island of San Juan. During the 1600's and 1700's, the fort had been the only structure that existed on the easternmost point of the island of San Juan. Unlike its massive sister fortresses—San Cristobal and El Morro—that formed part of the defenses of Old San Juan, San Geronimo was basically a small, square outpost surrounded by thick walls that stood on its own. Each of its sides measured no more than one hundred feet. Its barracks were nestled against its eastern wall; a thick, boxlike structure that had provided refuge from the elements to its undersized garrison and doubled as the fort's powder room. Parallel twin ramps rose at the opposite sides of the barracks, and climbed to an elevated platform—the barracks' roof—that faced the Condado Lagoon.

In its heyday, the diminutive fort, or *"fortin"* as it was called in Spanish, had been designed to provide a first line of defense to San Juan, to harass any enemy that attempted to approach the city from the lagoon. San Geronimo had served its purpose well. It had withstood Sir Francis Drake in 1595, been destroyed in 1598 by the Earl of Cumberland and, after subsequently being rebuilt, endured in 1797 several attacks and a continued two-week bombardment by a 13,000 man British army, including the Royal Marines that later became famous for defeating Napoleon in Egypt.

Peacetime, however, had nearly destroyed it. By the early 1900's it had been abandoned, having outlived its strategic usefulness, and fallen into serious disrepair. Recently, efforts to save it had gained momentum, and now it was being used as a tourist attraction. Such efforts had included assigning its management to the Grand Laguna Hotel, which in exchange for its upkeep, occasionally used it for private events of the resort. There had even been talks of opening a restaurant in the fort, but anticipating the public outcry against the use of a historical monument for such purposes, Governor Pietrantoni had vetoed the idea.

Not that the hotel needed another food establishment. The Grand Laguna boasted eight different restaurants, in addition to its convention facilities, including a French bistro, a Japanese sushi bar, a Morton's, and on the penthouse of the twenty-storied annex, "El Ajonjoli", one of the most exclusive local *nouvelle-cuisine* restaurants in the island. The hotel also contained ten boutique stores, a pharmacy, a small infirmary, a two-story gym and wellness center, an enormous casino, and two nightclubs, as well as a business center with two dozen offices and variously sized conference rooms.

Every modern convenience, including the latest technological advances in fire prevention, security surveillance, and communications had been incorporated into the hotel. Its emergency generators could produce sufficient power to satisfy uninterruptedly all of the electrical needs of the two towers for an entire month. An underground reservoir held enough water to keep the hotel operating at full occupancy during a period of two weeks, and had been designed to capture and process rainwater.

In summary, the Grand Laguna Hotel could operate as a self-contained mini community.

And for that reason, San Miguel had chosen to make it his operations headquarters during the San Juan campaign.

Capturing it had been surprisingly easy. The Autoridad de Acueductos vehicle on which he traveled had screeched to a halt at the vehicle arrival area, followed by two other vans. A parking attendant, garbed in a sky-blue, short-sleeved shirt and tan pants had given the government vehicle a hard stare but nevertheless approached it and opened its passenger front door. San Miguel had thanked him and stepped off into the hotel, unmindful about the half dozen armed men who poured out of the back of the van.

Ignoring the curious, somewhat alarmed looks of the handful of guests in the lobby who had risen early, San Miguel had cheerfully made his way to the reception area. Like everything else in the hotel, the front desk had been fashioned in glass and metal, resembling frothing waves. It was located at the western end of the lobby, and extended about a third of its length. Usually manned by six clerks, it was still being handled at that time of the morning by the three-person graveyard shift.

A good-looking attendant saw the tall, black-haired man approach the desk and smiled with curious anticipation. He smiled back at her, and leaned on the counter. Even though he was wearing a shirt with the Acueductos logos, something about his confident demeanor caused the attendant—bearing the nametag of Sandra Perez—to pause.

"Good morning," she said pleasantly.

"Good mor—" San Miguel began to answer, but a succession of thunderous explosions drowned his voice, and shook the building. The explosions seemed to originate very close to the hotel, and the attendant searched nervously for signs of their origin, but could find nothing awry. "Goodness!" San Miguel said, placing a hand over his chest. "Those charges came off louder than we expected!"

The attendant laughed nervously, and then became conscious of the import of the tall visitor's words. She gazed at him quizzically, not fully understanding what he meant.

"I'm sorry," she said after a pause, "what charges are you talking about?"

"Oh, of course," San Miguel said in an apologetic tone. "I forget that not everybody knows. I'm referring to the charges that destroyed the bridges connecting Miramar and El Condado to San Juan. I had no idea that they would make so much noise!"

The pretty attendant tilted her head slightly, still not understanding. She smiled uncertainly, as if she was being made the object of a joke she did not fully grasp. "What...Exactly, what are you talking about?"

San Miguel nodded sympathetically. "I can understand your confusion. Let me explain. My men," he said, directing his arm in a sweeping gesture towards the lobby, where about two dozen men holding semi-automatic rifles were now fanning out into the hotel, "placed explosive charges under the bridges to Miramar and Condado, and destroyed them. We are now taking over this hotel," he added in a firm but not unpleasant manner.

The attendant grew pale. Having directed her full attention to the tall visitor, she had not noticed until that moment what the rest of his associates were doing. There had been no screaming, no shots fired, no scuffles or protests. Like a cancer, the men were quietly spreading through the hotel, heading towards different areas, calmly rounding up the confused staff and guests and directing them to the center of the lobby.

Taking a deep breath, the pretty attendant moved her hand under the counter, searching for the alarm button. She was shaking so hard, however, that she could not find it. San Miguel leaned over the counter's top and briefly scanned its edge. He caught the attendant's wrist, and gently guided it to where the red button was located.

"I believe this is what you're looking for," he said, gazing directly at her eyes. "Press it."

Lucas felt a slight rumble under his feet a couple of seconds before the sharp staccato of several far away explosions followed. They sounded, by their speed, like a string of firecrackers going off, except heavier and more powerful, reminding him of the distant thud of artillery shells landing on a target.

Dozens of pigeons perched on the ledges of the surrounding buildings flew out of their high shelters, startled by the noise, and the few persons already awake and out on the streets stopped to look inquiringly at the sky. But their view was limited by the tall colonial structures that flanked the narrow sidewalks, and between the buildings they could see nothing but the blue sky of what promised to be a beautiful Sunday morning.

Strange, Lucas thought, unable to find a reasonable explanation for the disturbance. He waited for several seconds, but no further noise interrupted the morning's peace.

As he renewed his trek towards the *Joyero,* he made a mental note to find out in the evening news what had happened.

For one brief second, as a woman screamed and the reporters instinctively flinched, Police Superintendent Maldonado thought that the bombs in the Convention Center had been set off. He had been caught unaware, just as he had begun to tell to a female reporter from Telemundo who had thrust her microphone in front of his face—and whom he intensely disliked, even though he never ceased to admire her figure—that he had no idea who the "possible perpetrators" behind the plot to destroy the huge building were. But just as quickly, his brain registered that the blasts were too many, and that the noise originated from the wrong direction.

Confused, he searched for the source of explosions, and saw that a large column of black smoke was billowing from the direction of the San Juan Yacht Club, already beginning to rise into the sky. Other secondary explosions, the type that occur in big fires where smaller gas tanks ignite, continued to rattle the air, and echoed back from the cliffs of upper Miramar. Then he noticed the enormous gray cloud of dust expanding over the Condado Lagoon, like a huge, ghostly dome, and felt sick to his stomach.

They had been duped. Prestidigitation. Slight-of-hand. It had been used after all. But not by him. The Convention Center bombs had been a ruse. A trick to keep them entertained while the real damage happened elsewhere. How stupid he had been!

Maldonado quickly walked back to his car, ignoring the press of people who followed him, entered the vehicle, and shut the door behind him, motioning his chauffer—Beto—to hand him the microphone of the CB radio.

"Headquarters, this is Number One," he said, releasing the elongated "Talk" button without saying "Over", a lifelong habit that his men had learned to accept.

"*Yes, sir. Over.*"

"Can you patch me to Colonel Montañez, please," he instructed the police operator.

"*Yes, sir. Over.*"

Maldonado waited, nervously tapping his fingers on his right knee, while the throng of reporters outside anxiously tried to look through the tinted glass windows. Knowing better than to interrupt his boss, Beto said nothing.

"*I'm here, over,*" a calm, deep voice finally announced, after almost five minutes.

"Alejo, what can you tell me?"

Except for the Superintendent, no other figure in the Police Department had gained as much public recognition as Alejo Montañez. A tough, practical no-nonsense cop, the colonel had spearheaded during the past decade a surprisingly effective and fierce war on drug traffickers, including what was considered to be the biggest cocaine trafficking bust in the history of the United States, a twenty-two ton shipment valued in the streets at more than 700 million dollars. His close-knit force of select officers and detectives had been nicknamed "The Untouchables" by the local media. A giant of a man, towering a half head over Maldonado, he had established a close bond with the Superintendent, and many considered him to be the natural choice as the next Superintendent of the Department.

"*The information is just starting to come in,*" Montañez responded. "*The 911 services are clogged with phone calls, and our switchboard is about to collapse.*" The colonel paused, as if attempting to gather his thoughts and be as straightforward as possible. "*The picture is very fuzzy still. There is talk of explosions on the bridges to San Juan—*"

"Which of the bridges?" Maldonado interrupted.

"*All of the bridges, all of them,*" the colonel replied gravely. "*There are also reports of dead and wounded, but the numbers we're getting are still all over the place. From five to a hundred. We need to get a better grasp on that. I'm sending everything I've got to the bridges now, from both sides of the bridges, except for ten patrol cars that I'm keeping in reserve here in head-quarters for any contingency...*" Montañez paused again, then resumed his report. "*Wait, wait, we're getting something on TV...A helicopter from WKPA news that was covering the Convention Center is flying over the area now...*" He stopped again, as he watched the televised broadcast, and then whispered in a stunned voice: "*Shit...shit. It is all of the bridges, and...the San Juan Yacht Club...It's burning!...Jesus Christ! Who did this?...This is serious, Roberto. Can you get to a television set, over?*"

Maldonado nodded to himself. "I'll get one of the reporters to take me inside their broadcasting van."

"*I'm hauling ass towards the lagoon right now, over.*"

"Let's meet by the Miramar Bridge in an hour," Maldonado said, and not waiting for Montañez to confirm, he opened the door of his car, and was engulfed by the waiting press.

For a fleeting moment, the five men lay flat on the ground, too stunned to move. Then Daniel stirred, sitting up and removing his earplugs. At the distance, he saw the jogger stand on wobbly legs, and shook his head in amused disbelief.

"Lucky bastard," he muttered, chuckling. He started to look around him, but at that very moment an expanding cloud of dust and cement particles covered everything in sight, forcing him to close his eyes and cover his mouth. "Everyone all right?" he asked through his hands.

"I think I shit myself," a nasal voice with a slight Italian accent said to his right.

Someone else chortled, and then the men burst into laughter, releasing their stress. "That was some mother-fucking explosion!"

Daniel smiled. The gray haze continued to blow over them, becoming less dense. He saw Figueres, to his left, getting back up on his knees, and Sasha already standing up.

"Let's see what we did," Daniel said, as the dust began to settle. He began to climb the hill that had shielded them from the destruction, followed by the others.

He had never felt more alive. The adrenaline rushing through his body made him feel strong, quick, and agile, and enhanced all of his senses. *This, not justice, religion, or any other cause, was why he had joined San Miguel's gang. Let others die for what they believed. He would live for what he enjoyed.*

The clump of trees through which he had unreeled the wires connected to the explosive charges had sustained heavy damage. Many of their branches, and clusters of leaves had been shorn off or broken, and even some of the tree trunks had been splintered or shattered in half.

Nothing, however, prepared them for what they saw beyond the trees. To their right, the San Juan Yacht Club burned fiercely, as did many of the boats moored around it. On one large yacht, partially on fire, its crew was attempting to navigate through the conflagration, but Daniel doubted it would be saved. Small explosions, probably from the gas tanks of some of the boats, sporadically added to the mayhem and further fueled the flames. Nobody would be able to approach that area for the rest of the day, if not the week.

"Give me your binoculars," Daniel ordered Sasha, who was using them to gauge the damage to the bridges.

"We did good, Danny," the Byelorussian noted with intense satisfaction, as he handed his binoculars to Daniel. Sasha was part of what Daniel called "San Miguel's travelling circus", a cadre of about three dozen hard core veterans who had participated in several of San Miguel's covert actions during the last decade and a half. They hailed from different parts of the world, and shared no common characteristics except for their professionalism and intense dedication to the success of the group. Sasha was a Mongol who liked to dress like a cowboy, down to the tight dungarees, wide silver buckle, and high boots he was presently wearing.

Daniel focused the binoculars on the first of the three Miramar bridges, the one closest to the San Juan Yacht Club. He confirmed that the entire central span of the structure, about forty feet in length, had vanished. The detonations had been so powerful that they had cut through the re-bars embedded in the concrete, and the middle of the bridge had collapsed into the lagoon.

The second, older bridge had fared even worse, crumbling into the water at both ends. Unlike its sister bridges, it could never be repaired.

The third bridge also suffered heavy damage, showing a gap of more than thirty feet between its two extremities. A slab of concrete about ten feet long stuck out like a wide tongue from the San Juan side of the bridge, angling slightly downwards towards the water, still attached to the bridge by its steel reinforcement. However, any attempt to place any weight on it would send it tumbling into the lagoon. For all practical effects, the bridge had become un-crossable.

So had the Dos Hermanos Bridge, connecting the island of San Juan to the Condado sector. The explosive charges had severed the steel beams that supported the temporary structure, leaving only long, jagged pieces of metal that stuck out of the water like short quills from a giant sea urchin.

Daniel turned towards his men, who were beaming at him.

"Gentlemen," he said pleasantly, handing back the binoculars to Sasha, "I believe we have finished our work here. You have successfully separated San Juan from the rest of the island of Puerto Rico. Let's go have a drink."

The men whooped in exultation.

CHAPTER XIX

Colonel Calderon watched the first few policemen trickle out of the three-story building across the street, and lowered his binoculars towards the station's doors. As he expected, the volume of exiting officers rapidly expanded into a throng of armed men, many carrying shotguns or rifles, who hurried into the parking lot and headed for the more than a dozen vehicles parked in front of the station. The sight from the rooftop of El Falansterio reminded the veteran Venezuelan soldier of an anthill seething with fire ants, like the anthills that he and his younger brother used to disturb and burn with newspapers for sport when they were young children.

Calderon knelt and raised his right hand. Had any of the policemen below paused to look at the top of the buildings across the street, the colonel's dark outline would have been plainly visible. But they were too busy to notice, adjusting their bulletproof vests, checking their weapons, or simply looking for vehicles to crowd into.

Many of the apartments below Calderon's feet had stirred into life a couple of minutes earlier, when the earth had shaken from the explosions originating from the lagoon, and a great cloud of dust had momentarily obscured the sun. As the dust settled, some residents had leaned out of their balconies, and pointed at the column of smoke rising out of El San Juan Yacht Club, scarcely a half mile away, unaware that they were being seen from above. Faint electronic voices, either from radios or television sets, wafted out from some of the windows, as many of the Falansterians attempted to find out what had caused the commotion. More and more people began to walk out of the housing complex, chattering excitedly on the cell phones and heading towards the lagoon, to see first hand what had happened.

Calderon could feel the eyes of every one of his men. They were well trained and well briefed, and would not fire until ordered to. The police parking area was separated from the street by a tall fence of steel bars embedded into a one-foot high concrete base. Two exits, one at each end of the fence, provided the only way out from the parking area to the street. If the exits were blocked, the police would be trapped inside.

There were two additional exits in a lower level at the back of the building, used as a garage for vehicles that needed maintenance, but they were not connected to the main parking area. The Macheteros were supposed to render those inoperable. He had seen some of them moving during the night around the perimeter of the building, but—contrary to what El Alacran had promised him—had had no direct communication with them. He hoped that they would keep their end of the bargain, but if not, he had enough firepower to handle any strays emerging from the station's rear.

Traffic on Fernandez Juncos Avenue had started to slow down several minutes before the demolition of the bridges, as San Miguel's men had blocked the access to Miramar. Now, it was at a standstill. The stopped cars were wedged between the police station on one side, and concrete barriers that separated that part of the avenue from the lanes where traffic flowed in the opposite direction. Many of the trapped drivers had switched off their engines and opened their doors, stepping out of their vehicles and staring at the sky with concern, or speculating with those closest to them about what had just occurred.

One patrol car backed out of its parking spot and moved towards the exit closest to the right end of the station. Still, Calderon waited, holding up his hand. The police vehicle ventured halfway through the gate, but had to halt, unable to continue because of the stopped cars in the street. It switched on its siren, trying to create a path through the stalled vehicles, and as the siren's wail pierced through the street noise, the colonel shouted "Fire!" and dropped his arm. Sergeant Alfonsin, squatting next to him, immediately stood up to his full height, and as if to make certain everyone obeyed, repeated the order at the top of his lungs, first to one side, then to the other.

The roof of El Falansterio erupted in an earsplitting fusillade as its occupants unleashed their firepower on the open parking area below them. The two machine guns further to the right opened fire first, followed closely by the other two. The machine gun operators fired in short, deliberate bursts, taking their time to aim, the deafening blasts of their weapons adding to the already numbing din underneath.

At the parking area, some of the men continued to walk even after the firing started, the sound of the shooting partially masked by the blare of the patrol car's siren. Others mistook the abrupt, successive detonations with the loud backfire of the motorcycles that were being kicked to life by some of the troopers, while still others stopped, looking uncertainly around them for the source of the noise. A handful of policemen, army veterans mostly, ran for cover behind some of the parked cars.

Calderon saw two men drop straight down, like big sacks of potatoes. Then a diagonal line of holes sprang across the hood of the exiting patrol car, as one of the machine guns found its range. A scant second later, the entire front windshield exploded into a great shower of shiny fragments, and the car, smoke and a few flames billowing from its engine, slid slowly forward—its siren still wailing—until it bumped into a delivery van stuck on the street just a few feet away. Its left back door swung open and an officer, limping severely, tried to retreat to the main station building, but was cut down before he could walk half a dozen paces.

Everywhere men began to fall. The gunners fired methodically, concentrating on the targets chosen by their teammates, who doubled as spotters and helped feed the ammunition belts into the machine guns. The heavy caliber of the MAG's bullets tore through bone, tissue, and metal with devastating ease and efficiency. Police vehicles crammed with men became death traps, as they were picked out by the machine gun operators and riddled with bullets. One exploded in a large ball of fire. Nobody exited from the burning automobile. Hails of projectiles started to hit the windows of the building, and the shattered glass cascaded on those standing in the parking area below. In Fernandez Juncos Avenue, scores of motorists abandoned their vehicles and crouched between them, uncertain of where to hide.

One white-helmeted motorcyclist managed to reach the left exit, and signaled to a moving patrol car to follow him. A bullet sliced off most of the motorcyclist's arm before he could lower it, so that his forearm flapped backwards over the lower half of his arm, still attached to the rest of his body by a few tendons. Another bullet struck him squarely on the head a second later, shattering the helmet and its contents like an exploding watermelon. The motorcycle wobbled and toppled sideways, right into the path of the speeding patrol car. The patrol's driver tried to turn towards the exit and avoid the motorcycle, but as he did so was hit on the clavicle and lost control of his vehicle, crashing against the exit's gate. Two men crawled out of the car's shattered windows. One made it back halfway to the building before a bullet shattered his spine; the second dropped as he reached the station.

Some policemen fought back, firing blindly at the rooftop of El Falansterio, seeking refuge behind the parked cars or the two trees on the sidewalk. One police captain, oblivious of the perilous crossfire of the machine guns, walked from one pocket of resistance to another, trying to rally and organize his men, directing their fire for better effectiveness.

He lasted all of two minutes before he was shot through the neck by one of the Venezuelan snipers supporting the machine gunners.

Those who continued to fight fired mostly with their handguns at the rooftop of the buildings across the street, with very little effect. A few used their shotguns, but the ammunition scattered and lost its power long before it bounced off harmlessly from the buildings' concrete walls. They were no match for the rapid, heavy-caliber fire of the MAGs and the precise, high-power bullets of the Dragunov sniper rifles. One by one, the fighters were methodically identified by the Venezuelan spotters, pinned down by machine gun fire, and shot by the snipers.

The most successful resistance came from the small structure located next to the main police building. There, the half dozen or so policemen inside had barricaded the door, and sporadically fired from the side windows. As resistance dwindled in the parking area, the minute police station drew increasing fire from the Venezuelans until its Miami aluminum windows were riddled with holes and reduced to scraps of metal. Eventually, the police inside stopped shooting, either overwhelmed by the assault, or saving their ammunition.

There was one miraculous escape. During the height of the fighting, one man pushed himself out of the partially burning car that blocked the right parking exit, and after gathering his wits behind the open rear left door, suddenly sprinted towards the street. Several bullets dogged him as he zigzagged between the abandoned vehicles in Fernandez Juncos, one hitting a windshield so close to his head that it sprayed his face with bits of shattered glass and momentarily blinded him. The man dived behind a bullet-pocked red Mercedes, and waited for the intensity of the fire to wane. Then, as the shooters apparently sought for other prey, he crouched and darted from car to car, trying to reach the tall bushes that fringed the right flank of the police station.

About five minutes into the fight, a minivan that had been parked all night long in an alley next to the police station stirred into life, and slowly headed towards the rear of the building. As it neared the first of the station's two open back exits, the side door of the van opened, and a Machetero tossed a backpack deep into the basement's bowels. Then he repeated the procedure at the next exit, and sped away. The backpacks, in reality satchel charges packed with C-4, exploded a few seconds later. The force of the detonations spewed debris through the two open exits, and punched through the cellar's ceiling, destroying most of the floor above it. Used as the mechanics' workshop, the cellar contained a large gasoline tank, propane gas containers, and hundreds of flammable materials that ignited into a huge ball of fire.

The explosions occurred with such violence that they rocked El

Falansterio. Calderon scanned the street below him, and knew that the battle had been won. More than fifteen policemen lay sprawled on the concrete floor of the parking lot, soaked in crimson puddles of blood that spread unevenly on the pavement. A few were still alive, but many had been torn up beyond recognition by the heavy fire of his men. Possibly half a dozen to a dozen additional men were trapped inside some of the destroyed vehicles. One police car burned furiously, the stench of burned rubber thankfully masking the odor of the men smoldering inside. Another car, the one that had turned on its siren, continued to billow gray smoke from its engine.

The rear of the police building was also on fire, and the flames were spreading quickly. Soon, the fire would consume the entire structure. Fortunately, only the small old police station lay close to the burning building. With luck, the conflagration would not spread any further.

Calderon sighed. To continue fighting would be the equivalent of murder.

"Sergeant Alfonsin," the colonel said, taking a long swallow of water from a plastic bottle, "order the men to cease fire. Take half of your men, and gather the prisoners."

"Yes, sir." Alfonsin stood up to convey the order, once again screaming it at the top of his lungs. The shooting tapered off, and then stopped completely. As the noise ceased, the roar of the station's fire took its place. The siren of the police car continued to produce a sporadic, low-volume moan, as if the car was slowly dying.

Calderon stood up, to the protests of his sergeant, and dusted off his black clothes. He searched briefly for a small bullhorn that had been brought by one of his men, found it a few paces away, and scooped it up. He surveyed his men. Spent bullet cartridges were strewn over a great portion of the roof. None of the men had suffered as much as a scratch. Already Alfonsin was moving among them, selecting those who would descend with him to the parking area. Two of the snipers flanked the colonel, searching the burning building and its immediate vicinity for possible threats.

Calderon placed the bullhorn over his mouth, and pressed its red "speak" button.

"Men and women of the police, throw down your weapons and surrender. You have fought bravely and honorably, but to continue to resist will be suicide. We have no desire to kill you! You have five minutes to surrender!" Calderon paused, and waited for a response from the besieged survivors. "Corporal Caraballo," he said to one of the soldiers standing beside him, not taking his eyes from the station, "I think we can release Mr. Roman now."

"Yes, sir."

Caraballo unsheathed a long dagger from his belt, and walked to the stairwell where Archie sat propped against a wall, his feet and hands still bound by plastic cuffs, his mouth covered by a large rag. With one swift flick, the corporal cut each of the plastic restraints open.

Archie groaned, as he stretched his stiff arms, and removed the piece of cloth that had covered his mouth.

He felt exhausted. His bad right leg had throbbed all night with a terrible intensity, the pain gradually extending through his spine and exploding in a numbing headache. Even so, sometime during the early hours of the morning he had fallen into a deep, dreamless sleep. It was an involuntary defense mechanism he had acquired while serving in Iraq, where he would take short naps anytime and anywhere that the circumstances allowed it: a protective, automatic shutdown by his body, to recharge his batteries during times of high stress.

The explosions from the bridges and the San Juan Yacht Club had jolted him awake. Encased by the walls of the stairwell, he had been unable to see what had happened. The noise had tortured him because he knew that the men he had led into El Falansterio were somehow connected to the events that were unfolding outside. For the next fifteen minutes, and for the first time in many years, he had prayed to God that no one would be hurt because of him.

Then his worst suspicions had been confirmed as he had heard a siren and someone scream "Fire", and then the rooftop had been racked by the rattling discharges of multiple automatic weapons. He had had no difficulty in identifying the firearms that produced them. He had heard similar noises in a dozen firefights in Iraq, the repeated detonations of heavy caliber machine guns, discharged with deliberate, professional precision. A feeling of doom had overwhelmed him. MAGs were being fired into the street, and the damage they would inflict would be horrible.

And it would all be blamed on him.

He had been so concentrated on the disturbance outside, that he had not noticed the little boy who had climbed the stairs and was watching him, wide eyed with fear, three steps below the landing where he lay. Thin as a rail, barefoot, and wearing a white T-shirt and Toy Story underwear, the boy must have been no more than five or six years old.

Archie had tried to speak through the rag that covered his mouth, but had only managed to produce a few unintelligible moaning sounds that had terrified the child and sent him scampering down the stairs. He had cursed himself for his evident lack of subtlety, salty tears of frustration stinging his eyes. Minutes later the building had shuddered with two consecutive explosions. The firing had continued for a few more minutes, and then, miraculously, everything had stopped. A man, he was almost certain it had been the man who one of the younger cartel mobsters had addressed as "Colonel", had spoken through a loudspeaker, but he could only pick out some of his words, particularly "honorably" and "surrender".

A short interval later, one of the black clad men had appeared at the entrance of the stairwell, and cut his bonds.

"You are free to go," he had said tersely, then turned his back on him and disappeared.

Archie slowly got off the floor, the cramped muscles of his right leg burning like hot shrapnel. As he stood up, the man he had heard being called Alfonsin and six others rushed past him and hurried down the stairs, ignoring him entirely. They were all armed with rifles. For a moment, as he heard their footsteps recede down the stairwell, he considered running away as fast as he could from his captors and hiding in his apartment for a week, hoping that that day's incident would blow over. But he knew that would not happen. Wincing with pain, he stepped into the bright sunlight of the roof.

His eyes had to adjust for a few seconds, but then he saw a huge cloud of black smoke spiraling towards the bay from the direction of the police station, and he limped closer to the edge of the rooftop—all the way to where the colonel stood with his back turned to him—and tried to determine the origin of the fire.

His movements did not remain undetected. A short man with a rifle ordered him to stop, and aimed his weapon at him. The colonel turned his head briefly, and then waved the armed man away.

"Come," he said to the redhead, returning his attention back to the conflagration below.

Hesitantly, Archie walked closer to the edge of the building, gazing at the carnage below. The fire in the police station was burning out of control. A small number of policemen were running out of its main entrance, coughing and raising their hands in surrender, stepping over some of their dead companions, or trying to move away from the flames those that were wounded. Some of Alfonsin's men were already herding many of them into El Falansterio, presumably to the building complex's inner courtyard. Several vehicles had been destroyed, and a few of them were also aflame.

"You lied to me!" Archie said angrily to the colonel, tears streaming from his eyes.

Calderon looked at him, but did not answer.

"You lied to me!" Archie repeated, this time shouting.

Calderon sighed. "I did not lie to you. I only gave you part of the information, and you accepted it willingly, without asking about any further details, just to take the money."

Archie nervously searched his pants for the yellow envelope that the colonel had handed to him a few hours earlier, and found it in his back pocket. He held it out to Calderon.

"I never agreed to be paid for *this*," he said bitterly, gesturing with his head towards the police station. When the colonel failed to take the envelope, Archie threw it at his face.

Calderon's eyes hardened dangerously, a vein bulging on his broad forehead. For a moment his body tensed as if preparing to strike Archie, but then his attention was diverted by the faint noise of a helicopter. He searched the skies overhead, partly obscured by the haze of the conflagration, but could not find it.

"Over there, colonel," one of his men indicated, pointing to a dark spot in the air sandwiched between the columns of smoke rising from the San Juan Yacht Club and from the police station. Calderon placed a hand over his eyes, and spotted the faint outline of a small helicopter, possibly from one of the television news agencies. It was heading in their direction at breakneck speed.

"Caraballo!" Calderon said out loud.

"Sir!"

"Keep an eye on it. When it gets closer, scare it away."

"And if it doesn't scare away, sir?"

Calderon stared at the corporal as if the answer to the question was so obvious it required no answer. He turned back to Archie.

"What you do with your money is your concern. You earned it. You keep it or dispose of it, as you deem fit. It's yours," he said scornfully. "But if you value your life, you will remove yourself from this place now. Otherwise, I will have my men throw you off the roof."

Archie began to answer, but at the last moment checked himself, amazed by his own anger. For an instant, he had been willing to fight the colonel, even if it meant being thrown out of the roof. It seemed almost as if another person had taken over his body.

Physically and emotionally spent, he began to walk away. "May God forgive you," he said despairingly. "May God forgive us all."

"Don't judge me, Mr. Roman," Calderon called angrily after the red-headed man. "Everything we did here today was absolutely necessary, and for the greater good of your country."

Archie raised his middle finger into the air and continued to walk away.

Aristides Andrade carefully adjusted his tie, looking at his own reflection on the window of a parked car. Even though distorted by the curvature of the glass and blurred by the faint morning light, he felt satisfied by what he saw.

Gone were his wavy, cascading hair and his pharaonic beard. A short, metro-sexual cut, and a carefully trimmed goatee had substituted them. Gone as well were his faded jeans, sneakers, and nondescript shirt, exchanged for an expensive, tan-colored linen suit, a gold and red tie, and brown, square-toed leather shoes. Even his height seemed to have increased, a combination of elevator platforms, and a conscious correction to his usually stooped posture. El Alacran appeared to have just stepped out of one of the top-floor, executive offices of the Hato Rey financial district.

An orange cat darted out of the waiting area in the bus depot, looked at him, and meowed.

"Handsome, uh?" he said to the cat, pulling out from his breast pocket a set of Ray Ban glasses and slipping them on with flair. The cat meowed again, prompting a thin-lipped smile to appear on Andrade's humorless mouth. "I could get used to this, you know? I really could. 'Mr. Alacran', the Golden Mile banker...I like it!"

Andrade resumed his trek towards the municipal station, whistling a Shakira tune. The cat followed him for a few steps, and then flitted across the cobblestoned street.

Unlike the state police building in Puerta de Tierra, the municipal police station in Old San Juan was a modest, one story outpost occupying one corner of the large terminal where all of the buses in San Juan ended their routes. Most of the time, no more than ten policemen manned the station. Along with the reception area and its inner offices, it contained three cells, used to temporarily hold persons who had been detained in the old section of the town—mainly drunks—until they could be transferred to a larger facility. One of the cells now contained the rowdy youth who had discharged his gun in the San Sebastian celebrations the prior night.

Andrade's men had kept the facility under watch during the night. A new shift of municipal guards was scheduled to come in at eight in the morning, to substitute the skeleton crew of five policemen that had spent the night there. However, El Alacran imagined that after the destruction of the bridges, all personnel would probably be called back to duty. And even though many of the guards who lived in the main island would be stranded on the other side of the lagoon, there would be some who lived in the old part of town and who would be able to reach the station. Therefore, the Macheteros would have to act swiftly.

Andrade walked into the reception area of the station, a small room containing two benches and an elevated platform where the dispatcher sat behind a tall desk. Except for him and a man who slumped in one corner of one of the benches, leaning forward and covering his face with his hands, the room was empty. Nevertheless, the dispatcher did not notice Andrade come in, immersed in what seemed to be a tangle of radio conversations originating from several sources. Two telephones rang non-stop next to him, the callers either refusing to quit, or new calls constantly coming in.

El Alacran walked up to the desk, and waited patiently for his turn. The dispatcher, a middle-aged veteran with a thin, graying mustache and bushy, unnaturally black hair, looked up briefly but failed to acknowledge him, continuing to harangue one of his radio contacts.

Two other men, dressed in construction workers' clothes, sauntered into the receiving area. One of them moved next to the man who was covering his face with his hands, and quietly sat next to him. The other walked next to Andrade, and stood there without saying a word.

Andrade cleared his throat, earning a peeved look from the dispatcher.

"Hold on, over," he told his radio contact, then leaned forward. "Yes?"

"I've come to report a possible accident," Andrade said mildly, smiling.

The dispatcher gestured with his head towards the man standing next to him. "Is he with you?"

Andrade turned, and examined the man, who stood a head taller than him. Then he nodded. "Yes, I guess he is," he answered pleasantly.

"Look, I'm very busy here right now," the guard snapped back. "You *guess* this man is with you, and you want to report a *possible* accident."

"Yes," Andrade replied.

"What is the *possible* accident that you wish to report?" the dispatcher asked with apparent irritation and a hint of sarcasm, grabbing a small notebook and a pen.

"Yours," El Alacran replied, pulling out of his jacket an Uzi submachine gun, and pointing it at his head, "if you don't do exactly as I tell you to do."

The dispatcher stared with disbelief at the frail-looking gentleman standing before him. Andrade continued to smile, placing a finger over his lips and nudging his machine gun upwards to indicate to the guard that he should raise-up his arms. At the same time, Andrade's companion marched behind the desk and placed a 45 automatic on the dispatcher's head.

The conversation ceased, the only noise in the room originating from the two unanswered telephones and the ongoing radio conversations. El Alacran turned briefly to look at his accomplice in the back, darting a questioning glance at the man sitting in the corner, who continued to hide his face in his hands. The accomplice shrugged, stood up, and popped his head out of the door of the station. After a brief pause, he waved an arm, apparently beckoning others to come. Then he walked back to the sitting man, took out a handgun, and tapped his shoulder. The man sat up as if awaking from a dream, and after becoming aware of the situation, wordlessly raised his hands in surrender.

"Turn off the radio, please," El Alacran told the dispatcher.

The municipal guard did as he was told.

"Now stand up, open the entrance to the back of the station, and walk with me for a while," the Machetero instructed him, nodding towards the locked entrance that gave access to the rest of the station. As the dispatcher prepared to press a button under the table and buzz the door open, Andrade said, "Pssst! Just the door, no alarm buttons, okay? You press anything else and I'll kill you and everyone else inside. Understand?" The guard nodded, and placed his hand under the desk. The lock clicked open.

Just then, three more men carrying AK-47s entered the room.

"Let's go!" he told them.

The Machetero holding the gun to the dispatcher's head grabbed his collar and pushed him forward. El Alacran followed with two of the men carrying the AK-47s, while the rest remained in the reception room.

The swift break-in caught the men inside completely by surprise. The policemen were gathered around a small television set, watching the first scenes of the destroyed bridges broadcast from a helicopter. Pointing their semiautomatic rifles at them and shouting at them to surrender or see their dispatcher executed, the intruders easily overwhelmed the municipal garrison. The captured policemen were forced to lie on the floor, and their hands were tied behind their backs with plastic zip ties.

"Get the key to the cells and lock them up," Andrade ordered. He sat in front of the television set, and glimpsed at the images on the screen. The camera was focusing on the Dos Hermanos Bridge, showing a wide gap partially littered with shattered, twisted steel beams. El Alacran pursed his lips and resumed his whistling rendition of the Shakira song, tapping one of his fingers on the desk.

Someone from inside the cell block started shouting "Long live free Puerto Rico!" at the top of his lungs and screaming curses at the guards, telling them how he had "told them so", and how "now the lackey dogs of the American imperialists" would get their comeuppance. After watching the television broadcast for a couple of minutes more, Andrade stood up and walked into prisoners' holding area.

It was a small room, containing three cells each twelve feet wide by twelve feet long, and a narrow corridor to lead the prisoners in and out of the cells. The five captured municipal guards had been locked up in the cell closest to the corridor's entrance.

A young, stringy man sporting a goatee was standing in the next cell, beaming at a Machetero who was about to unlock his door. But his liberator suddenly stopped and stepped aside, letting Andrade take his place. El Alacran finished unlocking the door, and slid the cell door open.

The tall prisoner regarded him with curiosity, as if trying to reconcile the elegant, executive-style attire of the man standing before him with the Uzi submachine gun that he was carrying. Then his confusion transformed into a look of astonished elation, as he recognized the face of his deliverer.

"El Alacran! You are El Alacran?!" he asked, staring at Andrade with euphoric joy.

"And you are...Bergara...Alejandro Bergara, is it?" Andrade replied, staring at the prisoner with detached curiosity.

"Yes! Yes I am! I am honored to meet you, Alacran!" he exclaimed, taking a step forward and extending his hand to greet the Macheteros' leader. El Alacran failed to take it, regarding him with a humorless expression.

"You placed our entire operation in jeopardy," he stated in a dry, matter-of-fact tone.

Bergara flashed an embarrassed smile, shrugging, "I know," he said shaking his head, "I guess I was too excited, I over drank. I'm sorry. I won't do it again."

El Alacran raised his submachine gun with his left hand, and discharged half a dozen shots into the chest of the youth at point blank range, the deafening roar of the detonations drowning the surprised screams of Bergara and of the municipal guards imprisoned in the adjacent cells. The bullets shattered the prisoner's spine, causing the upper part of his chest to momentarily bend forward at an odd angle. Some of the fired shots exited through Bergara's back and ricocheted off the wall behind him, bouncing off the cell bars and other walls, and sending everyone except Andrade scurrying for cover. Several of the Macheteros in the next room ran to the cellblock in alarm, saw what had happened, and quietly returned to what they were doing.

El Alacran knelt next to the crumpled body of the FEPIsta, and examined his face. Bergara's eyes were open, and he wheezed as his lungs flooded with blood and he tried to breathe.

"You insignificant piece of shit!" Andrade whispered fiercely to him, and spit on his face. "Did you think this was a game?"

El Alacran stood up. "Take this filth out of here, and throw him in a dumpster," he said, addressing the Machetero who had handed him the cell key.

CHAPTER XX

Ship Security Officer Bates rapped his knuckles sharply on the heavy oak door, and opened it.

"Permission to enter the bridge, sir!" he said, making the two officers who were conferring turn. They regarded the new arrival with friendly inquisitiveness, which changed to perplexity as soon they discerned the two customs officers that followed him.

"Permission granted," said the taller of the two men.

"Captain," Bates said, approaching the two officers. "May I introduce you to Officers Rodriguez and Rivera, from the U.S. Customs Office," he said drily, not bothering to hide his displeasure with the situation. "Gentlemen, this is Captain Kristoffer Clausen," he said, curtly gesturing with his hand at his superior officer.

Captain Clausen extended his hand to the two customs officers, while raising an eyebrow quizzically. Six feet tall, blue eyed, broad shouldered, and sporting a full blond beard, the captain lived up to the preconceived image of his Viking ancestors. He clasped each of the agent's hands in turn, making both men wince by the strength of his grip.

"I'm very pleased to meet, you," he said affably, "although I'm a little bit surprised by your unannounced visit," he added, directing a brief, withering look at Bates.

"And this is the ship's First Officer, Dag Folstad," the SSO continued, directing the visitors' attention to the redheaded man standing next to the captain. Even though not more than 5'8" tall, Folstad seemed every bit as formidable as his superior officer. During the Viking era, Folstad would have been the man wielding a huge battle-ax who spearheaded the attack on his enemies. His arms were as thick as any normal man's thighs, his neck as broad as the mast of one of his ancestors' ships. Although clean-shaven, he emanated raw power, even when standing still.

He nodded stiffly at the two customs officers, saying nothing. The First Officer took an instant dislike of Rodriguez, a thin, sour-looking man who examined the bridge with a disdainful, almost bored expression while chewing gum.

What Folstad did not realize was that Rodriguez was taking stock of the rest of the personnel that was present on the bridge. The blue-carpeted room from which the enormous ship was controlled was surprisingly compact. Horseshoe-shaped and surrounded by windows, it contained only two leather swivel chairs located behind the navigation control station. Several large screens displayed radar, weather and navigation data, as well as actual images of the bow and the stern of the ship. In addition to the captain and the first officer, a short woman—also dressed in Navy whites—stood by what seemed to be the communications radio. A second uniformed man hovered over a wide chart table, making some entries on a notebook. Otherwise, the bridge was unmanned.

Rodriguez had enjoyed every moment of his short visit to the *Mardi Gras*. He, Rivera, and the other members of his group had traveled on her sister ship, the *Fiesta Tropicale*, in order to get a feel of the layout of the ship. He had never been on a cruise ship before then, and had relished every moment. He had taken great pleasure in the constant, almost unceasing flow of food, the self-contained, air-conditioned weather, and the luxurious, carpeted interiors. He had learned by heart most of the ship's geography, even befriending one of the waitresses on the fourteenth deck's open air café and getting a tour of the crew's living quarters.

When he had boarded the *Mardi Gras* that morning, he and Rivera had noted with extreme satisfaction that the two sister ships were in essence identical, even to the name of its bars and restaurants. From the Promenade deck, located on the fifth level, Bates had led them past the Zanzibar Lounge, and into the circular, multi-story main lobby. There, he had ushered them into one of the glass elevators, and they had zoomed up to 13th floor. They had traversed a long row of doors leading to some of the most expensive suites in the liner, and stopped at a locked iron door in the corridor's furthermost end. Bates had punched four numbers—4-7-9-8—which Rodriguez had instantly memorized, and the gate had buzzed open. It had given them access to a stairway to the right, some sort of storage room to the left, and straight-ahead, to the starboard entrance to the bridge. And just like that, Rivera and Rodriguez had penetrated the captain's domain and the central brain of the ship.

"Captain," Bates said, cutting to the chase, "these gentlemen are here to inspect our Security Certificate. They claim that the certificate was...illegally obtained, that it is...what was it that you said?" he asked, looking at the two customs officers, and then continued without waiting for an answer. "Forged! They are here to inspect it."

Captain Clausen's expression changed to one of deep puzzlement.

"Illegally obtained?" he asked, astonished, turning to his SSO for an explanation.

Bates opened his mouth to speak, but Rodriguez cut him off.

"If I could explain," he said courteously. "We received a tip that your inspection in Miami revealed several safety violations, that your ship in fact failed the inspection, and that the certificate was issued improperly after the inspectors—or some of them, anyway—were bribed."

"That is ridiculous!" Folstad, the First Officer, exclaimed with indignation. Captain Clausen raised his hand, urging his subordinate to be patient.

"I am really at a loss as to what this is all about," he said, trying not to lose his temper, "but I will do everything in my power to cooperate with you and get this sordid allegation out of the way as quickly as we can."

"Thank you, Captain Clausen," Rodriguez answered. "I am certain there has been a misunderstanding and that—" Rodriguez paused momentarily, looking at his watch. "Excuse me," he said, as he verified the time. He nodded imperceptibly at Rivera, who moved closer to the female radio operator. "Please forgive me, captain. As I was saying, I'm certain that, to put it in nautical terms..." he chuckled, "the accusations won't hold water."

Nobody laughed at the customs officer's lame attempt at humor.

"There is one more thing," Rodriguez said, almost as an afterthought, looking up at the tall captain.

"Yes?" Captain Clausen answered, trying to keep the irritation out of his voice. The short customs man chewed furiously on his gum while he fished out of his back pocket an index card. He looked at it briefly, as if to make certain it was the right one, and afterwards handed it to the captain.

"I need you to read this in the ship's intercom," he told Clausen.

The captain examined the card silently, and almost immediately looked back at Rodriguez with a bewildered expression.

"What is this?" he inquired angrily, passing the card to Folstad.

"It's plain enough," Rodriguez answered pleasantly.

Folstad scowled at the card, and read it out loud: "*Your attention, please. We have been advised that unknown terrorists have blown up all of the bridges connecting San Juan to the rest of the island of Puerto Rico. There is, at this moment, no possible means of getting to the airport or to most of the hotels in the island. The local authorities have stopped the further disembarkation of passengers or crew until the situation is stabilized, and their safety can be guaranteed. Until then, you need to remain on board. Presently, armed customs officers are boarding the ship to protect it from any attempt of sabotage. Please return to your cabins and remain there until further notice. All restaurants will remain open to serve meals, as they become necessary. Thank you.*" The First Officer flipped the card towards Rodriguez, who made no movement to catch it. "What kind of hogwash is this?" he said derisively. "We haven't heard of any sabotage."

"Just look out of the window," Rodriguez answered.

Clausen, Folstad and Bates turned their attention to the direction that the customs man pointed, and for the first time saw in the distance a large column of smoke rising from the east. They walked closer to the windows, to get a better view.

"What *is* this?" Bates asked with indignation, returning his attention to the obnoxious customs officer. "How do you know that the bridges were destroyed? I can only see a lot of smoke, and I've been over those bridges many times. They're made of concrete, which doesn't burn—" The SSO stopped talking as he saw Rodriguez armed with what he recognized to be a Beretta pistol. A dozen paces away, Rivera pointed a similar weapon at the head of the female radio operator. The man near the charts remained immobile, too scared to do anything. Bates turned pale, as he realized how easily he had been duped, and the consequences of his mistake.

"Trust me," Rodriguez replied, smiling, as the captain and the first officer stared at him in disbelief. "I have my connections."

"What is the meaning of this?" Folstad asked furiously.

"*What is the meaning of this? Tam-tam-taaaaan!*" Rodriguez mocked in a singsong voice, making Rivera snicker. "Doesn't he sound like one of those B-type movie melodramas? I suspect that your intelligence is probably as dense as the rest of your body, Falstaff, or whatever your name is."

Enraged, Folstad started to move towards Rodriguez, but Clausen stopped him, grabbing him by an arm.

"At least someone is smart enough on this ship to think things through," said Rodriguez, with quiet amusement.

Captain Clausen glared at the customs impostor. "What do you want?"

Rodriguez shrugged, and sat on one of the two swivel chairs. "That depends on what happens during the next couple of days. We may need to 'borrow' your ship maybe, maybe not. For the moment, I need you to call your people at the gangway, and tell them that they should let through eight of our...'officers' into the ship. Tell them you have received word of a terrorist attack to San Juan, and that they have been sent here to protect the passengers. Also, instruct your people not to let any more passengers off the ship. That's all I need for the moment." Rodriguez continued to smile.

Captain Clausen shook his head silently.

"No?" Rodriguez asked mildly. He aimed his Beretta at Bates and shot him twice, filling the room with the noise of the detonations and the smell of cordite. The two bullets thudded into the SSO's chest, close to his heart. The officer careened sideways, his head slamming onto the bridge's controls. The female officer began to scream hysterically, while Clausen and Folstad shouted with rage and fear, the latter running to where the SSO had fallen. Bates was not breathing, and Folstad desperately tried to revive him with CPR.

"Please call your security people at the gangway," Rodriguez repeated with a weary expression. When the captain hesitated, he added, "Don't make this hard on me, please! The girl is next. She screams too much, anyway. Screaming women make me nervous, and I would rather not kill anybody else. I made a bet with Rivera, here," he said, jerking his head in the direction of his associate, "that not more than…How many did I say, Manny?"

"Two," Rivera replied, still holding on to the woman's waist.

"Two," Rodriguez repeated. "That no more than two people would die in the taking of this beautiful ship. We're one person short. Please don't let me lose my bet."

"You bastard!" Folstad growled, while he continued pumping his fallen shipmate's chest with his powerful hands. Blood covered his arms up to his elbows. "You'll pay for this!"

"Honestly!" Rodriguez said with mock indignation. "Can't you use more original dialogue? I may kill you next for being so boring. By the way, you're wasting your time. He's dead." He waited for the captain to answer, but when nothing was forthcoming said, "Well? Will I have to lose my bet?"

Captain Clausen walked reluctantly to the ship's communication console, and lifted the phone. "Get me security at the gangway," he requested.

While the captain waited, Rodriguez pointed his gun at Folstad and made shooting sounds with his mouth, reminding the captain what would happen if he screwed up.

"Marcy!" Captain Clausen said hoarsely, as soon as the female security officer answered. "We have been…eh…contacted by the local authorities. Apparently, some unknown terrorists have blown up the bridges connecting San Juan to the rest of the island—" he paused, while Marcy expressed her dismay. "Yes, yes, it's terrible, I know. The authorities have asked us to hold up any further disembarkation of passengers until the situation...stabilizes. I will be making an announcement shortly, but I wanted to let you know. Don't let anyone off the ship until further notice. Let the others there know." He paused again, listening to his security agent. "Yes, I know this is going to create havoc...I know...I know. But safety must come first. And Marcy? In a few minutes, some armed security personnel from the local government are going to board the ship. They are going to give us additional protection. Let them through, please." Captain Clausen watched in despair as Folstad, sobbing, gave up his struggle to save Bates. "Thank you, Marcy," he said, hanging up.

"Well done," said Rodriguez. He retrieved a cell phone from his belt holster and speed dialed a number. He waited a few moments, and then shook his head. "The cell phone service is not working already. I'll have to use the other phone." He looked at Rivera. "Keep a watch on them while I go outside."

Rodriguez got off the swivel chair and walked to the right side of the bridge, where a door gave access to a small balcony. After he stepped into it, he shut the door behind him, took out his satellite phone, and extended its antenna. It took him thirty seconds to get connected to his number.

A feminine voice answered.

"Send the people in," he said, hanging up.

Returning inside the bridge, he picked up the card that Folstad had tossed on the floor, and handed it to the captain.

"Now, if you could please read this announcement over the ship's intercom."

They had not moved for a full five minutes, with no prospects that the traffic jam would end. Michelle's taxi was trapped in the innermost lane of the Fernandez Juncos Avenue, close to the end of the police station, and had nowhere to go. Several drivers had turned off their vehicles and stepped out of their cars, at first to see if they could find out what was causing the gridlock, and when that could not be determined, to commiserate with their stranded neighbors.

Don Moncho had kept his taxi's engine running and stopped his meter, refusing to charge his passenger for the idle time or to let her suffer from the heat. Michelle had continued trying to reach Doel in WKPA via her cell phone, but all of her attempts had been foiled by her editor's Pac Man-music message.

She began to get nervous. Her newscast was due to start at 9:00 AM, and she had to be at the station at least an hour before that. It would not bode well for her if she failed to get there on time. Management would never forgive her, regardless of her personal friendship with Doel and Correcaminos. She knew there were a dozen other candidates vying for better positions in the news organization, and that the door that had opened for her could just as easily be shut.

"There must have been some kind of accident further down the road," she said to Don Moncho, who had unfolded his newspaper and was reading it while he waited for the traffic to move. "It can't be that far away. I'm going to walk across the bridge, and try to get a taxi on the other side."

Don Moncho carefully set his newspaper aside, and turned to look at his passenger. He seemed confused, as if he had not fully understood what Michelle was saying.

"I have to get to the station..." Michelle tried to explain, feeling bad for her driver, while he stared at her uncomprehendingly through his thick glasses. She opened the door of the cab, and handed him a twenty-dollar bill. "I'm sorry to leave you stranded here, but—"

Michelle did not finish her apology, as dozens of thunderous booms drowned her voice. Her first instinct, as well as that of the others standing on the road, was to crouch, because the noise came with a shock wave that shook the ground. A woman nearby cried in alarm, and several others looked around apprehensively. It was an unexpected, overwhelming sound, the kind people experience when a jetliner crashes or when a massive earthquake makes buildings sway.

As the noise stopped, Michelle got out of the car, and searched for its source. At first, she could see nothing. Then a giant cloud of gray dust rolled towards them like a tidal wave, swallowing everything in its path. People sought refuge in their vehicles and stared uneasily at the thick haze that enveloped them. Some covered their mouths and brazened it out, quickly becoming streaked by the floating dust particles.

Michelle re-entered the cab and closed the door.

"What's happening?" Don Moncho asked, frightened.

"I don't know," Michelle answered uneasily, trying to sound calm.

Both stared in silence at the mysterious mist. Don Moncho took off his glasses and wiped them with a small lens cleaning cloth he kept in a pocket of his cab's visor, and then put them back on. For about half a minute, they could barely see the cars about them. Then the air started to clear, as the main cloud of dust soared over them.

"I'm going out," Michelle told Don Moncho. He said nothing.

The street was ominously quiet. Someone was coughing a few yards away, and the voice of a news radio station drifted out of a car near her, but otherwise, nothing disturbed the hushed stillness of the morning.

Patches of blue began to reappear in the sky, and then she saw a great column of black smoke coming out of the direction of the San Juan Yacht Club.

"Oh my God! What the hell is happening here?" she asked herself, surprised by how frightened her voice sounded.

Suddenly her cell phone began to ring in her hand, and she almost dropped it from the surprise. She looked at the screen, and saw with relief that it was Doel.

"Thank God!" she said into her phone.

"*Where are you?*" he asked. Even though he tried to keep the edginess out his voice, she sensed his concern. In the background, she heard several excited voices, and Correcaminos saying loudly to "*Tell her to get the hell back here*". Doel shushed him impatiently.

"Something has happened," she said.

"*I know that. The bomb threat in the Convention Center—*"

"The what? Were those the explosions I just heard?"

"*The bomb threat. Don't you listen to the news in the morning?*" Doel paused, as he absorbed his reporter's last words. "*What do you mean 'the explosions you just heard'? Where are you?*"

"I'm a few blocks from the San Juan Yacht Club. We've been in a traffic jam during the past twenty minutes." Michelle expanded the time they had been stuck on the road, trying to minimize how late she had left for work. "The cars are not moving. About five minutes ago there was this terrific explosion. No, more like many consecutive explosions, and now I see a great cloud of smoke. I thought it was coming out of the San Juan Yacht Club area, maybe the Army Corps of Engineers Building, but I guess it was the Convention Center, right?"

Doel remained quiet for several seconds, the background noise momentarily muted as if he had covered the speaker with his hand, presumably to find out what was happening.

"*No. It wasn't the Convention Center,*" he said at last. "*We're not sure of what's happening. We're just now getting garbled reports that there have been some explosions in one or more of the bridges to San Juan and Miramar.*"

Michelle held her breath, her heartbeat racing.

"*We haven't heard anything about the San Juan Yacht Club. Not yet anyway.*" Doel continued.

"And the Convention Center?" she asked.

"*Nothing has happened there yet. We're watching it on TV,*" Doel answered absently. Through his voice, she could hear the cogs of his brain turning. "*Now listen to me. If the reports we're just getting are true—*"

"They *are* true, Doel. I heard the explosions."

"Well, if they are true," Doel was not yet ready to concede to the fact yet, *"and we'll know soon enough from our news helicopter, then you're stranded in San Juan..."* He paused again, thinking out loud, *"which is...not necessarily a bad thing..."* Michelle heard an angry exclamation in the background, and knew that Correcaminos was arguing with her boss. *"Be quiet!"* he said, and resumed his conversation. *"Sorry, I got interrupted,"* he explained without any further elaboration. *"You are the closest reporter to whatever has happened. Can you go to the lagoon, and make a first hand report?"*

"I'll go right now," Michelle responded.

"Wait..." Again, Doel cut off the conversation for an extended time. When he returned, his mood was a somber. *"Michelle, we've just confirmed that the bridges have been heavily damaged. We're seeing the pictures of it now on television."*

"All of them?"

"All of them. Blasted by explosives...It's...It's important that you get there and see it from the other side. We'll try to land our helicopter with a portable camera, and you can make a live report."

"It will take me some time to get there, since traffic isn't moving."

"All right. Please be careful. We don't know what you'll find out there," Doel told her. Then he added, *"How's your phone's battery?"*

Michelle examined the phone's screen. "It's showing a full battery."

"Marvelous!" he said, trying to sound enthusiastic and less concerned than he really felt. *"I'm calling the station to patch you up live right now, so that you can give a report of what you experienced. We'll broadcast it on TV with a picture of yours, while we get that camera to you. That way we'll get a scoop on—"*

Michelle had to cover her ear as a police siren went off, insistently "whoop-whooping" somewhere behind her. When she turned, she saw a patrol car from the police station trying to make its way out of its parking area into the street through the nearly solid wall of stopped vehicles. For the first time, she observed that the immediate area outside of the station was seething with police officers. She had not noticed how close the taxi had stopped to the three-story police building.

"I didn't hear that last part," she shouted into the phone. "Where do you—"

The sky above her exploded in a massive roar. For a moment, she thought some idiot had lit up hundreds of firecrackers from one of the apartment buildings across the street. But then, she saw several holes punch through the hood of the exiting police car and its windshield disintegrate. Other policemen, she could not tell how many, crumpled unexpectedly unto the ground, while others ran in confusion, seeking cover.

"Oh my God," she whispered to herself. "Someone is shooting at us!"

"What? Please repeat what you said, I can't hear you!" she heard Doel say in the cell phone. *"I can't hear you very well. There's a lot of interference..."*

Several windows in the police building shattered into thousands of shards of glass that rained on the defenseless officers. One policeman, a scant dozen feet from Michelle, pulled out his gun and fired towards the sky. However, he only discharged his gun once before something struck him somewhere close to his right shoulder, producing a terrible "thwacking" sound. He fell to the ground, flailing like a landed fish.

"Doel! Someone is shooting at us!' she screamed into her phone.

"What?"

"SOME-ONE-IS-SHOOTING-AT-US!" she shouted as loudly as she could, crouching behind the cab.

"Who is shooting at you?! Why?!"

"I don't know!"

A stray bullet crashed into the rear glass of the cab, destroying it. Inside, Don Moncho looked back and moved his head from one side to another, unable to comprehend what was happening. Chaos reigned in the street. People were running aimlessly, abandoning their vehicles—pinned between the concrete barriers in the middle of the avenue and the buildings on the other side—to escape from the deadly hail of bullets falling from the sky.

Michelle crouched and crawled to the taxi's front door. She opened it, and pulled Don Moncho out of the vehicle. She sat on the pavement with her back against one of the cars in the next lane, and forced the old man to do the same.

"We have to get out of here!" she cried partially at him, partially at Doel. Don Moncho stared at her through his thick glasses, his scared, wide-opened eyes magnified out of proportion, and he nodded. Michelle spoke into her cell phone. "Listen, Doel. I don't have much time, and I can barely hear you, so record what I'm saying or patch me through to the station! The police station in Puerta de Tierra is under attack. There is heavy gunfire apparently coming from the buildings on the other side of the street!" She paused, got on her knees, and peered over the hood of the car towards the opposite side of the road.

Initially, she could not see from which apartments of El Falansterio the shooting originated. Then she noticed movement on the rooftop. There were men up there, barely visible from where she hid, mere shadows along the upper edge of the buildings. But then she distinctly saw a man with a rifle stand up, take very deliberate aim, and fire. She turned just in time to see a policeman tumble backwards, blood spurting from his throat every time his heart beat. She closed her eyes in horror, and brought the cell phone back to her mouth, her hand shaking so badly she could scarcely hold it.

"*Michelle! Michelle! Are you there?!*" she heard Correcaminos shout into Doel's phone, sounding sick with worry. Knowing him, he probably had wrestled the phone away from Doel.

"They're massacring the police," she said with as much breathless strength as she could muster.

"*Get out of there!*" Correcaminos said. "*Get out of there now!*" A brief pause followed where she heard her two friends arguing. Then Doel returned to the phone. "*You're patched through,* he stated curtly. "*We're recording and going to telecast what you say with a two minutes delay. Go.*"

Michelle breathed in deeply, trying to calm herself. Then she began to speak.

"This is Michelle Alfaro reporting, live on the scene. I am located in the middle of the Fernandez Juncos Avenue, in front of the Puerta de Tierra police station, where traffic has been stalled for the last twenty minutes. Five minutes ago, unknown persons opened heavy fire on the police, as it prepared to leave for the bridges in the Condado Lagoon. The gunmen appear to be stationed on the roof of the El Falansterio public housing buildings, and they are very well armed."

She heard the voice of Correcaminos—in its professional mode—interrupt her.

"*Do you know how many gunmen there are?*"

"It is difficult to tell, but there seem to be many of them. They are using fast, repetitive firing weapons, as well as rifles with telescopic sights."

"*Have the police brought the situation under control?*"

"No! The situation is *far* from under control. This is a terrible scene. There must be dozens of police down in the parking lot, who are either wounded or dead. I can see...two cars burning, and several others are riddled with bullet holes. *Oh!*" she shouted involuntarily. "I just witnessed a policeman on a motorcycle get shot in the head!" she managed to gasp through a stifled sob. "He's dead! He's dead!" Her voice broke down, despite her desperate attempts to keep her composure.

"*Get out of there, Michelle,*" Correcaminos urged her, forgetting he was participating in a delayed telecast, his emotions taking over.

Two stray bullets thudded into the roof of the taxicab, and Don Moncho began to stand up to look at the damage.

"No!" Michelle screamed, yanking him back down.

"My car!" he protested.

Another bullet pinged on the pavement less than a foot away from the old man's leg, and ricocheted onto the cab's front tire, ripping it open with a loud bang. Still holding on to Don Moncho's arm, Michelle tried to collect her thoughts. She took a deep breath.

"The police station is sustaining tremendous damage. Most of its windows have been destroyed, and you can see the shredded screens, the light fixtures, and the partitions hanging from the inside. Many drivers and passengers who were heading out of San Juan are trapped like me in the cross fire, and the bullets are hitting everywhere. Just now, two bullets hit the roof of the taxicab that I was traveling in, and its rear glass has been destroyed." She paused, trying to catch her breath, tears still streaming from her eyes.

"The police urgently needs reinforcements, Correcaminos," she continued. "They cannot survive this much longer."

A tremendous explosion shook the police station. The windows on the first floor exploded outwards, spewing debris in every direction. Then a second explosion rocked the street, even more powerful than the first.

"We have to leave!" Michelle shouted over the noise. "The police building is burning!"

"*Get out of there now!*" Correcaminos repeated, really concerned.

Michelle stood up, grabbing Don Moncho by the arm. She led him between the stalled cars, moving in the direction of Miramar to put some distance between the police station and them. As she ran she continued to speak into the cell phone. "The police building...it is now burning out of control. The two big explosions that you heard came from within the building and they...they have obliterated the first floor. It is impossible to tell how many people are still inside and what is their condition. Even from where we stand, we can feel the heat of the flames!"

She stopped as they walked past a minivan. She had heard a child crying inside. Looking through one of its windows, she saw a little girl, no more than three years old, still strapped to her infant seat. The glass of the side door window opposite to where she sat had been blown apart, and small pieces of glass were scattered everywhere. Michelle tried to open the door, but it was locked. She thrust her hand through the broken window, and after a brief search unlocked the door from the inside.

"Don't cry, baby," she said to the terrified girl after she opened the door. "I'll get you out."

As she got in, she discovered the figure of a woman crouching under the wheel of the van.

"Are you hurt?" she asked more loudly than she expected, fearing the worst.

Slowly, a woman raised her head and stared at her in utter panic. She said nothing.

"Are you *hurt?*" Michelle insisted.

The driver shook her head. She was a blond woman in her early twenties, dressed in tight jeans and a white blouse.

"Can you move?"

The woman nodded briefly.

"Why didn't you take your baby out of her seat?" she asked, uncomprehendingly.

"She's not my baby..." she mumbled. "I'm her babysitter."

Michelle lost her patience. Fueled by her own fear, she snapped back at the woman with intense anger. "So you hid and you left the baby *there*, you little shit?!" she said, glaring at the babysitter, who merely whimpered.

Michelle returned her attention to the little girl, who was holding out her arms towards her, terrified. She unstrapped her from her seat and picked her up. The girl clung to her neck with her arms, crying. As Michelle clumsily backed out of the van, she turned to the younger woman and said, "You either follow me, or you stay here by yourself. Frankly, I don't care either way."

It was not until she exited the van that she realized that the shooting had stopped. The blond babysitter tentatively opened the front driver's door, and looked around, as if awakening from a bad dream.

"Is it over?" she asked, filled with dread.

As if answering her question, a man spoke over a loudspeaker. Following the sound, Michelle saw a man standing close to the edge of El Falansterio's roof, holding a bullhorn. Something about his appearance unsettled her. It was not that he looked particularly sinister or evil. On the contrary, he was dressed in a simple pair of jeans and a dark shirt, and from the distance seemed to be fit and neatly groomed. It was his self-assurance—the authority with which spoke—that scared her. Reinforcing her mental image, two more men, each carrying a rifle, appeared at his side as he used his bullhorn. She listened, while the man finished stating his demands.

"Correcaminos," she whispered into her cell phone again. "Are you still there?"

"*Yes. We have you on the speakerphone. Doel and the rest of the crew are here with us also,*" the sportscaster responded. "*Are you all right?*"

"Yes. The shooting has stopped... A man with a bullhorn standing on the roof of El Falansterio is demanding that the police surrender. He's giving them five minutes to do it...Hold on..." Michelle raised herself enough to be able to see into the police station parking lot through the van's broken window. "They're coming out... They're coming out! I see several policemen and women staggering out of the burning station. They have their hands raised up in the air, and they are in terrible shape. The police are surrendering! I repeat, the police have surrendered!"

Michelle watched in silence as several armed men exiting from El Falansterio crossed the street and headed towards the station, not more than three cars away from where she and the others hid. "Some men carrying rifles have just moved into the parking area of the police station. I don't know where they came from, but I presume it's from El Falansterio. They are surrounding the policemen that surrendered and disarming them..." She stopped, observing the armed men handle the police.

They all wore black shirts and pants, similar to those of the man who had spoken through the bullhorn. And wrapped around the right arm of their shirts they bore what appeared to be green-colored words. She was too distant to read them, but they piqued her curiosity. There was something very familiar about them.

Still trying to figure out what the green words said, she observed one of the gunmen separate from the rest and check the fallen police officers. Twice he stopped and placed two of his fingers on the throat of a wounded policeman, as if to ascertain that they still had a pulse, and moved on. He avoided completely a trooper who had been shot in the head and who was obviously dead. But as he checked a fourth victim, the wounded man stirred. The armed man gently examined the downed officer's wounds. His expression turned grim as he pulled the wounded man's shirt open. Wearily, he drew a gun from his holster, placed it on the temple of the wounded man's head, and pulled the trigger.

Michelle recoiled in shocked horror, dropping her cell phone. She fell on her knees and hid her face in her hands, while the others watched her anxiously. The girl, transferred to the hands of her babysitter, looked at the others with quiet apprehension while she sucked her thumb. Don Moncho gently placed a hand over Michelle's back, uncertain of what had happened, and even less certain of what he should do.

Michelle thought she would faint. The images of the execution whirled in her head and did not let her think. Dazed and nearly hysterical, she tried to regain control of her emotions. She heard Doel's voice in the distance, and after a few moments realized it originated from the cell phone lying on the ground next to her. She picked it up, her hands quivering.

"Doel?"

"*She's back,*" she heard her editor whisper to the others with relief.

"Doel?"

"*I'm here, Michelle. You're doing an incredible job. Hang in there!*" he urged her, sensing her despair but not willing to give up yet on the momentous news story.

"They...they are executing some of the wounded," Michelle managed to say with a shaky voice. "One of the terrorists"—it was the first time she had used that term—"just shot a wounded policeman in the head."

Her report produced long silence at the other end of the line. Finally, Doel spoke. "*This is getting too dangerous,*" he said soberly. "*You need to go. Find a safe place, and call me back. I am sending our helicopter to rendezvous with you, and it will either pick you up and bring you back here, so you can give a first hand account of what you saw, or depending on the situation, film what's happening there, okay?*"

Michelle nodded, and said, "Okay."

"*Michelle,*" Doel hurriedly added before she could hang up. "*We're off the air now. I just wanted to say...I'm...we're very proud of you. I know your dad would be too. Please call me when you're safe.*"

Michelle heard Correcamino's voice in the background say, "*Not thanks to you, you cold-blooded prick!*" And then the communication went dead.

"Let's go," she whispered to the others, who were still crouching next to her. She looked at the babysitter, not bothering to hide her hostility. "Do you think you can manage to do your job?" she asked icily.

The young woman nodded.

Michelle turned to the old taxi driver, who still seemed distraught with the prospect of abandoning his cab. "You should take your hat off," she said, pointing at the white, immaculately clean Panama hat on his head. He had not removed it during the entire ordeal. Don Moncho directed her a disconcerted stare, as if she were suggesting that he get naked. "We need to attract as little attention as possible, and your hat is so shiny and beautiful, that it can be seen from a mile away without using binoculars."

Reluctantly, Don Moncho removed his hat, revealing his baldpate, with a few long hairs pasted across it. He cradled it tenderly on his chest, and gazed at Michelle through his industrial sized lenses.

"Okay then," Michelle got on her feet, and crouching behind the abandoned cars, began to lead the small group away from the burning station.

CHAPTER XXI

Lucas smelled the strong coffee brewing even before he slid *El Joyero's* heavy door open. The air conditioner was running, although not long enough to cool the store. Several old, beaten-up boxes littered the store, including the long, flat one that had stored the large, golden "Anniversary Sale" sign used in every anniversary sale since he remembered. Other boxes contained special items such as black velvet, headless busts and long, fingerlike props, used to display necklaces and rings; large plastic bags filled with decorative lights; and rolls of unused, gold anniversary wrapping paper left over from other years.

Most of the store's lights had not been turned on, so that the *Joyero* was enveloped in the peaceful but slightly creepy semidarkness that old establishments acquired with the passage of time. *There were ghosts here,* Lucas thought. Not the scary type of ghosts, but the kind that crept unbidden into your mind, bringing with them bittersweet memories from the long-forgotten past. He remembered the times when, as a young boy, he would visit the store with his best friend, Robert, and while the elders worked, the two children would play in the gloomy recesses of the store, inventing fantastic alien worlds and beings.

He could feel the presence of his grandfather here, pacing through the store that he loved so dearly. Don Jorge had possessed a subtle sense of humor, and would do quiet, practical jokes that would help lighten the dullest hours of the day. Lucas remembered how on one occasion his grandfather had dealt with a competing jeweler from La Alhambra, a huge jewelry store located just two blocks away on Cristo Street.

Periodically, the Alhambra's owner would come to "visit" Don Jorge. While they chatted, the man would furtively scan the prices of the jewelry on display, and later sell similar merchandise at lower prices in his store. Also, whenever his visits coincided with those of Lucas' grandmother

Margot, the man—who had harbored since his youth a secret passion for her—would recite to her love poems.

Don Jorge put up with the situation for several weeks, but after the visits increased in number and intensity, he decided to end them. As the man began to regale Margot with a passionate recitation, Don Jorge offered him a tumbler of wine. The man accepted it gratefully—never pausing in his fiery poetic delivery—while Don Jorge filled the tumbler to its very rim. The man suffered from a chronic condition where his hands shook constantly, and as he brought the drink to his lips, the wine began to fly out of the tumbler in every direction, spilling on his chin and his shirt. Then, his grandfather filled his own tumbler to the brim and, toasting Margot, drank from it without spilling a drop. Not saying another word, Don Jorge handed to the man a list containing the sales prices of dozens of items in the store. The man's face reddened and he left, never to return. Lucas smiled. He knew his grandmother had missed the poems.

"Good morning, Mr. Lucas," Antonio, the security guard, said as he exited from the back of the store with a dilapidated cardboard container.

"Good morning," Lucas replied, placing on one of the counters a shopping bag with additional supplies. "You started early today!"

Antonio smiled good-naturedly. "I thought if I got here early, we would leave early. I brewed some coffee."

"I know!" Lucas walked to the coffee machine, and grabbed his personal cup, a porcelain mug that read: *"Jewelers never die, they just lose their charms."* "I smelled it as soon as I got off my car in Doña Fela's."

Antonio laughed somewhat uncertainly, as if not sure that his boss was making a joke. *Not the brightest bulb in the marquee*, Lucas thought.

"What time did you get here anyway?" he asked, pouring some coffee into his mug.

"Oh, around six."

"Six? In the morning?" Lucas repeated in a surprised tone, adding some milk to his coffee. "You've already been here for almost two hours! What time did you get up?"

Antonio lived in the northern town of Manati, about an hour's ride from San Juan. He did not own a car, so he had to take a *"publico"*— publicly licensed cars or vans that squeezed into them as many passengers as they could fit, and charged them two dollars each way for the ride—after walking two miles from his home to the town's central square, or "plaza".

"At a quarter to four in the morning," he replied almost defensively.

"Wow! You should have slept here! How come you're so early? You *know* the Pietri sisters won't show up 'til eight, at least."

Antonio laughed again, in the infectious Goofy-like fashion that always made Lucas smile. The *Joyero* guard had been one of his grandfather's recruits. Originally hired by a security firm when he was eighteen years old, he had been a shy, sweet, awkward, and unremarkably-looking-and-sized *'jibaro"*—or hillbilly—who had been temporarily assigned to keep watch over *El Joyero de San Juan* during its operating hours. He had quickly gained the affection of Don Jorge and the *Joyero's* staff. When the security firm had notified that the young guard would be substituted by a bigger, tougher looking, more experienced employee, Don Jorge had refused to replace him, and offered him a higher paying job.

That had been nearly twenty-five years ago, and during that span of time Antonio had been adopted—if not legally, emotionally—by the Pietri family. The shy, sweet, awkward, unremarkably-looking-and-sized youth had grown into a shy, sweet, awkward, unremarkably-looking-and-sized adult, distinguishable from his younger version by a pencil-thin mustache, some scattered gray hair, and ten extra pounds.

As far back as Lucas could remember, Antonio had never missed a day of work. Every morning he would be in the store by 7:30, prepare the coffee for the Pietri sisters, clean the display counters, and escort Maria in her daily peregrination to the banks. At 9:00 AM he would open the store and place a wooden stool at the entrance, where he would perch whenever he grew tired of standing. Most of the *Joyero's* established clientele knew him by name, and they would greet him as they entered the establishment. He would also be visited by what he called his "sources of information", colorful characters from San Juan that he had befriended through the years and who kept him abreast of the latest gossip and rumors circulating in the old city.

Except on counted occasions—when he was off-duty like that morning—he would wear a crisply starched-and-ironed, white, short-sleeved shirt with a large silver badge—where the badge originated from, Lucas was not sure—and blue, neatly pressed pants. A black leather holster always hung from his waist, although its large flap remained closed and Lucas had never seen the type of gun that it nestled.

"It's just...I have a date this afternoon at five," Antonio confessed, casting his gaze to the floor, grinning embarrassedly.

Lucas nodded, trying to maintain a neutral expression. Antonio's love life had been the object of countless, oftentimes hushed discussions between the Pietri sisters, who could not understand how a fine man like him had not married.

It was not that Antonio did not go out with women. He dated often. But Lucas had met briefly some of the ladies that Antonio went out with, and had not been very impressed. For the most part, they were not plain, or ugly, and some were even quite voluptuous. But it seemed to Lucas that the relationships were doomed to fail from the outset; Antonio invariably favored sassy, self-centered women who failed to appreciate the shy, self-effacing gentleman who invited them out. Maria had summed it up once by telling him—as "gently" as Maria could be "gentle"—that he should be *"looking for more quality, and less quantity"*.

"Great!" Lucas managed to say, sipping more of his coffee. It was dark and rich and strong, and just what he needed to jolt his system from its still passive Sunday mode.

"Do you think we'll be out by then? I mean, by five?" Antonio asked hopefully.

"Believe me," Lucas answered sincerely. "You're not going to miss that date. Even if we have to drag the Pietri sisters away from the store kicking and screaming. It's a promise. But just in case, did you bring your gun with you?" he asked in a dead-serious tone.

Antonio's eyes momentarily narrowed in alarm, but then he realized that Lucas was joking, and he guffawed, Goofy-like. It was an infectious laugh that made Lucas feel good.

A long silence followed as both men began to unpack the contents of some of the boxes. Although Lucas knew that he should not pursue the topic any further, his curiosity eventually got the better of him.

"So tell me, is she someone new?" he ventured to inquire as casually as possible, keeping his eyes on the dilapidated box he was emptying.

"Who?...Oh! My date?" Antonio's cheeks and neck turned red. "Oh, no. Not new. We take the same *publico* every day to San Juan. She's..." he hesitated, as if considering whether he should say more.

"Oh, so she's from Manati also?" Lucas said, trying to keep the conversation alive. "Did you know her before she started...you know, traveling with you?" After all, Manati was not such a large town.

"No, no. I'd noticed her before, walking around town. How couldn't I? She's beautiful!"

The emotion in Antonio's words startled Lucas. He kept quiet, hoping the shy guard would continue his story.

"We had never talked...well, really talked, except to say good mornings and that sort of thing. Until two days ago...I didn't know what to say to her."

He stopped, having answered Lucas' question.

"And what prompted you to finally talk to her two days ago?" *There was a conclusion to this unique story,* Lucas thought, *and he would not let it taper off so easily.*

"I didn't talk to her, she talked to me!" he explained with more than a trace of wonder in his voice, beaming at Lucas and shaking his head with incredulity.

"All right Antonio!" Lucas laughed, and high-fived his shy friend, infected by his apparent happiness. Antonio's grin widened. "What did she say?" Lucas asked, before he could stop himself.

Antonio paused, his eyes reliving the moment she had first spoken to him, still relishing every second of the conversation.

"She asked me what it was that I wrote every morning, when we headed to work," he answered.

"You write on the way to work?" Lucas said, truly surprised. He could picture Antonio cramped in the *publico* with several other passengers, trying to write as the car speeded and turned through the local roads.

Antonio assented. "I write poetry. I can't write it while I'm working, so I use my free time coming here, and when there's enough light, when I return to Manati." He walked to his backpack, which he stored in a corner of Fannie's small office by the entrance, and returned with a black and white, hardcover notebook, covered in transparent contact paper. "In this notebook," he said, showing it to Lucas from a distance, and putting it away again.

Poetry! Who would have thought it, Lucas wondered.

"She was sitting next to me, and so I told her that I was writing poems, and she asked if I could show some of them to her. There were other curious people around. You know, the type that pretend not to hear but listen to everything you say, so I told her I'd read some of it to her in private." Antonio's cheeks went from red to deep crimson, as he realized how his last statement had sounded, and hastened to explain, "I mean, not read them in front of the others in the car. They're romantic, the poems are, so I didn't want to read them in front of the others."

"So you invited her to go out with you tonight."

Antonio hesitated. "Well...she invited me! To have dinner tonight. And I said sure, okay!" he said, pausing, and adding hurriedly, "I'm paying, of course."

Lucas smiled, genuinely pleased. "Congratulations. I think you will sweep her off her feet." He stared at the timid, tongue-tied guard, seeing him in a new light. He had know Antonio all of his life, and considered him to be a simple, likable, gentle man with a limited personality and not much depth in his thoughts. *And he had been wrong. Unconsciously, arrogantly wrong.*

"How long have you been writing love poems?" he asked, attempting to hide his thoughts by continuing to unpack a box that contained several of the headless, black velvet-covered busts, each wrapped in several newspapers.

"August 28, 2012," he answered without a moment's hesitation.

The precision of the response made Lucas glance up with amusement. "Any particular time?" he asked jokingly.

"Oh…I guess around eight at night," he answered after doing some mental calculations. It was Lucas' turn to consider if Antonio was joking, but the man was dead earnest.

"How can you remember the exact date and time?"

"That was the time of the day when Mercedes, you know—that's her name—Mercedes, first walked into the *publico*," he answered simply.

Lucas stared at Antonio with awe. For several years, the man had been writing love poems to the woman who traveled next to him to San Juan, and never directed a single word at her.

"I'm scared that she may not like my poems," he said, without stopping his work, not really concentrating on what he was doing.

Lucas waved his hand dismissively.

"Listen to me, Antonio. You have nothing to fear. When she finds out the poems are about her, she'll fall madly in love with you. Instantly! Unless she's in love with you already. You may end up marrying her, you know?… Love poems!" he said with admiration. "Honestly! That's just sheer genius!" He thought of trying it himself, and gaining some points with Jeannie.

Antonio grinned happily. Saying nothing, he returned to the attic.

The Pietri sisters arrived at *El Joyero* by 7:45 AM, about an hour earlier than Lucas had expected them. By that time, Lucas and Antonio had hung the "ANNIVERSARY SALE" sign on the back wall of the store, cleaned the glass display cases, unpacked most of the boxes, and dispatched two servings of Antonio's strong coffee. The two men had heard the sisters long before they engaged in their daily struggle to slide open the store's heavy door. They were debating heatedly some unknown subject, Evelyn asserting with apparent conviction something incomprehensible, and Maria reacting with a moan.

"Did you hear the explosions?" Evelyn asked Lucas, as he helped them open the door. "I suspect sabotage!"

Maria rolled her eyes. "Jesus, Evelyn! If it were up to you, we'd be invaded by terrorists every day of our lives!"

Fannie entered last into the store, and whispered to her son, "It's been this way since we left Michelle's apartment. I seriously considered jumping into the bay."

"You're early!" he answered diplomatically, kissing her and then kissing each of his aunts as they got rid of their purses and the packages they carried.

"But seriously, did you hear the noise?" Evelyn insisted, sounding very concerned. "We heard it just as we were in Michelle's apartment! It sounded like several explosions. Boom! Boom! Boom! Boom! Boom!"

"Some day her head is going to explode," Maria whispered to Lucas. Then she added more loudly, "Evelyn says it's the *statehooders*."

"The *statehooders*?" Lucas sounded amused, despite himself.

"I didn't hear any explosions," Antonio ventured to say with a tinge of concern.

"That's because your mind was elsewhere," Lucas told him with feigned innocence, making Antonio blush. "But I did hear some strange noise as I was heading here," he added. Evelyn regarded Maria with an *"I-told-you-so"* look, while the latter sighed.

"Honestly, Evelyn! Every day you come up with weirder and weirder stuff!" Maria lamented, failing to register the last exchange between Antonio and Lucas. It did not, however, escape Fannie's attention, who raised an eyebrow quizzically. "I'm starting to think that you really believe everything you say. And sometimes you even make sense, which scares me even more!"

"But listen, Lucas," Evelyn persisted, seeking a more sympathetic ear. "Doesn't it all make sense? The *PNPers* want statehood, but right now they're divided, and they're scared of the *populares* because the *populares* have never lost a plebiscite, right?"

Evelyn waited for Lucas to confirm her statement, and Lucas nodded dutifully, earning a withering stare from Maria.

"So they do some kind of sabotage," Evelyn suggested, lowering the tone of her voice for dramatic effect. "They make a lot of noise, and maybe cause some damage, something that will unite the *statehooders* against the...the...*independentista* threat. It makes sense, doesn't it?"

"Oh sweet Baby Jesus!" groaned Maria. Fannie and Lucas traded a quick glance and grinned.

"Why not?" Evelyn argued heatedly. "They do it to scare the majority of the people, so that they seek the safety of the United States! How do they seek it? Statehood, that's how! What do you think?" she asked Lucas point blank.

He had hoped not to get involved in the doomsday argument, but it seemed that he would not be able to avoid it.

"Well," he began to say hesitantly, "I—" but Antonio interrupted him.

"I heard that they had placed some bombs in the Convention Center," he said excitedly.

A surprised hush followed his statement. Intimidated by everyone's questioning looks, he said apologetically, "It's a possibility..."

"What bombs?" Evelyn interrupted.

"I heard it in the *publico* this morning, when we were driving to San Juan. They discovered them this morning. Six bombs! Everybody was talking about them. They surrounded the entire area!"

"Wait a minute, wait a minute, wait—*a—min—ute!*" Maria raised both of her hands in a "Halt everything!" gesture. "Who is *they* and who is *they*?"

"What?" Fannie sounded confused.

"I think what Maria means is—" Evelyn began to explain, but Maria cut her short.

"*They*, the people who placed the bomb," she said, addressing Antonio. "You said *they* had placed a bomb. Who is *they*?"

"The Macheteros," Antonio answered.

"You see?" Evelyn exclaimed triumphantly. "They're already blaming the *indepen...*"

"Wait!" Maria shouted, and then addressed Antonio in a more subdued tone. "And you said that *they* had surrounded the Convention Center, *they* being?..."

"God, Maria, even a five year old can answer that!" Fannie said with exasperation, looking at Antonio. "The police surrounded the Convention Center, right?"

Antonio nodded.

"Duh!" Evelyn added, prompting Maria to shake her head in despair.

"And the bombs exploded?" Fannie asked, genuinely alarmed.

Antonio raised his shoulders weakly, signaling complete ignorance. "They hadn't exploded when I got off the *publico*. At least if they had, we didn't hear anything about it..."

"Didn't the *publico* have the radio on?" Maria asked.

"At the beginning. Then the driver began playing a CD, and nobody asked him to put the news back on," he said.

Besides, Lucas thought to himself, *Antonio was busy talking to Mercedes.*

"I told you the noise we heard sounded like bombs going off!" Evelyn said. She seemed to be scared. "It had to be the bombs in the Convention Center." She turned to Maria. "Now do you believe me?"

Nobody spoke for several seconds.

"That's all we need," Fannie said worriedly. "A bomb scare just when we're about to start our anniversary sale."

"Those dammed *statehooders*!" Evelyn muttered angrily. Her-off-the-wall comment made Lucas catch his breath to stop from laughing. But he could not control himself, and chuckled. Other giggles followed, and then everyone, including Evelyn, burst into laughter.

"Well," Fannie said after the laughing had subsided, "let's hope that Evelyn is wrong. Can we find out what's happening?"

"I'll turn on the radio in my office," Lucas offered.

As he walked down the stairs to his repair shop, he could not help but feel uneasy. They all had laughed because of Evelyn's wild *statehooder* sabotage theory. But something was definitely not right, and the sooner they found out about it, the better.

Police Superintendent Maldonado walked between the rows of cars that had been abandoned by the panicked drivers in Ponce de Leon Avenue, at the mouth of the bridge connecting Miramar to San Juan. A tall man dressed in blue police fatigues and military boots accompanied him. About a half dozen other policemen trailed them at a respectful distance. The urgent wail of sirens, dozens of them, could be heard in the background.

The two men stopped by the automobile where the man shot by a terrorist had fallen. The shooting victim still lay on the hood of the blue Yaris, but he had been covered by a blue plastic tarp. Two detectives, a police photographer, and half a dozen other policemen were busy documenting the crime scene and making certain that no evidence was lost. A large area around the car and the car ahead of it had been cordoned off with wide, yellow tape.

One of the detectives saw them arrive and greeted them with the respectful familiarity that was accorded to superiors that were held in high regard.

"Alexander," Maldonado said, addressing the crime investigator by his first name. The police chief knew most of his detectives' names, a feat that was both known and appreciated throughout the force. "What do we have here?"

"The victim is a male in his thirties named Pedro Santana," the detective, a man in his thirties himself answered. "He was driving the Camry up ahead." Alexander nodded towards a white automobile stationed in front of them. "Apparently he got into an argument with some government worker who was at the bridge, and the worker shot him through the windshield twice, once on the chest, another time on the jaw and neck. We have several witnesses, including the owner of the Yaris."

The Superintendent stared briefly at the body. He was missing one of his shoes, but it was nowhere to be seen. It was probably under one of the cars. The taller man who had walked with Maldonado sauntered to the dead man's Camry and examined its windshield.

"They used a powerful gun, .40 caliber ammunition," the large man said, as the police chief approached him. "A Beretta, or a Glock probably."

"You bullshitter. You can't tell that from the bullet holes on the windshield," Maldonado observed as he continued walking towards the lagoon.

The tall man shrugged and smiled. "I cheated. I looked at the cartridges on the road." The two cartridges discarded by the gun lay in front of the car, circled in yellow.

The Superintendent abandoned the cars, and walked to the edge of the severed bridge. Quietly, he surveyed the grim scene before him. A column of billowing smoke rose to his left, as the San Juan Yacht Club burned unchecked. Some fire trucks stationed in San Juan were busy trying to quench the flames with very little success so far. Further away, more smoke rose into the sky. That one worried him even more, since it seemed to come from the area where the San Juan police station was located. Shortly after the blasts, Maldonado had received a report that the San Juan police station was "under heavy attack". The dispatcher had mentioned "many casualties" and described the situation as "desperate", and a few minutes later all further transmissions had ended. Now a cloud of thick, black smoke was rising from the area. A helicopter sent to investigate had to turn away after being struck by bullets.

All four of the bridges connecting San Juan to the main island of Puerto Rico had been seriously damaged. He could see that personally now. About a forty foot gap, maybe more, hindered the crossing of any of them. The main avenues heading to and from the bridges were gridlocked with stalled vehicles that had been deserted by their owners. Many of the cars had been destroyed, and from some smoke he observed in the Condado end of the lagoon, some seemed to have caught fire.

Even getting to ground zero had been an ordeal. Maldonado had been forced to abandon his vehicle and walk after driving out of the Convention Center area and stumbling onto a solid wall of unmoving cars. For the same reason, bringing medical help to the scores of people hurt either from the debris of the explosions or from the panicked fleeing that had ensued had been impossible, as the ambulances had been unable to get through. It had taken the Police Chief nearly half an hour to get to the lagoon.

Maldonado was dumbfounded. The damage was much worse than anything he had imagined. Most of the palm trees closest to the lagoon had been riddled with shrapnel-like debris, some of their thick trunks snapped in half. Other smaller trees and vegetation had been shredded to small pieces. Across the lagoon, many of the buildings closest to the Dos Hermanos Bridge showed curtains flapping like flags, sucked out by the wind through their broken windows.

"Who could have done this?" the Superintendent heard his large companion ask. There was anger and a promise of violence in his voice, as if he was already thinking about what he would do when he laid hands on the people who had caused such senseless destruction.

Maldonado cast a sideways glance at the man standing next to him. Colonel Alejo Montañez was a very big man, surpassing the police chief in height by a full three inches. Brash, honest, and fearless, he had become the Superintendent's right-hand man, a warrior willing to tackle any challenge regardless of the odds. His "Untouchables" were regarded to be the cream of the police force, a small, tight-knit group of veteran lawmen whose main task was to search and destroy drug traffickers in the island. Montañez was also Maldonado's best friend.

"I suspect we will find out soon enough," Maldonado replied bleakly, as he observed about a dozen of his men examining the damaged bridges.

"The Macheteros?" Montañez suggested. "They claimed to be behind the bomb threat of the Convention Center."

"Maybe, although this..." Maldonado shook his head in disbelief. "This would be something of a scale beyond anything they've done before. And they're supposed to be on the run, since the FBI captured Cacho."

"Have you heard from the Governor yet?" he asked, voicing his boss's main unspoken concern.

"No," Maldonado said drily. He looked at his watch. In a few minutes, it would be eight in the morning. "Nothing. I fear the worst. Have the federal authorities been alerted?"

"They have," Montañez confirmed. Then, trying to ease his friend's anguish, he said, "May I make a suggestion?"

"Will my saying no stop you from making it?" Maldonado said, smiling grimly.

"No."

"Then make it."

"We have a police boat tied up in Cataño," he stated, aware that his friend had full knowledge of the boat and that he was stating the obvious. Cataño was a town located across the bay of San Juan. A ferry operated during most of the day transferring passengers back and forth from the two cities. "Let me use it to find out what's happening. I'll take five of my men with me, just in case. We'll have La Fortaleza secured in no time," he said confidently, and then, as an afterthought, added, "Not that I think it needs to be secured."

Maldonado considered the colonel's proposal, and shook his head.

"No. Not an armed party. Send two plainclothes observers. We need to know what's happening before we move." Maldonado's cell phone began buzz. He flicked it open and paused, while he read the name of the caller. "I have to answer this," he told Montañez. "It'll only be a minute." Maldonado withdrew a few steps, spoke softly on the phone, and shut it off. "My wife," he informed Montañez, "calling to remind me about the dinner party tonight. I told her to cancel it." The Superintendent picked up the conversation where he had left it. "And I don't want you to be one of the men that goes there. I need you with me today, okay?"

"Yes, sir," the colonel replied, his attention already shifting to an aide running in their direction. Maldonado also looked at the approaching man.

"Sir!" the aide said loudly. He was carrying a portable telephone. "We have received an urgent telephone call from the Grand Laguna Hotel! They claim to be under attack from terrorists!"

Montañez stared at his friend as he took the telephone, and was surprised by how steady his hand held on to the receiver. His boss had nerves of steel, acting so coolly under such pressure.

"This is Maldonado," the Superintendent announced curtly, without any preamble. "Talk to me."

"*Good morning, Mr. Superintendent, thank you for answering the call so quickly. I know you are a very busy man right now.*"

Maldonado sighed impatiently. The caller sounded too calm to be reporting a "terrorist attack". "Yes?"

"*I wish to report that the Grand Laguna Hotel has been captured by terrorists.*"

"Where are you calling from?" the Superintendent asked, keeping in check his temper.

"*The Grand Laguna Hotel!*" the man answered, as if stating the obvious.

"And where are the terrorists?"

"*We are the terrorists!*" the voice said with exaggerated indignation.

Maldonado cursed. "Who *is* this?" he asked angrily.

"*We have already established that,*" the man answered in a patient tone. "*But if you need specifics, my name is Angel San Miguel.*"

Maldonado signaled Montañez to come closer. The colonel leaned next to his boss, trying to listen.

"*Are you there?*" the caller asked.

"I'm here," Maldonado replied. "But not for long. I have too many things to do to be listening to assholes like you." Montañez smiled.

"*Listen,*" the caller said in a pleasant voice. "*I can understand that you have doubts about the authenticity of this call, but you should have caller ID, and I think that you can verify that it is coming from the security office of the Grand Laguna Hotel. But if not, you can always trace the call back to me. I'm not about to hang up.*"

Maldonado and Montañez exchanged a questioning look. Then Maldonado nodded. Montañez called the aide to his side, and instructed him to verify the telephone number from which the call was being made.

"*I mean,*" the caller insisted in a perfectly reasonable tone, "*I could put the head of security on the phone and he could confirm what I just said, but then, you don't know the head of security of the hotel, do you?*"

"What do you want?" Maldonado asked.

"*That is too broad a question. For the moment, I just want to inform you that we, the people that you call 'the terrorists' that is, have captured the Grand Laguna Hotel and most of its guests. Our forces have also captured*" *the Mardi Gras cruise ship, docked in San Juan. No passengers are being allowed to disembark."*

Overwhelmed by the news, the Superintendent unconsciously lowered the hand that held the telephone to his waist, and then moved it back to his ear reluctantly.

"Hello, are you still there?" the caller asked for the second time, sensing a variation in the background noise.

"Yes," Maldonado responded soberly.

"Just making sure. You also probably know by now that we have captured your police station in Puerta de Tierra and the municipal police station at the bus terminal in San Juan. Regrettably, many of your men were killed or wounded, and some need immediate medical attention. We will allow you to collect them by helicopter at the empty lot by the piers, behind the police station. But if you try to use your helicopters for any other purpose, we will shoot them out of the sky. Is that understood?"

Maldonado nodded to Montañez, who ran to make the necessary arrangements. "How do we know this is not a trap to shoot down the helicopters?"

"It's a risk you'll have to take, isn't it?" San Miguel responded curtly. *"However, bear this in mind. We intend to make certain demands of you in the future—"*

"What demands?" Maldonado interrupted.

"All in its good time," the caller responded. *"We will not jeopardize those demands by playing tricks with you and shooting down your helicopters. As long as you only use them to pick up the wounded, of course."*

"I will send them as quickly as I can. How many wounded are we talking about?"

"Plan for two dozen men and women, seven of them seriously. As a gesture of good faith, we will also release seventeen men and women who surrendered to our forces."

Maldonado cursed under his breath, knowing their conversation was being recorded and would eventually be overheard by his men and the rest of the world.

"I will send the helicopters as quickly as I can," he repeated.

"Please do," the caller said evenly. *"The men need to be evacuated urgently."* The caller paused, as if to collect his thoughts.

"Are you the leader of the terrorists?"

"I will ask the questions for now, and you will listen," the voice said in the vexed but patient tone of a parent addressing an unruly child. *"You are doing well. Be patient!"*

Maldonado remained silent.

"Now listen carefully to me," the man said. *"At ten-thirty AM today, we*

intend to list our demands. We will do so in private, and you may or may not make them public, at your discretion."

"Why at ten-thirty?" Maldonado interrupted again. "Why not now?"

"No questions," the caller reminded gently. *"We will make our demands at that time. I will, however, make some suggestions to you now, and I hope that you follow them. Do not attempt to make any rescues or to enter the island of San Juan. This is our land now, and any hostile act will provoke swift and severe retribution."*

Montañez returned to Maldonado's side, having ordered the helicopter evacuation. He raised his thumb, indicating the helicopters had been sent.

"Secondly," the man continued, *"I would suggest that you do not hang up. When the news of the demolition of the bridges gets to the public—and I can bet it is already filtering out to the media—your telephone lines will be flooded, and getting calls through will become a nightmare. Keep this line open. Don't hang up. I will do the same here. Understood?"*

Montañez nodded emphatically at Maldonado, who agreed by assenting once. It made sense to keep contact with the terrorists. Even any unwitting noises or conversations could help the rescue efforts.

"I will keep it open."

"Thirdly, some fire trucks, apparently from the Puerta de Tierra station, are trying to make their way to the police station, and some are at the San Juan Yacht Club. Call them away, if you don't want your firemen to be shot at."

"But we need to control those fires!" Maldonado protested.

"The fires will not spread. Let the buildings burn down. I mean, it's up to you!" the caller said deferentially. *"But my men will not let the firemen get close to the buildings, and they will shoot if the firemen do so. They will not let the firefighters put out the fires anyway. So it's better not to put the firefighters in harm's way, do you understand?"*

Maldonado made a mental note of the caller's reference to "his men". *How many terrorists were there,* he wondered. *Was he dealing with an army?*

"I will ask them to withdraw," he said in a reluctant tone.

"Excellent! Then that's all for the moment..." the caller paused as if hesitating. *"No wait, there is one more thing,"* he said, as if he had just remembered one minor item in his "to do" list. *"We have captured the Governor and everyone in La Fortaleza."* The man waited, knowing the enormity of what he had just said and letting it sink in. Maldonado closed his eyes momentarily, allowing for a second his emotions to show. Montañez clenched his jaw, saying nothing.

"Is—" he began to ask, but was interrupted by the caller.

"He is fine. Two of his bodyguards are dead, but the rest of his staff is in good health. I just wanted to let you know, so that you have full knowledge of your situation. Do you understand?"

"Yes," Maldonado said, hissing out the short word as if it were laced with venom.

"*Good. Then our conversation is ended until ten-thirty. Goodbye.*"

Maldonado and Montañez stared at each other silently for several seconds, trying to digest the terrifying news they had just received. *How could something like that have happened? Who were those men? Where did they come from? What did they want?*

"Who is next in line when the Governor cannot perform his duties?" Maldonado inquired, breaking the silence.

"The Secretary of State, I think," Montañez answered, shrugging.

"Find out. Whoever he is, alert him of what's happening."

"Yes, sir."

"I'm thinking of establishing a command post at the San Geronimo Plaza." The San Geronimo Plaza Hotel lay at the tip of the Condado peninsula, opposite to the Grand Laguna Hotel, across the lagoon. Both hotels were separated by the reefs and the narrow passage of water that fed the waters of the Atlantic Ocean into the Condado Lagoon. "Make the necessary arrangements. I want you there with me."

Montañez nodded, waited briefly for additional instructions, and left when none came.

Maldonado walked closer to the bridge, and examined the destruction. The terrorists had been very professional. Their work had been swift, precise, and very effective.

His thoughts went back to the first call he had received through his cell phone. He hoped Montañez had not overheard his caller.

He would have to be very careful from now on.

CHAPTER XXII

Czecka alighted from the front passenger seat and walked to the back of the van, his oversized feet crunching on the gravel of the driveway. Before knocking on the door, he turned to the tall weeds growing in front of the abandoned house, opened up his pants' zipper, and peed. Only the splattering of his stream hitting the overgrown weeds and the chirping of the birds altered the day's peaceful silence. It was a beautiful morning. At one time, it had been filled with the clatter of explosions and gunfire and the wails of the sirens of fire trucks, but for the last fifteen minutes the clamor had abated. He liked it better that way. *Peaceful.*

A bee hovered close to his face, bothering him. With the flick of one of his enormous hands he captured the tiny insect and crushed it in his fist, discarding it into the urine-filled vegetation in front of him. One of the hidden lookouts in the vacant structure beyond chuckled, and was rewarded with a scowl. The lookout's merriment died out instantly.

Zipping up his pants, he walked to the back of the van, and knocked twice. One of its twin doors opened after several seconds, letting out part of the frigid air in its air-conditioned interior. A sleepy looking man holding an AK-47 peered at the giant, blinking in the sunlight.

"We're leaving," Czecka announced curtly. He placed two fingers on his lips and produced three sharp whistles. Immediately, two men emerged from the elephant grass that surrounded the wrecked house. Like the man inside the van, each was armed with an AK-47. They walked wordlessly to the waiting vehicle, and climbed in without acknowledging one another.

Czecka took one last glance into the van's interior, making certain that the cargo was still there. He had survived all of these years by not taking for granted even the most obvious parts of any plan. Satisfied with what he saw, he closed the door.

As soon as the giant settled into the passenger seat, the van's driver—Da'ud—slowly pulled the vehicle out of the driveway. The van turned left and traveled down the narrow street towards Fernandez Juncos Avenue. There it stopped for a moment, and the two passengers stared quietly at the twin infernos—one to their right and the other to their left—spewing huge curls of smoke into the morning sky.

The San Juan Yacht Club—the fire to their left—was the closest, and they noticed that the blaze originated not from one source but from many, some larger than others. Orange flames flickered through the foliage of the tall trees that separated the road from the marina, while scores of abandoned cars lay stranded in the two right lanes that headed towards the Miramar Bridge, jammed between the fire and the concrete barriers that lined the center of the road. A small crowd of no more than two-dozen people watched uneasily the conflagration from a distance, but there were no fire trucks or firefighters trying to control the flames.

To the right of the van, at a greater distance, the second fire blazed. Czecka could not see the burning structure from where he sat, but a thick plume of black smoke billowed high into the sky with no signs of abating. The van turned in that direction and began to move at a very slow speed.

The two lanes heading towards Old San Juan were empty. The few pedestrians that meandered on the sidewalk and among some of the abandoned cars stopped to stare warily at the passing vehicle. Just one block away from where it had entered Fernandez Juncos Avenue, the van passed by a small fire station. About a dozen firemen milled in front of it, chatting excitedly, and casting concerned glances at the two fires. They too stopped talking and stared with distrust at the moving van.

Just then, Czecka heard the repeated blares of a horn. Ahead of them, he saw a red pickup truck approaching them at full speed. A big Puerto Rican flag attached to a long piece of wood had been tied to the driver's doorframe, and flapped cheerfully on the wind. Three people stood on the cargo bay behind the truck's cab, one of them waving a shotgun.

Czecka extended his burly arm to the wheel, and began honking the van's horn.

"Show them your armband," he ordered Da'ud.

The driver raised his left arm, displaying his "Libre como el Coqui" black armband. The pickup truck increased the tempo of its horn, and the people at the back began to jump up and down in celebration. They cheered as they passed the van.

"Who are they? Da'ud asked.

"FEPIstas. Anti-American university students," Czecka replied. "They are keeping a watch over the locals."

"Who is keeping watch over them?" Da'ud said contemptuously. He began to slow down, as the burning building of the police station came into full view.

The entire structure was ablaze. In the parking area in front of the station, several police cars also burned, while at least a dozen dead bodies were strewn on the pavement, some so close to the conflagration that they were starting to smoke. About five men, all dressed identically in black and wearing the "Libre como el Coqui" armbands, looked on from the opposite side of the street. They were all armed with AK-47s and long range rifles.

The fire was so intense that as the van passed the building, Da'ud and Czecka could feel the blistering heat radiating through the window. The Arab whistled through his teeth with a mixture of dread and admiration. "Masha-Allah!" he whispered.

Czecka raised an eyebrow but said nothing. Sensing that his massive companion had not understood his remark, the Arab explained, "Just as Allah willed it."

The men in the street did nothing to stop the van. Not until after the vehicle rolled past the burning building did Da'ud notice that Czecka was holding in his right hand a .45 automatic pistol, which he had apparently pulled out of his holster and placed on his lap with surprising stealth for a man of his size.

They traveled down Fernandez Juncos Avenue for another block, passing to the right the new public housing buildings that were still under construction. Then they turned in that direction, entering a low-income area of mostly seedy-looking, three-story structures that normally seethed with the activity of its overcrowded inhabitants, but that looked eerily deserted that day.

The road rose steeply as it climbed northwards towards the Atlantic shore. Constitution Avenue, a wide, three-lane boulevard that started at the entrance of Old San Juan, also showed no signs of life. Czecka's vehicle cut across it, and continued its northward trek until it reached Luis Muñoz Rivera Avenue, where all the city buildings stopped, and the mighty Atlantic Ocean suddenly opened into view.

Perched atop fifty-foot cliffs, Muñoz Rivera Avenue hugged the northern coast of the island of San Juan past the Luis Muñoz Rivera Park, the twin bell towers of the Puerta de Tierra Church, and the white-marbled, high-domed Capitol Building. There, the cliffs disappeared from view, substituted by a small square where the statue of St John the Baptist—San Juan in Spanish—perpetually stood with an upraised arm, facing the Capitol Building as if scolding the legislature. And then, the plaza gave way to the gigantic, overlapping, and overlaying walls of the Fortress of San Cristobal.

Unlike other older, medieval castles, San Cristobal was not surrounded by one single wall, but by several sets of concentric walls that rose successively higher—and sometimes dropped abruptly—to its tallest, central fortifications. The walls themselves did not follow any particular pattern. Sometimes they protruded outwards at sharp angles, while at other times they receded, creating open, shelter-less areas that could be turned into killing fields for those who dared to attack them. Sometimes the walls would contain gaps that would lead to wide blind alleys— deadly traps where the invaders who wandered into them would be surrounded by defenders on almost every side. An armored concrete bunker and a small lighthouse—the most recent additions to the fortress—crowned the defenses of the fort, resting on its uppermost point. Both had been built by the Americans during World War II.

Like a huge, dormant alligator, the fortress straddled the northeast corner of Old San Juan on top of a hill that dominated the entire city. In its heyday, any army approaching San Juan on land from the east had to overwhelm the giant stronghold in order to get into the city. Its miles of crenellated walls required a substantial garrison to man and defend it, and San Cristobal had been just one in a formidable chain of fortifications that ringed San Juan. The city did not contain enough men to simultaneously man every wall in its massive defense system. Therefore, the Spaniards devised a system to move the troops from one location to another as they were needed, without exposing them to the artillery bombardments that usually supported an invasion; they constructed an underground web of tunnels that connected the two main forts—El Morro and San Cristobal—with each other, as well as with other strategic locations of the city.

Eventually, in the more peaceful times that had followed, those tunnels had been abandoned and sealed, and gradually forgotten. But the rumors of their existence had not escaped San Miguel's attention as he explored San Juan and pieced his master plan together. After he had confirmed their existence, the tunnels had become a central element in his scheme.

Czecka's van drove past the Capitol building and continued towards Old San Juan. To the right, the walls of Fort San Cristobal began to rise until they erased the view of the sea and loomed ominously over the small band of terrorists. Here the road dipped and curved towards the city, and in the middle of the curve, the walls of the fort opened up into a long rectangular space. That space, originally one of San Cristobal's killing fields, had been converted into a parking area where visitors could leave their cars to explore the fort.

The digital clock on the van's radio marked 8:35 AM as Da'ud veered into the allotted area for visiting vehicles. The fort would not open for another half hour. Already three other cars, a Jeep and two Japanese-built sedans, were parked close to the fort's admissions area. The van stopped next to them. Czecka got off the vehicle and hid his gun inside one of his cargo pants pockets. Two more seemingly unarmed men descended from the rear of the van. Together, they walked to the front entrance.

The modern glass door that gave access to the fort was locked and the room beyond it looked empty. Czecka tapped gently several times on the glass, and after a short wait a cute, curly-haired woman dressed in the grayish green attire and wide brimmed hat used by the U.S. National Parks Service rangers came to the door. She pointed at her watch, and then showed the men nine of her fingers, indicating the time when they should come back. Czecka responded by pulling out his .45 and aiming it at her head through the glass.

The woman ran. Czecka uttered a guttural sound—a curse in his native language, probably—raised his leg and kicked the lock of the door. The glass disintegrated into a thousand shiny fragments, allowing the other two men to rush through the opening. Czecka followed quickly behind.

The female ranger had rushed into the adjoining room, where a ramp led up to the admissions desk. She screamed for help, startling the two male rangers who were standing behind the counter drinking coffee. However, before she could reach them, one of Czecka's men tackled her from behind.

Czecka hurtled over the two fallen bodies, and dashed towards the counter. For a big man, he was surprisingly fast and agile. One of the rangers angrily began to ask what was the matter, but the giant intruder leaned over the admissions desk and punched him squarely on the face. The struck man collapsed to the ground like a house of cards.

The other ranger crouched behind the counter and struggled to open a locked drawer, seemingly looking for a gun. However, before he could find it, Czecka leaned over the counter's top, grabbed the man by the collar of his shirt, and lifted him off the ground, flinging him over the admissions desk into the wall at the opposite side of the ramp. The man landed with a sickening thud, and remained motionless.

"Tie up their hands," Czecka growled to his two companions. "Make certain nobody else is here."

Crunching over the broken glass, Czecka walked out to the parking area and signaled the van to approach. Da'ud brought his vehicle's engine back to life, and then backed the van as closely as possible to the fort's entrance.

As the van stopped, Da'ud leaned out of his window and shouted at his associate, "Everything is all right?"

Czecka did not answer. He moved to the rear of the van, and knocked twice sharply. When the door opened, he said, "Be ready," and shut the door. He returned to the admissions room, where his men had rounded up the three rangers and tied their hands behind their backs. The female and the man Czecka had tossed onto the wall were awake, both looking stunned. The ranger he had punched remained stone cold unconscious. Czecka squatted in front of the woman, who stared at the bald, hulking man in utter terror. He plucked a key ring attached to one of her pants' belt tabs, which contained several keys, and showed it to the frightened woman.

"Tell me what each of them is for," he said.

The female ranger regarded the bear-sized man with undisguised horror, but she said nothing. Czecka knotted his thin eyebrows into a scowl. He would have looked comical in other circumstances, but to the bound, helpless woman her captor's unstated anger terrified her.

Czecka grabbed her by her right forearm and turned her around roughly, so that he faced her back. He grabbed one of her bound hands, and took hold of her index finger.

"If you don't answer me," he said, as San Miguel had instructed him to say, "I will break your fingers, one after the other." He felt his prisoner's body shudder and grow tense, and suppressed the urge to smile. Without any further hesitation, the female ranger explained the use of each of her keys. When she had finished, Czecka spun her again by one arm and faced her.

"I will verify the information that you have given me," he said, staring at her dispassionately with his blue eyes, as if considering what to do with a used-up, disposable object. "If you have lied to me, I will break five of your fingers and ask you again."

Ignoring the female captive's loud assurances that she had told him the truth, he stood up and addressed one of his subordinates. "Take them to one of the fort's cells," he ordered.

Like most Spanish military facilities, San Cristobal contained several dungeons. One of the cells, located near the end of a tunnel that descended into the gloomy, windowless bowels of the fort, had become one of the central tourist attractions of the former garrison. It contained wonderfully detailed graffiti of three-mast ships, scratched into its walls by past cell dwellers.

The two conscious rangers were hoisted to their feet, while the third one was heaved by Czecka and placed like a sack of potatoes on the shoulder of one of his men. Both of Czecka's subordinates were big, hefty men, but next to their leader, they seemed scrawny and undersized.

"If you don't find me when you come back, I will be getting the surface-to-air missiles and placing them on top of the castle," he said, speaking more than he had probably spoken at any other given time in his life. It was all part of the script that San Miguel had made him memorize, intended to be heard by his captives. *'We must mislead them',* San Miguel had told him, and forced him to repeat the surface-to-air sentence until it had flowed out of its taciturn speaker's mouth naturally.

Satisfied with its delivery, Czecka turned and returned to the van.

It was time to tend to the real business at hand.

The area directly behind the Puerta de Tierra police station was an open-air dock with the approximate size of a football field. Normally, it was used to store freshly arrived automobiles until they could be distributed to the different car dealers in the island. But that morning, the space contained no vehicles. Instead, eighteen wounded police officers—fourteen men and four women—had been laid out on its pavement, close to the edge of the water, while the fire in the station raged just a block away. They had been placed on empty burlap sacks due to a lack of stretchers, carried there by the other captured policemen who had escaped the massacre with less serious wounds, and by some of the men who had ambushed them.

Under the watchful eye of half a dozen men dressed in black, the healthy captives had been allowed to sit next to their comrades. They had been provided with water bottles and their wounds dressed with makeshift bandages, but not much more. In two severe cases—a man who had been struck by a bullet in his groin and a woman who had lost an eye—the pain had been deadened with shots of morphine, but medical supplies were very scarce, and most field injuries had been treated at best superficially, or not at all.

Colonel Calderon stood among the wounded and the captured policemen, occasionally addressing some of them, at other times scanning the horizon for signs of the approaching government helicopters. He did not fear the men who surrounded him. He knew that whatever fight they had had in them had been crushed by their bloody defeat.

He saw a man kneeling by one of his wounded comrades, trying to give him water from a plastic bottle. However, the man's hands were shaking so badly that he could not manage to place the bottle on his companion's lips. Calderon crouched down and steadied the kneeling man's hand, noticing that the policeman lying on the floor continued to bleed slowly through a bullet orifice in his left thigh. *Hopefully, he will receive proper medical attention soon,* Calderon thought, *before his condition takes a turn for the worse.*

The wounded man gulped the water greedily until the bottle was empty, and then rested his head back on the pavement and closed his eyes.

Calderon stood up and continued to move among the prisoners. After a half dozen paces, he came upon a man sitting on the tarmac, his knees drawn up, his arms embracing them, staring listlessly at the San Antonio Channel. On his shoulders he bore the epaulets of a police captain.

"I'm sorry," Calderon said, squatting next to him. "I wish there could have been some other way."

The captain did not respond. He seemed to be in shock.

Calderon sighed and drew himself back to his feet. *The aftermath of war had never been pretty*, he told himself. But the doubts in his conscience would not be stilled.

Finally, he heard the distant "whop", "whop", "whop" of rotor blades, and confirmed that three helicopters were approaching from the east. Looking through his binoculars, he identified them as a Bell 407 and two Lakota choppers, each capable of carrying from six to eight men. *They would have to make several trips before they could carry everyone away*, he thought.

"Be ready," he warned his men, and calmly began to walk away, turning his back on the three aircrafts.

A few minutes later, the Bell helicopter touched ground, while the other two choppers hovered at a safe distance. Two paramedics dressed in green overalls jumped out of the helicopter, each carrying two collapsible canvas stretchers. Ignoring the guns pointed at them, they quickly evaluated the situation and organized teams of stretcher-bearers to carry the four most critical cases to the waiting aircraft. Then they ushered aboard three of the captives who could still walk, and the helicopter began to rise. At the same time, one of the waiting Lakotas dipped its bow and started to approach the evacuation area.

Calderon felt relieved. He did not have the manpower, the food, or the medical resources to take care of the captured policemen. Had they not been removed, he would have been forced to execute them.

Would he have been able to do it, he wondered? Fortunately, he would not have to find out.

CHAPTER XXIII

Yajaira beamed at Johnny Ray and handed him a large, silver microphone. She looked particularly fetching, her long, red hair undulating in the soft morning breeze, her full, feminine curves highlighted by a red tank top, dangerously tight jeans, and matching red sneakers.

Next to her stood Lebron, a full inch shorter than Yajaira, but nearly twice her girth. He too seemed elated, which slightly befuddled Johnny; the moments when the FEPI Secretary-General and the female Vice-president shared the same mood were scant, and far and in between. In honor of the occasion, Lebron had changed his faded *guayabera* to a more modern, orange-colored version.

Johnny looked at the time, and noticed it was nearly 8:50 in the morning. His broadcast had been scheduled to begin just after the explosions, but setting up the pirate radio equipment had proven to be a much more difficult task than he had imagined.

He, Yajaira, Lebron and the FEPI's top communications expert, a computer and ham radio techie nicknamed "Cerebrito", had been waiting since six-thirty in the morning inside an automobile parked on the open top floor of the Doña Fela parking building. In addition to his technical knowhow, Cerebrito—which literally meant "little brain" in Spanish but was also used as a slang term for being sexually aroused—was famous for lusting after every woman that came within the range of his eyes, as well as for the unusual amount of curly, crinkly light-brown hair that seemed to explode and cascade from every part of his body.

About a half hour into the wait, Lebron had begun to fret about the delay in the start of the operation and to dab his forehead with a handkerchief. Just when his constant complaints—endured with irritated silence by his companions—had threatened to shatter the fragile truce between him and Yajaira, the distant rumble of several explosions had quieted him down. Yajaira had jumped out of the car and trotted—her bouncy gait followed intently by Cerebrito—to the building's railing, leaning on it to see if she could observe any signs of the destruction in the distant horizon. However, she had been unable to see anything out of the ordinary from where she stood. Disappointed, she had walked back to the car.

That had set off Lebron again. The FEPI Secretary-General had begun to question the wisdom of the entire plan and the professionalism and the credentials of its leaders, and had even suggested that maybe it was for the good of their organization if the operation did not happen. As Johnny was about to tell him to shut up, his cell phone had rung, startling everybody. He had listened quietly for a few seconds, shut the phone, and looked dramatically at his expectant companions.

"They have blown up the bridges," he had announced solemnly, the monumental import of the news reflected by the somber amazement of his voice. The other three FEPIstas had kept a stunned silence for a few brief seconds, and then exploded in celebration, Lebron grinning sheepishly while Cerebrito pummeled his back, Yajaira and Johnny exchanging a long and passionate kiss in the front seat.

"Okay, okay guys! We have a lot of work to do," Johnny had breathlessly reminded his friends, pulling away—although reluctantly—from his vice-president. "We have to start alerting the cell leaders so that they can start doing their rounds."

There were a total of forty-eight groups or "cells" that would patrol the streets of Old San Juan and Puerta de Tierra, each composed by three students. They would be working in three eight-hour shifts, so that at any given time only sixteen cells would be officially on duty. Of course, the off-duty students would always be "on call" if needed, and they were encouraged to voluntarily join any of the official patrols, or to conduct further vigilance on their own.

The three FEPI leaders in the car had agreed to each alert five of the first sixteen cell leaders, except for Lebron, who had been assigned six. Their calls had been short; their passwords similar—"Green like the Coqui." In less than five minutes, all of the cells had been dispatched to their assigned areas.

After they had finished, the four university students had exited the car—an old beat up brown Volvo that belonged to Cerebrito—and opened its trunk. They had pulled out two metallic suitcases, one slightly larger than the other, and an elongated nylon bag. The cases contained a sixty-watt portable radio transmitter, electrical extensions, two batteries, and an antenna. If it worked properly, they would be able to broadcast in a VHF band over an area of fifty miles; not enough to cover the entire island of Puerto Rico, but enough to be heard by at least two million in-habitants in the main island. Word of mouth, news reports, and re-broadcasts would do the rest.

However, to spread its message effectively, the pirate radio station needed to be placed on the roof of a tall structure. The two tallest build-ings in Old San Juan were the Metropolitan Center, located in front of City Hall, and the Banco Cosmopolitano, situated next to the docks. They had chosen the latter, knowing that the Venezuelans would place a surface-to-air team on the Metropolitan Center to deal with any aircrafts that approached the city from the south or the east.

For three consecutive Sundays, they had kept the Banco Cosmopolitano building under close observation, becoming familiar with its security rou-tine. Much to their surprise, they had discovered that the bank used only one security guard to keep watch over its facilities—a sign of the difficult economic times—and that the guard spent a great portion of his shift sleeping behind the reception desk of the building's locked lobby. The watchman, probably in his sixties, substituted the night security guard at seven-thirty in the morning. Therefore, Johnny had planned to intercept him as he walked into the building, capture the late shift watchman, and tie up both men. Despite serious misgivings, he had brought the Glock that Emmanuel—San Miguel's associate—had given him in the Calle San Sebastian safehouse. It had helped that Yajaira had expressed how very aroused she felt when she saw him carrying the gun.

The delay in the demolition of the bridges had thrown their plans askew. By the time that the four FEPIstas reached the Banco Cosmopolitano Building, at nearly 8:00 AM, the morning guard had al-ready entered the bank and begun his shift.

They had quickly concocted a new plan, where Yajaira would knock on the lobby's glass door—where the guard usually took his nap—and trick him into opening it. However, the newly arrived watchman was nowhere to be seen. Growing desperate, they had begun to circle the building, searching for an intercom or doorbell they could ring, but could find none. Just as Johnny was considering blasting the lobby door open with a gunshot, the elderly guard had walked into the bank's de-serted atrium, still pulling up his pants' zipper.

The three male students had clumsily hustled behind a wall, and Yajaira had begun to rap urgently on the glass. The guard had looked up sharply, aware for the first time of the stranger knocking outside, and walked wari-ly to the door. His eyes had opened widely as he gazed at the voluptuous woman standing by the entrance. She had smiled prettily at him, and mouthed something incomprehensible. He had asked her to speak more loudly, but her words had come through as an unintelligible mumble. Motioning with a hand to wait, he had fished for his keys inside his pants pocket, and disengaged the lock at the bottom frame of the glass door.

The students had rushed into the lobby, shoving the door and knocking the guard down before he could straighten himself up. In an instant, Johnny Ray and Lebron had pinned him to the ground and dragged him out of sight, while Cerebrito and Yajaira hauled the equipment into the bank. They had bound the guard's hands and feet with rope, and left him behind the reception desk. Depriving him of his keys, they had managed after several tries to get the service elevator working, and taken the equipment to the penthouse. There, they had climbed a set of stairs that led to the open rooftop, and begun to set up the radio transmitter.

They had assembled the thirty-foot antenna that they had carried in the nylon bag in less than fifteen minutes, and secured power for the transmitter with two fifty-foot electrical extension cords that ran down all the way to a 120-volt outlet in the penthouse club lounge. Cerebrito had worked arduously and fast, and by 8:45 AM, the equipment had been up and running. To shelter the microphone from the noise of the wind coming from the bay, the transmitter had been set on a small table inside the stairwell.

Finally, at 8:50 in the morning, everything had been ready. Lebron dialed a private phone number, and an excited *"Hello!"* answered even before the first ring had stopped. The voice belonged to a young female volunteer who sat by a radio in the FEPI headquarters in Rio Piedras. "We're about to broadcast," Lebron informed her. "Let us know if you can hear us. Remember, we're transmitting at 95.5 megahertz."

"I'll be listening!" she responded breathlessly.

Lebron nodded to Cerebrito, who pressed the "play" button of a CD player connected to the transmitter. The tune of *"Verde Luz"*, a beautiful nationalistic ballad about Puerto Rico, began to play:

> *Emerald light from the mountains and the sea,*
> *Virginal Island of the corals,*
> *If I grow absent from your lovely shores,*
> *If I leave your silent palms,*
> *I must return. I must return.*
> *To feel your warm sand,*
> *To sleep on your riverbanks,*
> *My island, captive flower,*
> *For you, I want to return.*
> *With a free sky,*
> *With a single star,*
> *Maiden Island, I want to have,*
> *Emerald light from the mountains and the sea.*

It was a beloved song, one that tugged at the heart of every Puerto Rican, regardless of their political sympathies, and for that reason, it had been chosen to precede Johnny Ray's speech.

"Are you hearing the song?" Lebron whispered into his cell phone to his female associate at the FEPI headquarters, as the music played on. A loud, high-pitched squeal forced him to yank the phone away from his ear. "You're too close to the radio!" he said, grimacing. "You're creating feedback. Move away from the radio!"

The shrill noise quickly subsided, and the female voice said, "*Sorry! I can listen to the song clearly. Verde Luz, right?*"

"Yes! Thank you!" Lebron formed his thumb and index finger into a circle, and showed the okay sign to Johnny Ray, who nodded in return. Cerebrito raised his left hand as he stared at the digital gauge that showed the time left for the song to end, and after a pause began to lower a finger as each of its last five seconds passed. Yajaira took out her I-phone and began to video record the transmission, to circulate it later on Facebook and You-Tube.

Johnny briefly cleared his throat, smiled weakly at Yajaira, and as the last chords of the ballad faded, began to speak. He had not rehearsed his speech, merely jotted some ideas on a used envelope. But now, as the time came to address his country, he felt no need to refer to his notes. His heart had taken over.

"Men and women of Puerto Rico! We speak to you from a small corner in Old San Juan. There is nothing physically remarkable about this spot. It is bare, and windy, and lonely. But nevertheless it *is* remarkable, because it is *free*." Johnny paused briefly, to emphasize the last word.

"For more than one hundred years, our country has been occupied and oppressed by the United States. When in 1898 our island was captured by the Americans and kept as a trophy of the Spanish-American War, we had been granted autonomy—self-rule—by the government of Spain. But our newly found freedom, gained after three hundred years of tyrannical oppression by the Spaniards, was crushed under the military boot of the new world emerging power. Denying the liberties that its founding fathers had fought so hard to attain for themselves, the American Empire turned us into a colony, exploiting our economy, forcing their expensive goods on our markets while denying the entry of cheaper goods from other countries, drafting our young into their foreign war adventures, assaulting our values and culture to implant their own foreign values and ideals. Like ancient conquerors from another era, they marched into our country and took away our choicest lands to build their bases, depriving generations of our people of the use of hundreds of thousands of acres of our patrimony."

Again, Johnny paused briefly. He was in a rhythm now, his words flowing with eloquent deliberation, his growing indignation still kept in check but evident for all to hear.

"Who can forget how the American Navy systematically destroyed and polluted our pristine beaches in Culebras and Vieques, using them for target practice? Who can forget how in the 1950's, their drug manufacturers experimented with the women from our low income families, using them as guinea pigs, giving them birth control pills to see how they would work, without knowing what their side effects would be? And who doesn't remember how Filiberto Ojeda, after being shot and captured, was allowed to bleed to death by the FBI agents who refused to call for medical help? Our list of grievances is great, and continues to grow every day."

Now Johnny raised his voice, his anger showing.

"And what have we received in exchange? What have we acquired, out of this one hundred year...*relationship*? How have we benefitted from this...*association*, this shotgun marriage that our island has been forced to accept with that ugly, bearded man that *they* call Uncle Sam?" he asked with apparent disdain. "We have been given the honor of becoming U.S. citizens! Not Puerto Rican citizens—that we are not allowed to be—but *U.S. citizens*!" he said, his voice now dripping with contempt. "And what a great *honor* that has turned out to be! We have become a nation of second-rate citizens. *They* will let us die in their wars, but we have no representation in Congress. We cannot vote for the President, and we have no senators or representatives to protect our interests. We have no say whatsoever in Washington—except for the puny lobbying of our Resident Commissioner, whose only role in Congress is to grovel for the scraps that the federal government deems to toss out to him from its table! *They* will let us fight in their wars, but we have no control over our destiny. Washington decides our foreign policy; *we* cannot enter into any treaties, even if they would benefit us as a nation. It is *they*, not *us*, who choose who our allies and our enemies will be! *They* will let us fight in their wars, but treat us like foreigners, and discriminate against us, and look down upon us with alarm and distrust, even in our own land. We are despised when we emigrate to their cities, they look upon us as some kind of pest, and they classify us as a separate race, not white, not black, but "latinos", bunching us up with any other Spanish-speaking immigrants that happen to be in their country, no matter where they come from, whether legal or illegal. But of course, when it comes to *their* wars, *they* will let us fight in them."

Johnny Ray stopped briefly. He looked at his companions' faces, and noted by their enthralled expressions that they were moved by his words.

"For more than one hundred years, we have been denied the most fundamental right that we, as a people, are entitled to have. The right for which they fought their own war of independence. *The right to self-government, to self-determination, THE-RIGHT-TO-BE-FREE!*" he stated, stressing each word to its last vowel.

"For too long we have been denied our basic right to be a free nation. For too long we have been set on a path not of our choosing, but chosen for us by a foreign nation that has no legal or moral entitlement over us, no justification to dictate how we, *the people of Puerto Rico*, should run our lives." Johnny raised his voice deliberately, but pondered each word he said, careful that it would not degenerate into a tirade that would alienate his listeners.

"Today we say *ENOUGH!* Today we say *WE WANT OUR FREEDOM!* Our fight for freedom starts here *TODAY!* And to that effect, a group of Puerto Rican patriots has today struck our first blow for freedom by liberating the city of San Juan and declaring the existence of the Republic of Puerto Rico." Yajaira and Lebron burst into spontaneous clapping, but stopped it quickly after Cerebrito signaled to them that their noise was interfering with the broadcast.

"We now have absolute control of Old San Juan and Puerta de Tierra, and we are in the process of establishing a provisional government, until the rest of our country is liberated and elections can be held to establish a legitimate, Puerto Rican government. We wish to avoid any kind of violence, but we will not hesitate to defend ourselves if we are provoked. Right now, hundreds of brave volunteers, men and women alike, are in our streets, ready to resist any aggression that may come from the American Empire. No matter what the enemy will throw at us, we will prevail. Soon, the whole world will find out what is happening here, and many freedom loving countries will rally to our cause."

Johnny stopped briefly, surprised to feel tears rolling down his cheeks. He looked at Yajaira, and saw she was crying too, as was Lebron.

"*Men and women of Puerto Rico!* Today we officially declare our independence from the United States of America, as we are rightfully entitled to do. We have done our part, and will continue to do it as long as we have any breath left in our bodies! We have staked our lives and our fortunes in this enterprise! Now it is up to you to do the rest! *ARISE! ARISE, CHILDREN OF BORINQUEN! NOW IS THE TIME TO FIGHT FOR OUR FREEDOM! STRIKE AT OUR ENEMIES! FIGHT FOR OUR FREEDOM! RALLY TO OUR CAUSE!* March peacefully through our streets and demand our freedom! Boycott the federal government! Let the rest of the world know what is happening here! Together we can shatter the shackles of our oppressors *AND MAKE OUR COUNTRY FREE!*"

Johnny let his plea resonate for several seconds.

"Long live free Puerto Rico!" he said curtly, and signaled Cerebrito to start the music. The nostalgic chords of *Verde Luz* once again took over the broadcast. Yajaira and Lebron walked towards Johnny and embraced him.

"Did you record it?" Johnny asked his techie assistant.

As a response, Cerebrito activated his CD player, and the FEPI president's speech began to play.

"Great! We will replay it all day long, so that more people can listen to it as the word spreads around," Johnny said. He turned to Lebron. "I'm going to do a round through the city, to check on our people. I'll be back by noon and bring back some food. I need you to stay up here with Cerebrito. I will call you every now and then to give you updates on what's happening. Then you can broadcast those updates between the playing of my speech. Okay?"

Lebron looked as if he was about to say something, but thought better of it and nodded resignedly.

Johnny shifted his eyes to Yajaira, who stared back at him adoringly. "Ready? I need to display you to our troops," he said, only half in jest.

"Yes!" she answered enthusiastically, and began to descend the stairs.

Johnny shook hands with Lebron. "And so the adventure begins," he said to him cheerfully, and surprised by his optimism added, "May God help us."

Lebron considered his associate's words for a moment. "I can't rely on the help of God, because there isn't one," the dour Secretary-General answered. Then he flashed an uncharacteristic smile. "But if we pull this one out, I will light a candle in church every day for the rest of my life."

"Let's *go-o-o!*" Yajaira called up impatiently from the bottom of the stairs.

Slapping Lebron's shoulder, Johnny ran downstairs.

They headed east towards the Condado Lagoon, trying to put as much distance as they could between them and the burning police station. Still, the prospect of moving in that direction scared them. The dark gray, nearly black column of smoke churning from the San Juan Yacht Club had begun to spread over the sky like an ugly stain of oil in the sea, and to mingle with the haze from the other fire, covering the sun and casting the day into an unnatural gloom. The acrid smell of burning wood, tires, plastic, and fuel permeated the air, and flecks of light gray ash floated everywhere like tiny snowflakes, in ever increasing numbers. Every so often, they would hear the distant staccato of gunshots, sometimes a lonely discharge, other times two or three bursts, and once a prolonged string of machinegun-like rapid fire. It served to remind them of the need to stay hidden.

Michelle led the tiny band of refugees, zigzagging between the twin lines of driverless vehicles. Her aim was to move away from the black-uniformed gunmen that had destroyed the police station, cross Fernandez Juncos Avenue at a safer spot, and head towards the destroyed bridges. Depending on what they found, she could coordinate a rendezvous with WKPA's helicopter in one of the open spaces close to the Condado Lagoon, and hopefully do a live broadcast using the chopper's camera. Afterwards, the helicopter could fly them to safety, carrying the others across the lagoon, and taking her to the television studios.

Her companions followed her with tight-lipped resignation, Don Moncho walking in a stunned half-daze, the blond babysitter carrying her ward on her back and staring fixedly at the ground, too ashamed to look into the eyes of the others. Even the two-year old child, a bright-eyed girl who had identified herself to Michelle as Katherine Elizabeth Martinez, had settled into an exhausted silence, sucking her thumb and nervously shifting her gaze from one place to another.

About two blocks away from El Falansterio, Michelle signaled for the others to stop.

"Wait here," she said, and stooping behind a red Mercedes 300, she inspected the two empty lanes normally used by the traffic coming from Miramar to San Juan. A line of trees and ornamental bushes and some low fences fringed the opposite sidewalk. It was a convenient place for the small group to cross, offering them a place to hide if anybody approached them. Seeing no one, she took off her high heels and, holding them in her right hand, climbed over the concrete barrier that separated the incoming from the outgoing lanes, and sprinted across the road. She braced herself for the sound of a shot or a shout of alarm, but none ever came.

Reaching the other side, she hid behind a low cement fence that bordered the small parking area of a hardware store. For a full minute she stayed there and waited, listening intently for any type of movement. Then, her heart still pounding, she stood up and called to the others.

Just at that moment, she heard the remote hum of an engine, and in the distance noticed a dirt-colored van turn from a side street into the Fernandez Juncos Avenue and slowly roll in her direction. At the same time, Don Moncho popped up his head from behind the red Mercedes.

"Don Moncho!" she shouted. "Stay where you are! A car is coming!"

The old taxicab driver stared at her as if trying to figure out what she was saying. She motioned with the palms of her hands for him to stay still, and at last Don Moncho understood and nodded, his head disappearing behind the abandoned vehicle.

Michelle studied the approaching van, wondering if she should stop it and seek its passengers' help. However, something about the casual speed at which it traveled, seemingly unconcerned about the raging fires behind and in front of it, warned her to remain behind the fence.

A horn suddenly began to blare from the opposite direction, making her heart jump. Turning her head, she observed a red pickup truck with a large Puerto Rican flag moving at a fast clip down one of the deserted lanes. Three young men stood at the rear, holding on to the roof of the truck's cab. They seemed to be celebrating, one of them brandishing a rifle of some sort.

The van—a rust-colored beat up contraption that appeared to have escaped from the city dump—answered back with its own barrage beeps. A few moments later both vehicles whizzed past each other, exchanging friendly waves, hollers and cheers. A huge, dour looking bald man glared out of the van's open passenger window in Michelle's direction but did not see her. To her great relief, the two vehicles continued traveling towards their opposite destinations, the sound of their horns distorted as they increased the distance between them.

Michelle slowly stood up, realizing for the first time that she was still holding in her hand her high heels. She smiled, feeling foolish, and prepared to call the rest of her companions, when a male voice behind her startled her out of her wits.

"Well, well, well! What have we here?" it said in a happily surprised tone.

Michelle's heart sank. About a dozen yards away stood two men, each armed with a rifle. One, the tallest of the two by half a head, seemed to have walked out of a Cuban guerrilla movie, sporting a black beret, a heavy black beard, and long hair. He wore a U.S. military shirt, and olive colored pants that were tucked into a pair of black combat boots. A large dagger was strapped to his left ankle, while a gun without a holster was fitted into his belt.

The second stranger was a heavyset man with thick, hairy arms and short, muscular legs. Although shaven, his facial hair reflected the dark shadow of a heavy beard. His hair was partially hidden by a cap that read "American Idol", cascading from the sides in oily dark brown curls. He wore a white T-shirt a size too small that stretched over his barrel-like chest and accentuated industrial-sized love handles. Like his partner, he carried a gun and a combat knife, except that both were attached to his belt, semi-embedded in his right love handle. The two men wore black armbands that read "Libre como el Coqui" on their left arms.

These were not some of the soldier-like, black-uniformed gunmen that had just attacked the police station, nor were they some of the noisy youths she had just seen on the back of the pickup truck, Michelle realized, feeling very scared and trying not to show it. These were killers; hardened, dangerous men. She had met their kind before, when interviewing several convicted murderers in the Bayamon state prison for a television special. Men with "dead souls", she called them, men who could terminate or cripple a life with the same ease that they could flick off a light switch.

And now, two of them were standing before her, staring at her like two wolves eyeing a baby lamb.

"Why were you hiding?" asked the shorter, broader man, grinning widely and revealing a gap between his upper front teeth.

"I was afraid," she responded with as much firmness as she could muster. "I don't know what's happening today. The world has gone crazy—"

"She's sexy!" the taller man said, interrupting her. "Isn't she sexy, Adrian?" he asked his companion.

"Of course she is!" the shorter, barrel-chested gunman answered, slowly moving to her right, while his bearded counterpart followed his lead and moved to her left. "Don't you recognize her?"

"Recognize her?" the other man repeated with newfound curiosity, squinting in her direction.

Adrian shook his head with exasperation as he slowly continued to reduce the distance between him and the object of his attention. "That's Michelle...Michelle...Alfaro! Michelle Alfaro, the reporter from TV! That's you, isn't it?" he asked, ogling at her with undisguised lust. "I must apologize for him, he's a little slow," he explained, widening even more his grin. "Mean, but slow. That's why we call him 'Croma', short for 'Cromagnon'."

"She took off her shoes!" Croma said, ignoring what his companion had said. Obviously, he had no idea who Michelle Alfaro was, and did not really care. "I like her, she's sexy."

"Yeah, why did you take off your shoes?" the short gunman asked, ever edging closer to Michelle.

"Maybe she was taking all of her clothes off," Croma suggested, leering at her.

Adrian laughed.

"I was resting my feet," Michelle said, with a slight tremor in her voice, her mind racing at a hundred miles an hour. She knew the two men would come after her. Urged to do so by Correcaminos, she had taken a few personal defense lessons some months before, but that would be useless against two men. She carried a pepper spray in her purse, but she had left the purse by the cement fence behind which she had been hiding, and she knew that if she tried to retrieve it they would stop her.

"We need some rest ourselves," Adrian said. "We just ambushed a police car that was heading to the police station. We creamed them! We filled that car with so many holes that it looked like Swiss cheese!"

Croma began to giggle, amused by his partner's description.

"I think we've earned a rest break, don't you think so, Croma?" The squat American Idol fan cast a malevolent look at his friend, then returned his attention to Michelle. "Have you ever made it with a television celebrity?"

"I don't know," Croma answered laughing. "I never ask the women I have sex with what they do for a living."

Michelle realized that her only opportunity to escape would be to look helpless and frightened, and bide her time until she could reach her purse. It would not be necessary to pretend, since she was shaking badly despite herself.

"Please don't hurt me," she pleaded, her voice trembling.

"That entirely depends on you," Adrian answered, slipping his rifle's cartridge belt over his head, and turning to Croma. "I'll go first," he said, tossing his weapon at his companion, who let go his rifle to grab it.

It was the moment that Michelle had waited. Taking advantage of their momentary distraction, she turned and sprinted towards her purse. She snatched it and kept running, dashing towards the stalled cars, away from where the rest of her group lay hidden. She was a strong jogger, and hoped that with her head start she could outdistance the heavier, swarthier man, while his companion struggled with the rifle that he had been thrown. She heard Adrian shout, heard his labored breathing and his receding footsteps behind her, and knew that she would outrun him. Elated, she looked back and saw that the gap between them had already widened by about thirty feet. And then she tripped.

Had she been looking forward, she would have seen the stray dog dart out from a narrow opening between two of the concrete barriers that divided the road. Even so, it would have been extremely difficult to avoid it. The dog, a typical tan-colored mongrel, tangled between her legs and yelped, causing her to lose her balance. She fell hard on the pavement, scraping her hands and her knees. She cursed herself for being so stupid, and managed to get back on her feet, but by then Adrian had caught her.

He tackled her, falling on her with his full weight and pinning her to the ground. For a terrifying moment she tried to breathe but could not. Then air began to flow into her lungs. She tried to move, but her attacker held her by her wrists, and sat on her waist. He leaned his face towards hers, and smelled her so closely she could feel his breath.

"Just as I thought," he said, flashing her a grin. "You smell so sweet!"

He brought his face closer to hers and licked her on one cheek, while she shook her head trying to evade him. Laughing, he straightened up and released her left hand, grabbing her skirt and pulling it up. Panicked, she screamed and tried to scratch his eyes, but he avoided her easily. With deliberate slowness, he raised his hand and slapped her twice hard across the face. A thousand stars exploded inside her head and she nearly lost consciousness. As her sight failed her, her other senses seemed to sharpen. She could feel the heat of the road on her back and smell his sweat while he struggled to slide his hand up her thigh. In the distance, she heard someone—Don Moncho, she thought—shout angrily, followed by a grunt and the laughter of the other man.

"No!" she groaned, as he tried to kiss her once more. She pounded his back with her fist with little effect, and he slapped her again.

"Hurry up!" she heard Croma say in an amused, excited tone.

She felt her attacker's beefy fingers grab her panties and pull them down, and in her revulsion she screamed and tried to wriggle free from under him, stretching her free arm to push herself up. She could not, but her hand dropped on a curved, pointy object that she did not recognize immediately. Then she realized it was one of her high-heeled shoes.

She looked up and gazed at her tormentor, who continued to grin at her and made obscene flickering movements with his tongue. A strange calm overtook her as her brain instinctively grasped what she had to do. Time seemed to crawl down to a near dead stop, where she could distinctively feel every beat of her heart. Her outstretched fingers wrapped around the leather sole of her shoe, and her lips pressed into a thin, angry smile, momentarily causing Adrian to pause and stare at her with curiosity. Then she plunged the heel of her shoe into his right eye.

The man wailed with pain, groping at the eye with both hands, and rolling on the ground in agony. A few yards away, she heard Croma shout with anger and surprise. Shakily, she tried to sit up, but before she could manage it, the bearded gunman had grabbed her by the collar of her dress and begun to shake her.

"You treacherous bitch!" he screamed at her over Adrian's shrieks of pain, shaking her so hard that her teeth rattled. "Look at what you did to Adrian! You took his eye out, you bitch! Oh man, you're going to pay!"

Michelle began to black out, and knew if she was to survive she would have to stop her assailant then. She swung at his kneecap weakly with her bloodied heel but missed it completely. He grabbed her by the throat and started to choke her, making her gasp for air. Desperately, she tried to clear her head and to think about what she had learned in her personal defense class. Her mind replayed images of the television report where she had discussed the need for women to learn how to protect themselves from rapists.

But it was already too late. She could not think. Her strength had left her. She could barely raise her hands.

Suddenly she heard a "c-r-a-c-k", like a large stick breaking, and the grip around her neck instantly relaxed. Croma's body collapsed next to her, and she began to cough violently, urgently trying to breathe. A shadow covered her face as someone leaned over her and placed an arm behind her head, gently pulling her up.

"Are you all right?" a man she had never seen before asked her. He was young, probably in his late twenties or early thirties, and had reddest head of hair she had ever seen on a human being.

"Look out, look out!" another man shouted. Two shots followed, and Adrian's screams stopped.

Michelle tried to talk, but could only manage a groan. She began to sob disconsolately, and the redheaded man cradled her against his chest.

"It's okay. It's okay," he said gently. "You're safe now."

Another man, dressed in a khaki uniform, rushed next to them.

"We have to hide the bodies and go!" he said in an agitated voice. "Those shots may bring others!"

"Let's get her and the old man out of the road first," the redheaded man replied. The uniformed man nodded and disappeared.

"Can you walk?" he asked Michelle. She stopped crying and nodded, still coughing.

"There's a woman with a little girl..." she managed to say in a hoarse voice. Part of her upper lip felt numb. She touched it and winced from the pain.

"We have them," her rescuer said reassuringly. "Come on, I'll help you up."

For the first time, she noticed the body of Croma lying next to her.

"I think I broke his neck," the redheaded man confessed, as he assisted her to get up. "I hit him on the back of the neck with the butt of his rifle," he explained.

A few yards away he saw the uniformed man—a policeman, she thought—guiding Don Moncho towards the abandoned automobiles. Much closer, the body of Adrian lay in a pool of blood. In one of his hands he held a gun, while the other still clutched his right eye socket. She shuddered involuntarily as, aided by the redheaded stranger, she walked past him.

Michelle's rescuer guided her to a spot behind the cars, close to the Army Corps of Engineers building. There was no sign of the blond babysitter, or of Katherine Elizabeth. The man in the khaki uniform had returned to the street and, after making certain that no one was watching, had begun to drag Croma into the line of cars.

"Where are the others?" she asked.

"They're right over there," the redheaded man answered, pointing to some bushes about one hundred feet away. "Don't worry. I'll be right back," he promised, and rushed to help his companion.

"My purse!" Michelle called after him. When he stopped, she said, "If you see my purse, could you please bring it back? It has my cell phone."

He nodded and left. She watched him move away for a few seconds, and then she headed towards the bushes where her other friends hid.

CHAPTER XXIV

The Command Center in the San Geronimo Plaza Hotel was up and running by 9:30 AM. Several computers, as well as a telephone callboard and two wide screen television sets were installed in the Salon Carnaval, one of the large ballrooms of the hotel. About a dozen police personnel were busy setting up more equipment, and more were pouring in. Their numbers, in fact, would swell to about fifty, as the police intended to set up several lines to receive calls from anyone—particularly those on the other side of the lagoon—who could provide them with any kind of information about the terrorists. One of the hotel's underground parking floors had been emptied to make room for the police vehicles entering or leaving the area, and most tourists in the hotel—particularly those on the side of the San Geronimo Plaza that faced the Grand Laguna Hotel across the lagoon—had been evacuated to other, more distant resorts. Already, a SWAT team had set up positions on the roof of the Plaza, from where the Grand Laguna could be seen about two hundred yards away.

The press had been given limited access to the hotel, and allowed to set up their equipment in the lobby facing the Atlantic Ocean. Their broadcasting vans lined both sides of Ashford Avenue, the road that led past the hotel to the severed Dos Hermanos Bridge. Shielded by the San Geronimo Plaza from any possible snipers in the Grand Laguna Hotel, Ashford Avenue had been deemed safe enough to accommodate non-official vehicles.

Being an old hand at dealing with the press in emergency situations, Police Superintendent Maldonado had paused briefly to address the awaiting media before he walked into the Command Center. He had confirmed that the police station in Puerta de Tierra had been attacked and captured, admitting that he had acquired most of his information from the radio and television broadcasts, and alluding specifically to

Michelle Alfaro's live telephone report during the assault to the station. When asked who was behind the attacks, he had answered that he did not have enough concrete facts yet to make a determination. He promised to give periodic conferences in the lobby, starting with an extended situation report at 11:00 AM. Most important of all, he failed to mention his contact with Angel San Miguel. Refusing to speculate or answer any more questions, he had continued to the Command Center.

There, he met with the Fire Chief and with the head of the Civil Defense—both of who had arrived at the Command Center a few minutes after him—and briefed them fully about the situation in San Juan. The Fire Chief, a grizzled veteran named Francisco Oronoz, had listened quietly as Maldonado repeated his telephone conversation with San Miguel, and then burst into a string of expletives warning the Superintendent about the dangers of letting the fires burn unchecked. Maldonado had promised to bring up the subject again at the scheduled ten-thirty telephone conference with San Miguel, and to try to secure an agreement to allow the San Juan firemen to do their job. After the briefing, the two visiting agency chiefs had withdrawn with their respective staffs to separate areas in the ballroom to set up their own communication centers and to coordinate the further mobilization of their departments.

During the past hour, the Superintendent had tried to determine what police assets still remained in the island of San Juan and, if possible, how they could be consolidated and put to their best use. Of the six state police cars patrolling the old city at the time of the explosions, one had been ambushed as it rushed towards the Puerta de Tierra Station. The radio operators in the Police Communications Center in the Hato Rey headquarters had listened with impotent horror as the patrol's passengers were massacred, and then all contact had been lost. The other five police vehicles had been ordered to protect the Sheraton and the El Convento hotels in Old San Juan, and to fire upon any unidentified persons attempting to enter the hotels with any type of weapons. Maldonado had tried to communicate with the municipal police station, but to no avail. Unless some contact was established in the near future, he had to assume that he could not count on the organized help of the municipal police.

Even before getting to the San Geronimo Plaza, the Superintendent had managed to reach over the phone from his car the mayor of San Juan, Samuel Padilla, and briefed him fully about what he knew up to that time. The mayor, who lived in the outskirts of the city, had not been trapped in the island of San Juan. A long time critic of the Police Superintendent and supporter of former Governor Alarcon, Padilla had been very noncommittal, thanking Maldonado tersely and telling him that he would be setting up his own municipal emergency task force in Hato Rey. Just as tersely, Maldonado had promised to keep him abreast of any new information that he acquired. He expected to see Padilla on TV or in a press conference at any moment now, blasting him for his incompetence.

He had also managed to reach Special Agent in Charge Mario Franceschini, the head of the F.B.I. in Puerto Rico and the Virgin Islands. A contemporary of Maldonado, Franceschini was a Puerto Rican who had risen through the federal agency's ranks on his own merits and talent, and who had recently been appointed to head the local agency after the death of the Machetero's former leader, Filiberto Ojeda. Intelligent, quiet, and highly efficient, Franceschini had established an excellent working relationship with the local police and a personal friendship with Maldonado. Their conversation over the present crisis had been direct and to the point. Franceschini had pledged the full support of the F.B.I., and promised to contact Washington to request additional resources.

It had been Franceschini who had alerted Maldonado about an unlicensed radio manifesto being broadcast by a self-denominated group of "Puerto Rican patriots" who claimed credit for the destruction of the bridges and declared the existence of the "Republic of Puerto Rico". The broadcast was being repeated over and over again, and already several news sources had picked up on it and even replayed it through some of their own stations.

All police leaves and vacations had been cancelled, and because of the call for insurrection made by the terrorists on the radio, all security forces had been placed on high alert. So far, no violent acts had been reported in the main island, although there had been a few protests. But Maldonado knew that that could change at any moment.

Now, nearly forty-five minutes after his arrival to the San Geronimo Plaza, Maldonado paced impatiently inside of the commandeered ballroom, sipping from his third cup of coffee, as he waited for the 10:30 AM call scheduled by the terrorists. Contrary to what many of his detractors suggested, it was not true that the tall, somewhat portly Superintendent was an alcoholic. He was no stranger to liquor, but never drank during work hours, and on his free time he limited his intake to one or two glasses of scotch when the occasion arose. He was, however, addicted to coffee; drank it constantly, particularly during tense situations, and nowadays almost everything in his line of work qualified as a tense situation.

Colonel Montañez walked into the ballroom and stopped at its entrance, surveying the enormous hall. Illuminated by two, huge crystal chandeliers that bathed everyone in a subdued, yellowish light, the almost hangar-sized room cast the entire operation in a surreal, theatre-like atmosphere. Maldonado would have preferred a much smaller facility, but the Salon

Carnaval was immediately available and closest to the area of conflict. Besides, the hotel had allowed the police to use it for free.

Montañez located his boss, waved at him, and walked briskly in his direction.

"I have bad news and I have bad news," he said, trying to sound cheerful and failing miserably.

Maldonado sighed with resignation, and sipped more of his coffee.

"Just tell me," he mumbled miserably.

"The Secretary of State is next in succession, when the Governor cannot perform his duties."

"Arizmendi?" Maldonado said. Unlike others in the Cabinet, he had never referred to the Secretary of State as "Double A". Although not the best of friends, the two maintained a cordial if distant relationship, recognizing each other's talents and trying to keep out of each other's way. "He's a good man."

"He's also in La Fortaleza with the Governor. We just got hold of his wife, who was at a morning mass. She says he was spending the night there, helping the Governor prepare for his State of the Island address."

Maldonado winced, whether from the news or from the taste of the coffee, Montañez could not tell. "Damn. So who's next?"

Montañez maintained an ominous silence.

"Oh no..." the Superintendent said to himself, genuinely concerned, "not the Secretary of Justice, Rovira Melendez?"

"The one and the same," Montañez confirmed. "He could hardly hide his excitement when he found out that he was the next man in line. He said he would be here in half an hour, so that you could brief him personally on what has happened..." The colonel hesitated.

"And what else?" Maldonado inquired with a growing sense of doom.

"He told me that he plans to hold a press conference after he talks to you, to reassure the people."

"Great. That's just what we need."

There had been bad blood between Maldonado and Rovira Melendez from the first day they had met. During former Governor Alarcon's election campaign, Rovira had been one of Maldonado's greatest critics, accusing him of corruption, habitual drunkenness, and womanizing. Maldonado had refused to engage him, continuing to serve in his post until Governor Alarcon had taken over and demanded his resignation.

"He asked me for a four-motorcycle escort for his trip from his home to the hotel," Montañez added, smirking. "Initially he requested a helicopter, but I told him they were all busy evacuating the wounded from the police station. I provided the escort, of course."

"You did the right thing. We must protect the life of the Governor in these difficult times," Maldonado said so matter-of-factly that Montañez could not tell if he was being sarcastic. He looked at his watch. Five past ten. He would soon be talking to the terrorists. Hopefully, Rovira Melendez would get to the hotel after the conversation had taken place.

As if reading his thoughts, Montañez added, "We're taking him the long way...As you say, for his own protection."

That forced Maldonado to smile for the first time during that terrible day. Matters seemed to be going from bad to worse. The telephone report by Michelle Alfaro about the police massacre had shaken the entire police force. He could see it in the faces of the men and women working in the Command Center. The public did not know about the Governor's capture yet, or about the *Mardi Gras* or the Grand Laguna Hotel, but the television channels were continuously broadcasting scenes of the fires raging across the lagoon and of the destroyed bridges, as well as of the quarantined Convention Center, and speculating about the cause behind these events and the apparent absence of firefighters. The press was not stupid. He had forbidden, for security reasons, the use of helicopters to fly over the demolished bridges. But sooner rather than later, one or more of the news organizations would piece all the events together and reach their own conclusions, if they had not done so already.

Hoping to gain some time, Maldonado had instructed the Department's press secretary, Maria Noriega, to give a second briefing to the mounting number of reporters in the lobby. He had purposefully kept her in the dark about his conversation with San Miguel, so that she would sound as ignorant of the facts as she was supposed to be. Her instructions had been simple: to acknowledge the destruction of the bridges by means of unknown explosives and the fire caused by the explosions in the San Juan Yacht Club, to confirm the attack on the police station without any reference to the number and nature of the casualties suffered, and to repeat that the "authorities" were still trying to determine the extent of and the reasons for the attack. If asked about the Governor, she was to answer that she was not aware of any response yet from La Fortaleza. She had also been instructed to promise a full press conference at 11:00 AM, and not to answer any further questions at that time because her answers would amount to "pure speculation". She had returned flustered but alive, and given him a "thumbs up", "mission accomplished" signal.

Maldonado finished his coffee and discarded his paper cup in the trash. He examined his watch, noting it was almost 10:20 AM.

"Ten more minutes for the call," Montañez announced, after glancing at his own watch. "Should we get ready?"

Maldonado nodded, and both men began to walk towards the ballroom's exit.

As San Miguel had suggested, the telephone line between the Grand Laguna security office and the police had been kept open. It had been a good idea. Already, the phone lines and cell phone channels were experiencing serious delays from the hundreds of thousands of calls by people who had awakened to the news of the destruction of the bridges, and who were concerned about their friends or families in San Juan, or just wanted to talk about it.

A female staffer had been set up in one of the administrative offices located next to the Salon Carnaval to constantly listen for any stray conversations by the terrorists in the hotel that could be picked up over the line, and to hail Maldonado in case that the terrorists decided to talk ahead of the scheduled time. The call was also being recorded, and had been "conferenced" with audio experts stationed in the Hato Rey police headquarters, so that any sound coming from the connected call could be amplified and analyzed.

Maldonado stopped by the two policemen standing by the entrance of the private office, and greeted them by their names.

"If Rovira Melendez should wander into this corridor while we're inside," he told them, "usher him into the Command Center and tell him to wait for me there. Under no circumstances let him know where we are, is that understood?"

The two guards nodded, grinning conspiratorially.

The female attendant—a plump brunette with a round, friendly face and hair stretched and tied into a short bun—stood up as soon as the two men entered the office. The temperature in the room was bone chillingly cold, and she was wearing a blue police jacket.

Maldonado signaled her to place her hand over the receiver of the telephone, and then asked her in a low voice, "Anything yet, Yomaris?"

She shook her head.

"No noises, no conversations, anything?"

"No, sir," she responded. "I couldn't hear a thing on the other side. If I didn't know any better, I would have said that they had hung up."

Maldonado looked at his watch again. "Well, we'll find out soon, won't we? Less than five minutes to talk." He extended his right hand, motioning her to give him the telephone receiver. "Take a break," he told her. "There's coffee and pastries in the Command Center."

Yomaris thanked him and left. Maldonado sat on the edge of the desk where the telephone had been placed, and covering its mouthpiece, placed the receiver on his right ear. As Yomaris had indicated, he could hear nothing; not the mechanical noise of any equipment, or the shifting of chairs, or the squeak of an opening door.

"Do you believe in God?" he asked Montañez while they waited.

His friend looked up in surprise. "Yes," he replied. "And you?"

Maldonado took his time to answer. "Sometimes," he said at last. "There have been some times...some situations, where I don't think I would have been able to escape with my life without His direct intervention. But there are other times..."

"Like now?" Montañez suggested, raising one of his eyebrows.

Maldonado considered the question, taking a long time to reply. "I don't know yet," he answered finally.

The two men stopped talking, waiting for the connection to come to life. When it did, no noise preceded it. The man at the other end of the line just cleared his throat and began to talk, as if he had been sitting all along at the other end of the line.

"Superintendent Maldonado?" the terrorist suddenly said.

"This is he," Maldonado stated flatly. He pressed the speakerphone button on the telephone equipment, so that Montañez could listen.

"This is San Miguel. Thank you for answering so promptly," the man had said in a businesslike tone. Expecting the Superintendent not to answer, he continued. *"I will list my demands now. If you need to write them down, or think that I am going too fast, let me know, and I will repeat them."* The voice chortled. *"Although I'm certain that you are recording all of this, right?"*

"Just go ahead," Maldonado answered impatiently.

"Just go ahead."

San Miguel detected a trace of anger in the Superintendent's voice, and smiled at Daniel and George. The three men were lounging on high backed black leather chairs that bordered a round oak table in one of the conference rooms of the Grand Laguna Hotel's business center. The room was separated from the reception area by a glass, soundproof wall, next to which a man with an AK-47 rifle made certain that no one interrupted the ongoing telephone conversation.

San Miguel leaned closer to the speakerphone on the table. "Before listing our demands, I must remind you about our ground rules. First, no interruptions. I will state what we require of you, and you will listen. Secondly, no negotiations. We are not here to haggle. Either you comply with our demands, or you face the consequences for failing to do so. Understood?"

Maldonado did not answer. San Miguel could imagine him, listening somewhere in the San Geronimo Plaza—he had watched the television broadcasts and press conferences held at the hotel and knew he was there—grasping the telephone receiver with white-knuckled intensity, struggling to remain calm and not say something rash. From his seat, George opened his eyes widely and chuckled, covering his mouth to avoid being heard. Daniel remained motionless, his knees resting on the edge of the table, his eyes staring at the ceiling.

"I will take your silence to mean yes," San Miguel said gently, as if addressing a friend. "So, on to the demands. First: you will release Adalberto Cacho from the federal prison in Bayamon and fly him here in a helicopter."

"Cacho, the Machetero leader? You know that I have no jurisdiction over federal—" Maldonado began to protest, but San Miguel cut him off.

"Please, don't break our rules of engagement so quickly! I said no interruptions," he snapped back sharply. He waited, and when Maldonado failed to reply, continued in a more patient voice. "I know that you do not have jurisdiction over federal prisoners, and that the Americans can make life tough for you, so I'll give you the proper tools so that they will listen to you. Convey this message to the federal authorities. We now hold captive...give or take...about...over two thousand tourists here. If Cacho is not released and delivered to the Grand Laguna Hotel by...let's see..." San Miguel made a pause, as if looking at his watch, "by 2:00 PM today, we will begin to throw a tourist from the roof of the hotel every hour."

San Miguel stopped, waiting for a reaction, and heard Maldonado say, *"May God find the way to forgive you."*

"God, in His everlasting mercy, has given you and the Americans a way to avoid any executions," San Miguel answered in a disarmingly benign tone. Daniel grinned without taking his eyes off the ceiling. "If anybody dies, it will fall on your heads, not ours."

Again San Miguel waited, but Maldonado chose not to speak. *Wise man*, San Miguel thought. *No wonder so many people thought so highly of him. He would not underestimate him.*

"Secondly, none of the authorities, local or federal, will attempt to cross, fly into, land, swim to, or overfly the island of San Juan, or attack any of our freedom forces. Any violation of this condition will be met with violent force, and will result in more tourists being thrown off the roof of the Grand Laguna Hotel." San Miguel paused momentarily, and then said, "Are you with me so far? Do you need more time to write this down?"

"You know I don't," Maldonado retorted. *"Keep talking."*

"In order to conduct our fight for liberation, we have incurred in significant financial obligations that we need to repay. By the same deadline, you will transfer one hundred million dollars to the overseas bank account that I will give to you in our next conversation."

San Miguel heard Maldonado laugh bitterly, and smiled. He liked the man.

"I thought you were a bunch of freedom fighter idealists!" the Superintendent retorted. *"I guess you're freedom fighters that like to live well."*

"Freedom these days does not come cheap," San Miguel said pleasantly. "One hundred million dollars is within the means of your American friends, and they will pay it when their citizens start dropping from the roof of the Grand Laguna like ripe fruit."

Another silence ensued. San Miguel could almost hear Maldonado thinking. The Superintendent probably considered the terrorists' demands naïve; he would know that the United States would storm the hotel if its guests began to be killed. But to his credit, the police chief made no comment.

"Anything else?" Maldonado asked with a trace of irony in his voice.

"That's it...for the moment," San Miguel replied. "You have to agree these are very straightforward demands, don't you?"

"What do we get in return?" Maldonado asked, ignoring the last question.

San Miguel smiled. "What do you get in return?" he repeated. "What ever do you mean?" he asked innocently.

"If we comply with your demands, will you let your hostages go?" Maldonado went straight to the point.

"Which hostages, the ones in the Grand Laguna Hotel? Those in the *Mardi Gras*? Or are you referring to the Governor and his family?"

George chuckled again, while Daniel listened with his eyes closed.

"You know very well I'm referring to all of them," Maldonado answered, barely able to hold his anger in check.

"Well, to answer your question, in return for our demands, our hostages will stay alive. Depending on how events unfold we may release some or all of them in the near future, but that is solely at our discretion."

"That won't work, and unless you're very stupid, you know it," Maldonado insisted stubbornly. *"Listen to me—"*

"Like I said before," San Miguel interrupted, "it's all up to you. I'm not here to negotiate, just to tell you what our demands are. I think that you understand them, so there is nothing further to talk about. I suggest you continue to keep this channel of communication open. If you agree to our demands, simply talk into it. Someone will answer."

"We need to talk about the Governor—"

"All in due time, Mr. Superintendent. When our demands are met. For the moment, this conversation is finished."

San Miguel hit the "pause" button on the speakerphone, which effectively silenced their end of the line while allowing them to listen to any noises at the other end. He signaled to his two companions to follow him, and they exited the conference room, closing the door behind them. "Martin," he said to the armed man in the reception area, "please stay in the conference room, and let me know if I get any calls."

"Yes, sir."

The three men headed back to the hotel lobby.

"That went well," San Miguel commented as they walked. "Do you think I've provoked them enough so that they will attack us?"

"I would if I were them, boss," George said. "There's no way they can comply with our terms. I predict that they will try something before the end of the day."

"Let's hope they don't try it too soon. Remember, the earliest we can rendezvous with our transportation out of here is tonight at midnight," San Miguel said. He looked at Daniel, who seemed engrossed in his own thoughts. "You seem very quiet," he said to him.

"I was wondering..." he answered with a hint of hesitation. "That mole in the police station...our contact..."

San Miguel cast a sharp look at his second-in-command, warning him not to mention his code name. Daniel nodded slightly, understanding.

"Yes, the police mole. What about him?" San Miguel inquired guardedly.

"You said that he was a very high ranking officer of the force...and that when you met with him, you never saw his face."

"That's right," San Miguel replied, guessing where Daniel was heading.

"Do you think—"

"That the Superintendent may be the mole?" San Miguel finished the sentence for his companion. "I suppose it's possible," he said, answering his own question. "Unlikely—his voice did not sound like the one I heard at the meeting, although it was electronically distorted at the time—but possible. That would be something, wouldn't it? That the chief of the Puerto Rican state police has been bought off by the Colombian cartels? If he is the mole, he must be walking a very tight rope."

"Just as we are," Daniel reflected, directing a pointed look at San Miguel. "If our partners found out what we are doing..."

"Which reminds me, have we heard from Czecka yet?" San Miguel asked, shifting the conversation on purpose.

"No," Daniel answered. "But it's too early. I expect to hear from him in about another hour."

"Do you want me to check up on him, boss?" George volunteered. "I know my way around that fort."

"No," San Miguel replied. "Czecka can take care of himself. Besides, its time you got to La Fortaleza and looked after the Governor. I'll be going there now, so I can drop you off and at the same time check how things are going with Andrade, Johnny Ray, and Calderon."

"Right, boss," George answered brightly.

San Miguel turned to his other associate.

"I want you to also come with me, Daniel. We should be back here long before the two o'clock deadline. If Maldonado tries to reach me, I have left instructions with Martin to call me, and I'll talk to him through my satellite phone. Emmanuel will be in command of the hotel while we're away. If we're delayed, he knows what to do."

The three men reached the lobby of the hotel and found it eerily calm. Two men patrolled the reception area, while about a dozen slept on the lobby's couches, under the Chihuly chandeliers. Two others sat at the lower level bar, chatting quietly and sipping what seemed to be soda; drinking liquor had been strictly forbidden, and the order was being obeyed—for the moment. San Miguel did not recognize any of the men—they were Macheteros—but they wore their "Libre como el Coqui" armbands, and they knew who he was.

It had not been that calm just three hours before. The fire alarm had been activated, to prompt the hotel guests to abandon their rooms and descend to the lobby. They had come down in droves, through the stairwells and the elevators, some half dressed or in pajamas, and been intercepted by the armed men who now slept in the reception area. There had been surprisingly little violence as the scared tourists had been rounded up and deprived of their valuables and cell phones: a couple of scuffles by indignant, irate high-paying patrons who could not believe that a first class hotel would allow such type of treatment to its guests, and one death, an apparent heart attack from a flustered lady in her eighties. Some of the resort's personnel had fled when it realized what was happening, but a great portion of the employees had been captured or had volunteered to stay to help the guests.

About six men had been detailed to hunt for stragglers on a floor-by-floor basis, a daunting task that would take them the rest of the day to complete. So far, the search had yielded about two-dozen captives, many of whom had slept through the fire alarm.

Hundreds of frightened and angry men, women, and children, and scores of staff members, had been herded into the hotel's huge main ballroom. There, the real work had begun. The detainees had to be organized into more manageable groups who at different times would be fed or escorted to the restrooms, and at times help the captured staff members serve the food or clean up the holding areas, as the need arose. Emmanuel, the man who had run the San Sebastian safehouse during the past two months, had been designated to give some semblance of order to the hostage logistical nightmare. Fortunately, the situation would not last for long.

San Miguel moved towards one of the men patrolling the lobby, a small, frail looking young man garbed in green fatigues and sporting a D'artagnane-Dali-esque thin mustache and a pointed beard, who seemed incapable of harming a fly. Dozens of cars had been parked bumper to bumper along the entire border of the passengers' unloading area, to create a barrier behind which the hijackers could defend against a surprise land attack. The young Machetero maintained a watch over the approach to the hotel, making certain that any new arrivals wore the identifying armbands. The men who had placed the explosives on the bridges had continued to trickle into the hotel for about an hour after the charges had been set off, as had most of the men who had taken over the San Juan Yacht Club before it burned.

"How's it going?" San Miguel asked the feeble-looking revolutionary in a cordial tone, shaking his hand.

The man shrugged and took a swipe out of a water bottle he had kept in one of his pants pockets. At close range, he seemed even younger than his ridiculous whiskers—probably grown to give him more credibility—had led San Miguel to believe he was.

"It is a glorious day!" he said grandly. "The first day of our new, socialist republic!" Daniel and George exchanged a quiet, amused glance.

"It *is* a glorious day!" San Miguel repeated in a voice brimming with sincere enthusiasm, placing a hand on the Machetero's shoulder and beaming at him without any real conviction. "Have you caught any stray tourists?"

The man barked a short laugh. "They come out of the strangest places, like termites. Why just ten minutes ago, this American lady, a stunner of a woman," the man made suggestive, curvy motions with his hands, simulating the body of a woman, "you know what I mean? She walks out of the service elevator, over there," he pointed to a corridor at the end of the driveway, "looking very confused, and asks me where she could get a taxi to get to the airport! I think she mistook me for a bellhop. I almost took her to a closet, to give her another kind of a ride, if you know what I mean!" he added with a wink, smiling in what he thought was a manly, conspiratorial way.

She must have been a very confused woman to mistake the boy for a bellhop, San Miguel thought to himself. Had the terrorist leader really wanted the "revolution" to succeed, he would have been very concerned about the quality of his allies. The Macheteros' organization must be stretched to its limit when it relied on people like the bearded, shrimplike teen guarding the access to the Grand Laguna Hotel. But that was not of San Miguel's concern.

"Well, I hope you're able to rest soon," he told the guard, and then told George and Daniel, "Let's go."

Not bothering to say anything else, he climbed over the bumper of a parked Honda Civic and slid over it to get to the other side, into the bright morning sun of the valet parking area. His two companions followed.

The Machetero youngster had one thing right: it *was* a glorious day. The breeze from the Atlantic, carrying with it the sultry, ageless smell of the ocean, had blown the smoke of the fires away from the hotel and onto the Bay of San Juan. The sun shone through a cloudless, light blue sky over the Grand Laguna Hotel, with that clean, airy brightness that could only exist in the Caribbean Islands.

Tired but elated, San Miguel thanked God. So far, the operation had succeeded beyond his wildest expectations. Nothing had gone wrong.

And nothing would, not because his enemies were weak or stupid or unlucky, but because God willed it so, and therefore, so it would be.

And after that day, the world would never be the same again.

CHAPTER XXV

Governor Roberto Pietrantoni sat on one of the two padded rocking chairs that were located in the center of his office, and tried to calm himself down. For the last ten minutes, he had been trying to force open one of several double sets of doors that lined three of the sides of the hall-like room, with no success. Although the handles of the tall, ornate wooden doors turned and unlatched, they would not budge, the doorknobs apparently tied together by rope or wire from the outside.

The strangers who had infiltrated La Fortaleza had been very thorough. His desk and cabinets had been carefully searched, and anything that could have been turned into a weapon had been removed. That had included his silver letter opener, two pairs of scissors, and a commemorative flintlock pistol from a visit to Spain that he kept in one of his drawers. All means of communication had also been eliminated, his telephone lines cut, his cell phone confiscated. He was totally isolated, guarded by an armed man who stood watch outside of the main entrance doors, in the waiting room.

He did not know where his son Francisco was, or Francisco's friend, Alfredo, or Nereida, or even his friend Alberto Arizmendi. He was stunned, still trying to make some sense out of what had happened.

He had left La Fortaleza at a quarter after six in the morning for his usual morning jog through Old San Juan, escorted by two of his bodyguards. Double A, a non-athlete and late sleeper, had not accompanied him. He had followed the same route that he ran every morning, one that took him around the old city: uphill from La Fortaleza through Cristo Street to the open grounds of El Morro, then bordering the northern coast past the La Perla sector, and then down the steep incline of Norzagaray Street, past the looming walls of Fort San Cristobal, the proud statue of Christopher Columbus in Plaza de Colon, and the old colonial Tapia Theater. From there the course had taken him west back towards La Fortaleza past the busy cruise ship docks, the Doña Fela multi story parking building, the imposing U.S. Post Office and Federal Court building, and through the beautiful tree-lined promenade of the Paseo de la Princesa. There, the path had turned northwards at the Bay of San Juan—marked by the enormous fountain that commemorated the ancestral races of the Puerto Rican people—and continued under the high walls of the city that guarded La Fortaleza. Finally, he had run through the now perpetually open Gate to San Juan, and returned to the Fortaleza compound through the garage building.

For his bodyguards, the daily jog was always a security nightmare. There was no way that they could have protected the Governor, had a sniper decided to take him out. There were too many buildings, too many hiding places, and too much open space to keep him safe. They had repeatedly warned him about the dangers, but he had refused to stay locked up inside of La Fortaleza. The route was too beautiful to give up; it helped him to clear his mind in the mornings and to prepare for the rest of his heavy daily schedule. Regardless of the dangers that he faced, imaginary or real, he had never considered discontinuing his daybreak jogs as a real option.

That morning, he had confirmed once more to the men in charge of protecting him that their concerns were groundless. He had finished his circuit around San Juan without receiving as much as a disapproving stare—which he did receive every so often—and returned to La Fortaleza by 6:45 AM. He had asked Patria, the Executive Mansion's head housekeeper, to make certain that his Secretary of State had awakened, and returned to his room, where he had showered and dressed for breakfast.

He had planned for a quick breakfast, since he and Arizmendi had a full day of work ahead of them. He had hoped that Francisco and his friend Alfredo would already be up, so that he could spend some time with his son before losing him for the rest of the day. Knowing him and how excited he was with his visitor, he was certain that Francisco had been roaming La Fortaleza for at least the last two hours.

The walls of La Fortaleza were very thick, and isolated most of the noises generated in the other parts of the house. Therefore, the first sign he had noticed of trouble had been just as he had finished dressing after his shower. He had heard two loud bangs, followed by a heavy crash and a scraping sound on the door outside of his room. Thinking that Francisco had probably caused the ruckus—firecrackers had come to mind—he had quickly walked to the door and opened it.

The half-sitting body of Ray—one of his security guards—had fallen backwards towards the Governor's feet as the door failed to support him, striking his head hard on the floor's ceramic tiles. Pietrantoni had knelt instinctively, trying to help the hurt man, not knowing what had caused him to fall. It had not been until he had raised his fallen bodyguard's head and placed it on his lap that he had realized that the man was bleeding profusely from a wound in his chest. Ray had still been alive, but barely. Even though seriously wounded, he had held on to his gun and repeatedly tried to raise it from the floor without success.

Only then had the Governor noticed the short, lean man dressed in black standing at the other side of the hall. The man also held a gun, but unlike the bodyguard's, it had a long cylindrical silencer attached to it. The intruder had pointed his weapon at Pietrantoni with his two hands, while darting quick looks around him to make certain that no other security personnel was approaching.

The rattle of automatic weapons had unexpectedly shattered the tense silence between both men. It had come from the outside; multiple, rapid bursts of fire, mingling occasionally with isolated shots. The armed man had paid no attention to them, jerking slightly the muzzle of his pistol to make the Governor stand up.

"On your feet," the man had ordered when Pietrantoni failed to react. "Hands behind your head!"

"This man needs help urgently!" the Governor had protested angrily.

The armed man had walked to the fallen bodyguard and shot him twice on the chest. "Not any more," he had said.

Pietrantoni had shouted and instinctively backed away. "What are you doing!" he had yelled at the killer.

"Stand up," the intruder had snarled. "Do it now, or I will shoot you too."

The noise of the fighting outside had continued unabated. Reluctantly, his upraised arms shaking, the Governor had gotten back on his feet. "Who are—"

"Hands behind your neck, face the wall!" the armed man had commanded, ignoring him and moving closer.

Pietrantoni had obeyed, placing his hands at the back of his head, and turning towards the wall next to his room's entrance. The intruder had pushed him forward, so that the Governor had to lean on the wall, and patted his clothes hastily in search of hidden weapons.

"You will come with me," the man had said after he had finished.

"I don't know what you want, but you won't get out of this—"

"Be quiet!" the man had whipped the back of Pietrantoni's head twice with his pistol, hard enough to hurt him but not to knock him out. The Governor had staggered forward and covered his head with his hands. The armed man had grabbed him by the shirt and shoved him away from his room.

"My son..." Pietrantoni had implored.

"He is alive, as are most of the others in your household," the gunman had answered cryptically. "Now move!"

Pietrantoni had been led to his office, passing three other men armed with rifles. One was dressed in black like his captor; the other two wore civilian clothes. Somewhere along the way the shooting outside had tapered off, and then stopped entirely, filling the Governor with dread. He had hoped to find Francisco, Nereida and the others waiting for him. However, the office had been empty.

"You will stay here for the moment," the armed man had said. "For the well being of your son and your mistress, do not try to escape."

The intruder had begun to close the door, but Pietrantoni had placed his foot on the door's edge, stopping it from closing.

"Wait! Please! I need to see my son!" he had pleaded desperately.

The armed man had struck the Governor with his gun's barrel across the face, making him stagger backwards.

"You will see your son when we say so," he had answered, slamming the door shut.

That had been three hours ago. Pietrantoni had a massive headache. Two bumps had grown in the back of his head where the intruder had struck him, throbbing with every heartbeat. A long, bluish-purple streak had welled up on his face, running diagonally from his right ear almost to his chin. Twice he had heard the shuffling of feet, and had expected the doors to open and his son to rush in, and twice he had been disappointed. Fearing the worst, he had decided to slip out of the office and search for Francisco on his own. However, all of the doors had been hermetically shut from the outside.

What had happened? Who were those men? How many were they? What did they want? How did they get in? Surely, the police would have surrounded the area by now, but the terrorists—there was no other way to describe them—would be using him and the others as bargaining chips. He could hear no activity outside.

His hands shook slightly; his mouth and throat felt drier than dust. The mere thought of his son being alone with the violent men who had captured La Fortaleza terrified him and affected his concentration. He prayed to God that Francisco would at least be allowed to stay with Nereida. She would know what to say to keep him calm...*And Alfredo!* He kept forgetting about the other little boy.

He had to help them. He knew that the terrorists were playing psychological games with his emotions, hoping to break and use him, so he had to stay calm and not play by their rules or he would surely lose everything. If he was going to survive, if he was going to be of any help to his loved ones, he would have to shrug off his anxiety and clear his head.

He did not hear the men coming into the room until the door opened. Two men walked in. The first one he recognized immediately as the small lean man who had killed Ray. He had never seen the second one. He would have remembered. The Governor stood up.

The man was dressed in a beige linen suit and a wine and gold colored tie. His hair was cut short, and he sported a neatly trimmed goatee that gave him the appearance of a Wall Street lawyer. He was just as short as his companion, and thinner, almost to the point of emaciation. He seemed to carry no weapons.

The two intruders wore black bands on their left arms that read "Libre como el Coqui" in green letters. Pietrantoni had not noticed the armband before on the man who had locked him up in the office, but considering the circumstances, that was not surprising. The armband clearly stood out on the new arrival's light colored suit.

The man with the goatee examined the Governor with the same interest that a racehorse owner examines a newly acquired horse, his black eyes shining with pleasure. His companion looked at him nervously, as if the other man was not supposed to be there.

"Governor Pietrantoni," the well-dressed man said, walking towards him and extending his hand, "Aristides Andrade. It is a pleasure to finally meet you."

It took a couple of seconds for Pietrantoni to place the name, his image of El Alacran contrasting significantly with the small businessman standing before him. He had seen some blurry pictures of the Machetero leader before, each showing a completely different person in different garbs and hairstyles. Arizmendi had joked about him, saying that the man should have been nicknamed El Camaleon—the Chameleon—rather than the Scorpion. But meeting the Machetero face to face, Pietrantoni thought that the nickname fitted him perfectly. There was something very dangerous and venomous behind the puny man's gaze.

The Governor failed to take the proffered hand, and Andrade withdrew it with a humorless, knowing smile. The armed guard looked at him, uncertain as to what he should do.

"I see that you recognize me even with my new look," said El Alacran. "Good." He sat on the rocking chair opposite to Pietrantoni's, and motioned the Governor with his hand to do the same. Pietrantoni sat.

The man dressed in black moved closer to Andrade, and leaned to speak closer to his ear. "Forgive me for interrupting, sir, but San Miguel has specifically ordered not to allow anyone to see the Governor without his authorization."

El Alacran swiftly turned his gaze towards the armed guard, regarding him with malevolent amusement. He sighed. "I'm sure Mr. San Miguel will not mind my short visit to La Fortaleza. In fact, you should know that my men now outnumber his two to one, so La Fortaleza is now technically under my control, not San Miguel's." He smiled. "Not that it matters, because we are all allies," he added, raising a placating hand. "However, for your own peace of mind, by all means call San Miguel and let him know that I am here."

The armed man hesitated for a moment. Then he nodded curtly and walked out of the room.

Andrade waited until the man had left, and shook his head. "These Arab foreigners! They have been very helpful to us, but...well, they're foreigners. They are not Puerto Ricans, like me...Like you! You can't expect them to understand our idiosyncrasies or our problems, any more than we can understand what they're doing out there...in their wretched Palestine." El Alacran moved his hand in a languid, dismissive gesture. "But they have been useful, I must say that..."

El Alacran coughed and cleared his throat.

"Excuse me, Mr. Governor, something must have gone down the wrong side of my windpipe."

Pietrantoni maintained a tight-lipped silence.

"Yes," Andrade said, as if reading his thoughts. "I don't like you either, and there are a thousand things I need to do, so let's dispense with the chit chat and get right to the point." El Alacran stared right at the Governor. "I can see from your expression that you don't have a clue of what is happening, so let me fill you in."

He flashed another mirthless smile at his prisoner. "We have captured the island of San Juan. Our forces have blown up the bridges that connect San Juan to the rest of Puerto Rico and taken over the Grand Laguna Hotel and a cruise ship, I forget its name now...The *Carnivale*...the *Bacchanal*...No matter, it will come to me eventually. What matters is that we have neutralized the police forces in San Juan, so don't expect to be rescued any time soon. As of this morning, a new government has been established to run the new Socialist Republic of Puerto Rico. Your government is no more. And...that's it, basically. So what do you think?"

El Alacran's eyes shone with perverse pleasure. Despite his desperate attempts to look unfazed, Pietrantoni felt the blood rush to his face. *San Juan taken! Controlled by the Macheteros and foreign terrorists!* For several seconds words eluded him. Then his anger took over.

"You must be more stupid than you look," he said. "Do you really think the people will follow you, when the majority does not want independence?"

"And what does the majority of the people have to do with any of this?" El Alacran retorted scornfully. "The majority of the people don't know what's good for them! They wouldn't know it even if goodness itself bit them in the ass! The majority of the people did not choose to be occupied by your American imperialist masters, and the majority of the people has been oppressed and manipulated by Washington and a few of its lackeys ever since the first day they stepped on this island! *Majority!*" Andrade spat out the word as if it was poison. "Don't speak to me about majorities. The people in power decide who the majorities are, and right now we, the revolutionary government of Puerto Rico, we are the majority in San Juan."

The Governor shook his head. "You may hold Old San Juan and Puerta de Tierra by force, but you sure as hell are not the majority here or in the rest of the island. Do you really believe that the country will follow your terrorist movement?"

El Alacran's lips stretched into an involuntary smirk, but he maintained absolute silence, rocking back and forth on his chair.

Pietrantoni observed his reaction with growing curiosity, and then, with a sense of dread, he began to understand the real purpose behind the Machetero leader's actions "But...you...You don't really believe that this coup will be successful, do you?"

Andrade crossed his legs and stared quietly at Pietrantoni. "You never know, stranger things have happened before. The FEPI has planned demonstrations in the Rio Piedras, Mayaguez and San German campuses later today. And there will be acts of sabotage, you know, power outages, bomb threats, cars set on fire, that sort of thing." He chuckled. "But no, I don't think that the rest of the country will revolt," he said smugly.

"Then what—"

"Will we gain from all this? What indeed," Andrade reflected. Then, as if making up his mind, he leaned gently forward. "I will tell you what we will gain," he whispered. "First and foremost, we will get the federal government to release Adalberto Cacho from prison. It will be good to have our leader back."

El Alacran settled back into his chair and laced his hands with his fingers, waiting for the Governor to react.

"And what else?" Pietrantoni asked. "You said 'first'. What is the other reason?"

"I thought it was so obvious that I didn't have to mention it," Andrade responded, raising one of his eyebrows in mock surprise. "We destabilize your government, of course! We show the rest of our country and the rest of the world that we can do as we please here, and that nobody can stop us! I don't expect to win immediately, but eventually we will. Your colonial government will collapse on its own accord. Nobody will trust it. Our people, the *majority* of the people, will not stomach a prolonged terrorist campaign, and they will never recover from the shock they have experienced today," the emaciated terrorist gloated.

"You underestimate the resolve of our people," Pietrantoni retorted, his head throbbing so painfully that he thought it would explode.

"Do I? We'll see."

Andrade opened his jacket, revealing a large holster strapped to his chest. From one of his jacket's pockets he extracted a creased piece of yellow legal paper and fastidiously unfolded it, handing it over to the Governor.

"This is your resignation as Governor of Puerto Rico, your condemnation of the United States colonialism, and a plea to the rest of the world to free our country," El Alacran explained, while Pietrantoni examined the handwritten document.

"You expect me to sign this?" the Governor asked, when he had finished scanning the document.

"For your son's sake, yes," he answered, almost with a hiss. "And for the sake of your whore," he added with understated relish.

Unable to control himself, the irate Governor jumped on the scrawny terrorist and caused him to tumble back in his chair. Andrade hit a lamp and crashed into a small table, hitting the floor hard. The doors of the office burst open almost immediately, and the black uniformed guard rushed inside, surveying the scene with wide-eyed shock.

"Stop!" he yelled, pointing his gun at Pietrantoni.

El Alacran slowly picked himself up from the floor. Pietrantoni stood a few feet away from him, amazed by his own reaction.

"San Miguel wants to talk to you," the guard said to Andrade, showing him his cell phone. "You'll have to go outside, to get satellite reception."

"So you *do* love her," El Alacran hissed to the Governor, trying to smile but only managing to produce something that looked more like a snarl. "I believe I struck a raw nerve just now." Gently, he jerked his jacket straight. "That is why you will sign your resignation. Not only sign it, but read it on the radio, and do anything else that we tell you to do. The Macheteros are willing to sacrifice everything for this country. *Everything!* You are not. And that is why in the end we will win."

El Alacran walked past San Miguel's man and snatched the telephone from his hand. "I will be back this afternoon," he said as he exited the room. "Be ready to sign and record my little speech."

CHAPTER XXVI

The corpses of the two terrorists were dragged from the street and dumped in the back of a black Dodge Ram. They were stripped of their AK-47 rifles and several clips of ammunition, their knives, and their cell phones. Neither man carried any identification that could give any clues of who they were or where they had come from.

Michelle had steeled herself to examine the bodies at close range before they were hidden in the truck. She had gagged and almost vomited when she had knelt beside the man who had tried to rape her, not so much because of his empty eye socket and the blood caked over half of his face, but because of the stench of his sweat. Her head had momentarily reeled as the memories of the attack had flooded her brain. She felt dirty and violated, and could feel no pity for the dead man. On the contrary, she hated him, and hoped that he would go straight to hell.

"He won't bother you any more," the redheaded man told her, and she wondered if her expression reflected so clearly what she was thinking. She was a mess, she knew. Her upper lip was swollen, and even though she had not seen herself in a mirror, she knew that her eye makeup was probably spread over most of her cheeks. The palms of her hands and her knees were scraped raw and throbbed with pain. Even so, she felt more determined than ever to obtain as much information as she could to help clarify the strange events of that day.

Except for the black armbands that both men wore, her examination of the bodies yielded little information. She slipped one of the two armbands off, but could find no labels or markings that revealed its origin. She even spread some powder from her makeup compact case on a small round mirror that she carried in her purse, and fingerprinted the two dead men for future identification. Also, she photographed both men with her cell phone.

"We have to go," the man in the khaki uniform urged, looking over his shoulder towards the road, to see if anybody was coming. She nodded, and helped her companions stretch a blue plastic tarp over the back of the truck, concealing the two dead bodies. Then they withdrew into the wooded area next to the Army Corps of Engineers building, where the rest of the group had taken refuge. Don Moncho, the babysitter and the two-year-old toddler were hiding behind a large, flower filled semicircle of hibiscus bushes that rose to about the height of Michelle's chest.

She found the ancient taxi driver sitting cross-legged on the ground while the babysitter tended to an enormous bump on his forehead. Katherine Elizabeth watched with rapt attention, holding on to the old man's hat.

"How is he?" the redheaded man asked as he walked into the bushes, making the babysitter jump up in alarm.

Don Moncho saw Michelle and extended his arms towards her. "I thought they were going to kill you!" he said, his voice cracking with anger and relief. "I tried to stop them, but the bearded one hit me with his rifle."

Michelle embraced him. "Thank you, thank you, you were very brave," she said, kissing him lightly on the forehead. "Thank you all," she said, turning around and looking at the two strangers who had saved her.

It was the first opportunity she had had to examine her rescuers. She thought she had seen the redheaded man before, although she could not place him. He must have been in his early thirties, with dark blue eyes and a pleasant, almost handsome face that was covered with freckles. He was fairly tall, she guessed about five ten or eleven, and although he walked with a limp, seemed fit and athletic.

The other man looked no older than nineteen years old, if that. She now recognized the khaki uniform he wore as that of a police cadet in training, which explained his youthful appearance. His dark hair was cut very short, revealing a pair of ears that reminded her of the open doors of a Volkswagen Beetle. He had hazel eyes that were framed by thick eyebrows, a long, aquiline nose, and a thin-lipped mouth that, despite the anxious present situation, seemed to be always curved in a gentle smile. He also was tall—taller than the redheaded man—thin, and gangly, but he moved with a surprising fluidity that most men of his height lacked. He reminded Michelle of a younger version of the scarecrow in the Wizard of Oz.

"Are you two okay?" she asked the babysitter and the little girl. It was the first time she had addressed the babysitter in a normal tone.

"Yes, thank you," the girl's caretaker answered timidly.

"Since we're going to spend some time together, I think we should all learn each other's names," Michelle suggested. "I'm—"

"Everybody knows you," the redheaded man interrupted. "You're Michelle Alfaro, the reporter from WKPA TV." He smiled embarrassedly. "I've been a fan of yours for ages, well, I mean, not for ages, because you're very young, but..." If it was possible, his face grew redder. He stuck his hand out to her, and said, "Archie Roman, and I'd better just shut up."

Everybody smiled.

"Although I should tell you that I've seen you in the *Joyero de San Juan* many times." Archie did not tell her that he frequented the store to speak to his friend Antonio, the *Joyero's* security guard, and that he occasionally sold him illegal *bolita* lottery tickets.

Michelle examined his face, still trying to remember where she had seen him before. "I'm very glad to meet you," she said more formally than she intended. "I mean, I can't express enough to you how grateful I am for saving my life."

"He had it coming," Archie replied, surprising her with the bitterness that his voice carried.

"Yes, he did," she replied honestly. "But I'm sure there are many other people hiding that saw what was happening and didn't dare to do anything about it."

"You can't blame them," the rookie policeman said. "They're all scared." He spoke with a high-pitched voice, which added to his youthful appearance. He grinned at her tiredly. Even though he seemed to be trying to put on a brave face, his expression showed a mixture of exhaustion and sadness. "Hi, I'm Edgardo Negron, and *I* am the greatest fan that you have in all of Puerto Rico...In the world!" he said guilelessly, his eyes briefly shining at her with unabashed enthusiasm. "I have been watching you since I was a teenager."

"You *are* a teenager, for God's sake," Archie interjected with a slight smile.

Michelle noticed that Negron's clothes and even parts of his face were splattered dark stains of what could only be dry blood. He seemed unhurt, however, so the blood must have originated from moving the corpses of her two assailants.

"I'm Maribel...Maribel Albarran," the blond babysitter blurted awkwardly, glancing nervously at the others and managing a half-hearted smile. "And this is Katherine Elizabeth Martinez," she added pointing at the little girl still holding Don Moncho's hat, who shifted her huge eyes from one adult to another.

Negron searched his shirt pocket, and drew out a plastic bag containing four partially crushed vanilla wafers. Michelle noticed that Negron's hands shook slightly as he opened it and offered the wafers to Katherine.

The girl watched him briefly, and then grabbed the gift wordlessly, dropping Don Moncho's hat on the ground and sitting on her babysitter's lap. With surprising care, she extracted one of the wafers out of the package with two of her stubby fingers, and attacked it voraciously. Archie picked up the discarded hat, and handed it to Don Moncho.

"I'm taking care of her this week, while her parents are traveling in France," Maribel explained. She looked at Michelle apologetically. "I'm really sorry about back there. I panicked. I guess I—"

"It's okay," Michelle assured her, touching her arm lightly. "It's been a rough morning for all of us," she said. She tried to smile, but her upper lip felt heavy and dry, and she talked with a lisp. It made her feel self-conscious, as if everyone was staring at her mouth. She wondered if by the time she reached the WKPA helicopter and gave her televised report, the swelling would have started to subside. She hoped so. She did not want to look that way in front of millions of viewers. "This brave man here," she said, directing a loving glance and shifting the attention of everyone to the old man sitting on the ground, "is Don Moncho."

The taxicab driver acknowledged the introduction with a weak wave. Somewhere in the distance, probably in the San Juan Yacht Club, something exploded, momentarily stopping the conversation. Using his AK-47 to part the lower branches of the bushes behind which they hid, Negron scanned the street for movement. Next to him, Maribel anxiously examined the rookie's face for any sign of alarm, while Katherine munched on a wafer contentedly.

"I need to call the station," Michelle said, opening her purse and rummaging through it until she located her cell phone. "I made arrangements with WKPA to meet me...us...with their helicopter, somewhere near the bridges that were destroyed this morning."

Her statement was received with dismayed disbelief.

"What bridges were destroyed?" Archie asked with alarm.

"Didn't you know?" she asked, realizing as she mouthed her question that they probably didn't.

Archie shook his head.

"All of the bridges connecting San Juan to Miramar and El Condado were damaged. At least that's what my editor told me a while ago over the cell phone. I don't know the extent of the damage, but it seems there's no way of getting from one side of the lagoon to the other."

"Sweet Jesus!" Archie muttered. He plucked a large red hibiscus flower from the bush next to him, and began to pull away its petals. His mood seemed to darken considerably.

"I need to call the station to coordinate our meeting with the helicopter," Michelle repeated. "It's our best bet to get Katherine and the rest of us safely to the other side." The idea of seeking safety by leaving San Juan made her think, for the first time since the shooting had started, about her mother and her aunts. *Were they in any danger by staying in the old city? Surely, nobody would try to harm them, and they had enough common sense to stay in her apartment until the present emergency ended. On the other hand, they may not even be aware of what was happening.* She decided to call them right after she communicated with WKPA.

"Is that safe?" Negron asked, glancing at her over his shoulder, then returning his attention to the road.

"What, using the cell phone?" Michelle responded distractedly as she speed-dialed Doel's cell phone number.

"No," the rookie replied, "sending a helicopter to meet you. You don't know if there are...others, out there," he said, nodding with his head in the direction of the bridges.

Michelle barely listened to him. She waited for the call to connect, but instead the words "NO SERVICE AVAILABLE" appeared on her cell phone screen.

"What's that you said?" she asked absent mindedly, hitting the redial button and waiting for an answer.

"I said that it may be dangerous to land a helicopter in this area. These people, whoever they are, they're everywhere, like roaches coming out of the sewers. I don't think they're planning to leave anytime soon. They may shoot at us...or the helicopter, if it tries to land."

Michelle cursed under her breath as her call failed to go through for a second time.

Archie nodded grimly. "Negron has a point," he said. "These people are very well organized and very dangerous." He pointed to the thick column of smoke curling into the sky from the burning police station. "You *saw* what they did over there. That was no random attack. The police didn't have a chance. It was a perfectly executed operation. A military operation planned to the hilt. I mean, they used MAG machine guns and high-powered sniper rifles! Those are weapons you normally use in a full-scale war, for heaven's sake! The type they use in Iraq and Afghanistan. Any of them can bring down a helicopter."

Michelle, Maribel and Don Moncho listened with apparent dismay, looking very scared.

"How do you know?" Michelle asked him.

"What?"

"How do you know about the type of weapons they used to attack the police? Did you see them?"

For a moment, Archie looked flustered. "I was in the military," he answered finally. "Iraq. Believe me, I know the sound of those things."

Michelle stared at him with curiosity. It seemed she had touched a raw nerve with her last question. Maybe she had triggered some painful memory from the war.

"So you were there, during the shootout?" she stated more than asked.

"I live in El Falansterio. My balcony faces the police station," Archie answered. "I saw everything that happened. They were shooting from the roof, just above my apartment. I could hear them discharging their weapons, even shouting at each other. It was terrible," he said sincerely, his voice breaking. He had Michelle's full attention now. "Even in Iraq, I never witnessed anything like it. These are dangerous, military trained professionals. And now you say that they have destroyed the bridges..."

Archie finished dismantling the red hibiscus flower he had plucked from a bush, and tossed the leafless stalk away.

"If the bridges have been sabotaged as you say, then that means that whoever did this is trying to cut the island of San Juan from the rest of Puerto Rico," he concluded. "Not only that, but since they have wiped out most of the policemen on this side of the Metropolitan Area, and have openly taken to the streets, it can only mean that they intend to take over and keep Old San Juan. So I don't think that they will deal very kindly with any helicopter trying to land on this side of the lagoon."

"The Lord preserve us!" Don Moncho said in a shaky voice.

A shocked silence followed Archie's words. Maribel the babysitter produced an involuntary sob, and bit her lower lip to stop herself from crying.

Archie was right, Michelle thought. *What else could the events of that day point to? And then, there were the other bits and pieces of information she had come across during the last twenty four hours: the armbands carried not only by her attackers, but by the men dressed in black and by the drunk student arrested in San Sebastian...What was his name? Bergara...Alejandro Bergara. All showing the same slogan, "Free Like the Coqui." And the canned food that Bergara had carried in his backpack— enough to feed him for several days—and his extra sets of clothes; all of them now clear indications of the jailed FEPIsta's intentions to stay in San Juan for a long time.*

Who were these men? What did they want? Had Doel been there, he would have rapped his knuckles gently on her skull and urged her to *think! "Show me that your head is not just some pretty decoration sitting on top of your shoulders!"* he would have challenged. *"Marshall your facts. What have you got so far?"*

It wasn't that hard to figure it out. Bergara's threats about an impending "revolution", which had seemed like the empty boast of a drunken college student, had suddenly become a very frightening reality. As unreal and incredible as it seemed, Michelle had been caught in the middle of an armed revolution while she was heading for work. And unless Doel or Correcaminos knew something different, the odds that a helicopter—even a news helicopter—would be allowed to land unchallenged on San Juan were very slim indeed.

But even if Doel or Correcaminos knew something different, her efforts to contact them had so far been frustrated by a telephone system that refused to work. *Had the airwaves been jammed sometime after she had last spoken with Doel?* Michelle decided to try a different telephone number, and dialed *EL Joyero's*.

"Nothing," she said to herself, when the "NO SERVICE AVAILABLE" notice appeared on her screen.

"The system must be overloaded," Archie stated. "It happens during big emergencies. It happened in Katrina, and 9/11, and when that bridge in Minnesota—"

"Minneapolis? The bridge that fell down?" Michelle said automatically.

Archie nodded. "As people find out that a catastrophe has happened, they start calling their relatives and friends. It's natural. They want to know if they're all right, or to report what's happening, or simply to talk. I have this friend in the cell phone business. He says that most systems for cell phones are designed to handle the calls of about 18 percent of their subscribers at any given time. When a lot more people call, they create a spike. The system can't handle it; it gets congested, overloaded. Calls, anything that uses the ground station facilities for the cell phone system, even emails or texts get clogged up. It's...it's like molasses, trying to get through a funnel. Calls fail to get through. The system may even collapse and stop working entirely."

"And right now, the system is getting pounded with thousands of calls from people trying to find out what is happening here." Michelle completed Archie's thought with utter frustration.

She stored her cell phone back in her purse, and shifted her attention to the San Juan Yacht Club. Now that she was closer, she could make out several fires in addition to the large conflagration in the clubhouse, the smaller plumes of fumes intertwining with main whirling mass of smoke that rose into the sky. The wind was beginning to shift. The haze blanketing the grounds of the Corps of Engineers building had grown murkier, the heavy smell of the fire making it harder to breathe, and stinging her eyes.

She had been heading towards the lagoon hoping to meet WKPA's helicopter, but with communications down and the "revolutionaries" apparently in control of San Juan, that plan would not work. They needed to get out of there, or the smoke would soon overwhelm them. God only knew what toxic fumes they were inhaling already.

"So what do we do now?" she asked, more to herself than to the others.

"We need to find out what is happening," Archie stated. "That way we can determine what would be the best thing for us to do. Maybe we can locate a radio."

"You know what?" Negron interjected, taking off his police cap and brushing away the sweat on his forehead with one of his sleeves. He struggled from his sitting position back to his knees, and looked back at the others. "It's us that probably know more right now about what is happening here than the rest of Puerto Rico," he said, grunting. "I don't think anyone has a complete idea of what's happening here right now, except maybe for the terrorists. We need to find a refuge, where we can at least drop off the women, the baby and Don Moncho, and get some food and water. We—"

Negron suddenly stopped talking and swooned. He would have lost his balance had not Archie, sitting next to him, grabbed him by the shoulder and steadied him.

"Whoa, my friend!" the redhead said with concern. "You need to rest."

"Are you all right?" Michelle inquired solicitously, afraid that the stains on Negron's clothes had originated from a wound, after all.

The rookie policeman sat back on the ground and bent his legs in front of him, resting his arms and his head between his knees.

"I found him on the side street next to El Falansterio," Archie explained. "He was hiding inside one of the cars that were parked by the sidewalk."

Negron raised his head. His cheeks were streaked with grime and tears. Whether the tears had been caused by his exhaustion, by the smoke, by grief or by anger, Michelle could not tell.

"I was trying to redeem myself," he stated unexpectedly in what sounded like a half groan, without any further elaboration. Then, as he noticed the confused faces of his listeners, he managed a thin, tired smile. "It's complicated," he said with resignation, knowing that he would now have to explain himself. "But then, everything today is complicated, isn't it?"

The rest of the group stared at him, waiting for him to continue.

Negron took a deep breath and combed back his hair with his hands, his thoughts wandering a long way from the hibiscus bushes that hid him.

"Did you know that today was going to be my second day patrolling the streets? I mean, my second day *ever*? I got assigned to the morning shift, starting at seven. Yesterday I patrolled San Sebastian Street, and I thought, *this is great,* you know? When you wear a police uniform, most people treat you differently. They look up to you. They assume you know what you're doing. Especially the children. They look up at you with that...that...*Wow!* expression in their faces. It feels good. Special. I even got to arrest a shoplifter in a souvenir shop yesterday... It felt really good."

A black crow-like *chango,* curious about the food Katherine was consuming, alighted a few feet away from her, and cautiously approached her with several short hops. Negron picked up a pebble and tossed it at the bird, scaring it away.

"Today, I got in to the station at 6:00 in the morning, even though I wasn't supposed to be there until an hour later. There were rumors that they were short on personnel for the afternoon shift, and I wanted to talk to my sergeant first, to volunteer in case they needed more men. I could use the extra pay, and I didn't have anything better to do, so I volunteered."

The rookie's face darkened, as he recalled the morning's events.

"But then, sometime after seven, we heard some very loud explosions. *'Boom! Boom! Boom! Boom!'* Some of the my fellow officers walked outside of the building, to find out what was happening, others looked through the windows. Most of them came back in saying that they couldn't see anything, but that there was this big traffic jam in front of the station, which was pretty strange for that time of the morning. Then, about a minute later, the few of the people who had stayed outside came into the station, saying that a huge cloud of dust was covering everything outside. I looked out through one of the windows and true enough, it looked like one of those movies from The Mummy, where this sandstorm—the Mummy really, disguised as a sandstorm—covers the explorers that are trying to get into his tomb," he said solemnly.

Michelle was forced to turn her head away, in order not to laugh at the rookie's "Mummy" comparison. Nevertheless, she shuddered involuntarily, remembering the moment when the dust had engulfed her and Don Moncho in the taxicab.

Negron continued.

"While I was looking out through the window, I heard someone shout that Headquarters in Hato Rey had reported that the bridges had exploded. Around that same time our switchboard got flooded, almost instantly, with 911 calls. People from the buildings close to the lagoon were saying that the bridges had exploded. They were reporting broken windows and cars burning. We also got reports about civilians getting shot or wounded. It was utter chaos inside the station. Every available police officer on duty was ordered to get to the lagoon immediately, to assess the situation, and to secure the safety of the civilians. So we grabbed our equipment, and any kind of weapon we could lay our hands on, and ran outside. I personally got hold of a shotgun, besides Sally here," the rookie policeman slapped his black leather holster with his right hand. "My Smith & Wesson," he explained, "which I always carry. I call her Sally. We were armed to the teeth, like in a Stallone movie."

Negron stopped. He took a deep breath and shook his head in disgust. "In the Police Academy, I thought I had been prepared to deal with any emergency situation, but *this*..."

The rookie's brows knotted into an expression of deep anguish.

'We...my partner and I...' again he could not continue. He cleared his throat. "Did I tell you about my partner? Jerry's his name, although I call him 'Angel Guardian', because he sort of acts as my guardian angel. We were discussing what could have happened, wondering if this was some kind of terrorist attack. Officers were rushing us to any vehicles they could find."

"How many of you were there?" Michelle asked, automatically going into her reporter's mode. After the intense tragedy and misery she had personally experienced and witnessed that morning, she felt guilty, almost immoral, inquiring about the unfolding events as developing news; it was sort of like a pathologist doing an autopsy on a relative. But fate had given her the opportunity of a lifetime: to report first hand on an incredible, terrible series of incidents that would make world headlines for weeks to come, and could, in the process, make her famous. She could not let that opportunity pass. *If only her cell phone would work.*

"There must have been about thirty or forty of us," he replied. "Five trainees for sure, including me. Plus the regulars. There was not enough transportation, that's for sure, and everybody was cramming into the cars and the vans that were available. We didn't know what had happened, but we were angry and ready to kick ass!"

Michelle quietly examined the faces of the others around her. She had learned very quickly in her profession to look at the expressions of those who listened to the person that she was interviewing. Sometimes their reactions helped her determine what parts of the story would elicit the most interest from her television audience, and what further questions to ask. She would tailor her report accordingly.

The babysitter listened with an expression of dread—no doubt reliving her own panic in her minivan—while Don Moncho stared at the rookie with upraised eyebrows. She could not decipher Archie's face. The redhead's eyes were half-closed, his jaw clenched tightly, and he nervously twirled a twig from a hibiscus shrub between his right thumb and his index finger. Katherine, having finished the wafers, was playing with the plastic wrap that had enclosed them.

"Four of us squeezed into the back of a patrol car with all of our gear. You can imagine how tight that was, like sardines in a small can. We couldn't put on our seatbelts, but we were in a hurry, and anyway the lagoon was just two minutes away. Jerry and I went in the back of the car with two other regular policemen." Negron frowned. "I'd seen one of the other guys several times before but I can't...if you hit me on the head with a bat, I can't remember his name..." he paused, trying to come up with a name.

"It's not important," Michelle said impatiently.

Negron shrugged. "I know that Jerry called him 'Fart Face', because the guy always seems to be disgusted by someone or something. Anyway, we closed our doors and took off—I think we were the first to go, our siren going at full blast and all. I have to admit that we were all very tense, with the reports about the bridges and the wounded and all, but I was also very excited and pumped up. For me, a farm boy from San Sebastian, this was the real thing! You know, Die Hard, Lethal Weapon stuff. Kick-ass adventure!"

Once again Michelle caught herself smiling and trying not to laugh at the gangling youth's comparisons. She noticed a similar amused look on the faces of some of the others. Only Archie remained inexplicably detached, his eyes still shut.

"We didn't get very far, though," Negron continued, "because as soon as we cleared the gate we ran into a river of stopped cars blocking our exit."

The rookie made a pause in his story. It seemed apparent to his listeners that he had reached a very painful moment in his narrative, and that he was struggling to continue.

"Go on," Michelle urged him gently.

Negron nodded.

"The officer that was driving turned the siren on and tried to find a gap between the cars stuck in the highway. Some of the drivers in the cars blocking our way actually began backing up, to try to make room, and we slowly began moving forward, but then something rattled our car and shook it very hard... How can I describe it?" Negron thought for a moment. "Have you ever driven shift?" he prompted.

Michelle nodded.

"You know when you're learning to drive with the stick, and you don't shift your clutch properly, and the whole car shakes and the engine chokes? It was something like that, except with a tremendous clatter of metal, as if somebody was hitting the hood of our car with a hammer, very fast*! 'Clank, clank, clank, clank, plom!'* I remember I started to say '*What the hell is that,*' but I couldn't finish, because the windshield exploded and glass flew everywhere, and something that sounded like large angry wasps started striking everything around and in front of me. It took me a couple of seconds to realize we were being shot at...."

Negron's voice faltered, and he breathed harder. "Our driver got shot in the chest and lost control of the car. He was wearing his bulletproof vest, we all were, but whatever they were shooting went through it like tissue paper! The man to my left, Fart Face, fell on top of me, and I heard Jerry grunt as he took a bullet on his left shoulder. Our car crashed into the other cars blocking the street, and the other policeman sitting next to Fart Face, by one of the doors, opened it and ran outside. I never saw him again. I heard Jerry scream, and he told me to get out of the car and run! I tried to reach him but then...then...." The rookie rubbed his eyes and the bridge of his nose, unable to continue. He breathed in deeply. "His face disappeared," he whispered. "It burst like a water balloon! His face was here for one second, and then his eyes, his nose, his mouth...they became this big, bloody hole!"

Michelle saw Archie wince, while Don Moncho and Maribel, the babysitter, listened in stunned silence.

"After that, the rest of my time in there is just a blur. Fart Face was over me, and his weight pinned my legs for a while, but while I was trying to push him away he took two bullets that would have struck me. The men in front of the car were also hit many times. The noise that the bullets made when they hit them was terrible. Have you ever been hammering a stake on the grass with a hammer, and you miss and hit the ground and it goes *'thud'!* That's how it went when the men got hit, *'thud, thud, thud!'* Getting chopped up by the bullets."

Michelle now understood where the blood on Negron had come from. She also understood why the young rookie seemed exhausted to the point of collapse. She could imagine him struggling to move the body that was pinning him down, while his companions were being chopped to pieces, blood splattering everywhere. It was a wonder he had not lost his sanity inside the car.

"Some bullets came down through the roof. They made egg-sized holes, through which I could see the sky. One bullet whizzed past my left ear so close that I could feel its heat. I began to smell oil burning, and some smoke started coming out of the air conditioner vents. I panicked," he admitted, looking scared. "I started to push Fart Face off me, but he would not budge, no matter how hard I pushed. Then I realized that it wasn't Fart Face but the seatbelt behind me that was keeping me from getting up. It had gotten all tangled up with the back lacings of my bulletproof vest. So I untangled it, and then I lifted, and pushed, and kicked Fart Face away from me until I freed my legs."

Negron's brown eyes darted wildly from one place to another, as if he was searching for a way out.

"There was a lot of smoke in the car by then. It's funny, because the air conditioner was still working and it was cool inside the car, but with a lot of smoke," he said quietly. "I crawled over Fart Face's body, and tried the handle of the door. It gave way—it was open already—and the door moved, but I didn't open it all the way. Around that time, I realized that whoever was shooting was not shooting at the car anymore, and I didn't want to attract their attention until I was ready to go."

"Would you have stayed in the car pretending to be dead if there hadn't been any smoke?" Michelle asked, very conscious of her increasing lisp. The word "smoke" had sounded like "sthmoke".

Negron shook his head emphatically.

"There is no way I could have stayed there surrounded by the corpses of my friends and fellow officers. Have you ever smelled blood?" he asked her, in an edgy tone. "I mean, bucketfuls of blood? Human blood? I could smell it even through the smoke! And it came from my friends! Sweet Jesus!" he cried. "You know what was the worst thing? Their silence. My dead friends' silence. The screaming I could deal with. Their silence I couldn't take. It made me feel...I guess the word is 'guilty'... As if I had failed them by staying alive...As if they were judging me for not getting killed, like them."

A long hush followed.

"I'm sorry," he said apologetically. "I—"

"There's nothing you could have done," Archie urged, staring at him. "Nothing," he repeated emphatically.

"You don't have anything to be ashamed of," Michelle said at nearly the same time, placing her hand over one of Negron's. "If I had been in your shoes, I would have gone crazy."

"I doubt it," Negron answered with a grudging smile. "Anyway, just wait a bit. I may be breaking down shortly."

"So...What happened?" Maribel asked timidly, wanting to hear the rest of his story.

The rookie slowly stretched his legs. "I made certain that I placed my legs so I would not trip—it was harder than you think, believe me, with the little space left in the back of the car—then I pushed the door open, and I ran. I think that I surprised them, because nobody shot at me for a long while. At least it seemed like a long while. I sprinted from one car to another, at different intervals, and moved behind some of them, so the shooters were never quite sure where I was. I moved as fast as I could, which is very fast. I was a champion sprinter in my town, you know. 'The Flash from San Sebastian', they called me," he said with a sudden rush of pride. "A few bullets started flying past me and hitting stuff very close to me, but I don't think they were very interested in getting me. Besides, a voice inside of me kept telling me that no one was going to get me! It was as if God...God saved me inside that car, so why would He let me get killed now? It wouldn't have made any sense!"

"Hallelujah!" Don Moncho exclaimed, raising both of his palms towards heaven. "Glory to God!"

Archie opened his mouth to make a sarcastic remark, directing a doubtful glance at the old man and the rookie, but thought better of it, and just shook his head.

"I guess they lost interest in me completely after a while, because they stopped shooting in my direction. So I ran and I ran, as fast as Forrest Gump I ran. I even passed several people who were also fleeing the scene, heading towards Old San Juan. And I got to where there were no more cars on the road, almost four blocks away. And while I ran, I heard two tremendous explosions, and I looked back saw that the station was burning! I could still hear a lot of shooting, and I realized that my fellow officers and friends were still fighting and dying over there. And here I was, several blocks away, running away like a scared chicken!"

The rookie sighed.

"You know, ever since I was a young boy in San Sebastian, I always wanted to be a hero. Not a policeman, a hero. A superhero. Someone like Batman, who would fight for the good of the people of this island, who would run into danger without giving it a thought to stop an injustice. I wanted to be a man of honor, someone that others would look up to and count on."

Michelle regarded the young rookie sympathetically. She could perceive no guile or conceit in his words. She was listening to a rare kind of man: a pure idealist.

"So when I stopped running, and heard the fighting a few blocks away...man, I felt like shit," Negron said miserably. "Like I had been given the chance to step into the plate and prove myself, and I had stepped out of it and let the others take my place. I felt the others, the other people who were fleeing towards Old San Juan, watching me as if I was ...I don't know, a deserter, a coward! It felt...terrible! As if somebody had eviscerated me, torn out my entrails and left me empty. I felt like I was some kind of scrawny chicken who had run away squawking—"

"Okay, okay," Archie interrupted impatiently. "We get the idea! Get on with it!"

"There's nothing you could have done," Michelle repeated, trying to reassure the rookie policeman and directing a stern look at Archie, who shrugged.

"Maybe he would have felt better if he wasted his life and died with honor," Archie said sarcastically. "Probably would have gotten killed, if I hadn't found him."

"God moves in mysterious ways," Don Moncho said cryptically, looking as confused as ever through his thick glasses.

Anger flashed on Negron's face. "You don't understand!" he said to Archie. "They fought! My comrades fought! They made a stand! And I, the hero, ran away when they most needed me!"

"They needed a fucking army, Edgardo. Not just you!"

A frustrated silence followed.

"But you returned," Michelle said, trying to ease the tension. "You came back."

Negron hesitated, and then nodded tersely.

"Yes, yes, I suppose I did," he answered, forcing himself to continue the story. "I crossed to the other side of Fernandez Juncos, because I thought it would be harder for the enemy shooting from El Falansterio— that's where they were shooting from—to spot me straight from above, and I headed back to the fighting. My legs were shaking so hard that I could hardly walk, but it felt right, you know, like I was doing the right thing. I hurried, jumping behind fences and hiding behind bushes and parked cars...and as I got closer, I started thinking of a plan to save my comrades. I would climb up to the roof of El Falansterio, going up the stairs of one of the buildings behind the enemy, and shoot them one at a time, without their realizing it. Something like the movie of Sergeant York. You ever see that movie?"

"Sure," Michelle said, "with Gary Cooper."

Archie snorted derisively, prompting a scowl from Negron.

"You really should stop seeing so many movies," the redhead said. Michelle directed a withering look at him, warning him with her eyes to be quiet.

"But I was too late," the rookie said disconsolately. "By the time I got to about a block from El Falansterio, the shooting had stopped altogether. Somebody shouted something over a loudspeaker from the roof, but I couldn't understand what he said. By then I had managed to get to one of the side entrances of El Falansterio, but just as I was going to climb up, I heard many footsteps and voices coming down the stairs. I ran back out, where I found an unlocked car—"

"You were lucky!" Michelle interjected.

"I was," Negron acknowledged. "I ducked into the car just in time, because maybe five seconds later about six or seven men came running out of the building, carrying semiautomatic rifles, and rushed towards the police station. I was crouching in the back of the car, thinking about what I should do next, when Archie found me." He directed a peeved glance at the redhead. "I guess I wasn't hiding that well."

Archie smiled, despite himself.

"Part of your head could be seen through the glass," he told Negron. "It was just a matter of time before somebody saw you and shot you right there."

"So what happened?" Michelle asked.

It was Archie's turn to speak. "I looked around, and made sure that nobody was near us, and then I knocked on the glass. You should have seen his face of surprise!"

Negron grinned sheepishly.

"I convinced him to abandon his suicidal plans and to follow me into El Falansterio. I took him through several corridors of the complex, fig-uring the drug...the shooters were not going to use them," he added quickly, before Michelle asked him what he had been doing there. "My idea was to get him as far away from the station as quickly as I could."

"He saved me," Negron attested flatly, whether sarcastically or sin-cerely, Michelle could not tell. Probably the latter, since Negron did not seem to have a mean bone in his body.

"It was nothing," Archie expressed with surprising warmth, and con-tinued his story. "We left El Falansterio through its opposite side, and began moving towards the Puerta de Tierra Fire Station, thinking he could hide there, and that he also could be of help to the firemen."

"We hid behind anything we could find: trees, trash cans, cars..." Ne-gron said.

"And then we saw you," Archie said, regaining control of the story. "You were running like an Olympic sprinter, barefoot, down the middle of the street, high heels in one of your hands!" he said with undisguised admiration. "A frog-faced man and a Che Guevara double were chasing you. Actually, we heard you scream before we saw you."

"I saw her first!" Negron exclaimed proudly.

Archie raised an eyebrow. "That's true. He was the first to see you, and he started to run behind you. I followed. I saw Don Moncho come out from behind the cars that were stranded in the street to try to defend you." He looked at the old taxi driver. "You are a very brave man. They could have killed you!"

Don Moncho shrugged. "I fought in Korea," he stated proudly. "I faced much more dangerous men with the 65th Infantry than the punks who attacked my princess!"

It was the first time that Michelle had heard Don Moncho refer to her as "his princess", and it nearly moved her to tears.

"Well, you're a tough old man," Negron said. "That bearded freak hit you on the head with his rifle, and from the noise I heard I thought that you had cracked the rifle's butt!"

Don Moncho cackled with laughter, amused by the rookie's exaggeration.

Archie nodded. "He didn't crack the rifle's butt, but he got hit very hard! His eyeglasses flew out of his head, and he crashed on the floor."

"But I didn't lose consciousness," Don Moncho asserted defiantly.

"A tough old man," Negron repeated with unstated wonder.

"And a tough, beautiful princess!" Archie added, staring at Michelle with admiration. "You really did a number on the frog's face! Negron got to you as the Che Guevara wannabe was choking you and hit him with the rifle he had discarded."

Michelle shuddered. She remembered the distinct "crack" of the man's neck as it broke.

"He deserved it," Negron muttered under his breath. "Coward!"

"I asked Negron to look after Don Moncho and to take him out of the street," Archie said. "You must have passed out for a couple of seconds, because when I picked you up you kept looking at me as if you were wondering '*What am I doing here?*'"

"I was quite taken by the color of your hair," she said, only half jokingly.

Negron, Don Moncho and Maribel laughed. Archie blushed.

The haze originating from the smoke of the San Juan Yacht Club fire had continued to thicken with the passage of time. Michelle's throat felt sore and scratchy. She tried calling Doel again, but the words "NO SERVICE AVAILABLE" flashed immediately on the screen. She attempted a short text to Correcaminos—Doel never texted, but Correcaminos did—with the same negative result.

"Nothing?" Archie asked.

"It's worse than before," she answered. "We have to leave this place. This smoke is going to kill us. We need to find a place that is safe and where we can rest and drink some water."

"The Fire Station?" Archie suggested. "We were heading in that direction..." He stopped, and to everyone's surprise rapped his head with his knuckles. "Wait, wait, wait! I'm so dense, sometimes!" He crawled next to Michelle, and asked her, "Do you still have that cell phone we took from frog face?"

Michelle rummaged through her handbag and produced the phone she had stolen from the corpse. She gave it to Archie, who examined it briefly and then displayed it to her.

"This is not a regular cell phone," he said. "It's a satellite phone!" He pressed one of the keys, and the screen went on. It read "Radium", and below it "Registered". "I recognize this from one that a friend of mine owns." He did not tell her that her friend had been one of the principal contacts behind the illegal *bolita* gambling ring for which he worked. "You found it on which of the two men?"

"Each had one," she answered. "I got this one from the bearded one."

Archie muttered something to himself while he looked at the phone's screen. Then, as he began to understand why Michelle's attacker was carrying the phone, he whistled softly. "These people have thought about everything," he whispered.

"What do you mean?"

"They anticipated the cell phone problem," he stated simply. "Satellite phones don't use local ground stations to communicate with each other," Archie explained. "The telephone generates a signal that is received by an orbiting satellite, and that can be relayed via satellite to other satellite phones, or even to—"

"Truck!" Negron warned, looking through the bushes at the road, and grabbing his AK-47. The others crouched behind the shrubs, and waited quietly. They were well concealed and separated from the Fernandez Juncos Avenue by the rows of abandoned cars. Even so, Michelle felt a knot of fear rise up from her stomach to her throat.

In the distance, a white pickup truck leisurely traveled over the street towards the Condado Lagoon. A man on the passenger side surveyed the landscape rolling past him, while tapping with his hand on the door to the beat of some unheard tune. Like a ghost, the pale vehicle passed them and gradually disappeared into the haze.

"It's gone," Negron announced with apparent relief.

Michelle sat up, crossing her legs. She studied the satellite phone that Archie held in his hand. It looked like a boxier version of a cell phone, with a bigger antenna.

"So what you're saying," she said to Archie, "is that the terrorists were foreseeing the cell phone gridlock problem, and planned to bypass the local phone networks by using satellite communications?"

"Precisely."

"And could I use the satellite phone to call Doel?"

Archie considered the question, and tentatively moved his head from one side to another, conveying his doubts.

"Well...you could try...But...I'm not a satellite phone expert, but I suspect that it doesn't work like that. I mean, this Radium phone will generate a signal that will be sent to a satellite, and the satellite will send it back to earth. If you have another satellite phone with the capability to pick up that signal, then in theory you should be able to get through with no problem. But if you're calling a regular cell phone number, that cell phone will not have the capability of receiving that call. What will happen is that the satellite will send your call to the local network that handles Doel's calls, and then that network will relay the signal to his cell phone."

"And that system is already overloaded, so we're back to square one," Michelle finished Archie's thought in a disappointed voice.

"She's so smart!" Negron said admiringly to Maribel.

"I don't suppose you know anybody with a satellite phone..." Archie began to say in a tone that suggested he already knew the answer, but then he stopped and slapped his forehead. "But maybe I do!" he said in a surprised tone, opening his eyes as if he could not believe his own stupidity. Tapping his pants to find his cell phone, he pulled it out from one his pockets and hit the menu key.

He searched his directory of contacts, and looked for "El Chino", hoping that for some reason he had not erased the number. He looked first under the "C's" with no luck, but then, the name appeared under the "E's". He found two numbers under his name. The first one corresponded to El Chino's regular cell phone number. But under it appeared another, longer series of digits: a *satellite* telephone number.

Smiling, he looked at Michelle. "Let's try dialing this number on the satellite phone," her said to her.

CHAPTER XXVII

Czecka emerged from the small, low arched exit of the tunnel with the same startling implausibility of a clown climbing out of a tiny clown car. His shirt, drenched with sweat, clung to his broad back like a second skin. His nose, forehead, shaved pate, and arms were streaked with soot and dust.

How San Miguel's humongous henchman had squeezed through the diminutive entrance of one of San Cristobal's walls and walked nearly a mile through the dark, cramped, and muggy underground passages was a source of wonder to Da'ud and the other two men who had followed him. Had they not witnessed it with their own eyes, they would not have believed it.

They were all glad to be out of the tunnels. Da'ud was not a superstitious man. Nevertheless, the dark, slow journey through Old San Juan's dank, long-abandoned underground passageways had unnerved him. There had been faint, unexplained noises, echoes of footsteps, of things falling, of animals squeaking and squealing, and sometimes, even of voices. His common sense had told him that the sounds must have originated in the streets, several yards of dirt above him. But his visceral instincts warned him to be careful about the ancient spirits that lived below. There were things one did not dare to tangle with.

Luckily, Czecka had led the way, Da'ud thought. Any spirit or monster that dwelled in the tunnels would have been forced to go through him first. And that consoled him.

They had been dragging—and sometimes carrying—the device that they had unloaded from the van through the musty corridors for what had seemed to last an entire lifetime. Fortunately, for underground passageways that had not been maintained for centuries, the tunnels were in surprisingly good shape. They were made of red, plastered bricks, with arched ceilings that curved at a height of slightly more than five feet. The floor was nothing more than dirt hardened by the passage of feet and time, and in some areas water dripped from above, creating a muddy, slippery mire on which the device's wheels refused to roll. Sometimes roots stuck out through the ceiling or the walls, and at certain spots, parts of the brick wall had given way and partially crumbled, hindering their progress.

Periodically, the sides of the corridors had been interrupted by square openings, so narrow and low that even the short Spaniards who had garrisoned Fort San Cristobal would have been forced to crouch in order to fit through. The square openings gave access to minute spaces, rooms—if they could be called that—not large enough to accommodate more than three or four men at a time. It had been in front of one of these spaces that—after nearly an hour of strenuous pushing and pulling the device under the streets of Old San Juan—the men had finally stopped.

There, they had been forced to very carefully lean the device—a metallic, rectangular box about four feet high by two feet wide—in order to fit it through the tiny room's square opening. Da'ud and another of his associates had cradled it and carried it inside, setting it upright after it had crossed the narrow threshold. The Arab had then examined the device's control panel, and satisfied that it continued to work properly, had hidden the strange metal object under a black sheet of waterproof, breathable fabric that rendered it invisible from the corridor, and was difficult to detect even when a flashlight was directed at it. To identify the location of the device, one of the men had sprayed an "X" on the wall above the room's square opening with fluorescent paint, only visible when illuminated with ultraviolet light.

Satisfied with their work, the four men had trekked back to the city's surface. Czecka had again led the way, and Da'ud had covered the rear. Again, strange, unexplained noises had haunted their retreat, prompting the Arab to look apprehensively over his shoulder every few seconds at the overwhelming darkness that closed in behind him.

They had exited into a broad, dry moat; a wide, grassy corridor located between the huge, outermost walls surrounding San Cristobal and the second, even bigger set of walls that enveloped the humongous fortress. The moat was a blind alley, an exposed killing field boxed in on three sides by vertical, impossible-to-climb, four-story-high ramparts. Needless to say, any invaders who would have managed to get there would have become easy targets for the garrison manning the upper defenses.

There were other low arched openings, identical to the one that had been used by San Miguel's men, spaced along the base of the fort's outer wall. Most led to short tunnels inside the walls themselves that ended in narrow, slit-like windows facing the sea or facing the land approaches to the fort. They had been generally used as lookout outposts. However, they had also been designed to be used as mines during times of dire need. When the fortress was attacked, the tunnels had been packed to the roof with barrels of powder, and primed to be detonated in case that the enemy breached the outer defenses. Usually, the fastest member of the defenders would be chosen to run down the tunnel, light up the long fuse that ignited the stored powder kegs, and run back up, hopefully before the explosives went off. Any enemies overrunning the fort would be destroyed along with the outer walls. Fortunately for those defenders who were swift of foot, the San Cristobal defenses had never been breached, and the need to demolish the fort's walls had never materialized.

Nothing distinguished the gate that had been used by Czecka and his men from the other gates that led to the lookout windows. And yet, that gate had served an entirely different purpose: to establish an underground connection between the main fortress and El Abanico, a small fortification located about a hundred yards east of the outer walls of San Cristobal. Shaped like an open hand fan—thus its name, "El Abanico" or "The Fan"—with its broad, semicircular side facing directly towards the east, El Abanico had been designed to hinder the advance of any attackers by stopping them long enough to expose them to the withering artillery fire coming from San Cristobal.

The passageway from Fort San Cristobal to El Abanico ended in a small, underground chamber that had probably served, in part, as the latter's storage and powder room. A trapdoor on the chamber's ceiling connected the room to the garrison's quarters above. In ancient times, a ladder had connected the two chambers.

The main feature of the underground chamber, however, was a heavy, nail-studded, hobbit-sized door located in the back wall of the room. That door connected El Abanico with one of Old San Juan's greatest secret wonders: its ancient system of tunnels.

In its heyday, the undersized door must have been just one of several ways that the city's defenders could gain access to the web of tunnels under Old San Juan. It would have been foolish for the builders of the fortifications to limit to one single passageway their ability to move troops underground from one fort to another, a connection that lay outside of their main defensive walls and that could be overrun by the enemy. Other connections to the tunnels must have existed. However, with the onset of time, the other portals to the tunnels in San Cristobal and elsewhere had either collapsed or been sealed, and long since forgotten.

After the Spanish American War, El Abanico had been abandoned. The old outpost had been adopted as a makeshift shelter by some of the city's homeless, and had deteriorated quickly. The trapdoor opening to the underground chamber had rotted away, becoming an exposed dark hole that several subsequent generations had used as a garbage dump and latrine.

In 1959, the U.S. National Park Service had conducted certain structural repairs of the fort, filling in cracks in the masonry and improving the tiny bastion's drainage system. However, the underground chamber had remained untouched. Then, eight years into the new millennium, a team of Puerto Rican archeologists had "rediscovered" the forgotten room. About half a year after the team had begun sifting through the discarded artifacts in the chamber, it had come up to the long-lost door, covered by rubble.

It had been a startling discovery, largely kept secret to protect the city's fragile system of underground passageways from careless intruders and vandalism. For public safety, a new metal hatch had been installed, and the underground chamber in El Abanico had been shut under lock and key.

A few, unsubstantiated rumors had filtered into the press, but the information provided had been vague and speculative. "Tunnels had been discovered under the city. The government was contemplating restoring some of the tunnels, but tight budgetary considerations had frozen the project."

But San Miguel had followed up on the rumors. Claiming to be making a documentary for television, he had contacted several historical and cultural organizations in San Juan, attempting to uncover the truth behind the rumors. His persistence had paid off after several months of relentless investigation. There *were* tunnels under the city, he had confirmed with the Institute of Culture of Puerto Rico. And as a film documentarian for the National Geographic Society, he would be given limited access to them.

As he exited the last of the tunnels, Czecka stretched to his full, bearlike height and observed the ramparts that surrounded him. Behind him, Da'ud watched with silent amusement. It was not hard for the Arab to imagine him dressed as a privateer, a red bandana draping his bare scalp, an eye patch over an empty socket, his exposed chest crisscrossed by two wide leather belts holding several flintlock pistols, his right hand grasping a heavy, curved cutlass. *Somehow,* Da'ud thought, *despite his hulking body mass, Czecka would have made it over the walls of the fortress and butchered its defenders.*

The taciturn giant headed towards an aluminum staircase recently constructed by the National Park Service, and noisily climbed to the top of the fort's easternmost wall. A man who stood on the top of San Cristobal's castle-like lighthouse several hundred feet away turned his binoculars to stare at him. After a moment's hesitation the man waved and looked away in the opposite direction. He was one of Colonel Calderon's men, stationed there to operate one of the rebels' surface-to-air missile defenses, in case any hostile aircraft approached San Juan from the north. The man had been forewarned about the hulking giant's presence in the fortifications.

From where he stood, Czecka could see to the north the Atlantic Ocean, and to the east the marble-covered dome of the capitol building of Puerto Rico, as well as the high cliffs of the northern coast of San Juan. A brisk wind made the wide legs of his cargo pants flap like twin flags.

He pulled out a satellite phone from one of his pockets and plucked out its antenna, doubling it in size. In a matter of seconds, the phone's screen registered a satellite connection, and Czecka pressed the number 1, followed by the # symbol.

San Miguel answered after two rings.

"Good morning," San Miguel said cheerfully.

"It's done," Czecka replied with as much emotion as a rock.

"Excellent!"

San Miguel ended his conversation. Czecka returned his phone to his pants' pocket, and began to descend the stairs. It was time to get rid of the van.

The lobby of the San Geronimo Plaza buzzed with the noisy chatter of scores of journalists, cameramen, and technicians who waited for the press conference to begin. The low platform by the main bar—where the musicians played during happy hour—had been converted into an impromptu stage, a podium still emblazoned in glittering silver with the words *"La Revolucion del Merengue"* (*"The Merengue Revolution"*)—the name of the orchestra that played there—chosen as the spot from where the Police Superintendent would address the crowd. Scores of television cameras surrounded the speaker's stand, while several dozen radio and television news people holding microphones crouched and crowded around them, jockeying for the best positions. A few of the reporters were speaking to their cameras in front of the empty podium, in anticipation of the impending broadcast. Several policemen warily surveyed the scene, making certain that order was maintained.

Outside, the number of vans parked on both sides of Ashford Avenue, with their tall, extended transmission towers, had increased from half a dozen to fifteen, and more were due to arrive soon. Scores of long, black cables snaked over the sidewalks and part of the street in front of the hotel, making their way into its lobby.

The police had cordoned off the entire tip of the Condado peninsula with yellow tape, from the tip of the Dos Hermanos Bridge—close to where the explosives had been set off—past a residential building, and all the way down to the San Geronimo Plaza. The residents of the residential building had been evacuated in anticipation of a possible exchange of gunfire between the terrorists entrenched in the Grand Laguna Hotel and the police forces protecting the opposite side of the lagoon. Unaware of what was happening in the Grand Laguna, many of the residents had protested angrily as they were forced to leave their homes.

Correcaminos looked at his watch for what must have probably been the hundredth time. A couple of hours before, he had hitched a ride with the WKPA broadcasting van dispatched to the San Geronimo Plaza, and run into the lobby, fearing that the press conference had already begun. To his relief, he had discovered that the scheduled briefing was fifteen minutes late, and showed no signs of commencing.

The veteran newscaster had filled the time by detailing to his audience the events that had led to the present situation, by interviewing an ex FBI terrorist expert, and by trying unsuccessfully to talk to some of the officials who moved in and out of the lobby. He had also interviewed several politicians about the unauthorized radio transmission that was being broadcast from Old San Juan announcing the establishment of the Puerto Rican Republic. Of particular interest had been the expressions of Senator Miguel Moreda, the charismatic leader of the Puerto Rican Independence Party, who had condemned the violent acts of the rebels proclaiming the republic, but at the same time had sympathized with their misguided efforts to liberate Puerto Rico from its colonial masters. Senator Moreda had volunteered to speak to the rebels and negotiate their surrender, if they would so agree.

The preceding hours of nearly nonstop talking, coupled with his concern about Michelle, had taken a toll on Correcamino's nerves. Fortunately, Doel had managed to create and periodically broadcast a five-minute report displaying photographs and videos sent to the station by different viewers—most of it Twitter and Facebook photos that had been sent before the internet slowed down to a crawl—that showed some of the destruction caused by the terrorists. Those pauses had allowed Correcaminos to rest and reorganize his thoughts.

"I need some water," the sportscaster said to his technical assistant, a girl wearing shorts, flip flops and a huge pair of sunglasses set over the top of her head. He was instantly rewarded with a large Crystalia plastic water bottle. He took a long sip, and spoke into his microphone. "Is this feed still connected to the station?" he asked.

"I can hear you, Correcaminos," Doel responded through his earpiece. The news editor had remained in WKPA to coordinate the broadcast.

"What have you heard from Michelle?" Correcaminos inquired in a concerned tone.

"Nothing," Doel answered somberly. *"It's my fault. I should have anticipated the phone system overload."*

"Yes, you should have," Correcaminos said in an irritated voice. "I should have thought about it too, but you're the one that gets paid for thinking. I just provide the manly image that the viewers see, and do the broadcasting," he added in a half-hearted jest. Doel's silence confirmed to him that his joke had not been well received. "Listen," he said in a kinder tone, "I know that you are as concerned as I am..." His earpiece remained silent. "Are you there?" Correcaminos asked, making certain that they had not been disconnected.

"If you're going to ask if our helicopter can do an aerial search for her, forget it. The police has prohibited that anyone fly over San Juan. They say it's too dangerous, and I tend to agree. I imagine Maldonado will explain why in his press conference."

"I know that," Correcaminos answered patiently. "But I've talked to a contact in the hotel—"

"A contact?" There was a trace of ridicule in Doel's voice.

"Yes! What? Do you think you're the only one that has contacts in Puerto Rico, you pompous asshole?"

"You mean pompous ass, right? Because I am one and I don't care!"

"In your case I mean POM-POUS ASS-HOLE!" Correcaminos responded heatedly, emphasizing each syllable. The conversation stopped as the two friends tried to regain their composure.

"Look, I'm sorry, I'm not trying to mock you," Doel said. *"We just don't have time for any of these wild schemes of yours right now."*

"Just hear me out, please!"

There was a pause, and then Correcaminos heard Doel say, *"Go ahead."*

"I know someone here who can let us use one of the boats of the hotel. After the press conference, I can get on the boat—"

"No, no, no..."

"And get to the other side, to search—"

"FORGET IT!"

"You can't stop me from going," Correcaminos said after a long silence.

"I can't," Doel admitted in a steadier voice. *"But I need you right where you are, and if you go, all you will manage to do is put yourself in danger, and you will probably not find Michelle. San Juan is a big place, you know?"*

"Michelle was heading towards the lagoon when we last spoke to her. That narrows the search area."

"Rafael," Doel had never addressed his friend by the nickname of "Correcaminos", which he found ridiculous. *"I consider you a great reporter and a smart man...But sometimes...sometimes I wonder about you. Why do you think that the police has not crossed the lagoon in any boat so far? Why are they stopping everyone from doing so? Do you believe that it is for lack of interest?"*

Correcaminos considered his friend's question in mortified silence. Behind him, his technical assistant stirred and tapped him on the shoulder.

"I think they're coming out," she said, pointing at some movement behind the cloth-covered instruments of the *Revolucion del Merengue* orchestra.

"The Superintendent is coming out," Correcaminos informed Doel. "Get ready to transmit. But we have *not* finished this conversation."

"Concentrate on what you're doing," Doel warned his reporter. *"You're broadcasting in ten seconds, nine, eight, seven..."*

Correcaminos turned his back towards the podium and faced the camera, as he was bathed in the bright, sun-like glare of the spotlight that had just been turned on by his cameraman. He watched his assistant as she continued the countdown with her fingers, silently mouthing the number of seconds as they decreased. The red light on the camera went on as the countdown expired, and the newscaster frowned and began to talk.

Police Superintendent Maldonado walked onto the floodlit platform, followed by Secretary of Justice and Interim Governor Rovira Melendez, the Mayor of San Juan Samuel Padilla, the House Majority Leader Marisel Delgado, the President of the Senate Carlos Cortes, and several other members of the Governor's Cabinet and the Legislature. For a moment the room pulsed with hundreds of camera flashes, as the photographers attempted to capture the images that would headline the front page of the next day's newspapers. The group of grave looking dignitaries crowded onto the orchestra stage behind the Superintendent.

Maldonado briefly gazed about him, and cleared his throat.

"Good morning," he said, leaning into the podium's microphone. "The situation, as you will find out shortly, is very fluid and uncertain. Therefore, I will limit this meeting to a short statement, and I will take no questions at the end."

Maldonado took out an index card from his jacket, and placed it on the podium. He had never been a very good public speaker, preferring to conduct his work quietly, and as distantly from the press as he could.

"Today at around seven in the morning the three bridges connecting San Juan to the Condado and Miramar areas, four bridges if you count the old trolley bridge that was not in use any more, were damaged by explosives set up by an unknown group of terrorists. We believe that the Macheteros are involved, but there may be others. Earlier in the morning we had received a bomb threat to the Convention Center. We discovered several unidentified packages placed in the immediacy of the Center's main building, but in the last few hours we have been able to verify that the alleged bombs were fakes, probably placed there to keep our attention away from the bridges and to draw away part of the police from San Juan."

Maldonado's face reddened. It was evident that he blamed himself for falling for the fake bomb ruse. Behind him, Rovira Melendez scowled at the floor, giving the impression that he was struggling to keep his anger in check. The Superintendent cleared his throat again.

"As you are all aware, the State Police Building in Puerta de Tierra was attacked by a paramilitary group of heavily armed individuals a few minutes after the bridges were damaged. Many of you have probably heard, as I have, Michelle Alfaro's personal account of the shootout. As a result of the attack, the Police Building caught fire and the police personnel had to be evacuated. Our personnel sustained many casualties, which for respect to their families we are not yet ready to disclose. There is reason to believe that the Municipal Police Station in Old San Juan was also captured, although our information there...it's a lot sketchier. The San Juan Yacht Club is also burning. We think that that fire was a result of the explosions on the bridges."

Maldonado took a deep breath, and prepared to reveal the information to which the press still had no access. He was sweating profusely, and wondered if it showed on television.

"Around 9:00 in the morning the terrorists established a contact with the police, and announced that they would make their demands at 10:30 AM. I have just finished speaking to them, and have briefed the members of the Cabinet and the Legislature about the terrorists' demands."

For a moment the Superintendent hesitated, his hands holding on so tightly to the edges of the podium that his knuckles turned white.

"The terrorists have captured La Fortaleza, and hold hostage the Governor and his family and his staff, as well as Secretary of State Alberto Arizmendi." Maldonado was forced to stop when the lobby erupted with excited voices and shouted questions. He raised his hands and hushed the crowd back to silence. "We have been informed that the Governor is not hurt, although we have not been able to confirm it. For security reasons, I cannot tell you much more than that at this moment. The terrorists have also captured the Grand Laguna Hotel and the cruise ship *Mardi Gras*, docked in San Juan. They are demanding the release of the Machetero leader, Adalberto Cacho, and the payment of one hundred million dollars. If we do not comply with their demands by two o'clock this afternoon, they have threatened to publicly execute a hostage every hour from the roof of the Grand Laguna Hotel."

Another uproar ensued, as several reporters started shouting questions at the Superintendent. Maldonado failed to answer any of the proffered inquiries, staring patiently at the top of the podium until the noise subsided. "I am very busy, so I need to finish..." he stated in a low voice.

Some in the crowd began to hush those still talking to listen to the police chief.

"We are confronting a well organized, highly prepared terrorist organization that is set on fostering a revolution in Puerto Rico," Maldonado continued when the noise had subsided. "As of now, the island of San Juan seems to be under the control of the terrorists. To those viewers that live in Old San Juan and its surrounding areas and are watching this telecast now, I urge you to stay in your homes and away from the streets. Treat this as if you were dealing with a hurricane; stay in your shelter until the danger has passed. Help is on the way. We have been in close consultation with the FBI and the federal authorities, and they have offered their full cooperation."

Maldonado paused, and looked at the notes he had scribbled on his index card. "The National Guard has been activated, and along with our police force is patrolling our streets and making certain no other terrorist acts take place in the island. We urge the citizenry to remain calm, but to be vigilant. If you observe any suspicious activities, please report them immediately to the authorities. Which reminds me...Right now, it has become nearly impossible to communicate by telephone, cell phones and landlines included. This has been caused by the enormous number of calls that are being made, which our system cannot handle effectively. We need to restore our capacity to communicate. We urge you not to use your telephones unless they are needed for an emergency. This is no joking matter. By staying away from the phones, and alleviating the load to our telephone system, you may be saving the lives of some of your fellow citizens."

The Superintendent swept his eyes over the crowd of news people. Most of them were locals—there not having been enough time for the big guns from the national and international news services to arrive yet—and they seemed stunned and scared. He could not blame them. In one swift, daring move, a band of terrorists had effectively deprived Puerto Rico of an operating government and taken control over tens of thousands of its citizens. The damage suffered had been great, in the end to be tallied not so much by the physical destruction and loss of life that had already occurred—in itself terrible and unacceptable—but by the psychological harm inflicted on the inhabitants of the island.

Until that morning, when he had gotten out of bed, he had thought of his country as a stable, solid democracy, afflicted—yes—by crime and drugs, but impervious to the political instability that affected the so called "banana republics" and the petty dictatorships of many Central and South American countries. If any changes occurred to the Puerto Rican government, they happened at regular intervals, through the vote of the majority of its citizens. That perception of stability had been shattered that morning by the surprise attack of the Macheteros.

"The next few hours will be very difficult ones, where many of our fellow citizens will face real danger. As a Puerto Rican, speaking to Puerto Ricans, I assure you we will get through this. I ask all of you, here and at home, for a moment of silence for all of the police, men and women, who were killed or wounded this morning in the performance of their duty."

Despite the thousand questions that the reporters so desperately wanted to ask, they rose to their feet and maintained complete silence. Maldonado watched them quietly, noting several known faces among them, moved by their genuine sorrow. Then he nodded curtly.

"Thank you," he said, and he turned to leave.

The lobby immediately exploded with the clamor of a hundred shouted questions.

"Mr. Superintendent, who's in charge of the government?"

"Will you release the Machetero leader?"

"Will you give in to the demands of the terrorists?"

"What can you comment on the radio broadcast that announces the establishment of a Puerto Rican republic?"

"Do you have any plans for freeing the hostages?"

Maldonado ignored all of the questions, and continued walking. However, the Secretary of Justice, Walter Rovira Melendez, stepped up to the podium and calmly surveyed the crowd. The rest of Cabinet members and other politicians, who had begun to follow Maldonado, stopped and hesitated, finally opting to stay with Rovira. With the Superintendent gone, the reporters directed their questions to the Secretary of Justice.

"Mr. Secretary, who is in charge of the government?" someone shouted from the back. Rovira Melendez made an effort to search the person who had made the question, failed to find him, and shrugged. He was a tall and elegant man, who projected total confidence in his ability to lead and who seemed to thrive in challenging situations. Even though he was not smiling, his eyes flashed with what seemed to be amused enjoyment.

"Law Number 7 of 2005 expressly provides that in the case where the Governor of Puerto Rico is incapacitated to perform his duties, they will be assumed by the Secretary of State. Unfortunately, Secretary Arizmendi is presently a hostage in La Fortaleza, along with Governor Pietrantoni. The next in the line of succession is the Secretary of Justice. That would be me," he said with a self-deprecatory smile, as if ruing his fate.

Several shouts of "Mr. Secretary!" followed his statement. Rovira Melendez's eyes darted among the crowd until they settled on an attractive female newscaster from WIPR, the government owned television station.

"Yes, Rosa Sanchez," he said, nodding his head in her direction. Like Governor Pietrantoni, Rovira took great pride in remembering the names of those he had met before, and loved to show it.

"Mr. Secretary," the female reporter said. She was wearing a tight, emerald dress that accented her voluptuous figure and made her stand out among the mostly drably dressed crowd of reporters that surrounded her. "Will you be taking charge of the situation?"

Rovira Melendez straightened up to his full height, his every move projecting a confidence and leadership that had not been as apparent during the Police Superintendent's prior appearance.

"Well look, Rosa, like I said before, the law requires me to assume command while the Governor is incapacitated, and I will not shirk from that duty, however unpleasant it may be," he answered with just the right mixture of conviction and regret. "I have a lot of catching up to do, since I just learned from Mr. Maldonado—barely half an hour ago—what has been happening. That's just a few minutes ahead of the rest of you. I am still trying to understand how all of this could have happened without anyone, particularly our protection agencies, getting any prior hint of it. Nevertheless, this is not the time to ask questions about how this could have happened or been prevented, as much as it is to find out how we can get out of this mess."

From the beginning of Governor Pietrantoni's term of office, Rovira Melendez had openly criticized the appointment of Maldonado as Police Superintendent, even refusing to address him by that title. It was therefore not surprising that, at the very first opportunity that was offered to him, he would try to distance himself as much as possible from everything that had happened up to that moment, and in the process raise doubts about Maldonado's competence in the performance of his duties.

"I am establishing a command center at the Electoral Commission Building in Hato Rey. I believe that the Electoral Commission is ideally equipped with the necessary technological and communications equipment to deal with this...terrible emergency, and has the space to accommodate the various department heads that will be working under my supervision. From there, I will be able to coordinate and implement the necessary measures that a rescue operation of this magnitude requires."

"Does that mean that you will be taking over? That you will be assuming direct command of the rescue operations?" a reporter standing next to Ms Sanchez managed to ask before she could follow up with another question.

Rovira stared at the man with a slightly irked expression. It was a trademark gesture, used to express his displeasure whenever someone interrupted him. Nevertheless, he answered the man's inquiry.

"Like I said, the law requires me to take over," he responded, letting everyone know by the tone of his voice that he was assuming command reluctantly. "I wish it was Governor Pietrantoni who was here now answering your questions, and we must all pray for the welfare of him and his family. Mr. Maldonado will remain here, in this hotel, reporting to me and implementing the rescue efforts. But to answer your question, yes, I am taking over. I am ultimately responsible for the welfare of this island. I will be communicating shortly with President Powell and the federal authorities to brief them on what is happening in San Juan, and to bring them into the picture as quickly as it is possible."

A stream of shouted questions followed. Rovira Melendez searched the crowd and pointed to a tall, gaunt, middle-aged man wearing an electric blue suit.

"Alfonso Guevara, from—"

"El Nuevo Dia," Rovira finished for him, once again displaying his command over the names and faces of the attendees. El Nuevo Dia was the principal newspaper in Puerto Rico. "Yes, Alfonso."

"I have two questions. First, you have referred on several occasions to 'rescue' of the hostages, something that Superintendent Maldonado never mentioned. Is it your intent to rescue the hostages, or are you willing to negotiate some sort of deal along the lines they have suggested, for their release."

The Secretary of Justice grabbed the podium with both of his hands and leaned forward, regarding the reporter with a stern but slightly concerned look. He was a handsome man, prematurely gray on the sides and back of his head while retaining the original black color on the top of his head and on most of his wide mustache. He had dark gray eyes, which reflected the fierce, fearless personality for which he was known, and which every person either hated or admired but none took for granted.

"Alfonso, as you must understand, I cannot detail here what we plan to do. I will tell you this, however. We *will not* negotiate," he said, emphasizing every word by rapping the top of the podium with his knuckles after every syllable, "now or at any other moment, *anything* with any of the terrorists."

"My second question is closely related to the other, Mr. Secretary. Are you saying that you will not negotiate with the terrorists even if the life of the Governor is endangered?" the Nuevo Dia reporter asked.

Rovira Melendez smiled, not a cordial but a feral, *'I-would-like-to-see-them-try-that'* sort of smile.

"You must understand this. For the terrorists, Governor Pietrantoni is the goose that lays the golden eggs. They will not harm him. They would be sharply diminishing their negotiating powers if they did. I will never—"

"How about his child? How about Secretary of State Arizmendi, or the tourists trapped in the Grand Laguna Hotel or in the cruise ship, the *Mardi Gras*?"

Rovira Melendez's expression changed briefly to a one of pure anger, as he searched in the crowd for the person who had interrupted him. It was not difficult to identify the culprit, since everyone around him backed away, as if threatened to be struck by lightning.

"Mr...Correcaminos, is it not?" Rovira asked, reassuming his confident demeanor. "*Sports* reporter for WKPA, if I'm not wrong?"

Correcaminos acknowledged the Secretary's statement with a nod.

"Correcaminos," Rovira Melendez repeated with a mocking twinkle in his eyes. "Is that your real name?"

"No, sir," Correcaminos responded immediately, combing back with his hand his pomaded shiny black hair and beaming back at the Secretary with a friendly smile. "But getting back to my question, you're not concerned that the terrorists will kill somebody else, maybe someone not as important as the Governor, who only reduces the terrorists' negotiating power by a *tinsie-winsie* bit?" The newscaster showed to Rovira Melendez the tinsie-winsie space between his thumb and his index finger.

Rovira's expression darkened.

"You are embarking into the realm of pure speculation, Mr. Correcaminos. This is not like reporting scores in sports," he replied with a fierce smile, and turned to take the next question.

"You don't think that by announcing ahead of time, on television and radio, that you will not negotiate with terrorists and that you are preparing a rescue mission, you are sabotaging the police's chances of reaching a peaceful solution and endangering the lives of the hostages?" Correcaminos insisted, shouting his question over the voices of the other reporters.

The room went deathly still. The Secretary of Justice regarded the newscaster with the same interest of man trying to avoid stepping on dog turd.

"You seem to suggest that we should give the terrorists what they ask for," he said with quiet derision.

"No, sir. I suggest that you do not let the terrorists know ahead of time what you are proposing to do."

"You think that the terrorists are watching this news conference?" Rovira asked with incredulity.

"Is there any reason why they wouldn't?" Correcaminos asked. "I would, if I were them."

"You do have the makings of a terrorist," Rovira Melendez said, realizing his mistake and trying to make light of it. Some of the people in the room laughed nervously. "Well," he said, looking squarely at the cameras, "if any terrorists are watching—or listening—know this," he said earnestly. "If you dare to harm a single one of your hostages, I will make certain that we hunt each and every one of you into the ground. No matter under what rock you may have crawled. That is my personal pledge."

The Secretary of Justice cast a curt glance at Correcaminos and ignored him as the lobby thundered with the voices of every reporter in the room. *It had been touch and go for a moment,* Rovira thought, *but he had managed to control the damage and even gain some points by talking tough to the terrorists. He would have to be more careful the next time about who he chose to make the questions.*

As for Correcaminos, Rovira would deal with his impertinence later, once the present incident was settled. The second rate reporter should be more careful of who he antagonized. He should stick to the safer practice of goading boxing champions and challenging other sports stars. Rovira played *his* game for keeps.

Two minutes later, the Secretary of Justice finished his press conference, and walked out of the lobby followed by the rest of his political retinue.

Superintendent Maldonado gently grabbed Rovira Melendez by the crook of his arm as the Secretary of Justice exited the lobby of the hotel.

"I need to talk to you," he said to him in a subdued voice.

"What about?" the Interim Governor inquired in a peeved tone.

"It has to be in private," Maldonado said. He led Rovira to a nearby office, where a secretary who had just watched the press conference on TV stared at them with surprise. "We need to borrow your office for a few minutes to talk in private," Maldonado explained.

Both men remained quiet as the secretary got up from behind her desk and scurried away. As soon as she left, Maldonado turned and faced his companion.

"What the hell were you trying to do out there?" he asked furiously, barely managing to keep his voice down. "Are you crazy?"

"I was merely trying to do your job of informing the public, instead of running away," Rovira answered, unfazed.

"Jesus Christ!" Maldonado stared at the Interim Governor with disbelief bordering on disgust. For a moment, it seemed as if he was about to strike Rovira, but instead, he slammed his hand on a nearby desk. "That reporter from WKPA was right! Those terrorists are not stupid! They have taken over a hotel that has television sets everywhere! Do you really think that they were not watching us?"

"So what if they were?" Rovira answered unconcernedly. "Now they know who they're dealing with! You may think that the way out of this...mess, a mess that is mostly due to the incredible incompetence with which you run the Police Department, that the solution is to pull your pants down and offer the terrorists your ass! Well, you may be used to that, but I am the Governor now, and I won't do it! And if you feel incapable of dealing with the situation, quit now!" he shouted.

Maldonado grew pale. He knew Rovira Melendez's shouts had been heard outside. The Secretary of Justice was a tall man, but the police chief was just as tall, and of a much heavier build. He could have grabbed Rovira by the neck and crushed his windpipe without breaking a sweat. He did not, however, translate his intense anger into violent action. He was a veteran ex-policeman, trained to ignore personal provocation, and he would not take his enemy's bait now.

To save the hostages, Maldonado had to mount three rescue operations, hitting the Grand Laguna Hotel, the *Mardi Gras* and La Fortaleza simultaneously. Raiding only one or even two of the terrorist strongholds would expose the other captives to a swift and deadly retaliation by the remaining terrorists. Mounting an operation to liberate the hostages in any one of the three terrorist targets, without a significant loss of life, would in itself be a daunting proposition. There were countless examples, such as the Munich Olympics massacre and the attempt to liberate the captives in the American embassy in Iran, which showed how easily a rescue mission could turn into an unmitigated disaster. Mounting three operations of such a complex nature would require impeccable planning and execution, as well as an incredible amount of luck.

In order for there to be any possibility for success, Maldonado needed to gain time. Time to gather a sufficient number of trained men—which he lacked right now—who could carry out the three operations. Time to gather the necessary resources to carry out the rescue. Time to study the locations where the hostages were being kept, and determine the best ways to approach them. Time to obtain information about the terrorists and get a better idea of their strength and numbers. An improvised rescue attempt would only lead to tragedy.

He could rely on the Puerto Rico SWAT team, which had trained intensely to deal with hostage situations. But he only counted with a total of thirty-six men, hardly enough to handle one of the three hostage situations. The local head of the FBI, Mario Franceschini, had called him ten minutes before the press conference to let him know that one hundred

Navy SEALs from the Naval Special Warfare Group in Norfolk, Virginia were at that very moment being mobilized to assist the local government. However, that help would not materialize until late in the afternoon, at the very best.

The only way out was to gain time. And that time could only be gained by establishing a dialogue with the terrorists, where Maldonado could convince them to delay the two o'clock deadline that they had established, hopefully until nighttime, when a night raid would have the most chances of success. And if in order to gain that time it became necessary to give in partially or completely to the terrorists' demands, he would do it without hesitation.

But now, by announcing to the world that he would not negotiate with terrorists, the Secretary of Justice and Interim Governor of Puerto Rico had, in one master stroke, eliminated any opportunity to bargain for more time. In fact, Maldonado would not be surprised if the Macheteros, after listening to Rovira's words, would not wait until the established deadline and instead begin to execute hostages now. If he had been them, why would he wait?

For a moment, Maldonado felt tempted to accept the invitation to quit, and let Rovira Melendez take over. It would probably lead to disastrous consequences and the end of Rovira's political career. However, too many lives were at stake. He could not turn his back on the hostages or his country. Besides, there was another powerful reason why he needed to stay at the helm of the Police Department.

Rovira stared at him with a mirthless smile. "You won't quit?...No? I thought so. Then I suggest that you fall in step with me, and give me the deference and respect that I deserve as Interim Governor." He turned and started to walk towards the door.

"It's the man, not the title, that deserves the respect. Pietrantoni is ten times the man that you are, and the real leader of this country, and I intend to rescue him, no matter what the odds," Maldonado asserted quietly. "You will not be Interim Governor for long, be assured of that. So be sure to enjoy your fifteen minutes of fame, because you'll spend the rest of your political life in Governor Pietrantoni's shadow."

Rovira hesitated and stopped, as if tempted to reply. Then he waived his hand in dismissal and, laughing, left the room.

CHAPTER XXVIII

Lucas turned off the radio in his office, and sat for a long while staring at his tools, too stunned to react. He had just finished listening to the press conference held by the Police Superintendent and Secretary of Justice Rovira Melendez. The news had turned his world upside down.

Earlier that morning, the radio had reported unconfirmed rumors of damage to the bridges connecting San Juan to the main island. The amount of the destruction had not yet been determined. He had groaned, knowing what that would do to the traffic, and returned to the main floor to convey the bad news to the others and get back to the preparations for the anniversary sale.

The Pietri sisters had reacted with predictable dismay, concerned not just about the senseless violence and the identity of the perpetrators, but about what the obstruction of the bridges to San Juan would do to their anniversary sale. However, they had continued decorating the store, in the hopes that by Monday, most if not the entire problem would be resolved. The work had consumed their attention for the next two and a half hours, as the Pietris and their two male helpers embarked in the long and tedious process of placing marked down price tags on most of *El Joyero*'s jewels.

By 10:30 in the morning, Lucas was ready for a break. He had made espresso coffee in his workshop's espresso machine, and Antonio had been sent to La Bombonera to buy some *mallorcas*. As he prepared the coffee, Lucas had turned on his radio to catch up on the latest news about the damaged bridges. He had tuned into a discussion by two political analysts who were speculating about the identity of the bombers. One of them considered the Macheteros to be the prime suspects, while the second disagreed, pointing out that they usually did not operate in that fashion, preferring to rob banks and attack U.S. businesses in fast, limited, nighttime raids. Very little was said about the damage that the bridges had suffered.

The discussion had been interrupted by the announcement that a live press conference from the San Geronimo Plaza was about to begin. Lucas had listened in utter disbelief, as Police Superintendent Maldonado described the events of the morning, and Secretary of Justice Rovira Melendez announced that he was the Interim Governor of Puerto Rico.

A thousand thoughts raced through his mind. They—his mother, his aunts, Antonio and him—were trapped in San Juan until God knew when, apparently in the middle of an attempted *coup de etat*. The main police building in Puerta de Tierra had been destroyed—set in flames—possibly with a tremendous loss in human life. The Grand Laguna Hotel had been captured, and so had the cruise ship *Mardi Gras*—he had seen it when he had parked in Doña Fela's—and their occupants made hostages. The terrorists must have already been in the *Mardi Gras* when he drove past it.

And La Fortaleza! The Governor taken prisoner! How could that have happened?

It was then that the full import of the news struck him like a battering ram. *Alfredo! He had completely forgotten about him! Alfredo had spent the night in La Fortaleza! Lucas was supposed to pick him up that afternoon at three!*

The sudden realization of what had happened to his godson made him sick. For several minutes, he could not think straight, as a thousand thoughts assailed him. He tried to pray, to ask God to protect his nephew, but he could not concentrate to even do that. He kept hoping that somehow, some way, the young boy had managed to escape or been set free. After all, the Governor would be the Macheteros' main objective. An eight year old child would just be in their way. Maybe he had been set free with the Governor's son and the nanny—what was her name—Nereida. Maybe they had sought refuge somewhere in San Juan.

He wondered why his sister Vanessa, Alfredo's mother, had not called. He was certain that she would, had she felt that her son was in danger. She had to be aware of what was happening in San Juan. Michael, her husband, was a news bug who worked out of their home. Surely that day's news would not have escaped him.

Lucas dialed his sister's house phone number, and after a few seconds of silence, was rewarded with a strident busy signal. He tried twice more, and then called from his cell phone, obtaining a similar result. Growing ever more concerned, he dialed Michael's cell phone, and even his own home. He could not get through to any of the numbers.

It was the communications spike, he thought. Maldonado had warned the people to stop using their phones, except in cases of emergency. Either there were a lot of emergency cases, or nobody had paid much heed to Maldonado's plea. On the contrary, he imagined that the information made public during the press conference had probably caused the number of phone calls to increase even more.

Lucas' heart sank. Vanessa and Michael had probably been calling *El Joyero* all morning long. Vanessa would have called their mother anyway, once she learned about the situation in San Juan, even if Alfredo had been safe in his room. If she hadn't called so far, it had been because she couldn't get through.

He thought of his family upstairs, and the intense anguish that the news about Alfredo would cause. Knowing his mother, she would insist on going to La Fortaleza personally to get back her grandson. Fannie was a strong-willed woman, but the possibility that terrorists had kidnapped Alfredo or that he could be hurt would drive her insane. It would be too much for her.

The more he considered the situation, the more he realized that there could only be one way to handle the problem. *He* would have go to La Fortaleza, and try to get Alfredo released. The decision made him sick with fear, because it meant that he would have to approach the captured Governor's mansion and somehow convince the terrorists to return his godson to him. He would argue that Alfredo was of no value whatsoever to them, and that it would simplify their lives to let him go. *After all,* he told himself trying to bolster his own sense of confidence, *if these were pro-independence revolutionaries, they would not make war on children or neutral civilians.*

Of course, they could shoot him before he got to talk to any of them, a prospect that filled him with mind numbing fear. Not so much the fear of getting killed—he had faced death in Somalia several times, and gotten to accept its inevitability—as the fear of not seeing his loved ones again. That morning when he had left for work, he had given little thought to the moment when he would come back to Jeannie and his children, Sofia and Gabriel. His eventual return had seemed like the most natural, obvious thing in the world. The notion that he might never see them again had never crossed his mind. His main preoccupation had been how much of his only free day of the week would be spent away from them and in the preparation for the Anniversary Sale, a sale that now seemed doomed to fail.

Now, he could not even get in touch with Jeannie. He could not even tell her how much he loved her, and how much he was thinking of her and the children. *If he was killed, without being even able to say goodbye, how would they feel, especially Jeannie?*

He was being overly dramatic, he told himself. When he was a Ranger, he had been taught to concentrate on the mission, to visualize in a clear and concise manner his objective, and plan the most effective way to attain it. Any other thoughts were superfluous and would serve only to jeopardize his chances of success. He should not think about himself but about Alfredo. He could not abandon his godson.

Lucas opened the notebook where he logged the deadlines for jewelry repairs and tore off a blank page. He began to scribble on it furiously, finishing ten minutes later. He folded it, and wrote on one of its sides "To Jeannie," placing it into one of his jeans pockets.

He intended to give it to Antonio, the only person on whom he would confide his plans to rescue Alfredo. He would ask Antonio to wait for him in the store for an hour after Lucas left for La Fortaleza. In case Lucas did not return, Antonio would be in charge of taking the others back to Michelle's apartment, and staying with them until the emergency ended. He had decided, if the terrorists refused to release Alfredo, to offer himself in exchange for his godson. A *quid pro quo*. That should satisfy the Macheteros. In that case, he would make Alfredo run to *El Joyero*, located just three blocks away from La Fortaleza. There was always the grim possibility that the terrorists would just opt to make him a prisoner and keep Alfredo, but that was a chance that he would have to take. And if that happened, at least Alfredo would be with him. So it was a worthwhile risk.

Having made up his mind about what he was going to do, a strange calm overtook him. He exited his workshop and closed its solid metal door, securing it with a padlock, and climbed the steep steps that led from the cellar up to the main floor.

And unexpectedly, he walked into a holdup.

The entrance doors to *El Joyero* were wide open, the fountain in the Plaza de Armas fully visible from where Lucas stood. Two men and a woman—all of them very young—had somehow gained access into the jewelry store. The largest of the three, a sandy-haired, heavily muscled male wearing a tight-fitting T-shirt with a green Taino Indian motif, was pointing a gun at Fannie. The second intruder, a short, bulky, boyish-looking man with nervous eyes, stood partially behind his armed companion, apparently listening to the ongoing conversation. The female, a blonde with short hair, red pants, and the figure of a boy, stood with her back towards him. She turned towards Lucas with a startled expression, revealing beautiful blue eyes and pouting lips.

"Oh shit!" she screamed, backing away a couple of steps, then laughed at her own reaction. "You surprised me!" she told Lucas pleasantly, placing a hand on her chest.

From his mother's dismayed face, Lucas could tell she had hoped he had remained downstairs. Next to her, Evelyn looked terrified, staring at the intruders and opening and closing her mouth several times, as if about to speak. Even though taller than Fannie by almost a full head, she stood behind her.

That was not the case with Maria. She had squared off in front of the heavyweight intruder, and glared intently at the three youths. Antonio stood close by her, one of his arms extended to the side, as if keeping Maria from advancing towards the two men in front of them. Apparently, she had been in the middle of a heated argument when Lucas had walked in. A white box with *mallorcas* from La Bombonera lay on a display counter close to them. When the blond woman retreated, Antonio had turned his head and given Lucas a look of utter despair. He seemed to be on the verge of tears.

"Mr. Lucas," he began to say apologetically. "I'm so sorry! I didn't see them until I had opened the door to the store. They hit me in the back and forced their way—"

"Quiet!" the man with the gun shouted at him in a belligerent tone. Then he nodded at Lucas. "You! Where did you come from?"

Lucas stared at him in silence. The man was obviously an amateur, and if forced to fight, Lucas could probably take him. But he was too far away, and there were too many people in the store that could get hurt. He raised his hands and began to approach the armed man as he spoke.

"Downstairs, I came from my shop downstairs," he replied calmly. He noticed that the muscle-bound gunman did not seem to be bothered by the steps Lucas had taken, and continued to close the gap between them.

"Is there anybody else down there?" the man asked. Next to him, the blond girl continued to smile, eyeing him in a flirtatious way.

Lucas shook his head. "No. I'm the only one." He moved next to Antonio, who was standing closest to the armed intruder.

"I'm sorry," the *Joyero's* guard whispered again to his boss, looking distraught. "It's my fault."

"Shit, I told you to be quiet!" the gunman shouted at him. "Junior!" he said, addressing the portly youth standing next to him without taking his eyes from Lucas and Antonio. "Go downstairs and check out if there's anybody else down there."

Junior regarded his brawny leader dubiously, prompting the thin girl to laugh.

"He's scared! You want me to do it?"

"No, *he* should do it. *Do something* for the cause," he sneered. "What's the matter with you, are you going down? Or is Viviana right?"

"I'm not armed," Junior replied plaintively.

Viviana hooted with laughter.

"I'll do it, Victor," she insisted.

"I said NO!" he screamed at her, making her cringe. "I said Junior should do it, and he *will* do it. I'm the cell leader in this group, and he will follow my instructions. Now go and search below," he said to his nervous associate, grabbing him by the arm and sending him scurrying towards the basement past Lucas. "If you find anybody, just tell them I have his friends here and that I'll kill them if they don't surrender." He turned to Lucas. "And you'd better not be lying about who's down there, or I'll shove this gun down your pretty mouth and break your pretty teeth."

Victor watched Junior disappear into the stairwell.

"Sheeesh!" he muttered disgustedly to himself, turning his attention back to his captives.

Lucas noticed the black armband attached to the cell leader's left sleeve, bearing the words "Free like the Coqui". He saw that the blond girl also wore one.

The man with the gun directed a half appraising, half-mocking look at him. Lucas recognized his type; the typical schoolyard bully: big, overdeveloped, and instinctively cruel.

"You like it?" Victor asked, pulling his armband and smiling at Lucas derisively. "Only the freedom fighters can use them."

"Freedom fighters my ass!" Maria interjected angrily. "He's just a common crook, it's what he is! He wanted me to open the safe and hand him our money. Precious freedom he's fighting for!"

Victor's lips curled into an unpleasant sneer, but his face reddened.

"We're just liberating the wealth that your kind has hoarded for so long," he asserted, winking at Viviana.

"But look, Mr. Victor," intervened Evelyn, talking to the heavily muscled gunman in a reasonable voice, while casting a reproachful look at her sister, "there's not enough money in the safe to make it worth opening."

It was true, thought Lucas, *but the vault also held some of the Joyero's most precious jewels.*

The heavy steps of Junior coming up the stairs interrupted the conversation.

"The man was telling the truth," he said to Victor, as he cleared the last steps. "There's no one down there. Just a metal door, locked from the outside with a padlock."

The beefy cell leader acknowledged the information with a nod and resumed his discussion with his captives.

"You're lying, bitch," he said to Evelyn scornfully. "I can see it in your eyes. You don't want to share your grubby money with the working class. You're a jewelry store. You're swimming in money. Everybody knows that."

"That's not true. We're—"

"Don't try to reason with him," Maria said to Evelyn, looking straight at the gunman defiantly. "He's just a punk with a gun who has less brains than a hairy monkey!"

Viviana snickered, amused by the comparison.

Victor's expression turned dangerous.

"I'm just about tired of your fucking bickering, slut!" he growled at her, cocking his gun and placing it on Maria's forehead. "Open that safe NOW! Or I'll blow your fucking brains out!"

Maria stiffened but she refused to move, clenching her jaws tightly.

"I'll do it," Fannie said quickly, and began to head towards the large safe at the back of the store.

"NO!" Victor bellowed, and his female companion stepped in front of Fannie, holding her by the shoulders and smiling.

"What difference does it make?" Fannie asked desperately, turning towards the gunman. "Can't you see that she's terrified? I'll get you the money."

"I said no!" the armed man pressed the barrel of his gun on Maria's temple. "I told the bitch to do it, and she *will* do it, or I'll blow her head all over the rest of you!"

Maria swallowed hard, and looked past the muzzle of the Glock at the face of her tormentor, the irises of her eyes shaking wildly, as they did when she felt scared.

Lucas edged closer to the enraged youth, trying to get past Antonio, who was partially blocking him.

"Do it, Maria," he urged his aunt earnestly.

Her two sisters regarded her with frightened faces, Fannie silently mouthing a prayer, while Viviana continued to watch with fascination, as if viewing a reality show on TV. Further away, Junior stood by the top of the stairway, grasping the stairs' railing, an expression of horror etched on his round face.

"Maybe we should just go," the latter suggested half-heartedly. "We have a lot of things to do."

"Then by all means go ahead and do them!" Victor snorted. "I want to see her open the safe."

Maria continued to stare at him, refusing to move. "I would rather rot in hell," she said slowly, her words brimming with visceral contempt.

"Would you?" Victor reached out with his free hand and grabbed her hair, pulling her towards him. "Would you like me to send you to hell?!" he shouted at her face.

"You leave my sister alone!" Evelyn cried furiously, and pounced on the gunman. Surprised, he let her slap him twice, then easily swatted her away with the back off his left hand, throwing her on the floor.

It was the moment that Lucas had been waiting for. He began to move forward, but before he could act, Antonio stepped in his way and jumped on Victor.

He landed on the muscular intruder just as the latter, sensing his attack, turned his gun towards him. Antonio could have stopped, but let himself fall forward, wrapping his arms around Victor's neck. The gunman fired wildly three times as he and Antonio fell to the floor together, the noise of the detonations reverberating in the small store. The *Joyero's* guard desperately clung to his adversary's arm, pinning it to the ground. Victor tried to pull Antonio away from him, but by that time Lucas had reached him.

Lucas stepped with all of his weight on the gun, crunching Victor's fingers between the floor and the weapon's metal trigger. The muscleman grunted and released the pistol, which spun on the floor a few inches from his head. Antonio sat up, and slowly struggled to get back on his feet. Victor groped for the gun, but Lucas sat on the man, and grabbed the top of his wrist. With a quick, effortless move, Lucas pulled upright the muscleman's left forearm, and shoved Victor's wrist downward with his two hands. There was an audible "snap" as his adversary's wrist broke and his hand went limp.

Victor shrieked with pain, rolling in agony on the floor. Viviana stared for a moment with amazement at Lucas, and ran out of the store, followed closely by a terrified Junior.

Antonio leaned clumsily and grabbed the gun, handing it to Lucas. Then he collapsed on the floor.

His white shirt and dark pants were drenched in blood. Lucas knelt next to him and ripped open his shirt. There were two puncture wounds in his belly, one close to his navel and the second on the upper left side of his abdomen. Blood continued to seep from the latter in large quantities, puddling around the fallen man, soaking Lucas' knees.

"Call 911!" Lucas cried, shouting over Victor's moans of pain as he looked around to find something to staunch the flow of the blood. He grabbed a cleaning rag from a nearby counter and pressed it gently on the wound. Antonio looked up at him, looking pale.

"I'm sorry," the *Joyero's* guard whispered. "I let you down. I should have checked before I opened the door."

"What are you talking about?" Lucas said to him gently. "You did great! You saved all of us." Blood kept oozing out of the bullet wounds. Lucas felt scared. He had seen wounds like that before in the battlefield. If the bullet had hit the spleen...He grabbed one of Antonio's hands and squeezed it.

"I can't get through!" Fannie said in a shaky voice.

"Keep trying," Lucas urged her calmly. Maria and Evelyn knelt next to their friend. Maria ran her fingers through his hair, while Evelyn, with one of her eyes nearly closed shut by the blow she had just received, watched with helpless tears streaming down her cheeks.

"I don't feel too good," Antonio said. He had continued to lose color, even from his lips, and had started to shake.

"You'll be okay, old friend," Lucas told him.

"Pray for me."

The prayer came naturally to Lucas. He had prayed it thousands of times while he had served in Somalia.

"The Lord is my shepherd, I shall not want," he whispered, and the others around him took up his words. "He makes me lie in green pastures. He leads me beside still waters. He restores my soul."

Antonio listened to him quietly, watching his face intently, his lips silently mouthing Lucas' prayer. His breathing became more labored.

"Even though I walk through the valley of the shadow of death, I will fear no evil; for You—" Lucas felt his words choke in his throat, and he struggled to continue. "You are with me; Your rod and your staff, they comfort me."

Lucas heard footsteps rush into the store. With the corner of his eye, he saw his mother move towards the new arrivals. There was some muted discussion, but he did not pay any attention. Antonio's eyes had become unfocused. The grip of his hand slackened.

Tears blurred Lucas' eyesight. "Surely goodness and mercy shall follow me all the days of my life; and I shall dwell in the house of the Lord...forever."

Maria sobbed disconsolately, while Evelyn covered her face with her hands.

Lucas released Antonio's hand and placed it on his chest; then he gently closed the *Joyero's* guard's eyelids. "Goodbye, my friend," he whispered.

Behind him, somebody placed the barrel of a firearm between his shoulder blades.

"Hand me over your gun," a man's voice, bereft of all emotion, ordered him.

Confused, Lucas began to turn to ask the man what he was talking about, and then realized there was a gun tucked in his waist. Apparently, he had placed it there when Antonio had handed it to him.

"Slowly now," the man behind him said. "Grab it by the end of its grip with your thumb and your index finger."

Lucas did as he was ordered. A few feet away, he saw Fannie talking to a couple, a young man and a redheaded, voluptuous woman, who were listening to her with great attention. He also noticed that Junior and Viviana had returned, and were helping the ailing Victor to climb back to his feet.

"Get up," the voice behind him said evenly, without any trace of hostility.

Lucas stood up and examined the man who had spoken to him. He was about his same height and age, with wavy brown hair and the trim, fit build of an athlete. The man appraised him with the quick professional air of an army sergeant, and directed to him a not altogether unfriendly nod. It almost seemed like the salute from one warrior to another.

"I'm sorry about your friend," the man said. "I'm going to have to frisk you. Spread your feet, lean against this counter," he ordered.

The man moved his hands swiftly over Lucas' clothes.

"He's clean," he said over his shoulder.

"I imagined as much," a taller man, standing near the back of the store, answered, as he examined the array of pearl necklaces and rings stored in the glass display cases that surrounded him. "Beautiful," he said to himself, and reluctantly abandoned his casual perusal of the *Joyero's* merchandise. He walked past Lucas, ignoring him completely, and approached Fannie, who looked very small and vulnerable next to him. Lucas instinctively moved towards her, but the man behind him placed a hand on his shoulder and stopped him. Nobody spoke as the muscleman with the shattered wrist was brought before the couple that had been interviewing Fannie.

"Did you do this?" the redheaded voluptuous woman asked Victor, pointing at Antonio's body.

"It was just a joke, we were just joking" Victor answered sullenly, still smarting from the pain. Then, realizing he had said the wrong thing, added, "They provoked it when they attacked me."

"You're lying," the young man standing next to the redhead said. "You son of a bitch, is this how you pretend to win the people of San Juan to our side?" he shouted angrily.

"No! What Victor says is true!" Viviana, standing next to Victor, interjected. "They started the fight without any provocation!" The blond girl directed a venomous look at Lucas.

"It's not true!" Fannie protested with fierce indignation, tears streaming down her cheeks, her pent-up emotions overflowing. "This man *murdered* Antonio! He would have killed my sister if Antonio had not defended her."

"Junior?" the young man turned to the nervous youth who had helped Victor get back on his feet.

Junior licked his lips, and looked at Viviana. "I was downstairs when it happened, Johnny. I didn't see what happened," he mumbled.

The man addressed as Johnny looked at the taller man who had joined them, as if seeking guidance. The tall man grimaced, signaling his reluctance to intervene.

"I think, Johnny," he said pleasantly, "that we are in the middle of a revolution, where this type of thing unfortunately happens. But if you want to find out who is to blame—"

"I do," Johnny interrupted. "This may be a revolution, but that does not give anyone the right to kill or steal from people who are not our enemies," he said with evident indignation.

"In that case," the other man continued, showing no signs of being bothered by the interruption, "and in light of the conflictive versions given by the witnesses, you will have to interrogate each of them later in more detail, to see who's lying. Unfortunately, your time is too important to do that now." The man looked around him. "Is there anywhere where we can...keep these people locked up until we can question them properly?"

Junior raised his hand timidly, as if answering a teacher in his schoolroom. "There's a shop in the cellar that can be locked from the outside. We can keep them there."

"What if he has a spare key?" the man behind Lucas asked, nodding at him.

"It's a solid metal door. Even if they had a spare key hidden somewhere, they would not be able to reach the padlock on the other side of the door."

"Good," the tall man said, as if Junior's information settled everything. "Daniel, give this gentleman the gun you just retrieved, so that he can escort these people to the cellar." The tall man walked to the box of *mallorcas* that Antonio had purchased just half an hour before. "La Bombonera," he said, reading the logo on the box. "Great pastries! I think that our detainees should take this with them, to mitigate their hunger while they wait." The man looked down at Fannie and smiled affably. "I'm sorry for the inconvenience of locking you up, madam. I promise it won't be for long."

"What about Antonio?" Lucas asked stiffly.

"Antonio?" For a moment the tall man seemed to be at a loss. Then he realized that Lucas was talking about the dead man on the floor. "I'm afraid there isn't much you can do for him now."

"May I at least cover him up?" Lucas insisted stubbornly.

The young man who had been interrogating Victor nodded. Lucas stared at him briefly.

"Is there anything to cover him with?" the tall man asked, with a hint of impatience in his voice. It was evident he was in a hurry to continue on to the next subject in his agenda, whatever that was.

Lucas took a step toward the small swing door that gave access to the narrow space behind the counters, but then remembered that he was not allowed to move. Stopping, he pointed to the display counter closest to the door, which contained several trays filled with gold charms.

"Look in the shelf under the display," he said. "There are some large cloths there that we use to cover the merchandise."

After briefly struggling with the door's lock, Junior moved behind the display counter, squatted, and came up a few seconds later with two swathes of green, velvety cloth. He gave them to Lucas, who knelt next to Antonio's body and with great care covered him up.

"We have to go," he whispered to Maria, who still knelt by her friend's head, weeping. She nodded briefly, and with Lucas' help stood up.

"After you," Junior said, waving his gun at them. From the way that he grabbed it, it was evident to Lucas that his knowledge of firearms originated from old spaghetti westerns. He was convinced that he could disarm him in the cellar, but then he would place the rest of his family in danger, when Junior failed to reappear.

"But what about the body? Are you just going to leave him lying there?" Evelyn protested with indignation, her left eye completely shut. She could not bear abandoning someone who had been a beloved member of the Pietri family like a piece of discarded litter. "And the store?" she asked with dismay, as it slowly dawned on her that there would not be an anniversary sale. "If you lock us up and leave the door open, the people from the street will steal all of our merchandise."

The tall man sighed. "We'll take care of the body, and lock up the store," he assured her in a barely civil tone.

Evelyn opened her mouth as if to speak again, but Lucas pressed her left arm with his hand, and she said nothing. Resignedly, she followed her sisters and her nephew into the cellar, closely guarded by their nervous, chubby guard.

CHAPTER XXIX

"We need to talk somewhere in private," Angel San Miguel told Johnny Ray, as they watched the small party disappear into the jewelry store's stairwell.

"How about over there?" Daniel suggested before Johnny could answer, pointing at a tiny office near the entrance of *El Joyero*.

"Yes, yes, let's go in there," agreed Yajaira, staring squeamishly at the dead body on the floor, grateful for the invitation to move away from it. Even though covered by a large cloth, a big puddle of partially clotted blood was still visible around his waist.

Johnny regarded Viviana and Victor with evident distaste.

"I want to talk to you two here when I come out of this meeting," he said to them, paying no heed to Victor's obvious discomfort. "This incident is far from over."

San Miguel, Johnny, Yajaira and Daniel squeezed into the small office. An irregularly shaped desk that could accommodate only one seat took most of the space. The men remained standing, allowing Yajaira to take the chair.

"You know, that boy needs medical attention," San Miguel said referring to Victor as he pulled back the chair for Yajaira, while watching Daniel close the door behind him. "Calderon has a medic with him. He can probably help him."

"I should let him stay that way," Johnny answered irritably. "I've known him for about a year, not that well, but enough to know that he's a bully and a liar. Now he's a murderer. I should have never let him form part of this operation!" he said, clearly upset. "How are we going to get the people on our side if we start killing and terrorizing them?"

"We didn't have enough people," Yajaira said, trying to soothe him. "We had to use those we could get."

Daniel picked up from the desk a golden turtle that had a magnifying glass where its shell should have been, and looked through it curiously. It was the only decoration on the desk, except for some picture frames holding photographs, presumably of relatives of the storeowner.

"That jeweler guy really did a number on his wrist," he said with more than a tinge of admiration in his voice. "I can stake my reputation that he is ex-military, possibly Special Forces."

"You should not be so hard on yourself, Johnny," San Miguel said, ignoring his associate's comment. "The FEPI patrols are doing great work. We passed two of them while we were heading in this direction. They were very disciplined and alert, and have maintained the order in the streets. Fortunately, most people are keeping to their homes. That makes everything easier." He smiled at Johnny. "By the way, I heard your radio broadcast. Masterful!"

Yajaira beamed at Johnny, who looked somewhat mollified by San Miguel's words.

Daniel raised a hand, signaling everyone to be quiet. For several seconds nobody spoke, listening intently. Then Daniel shrugged.

"Forgive me," he said. "I thought I heard some woman's voice. It must have been a trick of my imagination."

He paused, and made one final effort to hear.

"Somebody on the sidewalk outside, perhaps?" Yajaira ventured.

"Perhaps..." Daniel replied absently.

"Yes, well, I wanted to talk to you before the others got here," San Miguel said to Johnny, "because I consider you to be the true soul of this movement." Yajaira nodded emphatically, while Daniel struggled to keep a straight face.

"At this stage of the proceedings, securing the help of the Macheteros is essential for our success," San Miguel continued. Johnny indicated complete agreement with his head, although unconsciously raising an eyebrow, wondering where the discussion was heading. "So far, everything has exceeded our greatest expectations. Calderon and Andrade's men have neutralized the police forces in San Juan much more easily than we anticipated. There have been some police casualties, but that is inevitable."

Johnny nodded, waiting for San Miguel to continue.

"Your people are in effective control of Old San Juan and Puerta de Tierra," again Johnny nodded, "and my men and the Macheteros have captured the Grand Laguna Hotel and the *Mardi Gras* with no loss of life whatsoever. We have also captured the Governor and the Secretary of State, and the last I heard from Andrade, he was talking to Governor Pietrantoni to convince him to recognize the birth of the Puerto Rican Republic, and to resign from his office."

"That is wonderful!" Yajaira exclaimed enthusiastically, smiling and looking very attractive. Emotional tears started brimming from her large, doe-like eyes, prompting her to pry out of one of her tight pants pockets a plastic pack of Kleenex and to fish out with her long, red-lacquered nails one of the tissues. She blew her nose daintily, unconsciously tapping one of her red sneakers while she composed herself.

San Miguel paused, and then looked straight at Johnny with his most sincere expression.

"I have to be honest with you," he said. "When we started all of this, I thought that our chances of holding on to San Juan were less than fifty-fifty." In fact, San Miguel had never believed that they could hold on to San Juan for more than a couple of days. "My principal aim was the same as yours: to send a message to the Americans that Puerto Rico could never become a state, that it would never be assimilated by them. To create such a mess that they will end up wanting to get rid of the island for their own good."

"That was my idea too," Johnny confirmed, moving his head emphatically.

"I think that objective has definitely been achieved, don't you?"

"Yes," Johnny agreed, smiling happily, "yes, I think it has."

"It has," San Miguel repeated. He frowned. "And now, the more difficult objective is also within our grasp. I was watching television in the Grand Laguna and we're already on CNN. Portions of your radio message were quoted. We are officially world news!" he said with measured enthusiasm. "If we can only hold on for a few more days, Venezuela, Cuba and Iran will create enough support from other countries to bring the matter to the United Nations Security Council and embarrass the Americans. We will draw the attention of the world to the plight of your country, and I doubt that the Americans will conduct any violence against you, once the gaze of the world sets upon them."

Johnny's eyes brightened. San Miguel's words only confirmed the feeling that had been consistently growing in his heart all day long, a feeling that he could sense in the hearts of his followers as well. The FEPIsta volunteers had been supposed to wear ski masks, in order not to be recognized if the revolt failed. But almost from the outset, most of them had discarded them, and shown their faces openly and proudly. It was as if they could sense the impending success of the revolution, and were not afraid of being identified any more.

San Miguel observed him, almost reading his thoughts. He did not feel guilty playing mind games with the FEPI president. *Johnny was a big boy, and knew—or should have known—what he was getting into.* Besides, San Miguel was certain that Johnny was also trying to use *him* for his own private ambitions.

The university students gave credibility to San Miguel's operation, and allowed him to do *his* work—*God's* work—so much more easily and unobtrusively. As the FEPIstas paraded through the streets making noise and waiving their flags—and keeping the terrified residents in their homes—they diluted the risk of the leaders being identified or isolated, and confused the Puerto Rican authorities about the real number of effective fighters in San Juan.

So even though the FEPI was not essential for San Miguel's plans to succeed, it still provided a substantial edge to the operation. Therefore, it behooved on San Miguel to keep Johnny happy, at least for the time being. However, it would take all of San Miguel's persuasive talents to keep Johnny happy after the news he was about to receive.

"We still have a long way to go," Johnny said with cautious optimism.

"Yes," San Miguel acknowledged immediately, grateful for the opening that Johnny's comment had just provided to him. "That's why the participation of the Macheteros will be crucial in the next twenty-four to forty-eight hours. Even though they have limited numbers, their reputation and experience serve our cause as if they were a thousand men." He paused, hesitating noticeably.

"Somewhere, there is a 'but' in what you're going to say next, isn't it?" Johnny asked warily.

San Miguel nodded with a pained expression. Yajaira leaned forward, to listen with concerned fascination.

"Yes," he answered starkly. "Have you heard today's news?"

Johnny shook his head slowly. "I've been too busy," he explained.

"I imagined as much. Let me put you up to date." San Miguel rubbed the bridge of his nose as he gathered his thoughts. "As you know, El Alacran's main condition to help our cause was that we demand the release of his leader, Adalberto Cacho, do you recall that?"

"Of course," Johnny replied. "It seems like the obvious thing to do."

San Miguel nodded. "What I'm about to tell you must be kept strictly confidential, do you understand?"

Johnny agreed with his head.

"Last night, Andrade came to see me at the bridges, while we were setting up the explosives. He asked me how I intended to get the federal government to release Cacho from prison. I told him that, as we discussed in our meeting in San Sebastian, we would offer to exchange some of our hostages for him."

"I remember," Johnny said. He recalled a very general conversation in the San Sebastian house about how they would use of the hostages from the Grand Laguna Hotel to negotiate their demands with the federal and local authorities.

"When I told him about my intentions, Andrade reacted very negatively. He said that the federal government would never agree to such an exchange, regardless of the number of hostages that we offered. He said that such a 'limp' offer...'Limp' was the word he used, wasn't it, Daniel?"

"Limp," Daniel confirmed.

"That such a 'limp' offer would make us look weak and encourage the authorities to make unacceptable counter demands."

Johnny considered San Miguel's statement. "There's only so much that we can do," he reflected sensibly.

"That's what I told him, almost word for word," San Miguel said. "But Andrade wouldn't accept that."

"So what did he want, for us to break into prison and rescue Cacho?" Yajaira snickered.

"No, he wanted something much more dramatic. He wanted us to threaten the government with the execution of a hostage every hour until Cacho was released, starting at ten in the morning," San Miguel said in a doleful voice, his face reflecting the distress that El Alacran's demand caused him.

Johnny stiffened as if he had been slapped. Sitting in front of him, Yajaira gasped. Daniel stared at the floor.

"You said no, of course," the FEPI leader said.

San Miguel opened his hands in a helpless gesture.

"I pleaded with him, I begged him to reconsider, I told him this could affect the way that the world perceived our revolution, that it would reduce the sympathy to our cause! He refused to listen. He said that if we did not act as he said, the Macheteros would withdraw from the operation!"

"But that is blackmail!" Yajaira exclaimed indignantly. "He can't do that to—"

"I'm afraid he can," San Miguel interrupted her, unwilling to waste any time in useless chatter.

Johnny was wise enough to wait for him to continue.

"Worse of all, he demanded that the executions be made in public," San Miguel disclosed, looking miserable.

Yajaira snorted in derision, but Johnny, standing behind her, pressed her shoulders and she aborted her comment.

"What kind of public execution?" the FEPI president asked with hardly disguised dread.

"He wants us to throw the hostages from the roof of the Grand Laguna," San Miguel said wretchedly.

"No, no, no, no!" Johnny said angrily, increasing his volume with each "no". "Is he crazy? The world press will crucify us! They'll forget about the justice of our cause! They will call us terrorists, and they will be right to do so!"

Precisely, San Miguel thought. *That had been his intention all along, although Johnny would be the last to find out about it.*

"I told him as much. But in the end, he would only agree to put off the executions until two in the afternoon."

Johnny shifted uncomfortably on his feet. "Keep delaying, invent some excuse!" he suggested.

San Miguel shook his head sadly. "Andrade forced us to make the demand to the local authorities this morning. They have been made public."

Johnny looked at San Miguel in shock.

"You made the demand just as Andrade wanted?"

"We had no choice."

Johnny's eyes lost their focus, as he began to think of the possible ramifications of El Alacran's demand. *Hopefully, the authorities would take him seriously and cave in. But if not?*

"And you say that the demands were made public?" he asked.

"I tried to keep them private, to minimize the publicity. Unfortunately, the Police Superintendent held a press conference after I spoke with him and made them public."

Johnny grew pale, while Yajaira looked scared.

"Maybe they will release Cacho," the latter said.

"The Interim Governor has already rejected any further negotiations," San Miguel said with chilling finality.

Johnny looked at the faces around him with a terrified expression, as if suddenly the room had become too small for him and he had to leave.

"So what do we do now?" he asked helplessly to no one in particular.

San Miguel and Daniel exchanged a quick look.

"What do you think we should do?" San Miguel asked gently. "If we back out now, they will think that we are bluffing, that we will not back up our demands, and attack us. We will fight, but they will overwhelm us, and there will be a great deal of loss of life."

"This is worse than I thought," Johnny said disconsolately.

A long silence ensued.

"As the student of history that you probably are, you should know that in every revolution there will inevitably be casualties," Daniel said, contributing to the conversation for the first time. "I may sound like a cold blooded bastard, but the notion of bloodless coups and wars without civilian casualties is something that only your technology oriented generation has come to expect. Wars and revolutions bring violent changes. They are dirty, deadly, and bloody affairs where sometimes—usually—atrocities occur. The trick is to kill as little civilians as you can."

San Miguel raised an eyebrow and glimpsed at Johnny and Yajaira apologetically.

"Daniel has never distinguished himself for his subtleness, but he is right. As hard as it is to accept, if we are to keep our opportunities of success alive, we have to carry through on our threat. Believe it or not, it is the less bloody of the alternatives."

"It is a *terrible* alternative," Johnny said sullenly.

"I know," San Miguel answered, "but we all knew that this was not going to be simple." He fixed his eyes on the FEPI president, staring at him with a mixture of sympathy and sternness, and clenching his jaws in order not to smile.

Manipulating him was so easy!

"Johnny, you did not get to the position where you are today by making simple choices. None of us did. You are on the verge of achieving what no other patriot in the history of your country has ever achieved. Independence for Puerto Rico! Hundreds of persons who have taken the selfless commitment to fight for their country's independence rely on you. Do not let them down."

A tense hush followed San Miguel's plea, as Johnny pondered his reply. Daniel tapped his fingers softly against the wall on which he was leaning, while Yajaira unwrapped a piece of gum she had taken out of her pocket, and began to chew on it furiously.

"I really don't have any choice, do I?" Johnny stated miserably.

"You always have a choice," San Miguel answered. Even though he knew what Johnny's choice would be, a cruel streak in his nature did not allow him to let off the FEPI student that easily.

"We cannot give up on our revolution," Johnny said with reluctance after a further pause. "I will not oppose the executions...not yet, anyway. But if it becomes clear that the Americans will not relent, and that the death of the hostages is achieving nothing, I will stop it, I swear it."

San Miguel nodded slowly. "I think that is a fair alternative. If it comes to that, I will back you up." He extended his hand to Johnny who, now that he had made his decision, shook it gratefully.

"Thank you," Johnny said. "I know that this is hard for you as well."

"It is," San Miguel responded without hesitation, looking directly into Johnny's eyes. "Very hard. We should go," he added as an afterthought. "We have much to do, and I still have to meet with Andrade and Calderon before I return to the Grand Laguna Hotel. I will take up the matter with them again, and see if I can convince Andrade to relent. But don't count on it too much."

"I don't envy what you're going to have to do," Johnny said in a commiserating tone.

For a heartbeat, San Miguel seemed confused. He recovered quickly, however, as he realized the FEPI president was talking about the execution of the hostages. Their deaths had not worried him at all. After all, it had been his idea. Andrade had had no say in the demands, although he doubted that the Machetero would disagree with his ultimatum to the public authorities.

"Thank you," he said, without missing a heartbeat, and moved out of the office as Daniel opened the door for him, and followed him.

Outside, Victor, Viviana and Junior stopped talking, and waited nervously for their leader to emerge.

Lucas sat at his worktable, desperately trying to collect his thoughts. For the last ten minutes, they had been listening to the voices of the tall man, the young couple and the man who had disarmed Lucas, casually discussing plans for the execution of hostages—throwing them off the Grand Laguna Hotel's roof no less—and the violent takeover of the government of Puerto Rico.

They had followed the conversation in rapt attention, looking at the ceiling above them, from where the voices seemed to have magically emerged, and not daring to move until long after the last words had been spoken, and the terrorists had finished their meeting.

They had almost been discovered.

From *El Joyero's* main floor, Junior had escorted them down the steep stairway into Lucas' repair shop. The nervous FEPIsta had briefly searched the room, forcing Lucas to remove the welding torch that the latter used to repair jewels, and then closed the heavy metal door behind them, leaving them locked inside. A rattling on the door had let the prisoners know that the padlock had been fastened outside.

"We'll be back as soon as the situation is under control," Junior had assured his captives, not sounding very convinced.

A mood of desolation and unreality pervaded the small room. Maria slumped onto a chair and cried without stopping, while Evelyn talked mostly to herself about what they would do without Antonio. It was Fannie who had concerned Lucas the most, however. As she had entered the room, her legs had nearly failed her, and he had half-carried her to his chair, where she had silently held her head between her hands.

He had turned on his small espresso machine to make her some coffee, when the voices had begun to filter into the room.

"What is that? Who is speaking?" Evelyn had asked in a surprised voice, and Lucas had gently shushed her, pointing at the opening in the ceiling.

"Don't say a word," he had whispered urgently to his aunts and his mother. "You see that hole? It's connected to Fannie's office. They must be using it."

The Pietri sisters had stared with horrified fascination at the spot above their heads where Lucas was pointing, and kept a tense silence as they listened to the ensuing conversation.

"What are we going to do?" Maria asked in an anguished whisper, several minutes after the voices upstairs had receded.

"Those people are very dangerous terrorists!" Evelyn said in the same voice. "I told you this morning something strange was happening when we heard those explosions!"

Maria seemed ready to snap back with a sarcastic reply, but reconsidered and stayed quiet.

"What do we do?" Fannie asked. Then, looking straight at his son, she said, "They have Alfredo, don't they?"

Maria and Evelyn looked shocked. In the tension of the moment, they had completely forgotten about their grandnephew, and failed to register that he was still in La Fortaleza. Even when the tall man had announced that they had captured the Governor, they had not considered the full implication of what that meant. Now they all looked at Lucas inquiringly, waiting for him to answer his mother's question.

"I had just heard about the capture of the Governor when I came upstairs and found you with those people," Lucas said, omitting the fact that he had not intended to tell them about it until he had tried to get Alfredo out of La Fortaleza. He saw the terrified faces of his mother and his aunts and tried to reassure them. "Don't worry about Alfredo. These... people may be a lot of things, but I don't think they will hurt the children. There's enough grownup hostages as it is."

Evelyn made the sign of the cross and whispered, "Jesus, Mary and Joseph, protect him!"

"My idea was to go to Fortaleza, and ask them to return Alfredo to us."

"Just like that?" Maria asked, addressing him as if he was insane. Being the youngest of the Pietri sisters, and having lived with Lucas' parents from a very young age, she treated him more as a younger brother than as a nephew. "Then we'll have two hostages instead of one. Brilliant!"

"So what do you suggest? Call the police?"

Maria stared at him angrily, then looked away.

"Whatever we do, we have to get out of here *now*. I don't think those people are going to be back any time soon," Lucas said to them.

"Maybe we can talk to this Johnny guy, the young person who defended us upstairs," Maria said, prompting the others to nod in agreement.

"He seemed like a reasonable person. He can probably arrange to have Alfredo returned to us."

Lucas shook his head. "The people who are in La Fortaleza are not Johnny's people, and I doubt that he has any say over them. He can't even control his own people, for Heaven's sake! The FEPI is just patrolling the streets. You just heard it yourselves. The Macheteros are the real people in charge. Besides, do you really think he is going to take the time to help us when he was so pressed with so many other matters that he couldn't even ask his people what had happened in the store?"

"But the fat one, what's his name?" Fannie said, scared about what her son was proposing.

"Junior?"

"Junior. He promised that they would come back soon. Maybe we should wait for them, and see if they can help us," she pleaded.

"Mom," Lucas stared straight into his mother's eyes, "they *killed* Antonio! These people are not our friends! And as time goes by, the situation will only become worse! The government has not agreed to the demands of the terrorists. The terrorists will start killing the hostages soon, and the government will try to rescue them! There will be a lot of fighting on both sides. We have to get Alfredo out of La Fortaleza *now!*"

"What are you going to do, anyway?" Maria asked him. "We're locked up in here. There's no way of getting out."

"I may know of a way out," he answered.

"At least, let's try to talk to them before you go out there on your own," Fannie urged her son. "If they say no, well...then...do what you think you must do," she said helplessly.

Lucas brooded over his mother's request. He sighed resignedly.

"I'm willing to do this," he said. "I'll cry to the people upstairs that we need to talk to them. If there's anybody there, they'll hear us. If they answer us, I will try to convince them to help me get Alfredo out of La Fortaleza. Okay?"

The Pietri sisters nodded.

Lucas walked to the metal door and began pounding his fists on it. "Hey!" he shouted at the top of his lungs. "Is anybody out there? We need some help here!"

He continued pounding the door and screaming for several minutes, pausing periodically to listen for any sign of activity on the other side of the door. There was none.

"They've all left," he said to Fannie. "They've left us alone here."

Lucas knelt next to her mother.

"Fannie," he said softly, calling her by her first name as he did when he tried to lighten the mood. "It will be all right."

She tightened her lips and closed her eyes, shaking her head in despair.

"This is crazy!" Maria said from where she sat. "How are we going to get out of here anyway?"

"I have a key," Lucas said.

"Yes, but you can't get to the lock, remember?"

"Not from here," Lucas answered.

He walked to his worktable, grabbed it by the edge, and pulled it back until he had access to the plywood-paneled wall behind it.

"I don't know if you remember, but Robert and I used to play in the cellar when we were young."

A small, nostalgic smile appeared on Fannie's face. "I remember," she said.

Lucas grabbed a large screwdriver, and began to hammer it into a joint between two of the plywood sheets with a ten-pound hand weight he kept in the room. After a third of the screwdriver had been driven in behind the panel, he pulled the screwdriver towards him, using it as a lever to separate it from the other plywood sheets.

"There used to be this narrow crawl space..." he said while he pulled, "that looked to us like a small tunnel..." He grunted as the nail holding the plywood began to give way. "...Never could tell exactly what it was for. Probably left there to accommodate air panels or pipes that the building could need in the future, I don't know."

With a loud crunch, the upper corner of the plywood separated from the sheet next to it. Lucas put on a pair of leather gloves and grabbed the separated corner, pulling it back with all his strength. The plywood sheet made a loud, crunching noise and separated abruptly, making him lose his balance and stumble backwards.

He moved back to the panel immediately, and finished pulling the wooden plank from the wall.

"*Voilà*," he said, pointing at a small, rectangular space located at the base of the wall that must have been no wider than two feet by three feet high. The space seemed to continue behind the concrete wall of the office. "The entrance to our secret passage. It goes all the way to the central stairs of the building."

"Do you fit in there?" Maria asked dubiously.

Lucas walked to the opposite side of the room, and took down from the wall a flashlight that was hanging from a nail.

"We'll find out soon, won't we?"

CHAPTER XXX

Czecka strode to the back of the van and pulled open its twin doors.

"Out," he ordered his men, and circled the vehicle to the driver's side, where Da'ud waited outside. In front of them, the fire raged unchecked, generating so much heat that it almost singed their skin and made their eyes water and their throats hurt.

They were in the open space behind the Puerta de Tierra police station, the same area where—just over an hour before—Calderon's men had allowed the police to pick up the wounded in their helicopters. The police had long since left, and so had the Venezuelans. Except for Czecka's tiny group, the lot was deserted.

Because of the lines of abandoned cars blocking Fernandez Juncos Avenue, it had taken them much longer to get there than they had expected. They had been forced to drive the van over the sidewalk, having to negotiate past "NO PARKING" signs, side street curbs and trees, knocking down trash containers, mailboxes, and even an inconveniently bolted-to-the-floor aluminum bus stop bench that had blocked their way. Finally, nearly forty minutes after invading the sidewalk, the large, rust colored, highly scratched and dented vehicle had made it through to the corner of the narrow side street that bordered the western side of the burning building.

There had been no possibility of driving the van into the station's parking area. Not only did several destroyed police vehicles block its two entrances, but the blistering heat made it impossible for the van to get much closer. Instead, Da'ud had veered to the right, into the side street adjacent to the station, driving at full speed past the conflagration to avoid getting cooked alive. The Arab driver had steered his vehicle directly into the large, now empty lot where the helicopters had picked up the wounded policemen, not stopping until he reached the edge of the water.

There, Czecka had jumped out of the van and walked back towards the burning building, examining it from a prudent distance. Large, orange flames continuously swelled out of the two gates in the lower floor of the station and flickered from every window in the floors above, licking the concrete walls above them and trailing swirling plumes of black smoke. Despite this—Czecka noted with quiet satisfaction—only a few scattered, mostly small, blackened and unrecognizable chunks of smoking debris littered the narrow back road between the smoldering building and the empty lot where he stood. Otherwise, the street was clear of any major obstructions.

Czecka made his way closer to one of the exits of the empty lot. About thirty yards from the exit, at a slightly diagonal angle, lay one of the two open entrances to the cellar of the burning police station. It would be easy to drive the van into the building from that spot.

Covering his face with one of his arms, the humongous man ran to where a bumper-sized piece of debris interrupted the path between the station and the empty lot, and dragged the smoldering chunk away, feeling the searing heat of the conflagration on his back and thighs. Then he quickly backed away to the relative safety of the empty lot, and signaled with his arm to the waiting van to approach him.

"We will do it from here to there," he informed Da'ud, pointing with his huge, beefy hand at the open gate of the station, and walking away to let out the men in the back of the vehicle.

The Arab nodded, mostly to himself, and slowly edged the van forward, pointing it toward the garage entrance. As he did so, he carefully turned his steering wheel until a red mark at the top of the wheel was aligned with a similar red mark on the dashboard, showing that the tires of the van were straight. He then slowly backed away, carefully keeping the two red marks even, to make up for the distance he had traveled forward to straighten the wheels, and to escape the scorching heat that filtered through the glass of his windshield and closed windows. Placing the vehicle in "Park", he leaned forward, and pulled out from under his seat a wooden stick. He pressed down on the accelerator, and wedged the stick between the depressed pedal and the driver's seat.

"It's ready," he shouted to Czecka over the roar of the Raptor V-8 engine, as the uncommunicative giant approached him. "Do you want me to do it?"

"No," Czecka answered, not wasting any further words.

The van vibrated violently, its 400 horsepower barely held in check. Czecka wanted to make certain that nothing in it would raise any suspicions, if for any reason its charred remains were later examined. The wooden stick holding down the accelerator would be consumed by the fire, after the vehicle speeded into the burning building.

Czecka stared at the station. The flames enveloped most of the walls of the structure. The upper floors of the building would not hold up for long. Because of the special features of the van—the steel sheets and lead lining on its walls, and the puncture resistant wheels, among others—San Miguel had decided to keep it hidden in La Perla until the damaged bridges had been restored to their full use. Then he had planned to transfer the van to a remote location of the island, and dispose of it there.

La Perla was a rocky strip of land encapsulated between the Atlantic Ocean and the northern walls of Old San Juan. A prime piece of real estate, it had been occupied by squatters since the nineteenth century, and eventually become a community unto itself, operating outside of the boundaries—and the walls—of the old city. Avoided as a dangerous place even by the local police, illegal drug trade had flourished there for decades, and drug kingpins had lorded over the community as its *de facto* rulers, ruthlessly eliminating the competition while securing the loyalty of its residents by dispensing generous gifts—paying even for the residents' medical and other types of expenses. Recently, the police, community leaders, and social reformers had challenged the hold of the drug lords over the community. However, strong pockets of the isolated neighborhood remained under their control.

San Miguel had contacted a local drug chieftain called "El Gordo Purcell", and secured a private garage where the van could be stored under Purcell's protective vigilance until it could be moved away. San Miguel had not wanted the vehicle to be discovered and examined by the police or even worse, by the federal authorities. But the accidental conflagration of the police building had provided him with the unique and unforeseen opportunity to dispose of the vehicle in an effective and immediate fashion. He had contacted Czecka, and ordered him to—"if feasible"—plunge the van into the fire, where it would burn with countless other vehicles, and be covered by the flaming rubble of the collapsing building. The probabilities that anyone would take the time to examine the burned wreckage of the van and find something there that would reveal any significant information about the device that the van had carried, would be infinitesimal.

Czecka stretched his right leg and pressed the brake pedal, while keeping the other foot outside of the van. He reached for the gearshift, and slid it from "Park" to "Drive". The van lunged slightly forward as its transmission allowed it to move, but its brakes held it in check. Then, heaving himself backwards, he released the brake pedal, and let the vehicle go.

The van rushed forward, heading directly towards the garage entrance. At the last moment, it began to veer slightly to the left and Czecka held his breath as he thought that it would hit the left side of the entrance. But in the end, it missed the wall, passing so close to the garage door's frame that its side view mirror was sheared off, then disappearing into the roaring blaze. A noisy crash of metal and glass and the screeching of the van's wheels followed its entry, as the vehicle's revved up engine continued to push against the debris inside.

Czecka stared into the fire until the van's gas tank exploded with a loud "whumph". For the next half hour, he watched the building burn from a safer distance, braving the smoky haze that blotted the sun from the sky. Finally, the two upper floors of the station caved in on the lower level, covering the garage entrance and the small street behind it with a mountain of smoldering debris.

Grunting with satisfaction, Czecka began to walk towards the Grand Laguna Hotel, followed by his men.

John McFadden made his living by traveling alone in cruise ships, preferably in cruises lasting seven days or longer. At two years over forty, he still looked fit, although lately—due to the abundant, never-ending and surprisingly good food thrust at every waking hour upon him—he had gained about five pounds over his ideal weight that had stubbornly refused to dissipate despite his continuous visits to the ship's gym. He still retained his innocent-but-mischievous good looks, however, which—combined with his Australian accent—seemed to make him irresistible to most women. Therefore, the extra weight did not trouble him that much. In fact, business continued to flourish. In the last cruise, he had actually been forced to choose between several prospects who had expressed interest in his company.

John was in the escort service business for lonely—or not so lonely—women who traveled in cruise ships. Some called him a gigolo, and he did not mind it; in fact, he took pride in being in the position of providing companionship to women who desperately needed it, in exchange for monetary remuneration. He considered himself to be among the best in the trade, and his clientele confirmed it. Those women who chose to be with him, usually ten or more years his senior, were made to feel like royalty, even though he was very upfront with them about his occupation. He would literally wine and dine them—with their money—take them dancing, and rub suntan lotion on their backs in the pool deck.

Most importantly, he talked to them. He actually listened to what they said and thought, and gave them his honest opinion about their problems. When he had started the business, he had been amazed at how many women were starved for personal attention, and how little sex his job required. It was company that most women wanted, and he provided it unconditionally.

On the *Mardi Gras* cruise he had provided his services to a very fit, seventy something divorcee—she had never revealed to him her true age—whom he had escorted twice before in other cruises. Like him, she was a habitual traveler in the gigantic ships; she had more than one hundred and fifty cruises under her belt, and was treated by the captain and his crew as a sort of mini celebrity. She called herself the Countess of Gilly, and conducted herself with the dignified manners of royalty, so she very well may have been a countess, as far as McFadden was concerned. She was French, anyway. And very generous. Her tip alone would pay for his next trip.

That morning he had risen at 6:45 AM. He had a late connection to fly to Miami, and had made arrangements to disembark with the last group of passengers. Nevertheless, he had agreed to have breakfast in the Countess's fourteenth deck suite, not only because it was good business—he expected to accompany her in other future cruises—but because he actually enjoyed the company of the royal traveler.

As always, he had decided not to take the elevator from his eighth deck cabin, but to use the stairs for the exercise. The Countess's suite was located in the middle-forward section of the cruise ship, which meant he had to walk through the ship's casino and English pub in order to reach the forward stairway. As he did so, he stopped briefly in the pub to say goodbye to an English couple he had befriended during the trip. Their time to disembark was fifteen minutes overdue, and they were waiting for their group to be called.

While they talked, the ship's intercom system chimed three times, followed by the captain's voice.

"Your attention, please," it said. *"We have been advised that... unknown terrorists have blown up all of the bridges connecting the island of San Juan to Puerto Rico."* The captain paused, and it seemed to John that even though he spoke in a deliberately controlled tone, he could not mask the stress behind it. *"There is, at this moment, no possible means of getting to the airport or to most of the hotels in the island. The local authorities have stopped the further disembarkation of passengers or crew until the situation is stabilized, and their safety can be guaranteed. Until then..."* the captain seemed to hesitate, *"until then, you need to remain on board. Presently, armed customs officers are boarding the ship to protect it from any attempt of sabotage. Please return to your cabins and remain there until further notice. All restaurants will remain open to serve meals, as they become necessary. Thank you for your patience."*

Confusion followed the announcement. Concerned passengers mobbed those members of the crew that were nearby. It did not reassure them to see that the crew seemed as confused as they were. People milled about everywhere, talking excitedly and speculating about what was happening. Very few obeyed the captain's instructions to return to their rooms.

John said goodbye to his British friends, and continued towards his appointment with the Countess. If he was to spend any time waiting in a room, he would rather do it in her ample suite. As he prepared to ascend the stairs, he noticed through a window two U.S. Customs men armed with semiautomatic rifles enter the ship through the Promenade Deck, a few floors below him.

The corridor that led to the Countess's suite was deserted except for two room stewards who were busy cleaning up a chamber from one of the passengers who had already left. John wondered what the stewards would do when the passengers returned to the room.

He knocked on the Countess's door, and she opened it almost immediately.

"Bon jour," she said pleasantly, kissing him on the cheek. "Breakfast is already served, and getting cold. Come in, come in, *s'il vous plait.*"

In her time, the Countess of Gilly must have been a stunning woman. Even at seventy, she managed to maintain a thin, attractive figure, and when she smiled, her face lit up with the unrestrained mirth and energy of a teenager. Her eyes were transparent blue, and seemed to take in everything with amused interest.

McFadden walked into an ample, blue-carpeted living room containing three overstuffed light yellow sofas, a low central glass table, and a wide walnut cabinet that supported a sixty-inch flat screen television set and every other modern electronic convenience. She grabbed his hand and walked him into the dining room, which opened to a wide balcony with ceiling-to-floor glass windows, showing the Bay of San Juan. The dining room table, which could seat up to eight guests, had been set up with elegant cutlery and silverware for two.

A jar of orange juice, a plate filled with slices from various tropical fruits, a large coffee pot, three different jams and butter, and a large breadbasket covered by a napkin cloth had been placed on the table. An open bottle of champagne was kept cold in a silver ice bucket, part of its content already mixed with the orange juice in two high fluted crystal glasses.

"Mimosas!" John said happily. "What better way to start the day!"

"I took the liberty of ordering a special breakfast for you," the Countess said, pointing at a covered plate on John's station.

John uncovered the plate, finding scrambled eggs, half a dozen strips of bacon, and hash browns.

"You pamper me," he said smiling.

"*Vraiment,* I can't understand how you can eat all of that greasy food," she said. "It is full of cholesterol and it will kill you sooner rather than later."

"Not everyone can hope to live as long and look as beautiful as you do," he answered, meaning it. Ever since they had known each other, they had engaged in platonic flirting, which had never progressed beyond that. Had she been ten years younger, it could have been another matter.

He took the two *mimosa* glasses by their stems, and gave one to the Countess. "*A votre santé,*" he said, clicking the glass and taking a sip from it. As he savored his drink, he looked out of the windows into the bay. To his left, he could see two large columns of smoke rising from the city. It seemed like two large fires were burning somewhere. He wondered if it had anything to do with the announcement of the captain. If so, more than the bridges had been destroyed.

"It appears that we are to remain here for a while longer," the Countess said, standing next to him and staring at the fires. "So come, eat your breakfast before it gets cold."

"I'd rather stay here than anywhere else," he replied, trying not to show any of the uneasiness that he felt, and sitting at the table.

"Maybe the ship will continue to travel elsewhere, where it's safe," she suggested.

He shrugged. "Maybe. Although it would alter the connection arrangements for most of the passengers." He lifted the cover from his plate, and attacked his food with relish.

They spoke little as they ate. It was one of the aspects of their relationship that he enjoyed; no forced conversations or awkward pauses. Several times, they heard the muted voice of the intercom outside, and once John stood up and opened the door to the corridor to listen to what was being said. Passengers were being urged to leave the public areas and return to their cabins, or risk being detained by the customs officers.

"More of the same," he told the Countess as he returned to the table. But the announcement on the intercom bothered him. *Why stay in the rooms? That did not make any sense whatsoever. Why couldn't the passengers be allowed to use the facilities of the ship? It wasn't as if the terrorists were roaming the ship's corridors.*

"Something is troubling you," the Countess said, looking shrewdly at him.

John pondered what to say for a moment, and was about to speak when an urgent rap on the door interrupted him. He began to stand up, but the Countess got up before him.

"Eat your breakfast before it gets cold," she insisted in an almost motherly fashion, and walked quickly to the door.

John chewed on a piece of bacon, while listening to the hurried voice of the man who had apparently knocked on the door. He could not understand his words, but they sounded insistent. He heard the Countess answer something, the man respond with even more urgency, and the door slam shut.

"What was it?" he asked as he heard the Countess return.

"We have a visitor," the Countess announced in a neutral tone.

John turned and saw a man wearing the dark blue blazer and white pants of the crew enter the dining room behind the Countess. John recognized him immediately as one of the dining room managers of the Four Seasons Restaurant, a slight, thin, effeminate-looking, perennially smiling Filipino man to whom he had spoken several times while in the company of the Countess. This time, however, he seemed very upset, sweating profusely and breathing very heavily. John looked at the Countess quizzically, but she raised one of her eyebrows, silently letting him know she did not fully understand why the man was there.

"You remember Ernan, don't you, John?" she said. "Maybe you can explain to John what is the matter," she suggested helpfully.

"Please forgive me for barging in here so unexpectedly. I did not know where to go," the man said with such distress that he seemed to be on the verge of crying. He tried to speak, and swooned, holding on to a chair. John noticed that his right hand was bleeding, and quickly stood up to grab him. He led the wounded man to a chair and made him sit.

"Here," the Countess said, pouring him a glass of champagne. "This will make you feel better."

Ernan accepted the glass gratefully, but his left hand was shaking so badly that he had trouble bringing it to his lips. The Countess held it for him, and he took several swallows.

"You are hurt," she said. Placing the glass on the table, she moved behind him. "We must remove your jacket, to see your wound. John, would you be so kind to call the ship's infirmary?"

"No!" Ernan said, shaking his head wildly. "They will be expecting the call, and come to kill me!"

"Who is *they*?" John asked gently.

"The pirates!" he answered. "Pirates have taken over this ship!"

Ernan stopped talking and grunted, as the Countess removed his jacket. His right-hand shirtsleeve was soaked with blood below his elbow all the way down to his hand. The Countess carefully rolled up his sleeve, exposing a deep gash on his forearm. Fortunately, it had not severed any major blood vessels.

"I will get some alcohol," she said, and hurriedly walked to her room.

"Who did this?" John asked Ernan.

"Pirates," he stated again. "After the captain announced that the passengers had to remain on board the *Mardi Gras*, we got flooded with people asking that we open up the Four Seasons Restaurant, to serve breakfast. I tried to reach the captain on the bridge to get his authorization, but I could not reach him. I imagined that everybody was trying to talk to him at the same time, and that I would have to go up to the bridge to talk to him in person, so that is what I did."

The Countess came back, carrying a small plastic bottle, a washcloth, and some large bandages. "A world traveler must always be prepared," she said, pouring some alcohol out of the plastic bottle into the towel, and lightly applying it to the wound. After cleaning the gash—which extended nearly from the end of his elbow to his upper wrist—she applied some antibiotic cream, and began to cover it with gauze.

Ernan winced, but he continued. "When I got close to the bridge, it's door opened, and a man backed out of its door, pulling something. He was wearing a uniform, it said United States Customs on the back, and what he was pulling was so heavy, he did not see me at first. I thought he might need some assistance, and moved towards him, and that's when he heard me." Ernan shuddered involuntarily. "The man released one of his hands and turned, and as he did, I saw that what he was pulling was a man. A dead man! His eyes were open, and I recognized him, it was Bates, the security officer."

John and the Countless listened in absolute silence, too shocked to say anything.

"I stood there paralyzed, not knowing what was happening. Then the man shouted at me and pulled out a gun, and I ran. The man fired several times, but he missed me, or so I thought," Ernan said, looking at his wound. "I didn't feel this until later. I dodged into a corridor, and heard him following me, so I ran as fast as I could and doubled back into the corridor where he had been. I ran back to Mr. Bates, and saw he had been shot twice in the chest. Then I heard footsteps, and I hid inside a closet close to the body."

Ernan was shaking so much that John feared he would faint.

"I left a crack of the door open, to be able to see what was happening outside. And then I saw the same man who had shot at me grab Mr. Bates by both hands, and begin to drag him towards me, and then he stopped, and looked at the floor and at the closet where I was hiding, and then he took his gun out and walked directly to where I was hiding."

Ernan shuddered, and the Countess gently placed her hand on his shoulder.

"He opened the closet's door as I grabbed hold of something metallic, I think it was a vacuum cleaner metal extension of some sort, and he pointed the gun at me, but I screamed and I hit him on the head, hit him with all my strength, and he fell backwards, and I kept hitting him and screaming until his face was all bloodied up and he didn't move any more! Then I heard more voices and footsteps of people coming, and I ran up the stairs to this floor. I remembered you were in this suite, our VIP passenger, so I knocked on your door praying that you were here. I thank God that you were!"

He looked desperately at the Countess. "They are looking for me, I know it, and if they find me they will kill me! I need your help, please!"

John and the Countess exchanged a quick look. What the man said seemed unbelievable, a US customs officer assaulting a member of the crew and dragging the body of another? And yet, Ernan could not have faked his distress. The Four Seasons dining room manager was thoroughly terrified. And he was wounded. He could have faked the wound, but for what purpose?

It all added up, McFadden thought. The captain ordering everybody to their cabins, the refusal to let any passengers off the ship, the customs men roaming the decks with semiautomatic weapons. The *Mardi Gras* was being hijacked.

Which meant that if Ernan was found in the Countess's suite, they would all be in grave danger. John pressed his hand over the Countess's arm, letting her know they needed to talk.

"Will you excuse us for a minute? Please, have some food," he said to their disturbed visitor.

John and the Countess walked into her room's large, marble decorated bathroom, and shut the door.

"We have to get rid of him," he said to her, as soon as they were out of hearing range.

"What do you mean? The man is wounded! They are looking for him and it is possible that they may kill him!" she protested. "We can't throw him out!"

"You don't understand," John said gravely. "There is nowhere here where we can hide him. They will be looking for him. He may have even left a trail of blood to this cabin. The only thing we will achieve by keeping him here will be to put our lives at risk!"

The Countess regarded her companion with a look of stubborn disappointment.

"What you suggest is the same as if the Nazis came looking for Jews, and we turned them over to them. Do you know that I am half-Jewish?" She stared at him and slowly turned her head. "No, you did not know, *n'est ce pas?* My mother was a French Jew. She survived the war because some very kind people risked their lives to hide her."

"It's not the same," John countered weakly.

"I can't see the difference," she replied angrily. "If you are so concerned, go back to your—"

She stopped, as someone knocked loudly on the suite's door. John opened the bathroom's door, careful not to make any noise, hoping that whoever was outside would think the room was empty. It was no use. The knocks continued, this time as loud bangs.

"Go!" the Countess ordered John. "Hide Ernan, while I deal with the people outside!"

The Countess walked to the suite's door, took a deep breath, and half-opened it, looking outside.

A woman waited in corridor. She wore jeans and a blue shirt that had stenciled in black letters over her right breast the words "US Customs". A similarly colored cap, bearing the same logo, covered her short blond hair. On her hands, she carried a rifle of some sort, as well as a holster tied to her belt. She must have been in her low thirties or maybe high twenties, although it was difficult to tell because of the hardness of her brown eyes. The woman regarded the Countess with amused curiosity, and tried to push the door further in, but could not because of the Countess's foot.

"I am looking for a man who assaulted one of our officers. Please let me in," she said, again trying to force her way past the Countess, and again encountering resistance.

"There is nobody here except my friend John McFadden, who is having breakfast with me, but if we see anybody—"

The customs woman pointed her rifle at the Countess, and nudged it into her stomach.

"Then maybe you can explain the blood on the handle of the door," she replied with a half amused smile.

The Countess stared at lock of her door, and confirmed it was stained in crimson, as was part of the door itself.

"I don't...know who did this," she answered helplessly. "The person you are looking for must have tried to get in and left."

"He's here all right," the blond customs woman replied, her grin widening. "I followed his blood stains to this door, and they don't come out of here. So move!"

The woman jabbed her rifle hard into the Countess's stomach, making the old woman double up in pain, and walked past her. She continued into the dining room, where she saw a man sitting at the table having breakfast. He looked over his shoulder when she entered, and stood up next to his chair, looking startled.

The customs officer pointed her rifle at him.

"Hands above your head, sweetheart," she said, examining him briefly for signs of an injury, then darting her eyes from one side of the room to another. "Are you alone?"

John slowly raised his hands, and placed them on his head. "No," he answered. And after a pause, added, "The Countess of Gilly is here with me."

"The Countess...*that* old lady?" the woman said, with a faint trace of surprise in her voice.

"Is something wrong?" John asked, in a concerned tone.

"Who else is here?" the woman said, ignoring his question.

"Besides the Countess? No one."

The customs woman continued to scan the room. Deciding there was nowhere to hide, she motioned John towards the bedroom with her weapon.

"Move."

Even though opulent and large, there were not too many places in the master bedroom where a man could hide. The large mahogany double-door closet only contained enough room to store the astonishing array of clothes and shoes that the Countess carried with her, and the cabinet under another wide screen LCD television was subdivided by shelves that made it impossible for a grown man to hide. A quick search below the bed revealed three pieces of matching, leopard printed luggage. The space under the desk was open and empty.

"There's no one here," John insisted.

The woman nudged her head towards two extra bunk beds that were folded against the inner wall of the room.

"Open them," she said.

John approached the two bunk beds and opened the lower one. It was empty.

"Satisfied?" he asked.

"The other one," the woman ordered, pointing her gun at him.

John pulled on the strap on the side of the upper bed, but it would not swing open.

"Do it!" she shouted at him, making him cringe. He pulled harder and, reluctantly, the bed gave way until it opened. There was no one there.

John gestured with his two hands towards the empty bed, like a model in a television game show showing a prize. For a split second, the US customs woman looked bewildered. She recovered quickly, however, and directed John to move out of the bedroom into the living room.

"You first," she told John.

He ambled past her and she began to follow, when something on the blue carpet caught her eye.

"Wait," she said, and knelt beside what seemed to be a small, dark spot next to the king-sized bed. She rubbed it with her thumb and index finger, and examined it. The tips of both fingers were red.

Standing up, she grabbed the bed's quilted cover and pulled it down.

Ernan was lying across the width of the bed, behind three pillows.

With a shout of triumph, the customs officer leveled her semiautomatic rifle at the terrified crewman. "You killed one of our people," she said with a sneer. "Now it's your turn!"

John realized she was about to shoot the Filipino on the bed, and jumped on her before she could press the trigger. The woman, however, was far too quick, and as he tried to grab her she turned and struck him hard with the butt of her rifle on the solar plexus. John gasped with pain and fell to his knees. The woman gripped him by the hair, and was about to crunch her knee into his face when Ernan tackled her from the bed, screaming like a madman. They fell on the floor in a tangle of arms and legs, the woman still holding on to her rifle.

John tried to get back on his knees and rejoin the fight, but could barely breathe. With the corner of his eye, he saw Ernan and the woman roll on the floor, both exchanging blows, Ernan receiving the worst part of them. Then a shadow rushed past him, and he realized that the Countess, too, had joined the fight. He heard the noise of curses, grunts, and kicks, but lost sight of the others as they rolled behind the bed.

After several seconds, John finally managed to push himself up with his arms from the floor. Leaning over the bed, he saw the woman flat on her back, choking Ernan by the throat. The Filipino was frantically trying to pull her hand away, but could not free himself from her stranglehold, even with both of his hands. The Countess sat on her waist, trying to pin her left hand to the floor, while receiving a tremendous pounding on the back from the woman's knees. The customs agent seemed to be slowly squirming from under the old woman.

"Heeeeelp!" the agent began to scream at the top of her lungs, over and over again. "Heeeelp!"

Terrified that she would be heard, John stumbled onto the bed and grabbed a pillow. He staggered past the Countess, and pressed the pillow on the woman's face, stifling her cries. The customs agent released Ernan's throat, and the Filipino fell sideways on the floor, coughing violently. The woman fumbled for the gun in her holster, but John gripped her wrist, preventing her from drawing her weapon. With only one hand pressing the pillow, however, John could not prevent the woman from turning her head sideways and renewing her wild screams for help.

"Damn it!" he muttered, astonished by the strength of the woman. Then Ernan crawled to them and clutched the pillow, pressing it hard against the agent's face.

The woman freed her wrist from John's grip and again tried to draw the gun from her holster, but again John stopped her.

"Do you give up?!" he shouted at her, but if she heard him she continued to struggle, and almost freed her hand yet again. "Do you give up?" John repeated more urgently.

The woman began to kick both of her feet more rapidly, and to frantically buckle her waist up and down, making the Countess bounce as if she were riding a wild bronco. Then her movements began to weaken, until her hands and legs went limp.

"I think she's suffocating," John told Ernan. "Release the pillow!"

But the Filipino man kept pressing the pillow down, his eyes blinded by fear and rage, his brain failing to register any words.

"Ernan!" John shouted, and when the Filipino failed to respond, he pushed him away. Hurriedly, the Australian removed the pillow from the woman's face. Her brown, hard eyes were open, her mouth stretched into a wild grimace, and she was not breathing. He tried to feel for a pulse on her neck, like he had seen doctors do in the movies, but could feel nothing.

"Oh my God," he said in a horrified voice. "I think we killed her!"

The Countess tried to stand up but could not.

"Please help me," she said to John, extending her arms towards him. Almost zombie-like, John took her hands and pulled her up.

"Are you all right?" he asked her. She rubbed her back and nodded.

"Get her gun," she said, "just in case she wakes up."

"But she's dead!" he protested.

"I hope so, sincerely," the Countess answered, staring at her distrustfully. "She was a terrible woman!"

John picked up the semiautomatic rifle, and pulled a .45 automatic from the dead woman's holster. Beside him, Ernan stared at the body as in a daze.

"They will be looking for her," John said anxiously. "It won't be long until they follow Ernan's bloody trail here, as she did!"

"Then we will have to hide her and go somewhere else," the Countess responded while rubbing her back, as if that would solve all of their problems. "Ernan, you know this ship better than us. Do you know where we can hide?"

The Filipino thought for a moment, and nodded.

"This is a big ship," he answered, already mapping a route in his head. "The pirates cannot be everywhere. The crew's quarters will be a good place to hide. Also, there are many passages throughout the ship that avoid the public areas and are used by the crew to move about. I think we can use those. Especially now, that the pirates are busy guarding the passengers."

The Countess looked at John for his approval. He shrugged, unable to think of anything better to say. The events of the last few minutes had overwhelmed him. From wrapping up a wonderful cruise, he had ended up killing a terrorist and placing his life in terrible jeopardy. They should have sent the Filipino away while they still had a chance. Ernan would have done exactly what the three of them would now have to do: hide in the ship. But now, now it was too late.

The Countess stared at him with her clear blue eyes, as if reading his thoughts.

"You can still go back to your cabin and stay there if you wish," she said. "Ernan and I are compromised, he because he was seen and wounded, I because they will find the body in my cabin. But you..."

"We can always throw the body overboard from the balcony," John suggested lamely.

"And risk that one of the terrorists sees it fall from above? Or that they see the body floating in the bay? No, *mon cher,* go! We will hide the woman here, somewhere, and hope they will discover her...later rather than sooner."

John considered the Countess's suggestion briefly. She was right on all counts. If he got to his cabin, nobody would know he had participated in the killing of the terrorist woman or helped the Filipino escape. Anyway, how would his staying with the others help them in any way whatsoever? God knew that he was not a fighter. His struggle with the customs woman had confirmed that. And a group of three people would run a bigger risk of being detected than two. If anything, he would be a hindrance to them.

"Go, go," the Countess urged him, waving her hand as if shooing a cat. "We will be all right in the decks below."

John sighed and shook his head.

"We're all in this together," he replied, not believing the words that were coming out of his mouth, even as he was saying them. "I can't...I'm not leaving you behind."

The Countess regarded him with deep affection, and kissed him on the cheek.

"You are a very brave and gallant man," she said smiling.

"I thought you knew me better than that," he said, smiling back at her.

"But I do," she replied. "I do."

They carried the dead woman between the three of them, John grabbing her by her armpits, Ernan and the Countess each picking up a leg, and lay her across the bed's headboard, where the Filipino had previously hidden. They placed the bed's three pillows over the outstretched body, and covered it with the bedspread. The made-up king-sized bed looked normal, except for its overstuffed pillows.

They did not tarry long in the suite. Collecting a few water bottles and some crackers wrapped in plastic, they gathered by the cabin's door and listened for noises outside. Then John opened the door and casually stepped into the hallway. He walked several steps in the direction of the stern, as if searching for a steward, and stopped in front of a door with letters stenciled in black that read "For crewmembers only". There was no one in sight.

Looking back, he saw the Countess's head sticking out from the half open door of her suite, and signaled her to approach. He pushed down the handle of the door leading to the crew's stairway and it gave way, opening inwardly. He listened for a moment and, hearing nothing, stepped inside. Less than a second later, Ernan and the Countess joined him, carrying the weapons of the fake customs agent.

Silently, they began to descend towards the bowels of the *Mardi Gras*.

CHAPTER XXXI

"Frigorifico El Coqui," a female voice answered.

"Hello!" Archie said excitedly through the satellite phone. "Can you hear me?"

There was a pause at the other end, and then the female voice said, *"Yes?"*

"Listen, this is very urgent. I need to talk to El Chino."

Another pause followed. Then the female voice said, *"I'm sorry, but El Chino is not here right now. Call him later."*

"Wait, wait, don't hang up!" Archie urged a little too loudly, and cringed, knowing he would antagonize the woman who had answered his call.

"Yes?" the female hissed impatiently.

"It's very important that I talk to him, I—"

"I told you already, he's not here!"

"...know that he's there. He's always there—"

"I'm going to hang up!"

"Wait!" he shouted urgently. He was painfully aware of the anxious stares of Michelle, Negron and the others. "Wait," he said in a lower voice.

"Yesss?" the woman repeated, clearly at the end of her patience.

Archie looked away from the others and cupped his hand over the mouthpiece.

"Tell El Chino that this is El Colorao. Tell him that this is a matter of life and death, and that if he doesn't come, the police may come by his house," he whispered fiercely.

There was no answer. Archie could tell that the woman had not hung up, because he could hear in the background voices, either from the radio or television, talking about the bridges. Therefore, he waited.

He had called the only satellite phone number that he knew, that of El Chino ("The Chinaman"). El Chino was a big, fat, hairy man who did not look at all Chinese. He lived in an old apartment building in Miramar, close to the Condado Lagoon, which he would share with different women. Once a week, Archie would deliver to him the proceeds of his *bolita* sales—*bolita* being the illegal lottery played in Puerto Rico. El Chino would always complain about Archie's meager profits, but valued "El Colorao"—as he called Archie—for his conversation. He would sit with his redheaded business companion for hours, and chat about crime and politics, two of his favorite subjects, or show Archie the latest technological gadgets that he avidly purchased as soon as they came into the market.

Some two months before, El Chino had displayed to Archie his new satellite phone.

"With this," he had told El Colorao, "I can make a call from anywhere in the world!"

"But you're always here!" Archie had argued.

El Chino had directed to him an offended look. "I travel," he had said vaguely. "And if I ever need it, it will be here." He had given Archie his satellite's phone number, in case he ever needed to communicate with him "while he was away". Archie had entered the number into his cell phone directory, and quickly forgotten about it.

Until now. Archie had dialed El Chino's satellite phone number, and hoped that the gadget was not buried in some drawer, along with so many of the fat man's other technological wonders. To his surprise, the phone had been answered after the second ring. The woman who answered—he had never spoken to her before—had used El Chino's fictitious business name, *Frigorifico El Coqui.*

Finally, Archie heard some activity at the other end of the phone, followed by a heavy wheeze.

"Hello," El Chino's gruff voice said, sounding more like *"Yeh-low".* *"Colorao, is that you?"*

"Yes, how are you, Chino?"

"Blanquita told me you're threatening to call the police on me," he said with a half-laugh.

"She was threatening to hang up on me," Archie explained. "You know I wouldn't do that to you."

"I know, I know," he said, then lowering his voice he added conspiratorially, *"It's very hard getting good help these days, you know what I mean? Anyway, it's my fault. I told her I didn't want to be bothered. I've been watching the fires on TV. Have you seen them?"*

"Seen them? I'm between them!" Archie replied, turning back his head towards the rest of the group, and raising his eyebrows at Michelle. "Listen, that's what I'm calling you about."

"Why are you using my satellite phone?" El Chino interrupted.

"Have you tried to use the regular phones today?" Archie asked.

"No, come to think of it, you're the first call I've received all morning. Not working, are they?" he immediately concluded.

"No," Archie confirmed, and before El Chino could engage him in any additional small talk, he said, "We were lucky you didn't have your phone packed away somewhere."

"There's nothing lucky about it. I never buy stuff to keep it packed away. I keep this one in my penthouse terrace, where it can pick up calls, you know?"

It made sense. In a drawer, the satellite telephone would become a useless scrap of technology.

"Listen, Chino," Archie said tentatively, "I need a special favor from you."

"Uhum," El Chino responded noncommittally.

"We're trapped here, in San Juan. When I say I'm between the two fires, I mean it, literally. Some people have even tried to kill us."

Archie waited for some sort of response from El Chino, but just got another *"Uhum"*.

"I'm with a group of people here, and we're trying to escape from some terrorists. I have a child, two women, and an old man with me. One of the women is Michelle, Michelle Alfaro, the reporter from WKPA, and she has some vital—"

"Really?!" El Chino asked excitedly. *"Michelle Alfaro? Put her on! I want to say hello to her."*

Archie closed his eyes in exasperation.

"El Chino wants to say hi to you," he told Michelle, handing her the satellite phone. "Make it quick, so we don't lose the signal."

Michelle grabbed it, and quickly spoke into it. "Hello? Hello? Mr. Chino?" she said, while Archie watched her impatiently.

Next to her, Negron mouthed to Archie the words: "Who the hell is this guy?" while the babysitter smiled and Don Moncho looked confused.

"Hi, this is Michelle Alfaro."

"Wow!" El Chino exclaimed. *"It really is you! I just want to tell you how much I admire your work. You are a wonderful reporter! I loved that—"*

"Thank you," Michelle said, trying to cut the conversation short, while Archie glared at the ground. "You are very kind, but now we really need your help."

"Uhum," he responded, immediately assuming his business tone.

"I need to get in contact with my editor in WKPA, and the telephones don't work."

"Yes," El Chino replied, a little less guardedly.

"We can only get in contact with him via a satellite telephone, but the only person with a satellite telephone that we know is you."

"So what do you want?" he asked suspiciously.

"I need somebody to go to the station and tell them to call us at this number. Call us with a satellite phone. Do you have the number on your screen?"

"Hold on a moment," there was a pause, while El Chino looked at the screen of his phone. *"I see here a...one, two, three...fourteen, fifteen, sixteen digit number. Is that it?"*

"I imagine so," Michelle said uncertainly, "but we don't know our phone number."

"Does your editor have a satellite telephone?"

"No, but there must be one somewhere in WKPA."

"Mother of God!" El Chino cried. *"Put El Colorao back on!"*

"El Colorao?" Michelle looked at Archie, smiling wickedly. "It's for you," she told him.

Archie blushed, red splotches covering his neck and cheeks.

"Yes, Chino," he said after he had picked up the phone.

"That lady reporter is not very bright, is she?"

Archie darted a glance at Michelle, and smiled despite himself. "No, she isn't," he said.

"But she's beautiful, so listen, this is what I'm going to do. I'm personally driving to WKPA." Archie raised an eyebrow in surprise, since he knew that El Chino hardly ever abandoned his house. *"I will bring my satellite phone with me, and give it personally to her editor...What's the editor's name?"*

"What's your editor's name?" Archie asked Michelle.

"Doel Reyes," she answered. "If you can't get him, ask for Correcaminos."

Archie repeated the two names to El Chino.

"It may take me some time to get there, since traffic around here is not in its optimum condition, with the bridges down and everything, but I'll get there. If you don't hear from me in an hour, call this phone again. Okay?"

Archie nodded. "Okay. Thank you, Chino. You don't know what this means to us."

"Yeah, well tell Michelle that I expect to get her autograph for this," he said laughing, and hung up.

"If he gets us through to WKPA, I'll kiss him on the mouth," Michelle said, after Archie had repeated El Chino's request.

"You haven't seen El Chino, have you?" They all laughed, not so much at Archie's comment but because of the elation they felt after managing to communicate with the "outside" world, after confirming that a safe, orderly society still existed beyond San Juan, and that though stranded, they were not alone.

The roar of a truck speeding towards the lagoon brought all of them back to reality.

"We can't stay here," Michelle said. "We need to get Katherine Elizabeth somewhere safe. At least, safer than where we are now." She pointed at the two-year-old girl, who was sitting on her babysitter's lap and nearly falling asleep.

"We were going to the fire station when we met you," Negron, the young police rookie said, renewing Archie's prior suggestion. "We can still go there."

"That's an alternative," Archie agreed. "The only thing is that we would have to go back a couple of blocks in the direction of the police station, close to where you were attacked," Archie reminded the others. "I'm not sure that we want to go that way again."

Silence followed Archie's statement, as they considered what other alternatives they had. Finally, Michelle spoke.

"The Lazaros," she said.

"What?" Archie asked.

"The Lazaros!" Michelle repeated, becoming more animated. "I have a friend. Her name is Puchi Lazaro. Her parents live in the Condominio Laguna Vista. I've visited them there a couple of times with Puchi. If they're there, I'm sure that they will help us."

"Well, at least it's very close," Archie said, looking directly at the building.

The Laguna Vista Condominium stretched opposite to where they hid, across the Fernandez Juncos Avenue. It was a huge, modern, luxury residential building with a curved, flowing design that had been constructed on an elongated piece of land between the Constitucion and the Fernandez Juncos avenues. Relatively new, it had been the object of great controversy, since it lay close to the path of the airplanes landing in the neighboring Isla Grande Airport. Several politicians from the Commonwealth Party had accused the Planning Board of granting the construction permits without considering the hazards that the building posed, and some had even demanded that the building be condemned and demolished. By that time, however, the condominium had been finished, and several families had moved into it, making the whole matter moot.

Even though the Laguna Vista was near, in order to get there Michelle's group would have to cross Fernandez Juncos Avenue, plus two other lanes used exclusively by the Metropolitan Bus Authority for the transit of its buses. Once there, the refugees would have to circle around the elongated building, since its entrance lay on the other side of the structure, facing Avenida Constitucion.

Most of the walk to get there would be exposed, with nowhere to hide. Even worse, they would not be able to see anyone on the other side of the Laguna Vista until they rounded the building. There was no reason why anyone should be there, but then again, there was no reason that the terrorists should be anywhere in San Juan.

Archie and Negron volunteered to scout ahead of the group, but because of Archie's limp, Negron was chosen to do it. The rookie policeman took off his shirt and hat, and covered the waist of his pants with his T-shirt, making it harder to be identified as a police officer from the distance. He tucked his service gun, the Smith and Wesson he called Sally, under his waistband so it would not be seen, and stepped out of the bushes.

"Let's go," he said to the others, sounding excited.

They moved quickly until they reached the abandoned stream of automobiles that clogged Fernandez Juncos Avenue in the direction of Miramar. There they stopped, and studied the open space beyond the stalled vehicles and the street concrete barriers.

"Don't take any unnecessary risks, okay?" Archie told the young policeman. "Just run in a straight line until you reach the other side, and stick as closely as you can to the building, so you'll be harder to spot."

"Nobody will see me," Negron answered with a self-assurance that bordered on arrogance, and sprinted across the street.

Michelle had never seen anyone run like him before, except in television cartoons. His long, gangly legs moved at a prodigious speed, and he pumped his arms in an exaggerated fashion, while keeping the trunk of his body vertically straight.

"He does look like Forrest Gump, doesn't he?" Archie said, laughing. "You should have seen him when he saved you."

Michelle could not suppress a chuckle, despite the tension of the moment.

Negron made it to the other side of the avenue, and made an exaggerated wave with his right arm.

"Oh Christ," Archie muttered, "he's going to let everyone around us know that we're hiding here!"

Negron moved closer to the building and, crouching, began to jog along its edge in the direction of the lagoon, until he disappeared from sight.

"I hate people who are so self-confident!" Archie said, half in jest, half dead-earnestly.

"Perhaps he thinks that if God spared him from getting killed in the police car, He will certainly not have him killed crossing the street," Michelle said, casting a sideways glance at his redheaded companion.

"Hallelujah!" Don Moncho whispered from behind them.

Archie looked at her skeptically, saying nothing.

"You don't believe in God, do you?" she said, more as a statement than as a question.

He hunched up his shoulders in a hesitant fashion, and shook his head. "No, not much."

"Not *much*?" Michelle repeated with a hint of mischief in her voice. "Is that like not believing in Him most of the time, but believing in Him in some isolated occasions?"

Archie regarded her with a half smile. "You know, I'm beginning to understand why reporters alienate people."

"Do I alienate you?" Michelle asked, looking straight into his eyes. She looked so beautiful, even with her swollen upper lip, that he was forced to look away in order to concentrate on what Negron was doing.

"Well?" she insisted.

"Here he comes," Archie said instead, relieved by Negron's reappearance.

The rookie jogged back to the spot directly in front of them, and signaled them to approach him.

"*Let's go!*" Archie urged.

Taking one last hard look in every direction, Archie led the small group across Fernandez Juncos Avenue. Maribel carried Katherine Elizabeth in her arms, while Michelle helped Don Moncho.

"The other side is clear," Negron told them when they reached him. "Follow me."

They moved around the building as quickly as they could, through a landscaped garden of red Maltese cross and yellow bellflowers, through tall bushes hiding the building's central air conditioning system, and past the Laguna Vista's curved, easternmost end, until they reached its northern façade. There, the group was forced to travel through an open area where only a few scattered palm trees grew, and where a high concrete wall protected the building from the outside world.

They continued circling the Laguna Vista, expecting the noise of an approaching truck to shatter the eerie silence of their surroundings at any moment, but nothing stirred except for the fronds of the palms in the wind. To Michelle, it looked like one of those end-of-the-world movies, where everyone but a lucky few had disappeared from the face of the earth. Usually, the Avenida Constitucion would be buzzing with heavy traffic, even on Sundays. That day, the only discernible activity was the occasional distant cry of a seagull over the lagoon, and the noise of the breeze stirring the trees.

They moved in an Indian file, led by a very alert Negron and guarded in the rear by a nervous Archie, until they finally reached the condominium's gate. An air-conditioned guardhouse controlled the building's traffic with a wooden, red-and-white-striped barrier, but the guardhouse was empty.

The group skirted the barrier's arm, and walked into the parking area. They stopped at the entrance of the lobby, a sparsely furnished, wide marbled-floor hall separated from the outside by a glass wall, and examined the intercom's list of residents. Andres Lazaro, Michelle's friend's father, appeared listed under "PH-2".

"This one?" Negron asked, and pressed the intercom button next to the "PH-2" number before Michelle could answer.

"Yes," she said patiently, after the fact.

They waited a full minute without getting a response. Negron pushed the button again, this time longer.

"They're not home," Maribel, the babysitter, said bleakly.

"Or maybe they're scared to answer," Michelle said, as she watched Archie walk into parking area. "Where are you going?" she asked. He didn't respond, gesturing with his hand for her to wait.

Studying the wall beyond the row of parked cars, he stopped in front of a silver Mercedes W 211 and confirmed it occupied one of the two parking lots designated with the letters "PH-2". A white Lexus GX11 SUV occupied the second lot.

"Your friend's family has a lot of money, doesn't it?" Archie said, pointing at the two vehicles. "Their cars are here, so they must be in."

"They're not answering," Negron said. "So what do we do?"

Archie walked back to the intercom and searched for the apartment's number. "This usually works," he said, punching the beat of "A Shave and a Haircut" on the button with his thumb.

"*Who is this?*" a man's voice inquired after a few seconds.

"Don Andres?" Michelle immediately said, leaning closer to the intercom.

"*Yes,*" the man answered doubtfully, as if not recognizing the voice.

"Don Andres, this is Michelle, Michelle Alfaro, Puchi's friend? I need—"

"*Michelle? What are you doing out there? Come in, come in! I'll send the elevator to pick you up.*"

The glass door giving access to the lobby buzzed for a few seconds, and Negron pushed it open. With a great sense of relief, the refugees entered the frigid, air-conditioned, clean-smelling atmosphere of the reception area, and waited for one of the elevators to come down.

"Thank God," Michelle whispered to herself, watching the digital display that showed the floor location of the various elevators begin to change. "The worst is over."

"Gentlemen," Colonel Alejo Montañez said to the small group of men clustered around the table, gesturing at the wall, "this is our objective."

Police Superintendent Maldonado observed the projection of the Google Earth image that showed the Grand Laguna Hotel. The five-star resort had been built on a tiny peninsula, where only its western side was connected to the island of San Juan. The shallow waters of the Condado Lagoon covered its southern boundary, while the boisterous waves of the Atlantic Ocean crashed against its northern and eastern shores. Shallow reefs rimmed the entire coast around the hotel, making its approach by water impossible.

Next to him sat Special Agent Mario Franceschini, a balding, gray-haired man with quick intelligent eyes, a wide forehead, and thin lips that always seemed settled on a friendly smile. He headed the FBI in Puerto Rico, and represented the federal government in the rescue operations. Until Montañez had started the briefing, Franceschini had been studying the two men occupying the two seats opposite to him, and thinking how different both of them were.

The first of them, the man sitting closest to the wall where the Google image was being projected, was Captain Camilo Gomez, a career officer who headed the Puerto Rican SWAT team. Black-haired and clean-shaven, lean, athletic and of a medium build, he personified what a police officer should look like. He was dressed in his dark gray and black camouflage SWAT uniform, including a bulky bulletproof vest that made it difficult for him to sit.

Captain Francisco Ramirez, the officer who had handled the bomb threat at the Convention Center that morning, occupied the second chair. Contrary to his SWAT counterpart, Ramirez was basically a political appointee from the Alarcon administration. Tall, prematurely grayed, and distinguished looking, he contrasted markedly with the rest of the officers sitting around the table for his overbearing confidence and abysmal lack of common sense. From the hostile vibrations that he was sensing from Maldonado, Franceschini guessed that Ramirez was there at the insistence of the Secretary of Justice Rovira Melendez. Sent there to keep the Interim Governor informed about what the Superintendent was doing.

"The keys to any successful rescue are speed and surprise," Montañez, standing next to the projection on the wall, said. "In the Grand Laguna Hotel hostage situation, because of its particular location and our lack of access to the island of San Juan, we basically will have neither."

"If we attempt a daytime rescue in the Grand Laguna Hotel, there will be no surprise factor," Captain Gomez asserted gravely, tapping nervously the surface of the table with a pencil. "We need to negotiate with the Macheteros for more time, until it's nighttime."

"We don't have that option any more," Maldonado interjected, casting a hostile glance in the direction of Ramirez. "Our Interim Governor took it off the table during the press conference."

To his credit, Ramirez opted to remain quiet.

"That puts us in a very difficult position," Gomez continued. "We don't have enough intelligence to know even where in the hotel they are keeping the hostages, if they are keeping them all in the same place."

"It's a lot worse than that. You have to consider that the hotel is only a part of the picture," Montañez reminded the others. "Even if we are successful in freeing the hostages in the hotel, the terrorists will still be able to take reprisals against the other hostages that they hold in the *Mardi Gras* and La Fortaleza."

"We can't mount three rescue operations at this moment, particularly with the little information that we have," Gomez said. "I don't have the men to do it. In three hours, the Navy Seals will be here. Then we'll be in a better position to conduct simultaneous rescue operations, at night. It will improve the odds of the rescue significantly."

"The FBI can provide two dozen agents that can help in the rescue effort, even though our training in nighttime amphibious operations is minimal at best," Franceschini volunteered.

"Can't we threaten to execute their Machetero leader, what's his name? Cacho, Adalberto Cacho, if they harm any of our hostages?" Captain Gomez asked.

Maldonado regarded the young SWAT officer in shock, surprised by his naïveté. "I will take that as a joke. We don't do that type of thing. This is not the Wild West, you know. We have a Constitution that protects Cacho's rights, despite what we may think of him."

Gomez smiled. "Forgive me, Mr. Superintendent, but I did not explain myself well. I didn't mean that we actually carry out his execution, but that we *threaten* to execute him. The terrorists are people who don't respect the law, who really don't care that much about the Constitution. They're people who are used to taking things into their own hands. We could bluff them, and say that we will kill Cacho if they kill any of the hostages, and if we do it with enough conviction, they might believe us. At worst, it would make them think twice before they did anything. Anyway, what have we got to lose?"

Maldonado and Montañez exchanged an amused look. The SWAT captain showed a lot of initiative and imagination. The Superintendent made a mental note to keep track of the young officer's career for future reference.

"It's worth a try," he conceded. "However, I believe that the terrorists we're dealing with are intelligent and well-informed, and that they won't fall for our bluff. We need to prepare for the worst."

"We can always try to prevent the terrorists from throwing someone off the roof of the hotel," Gomez said, prompting Maldonado to stare at him questioningly. "What I mean is, sir, the Macheteros want to make the executions as public as possible, right? That's why they're planning to throw people off the roof, so that everybody in the world, all the news services, will broadcast it."

Maldonado nodded in agreement.

"So that means that they will try to march someone to the edge of the roof and push him off," the young captain said.

It was a terrible image, one that would define the face of terrorism for years to come.

"The hostages won't jump off the edge voluntarily," Gomez said, not trying to sound facetious, "which means that one or more of the Macheteros will have to force them to walk to the edge of the building, and push them off. So we place our best snipers on the roof of this building, the San Geronimo Plaza, and on the roof of the condominium next to us, and we shoot the terrorists before they can push the hostages off."

"Of course, that will not prevent the terrorists from shooting the hostages out of our sight," Montañez said, "except it won't be as dramatic as seeing someone fall from the Grand Laguna Hotel."

"And it may prompt the terrorists to kill more hostages just for interfering with their plans," Franceschini added.

"Quite," the young captain acknowledged.

"But if it comes to that, we'll still do it," Maldonado said. "We'll have snipers ready to shoot anybody that attempts to push a hostage over the edge of the roof."

Silence followed, as everyone considered the ramifications of the course of action that they were discussing. A clock in the room imitating the Big Ben chime tolled twelve times, announcing the beginning of the afternoon.

"I don't want to sound cold-blooded," Montañez said hesitantly. "But it all may come to what is best for the greatest number of the hostages."

"What do you mean?" Maldonado asked.

"Our best chances of success hinge upon a night raid," he said, and stopped.

"Go on," Maldonado urged.

"To try to go in during the day, without even knowing where the hostages are, and without taking into consideration the hostages at the other locations, would be irresponsible, and amount to a kamikaze attack."

"We could probably narrow down the places where such a large number of hostages could be kept together, like the lobby of the hotel and the big ballrooms where the conventions are held," Captain Gomez prompted, "but even then, the terrorists could kill hundreds of hostages before we got to them. Remember the Munich Olympics, where the police knew exactly where all of the hostages were located at all times, and even so, the terrorists managed to kill every single one of them."

"So what are you saying?" Maldonado directed his eyes to his old friend, already suspecting what he was going to suggest.

Montañez swallowed hard. "Barring that we can negotiate an extension of time to comply with their demands, and discarding an all-out attack, the best option we may have is to do nothing until nighttime."

"Even if it means that the terrorists carry through with their threat, and they throw off the roof ten to a dozen hostages before we attempt a rescue?" Ramirez, speaking for the first time, asked in a shocked voice.

Montañez took a long time to answer.

"It would be a terrible alternative, I know," he replied at last, "but one we need to consider. Want it or not, these people have for some unknown reason declared war on our citizens, and in wars, it's impossible to save everyone. We fight for the greater good, and to minimize—and I stress the word 'minimize'—the number of casualties that our enemies can inflict." The police colonel stared straight at Ramirez. "I agree with Captain Gomez that an all-out day attack will probably end in disaster and heavy loss of life, not only of the hostages, but of the rescuers. Our best alternative is to negotiate for time, and try to secure the release of some of the hostages...But that alternative has been negated by Rovira Melendez. So we must consider *all* options, and that includes our willingness to let the terrorists kill some of the hostages, for the greater good of the others."

Captain Ramirez cleared his throat, and everybody looked at him. "I have been instructed by the Governor—" he began to say.

"*The Governor*?" Montañez asked in a derisive tone. "You mean that *the Governor* has been rescued already?"

Ramirez's face reddened with anger.

"Interim Governor Rovira has asked me to remind all of you that we cannot appear to be weak or indecisive, and that we must not allow any hostages to be killed, since it will reflect very badly on the Police Department."

Only Montañez, the Superintendent's longtime friend, and Franceschini, an expert interrogator trained to observe and interpret expressions, knew how close Maldonado came to react in a violent manner, and how he struggled to maintain his composure. For a moment, the Superintendent's knuckles turned white and the veins of his neck stuck out like those of an angry bull. Then the moment passed, and the chief of the police turned to Montañez, without replying to Ramirez's last statement.

"The alternative that you have outlined is the soundest, less risky one, and I know—because I have known you for years—that it has not come as an easy thing for you to propose. But I also know that our country would never recover emotionally from watching on TV a dozen hostages being methodically thrown off the roof of the Grand Laguna, while we do nothing about it. It is contrary to what we, as Puerto Ricans, would do, and I think that the people would never forgive us...or trust us, if we just watch with our arms crossed while some helpless hostages are killed like cattle."

Montañez and the others nodded in agreement.

"Unfortunately," Maldonado continued, "Rovira Melendez is a very smart man who does not have the same scruples that we have, and who has chosen to do political posturing, instead of thinking about the human lives involved, the lives, as you point out, Alejo, not only of the hostages in the Grand Laguna Hotel, but of those in the *Mardi Gras*, La Fortaleza, and those of our men."

Ramirez shifted uncomfortably in his chair, and stared fiercely at his own hands. The Superintendent knew that everything that he was saying would get back to the Interim Governor, and in a perverse way hoped it would do so, word for word.

"So...what do we do?" Ramirez asked in a somewhat petulant tone.

Maldonado walked to a small table containing refreshments, grabbed a plastic cup, and after scooping some ice, picked up a can of diet coke. Montañez suppressed a smile, amused by the Superintendent's lame attempt to limit his consumption of calories through the use of dietary drinks. He had seen Maldonado eat.

"What do we do?" the Superintendent repeated pensively, as he sat down and flicked open the can of soda. "I don't know. It's a decision that the Interim Governor will have to make, and that you will have to discuss personally with him," he responded, taking a sip of his soda and relishing more than he should Ramirez's shocked reaction.

"But that means that I'll have to—"

"Travel to the Elections Board Building in Hato Rey?" Maldonado interrupted. "Most assuredly. We have established an open television feed with the Elections Board, which can be used to communicate with Rovira. It's true that the image is scrambled and unscrambled at the government headquarters, but there's no guarantee that somebody may intercept it and manage to unscramble it. So I suggest...no, I insist that you go to Hato Rey and talk to the Interim Governor personally."

"This is ridiculous!" Ramirez protested. "Just because you have a private quarrel with Rovira Melendez—"

"I do have a private quarrel with Rovira Melendez," Maldonado acknowledged, cutting off Ramirez again. "But this has got nothing to do with it. The decision we have to make is beyond my pay grade and authority.

It's a policy decision, too important for anyone to make except for the...Interim Governor...Especially after he publicly decided to deny us the negotiations option. I need someone—not essential to the rescue operations—to go to Rovira and let him know what our alternatives are. That non-essential person is clearly you. Now to remind you, and so there is no confusion, there are three basic options."

Maldonado took another sip from his coke, placed his cup on the table, and raised his index finger.

"Number one: do nothing until nighttime, even if it means that the terrorists get to execute some of the hostages. The downside, beside the loss of life, is that Rovira Melendez's...administration...will look cruel and callous, or worse, it may look powerless and indecisive, like it can't do anything to stop the executions."

Maldonado raised a second finger.

"Number two: shoot at the terrorists when they climb to the roof, and hopefully stop them from throwing one or more of the hostages off the building. There is a downside to that one too. It may not work. We may hit by mistake some of the hostages. And if we stop them, the Macheteros may still kill the hostages some other way. Or even kill more hostages than they threatened to kill originally, because we frustrated their initial attempt. Frankly, if I was a terrorist, that's what I would do." The Superintendent looked at Ramirez. "Are you getting this?"

"Yes," the captain answered sullenly.

"Good. And number three," Maldonado raised his middle finger, "an all out rescue effort by SWAT, but only directed at the hotel, with all of the variations we've discussed before. So go." Maldonado waved the hand with the three upraised fingers dismissively. "Brief the Interim Governor."

Captain Ramirez stood up, picked his cap off the table, and abandoned the room wordlessly, with as much dignity as he could muster. *It had not been a good day for him,* Maldonado thought, feeling no pity whatsoever. He waited until the captain had left, and then resumed the discussion, speaking to Franceschini and Gomez.

"Now, before you arrived to the meeting, Colonel Montañez, Ramirez and I had spoken of a possible plan to rescue the hostages in the Grand Laguna Hotel, in case we cannot delay the executions. It is a desperate plan, and very dangerous to our men, but...unless anybody can think of anything better, it's the best we can do at this moment."

Maldonado nodded at Montañez, who cleared his throat.

"If we decide to storm the Grand Laguna Hotel during the daylight hours, we will have to rely on speed. We have secured three rubber rafts that can hold up to eight men each."

"How many horsepower?" Captain Gomez inquired.

"I believe each raft is equipped with a 250 HP outboard engine," Montañez replied. "So those boats will almost be able to fly over the water. They'll get from our side of the lagoon to the edge of the hotel in three minutes or so." He paused, making certain that Gomez was reassured by his answer.

"The distance over the water is relatively short," Franceschini added, as if to reassure the others.

"The smoothest and shortest way to get to the hotel is directly across the lagoon," Montañez confirmed, "from our staging area here," the colonel moved closer to the Google map projection, and pointed to a spot on the Dos Hermanos Bridge that had not been destroyed by the explosions, "to here." His hand moved in a direct line over the shallow waters of the lagoon to an area south of the small Spanish fort of San Geronimo.

The other men in the room examined in silence the route traced by Montañez. To Gomez, it made no sense. The terrorists had severed the section of the bridge closest to the Condado area. The colonel had suggested that the rescue operation be launched from the structure that existed beyond the gap created by the explosions. In order to do that, the SWAT team would first have to cross over the demolished portion of the bridge.

"I'm sorry," Captain Gomez said awkwardly, "but how do we get to the rescue staging area? Isn't the bridge cut off by the explosives?"

Montañez looked at the spot that the captain was pointing, then realized why he was confused.

"Oh, we don't actually *start* from that point. The rafts will start from behind the bridge, from the side of the lagoon that's behind the bridge." The colonel pointed on the projected Google image to an area that showed a building facing the eastern section of the Condado Lagoon, across the street from the San Geronimo Plaza Hotel. "Do you see the two tennis courts behind this building, close to the lagoon's shore? That's where your men will gather and board the rafts."

It was a good spot. The courts, blocked from the view of the Macheteros in the Grand Laguna Hotel by both the San Geronimo Plaza Hotel and the apartment building to which the tennis courts belonged, would allow the SWAT rescue team to make its preparations without being detected by the terrorists.

"The ideal staging area for the assault would have been from the small beach next to the San Geronimo Plaza, but then your men would be fully visible from the Grand Laguna, and the terrorists would guess ahead of time what we're planning to do," Montañez added.

"If they haven't guessed already," Franceschini interjected. "These people are very smart. I think you can safely bet that they will be expecting us to do something like this."

"Of course," Montañez said. "And we must all depart from that basis."

They all nodded.

"When...if the rescue operation starts, your boats will go full throttle under the bridge and head like sinners escaping from hell directly towards the hotel," Montañez continued. "You are to stop for nothing or no one. If any of your men, God forbid, falls from a raft, you will leave them there. Our snipers...some from your SWAT team, and some from the Police Department, will be providing covering fire from the roofs of the San Geronimo Plaza and the condominium closest to the lagoon."

"Will that be enough?" Gomez asked, concerned about his men. "I mean, we will be completely exposed to any enemy fire. If they are waiting for us, our loses could be significant."

"We know," Maldonado said, before Montañez could respond, "but we will try to improve the odds with one more surprise for the terrorists, right Alejo?"

"Yes," Montañez answered. "We have secured from the National Guard some smoke canisters. When our attack begins, two police helicopters will fly over the Grand Laguna area and drop them along the shore. Hopefully, it will provide additional cover for your rafts. One of the helicopters will then give your men more cover fire from above, shooting at any snipers that the terrorists may have, while the other will fly to your landing area and have five of your men rappel down to secure your beachhead. Any questions so far?"

A brief silence followed as the men around the table digested the information imparted to them by the colonel. Gomez tentatively raised his hand.

"May I propose a small variation?" he asked.

"Go ahead."

"It's about the helicopter providing additional cover. Depending on the hostile fire it encounters, the helicopter could approach the heliport on the rooftop of the Grand Laguna, and drop three of my men on the rooftop. If there are any hostages stranded up there, my men could protect them, and mount a second attack from above."

Montañez looked for approval from Maldonado, who nodded.

"Getting out of the rafts will not be easy," the colonel said, continuing to outline his plan. "The entire shore of the Grand Laguna Hotel is lined with large volcanic rocks that have razor-sharp edges, and they will slow you down. We will continue to provide you with covering fire from the rooftops of the buildings and the helicopters until you're securely ashore," he said directly to Captain Gomez. "Now, as soon as your men are off those rafts, the boats will return to pick up more men. Those will be my men, by the way," he added with a smile. "I will be going with them."

From Maldonado's mildly irritated expression, Franceschini deduced that the last bit of information had not been previously discussed by the two men, and would be the object of further conversation.

Montañez paused for questions, and when he got none continued.

"As soon as you land, you will split your men into two groups. One group will head towards the lobby, the second to the ballrooms," he said, addressing Gomez again. "It goes without saying that speed is of the essence. From the moment you hit the ground, it will be your show exclusively. You'll have more knowledge of what is happening than any of us back here. You have been provided with a diagram of the lower floor of the hotel, and your men have copies of it as well. Have them study it carefully. We can't afford losing time because some of the men got lost along the way."

"Yes, sir," the SWAT captain answered.

Montañez switched off the projector, and sat down. Maldonado stirred in his chair, and stood up to address the group.

"As you can see, our plan is far from perfect and the risks are very high. However, the stakes are even higher. You and your men," he said to Gomez, "are the best that we can offer, and therefore, I have no choice but to put you in harm's way. Colonel Montañez and I, and I'm sure that Franceschini as well, have full faith in you. I wish that I could give you additional advice that could help you, but I can't. I would ask God to bless you," he said, smiling ruefully and directing a covert glance at his friend Montañez, "but I'm not sure that my standing up there is that good. It may turn out to be more of a curse than a blessing."

Everyone smiled.

"But as much as I am concerned about this operation, I am a lot more concerned about what happens afterwards. Because even if we are one hundred percent successful, even if we save every single one of the hostages in the hotel, the terrorists will still hold the Governor, his family, and the *Mardi Gras* as hostages."

A gloomy silence followed his statement.

"We may be a bit fortunate in that they are probably experiencing the same communications problems as the rest of us. Which means that they may not be able to communicate by cell phone, and that they may have to rely on runners coming in and out of the hotel. Let's hope so. Once the SWAT team lands, and we drop the men on the roof, the helicopters will fly around the hotel, trying to intercept any messengers that attempt to leave the hotel to warn their comrades about what is happening."

"They may have walkie-talkies," Gomez mentioned.

Maldonado nodded. "I'm trying to get some jamming equipment from the National Guard right now. If we get it in time, I will send it to the SWAT team. We may gain some time from a communications breakdown, but somehow I suspect that will not be the case, and that the other hostages will be at the mercy of whatever reprisals the terrorists want to take on them." The Superintendent unconsciously loosened the knot of the tie under his thick neck, as if feeling the pressure.

"It may also be," Montañez suggested, "that the leaders of the Macheteros are in the hotel. If we capture them, we may leave the rest of the terrorists in disarray."

"Which may be a good thing or a bad thing, depending on how trigger-happy those other terrorists are," Maldonado interjected.

A long, contemplative silence followed. The operation that they were discussing was terribly dangerous, and a thousand things could affect it. Each man in the room considered what else should be said, but none of them could think of anything to add.

"Captain Gomez," the Superintendent said finally, turning to the SWAT officer, "you and your men have a lot of preparing to do."

"Yes, sir," the captain bolted upright from his chair, looking embarrassed, and saluted the Superintendent.

"I don't know for sure if you'll get the green light for your rescue operation, but I wish you the best luck in the world." Maldonado clasped the captain's hands between his two beefy paws and shook it warmly. "Take good care of yourself."

"Thank you, sir," the young captain responded, turning to shake Franceschini's hand as well, while receiving a slap on the back from Montañez.

"Be brave," the latter said, "but most of all, be smart. The graveyard is full of stupid brave men."

"I will try to live up to your standards, sir," Gomez responded with the open hero worship that most of the force accorded to the leader of the "Untouchables".

"I never cease to be amazed at the great caliber of men we keep recruiting into the force," Montañez said in an admiring tone as he watched Gomez stride out of the room. "These youngsters are smart and talented, and could get a job anywhere. And yet, they're willing to risk their lives every day for the low salary that they get paid."

"*You* should know," Maldonado said, and thought he saw his old friend blush.

"Somehow, I suspect we're not going to hear from Rovira Melendez," Franceschini said thoughtfully to Maldonado. "If I were him, I would just avoid talking to you during the next few hours. I'd let the events play out by themselves. You'd be forced to make your own choices. If they go sour, it's your fault. If they succeed, it was due to his skillful leadership."

The Superintendent smiled bitterly.

"I know, my friend. I expect that's exactly what he's going to do. But it was worth it, getting rid of Ramirez, wasn't it?"

The three men laughed.

"I have to go," Montañez told Maldonado abruptly. "I've got to make the arrangements to get those SWAT men on the helicopters, prepare my men for the assault, and see if I can secure that jamming device from the National Guard. It's going to be a busy two hours—" Montañez started to get up.

"I don't want you to go rogue on me," Maldonado warned his subordinate before he could finish standing up.

"Pardon me?" Montañez stopped on his tracks and looked questioningly at his friend.

"That idea of you leading the second wave of rescuers on the rafts. It's not going to happen."

Montañez paused, as if considering a reply, then simply nodded.

"I mean it," Maldonado growled, as his friend tried to reach the exit. He stared hard at him, all humor gone from his eyes. "I will need you to be close to me during the rescue operations. Your advice will be invaluable. Understood?"

Montañez hesitated, and then answered soberly, "Understood."

Maldonado and Franceschini quietly waited for the police colonel to close the door behind him. Then Maldonado turned to the FBI agent, and asked him in a confidential voice, "Are your men ready?"

Franceschini shifted his chair to face him.

"The National Guard is providing us with three Blackhawk helicopters," he answered. "Right now, they're in a hangar in the Isla Grande Airport, just across the Puerta de Tierra police station. They're ready to fly the moment you tell us to do so. I can contact them by walkie-talkie from the hotel. There will be eleven of my men on each of them. One will unload the men in La Fortaleza's gardens, and if conditions allow, on its roof. The other two will approach the *Mardi Gras* and try to land agents on its upper deck and on the dock where it's berthed. I've gotta tell you, it's going to be wild and unpredictable, but if push comes to shove, we'll do it."

"Good. Let's hope we don't have to use them just yet," Maldonado said. The idea of the FBI charging wildly into the cruise ship and the Governor's Mansion terrified him. Information and expert manpower were key in the effective rescue effort. Until they obtained more of both,

Maldonado had to somehow extend the precious little time that they had left.

"We have received via email the blueprints of the *Mardi Gras* from its parent company in Miami, and we're analyzing them right now, so that our rescue teams will become familiar with its layout," Franceschini stated, reading the Superintendent's thoughts. "Also, one of my men worked in the La Fortaleza security detail for three years before he transferred to the FBI, and he knows the place inside out. He's briefing the Fortaleza team now. So we won't be completely blind when we go in."

"Excellent," Maldonado said. "It's good to have you on our side."

Franceschini smiled despite himself, flattered by the Superintendent's praise.

"Of course," he added cautiously, "it would be infinitely better if we did it at nighttime."

"You sound like my wife," the Superintendent said wryly.

Franceschini laughed. It was an open secret that despite Maldonado's constant complaints about his forty-year marriage, he still was madly in love with his wife.

"There is one way you could extend the time," the Superintendent said. "You could use your contacts to convince the President to release Cacho. It's not Rovira Melendez's prerogative to release him anyway."

"I've already thought about it, and I am working hard to make it happen," Franceschini replied smugly.

It was Maldonado's turn to chuckle. "You FBI guys are really smart, aren't you?"

"We had to be able to survive J. Edgar Hoover," Franceschini answered, only half in jest. Then he added, more soberly, "It will not be easy, you know. We're asking the President to release one of the men that topped the "Most Wanted List" for several years. He will be laying his political neck on the line if he agrees to send him over to the terrorists, and then the man escapes and causes more damage."

"Let's hope the President has more of a backbone than our Interim Governor," Maldonado ventured.

Franceschini gazed seriously at his counterpart.

"You haven't told the others about any of this?"

"About the additional rescue operations? Not even Montañez," Maldonado replied. "As you know, we have leaks."

It was true. Two and a half months before, Maldonado had reluctantly requested the FBI to secretly investigate the top thirty officers of his department, after receiving a tip from a reliable informant that the police force had been infiltrated by a well-placed mole. Other signs had also pointed in that direction: covert anti-drug raids where the suspects had been forewarned and disappeared just before the police got to the site, and an increasing flow of drugs into the island despite the heroics of the Untouchables. A couple of anonymous tips had even claimed that some members of the Untouchables might be part of the cartel infiltration, although no evidence about any such involvement had been discovered.

The FBI had mounted an intense covert investigation of the police top brass. But it had yielded nothing. And even more disturbing, only two days before, the severed head of the original informant who had tipped Maldonado about the mole had been found in a trash can in the Llorens Torres public housing complex, wrapped in a newspaper. The gruesome discovery had profoundly shaken the Superintendent's confidence. Only a handful of men had known the identity of the informant. They had included Captain Ramirez, his personal secretary Eloy Mestres, the head of the Anticorruption Division Baltazar Matos, and Colonel Alejo Montañez.

Not surprisingly, Maldonado's suspicions had zeroed in on Captain Ramirez, the political appointee. In addition to the FBI investigation, the Superintendent had ordered the police surveillance division to secure a court order to tap all of his telephones and to keep him under constant watch around the clock. Just that morning, Maldonado had received a report indicating that the taps and the surveillance had detected no illegal behavior. The news, received as he and Montañez were inspecting the damaged bridges, had unsettled him. *If not Ramirez, then who?* The other three suspects were, as far as he was concerned, loyal, solid, honest policemen who had risen through the ranks and served honorably in the force for decades.

Maybe Ramirez was being cautious. Maybe he had made no overt move within the last few days, being extra careful after Maldonado's informant had been discovered in a trash can. Maybe the informant had made a mistake, and there was no mole in the force. Maldonado sincerely hoped so. *Because the other alternative would be something too terrible to contemplate.*

"How do you know it's not Montañez?"

Franceschini's question startled Maldonado out of his thoughts. *Was the man psychic?*

"I trust Montañez with my life," he answered more fiercely than he intended. "When you were a teenager watching Hawaii Five-0 on TV, Montañez was risking his life every day to keep criminals off the street. One of his sons was killed by a disgruntled drug dealer, and he has survived two assassination attempts by drug gangs. He is probably the bravest, most unselfish man I know. Don't ever question his loyalty!"

Franceschini raised his hands placatingly in a gesture of surrender.

"Okay, okay! I'm not accusing him of anything!" he said apologetically. "I just..." he shrugged. "We can't take anything or anyone for granted, not with the modern cartels or even the local drug gangs. As you most of all people are aware, they have tremendous monetary resources, and a long arm that can reach nearly anyone nowadays."

"Not Montañez," Maldonado assured him with a half-growl.

Franceschini sighed. "I trust and abide by your judgment, which most of the time has proven correct," he said in a chastised tone. "Besides, we haven't been able to pin anything on him. If you vouch for him, that's good enough for me."

"I *do* vouch for him," the Superintendent stated in a manner that admitted no further discussion.

"So I should stop my surveillance of him?" Franceschini asked, cringing inwardly in anticipation of the Superintendent's furious response. Instead, he got silence.

"No," Maldonado responded eventually, finishing his coke in several long swallows and standing up. "I may trust him with my life, but I'm not the Pope."

"Excuse me?" Franceschini asked, totally bewildered.

"Infallible," Maldonado replied curtly, and began to walk away. "I'm not infallible, like the Pope. I may trust Montañez, but I may be wrong," he said over his shoulder.

And in that case, it would break his heart.

CHAPTER XXXII

Angel San Miguel sat wearily on one of the benches of the Plaza de Armas, listening to the crisp, liquid sounds produced by the Fountain of the Four Seasons, just a few feet away from him. Even though the sun had climbed to its midday point, the day's temperature remained surprisingly pleasant, as a mild breeze rustled through the trees in the square and blew a fine mist from the fountain in his direction.

"This is nice," he told Daniel who, after scrutinizing the surrounding buildings, slumped next to him.

"Tired?" San Miguel asked. "Maybe you should take a nap."

"The device has been placed," Daniel said flatly, not bothering to respond to his associate's question. "Our mission here is almost finished. Do we still need to throw the tourists off the Grand Laguna Hotel?"

San Miguel pondered the question, placing his hands on his knees and stretching his back. He nodded.

"A few," he answered. When Daniel said nothing, he added, "The device is, as you say, our main objective. But so is what we're doing here today." He waited for Daniel to say something, and when he failed to do so, continued. "You don't get it, do you?"

Daniel laughed softly. "Oh, I get it. Your present goal is the same goal you've always had: to inflict terror in any and every possible way."

San Miguel directed him an amused stare.

"Something like that," he acknowledged, meaning to end the matter there. Then, casting a second look in his companion's direction, he yielded to the temptation of expanding his answer.

"Oh, oh," Daniel said before San Miguel could speak, "here comes the lecture from the professor."

It was a humorous but not entirely inaccurate comparison. Daniel was convinced that San Miguel would have made a great college professor—

the type that is revered by his students and fellow colleagues—had it not been for his innate cold-bloodedness.

"You must understand," San Miguel said gently, "that we are engaged in a war against the superpowers of the world. We lack the vast resources that they have at their disposal. Our basic tool is—"

"Terror," Daniel said in unison with his associate.

"Terror," San Miguel repeated, assenting. "It is the only way we can destabilize the capitalist, Jewish-run institutions entrenched in every major government, and restore God to the world."

"The device will certainly cause that terror," Daniel interjected.

"Indeed it will," San Miguel agreed. "It will shake the foundations of every secular state in the world."

"So—"

"Why execute hostages from the roof of the Grand Laguna Hotel? Think about it. Even you, who have been involved in this business for years, and have witnessed death in its many manifestations, can picture the horror of seeing some civilians being thrown from the roof of a building. Think how it will play before the millions of people watching it happen live," he said, his eyes brimming with excitement, as the professorial terrorist imagined the moment.

Daniel watched San Miguel with fascination.

"Those people will never feel safe again, because what happened to the hostages in the hotel could easily happen to anyone, including themselves or their children or their parents or their friends! Think of the tremendous leverage and credibility it will give us the next time we demand something from those governments."

"So why not kill them all?" Daniel asked perversely, just for the sake of argument. "Are you perhaps afraid of God's punishment?"

"Only if God punishes those who do His work," San Miguel replied without flinching. "God understands that what we do is just and necessary, however unpleasant it may seem. It is a justifiable evil, required to be done in order to rid the world of its secular overlords."

Daniel felt the hairs at the back of his neck rise. Angel San Miguel was one of the most intelligent, rational, and charismatic men he had ever known. But when he began to talk about religion, his religious zeal overwhelmed all of his other qualities. It creeped Daniel out.

"But to answer your question, there is no need to kill all of the hostages. The execution of one or two will be enough to have the visual effect that we desire," San Miguel said, as if considering the best way to market a product. "Contrary to what you may imply, I'm not a butcher, and you know it. I don't kill for the sake of killing. I just do what needs to be done, that's all. Besides," he added as an afterthought, "what happens to the rest of the hostages will be up to the Macheteros, who will end up guarding them when we leave."

San Miguel stopped, and his eyes lit up again as he imagined the aftermath of the executions.

"People will have nightmares about it, about the way tourists who came to a Caribbean island paradise to enjoy its warm beaches ended up splattered on the concrete pavement of their resort. And when the terrorists disappear, and the world begins to feel safe again because the killings are over...that's when the device will bring new terror into their lives, only a thousand times worse."

San Miguel slapped his friend's knee enthusiastically.

"Terror will do it, Daniel. Terror! The people's trust that their governments can protect them from situations like this will evaporate, and the terrorized citizens will force their rulers, what's left of them anyway, to come to terms with us. Because otherwise, they will never feel safe again."

San Miguel spoke with a passion that Daniel had never witnessed before. His surprise must have been reflected on his face, because San Miguel stopped speaking, and blinking embarrassedly, withdrew behind his professional, professorial façade.

"In any event, we need to keep the local authorities distracted until our rendezvous tonight," he said pleasantly, gazing at the square.

Hundreds of blue and gray pigeons hobbled about scavenging for food, their plump bodies doing a fair imitation of the Charlie Chaplin walk. Normally by that time of the day, they would have been well fed, the pavilion that sold espressos to the tourists and corn for the pigeons having been open for business for several hours. Today, however, was different. Few businesses had opened, and most of those had closed after the city began to realize what was happening and the FEPI patrols began to roam the streets. Most *sanjuaneros* had remained in their homes behind locked doors, glued to their television sets to find out what was happening outside. A few daring or desperate souls had braved going out, mostly to stay with somebody else for company or with a bigger television set, to obtain some desperately needed medicine, or to find food in some restaurants like La Bombonera, that had refused to close.

San Miguel looked at his watch.

"Andrade should be here any moment now," he said to Daniel. "I got a call from George a few minutes ago. He told me that—" he stopped, as the ringtone of his satellite phone—the soothing sound of a bubbling brook—interrupted him. He scanned the screen, then stated with relish, "Ah! An unexpected caller! Hello!" he said brightly, pressing his "TALK" button, "Rafael Soriano here!"

Daniel stared at him curiously, a half smile gradually appearing on his lips. San Miguel listened intently, only saying "aha" when the speaker on the other side paused. Twice he looked at Daniel, raising his right eyebrow humorously, as if anxious to finish the conversation. Then he motioned with his head in the direction of the State Department Building, alerting Daniel that El Alacran was approaching. He continued to listen, and ended the call wordlessly as Andrade closed in.

Daniel had already risen from the bench to greet the Machetero leader and give his boss time to finish his telephone conversation.

"El Alacran, I presume," Daniel said playfully, extending his hand to shake that of the newcomer. Andrade stared at him as if being offered to hold a quaint artifact, then acknowledged it with a limp handshake.

"I hardly recognized you with your new clothes and haircut," Daniel stated.

"Mr. Andrade!" San Miguel exclaimed, genuinely surprised by the radical change in his appearance. "Why, you must tell me the name of your fashion adviser! He has transformed your image!"

El Alacran's eyes shone brightly with malevolent intensity, whether from pleasure or anger, San Miguel could not tell.

"What news do you bring from La Fortaleza?" San Miguel inquired, even though he had been fully briefed by George via satellite phone, just fifteen minutes before. In fact, the news had been mildly upsetting.

The capture of the Governor's Mansion had been a joint operation between his men and the Macheteros. Four of San Miguel's men had scaled the outer wall of La Fortaleza, infiltrated its gardens, and from there mounted an attack on the palace, killing all but two of the security men inside the building. The Macheteros had simultaneously occupied the roofs of the buildings closest to the main entrance to La Fortaleza, and ambushed the security detail stationed at the gate, killing one and pinning down the others with heavy fire until San Miguel's men disposed of them. Finally, the two groups had conducted a mopping up operation, eliminating the remainder of the Governor's security force, which had taken refuge in the garages close to the Gate of San Juan.

The plan had called for four men from each group to occupy La Fortaleza and keep watch over the Governor and his family, but El Alacran had unilaterally altered that ratio. By 10:00 AM, a dozen Macheteros had moved into La Fortaleza and quietly taken over. San Miguel's men had been integrated into the occupying force, but assigned marginal positions, separated from each other and away from the Governor. For all effects—George reported to San Miguel—La Fortaleza had become a Machetero stronghold. San Miguel had instructed George to remain close to the Governor, and to report any unusual activity.

"I met with Governor Pietrantoni," Andrade said matter-of-factly. "We discussed his public resignation."

A nearly imperceptible flicker of movement under the Machetero's half-closed eyelids betrayed his curiosity about San Miguel's reaction to his last statement. There was none.

"Of course, you already heard about it," he said, with a tinge of annoyed disappointment.

San Miguel acknowledged the question with a slight nod. "That, and a few other things," he replied, the previous cordiality in his voice quickly dissipating.

Looking at both men, Daniel was struck by the marked differences between them. San Miguel towered nearly a foot over the diminutive Andrade. He was also the strongest and most vibrant of the two men. And yet, it was Andrade who projected the greatest threat. Like its namesake—the scorpion—he radiated an aura of deadliness, as if perennially poised to strike and inject his venom into anyone who dared to stand in his way.

"Please update me on those *other things* that you heard about," Andrade said in an ironic tone.

"It seems," San Miguel said looking down at his counterpart with the patient irritation of a teacher chiding a young student, "that the Macheteros have taken over La Fortaleza."

Andrade raised an eyebrow in mock concern. "Oh? Isn't that what we were supposed to do?"

"We were supposed to keep the Governor under joint custody," San Miguel reminded the Machetero.

"Aren't we?" Andrade asked.

"In name only. You have almost tripled the number of men we each agreed to keep in La Fortaleza, and my men have been excluded from any real access to the Governor."

A faint, mocking smile appeared on Andrade's lips.

"As you said two nights ago, it is your intention to transfer control of this...revolution to the Macheteros as soon as Adalberto Cacho is released by the Americans, no?" he said, opening his arms in a gesture of pure innocence. "So what is the problem with accelerating part of the transfer by a few hours?"

"Adalberto Cacho has not been released yet," San Miguel pointedly reminded Andrade, "and there is a distinct possibility that he may not be released. I am in charge for now."

"I have absolute faith in your powers of persuasion," El Alacran said, his smile widening to something akin to a grimace. "I am certain that you will convince the '*gringos*' to release Cacho."

For a fraction of a second, Daniel thought that San Miguel would lose his patience and let his temper get the better of him. Instead, the terrorist leader drew out from his shirt pocket a plastic box of TIC-TAC mints, and offered it to Andrade, who refused them politely.

"About how many men do you have in La Fortaleza?" San Miguel inquired as he shook the small box and extracted two white mint pellets that he popped into his mouth.

Andrade shrugged. "Twelve, maybe fourteen. You may have a more accurate number, perhaps?"

"Two nights ago you said that you counted with a total of thirty-seven Macheteros for the entire San Juan operation," San Miguel stated, ignoring El Alacran's last question. "So with these additional eight or ten men in La Fortaleza, that would increase the total number of your men in San Juan to about forty-seven?"

"More or less," the Machetero leader answered, his eyes sly and unrepentant.

"So your initial estimate was wrong?" San Miguel inquired patiently.

"I may have miscalculated," Andrade said, evidently pleased by his counterpart's discomfiture.

"Any further revisions to your numbers that I may need to know about? It would be useful to know how many men we can count on."

"There may be two or three more," Andrade answered vaguely. "Not much more than that, though."

A strained silence followed. Daniel, thoroughly enjoying the exchange, tried not to smile. In a contest of wills between the two men, he would still place his money on San Miguel, but just barely. He wondered how Adalberto Cacho, the Machetero's maximum leader, could be a more formidable leader than El Alacran. That would be something interesting to behold.

"Well, your men, however many they are, will get a chance to fight for their country sooner than they think," San Miguel told Andrade, switching topics on the Machetero. "I've just received detailed information about the police and FBI rescue plans, if we decide to execute any hostages."

"You received information from your source inside the Police Department?" El Alacran asked with newly found interest.

"I will brief you on the details when Colonel Calderon gets here," San Miguel said ignoring the question. "I expect to head back to the hotel in about..." he glanced at his watch, "half an hour, after I brief you and Calderon. You're welcome to ride back with us."

San Miguel turned on his heels and walked away. Andrade watched him go in silence.

"That was abrupt," he said to Daniel. "Is he always like that?"

"Only with people he doesn't like," Daniel answered pleasantly.

If his remark offended Andrade, he did not show it.

"I think San Miguel is either going to have an espresso in Starbuck's, or return to the hotel" Daniel said. "Shall we join him?"

Lucas' greatest fear was that the trapdoor at the end of the long, cramped space would be locked. That would be very bad. There could be no way that he could back out from the spot into which he had crawled. As a seven year-old boy, when he and his best friend Robert had played at being space explorers or intrepid archeologists, the small passageway, though tight, had been their portal to adventure, a wondrous connection that transported them to alien worlds or lost, mummy-infested tombs. It had led from what was now his repair shop to the dark, dungeon-like stairwell that rose from the basement of the Metropolitan Center all the way to its roof.

A square, rickety plywood trapdoor with a wooden latch had kept the other end of the "tunnel"—as they referred to the narrow duct—shut. Before starting their adventures, they had always made certain that the wooden trapdoor—or "portal"— was unlocked, a lesson they had learned the hard way after their first unsuccessful attempt to travel through it.

But when Lucas was a seven-year old boy, the "tunnel" had been wide enough for him and Robert to crawl through. Now, thirty years later, Lucas had found the pitch-black duct impossibly constricting. He had only been able to squeeze into it by raising his arms over his head and wiggling into the narrow space sideways on his right side.

Progress had been slow and surprisingly painful. He had only been able to move inches at a time, by flexing his knees until they were stopped by the wall, wedging his toes against it, latching his fingers onto any uneven edges or cracks in the masonry for additional leverage, and shoving himself forward.

It had taken him more than thirty minutes of straining every muscle in his body to scrape, pull, and scratch his way through the fifty-foot distance between his repair shop and the "portal" in the building's stairway. At times, he had felt odd stirrings on his arms, his neck, or his back, and tried to banish from his mind what caused them. Finally, exhausted and drenched in a sweaty mixture of grime, cobwebs, and God-knew-what-else, he had stopped before the very same square door that years before had led him to so many foreign and alien worlds.

He had paused, trying to regain his breath. He could barely wait to get out of the musty, hot hellhole into which he had crawled. He prayed to God that the trapdoor had not been changed; that it had not been secured from the outside with a stronger latch, or with some sort of crisscrossing locking device, or worse, with a strong padlock. He imagined himself stuck in there permanently, stuffed forever inside the building's wall, and could barely hold back a visceral surge of panic.

Inhaling deeply, he pulled his right fist as far back as he could and rammed it against the small wooden door. It rattled but did not open. He felt a mixture of encouragement and fear, and prepared to try again. Behind him, he heard his mother ask worriedly, *"Are you all right?"* and managed to answer, "Yes," in what he thought was his calmest-possible voice.

Bracing his back against the wall, he placed the palms of his hands on the door, and shook it violently several times. To his relief and surprise, it gave way with ease, swinging outwards with a loud creak. He felt the cooler air of the stairwell flow over his face and breathed it gratefully, not even minding the faint, sickly-sweet smell of garbage that sifted into the duct from two plastic bags leaning against one of the walls.

Grabbing the edges of the open trapdoor's frame, he pulled himself out of the narrow space and dropped on the floor, less than a foot below.

"I'm through," he called back through the crawlspace, amazed at how small it looked. "I'm going to open the gate from the stairs and get you out."

He heard someone answer *"okay"* at the other end of the "tunnel", probably Maria. From his right pocket, he pulled out a ring of keys. A regular wooden door had originally connected the basement of *El Joyero* with the Metropolitan Center's inner stairway. However, after a botched burglary attempt, the Pietri sisters had installed a wrought iron gate that covered the door from the outside.

The gate was secured with a thick padlock from the inside of the jewelry store. During a rare inspection by the Fire Department, a fire marshal had indicated to the Pietri sisters that the exit to the stairway could not be blocked in any way, and that the gate could not be locked. The sisters had explained to him that eliminating the gate would expose *El Joyero* to further burglary attempts. After much discussion, a compromise—not entirely within the letter of the law, but practical—had been reached, where each employee in the store would carry a copy of the key to the gate's padlock. Also, two additional keys had been made available, one kept in Lucas' shop and the other hung from the wall, immediately next to the exit, inside the jewelry store.

Lucas found his copy of the key and walked to the wrought iron gate, still feeling very stiff from his prolonged enclosure. His fingers and hands were scraped raw from his attempts to pull himself through the duct, his pants ripped at the knees and stained with blood.

Almost immediately, he realized that it would be impossible to open the gate from the stairwell. The padlock was located on the opposite side. The gate's grillwork was set in a thick, ornate pattern that did not allow his fingers to slip through to reach the padlock, much less the hand holding the key. There would be no way that he could fit the key into the padlock from that side of the gate, in order to open it.

"Shit!" he whispered, already knowing what he would have to do, and dreading it.

He walked back to the duct, and popped his head inside it. "Listen!" he hissed. "I can't open the door from this side! I'll—"

"Come back!" Maria answered, more loudly than he cared to listen.

"I will, but not through the tunnel," he answered. "I'm going around. Up the stairs and through the entrance of *El Joyero*. Then I'll get you out."

"You're—" Maria began to say, even more loudly, but Lucas shushed her sharply. "You're crazy!" she said in a more subdued volume. "They'll see you and kill you! Come back through the tunnel! We'll wait here until they unlock us."

"*You're* crazy! I'm not crawling in there again. Don't worry! It'll be all right! I'll be there in a couple of minutes."

Maria began to protest, but Lucas ignored her, closed the "portal's" gate, and began to climb the stairs to the street level lobby.

The Metropolitan Center occupied an entire block of the city, and was subdivided in two distinct sections. The commercial area—nearly two thirds of the entire building—contained the street level stores with several floors of office space above them. The residential section—the westernmost side off the building—was occupied by large, old-style apartments with balconies facing the Plaza de Armas. Each section of the building had its own separate entrance, lobby, elevators, and stairways. Although a commercial establishment, *El Joyero de San Juan* was located below the residential apartments.

The stairway that Lucas now used led to the residential area's lobby, and not to the wider, more open lobby in the commercial area. For security reasons, the residents' lobby was separated from the street by a massive, wall-to-wall, ceiling-to-floor decorative grillwork with a gate that required a key to open from the outside, but which could be opened from the inside by the simple turn of a small, round, ancient brass doorknob. Like the gate connecting the basement of *El Joyero* to the stairway, the grillwork had been crafted in ornate patterns with thick, iron patterns set so closely together that they permitted nothing wider that a finger to fit between them.

Looking in from the sidewalk or the plaza outside, no one could see a person standing inside the lobby. But from where he stood, Lucas could gaze out onto the square through the narrow spaces in the grillwork.

The first thing Lucas noticed was the tall man who had entered into the jewelry store earlier that day and his shorter, more athletic counterpart. The younger man called Johnny and the three thugs whom Johnny apparently commanded were nowhere to be seen.

At that moment, the tall man was talking to a much smaller, almost diminutive male dressed in a business suit. Like the others, the small businessman wore a black armband on his left arm. The tall man was making no hostile or menacing gestures, and the man in the business suit hardly spoke, but he could sense, even from where he stood, the tension between the two of them.

Something about their exchange fascinated him, in the same perverse way that people are fascinated by shows of great white sharks lurking in the water. The tall man radiated the authority and charisma of an aristocrat, or of a chief executive officer in a giant corporation, even though clad in jeans and a shoddy, short-sleeved shirt with the Aqueduct and Sewers Authority logo imprinted on its pocket. The smaller man, on the other hand, looked awkward and ill at ease in his Wall Street attire, as if he was wearing a disguise that did not quite fit him. And the tall man's companion, the man who had disarmed Lucas in the jewelry store, was watching the conversation of the other two with catlike amusement.

The discussion continued for some time, and then the tall man turned around and began to walk away. After a brief exchange of words, the other two terrorists followed.

Apart from the three men, Lucas observed two other persons in the background, both males. One—a local vagrant that made grasshopper figures from palm fronds and sold them to the tourists—was sitting under one of the arches of the city hall entrance. The second, a teenager, walked quickly through the square, casting wary glances about him and trying to look as inconspicuous as possible; probably a store or fast food clerk released from work early and trying to return home.

Lucas took a deep breath. If he was going to free the others, now was the moment to do it. Twisting the brass knob, he pushed the gate open, and stepped into the sunlight, which dazzled him for a moment. He turned left, in the direction of the jewelry store, and nearly froze when he discovered two armed men standing at the far corner of the Metropolitan Center, about thirty yards beyond *El Joyero's* entrance. Both were wearing armbands. Trying not to appear self-conscious, he willed himself to keep walking in their direction, mostly staring at the sidewalk beneath his feet. He fought the urge to sprint to the store, and managed to stay calm, covering the remaining distance in what he hoped looked like a casual stroll.

The men regarded him disinterestedly for a moment, and then resumed their subdued conversation. *He would have to be more careful,* he chided himself as he got to *El Joyero's* gate. He began to think about what he would do if he entered *El Joyero* and ran into Johnny or any of his men, and readied himself for a fight. But as he got to the door and looked through its glass panel, he confirmed that the store was empty.

He opened the gate easily—it had not been locked—and quickly slid inside, shutting the door behind him. Antonio's body still lay there, covered by the two swathes of green cloth, his shoes sticking out from under them. Lucas had never noticed how worn they were, and felt his heart break for the soft-spoken, gentle guard who had confessed to him, just that morning, that he had fallen in love. He knelt briefly, and placed his hand on Antonio's chest.

"Goodbye, old friend," he whispered affectionately. "I don't rightly know what we'll do without you."

Intense anger surged within him, anger that he had not allowed himself to feel while he had to protect his family. He tried to drive it from his mind but couldn't. He knew that giving in to it would not help him and would cloud his thinking, but he could not help it. Tears clouded his eyes. *How could they have done this to such a good, decent man? How could God have allowed it?*

Feeling guilty about leaving him behind, Lucas stood up and descended the stairs at the back of the store to get to the basement. He wiped off his tears with his sleeve, and opened the padlock latched to the door of his repair shop.

The three Pietri sisters were huddled around his desk's telephone, listening intently. His mother, Fannie, held the receiver to her ear, while the other two tried to listen.

"You got through?" he asked with amazement.

Maria looked back and hushed him. "It's Vanessa!" she said. "She kept trying and trying, for hours! And suddenly, the phone worked!"

Lucas heard his mother say "uhu, uhu" several times into the receiver. She turned her green eyes to him, looking very scared.

"Your brother is here now," she said into the mouthpiece. "Talk to him."

Fannie handed the receiver to her son, her hand shaking visibly. She seemed suddenly old and frightened, as if she had been cornered into a blind alley, and he understood immediately why. His sister Vanessa had probably called to find out if Alfredo had returned from La Fortaleza to the jewelry store, and probably disintegrated emotionally when she learned that her son had not made it back.

Fannie's expression was one of helpless despair. She knew that every minute that her grandson spent in La Fortaleza constituted an unacceptable risk to his life. But at the same time, she had come to the frightening realization that the only way to get Alfredo back was by allowing Lucas to go look for him.

"Hey..." Lucas said into the phone, unable to say anything else.

"Lucas!" he heard his sister say, her first word a mixture of agonizing grief and new found hope. *"Lucas!"* she repeated, struggling to remain coherent, and then she began to sob uncontrollably. *"They have my baby!"* she bawled, unable to contain herself. *"They have Alfredo! My baby! I don't know what to do!"*

Lucas remained silent as he tried to steady his breathing. He did not want his voice to betray his anguish.

He loved his sister dearly. They were Irish twins: siblings born within less than a year between them. As far back as he could remember she had always been there. He had been her protector when bigger kids bullied her; she had been her staunchest childhood companion and accomplice, following him blindly into his wild, imaginative, and sometimes dangerous schemes—from which they had emerged miraculously unscathed—and on two occasions she had even acted as his go-between with a couple of girls that he liked but did not dare to talk to. The day before Vanessa got married, Lucas had taken his future brother-in-law Michael on a very long car ride and described to him in great detail the various ways in which he would hurt him if Michael failed to treat Vanessa right. The two siblings had made each other the godparents of their children.

"Vanessa," he forced himself to say as calmly as he could, "don't worry. I'll go to Fortaleza and get Alfredo."

"You will?" she asked, wanting to believe that he could manage it, her voice instantly filling with relief. *"Do you think he's all right?"*

"Of course he's all right," Lucas answered with all of the conviction that he could muster. "These are a bunch of *independentista* students acting out a fantasy. They won't hurt children."

Vanessa sniffled, and Lucas heard her blowing her nose. *"You really think that? You're not saying it to calm me?"*

"Yes, I really think that," he answered, not really believing it. "I'll just go to La Fortaleza, and ask the people there to release him. He doesn't play any role in their plans. There's no reason to hold him."

"Yes! Yes! That's what I think too!" Vanessa said, her hopes renewed. Then he heard her say something sharply away from the telephone.

"Hello, are you there?"

Lucas heard his sister shush someone, and after that she spoke to him again. *"It's Michael. He's like...like...like a crazy man! He's got two guns and a shotgun, and he wants to go to San Juan to get Alfredo."*

"Put him on."

Lucas listened as Vanessa said to her husband, *"He wants to talk to you."* Almost immediately, Michael's gruff voice came into the line.

"Hello!" he said abruptly.

"Hey, big guy, what's this I hear about you coming over to San Juan?" Lucas asked, with what he hoped was the right mixture of humor and alarm.

"They have my son, Luke. Those independentista assholes have my son," he said bitterly. *"If any harm comes to him..."* Michael stopped, unable to continue.

"Listen to me," Lucas said sternly. "There's nothing you can do from where you are. The bridges are down. How do you intend to get here, for God's sake?"

"I'll find a way," Michael said in sullen voice. *"Even if I have to swim across the lagoon."* Lucas did not doubt it. When provoked, his brother-in-law turned into an angry, dangerous man with the single-minded drive of a pit-bull.

"Don't," Lucas said sharply. "I'm here already, and I'll get him."

"I'll come with you," Michael offered, meaning it.

"And make me wait until tomorrow? You're not being rational, Mike! Suppose you make it through—"

"I will," Michael interrupted.

"It will take you forever to get here! And then what? You sound like a lousy gringo, and they hate gringos! They'll shoot you and probably shoot me in the process!"

Michael maintained a stubborn silence.

"You're not being reasonable, Michael," Lucas repeated, pressing his advantage. "The only thing you'll achieve by coming here is to let off some steam before you get all of us killed! I'll do it, Michael. I'll get Alfredo out." As he spoke, he watched the scared faces of his mother and aunts, and felt his heart go out to them.

"I don't want you to risk your life," Michael said, his voice filled with conflicting emotions.

"Then don't come," Lucas replied. "Take care of my sister. She's too distraught. She needs you, Michael."

A long pause followed. Then, thoroughly beaten, Michael said, *"Okay, but if they give you any grief, call me, and we'll get him back together."*

Lucas would have smiled at his brother-in-law's irrational words if the moment had not been so desperate. "I'll call you as soon as I have Alfredo," he said instead.

"Thank you, Lucas," Michael said, unable to hide his misery. Lucas was about to hang up when he heard Vanessa shout, *"Wait!"* and suddenly Jeannie was talking to him.

"Lucas!" she said, her voice reflecting her utter despair.

It took him by surprise. He started to speak, but choked, and gripped the phone helplessly. "Jeannie," he said hoarsely, unable to conceal his anguish any longer. "I love you," he whispered.

"I know," she answered. She was crying. *"I know,"* she repeated.

"I can't leave Alfredo with those men..." he tried to explain.

"I know," she said again, and in the urgent silence that followed, they exchanged a thousand unsaid words and feelings.

"Wait for me," he said, feeling stupid as he said it.

She sobbed. *"I will."*

"Tell Sofia and Gabriel that I love them...that I'll see them soon."

"I will," she repeated in a barely audible voice.

"I will come back, Jennie," he promised earnestly.

"I know you will," she said with a conviction that surprised him. She cleared her throat, forcing herself to speak calmly. *"You are a survivor,"* she said fiercely, *"and you will find a way."*

Lucas nodded, his flagging spirits buoyed up by his wife's brave words. "I will come back," he repeated, more to himself than to Jeannie. "You just wait for me, okay? I have to go now, honey," he added gently.

He heard Jeannie gasp, and she said quickly, *"Wait!"*

"I'm here," he answered.

She said nothing for several seconds. *"I just wanted...I wanted to hear you, to be with you a little longer,"* she explained apologetically. *"Please forgive me...I'm being silly! Go!"* she said in a husky, toneless voice.

"I love you, Jennie. You are the love of my life," he said, closing his eyes and picturing her in his mind. She would be leaning forward, holding on to the phone as if it were a lifeline, probably wearing flip-flops and one of her many shorts. He longed so badly to be with her at that moment.

"I love you too," she whispered, and hung up.

CHAPTER XXXIII

"Your attention please, all passengers are urged to go immediately to the Stardust Theatre for the latest briefing on the onshore situation. I repeat, please go immediately to the Stardust Theatre for the latest briefing on the onshore situation."

The PA system echoed through the multistory metal staircase, startling the three fugitives.

"They're gathering the crowd. They're probably looking for us," John said apprehensively. "How much longer to the crew's quarters?"

They had descended nine flights of stairs making so much noise on the metal steps that he thought they would rouse the entire ship. Fortunately, they had not run into a single person.

"Two more floors," Ernan, the wounded steward indicated.

Just then, someone in one of the flights above them opened one of the doors into the stairway, and shouted, "Anyone in here?"

The fugitives stared upwards apprehensively, remaining very still. The person above them waited several seconds, and then slowly began to descend the steps.

"Merde!" the Countess whispered, and started to run down the stairs. Her two companions followed her instantly.

"Wait!" the man who had entered the steps shouted, accelerating his descent. "Halt right there!"

He could not have been more than two decks above them, and seemed to be gaining. John panicked and rushed past the slower moving Countess and Ernan. His instincts of preservation urged him to move on and leave his companions behind. But then he stopped, and let the others pass him.

He was carrying the rifle they had captured from the dead female terrorist, but had no idea how to use it. He looked nervously upwards, to the steps they had just descended. From where he stood, he would be able to see the feet of their pursuer when he reached that flight of the stairs.

The Countess and Ernan stopped a few steps below him when they saw he was not following them, but he urged them on. "Go!" he said hastily, "I'll be with you in a second! Hurry!"

As his two companions resumed their swift descent, John saw two legs shod with military boots appear on the steps above him. Without thinking of the consequences, he thrust the barrel of rifle through the open banister and held on to the rifle's butt.

Caught unaware, the man rushing down the stairs had no time to avoid the sudden obstacle. His feet tangled on the rifle's barrel, nearly ripping the weapon from John's hands. The terrorist flew through the air and landed heavily on the stairs, the gun that he carried clattering noisily on the metal steps. He continued to roll down the stairway until he struck the wall at the end of the flight.

John ran like a madman down the stairway behind the others, not bothering to see what had happened to his pursuer. However, he could not find the Countess or Ernan, and nearly passed them by before a door opened and a hand grabbed him by the arm.

"This way!" Ernan hissed, leading him without a second's waste through a long corridor where the Countess waited.

"Well done, *mon cher!* Did you kill him?" she asked.

"I don't know," he answered honestly. "I didn't wait to find out. I don't think he was following me when I ran down, though."

"There's no time to talk here!" Ernan interrupted. "Follow me!"

Unlike the passenger levels, the corridor was not carpeted, but covered by a blue linoleum-like material. Its walls were decorated with bulletin boards, one next to the entrance of each cabin. The cabins must have been very narrow, John noted, since their doors were much closer together than those of the higher decks.

"I hate to be a spoilsport," he said, "but when they find the guy that I just tripped in the stairs—"

"If they find him," Ernan said.

"Or if he was just knocked out," John continued, "the first place they will search are the areas close to where that man found us."

The Countess looked back at John with distress as she considered his gloomy prediction.

"We can hide in the laundry room," Ernan indicated, as he continued to lead them down the corridor. "The washing machines are huge, and we can hide inside of them."

John stopped abruptly. "Wait, wait, wait, wait! That's your plan? To hide inside the washers? Are you crazy?!"

Ernan looked at him half-defiantly, half-chastened. "It's just until they do the search. Then we can hide in one of the cabins."

"We need a better plan!" John said to the Countess, beginning to panic. "We need a plan to get out of this ship!"

The Countess nodded several times. "Yes, *mon cher*, I agree. But first, we must get out of this corridor."

Ernan took the Countess's words as a signal to keep moving, and renewed his march, forcing the others to follow. John continued to protest softly, mumbling to himself. He was so upset that he never felt the stranger following them until it was too late.

"Halt!" a male voice cried, startling John so much that he dropped his rifle. "Don't move! Hands against the wall now or I will shoot you!"

The three fugitives obeyed immediately, scared and bullied by the aggressive tone of their unexpected pursuer.

"Eyes and hands towards the wall! Spread your legs!" the man said heatedly. Then he paused for several seconds. "Ernan?" he finally said, in a tone of surprised recognition. "Ernan, is that you?"

The Filipino steward turned his head and smiled. "Harshad! Thank God! It's okay. These people are my friends! They saved my life!"

Ernan backed out of the wall, and embraced the man who a moment before had screamed at him. The Countess and John watched with quiet curiosity.

The man embracing Ernan stood more than a head over the smaller Filipino. He wore a set of the maintenance crew's white overalls that were either several sizes smaller than his girth, or which he had outgrown by overeating. The white garment contrasted markedly with his bronze skin—which bulged from an orange shirt's short sleeves—and with his curly, shiny hair, so dark that it almost seemed blue. A thick, walrus-like mustache covered most of his mouth, and was matched by equally bushy eyebrows that nevertheless failed to diminish his huge, round eyes.

To John, the face seemed terribly familiar, although he was certain that he had never gazed upon the man before. He tried to place him, and then in a flash it came: he looked like "Animal", the wild drummer from the "Muppets".

"Harshad!" Ernan repeated delightedly.

"So these are your friends?" Harshad confirmed in a distinct accent, whether Hindu or Pakistani John could not tell, regarding John and the Countess with newfound appreciation.

"They saved my life!" Ernan explained once more. Turning towards his two companions, he added, "This is Harshad, the best electrician—"

"Connie is pretty good," Harshad interrupted, shrugging.

"Bah! Compared to you, Connie is not worthy of carrying your toolbox," Ernan said, beaming at his friend.

John listened to the nonsensical exchange with growing impatience, aware that they were plainly visible to any less friendly persons who wandered into the corridor. In the meantime, the Countess shook the electrician's extended hand and, smiling, kissed him on the cheek.

"I'm very pleased to meet you," John said when his turn came. "I don't want to sound like an alarmist, but shouldn't we get going?"

They all looked at him, as if he had disrupted a social gathering.

"Of course," Harshad said eventually, frowning. "There is a meeting of the crew...well, some of the crew, to plan how we can take the ship back."

"Take over the ship from the terrorists?" Ernan exclaimed, in a doubtful tone. "We were going to hide in the laundry room, but...I guess it would be better to join you. Where is the crew meeting?"

For the first time, John noticed that Harshad had no weapons. He was about to point this out to the others, but the big Indian cut him short.

"We're meeting in the deck's mess hall," he replied. "I am one of the lookouts, in case anyone like you or the terrorists show up."

"We should go there, then," Ernan said to the Countess. He slapped affectionately the electrician with his wounded arm, wincing with pain afterwards. "Lead the way."

"But you have no guns!" John finally managed to put in. He did not like the turn that the discussion was taking. They were supposed to be searching for a way to escape. Now the overgrown Indian was talking about retaking the ship from the terrorists, apparently with no guns.

Harshad smiled ruefully. "We have your guns now," he said, as if that made all the difference in the world.

"Tell me something," John said, trying not to show his growing sense of unease. "How exactly were you planning to stop any terrorists that came your way? I mean, without any guns?"

"Well, the same way I stopped you," Harshad answered with a logic that admitted no discussion, opening his eyes wider than before to give more emphasis to his words. He was a dead ringer for the Muppet's "Animal" character. "It is a known fact that terrorists are stupid. If I fooled you, who are a lot smarter, a fact clearly demonstrated by your escape from the terrorists, then the terrorists will collapse with our counterattack!"

John's head reeled with the implications of Harshad's logic. *Was he for real?* The worst part was that both Ernan and the Countess were nodding, as if agreeing with the electrician's conclusions. *First Ernan had planned to hide inside the crew's washing machines, and now this?*

"We have to go," he said, looking apprehensively towards the end of the corridor.

"I must stay here to stand guard," Harshad assured them, silently eyeing John's rifle.

"You can have it," John said, handing it to the Indian electrician. "I don't know how to use it."

"Thank you most kindly!" Harshad said gratefully. "I will figure out how it works!"

John groaned inwardly. *They would all surely die,* he thought.

Ernan renewed his march into the central portion of the ship. They walked past scores of additional cabins with closed doors. Once, the Filipino stopped briefly to point into a large interior room with no door, painted in light green, illuminated by bright neon lights, and radiating hot air.

"The laundry room," he indicated.

John poked his head inside and saw three huge, white, boxlike machines that rose from the linoleum floor to the aluminum-lined ceiling, each with a central hatch with a round glass window. They could certainly hold a person inside, although once locked, he was not certain how they would be able to get out. He shuddered involuntarily, thinking about it, and promised himself that he would never crawl into one of them.

The mess hall lay at the end of the corridor closest to the ship's stern. Its access was controlled by a glass sliding door that opened with an automatic eye. John could not perceive any human activity from the outside, and wondered if Harshad's associates had left.

The automatic door did not work, as Ernan found out the hard way when, expecting it to glide open, he bumped into the glass. It was not a hard bump, but it caused a nervous-looking man on the other side of the door to pop out from behind the wall to the right.

Like Ernan, he was a Filipino, slightly taller and younger, but just as thin. He examined the three people standing opposite to him with an unfriendly expression, then seemed to recognize Ernan and acknowledged him with a shy, conspiratorial wave, pulling the door open. Again, Ernan was greeted by his own name, and was received as warmly as he had been by Harshad.

The crew's mess hall looked like a no-frills high school cafeteria: three-dozen, long, aqua-colored plastic-topped tables spread to the left of the entrance, while to the right, a glass-covered buffet with an aluminum track for trays followed the contours of the serving area, looking like a large, inverted "C".

About twenty people were standing behind the serving area, close to the kitchen doors, not visible to the new arrivals until they had walked into the mess hall. Most of them were men, with a sprinkle of about half a dozen women. Many wore the white overalls used by Harshad, but there were also a few dressed in the black pants and vests that were sported by the restaurant waiters, or in the more formal black jackets of the floor managers. A few were clad in civilian clothes, including the crew-cut man who seemed to be presiding over the gathering.

The Filipino who had opened the automatic glass door closed it back manually—it had been disabled, he explained, in order not to allow anyone to walk into the cafeteria—and ushered the Countess and her two companions behind the serving area, to join the others. The crowd fell silent as they approached, and parted to let them through.

The man that was speaking regarded them with interest and smiled broadly; *a full-toothed, crocodile smile,* John thought to himself, instantly disliking the man. He was heavily muscled, of a medium height, and wore his clothes—a black T-shirt and faded jeans—especially his shirt, like a second skin. His eyes were ice blue, interrupted by a broken nose and followed by a broad hairless mouth.

"Welcome," he said in a mildly questioning tone that did not reflect the mirth of his toothy grin. "And you are—"

"Ernan Castellanos, as many here know" the Filipino answered before the other two could say anything. "This is the Condessa of Gilly, and her companion friend, Mr. John." The latter cringed inwardly at his given name. "We have escaped from the pirates, after killing three of them," Ernan announced proudly, causing the crowd around the three new arrivals to break into an excited buzz.

The crew-cut leader raised a hand to silence the assembled crewmembers.

"You killed three of the hijackers?" he asked, casting an appraising glance at the slight Filipino man, the old Countess and her "companion friend" as if doubting Ernan's assertion. "That's a very impressive accomplishment, mate. Would you care to tell us how you did it?"

John recognized the man's accent as heavily Australian, but could not quite place from what part of the country.

"Well," he began to explain, "we're not sure if we killed the third—" but Ernan took over.

The Filipino retold his story in great detail, enhancing the exciting parts and expanding his role in the events. His audience listened spellbound, reacting excitedly during the fight and escape sequences, but mostly letting their fellow crewman tell his story. The Australian grabbed a slice of pizza from one of the serving trays, and wolfed it down while Ernan spoke.

"You were very brave," the Australian said after Ernan had finished. "But by killing three of them, you've sort of stirred the hornet's nest, which underscores our need to act quickly."

"Act quickly? In what sense?" John asked, managing to say something without anyone interrupting him.

"You from Australia?" the crew-cut man inquired.

"Sydney," John confirmed.

"A city boy! I'm from near Cairns myself," the man said, extending his hand. "Roy White."

John shook his hand, wincing at the unexpected pressure of the man's grip.

"Yes, well if you've heard the PA announcements, it seems like they're looking for you, the hijackers are, that is," White said in an oddly chipper fashion. "That means they'll be conducting a search of this area soon. We'll have to act pretty fast."

"I understand that," John said, cutting off Ernan. "But what do you mean by act?"

"We need to recover the control of the ship," the crew-cut Australian answered, as if it were the most obvious course of action. "You've already killed two, maybe three of them, from what I've heard, and you captured their weapons…" White searched for the gun and the rifle that Ernan had mentioned in his story. "By the way, where are the weapons?"

The Countess raised her skirt, and from the rim of one of her nylon stockings produced a gun, handing it over to the Australian.

"I was trained in the use of handguns by my former husband," she said, smiling, "but if any of you gentlemen prefer to use it, you are most welcome to have it."

"We gave the rifle to Harshad," Ernan added. "He's keeping watch with it."

White nodded, accepting the gun. John stared at him, exasperated by the futility of the entire exchange.

"I don't want to strike the odd note here," he said, his Australian accent unconsciously thickened by his distressed mood, "but I think you're all being very optimistic if you think that you can wrestle away the control of this ship from heavily armed, and possibly highly trained terrorists with just one gun and one rifle."

"What would you propose?" White shot back, frowning earnestly.

The question took John by surprise. *What could they do?*

"Well, for one thing, has anyone tried to contact the authorities? They must have people who specialize in this type of thing."

"All the phones are busy," one of the several Filipinos in the crowd attested. "We can't get through."

The response stymied John. *They couldn't get through?*

"We can't rely on the authorities," White confirmed, guessing what his fellow Aussie was thinking. "Haven't you watched TV?"

John shook his head.

"The terrorists haven't just taken over this ship, they've taken over all of bloody San Juan! Maybe all of Puerto Rico! This is a bloody revolution, mate!"

John exchanged a glance with the Countess, who looked as surprised as him.

"How about the internet?" he asked desperately.

"Slow as molasses. We can't get through," White answered, smiling toothily again. John's dislike of the crew-cut man continued to increase. He seemed to be enjoying himself immensely.

McFadden's idea had been to escape from the ship, by either jumping off it or climbing down a rope into the water. But if he suggested that now, he would probably be branded as a self-centered coward who only thought about himself and did not care about the rest of the passengers and the crew in the ship—all of which was pretty much true. Not that he minded that much if he was called a coward. He had never given a rat's ass about what others thought about him. But it was not good business, abandoning the Countess and running away. And gauging the emotional state of the group that surrounded him, he would not put it beyond any of them to cause him physical harm if he announced that they could go about the rescue of the ship without him.

Apart from his own personal considerations, it bothered him that a heroically inclined idiot had come to be in charge of the remaining group of crewmembers. White was a dangerous leader, one of those gung-ho, do-or-die types of people who would not think twice about taking tremendous risks, instead of laying low and waiting for the opportunity to escape. John would have to be careful, and try to steer the plan of action into a saner, safer course.

"It is going to be difficult to capture the ship if we don't even know how many terrorists there are on board," he suggested cautiously.

"Larriaga," White said to a wiry, black haired man in the crew's uniform, "how many armed men did you see coming into the ship up the main ramp?"

"I saw twelve terrorists come aboard this morning," the man answered.

"More may have come on board since then," John pointed out.

"We have been keeping watch from one of the cabins next to the boarding ramp for the last hour, and the only movement has been one man getting off the ship and coming back on, twice," Larriaga replied, to John's intense mortification. "And we have to subtract the three terrorists that you killed."

"Granted, there *was* a window of time—about an hour and a half's worth of time—where nobody was watching the ramps," White conceded, "so for safety's sake we must assume that there are more of them out there...But I don't really think so."

"But if, as you say, San Juan is under terrorist control," John insisted, knowing that he could push his misgivings only by so much, or he would risk antagonizing the crowd and losing whatever little influence he had, "then that means there are a lot more terrorists out there who may come into the ship at any moment, even when we are trying to recapture the ship. Some are probably a stone's throw away, ready to jump in if they are warned by any of their onboard companions."

White nodded in agreement. "What my fellow countryman says is right," he told to the rest of the people gathered around him. "That's why we need to act very quickly, before more of the hijackers climb on board."

John, who had started to nod in agreement, stopped and looked at the crew-cut Australian in horror.

"I suspect," White continued, "that the hijackers did not take over this ship just for...to create terror, but to use it as a means of escape if their revolution fails. And if that's the case, then the more we wait, the greater the chances are that the ship will be flooded with more of them trying to escape."

John cursed himself inwardly for unwittingly giving White an additional argument to continue with his suicidal plans. The sobering scenario proposed by the Australian made sense. If the rest of the terrorists that allegedly had taken over San Juan poured into the *Mardi Gras* and pulled out of port, God knew where the hostages would end up, and in what condition. The problem was, however, that retaking a ship from at least a dozen vicious, well-trained paramilitary men seemed like an even more daunting scenario, one that would get them all killed.

It all left him with one simple solution: he would have to escape the ship alone, when nobody was watching, and take his chances when he got ashore. He felt sorry for the Countess and the hundreds of hostages who would be left behind, but in any event, he was certain that his participation in the rescue activities, whatever that would be, would not make any difference in the outcome of the operation.

For the moment, however, he would have to play along with the others and wait for the opportunity to escape.

Interpreting his silence for acquiescence, White began to delineate his plan. John listened attentively, and realized within seconds that it would not work. He had seen it all happen before in a dozen war and spy movies: a group would create a diversion in the deck below the ship's theater, drawing the attention of most of the terrorists, while a selected group would overwhelm anyone guarding the theater's second floor.

They would then free the hostages, take the weapons of those terrorists that had remained in the theatre, and fight off those who had wandered into the lower deck.

It was a recipe for disaster. The terrorists were not stupid. They would be on high alert, particularly after some of them had been killed. And even if the crew managed to overwhelm whomever was stationed in the Stardust Theater, what would it do after that? It would all end in a shootout, where the rescuers would have little opportunity of prevailing, and where many of the hostages would get killed.

Once more he felt tempted to make public his misgivings, and once more he decided against it. He feared that any participation in the ongoing discussion would only lead to his gaining a prominent part in its execution of whatever half-witted plan they were concocting, something that he clearly did not desire.

He felt the desperate urge to smoke—he had nearly kicked the habit, but still felt the need to consume cigarettes during moments of significant stress—and unconsciously patted his pockets searching for a cigarette pack. Instead, he felt the bulge of his cell phone in one of his pockets.

It was a satellite phone. Because of his travels all over the world, he had found it very convenient to own one, its rates being cheaper than those usually charged by the cruise lines for calls made through the ship when it was traveling overseas.

And then it came to him: a plan to escape, using his satellite phone as a cover. It would involve some danger, but significantly less than the kamikaze attack proposed by his Australian counterpart.

"Has anyone attempted to contact the authorities with a satellite phone?" he asked, momentarily stilling the rest of the conversation. No one, including White—to John's secret satisfaction—answered. "No one?" He raised his telephone, for everyone to see.

"Why should it be any different than the other cell phones?" White asked, somewhat peeved. He had been finalizing the details of the hostage rescue with the others.

"Because it's not connected to the local communications systems. It goes directly to a satellite in space orbit," John replied. "If the terrorists knocked out the local communication systems in San Juan, the satellite communications would still not be affected."

Everyone's attention turned to White, to see what he said about McFadden's suggestion.

"It's worth a try," the former said with a hint of reluctance. "Who would you call?"

John pondered on the question for a moment.

"We can't call anyone here who doesn't have a satellite phone, since they will be in the same situation that we are. However, I could call information, and have them get me the number for the FBI or Homeland Security in Washington."

The crew-cut Australian considered McFadden's recommendation, and nodded.

"All right then. Make the call."

John shook his head.

"It's not that simple. We need to make the call from an open space, where my phone can link up with a passing satellite. I can't make the call from inside the ship."

"The crew's terrace!" Ernan proposed immediately.

"That may do, although you'll be visible from the upper decks," White said. "If you're willing to risk it..."

"I am," John answered with a relief that the others mistook for enthusiasm. "I think the possible benefits more than outweigh the risks, don't you?"

White slapped his fellow countryman on the back enthusiastically.

"You're a brave man, John!" he said, genuinely moved. "We'll wait for you here, working on the details of the rescue. You will need someone to guide you to the crew's terrace."

"There's no need," John answered a bit too quickly. With the corner of his eye he saw the Countess staring at him strangely. "No use dragging anyone else with me. Just tell me where to go, and I'll get there myself."

"It's better that somebody that knows the ship and the crew's quarters take you there," White insisted. "If you get lost, you could end up in the wrong place."

John was surprised by his Australian counterpart's apparent concern. Others in the crew nodded. It made him feel uncomfortable and guilty.

"I will take him," Ernan volunteered, and turning towards John added, "I'm here because of you. I can't abandon you now."

John got ready to object again, but he bit his lower lip and remained silent. *It was no use,* he thought. Protesting too much would only raise suspicions. He would have to go with Ernan, and make the call. He would fill in the Filipino on whatever information he obtained from his call—who he would call exactly, he was still not certain—and then get "lost" as they returned to the crew's mess hall. That way he would help them, by establishing a link between the crew and the authorities, and avoid participating in their crazy rescue attempt.

Not that he had figured out yet how he would escape. He would have to make that determination once he got to the terrace. He would probably jump for it, the terrace being not more than three or four decks above the water. He was a strong swimmer, and felt certain that he could hide under the docks before any terrorist found out what had happened. From there he could wade undetected away from the *Mardi Gras* to a spot in the waterfront where he could climb out of the water and find some place in the old city where he could be safe until the emergency blew over.

"Okay," he said resignedly after a short pause. "Although I still think that I can find my way without placing anybody else in harm's way," he insisted half-heartedly, this time just for the effect.

"We're all in harm's way," White said grandly, managing a wistful smile.

"I'd like to go with you too," the Countess said, directing a sharp glance at her cruise companion.

Few people knew John as well as the Countess of Gilly. They had traveled together in several cruises, and developed the kind of easy, comfortable relationship that only good friends could have. For John, the relationship bordered on the closest thing that he could call affection; he appreciated the old woman's combination of charm, wit, and pure spunk. But for that same reason, her suggestion now made him nervous. She, better than anyone, could read his mind, and she, better than anyone, knew that he was not the type of person who would voluntarily risk his life for others.

"Are you sure?" he asked her, not daring to look into her eyes. "I can't bear to place you in danger—"

The Countess regarded him with a cold, mirthless smile. "Like our friend White said, we are all in harm's way."

John had expected White to object, but the Australian said nothing.

"Are you ready then?" Ernan asked, sounding edgy.

John nodded.

"May you be safe from all harm, my friends," White said. Others in the crowd added their thanks and well wishes, a few slapping John on the back, and two rubbing Ernan's head for good luck. The same man who had opened the automatic glass door when they had entered the cafeteria now opened it for the two men and their female companion to slide through.

Ernan began to walk in the direction they had originally come from, which immediately alarmed John. The Australian gigolo was about to question the wisdom of using that route, when his Filipino guide stopped in front of a door with an elongated horizontal handle.

"These stairs are a short-cut to the crew's deck. I will open the door just a crack and listen, in case there's somebody on the other side who should not be there," he said in a hushed voice.

Ernan pushed down the metallic handle with exaggerated care, but the bolt made a loud *"crack"* as it was unlocked that reverberated in the stairwell beyond.

Well, thought John to himself, *that takes care of the stealth.* They listened for several seconds, and not perceiving any noise that could reveal any hostile activity, they walked in. They traveled up a narrow stairway that snaked its way to the deck above. Unused by passengers and probably by most of the crew, no attempt had been made to conceal the various pipes, air vents, and cables that cris-crossed its sides and ceiling. Thick white paint had been carelessly slopped over its railings and walls with the sole purpose of preventing corrosion, only the aluminum steps and a few ducts and cables retaining their original colors.

"We must move quickly," Ernan said urgently.

John agreed. Any movement, no matter how careful, would be magnified in that echo-bound stairwell. The faster they got out of there the better.

Reaching the next landing in the stairs, they turned left and entered a short, even narrower, more cluttered corridor that ended in an oval hatch. As before, Ernan pushed down with deliberate care the door's latch, this time managing to make very little noise. Looking through a narrow crack of the open hatch, he perceived no movement. Still, he could only see a little distance into the red-carpeted corridor on the other side.

"The deck is to the right, just a few feet away," Ernan indicated. "There's a glass sliding door that gives access to it."

"I'll go alone," John stated.

"No!" the Countess interjected fiercely. "We must all go!"

"No, listen to me!" he answered just as fiercely. "It makes no sense for the three of us to go out there. It will only increase the chances of our being seen!" He looked at Ernan for support, but the Filipino merely shrugged weakly. "I will make the call, and I will come back to tell you what I find out," he said directly to the Countess, then added, "I promise."

The Countess stared directly into John's eyes, as if trying to read his thoughts. Her blue eyes brimmed with tears, and she wiped them off with the back of one of her veiny hands. For the first time through the entire ordeal, she seemed old, frail and scared. He could not understand her. Less than an hour before, when they were in her suite, she had been willing to let him go, and take her chances with Ernan. Now that she sensed his intentions to bolt from the ship, she seemed unwilling to lose him from her sight. It almost felt as if, having been assured by John that he would stay by her side, she had pinned all of her hopes to escape on him, and was now realizing that she would be left alone.

"I promise," John repeated, and choosing his words very carefully, said, "I will come back to tell you whatever I can find out."

"Very well," the Countess answered bitterly. "Go, and do what you have to do." She spoke in a very thick French accent.

"Once you go through that glass door, you will be exposed to view from the upper decks," Ernan told him. "Stay as close as you can to the wall, so that you will be visible only to those who lean over the railing. Also, stay away from the glass door, or you might be seen from the corridor."

John nodded.

"I will watch for any approaching pirates from here," Ernan added reassuringly, but John knew that if anyone came, there would be no time to warn him.

Without saying another word, he stepped out through the hatch. He saw the glass door to the deck immediately, scarcely ten feet away from where he stood. It was clouded by dry sea spray, but he could still see the beautiful blue winter sky of the Caribbean showing through it.

This time, the door opened automatically, exposing John to a surprisingly strong breeze that tussled his hair and puffed up his shirt. He stepped outside and briefly examined the area, making sure that he remained close to the wall next to the exit.

The deck was shaped like the half of an egg, following the contours of the stern—or rear—of the ship, its floor covered with light colored teak wood. About thirty blue, plastic long chairs were spread over it, as well as half a dozen white, small, round tables with similarly colored, regular-sized seats. The deck stood more than forty feet above the surface of the bay—a higher drop than John had anticipated. Still, he was certain that he could manage a jump from that height.

He slid his satellite phone out of his pocket, and extended from its side its antenna. After just a couple of seconds, it registered contact with a satellite. On the phone's screen, he searched the "Menu" for "Information", and selected a "Satcom Direct Communications" preprogrammed thirteen-digit number. Almost immediately, a pleasant female voice answered the call.

"Satcom client assistance, how may I help you?" she asked.

"I need the number for the FBI in Washington," John whispered.

"I'm sorry, but you'll have to speak more loudly. There seems to be a lot of noise in your end," the female voice said.

It was true. The wind was blowing in strong spurts, creating a vacuum cleaner noise in his receiver.

"I need to get the number for the FBI in Washington!" John repeated more loudly than he intended, feeling alarmed by the noise he made.

"Thank you," the woman said cheerfully, not registering any curiosity or concern in her voice. *"Would you like me to patch you through?"*

"Yes, please," John answered gratefully.

The call was placed on hold, and shortly thereafter the line purred intermittently as the satellite link was redirected to Washington.

"This is the Federal Bureau of Investigation in Washington, DC," a prerecorded female voice answered. *"Please listen to the following choices in order to make an adequate selection. To report information on select major cases, please dial #1 now."*

John did not wait for the other choices to be listed, pressing #1. Almost as if someone had been waiting next to the phone to pick up the call, a voice—this time that of a male—answered instantly.

"FBI Major Case Contact Center, how may we be of assistance?"

"Hello? Can you hear me?" John spoke over the noise of the breeze.

"I can hear you fine," the man at the FBI call center answered.

"My name is John McFadden. I'm a passenger in the cruise ship *Mardi Gras."* John waited for the man on the other end of the line to react.

"Yes?" the man said tentatively.

"The *Mardi Gras,* the ship that's been hijacked in Puerto Rico?"

There was a short silence, as the FBI contact absorbed the information.

"You're on the Mardi Gras right now?" he asked cautiously.

"Yes, yes, I'm on board the ship right now!" John answered impatiently.

"How can we verify that this is not a prank call?" the FBI man asked. John heard the scraping sound of a chair and the shuffle of paper over the man's voice.

"Check the ship's list of passengers! My name is John McFadden. I was in room 864, in the Pacific Deck," he urged the man.

"Hold on," the FBI man said, a little more urgently. John heard another voice whisper something unintelligibly.

"Hurry, please! I am calling you from an open space through my satellite phone and I can't stay here much longer without being seen!"

"I'm patching you through right now!" the voice at the other end said.

John waited, staring up. He felt very vulnerable, even standing against the wall. He expected someone to appear at any moment through the automatic sliding door. Finally, his phone came back to life amidst the hubbub of several voices.

"Hello? Mr. McFadden? Are you there?"

"For the moment, yes," John answered nervously.

"This is Special Agent Tom Moylan. I'm here with agents Brown and Medina." Two other voices, one of them female, briefly greeted him. *"Please tell us what is your present situation."*

"I'm calling from an open deck. It's the only way I can use my satellite phone since regular cell phones are not working," John explained, "So if you lose me, it may be because I've been discovered."

"We understand," Moylan said. *"Can you tell us what is happening in the ship?"*

"It's been taken over by armed terrorists..." John tried to steady his nerves and to speak as coherently as possible, but for some reason, talking to the FBI to describe the situation only seemed to make him more anxious. "The terrorists are armed with rifles and handguns. They have ordered everyone to go to the Stardust Theater, that's the main theater of the ship—" John thought he heard a noise above him and for several heart-stopping seconds he ceased to talk, leaning hard against the wall and craning his neck upwards.

"Hello? Hello? John, are you there?" Moylan asked, increasing the volume of his voice but keeping it calm.

"I'm here!" John said in a whisper, and then realizing that he had probably not been heard, repeated it more loudly. "I thought I heard someone."

"How come you're not in the Stardust Theater with the others, John?" Moylan asked him.

"So far, the terrorists have deceived most of the passengers and the crew into believing that they are the police, that they were sent to the ship to protect it from the terrorists in San Juan. This is a big ship, so it's very difficult for them to control all of the people in it."

"How come you weren't fooled?" said Moylan.

"That's besides the—" John began to protest angrily the interrogation to which he was being subjected, but stopped himself. "Listen, I don't have much time. One of the people with me saw a body being dragged from the bridge, and ran away. Unfortunately, he was seen and followed, and he sought my help. We had to kill one of the terrorists to defend ourselves."

"Was the body that of the captain?" Moylan inquired.

"I'm not...I don't think so," John said, concentrating really hard. It had been the captain who had spoken over the PA system urging the passengers to go to the ship's theatre.

"You said you killed a terrorist?" Moylan casually stated next, keeping his interviewee on track.

"Yes, two, maybe three. We didn't wait to see if the other was dead," John responded.

"Did you take any of their weapons?"

"A rifle and a gun."

"Do you know how many terrorists there are on board?" Moylan asked after a pause.

John searched his brain, trying to recall what White had said about the number of the terrorists. "At the last count there were twelve, minus the two or three that were hurt or killed. There may be more at the dock…In fact, there *are* more at the dock, since there have been some comings and goings to and from the dock all day long. I'm afraid that more will come soon."

"*This is agent Brown,*" a female voice said. "*Do you know where the terrorists are located in the ship?*"

"All over," John answered. "They are looking for those like me who have not gone to the theater."

"*How many of you are there?*" Moylan picked up the questioning again.

"About twenty, two dozen of us that I know of, mostly crew. They are planning to try to rescue the hostages from the terrorists," John said. He heard the three agents at the other end exchange several hushed words.

"*No, no, John,*" a third voice, presumably that of Agent Medina said. "*That could end in real disaster. You can't take on the terrorists with a rifle and a gun. These are professional killers.*"

John nodded, in absolute agreement.

"I know," he said. "I've told them as much! But they're decided. They're afraid—with reason—that more terrorists will board the ship and that then there will be no chance to do anything."

John heard more whispering at the other end.

"*John,*" Moylan said, "*it's a genuine concern, but trying to take on the terrorists is just too dangerous. It could end in a disaster. You have to get back to them and tell them that—*"

"They won't listen to me, and I don't blame them. They're scared of who else may come on board, or that they may be discovered."

"*You have to try, John. We'll be sending a rescue force soon, but it will take time. We need more intelligence on what's happening, so that our people know how to take the enemy out!*"

John shook his head. *More intelligence? They were running for their lives, for God's sake! Leave it to the FBI to suggest that they gather more intelligence.*

"*John…are you there?*" Moylan asked.

"Where else?" he answered angrily.

"*You must get back to your people and convince them to hold back. It's essential that you do that. Do you understand?*"

Yes, he understood, *but he was not going to do it.* The most he would do is explain the situation to the Countess and Ernan, and let them try to explain it to the others. It did not have to be him, anyway. Ernan probably had a lot more influence on his fellow shipmates. John would even give him his satellite phone, so he could communicate directly with the FBI.

"I understand," he answered, trying to end the conversation.

"Where are you now?" Moylan inquired. *"You said you were in an open deck. You think that later during the day, our people could climb into that deck to get into the ship?"*

"It's four decks from the water," John responded. "You would need a rope."

"Do you think your people can find one?"

"Maybe...I don't know," he answered, confused.

"Okay, let's do this. See if you can hold off your people..." John grew more and more impatient. *When did the crewmembers suddenly become "his people"?* "...from attempting to rescue the passengers. See what additional information you can get on the whereabouts and number of terrorists, and see if you can find a rope. We will talk again in an hour—What time is it? Close to noon your time? We'll call you at 2:00 PM, if that's okay with you."*

"No, it's not okay with me!" John answered desperately. "I may be dead or captured by that time! The deck may be full of terrorists in a minute! It's not okay with me!"

There was a lull in the conversation. Then Moylan said, *"John, I understand what you're going through...what you've gone through. I truly do. I know that what we're asking you to do is not easy. I'd be scared shitless if I was in your position. But a lot of lives depend on what you do in the next few hours. You've done great so far! You've already given us a lot of important information. Help is on the way, I promise. But you have to help us set up the rescue operations. You are our only eyes in there right now. We need your help!"*

John maintained a bitter silence. *It was not fair. They were pressuring...no, blackmailing him emotionally. Well, he would not fall for that. He would play their game, and pass the responsibility to White, who wanted it so badly anyway.*

"I will do what I can," he said non-committally.

"Write down this number," Moylan instructed him, and gave him a direct telephone number to which he could call. John entered the number into his phone's directory. *"Thank you, John,"* the FBI man said. *"May God guide you in this critical time."*

The Australian hung up without saying goodbye. Poking his head sideways, he saw through the glass door that the corridor was empty and returned to the hatch where Ernan and the Countess waited. The Filipino nearly had a heart attack when John pulled back the door unexpectedly, and nearly dragged the small man–who was holding on to the door's handle—into the corridor.

"I spoke with the FBI," John informed them as he walked into the narrow alley where the other two hid. He crouched next to his two companions, who looked at him anxiously. Ernan continued to keep watch through a thin crack of the open hatch, in case somebody approached them from the corridor.

"I told them what the situation was in the ship right now, and what a group of us is planning to do about it."

He repeated to them his telephone conversation with the federal agents, sparing no detail. The Countess and Ernan listened wordlessly, nodding at times, looking doubtful at others.

"You must convince them not to attempt the rescue, Ernan," John said to the Filipino at the end of his story.

Ernan assented emphatically. "You and I will convince them. We must help the FBI in any way that we can."

"You will have to start without me," John told his companion, smoothly shifting gears in the conversation. Both the Countess and the Filipino stared at him with surprise. "It will only be for a moment," he hurried to add, shifting his eyes from one face to the other. "While I was talking to the FBI, I think I saw a rope tied to the railing of the deck which may be useful to us. I completely forgot about it until now. I'm going back to check if it's really there, and try to recover it," he explained.

"We will wait for you," said Ernan.

"No!" John retorted. "We mustn't lose any more time! The crew may decide to act without us at any moment. Here!" John handed his satellite phone to Ernan, who received it reluctantly, as if it were some strange technological artifact from an alien world. "I've already marked the FBI's contact number. All you have to do is press the 'Transmit' button. If you lose it, it will be in the directory, under FBI. But remember, you must be in an open area to get reception."

"But if you're coming back, why don't you keep it?" Ernan asked, offering back the telephone to its owner.

"I will. It's just a precaution, just in case something happens to me," John replied.

"You should leave the rope where it is," the Countess said, not taking her eyes from his friend's face. "If what the FBI said is right, they will use the rope to climb to the crew's deck anyway!"

"Maybe," John was slow to answer, "but if the terrorists for some reason later occupy the deck, we will be left both without a place for the FBI to climb *and* the rope. Better be safe than sorry, and make certain we at least have the rope. Now go! Hurry! Talk to the crew! I will be with you shortly!"

Not waiting for a response, John took a quick glance through the crack of the semi-open hatch, and stepped back into the corridor, leaving behind his two confused companions.

The glass door to the deck swished open as he approached it, allowing him to re-enter the deck. He turned to his right, staying close to the wall, and walked until he reached the ship's railing. It would be a long drop by any means, the equivalent of jumping from a forty-foot cliff. The *Mardi Gras* was moored too close to the dock for him to jump from that side. He would have to get to the rear of the ship, in order to make a safe jump as close to the docks as he could. From that spot, he would be exposed to anyone on a higher deck looking in his direction, but it would only take him a few seconds to dive into the murky waters of the bay and disappear under the docks.

The terrorists would not spend a lot of effort trying to locate a stray tourist. After all, he was just a tiny fish slipping through the huge net of the terrorists. They could not afford to expand their already overextended resources just to catch him.

He felt badly for the others, especially the Countess, but realistically, what else could he do? It was not like his staying there would make any difference. He had placed the crew in contact with the FBI, and hopefully, they would be steered in the right direction.

Walking at a normal pace in order not to arouse any suspicions from any casual onlooker, he reached the rear of the ship, and leaned over its railing. The water below glistened with the cheerful, golden reflections of the afternoon sun, almost as if beckoning him to jump. His hair stirred in the brisk breeze of the sea.

It was time. He considered taking off his shoes, but decided against it. He was a good enough swimmer, and would certainly need them later. He placed one leg over the railing and the other on one of the railing's lower balustrades, and braced himself for the jump.

The soft hiss of the glass door stopped him. Startled, he looked back and saw the frail outline of the Countess of Gilly, her face a mask of disappointment and grief.

"So I was right," she said, more to herself than to her companion, "you *are* running away."

John felt his face heat up, a mixture of shame and anger. "I am not a hero," he answered weakly. "I never pretended to be one."

She wiped away a tear and saying nothing, turned to leave. And as she did, she screamed in terror, as a pair of burly arms enveloped her, and two other men rushed out of the corridor towards the deck.

John stared at them long enough to see their guns. Then, taking a deep breath, he plunged headfirst into the bay.

CHAPTER XXXIV

Doel Reyes sat in the control room behind the director, watching the dozen monitors that showed the images of various areas around the Condado Lagoon and the docks of Old San Juan. Two of the small screens showed the fires at the San Juan Yacht Club and the Police Station, still blazing at a high intensity. At the yacht club, some of the larger boats—the lines that had held them to the docks burned by the flames—had floated away and begun to drift into the San Antonio Channel, carried away by the receding tide.

"Like floating Viking funerals," Doel muttered to himself, as he watched the million dollar-white hulled vessels slowly wander off their piers, their decks and superstructures totally enveloped in black smoke and orange flames.

"What?" the director asked distractedly without taking his eyes off the monitors, while dispensing continuous instructions to his cameramen.

"Nothing," Doel replied. "Just thinking with my mouth open."

'Well shut it," the director said to him, with the rough familiarity that only good friends could share. Like with Correcaminos, the two men had worked together for many years.

Two of WKPA's cameras covered the Grand Laguna Hotel with extreme telephoto lenses, as did hundreds of other news services that by that time had converged from all over the world in the Condado area. The first one showed the two structures that comprised the hotel: the dazzling, very tall, spiral tower of crystal that the locals had dubbed as "The Screw"—rising forty stories into the sky—and the shorter building with the façade of a surging tidal wave that housed the ballrooms and the convention facilities of the resort.

The helipad, where VIP guests of the hotel were routinely flown from the airport to avoid San Juan's heavy traffic, had been constructed on the roof of the smaller of the two buildings, so that whenever a helicopter landed, it seemed to rest on the crest of a giant, rolling wave. The telephoto periodically swept over the two buildings, trying to detect movement in their empty balconies, halls, and gardens, with no apparent success.

The second of WKPA's long-range lenses focused exclusively on the large, red circle—looking very similar to an oversized "Target" logo—that marked the site of the helipad.

The landing site for the helicopters in the lower of the two buildings—as opposed to the spiraling tower of "the Screw"—was the most logical place where the hostages could step onto the roof, and be pushed to their deaths in full view of the television cameras. At twenty stories high, the helicopter pad was not visible from the street level. To cover it, WKPA had managed to place a camera atop the Condado condominium that faced the Grand Laguna Hotel across the lagoon and from which all residents had been evacuated.

The helipad itself rested on a squat, windowless structure about forty feet wide by forty feet long that rose one story above the remaining area of the roof. Any guests alighting on it were led down a set of stairs to a small, air-conditioned room with two, bronze-doored elevators that connected the landing platform to the luxury suites and the rest of the hotel. The area had been designed to protect the privacy—and sometimes the identities—of the scores of movie celebrities, politicians, and other famous people who visited the Grand Laguna Hotel regularly, and had proven to be a very effective and paparazzi-proof method of catering to that exclusive clientele.

There was also a blue metallic door in the landing pad structure that opened towards the lagoon. The door provided access to the rest of the rooftop of the building: a flat open area as large as a soccer field, covered with a silver-colored coating that was occasionally dotted with small black areas where rainwater had ponded or soot had accumulated. Except for the helipad, no other structures, fences or restraining elements bordered the outer boundaries of the twenty-story building. Anybody marching out of the helipad structure onto the rooftop and continuing to march in a straight line would eventually step into the void beyond the building's edge.

What Doel could not figure out was how the terrorists would manage to walk the hostages to the rim of the hotel and force them to jump. Assuming that one of the Macheteros used the hostage as a shield, he would be exposed to SWAT's sniper fire from the San Geronimo Plaza once his captive had been hurled to his doom. Maybe the terrorists would hide behind the metal door of the helipad structure, and give the hostage the alternatives of jumping or getting shot on the spot. But that made no sense. The hostages would probably refuse to move, or collapse from fear, or try to run away. And the shocking effect intended by the terrorists—that of showing to the rest of the world a guest dropping from the roof of a luxury hotel and smashing onto the concrete below—would be lost.

So how would they do it?

A telephone handset lodged in the control room's console began to emit demure, muted beeps, a yellow light below it flashing on and off. The director's assistant picked it up, listened for a few seconds, and turned to Doel.

"Do you know anyone going by the name of 'El Chino'?" he asked.

Doel continued to stare at the monitor screens, barely paying any attention. "What?" he said distractedly.

"El Chino," the assistant repeated, in a peeved voice, wanting to get rid of the handset. "Do you know anyone named 'El Chino'?"

Doel frowned, searching his memory. "El Chino...el Chino...I know a Chirino...Daniel Chirino..."

The assistant director repeated the name into the handset, waited a moment, and said, "No, this is 'El Chino'. He says he spoke to Michelle about an hour ago."

Doel immediately tore his eyes from the monitor screens and extended his arm towards the assistant director, motioning impatiently with his hand to give him over the phone.

"Michelle? He spoke with Michelle? Put him on!"

"No, no. He's not on the phone. He's here, in the reception area. He says he brings a message from Michelle—"

Doel stood up, his lean frame quivering with excitement. "Well why the hell didn't you start with that piece of information? Bring him in, bring him in!"

"Not here!" the director said over his shoulder. "And please shut up! I can't hear my crew."

"Tell security to bring him to Studio B. I will meet him there," Doel said in a more subdued tone, as he exited the control room.

Studio B currently contained several rooms of the huge, Victorian style mansion used in the soap opera "Son of Renzo, the Gypsy", including the mansion's foyer, a grand staircase, a wall-to-wall book-lined study, a dining room with a twelve-chaired table set and an elaborate glass chandelier, two heavily draped bedrooms, and a balconied terrace that opened up to the edge of what were supposed to be a manicured lawn and gardens. Doel chose to meet his visitor in the "study", and pulled a high-backed leather chair from behind a large, ponderous mahogany desk for his guest to sit in.

The visitor walked in a minute later led by "Magnum", the oldest security guard in the station. "El Chino" did not look Chinese. The man was huge, both in height and in girth. *Three Magnums would have fitted inside of him,* Doel thought.

He wore a wine-colored—was it polyester?—sports jacket and a wide, shiny psychedelic-patterned tie that did not quite manage to hide the stretched, open collar around which it was knotted. Doel imagined the shirt buttons under the tie straining to capacity, if some had not already popped out of their restraints. A pair of ivory-colored slacks covered his trunk-like legs and cascaded over immaculately white, patent leather loafers.

It was his face, however, which claimed Doel's immediate attention. His hair, jet-black, grease-shiny and plastered to his skull, had been cut in the old fashioned, Moe-of-the-Three-Stooges style, as if somebody had placed his head inside a large kettle and snipped the hair away around the metal pot's circumference. Straight, vertical bangs covered his forehead almost to the edge of his eyebrows, highlighting his most prominent facial feature, his eyes. There was nothing dull or sluggish about them. Dark and shiny, cunning and distrustful, they seemed to move with a will of their own, darting from one spot to another, absorbing every detail of anything upon which they happened to alight. Doel likened them to the eyes of a rat, of a man who felt infinitely more at ease prowling through a dark alley than strolling on an open sidewalk.

The portly visitor seemed to be dazzled by his surroundings, taking in with apparent relish the great, somber settings that served as backdrop for the soap opera's implausibly beautiful cast of characters. He pretended not to notice Doel until he had almost stumbled into him. Then he gazed at him benignly, and smiled.

"This is where Lady Hastings poisoned Maladroit, the hunchback butler, isn't it?" he said, pointing at an ornate Persian rug laying half a dozen paces from the desk where the news editor waited. Doel had no idea. "That is one nasty lady. Although Maladroit had it coming, if I may say so!" The huge man turned his head to another corner of the cavernous studio. "And that is where Renzo lives!" he exclaimed with pleasure, pointing to a gypsy wagon hidden in what was supposed to be a dense forest. "The question is, is he really cursed as the *pitonisa* claims, or is everything that happens to him a coincidence?"

"I don't believe in coincidences," Doel responded, signaling with his head to Magnum that it was okay to leave—a gesture that did not escape the visitor's inquisitive eyes.

"Mr. Chino? I am Doel Reyes, news editor for WKPA news…Michelle Alfaro's boss." The news editor's hand was engulfed by El Chino's beefy grip, and shaken warmly.

"Please, just call me Chino. This has been quite a day for me, first Michelle and now walking into the studio where Son of Renzo is made," the obese man said, shaking his head in wonderment. "It all looks different here," he added, looking around him. His voice did not reflect any disillusionment, but admiration. "Smaller...less real...Great job! Great job!"

Doel bobbed his head side to side, Indian fashion, not entirely certain of how to respond.

"You have been in contact with Michelle, the receptionist said?" he inquired, attempting to steer the conversation away from the soap opera. The oversized man stared at him with a faintly puzzled expression, and then his brain seemed to "click" into the business at hand.

"Yes..." he answered at first uncertainly, gaining momentum as he focused on the purpose of his visit. "I spoke to her..." he looked at a watch that looked puny on his fat wrist, "a little more than an hour ago."

Doel examined the man's face, trying to detect any signs of deception. Now that he was closer, El Chino reminded him of a pig. Heavy, hairless jowls covered most of his face below his dark, intelligent eyes, partially hiding the corners of his mouth beneath their fleshy folds. His nose was surprisingly small and round, like a coat button.

"May I ask what is your connection with Michelle?"

"My connection with Michelle?" El Chino mischievously raised his eyes, as if searching his memory. "I have no connection to Michelle," he confessed at last with a rueful smile. "I mean, if you ask like in 'Six Degrees of Separation', then I am...one degree of separation." He stared at Doel with evident glee.

The interview was definitely not going well, Doel decided. However, he had no choice but to plod on.

"In other words, you know someone who knows her?" If El Chino wanted to play "Six Degrees of Separation", Doel would play along.

"Precisely."

"Where is Michelle?" Doel asked patiently, hiding his exasperation.

"Why, in San Juan of course," El Chino replied, as if stating the obvious.

"Then how—"

"She called me!"

"She called *you*!"

"Well, not exactly her. Archie...a friend of mine called me, and then put her on the phone. She asked me to contact you, Doel Reyes. You said that that was you, right? She is such a lovely woman—"

"Wait!" Doel continued to scrutinize his visitor's expression, attempting to determine if he was telling the truth. "Please don't be offended, but why would Michelle call *you*? Why call not me, her boss?"

El Chino sighed, as if his patience was running thin.

"Oh, she couldn't get through to you! She tried to. She told me so. *I* couldn't get through to you either! That's why it took me so long to talk to you. I had to come here all the way from Miramar to see you. Do you have any idea how bad traffic is right now?"

El Chino searched for a place to sit, apparently not used to supporting his heavy frame for an extended period of time. "May I?" he asked Doel, pointing at the padded leather chair that Doel had pulled out from behind the desk a few moments before.

"Please!" Doel swiveled the chair in his direction.

El Chino sat with a sigh of relief, his eyes gleaming with grateful pleasure. The chair protested the unanticipated strain with a prolonged creak but held, to Doel's relief.

"This is where the Mendozas plan their evil deeds," he said, his plump hands caressing with reverence the handles of the chair. "They should all be tied up and thrown into the sea, that wicked family. I can't fathom how Marianna has not seen through their deceit, which is fairly obvious. Sometimes I wonder about that girl's common sense." El Chino shook his head with real concern.

Doel remained silent, waiting for his visitor, who lounged on the "Mendoza" chair like a beached whale, to resume his story. He still had not decided if El Chino was sane, a delusional television nut, or a practical joker. Probably a little bit of all.

"So she got through to you..." Doel prodded, when nothing was forthcoming. "How exactly?"

Once more, El Chino seemed to force himself out of the reverie into which he had drifted, and refocus on the real purpose of his visit to the television station. One of his hands reluctantly parted from the chair's padded armrest, and disappeared briefly into his wine-colored jacket. When it emerged, it held a portable telephone.

He showed it to Michelle's boss as if it were the most precious object in the Universe, holding it between his thumb and his index finger. Doel stared long and hard at the produced gadget, not grasping its significance. Then, as he read the word "Radium" imprinted over the phone's dial pad, he finally understood, slapping the desk with gleeful wonder.

"A satellite phone!" he said out loud.

Michelle had found a way to communicate with him after all.

The contrast was surreal. One instant she had been hiding, her throat parched, fearing for her life. The next she was sitting with a glass of cold lemonade in her hand, on a plush couch in the air-conditioned, marbled-floor living room of the Lazaros' penthouse, looking out through glass doors that led onto an open terrace facing the Condado Lagoon. The sun shone brightly on a blue, cloudless sky, the smoke from the burning, adjacent San Juan Yacht Club dispersed by the sea breeze, away from the Laguna Vista Building and west towards the San Juan Bay.

The Lazaros, Andres and Rosa, had welcomed the refugees with the same warmth and cheerful familiarity they would have accorded to close friends attending a dinner party. Andres, a very successful corporate lawyer in his sixties, had opened the door carrying a snub-nosed Smith and Wesson .38 revolver, "just in case". A cheerful, vigorous man with a thunderous voice, he had ushered them into the apartment, and listened carefully to their disjointed versions of the morning's events, somehow distilling the relevant facts and quickly grasping their present situation. Rosa, ten years younger than her husband and still a considerably attractive woman, had fussed over Michelle's injuries and quickly led her to clean and dress her cuts and scrapes.

Michelle had been shocked by the face that had stared back at her in the bathroom mirror. Not only had her upper lip ballooned over much of the rest of her mouth, but also the bridge of her nose had swelled up like that of a beat up boxer, and was already beginning to turn yellow.

"I look awful!" she had said to herself, tears brimming in her eyes, except it had sounded something like, "I luc ophul!"

Mrs. Lazaro had snatched a plastic bottle of alcohol, some gauzes, and a tube of antibiotic from the bathroom's vanity and placed them on the sink's marble-topped counter.

"Do you think you can take care of yourself while I tend to your friends?" Rosa had asked. Michelle had nodded, not wanting to say "Yeth".

Fifteen minutes later, she had joined the others in the living room, where Mr. Lazaro had immediately placed a glass of lemonade in her hand. There she had learned about the assault on the Grand Laguna Hotel, the capture of the *Mardi Gras*, and the seizing of La Fortaleza.

Michelle drank the lemonade gratefully, noticing for the first time that her hands shook slightly. She thought it was the best lemonade she had ever tasted. Her companions sat scattered over the furniture of the bright, ample room, similarly equipped with tall glasses of lemonade, or munching on thick chocolate and vanilla cookies that Mrs. Lazaro had quickly produced. Only Negron had refused to rest, walking through the living room's glass doors to the open terrace, and gazing with subdued wonder at the breathtaking view that extended before him. Michelle suspected that the rookie policeman had never been on the twenty-fourth floor of a luxury apartment, and was finding the new experience exhilarating. He had volunteered to take with him the satellite phone, in case it received a call.

Archie sat on the sofa next to her, his eyes riveted on the fifty-two inch flat screen television set that showed varying images of the burning buildings and the Grand Laguna Hotel, its volume turned down to a barely audible level in order to accommodate the newcomers.

The news of the hostages taken by the terrorists in the hotel and the impending threat of their execution had shocked and unsettled Michelle, but at the same time stirred her journalistic instincts. Periodic news summaries showed the destroyed bridges from above, each bridge showing a wide gap with collapsed chunks of concrete that disappeared into the water. She could have probably walked out into the balcony and seen them from where Negron was standing, but felt too tired to do so.

Don Moncho rested on a sofa closer to the table holding the food, quietly consuming the sweet munchables that Mrs. Lazaro had produced, one at a time. Katherine Elizabeth was being pampered by Mrs. Lazaro, who had brought her a Barbie doll and was gently wiping the little girl's face with a wet towel. Katherine's babysitter, Maribel, watched tiredly from an adjacent chair, struggling to stay awake.

"This is such a disgrace," Mr. Lazaro lamented loudly, as he watched the TV. "What are those people thinking? This will set back the independence movement by a hundred years! And then, to top it all off, we have in this moment of great crisis our idiot Secretary of Justice, Rovira Melendez, acting as our Interim Governor! Good God! What have the Puerto Ricans done to deserve this?" he shouted angrily, prompting a disapproving "Shush!" from his wife, who motioned with her head towards Katherine Elizabeth. Lazaro grimaced apologetically, but the two year old did not seem to notice, concentrating all of her attention on dressing with a tight, golden nightclub dress the Barbie she had been handed.

"I'm sorry," he said in a softer voice. "Pompous assholes like Rovira upset me." He looked around him at his visitors. "I hope he's not a friend of any of you."

No one claimed his friendship.

"He was one of my students in Law School, did you know?" Lazaro said to Michelle, "and I'm not proud of it. Took the Evidence Law course with me—the only course he took with me, because he got a C, and I was an easy grader. Not that he's stupid. He's not. He's actually very smart. Cunning, more than smart. But he's also arrogant and lazy. And that's a dangerous combination. Almost as bad as stupid, arrogant, and lazy. Wouldn't study, because he thought he knew it all. Would ignore the case law, and interpret the rules of evidence his way, sometimes basing his arguments on the flimsiest of assumptions." Lazaro harrumphed, clearing his throat. "He practices his politics the same way, God help us."

Negron slid open one of the terrace's glass doors and stuck his head into the living room.

"I have a phone call for you," he said to Michelle, holding the satellite telephone away from the door so that communications would not be cut off. "It's your boss!"

Michelle nearly jumped out of the sofa, feeling very stiff and tired. She heard in the background Mrs. Lazaro say, "My goodness! It's already well past noon! Almost one o'clock! You people must be famished! I'll make some sandwiches for all of you."

Michelle stepped into the terrace, followed by Archie. Negron handed her the phone, but stayed to listen to the conversation.

"Hello?" she said excitedly. "Doel?"

"Michelle! Thank God!"

Doel held onto El Chino's satellite telephone with both hands, as if holding on to Michelle herself, his expression one of genuine relief. He was alone on the rooftop of the television station, having abandoned his corpulent visitor in Studio B in order to talk privately to Michelle. Not that El Chino minded. The day's rehearsal for Son of Renzo had begun—despite the major emergency in San Juan, the show had to go on—and he had been allowed to watch them from a corner of the studio. El Chino would be entertained for hours. Nevertheless, Doel had asked one of his staff members to get him two additional satellite phones. He had connected the telephone to a portable recorder, in order to preserve the reporter's words.

"Doel, I—"

"First things first!" Doel interrupted Michelle. "Are you all right?"

"I am fine!" she answered, but it sounded to his boss like *"I em phuine."*

Doel frowned. "You don't sound 'phuine' to me! What happened?"

"I have a listhp," Michelle said in a mortified tone. She quickly summarized the events of the last few hours, while he listened quietly, occasionally taking notes in a small notebook.

"That was too close for comfort," he said when she had finished, sounding very concerned. "Have you heard about the terrorist demands?"

"Yeth," she confirmed.

"We don't know what is going to happen. The terrorists in the Grand Laguna said they would start executing hostages from the roof of the hotel at 2:00 PM, every hour. That's about an hour from now."

Doel hesitated, his mind racing at a hundred revolutions per seconds. She had been through hell in the past few hours, and he hated to place her in any additional danger. Her account of the events that had led her to the penthouse of the Laguna Vista would be more than enough to broadcast immediately in an edited fashion—not disclosing her present location—and to use in a news special after the emergency ended. But there was an opportunity to do so much more, to broadcast from the very heart of what was proving to be the news event of the decade, if not the century. It would turn her into a major newsperson, barring any unfortunate occurrences.

He shook his head, hating himself. He would leave it up to her.

"Now listen," he said gingerly, taking a deep breath. "Correcaminos is going to hate me for this but...You are the only reporter on that side of San Juan. The only one who can give a firsthand account of what is happening there..." He stopped, trying to choose the best way to continue.

"You want me to get closer to the hotel," she finished for him. It really had sounded as *"You wand me do ged clother do de hodel,"* because of her swollen lip, and Doel was forced to smile despite his misgivings. There was a pause. *"I'm trying to see if I can locate the Grand Laguna Hotel from where I am... No...no...I'm leaning over the balcony's railing as far as I can, but even so, I can hardly see the hotel. To really see what is happening, I'll have to get closer,"* she explained. *"But I'm way ahead of you,"* she added. *"I'm thinking of seeking an interview with the terrorists in the hotel—"*

"No! That would be too dangerous! Just get as close as you can and report what you see."

"Your cameras can do that from the other side of the lagoon," she pointed out to her boss.

"There is no guarantee that those people will not take you as a hostage or throw you off the roof!"

"I know," she replied in a reasonable tone. *"I'm not suicidal. I will play it by ear. I will get closer to the hotel, and then decide if it's safe to seek an interview.. If I sense any danger, I will keep my distance."*

"No. There is no way that you will know how reasonable those people are until you talk to them. And by then, it will be too late."

"Doel, lithen to me!" she pleaded, her lisp more evident the more upset that she got.

"No! You can't even talk well, for God's sake!"

"Lithen to me! Those people want publicity. I can give it to dem."

Doel paused. *She was right, of course.* But throwing a nosy reporter from the roof of the Grand Laguna Hotel would also get them a lot of publicity. It would really get the attention of the world press. *It was just too risky.* He decided to try another tack.

"You realize that once you're in there with them, you won't be able to report whatever you want to say whenever you want to report it. They will control what you say."

There was silence on the other end, as Michelle considered Doel's argument. Doel took the opportunity to press his case further.

"You don't have to *prove* yourself by risking your life. You've already obtained information that is essential to the police. We now know that they probably communicate by satellite phone. I will let Maldonado know this. Maybe the FBI or the police can intercept their calls. You will be more useful to us if you can describe what you see freely..."

As Doel spoke, he sensed that Michelle was not paying a lot of attention to his words. He had seen her like that a thousand times before, where he would say something to her and send her brain spinning.

"Okay, okay, I'll think about it!" she said hurriedly. *"Can you wait one moment? There's something I have to check."*

Doel sighed. Through the years, he had come to know Michelle well. He now knew by her abrupt change in the conversation that he had to wait and allow her to "check" whatever had attracted her attention.

"I'll wait," he said resignedly. "But don't take too long. You never know how long we'll stay connected."

"I won't be long," she promised, and he was placed on hold.

Doel leaned against the outside wall of the roof's stairwell and considered Michelle's idea. Interviewing the terrorists would be a definite coup. It could even, if they wanted to play up to the television audience's sympathy, convince them to delay the execution of the hostages. And if anybody could pull it off, it would probably be Michelle.

On the other hand, one of the terrorists had nearly raped and killed Michelle. They had also wiped out without any kind of moral compunction the police station in Puerta de Tierra, massacring dozens of police officers. Men like those would not hesitate to rape or kill Michelle if they thought that it furthered their cause or considered her a security threat, or merely disliked her. *It was too risky.* When she took him out of "hold" he would forbid her from pursuing her idea.

The phone's receiver came back to life. *"Doel, are you still there?"*

"Michelle, about seeking an interview with the terrorists—"

"Yea, yea, it's too risky. I know. Archie and Negron agree with you."

For the second time in the conversation, Doel felt intense relief.

"But listen," she said before he could say anything else. *"That thing you said about the satellite phones, that the terrorists are using them to communicate. Archie mentioned the same thing before when we called El Chino, but it didn't click on me at the time until you repeated it—"*

"What didn't click on you at the time?" Doel had lost the thread of the conversation.

"To look for other telephone numbers in the phone's address book! If they're using the satellite phones to communicate, they could have some numbers where they can reach some of their other associates. And if there were..."

"Maybe the authorities can intercept any calls made from those numbers!" Doel finished her sentence excitedly.

"Can they?"

"I don't know. I imagine that the Federal Government...The FBI or the NSA must have the means to do it. Were you able to find any telephone numbers in the satellite phone's directory?"

"I hit the menu button while I had you on hold, and located the address book. There was only one telephone number listed, with no name next to it, just a number symbol and a number one next to it. There were no other numbers listed on 'Sent' calls, except for El Chino's, and no numbers listed in 'Received' calls. It's as if the phone had never been used before."

It probably hadn't, Doel thought. The telephones must have been distributed to the terrorists recently, and were not supposed to be used except in emergencies.

"Did you dial the number?" he asked.

"I was very tempted to do so but I didn't," she answered. *"I followed your advice about not acting on impulse and thinking things through. I figured that if I dial that number, and then I can't identify myself properly to the contact person that answers it, he or she will stop using that number, and we'll blow any chance of intercepting any other calls that other terrorists may make. What do you think?"*

Doel smiled. "I think you've done great!"

"Do you have something to write down the number?" Even though Michelle tried to maintain an even voice, he could sense her excitement.

"Are bananas yellow?" he answered.

Michelle proceeded to give him what seemed to be an interminable telephone number, and made him repeat it.

"I'll give this to the Superintendent immediately," Doel said. "I'll also give him your phone number, in case he wants to talk to you."

"How will you get through to him?"

"His headquarters are in the San Geronimo Plaza, and we have a mobile unit there," Doel responded. "We can use the feed line from our mobile unit, the one we use to receive the video we get from our cameras in El Condado. Correcaminos is there right now. I'll get him to talk to the Superintendent and bring him back to our mobile unit, where I can brief him on what you have found out so far."

"I'm going to get as close as I can to the Grand Laguna Hotel, and report what I see," Michelle said. She paused, and Doel heard several voices in

the background. *"Negron, the policeman I told you about, and Archie, the redhead, have volunteered to come with me,"* she added.

He should have felt relief that two men would accompany her, but he did not. If they were discovered, he suspected that there would be very little that the two men would be able to do.

"Now pay attention to me," he said in his most fatherly tone, not intending at all to sound fatherly. "You must be very careful. Don't take any foolish risks."

"Just intelligent risks," she said seriously, mocking him.

"You know what I mean, don't joke about this! These are very dangerous men—"

"I know, I know," Michelle said in a loving, gentle tone. *"I almost got killed today, remember? I'm not going to take any stupid risks. I'll call you as soon as I have something new to report, if the phone is working."*

"You'll call me every hour on the hour, to let me know that you're all right," Doel corrected her. "Anyway, our regular telephone system is slowly starting to get back to speed. Some cell phone and landline calls have been able to get through. Our station is running a public service announcement every ten minutes urging people not to use their telephones unless it is absolutely necessary to do so, and people are starting to heed to our requests. So if you can't get through to us via your satellite phone, try your cell phone instead."

"I'll do my best," she responded, speaking with an upbeat tone, but sounding very young and vulnerable. It conjured in Doel's mind the image of her as a six-year old child, when she would visit the station to watch her father direct shows or appear in television dramas.

"I mean it. If something happens to you..." he had to stop, surprised by his own emotions.

"Don't you go mushy on me!" Michelle said sternly, half in jest, half seriously. *"That's Correcamino's job. Your job is to urge me on, right?"*

Doel failed to answer.

"I love you," she said sweetly.

"And I love you too. You know that, right?"

"Yeth."

CHAPTER XXXV

The grand ballroom of the Grand Laguna Hotel was a massive hall that could comfortably fit, when all of its sections were open, over two thousand people. Five massive chandeliers hung from its ceiling, more for decoration than for the actual lighting that was provided by hundreds of recessed lights. Polished, parquet floors gleamed unnaturally, reflecting blurry images of anything placed above them. A large stage covered about one third of the wall opposite to the half dozen, double-doored entrances that gave access to the room.

At one in the afternoon, the hall was filled to capacity. The processing center—a long table set up on the stage behind which sat two men and a woman—had still not finished tallying the total number of men, women and children that had been herded into the ballroom, but the female, a heavy, brown haired, twenty-year old university student, estimated the number of captives packed into the hall to range between two thousand to two thousand three hundred.

The "interviewers", as the FEPIstas sitting behind the table on the stage called themselves, relieved each hostage from any wallets, purses, cell phones, identifications, money, or other objects that they still may have possessed, asked them their names, age, occupation and place of provenance, noted the information in alphabetized notebooks, and assigned each of them a number. Afterwards, all but those hostages who had background in any medical professions were released to sit wherever they could find a spot on the floor, no chairs having been made available for them. Doctors and nurses were assigned shifts to treat any persons—hostages or revolutionaries—who required medical attention. Those still waiting to be interviewed stood in a long line that followed the contours of the hall.

A second line of hostages had formed at one of the exits located farthest from those waiting to be interviewed, containing between fifty to one hundred persons at any given moment. It corresponded to those hostages that needed to go to the bathrooms, which were situated outside of the hall. Every five minutes, a group of about twenty people would be escorted by an armed guard to the sanitary facilities.

Meals were distributed from two long tables located near the central doors of the ballroom, according to the numbers assigned by the "interviewers". The hostages were called in groups of one hundred, and received sandwiches, snacks, and beverages prepared by the hotel's staff. Blankets, sheets, and pillows were distributed by half a dozen of the FEPIstas, who treated the prisoners as humanely as possible, trying to keep the frayed nerves of the enormous crowd under control.

Macheteros carrying Uzi submachine guns were in charge of security, maintaining three men at the main entrance at all times. Except for two fights among the nervous hostages, one a shoving match between two men arguing about politics, and the second a real, hair-pulling, eye-scratching, free-swinging-and-kicking brawl between a teenage girl and an older, heavily breasted woman, the mood in the enormous hall had been relatively peaceful. The scared, indignant din of the hostages as they had been led at gunpoint into the ballroom had given way to a subdued, muted hum of resignation.

Mark Sampson, the Florida representative who had been surprised by the explosions as he jogged in the direction of the destroyed bridges, had been one of those treated by the captured medical personnel, in a makeshift infirmary near the entrance to the hall. Although not seriously hurt, he had suffered several cuts and bruises that had been washed and bandaged by one of the nurses. Fortunately, he had apparently escaped permanent damage to his hearing, the humming in his ears nearly disappearing.

As he moved into the room, he had examined with hidden alarm the armed, mostly longhaired, bearded armed men garbed in Cuban army-style fatigues that guarded the doors of the hostage holding center. He had resolved to remain anonymous, knowing what a valuable resource a Florida lawmaker—particularly the Speaker of the Florida House of Representatives—could be to the terrorists. Fortunately, he had been detained as he had returned to the hotel in his running shorts and T-shirt, while he was not carrying any identification with him. When questioned by the female "interviewer", he had lied and said that he was a car salesman from Rome, Georgia. He had been briefly scared out of his wits when she had stared at him for several seconds, as if trying to place his face—after all, he was a known political personality, and a picture of him had appeared on page 4 of the local newspaper, El Nuevo Dia, just two days before—but then she had allowed him to join the other interviewed prisoners in the hall. He had been assigned the number 1,576.

He had quickly located his aide, a busty, twenty-three year old woman called April, and sat on the floor, in the space she had saved for him. April was a Georgia Tech major in journalism, and she was a stunning looking brunette with a Barbie doll-like figure, unnaturally light blue eyes, and a constant, sexy pout on her lips. She was wearing the blue denim short shorts and white tank top with which she had expected to receive Mark when he returned from his jog.

During the terrorist takeover of the hotel, she had been taken hostage as she had descended in one of the elevators from her room to look for her boss, and been led directly to the grand ballroom. Mark had arrived several minutes later, still dazed from the explosion. She had seen him being directed to the medical personnel as she waited in line to get interviewed, and made a movement to follow him, but Mark had surreptitiously waved her away, gesturing with his head to stay where she was.

This was the first opportunity she had had to talk to him.

"That was very brave of you," she told him as, grunting, he slowly sat on the floor next to her. He looked at her with confusion.

"What?" he asked.

"Ordering me to stay away from you, not to attract any undue attention to me, even though you were in pain and needed help," she answered, her eyes reflecting the absolute worship in which she held him.

"Oh, it's nothing," he said modestly, staring into her lovely eyes and for a moment lamenting the interruption of their plans for that morning, despite their desperate situation. *What a waste,* he thought wistfully. *It would have to wait for some other time.*

In reality, it had been the other way around. Mark had waved her away because he knew that such an attractive woman walking out of a line to join him would inevitably draw attention *to him*, and he had to be very careful. If any of the terrorists discovered his identity, they would use it to their advantage. He was, after all, a very important man who, even though he would be willing to die for his country and his constituents, knew that he could render a far greater service to them by remaining alive.

"What number did they assign to you?" he asked April in a barely perceptible tone.

"Five hundred and forty three. And you?"

"Fifteen seventy-six," he said.

"Why, that's two hundred numbers away from America's Declaration of Independence!" she said with genuine delight. "It's a sign! You are bound to do great things!"

He nodded half-heartedly, worried that her enthusiasm would carry her away, and that she would expect him to do something about their present ordeal. His fears were not unfounded.

"Do you think there is something you can do to end this situation?" she asked hopefully.

"Maybe," he answered guardedly, barely stopping himself from rolling his eyes in despair. *What did she have in mind? That he took on all of the terrorists, single-handed?*

A small baby boy that could not have been more than a few months old began to cry a few feet from them, prompting his desperate-looking mother to bounce him gently in her arms. The father, a quiet man with a military crew cut, cuddled his wife and his child placing one arm around them. Mark heard April say "Awwww!" and welcomed the distraction.

He shifted his eyes in the opposite direction, and was shocked to see an old man staring directly at him in deep concentration. He was sitting almost diagonally across him, maybe four arms lengths away. Mark knew that stare. The man was trying to place his face.

He had the appearance of a malevolent gnome; bald, shiny pate fringed by silver, nearly invisible hair; large, bat-like ears with coarse, gray tufts of hair; a long nose that seemed to have melted over his upper lip; and dark, curious eyes. A portly woman in her late sixties or early seventies—about the same age of the man—sat with a permanent grimace of discomfort etched on her face. She wore a wide "Mumu" dress with a red flowery design, pointy eyeglasses rimmed with fake diamonds, and sandals that revealed the blue veins in her feet. Mark turned his head away, silently praying that the man's interest would shift from him to somebody else. It did not.

"You're that guy from Florida, aren't you?" the man shouted nearly at the top of his lungs.

Mark kept looking in the opposite direction, hoping the old man would stop talking to him.

"You!" the old man said even more loudly, prompting those around Mark to gaze at him curiously. Even April was staring at him. "The man sitting next to the girl with the white tank top!"

Mark finally directed his attention to the man. "Me?" he asked weakly, pointing at himself.

"You'll have to speak louder!" the old man indicated just as loudly as before. More people were looking to see what was the source of the noise. The man cupped his right hand over his ear. "You'll have to speak more loudly! I'm nearly deaf!"

"He's deaf!" his plump wife repeated just as loudly with a nasal voice, pointing at his husband. "He talks this way all the time!"

Mark nodded with a frozen smile, cringing inwardly. He decided to crawl towards the man, hoping that their proximity would lead to a more subdued conversation.

"You look like that fellah from the Senate in Florida!" the old man yelled as Mark approached him. "...Er...what's his name, Flora?"

Flora pushed her eyeglasses to the top of her nose and moved her face to within a foot away from Mark's face, squinting.

"Oooooh, you mean the Fort Myers politician...eh...eh...Frank Wallace!"

"No, no!" the old man shook his head, waving his hand dismissively. "Not Frank Wallace!...He's old! The guy from the Senate! The good looking guy!" He turned impatiently towards Mark. "What's your name?"

Mark considered lying, but thought better of it. A denial would probably not satisfy his deaf tormentor, and provoke a further, high-decibelled discussion about his identity. Already, one of the two male interviewers sitting on the stage had briefly interrupted his writing and directed a peeved glance in their direction. The Florida representative could not afford a lot more of that type of attention.

"Mark Sampson," he answered reluctantly.

"Mark...Mark Sampson! That's it!" the man boomed with intense satisfaction, after staring intently at Sampson's lips. "What did I tell you, Flora? The President of the Florida Senate, right? Tea Party guy!"

"Not the Senate, Fred!" his wife said, correcting him. "The House! The House of Representatives!"

"Oh yea, the House!" The man extended his hand and shook Mark's warmly. "Glad to meet you! Fred Lyons, accountant from Miami. I'm one of your constituents. And this is my wife, Flora."

Flora reached out from where she sat, touching Sampson's hand with the tip of her fingers. "How do you do?" she said, unconsciously fixing her hair with her other hand.

"We voted for you! It's about time we stop those socialist bastards," Fred said enthusiastically. "Great job you're doing in Tallahassee! Not touching Medicare, though, are you?" He switched his attention towards the representative's female companion. "That is one gorgeous woman!" he shouted. "Is she your wife?"

Several people seating close to them turned to examine the object of Fred's admiration, and Mark felt his neck and face redden.

"Oh no," he answered quickly, attempting to cut the subject short, "that's my public relations aide!"

"You'll have to speak more loudly! I'm almost deaf!" Fred shouted, cupping his ear with his hand again.

"He can barely hear you!" Flora confirmed, leaning forward and speaking almost as loudly as Fred.

"I can barely hear you!" Fred repeated. "We were going to sail out tonight in the *Mardi Gras*, island-hopping hopping in the Caribbean, shopping, some nude beach tanning in St Martin's, you know? But I guess these people," he jerked a thumb at the terrorists sitting on the stage, "won't let us go! Unless some of your people can do something about it!" He looked at Mark, expecting an answer, but the Florida representative just stared back at him with an uncomprehending expression. "Nothing, uh?"

Mark cursed his luck, casting nervous glances at those closer to him. They all seemed to be listening with a great deal of interest. With the corner of his eye, he caught a brief glint of daylight, as the door of the ballroom furthest to the right opened and closed quickly and three men walked in. He returned his attention to the old accountant, resolving to end his conversation as swiftly as possible.

"So what important government business brings you here?" Fred asked, receiving a nudge in the ribs from Flora's elbow. She gestured with her head towards the stage, and placed a finger on her mouth. Mark directed a grateful look at her.

"My wife thinks I'm being indiscreet," the old man confided to his newly made friend in a very loud whisper. "I'll shut up!"

Mark swallowed hard, and observed warily as the newly arrived men made their way among the prisoners to the stage. Their leader, an athletic, trim-looking man in his thirties, climbed the stairs to the stage past the line of hostages still waiting to be processed, and approached the table. His two companions waited at the foot of the stage.

Despite his cheerful, almost unassuming demeanor, the new arrival exuded an unmistakable aura of ruthless efficiency and danger that made all of those he passed stop talking and follow his progress with a presentiment of doom. Silence spread over the crowd like a large ripple in a pond, so that by the time he reached the seated interviewers, nearly the entire grand ballroom had become quiet.

The terrorist placed both of his hands on the table and leaned forward, chatting pleasantly in a low voice with the three FEPIstas for a couple of minutes. Then he moved away and, crossing his arms, stared silently at the crowd.

"They're letting us go!" Fred whispered to Mark, his megaphone-like voice resonating throughout the noiseless hall.

A thin, amused smile appeared on the new arrival's lips, as if he thoroughly enjoyed the unsolicited comment. The FEPIsta sitting furthermost to the right of the table—a tall, skinny youth with thick eyeglasses, a few long facial hairs and long limp hair—cast Fred an evil glance and pushed back his metal chair, standing up. He briefly conferred with his other two associates—a heavy female with an oversized black T-shirt that still managed to show the various folds of her stomach, and an older gentleman with a Lenin-like goatee—and compared the entries they had made in their respective records. After scribbling several words on his pad, the tall FEPIsta stood and showed his notes to the man standing in front of the stage, who examined them for a pair of seconds and shrugged. Then the FEPIsta addressed the crowd.

"Your attention, please. I will now read several numbers, and as I do, you will stand up. When I finish, those called will be instructed what to do next." He looked around not so much to answer any questions as to assert his authority, and proceeded to announce the selected numbers.

"Number forty-eight!" he said, instantly looking up.

A middle-aged man with a white undershirt, gray business suit pants, and half of his face unshaven—apparently taken from his room as he was doing his toilette—slowly rose to his feet in one corner of the hall, and warily stared at the stage, blinking repeatedly as if under a spotlight.

Satisfied, the FEPIsta looked back at his list.

"Number six hundred and two!"

A thin, teenaged girl wearing braces sprang up from her resting place, close to the stage, as her mother, sitting next to her, watched in anguish. A bald man with a pronounced paunch raised a hand and began to push himself off the floor, presumably the girl's father.

"A question!" he said, even before he finished getting up. "What is—"

"Quiet!" the FEPIsta shouted. "You have not been called, and this is not a question-and-answer session. Remain sitting, or we will force you to do so!"

The man flopped back on the floor, and grabbed the standing girl's hand.

"Number seven hundred and seventy-nine!"

The woman holding the baby who sat close to April and Mark turned to her husband and whispered, "That's me!" with a shaky voice. She tried to hand the baby to his father, but he stopped her.

"I'll stand," he told her reassuringly, and before she could say anything else, got off the floor.

The interviewer reading the numbers watched him with a tinge of uncertainty, but then he returned to his list.

"Number one hundred!"

"Here!" A man with a ruddy complexion, white hair, and a bulbous nose, garbed in a priest's brown cassock, waived his hand and calmly stood up. He smiled reassuringly at the scared teenager.

"Number five hundred and forty three!"

April flinched as if she had been prodded by an electric cattle prod. She looked at Mark expectantly, but he turned his eyes away. Nervously, she stumbled up to her feet. The FEPIsta announcing the numbers examined her with an appreciative glance.

Mark felt his mouth dry up in a matter of seconds, his heart pounding savagely in his chest. He feared that she would cry out his name at any moment. His eyes briefly met those of Fred, and the latter conveyed with them—as none of his previous loud statements could have—his surprise and utter disgust. Mark kept his gaze fixed on the floor, trying to avoid any visual contact with his aide. He could not avoid seeing, however, April's magnificent legs and painted red toes, and the shadow of her shaking hands over them.

Damn it, he thought, *he had never imagined that his dream weekend could end up this way!* He prayed to God that He would save him from that terrible ordeal, and promised that he would never embark in another adventure like that one again.

April would be all right, he told himself. To take her place would have been crazy and dangerous. It would have been tantamount to handing to the terrorists an additional weapon, another means with which they could blackmail the government authorities. What Fred—the deaf accountant— and others around him did not understand was that he had to consider the common good first, before giving in to any personal concerns.

Five more numbers were called. Two were women, three were men. Their backgrounds were varied, ranging from a high school math and gym teacher, a corporate lawyer, a computer programmer, an airline pilot, and a construction project manager, among others. Most were aged between twenty to forty years old, except for the teacher—a sixty-four year old woman who was celebrating her thirtieth year as an educator courtesy of her students—and the construction manager—a strapping six foot four inches tall southerner who had decided to enjoy the beach for a few days before he returned to work in his next project.

After the interviewer exhausted his list of numbers, he turned back his head and said something to the man standing behind him, who shrugged.

"All those selected will form a line and follow this man to the corridor outside of the ballroom," he pointed to the newly-arrived man, who acknowledged the reference to him with a friendly wave. "That is all."

As the ten hostages were led away, April cast one last, desperate look at Mark. He was staring intently at the parquet floor, as if preoccupied with its polish. With a deep sob, she walked away and joined the others as they were led outside of the ballroom. After she had left, Mark stood up and, failing to look at anyone around him, moved to the opposite end of the hall.

Daniel watched silently from the stage of the grand ballroom as the hostages were called and made to stand one by one. He had asked the FEPI interviewers to choose five men and five women at random. Nobody except him, not even the interviewers, had any idea for what the hostages were being selected. He wondered if the FEPI activists, regardless of their patriotic fervor, would have so readily complied with his request had they known what Daniel had planned for the hotel guests.

He had arrived at the Grand Laguna Hotel scarcely ten minutes before, crowded in an old Buick Regal with San Miguel, Colonel Calderon, Johnny Ray, Yajaira, and Andrade. Had the government authorities somehow managed to destroy the vehicle with a drone—not that there was much chance about that—they would have deprived the San Juan occupying force from its entire leadership.

The trip had been quick and uneventful. Few of the residents of San Juan were venturing into the streets, and except for the trucks used by the FEPI patrols, vehicular traffic was nonexistent. The entire drive to the hotel had taken less than ten uneasy minutes, during which none of the passengers except Yajaira had uttered a word. She, on the other hand, had not stopped talking—nonsense for the most part, a stream of consciousness probably spurred by her nervous exuberance.

Czecka and his men had been waiting at the lobby. Daniel had spotted his towering frame even before the car rolled into the lobby's curved drop-off area. He had been inexplicably pleased to see the moody giant, even after the latter ignored him as he got off the car.

San Miguel had directed the others to the conference room in the business center, where the telephone connection with the Police Superintendent was still kept open. Then he had grabbed Daniel by the elbow and, followed by the hulking presence of Czecka, had huddled with his associates in a quiet corner of the lobby.

"Welcome back!" he had said brightly to Czecka. "I presume you were able to dispose of the vehicle?"

Czecka had produced something like a grunt and left it at that. San Miguel had not deemed it necessary to inquire about the details. Instead, he had turned his attention to Daniel.

"Your time is fast approaching. It's less than an hour to 2:00 PM. Are you up to it?"

When the operation was being conceived, it had been agreed early on that Daniel would be in charge of executing the hostages. Normally, Czecka would have been assigned that task. However, this time his immense bulk precluded him from doing it. Therefore, the responsibility had fallen on San Miguel's second in command, even if it meant placing Daniel—San Miguel's most precious asset—at serious risk.

Daniel had shrugged indifferently.

"That's not exactly the response I was expecting," his mentor had expressed with a sour smile.

"Have I ever not been willing to implement any of your schemes?" Daniel had responded in a somewhat peevish tone.

"The stakes have never been this high," San Miguel reminded him.

It was true. The execution of the hostages in front of every news media in the world was a critical stage of the plan, designed to outrage the viewing audience and eventually erase any sympathies that any misguided person still harbored in favor of the present coup. It was supposed to expedite the inevitable collapse of the takeover, by forcing the government authorities to act as speedily as possible. With luck, order would be re-established by the morning of the next day. Of course, none of San Miguel's allies knew this.

Daniel would be key in bringing the operation to a quick end. He had no qualms about the danger to which he would be exposed when he herded the prisoners to the top of the Grand Laguna Hotel. Placing his life on the line infused him with the adrenaline high that that he relished and lived for; it was the main reason why he had stuck to San Miguel and had participated in all of his wild schemes for the last thirteen years.

Nevertheless, he did not relish the idea of throwing innocent people from the roof of the hotel. Killing in the heat of battle posed no problem for him. He had at least shot, stabbed, or blasted to pieces three-dozen people in his long-lasting affiliation with San Miguel, and a few others before that. But the cold-blooded execution of hostages gave him pause.

Not that anyone was completely blameless, according to San Miguel. Every citizen from the so-called affluent countries—particularly the Americans—were guilty of callously exploiting the poor of the world, and keeping them in extreme misery and poverty. To maintain their impossibly high and wasteful standards of living, they promoted an unbridled consumerism and a Godless belief in American capitalism, smothering any weaker cultures that happened to stand in their way, and depleting the natural resources of their weaker, impoverished third-world neighbors. Not a single American, San Miguel had argued time and again in a calm and civilized fashion, deserved Daniel's pity.

Daniel did not care for any of that talk. He was there basically for the thrill of it, and the killing of innocent—and if not innocent, at least helpless—victims did not thrill him in any way or fashion.

"You can count on me," he had assured San Miguel unenthusiastically.

The latter had given him a hard stare, then slapped his shoulder and nodded with satisfaction.

"I know I can," he had said with conviction. Then he had added, "May God guide you and be at your side."

Daniel had suppressed a chuckle. San Miguel knew how he felt about *"God"*. God had been the object of many debates between them. *He is trying to provoke me,* Daniel had told himself, *trying to see how I react under the present stress.* He had not taken the bait. Instead, he had lowered his head and walked away under the watchful gaze of his boss.

He had chosen Da'ud—the bearded Arab driver who had helped Czecka deliver the "device" to Fort San Cristobal—and Figueres—the explosives expert who had helped him set the charges in the bridges and who had trained suicide bombers in Palestine and Afghanistan—to come along with him. Both were ruthless, dedicated killers who would not hesitate to carry out their assigned tasks, no matter how unsavory, when the time came.

The three university students interviewing the hostages on the stage had met him earlier that morning, and knew that he was one of the top ranking leaders of the revolt. Therefore, when he had asked them to randomly choose five men and five women from different backgrounds and age ranges, they had not questioned his request.

As he watched the selection of the hostages by the FEPI interviewer, he had considered in silence who he would most likely choose to throw off the hotel's roof. The plan required that the execution generate the greatest amount of public outrage and indignation possible. If carried out right, it would actually save lives, since the more outrageous the act, the more pressure would be placed on the authorities to act, and the faster the hostages would be rescued.

Daniel caught himself justifying his actions and snorted derisively. He sounded more and more like San Miguel, who distanced himself from the violence he generated by explaining it as a justifiable evil, as a sacrifice for the greater good or—even worse—to serve God's will. He would leave the justification to others, and just do his job. So he had focused instead on observing the guests who had been selected.

The teenage girl must not have been older than thirteen. Unlike others of her kind—most of which their elders would probably throw off the roof of the Grand Laguna Hotel voluntarily—this one still appeared to retain the sweet innocence of her younger years. Blond, curly hair cascaded over her shoulders, and a rebellious lock covered most of her eyes every time she nervously turned her head to talk to one of her parents. She wore braces on her teeth, a bracelet with tiny colored hearts on her left wrist, and held on tightly to a pocket book—probably one of the vampire novels in vogue—whose title he could not discern.

She was thin, awkward, and flat-chested; the blossoming of her womanhood still nothing more than a hopeful promise of things to come. Her father clung to her right hand as if his own life—or maybe hers—depended on it. Daniel thought that if her daughter's life was snatched from him, the man would die from grief.

To sacrifice such an innocent, scared girl would be heartless and cruel. It would break the heart of every father who witnessed the execution either on live TV or in the hundreds of replays, at normal speed and slow motion, that would surely follow. It would damn any remote prospect that the revolt that San Miguel had fostered would succeed. It would be, in other words, perfect for San Miguel's plans.

Such a crime would horrify and shock even the most hard-hearted of their pro-independence allies. Any claim for sympathy to their cause would be automatically wiped out. The *independentista* rebels would be shunned as child killers. But for that same reason, killing the young girl would probably offend the FEPIstas and the Macheteros. They would accuse San Miguel of dooming their revolution on purpose, and they would be right. Daniel could not afford to antagonize the forces that were holding on to Old San Juan. *Not yet, anyway.*

The priest was another interesting choice. He seemed at first glance, unlike many other religious men he had met, to be a genuinely good and humble man who—like San Miguel—happened to believe in God. Although what such a man, dressed in a simple brown robe and sandals, was doing in a luxurious hotel like the Grand Laguna was perplexing to Daniel. Visiting, maybe, or enjoying a gift by his parishioners? There had been genuine concern behind his gray eyes when he looked at the teenaged girl, but very little fear for himself, as behooved any man who believed in the "ever after".

The television image of a saintly man being marched to the edge of the roof of the hotel and sacrificed to the gods of war and revolution would galvanize the religious watchers, and create a tremendous pressure on the government to act immediately. Puerto Rico, a mostly Catholic country, would see the execution of a priest as an expression of Communist zeal that would immediately scare away any possible support for the *independentistas'* revolt. Puerto Ricans had seen what had happened to the neighboring island of Cuba, and were terrified that anything similar would happen in their own country.

Any act against a member of a religious institution would be disastrous to the present "revolution". By the same token, however, any such act would instantly raise suspicion among their *independentista* allies about San Miguel's operation. Like the killing of the teenager, the execution of the priest would probably be perceived by the FEPIstas and even the Macheteros as a too inflammatory action that would harm their cause. A less controversial choice had to be made.

By the time that the tenth number had been called, Daniel had narrowed his choices to two.

The first had been a woman in her upper twenties. Daniel had held his breath when the statuesque brunette had stood up. Every man in the ballroom had reacted the same way. The woman belonged in a Playboy centerfold. Her brief panicked glance at the man sitting close to her did not escape his attention. Unlike the military-looking man who had obviously taken the place of his wife, the brunette's companion had looked away and abandoned her to her fate.

It would be a shame to kill her. He knew, by the looks of the couple, that she was not the man's official mate and that she would jump without hesitation at the opportunity of becoming Daniel's temporary lover in exchange for her life. Killing her, on the other hand, would cause quite a great deal of commotion and horror. Her execution would violate the Puerto Rican *machista* code of conduct, which required that men be gallant to their ladies—especially beautiful ones. Her death would have the desired effect.

Which brought him to his second prospect: the brave father who had taken the place of his wife. By his bearing, fitness, and haircut, he could tell immediately that the man had served or was serving in the military. Maybe he was taking a vacation before he returned to active duty. It was the type of man that he respected and could relate to, even if in this case the man would probably be his enemy if they met in a battlefield. Taking his life, while the cowardly companion of the brunette lived, offended his sensibilities.

But he seemed like another perfect choice. To the independence movement, he *was* the enemy, a representative of the very army that kept their country subjugated. His execution would infuriate the pro-statehood faction of the population, be guardedly condemned by the moderates of the independence movement, and be applauded by the radicals. It would create quite a stir in the United States, when one of its finest and bravest was viciously put to death. And it would horrify the rest of the world.

The group had ended being composed by four women and six men, confirming his suspicion that the young military man had taken his wife's place.

Daniel climbed down from the stairs on the stage and walked to the head of the line that had begun to be formed by the hostages. Da'ud and Figueres quietly assumed positions on both flanks of the gathering prisoners.

"Follow me," Daniel said to the half-shaven man standing in the lead.

The line slowly snaked its way through the hundreds of sitting captives, and exited to the outside corridor.

Daniel guided them in the direction of the hotel's ornamental gardens, and then turned to his left. He continued until he reached a narrower passage that led to the lobby, and went into it. He stopped almost immediately between the two elevator doors that gave access to the VIP guest rooms. Da'ud and Figueres made all of the hostages turn and face him.

"I will not lie to you," he said without any kind of preamble. "The next hour will be a bit difficult for all of us." He could not help but watch the brunette as she drew in air sharply, making her breasts heave. "But if you follow my instructions, you will be all right." He lied easily. It was only a partial lie, after all.

Daniel nodded towards Da'ud, who moved to a small table placed next to the first elevator door. There was a large, brown paper grocery bag on the table. The Arab began to extract from it long strips of black cloth.

"You are going to be blindfolded," Daniel informed his prisoners.

Except for a squeaky sob from the brunette, the announcement was followed by deathly silence, as the captives realized the gravity of their situation.

"We are going to bargain with the Puerto Rican and federal authorities," Daniel explained. "To induce them to negotiate, we will show them some of our hostages. Those hostages will be you."

The young teenager began to weep, while next to her the math teacher, a barrel-chested, mannish-looking woman who looked tougher than some of the terrorists, glared at Daniel. The sexy woman's mouth moved incoherently, as if saying words without producing any sounds, as did the priest's mouth, obviously in prayer. The man with the military haircut maintained a neutral expression, but his eyes reflected concern, as did the expression of the construction worker. However, it was the computer programmer, a short, stocky man with blond hair, manicured eyebrows, and a deeply furrowed chin, who reacted the worst, falling on his knees, covering his face with his hands and blubbering incomprehensible phrases.

Daniel stared at him, unable to hide his contempt.

"Stand up," he ordered to the terrified man, who continued to bawl out loudly. He nodded to Figueres, who approached the man, grabbed him by the ear, and pulled him up, oblivious of the man's shrieks of pain.

Daniel approached him and said calmly, "Be quiet, or I will hurt you."

Shaking, the man stopped moaning and sobbed quietly.

"As I was saying, we will be showing you to the authorities and the news media. Before long, you will become celebrities, when your faces are shown all over the world."

He had made that up as he spoke, trying to allay their fears, although it would probably turn out to be true as families or friends watching the broadcast identified their blindfolded faces. In order for the execution to happen smoothly, he needed the hostages to be calm.

"After you are blindfolded, we will take you to the roof, where you will be able to be seen best."

The computer programmer howled with fear, and began to say that he was afraid of heights. Figueres moved behind him and delivered a short, nasty chop to his right kidney. The man dropped straight to the floor, gasping for air.

Daniel continued talking as if nothing had happened. "At all times, you must listen to me and follow my instructions without hesitation, so stay alert! Your safety will depend on this. Anybody who disobeys me will be severely punished. Any attempt to resist or escape will be punished by death."

Figueres began to tie a blindfold on the half-shaven man, who offered no resistance. The teenage girl shook uncontrollably, but remained quiet.

Daniel looked at his watch and saw it was already five minutes past the half hour. *Twenty-five minutes to go.* They would have to hurry, or they would be late. He needed the hostages' cooperation.

"As I told you before, if you follow my instructions you will have nothing to fear, and you will be out of this before you know it."

On the floor, the computer programmer continued to breathe hard, but had quieted down. *Maybe I should throw him off the roof,* Daniel thought.

One way or another, the first hostage would die in less than half an hour.

CHAPTER XXXVI

"I need to speak with Superintendent Maldonado."

Correcaminos, not a tall man, stood a head shorter than the two burly policemen barring his way. The disparity between the three men was enhanced by their appearance. Correcaminos was wearing an immaculately pressed, tan Armani cashmere suit, with a pink and light blue silk tie, and brown, Enrico Bruno lambskin half boots, in stark contrast to the two police officers' fatigues, long, wooden batons, military boots, and black berets. His rich dark hair was combed backwards, and glistened with the rich pomade that he regularly applied to it.

He had interrupted their conversation, and could feel their hostility towards him like a wave of heat radiating from the open door of an oven. He could hardly blame them. They had been fending off frenzied requests from news reporters, politicians, and even some private citizens to talk to their boss on all sorts of urgent matters.

"The Superintendent is very busy right now, but if you want to wait, you can take a seat with the others," one of the two policemen, the larger of the two—bearing the nametag of Colon—answered offhandedly, and returned to his conversation with his partner.

Eight other persons, all of them men, were already sitting on the three sofas that lined the walls of the small waiting area—the "limbo room", as Correcaminos called it, "where innocent souls who could not get into Heaven were sent to wait forever". Two of the waiting men who Correcaminos recognized as flunkies from other local news outfits, lingered there in the hope that something worth reporting would happen. A third was a newly arrived American reporter from CBS News who probably relied—so far unsuccessfully—on his national prominence, hoping it would impress the small island police chief sufficiently to get him an exclusive interview. The other five he did not know.

"I'm not here to interview the Superintendent," Correcaminos explained patiently. He had dealt with nervous people before—mostly athletes but a few policemen as well—and learned that the best way to obtain results was to remain as calm and low key as possible. "I have important information about—"

"I'm sorry," Colon interrupted, "but nobody is allowed to bother him now."

Correcaminos sighed, sizing up the man before him. The policeman must have been over six feet and a few inches tall, and probably weighed close to two hundred fifty, maybe two hundred sixty pounds of mostly pure muscle. He bore the yellow patch on his left shoulder that identified him as part of the "Fuerza de Choque" or Tactical Operations Division, the shock troops used to break up riots and other acts of civil unrest. He wore a tight fitting, short-sleeved blue shirt which bulged with the man's biceps. His eyes reflected an intense dislike for the dandified, pesky little man trying to circumvent the established procedure.

The newscaster cast a quick glance at the others in the room, and saw that they were listening with interest to his conversation, ready to jump out of their seats if he was allowed to go through. Colon knew that too, and he was not about to let it happen.

It was important that Correcaminos got his message through to the Superintendent, but at the same time he could not state out loud what the exact purpose of his visit was, or describe what Michelle was doing, since the others in the room would hear it and her security would be seriously jeopardized.

He tried an oblique approach. "May I talk to Special Agent Franceschini, then?" he asked, directing his request at the other policeman surnamed "Agostini", who seemed to regard him with less open hostility.

"You'll have to talk to the FBI directly," Colon answered for Agostini, stepping between his fellow officer and Correcaminos. "Now please remove yourself from this access."

"Is there anyone else I can talk to?" Correcaminos insisted as calmly as he could.

"No," Colon answered, ostensibly placing his hand on the hilt of his nightstick. "Now move along."

Correcaminos shrugged, but remained standing where he was. He moved his left hand into his jacket, prompting the policeman to take a sudden step backwards. The television reporter brought out his mobile phone and casually began to flick through its contents. Colon resumed his previous position, and glared at the pretentious intruder.

"What *are* you doing, mister?" the policeman asked angrily.

Correcaminos raised his right hand in a "hold it" gesture, and continued to rummage through the contents of his cell phone. "I'm looking for an application that may help us," he said, concentrating on his screen. "Ah! Here it is! 'How to deal with police assholes'! That should be of help."

Colon snarled at the reporter and grabbed him by the scruff of the neck, nearly raising him off the floor, and slamming him against the doorframe. Several of the persons in the waiting area stood up in shock. Correcaminos did nothing to defend himself, letting his arms hang at his sides, while Agostini, with a half grin on his face, moved to separate the two men. He whispered something in the ear of his partner, who after some hesitation slackened his grip on the reporter and let him go.

"Now listen to me, you son of a bitch," Correcaminos whispered to the angry policeman, "you have just attacked a member of the press in front of several witnesses, and this could develop into a serious public incident. I also recorded the incident with my phone." Correcaminos seriously doubted that with all of the news events happening around them, the roughing up of a smart-alecky newsman would amount to anything, but he spoke with absolute conviction and pressed his temporary advantage. "I am bringing confidential information that will help your fellow officers save lives. I will not leave until I talk to someone *in private*. If after I talk to that person he still thinks that I should go, then I will go. Is that a deal?"

Colon hesitated, his face reddened with anger.

"I'll talk to him," Agostini said, still smiling.

Colon considered the offer. Finally, he nodded once.

"Right here, in the corridor behind me," he said. He moved aside and let Correcaminos slide past him. There were vocal protests from the others in the room, but Colon closed the gap and took out his nightstick, slapping it on his hand.

It took Correcaminos very little time to summarize to Agostini Michelle's situation and to outline her plan of action. Agostini listened with growing interest, saying to him at the end, "Wait here, I'll be right back." He whispered something to Colon, who directed an unfriendly glance at the reporter, but said nothing.

Agostini left immediately.

Correcaminos exhaled with newfound relief. It had been risky, but it was not the first time that he had successfully used that tactic. He called it the "play one friend against the other" ploy: ridiculing with humor one member of a hostile group to gain the sympathy and lighten the mood of the others. It had worked with a high degree of consistency in the oftentimes highly charged atmosphere of sports locker rooms, so there had been no reason why it would not have worked now. Had he been arrested, he would have made his one allowed communication to Doel, to ask him to take over.

He felt elated by the news of Michelle's safe reappearance, although the story about the attempted rape had been less than reassuring. He had let Doel have a piece of his mind for convincing her to expose herself to further danger, but at the same time appreciated the news director's intentions. If Michelle pulled this off, her future in the news business would be assured.

Agostini returned after five minutes.

"The Superintendent is going into a telephone conference right now," the policeman said, "but he'll see you when he finishes. I will take you to the Command Center."

Correcaminos began to follow Agostini, but stopped and tapped Colon on the shoulder. The large man turned and faced the reporter. Correcaminos handed him a card that he had pulled out of his wallet.

"This is the address of my gym. It has a boxing ring. I usually train there during the weekdays, at six in the morning. If you ever want to finish what you started today, look me up. I'll be glad to oblige"

Colon stared at the card, and then at the small man who was offering it to him. He searched the reporter's face for signs that he was joking, but saw he was dead serious. He took the card and carefully placed it in one of his shirt pockets. His eyes reflected curiosity and newfound respect.

"I may take you on that offer," he called uncertainly after Correcaminos, who had begun to follow Agostini.

"I'll be waiting," Correcaminos responded without looking back as he disappeared from sight.

From the limited information he had received from Officer Agostini, Police Superintendent Maldonado wished he could have had the opportunity to meet with Correcaminos before he had been called away urgently to answer a call from the terrorists through the direct line established with the Grand Laguna Hotel. Maybe the WKPA reporter could have given him news that could have been useful in the upcoming telephone conversation. But it was too late now.

He had spent the last twenty minutes getting the latest updates on the hotel rescue preparations from Franceschini and Montañez. The latter's report had been brief and to the point: the boat assault force, the helicopters, and the SWAT snipers were ready and awaiting his orders to go.

Franceschini's conversation had lasted longer. The FBI agent had confirmed that his men were ready to storm La Fortaleza and the *Mardi*

Gras, if the circumstances so required it. But then the talk had shifted to Franceschini's efforts with the federal government to secure the release of the head of the Macheteros, Adalberto Cacho. His release could be used by the Superintendent as leverage to stop or delay the threatened execution of the Grand Laguna Hotel guests.

However, as far as Maldonado was aware, the only way to free Cacho from federal prison was via an official pardon by the President of the United States. That involved absolving him fully from any crimes for which he was serving time, a daunting proposition for a man who had topped the FBI "Most Wanted" list for several years.

If he pardoned Cacho, President Powell would be placing his political career on the line, hoping that any additional time bought by Cacho's release yielded positive results, a very uncertain premise at best. The President would almost certainly be accused of encouraging future terrorist acts by yielding to the Macheteros' present demands. And if—God forbid—Cacho participated in new terrorists acts and subsequently escaped, the press and Powell's political opponents would have a political field day, and Powell's chances for reelection would be seriously jeopardized.

It was therefore with very little hope that Maldonado had asked Franceschini if he had any news from Washington about the issue. To his surprise, the FBI Special Agent had given him a glimmer of hope. The President would definitely not pardon a proven criminal like Adalberto Cacho, he had replied. It would wipe his criminal record clean, and allow him to walk away as an innocent man—barring he committed any new crimes. But—Franceschini assured Maldonado—the Justice Department was frantically studying other laws whose interpretation could be "stretched" to allow the release of Cacho without pardoning his crimes, in the hopes that he would be captured later, after the revolt collapsed.

One promising alternative was Section 3582(c)(1)(A)(i) of Title 18 of the United States Code, which allowed for the modification of an imposed term of imprisonment when "extraordinary and compelling reasons" warranted the release of a prisoner. Usually, it was used in cases where the inmate was suffering from some disease that did not allow him to provide for self-care in a correctional facility, or when another member of the inmate's family who was the sole provider for his children died and became incapacitated. In such cases, and after following a complex procedure, the prisoner could be released under certain modified conditions. There were no express limits on what the "extraordinary and compelling reasons" to release a prisoner could be. Releasing Cacho in order to stop the execution of hostages could certainly be considered to be an extraordinary and compelling reason.

The legal procedure for the release, though complicated, could be expedited, Franceschini explained. But there was one particular legal provision that the Justice Department was still struggling to deal with. Section 3553(a)(2) of the law established that in order to authorize the reduction of the jail term, the court had to determine that "the defendant is not a danger to the safety of any other person or the community." The lawyers of the Justice Department were still figuring out how to deal with that seemingly insurmountable condition, as well as exploring other legal alternatives.

It was the main difference between a country ruled by law and the constitution, and a dictatorship, Maldonado had thought. In a dictatorship, all that the dictator had to do was to order the release of the prisoner, and that would be the end of that. In Puerto Rico, the rights of *any* inmate could not be affected unless the authorities complied with the applicable legal process. *It was a tempting argument in favor of expanding the powers of the executive, and limiting the red tape of the courts*, Maldonado reflected. *But then, bastards like Rovira Melendez could end up wielding unlimited power.* Considering the alternatives, he preferred the red tape.

As he walked towards the small office where the connection to the Grand Laguna Hotel was located, Maldonado prayed to God for calm and inspiration. Montañez and Franceschini flanked him, giving him reassurance.

When he entered the office, Yomaris—the policewoman monitoring the call—stood up. "They're waiting," she whispered, and left the room. Maldonado sat on the seat behind the desk where a speakerphone had been installed, while Franceschini half-leaned, half-sat on one of the desk's corners. Montañez remained standing with his arms folded across his chest.

The Superintendent breathed in deeply, his heart pounding furiously. During the last hour, he had rehearsed maybe a hundred times with his staff, with negotiating experts, and in his head the conversation that was about to take place, and he still felt unprepared for it.

"This is Maldonado," he said, switching off the "Mute" button on the speakerphone to which the line had been connected recently, and breaking the silence. He heard the faint murmur of hushed voices on the other side of the line, and then a man said, *"Mr. Superintendent, it is good to hear you again."*

It was San Miguel, the same man to whom Maldonado had spoken before. The greeting carried no gleeful or mocking overtones. It was spoken in the courteous, guarded tone of a businessman addressing another.

"Do you have any news for me?" San Miguel asked matter-of-factly.

"We are still working on your requests," Maldonado answered, looking up at Franceschini, who nodded slightly. It had been the vague answer that they had agreed to give to the anticipated question.

"I am sorry to hear that," San Miguel said with what appeared to be sincere regret. *"It will be two o'clock soon, and we will have to start executing our prisoners."*

Even though Maldonado had expected that answer, he was shocked to hear it.

"Listen," he said earnestly, "your requests take time! There are legal procedures to follow. We can't just release Cacho with the snap of a finger!"

"That is not our problem," the man replied evenly.

"We need more time!"

"Do you? I don't believe you're doing anything. Your Interim Governor said that he would not negotiate with us, just a few minutes after I last spoke with you. Despite that, we have kept our deadline, even though we already have your response. What has changed since then? I think that we have been more than reasonable, don't you?"

Maldonado bit his tongue, his rage threatening to overwhelm his common sense. *Reasonable?! The Macheteros had already caused dozens of deaths and paralyzed the island. They had seriously damaged San Juan's infrastructure and were threatening the life of thousands of helpless hostages, including the Governor, and he called himself reasonable?!* But instead of screaming into the telephone, he said, "The Interim Governor has no say in the release of Adalberto Cacho. Cacho is a federal inmate. As such, his fate is determined by the President of the United States."

"Then let it all hang on the President's conscience," San Miguel replied.

"The murder of any of your civilian prisoners will be on your conscience...if you have one," Maldonado replied bitterly. Then, with a flash of anger, he added, "May God forgive you."

His last words seemed to strike a chord. For a moment, San Miguel seemed to lose his composure, replying sharply, *"God has nothing to forgive. I am doing His will."* He recovered quickly, however, adding, *"The executions will continue. You leave us no choice."*

"Just give us two more hours!" Maldonado pleaded.

There was a long pause where the phone seemed to die. Maldonado was about to order Montañez to seek a telephone technician, when the stranger's voice came back on the line.

"No," the man said. *"Regrettably, you are not taking us seriously. It is now...twenty-six minutes to two PM. You have very little time left. Talk into the telephone if you have any further news. We will hear you. Goodbye."*

Maldonado glared at the speakerphone, as if were alive. Most of the color had drained from his face. Slowly, almost in a daze, he stood up from his chair and walked out of the office into the outside corridor. His two companions followed him.

"Alert Captain Gomez and the SWAT teams covering the roof," he said to Montañez as soon as he had shut the office's door. "We start the rescue as soon as one of the hostages steps on the roof. And I want all television images showing the hotel and its surrounding areas blacked out as of now!"

"Yes, sir!" Montañez turned on his heels and hurried towards the command post set up in the Salon Carnaval.

"How about the other rescue operations?" Franceschini inquired, referring to the *Mardi Gras* and La Fortaleza. Maldonado considered the question for several seconds. He knew that regardless of what they did, lives would be lost. The trick was to choose the alternative that saved the most lives. Once Captain Gomez stormed into the Grand Laguna Hotel, all of the hostages would become legitimate targets for the terrorists, not just in the hotel, but also in the *Mardi Gras* and the Governor's Mansion.

But the man on the telephone had only referred to the captives in the Grand Laguna Hotel, not to the others. Maldonado doubted that the Macheteros would kill all of their hostages in retaliation for the SWAT team's rescue attempt. It would leave them without any leverage to negotiate. The terrorists would not be that stupid. His gut feeling told him that even after the Grand Laguna was attacked by Gomez's force, the hostages in the cruise ship and in La Fortaleza would not be harmed. At least, not immediately. Besides, there was a real possibility that the terrorists in the hotel would be unable to communicate with their other counterparts. But it was all a calculated risk. If he turned out to be wrong, the toll in human lives would be too terrible to contemplate.

He had to make the decision *now*. By not ordering the other rescues, he could be allowing the terrorists in the other two locations to dig in and make any subsequent rescue attempts a lot more difficult. *But wouldn't the terrorists have prepared by now anyway?*

"Alert your men to be ready," he told Franceschini, "but hold off until I say so. Let's see how our rescue attempt on the Grand Laguna progresses. If we are successful, we may have to move on the other locations. When the terrorists in the *Mardi Gras* and La Fortaleza hear that we captured the Grand Laguna Hotel, they may decide to go out in a blaze of glory and kill everyone they hold. We may have no choice but to move on all fronts, even though I would prefer to wait and conduct the rescue operations under the cover of darkness. Do you agree?"

Franceschini nodded slowly, mulling over the dilemma in his mind. "I do. I don't think there's a right or wrong solution to this problem, regardless of what we end up doing. However, your instincts have always been good, and I will abide by them, whatever they are," he said finally. "I would hate to be accused of creating another Waco because we acted hastily, but then again, it's so easy for armchair generals to predict the next day what the right move would have been, with the benefit of hindsight, instant replays, and no risk for them." The FBI man stood up. "You know, of course, that if we're wrong, they're going to crucify us, don't you? Especially you."

Maldonado assented.

"They will crucify me regardless of what happens," he replied. "I don't expect to keep my job after this is over."

And he wasn't that sure that he wanted to keep it, anyway, he thought to himself.

Angel San Miguel pressed the "Pause" button on the intercom and sighed.

"I am impressed," El Alacran said softly from his end of the conference table. "I think you handled that very well."

San Miguel acknowledged the rare compliment with a curt nod.

Funny, thought Johnny Ray, *how everybody had ended up sitting in the same relative locations where they had sat two nights ago in the Old San Juan safe house.* He watched Yajaira twirl her hair nervously with her long, exquisitely manicured nails.

He had spoken twice with Lebron, his Secretary-General—who still had not moved from the rooftop of the Banco Cosmopolitano Building—using the satellite phones. Lebron had filled him in on the limited reports he had been able to gather via telephone from the student patrols that roamed the streets, and Johnny had updated the Secretary General on his conversation with San Miguel.

So far, everything had proceeded as expected. Most of the population in Old San Juan and Puerta de Tierra had stayed in its homes, too scared to come out. Thus far, there had only been three violent incidents since the takeover that morning, including the one that he had personally witnessed in the jewelry store in the Plaza de Armas.

That last one still weighed heavily in his mind. He made a mental note to tell Lebron to get some food and water to the shopkeepers who had been locked up in the basement of the store. He would keep them there until his grip on the city solidified. He could not afford to let them go and have them spread the rumor that his people were committing atrocities on the civilian population. Eventually, when matters settled down, he would let them go.

He did not have that much of a grasp on the other two incidents. Apparently, in one, an old lady had attacked one of the patrols with a rolling pin, and in the subsequent scuffle had been tossed to the ground and tied up. He had ordered Lebron to have her released. The second occurrence had involved the attempted rape of a young woman by one of the students on patrol. The FEPIsta had been reprimanded, disarmed, and let go to find his own way home. Like the jewelry store affair, the incident had been very unfortunate. However, considering the circumstances and the more than one hundred thousand inhabitants in San Juan and Puerta de Tierra, the events had been surprisingly few. Soon, hopefully, some of the scared citizens would begin to rally to their cause.

Colonel Calderon sat, as he had during their last meeting, in front of him. He had barely spoken except to greet the others, keeping to himself and looking—if not concerned—absorbed in his own thoughts. Johnny had heard about the massacre in the Puerta de Tierra police station, and lamented the excessive loss of life. The Macheteros had ambushed one other police vehicle as it rushed to aid the officers trapped in the station, and all of their occupants had been killed. He knew that it had been inevitable, the necessary evil that happened in an armed revolution, but he disliked it anyway.

And now the most disagreeable of all the incidents was about to take place. He directed a covert glance at El Alacran, the main supporter of the impending executions, and wondered if he was enjoying the moment. It was hard to say. Even without his long, goat-like beard and frizzled mane of hair, his face still reflected the same emotional intensity of a blank wall. Only his dark eyes gave any indication that a live man dwelled behind his expressionless façade. At that moment they shone with intense amusement—or was it malice—as they contemplated San Miguel.

Johnny had admired Andrade since he had become aware of his existence in high school. He had considered him to be a genuine freedom fighter, second only to Filiberto Ojeda and Adalberto Cacho, the two former Machetero leaders. But after interacting with him, he had begun to wonder about the real motivation behind his acts. The man seemed incapable of human emotions. How could such a dead fish champion such an emotional cause as the independence of Puerto Rico?

As if listening to Johnny's rambling thoughts, El Alacran directed a flickering glance in the FEPIsta's direction, and a thin, graceless smile formed on his lips. Johnny avoided him, casting his eyes at the table's top.

"Maybe..." he heard himself say, "maybe they *do* need more time."

Everyone's attention focused on him except for Czecka's, who stood behind San Miguel, a looming, silent presence that did not need to speak in order to be felt.

"I am certain that they do," San Miguel responded. "Superintendent Maldonado, or that jerk who is the Interim Governor, for that matter, do not have the power to release Cacho, I know that. But he won't get the authorization for the release in two hours, nor in ten hours, nor in a week. He won't get it until the federal government takes us seriously."

"Which *un*-fortunately—El Alacran stressed the first vowel of the word with deliberate slowness—will not happen until we start executing the hostages."

"Unfortunately, yes," San Miguel repeated, sounding truly distressed about what was going to happen.

A long, uncomfortable silence followed. Johnny took a quick look at Colonel Calderon. From the concentrated way that the Venezuelan soldier fidgeted with a paperclip, he could tell that the colonel did not feel very happy about the killing of helpless civilians either. It also told him that there was not much that anyone could do about it.

Yajaira looked at her companion as if waiting for him to say something else, and then tensed her body and prepared to speak herself. But Johnny stopped her, pressing her hand and shaking his head imperceptibly.

"May at least the Puerto Rican hostages be spared?" he asked. "It will do a great deal of damage to our cause if—"

"I've already given instructions to Daniel to that effect," San Miguel interrupted, sympathetically acknowledging Johnny's concern. He had given no such instructions, of course, and chided himself for not thinking of that before. Executing a Puerto Rican would definitely kill any remote chance that the revolt was successful. He should have instructed Daniel to make certain that one of the locals was put to death in front of the entire world. It was a pity no such instructions had been given. *An opportunity wasted.* But maybe Daniel had thought about it. Time would tell.

"We will reconvene in one hour," he said, scanning the faces around him for any further questions and nodding with satisfaction when none were asked. "Good luck to all of us."

CHAPTER XXXVII

For nearly two decades, the Golden Triangle had been at the forefront of every Pro-statehood and Popular government's agenda. The project involved the restoration and development of three key areas close to the Condado Lagoon—each designated as a corner of the "Triangle"—by making them more attractive to tourists and local residents. Each incoming administration tweaked and refined the thousands of details involved in the ongoing venture, but the main concept remained the same: to create three interlinked locations that could compete head-to-head with mega tourist attractions such as Downtown Disney or Miami's South Beach, and that would have no equal in the Caribbean.

The Convention Center District constituted one—if not the principal—of the three angular corners of the Golden Triangle. It not only included the gigantic convention building per se, but also two luxury hotels, and a grand canal. Plans were already approved for the construction of shops, restaurants, nightclubs, a movie complex, a multistory office building, a park, and a museum, as well as scores of residential row houses and apartment buildings. The Great Recession had delayed by several years the full development of the district, but had not managed to derail it. Governor Pietrantoni in particular, considered the Convention Center District to be of crucial importance for the continued growth of the tourism industry in Puerto Rico.

The second angular corner of the Triangle was situated north of the lagoon in the Condado area, where two of the oldest and largest hotels in San Juan—La Concha and El Condado—had been gutted, modernized, and refurbished. The two hotels were separated by an enormous, open plaza facing the sea that occupied the area of the old convention center, and surrounded by scores of brand new, lavish condominiums. This was a neighborhood where many of San Juan's best restaurants were already located, and which would therefore benefit from and supplement the massive infusion of tourists and new residents expected to flood the area.

The last corner of the Triangle corresponded to a small abandoned base previously used for the housing of U.S. Navy officers. About the size of a city block, it was located close to the Grand Laguna Hotel. It had been the last of the three elements of the Golden Triangle to be developed, but was well on the way to being the fastest to be finished. Several luxury residential and rental apartment buildings had substituted the abandoned Navy units despite massive protests by conservationists and nationalists who claimed that the land was part of Puerto Rico's patrimony, and that it could not be ceded to private interests. As part of the project, a long walkway had been constructed along the westernmost shore of the Condado Lagoon, connecting the Grand Laguna Hotel all the way to the Miramar and Dos Hermanos Bridges. Like the other two angular corners of the Triangle, restaurants and shops were already being built, slated to open in the near future.

It was through this last area that Michelle planned to approach the Grand Laguna Hotel. Three months before, she had participated in a short news feature for television where she had discussed with the developers the plans for the area and showed the progress of the construction of the new facilities. Along with a cameraman, she had toured the construction site and been allowed to film the work under way.

At the time, only a ten-story building to provide parking for the upcoming facilities had been finished. Four centrally located elevators and two sets of stairs at each end of the building—still not open to the public—would connect the parking floors to an open pedestrian walkway and to several internal courtyards where the shops, offices and restaurants would be located. When finished, the walkway or "promenade"— as the developers had dubbed it—would also be linked to half a dozen other narrower passageways leading to the surrounding condominiums and to the lagoon. One of those particular passageways would connect directly with the Grand Laguna Hotel. Michelle was convinced that the less risky manner to reach the hotel was through the latter corridor, even though the last time she had visited the construction, corrugated metal sheets had blocked the corridor's entrance.

Their host, Andres Lazaro, had adamantly objected to her plan. It was crazy, too risky and too dangerous, he had pointed out correctly. They should all wait in the Laguna Vista Condominium until the situation blew over. There was food for everyone to last for several days, and ample room to sleep. Like in the times of a hurricane, the Lazaros had filled their bathtubs to the brim with water in case the water supply was cut off, although the building's immense water cistern would not run out of the precious liquid for a week. An emergency generator could like-wise supply power uninterruptedly for five days, at least in theory.

In any event, he had argued, he doubted very much that the revolt would manage to survive more than a couple of days. The Americans would not allow it.

When Michelle had stubbornly insisted on leaving, Lazaro had of-fered her his Smith and Wesson .38 revolver. She had refused, telling him that he could need it. He had laughed.

"What for?" he had said. "To take on the rebels? This old fart? They won't do anything to us. You should be the one to worry. You are heading straight into the wolf's mouth. The very least you can do to set me at ease—and it will still not set me at ease very much, let me tell you—is to accept this gift from me. You can give me credit later in your news re-port."

In the end she had accepted. Mrs. Lazaro had also convinced her to change into a pair of her jeans and a T-shirt, to substitute her torn and dirty dress. The jeans had fit Michelle adequately enough—she was slightly taller and leaner than Mrs. Lazaro—as had the white Polo shirt with an open neck.

The shoes had been more difficult to substitute. After the rape at-tempt, she had never found one of her high heels and had discarded the other. She had walked to the Laguna Vista on her bare feet. Mrs. Lazaro had offered her a pair of sneakers, but Michelle was two sizes larger than her host, and they would not fit. The babysitter's sandals had also proven too small. Michelle had been forced to settle for a pair of beach flip-flops that barely reached the end of her heels.

Negron had also shed his police cadet khaki uniform. Unlike Michelle's clothes, his substitute apparel—picked out of Mr. Lazaro's closet—hung on him in folds and made him look like an elongated prune. Andres Lazaro wore extra large shirts and 40-inch waist pants. Negron's gangly frame shot off the ground like a corn stalk to a height of over six feet—three inches taller and forty pounds lighter than Lazaro— and his waist measured thirty-one inches. The borrowed pants crumpled around his hips, held up exclusively by his black police-issued belt; the shirt, made of a rayon-like material with an unremarkable tannish color, drooped like a deflated balloon over his narrow shoulders.

When Negron finished changing and walked out of Lazaro's room, Michelle suppressed a laugh, while Archie struggled to remain silent. The latter's meaner instincts prevailed, however, and he said with a smirk, "The Wizard of Oz called. He's finally found a brain for you."

Negron stared at him confusedly for a brief moment, then smiled de-lightedly as he got the reference. "Oh, you think I look like the scarecrow!

That's funny! And I guess Michelle is Dorothy! And that would make you—"

"The Cowardly Lion," Archie prompted preemptively.

"I was thinking more of a Munchkin, but okay," the rookie policeman answered, directing a covert glance at Michelle to see her reaction. He was pleased to see her smile. "Anyway, the shirt is wide enough for me to hide my gun inside it, along with the holster." Negron unfastened two buttons close to his stomach and opened his shirt, showing his holster strapped right under his thin ribcage.

"There is one more thing," Michelle said. Out of her purse, she pulled out the black armband she had slipped off the arm of Croma, the dead Machetero. She shuddered involuntarily.

"What is *this*?" Lazaro asked as Michelle handed it to him, holding it with great care and examining with curiosity the phrase written on it. "Libre como el Coqui..." he read to himself with wonderment.

"Both terrorists that attacked Michelle wore them," Archie explained.

"I also noticed those on some of the men patrolling the streets," Negron confirmed.

Michelle nodded. "And the drunk U.P.R. student who discharged his gun into the air last night, in the Fiestas de San Sebastian, remember? He was carrying one in his backpack," she added.

"Which means," Lazaro concluded, finishing the thoughts of the others, "that these people...whoever they are, they're using the armbands to identify each other."

"Not necessarily," interjected Archie. "They may be wearing them to give publicity to their cause—"

"Which is?" Negron fixed his eyes mischievously on the redhead. "What? To live free like the coquis?" Again he shifted his eyes to Michelle, seeking some sign of a smile. It was evident that both men were vying for her attention.

Lazaro shrugged. "Maybe," he said, responding to Archie's suggestion. "Although for the most part they have stayed out of sight, so I don't see how their armbands can give them any kind of publicity. I believe that they're using them because there are so many of them who don't know each other, that they need them to know who's who in this mess."

"Whatever the reason," said Michelle, picking up the thread of the conversation, " I think one of us...You, Negron, should wear it."

Negron pointed at himself with a quizzical expression, feigning surprise but clearly pleased that she had chosen him.

"Yes, you. I think that you should wear it," she indicated in a tone that admitted no contradiction. "It may distract any terrorists that see us. The armband may make them believe that you are one of them." She shook her head with mortification. "I should have taken the armband from the other dead terrorist. I should have thought about this sooner. It's too late now."

"Why me?" Negron asked, genuinely mystified. "Why not you or Archie?"

"Haven't you noticed the men in the trucks?" Michelle responded. "They all seem to be very young, about your age." Negron seemed to be deflated by the age reference, as if she was considering him to be too young, and therefore not worth taking very seriously. "And I haven't seen any women wearing them so far. Your appearance fits better with the demographics of the terrorists than Archie's or mine."

"What about the Macheteros that attacked you?" Negron said. Michelle could not help but notice how more and more often they were referring to the terrorists as the "Macheteros", despite any real evidence that the men involved in the takeover in fact belonged to that group. However, the terrorists had demanded the release of the top Machetero leader as one of their conditions to stop the execution of the hostages, so the reference to the group was not unreasonable. "They seemed to be in Archie's age group."

"Which would be..." the redhead prompted.

"Old," Negron responded.

"True," Michelle said, then added for Archie's benefit, "*They* seemed *older*. But they were the exception, and they had the appearance of cold-blooded killers. Archie's appearance is not very intimidating...No offense intended, Archie."

Negron smiled delightedly, while Archie looked unhappy.

"Besides," Michelle continued, "all modesty apart, I have a very recognizable face. Anyone taking a close look at me would begin to wonder what I was doing there. If that were to happen, it would be better that you were wearing the armband and that you claimed that you have captured me."

The corners of Archie's mouth curved slightly upwards, in an impish grin.

"Believe me. Right now, nobody will be able to identify you," he said, adding with relish, "No offense intended..." It was a retaliatory remark for Michelle's prior comment, but he regretted it immediately when he saw her hurt expression. "I mean," he added hastily, trying to lessen the impact of his last words, "not that you still don't look beautiful, because you do. Just a different beautiful."

He meant it. He had been smitten by the WKPA reporter, and was prepared to defend her to the death and against all odds. At least, that's the way he felt. But Michelle fixed him with an angry look that made him burn behind his ears and caused him to momentarily lose his ability to speak.

"Children, children," Lazaro warned sternly, and only half in jest. "Behave!"

Just then, Mrs. Lazaro walked back into the living room, carrying a black scarf and a long piece of black cloth. "These may pass as armbands if viewed from a distance," she said, holding them up for the others to see.

"That is brilliant!" Michelle said excitedly. In no time, Mrs. Lazaro had pinned the scarf on Michelle's arm, and the other piece of cloth on Archie's.

Time was running short. If the terrorists really meant to carry out their threat, they would begin to push hostages off the Grand Laguna's rooftop within the next half hour. They had to leave now.

Don Moncho, the babysitter Maribel, and Katherine Elizabeth would stay behind. Don Moncho had not spoken a word since he arrived at the apartment, settling on a padded chair in front of the television screen and watching the broadcast unfold with a lost, dazed expression. Michelle approached him and knelt by his side. She felt terrible for him, knowing how his world, centering on his immaculately kept taxicab, had been shattered that morning.

"I'm leaving now," Michelle told him gently. "You should stay here until matters get back to normal."

Don Moncho shifted his eyes to her face, and he grasped her hands between his own. Michelle had never noticed before how long and delicate his fingers were.

"I can't go with you," he said, expressing wordlessly through his thick lenses his frustration at being unable to help. "I'm too old. I would be a liability for you. I can't move fast enough now, as I did at one time, not without my taxi," he explained miserably.

"I know," she answered.

"Be very careful out there. Those two boys that are going with you mean well, but they're a little goofy."

Michelle smiled. Don Moncho kissed one of her hands, and released them.

"May God walk with you, my princess," he said.

Michelle found Maribel in the dining room, feeding Katherine Elizabeth small pieces of a pizza slice that Mrs. Lazaro had warmed up for her. The two year old grinned at her, briefly showing the contents in her mouth.

"I'm leaving," she said to Maribel. The babysitter looked up tiredly, and nodded.

"I'm sorry for the way I behaved," she said. "You saved me today. If anything had happened to Katie because of me—"

"But nothing happened," Michelle replied, not allowing her to dwell on the subject. "What matters now is what happens next."

"I won't fail her again," Maribel promised, and Michelle believed her, although she hoped the babysitter would never be put to the test again. She kissed Katherine Elizabeth, who planted her wet, garlic smelling lips on her cheek, and returned to the living room, where her two companions and the Lazaros waited.

Mr. Lazaro looked through the apartment door's peephole, to make sure that no stranger was waiting there, and then opened the door.

"This is your home," he said to his three departing guests. "You may return here whenever you want or need to." He embraced Michelle and shook each of the men's hands, while Mrs. Lazaro kissed each of them. There were tears in her eyes. Lazaro pressed the elevator button to go down.

"We have no words to thank you enough," Michelle said to the Lazaros. "You have been so kind to us. God bless you."

"I'm not sure if I should thank you for lending me these clothes," Negron added with a half smile, making everybody laugh. "But hopefully I'll be able to return them to you."

"Washed and pressed, I hope," Lazaro answered lamely as the elevator door opened with startling suddenness.

Michelle and her two companions stepped in, and descended in meditative silence towards the lobby.

"Let me go out first," Negron said to the others as the door opened.

The frigidly-air-conditioned, marbled-floored reception area was as devoid of life now as it had been at the moment when they had first stepped into it...*When had that been? Only an hour or so before?* It seemed like a much longer time than that to Michelle. Through its glass walls she could see the abandoned guardhouse in the parking area. Nothing moved, except for the palm fronds swaying in the wind.

They hurried out of the lobby and, staying behind the concrete wall that surrounded the building, walked towards the barrier arm at the gate. The guardhouse next to the barrier was locked and definitely empty. They stood partially behind it, and examined the landscape looming ahead.

Constitutional Avenue stretched before them, five lanes wide. It was the longest and broadest thoroughfare in the island of San Juan, running several miles from the end of Fortaleza Street and the Plaza de Colon at the eastern edge of Old San Juan proper, past the island's Capitol building and the Luis Muñoz Rivera Park in Puerta de Tierra, and finally joining Fernandez Juncos Avenue at the bridge closest to the San Juan Yacht Club. On the other side of the street, and partially hidden by dozens of huge, multi-rooted ancient banyan trees, lay the domed marble building of the Supreme Court of Puerto Rico.

The entire scene reminded Michelle of the movie *"On the Beach"*, where due to a nuclear catastrophe, the entire city of San Francisco appeared, except for a few stray pieces of paper drifting in the wind, lacking any sign of humanity. It had terrified her as a child, causing her nightmares, and this terrified her now.

"It all seems pretty empty to me," Negron stated in a casual voice, and before Archie or Michelle could stop him, he stepped out into the wide boulevard. Michelle began to follow him, but Archie stopped her with his arm just as the rookie policeman paused in the middle of the street. With an exaggerated smile, Negron turned and waved to someone to his left, raising his right arm high into the air so that his black armband would show.

Archie peered from behind a cement column near the building's entrance, opposite to the guardhouse, and saw the object of Negron's attention: the faraway figure of a man, maybe two blocks away, holding on to what seemed to be a rifle.

The distant man hesitated, and then waved back.

"Come on, fellow terrorists..." Negron muttered under his breath, looking back at his two companions, a forced, foolish grin etched on his face. "Follow me..."

Michelle strode boldly onto the avenue, her flip-flops flapping lustily on the pavement. Cursing under his breath, Archie followed.

The man with the rifle stared at them with renewed interest, and for a moment it seemed that he would head in their direction. He raised his arm and shouted something, beckoning them to approach him.

"We have to go to the hotel!" Negron answered, cupping his hand on his ear and continuing to walk towards the banyan trees that flanked the Supreme Court building. "I can't hear you!!" he shouted even more loudly, and said again, motioning with his arm towards the Grand Laguna, "We have to go to the hotel!"

The armed man took a couple of faltering steps towards the three strangers, but by that time they had disappeared into the woods. He did not follow them.

The three friends huddled behind a massive banyan tree, nervously searching around them for further movement.

"Well that was exciting!" Negron said breathlessly, beaming at the others.

"You asshole!" Archie muttered furiously, barely holding his voice in check. "Who do you think you are, Indiana Jones? You could have gotten us all killed!"

The rookie policeman stared at his redheaded companion with the uncertainty of a person who is not sure why he is being insulted, and who is making up his mind whether to ask for an explanation or get angry. Sensing a quarrel, Michelle stepped between the two men.

"Don't you see what he's doing?" Archie insisted, venting his rage. "By pure, dumb luck, he manages to survive a massacre where all of his companions get shot to pieces, and now he thinks he's immortal! So he walks carelessly around without taking any precautions, probably believing that he has been chosen by God for some higher purpose, and in the process, if we get killed, well, that's just too bad!"

Negron's pleasant face darkened, and he stepped swiftly forward and irately grabbed Archie by his shirt, despite Michelle's attempts to keep the two men apart.

"Stop it! Stop it!" she shouted, pushing Negron away with both hands. Negron let go and backed away, breathing heavily.

"What *is* it with this guy? Who does he think he is?" the youngster asked Michelle, refusing to talk to Archie. "He doesn't let up! Constantly criticizing everything I do!"

"Because you act stupid, you stupid *jibaro* from San Sebastian!" Archie replied crossly, emphasizing the word *jibaro*, the equivalent of a Puerto Rican hillbilly.

Negron and Archie moved towards each other, but Michelle kept them apart with her outstretched arms. She knew they could have easily overpowered her, but that they would not dare to push her away.

"*I said stop it!* Are you two crazy?"

Michelle talked to the two men, looking from one face to the other.

"Archie, you shouldn't talk to Negron that way! We're on the same side, remember?"

"I should have never rescued him from the car where he was hiding," Archie said bitterly.

"*Enough!*" Michelle cried at Archie. "If you want to waste any more time airing your...your...petty grievances, do it some other time and place or leave us now! The lives of a lot of people may depend on what we do next, and so far we've only managed to insult each other and waste precious time!" She turned to Negron, who winced even before she spoke. "As to *you*," she said to the rookie policeman, "Archie is right. We act as a team. Stop making unilateral decisions. Wait for instructions."

"I got us across, didn't I?" Negron responded sullenly.

Archie opened his mouth to reply, but opted to keep quiet, shaking his head in frustration.

"Yes, and you kept a cool head in the face of a possible disaster. But we may not be as lucky next time. You didn't give us enough time to make certain that nobody could see us. You only looked in the direction of the Grand Laguna, and forgot to look the other way. So we have to be more careful next time. All of us. Okay?"

Negron nodded, grudgingly. He stared briefly at Archie. "After all of this is over, Woody Woodpecker..." he said, leaving the rest unsaid.

"After all of this is over," Archie agreed undaunted.

Michelle groaned and began to walk away through the densely wooded grounds, followed quickly by the others. To their left, just a few yards away, they could see the tall, iron-bar fence that separated the Supreme Court from the trees, and beyond that the Supreme Court building itself and an annex housing the court's library and several administrative offices. They detected no movement there, not very surprising, since it was Sunday and the bridges into the island of San Juan had been cut off.

They crunched their way over a thick carpet of dead, dry leaves, fearing that the noise would give them away, and finally reached the end of the trees and faced their next obstacle, Luis Muñoz Rivera Avenue. They were close to the spot where the highway, four lanes wide, curved northwards and headed towards the main entrances of the Grand Laguna Hotel and the Hotel Normandie. The latter was a smaller, steamboat-shaped hotel that had been forced to close down a couple of years before due to the recession and the intense competition from its humongous neighbor. From there the road again curved to the west and ran past the Luis Muñoz Rivera Park, bordering the edge of the cliffs that faced the Atlantic Ocean all the way to Fort San Cristobal and the entrance to Old San Juan.

The parking building to which they headed stood on the corner where the Muñoz Rivera Avenue turned north and headed towards the Grand Laguna Hotel. After they crossed it, they would have to walk half a block on an open sidewalk before reaching the only entrance to the parking building.

The group paused by another large banyan tree and searched the avenue thoroughly for any kind of activity. They saw no one.

"*Now* may I be allowed to cross?" Negron inquired peevishly.

"Just follow me," Michelle answered, and began to walk across the wide avenue at a fast clip, chased by the others. They made it to the opposite sidewalk without incident, and continued their trek towards the parking garage's gate.

They did not speak, feeling terribly vulnerable and exposed, listening intently for noises that would betray the approach of their enemies. To their right they could see the tall column of black smoke rising from the still burning San Juan Yacht Club, bending away from them towards the bay. They could also see the Condado Lagoon in front of them, but because they were level with the bridges, they could not perceive the damage that the bridges had suffered. Debris, mostly in the form of pebbles, chunks of concrete, clumps of dirt, and tattered shreds of vegetation, were strewn all over the sidewalk, the road, and everything else as far as the eye could see. The few automobiles parked on the street were pocked with dents of various sizes, many of their windows cracked or shattered.

No one challenged their progress. The two tollbooths that controlled the double-gated entrance to the parking building were as empty as the guardhouse in the Laguna Vista. The three friends walked past the barrier arms in the access gates into the relative safety of the neon-lit first floor of the parking area. Mostly reserved for the valet service, there were no vehicles visible except for a motorcycle protected by a silver vinyl cover, and a delivery van for a flower shop called "Capullos de Aleli".

Michelle paused in order to get her bearings. Then she headed to her right, towards the back end of the parking area, her flip-flopping footsteps reverberating in the windowless, empty space. She reached a stairwell that connected to the upper levels of the building, so recently finished that it still smelled like fresh concrete.

"If I recall correctly, there is an overpass one floor above us that connects the parking level to the commercial area under construction," she whispered to her two companions.

Quietly, they climbed the stairs and reached the second floor landing. There were more cars there, probably belonging to some of the nearby condominium residents or to their guests. To the right, a narrow pedestrian bridge connected the parking building to what seemed to be a corridor in the second floor of a commercial area. The corridor continued for about the length of a football field, one of its sides lined with large, unfinished spaces, possibly intended for shops or offices, the other open to an internal courtyard one floor below. When the construction was finished, an aluminum railing would line the rim of the corridor closest to the courtyard, but for now it remained rail-less.

Strips of yellow tape, of the type used to cordon off crime scenes, had blocked the small bridge connecting the parking building to the commercial construction site, but somebody had torn them off and they lay on the floor. As the group moved over the overpass, the courtyard below—or plaza, as it was called in Puerto Rico—became visible to them. It had the shape of a wide rectangle, framed in its entirety by what would be two floors of shops and restaurants. An ornate wrought-iron framework served as the courtyard's ceiling, presumably to be supplemented later with a retractable roof or some type of transparent cover. Construction was far from finished, but already the plaza showed the footprint for one grand and two smaller fountains, and dozens of planters for trees and decorative plants.

"Wow!" Negron said softly. "Sweet! I'll take my girlfriend on a date here when this is finished..." He directed an embarrassed look at Michelle. "That is. When I have a girlfriend..."

Archie rolled up his eyes in despair.

"There are several corridors in the lower courtyard," Michelle said. "They connect to the nearby condominiums, the lagoon, and Muñoz Rivera Avenue. There's also one that leads to the hotel. If I remember correctly, they were all blocked with metal sheets while the construction is going on, so it will not be easy getting through them, but at least the terrorists won't expect anyone to come from this way."

Archie nodded with a concentrated expression, already trying to figure a way to open the blocked passage.

"Where is the corridor?" he asked.

Michelle pointed to a spot on the second floor further ahead, across the courtyard. "We have to hurry," she said, and began to walk in that direction. "What time is it, anyway?"

Negron glanced at his wrist and whistled softly. "My watch says it's one forty three already," he began to say, but stopped as voices, then footsteps of persons climbing up stairs, came suddenly from below. "Hide!' he whispered.

Searching frantically about them, they scurried into a dark room to their left. It's front wall, designed to hold display windows, had still not been constructed, but they managed to squeeze behind a small mound of bags of cement inside.

They hid just in time. Two men emerged from a stairwell just a few yards ahead of them, and walked into the corridor where the others had just been standing. From her hiding place, Michelle could barely make the outlines of the strangers through a crack in the bags. One of the men was considerably taller than the other and somewhat leaner, and he seemed to be doing most of the talking.

"I would come with you," the tall man was saying in a friendly, pleasant voice, "but I have to remain close to the direct line with the Superintendent. He may call us at any time."

Negron exchanged a look of curiosity with Michelle, and tried to raise his head from behind the cement bags, but Archie pulled him down.

The two men stopped by the farthest corner of the room where the others hid.

"I understand," replied the shorter of the two men.

"Now remember," the taller person said. "Our intelligence sources have let us know that the attack will come in fast boats over the lagoon. They will also use two helicopters, to throw smoke canisters and to try to land on the roof of the hotel to save the hostages. You must be able to stop both—"

A crackling, electronic noise interrupted him. The shorter man apologized, and plucked out of a small holster strapped to his belt a rectangular object with an antenna that looked like a walkie-talkie. The man raised the communicating device to his ear and responded, "This is Alpha One, over." He listened for several seconds, and then said impatiently, "Why are you bothering me with this?" He listened again, answering, "I'm *not* in Plaza de Armas and I'm pretty busy right now." Again he listened.

"What is it?" the taller man asked.

"My men in the Metropolitan Center, in San Juan. They have captured someone who was sneaking about, on the rooftop of the building. The prisoner says he wants to talk to someone in command, something about releasing a child in La Fortaleza. My men don't know what to do with him. They don't even have anything to tie him up. They're calling me for instructions."

The tall man signaled his companion with his hand to give him the walkie-talkie. "This is San Miguel," he said. "You can't be distracted from your mission, and you can't release him. He's too much of a security risk. Kill the prisoner, over." San Miguel listened to a short reply, and then replied, "Yes, that is what I said. *Kill him.* Do it quickly. Over and out." He handed back the walkie-talkie to his companion.

"I'm sorry for the interruption," the shorter man said, placing the walkie-talkie back into its holster. "Sometimes I wonder about the common sense of some of my men."

"Don't worry. I know your men are professionals. They've shown it several times today already."

"We will not fail you," the shorter man assured his counterpart.

"You did a fine job at the police station," the taller man said. "But we now need a repeat performance. This is the defining moment of this revolution. This will determine if we fail or win."

Negron gasped and he began to fumble with his shirt buttons, trying to reach the gun under his shirt. Realizing what he was about to do, Michelle grabbed his wrist and placed her other hand over his mouth, shushing him gently, and in the process, losing track of part of the conversation.

"...You have nothing to regret. You did what you had to do," the taller man was saying in response to something his companion had said a moment before. "Sometimes, the greater good requires us to do things that we do not like to do, and I completely understand how you feel. I admire and respect you for it, in fact. I would not like to be associated with anyone who kills for the pleasure of it." The taller man paused. "But," he said, raising his right hand and wagging gently a finger at his shorter counterpart, "you must not let your emotions get in the way. When the attack comes, you must crush it completely, so that they will not think of doing it again."

"Yes, yes, of course. I understand," the shorter man answered. "Our men are ready, and I will lead them personally. None of the attackers will reach this side of the lagoon."

The tall man extended his hand to his companion and shook it warmly.

"May God be with you," he told him.

"May God be with us all," the shorter man said in reply, and began to walk away towards one of the corridors that connected to the surrounding apartment buildings.

"Oh, and Calderon!" the taller man shouted suddenly after him. "In case anything happens and we can't talk in the next few hours, remember that you and your men must withdraw from the hotel and meet us at the rendezvous point before midnight tonight."

The man addressed as "Calderon" paused for a fraction of a second, as if considering asking the taller man a question, but then seemed to think the better of it and said, "Yes, of course," renewing his trek into the corridor.

Michelle continued to hold on to Negron's wrist, fearing the young policeman would rush after the killer of his fellow officers. Even in the dusty semidarkness of the room, she could see him struggle with his instincts, tears of anger running down his cheeks.

As the footsteps receded, Michelle slowly stood up and leaned against the heavy cement bags. She felt stunned, and dazed, and scared. Ever since that morning, she had tried to imagine who could have been behind the destruction and carnage that she had witnessed, secretly hoping to interview them or expose them to her viewing audience. Now, only a few steps away, she had stared directly at the face of evil, and it had shaken her to the core. The men who had stopped in front of them had chatted about their plans to massacre the police rescue force in the same casual tone they would have used discussing the weather. They were monsters, let lose on the people of San Juan.

"We have to stop them," Negron said urgently, still kneeling on the floor. "I'll go after the one that went that way," he said to Archie, pointing at the corridor through which the shorter man had disappeared, "you go after the tall one."

Archie stirred from the spot he was hiding behind the bags, and pushed himself off the floor, brushing the gray construction dust off the knees of his pants. He stared wildly at the police rookie, not really seeing or listening to him but lost in his own thoughts, as if struggling to focus on what he was saying. Then his eyes regained their concentration, and he glared at his younger companion.

"Follow them? And if we get to them what?" he asked, barely able to keep the irritation out of his voice.

"Arrest them! Take them with us!" Negron answered as if stating the obvious. "Shoot them if we must!"

"We'll have to, because they won't come with us voluntarily."

"Then shoot the bastards, God damn it! They murdered dozens of cops, they destroyed the bridges, they...they are going to throw people off the roof of the Grand Laguna in a just few minutes! What's so wrong about killing them if we have to?" Negron said indignantly. "If you're too scared, I'll do it."

"You bet I'm scared!" said the redhead. "But you're crazy! What do you think will happen if we start shooting at them, eh? Do you think the others won't hear? Do you think they won't shoot back? We'll be dead in a matter of minutes! And what will we have accomplished?"

Negron shrugged, shaking his head in frustration. "We'll shoot them and run..." he said, pleading his case directly to Michelle. "We can—"

"You are such an idiot," Archie said, waving his hand dismissively in disgust. "Listen to me, you silly hillbilly. Colonel Calderon is a well-trained fighter who will hear you coming long before you see him, and who probably won't need any help from his friends because he will kill you first. Trying to stop him is like going in a kamikaze charge that will only help the terrorists."

For a fraction of a second Michelle stared at Archie with curiosity, but then her attention shifted to Negron. "Archie's right," she said to him in a less hostile but firm tone that permitted no further discussion. "They're gone anyway," she added, as she fumbled for the satellite phone she had pushed earlier into one of her jeans pockets. "We have to warn the Superintendent. If what those terrorists said is right, and a rescue attempt by the police is imminent, the only way to save them is to stop them from coming."

Michelle finished pulling out the stubby cell phone from her pocket, and pressed the power button on. She had turned off the satellite telephone to save the battery. The word "Radium" appeared on an otherwise bare screen, followed by the date and the time. She did not see the words "Searching for network..." and began dialing the number she had received from Doel. Almost immediately after she pressed the green "Send" button, the words "No connection to network," flashed on the screen.

She cursed in frustration, realizing that the phone could not work in an enclosed space. "We need to get into the open in order to contact Doel," she stated. "How are we doing on time?" she asked Archie.

"We have less than ten minutes," he said after looking at his watch.

"Then we have to run!"

Archie looked at her, and after a second's pause nodded. "There was an elevator door next to the stairs in the parking building. Maybe it will take us to the roof," he suggested.

Michelle walked out of the room without saying another word, heading back towards the pedestrian bridge. Archie followed her, limping noticeably. Negron continued to sit glumly on the floor for a moment, and then jumped up and followed also.

"You know one of those men," Michelle told Archie quietly, as they walked towards the elevator.

Archie stared at her in alarm and confusion, not understanding how she had come to that conclusion.

"You called one of them by his military title, just a moment ago. When you were arguing with Negron," she stated. "Colonel Calderon, you called him. How did you know he's a colonel? Did you know him from somewhere?"

For an awkward moment, Archie regarded her with a blank expression, as if desperately grasping for an answer. "I don't know for sure," he answered unconvincingly. "I may have heard his voice during the shootout in El Falansterio..."

They stopped as they crossed the pedestrian bridge and reentered the parking building. As Archie had indicated, there were two elevator doors next to the stairs' landing. Michelle pressed the "Up" button on the wall, all of the time watching his companion's face, unable to conceal her doubts about his explanation. "You overheard his rank during the shootout in El Falansterio?" she asked incredulously, but then shut up as Negron reached them.

"I'm sorry," the young policeman said. "I sometimes let my emotions carry me away."

"I'm sorry too," Archie said, managing a half smile. "I shouldn't have been so hard on you."

The elevator's door "pinged" open and the three friends quickly walked in. Michelle considered pursuing her question, but decided to do it later. She did not want to become involved in another argument at that moment. However, she felt uneasy about Archie's nervous evasiveness.

Negron hit the button to the uppermost floor, and they began to rise. The outer wall of the elevator was made of glass and, after clearing the second floor, the courtyard and the buildings beyond it immediately became visible. Then, as the elevator rose even higher, the rooftops of some of the lower buildings bordering the lagoon and the lagoon itself came into view.

Michelle could see as far as the Atlantic, its waves rolling to crash on the reefs that marked the beginning of the blue, still lagoon. It was a beautiful sight, but a somber one, showing the gaping hole on the Dos Hermanos Bridge that had connected Condado to San Juan, its twisted metal frame collapsed in the water, many of the cars caught in the explosion still clogging the access to the Condado peninsula.

"Look over there!" Negron said, pointing at a short concrete wall that rimmed the edge of the lagoon, close to the hotel. More than a dozen men, some of them holding automatic rifles, sat with their backs against it, not moving. They would not be visible from the buildings in the Condado area.

"And there!" said Archie, pointing to the roof of one of the condominiums closest to the lagoon. Behind a stairwell waited two men, holding on to what seemed to be a very long bazooka, apparently engaged in a friendly conversation. "There must be others that we can't see," the redhead added. He squinted, trying to make out what was the weapon the men were holding. "It looks like some sort anti-aircraft device," he murmured. "Wish I had some binoculars. Jesus! Those people have a lot of sophisticated weapons! If that is what I suspect it is...Well, let's just say that the police better not try to do anything from the air!"

The elevator door opened unto the rooftop level of the ten-story building. It looked completely empty.

"Let's make that call," said Michelle, stepping out.

CHAPTER XXXVIII

As a child, Lucas must have played in the dark, dungeon-like stairs that connected the jewelry store's cellar to the Metropolitan Center's residential area more than a hundred times. It was a spooky, windowless place that smelled of garbage and humidity, and therefore the perfect place to use as the evil monster's lair. On many occasions he and his childhood buddy Robert had heard strange noises—footsteps or muted voices—coming from above, and had shuddered with pleasure, anticipating the sudden appearance of strange, evil beings.

Even now, as he, his mother and aunts steadily climbed the stairway towards the apartment floors above *El Joyero*, he could not shake the creepy feeling of being watched, and would stop occasionally to listen for noises. But there were none, his childhood ghosts apparently content to watch them in silence.

Their progress had been slow. The Pietri sisters were not in their best physical shape—except for Evelyn, who supplemented her income by teaching ballet at night in her house—and Fannie suffered from severe arthritic pain in her right knee, so that every upward step required her to expend great effort.

There were two apartments per level, starting on the second floor. Don Jorge Pietri, founder of *El Joyero*, had lived in the fifth floor from the day that the building had been inaugurated, long before the jewelry store had opened. During the early days, he had operated from a small office in his apartment, where he received his clients strictly by appointment. Later, when the business increased, he had taken over the commercial establishment below. After his death, the Pietri sisters had sold the apartment, much to Lucas' regret. It had been an ample dwelling, with tall ceilings and four enormous rooms, the type of apartment that was no longer constructed in Puerto Rico. It would have been perfect for Lucas and his family.

It took them nearly twenty minutes to get to the fifth floor. When they reached it, Lucas went not to the door that had belonged to his grandfather, but to the one on the opposite side. He waited for his mother and aunts to catch up with him, raised the brass doorknocker on the door, and knocked sharply three times. They waited, the three Pietri sisters staring expectantly at the door. When nothing happened, Lucas knocked again. This time, a muted female voice answered.

"I'm coming, I'm coming!" it said, sounding grouchy. Then, closer to the door, the woman asked, "Who is it?"

Fannie answered, "Francesca, it's me! Can you open the door?"

"Fannie? Fannie Pietri?" the woman asked in a more friendly tone, recognizing the voice.

"Yes! I'm here with Evelyn, and Maria, and Lucas. You remember Lucas, don't you?"

"Of course she remembers Lucas," Maria whispered. "It's not as if she hasn't seen him for years!"

Fannie shushed her.

"Hold on," Francesca said. There was a pause, then the rattle of chains—three in total—as she began to unlock her door. The chains gave way to the more solid "click" of a double metal lock, and then the door opened a crack, still hampered by another chain.

"Fannie!" the female voice said with delight. The door shut momentarily, and then a woman in her mid-seventies opened the door, holding in her left arm a shotgun that apparently she had been carrying all along. She leaned the weapon against the door's frame and embraced Lucas' mother.

Francesca was a tall woman even in her elder years, only about two inches shorter than Lucas. She was wearing a light, sky-blue robe and pink, fuzzy slippers, her brown hair bunched up over her head in a tall bun riddled with bobby pins. She had gained some weight with age, but her robust body still kept the curves that in her younger years had driven men crazy.

Lucas had known her since he had had use of reason. She was an optometrist, who kept her office in her apartment, and who—like Lucas' grandfather—attended to her clients on an appointment basis. Not surprisingly, she had been the family optometrist and Lucas' optometrist until he had joined the army. When he and his sister Vanessa were very young, she had owned a female Chihuahua named Chiquita that had terrorized them, barking non-stop every time she saw them, and making them climb on any nearby furniture whenever Francesca did not lock her dog in an adjacent room.

Francesca had been a beautiful woman who had never married, but whose romantic life had been the subject of numerous conversations over the dinner table between the women of the family. Despite a purely rumored promiscuous past, and even some fleeting rumors about her and Don Jorge Pietri, the family had always considered her a friend.

"Lucas!" she said fondly, kissing him on the cheek after greeting the sisters and ushering all of them into her apartment. "I haven't seen you for ages!"

Francesca closed the door and began to slide the security chains back into their slots. "You can't be too careful, with all of these hoodlums running lose around San Juan." She pointed to her living room TV, still a large, box-like television set that must have been at least twenty-five years old. "Have you seen everything that's happening? Any time soon, those bastards are going to start throwing people off the roof of the Grand Laguna! Barbarians, that's what they are!"

"They killed our guard, Antonio," Evelyn informed her quietly.

Francesca stopped talking and looked at the sisters in shock. "Antonio?" she asked with disbelief. "That quiet, lovely man who wouldn't hurt a fly? Why? I'm so sorry!"

"They tried to rob *El Joyero*," Maria explained. "He tried to stop them, and they shot him."

"We were locked up in the cellar," Evelyn said, "so that we wouldn't tell anybody."

"They captured Alfredo," Maria said at the same time.

"They have him in La Fortaleza!"

"We don't know anything about him!"

Francesca listened wordlessly, trying to make sense of the barrage of breathless information fired at her.

"Please!" Fannie cut in. "We're not making any sense."

"Alfredo...Your grandson?" Francesca asked uncertainly.

"He was spending the night with the Governor's son," Fannie said, nodding, and Francesca's eyes filled immediately with dread.

The optometrist crossed herself. "God help us!" she said, and then, looking at her visitors, she added, "But you must be exhausted. I'm making some coffee. Sit, please, sit." She motioned with her hand towards the overstuffed sofa and chairs in her living room.

Lucas looked at her with embarrassment. "I'm sorry to impose on you in this way, but I need to leave them someplace where they're safe while I go to La Fortaleza to get Alfredo. I'm going to ask the revolutionaries to return him to me."

Francesca took so much time to answer that he thought that she would say no.

"He's crazy," Maria interjected. "Talk some sense into him!"

Francesca turned her eyes on Lucas. He could still see in them a reflection of the beautiful woman that had caused so much gossip decades before.

"No," she said, finally understanding. "I've been listening to the news. These people are dangerous. They won't give up without a fight. Lucas is right in trying to get Alfredo out of La Fortaleza before any of the fighting starts there."

Maria looked mortified, but said nothing.

Loud noises, a mixture of car horns, the revving of motorcycle engines, and excited shouting suddenly rose from the plaza below. Francesca and her visitors walked into her office, and carefully peeked through its two windows. Preceded by two motorcycles, three trucks of various shapes and makes had entered from Calle San Francisco, the street that encircled Plaza de Armas, and stopped in front of the City Hall. They carried between them more than two-dozen men and women— mostly students by their appearance—waving Puerto Rican flags, and here and there brandishing different types of weapons.

The jubilant revolutionaries began to stream out of the vehicles and their back cargo holds. They were in a festive mood, shouting anti-American slogans ("Con nosotros no se juega, to's los Yanquis van pa'fuera!" "You don't fool around with us, all the Yankees have to go!"), laughing, and exchanging friendly insults. One of the vehicles began to boom salsa music through a massive speaker system, and two women began to dance with each other in the middle of the square.

Two of the men from the leading truck headed directly towards "La Sandwichera", a small cafeteria located next to the city hall, and began kicking its padlocked door. When they failed to break it down, a third student took out a crowbar from the pickup truck's tool box and wedged it between the restaurant's door and its frame. The three men pulled and the doorframe splintered unexpectedly, causing them to fall on top of each other, to the intense merriment of others who were watching. A cheer broke out as the door was flung open and half a dozen men rushed inside. Moments later they emerged carrying scores of paper-wrapped loaves of "pan de agua" and "pan sobao", as well containers full of cheese and sliced ham and pork used to prepare some of the sandwiches sold by the cafeteria.

The greatest cheer, however, was reserved for the man who exited "La Sandwichera" holding up four six-packs of beer in his upraised hands, and began to pitch cans to those around him.

"The looting has started," Francesca said with calm dismay.

"Punks!" whispered Maria, next to her.

The mood got rowdier as a fourth truck noisily made its entrance into the square, and more alcohol was carried out of the cafeteria. Two male residents foolishly tried to walk through the square, trying to remain anonymous in the crowd, but were easily identified because they wore no armbands. They were detained and questioned by some of the more zealous revolutionaries, then jostled and harassed, and finally forced to seat on the floor in the center of the square with their hands on their heads, apparently placed under arrest.

Lucas shook his head. "I have to go," he said to no one in particular.

Francesca cast him a sideways glance. "From the looks of it, if you walk out of this building now, those idiots down there won't let you go very far. I would wait a while, to see if they leave."

Evelyn and Maria echoed their approval.

"And the people who killed Antonio might be down there," Fannie added. "If they recognize you—"

Somebody with a gun fired a shot into the air, startling the others and provoking a new bout of laughter and shouted obscenities.

"I'll have to risk it," Lucas replied. "I can't wait any longer."

He stared at the revelers below, to see if he recognized any of their faces, but could not distinguish their features from that distance. He knew that sooner or later he would have to engage in a dialogue with the revolutionaries, but he worried that he would not get very far with the crowd below. If he could get to La Fortaleza, his chances of being heard by somebody who was actually in charge would increase significantly.

"I can try to use the stairway at the back of the building, the one that comes out to Fortaleza Street, right?"

"Yes," Francesca answered, "but that's located in the commercial section of the Metropolitan Building, and it's not connected to the apartment area."

Lucas considered the problem briefly. "I could always go to the roof. There's a wall separating this area from the commercial section, but it shouldn't be too hard to get over it, and walk to the other stairway."

"If the door is not locked from the outside?...I suppose so," Francesca responded. "But you know about the administration of this building. It's run by that dragon lady, what's her name...Alfonsina! And she locks everything...except her foul mouth."

"Well, it's worth a try," Lucas said. "If I can't get to the stairs, the only thing I'll lose is time, the same time I'm going to lose waiting for those people down there to move out from the square."

He walked back to the living room, followed by all of the ladies. Francesca walked to the apartment's door, and placing a finger on her lips, listened for noises outside. After a pause, she removed some of the security chains, opened the door a crack, and looked at the corridor.

"It's free and clear," she whispered, and began unfastening the last of her numerous anti-theft devices.

Feeling miserable, Lucas decided to make his farewells as brief as possible. He embraced his aunt Evelyn, who patted him on the back and said to him gently, "Don't worry! These people are after the Governor. This is all a conspiracy to stop statehood from happening, and everybody knows you're not a *statehooder*. They won't harm you or Alfredo."

Maria clung to him with tears in her eyes. When she separated, she frowned at him and muttered, wiping her eyes, "If you do anything stupid, it won't be the terrorists that will kill you!"

He turned to his mother last, and kissed her. "It's okay, mom. Don't worry!" he said, grabbing her by the hands. She nodded, unable to speak, her eyes reflecting the intense pain and terror that she felt in letting him go. "Take care of the others. I love you," he told her.

Fannie breathed in deeply to gather her strength. "I love you too," she answered with an unsteady voice and, with the tip of her fingers, made the sign of the cross on his forehead, as she had done every day since he was a child when she put him to sleep. "May God keep and bless you," she said.

"Amen!" Francesca concluded forcefully. "You must visit me for a longer spell than this, when this is over," she said brightly.

Lucas nodded and pecked her cheek. "You will take care of these ladies?"

"We'll have a pajama party while you're gone. I have an unopened bottle of Johnny Walker, green label, that I have been saving for a special occasion. I know Maria is an alcoholic, and Fannie can drink the rest of us under the table." She stared at Evelyn with exaggerated pity. "I guess I can get some juice for her..."

"I can drink too!" Evelyn protested indignantly.

Lucas smiled, trying not to look at his mother, knowing that if he did it would break his heart.

"Don't get too rowdy. You don't want to attract the attention of the people below!" he said.

Francesca grabbed the shotgun that was still leaning against the doorframe by its barrel and looked at Lucas with a glint of mischief. "If any of those morons tries to get through this door, he'll come through with a large piece of him missing!"

Lucas stepped into the outside corridor, and waited for the door to close. He listened, as Francesca began to fasten her various chains and locks, and then began to run up the stairs, two steps at a time. He reached the end of the stairway and the rooftop door in a couple of minutes, and pushed the door open, heaving against the strong breeze outside. The door slammed shut as soon as he stepped out and let it go.

Apart from the structure housing the stairs and a few rusted television antennas, the roof was bare of any furniture or mechanical equipment. It was a glorious, cloudless day, the type that urged people to stay outside. Had it not been for the heavy gusts of wind sweeping intermittently over the building, he could have had a picnic in the shadow of the stairwell.

A tall wall, about eight feet high, divided the western half of the building from its commercial counterpart. Lucas would have to climb over it to get to the other side and reach the stairway that went down to Fortaleza Street. He had not attempted to climb that kind of an obstacle since his Ranger days, and hoped he could still manage to do it.

Withdrawing several yards, he ran towards the wall and jumped, placing one foot on its smooth surface and trying to grab its upper edge, but missed and toppled backwards, nearly falling flat on his ass.

"Shit!" he whispered.

He paused to catch his breath, searching the wall to find any cracks that he could use to his advantage. A five-foot concrete fence enclosed the other edges of the building. Had any of the lower fences been directly connected to the eight-foot central wall, he could have climbed onto them, and from there jumped over the taller wall to the other side. However, streams of razor sharp barbed wire, partially embedded into the concrete, made it impossible for anyone to reach the central dividing wall from its lower counterparts. Lucas had no alternative but to jump for it, or go back to Francesca's apartment and get a ladder or something from which he could climb. Having just said goodbye, he dreaded the latter alternative.

Separating himself from the median wall, Lucas sprinted for a second time towards it and hit it at a slight angle, trying to push himself up with his right foot. This time, he caught the upper edge with his fingertips and held on to it. Flexing both of his arms with every ounce of strength left in his body, he slowly pulled himself up until his chin cleared the edge. Then, breathing in deeply, he swung his right forearm over the wall and wedged it over the top, between his ribs and his shoulder. He followed with his right leg, resting his entire body on the edge.

"I'm so out of shape..." he said softly, panting for breath.

Allowing himself a few seconds to recover, he let his body swing down to the other side, landing hard on his feet.

"Hey! Hey! Hey!!" somebody behind him suddenly shouted, startling him out of his wits. "Where do you think you're going?"

Lucas began to turn, but the stranger screamed, "Stay where you are or I will shoot you!"

Lucas stopped and raised his hands in the air, even before he was instructed to do so.

"Hands behind your neck, and don't move!"

Lucas did as he was told, staring at the smooth face of the dividing wall. He had detected a slight foreign accent in the man's way of speech, but he could not quite place its origin.

"Cangiano! Search him for weapons," the stranger said.

Lucas heard footsteps approach him, and then he was pushed forward.

"Lean against the wall, arms and legs open," a second, younger voice said calmly.

Again, Lucas did as ordered. However, he shifted his feet slightly to be closer to the wall, so that he was hardly leaning against it. The man behind him frisked him with professional efficiency.

"He's clean," he said.

Lucas sighed. He felt stupid, for failing to check if there was anybody on the commercial side of the rooftop before jumping down from the wall. It was an obvious and careless mistake.

"Who are you? What are you doing here?" the man with the gun asked, his voice sounding closer as he talked.

Lucas tried to turn his head to speak face to face with the stranger, but the man stopped him.

"Ah, ah, ah! Stay as you are please."

Something hard pressed the Puerto Rican's spine.

"This is to let you know that the gun is real," the man said, so close to him that he could hear him breathing. "Now speak. Who are you?"

"My name is Lucas Alfaro."

"What were you doing when you fell out of the sky?"

Cangiano snickered at his friend's joke.

"Who are you hiding from, ah?"

"I was trying to get to the stairs on this side of the building to get down to the street," Lucas answered. He had considered his options, and decided that his best chance of success would be to tell the truth and convince the two men to help him. Therefore, he tried to sound as composed and rational as he could.

"What, there are no stairs on your side of the building?" the gunman asked in a mocking tone.

"Not leading to the back of the building," Lucas confessed, and swallowing hard added, "I was trying to avoid the crowd in the plaza."

"Why? Are they looking for you? What did you do to them?"

"Nothing. I've done nothing to them," he answered. Lucas noticed Cangiano as the latter came into his peripheral field of vision, standing a few feet away to the right. He immediately recognized him as one of the black-clad men he had mistaken for musicians in the Doña Fela parking building the night before. About Lucas' height, clean-shaven and closely shorn hair, Cangiano was listening silently to the conversation, which probably meant he was the other man's subordinate.

"Then why are you trying to avoid them?" the man with the gun asked.

"Have you seen them? They stop everybody who is not wearing an armband, beat them up, and arrest them."

There was a pause, and Lucas saw Cangiano glancing involuntarily at his own armband.

"Anyone wandering around should be detained," the man behind Lucas said. "They have no reason to be taking walks in San Juan in the middle of a revolution. Or jumping over walls on roofs of buildings."

"I'm sorry, I didn't mean to startle you. I just need to get to La Fortaleza as quickly as I can," he said, knowing that would definitely capture the attention of the two men.

"La Fortaleza?" the gunman tried to sound mildly amused, but could not conceal his curiosity. "This gets more interesting by the second. Go on."

"My son stayed overnight in La Fortaleza." Lucas lied about his relationship with Alfredo, to make it more personal. "He's a classmate of the Governor's son. When they captured the Governor this morning, they also captured him along with the others. He's eight years old, just a small boy, and he must be terrified. He has no value whatsoever for the revolutionaries. I am going to La Fortaleza to see if they are willing to give him back to me."

The gunman considered Lucas explanation in stony silence.

"Surely, if you have any children, you must understand how desperate I am," Lucas pressed on. "If anything happens to my son, I'll...I'll...I'll go mad! I need to talk to someone in authority who can help me!"

"Be quiet!" the gunman ordered, as if trying to think. It was evident that Lucas had struck a cord. "What are we going to do with you?" he asked, more to himself than to his prisoner. "We can't just let you go. For all I know, you may be a spy, working for the Americans, and your story is a lie—"

"It is not a lie," Lucas interrupted. "Call La Fortaleza. Ask if there is a boy there called Alfredo, eight years old."

"I can't call La Fortaleza, and you probably know that," the gunman replied. The man paused, as if pondering what he should do. "Cangiano," he said to his companion, "do we have anything we can use to tie him up while we resolve this matter?"

"Negative, corporal," Cangiano answered.

The gunman cursed.

"Can't you contact anyone who *can* reach La Fortaleza?" Lucas urged, his hopes buoyed by the corporal's hesitation.

"I told you not to talk to me," the "corporal" said, prodding the tip of his gun into Lucas' back.

"Maybe we should call the Colonel," Cangiano suggested.

"Shut up and let me think!" The reference to a military rank raised all sorts of questions in Lucas' mind, and would be valuable information that he could later pass on to the police. On the other hand, the fact that military personnel seemed to be involved raised his hopes that there would be somebody in control that would act more rationally and less impulsively than the students roaming the streets. It was evident that the "corporal" did not want to bother the "colonel". On the other hand, he seemed at a loss about what to do. "All right," he conceded grudgingly, "call Colonel Calderon on the radio."

Lucas saw Cangiano walk away and heard him rummage through something. Then the soldier began to say, "Alpha One, Alpha One, this is Alpha Seven, over!" as he walked back to where Lucas and the corporal were standing. He was holding a walkie talkie.

A few seconds later the radio crackled into life.

"This is Alpha One, over!"

The corporal snapped his fingers, apparently signaling Cangiano to hand him the radio. He did not let up the pressure of his gun on Lucas' back.

"Alpha One, this is Corporal Lopez. We have caught a man who jumped into the roof. He says that his son is part of the hostages in La Fortaleza. He...he says...he wants to go to La Fortaleza to ask for the release of his son. We don't know what to do with him. We have nothing with which to tie him up, and we can't keep a constant watch on him. We need instructions, over."

"Why are you bothering me with this?" the radio replied.

"I'm sorry, sir," Corporal Lopez did not even wait for the word 'over'. I thought that since you were in the Plaza de Armas, you could send somebody to—"

"I'm not in the Plaza de Armas, and I'm pretty busy right now!" the colonel interrupted.

Lucas felt his hopes evaporate. He had hoped that the corporal would help him get Alfredo back, but from what he could gather from the conversation, all that Corporal Lopez was interested in was to find a way to get rid of him. He was a hindrance to the two men on the rooftop, a bothersome distraction for which they had no solution. And now their commander, the only person who apparently had the authority to help Lucas, seemed about to wash his hands off him because he was "too busy".

He could not afford to be detained. Every second of delay increased the risk that his godson would be hurt.

Lucas tried to gather his wits, knowing that the next few minutes would be critical for his survival. After the colonel finished talking to his two captors, Lucas would somehow have to convince them that it was to their best advantage to let him go. He would explain that he had no particular interest in the outcome of their revolution, and that he was indifferent to the fate of the Governor—which he wasn't, except that he cared more about the fate of Alfredo. It would be very distracting for the two terrorists, he would argue, to keep him under constant watch, and much simpler to allow him to leave. There would be no threat to their security, since he had no means to talk to any of the government authorities. Also, he would remind them, by walking voluntarily into La Fortaleza, he would become a prisoner of the much larger garrison there—*it had to be larger, he guessed*—if the Governor's guardians determined that he was a security risk.

All of these arguments he marshaled in a fraction of a second, as he waited for the radio dialogue to end. But then the walkie-talkie came back to life, and a new voice spoke, shattering his plans.

"This is San Miguel," the new voice said. *"You can't be distracted from your mission. Kill the prisoner, over."*

For Lucas, the time after those words were spoken passed in excruciatingly slow motion, as his brain went into overdrive. He heard the corporal take in a sharp breath, and felt the muzzle of the gun slide down slightly to the middle of his back, as if his captor's hand had shaken involuntarily. Simultaneously, another portion of Lucas' consciousness recognized the voice that had just spoken through the radio, and automatically tried to place a face on it.

"Excuse me sir?" the corporal asked uncertainly, as if disbelieving the order. "Did you say kill him? Over."

"Yes, that is what I said," the stranger answered, his words striking Lucas like actual, physical blows. *"Do it quickly. Over and out."*

During the Ranger days, Lucas' combat instructor had pounded into his head the need to act on the moment, to practice his combat moves until they became second nature, automatic responses integrated into his mind and body like the very act of breathing. *"You're dead!"* he would scream into Lucas' ears when he failed to react on time. *"Your survival depended on a small window of opportunity and you blew it!"* he would drone on and on, as he made Lucas repeat each move. *"One critical split second before your enemy decides to act! That's the difference between a dead and a live Ranger!"*

Lucas had practiced, and practiced, and practiced again, until he could react without thinking, until his conditioning made his body move faster than his thoughts.

Now, the impatient orders crackling through the walkie-talkie triggered his long suppressed instincts. In the heartbeat that followed the last of the radioed words and the corporal's response, Lucas righted himself and pivoted his body, moving his right foot sideways and stepping out of the extended gun's line of fire. Before the distracted corporal could react, he grabbed the gun's barrel and twisted it down and back sharply, away from him and towards the foreigner. He heard the corporal take a quick intake of breath, and felt the hold on the gun slacken, as the terrorist released the weapon to ease the pain in his fingers.

It was the natural reaction that Lucas had been trained to expect, and he took full advantage of it, snatching the weapon away, and instantly swinging it sideways. The gun's handle smacked into his foe's exposed left temple, causing the man to grunt and drop to his knees. As the corporal tried to regain his bearings, Lucas whipped him twice more with the pistol's grip. He felt something wet and warm sprinkle his hand—whether blood or spit he could not tell—and saw the foreigner pitch forward holding his face.

It all happened in less than two seconds, and Lucas did not wait to see the man hit the ground, focusing instead on his next threat. Cangiano had watched with horrified surprise the quick exchange of blows, and realizing that it was too late to help his companion, decided to charge the Puerto Rican intruder before he could use the captured weapon on him.

He tackled Lucas as he was trying to grip the gun to fire it, knocking it off his hands and toppling with him to the ground. The gun clattered over the roof's surface, coming to a stop several yards away. Lucas bore the brunt of the fall as Cangiano landed on his stomach, driving the air out of him. As the Puerto Rican struggled to breathe, Cangiano sat on his waist and squeezed his hands around his neck, shutting off his source of oxygen with his thumbs. Choking, Lucas panicked and tried to tear his assailant's hands from his throat, but the young terrorist was too strong and pressed harder. Then Lucas' training took over, and he viciously jabbed his enemy's windpipe with the edge of his bent fingers, causing him to gag and momentarily sit back, releasing Lucas' neck.

Knowing he had only seconds before the terrorist recovered, Lucas raised his two legs and wrapped them around Cangiano's head, dragging him down sideways and causing him to crash to the ground. Then, bringing back up his right knee, he aimed his heel at the soldier's face. He struck him on the mouth and chin and his head snapped back with a sickening crunch. Cangiano went limp immediately, his hands falling to his sides.

Lucas lay on the hot surface of the roof, coughing violently and straining so hard to breathe that his stomach muscles hurt. With the corner of his eye, he caught a glimpse of a shadowy figure moving in his direction, and he instinctively raised both of his arms to protect his head like a boxer, just in time to deflect a kick from Corporal Lopez's iron tipped boot. He felt a sharp pain explode in his right forearm and shoulder as they absorbed the force of the blow, hearing the corporal grunt as he struck him.

Lopez tried to kick him again, but Lucas rolled away, making him miss. Roaring with frustration, the corporal pressed forward and tried to kick him again, but Lucas kept rolling out of his reach, increasingly enraging his assailant. After his third miss, the corporal switched tactics and hurried forward, raising his leg to stomp his fallen foe on the face. But this time, Lucas surprised him, rolling towards him and causing him to trip. Lopez stumbled over his body and staggered several steps forward, trying to regain his balance. It gave Lucas enough time to stand up and raise his fists in a defensive position, his right arm still throbbing from the kick it had received.

The two men eyed each other warily, standing sideways in the classic combat stance. Lucas was still breathing hard, not fully recovered from Cangiano's chokehold. The corporal had a nasty welt on his left forehead, and his left eye had begun to swell, forcing him to expose the right side of his body to Lucas, rather than his left, in order to be able to see better. It was an awkward pose for him, Lucas realized, one that would hamper the terrorist's ability to fight. The two fighters slowly moved in a circle, searching for openings in each other's defenses.

"Military training," the man grudgingly observed.

Lucas nodded. "You too," he replied.

"You killed Cangiano," the corporal stated angrily.

He was trying to kill me, Lucas thought, but said nothing.

"You fight well," the terrorist acknowledged without any bitterness. "It's a shame that I have to kill you."

"We don't have to fight," Lucas replied without any real hope. He saw the gun he had lost—he recognized it as a SIG Sauer semi-automatic—lying on the shiny waterproofing coating of the roof, a scant three yards behind his enemy. Lopez watched him with interest, and began to bounce on the balls of his feet, boxer-style. Lucas mirrored his enemy's movements, moving to his right, trying to get closer to the weapon.

"But we do have to fight," the corporal replied, reducing the distance between them. "I can't let you go, I have my *orders!*"

With his last word, he attacked with a lighting quick kick to Lucas' head. Lucas barely avoided it, stepping to one side, then ducking as the corporal followed with a second, roundhouse kick that grazed his cheek. Lucas countered immediately, aiming a short kick at the corporal's right leg that would have shattered his knee, but the corporal moved back quickly and withdrew, bouncing again on the balls his feet.

Lucas did not wait to press the attack. He feinted a jab with his right arm, which his opponent blocked immediately, but which allowed Lucas to move in and hit the corporal on his left cheek with a short punch. The corporal tried to retaliate by swinging his right fist towards the Puerto

Rican's face, but Lucas' upraised arms and close proximity caused his enemy's blow to land harmlessly on his forearm.

Almost simultaneously, Lucas swung his right fist at the corporal's face. It grazed his nose and upper lip, but otherwise missed his face entirely. However, Lucas immediately swept his arm back in the opposite direction, and with the terrible force of a hammer caught Lopez's right temple with his elbow.

The corporal reeled backwards, his vision blurred, swinging wildly as he struggled to remain conscious. Lucas attacked again, landing two quick punches on the chest and one on the stomach, each punctuated by sharp intakes of breath from Lopez as the blows landed on him. The corporal lurched forward, and desperately latched onto his opponent's waist, much like a boxer trying to avoid a knockdown. Lucas tried to hit his face with his knee, but the corporal held on for dear life, pushing Lucas with his body and keeping him off balance.

For several seconds both men remained locked in a grotesque dance, stumbling in different directions. Then suddenly, the corporal released Lucas and ran away. It took Lucas completely by surprise. He had never expected Lopez to flee. Then he saw where the man was heading and understood, a second too late, what the corporal intended to do.

He was running towards his gun. Somehow, he had seen it during the fight, and he now made a frantic dash to retrieve it. Lucas sprinted after him but knew he had no chance of reaching the weapon first.

As Lopez rushed forward, he took a quick glance over his shoulder to get a fix on his adversary's position, and seemed to momentarily lose track of the weapon. Then he found it, turned, and fired.

Lucas had seen the terrorist look back and instantly guessed his intentions. He shifted slightly to his left, losing a fraction of a second, but hoping that Lopez would initially aim in the direction where he had last caught a glimpse of him. He saw the corporal briefly fumble for the gun, and dove at him as he turned to fire.

He was so close to the corporal when the shot went off that he saw the flame shoot out of the gun's barrel, its deafening, point-blank detonation shrouding the rest of the sounds around him. He braced for the impact of the bullet but none came, and caught a glance of the surprised terrorist's face just before he rammed into him.

He had aimed for the corporal's waist, but barely made it to his knees. Firing a second wild shot into the air, the terrorist fell backwards and landed flat on his back. Lucas landed on him and immediately reached for the hand holding the gun, and for a terrifying moment could not find it. But as Lopez aimed it at his head, Lucas grabbed hold of the gun's barrel, and for the second time twisted it backwards and out of the corporal's hand.

Lucas saw his enemy move his mouth as if venting his frustration, but his ears still rang from the blast of the last shot. Lopez hit him on the back with his fists but his punches carried very little momentum from his awkward position, as he tried to wriggle free from the Puerto Rican's hold.

Lucas obliged, rolling away and rising to one knee. As he got back on his feet, he discovered that the corporal had managed to reach Cangiano, and was attempting to draw the gun out of the fallen terrorist's holster.

The words "Don't do it or I'll shoot you" formed in his mind as he aimed his ZIG Sauer with both of his hands directly at Lopez, but Lucas only managed to shout out the word "DON'T!"

The corporal paid him no heed, either not hearing the warning, or gambling on the likelihood that Lucas would hesitate to shoot him. But Lucas had locked him in his sight, and at that close range it was impossible for him to miss. He fired twice as the corporal began to turn in his direction.

One of the nine-millimeter bullets struck the corporal on the left shoulder, and the second squarely on the chest, causing him to topple forward over his left knee. He smashed his head on the floor, his hands unable to hold him, and lay there, his ass sticking upwards like an ostrich trying to hide his head in the sand.

Lucas stood up and approached him cautiously, still pointing his gun at him, his heart pounding violently. *Surely, the revelers in the plaza below must have heard the shots fired and would be rushing up the stairs at any moment,* he thought. He kicked the gun away from the prostrate terrorist, and when he did not stir, knelt and felt for a pulse.

He was dead.

Lucas walked quickly to the edge of the rooftop that faced Plaza de Armas, and carefully stared down at the square. The young revolutionaries that occupied it still went calmly about their business, showing no signs of alarm. A few were sleeping under the shade of the trees surrounding the plaza. Not knowing where the shots came from, they must have ignored them or thought that they had been fired by other groups celebrating their newly earned independence, Lucas thought.

He remained at the edge of the building for a couple of minutes, trying to ascertain that no one would try to investigate the rooftop detonations. Then he withdrew and approached the body of Cangiano. A cursory check of his pulse revealed that the man was still alive, to Lucas' great relief. Dry red blood masked most of his mouth and lower face, and his jaw seemed bent at a slightly odd angle—probably broken by his kick—but he was still breathing.

Lucas removed the strings from the soldier's boots, and used them to tightly bind his hands behind his back, as well as his ankles. Then he grabbed the foreigner under the armpits and pulled him to the shaded area under the stairwell's roof. He was certain that Cangiano would eventually break loose from his bonds, but by that time, Lucas would be long gone.

Feeling very tired, the ex Ranger sat down next to the unconscious soldier and leaned against one of the stairwell's walls to catch his breath. His hands were still shaking. During his army days, he would have shrugged off what had just happened and walked away from it to his next mission without much further consideration, if anything feeling exhilarated for a job well done. He had been younger then, brimming with self-confidence, feeling indestructible as most young people felt. He had been unburdened by the concerns that came from raising a family.

Everything was different now. He had a lot more to live for. The mere idea of never seeing Jeannie or the children again terrified him.

His thoughts raced in a hundred different directions. He had just killed a man and injured another severely. In his world, up to a few hours ago, that would have provoked serious civil repercussions. He could have been charged with murder or aggravated aggression, and even though it had been in self-defense, he would have been forced to go to trial and prove it.

But now they were in the middle of a revolution, where civil order and law enforcement had ceased to exist, where scores of policemen had in fact been massacred, where tourists were being executed. The world in which he lived had been turned on its head. When the revolution collapsed—and he was certain that it would—and the local authorities found the dead bodies on the rooftop with his fingerprints stamped all over the place, would the law go after him? Would he have to volunteer to the police what he had just done?

He tried to banish these thoughts from his head but could not. It was obvious that he had undertaken a task that was just too big for him to handle. The terrorists would not give up Alfredo voluntarily. Why should they? If the solution of the terrorist high command to his unintended intrusion in the rooftop had been to have him executed, how could he expect to walk into La Fortaleza and get his godson back? The revolutionaries were preoccupied with much larger stakes, and would consider him to be a hindrance, to be disposed of in the most expedient and less troublesome way.

His resolve began to falter, and he considered returning to the safety of Francesca's apartment, a few feet below. He had promised his sister Vanessa and his brother-in-law Michael that he would rescue Alfredo, but to pursue that course of action now would amount to committing suicide. They had to understand there was only so much that he could do. He had tried his best and failed.

Cangiano groaned and stirred slightly but did not regain his consciousness. Lucas stared at him with curiosity. The man did not fit his image of a Machetero, or of any kind of terrorist or *independentista* for that matter. His appearance, as well as that of the corporal, suggested a man in the military service. Well, that, and the fairly obvious fact that they had addressed each other and one of their superiors by military rank. *Duh,* as Alfredo would have said to him.

The image of his godson made him smile and helped him focus his thoughts. *That kid was something else. A one of a kind original.*

Lucas breathed in deeply. *There was no way he could abandon him to the terrorists,* he thought resignedly. Matters in La Fortaleza were bound to deteriorate as the day progressed. He had to get his eight year-old nephew out of there as quickly as he could.

But how? He had already discarded the open, let's-reason-this-thing-with-the-terrorists approach, after his recent experience with the two rooftop terrorists. And a Rambo-let's-kill-everybody-in-sight-and-get-Alfredo-out solution would only lead him and Alfredo to certain death. That left as the only alternative sneaking unnoticed into La Fortaleza, and somehow stealing Alfredo away from the terrorists. *Not a very viable alternative either.*

Lucas stood up and searched the area around the stairwell. Propped against the opposite side of the stairwell's door, he found two backpacks, an elongated bazooka-like weapon with a bulky trigger mechanism, and two green, metallic cases. A speedy search of the backpacks yielded several packets of MRE's (meals ready to eat), a bottle of 50 SPF suntan lotion, a dozen plastic bottles of water, and a box of 9mm caliber bullets. One of the backpacks also contained a basic first aid kit, adequate to deal with flesh wounds and other non-life threatening injuries. He could find no documents or personal objects that could shed some light on the provenance of the two men.

The elongated weapon—about six feet in length—and the two rectangular, metallic cases were another matter altogether. It only took Lucas a cursory glance to identify the strange bazooka-like instrument as a surface-to-air missile launcher, probably a Grinch or an SA-24 of Russian origin. Each metal case contained two missiles, each about a yard long, latched to the case by aluminum claws and padded with dark-gray foam. Cyrillic words engraved on the missiles confirmed his guess about the origin of the weapon and the ammunition.

Lucas whistled softly, immediately understanding the reason why the two terrorists had camped on the rooftop of the Metropolitan Center. Until that moment, he had thought that they were lookouts, posted on the tallest structure in San Juan in order to detect and warn their colleagues on the ground about any suspicious movements or any airborne approach. But this was a game changer. The two men he had fought were professional soldiers, trained to bring down any aircraft that wandered into Old San Juan's airspace.

Just who were those men? Lucas asked himself with alarm. *How did they get hold of those missiles?*

For a fleeting moment, he thought about turning the weapon against the terrorists. A ground-to-air missile could cause a lot of damage even against a stationary target. He was certain that the launcher contained a laser beam that could guide the missile to a target.

But just a quickly, he discarded the idea. He did not have a definite idea as to how to load and fire the weapon. And even if he figured it out, what would he do? *Punch a hole in La Fortaleza? And then what?* He could end up killing the Governor or worse, Alfredo.

Making up his mind, he grabbed the launcher and walked to the stairwell, stopping in front of one of its corners. He held the launcher by one of its ends, much like a baseball player holding a bat, and swung it with all his strength against the stairwell's concrete edge. The launcher bounced back violently, vibrating in his hands and almost causing him to lose his grasp on the weapon. He examined it and saw a small dent on its cannon-like barrel.

He tried a different approach, this time aiming his swing so that it would be the weapon's large trigger mechanism that would smash against the concrete edge. On his third try, the trigger shattered, turning the launcher into an unusable scrap of metal. Satisfied with the damage, he considered what to do with the cases, and decided to leave them there. Without anything to launch them, there was not much that the terrorists could do with the unused missiles.

Disabling the Grinch made him feel better. It gave him a sense of purpose, of fighting back against the terrorists that had kidnapped his godson. It helped him focus his thoughts.

Lucas snatched the box of bullets and returned to where he had left Cangiano. He unfastened the unconscious man's webbed belt, which held an empty holster and a pouch of ammunition, and removed it from his waist. The pouch contained three clips, each holding nine bullets. Placing the clips in one of his pockets, he then opened the ammunition box and poured the bullets into the ammunition pouch.

His eyes were drawn to the armband on the terrorist's sleeve that read in Spanish "Free Like the Coqui". He pulled on the black armband, and confirmed it was not sown to the sleeve.

"Libre como el Coqui."

Obviously, the armband was intended to identify Cangiano as a sympathizer of the uprising. But was that its only purpose?

Something about the two men on the rooftop did not fit the *independentista* profile. They did not seem to belong to the same category as the youths—probably FEPIstas—who had barged into *El Joyero* and shot Antonio. For one thing, their accent was not Puerto Rican. Colombian, maybe, or Venezuelan, but definitely not Puerto Rican. And that equipment! Sophisticated ground-to-air weaponry of Russian manufacture. He doubted that the radical faction in the independence movement—even with the participation of the Macheteros—was capable of obtaining that type of combat weaponry.

If the group that had captured Old San Juan was indeed run by the *independentistas*—and he harbored serious doubts about that—then it had secured the aid of outside elements, either mercenary forces or professional volunteers or both, to bolster its strength. Furthermore, the group would have to be formed by a significant number of men; a force of sufficient size and strength to be able to hold on to the small island of San Juan after its police force had been neutralized. And the odds would be that not all of the members of the group would know each other. Thus, the "Free Like the Coqui" armbands really served as a means of identification between the terrorists.

A crazy plan to get into La Fortaleza began to form in Lucas' mind. It was simplistic and incomplete, its details to be completed as the facts developed, but it was the best option that he had thought of so far. It would involve using the ground-to-air launcher after all, although not in the technical sense of the word.

He untied Cangiano's hands and feet and stripped him of his armband, jersey and jeans, re-binding his extremities afterwards. Then he changed into the removed clothes. It was a tight fit, Cangiano being leaner and slightly shorter than Lucas, but it would pass muster. Finally, he slipped the "Libre como el Coqui" armband over his left sleeve.

Taking a last look at Cangiano, he returned to the disabled launcher and picked it up, slipping its leather sling over his head and letting it rest diagonally over his left shoulder. Afterwards he grabbed hold of one of the two metal cases containing the surface-to-air missiles and, losing no more time, walked to the commercial area's back stairwell, located on the southeast corner of the roof. He was prepared to blast the door if it was locked, but it swung open with a simple push.

He paused, hesitating for the last time before embarking in what was surely a suicide mission. Then, as he stepped into the shadowy bowels of the stairs that would lead him down to Fortaleza Street, he made the sign of the cross and whispered, "God help me".

CHAPTER XXXIX

John McFadden dropped headfirst into the bay, striking the water's surface with much more force than he had anticipated. It had been years, decades actually—since his lifeguard job as a teenager—that he had dived from any significant height, and the length and speed of the jump surprised him, for a moment making him overcompensate and almost fall flat on his back. As it was, he plummeted into the blue-green water with his body tilting slightly backwards, hitting it so hard that it drove back his extended hands and stung his shoulders and the rear part of his legs like a thousand needles.

He plunged into the cool, murky water with the force of a torpedo, swiftly descending a dozen feet before his body began to slow down. The rushing sound of the wind while he fell stopped abruptly, substituted by the liquid, bubbly noises of the bay. As he regained his bearings, he looked upwards towards the surface, expecting the telltale linear white streaks of bullets entering the water that he had seen in a hundred different movies, but none came. Either the terrorists were waiting for him to emerge, or they did not care enough about him to shoot randomly into the water in the hopes of hitting him.

He could not see more than a few yards ahead of him, and for a panicky moment, was unable to decide which way to go. He heard his heart thumping in his chest, whether from the fright or from the effort of swimming underwater, he could not tell. It was essential that he headed in the right direction. If he emerged where the terrorists could see him, he would get shot. He had to get under the adjacent dock.

He quickly replayed the jump in his mind. He had dived from the end of the *Mardi Gras* and moved away from the stern of the ship. If he had maintained that direction, the dock would be somewhere to his right. He knew how easy it was to lose his bearings underwater, and that he could be heading away from his intended objective, but he had very little choice. He turned right, and began travel forward as fast as he could, thrusting himself forward with his arms in wide arcs, while simultaneously kicking with his legs.

Still, he found no signs of the dock. Soon his lungs began to beg for air. The shadowy figure of an elongated fish moving ahead of him paused for a moment—as if studying him—and then scurried away, quickly disappearing into the gloom beyond. The muted noise of the water flowing past his ears mingled with clicking sounds, periodic metallic clangs and a constant whirr, presumably coming from machinery on the dock or from the massive cruise ship somewhere above him. But still he could not locate any of them.

He began to despair, as his oxygen supply faltered. He had been swimming underwater now for almost a minute at a fair clip. He should have hit the docks long before that. Alarm bells began to ring inside his head as his body rebelled, and he struggled against his instinct to open his mouth and attempt to breathe. There was no choice but to surface and run the risk of getting shot. Otherwise, he would drown.

Just then, he noticed a dark area to his distant right. It was too large to be anything but the ship or the docks. *Could it be that he had been completely disoriented? That he had been swimming parallel to the docks, rather than towards them?*

With a supreme effort he veered to his right again, and frantically began to kick and paddle in that direction. Almost immediately, a column encrusted with barnacles appeared before him, so abruptly, in fact, that he almost smashed headfirst into it. He swam past it, and headed towards the surface. It seemed impossibly far away, and his desperate ascent frightfully slow. But then his head burst out of the water, and he breathed in the sweet, wonderful air that had been denied from him for so long. He did not even mind the mild smell of diesel and the slight stench of stagnant seawater that came with it.

He could not have planned for a better place to emerge. The dock's concrete underside extended to his left and right, supported every ten feet by wide, barnacle-covered piles, every so often a rusted rebar showing through the concrete. At its outer edge, the dock cleared the surface of the bay by a scarce six inches, highlighted by the bright sunshine streaming into the blue-green water from the outside. But under the dock, the separation between its bottom and the water's surface rose to nearly five feet, creating an enclosed, concave space where the sounds of the small waves lapping the piles were amplified a hundredfold.

It would be impossible for the terrorists to find him there, unless one of them jumped into the water and swam under the dock. He doubted that they would go through the trouble of doing that. All he had to do now was to move under the concrete cover as far away as he could from the *Mardi Gras,* and take advantage of any ladder or rope close to the water to climb out. He would still have to be very careful, since he suspected that there would be terrorists patrolling the streets of the city. But he knew Old San Juan fairly well, and even had some friends in San Justo Street that would provide him shelter until the whole affair blew over.

He should have felt elated, having escaped from the clutches of very dangerous terrorists, but he did not. His last image of the Countess, as she got dragged away by her captors, troubled him greatly. He could not banish her face from his mind, seeing her expression not so much of fear as of hurt and disillusionment because of his betrayal.

Well what had she expected, anyway? Did she really think that he would go back and try to free her from those professional killers? He had never been under any delusions of being a hero. He was a professional gigolo who was kind to older women and who enjoyed his work. His staying aboard would not have helped her in the least, and probably gotten him killed. The Countess would be all right. She would be taken with the rest of the hostages and kept there until she was rescued.

John began to swim slowly through the dock's underbelly, trying to disturb the water as little as possible to avoid the possibility that the ripples on the water would betray his progress. He wanted to get out of the bay as quickly as possible, not only because of the terrorists, but because he did not know what marine life lurked in the murky waters where he was swimming. That elongated fish that he had glimpsed underwater had seemed eerily similar to a barracuda.

He had done his best, he told himself. He had contacted the federal government. The rescue was now in the hands of the professionals, as it should be—Navy SEALs or the Delta Force or whatever they were using these days to rescue hostages, probably the same men who had killed Osama Bin Laden. He hoped that Ernan, the Filipino waiter to whom he had given his satellite phone, had gotten away...and that he had returned to his companions to convince them, including that moronic fellow countryman of his, Roy White, not to attempt a rescue by themselves.

The last thought weighed heavily on him, and he cursed himself for his overactive imagination. *But what if Ernan had been captured? Who would let the others know that help would be forthcoming? Those well-intentioned crewmen would probably be massacred, and cause the death of many of the hostages as well.*

Damn it!

John paused, floating on the water. After a few seconds he renewed his swimming, only to pause again.

Damn it!

There wasn't anything that he could really do. He was off the boat. Climbing back on it would be impossible. There had been a rope on the terrace from which he had jumped, part of a scaffolding that the crew used to paint and clean the outside hull of the ship. But it had not been tied to the railing, nor was it dangling from the ship's side. The only other ropes attached to the ship were the thick lines holding it next to the dock. But trying to climb into the ship using one of those lines, even assuming that he could get to them, would leave him in plain view of every terrorist on board the ship. They would use him as target practice.

For the third time, he continued to swim away. But with every stroke that he took, his sense of shame increased. He could not banish from his thoughts the Countess of Gilly. Why, he couldn't understand. *She was a client, for God's sake. A good client, but a client nevertheless.*

And a good friend.

He couldn't just leave her there. He had had no choice but to jump when the terrorists came. Anything else would have been stupid. But he could not abandon his friend without at least making a last attempt to get back on board.

With a sense of dread he turned back and began to paddle towards the *Mardi Gras.*

One last try.

He would look for a way to climb back into the ship. It would be impossible, of course, but his conscience would be salved.

Soon, he reached a point under the dock where the white hull of the cruiser could be seen directly across from the lower edge of the pier. He moved behind one of the piles closest to the edge, and ever so carefully pulled his head from under the dock and peered outside.

About five or six decks up he saw the main gangway, a long, enclosed structure of steel and plexiglas that zigzagged its way, going up diagonally, from the terminal to the ship. It was designed to hold scores of cruise ship passengers at the same time, and could only be boarded from the dock. Therefore, it would be impossible for him to get on it unless he went to the port's terminal building and passed through the admissions center.

But to his surprise, he discovered a smaller walkway that was connected to a small opening in the hull of the ship. A simple, uncovered gangway with handrails that leaned upwards at a gentle slope, connected from the edge of the pier to an entryway in the *Mardi Gras,* hovering about five or six feet above the surface of the bay. It was made of steel, designed to hold forklifts carrying cargo in and out of the ship. It was close to the prow of the ship.

John swam to the ramp and examined it. It was not being watched by anyone. As he neared it, his heart began to pound wildly. Right under the walkway, between the ship and the dock, was a huge, black, conically shaped rubber object. The black object was attached horizontally to the edge of the pier by a large chain that ran through a wide hole in its center, from one side to the other.

It was one of the dock's enormous rubber bumpers, designed to serve as a buffer between the hull of the visiting cruise ship and the concrete edge of the dock. The bumper must have been almost eight or nine feet long, and about four feet wide. From where John was looking, he could stretch his arm and grab the rim of the chain running through the bumper's hole.

He continued to float near the bumper, unable to make up his mind about what he should do. As far as he could see, the entrance to the ship was clear. There would be a critical moment when he would be partially exposed to view, as he climbed onto the bumper and from there to the ramp, but anyone looking from the ship would have to lean over the side to see him. It would get riskier when he got into the ship, since he would have to find his way back to the crew's cafeteria through a maze of corridors he did not know.

He shook his head, thinking how unlike him it would be to get back into the ship from which less than an a half hour before he had escaped, and still not believing it, grabbed the chain, first with his right hand and then with both. *What a dumb jackass he was,* he thought, pulling himself up and trying to place a foot on the bumper's hole. He missed the first time and his foot splashed back into the water, making more noise than he cared for. He hung on to the chain quietly, waiting for someone to investigate, and when nothing happened, tried again. This time he was successful, planting his right foot on the inner edge of the bumper's hole.

The inside of the large rubber cone was slimy and slippery, and he almost lost his footing, but then he placed his left foot in the hole and, with great difficulty, slid his right elbow over the chain. Slowly, he pulled himself forward, bracing his legs on the bumper, until he was crouching upright, his head level with the upper edge of the dock, the ramp to the ship less than a foot away. He saw no one either in the terminal or inside the ship's entrance, and holding on to the ramp with his left hand, stepped on top of the rubber bumper. He turned and stumbled onto the ramp, quickly scrambling into the ship's hold, where he hid behind some boxes.

Breathing hard from the effort—*after all, he was no longer a spring chicken*—he sat down and waited for his heart to settle down. He was dripping wet. He felt stupid and sentimental, two adjectives with which he had strived never to be associated.

Finally, he stood up. "Hold on, Countess," he said resignedly, "I'm coming."

The news about the terrorist takeover of Old San Juan and the terrorists' threat to execute the hostages had gone viral. All the major networks in the United States, as well as countless stations in Europe, South America, Australia, and Asia, had interrupted their regularly scheduled programs to broadcast the events unfolding around the Grand Laguna Hotel. By two o'clock in the afternoon, the whole world was watching.

Like in many other situations where terrorists had threatened the lives of hostages, the images being transmitted had quickly engaged mass media attention and speculation. The spiraling tower of the hotel, relatively unknown outside of Puerto Rico, suddenly became a familiar sight to hundreds of millions of viewers. Scores of pundits, both from the left and the right, conjectured about the origins of the terrorists, ranging from Al-Qaeda to the Macheteros to North Korea, and blamed the present or former American administrations for their lack of vigilance, tolerance, and efficiency.

As the terrorists' deadline approached, many long-distance cameras began to focus on the helipad of the Grand Laguna, its boxy structure distorted by the heat shimmering from the rooftop. It was used as background or placed in a small box in the television screen, while news anchors and commentators discussed what was about to happen.

Superintendent Maldonado had ordered a blackout of the transmissions, knowing that the terrorists would be watching the movement of the rescuers through the television, and had managed, for exactly six minutes, to take the image of the Grand Laguna Hotel and the Condado Lagoon off the air. But at eight minutes to two, the Interim Governor of Puerto Rico had countermanded his order, contacting the Superintendent through a direct, private feed of one of the affected networks, and then appearing in a public broadcast to assure the world that Puerto Rico, contrary to other regimes of the world, would not interfere with the right of its citizens or of the rest of the world to know what was happening.

Maldonado had gone into a wild rage. In a private telephone conversation, he had threatened Rovira Melendez to go to the Elections Board Building, where Rovira had set up his headquarters, and "personally beat the living crap out of him" if anything happened to any of his men because of his meddling. Rovira Melendez had laughed, further infuriating the Superintendent. By four minutes to two, the helipad had returned to the screens of the world media.

Many of the cameras had focused their attention on the blue, metallic door located on one of the walls of the structure that held up the landing strip. By necessity, anybody stepping onto the rooftop would have to come out of there. The door conveniently faced all of the hotels across the lagoon where the news and television services had set up their observation posts.

As the remaining time dwindled to a minute, the news anchors and commentators vanished from sight—the news stations showing only the Grand Laguna rooftop—and spoke in hushed tones, as if witnessing a golf player trying to drive a very long put. At ten seconds, many showed the digital numbers ticking off in a corner, and slowly closed in with their cameras on the door, some of them so closely that its round doorknob could plainly be seen in the television screens.

But then the countdown ticked its way past zero, and the door did not budge.

Montañez looked questioningly at Maldonado, his expression a mixture of anguish and confusion. He, the Superintendent, and Franceschini were in the cavernous ballroom where they had set up their command center, along with dozens of other aides and officers, watching in trans-fixed silence a giant television flat screen provided by the hotel.

More than a minute passed beyond the deadline established by the terrorists, and still no one stepped out onto the roof of the Grand Laguna Hotel. Some of the commentators, after remaining silent for nearly half a minute, renewed their verbal reporting, still speaking quietly, their words hovering between subdued hope and puzzled skepticism. One urged their viewers to pray for the safety of the hostages.

"Do you think they changed their minds?" the police colonel asked.

Maldonado did not answer. He prayed to God that was the case, but did not think so. It could be that the watch of the person in charge was slow.

"Tell Captain Gómez to remain on standby," he said. "He goes as soon as we give the order."

Montañez nodded, and picked up his walkie-talkie to relay the order.

San Miguel patiently looked at his watch, then back at the small televi-sion set that had been brought into the conference room. Johnny Ray and Yajaira sat next to him, their eyes traveling back and forth between the television screen and their silent leader.

The deadline had come and gone by more than three minutes, and still no hostage had appeared on the TV screen.

San Miguel sat stiff as a board, the only sign of his intense irritation being the nervous tapping of a pencil on the oaken surface of the conference room table.

Four minutes! Now the NBC news reporter dared to optimistically surmise that *"the terrorists may be having second thoughts, considering how the threatened executions may turn world opinion against them."* San Miguel saw Johnny Ray wince with the reporter's words, and turned to Czecka, the only other person in the room.

"Czecka," he snapped, in an irritated voice. "Go to the roof and find out what's holding up Daniel, won't you?"

San Miguel's bear-like associate strolled out of the boardroom, closing the door behind him with unexpected gentleness.

"There's always something, isn't there?" San Miguel said to his two guests with a thin, wistful smile. "It's all for the best," he stated reassuringly, not sounding reassured at all. "It will be even more shocking for the authorities to see one of the tourists die after their hopes were raised by this...delay." Noticing their dismay at his last statement, he hastened to add, "In the end, it will make them cave in faster to our demands, and help save lives. It will all work out to our advantage."

Doel finished his satellite phone conversation with Michelle from the open courtyard next to the WKPA station building, and dashed towards the studio inside. He had been called urgently away from the control room just minutes before the two o'clock terrorist deadline, after his aide had told him that Michelle was calling, and that she could not wait another second.

She had given to him a word-for-word account of the conversation that she and her companions had overheard as they tried to get closer to the Grand Laguna Hotel. If what she said was correct, then the police was about to attempt the rescue of the hostages, and the terrorists had somehow found out about the attack, and were prepared to repel it. What surprised him the most was the amount of detail that the terrorists knew about the impending rescue attempt, including the number of helicopters involved. If what the Macheteros had said was true, then they had an insider within the higher echelons of the police, someone of sufficient rank to have access to the fine points of the rescue mission.

A mole in the Police Department, and WKPA had the exclusive information. What a scoop! But first, he had to get hold of the Superintendent and warn him that his men were heading into a trap.

Doel ran up the stairs to the control room, where the news show director, his assistant, and Doel's two aides were glued to the main television screen. The clock overhead marked the time as five after two.

"What's happening?" Doel asked as he walked towards the huddled group.

"Nothing," one of his aides, Erasmo, answered in a baffled tone.

"Nothing? What do you mean nothing? It's way past two!" Doel pushed aside his other aide, and sat next to Raul, the program director. "There's nobody on the roof!" he whispered.

"Thank you," Raul said testily, as his friend stated the obvious.

"They haven't come out yet?" Doel asked incredulously.

"No."

"Has the police started a rescue attempt?"

"Not that we know of," Lydia, the other aide answered.

Doel considered the information while looking at the various monitor screens of the cameras that were surveying the Grand Laguna. *Had Michelle been wrong?*

"No," he answered himself, prompting a curious look from the director. "Okay, folks!" he said to the others. "I need to contact the Superintendent right now!"

Correcaminos sat in one of the administrative offices contiguous to the grand ballroom where the police had set up its center of operations, inwardly simmering at the delay in meeting with Superintendent Maldonado. The two policemen sharing the room with him, including the one that had led him there, were riveted to a computer screen showing a live feed of the Grand Laguna Hotel.

"Do you think it will be long before the Superintendent sees me?" he asked impatiently.

Neither of the policemen answered.

Suddenly, his cell phone began making a strange "waku, waku" noise, the ringtone that Correcaminos had assigned to his friend Doel. One of the policemen glanced back over his shoulder, laughed, and returned his attention to the computer.

"Doel!" Correcaminos said in a muted voice. "You got through to my cell phone!"

"*I know, you dummy!*" Doel answered. "*The spike on the connecting circuits must be dropping. I first tried to send someone from the mobile unit to talk to you, but they turned him back. Said that you were with the Superintendent, and wouldn't let him in. So I tried your cell phone, and it worked, thank God!*"

"I'm still waiting to meet him," Correcaminos informed Doel. "The Superintendent won't talk to anyone at this moment. It's ten minutes beyond the deadline of the terrorists and nothing has happened. I don't—"

"*Now shut up and listen to me, before we get cut off!*" Doel interrupted urgently. "*This is a matter of life and death!*"

Correcaminos listened quietly while Doel briefed him on his conversation with Michelle. As he gathered the details, he watched the two policemen in the room. Both had their backs turned to him, enthralled by the broadcast.

He considered trying to alert them about the information Doel had just given him, but decided that too much time would be wasted, and that there was a risk that the policemen would still decide to wait for the Superintendent to call him.

Slowly, he pushed himself off the chair where he was sitting, and backed up towards the office's exit. As he turned the door handle, it clicked, but neither of the two men stirred. A few seconds later, he had stepped into the corridor outside.

"Take off your blindfolds," Daniel ordered angrily to the seven hostages who still had them on.

They were standing inside the helipad building, next to the elevators, facing their captor in one long line. Some, like April and the teenaged girl, were so terrified that they had trouble removing them, their hands shaking uncontrollably. Others, like the blond computer programmer and a chubby, pear-shaped corporate lawyer wearing Harry Potter-like glasses, stared directly at the floor, apparently fearful of catching the attention of the terrorists. That was not the case with the female gym and math teacher, who made it a point to express her defiance by staring contemptuously at her captors, while the white haired Franciscan and the half-shaved, half-dressed businessman examined the unfolding situation with undisguised concern.

Set apart were the young father with the military crew cut; a tall man in his late forties wearing a Trans Global Airlines uniform; and the construction manager: a sunburned man with disheveled, dark gray hair, almost as tall but twice as heavy as the Trans Global Airlines employee. They were guarded by a tiny, frail-looking Figueres, whose upper lip was swollen, the thin, blondish wisp of hair on his chin drenched in sweat and blood. Despite his injury, he seemed to be amused by either Daniel's evident discomfort or by his knowledge of what would follow.

Daniel walked to the crew-cut father, grabbed him by the shirt, and pulled him out in front of the others. Without saying a word, he drew out his gun and shot his hostage on the right thigh. The young man instantly dropped to the ground, groaning and grabbing his leg. Several of the hostages screamed, and the priest leaned forward to aid the fallen man, but Daniel turned his gun on him.

"Stop, Father," he said evenly, not raising his voice. "I don't want to shoot you as well. This is what happens to anyone who interferes with us. The next one gets it in the head. Now put your blindfolds back on."

Standing beside him and pointing an Uzzi at the larger group of hostages, Da'ud thought that Daniel was doing a great job in keeping his anger in check. For a moment things had gotten dicey, but thanks to his quick reaction they had been able to regain control of the situation.

It had happened suddenly and without warning. Figueres had brought out the first batch of five prisoners in the elevator. As they had stepped out and walked close to the emergency stairs, the Trans Global Airlines employee had suddenly turned and pushed him. Figueres had rolled down the stairs, banging his mouth on one of the steps. The airline man, whose blindfold had apparently not covered his entire field of vision, had torn the black cloth off his eyes and jumped over the fallen terrorist, running down the stairwell.

Figueres had recovered immediately, sitting and pointing his handgun at the back of the fleeing prisoner. He would have shot him had the young father with the crew cut not grabbed his wrist and deflected his weapon. Figueres' shot had gone wide, ricocheting off the wall, and nearly hitting the airline man on the head. The young man and Figueres had continued to struggle, and had been joined a second later by the construction manager, who had also freed himself from his blindfold. They had managed to pin the terrorist down, and were shouting at the other prisoners to run, when the elevator doors had opened again.

Daniel had been the first to come out. A quick look had told him all that he needed to know. Two of the hostages from the first group, the blond computer programmer and the teenager, were in the room with their blindfolds still on, too scared to do anything, while the muffled sounds of a struggle welled up from the stairwell in front of him.

Drawing his gun, he had run to the edge of the stairs and pointed it at the group still fighting at the bottom of the stair's landing.

"Let him go!" Daniel had shouted at the two hostages, and the men had obeyed immediately, cringing and raising their hands over their heads.

"The pilot is running down the stairs!" Figueres had said to his leader, wiping his lip and wincing with pain.

"You two, get up here now!" Daniel had screamed at the two hostages in the stairs. As they did so, he had walked back to the elevator and pressed the "DOWN" button.

"Take care of the prisoners," he had said to Da'ud while the elevator door opened, and then, as he stepped in, had added in a louder voice to Figueres, "Go get the pilot!"

Making a mental calculation, Daniel had pressed the elevator button to the ninth floor. The helipad was located on the twentieth story—the twenty-first story, if the lobby was counted—of the building. The fugitive would be trying to escape from the hotel by running down the stairs at that very moment. There was an outside chance that he would hide in one of the floors in between, but if the man was smart, he would know that once his escape was known, the building would be searched and he would be found—and killed. His best chance of survival would be to get out of the hotel *now.*

The elevator had stopped at the ninth floor, and Daniel had run to the door of the fire escape. He had taken great care about not making any noise, and slipped inside. He had been greeted by the hurried noises of more than one set of footsteps descending in his direction. Suppressing a chuckle, he had pointed his gun at the upper landing and waited.

It had taken the fleeing man another two minutes to reach the landing between the ninth and the eighth floor. Daniel had shouted at him to stop the moment the hostage had turned the corner, and the latter's surprise had been so big that he had tripped and fallen most of the way down to the eighth floor.

Daniel had kicked the pilot once for good measure, and then forced him back to his feet.

"You stupid fuck," he had said to the dazed hostage, and grabbing him by the back of his shirt's collar, had led him back to the elevator and up to the twenty-first floor.

Now, as the hostage with the crew cut agonized on the floor, Daniel leaned forward and whispered to him, "Take off your belt and make a tourniquet around your thigh. I will deal with you when I come back."

Da'ud smiled. The bald, bearded Arab had worked with Daniel long enough to know how deviously his mind worked. His boss was a romantic at heart who admired courage. Da'ud had seen Daniel's hidden admiration when the young man had volunteered to take the place of his wife. By shooting him, Daniel had guaranteed that the new father would not be the one thrown off the roof.

The light over the elevators' entrance lit up with a "bing" and the door slid open at its center. The hulking presence of Czecka stepped out, making the elevator's floor shake.

The giant terrorist calmly surveyed the scene, his eyes barely pausing on the wounded man. Without uttering a word, he pressed the "DOWN" button outside of the elevator, and stepped back into it when its doors opened.

"Tell San Miguel that he should have more faith in me," Daniel called after him, as the doors closed.

At 2:16 PM, when most of the newscasters had returned to the forefront of the screen to speculate why the terrorists had failed to make their scheduled appearance and many of the viewers were taking a bathroom or food break, the blue door of the helipad shook slightly and then swung open. All of the chatter filling the airwaves stopped immediately and the newscasters disappeared from view, as the cameras focused on the helipad. For a few, tense seconds, nothing else happened. Then, from one of the edges of the door, a figure appeared.

It was a small woman or a girl—from the distance it was difficult to tell—her face covered by a large black blindfold. She was moving sideways rather than forward, and it soon became apparent why. Her right arm was crossed over her stomach, linked to somebody else's arm, and as she emerged into the afternoon's light, another person followed her. It was a priest. Some of the commentators immediately identified his brown garb as Franciscan, and wondered out loud what was happening.

Both of the priest's arms were also crossed over his stomach, his left arm linked to the girl's right arm—it was now evident that it was a teenager—his shoulder pressed against hers, both facing forward towards the lagoon. Like the girl, his face was blindfolded, wisps of his white hair flickering over the upper edge of the black cloth as they were moved by the wind.

The two hostages continued to move sideways in short awkward steps until a third blindfolded person emerged, this one a half-dressed man with disheveled hair, wearing a T-shirt and the striped pants of a business suit. He held on to the priest's left hand with his right hand, his left shoulder pressed against the priest's right.

And so it continued. One of the newscasters from CNN noted it first, his voice choked with emotion. It was a human chain, formed to shield the terrorists from any snipers stationed on the roofs of the buildings that faced the Grand Laguna Hotel across the lagoon. A succession of hostages continued to emerge from the helipad's exit, moving clumsily shoulder to shoulder to their left, their arms linked together, like a line of uncoordinated dancers whose choreography had gone terribly awry.

The man in the T-shirt was followed by a short blond man, and he by a robust older woman, taller and more athletic than either of the two men who preceded her. Next came a fat man with thick glasses hanging from his upper shirt pocket. A statuesque brunette, clad in short shorts and a tight-fitting white tank top, continued the procession. She held hands with a tall—the tallest in the group—sunburned man apparently in his sixties, and finally a man wearing an airline uniform.

As the Trans Global pilot exited, he whispered something monosyllabic into the ear of the woman to his left. She, in turn turned to the man next to her and uttered something just as short to her companion, who repeated the words to the tall brunette next to him, and so on to the last person. As each person spoke, he or she stopped shuffling sideways until the entire line stopped moving.

For a moment nothing else happened. The hostages stood completely still, their arms still locked to each other, the strong wind that flowed from the sea flapping against their clothes and messing their hair.

It was a heart-rending scene, nine random guests, standing on the hotel's rooftop, blindly paraded like criminals about to be executed, their half-covered faces unable to express the terror that they undeniably had to be feeling. They had visited the Caribbean to relax from their everyday pressures and to spend time with their families and friends. Instead, they had been kidnapped and were about to be slaughtered by people they did not know, in the name of an ideology or cause completely foreign to them.

The television cameras detected movement behind the hostages: three crouching figures who spread evenly among their captives. There were short, fractional glimpses of their faces, which had not been hidden. One seemed to be heavyset and bald and sporting a heavy, square-cut black beard. The other two were more difficult to tell apart, both darting from one place to another behind their human shields, like puppeteers preparing to put on a show under the cover of the theater curtains. It was impossible to tell what type of weapons they carried, or for that matter, if they carried any at all. It was also impossible, at least for the moment, for any of the SWAT or police sharpshooters to acquire a decent target.

Without warning, the entire line of hostages moved forward. They moved in unison, pausing after every step, as if marching to the deliberate, shouted cadence of a drill sergeant. The terrorists moved closely behind, continuing to stay out of sight. Along the way, some of the hostages began to move out of step, as some advanced more than others, and the line suddenly stopped. Like sheepdogs, the hidden gunmen scurried behind the captive civilians, pushing and prodding them until the semblance of a line was restored. Then the line renewed its intermittent, unstoppable march towards the edge of the Grand Laguna's roof.

Maldonado watched with growing horror as the distance between the hostages and the end of the roof dwindled.

"Anything from our SWAT snipers?" he asked anxiously Montañez, who was holding a portable radio.

The colonel shook his head. "Negative, sir. They don't have a clear line of fire. The Macheteros are too well covered"

"God protect us!" the Superintendent shook his head in despair, as the line got dangerously close to the building's edge. Everyone in the room was staring at him, waiting for his next instructions. And still he balked, every fiber in his being telling him that ordering an all out assault on the hotel would be the wrong thing to do.

Then the hostages stopped moving, holding their ragged line at less than two feet from the chasm before them.

Maldonado leaned heavily against the table in front of him and closed his eyes. "Order Gomez to attack," he said quietly.

Montañez instantly pressed the "SPEAK" button of his walkie-talkie, and said, "Windmills one and two, this is Quijote, over!" He waited, while the two teams acknowledged the call, and then said, "You are cleared to go! I repeat, go!"

"Ah! There they are!" San Miguel exclaimed, unable to conceal his delight as the hostages began to emerge from the helipad structure onto the open rooftop.

Barely two minutes before, Czecka had returned to the conference room and whispered into his leader's ear what he had just observed on the twenty-first floor of the hotel, relaying at the end of his narrative Daniel's shouted message. San Miguel had nodded, and summarized the information he had just received to Johnny Ray and his female companion. With the corner of his eye, he had observed their reaction while pretending to watch the TV. Johnny was perspiring profusely, while trying his hardest to look unconcerned. Yajaira was visibly shaking.

Welcome to the real world, San Miguel thought with perverse pleasure. *Not as pretty and heroic as you thought, is it?*

"I wish..." Johnny whispered weakly as he watched the blindfolded prisoners, letting his words drift into the helpless silence of someone who realizes that there is nothing that he can do to change what is happening.

"What?" San Miguel asked.

"Nothing..." Johnny finally replied.

San Miguel smiled at him reassuringly. *The FEPI leadership was crumbling faster than he had expected,* he thought to himself. Soon, he would be unable to trust Johnny Ray or Yajaira. However, the FEPIstas had a legitimate role to play, at least until nighttime. Until then, he would have to lead his guests by the hand.

And watch them closely.

CHAPTER XL

Captain Gomez and his men had been sitting on their three large inflatable boats for the last half hour, their 250 horsepower Yamaha outboard engines idling impatiently. Each of the gray boats contained eight men, clad in their dark blue SWAT combat uniforms.

He felt very uneasy about the bulky garb that he wore, which included—in addition to his helmet—a heavy bulletproof vest, shoulder pads, and shin and knee armor plates. He also carried, strapped to his right thigh, a large, unwieldy canvas pouch containing smoke canisters and flashbang grenades—the latter designed to produce 175 decibels of noise and 2.5 million candela of light to stun the enemy—and ammunition for his various weapons. A holster on the right side of his belt secured a Glock .40 pistol, while an MP-5K compact sub machinegun hung from a harness on his left shoulder.

Although he and his men were wearing special flotation devices—compact life preservers that had been integrated to the bulletproof vests—he did not fancy crossing the lagoon with his heavy clothes and paraphernalia. If for any reason he fell into the lagoon, he would be in deep trouble. In the sixteenth century, the Duke of Cumberland had nearly drowned in two feet of water after he had fallen with his armor while attempting to cross a shallow part of the lagoon into San Juan. Captain Gomez did not want to suffer the Duke's same fate. He and his men would be crossing waters with an average depth of ten to twelve feet. Even if the flotation device maintained them above water, which he seriously doubted, they would barely be able to move, floating like oversized corks in front of the Macheteros' sights.

He had been assured by the Coast Guard, which had provided the inflatable barges on which his team would do the crossing, that the boats were made of Armorflate, a material capable of withstanding ballistic projectiles of up to 7.62 mm, the equivalent of the ammunition used by the AK-47s. Hopefully that, combined with the cover provided by the National Guard smoke canisters and the sniper fire coming from the neighboring rooftops and the helicopters, would be enough to guarantee the SWAT team a safe passage over the lagoon.

He looked at the seven other men sitting on the raft with him. They had been waiting with the excited impatience that only young, highly trained personnel could muster in the face of a dangerous assignment. They had burst into spontaneous applause when Gomez had informed them that they had been selected to rescue the hotel hostages, and then, under the ever-watchful eye of Sergeant Abe Cordero, had channeled their excess energy into getting ready for the assault.

Like their captain, each man was fully armed. Most carried M16-A1 assault rifles, and a few—the sharpshooters—were equipped with Remington 700 rifles with long-range telescopic sights. Each of the three boats carried an assortment of other tools and weapons, including short steel battering rams, tear gas guns, and even a couple of ballistic shields.

But the deadliest weapons were the men themselves. Most in their late teens and early twenties, they had been selected from the best members of the Police Department and placed under the command of Captain Gomez, a decorated veteran of the Iraqi War. From the outset, Captain Gomez had set his mind in creating an elite unit that would rival or surpass any other in Puerto Rico, including the island's most famous outfit, Montañez's Untouchables. To attain his goal, Gomez had recruited the services of retired ex-Navy SEAL Abraham Cordero, another hardened veteran of the Iraqi and Afghan wars, who had taken it as a personal challenge to weed out any suspect or weak links from the group, and to whip those who survived the first two weeks of training into a formidable fighting force.

During the past year, the team had intervened in about two dozen hostage situations, most involving domestic squabbles, two dealing with bank robberies in progress, and one with a car hijacking by an escaped convict. Except for one case, a tragedy where an estranged husband had killed his wife, his two children and himself before they could gain access into the wife's house, their success rate had been phenomenal.

Nothing, however, compared to the mission that they were about to undertake. *This was the stuff that happened only once in a lifetime,* Captain Gomez thought, *the kind of stuff that his men only dreamed about, but never got to see.*

As the two o'clock deadline neared and the preparations ended, the good-natured banter of the men gave way to contemplative silence. Then, the time to stage the attack passed, and the men began to get edgy.

Some started to wonder out loud if the mission had been called off, while others cast expectant glances at their superior officers.

Sergeant Cordero, sitting in the last of the three boats, had sensed the growing nervousness of his men, and at ten past two had stood up and, with a covert wink to his captain, had addressed the others.

"Now listen up!" he had said loudly. "We are about to go at any moment, so remember your assignments. Group A, that will be the captain and boats one and two, will head directly to the lobby of the hotel. Group B, that is my group, will join with our platoon coming across in the helicopters, and hit the convention area."

He paused, as all of his men listened intently.

"Now...some of us may have to pass one or two of the bars in the hotel along to way to our objectives," he said with a deadpan expression. "*Do not,* I repeat, *do not* stop there to consume any alcohol." There were several jeers and catcalls among the men. "I repeat, any lush stopping at the bar will be severely punished!"

Gomez felt the tension ease, as some of his men laughed at or booed the sergeant. One man shouted, "Hey captain! Maybe we should let the sergeant take on the terrorists by himself!"

"That's right!" another man said. "That way he'll bore *them* to death!"

The portable radio lying on the lap of the man sitting next to Gomez crackled suddenly into life, making the radioman jerk slightly his legs with surprise. *"Windmills one and two, this is Quijote, over!"*

"This is Windmill One, over," the man acknowledged immediately.

"You are cleared to go! I repeat, go!"

Captain Gomez stood up and faced the other two boats. He raised his right arm and pumped it up and down three times. The men cheered, but their noise was drowned by the powerful outboard engines, as they were revved up to their maximum power and the rafts immediately surged forward.

Colonel Calderon watched the television set as the hostages walked onto the rooftop of the Grand Laguna Hotel. *American entertainment!* he thought with amazement. *They would show their own mothers getting shot, if it produced enough ratings!*

He had been anxiously waiting for something to happen for the last fifteen minutes, sitting in the living room of one of the three luxury apartments facing the Condado Lagoon that his men had commandeered. All three were next to each other, on the fourth floor of two contiguous buildings. The Venezuelans had established three machine gun positions, one on each of the apartments' main balconies.

They were perfect, impregnable positions, which dominated the area of the lagoon from where the three SWAT inflatable boats would by necessity have to approach the hotel. At the same time, the balconies were not visible from the roofs of the San Geronimo Plaza Hotel and the condominium where the SWAT sharpshooters had been placed; they were blocked from the snipers' view by another building that was built closer to the hotel and further into the lagoon.

Only from a helicopter would Calderon's men be visible to their adversaries. And if any helicopters came—as their intelligence source had warned would be the case—they would be in for a terrible surprise.

So would the SWAT snipers stationed on the roofs of the buildings across the lagoon. Unlike the Colonel's group, Sergeant Alfonsin and six of Calderon's best sharpshooters had occupied a nineteenth floor penthouse apartment in the next building. From there, the SWAT snipers were plainly visible. For the past hour, Alfonsin and his men had followed through the telescopic lenses of their Russian-issued Dragunov rifles—from behind the curtained windows of the penthouse—every movement of their SWAT counterparts. Had they not been under strict orders not to give away their positions until the rescue operation began, the Venezuelans could have easily picked off a handful of the police snipers.

Calderon leaned back on his overstuffed chair and shouted, "Caraballo! Warn Alfonsin and the others that the attack is forthcoming. Let me know when you spot anything."

"Yes, sir!" the corporal answered. He was lying on the floor of one of the balconies, staring at the Dos Hermanos Bridge with a pair of binoculars.

Calderon sighed resignedly. He had instructed his men on repeated occasions that he did not want to be addressed in any way that hinted his military rank, in case they were overheard. But it was probably easier to ask for the sun not to shine. To his men, he was the Colonel, and it would be inconceivable for them to call him anything but "sir".

He continued to watch the terrible scene unfolding in the television screen, where the hostages were methodically being marched to the edge of the roof of the Grand Laguna Hotel. The entire affair seemed absolutely surreal. He had never thought that he would conduct a battle from an opulent, marble-floored, air-conditioned apartment decorated with antique furniture and museum-quality paintings.

He had seen the panic in the owners' faces as he and his men had broken into their apartments, and had promised that nothing would happen to them and that he would do everything in his power not to damage any of their belongings. It had not been an empty promise. He intended to avoid as many civilian casualties as he could, and he had instructed his soldiers to treat their prisoners humanely, and to respect their property. For their own safety, the two residents of the apartment he was presently in—a middle aged married couple—had been locked up in their master bedroom, facing away from the lagoon.

"Here they come!" the corporal suddenly announced, not taking the binoculars off his eyes.

Calmly, Calderon stood up and walked towards the balcony.

The three inflatable boats surged from under the Dos Hermanos Bridge almost simultaneously, traveling at a furious speed towards the opposite shore, leaving parallel wakes of white foam behind them. The high-pitched whine of their outboard motors shattered the atypical stillness that had pervaded over the lagoon area and its environs after the destruction of the bridges. The noise, however, was drowned almost immediately by the heavy, choppy drone of the two Bell police helicopters that swooped over the advancing SWAT teams and then turned sharply towards the Atlantic, to begin their short run along the coast bordering the Grand Laguna Hotel. Some of Gomez's men cheered and waved, encouraged by the display of speed and power.

It took several seconds for the news media, focused on the hostages atop the hotel, to realize what was happening, but then their cameras switched to the action below, as their commentators breathlessly described what was apparent for all to see.

Sergeant Alfonsin heard the approaching engines, and took one last look at his men. They were all positioned along the three windows of the penthouse that faced the San Geronimo Plaza rooftop and its neighboring condominium, following the movement of the SWAT sharpshooters through their telescopic lenses.

"You may fire at will," the Venezuelan sergeant said calmly.

A volley of detonations followed his words, as the Dragunov rifles went off in an initial massive volley. Looking through his binoculars, Alfonsin saw a dark-uniformed man on the San Geronimo Plaza rooftop who had stood up to follow the progress of the boats, lurch abruptly and fling sideways the long-barreled weapon that he had been holding in his right hand, and another man who was apparently shifting to a better location, stop in mid-stride, holding his left shoulder and dropping out of sight. A few puffs on the low concrete wall that edged the rooftop of the San Geronimo Plaza marked where some of the other bullets had struck, prompting some of the police snipers nearby to look around them confusedly and duck for cover.

As he shifted his attention to the roof of the condominium, Alfonsin saw that two other men had fallen. One was writhing on the floor, while the other lay still, a few steps away from the one that had been wounded. The situation there was more desperate, since there was no barrier or wall around the edge of the fifteen-story high roof behind which the men could hide. The eight snipers that had taken their positions there had been lying flat on the floor, propping their rifles on short bipods, waiting for the assault to begin. Now, as they came under fire, they had nowhere to retreat except to the stairwell in the center of the rooftop.

"Pick your targets carefully," Alfonsin instructed in a monotone voice, walking from one room to another as the shooting by his men fell into a more sporadic, deliberate pace. "Fire when ready. Don't let them see you."

The sergeant noted with satisfaction how steadily and efficiently his men were operating. All the months of hard drills and practice were bearing fruition. President Chavez had been right when he had prepared the Venezuelan Army to fight off any imperialist invasion. With the proper training and equipment, his men could defeat anyone, even the all-powerful Americans.

Correcaminos barged into the command center unchallenged, and saw the Superintendent of the Police standing several yards away, next to a large television flat screen. Of the more than half dozen men close to him, he recognized the tall, still athletic figure of Colonel Montañez, holding next to his face a walkie-talkie.

"They're on their way," Correcaminos heard the colonel say, and guessing what it meant, redoubled his pace towards the police chief.

"Superintendent Maldonado!" he shouted several times as he continued to approach the group, finally prompting several of those huddled around the television set to look back in surprise at the source of the commotion. Behind him, the two policemen who had been supposed to keep him in their custody rushed towards him and grabbed him by the arms. A brief scuffle followed, where Correcaminos was pinned to the ground and his hands were handcuffed behind his back.

"Please!" he shouted, his face pressed to the parquet floor. "This is urgent! You have to call your men back! They're heading towards a trap!"

The reporter's words managed to pry Maldonado's eyes from the television set. He motioned to the two policemen holding Correcaminos to bring the handcuffed newscaster to him.

Correcaminos was quickly lifted off the ground by his two arms and half-carried, half-dragged to the Superintendent. As he got closer to the television screen, he noticed the images of three inflatable boats heading at full blast towards the opposite shore of the lagoon. Those around the police chief stepped out of the way to let the new arrival through.

Maldonado received him with a withering stare, not saying a word.

"I'm sorry to bother you, Mr. Superintendent," Correcaminos said urgently, watching as the enormous television set now showed two helicopters joining the assault. "But you have to call your men back! They're heading into a trap! The Macheteros know that they're coming, and they're waiting for them!"

Several groans and expressions of disbelief interrupted him, but Maldonado raised a hand and stilled them.

"How do you know that?" he asked, his voice filled with understated dread.

"Michelle Alfaro overheard the terrorists—" he stopped, knowing how incredible his own account sounded. "She was hiding near the Grand Laguna Hotel, and two terrorists spoke about the rescue operations. They know you are coming."

"How do they know?" a balding, smaller man standing next to Maldonado asked. Correcaminos recognized him as Mario Franceschini, head of the FBI in Puerto Rico.

"Michelle doesn't know how. The terrorists spoke of intelligence sources—"

"That's impossible," Franceschini exclaimed, examining with curiosity the reporter's face. "How could you talk to her? There's no way of communicating with her if she's in San Juan!"

"There is!" Correcaminos replied. "But there's no time to discuss that now. Listen, they knew you are going to use two helicopters and throw smoke canisters—"

Maldonado interrupted him.

"They know!" he said, realizing that the information that Correcaminos was disclosing could only be known by an insider.

"They must have observers close to where our men got ready!" Franceschini suggested, trying to seek an explanation for the security breach. "We must warn—"

"Sir!" Montañez interrupted, as he listened again to the walkie-talkie. "Our sharpshooters on the rooftop report that they are under attack by heavy sniper fire! There are several men down."

Maldonado took a step closer to the television screen and watched as the helicopters closed in on the shore of the Grand Laguna Hotel, to begin dropping the smoke canisters.

"Call our teams," he said to Montañez. "Tell them to withdraw. *Now!*"

The first of the two helicopters banked over the reefs that separated the waves of the Atlantic Ocean from the Condado Lagoon, the reefs where the dog turned into stone waited for his drowned master to return. It whizzed over the rooftop of the Grand Laguna Hotel where the blindfolded hostages stood, so close to them that some of them cringed back, frightened by the noise and the wind that the whirling blades of the flying machine generated. Then, with its side door open and a gunner standing behind an M240 machine gun mounted on a pivot, it slowed down and began to descend towards the beachhead where the three inflatable boats were scheduled to land.

"Get the smoke canisters ready!" the pilot instructed the crew. "SWAT team, prepare for descent!"

Two of the six SWAT police officers grabbed green, spray-paint sized cans from a cardboard box containing dozens of them. On top of each of the cans was a round, ring-like safety pin that secured a lever extending over the canister's entire length. Once the safety pin was pulled out, the lever would be free to separate from the canister, setting off the smoke bomb's fuse. The men jerked out the safety rings but held the levers in place by pressing them down with the palms of their hands. Quietly, they waited for the order to start dumping the canisters down.

As the pilot continued to guide his helicopter down, he picked up radio chatter from the SWAT sharpshooters, and was surprised to hear that they were being attacked. So far, he had encountered no opposition, despite being much closer to the terrorists. He resolved to sweep by the buildings next to the hotel after he disposed of the smoke canisters and the SWAT personnel, and to try to engage the Machetero snipers with its heavy machine gun.

The helicopter continued to hover over the beachhead, and the pilot searched for the approaching boats, finding them already mid-way across the lagoon. He prepared to give the order to disperse the canisters, when his radio came to life.

"Windmills One and Two, Windmills One and Two, abort the mission and return home! I repeat, abort the mission and return home, over!"

"What the—" the pilot whispered. *Abort the mission? Were they crazy? They were already there!* He flicked on the "SPEAK" button on his control panel, and broke his radio silence. "Quijote, Quijote! This is Windmill Two. Can you repeat your order? Over?"

But it was already too late.

From the top floor of the parking building, Michelle, Negron and Archie could see—over the half-dozen, four-story condominiums in front of them—the Dos Hermanos Bridge and the lagoon. A taller building, probably close to twenty stories high, blocked their view of the Grand Laguna Hotel. They had waited there, spying on the group of terrorists hiding behind the stone fence that bordered the edge of the lagoon and on the two men armed with the long, bazooka-like weapon stationed on the roof of one of the lower buildings.

Aware of the terrorists' two o'clock ultimatum and of the upcoming rescue attempt, they had lingered on the ten-story parking lot to see what would happen. However, at ten minutes past two they had not seen or heard anything that even remotely hinted either the killing of any of the hostages or any effort by the police to storm the Grand Laguna Hotel. In fact, the armed terrorists that sat under the shadow of the stone fence bordering the lagoon seemed to be bored out of their wits. That would not have been the case, Michelle thought, if they had witnessed someone plunging to his death from the rooftop of the hotel and splattering on the sidewalk in front of them.

"Maybe the terrorists have backed down," Negron suggested half-heartedly. "Maybe the police have reached some sort of an agreement with them." After his outburst with Archie, the rookie policeman had made a conscious effort to calm down. He stared down at the men leaning against the stone fence. "You know," he said casually, "if I had a rifle, I could probably shoot a couple of those guys from here." He mimicked holding a rifle with his hands, and aiming at the terrorists went "Ptewn! Ptewn!"

Michelle smiled. Despite her swollen lip and nose, Archie thought that she was the most beautiful woman in the world.

"Maybe their watches are slow," he joked.

"Maybe they don't have watches!" Negron suggested, taking a deep sip from his water bottle.

"Maybe they forgot about it," Archie said, beginning to snicker.

"Maybe they asked for volunteers!" His own idea seemed so funny to him, that Negron snorted some of the water through his nose.

The three friends began to laugh until tears ran down from their eyes, releasing their pent up tension.

"Really, you two are awful!" Michelle said as they began to settle down, wiping away her tears with her hands. Her watch showed it was a quarter after two o'clock. "I think I should call Doel and find out what's happening," she added, sobering up quickly.

The shrill noise of revved-up engines interrupted their conversation. Negron, who had just sat next to his two companions, immediately stood up and stared over the edge of the parking lot's wall, just in time to see three boats spring out from under three different arches of the busted Dos Hermanos Bridge.

"Look!" he cried out excitedly, as Michelle and Archie scrambled to their feet to see. "And there come the helicopters!" he added, as the two aircrafts zoomed into view, flying briefly over the advancing vessels, and then turning northward and disappearing from view behind the tall building next to the hotel.

Further below, the waiting gunmen stirred, grabbing their weapons and crouching behind the stone wall where they were hiding. Michelle heard the distant sound of shots, but could not see anyone shooting. Then one of the helicopters reappeared, much closer to the Grand Laguna's southern shore, decreasing both its speed and altitude, as if about to land or drop something.

With the corner of her eye, Michelle saw one of the two men stationed on the rooftop of the building in front of her move out from behind the building's stairwell into the full view of the descending helicopter. He carried the long, strange looking weapon over his right shoulder, and seemed to be following the hovering aircraft through the weapon's sight.

Horrified, Michelle began to understand what the man was attempting to do. Next to her, Archie muttered, "Dear God!" while Negron groped for his gun, even though they were too far for the rookie policeman to hit anything.

Suddenly, the bazooka-like weapon emitted a loud popping sound, its rear raising a small cloud of the dust that had collected on the surface of the roof, its front spitting out a long, black projectile that for a split second shot upwards like a javelin, leaving no trail behind it. Then a bright, yellow flame roared out of missile's tail, thrusting the missile forward at a prodigious speed.

Barely a hundred yards away, the Bell helicopter had no time to react. The heat-seeking missile zeroed in on the chopper's Rolls Royce engine, its guidance system slightly adjusting its course, its progress marked by a thin, arching trail of smoke. In less than two seconds, it slammed into the helicopter underneath its rotor, where the aircraft housed its turbine. The missile ripped through its target's graphite skin and embedded its plastic-explosive warhead into the engine. And then, milliseconds later, it detonated.

The top of the helicopter burst into an enormous ball of flame, the clamor of the explosion reverberating over the entire lagoon and rattling the surrounding buildings. Even though the lower portion of the helicopter's cabin survived the initial impact, its eight occupants—the six SWAT police officers, the pilot and the copilot—died instantly, their bodies riddled by the fragments of the missile, the engine, and the shredded fuselage of the aircraft. Two of the blades of the main rotor shot up into the air, spinning wildly before they splashed into the blue waters below, one of them falling less than ten feet from one of the advancing inflatable boats.

Michelle and her two companions shouted with dismay and watched in disbelief as the flaming wreck of the police helicopter plunged vertically out of the sky and crashed onto the rocks edging the hotel's southern shore, where it continued to burn. Unexpectedly, the second helicopter soared into view, flattening the smoke of its downed sister ship into a dirty brown haze. Multiple popping sounds, similar to those made by a movie popcorn machine or a long string of distant firecrackers, abruptly filled the air. Michelle could not initially place them, but then she looked at the incoming boats, and saw multiple splashes dotting the surface of the water that surrounded them. At the same time, the men hiding behind the stone fence stood up and opened fire.

"They're going to shoot down the second helicopter!" Negron shouted, pointing at the two men on the roof of the building below them. The one holding the weapon had dropped to one knee, while the second one was busy loading another missile.

The rookie policeman raised his gun, and holding it out with both of his hands, rested his arms on the edge of the concrete fence behind which they were hiding. It was a Smith & Wesson M&P.40, the official service weapon of the Puerto Rican Police Department, chosen because of its power and reliability. But he was between sixty and seventy yards away from the men loading the surface-to-air missile launcher, a long distance to hit a target with a handgun.

Negron, nevertheless, took careful aim and, slowly and deliberately, began to shoot at his intended targets, pausing a couple of seconds between each round, and adjusting his aim as he watched where the last shot landed. Michelle covered her ears, and thought that the gun's heavy detonations would surely attract the attention of every terrorist around them. However, the Smith & Wesson's noise could not compete with the din of the pitched battle taking place below them.

Inexplicably, the second police helicopter continued to hold its position over the flaming remains of its counterpart.

"What are they waiting for?" Michelle asked testily, as she watched the two terrorists working on the launcher. "Don't they see they're about to be blown out of the sky?"

"They probably don't," Archie replied. "They're busy looking for survivors."

Michelle failed to hear him as Negron fired again. Then the helicopter began to move away, almost reluctantly at first, but subsequently picking up speed as it withdrew to the Condado area. Almost as if on cue, the man placing the new missile in the launcher slapped his companion twice on the back, signaling that he was finished. The launcher's operator immediately stood up, and pointed his weapon at the sky.

"Hell!" Archie muttered, as Negron continued to fire.

But just then, the man holding the weapon cringed back and crouched close to the ground, as the last of Negron's shots hit the top of the open metal case that held the missiles, slamming it shut. The two men handling the missile launcher looked about them apprehensively, and crouched for cover. Negron shouted in triumph, and started to jump up and down, wielding his gun and shouting at the two men.

"Get down!" Michelle told him urgently. "You want them to see us?"

"Yes!" he shouted. "Yes! That's exactly what I want!"

Next to him, Archie was laughing.

"That was really a lucky shot, you know that?" he said to the rookie policeman.

"Lucky my ass!" Negron answered, still jumping and hollering at the two confused men. One of them finally saw him, and pointed him to his partner. Negron aimed his gun at them and began firing at them again. The men immediately took cover behind the rooftop's stairwell.

"Lucky shot? What do you mean?" Michele asked, perplexed but smiling, infected by her friends' sudden exuberant mood.

"See that green metal case on the floor there?" Archie directed Michelle's attention to a longish, rectangular shape lying flat on the floor of the rooftop where the two terrorists were hiding. "That's an ammunition box, the box from where one of those guys took out the rocket that he just loaded into the launcher."

"Okay..." Michelle said uncertainly.

"It was open a few seconds ago. One of Negron's bullets hit it and shut it down. It must have scared the crap out of that terrorist." Archie shook his head and glanced at Negron, who had just fired the last bullet of his fifteen-cartridge clip. "What a lucky shot!"

"Luck had nothing to do with it, my friend," the rookie answered proudly, beaming with intense satisfaction. "That's what you call real shooting."

"Yea, right! As if you were aiming at the case!"

Negron shrugged. "I might have."

"Well, whatever you aimed at, you saved that helicopter," Michelle said, looking at the lagoon and confirming that the chopper was gone. However, what she saw terrified her. During the time she had focused her attention on the helicopter and the neighboring rooftop, the situation on the lagoon had changed drastically. Only one of the inflatable boats remained visible, and it was retreating towards El Condado. Something was burning in the middle of the lagoon, presumably another of the rescue crafts, and there seemed to be debris strewn over various parts of the water, some of it looking suspiciously like floating bodies, although it was too far to tell.

"Shouldn't we be going?" she said to the others. "Those men are going to tell their friends where we are, and they are going to come for us."

"That makes a lot of sense to me," Archie said. Negron failed to answer, continuing to feed bullets into his ammunition clip. Smiling, Archie grabbed him by the arm, and dragged him away.

"Captain!" the radioman called out over the din of the boat's engine. "They're calling us back!"

"What?" Gomez asked in total disbelief. "What do you mean?"

"Quijote has ordered us to withdraw immediately, sir."

Gomez considered the order briefly. *It didn't make any sense. They had not come under any hostile fire yet!* Already the first helicopter had reached its primary target, and was poised to start dropping the smoke canisters over their intended beachhead. But he knew that Maldonado would not have issued the order lightly. Gomez had no choice but to withdraw.

"Call the other boats," he said, turning to his radioman. "Tell them that we're—"

A deafening explosion shrouded his words. Gomez looked in shock as the helicopter's upper section disintegrated and its decapitated frame crashed onto the rocks below in a mighty ball of fire. Then the water around the raft began to boil with dozens of small jets of water, followed by the rattle of machine gun fire.

Suddenly, the boat was struck several times in rapid succession, each hit punctuated by a heavy thud and the hiss of escaping air. One of the men sitting near the bow grunted and fell, holding his thigh and screaming in agony. The man sitting next to him tried to help him and got shot in the back. A bullet whizzed past Gomez's head, its angry whine instinctively causing him to raise his hand as if to swat away a pesky bee.

They were under heavy machine gun attack. The terrorists had been expecting them. The bullet-resistant boats were being torn to shreds by heavy caliber, armor piercing bullets. *They had been betrayed,* Gomez thought bitterly.

Behind him, he heard his radioman calling urgently to the other boats, "Windmill one to teams two and three! Windmill one to team two and three! Withdraw, withdraw, withdraw!" Gomez looked to his left, and saw that the second boat's engine was on fire and that some of his men were jumping out of the raft in order not to get burned.

"Head that way!" he shouted to his navigator, pointing at the burning vessel. The man nodded and turned the tiller in the direction that his captain had pointed. However, a scant moment later he yelled in pain as a bullet struck him on the wrist and almost tore his left hand off, leaving it hanging by a few strands of muscle. Incredibly, the wounded man grabbed the tiller with his other hand and kept the boat on course.

Gomez jumped next to him and took over, while another of his men helped the navigator deal with his terrible injury. The other men on the boat grabbed hold of their M16's and began to fire back, unsure of where the fire was coming from.

The young SWAT captain revved up the engine to maximum power, feeling how the inflatable boat got progressively heavier as it lost its buoyancy. Even so, he managed to zigzag his way to the burning craft without suffering further casualties.

The fire in the burning boat was worse than it seemed. The fuel tank had ruptured and flooded the inside of the barge, and the gasoline was burning fiercely inside, radiating so much heat that Gomez could feel it several yards away. It was Sergeant Cordero's barge, and he had been able to maintain the discipline of his men in the water. As the rescue boat moved between them, the men in the lagoon began to climb in, helped by those on board.

Cordero had made certain that his men stayed hidden behind the burning raft, so that they would be less visible to the terrorists shooting at them from the shore. Even so, bullets sped past the stricken SWAT team everywhere. Most of the men being picked up were wounded. One of them, a youngster that Gomez knew as Severiano and who had been shot in the lungs, was spitting blood and would probably not make it to the shore. Two had received second-degree burns in various parts of their bodies. Three would never climb aboard, killed during the opening minutes of the attack, their bodies dragged by their comrades out of the abandoned boat so that they would not burn in the fire.

By the time all of the survivors had been picked up, the inflatable boat was listing to one side. Cordero was the last man to climb on board, grabbing hold of Gomez's outstretched arm.

"Pascual," the SWAT captain ordered to the man who had been helping the wounded navigator. "Take over the tiller and push it for all that it's got back to El Condado."

"Yes, sir."

Gomez exchanged a quick look with Cordero but neither spoke, their eyes silently expressing their intense grief and anger. *Somebody had betrayed them,* Gomez thought as he moved to make room for Pascual. *Somebody had let the terrorists know the exact place and location of their attack. The terrorists had been waiting for them. He did not know who or how it had been, but he would make certain to find him.*

As the sinking boat increased its speed, Gomez found a spot next to his sergeant and began to sit down. Then something crashed into his helmet and he felt himself fall. As blackness enveloped him, he thought how cool the water felt on his face.

El Alacran stared from behind the stone fence at the retreating enemy and grunted with satisfaction. He had not felt so alive in years, decades probably.

The intelligence that San Miguel had received from his man inside the Police Department, whoever he was, had proven to be as solid as concrete. He could not help but think what the Macheteros could do with a mole like that. Maybe, with enough time, he could persuade San Miguel to reveal his source.

In front of him, the lagoon burned like a small corner of hell. The rescue attempt had been repelled with dreadful loses for the police. The withering fire of the Venezuelans from the buildings behind had been no match for the local authorities. Andrade and his men had not really been needed. Even so, he had not minded the wait behind the wall. It had given him a front-row-seat to the spectacle not only in the lagoon, but also to the show that was about to start from the rooftop of the hotel.

The Macheteros had snuck up unobserved behind the stone fence that bordered the lagoon by taking advantage of a portion of the lagoon's walk that had been canopied by the construction developer to protect the public from falling debris. Andrade and ten of his men had crawled behind the wall, and waited for the attack to begin. There had been a brief period of doubt, when the two o'clock deadline had expired and he had wondered if the whole exercise had been a bluff by San Miguel. But then the attack had started in earnest, and the entire world had watched how the Macheteros had beaten back a full scale assault by the Puerto Rican puppet government.

The fact that most of the fighting had been done by the Venezuelans did not trouble him at all. Most of the broadcasts he had been able to watch speculated that the Macheteros were behind the entire event, and the world would certainly believe them. From nearly being wiped out by the FBI a few years before, his group would now become a household name, as well known as Al-Qaeda.

He still wondered, though, why one of the helicopters had been allowed to escape. Shooting it down as well would have been even more shocking to the television viewers, and therefore more effective to the revolutionaries' cause. And he also thought that the rescuers on the rafts had been allowed to escape with a lot less damage than that which could have been inflicted on them. He and his men had tried to kill as many of the rescuers as possible, opening fire from behind the stone wall and shooting until they had nearly run out of ammunition, but their line of sight had not been as good as that of the Venezuelans and, *let's face it,* the Venezuelan soldiers were better shots than his men. It had almost seemed as if after inflicting the initial casualties on the police, Calderon's group had decided to shoot generally in their direction and allow them to retreat. El Alacran was not aware of how many of the invading force had been killed—he could see a few bodies floating in the water—but he knew that there could have been a lot more.

It did not matter that much in the grand scheme of things, however. The execution of some of the hostages would seal the Macheteros' claim to fame. Nobody watching would ever forget the sight of helpless guests getting pushed out of the roof of the luxury hotel in which they had been staying, in plain sight of the government that was supposed to protect them. It would certainly show the inability of Puerto Rico and the United States to save its citizens from the acts of a few armed revolutionaries, and encourage people everywhere to stand up against the American capitalistic oppression.

"You better take cover behind the wall," Andrade told his men as the action wound down, following up on his own suggestion and sitting in the shadow cast by the four-foot high stone barrier. "After what has just happened, those SWAT snipers across the lagoon will be itching to shoot anything that wanders into their cross-hairs."

El Alacran wiped the sweat off his forehead. *It was getting too hot,* he thought, fanning himself with a hand. He hoped the people on the roof would get their act together, and start the show soon.

The sounds of gunshots tapered off gradually, and then ceased altogether, and the nine hostages continued to stand at the edge of the building. Since the pitched battle had started more than twenty minutes before, they had endured the terrifying noises of the invisible fighting happening all around them, occasionally recoiling from nearby or loud explosions, constantly warned by the men behind them to stay as they were.

Daniel could have easily disposed of one of his captives while the rescuers were being massacred, and then withdrawn with the others safely back to the helipad during the on-going chaos, but then the execution of his single hostage would have lost much of its intended effect; it would have become just one more in the string of casualties inflicted during the firefight.

It had been better to wait. To regain the exclusive attention of the news media airing the event.

That time had come.

Daniel moved behind the line of hostages until he reached the one furthest to the right, the tall airline employee who had tried to escape. Standing on his toes, he whispered in his captive's ear, startling him, "Now listen very carefully to me. I am going to release you, to send a message to the local authorities. Are you willing to do it? Please nod your head if you are."

The tall hostage nodded anxiously, saying, "Yes...yes."

"Very well," Daniel replied calmly. "Release the hand of your companion and turn around to face me. I will take your blindfold off."

The airline employee did as he was ordered and turned to face Daniel, waiting for further instructions. Even though most of his face was covered by a thick, black cloth, he exuded through it raw, almost palpable fear. He raised his shaking hands to remove his blindfold, but Daniel stopped him.

"Leave your blindfold alone! As I said before, *I* will be the one to remove it. Do you understand?"

The man nodded, whispering apologetically, "Yes, of course. Please forgive me."

"Okay," Daniel said, standing sideways in front of him, still covered from the SWAT snipers by the other hostages. Saying, "Time to go!" he tore the black cloth from the man's face, and kicked him on the chest. The hostage staggered backwards, his face a mixture of surprise and dismay. His left foot missed the edge of the rooftop, and for an endless moment, he struggled to regain his balance, his arms cart-wheeling wildly in the air. Then, he looked backwards and screamed in terror, falling into the void behind him.

The tall man who had stood next to him groaned, while April sobbed uncontrollably. The line of hostages tensed, grasping to each other for support.

"Stay as you are!" Daniel warned behind them. "You are in no danger *if*," he paused deliberately on the word "if", "*if* you follow my instructions. The pilot attacked one of my men, even though he had been warned what would happen to him if he disobeyed. He got what he deserved. Now we are all going to start moving together to get back inside the hotel, and we will do it the same way that we got out here, except by taking steps backwards, on my count, one step at a time! Is that understood?"

He paused, to let his prisoners assimilate his words.

"So ready?...One!"

CHAPTER XLI

His heart thumping wildly in his chest after running over the boarding ramp, John entered a large, rectangular warehouse-like area in the bowels of the *Mardi Gras* filled with rows of mostly plastic-wrapped crates and palates. They were stacked neatly, nearly all the way up to the ten-foot ceiling, and through the dull, transparent covering material, he saw that they contained canned and bottled food items. Ambling through its canyon-like corridors, he discovered at one end of the room two smooth, thick aluminum doors, which he determined belonged to some of the massive refrigerated areas where the frozen food was stored. Near them, he noticed the doors to an elevator, probably used to transport food up to the kitchens in the upper decks, and not accessible to the public. There was also a smaller door with an elongated hatch, which he quickly discovered led to a set of narrow stairs that climbed upward. Another door at the opposite end of the warehouse gave access to other smaller storage compartments that contained beverages in plastic bottles, toilet paper, soap, and other sanitizing equipment, as well as spare towels, office equipment, and even dozens of orange-colored lifejackets.

One particular room puzzled him for a moment. It looked like a large refrigerating room, with an aluminum door framing its entrance. In its chilled interior, he only found four long, rectangular metal slabs, stacked over each other in two parallel rows. He quickly realized it was the ship's morgue, and its sight made his skin crawl. "Shit!" he exclaimed with horror. "Shit, shit, shit!" He quickly got out of the room and shut the door behind him. "I will not end up here," he promised himself, but had trouble banishing the gruesome image of his body resting on one of the drab, cold tables.

He soon found out that there were no connections between the storage areas into which he had wandered and the crews' living quarters. *It had obviously been designed that way,* he thought, *to prevent personnel from stealing ship supplies.*

He doubled back to the large food warehouse, and walked to the narrow stairway's access hatch. Stepping inside, he listened for movement, and shut the door behind him. He began to climb slowly, but just about halfway to the first landing, he heard the hinges of a door somewhere above him swing open, and footsteps move hurriedly over the stairs' metallic surface.

Retracing his steps as quickly and quietly as he could, he returned to the hatch he had used to enter the stairwell, but to his great horror discovered for the first time that the door was locked from the inside. A panel with numbers on the wall next to the hatch, with a slit to slide an ID card, was the only means to gain access to the other side. Panicking, he leaned against the wall under the stairs' steps and stared upwards, waiting for the descending person to appear.

"Did you find any other stragglers?" the hoarse voice of a man asked. It sounded as if it came from a couple of decks up.

"Nothing," another voice answered, this time, surprisingly, that of a woman.

"I think it's a waste of time. Anyway, Michael wants us to go to the theater, to start interrogating and dividing the hostages and to organize the crew."

"I just have two more flights of stairs to finish," the woman said, making John curse under his breath at her feminine diligence.

"Forget it! You'll be wasting your time, and Michael wants us now. If there's anyone out there, let him enjoy the ship for now. Come on!"

There was a silence as the woman hesitated, then the sound of a few hurried steps, and the metallic clang of a door shutting down.

John exhaled softly, enjoying his reprieve. *He would have to be more careful if he wanted to survive.* He climbed seven decks, trying to place some distance between him and the searchers, and decided to chance a peek through the door. He was amazed to find himself in the ship's casino.

Keeping himself low, he stepped into the plush red carpet of the silent gaming establishment. He was in the slot machine section, where several rows of the machines glittered with thousands of colored lights and showed graphics of movies, card games, and jewels, their sparkle enhanced by the shiny, mirror-like walls and ceilings that surrounded them. The machines extended in various narrow concentric corridors that interrupted the flow between the two casino exits, designed with the express purpose of making it harder for passengers to walk straight through the gaming hall. John could not have asked for better cover as he moved towards the rear of the ship.

He knew where he was now. He was not a gambler, and spent little time in the cigarette-reeking gambling facility. However, he had cut across it often to get from one end of the ship to the other, and knew where its various exits were located. If he continued moving aft, he would reach the grand staircase that connected the ship's decks. And from there, he would be able to reach the crew's living quarters.

His watch told him it was ten minutes to two in the afternoon. If Ernan had escaped the terrorists who captured the Countess, John would still have time to make the 2:00 o'clock telephone conference, and help dissuade that madman White from trying to take over the ship.

But he had to hurry.

The end of the casino opened up to a small rest area decorated with an anchor and containing the restrooms. From there, the deck continued to the Red Lion, a cozy place decorated like an English pub with a grand piano, where John and the Countess had listened to an Elton John and Billy Joel impersonator until the wee hours of the night.

John sprinted from the casino to the shadows of the empty bar, hiding between its tables. From there he could see the grand staircase, its wide, glass-like steps cascading down from the upper deck, then splitting into two smaller stairways at each side to continue on to the mid landing. It was a luxurious, open area, where he would be in plain view of anyone who happened to be on the levels above or below him.

Nevertheless, he would have to chance it. He had heard the man and the woman in the stairway talk about a meeting in the theater, which hopefully would mean that no terrorists were wandering through the immediate area. *It had to be now.*

Steeling himself for the tension of the next few minutes, he stood up and strolled towards the staircase, turning his head from one side to another, hoping that he would discover anyone walking near him first, before they discovered him. He felt naked and exposed, and his legs shook from the strain.

As he descended, his almost panicked state of mind made him increase his speed until he was running down the steps, two at a time. At one given moment he thought he heard a noise behind him and looked back, tripping and falling headfirst down the stairs. Fortunately for him, the sixth deck's landing was carpeted and only two steps below, but he still hit the floor roughly, hurting his right knee.

Afraid that the noise of his stumbling misstep would attract unwanted attention, he rose up immediately and, ignoring his pain, rushed down to the fifth deck. There, the grand staircase ended. The only way to continue down was by moving through one of the ship's two parallel corridors further into the ship, or by using the stairwell that indicated on its hatch, in black stenciled letters: "AUTHORIZED PERSONNEL ONLY". It was the same stairwell that John, the Countess, and Ernan had used to gain access to the crew's open deck on the stern of the ship, and the one he opted to use now.

He did not pause on the fourth deck to look into the corridor that led to the open space at the rear of the ship from where he had jumped, but continued down to the third deck. There, he slowly opened the exit door and peeked into the corridor beyond. To his great relief, he saw the entrance of the crew's cafeteria a few yards to his left. It felt strange and changed, as if he had been there a decade before, not just slightly more than an hour.

On his prior visit, he had come down a stairway located closer to the center of the ship. This time, his walk would be a lot shorter and less perilous. But as he stepped out of the stairs and prepared to head towards the cafeteria, he noticed further into the ship something strange lying on the corridor's floor. Initially, it looked like a discarded piece of luggage. But then he realized it was the upper torso of a body, sticking out from the open door of one of the cabins.

"Oh no!" he whispered, and ran towards the fallen man.

He knew who it was before he saw his face. His blood-covered overalls still seemed too small for his wide girth, his thick arms bulging from his short-sleeved orange shirt. He was the electrician, Ernan's Indian friend, who had stopped them as they had made their way through the corridor, and to whom John had given his rifle. *What was his name?*

"Harshad," John said softly to himself, feeling an inexplicable sorrow for the man he had hardly known.

He lay face down on the floor, apparently shot in the stomach, from under which a large puddle of blood had spread like black wine on the blue linoleum floor. Dozens of brass bullet cartridges lay strewn all around him, and the door of the cabin where he had hidden, as well as the walls around it, were riddled with bullet holes. There were more blood stains in the corridor, not only on the floor but smeared on the walls, as if others had been wounded. Obviously, there had been an intense firefight, where the Indian electrician had fought until he had been wounded or run out of bullets.

John knelt next to Harshad and, with some difficulty, turned his body so that it would face the ceiling. Harshad's eyes were open, but seemed unnaturally calm, as if he had peacefully waited for death to overtake him. John closed them, as he had seen actors do to the eyes of people who died in the movies, and found to his surprise that they closed very easily.

"Rest in peace, my friend," he said, and looked for the rifle, but could not find it.

He stood up and renewed his trek towards the crew's cafeteria, dreading what he would find there. His fears were justified. The glass door that gave access to the dining facility had been shattered, its shards strewn like spilled ice over the entrance floor. And like the cabin where Harshad lay, the walls were covered with dozens of bullet holes.

John paused to listen for activity within the eating area but could not perceive any. *Quiet like a tomb*, he thought, and instantly tried to banish that image from his mind. His shoes crunching over the broken glass, he entered the cafeteria.

The terrorists had been there. Several tables and chairs were overturned, and part of the aluminum track for the trays in the buffet serving area had collapsed. Worse of all, two more men lay sprawled on the floor. John walked to the one closest to the entrance, a man dressed in a waiter's uniform, but quickly stepped back in revulsion, as he discovered that the back of his skull was missing.

A thick trail of blood led to the feet of the second man, like the trail left behind by a slug on concrete pavement. The man was half reclining against a counter, and had obviously dragged himself there after he had either been given up for dead by the terrorists, or abandoned by them to bleed to death. John recognized him immediately; it was his fellow countryman, White. His tight, black T-shirt was soaked in blood, its smell pungent even from the entrance of the cafeteria. Like in Harshad's case, there were several cartridges scattered throughout the floor.

John made his way to the fallen man and leaned to place two of his fingers over White's neck to feel for a pulse. To his surprise, the Australian stirred to the touch, raising his eyelids and staring tiredly at John. A glint of recognition flickered in his eyes.

"They...took my...my gun..." he barely whispered, his lips dry and bloody.

John stood up and searched the serving area. Locating a cup, he rushed behind the counters and filled it with water from the kitchen's faucet. He returned to the wounded man, and placed the cup on his lips, tilting it slightly to let him sip some of its liquid.

"The others," John said softly. "Ernan, did they take them?"

White looked up at him gratefully for several seconds and then exhaled, never to breathe again.

"Christ!" John muttered, feeling scared and utterly alone. "Why the hell did I return?"

The terrorists had won. They had wiped out the last remnants of any real resistance, and they would wipe him out too if they caught him. There was no way that he could contact the FBI now. The terrorists had his satellite phone. He should have swum away.

But still, the face of the Countess haunted and tormented him. She had trusted him, her silent eyes had screamed at him, and he had betrayed her. He could not let her down again. *Not yet, in any event.*

He decided to spy on the terrorists. They were going to...what was it one of them had said? *Organize. Organize and divide the hostages.* He would try to see where, if anywhere, the "divided" hostages were taken, and to obtain a rough estimate of the number of terrorists on board. After all, he had traveled thirty-two times on the *Mardi Gras*, and knew it better than any of the terrorists. He knew of ways to sneak into the Stardust Theater that only the ship's stage technicians knew about. It would be very risky, but he was certain that he could slip into the theater, and take note of what the terrorists were up to. Any information that he acquired would be of some value to the rescuers who hopefully would soon come to the ship.

He would spy on the terrorists for a couple of hours, he decided, and then jump from the ship again and try to get that information to the FBI, somehow. And this time, when he jumped from the *Mardi Gras*, he would not be abandoning the Countess but actually be trying to help her. And maybe her accusatory expression would fade from his mind.

John got back to his feet and exited the cafeteria. Now that his mind was made up, he felt relieved and more excited than afraid. Somehow, irrationally, he felt certain that the terrorists had finished their business in the third deck, and that they would not return. It was therefore a surprise when, as he walked through the corridor, he heard a strange noise ahead of him.

At the beginning it could have been one of the thousands of sounds produced by a giant cruise vessel. A metallic *crack* echoing on the empty passageway. But then he heard the definite, unpredictable, imprecise, banging sounds that only a human being could make; the noises produced by somebody ahead of him apparently attempting to handle some kind of equipment. Whoever he or she was, he had not seen John, and was not visible from the corridor. The noise, now plain and obvious, seemed to be coming from one of the cabins not very far away from where he stood.

John considered retreating to the cafeteria, but decided it would be the first place the returning terrorists would search. Instead, he hurriedly tiptoed his way to the cabin where Harshad's body lay, and entered it.

He quickly realized there was no real place to hide there. If the hijackers headed his way, he would have to hole up in the cabin's tiny bathroom and hope that they would not search the room.

Still, he felt curious about the identity of the noisemaker. The first sounds he had heard had been loud but sparse. But with the passage of time, the banging increased in intensity and urgency, as if the person making it was struggling with a machine. Leaning over Harshad's legs, John peered briefly outside, but still could not perceive any activity in the corridor.

The pounding seemed to be coming from somewhere very near, not more than half a dozen cabins away. And whoever was doing it seemed to be absolutely concentrated in whatever activity he was pursuing, and oblivious of the rest of his surroundings.

Unable to resist his curiosity, John walked out of the room and slowly made his way further into the ship. It took him no time to determine that the racket was coming from a large open entrance to his right. Stopping by the doorframe he paused and, taking a deep breath, took a quick peek.

He found himself looking into the crew's laundry room, and it was empty. And yet, the noise definitely originated from there. Puzzled, he walked into the room, and confirmed that there was nobody inside. However, the pounding continued unabated, apparently coming from behind one of the giant washing machines.

And then, at last, John understood, and laughed. "I am so stupid I should die!" he said to himself, and rushed to the washing machine nearest to the wall, pulling its handle and opening its door.

A slight man drenched in sweat stuck his head out and greedily breathed in the cool air of the laundry.

"Ernan!" John exclaimed with delight.

"Mr. McFadden!" the Filipino man shouted joyously, extending his arms out of the mouth of the washing machine. John pulled him out and helped him get back to his feet. "God is good! You are alive!" Ernan embraced his rescuer gratefully. "I thought that they had captured you!"

John nodded, smiling embarrassedly. "I escaped. It's a long story. Tell me, what happened after we last spoke?"

Ernan's face darkened. He seemed reluctant to relive the moments that had forced him to hide inside the washer. "After you left, the Countess and I waited, not wanting to leave you alone. I know that you told us to go ahead, to go down to the cafeteria without you, but we didn't want to abandon you. The Countess, she was particularly troubled. She has a great fondness for you. She wanted to follow you, and we argued. '*No*', I said. '*Mr. McFadden told us to go back to the others!*' But she would not listen. '*I must see what he is doing*', she said to me. Before I could stop her she ran out of the door."

The Filipino sounded upset and distressed.

"I really tried to stop her," he said apologetically. "But she is...well, you know her better than I know her. She is a very headstrong woman. Very headstrong! She would not listen to me."

"So what happened?" John asked, trying to hasten the Filipino's story. By overstaying in the laundry room, they were inviting trouble.

"She went after you. I sat down and waited. I could not see her through the narrow slit of the door that I had left open, so I...I stopped looking through it altogether, and just sat there and waited. I could hear her talking, I'm not certain what she was saying, so I tried to listen better. But then very unexpectedly two pirates walked past the door, and I heard the Countess scream..." Ernan shook his head with despair. "You must think I am a coward," he said bitterly. "And I am...When I heard her scream I fled down the stairs. I feared that if they found me they would kill me, so...I ran. I left her and you behind and I ran." His eyes filled with tears.

"There was nothing that you could have done, Ernan," John said. "It was your duty to warn the others and not to let the phone fall into the hands of the terrorists. You still have the phone, don't you?"

Ernan patted his pants, pushed his hand into his right hand pocket, and pulled out the satellite telephone. He handed it reverently to its owner.

"Thank you," John said appreciatively. "You did well." He flicked it open to check its battery power. It still had most of its charge. *So everything was not lost,* he thought with relief. He would not have to jump off the ship again to talk to the FBI.

The FBI! Suddenly, he remembered the 2:00 o'clock call and looked at his watch. *It was 2:25 o'clock already!*

"Did the FBI call?" he asked the Filipino.

Ernan moved his head negatively.

The answer surprised John, but then he realized that Ernan had been inside the ship at the time that the agents were supposed to call back, and that the satellite phone needed to be in the open in order to receive or transmit calls. They had probably been trying to reach him during the past half hour.

"What happened to the others?" he asked Ernan.

"When the pirates captured the Countess, I ran back down to my friends. I told Harshad that the pirates might be coming, and then I went to the cafeteria to talk to the others, as you instructed me," he answered. "I told them everything you said that I should tell them. That they should wait. That help was on the way. That you had spoken to the FBI, and that they said that we should not try to rescue the passengers by ourselves. But every one of my words was wasted in their deaf ears. The Australian, White, said that it was now more urgent than ever to rescue you and the Countess. They would not listen to me," he said dejectedly.

"White was itching to fight the terrorists," John consoled his new friend. "He wouldn't have listened to me or anybody else."

"I am sure that he would have listened to you," Ernan stated with conviction. "I decided to come back to the fourth deck and see if somehow you had escaped, and I was right, because you did and here you are!"

John thought about confessing to his friend how he had managed to escape, but decided keep it to himself, in order not to distract him.

"So then what happened?"

"I left the cafeteria, and had just walked past Harshad when I heard many footsteps and voices coming from the stairs that we had taken to go to the fourth deck. Harshad heard them too, and told me to hide, so I ran inside this cursed laundry room."

John suppressed his desire to smile. It had always been Ernan's idea to hide in the laundry room. In the end, he had gotten his wish.

"They must have been about to enter the corridor, because the shooting started just after I ran inside here. The noise was very, very loud, and Harshad held them off for a long time. But I knew it all would be a matter of time. The pirates had more guns and the firing noises coming from their side was tremendous. I was afraid that at any moment they would come into the room, so I hid inside one of the washing machines and shut the door."

Ernan looked around the room, searching for water. He was drenched in sweat. He walked to a refreshment vending machine, and fishing some change out of one of his pockets, bought a can of Dr, Pepper, and drank from it greedily. *It was all so surreal,* John thought.

"Please forgive me," the small Filipino said. "It was very hot in there, very hot. And I was so scared, listening to the shooting outside. I was afraid that they would find me and shoot me right in there, inside of the washing machine. But what really terrified me was when the shooting stopped, because it meant that the pirates had captured or killed Harshad, and that they were coming."

John listened quietly, picturing the small man lying still inside of the shadowy bosom of the washer, unable to see what was happening outside the laundry room, expecting to be discovered at any moment. He could still see the fright in the man's eyes.

"I have never prayed so hard. I am not a very religious man, but today I felt closer to eternity than never before, and I'm sure that my prayers covered me like a blanket and saved me, because the pirates never came into this room." He paused to drink some more Dr. Pepper. "I heard some more shooting later, farther away. In the cafeteria, I guessed. Then it stopped again and there was much shouting, angry shouting, scared shouting. I couldn't understand the words, but it kept getting louder, until it felt as if they were right here, outside in the corridor. After a while the shouts—they sounded more like curses to me—got less and less loud until they stopped completely, and then there was just silence. I decided to wait at least half an hour, to make certain that the pirates had left, but time would not pass. That was the worst part, waiting. I had nothing to do, nothing to distract me except my thoughts. I wondered what had happened to the others, and I thought about what would happen to me, and somewhere along the way I must have fallen asleep, because I woke up in this stifling heat where I could hardly breathe. Then I tried to open the door, but I couldn't! I started to push it and kick it, and it wouldn't budge, and I asked myself, for this you have been saved from the pirates? To have me die like this?"

Ernan stared at John, and smiled shyly.

"Pathetic, isn't it?"

"Not at all," John answered, not quite sure about what the Filipino was talking about.

"I should have trusted my instincts. I knew you would save me."

John smiled back at him.

"Your instincts are better than mine."

Ernan crossed himself. "Do you know what happened to the others?" he asked half-heartedly, afraid to find out.

"Harshad is dead and so is White," John replied, breaking the bad news quickly. "Both of them died fighting. Also another man I did not know. We must assume that the others were taken by the terrorists, and that they took them to the theater."

John had expected Ernan to break down emotionally, but the wiry Filipino acknowledged the news resignedly, quietly wiping his eyes with his sleeve.

"We have to contact the FBI," John continued. He was not very enthused with the idea, since it meant, unless Ernan knew of a different place, that they would have to place the call from the open terrace from where he had jumped.

As he suspected, the Filipino confirmed that there was no other nearby place. The open terrace would have to suffice. John would make the call from there, and hope that the telephone number that Agent Moylan had given to him would get them through to the FBI.

And so, taking two bottles of water from the vending machine—this time neither of the two men had change, so they ended up smashing the glass—they headed back up to the fourth deck, using the same narrow stairway that they had used before.

"Now listen very carefully," John whispered to Ernan as they reached the exit to the fourth deck. "If anything happens to me, you run, you understand?"

Ernan stared at him, and assented without any great conviction. John opened his mouth to extract a promise from the Filipino that he would do as he was told, but gave up on the idea. Instead, he took a fast peek into the corridor from behind the door and, finding it clear, stepped out and darted towards the terrace.

The glass doors swished open and the cool breeze of the bay rushed to greet him, messing up his hair. He moved sideways and lay flat against the wall. Extending the antenna of his telephone, he waited for it to register a satellite signal. This time it took more than a minute, but a few seconds later Moylan's voice responded.

"Moylan here," the FBI man's voice answered before the second ring. *"Is that you, John?"*

"It's me," the Australian answered softly.

"I have you on the speakerphone with Brown and Mendoza. We had given you up for lost!" the FBI man said, relief evident in his words.

You don't know how close you are to the truth, John thought to himself. "Things have gotten complicated," he said instead. "The terrorists have captured most of the remaining crew, and have killed at least three people. The only persons not yet captured are me and Ernan, a *maitre de* of the ship."

"I'm very sorry to hear that," Moylan responded. *"Are you all right?"*

"I'm fine," John answered impatiently. "Now listen carefully because I may not have much time. So far, the terrorists have kept the passengers and the crew in the Stardust Theatre. However, I overheard two of them say that they were planning to separate and organize them."

"That means that they may be planning to spread the hostages to make a rescue more difficult," the female agent, Brown, said, more to her two companions than to John.

"Did you hear that John?" Moylan asked. *"This is not good news. We need to know—"*

"Yeah, yeah, you need me to get more information on where they are being taken," John said, stopping Moylan from restating the obvious. "I know."

"I'm sorry, John. I really am. I know that I'm asking a lot from you. But every bit of information that we get will save lives."

He felt tempted to ask: *How about my life, you moron?* But he bit his tongue. "I understand that, and I will do what I can. I have to go now, but I wanted to tell you something else."

"Go ahead."

"In addition to the main gangway for the passengers, there is a second, smaller gangway that is presently open at the same level of the dock, close to the bow of the ship. It is used to get supplies into the ship, and it leads to one of the ship's storage areas. I don't know how much longer it will remain open and unguarded, but it's open now. It's another way to get into the ship."

John heard Moylan mumble something to the other two agents, and then his voice returned to the phone.

"We'll be looking into that right now, John. That's great intelligence. Thanks!" he said a little bit too enthusiastically.

"I will call you if and when I can with whatever additional information I can get. But I can't promise you anything."

"We understand. You've already done more than your share. Just hold on for a few hours more. Help is on the way. Good luck!"

John switched off his contact. *More than his share,* he thought, feeling no satisfaction. That was something he had never been told before. He had always prided himself for doing just what was necessary. *Only idiots did more than their share.*

John folded his antenna and turned his phone off. Making certain that no one was in the corridor, he exited the terrace and began to walk back towards Ernan.

Only idiots, he repeated to himself.

CHAPTER XLII

Lucas pushed the exit door at the emergency stairs in the Metropolitan Center, and stepped out onto Fortaleza Street. He stood for a moment under the old-style green metallic canopy that marked the entrance to the Marshall's store occupying the basement of the building, and casually scanned the area around him. Normally, the one-way street would be jammed with automobiles heading east, in the direction of Puerta de Tierra and Miramar, or planning to turn south, towards the city parking buildings and the docks. The noise of their engines would occasionally mix with the impatient blast of a horn and the shrill squeal of a brake, filling the small, canyon-like street that flowed between the parallel rows of mostly three-storied buildings with the echoes of a discordant traffic symphony.

At that time of the day, the sidewalks would be clogged with busy shoppers, both tourists and locals; office workers, mostly from the scores of state and municipal agencies located in the old city; a sprinkling of beggars, many sitting in predetermined intersections; and the actual residents of the city or *sanjuaneros*, some of them leaning from their balconies and lazily inspecting the crowd below. The McDonald's housed in the colonial-style building in the corner of the other side of the street would be brimming with hungry clients, while a lottery vendor—taking advantage of the canopy's shade—would display on a wooden bench his pre-printed tickets to prospective clients searching for "lucky" numbers. There would be busy merchants and messengers on motorcycles, police making their rounds, and children returning from school or skipping classes.

But that afternoon, the street was deserted. *As empty as the promises of a politician,* his grandfather would have said. He missed the old man.

Lucas adjusted the leather strap of the missile launcher over his shoulder, and began to walk towards the Governor's Mansion, just three blocks away. From where he had emerged, the street sloped gently upwards, past some of the oldest buildings in the city, now mostly occupied by stores and fine restaurants.

He had always enjoyed strolling through that part of town, every structure carefully preserved, with dark, wooden balconies and large, interior courtyards, each establishment painted in bright, different colors, as if celebrating their continued existence and individuality through the various centuries of the city's long history.

He knew that with the launcher sticking up at least two feet over his head, he would attract attention from very far away. It made him feel very vulnerable, as if he was walking down the street with a sign that read "LOOK AT ME" in bold letters. But he was also banking on his visibility to keep him safe. Anyone watching him from a distance would know that he was not trying to hide, and hopefully allow him to continue his journey without getting shot.

To make it more obvious, he traveled through the middle of the street, hoping his overt approach would dissipate any doubts about his open intentions. He was also relying on his black armband and the stolen clothes, praying that they would make him pass as one of the revolutionaries, and that he would not meet anyone who could recognize him.

As he passed La Barrachina Restaurant—*the birthplace of the Piña Colada*, a plaque at its entrance advertised—the faint outline of the tall wrought iron gates of La Fortaleza began to solidify before his eyes. It surprised him to see them intact. He had imagined that the Macheteros had broken through them in order to capture the Governor's residence, but apparently that had not been the case. He wondered how they had done it. He was still too far away to see anyone, but assumed there would be people guarding the entrance, if the radio reports were true.

He could still not believe what he was doing. He had reviewed in his head what he would say a hundred times, but still felt highly uneasy about his own imaginary responses. He would have to speak with a foreign accent, a made-up foreign accent, since he had never been very good at imitating the speech intonations of Spanish-speaking visitors from other countries. Mexican he could do, and a passable Argentinean as well, but the men he had fought had been neither. Their enunciation had sounded more Central American, so he would just have to invent an accent and trust that his interviewers were just as ignorant in foreign accents as he was.

He would tell them that the colonel—there had been a colonel in the walkie-talkie conversation—had been concerned about a helicopter assault on La Fortaleza, and that he had been sent to protect it from the roof. He hoped they would not notice the dents and shattered trigger of the missile launcher.

What he would do after that was uncertain. If he was allowed to enter La Fortaleza, somebody would probably lead him to the roof. He would have to be very alert as he walked through the Governor's Mansion, trying to determine where the hostages were. With luck, he could try to start a conversation with his guide and steer it to the prisoners' whereabouts. At the very worst, he would have to come down from the rooftop after he was led there, and search the mansion himself.

La Fortaleza was plainly visible now, its high neoclassical façade marking the end of the street. He counted three men, one standing outside of the gates, two lounging in the security guardhouse. Surprisingly, the man in front of the gate did not notice him until he was less than fifty feet away. Looking slightly startled, the guard placed two of his fingers in his mouth and produced a sharp whistle, making his two other companions to look up. He quickly slipped his AK-47 from his shoulder and began to walk towards the unannounced arrival.

Lucas placed the metal suitcase holding the missiles on the cobblestoned street and opened both of his arms widely, with the palms of his hands facing forward, to show that he was not holding a gun. He stopped, letting the guard—a wiry, clean-shaven teenager wearing a white T-shirt and jeans—approach him.

"What do you want?" the young lookout asked in a distrustful, semi-hostile tone, his eyes darting from the long, strange weapon that Lucas had strapped to his back, to his "Libre como el Coqui" armband, to the suitcase on the road.

"I've been sent to La Fortaleza, in case your government sends any helicopters to rescue the Governor," he answered, trying his best to mimic the singsong accent of the two soldiers he had met on the rooftop of the Metropolitan Center, and thinking what a terrible job he was making of it. He saw another of the guards trotting towards him and tried not to seem nervous.

This was a critical moment. For all he knew, the Governor could already have been dead, and then his explanation as to why he was there would make no sense. He had left the strap of his holster unlatched and the safety of his ZIG Sauer off, in case he had to draw his gun quickly and shoot his way out of there. Very slowly, he lowered his hands, to get them closer to his gun.

The young revolutionary snorted derisively. "*My* government?" He spit on the ground. "Certainly not *mine*."

Lucas managed a complicit smile, hoping it looked genuine. The second man arrived, examining Lucas even before he stopped. He was big and fat, a tall man nearing the three hundred pound milestone, his stomach bulging ostensibly over his belt. His hair was cut very short, as if shorn by a barber's shaving machine, seeming more like an extension of the three-day stubble that covered his jowls.

"What's happening? Who is this guy?" he asked his companion between long breaths, not prying his eyes from the stranger's face, in an uncharacteristically high-pitched voice.

"He says he's here to protect us in case the police tries to attack us with helicopters."

The fat Machetero stared at the rocket launcher. "Are you one of the Venezuelans?" he asked.

"Yes," Lucas answered gratefully. He had no idea about how a Venezuelan spoke, but guessed that neither did the others.

"Follow me," the fat Machetero said.

As Lucas approached the guardhouse, he could see behind the gate the bodies of two men sprawled on the floor, amid large puddles of blood. *Security men from La Fortaleza,* he thought, shuddering and diverting his eyes from them.

"What's the matter?" the young Machetero asked, snickering. "You scared of dead people? What a great soldier you are. Don't worry, we'll be getting rid of them soon. They're starting to stink."

Lucas did not bother to respond. As he entered the guardhouse, it struck him that he had not visited La Fortaleza since he was in grammar school, when his class had been brought to the Governor's Mansion on a field trip. He hardly remembered anything, except for a room where President Kennedy had slept, the display of a moon rock under a glass case, and a large, broken clock, struck by the outgoing Spanish governor to forever mark the time when the United States had taken possession of the island from Spain. All very interesting, but of little use at that moment.

The guardhouse was a narrow, air-conditioned structure with a metal detector. At the other side of the table where visitors placed their cameras, purses and other objects for inspection, was a console with six television screens. Lucas watched with interest that the cameras seemed to be focused on the areas surrounding the front gate and the garages of La Fortaleza. None showed the gardens behind the mansion. It was important information to know when he got his godson out.

The Machetero in the guardhouse, however, seemed more interested in watching a small television screen that was showing the Grand Laguna Hotel than keeping track of what was happening in his immediate area. Probably close to his fifties, the man sported a neatly trimmed beard of white hair, which framed restless blue eyes and a thin, skeptic smile, giving him an aura of authority that his two other companions lacked.

"You should see this!" he said to the arriving men. "All of the cameras are showing the roof of the Grand Laguna, waiting for the first hostage to take a dive." He shook his head in wonderment. "Isn't modern technology something else?"

"Haven't they thrown down anybody yet?" the younger Machetero asked.

"Supposedly at two. That was about ten minutes ago, but nothing has happened yet," the white-haired Machetero answered, already more interested in Lucas. "What do we have here?" he asked with the professional tone of a mechanic getting ready to check a stalled car.

"This gentleman is from the Venezuelan outfit," the fat man explained. "He has been sent over to protect La Fortaleza, in case the police try to get here by helicopter."

The white-haired Machetero stared at Lucas as he fished out of his pocket a cigarette pack. "Protect La Fortaleza? From where?"

"The roof," Lucas answered.

The guard nodded slowly, as if digesting the information.

"With that thing?" he asked, jerking his head at the missile launcher.

"Yes."

"How come they're sending you now? Why didn't they think of this before?"

Lucas shrugged.

"I don't know," he answered.

The bearded Machetero raised one of his eyebrows in a deliberate gesture that he must have practiced a thousand times. "You don't know?" he said with a hint of disbelief.

"I never question my colonel's orders," Lucas answered, looking directly at his interrogator's eyes. His tone was soft and polite, and yet it carried a distinct undertone of violence. "I just follow his orders. But if you want to find out, contact him."

The Machetero blinked and laughed. "You don't have to get upset, mister..."

"Fidel. Fidel Maestes," Lucas answered, mouthing the first names that popped into his mind.

"Mr. Maestes." The Machetero extended his hand and Lucas shook it. "Good to meet you. Ruben Escudero, at your service. Your Venezuelan accent is very similar to that of Puerto Rico."

Lucas cringed inwardly, but managed to smile.

"Another bond between our two countries," he said curtly.

"Quite."

A short, awkward silence followed.

"Shall I take him up to the roof of La Fortaleza?" the portly Machetero asked.

"Do you know how to get to the roof of La Fortaleza, Alberto?" The bearded man directed an amused glance at Lucas, as if secretly saying to him, *"Do you see the bunch of morons that I have to deal with?"*

Alberto shook his head.

"Then how are you going to get him up there? No. Take him to Tino. He'll get the necessary clearance from our superiors." Ruben returned his attention to Lucas. "I apologize for the double-checking, but we can't take any risks. Not with the Governor here, you understand?"

Lucas nodded. For the second time that day, his hopes had been raised only to be dashed a second later. He forced himself to remain calm. He had managed to fake his way through the outer security perimeter of the terrorists, and he would fake his way inside as well. And if he didn't...well, the strap of his holster was still unlatched.

Ruben waved his hand lazily towards the metal detector, and laughed as it buzzed when Lucas and Alberto walked through it. "That machine must be having a nervous breakdown after swallowing so much metal."

"Not so much as the metal those helicopters will swallow if they try to land here," Lucas said in his fake Venezuelan accent, playing his role to the hilt. The improbable image of Jeannie playing the game of *Balderdash* popped in his mind. *"If you want them to believe your bluff,"* she had told him after nobody had voted for his definition of a word, *"you can't exaggerate the role you're playing."* Just now he had sounded so fake that for a moment he feared the others would see through his pretended bravado. But fortunately for him, they all seemed to be concentrated in their own personal concerns. He would follow Jeannie's advice next time.

The Governor's Mansion now loomed before him, a huge, multi-balconied, light-blue, L-shaped structure, its cornices, plaster decorations, and long, shuttered windows fringed in white to highlight its elegant architecture. As he strode over the vast space in front of the building, he stepped on broken shards of glass, and for the first time he noticed that some of the mansion's windows were shattered by bullets. Close to the arched-roof entrance that led to the mansion's main stairway and the inner courtyard, he saw an American flag crumpled on the ground, alongside another white flag bearing the shield of the city of San Juan, apparently discarded by the revolutionaries.

Looking upwards, he noticed that of the three flagpoles rising from the top of the main building, only two flags now flapped in the wind. One was the official Puerto Rican flag. The second showed an emblem divided into four squares by a white cross, its upper two squares colored in blue, its lower two in red, a white star emblazoned on its left upper corner. It was the flag from the Grito de Lares, a short-lived revolt in the nineteenth century that had been crushed by the Spanish Government and had since been adopted as one of the principal symbols of the independence movement.

"Soon, every flag in Puerto Rico will be like one of those two," Alberto observed with pride, as he noticed Lucas staring at the flagpoles.

Lucas felt tempted to ask which of the two flags the Machetero preferred, but opted to remain quiet.

As they walked under the arched entrance, he glanced at the main stairway, extending upwards to his left into the Governor's palace. It was as beautiful and impressive as his sister Vanessa had described it the night before. The upper steps were made of marble and edged with mahogany, the vertical risers below each step covered with fancifully patterned porcelain tiles. Its banister was also made of mahogany and supported by ornately shaped marble posts. The walls were painted in pale yellow, and like the outside of the building, were decorated with fanciful bas reliefs portraying arches, columns, flowers, cherubim and the busts of well-endowed, scantily dressed women. Its ceiling rose up three stories, and was crowned by a dome illuminated by small windows with delicate glass patterns.

"Nice, eh?" Alberto said, reading Lucas' face again.

"Very," he answered. He tried to listen for sounds coming from within, but heard none. "I guess you're keeping the hostages in La Fortaleza under very tight security?"

"We have to," Alberto answered. "After all, it's the Governor of Puerto Rico...for now, anyway."

Lucas decided to chance it and ask point blank for the information that he wanted. "Where do you keep them?"

"Them?" Alberto glanced casually back at him, but kept walking.

"The hostages. Where do you keep the hostages?"

"Oh! We keep the Governor in his office. The others, I'm not so sure. I haven't dealt with them."

So much for that source of information, Lucas thought, totally frustrated.

The fat Machetero began to climb the stairs, huffing and puffing as he did so, the sound of his heavy footsteps echoing from the walls. After fourteen steps, the stairs reached a landing with wooden shuttered windows and turned to the right, renewing its climb towards the first floor. A man sat at the upper end, on a 17th century, French-style, elaborately carved armchair upholstered in blue silk, which he had obviously dragged from another room. He wore an intensely red T-shirt and a matching beret, which contrasted with a bushy, jet black, Castro-like beard. One of his legs rested over one of the chair's arms, an AK-47 rifle resting across his thighs while he ate a banana.

"I'm looking for Tino," Alberto told him without any introduction.

The man raised his hand and pointed to his left.

"He's in the Governor's office, with the black guy."

Alberto nodded and shuffled past the sitting guard. He turned left, guiding Lucas through a corridor until they reached a large, high-roofed room with heavy wooden beams that crossed its ceiling from one end to another. Its floor was made of small white, gray, and black polished marble squares, and it was sparsely decorated, its principal wall holding a large, embroidered tapestry bearing the shield of San Juan. A small staircase at the back of the room connected to the building's lower level. The room was meagerly furnished by La Fortaleza standards, looking almost like a small ballroom, with elegant high-backed furniture close to its two opposing windowless walls, and a carved mirror table decorating the only wall with a window.

Two tall, ebony colored wooden doors dominated the hall's fourth wall. They were shut, and a man chewing gum and holding a sub machinegun stood guard in front of them. He must have been in his early thirties, with short, badly shorn hair and a long scar running from his right ear and disappearing under his shirt from his neck.

"I'm looking for Tino," Alberto announced from a distance.

"Good luck," the guard answered, his attention focused on the funny, tube-like weapon that the man behind his comrade-in-arms was hefting. "He's been in there for about an hour now," he said, jerking his thumb in the direction of the dark-paneled doors behind him.

"Maybe we should wait," Alberto said uncertainly.

It was not what Lucas wanted to hear. He could not afford to stay there and wait. The two Venezuelans on the roof of the Metropolitan Center were bound to be discovered sooner or later, and after that it would only be a matter of time before they tracked him down. *He had to act, and act now.*

"I can't wait," he told the two Macheteros flatly, surprising them with the urgency and forcefulness of his voice. "I was sent here on an emergency basis, because there is reason to believe that a helicopter assault by the police or the federal authorities is imminent. This weapon that I carry can shoot down any enemy aircraft that dares to fly anywhere close to us. But I need to get to the roof of La Fortaleza, and I need to do it now! It will do us no good to send me up there after they have landed."

Alberto breathed in deeply. "I think maybe...I guess we could knock on the door and talk to Tino. This shouldn't take that long anyway." He glanced nervously at the other Machetero, who frowned and continued to chew gum at a more furious rate.

"It's up to you," he said in a neutral tone. "You know the facts much better than I do." In reality, he meant, "You're on your own."

The portly terrorist placed his right hand tentatively over one of the doors, hesitated briefly, and tapped it timidly. Leaving his hand there, he waited for about half a minute, but nothing happened. He darted a quick look at Lucas, and prepared to knock again when the other door suddenly opened.

A tall man with pronounced cheekbones and a skull-like expression stepped into the doorframe. He was dressed in black military fatigues, and carried two guns strapped by a gun belt to his waist, cowboy fashion. His eyes were dark and brimming with unstated anger, so much so that it took them several seconds to focus on Alberto.

"Tino!" the fat man attempted to sound more cheerful than he actually felt, but instead sounded apprehensive. His angry superior failed to acknowledge the greeting, and waited in silence for his plump underling to state his business. "I need your permission to allow this Venezuelan soldier to climb to the roof," he stated simply.

"Why should I do that?" the tall man snapped. The guard standing at the door could not suppress a snort of laughter, nearly losing his gum.

"Because he has been sent—" Alberto helplessly began to explain, but Lucas cut him short.

"I have been ordered to get to the roof of La Fortaleza because of a possible assault by helicopter."

Tino shifted his gaze to Lucas, as if noticing him for the first time. For a moment, he seemed to drift back into the private thoughts that were tormenting him. Then a thin smile appeared on his lips. "Come in," he ordered Lucas abruptly. "Not you," he added in a peevish tone, as Alberto began to follow. "You can go back to the gate."

Alberto hesitated and, nodding, left.

Lucas walked into what must have been the biggest and most luxurious office he had ever seen. Two large crystal chandeliers hung from its ceiling, while tall, bas relief columns, crowned with gold leaf ornaments, rose from the floor to the roof between multiple sets of doors. A beautiful carpet, highlighted in soft pastel colors and showing a combination of whimsical, geometric patterns, covered the entire floor. The furniture was elegant and classic, the center of the room dominated by a round table surrounded by two wooden, cushioned, rocking chairs and two small sofas.

"What is it? Who's there?" asked what seemed a to be disembodied voice, prompting Lucas to look into the office. He discovered a black man slumped almost horizontally on one of the sofas, reclining upright on one arm against one of its armrests. His first impression of the man was that of a round-faced cherubim who had strayed too far from Heaven and got singed in Hell. A smile showing perfectly white teeth stretched under his plump cheeks from one ear to the other, giving him a distinctly harmless, happy-go-lucky air, like that of a tourist who had just wandered into the room and engaged its Machetero occupant in a casual conversation. There was something about him, however, that Lucas did not like. Something about his intensely watchful eyes that warned him that there was more to this man than he cared to show.

As Lucas entered into the room, the man examined him with amusement, and emitting a deep, rumbling chuckle, said with mock horror, "Lordy, lordy! From what trap did this mouse spring?"

"This gentleman says that he has been ordered to move to the roof of La Fortaleza, to protect us with his weapon from any helicopters that decide to attack us," Tino said, wrinkling his nose at the reclining man. From the first word that he uttered, it was evident that the cadaverous-looking Machetero leader intensely disliked the man he was addressing.

"Really? That's interesting," the reclining man said, his grin widening, if that was possible. "Then allow him to protect us."

"Not so fast!" Tino answered, not hiding his irritation. "I am in command here and I have not been told anything about this man. I need to talk to El Alacran. Get his clearance."

The mention of El Alacran surprised Lucas and shook his self-confidence. He had heard on the radio that the revolutionaries were demanding the release of the Machetero leader, Adalberto Cacho, and like everyone else had suspected that the terrorist group was behind the events of that day. However, it was one thing to suspect their involvement, and another to confirm it. Like Cacho, El Alacran held a permanent position in the FBI's most wanted list, and was deemed the more ruthless of the two men. His being in charge of the San Juan revolt was grim news indeed.

Lucas unconsciously moved his hand closer to his gun's holster, and to his alarm noticed that his reaction did not escape the keen eyes of the black man with the Cheshire cat-like smile. The man, however, did not react, but instead laughed out loudly, earning a venomous look from his Machetero counterpart.

"I fail to see what you find so funny," Tino said.

"*You* are, my friend," the cherubic-faced man answered good-naturedly. "You keep saying that you're in charge, but you keep relying on others for instructions."

"That's too bad—" Tino began to say, but the black man interrupted him.

"For one thing," the grinning man continued, "you say that Mr. Alacran gave you 'instructions' to take the Governor here to the Grand Laguna Hotel." The man pointed to a large desk at the end of the room, and for the first time, Lucas realized that the Governor of Puerto Rico was seating behind it. His appearance shocked him. Even though he did not show any visible bruises or injuries, he seemed to be on the verge of exhaustion. "My boss told me to keep him under tight observation here, right where we are now. 'In the Governor's office', he said. This *is* the Governor's office, ain't it?"

"I don't care what—"

The black man chortled, and shook his head.

"And then," he continued, as if the Machetero leader had not spoken, "you won't let this man do his job until you talk to El Alacran." He turned his gaze towards Lucas. "But El Alacran ain't your boss, is he now, boy?"

Lucas shook his head.

"So El Alacran has no business knowing who sent you here, does he?" the black man asked him again, prolonging his question with another chuckle.

Lucas felt a wave of relief as Tino hesitated and said nothing.

The black man stood up, and slowly walked towards his counterpart. "Now, I'm not saying that you can't send the Governor to the hotel, but I'm not saying that you can, catch my drift?" he said, apparently renewing the discussion that he had been having with Tino before Lucas walked into the office. "The only person who can say that is San Miguel, and he's busy right now, throwing tourists off the roof of the hotel and all that stuff. So is El Alacran, as far as I know. So we sit tight, you and me, you understand? We wait for further instructions." The black man pointed at the Governor. "And when the time comes, I'll help you move him...If he has to be moved." He slapped the thin Machetero leader on the back in a friendly fashion.

Tino scowled, and for a moment it seemed as if he was about to send the other man to hell. In the end, however, he settled for a dissatisfied grunt. "I will wait for now," he stated, "but if we don't hear from Andrade soon, I will take matters into my hands."

The black man stared at him with amusement and shrugged. Then with a lightning quick move he drew his gun from his holster. During the split second that followed, it seemed that the man would shoot the disgruntled Tino, but then he turned and pointed his weapon at Lucas. He smiled.

"I still haven't figured out what to do about you," he said with a snicker. "Please raise your hands over your head." He saw Lucas hesitate, and shook his head good-naturedly. Lucas did as he was bid. Behind the armed man, he saw the Governor for the first time raise his head and watch what was happening with some interest. "I haven't seen you before, so I guess we better start from the beginning. Who are you, friend?"

"My name is Fidel Maestes," Lucas responded, and knowing that his life depended on it, added with all the self-assurance that he could muster, "private first class, First Hugo Chavez Anti-air Missile Battalion." It was all made up, but he suspected that the others would be unable to tell.

"Nice to meet you, Fidel Maestes," the black man replied. "I'm George. Who sent you here?"

"My colonel, sir," Lucas answered immediately. "He has received information that—"

"Yeah, yeah, I've heard that part before. What's the name of your colonel?"

Lucas knew that he was caught. He thought of drawing his gun but just as quickly discarded the idea, realizing he had no chance. He decided to brazen it out. "Colonel Martinez, sir. You can call him if you doubt me."

George chuckled, flashing his white teeth. "There is no need to call Colonel Martinez," he said.

"I would call him to make certain," Tino prompted in a critical tone.

"Like I said, there is no need to call Colonel Martinez. And that's because he doesn't exist!" George answered, producing a throaty rumble that culminated in a bout of laughter. "The only Colonel I know in this place is Colonel Calderon!" he said between guffaws. "This boy here, he's no more Venezuelan than I am Swedish, that's for sure."

Tino directed a wrathful stare at the fake Venezuelan soldier, whether caused by the deception or by the fact that he had looked like a fool in front of George, Lucas could not tell.

"I *knew* that he was not telling the truth! That's why I wanted to check with El Alacran in the first place!" the furious Machetero exclaimed, as if it had been due to him that the ruse had been uncovered. "Sebastian!" he shouted to the guard standing outside. He waited until the door opened, and then slapped Lucas, telling to the incoming sentry, "This man is a government spy! Disarm him, take him outside and shoot him!" He spoke triumphantly, as if it had been him who had discovered the deception.

Lucas automatically considered his chances of escaping, but decided to wait. The odds of taking out three armed adversaries were piss-poor at best, and he could not shake away the feeling that George alone would give him more trouble than half a dozen men. He would have to bide his time, and wait for a better opportunity.

"You boys will *not* take him out and shoot him," George stated quite forcefully, looking straight at the other two men and speaking with uncharacteristic authority. "Don't you think that we need to find out how the hell he got hold of that missile launcher?" The black man approached Lucas and deprived him of his gun, slipping it into his belt. Then gingerly, almost as if afraid of being contaminated, he slipped over the prisoner's head the leather strap of the missile launcher, and handed the weapon to

Tino. "And seems to me, that there may be other of them…uhm…'spies' trying to…uhm…infiltrate us to save the Governor, don't you think?"

Tino's sunken eyes blinked several times, as he considered the matters raised by his obnoxious companion.

"Very well," he relented. "I will interrogate him before executing him."

George held up a hand. "If you don't mind, I'd love to do the initial interrogating myself." He pulled out of a holster strapped to his ankle a long, gray knife, and his round cherubim face lit up with one of its all-encompassing smiles. With careful, almost loving care, he slowly moved the blade in front of Lucas' nose. "This here is BD, a close friend of mine and a very *sharp* interrogator." The black man laughed at his own joke. "This honey has never failed me yet," he said, in a soft but feral tone.

Tino seemed to be taken aback by the black man's request. His expression reflected an intense reluctance to let George take over the interrogation. He hated the little man, and instinctively wanted to refuse anything that he requested. However, it made no sense to argue with him at that moment. He would allow George to start the interrogation. If he succeeded, Tino would always get part of the credit, and if not, well…the black man would be the one who had failed.

The cadaverous-looking Machetero nodded once, signaling his reluctant agreement. George slid his knife back into his holster, and rubbing his hands with glee, said, "Good! But first, I need to talk to my men. You don't mind waiting for me, do you? I'll be back in less time than what it takes for a smelly fart to fade away," he said, chortling, and starting to stroll towards the office's exit before his counterpart could reply.

"Half an hour!" Tino called after him, unable to conceal his annoyance. "Half an hour is all I will wait! If you're not back by then, I'll start the interrogation!"

George waved absently with one of his hands, saying as he walked out of view, "Tie him up! You don't want him to bolt!"

For a second time, Lucas considered trying to escape. His odds had improved significantly with the momentary departure of George, but Sebastian, the guard who Tino had led into the office, was pointing his submachine gun at him from the open office doors, furiously chewing on his gum. There was a chance, if he moved fast enough, that he could grab Tino and use him as a shield, or maybe cause him to be shot. But George had taken his gun away, and there would be no way to defend himself from Sebastian's submachine gun. Besides, in the chaos that would surely follow, the Governor could get hit by a stray bullet. He would have to bide his time.

"Take him outside. I don't want him close to Pietrantoni," Tino ordered. "I will keep him covered while you tie him up."

He turned and faced the Governor, who had witnessed the entire incident without mouthing a word.

"And you!" he added, sternly pointing a finger at the captured leader. "Remember we'll be outside of the office, and that if you try to escape, your son, your lover and your staff will suffer the consequences." He smiled, an unpleasant, toothy grin. "Practice your speech of resignation. I'll be back later, to pick you up and drive you to the Grand Laguna Hotel."

CHAPTER XLIII

Interim Governor Walter Rovira Melendez strode to the podium bearing the shield of the Commonwealth of Puerto Rico, set up on a small, elevated stage at one end of the pressroom in the Electoral Commission Building. He had no trouble weathering the storm of flashes from the cameras that erupted, like a massive round of artillery fire, as he exited the Electoral Board's conference room. He would have been a bit concerned, in fact, by any lesser display of journalistic interest.

Tall, silver-haired, and handsome, he cut a dashing figure; the image of what a strong leader should be in moments of great need. Hated by many, revered by the rest, he had earned the well-deserved reputation of a tough, shrewd politician who never shirked from a fight and who actually seemed to thrive in direct confrontations.

That afternoon was no exception. After what was already dubbed as the "Condado Lagoon Massacre", he had called a press conference "to discuss the present status of the crisis affecting the city of San Juan". As he walked onto the stage, he was followed by the Governor's Cabinet, a train of somber, tired-looking executives who collectively kept their eyes on the floor.

Rovira stopped behind the podium, placing his hands on its edges, and calmly gazed at the hundreds of expectant faces jam-packed into the large meeting hall. Flashing a brief, wolfish grin, he stared directly into the television cameras clustered in the center of the room.

"I will give..." he paused to clear his throat. "I will start by giving a brief statement about the hostage situation in San Juan, and then open the floor for questions."

Rovira tapped several index cards that he carried in his left hand into a neat square, glanced at them as if having second thoughts, and then shifted them to one side, addressing the crowd without them.

"At approximately 2:15 PM today, a group of terrorists—which we believe to be part of the terrorist organization known as 'the Macheteros'—marched several hostages to the roof of the Grand Laguna Hotel with the intent of publicly executing them. At that moment, a contingent of SWAT police officers attempted to rescue the hostages, but despite their valiant efforts and sacrifice, were repelled at a great cost of human life. One hostage was also killed, but the rest were brought back into the hotel, no doubt because they were intimidated by our show of force and resolve."

Rovira Melendez stopped, continuing to stand ramrod straight. He regarded his audience with serene dignity, the kind of regal attitude akin to that of the Lion King, perched on a high rock, reviewing his subjects below. His eyes flashed with what seemed to be hidden tears. The reporters waited in respectful silence for him to continue, the stillness in the room becoming oppressive and stifling.

"As acting governor of Puerto Rico, I take full responsibility for everything that has happened. The names of the victims have been withheld until their next of kin can be notified. Our hearts and deepest sympathies go to them." He lightly tapped the small stack of index cards on the podium, as if reflecting on what else to say, and then stated, "I will now take your questions."

A gaggle of hands instantly shot up into the air, accompanied by the discordant chorus of a hundred shouted queries, each desperately competing to attract the amused attention of the Interim Governor.

Rovira Melendez gestured with his head to a small, balding man with several strings of hair running over his shiny pate. "Mr. Martin, like the singer, Ricky Martin, isn't it? From the San Juan Star."

"Yes, sir. Thank you, sir," the man answered with a deceptively mousy voice. "In light of what has just happened, what do the local authorities plan to do?"

"You don't expect me to tell to everyone watching us on TV what I am about to do, do you?" Rovira responded, raising an eyebrow with mock concern. "After all, there may be some viewers out there who are not so friendly to our cause."

Soft laughter rippled through the hall. The reporter shifted uncomfortably on his chair, and shrugged, in a half-chastened gesture.

"Will you now negotiate with the terrorists?" he shouted over the rising noise of other questions, but Rovira ignored him and pointed to someone else in the middle of the crowd. A portly man in a rumpled, tan linen suit stood up, quieting the rest of the reporters.

"Mr. Franklin, from the Associated Press," Rovira said evenly.

"Sir," the man, a thirty-year veteran with the hanging jowls of a bulldog, looked at a tiny notepad that he held in his right hand. "You began this press conference by saying that you—and I want to quote you directly, so that there is no confusion—that you would "give a brief statement about the hostage situation in San Juan…"

"Yes," Rovira acknowledged.

"But your remarks, and they were very brief indeed, have been limited to the hostage situation in the Grand Laguna Hotel. You have not said a word about the situation of the Governor in La Fortaleza, or about the hostages in the *Mardi Gras*. Or for that matter about the rest of the residents in Old San Juan."

"And the question is…" Rovira interrupted impatiently, barely able to keep the irritation out of his voice.

"What, if anything, can you tell us about the rest of the hostages?"

The Interim Governor stared directly at the reporter. "I could tell you a lot of things about the rest of the hostages, but it would be premature and irresponsible on my part to do so at this moment. I can assure you, though, that Governor Pietrantoni is still in good health."

"Have there been any communications between you and the Governor?" Franklin managed to sneak in before other queries were shouted.

"No."

"Any negotiations for his release?" Franklin insisted.

Rovira shifted his feet, squaring up his body like that of a boxer about to begin pounding his opponent. "I have made it clear from the outset," he said in a grave tone pregnant with unstated anger, "and I will repeat it one more time for the record, that it is not my intention to negotiate, *ever*, with the terrorists. If we do that, we might as well let them run our government. I know that this is not very popular with some of you, but I am not here to be a popular figure."

Rovira ignored the uproar that followed and turned to a round-faced man with a smug complacent expression, sitting in one of the central seats of the front row. Unlike his Associated Press colleague, he was immaculately groomed and dressed, and barely stirred when the Interim Governor acknowledged him. His name was Carlos Padilla Cintron, a political analyst for the Teledifusora Broadcasting Syndicate, a television and radio conglomerate that owned several broadcasting stations in Puerto Rico, Miami, and New York.

Both Padilla and the Teledifusora Syndicate were—and for years had been—strong, vocal supporters of Rovira Melendez, of former governor Oreste Alarcon, and of the statehood movement in the island, and as such were granted special privileges by the Secretary of Justice. That night he had been admitted into the pressroom privately, before the rest of the press corps, and allowed to seat in one of the best seats in the hall.

"Mr. Padilla," Rovira Melendez said in a pleasant, friendly tone.

"Thank you, Mr. Governor. It seems to me," the political analyst began to say in an academic, almost professorial fashion, "that the government's attempt to rescue the hostages in the Grand Laguna Hotel was based on a naïve, half-baked, poorly-conceived and amateurish rescue plan at best. Were you consulted or did you discuss the feasibility of such plan before it was put into effect?"

"As I said before," Rovira Melendez responded, "I take full responsibility for what has happened."

"Which, with all due respect, Mr. Governor, is very noble on your part. But the fact remains, sir, that you are not a policeman or a military man, and that you must largely rely on the judgment of the professionals that *supposedly*," Padilla stressed the last word, "have the experience and the technical know-how to conduct a complex operation of this nature."

Rovira Melendez shrugged non-committally.

"My query to you, sir," Padilla continued, "is if in light of the terrible fiasco that just happened, where you lost so many of your men and accomplished nearly nothing, and where the government intelligence sources failed dismally to anticipate the crisis that we are now facing, if in light of all that, Superintendent Maldonado still enjoys your confidence to lead the rescue effort, or whether you are planning to substitute him." Padilla turned his head briefly towards the other members of the press, as if to emphasize his point.

The Interim Governor gazed at the political analyst with the pained expression of a man who is not entirely at liberty to express himself. For a moment he hesitated. Then he breathed in deeply and said, "Now is not the time for finger pointing, or to try to find out who is at fault. Obviously, this crisis has revealed some serious flaws in our security system, particularly in our police forces, that we will have to investigate and address after this incident is over. But like in the days of the Wild West when the Indians attacked a wagon train, everybody in the caravan now needs to pull together into a tight circle and fight the Indians off. While the attack lasts, we will not throw out any wagon, no matter how incompetent or lazy its occupants are. Not now."

Rovira paused and smiled confidently at the sea of faces seating before him.

"Once we are safe, that is another matter. Then we will conduct a full investigation and get to the bottom of this mess. But not now."

Padilla Cintron harrumphed loudly, and managed to say before the others drowned his voice, "Spoken like a true diplomat!"

"You'd better take a look at this," Montañez muttered to his boss as he watched the large flat TV screen in the command ballroom.

Maldonado and his second in command had spent the last half hour attempting to deal with the aftermath of the failed rescue and to restore order to their badly battered forces, while at the same time trying to make some sense of what had happened. Through it all, the Superintendent had kept a brave face, listening to the grim reports, taking whatever measures were necessary to secure immediate medical help for his wounded men, and making certain that the rest of his officers were kept out of harm's way.

His cool display of leadership had helped to rally his men. However, for the handful of people who knew him well, like Montañez, it was apparent that the great man was in shock. After frantically calling the rescue force to withdraw, he had been forced to helplessly watch it get butchered by a superiorly armed enemy that had anticipated every move of the approaching SWAT team. Montañez knew how deeply Maldonado cared for his men. He knew that what he had witnessed would permanently scar his soul and haunt him for the rest of his life. Still, the Superintendent had managed to keep a calm façade throughout the ordeal, the only hint of his internal turmoil being the anguished comment to his second in command that, "I should have listened to my instincts."

It had been shocking to Montañez as well. The destruction of the helicopter had numbed him. He had expected the terrorists to put up a stiff and deadly resistance. After all, these were dangerous and well-trained men. But it had never crossed his mind that they had access to ground-to-air missiles.

Maldonado directed his attention briefly to the flat screen television, where the Interim Governor was holding court before the world press. He grunted with disgust, and returned to the telephone conversation that he had interrupted, ending it a minute later.

"That was Lieutenant Pabon from the Presbyterian Hospital. She says that officer Severiano is in critical condition, with two bullets in his right lung, but that they've managed to stabilize him. His family just got there, and they're asking for a priest." Maldonado stopped talking for a moment, fearing that his voice would break up.

"I know someone," Montañez prompted. "I'll call him right away. How about the others that were wounded?"

"There are eight others. They are not in any serious danger, thank God."

"Thank God," Montañez repeated.

"But seven of our men are still missing, including Captain Gomez and his sergeant, Cordero.

"Shit," Montañez whispered. "I really liked him," he said, referring to Gomez.

The Superintendent cleared his throat and drank from a glass of Coke that one of his aides had placed on the table in front of him. There had always been dark circles under his eyes, but in the last few hours they had grown alarmingly darker, giving him the appearance of a disgruntled owl.

"You keep telling me to watch this clown every time he appears on TV," he complained to Montañez, nodding at the flat screen. "Enough already! I don't have the time or the desire or the stamina to see him."

"You should be aware of what he's doing," Montañez answered, un-ruffled by the rebuke, knowing that he was one of a handful of friends that could safely nag the Superintendent—up to a point. "He's setting you up. Making the bed on which you will have to lay eventually."

"I know what he's doing, and truthfully? I don't give a shit!" Maldonado snapped back, more bitterly than he intended. "It's in his nature. It's what I expect from him." He was more concerned about what the people who were supposed his friends were doing. *Those were a lot more difficult to predict.* "The Judas among us—" he muttered unaware that he was mouthing his thoughts, prompting a curious glance from his second in command.

Fortunately, an aide—a blond, shapely female showing her curves through a uniform too tight for her body—interrupted him, showing him a walkie-talkie. It was a sign of his distraught state of mind that he did not give her a second glance, Montañez thought.

"Special Agent Franceschini wants to talk to you," the aide said to his boss. The FBI agent had been absent from the command center during the last fifteen minutes.

Maldonado extended his hand and grabbed the portable radio.

"Mario? What have you got?" he asked without any sort of introduction.

The radio crackled with Franceschini's crisp voice.

"I bring you good tidings, my friend," the FBI agent announced.

"Rovira Melendez has been kidnapped by the terrorists?" Maldonado asked in a deadpan voice.

Franceschini laughed. *"Nothing that dramatic, but just as good. The Justice Department has found a loophole to release Alberto Cacho."*

Maldonado's pulse quickened. "Go on."

"There is a provision in Title 28 of the U.S. Code, section 570.32 of the Judicial Administration Act, having to do with the Bureau of Prisons. It gives the authority to the warden of a penal institution to grant...er...furloughs..."

"Furloughs?" Maldonado asked in a surprised voice.

"Yes, furloughs to prisoners when...I have the text here..." Franceschini be-gan to read from the statute's text, *"An inmate may be authorized a furlough:*

(1) To be present during the crisis in the immediate family, or in other urgent situations..." The FBI man stressed the last part of the sentence.

"That is *really* stretching the law! I don't think that the phrase 'other urgent situations' contemplated releasing a known terrorist in order to stop the execution of hostages." Maldonado said, smiling despite himself.

"What is more urgent than that?" Franceschini replied with a short laugh. *"Hell, it's probably an illegal interpretation! I know that and you know that,"* he added. *"But it's all we've got! And by the time anyone thinks of challenging what we did, Cacho will be out of jail."*

Maldonado shook his head in amazement. He hoped that Franceschini was using a secure frequency to communicate with him. Knowing the special agent, he knew he did not have anything to worry about on that scope.

"And you say that *who* has the power to issue the furlough?" he asked.

"The warden of the jail! Can you beat that?"

"Do you think that the warden of the Guaynabo federal prison will agree to that?"

"He already has," Franceschini answered. *"Let's just say that he was 'convinced' to issue it by some very 'powerful arguments'."*

"I bet they were," Maldonado said. His head was throbbing now, as he considered all of the ramifications of the news he had just received.

"I guess that takes me out of the picture and makes you the chief negotiator with the terrorists," he said, feeling both relief and, to his own surprise, more than a small degree of disappointment.

"You guess wrong, my friend," Franceschini answered in the same cheerful voice that he had used to deliver his initial news. *"You continue to direct the negotiations and the rescue operations."*

"I don't understand," Maldonado said sincerely. "Didn't the federal authorities see what just happened? Why would they be willing to let me stay?"

"Well, I spoke directly with the...This is an encrypted radio frequency, by the way, but you never know. So let's just say that the powers that be were somewhat nervous to let you stay, but that I convinced them otherwise. I vouched for your competence and dedication, and told them that right now, at least until tonight, most of the security forces are men fiercely loyal to you. That they would not take it well if we removed you and placed an outsider in charge."

That made sense, Maldonado thought, *although Franceschini could have made just as good arguments to have him removed.*

"You're not exactly an outsider, you know," he said to Franceschini.

"But I am! The Police Department is your department. I told them that if Washington removed you, it would be interpreted as a slight to the entire force and that it would demoralize your men."

"I think you overestimate my importance in the Department."

"Maybe," Franceschini said with a dry chuckle, *"but I convinced them anyway. Don't misunderstand me. They're still very nervous, and I don't blame them. If nothing good comes out of the release of one of the top terrorists in the country, the Administration will be in very hot water. So they want me to oversee you, so that I let them know what we are up to."*

"Does that mean that we negotiate?" the Superintendent asked cautiously. After all, Washington had no authority over him, and negotiating with the terrorists would be considered to be a gross insubordination on his part that could lead to his removal.

"That depends," Franceschini answered. *"How much do you want to piss off Rovira Melendez?"*

Maldonado grinned. "He'll fire me for sure," he said, anticipating with perverse pleasure his open defiance to the Interim Governor's express orders. "If that happens, you have to promise me that you'll take over and not back out of any negotiations that I carry out."

"No need for that. I think that even as we speak, the President is taking care of that glitch for you. I think your ass will be properly covered."

It was too good to be true, Maldonado thought, visualizing Rovira's shocked expression when his refusal to negotiate with the Macheteros was overridden by the President of the United States.

"What happens if Adalberto Cacho escapes?"

"It will depend on what we can accomplish by his release. A C-17 Boeing Transport should be touching ground in San Juan's International Airport within the next hour. It is carrying two Navy SEAL teams, each forty men strong. They'll be ready to strike the terrorists tonight, alongside your men. Also, the first elements from the Navy's 2nd Fleet will be reaching the coastal waters of San Juan sometime tomorrow in the very early hours of the morning, and will help the Coast Guard to seal the waters around the city. So the odds that Cacho will escape are slim," Franceschini explained.

"What about implanting some tracking devices on him?" Maldonado suggested.

"It goes without saying," Franceschini responded, as if the Superintendent had stated the obvious. *"We're placing two devices on his clothes, but let's face it, Cacho's not stupid or he wouldn't have evaded us for so long. We have to depart from the basis that he'll remove his clothes as soon as he gets to San Juan for just that reason. At lunchtime, though, we managed to have him swallow another device with his vitamin supplements. You know, just in case we did release him."*

"Or give him a furlough?" Maldonado asked sarcastically.

"Or give him a furlough," Franceschini confirmed matter-of-factly, not acknowledging the Superintendent's tone. *"God knows how long that will work, though."*

Maldonado considered all of the information he had just received, and imagined a thousand ways in which what he was about to do could ruin the rest of his life. Nevertheless, his decision was already made.

"How long before we can get Cacho out of jail and delivered to the Grand Laguna Hotel?" he asked.

"How long will it take for you to send a helicopter to the Guaynabo federal prison?"

"It'll be there in fifteen minutes."

"Cacho will be ready."

Angel San Miguel sat at the head of the long conference table in the business center and tiredly stretched his arms over his head. He was alone in the room.

He preferred it—even more than that—wanted it that way. Fifteen minutes before, he had suggested to Johnny Ray and his female companion to grab a quick nap in one of the many, empty hotel suites, assuring them that he would alert them about any new developments, so that they could participate in them, a promise that he did not intend to keep. To his credit, Johnny had hesitated, unhappy to abandon the playing field at the peak of the game. But a pleading look from his busty companion had crumbled his resolve and kindled another kind of interest in his eyes. Johnny had left, promising not to "sleep" for more than an hour.

He had kept Colonel Calderon and El Alacran away by warning them that he had received new information from his mole about another impending attack, this time by the FBI—another fabrication. The two leaders had chosen to stay with their men, moving them to new positions and preparing them to crush the new federal invasion.

Which only left San Miguel to answer any calls that the Puerto Rican government authorities decided to make. And from the information he had just received from 'Ramon'—his mole—that call would come soon.

Everything had proceeded according to plan, something that even he had not expected. *Just a few more hours, and the most critical phase of his operation would be over.* However, he could not run the risk of having others interfere with the negotiations that he was just about to undertake. Those he had to handle alone.

As if sensing his impatience, a voice suddenly spoke out of the intercom in the center of the table. San Miguel recognized the voice immediately. It was that of Superintendent Maldonado.

Still, he did not answer immediately. *Let him sweat it out.* He took a sip from the coffee in the plastic cup laying in front of him, and noted the time marked on his watch. It was 2:45 PM, fifteen minutes before the execution of the next hostage.

Maldonado's voice called again, more insistently. This time San Miguel hit the "MUTE" button on the star-shaped intercom and spoke.

"Mr. Superintendent," he said casually, much like a businessman greeted his partner after a short lunch.

"This is he," the voice at the other end of the line answered.

"I would be lying if I told you that I was not expecting your call," San Miguel said truthfully. When the Superintendent failed to respond, he added, "I suppose there is something you want to say."

The lull on the other side continued. Then Maldonado answered sheepishly, *"Yes."*

A thin smile escaped from San Miguel's lips, as he imagined the Superintendent glaring at his speakerphone and trying to control his anger.

"It is now...forty seven minutes to three PM. If we are to accomplish anything before another hostage dies, I suggest that you hurry up and state what's in your mind."

"I have been authorized..." Maldonado hesitated, then blurted, as if spitting out some foul tasting brew, *"I have been authorized to release to you Adalberto Cacho if you stop the execution of any other hostages, and if you release the Governor and his family."*

San Miguel silently punched the air in a rare display of emotion. His voice, however, did not reveal any of it. "That is quite a demand. What about the money?"

"We can't get the money until tomorrow afternoon at the earliest. This is a Sunday, remember? Even if we had access to the type of money that you demand, there is nobody to talk to about it," Maldonado replied.

"That is simply unacceptable," San Miguel stated with mock indignation, his thin smile widening.

"Well, that's all that I can get for the moment!" Maldonado countered, no longer able to conceal his rage. *"Now listen to me! This offer stands as long as you don't murder anybody else. You kill just one more person and Cacho will rot in jail for the rest of his life."*

"I have not killed anyone," San Miguel responded with a sincerity that surprised even him. "Any deaths that have occurred are of your own doing. I warned—"

"Fuck you!" Maldonado interrupted violently. *"Fuck you to hell, you cowardly son of a bitch! How dare you tell me that you have no blame in the murder of my men? Regardless of what happens, I will hunt you down! I will find you if it's the last thing I do on this planet, do you hear me?"*

San Miguel waited patiently, letting the Superintendent vent his rage. He was not offended. He supposed that if the roles had been reversed, he would have been tempted to act in a similar fashion. But he was certain that in the end, he would have accepted God's inevitable will, and moved on to his next task.

That, he thought, *was the real difference between them.* Personally, he did not consider Maldonado to be an evil person, but rather a confused, honest man trapped by the corrupt, secular society in which he lived. Unfortunately, he would ultimately be condemned for the sins of the others, but that was part of the price of living in a godless culture.

"This is what I'm willing to do," San Miguel said, interrupting Maldonado. "Releasing the Governor is out of the question, at least for now. I am willing, on the other hand, to temporarily suspend any further executions until tomorrow noon if you deliver to us Cacho within the next half hour. However, if we have not received the payment for the expenses that we have incurred by that time, the executions will re-commence."

A long pause followed, as Maldonado considered the terms of the counteroffer. San Miguel waited patiently, knowing that the Superintendent had no real choice.

"I will need at least one hour to produce Cacho," the Superintendent said at last.

"I will give you until four PM, no more," San Miguel countered, looking at his watch. "After all, he's in the Guaynabo federal penitentiary. That's less than ten miles from here, as the crow flies. Do we have a deal?"

"Yes," Maldonado answered grudgingly.

"Excellent!" San Miguel exclaimed with genuine pleasure. "Now Mr. Superintendent, I am under the impression that this change in the tone of our negotiations does not meet the approval of your Interim Governor. Am I correct?"

Maldonado did not respond.

""As I thought. You are a brave and reasonable man, and I have no time to deal with fools. Therefore, tell your Interim Governor that there is another condition to our truce."

"We have already agreed to a truce," the Superintendent protested.

"One more condition," San Miguel repeated.

"What is your condition?" Maldonado asked warily.

"That I will only talk to you, do you understand? More than that. Tell your Interim Governor that I follow the news on television like any other viewer, and that if I find out that you have been replaced or fired, I will renew the executions immediately. I know that these conversations are being recorded. So if this Rovira character has any doubts about this condition, just play him back this recording. Is that clear?"

"Yes," Maldonado answered curtly.

"This is no trivial request. The moment anybody else starts to negotiate with me, I will start throwing hostages off the roof. And if the Interim Governor decides to order any other rescue of any of the hostages, tell him that he'd better be successful. Because if he's not, we will execute thirty hostages in the hotel, thirty in the cruise ship, and the entire staff in La Fortaleza. Do we understand each other?"

"I think you have made yourself sufficiently clear," the Superintendent replied, beginning to show his irritation. Then he added, *"There is another condition."*

"Name it," San Miguel said immediately, unable to hide his curiosity.

"The bodies of some of my men, those that haven't been dragged out to the sea, are still floating in the lagoon," the Superintendent said, the deep pain tormenting him evident despite his attempts to speak in a neutral voice. *"I need a cease-fire to recover them."*

"Of course," San Miguel answered without any hesitation. "Just give me fifteen minutes to warn my men not to shoot at the recovery party. Tell your men not to get too close to our shore, though. You have until four thirty to pick up your men. Is there anything else?"

"No," Maldonado responded.

"Then our business is finished for the moment. Let's hope that everything happens as planned."

San Miguel hit the "MUTE" button and fell back on his chair, yawning before he stood up. He walked to the conference room's exit and opened the door, nearly bumping into the massive frame of Czecka, who had taken it upon himself to stand guard outside.

"You're here!" San Miguel said pleasantly, pretending to be surprised. He was not. Of all of his men, none was more loyal to him than the sequoia-sized man standing before him. Ever since he had rescued him from a bouncer's job in a strippers' club in Russia eight years before, the mute giant had followed San Miguel around the world with the same devotion of a small puppy.

Czecka knotted his thin eyebrows, as if inquiring where else he should be.

"I'm glad you're here, anyway," San Miguel said cheerfully. "Please go get Daniel before he throws anyone else off the roof and tell him to stop. Then warn Colonel Calderon and Andrade that the police is going to pick up their dead from the lagoon and that they should abstain from shooting at them, unless they get close to our shore."

Czecka nodded and started to walk away.

"Oh! And Czecka!" San Miguel called after him. "Bring them all back with you. Johnny Ray too, and his woman. I have news to tell them."

San Miguel watched Czecka leave, then went to the automatic coffee dispenser, served himself some more black coffee, and began to drink it unsweetened. The moment itself was sweet enough for him. He could picture the embarrassed faces of all those members of the Group who had mocked him and called him a lunatic when he had discussed his plans and requested their collective blessings. More than their blessings, their support. Fortunately for him, the elite members of the Group—not the majority but the most powerful—had backed him up, and that had been enough. After all, the Group did not operate like a mob-run democracy, but by God-fearing men with a far-reaching vision, men who were not afraid to take whatever risks were necessary in order to destroy the great evils afflicting the world.

With faith and work he had done what so many had tried to do through the centuries and failed to accomplish. He had conquered San Juan.

And soon, unfortunately, he would have to destroy it.

CHAPTER XLIV

The phone rang so unexpectedly that it startled Michelle and she nearly dropped it on the floor. They had decided to approach the Grand Laguna Hotel from a different direction, after discovering that the original route they had chosen was crawling with dangerous men. At one moment, while they walked through a corridor towards the place where they had overheard the terrorists talking, they had nearly stumbled into four men running up the stairs, dodging them at the very last moment by scampering into a door-less maintenance closet.

Unable to continue without being detected, they had backtracked to the exit of the parking building and, after ascertaining that there were no terrorists in sight, walked back out into the sunlit sidewalk of the Luis Muñoz Rivera Avenue. They had turned the corner and headed north in the direction of the abandoned Normandie Hotel and the entrance road to the Grand Laguna Hotel grounds. Walking at a breathless, jog-like pace, dreading that one of the trucks carrying armed men would appear at any moment from around the avenue's bend, they had made good progress through the abandoned street until the telephone started to ring; a loud, distinct, old-fashioned telephone ring that resonated with unwelcome intensity in the abandoned area.

"Jesus Christ!" Archie hissed. "Turn that thing off! You're going to get us killed!"

Michelle had been carrying the satellite telephone in her hand, in case she received an emergency call. Crouching behind one of the cars parked on the street, she desperately looked for the green "ANSWER" button, found it, and pressed it. "Hello?" she answered cautiously.

"Is this Michelle Alfaro," a deep man's voice asked.

"Yes."

"This is the Police Superintendent. I was told that you were expecting my call," the man said without any further introduction.

"How do I know it's you?" Michelle asked. Both Archie and Negron were watching her intently.

"We have to get out of here..." Archie whispered to her.

"Your friend, Rafael Frontera, is standing next to me."

Michelle tried to process the familiar sounding name in her brain. *Rafael Frontera...*

"You mean Correcaminos?" she said, when she finally made the connection.

"Yes, Correcaminos," the man repeated. In the background, she heard Correcamino's voice shout *"Hello, beautiful! How are you?"* and she smiled. With the corner of her eye she watched Negron move towards the other side of the sidewalk.

"Mr. Superintendent, I am very happy to talk to you," she said breathlessly.

"Frontera says that you can help me," Maldonado said abruptly. *"That you can help us get some information on the situation in the Grand Laguna Hotel?"*

Michelle took a deep breath. "Well, we tried to get into the hotel through the new construction close to the lagoon, but it is crawling with terrorists. After the last attack, they seemed to be moving to new positions."

"Of course," Maldonado muttered, seemingly to himself. *"Go on."*

"So now we are trying to approach the hotel through its main entrance and see if we can get closer."

"Won't that be guarded as well?" Maldonado asked doubtfully.

"Maybe, but they seem to be more focused on what is happening on your side of the lagoon than where we are," she responded. She heard Maldonado grunt, apparently in agreement.

"Anything that you can tell us about them will be of crucial importance to us. The number of men you see, their location...We don't even know where the hostages are."

"We will do our best," Michelle promised.

"I just got hold of this satellite telephone," Maldonado said. *"I will have someone outside of the hotel at all times, in case you can call me. Can you write down the number?"*

"Yes, yes, of course." Michelle felt Archie tugging her arm as she prepared to enter the number into her phone.

"Somebody is coming!" he whispered urgently, pointing towards the portion of the avenue beyond the Normandie Hotel that curved westward, towards the sea cliffs of Puerta de Tierra and Old San Juan. She heard the distant sound of an engine approaching.

"We have to go. A vehicle is coming! Can you give me your number?"

Michelle listened while Maldonado began to recite the number, and tried to memorize it. Not willing to wait any longer, Archie grabbed her by the arm and began pulling her back towards some trees growing between two buildings, where Negron already waited.

"Hurry!" the rookie policeman urged, staring worriedly towards the road. A white pickup truck traveling contrary to the normal flow of traffic became visible as it left the cover of the trees lining the road and turned in their direction. A second later Archie and Michelle reached the tree thicket and lay flat on the ground.

Uncertain if they had been seen, Negron drew out his gun and held it with both hands in front of his face. But the pickup truck drove past them and continued in the direction of the lagoon, the three men who were standing on its back too busy talking to each other.

Michelle continued to repeat to herself the sixteen-digit number that the Superintendent had given her, while trying to enter it into the satellite phone's memory. Soon, Archie and Negron were repeating it in unison, making her smile and then snort.

"Stop it!" she said indignantly, as she entered the last of the numbers in her phone.

"Schtop it!" Negron repeated, mimicking her lisp, and earning a venomous stare from his female companion. "I hope the Commissioner understood some of the words you were saying, because from where I was standing it all sounded like 'sthps' and 'lths' to me."

Michelle laughed involuntarily, slapping Negron on the shoulder with the back of her hand, and saying again, "Schtop it!"

"There's someone inside that business," Negron informed the others, pointing at a cafeteria to his left called "El Palacio del Pavochon". "Maybe we can gather some information inside."

The young rookie stood up and, followed by Archie and Michelle, sauntered to the food establishment's glass door, but it was locked. However, its lights and an old, boxy television set installed above the serving counter were turned on. Negron knocked on the door, and when nobody answered, banged it with his fist.

Someone peeked from behind the counter. At first, he did not move, examining the strangers with distrust, but then his eyes lit up with recognition, and he stood up and walked hurriedly towards the entrance, pulling out of his pocket a tight bunch of keys. He picked out the right key with miraculous effortlessness, and unlocked the door.

"Get in! Get in!" he said, letting them through and re-locking the glass door behind them. He quickly walked past them and led them into the kitchen.

"You're Michelle, the reporter, right?" he asked his female visitor.

She nodded. The man must have been in his mid fifties, with dark, greasy hair and an equally dark and greasy mustache, and beefy, freckled arms that stuck out of a sleeveless white wife beater. A sort of fat Saddam Hussein in undershirt.

"I was wondering where you were, since I haven't seen you on TV all morning."

Archie and Negron exchanged a humorous look, as if saying, *"Here we go again!"*

The man was nervous, and talked non-stop. "I was watching what those terrorists were doing in the Grand Laguna Hotel, and it's terrible, terrible! Have you watched the TV? They've killed so many people already! I live upstairs of the restaurant, and I opened up at six in the morning without realizing what was happening, to prepare breakfast, you know? Who would have told me that this was happening, right here, next door to me! I had some people that came in this morning—the usuals, you know?—and nobody suspected anything. But after the explosions! Everybody left! Some didn't even pay what they had eaten! And afterwards those armed men on the trucks started driving by, screaming and honking their horns! I had to close. I wasn't going to get held up by any of those punks!"

The man took a small paper napkin from a large stack lying on top of another stack of plastic plates and wiped his forehead. He looked at Michelle's two companions, as if seeing them for the first time.

"Are you going to interview the terrorists?" he asked her. "I'm joking, of course," he added for her benefit before she could answer.

"No," she answered. "No. We are trying to get closer to the Grand Laguna Hotel, to see what the terrorists are doing."

He looked at her as if she was crazy.

"Are you trying to commit suicide? The three of you?"

"We've discovered that she is suicidal. That's why we're with her, to prevent her from killing herself," Archie asserted with a straight face, prompting the cafeteria owner to look doubtfully from one face to another.

"He's kidding," Michelle assured him, kicking Archie in the shin and making him back away from her. "But we may be able to help the hostages in the hotel if we get closer to it. Do you know of any way we can do that without being seen?"

"Besides using the service alley, no."

The answer thoroughly confused the three friends.

"What do you mean, the service alley?" Michelle asked uncertainly.

"That I don't know of any way of getting closer apart from using the service alley," the man responded, as if stating the obvious.

"What service alley are you talking about?" Archie asked.

The man walked to the back of his kitchen, and opened the back door. "This one," he said, pointing with his arm.

Negron walked right behind him and looked outside. He saw a narrow alley, flanked by buildings at both sides, that was wide enough to accommodate the width of a supply van. It ran parallel to the road further up north that led to the lobby of the Grand Laguna Hotel.

"Where does this end?" the rookie policeman asked the cafeteria owner, as Michelle and Archie joined him.

"How should I know?" the man answered. "I've never walked to the end of the service alley, so I can't say."

The group stepped into the alley and examined it. It ended about two blocks away, capped by a six-story building with long, horizontal open spaces between each floor.

"Isn't that the hotel's parking building?" Negron asked.

The cafeteria owner shrugged. "Could be," he said indifferently.

"It looks like the parking building to me," Michelle confirmed.

"Well, it's a way to get closer to the hotel grounds," Archie suggested. "Do you think the terrorists may be watching this way?"

Again, the cafeteria owner shrugged, this time saying nothing.

"It's much better than trying a frontal approach," Negron suggested cautiously.

Michelle turned to their host and shook his hand enthusiastically. "Thank you so much!" she said. "You have been of great help!"

The man smiled uncertainly. "So you're going to the hotel?"

"That is the general idea, yes," Negron answered, mouthing behind the man's back to the others, *"Is he slow or what?"* and prompting Michelle to open her eyes wide in reproof and Archie to laugh.

"Well. if that's what you want...But I still think it's very dangerous. Would you like some food for the road?" the cafeteria owner offered.

"What do you have?" Negron asked immediately, adding afterwards. "Hey, we don't know how long it's going to be before we get a chance to eat!"

"I could prepare you some Cuban or Midnight sandwiches, or ham and cheese or club, or cheese, fried egg and bacon if you prefer."

"A Cuban sounds great to me!" Negron said gleefully. "But hold the pickles! I hate pickles."

"Since we're at it, I'd also like a Cuban sandwich to go," Archie said.

The man nodded and looked at Michelle.

"You are so kind," she said gratefully to him. "I would love a Midnight sandwich."

"I have ice cold beer!" the cafeteria man suggested.

"It'll get warm by the time that we drink it," Michelle said.

"I could have one right now!" Negron said.

"Me too," said Archie.

"Medalla all right?" the man asked, as he began to walk into the kitchen.

"Better still!" Negron exclaimed with delight, whispering to the others, "I was wrong about this guy!"

"So..." the man paused, as if marshalling his thoughts. "The two Cubans and the Midnight sandwiches. That will be twelve dollars, plus...eight for the Medallas. That's twenty dollars total."

Negron chortled and looked at his two companions, raising his eyebrows.

"You thought it was going to be free, eh?" Michelle whispered to him when their host reentered the kitchen.

"You have any money?" Negron said.

The three friends laughed.

He awoke to a throbbing pain that threatened to split his head open, punctuated by periodic flashes of light that pierced his closed eyelids. As consciousness began to drift back in, he became aware that the lower part of his body seemed to be floating away from the rough, rocky surface on which his upper chest rested, slowly rising and falling as if with a will of its own. His ears echoed with the roar of crashing waves, which would surge irregularly in intensity, sometimes sounding as if the water was about to sweep him away.

When he opened his eyes, the brightness blinded him, blurring his vision and filling his eyes with tears. He felt nauseous, and struggled not to throw up. As he stirred, he realized for the first time that he was submerged in water up to his waist. He tried to get up on his knees, and would have floundered had not a strong hand gripped his right arm.

"Steady, sir!" Captain Gomez heard a familiar voice say over the noise of the sea. "You have a nasty bump on your head!"

Gomez turned his head slowly towards the source of the sound and through his fuzzy vision saw the face of Sergeant Abe Cordero.

"How do you feel?" the sergeant asked with concern.

"I..." the captain paused, feeling his throat burn. It felt as dry as parchment. "Not so good," he said hoarsely.

"Have some water," Cordero said, unscrewing the cap of his canteen and helping Gomez to sit.

The SWAT captain drank several gulps greedily, looking around him as he did so. They were resting on brown volcanic rocks that seemed to be part of a reef. Behind him, a smooth, clay-colored wall extended upwards twenty feet or more.

"What happened?" he managed to ask.

"A bullet hit you on the helmet. Fortunately for you, it was only a glancing blow or it would have drilled a hole through your helmet and your head. As it was, it dented the helmet and knocked you out."

The veteran policeman showed Gomez his helmet. It had a dent about the size of an egg on its upper left side.

"You fell out of the raft, so I jumped in after you," Cordero explained in a normal tone, as if abandoning the relative safety of the boat on which he had been traveling and diving into the bullet-riddled lagoon were part of his normal daily chores. "I think the rest of the men in the boat made it back to the other side."

Gomez took another swallow from the canteen and looked around him. He tried to turn his head but winced from the pain, and rubbed the back of his head.

"Where are we?" he asked.

Rather than answering, Cordero helped him to turn around and lean against the clay-colored wall. For a moment, he was disconcerted. He was inside a trench of jagged, volcanic rocks, into which water from the sea flowed in and out with the incoming waves. As he glimpsed over the edge of the trench, he realized that he was facing the Condado area and the Dos Hermanos Bridge from the opposite side of the lagoon. A tongue of flat rock and sand, no wider than twenty feet, extended from the edge of the trench fifty feet into the lagoon, with some small brushes clinging desperately onto its surface. Directly across them, like a set of jagged teeth, lay the reef that separated the lagoon from the Atlantic Ocean, where the stone dog continued to wait for the return of his drowned master.

"We managed to reach the San Geronimo fort," the sergeant responded. "After I got to you, I pulled you behind the raft that was burning, and used that as cover to keep us out of sight from the terrorists. They stopped shooting a few minutes later. Because of the smoke and the wreckage, I don't think that they realized we were still there, behind the floating debris. The current carried us close to the fort, towards the sea. It was a strong current, and I thought that we were going to be swept out into the ocean. But lucky for us, we were drifting close to these rocks, and I managed to pull you here, into this trench with me. That was just about an hour ago, before you regained your senses."

Gomez stared gratefully at his sergeant.

"If it wasn't for you, I'd be floating in the Atlantic. I owe you my life," he said to him.

Cordero shrugged, "I'll settle for a drink of Scotch and a steak when we get out of here. Besides, captain, I have the feeling that you would have woken up and made it back to shore. Not sure where, but I'm sure you would have made it back. So I'll take the steak and the scotch and be grateful about it."

The splashing sound of someone pushing his way through the water in the trench interrupted him, making him and Gomez turn their heads towards the opposite side of the trench. Gomez saw another man in SWAT uniform approaching them. He was leaning against the wall, skipping towards them over the jagged rocks of the ditch.

"I forgot to mention," Cordero said, "Tavarez also made it here with us."

A lanky, dirty blond haired man who seemed to be no more than sixteen years old waved from a few yards away, an M16 strapped to his shoulder.

"There's more reefs and water on the other side of the fort as well, sarge," he reported to Cordero. "But it shouldn't be too difficult to cross it."

"Raymond?" Gomez asked curiously. "Raymond's here? How the hell did he get here?"

"I fell off my boat, captain," the youngster answered brightly.

"Is he hurt?...Are you hurt?"

"He fell off the boat before the shooting started, sir," Cordero said with a smirk, as the young SWAT officer closed in.

"The boat hit a large wave, apparently, sir," Tavarez explained sheepishly. "I bounced out of it. I began to swim towards the Grand Laguna when I saw the boats turning back. I raised my arm, so that one of them would pick me up, and sure enough, one of them headed in my direction. But then it started to burn. By the time I got to it, another boat had picked up the survivors and left, and you and the sarge were the only ones left." He sighed. "I'm sorry, sir."

"About what?" Gomez asked confusedly.

"About falling out of the boat."

"You should be!" Cordero snapped back at him. "You should have held on better to it! What did you think, that you were going on some kind of kiddies' ride?"

"Did anybody else get stranded?" Gomez asked the sergeant.

"Except for this klutz? None that I know of, sir."

"So we are the only people who made it to the other side?"

"Yes, sir."

Groaning, Gomez managed to find footing on some of the rocks in the water and, staying close to the fort's wall, partially stood up. He considered their situation and wondered how they could make the most of it.

He and his two men were lying inside a rocky, partially water-filled trench that extended throughout the bottom of the east wall of the small fort of San Geronimo. Almost directly behind the fort, about two hundred yards away, was the Grand Laguna Hotel complex.

The wall of the fort, about twenty feet high, shielded them from the view of the terrorists in the hotel and the surrounding buildings. However, it was not so much being seen by the terrorists that worried the young captain. He and his men were facing all of the cameras that the news media had placed on the buildings in the Condado area. If they climbed out of the trench and any alert cameraman discovered them moving about the base of the San Geronimo wall, their image would be broadcast to the entire world, and the terrorists would find out exactly where they were.

Fortunately, the afternoon sun had begun to cast the shadow of the wall over the trench, which was good, because it protected them from the day's heat and helped to further conceal them from view, their blue-gray uniforms blending perfectly with the shaded area. If they were lucky and did not move around too much, they would not be seen. That was, if they had not been seen already.

More importantly, most of their weapons and equipment were intact. His Glock was still in his holster, and his MP-5K submachine gun still hung from his belt. The grenades and ammunition held by the canvas bag strapped to his right leg were still there as well, and a quick examination of Cordero and Tavarez revealed that they were similarly armed.

The flotation-bullet-proof vest devices that they wore had worked after all. Gomez and his men had not drowned, despite all the gear that they carried. If they got into a firefight, they would be able to fight back, and in the process, do some damage. He kept praying that there would not be any terrorists on the walls of the fort above them, but he remembered, from his Boy Scout days, that to get to the fort's walls and look down at them the terrorists would have to stand in an open-air platform, and would be ripe pickings for the police snipers on the other side of the lagoon. He hoped that was the case, anyway.

"Do we by any chance have a walkie-talkie?" he asked Cordero, who had crawled next to him.

"No, sir," the sergeant responded.

"That's a shame," Gomez said, looking at his watch. The time was close to 3:50 PM. It was wintertime, which meant that the sun would go down around six in the afternoon. If they could communicate with police headquarters, they could coordinate a new rescue attempt under the cover of darkness.

He could flash an object in the direction of the San Geronimo Plaza and try to communicate in Morse code, but that would not be very smart. At the very least, they would alert the world press of their presence there, if not the Macheteros.

As he pondered on the problem, he heard the faint noise of engines coming from the lagoon. Straining his eyes, he saw two small motorboats slowly moving over the water several hundred yards away.

"Are those ours?" Gomez asked.

Cordero opened his satchel bag, and rummaging through it briefly, pulled out a set of small binoculars.

"They seem to be," he said, after watching for several seconds. "They've been there for some time now."

"Why aren't the Macheteros shooting at them?" Tavarez asked. "Do you think it's over?"

Cordero continued to watch in silence, as one of the boats stopped. As they pulled a body out of the water, he finally understood.

"They're picking up our dead. None of our men are crossing the lagoon to go into the Grand Laguna Hotel, which means that the Macheteros still hold it. This must be a truce. The Macheteros must have granted them some sort of truce to pick up the dead and the wounded."

Tavarez stood up and started to wave. "Hey!" he shouted, "we're here!"

"Sit down and be still!" Cordero ordered sharply. "They're too far away and they won't hear you! All you'll manage to do is attract the attention of the Macheteros."

Tavarez backed up against the fort's wall and slid down. "Sorry, sir," he said to the captain, avoiding the look of his irate sergeant, "I didn't think it through."

"Next time don't think. Just do as you're told," Cordero hissed at him angrily.

"Yes, sir."

Suddenly the noise of a different type of engine permeated the air. The three SWAT officers instinctively looked up at the sky, and saw a helicopter flying towards the hotel.

"That's one of ours," Tavarez said, this time staying where he was.

The men watched in silence as the police chopper approached the Grand Laguna Hotel. It flew very quickly over the fort, and was lost from their sight. Whatever it did took only a few minutes, and then it flew back over the fort and headed in the opposite direction until it disappeared from sight.

"Do you think the terrorists are giving up?" Tavarez whispered, even though there was no way that he could be overheard.

"To the four or five men that the helicopter may have carried?" Cordero asked sarcastically. "After destroying us when we attempted to cross? What do you think?"

"I would say no," Raymond answered innocently.

Gomez said nothing. He knew what the helicopter had carried, or rather *who* the helicopter had carried. *So Maldonado had managed to gain some time after all,* he thought.

The three policemen watched with a growing feeling of helplessness as the boats circled around in the lagoon, stopping twice to pick up bodies floating in the water. One of the crafts at one moment speeded up and briefly headed in their direction, but turned away before it came near enough to notice the stranded men. Another boat raced out of sight after recovering a man from the water, possibly—Gomez hoped—after finding him alive. A half hour later, the boats had disappeared under the Dos Hermanos Bridge.

"So what do we do now, boss?" Cordero asked his captain.

Gomez took a long time to answer.

"Well...we're on this side of the lagoon, and our mission hasn't changed..." he paused again.

"Do you think the Superintendent will try another rescue tonight?"

Gomez thought about it and nodded slowly. "I know he will."

"We could help clear the way for the others..." Cordero suggested.

"We could sneak out of here when it's dark and take out their lookouts."

Cordero nodded. Tavarez, still stinging from the prior rebuke, listened quietly.

"Did you bring your silencer?" Gomez asked his sergeant.

"With all due respect, sir. Have you ever known me not to bring my silencer in a rescue operation?"

The three men smiled.

"We've got to think this through," Gomez said more to himself than for the benefit of the others. "We can't communicate with central command, and we don't know if or when a second rescue attempt is happening. We need to coordinate with them, if we can."

Another meditative silence followed.

"May I say something, sir?" Tavarez ventured tentatively.

"Go ahead," Gomez answered.

"I can swim to the other side of the lagoon and alert central command that we're here," he said, pointing at the San Geronimo Plaza Hotel.

His two superior officers stared at the Condado area. The distance to swim between where they were and the other side was not a considerable one. A strong swimmer could make it with little trouble. However, the breach to be gapped was the area where the waters of the lagoon met the sea, and the currents, depending on the tide, could be dangerous and overwhelming.

"The risk that they will see you is too big," Cordero said. "Besides, what use will it be that you get there? The Superintendent will know that we're here, but he'll still be unable to talk to us."

"I was thinking of crossing when it gets dark, sir," Tavarez replied. "It will be very hard for them to see me then." He thought for a moment. "You're right about it not being a very useful thing to do, though. If we can't communicate..."

Gomez continued to stare at the strip of hotels facing them across the lagoon. From where he was sitting, he could see the rear of the San Geronimo Plaza Hotel.

"You know..." he said in a pensive voice. "It could be of more help than we imagine. Suppose that Raymond makes it to the other side, he could help coordinate any rescue mission that they may be planning. They could use a flashlight from their side to communicate with us."

"The terrorists will see it," Cordero said doubtfully.

"They may, but if it's just a few flashes, the chances are that they'll miss them, or if they see them, that they won't know to whom they're directed or what they mean. I'm not talking about using the Morse code, but that they send us a signal with a predetermined meaning," Gomez said, becoming more enthusiastic as he spoke. "For example, and this is just an example, one flash followed by a pause, followed by another flash, could mean that no rescue operation is in the works. Three flashes means the contrary. If it is three flashes, then it could be followed by a pause, and then flashing the number of the time that the rescue operation will happen. For example, nine flashes could mean nine o'clock, ten flashes ten o'clock, and so on."

"It could be dangerous. If any of the terrorists tie the flashes to the time of the rescue, it would be very bad," Cordero interjected, already focusing more on the details of the plan than objecting to it.

"We can agree to add or subtract from the number of flashes. For example, to know the time, we can agree to subtract two hours from the number of flashes that are made. If the flashes are eleven, we will know that the attack will be at nine."

"And what would be our role?" the sergeant asked.

"To create a diversion," Gomez answered. "Like I said before, we could eliminate their lookouts, clear the way for the assault."

The ex Navy SEAL considered the plan and slowly moved his head contemplatively from side to side. "It would be nice paying them back for what they did to us today..." he said, cracking a smile.

Gomez looked at Tavarez.

"Are you sure you can make it?" he asked him. "The least thing in the world that I want is to send one of my men to be swept out to sea."

"I'm better suited for this than Tavarez," Cordero interjected, before the youngster could answer. "I'm a very strong swimmer and got trained for this sort of mission."

"If I may respectfully say something," Tavarez replied, his eyes flashing with mischief. "I believe that you *were* trained for this type of mission, but I also believe that was many years ago. You're not as young as you were when you were a Navy SEAL," Tavarez raised a hand pleadingly, anticipating the wrathful reply of his sergeant. "No disrespect meant, sarge. You're still in good shape...for your age. But you should know that until a year ago, I used to snorkel among those rocks—he pointed to where the stone dog sat waiting for his master—and catch small fish with a butterfly net, to sell to the pet shop aquariums. I know the currents and the undertow. They are strong and dangerous, and sometimes it is better to avoid them altogether and not get into the water. But I can handle them. Besides, as you said, you will enjoy more taking out a few of the Macheteros than swimming to the other side."

Gomez laughed. "I think Tavarez may be right," he said.

"I think Tavarez thinks too much for his own good," Cordero snarled.

Gomez's spirits began to rise. An hour before, his life had been turned upside down, his unit decimated and humiliated. Now he had the opportunity to strike back at his enemies, and he would devote every fiber of his being to doing so.

"We have roughly about two hours before nightfall," he told his men. "Let's plan the details of this thing."

CHAPTER XLV

The warden of the Guaynabo federal prison, a balding, heavyset man who seemed much older than his forty years of age, observed as the two guards ushered Adalberto Cacho into his office. The Machetero leader had changed from his prison uniform to the jeans, gray polo shirt and Nike sneakers with which he had been arrested at the Hiram Bithorn Stadium game between the Dominican and Puerto Rican national baseball teams. What was it about all of these communist revolutionaries that endeared them so much to the most American of all sports was something that the warden would never understand.

Dressed in civilian garb, and with his full head of brown hair cut short, Cacho could have passed for a professional businessman or a lawyer returning home after spending some leisure time watching his favorite team play. He fitted the mold of the typical "blanquito del Condado"—a Puerto Rican expression meaning literally the "white guy from the Condado area", applied to those wealthy upper class individuals who led a life of luxury and usually did not mix with the lower class.

His outward façade did not hint anything about the man behind it. His clean-shaven face retained a roundish boyishness that made him seem—contrary to the warden—much younger than his nearly fifty years of age. He stood at five feet ten inches tall, and weighed about one hundred and eighty pounds; not thin but, except for some incipient love handles around his waist, fit and healthy looking. He moved with a confident stride, and could have been equally at ease wearing a priest's cassock or a banker's striped suit.

If anything could have raised any suspicions that the man standing before him had been the head of the ruthless Machetero organization and one of the ten most wanted men of the Federal Bureau of Investigation, thought the warden, it would have to be his eyes. Nothing seemed to escape their intelligent, silent analysis.

Now, however, as they were fixed upon the few personal items lying on the warden's desk, they reflected mild surprise and a great deal of curiosity.

"Warden Travieso," the prisoner said courteously, nodding gently at his host.

"Mr. Cacho," the warden acknowledged.

"I hope that you are doing well."

The warden inclined his head slightly. "I am well, thank you. Are you aware of what is happening in San Juan?"

Cacho tried not to smile, but could not conceal his amusement, curving his lips in a poorly hidden smirk.

"I saw something on TV before it was blacked out by the jail censors," he answered.

"And are you aware of the terrorist demands?" the warden inquired, not taking his eyes off the prisoner's face.

"Only the rumors that I've heard," Cacho answered vaguely.

Those rumors must have come from some of the guards, the warden thought to himself. The free inflow of information coming into and going out of the inmate population through the prison's security personnel was a constant problem with which Travieso had to deal.

"What have you heard...exactly?"

"Exactly? That the terrorists are requiring my release from prison," Cacho answered.

"What else?"

Cacho considered the question for a moment. "Nothing else," he replied.

"Were you aware that the terrorists...the suspicion is that they are Macheteros," the warden said, searching the prisoner's face for some reaction and detecting none, "that the Macheteros will execute a prisoner every hour until you are released?"

"No. That I had not heard," Cacho said, his expression showing no guile.

"You haven't heard any rumors about that?"

"No."

"They have already killed several people," the warden said, somewhat misleadingly, as if implying that several people had been executed to secure his release.

Cacho raised an eyebrow in mild surprise, but did not say anything. The warden continued to look at him for several seconds, and then sighed. He motioned with his head at the few objects on his desk. There was an imitation alligator skin wallet, a set of aviator sunglasses, and a pack of spearmint gums.

"These are the articles that you carried on you when you were arrested at the Hiram Bithorn Stadium. You may have them back." The warden continued to observe him, his expression a mixture of disgust and resignation.

Cacho walked to the desk and examined the wallet. It contained a total of forty-three dollars, and the photo a little girl not older than ten years old—his daughter.

"My driver's license?" he asked.

"Was a forgery and has been confiscated," the warden stated in a tone that admitted no discussion. "So was the gun that you carried," he added.

Cacho's mouth soured into another smirk. "You're letting me go?" he asked.

"I'm granting you a three day furlough so that you go to San Juan and stop the killing," the warden answered with a straight face.

The Machetero leader's face showed genuine surprise, his eyes lighting up with the same amused interest of those of a cat that discovers a mouse in the distance. "A furlough..." he repeated uncertainly.

"Yes, the law allows me to grant furloughs to prisoners in times of emergency, and I am granting one to you now," the portly man said with surprising dignity. "I expect you to return in three days' time, after you have ended the hostage emergency."

"And if I don't return?" Cacho asked distrustfully, as if expecting a punch line.

"If you fail to return...you will be in violation of your furlough, and you will become a fugitive of the law," Travieso answered plainly, a hard edge in his voice. "San Juan is surrounded. There is nowhere that you can really go. If you hide, we will find you. So do the right thing. Stop the killing of innocent people."

Cacho stared at the warden with exaggerated innocence.

"I give you my word that I will do the right thing," he promised with a slight smile.

The warden shook his head sadly. It was the type of vague answer that he had anticipated.

"A helicopter is waiting for you outside. The gentlemen waiting outside of my office will escort you there."

Cacho nodded, and without saying another word began to walk towards the office's door.

Travieso watched him go, saying to himself as the Machetero leader exited the room, "May God have mercy on us all."

Although John McFadden devoted most of his time while at sea to the company and entertainment of more mature women, during his extended travels he had occasionally dabbled in a few, discrete, non-business-related trysts with other women on board, particularly crewmembers and showgirls. A shapely, black-haired Nicaraguan professional dancer named Maria de los Angeles Sequeira, who had formed part of the ship's chorus line for six months in 2013, had been one of those trysts.

It had been a hot and heavy affair, the type that flares up in a millisecond with the heat of a thousand suns, and burns out just as quickly. While it had lasted, however, he had been granted free access to the backstage of the Stardust Theater, and allowed to wander through its maze-like recesses while his leggy companion practiced.

Being curious by birth and daring by nature, he had explored every corner of the place, even sneaking up to the catwalks above the stage, where some of the spotlights and props were set for the various onboard productions. From there, he would watch the rehearsals taking place below, and wait for Maria to finish. Had he been caught, he would have gotten his paramour fired and probably been banished from the ship. However, those who had spotted him were Maria's friends, and had preferred not to see him.

To avoid having the artists enter the theater through its main entrance, a door had been set on the ship's fifth deck—close to the bow—that gave direct access to the dressing rooms. Maria would sneak John into the theater through that door. The fifth deck entrance was never locked, a sign over it reading "AUTHORIZED PERSONNEL ONLY". The door led to a small corridor that divided into three parts: the men's dressing quarters to the right, the ladies' quarters to the left and, at the end of the corridor, another closed door that opened to the back of the theater's stage. Stairs climbing to the catwalk were conveniently located just a few feet away from that door.

To get to the Stardust Theater, John and Ernan had walked through the entire length of the ship. The Australian had attempted to convince his Filipino friend to remain hidden while he scouted the theater, but Ernan would not hear about it. The waiter argued rather forcefully that they should stick together to help each other, while John pointed out that it would be less risky for one person to sneak into the theater than for two. In the end, Ernan had prevailed. He had been terrified to be left behind, preferring to walk into the terrorists' lair than to stay alone again.

This time, John had opted to walk straight through the sixth deck's corridor rather than taking a more roundabout route to the ship's bow. He had reasoned that most of the terrorists were in the Stardust Theater, and that after they had eliminated the surviving pocket of resistance in the crew's quarters, they would not be very concerned about the few strays that could still be roaming in the ship. Any lookouts would probably be posted on the ship's upper decks, to detect any possible assault coming from the outside.

Nevertheless, the walk through the long interior passageway of the sixth deck to the bow of the ship had been nerve wracking. Most of the doors along the corridor—belonging to passenger cabins—were closed and locked. That meant that if any terrorist made an unexpected appearance on the red-carpeted passageway, John and Ernan would have nowhere to hide.

To enhance their chances, the two stowaways had decided to use as cover one of the abandoned supply carts of the cabin attendants, pushing it in front of them through the long, empty corridor and hiding behind it. Twice they had stopped, imagining the sound of voices and approaching footsteps, once ducking into an open cabin that had been in the process of being cleaned at the time that the hijack took place. Both times had proven to be false alarms, the result of their overactive imaginations.

They had abandoned the cart next to the stairway closest to the bow of the ship, reserved for the use of the crew only. From there, they had descended to the fifth deck, reaching a door with a porthole that gave access to the outer promenade. There they had paused. John had stood up on his toes and looked through the porthole, searching as much as he could for movement outside.

"I don't see anyone", he whispered to Ernan, "but that doesn't mean that nobody's outside. Shall we chance it?" And without waiting for a reply, he opened the door slightly and peeked through the narrow gap between it and the doorframe. The wooden deck seemed deserted, a long row of unoccupied reclining chairs retreating nearly all the way to the stern of the cruise ship. "Let's go!" he said, and the two men stepped onto the deck, and scurried towards the bow.

The entrance to the backstage area had not changed since his last visit there a year ago, except that someone had pasted a sticker on the "AUTHORIZED PERSONNEL ONLY" sign reading "Anyone trespassing will be shot". John did not find it amusing.

"Stand back," he said to Ernan, and knocked softly on the door.

"What are you doing?" the Filipino asked in a terrified tone.

"Can you think of a better way to find out if anyone is on the other side?" John answered quickly. "If the door begins to open, we run!"

No one answered, and with his heart pounding, the Australian gigolo turned the long latch of the access door and slowly pushed the hatch open.

The short corridor was empty, all of its doors closed. A bulleting board on one of the walls contained several photos, yellow post-its with messages, and ship notices. The door at the other end of the short passageway, leading to the backstage area, was decorated with several silver and gold stars. Otherwise, the place showed no signs of human activity.

John entered the corridor and headed directly to the backstage access, followed by Ernan. This time, he opened the door just a crack, and listened.

Somebody, a man's voice, was talking through a microphone or a megaphone, but John could not make out what he was saying. Grabbing Ernan by the elbow, he pushed the door further and slid inside the theater.

A huge black curtain about five feet from the door blocked the view of the stage beyond. Several scenery props—skyscrapers lit at night, a sunny beach, a hot dog stand, and a Taj Mahal-like palace, among others, as well as a life sized bus mounted on wheels and cut in half lengthwise— lined the wall opposite to the curtain or hung suspended by wires from above, waiting to be used.

John pointed with his hand to a narrow steel stairway that rose steeply to the catwalk, more than forty feet up. It was located left of the door they had just exited.

"That's where we're going," he told Ernan. "You have to be careful, because some of the steps tend to squeak when you step on them. Try to place your feet away from the center of the steps. That's where they buckle and squeak the most."

The Filipino looked up apprehensively, and nodded.

The two men began to climb with exaggerated care, pausing whenever one of the steps creaked. As they got higher, the words spoken through a microphone became clearer, until they could be understood. The person speaking was definitely a male, with a foreign accent. John recognized him first, having spoken with him several times during his various cruises on the *Mardi Gras*. It belonged to Kristoffer Clausen, the ship's captain. He sounded exhausted and defeated.

"...I know that many of you are tired and hungry. There are fourteen hundred and thirty nine passengers on this ship, plus a crew of five hundred and seventy. I don't know how many are here, but as you can see, we are pretty crowded." There was a feeble murmur of agreement, but the crowd quieted quickly. "As captain of this ship, my foremost responsibility is to my passengers and my crew. The people who have taken over this ship are dangerous and well armed, and they will not hesitate to shoot anyone who resists them. The *Mardi Gras* is full of women, children, and elderly people...and I cannot afford to have any one of them to be hurt."

The captain paused, as if taking a deep breath.

"Therefore, I urge you to cooperate, and not try to escape or resist...I have been...assured," Captain Clausen could not hide his dislike for the hijackers of his ship, and it was reflected in the tone of his words, "by these...gentlemen, that if we follow their instructions to the letter, nobody else will come to harm."

John and Ernan reached the catwalk and slowly walked towards its center. As in the rear of the stage, several props made up mostly of cardboard with wooden frames hung in different places from wires, including five lampposts and, behind the catwalk, an enormous quarter moon covered in glitter.

With excruciating care, the two friends looked over the catwalk's railing. They could see the captain standing on the stage, flanked by two men, one of them holding an AK-47 semiautomatic rifle. They could also see the first four rows of the theater, brimming with hostages that spilled onto the aisles and the carpeted floor in front of the stage.

Darkness covered the two stowaways hovering above the stage, but even if all of the theater lights had been on, John doubted that the crowd below would have been able to see them. Every eye in the theater was riveted on the men on the stage; most of the hostages' faces reflecting fear and deep gloom. The Australian tried to find the Countess of Gilly, but failed to spot her among the visible rows.

"This applies to my crew as well," the captain continued. "We have set up, in the conference room directly below us, a provisional infirmary for anyone who may require medical help. Dr. Freedman and his two nurses are there right now, attending to a few of our passengers. Other members of the crew have been or may be required to perform their duties at different times. The cooks and the restaurant staff have already been called to make food for all of us. I will let the others in the crew know when or if they are needed."

Captain Clausen lowered the microphone and spoke to the only man standing next to him who was not holding a rifle. The exchange was short, but the captain shook his head emphatically after a few seconds. The hijacker, a short, thin man, snatched the microphone from the captain's hand and spoke directly to the passengers.

"Our captain understandably does not want to convey this part of the message to you, so I will do it instead," the man said with an unpleasant, nasal voice. "Within the next ten minutes, we will start taking groups of two hundred passengers and crew up to the Windjammer Cafe on the twelfth deck. You have been assigned numbers, so as you are called you will gather, *in numerical order*"—the man stressed the last phrase—"on that exit over there"—the terrorist pointed with his right hand towards the right end of the theater—"and form a line. Once the line is ready, you will follow your guide and walk up in an orderly fashion to get your food. When you get upstairs, you will have ten minutes to serve yourselves from the buffet tables and bring the food down here. Ten minutes! What you don't get by then, you don't get. Don't worry. Like the captain said, there is a staff of cooks and waiters up there that will ensure you get your food. That way everyone will have eaten in a couple of hours."

The terrorist looked around the theater, causing several of the faces in the crowd to nervously cast their eyes to the floor.

"Now I believe in honesty, since honesty avoids accidents, isn't that right?" he asked.

There was no answer, so he raised his voice. "I *said*, isn't that right?"

This time he received a half-hearted response from the crowd.

"Right!" he repeated with conviction. "So I will be honest with you. A line of two hundred people is a long line. There is the possibility that if some of you decide to...er...separate yourselves from the line and run somewhere else in the ship, you might be able to make it, to escape from the line. But you should know this. There is *no* way you can escape from this ship. There are men guarding the exits and men on the dock. So at best, you'll only manage to hide in the ship for a while and skip your lunch until we find you, and PS, we *will* find you!" he said loudly, and then lowering his voice added, "And *kill* you."

The theater was very still now.

"But wait! There's more!" the thin man said, in a tasteless imitation of a television commercial where the offer is improved if the caller calls immediately. He paused to chuckle at his own wit. "If you manage to escape, the hostage with the number before yours and the hostage with the number subsequent to yours will also be executed for letting you escape! So everyone, watch your neighbors! Because your lives will depend on them, literally."

The short, thin man handed the microphone back to the captain, who stared at it in a half daze, as if it was a strange object. Reluctantly, he grabbed it back and spoke.

"Please don't be alarmed, ladies and gentlemen. Just follow the instructions, and no harm will come to any of you. I will be walking with some of the groups..."

With unexpected abruptness, John heard a phone ring. It was a shrill, old-fashioned ring, the type that for so many years had been the only ringtone available to telephones around the world; loud, high-pitched, and strident enough for everyone to hear. And it was coming from one of Ernan's pants pockets.

John stared with incredulity at his companion, who in a panic struggled to pull out the phone to stop it from ringing, but could not manage to pry it out from his pocket, wedged between his wallet and his keys.

"I thought cell phones weren't supposed to be working!" John hissed fiercely at his companion.

"So did I!" Ernan answered desperately, still unable to grab the hellish device.

The captain, who had continued to address the hostages, stopped talking, and several people, including the two men standing next to him, began to look around.

"Shit!" John whispered, pulling Ernan away from the railing. The phone rang two more times and stopped, still lodged in the Filipino's pocket.

"Where was that coming from?" John heard the voice of the thin man ask.

"I think it came from somewhere behind the stage," another voice, gruffer that the thin man's, answered. "Want me to look?"

"What do you think? Of course I want you to look!" the thin man answered.

The man with the rifle disappeared into the thick curtains at the back of the stage. Ernan looked at John with an expression of utter terror. The only way the two of them could get down from the catwalk was through the metal stairs that they had just climbed. If the armed terrorist now searching the backstage decided to climb, they would be trapped.

"What do we do?" Ernan asked, frightened out of his wits. He knew that the terrorists would be looking for the wounded man who had killed one of his men, and that if they caught him they would execute him.

John tried to calm him. "Be still," he whispered. "Maybe they won't think of coming up here."

Ernan's hands shook badly. His eyes looked pleadingly at John, as if expecting his Australian friend to save him from their predicament. They could hear the armed man roaming below, although he appeared to be searching an area distant from the catwalk's stairs. Just then, the cell phone began to ring again, its sound reverberating throughout the theater.

Once more, Ernan frantically began searching his pocket for the source of the noise until he finally managed to grab it. As he pulled it out, the ringing noise increased, prompting many below to look up.

At his wit's end, the Filipino opened his cell phone to shut it off, but John snatched it off his hand, walked several steps towards the catwalk's stairway, and placed it on the floor, letting it ring.

Ernan looked at his companion in shock, thinking him crazy. He began to pace towards him, but John quietly rushed past him and examined the large half moon hanging next to the catwalk.

"What are you—" Ernan began to protest, but John shushed him, placing a finger on his lips.

The Australian pulled the half moon towards the railing, and beckoned Ernan with his head to approach him. When the Filipino failed to respond, he hissed at him angrily, "*Come on* already!"

At last Ernan reacted, hurrying to his friend's side.

"Get in!" John told him, pointing to a seat attached to the back of the half moon's glittering frontal façade. "I've seen this used before in some of this ship's shows. They lower an exotically dressed singer as she sits and swings from behind the moon. If you sit on it, and position your body along the contours of the half moon, nobody will be able to see you from the catwalk."

Ernan opened his mouth to say something, but just then they heard the noise of footsteps ascending the stairs.

"Hurry!" John pleaded. He did not have to ask again. Climbing over the railing, Ernan sat on the chair behind the moon.

It was John's turn, but both men could not fit in the same seat and hope to remain unseen. He only had one opportunity before the terrorist got there. There was a metal bar at the bottom of the chair that served as a footrest. Stepping over the catwalk's railing, John slipped his legs through the seat's footrest, and still holding on to the catwalk with one hand, grabbed Ernan by the waist with his other arm. "Don't make a sound!" he warned him, and gently let go. He bent his knees so that his feet would not dangle below the moon, and waited.

The moon oscillated outwards, swung back towards the catwalk, and then stopped about two feet from the railing. Almost at the same time, the cell phone stopped ringing. For the next couple seconds, all that John could hear was the hurried metallic clatter of the terrorist's feet climbing the stairs, and the wild thumping of his heart. He listened intently as the noises in the stairway abated, giving way to slow, cautious footfalls. These too stopped after a couple of seconds.

"If anybody is up there, you'd better come down now!" the armed terrorist shouted, sounding somewhat winded. "I will shoot if I find anyone up there!"

There was a long pause, and then more measured footsteps that stopped abruptly.

John closed his eyes, and instinctively held his breath. He heard the terrorist say, "Hmmm!" followed by several, more confident footsteps that continued until he seemed to be standing next to the moon.

"Find anything?" John heard the thin man shout from below. He did not dare look down, afraid that he would be discovered.

"Yes, a cell phone!" the man with the AK-47 replied, sounding so close to the two fugitives that he made Ernan flinch. John pinched him on the back, warning him to be still.

"What?" the thin man asked.

"A phone! A cell phone! There was a cell phone lying on the floor. Somebody must have dropped it or left it there some time before, because there's nobody here now!"

"Are you sure?" the thin man asked.

"Unless he's Harry Potter flying on a broom!" the other terrorist answered, laughing at his own joke. "The ringing is from the cell phone, but there's nobody here. It must have been here for some time. I can't imagine anybody being so stupid as to let the phone ring so it would lead us to him, can you?"

There was a pause below. "I don't know," the thin man said eventually. "Are you sure there's no other way of getting down from there?"

The terrorist on the catwalk took some time to answer, as he looked around him. John prayed that the moon and the surrounding darkness would provide them with enough cover to hide them from the searcher's eyes.

"No!" the man at last confirmed. "There's not even a rope that a person could use to slide down."

"Okay, then come back down."

"Hey! There's a nice view from up here!" the terrorist shouted. And then, quite unexpectedly, he farted loudly, making John wince with disgust. "I'm coming down!"

The two friends remained motionless as the footsteps of the terrorist receded. It was very cold, up there. The half moon prop was located near a large air conditioning vent that discharged its frigid air directly on the two fugitives. And yet, John felt his shirt clinging to his back like a wet cloth.

That had been too close of a call, he thought. *His luck was bound to run out. He would have to be more careful, and never place himself in a position where he did not have a clear route of escape.*

He wondered why Ernan's cell phone had rung. Probably, the initial spike in telephone calls that had overloaded the local telephone system had leveled off—or whatever it was that happened to spikes—and the phone service was returning to normal. That was good, except that they had just lost Ernan's cell phone.

Nevertheless, it had been a necessary sacrifice. By placing the cell phone on the catwalk and letting it ring, he had managed to create the impression that the personal communications device had been abandoned or dropped by its careless owner, probably one of the theater's lighting technicians.

He worried sick about the Countess. She had not been visible among the hostages sitting on the first few rows of the theater. He knew that that meant nothing. It was a large theater, and only a fraction of those crammed into it were visible from the catwalk. Still...he could not shake the hollow feeling of fear at the pit of his stomach. If the terrorists had found their dead female comrade in the Countess' cabin—after all, it would not be so hard to identify her as the suite's occupant—their revenge would be swift and terrible.

On the other hand, the Countess was a tough, old broad who, unlike Ernan, had the ability to think on her feet and take care of herself. The odds that the terrorists would find the body of the terrible woman that Ernan had suffocated with a pillow were small, at least until the next day, when the body started to stink. There were not that many hijackers on board to conduct a room-to-room search—at least not so far—and those that were there had their hands full keeping the passengers and crew under control. Chances were that the body of the woman had not been found.

John heard the gruff voice of the man with the AK-47 somewhere in the theater below him, yelling at some hostages that apparently had not lined up in numerical order, and finally felt safe enough to move. He stretched his arm and reached for the catwalk's handrail, and brought the moon closer to the floating platform. Gingerly, he slid off the chair's footrest, helping Ernan to climb out after him.

"Now do you understand why I wanted you to stay hidden while I investigated what was happening here?" he said softly to the Filipino, without any hint of recrimination in his voice. His body felt sore from the unnatural position that he had been forced to adopt while hiding behind the moon. "If you stay with me, you will be taking all sorts of risks. Do you still want to hang around with me?"

"More than ever!" the maitre answered emphatically. "You were awesome, Mr. McFadden!" There was something akin to hero-worship in Ernan's eyes.

John was forced to smile, despite of himself. "That's the first time a man has said that to me," he said.

The two friends leaned over the railing of the catwalk that faced the seats of the theater, and found that the terrorists and the captain had abandoned the stage.

"So now that we know what they're doing, we call the FBI, right?" Ernan asked with no real enthusiasm behind the question.

"That's why we're here," John answered wistfully, even though every instinct in his body still screamed at him to stop pretending to be a hero and to jump off the ship again. *How much longer could they last,* he wondered? *He had burned enough luck to win a dozen lotteries. It was bound to run out.*

Taking a last peek below, he began to walk back towards the stairs of the catwalk. He stopped at the top of the flight of steps, and sighed. They would have to risk their lives again, in order to make a call from an open spot.

What the hell, he told himself, as he began to quietly descend from his lookout post, followed by his nervous Filipino sidekick. *There was nothing else to do but to finish what he was doing. And the sooner it happened, the better.*

CHAPTER XLVI

"Move!" Tino shouted angrily, placing his foot on the lower back of the captured stranger and shoving him. The prisoner surged forward and crashed into a small round table in the waiting room, a small porcelain flowerpot on it falling onto the black and white tiles underneath and exploding into a spray of shards. The fake Venezuelan's head struck the wooden armrest of the wicker sofa next to the table, suffering a small gash on the forehead that slowly began to bleed.

The prisoner tried to steady himself by placing his hands and knees on the floor, but the Machetero kicked him again, this time near the ribcage, causing him to grunt.

"Stand up, worm," he shouted, the thin lips on his skull-like face twisting into a crooked, almost crocodilian smile. "You're about to learn the terrible mistake that you've just made, trying to sneak into La Fortaleza."

Tino gazed at the impostor with contempt, as the prisoner was made to sit on a chair in the center of the waiting room outside the Governor's office. The Machetero's cheeks still burned from the massive loss of face that he had suffered in front of the arrogant black American, that grinning monkey, George. He had been made to look like a fool, his authority seriously undermined. *If word of how he had initially been deceived ever got back to El Alacran, he would be in deep trouble.*

Tino had initially agreed to let George start the interrogation, but George had opted to abandon them to engage in a private conversation with his boss. It was true that Tino had told George that he would wait half an hour for him, but that had been fifteen minutes ago, and he had since changed his mind. Time was of the essence. He could not afford to waste any more of it. Besides, he would not allow the American thug to steal away his thunder.

He would interrogate and obtain the information from the trapped spy now, and convey it to Andrade before George returned. That way, he would regain control over the entire affair, and the black man would become irrelevant. There was still time, but he would have to hurry.

"Tie his hands behind his back," he said to Sebastian, who kept the prisoner covered with his submachine gun.

Tino drew a gun from one of his twin holsters and aimed it at the impostor's head. From his black shirt's front pocket, he fished out a square metallic object and held it with two of his fingers in front of the prisoner's face. It was a multiple-use steel gadget containing several imprints to unscrew bolts, twist screws, and even uncork bottles. Among its prominent features was a sharp, serrated side that could be used as a saw.

"I don't know who you are," the skull-faced terrorist told his captive, "but I will start sawing off your fingers one by one for every question that you do not answer or that I think is a lie..." Tino stopped talking and directed a vexed look at Sebastian, who had not moved since he had been ordered to tie up the prisoner. Instead, the guard stood a few paces behind the chair where the apprehended impostor had been made to sit, quietly listening to Tino's conversation while furiously chewing on his gum. "Is there something you didn't understand about what I just said?" Tino asked in a peeved voice.

"What should I use for a rope?" Sebastian asked, not pausing on his gum chewing.

Tino stared at him with an exasperated expression, saying nothing. Understanding the wordless response, Sebastian slipped the leather sling of his submachine gun over his shoulder, and began to search the hall for something that he could use. Finally, after several seconds, he located a braided chord that hung from one of the heavy silk drapes adorning the windows of the hall and, flicking open a switchblade, walked towards it.

Tino diverted his attention from his prisoner to Sebastian for only a scant second, uncertain about the wisdom of his companion's choice, but it was all the time that Lucas needed to act.

With the deadly speed of a snake, he struck Tino's scrawny neck with the ridge formed between the open thumb and index fingers of his right hand. He delivered his blow in one short, violent chop, hitting the Machetero's Adam's apple, driving it into his larynx and instantly blocking his intake of air. Tino dropped soundlessly to his knees, his mouth open, gasping soundlessly like a fish tossed out of the water onto dry land, his eyes bulging as his lungs vainly struggled for air. The serrated metallic object fell out of his left hand and onto the hall's thick, central Persian rug at the same time that Lucas stripped away his gun from his other hand with embarrassing ease.

The attack occurred so swiftly and quietly that Sebastian, cutting the drapery's chord with his back turned towards them, did not realize what had happened until he turned around with the severed chord in his hand.

"Don't move," Lucas warned him, his gun—a 357 Magnum—aimed directly at the terrorist's chest. The man stopped chewing gum, and raised his arms in the air. "Don't say a word. Drop your knife and turn around. Open your arms and legs and lean against the wall."

Sebastian obeyed without hesitation, his head turned to the ground in utter frustration. Approaching him carefully, Lucas pulled the chord out of the Machetero's hand, and crouched briefly to pick up the discarded knife. It was the classical pointy, double-edged switchblade used in every Hollywood gang movie since time immemorial, except it had a carved black skull at the bottom of its ivory-colored handle.

"Lay down on the floor and place your hands behind your back, your right wrist over your left wrist."

Lucas strained his ears, trying to pick up any sounds of people coming in his direction, but failed to detect any activity.

"Hurry," he ordered the man, fearing that George would return at any moment. While Sebastian finished stretching on the floor, Lucas made a loop with the cut chord. A few feet away, Tino writhed on the carpet, his face slowly turning blue, his tongue drooping out of his mouth.

Placing a knee on Sebastian's back, Lucas pressed the base of his neck with the sharp point of the switchblade. "Don't move, or I'll sever your spinal chord with one quick cut, do you understand?"

"Yes," the terrorist replied with a heavy grunt.

With his other hand, Lucas pushed the Magnum into his belt, and then slipped the looped chord over the terrorist's crossed wrists. Leaving the switchblade on Sebastian's neck, he quickly pulled the chord from both ends and pinned the wrists. This was a critical moment, since the Machetero could have attempted to roll over and fight back, but he did not even stir, allowing Lucas to securely bind his hands. His ankles were next, tied with the same rope so that his legs rose perpendicularly from the floor.

Lucas took another look at Tino, and saw that his body had stopped moving.

"Don't make a sound or I'll cut your throat," he whispered menacingly into Sebastian's ear. He walked to the silk drapes from which the terrorist had cut the chord, and with the aid of the switchblade ripped off a long strip of cloth. Then he returned to the downed terrorist and he lowered his head, so that his eyes were nearly level with those of Sebastian on the floor.

"I still have my doubts as to whether I should just kill you, or let you live," he said casually. "I mean, if somebody releases you, what will keep you from coming after me?"

Sebastian blinked several times in terror, but to his credit said nothing.

"I need you to cooperate with me and answer a few questions," Lucas said to him. "If you do, I may let you live."

The terrorist moved his head affirmatively several times, sliding his cheek on the floor tiles. "Tell me what you need to know, and I'll answer...if I can." Noting Lucas' skeptic expression, he added, "I'll answer, I'll answer! I swear!"

"How many more of your men are occupying La Fortaleza?" Lucas asked, trying not to make obvious his interest in his godson.

"I'm not sure." Sebastian did a quick mental count, anxious to please his captor. "There's fifteen of us plus...five of them," he said at last.

"What do you mean, *'us'* and *'them'*?"

" 'Us' is us, the Puerto Ricans. 'Them' is the foreigners who are helping us," he explained, as if it was obvious.

"You mean Americans, like George? Or Venezuelans?"

"Americans, Arabs, South Americans, you name it..."

Lucas considered the terrorist's unexpected answer, his curiosity aroused. *What the hell was happening in San Juan? Who were those people?* He did not have any time, however, to dwell any more on the subject, and decided to press on. Trying not to show his anxiety, he asked, "Do you keep any other hostages in this place?"

"In La Fortaleza? Of course!"

"Where are they?"

Again, Sebastian hesitated. "I'm not sure," he answered guardedly, but when Lucas moved the switchblade closer to his neck, he added, "I haven't been with them! I think somebody said they were in a hall with mirrors."

"And do you know where that hall with mirrors would be?"

Sebastian shook his head with great emphasis. "No," he said, closing his eyes in despair.

Lucas kept silent, hoping his prisoner would volunteer additional information, but he did not. Time was running short. He had to move on.

"Spit out your gum," he said finally. Sebastian complied immediately, spitting out the gum with a subdued 'pop', and sending it scurrying like a live pink insect over the floor all the way to the wall. Lucas ripped the cloth again, pushing part of it into the terrorist's mouth, then binding the rest of it tightly around his mouth and head. Grabbing the bound Machetero under the arms, Lucas dragged him behind one of the heavy curtains that decorated the windows.

Next, he walked back to Tino, and examined him at a closer range. He did not have to take the fallen man's pulse to determine that he was still alive. The bluish tinge of his face had faded into a more grayish complexion, and a half rasping, half wheezing sound emanating from his mouth confirmed that the Adam's apple had shifted back to its place, at least partially, to let in some air. The skull-faced man would have serious problems trying to get understood during the next few weeks, Lucas noted to himself with perverse satisfaction, but he would live.

It had all felt like déjà vu, a repeat performance of his prior encounter with the terrorists on the roof of the Metropolitan Center. Except that this time, it had been so much easier.

In fact, the ease with which his military combat instincts had resurfaced had both amazed and unsettled him. He had thought them long and deeply buried under the thick strata of his peaceful civilian years. It was true that he had kept himself physically fit, more as a matter of health and personal vanity—more vanity than health—but he knew that he was a pale reflection of the lethal fighter that the Rangers had trained two decades before. It had never occurred to him that it would all be still there, dormant, a little rusty perhaps, and slower, but intact. Now he realized that his fighting instincts had not been buried under the thick strata of civilized living after all, but that it had been the other way around. A thin veneer of civility had barely kept them hidden all that time.

The best—and worst—part of it all was that he never felt more alive. It was as if the weight of all of his personal responsibilities had been temporarily lifted so that he could concentrate exclusively on the problem at hand. His senses—sight, hearing and even smell—seemed to have heightened as the situation grew more precarious. He felt strong, and quick, and fully aware of his surroundings, probably the result of the immense amount of adrenaline rushing through his body. His thinking was clear and focused, divested of all distractions, devoted to one single purpose: getting his godson out of there alive.

Surprisingly, he no longer felt any anger towards the terrorists; they had simply become his adversaries, competitors in the dangerous, dirty game that they were all playing. And if in the process they were wounded, maimed, or killed, those were part of the rules that everyone playing the game was expected to accept and understand. Including him.

He did not bother to tie up Tino. The man would not get up for a very long time, and by then, George would have returned. He needed to act fast. His best bet would have been to find Alfredo and brazen it out of La Fortaleza, but that alternative was gone now. He had found out that his godson was in a hall with many mirrors, but he had no idea where that was. He could not afford to get lost within the walls of the massive Executive Mansion. He would have to get help.

Lucas unfastened Tino's holster and placed it around his waist. Then he grabbed the unconscious terrorist by the scruff of his shirt's neck and dragged him behind another of the heavy drapes adorning the windows of the waiting room, hoping that George would fail to notice the two hidden men upon his return, and would think that they had moved Lucas someplace else. Of course, the lack of a guard in front of the Governor's office would immediately suggest to him that something was seriously wrong, but it would buy some time while George figured out what had happened.

Pausing again to listen, Lucas walked to the twin mahogany doors of Governor Pietrantoni's office, and tried to twist the door's handle. It was locked, but a skeleton key stuck out from its keyhole. He twisted it and it clicked, one of the tall paneled doors giving way to his push.

Cautiously, he ventured a look inside the cavernous office, calling out softly, "Governor Pietrantoni—"

He had just enough time to duck, as he saw a shadow whiz towards his head. Something heavy struck the door a couple of inches above him, and bounced painfully onto his right shoulder. It was a statue, slightly smaller than a baseball bat, and the Governor was pulling it back to swing it again.

"Wait!" Lucas said urgently. "I'm a friend!"

Pietrantoni eyed the man who had just barged into his office with distrust, and with a flash of recognition, lowered the object—a big wooden statue of St. John the Baptist—that he was holding.

"You're Maestes, the man they took away a few moments ago," he said, staring distrustfully at the guns that Lucas was wearing strapped to his waist. "How come—"

"I escaped," Lucas answered. He had never met the Governor before, and found him, in his jeans and worn sweater, to be much taller than he had imagined. And leaner. "Mr. Governor, there's no time to waste," he said with urgency, "George may be back at any moment."

Pietrantoni listened quietly to his visitor, doubt etched on his face.

"My real name is Lucas Alfaro," Lucas continued, trying to gain his trust. "I work in the *Joyero de San Juan*." He watched with relief as the Governor's skeptic gaze softened to one of surprise.

"You're Michelle Alfaro's brother..." Pietrantoni said, in a tone that started as a question but ended as a definite, slightly surprised statement, as if he were assessing some legal issue and had just come upon the answer. He placed the heavy St. John the Baptist's statue on the floor, and extended his hand. "Of course, now that you mention it, I can see the family resemblance! And you are Fannie Pietri's son," he added, the consummate-politician-with-a-privileged-memory-for-names-instinct briefly taking over.

Lucas nodded and shook the Governor's outstretched hand. He was used to being identified as "his-famous-sister's-brother". Decades before, when his father had been a famous television actor and director, he had been "Mario Alfaro's son". It was nevertheless strange to be associated as "Fannie Pietri's son".

"But what are you doing here?" the Governor asked warmly, a glint of hope lighting his otherwise somber mood.

"It's a long story, and we don't have much time, sir," Lucas answered, deciding to come right to the point. "I came for my godson," he said, and seeing the confusion on Pietrantoni's face, added, "Alfredo, Alfredo Del Valle." The Governor's expression remained a blank. "Your son's, Francisco, friend?"

Finally, Pietrantoni grasped the purpose of Alfaro's unexpected appearance in his office, and with that came a look of astonishment mixed with great concern. His face grew pale, as the fear for his son's safety, momentarily pushed into the background, resurfaced to nearly overwhelm him.

"You penetrated the lines of the terrorists to find your nephew?" he said, utterly amazed. "How—"

"Do you know if he's all right?" Lucas cut him short, aware of the dwindling window of opportunity before the rest of the terrorists in La Fortaleza became aware of what was happening.

Pietrantoni considered the question and moved his head affirmatively. "They have assured me that my son and her governess, Nereida, are alive, so I must assume that Alfredo is too."

It was not the reassuring answer that Lucas had sought, but he had no time to dwell on it. He looked at his watch; almost twenty minutes had passed since George had left. The black terrorist would soon be back.

"I need to go," he said. "I got a description of where they keep the other prisoners."

"Where?"

"The Machetero outside said that they were in a hall with mirrors. Do you know where that is?"

"Yes," the Governor nodded again. "The Hall *of* Mirrors," he said, correcting the way that Lucas referred to the room. "It's the room where we hold most of the official state ceremonies. It's a large room, so it would be the natural place to assemble many people, which means that they probably are keeping all of the hostages there, together." He pointed to the back of his enormous office. "The best way to get there would be through that way."

It was Lucas' turn to look confused.

"You see those double doors to the left of my desk? If we could use them, we could cut across an adjacent room and walk directly into the Hall of Mirrors," Pietrantoni explained. "But the terrorists shut the doors from the outside. They wrapped the door handles with wire or tape, all the doors of the office except for this entrance, so I couldn't escape. So we'll have to take the longer route."

Lucas noticed that the Governor had begun to use the collective *"we"* word when discussing the rescue attempt. It instantly filled him with dread and dismay. It was one thing to attempt to slip away from La Fortaleza with a boy who had no strategic value for the Macheteros. It was quite another to help escape the Macheteros' main hostage—and his family, for that matter—since the Governor would refuse to leave his son, and probably his son's nanny, behind. The latter scenario was a game-changer. It would mean that if they attempted to escape, every terrorist within miles would try to hunt them down.

On the other hand, the Governor's intimate knowledge of La Fortaleza would be invaluable, and could give them the only real chance of getting out of there alive. And there was one more thing. He could not abandon the man and his family to their own fate. Had the positions been reversed, he would have been desperate to find his son. Still, the moment that he helped the Governor escape, the odds of slipping out of La Fortaleza with Alfredo unnoticed would drop to zero. It would also increase the possibility that Francisco, Nereida, or even the Governor would get injured or killed as they tried to escape.

He decided to state his concerns to the Governor and let him decide. After all, if Pietrantoni opted to stay, there was a good probability that he would later be rescued, or at the very least released if the government agreed to the Macheteros' demands.

"You may choose to come with me," he began to say, "or you may stay here and —"

"Of course I will come with you! Anything else would be out of the question!" Pietrantoni replied coolly, not allowing Lucas to finish. His eyes hardened, regarding Lucas with barely suppressed indignation, as if he had been offended. "I am the Governor of Puerto Rico. I owe it to our people to escape, if I can, not to sit here and cringe...And I have to get my son out of here before these people do anything to him."

"I understand, believe me I do," Lucas answered embarrassedly. "But you may be placing your son in even greater danger if we try to break out of here."

Pietrantoni opened his mouth to snap an angry response at Lucas, but then noticed his companion's discomfort, and sighed. "Please forgive me. I may have come on too strong," he said, the edge in his voice softening. "This has not been the best of my days, I'm afraid. However, you must understand that these criminals are using my son as leverage, and that I will never allow. We either escape together, or they kill me trying.

Nothing else is acceptable. Again, my apologies for snapping back at you. My nerves are a little bit frayed."

Lucas nodded. "Considering the circumstances," he replied with a thin smile, "I think you're doing pretty well."

The Governor grinned gratefully, attempting to put on a brave face, only the slight tremor of his right hand, as he combed back his hair, betraying his nervousness.

Lucas pulled out one of the two guns that he had appropriated from Tino and handed it to Pietrantoni.

"Do you know how to use this?" he asked him.

"That's a Magnum .357 revolver," the Governor answered, provoking a surprised stare from his companion. "When I was a federal prosecutor, I found it convenient to learn how to use and to carry a firearm. We were not exactly popular with a lot of people, you know? I used to go to the Police Gun Range in Puerta de Tierra twice a week." He weighed the revolver in his hand. "This is heavy artillery. It must have a wicked kick."

"Ever fire one?"

"A couple of times, just for fun. I had a Glock G21, really nice pistol."

"You'll find the locking mechanism on the left hand side, close to the trigger. I disengaged it just now," Lucas said, with newfound respect. "Be very careful with it."

The Governor pushed the cylinder of the gun and it flipped open. He checked if it was loaded, and then closed it again. "Five bullets. That's not much." He brought up the revolver with both hands, and aimed it at his desk.

"It will do," Lucas answered distractedly. He thought he had heard a slight noise outside of the office, like the muted shuffle of footsteps, and took a quick peek through the open door. He found both the waiting room and the corridor that led further into La Fortaleza devoid of life, however. *His nerves were beginning to play tricks on him*, he thought.

"Just make certain that you aim before you shoot, to make sure that you're shooting at the right people. Don't worry if you miss. The noise that you make will be as effective as the bullets you fire. I still haven't met a person who doesn't run away, flinches, or ducks for cover when somebody starts shooting. After that happens, I'll help you."

A look of curiosity appeared on the Governor's face, as if he was about to ask Lucas, *"Who are you? How do you know so much about guns?"* But to his credit, he settled for a nod.

"When we get out of this office, we will be very visible to any lookouts that are roaming around. The last thing we want to do is get into a firefight before we reach the hostages. That would be very bad."

Lucas hesitated before continuing.

"So even though I don't particularly like it...I am going to ask you to march in front of me, with your hands behind your back, as if they were tied or handcuffed together."

Lucas saw Pietrantoni arch an eyebrow.

"I know, it's a cliché movie trick, but it's the best I've got. Don't worry. I will be covering you at all times, and you will be holding your own gun in your hand, behind your back. In reality, it will be you leading me to the Hall of Mirrors. If anyone stops us, that's what I'll tell them, that I've been ordered to take you to the Hall of Mirrors with the rest of the prisoners."

The Governor stepped in front of his companion without saying a word. Lucas studied him guardedly. *If Pietrantoni was scared, he managed to hide it well.*

"If we meet anyone along the way, you keep walking, understand? You keep walking unless I tell you to stop."

Pietrantoni assented. Already, he had placed his hands behind his waist, holding the Magnum with its barrel pointing towards the floor. That was good. Lucas did not want to get shot. *It was time to go.*

"Are you ready?" he asked, taking a deep breath.

"No," the Governor answered, a hint of humor in his voice, "but what the heck? I've been doing stuff I don't want to do for years now." He straightened himself up, preparing himself for the upcoming ordeal, and cast one last glance at Lucas. "Just don't use me as a shield, okay?"

"I will do my best not to, Mr. Governor," Lucas answered, trying to inject some humor into the tense conversation, and failing miserably.

He opened one of the office's tall doors, and allowed Pietrantoni to walk out, following him with his gun pointing at his back. The two-man procession turned right, and began its perilous trudge into the bowels of La Fortaleza.

The carpeted corridor that led further into the mansion looked completely abandoned. Nevertheless, Lucas felt that they were not alone. It was as if La Fortaleza exuded a thick aura of its own, invisible to the naked eye, and yet as palpable to the senses as the gun Lucas held in his right hand. It felt as if the souls of the uninterrupted line of governors who had lived there during its five hundred year history, since the time of Ponce de Leon, watched the Governor and his companion as they marched in wary silence, curious about what the two of them were about to do.

As he followed Pietrantoni, Lucas could not help but wonder if any of the previous tenants of the Executive Mansion would have dared to do what the present Governor was doing. Muñoz Marin would have, and Ferre, and certainly Alarcon who, despite all of his faults, seemed to be scared of nothing. Just a few hours before, Lucas would have not placed Pietrantoni in the same category as the others. His impression of the present occupant of La Fortaleza was that he was a weak-willed politician who was easily manipulated and pushed around by the likes of Rovira Melendez and "Double A" Arizmendi, more of an ivory tower intellectual who did not like to get his hands dirty than of a man about to attempt to free his son from a bunch of armed terrorists. Pietrantoni was proving him wrong.

In fact, during the very brief time that he had known him, Lucas had developed a grudging admiration towards the gaunt, professorial-looking, and surprisingly candid political leader that had agreed to march, without a word of protest, in front of him. He liked him. They may not have shared the same political ideals, but the man had courage to spare.

Which was good, because he would need it soon.

George felt Tino stir under him, and instinctively placed his hand on the hilt of his dagger. If necessary, he would use it to silence the unconscious man. But the Machetero stopped moving as abruptly as he had started, his jerky movements apparently caused by an involuntary muscle spasm.

Standing on his toes—so that his shoes would not be visible—he spied towards the Governor's office from behind the drapery that covered him and Tino. Through a narrow crack in the curtains, he watched silently as one of the office doors opened and the chief executive himself exited, followed by the man who called himself Maestes. For a brief moment, he was surprised to see Maestes pointing a gun at the back of the Governor—after all, he had assumed that the impostor was there to rescue Pietrantoni—but then he noticed the other gun that the Governor carried and partially hid with his hands, and saw that his wrists were untied. He chuckled softly. *Such a naïve, worn-out trick!* But it had momentarily fooled him.

They would be trying to rescue the other prisoners, he surmised. That was stupid and suicidal. Had it been him, he would have run away by himself. However, he could not blame the Governor. If his son had been the one kidnapped by the Macheteros, he probably would have been as anxious to rescue him as Pietrantoni was. But that was beside the point. The issue was that the Governor would be risking his life, and that his odds of surviving—no matter how good Maestes was—would be less than those of an ice cream cone in hell. He had to make a decision, and make it quickly.

The Governor was a very valuable commodity, *the* most valuable hostage they had. The men guarding La Fortaleza would avoid harming him, unless instructed to do so. But in a gunfight, men tended to shoot first, and look who they were shooting at afterwards. If things got violent, Pietrantoni's life would be worth less than a Mexican nickel.

*And then there was that Maestes guy...*Something warned George that he would be a tough man to take down. And if he tangled with Maestes, he would probably have to fight the Governor as well. It was not a good alternative.

He turned his head to his left and, placing his index finger across his lips, warned Hassam, who was hiding behind the next set of drapes, to be still. George considered the Afghani as the most reliable man of the four San Miguel followers who had occupied La Fortaleza. He would need someone reliable at his side when the killing started.

The unexpected reappearance of Maestes had added an unpredictable factor into an already volatile situation. Somehow, this man had managed to single-handedly beat the crap out of two Macheteros while being unarmed and guarded at gunpoint—not an unimpressive feat, even if George's opinion of the Macheteros was not high.

But his escape was not necessarily a bad thing. If handled properly, Maestes' combat experience could be of great use to George. It could fit beautifully into San Miguel's plans.

If handled properly...

George wished he had been able to consult about Maestes with San Miguel, but in order to do that he would have needed to be in an open space—a rooftop, a courtyard, somewhere without walls or a roof where his satellite phone could operate. Anyway, he had no time. He had to follow the Governor and Maestes as soon as they disappeared from his sight.

He had spoken with San Miguel only twenty minutes before, after he had left the Governor's office. He had descended the main staircase, and turned left into the central atrium of La Fortaleza, a wide, square-shaped, roofless area enclosed by the Executive Mansion's wings. From there, he had headed west, skirting past some sort of dig or excavation that apparently had been taking place in the center of the atrium, and walking through the gate of the massive western wall that in prior centuries had protected La Fortaleza from the scores of invaders that had attempted to capture it. In its day, the western wall, flanked by two tall medieval looking towers, must have constituted a formidable barrier for anyone daring to attack the governor's seat of power. However, the prior night it had been easily breached by just four of his men.

From the gate, he had exited onto the palace's gardens, passing a couple of Macheteros who eyed him warily. Out of hearing, he had managed to reach San Miguel via satellite phone. Well, not exactly San Miguel, but Pepe—nicknamed "Pepe Cojones" or "Pepe Big Balls" for his fearless

exploits—whose main function was to stay in the open by the Grand Laguna Hotel, and receive any calls that anyone directed to San Miguel's
satellite phone. It had taken roughly ten minutes for San Miguel to get to
the phone, a lot more than George had estimated, and he had begun to
worry—foolishly, as it now turned out to be—that Tino would use his
delay as an excuse to start the interrogation of the prisoner on his own,
and botch up the whole thing.

"This is Pedro Martinez," San Miguel's voice had abruptly responded.
He had sounded in good spirits. *"How are you, Marc Anthony?"*

George had been unable suppress a chortle. "Well, you know how it
is with Cleopatra and everything."

He had not waited for a reciprocating laugh from his boss, knowing
that the latter would not be amused. George enjoyed baiting him,
though. He knew it made San Miguel uncomfortable, and he derived a
perverse pleasure from it.

"I'm getting some heat from some of the ah...workers here, in the
warehouse. They want to move the package to your place," he had informed his boss.

There had been a pause. Then San Miguel had answered, in a pleasant, reasonable voice, *"I suspected that they would want to do that, but I
don't want the package brought up to our offices here. It will only complicate
matters."*

"Shall I wrap up things down here then?" George had asked.

"Just sit tight for the moment," San Miguel had replied. *"If the others insist on sending the package, fire them."*

"I will do that, boss. Nice talking to you."

"And to you too," San Miguel had responded, terminating the conversation before George could make another of his wisecracks.

As he watched the Governor and Maestes disappear into the corridor,
George thought how lucky he had been. Had he been delayed further in
his conversation with San Miguel, he might have run into the two men as
he returned to the Governor's office; had arrived there earlier, he might
have caught Maestes disposing of the two Macheteros. Either way, George
would have been forced to make a split-second decision regarding
Maestes' future. Now he could just follow him, and figure out what to do.

After finishing his conversation with San Miguel, George had made a
round through the mansions' outside grounds, where El Alacran had
posted San Miguel's four men. He had quietly informed them that the
Macheteros intended to move the Governor to the Grand Laguna Hotel,
and warned them that if that was the case, they would have to stop the
Macheteros from doing so. In other words, that they should be ready to
fight at any moment.

Despite the more than the three-to-one odds against them, his men had received his instructions with surprising enthusiasm. They had been offended, one of them had said, assigned to the menial task of policing the outside grounds of La Fortaleza, when it had been they who had captured the Executive Mansion. George also suspected that his men were bored out of their minds, and were excited by the prospect of a firefight.

George had asked Hassam, the most efficient of the four men, to return with him to the Governor's office. As they neared it, however, George had discovered that nobody guarded the office doors.

For one panicky moment, he had suspected that Tino had taken advantage of his absence to spirit the Governor away. But as his eyes alighted on the floor of the reception area, he had quickly pieced together most of what had truly happened. Even though the furniture was still in place, there were fragments of a broken vase strewn over the black and white tiles that bordered the central rug in the room, next to the room's sofa. And two of the drapes that had been tied back to allow light to filter through the room's windows had been freed from the chords that bound them, spreading over the window frames and darkening the hall. On a hunch, he had dropped on one knee, and confirmed that there were horizontal shadows behind the curtains; no doubt the bodies of those who were supposed to have been guarding the Governor.

Warning Hassam to be quiet, he had drawn out "BD"—his seven-inch black dagger—and carefully pressed his ear on one of the office's paneled doors. Immediately, he had been able to discern the murmur of male voices coming from the inside.

"Follow me," he had whispered to his Afghan companion, and led him to the curtains on the opposite side of the reception room. "Keep an eye on the office doors," he had instructed Hassam. "If they begin to open, hide behind the curtains."

Gingerly, he had pulled one of the drapes to one side. The sight of Sebastian—the gum chewing Machetero who had stood guard outside the Governor's office— had made him chuckle with childish glee. The man's wrists and ankles were bound by the chord of a curtain, his mouth gagged by a shredded piece of cloth. Sebastian had stared back at him with a terrified expression, and when he had recognized the new arrival, had begun to struggle violently to free himself from the ropes.

"Why lookee here, Hassam!" George had said in a low, amused tone. "If it isn't a hog, all tied up and ready for the slaughter!"

Hassam had directed a quick, disdainful look in the direction of the downed man, and then turned back to watch the office.

George let the tip of his dagger rest on the floor, scarcely an inch from the Machetero's eyes. "Be still, my friend," he had said to him gently. "I don't want the people inside the office to hear you. It might make me nervous and..." The tip of the knife slipped suddenly towards Sebastian's wide-open eyes, stopping just before it nicked its left eyeball. "There! You see? Just thinking about it has already made me shaky!"

Sebastian stopped squirming immediately.

As he expected, George had found the unconscious body of Tino hidden behind the second curtain, his scrawny neck swollen and discolored, a tortured, rasping wheeze coming out of his cracked lips. George had only taken a couple of seconds to examine him, foregoing his usual chuckle, his round, expressive eyes narrowing into malevolent slits.

"Get yourself behind that curtain," he had hissed to Hassam, pointing to the drape shielding Sebastian's body. He had followed suit, taking cover behind the other curtain, his sneakers nearly stepping on the fallen Machetero's face.

While he waited, he had thought further about Maestes. The man puzzled him. From his brief encounter with the intruder and from his cursory inspection of the reception area, George could definitely tell that the stranger was a very dangerous man, one that had probably received training from one of the few, specialized military forces that operated in the world: the U.S. Navy SEALs, the Green Berets, or the Rangers, the British SBS, the Israeli Sayeret, or the Russian Spetnaz, basically. Most probably, one of the American units. Yet at the same time, that dangerous man had displayed a mystifying weakness.

Knowing how little time he had to get the Governor out of La Fortaleza before he was discovered, Maestes had lost precious minutes—life and death determining minutes—tying up one Machetero, when he could have easily killed him and Tino. *That* made no sense. If anything, it told George that the intruder, despite his fighting prowess, suffered from one serious flaw: he still valued human life. It was a serious flaw, one that would eventually get him killed, and one that George could exploit, if needs be.

As the Governor and Maestes abandoned the office and disappeared from his line of sight, George turned his head towards Hassam and made one quick, cutting gesture across his throat, getting a nod of acknowledgment from the Afghan. Then, he knelt next to Tino, placed BD at the nape of his neck, and plunged the dagger into his head.

Tino's body jerked twice, as if being pulled by ropes from both ends, and then went limp. George wiped his knife clean on the drape, and slipped it back into its holster. When he looked back at Hassam, he saw that he had also finished his business, a crimson puddle of blood spreading over the tiled floor from a trembling Sebastian's slit throat.

"All right," he said, with the same calm satisfaction of a mechanic who has finished fixing an engine, "let's go follow these people."

CHAPTER XLVII

The Lakota helicopter hovered gracefully over the glittering surface of San Juan Bay, its four passengers quietly surveying the landscape below them. In the late afternoon, the sun glistened over the bay's murky water like melting gold over a flat pan. To the north, El Morro Castle loomed like a giant, coiled dragon, guarding the entrance to the bay, while further to the east, the twin white towers of La Fortaleza shone like an enchanted fairytale castle.

The helicopter avoided flying over the captured island of San Juan, flying south of the San Antonio Channel over Isla Grande and the Convention Center, bypassing the two plumes of smoke still rising from the smoldering ruins of the Police Station and the San Juan Yacht Club. No ships disturbed the surface of the bay or its ports, a first in Puerto Rico's more than five hundred year history.

Adalberto Cacho watched from his window in absolute silence, his eyes scanning with mild curiosity the ancient, multi-colored buildings that dotted the southern boundary of the city of Old San Juan. He seemed to take special notice of the only cruise ship still moored on one of the city's piers, and then of the demolished bridges, as the Lakota abruptly veered north and flew over the Condado Lagoon.

From the air, the damage was clearly evident. A wide span in each of the three major bridges had caved into the waters of the lagoon, some large chunks of the demolished concrete still hanging vertically from their reinforcing steel rebars. The fourth bridge—the oldest and narrowest—was destroyed nearly in its entirety.

The island of San Juan had been cleanly severed from the rest of Puerto Rico, Cacho noted. It would take a major feat of engineering to reconnect it to the mainland.

The helicopter decreased its speed and started to descend. As it did so, it began to turn, so that its left side faced the Grand Laguna Hotel.

The large red circle painted on the surface of the landing pad began to loom larger and larger as the chopper slowly slid diagonally towards it.

For the first time, the descending passengers noticed the presence of several men on the rooftop, hiding behind the back wall of the helipad, not visible to the SWAT and police snipers nestled on the roofs of the Condado buildings across the lagoon. There were at least a dozen men, pointing their semi-automatic rifles at the helicopter, plus a man shouldering an ominous-looking, bazooka-like weapon.

"Time to get out," said one of the two U.S. marshals that had accompanied Cacho in his flight out of jail, not hiding in his voice the contempt that he felt towards his prisoner. He looked tough, with the pug nose of a boxer past his prime, sporting a short crew cut, and wearing a white, short-sleeved shirt. And in his hands he held a single barreled shotgun that he pointed at the Machetero. He eyed Cacho with an itchy intensity, as if waiting to find an excuse to blast him out of the aircraft.

As the helicopter touched ground, the door next to where the prisoner sat rolled back, exposing the passengers to the noise and the wind generated by the rotor blades. Two men hiding inside the helipad's stairwell rushed towards the chopper and grabbed each arm of their newly liberated leader. Cacho did not pause to look at them, letting them lead him away, as the speed of the helicopter's blades began to increase in momentum and the whine of its turbine mounted to a deafening pitch.

By the time that Cacho reached the stairs of the helipad, the Lakota had risen more than fifty feet into the air and begun to fly away back towards its base in Isla Grande. The Machetero leader watched it go, and then glanced at the two men who had helped him get off the chopper.

"Iglesias!" he said with genuine surprise to the first of the men, an older, white-haired gentleman with a more than decent physical build, who looked more like a high school coach than a terrorist. "I was afraid that they had captured or killed you."

"Me? No!" the older man answered, staring at his leader with a half-embarrassed, half-fearful look. He had been with Cacho on the day that Cacho had been apprehended at the Hiram Bithorn Stadium, watching the baseball game. It had been Iglesias who had warned him about the unusual number of police officers that had suddenly begun circulating among the rowdy crowd of spectators. They had decided to split, and the last time that Cacho had seen him, Iglesias had begun to run towards one of the stadium exits, followed by several agents. Two plainclothes policemen had arrested Cacho a few minutes later, wrestling him to the ground as he tried to climb over a chain link fence.

"It's all right," Cacho told the older man, placing a hand on his shoulder, sensing his guilt about having escaped while he had been captured. "You did what you had to do."

He directed his gaze to the second man, and after a brief pause, burst out laughing. "Andrade! Is that you?" he exclaimed with amazement. "My God! You almost look like a lawyer!"

"The things I do for you," El Alacran replied.

The two men embraced. For the very few people on the planet that knew both of them, the close friendship between the two Machetero leaders had been a source of mystery and wonder. Cacho was a very personable, expressive, and charismatic type of leader, an eloquent speaker who instilled unabashed admiration and loyalty—some would call it love—in his followers. He could be stubborn and ruthless and manipulative at times, and he took impulsive risks—as he had plainly shown when attending the baseball game at the Bithorn Stadium—that sometimes got him into trouble. However, he managed to lead by the force of his personality. Had he not been a terrorist, he would have been a politician.

Andrade, on the other hand, seemed to have crawled out from under a rock—hence his nickname, El Alacran. Most of the time, he spoke in a low hiss, avoiding direct eye contact, mostly spewing sarcastic remarks or understated threats. He would give in to irrepressible bouts of fury, and usually took matters into his own hands with violent results. Where his counterpart led with charisma, he led by fear.

The two men could not have been more different from each other. And yet, a genuine bond of affection existed between them. It was not unusual to find them talking for hours, discussing strategy, arguing politics and ideology, or even exchanging friendly insults. In that relationship, Cacho had always assumed the leadership role, and Andrade had never challenged it, even though among their followers, many wondered if the latter was the more effective revolutionary.

"Quite an interesting thing you've started here," Cacho said to Andrade as the two separated from their embrace. He towered over his friend by nearly a head's difference. "We're a little over the top, aren't we?"

El Alacran shrugged. "It worked, did it not? You're here."

Cacho stared at him for a moment, as if considering asking him more questions, but decided to shelve them for later, nodding.

"Anyway, we didn't organize this," Andrade continued.

"Oh?" Cacho raised his left eyebrow quizzically, one of his cultivated trademark expressions.

El Alacran shook his head. "No. We're here for the ride. Come," he said, pulling his friend gently by the arm, intending to lead him down the stairs, "I'll brief you about the main details as we're coming down."

"Not yet, Aristides," Cacho stopped him. "I suspect that these clothes have more 'bugs' in them than a beggars' convention. I need to get rid of them before we can talk."

"Then we should proceed to 'de-bug' you as quickly as possible," Andrade murmured, just in case the "bugs" could overhear him, "because there is a lot I need to tell you."

Placing an arm over his shorter companion's shoulder, the Machetero leader began to descend the stairs.

Johnny Ray and Yajaira waited for the arrival of the freed Machetero leader in the Grand Laguna's main lobby, along with nearly every other leader of the revolt and many of the men who had occupied the hotel. There was a spontaneous cheer when someone announced that the helicopter carrying Cacho had just alighted—fifteen minutes early—on the hotel's rooftop, followed by the excited chatter of people expecting a celebrity.

Johnny cast a sideways glance at his female companion, and found her strangely subdued. She had been that way during the past few hours, and when at San Miguel's suggestion they had locked themselves up in one of the hotel suites, she had dashed his hopes of having brief, wild sex by taking a quick shower and promptly falling asleep.

"Are you all right?" he asked her softly, gently caressing her back, between her two shoulder blades.

She looked at him and nodded slightly, returning her gaze to the elevator doors from where Cacho was bound to exit.

"Are you excited?" he insisted.

She nodded again briefly, keeping her eyes on the elevators, not really appearing to be excited at all. On the contrary, her arms were crossed closely over her chest, as if trying to ward off a chill, and she stood in a somewhat slumped position, contrary to the perky, breasts-forward stance that she usually adopted on important occasions.

It seemed to him as if she had almost given up, as if she had finally realized the enormity of what had happened and what little control they—Johnny and her—had over the ongoing events. She had been forced to accept the fact that the revolt had never been theirs to lead, and that their role in it was becoming less and less important as the affair unfolded.

He could not blame her. He felt the same way. What had seemed like a glorious, adventurous enterprise had become tarnished with the blood of many people. It was true that most of them had been combatants, policemen representing the imperialistic regime that had kept Puerto Rico pinned under the American boot for so many years, and that in a war, casualties were to be expected. But too many people had died. And he could not see an end in sight to the fighting.

Even his own FEPIstas had committed excesses of power. He could not drive out of his mind the image of the man who had died in the jewelry store. The explanation given by his people had sounded false and hollow. In addition to that, there had been several instances of looting in the city. He felt that he was losing his grasp over the situation. The revolution was taking a life of its own.

He had also expected that the tremendous risk that he and the rest of the freedom fighters were undertaking on behalf of their country would be appreciated by a majority of his countrymen, and galvanize many of them into action. He had spoken with Lebron, still transmitting Johnny's speech from the rooftop of the Banco Cosmopolitano Building in Old San Juan, just a half hour before. The FEPI Secretary General had asked him if he had heard about any reaction to their broadcast from the outside world, of any student or independence demonstrations in support of the uprising. Johnny had confessed that he had not, but had added that it was not likely that such things would be reported in the news. Privately, however, he doubted very much that anything was happening. The population in Old San Juan had not rallied to their calls. Everyone had kept to his home. The people's apathy weighed heavily on his soul.

"This is a historical moment!" he heard San Miguel say, and then realized that he was talking to him.

"Yes," Johnny replied, forcing a smile. He desperately searched his mind for something else to say, but could think of nothing, so like the rest of the people he fixed his eyes back on the elevator doors.

The execution of hostages from the rooftop of the Grand Laguna Hotel had been a serious mistake. It had scared the viewing population, he thought. It had portrayed them as terrorists, instead of liberators. It had been a setback to the revolution. At the same time, it had been the catalytic agent that had finally forced the local authorities to free Adalberto Cacho.

He did not know what to think any more. *Maybe things would change. Maybe, in all revolutions, there were moments like this.* He would have to wait and see.

The bell of one of the elevators made a musical "ding" and its silver, mirror-like doors opened. The crowd instantly grew silent, and then burst into cheers and applause, as El Alacran, another Machetero, and Adalberto Cacho walked into the lobby.

San Miguel watched with intense satisfaction as Cacho wandered into the reception area, acknowledging the thunderous ovation from the waiting crowd. He was surprised to see even some of his men applauding, whether caught in the emotion of the moment, being courteous, or just mocking him, he could not tell. He noticed Andrade whispering something into the Machetero's leader ear as he approached, and saw Cacho's eyes immediately turn towards him.

It was not difficult to pick San Miguel out from the crowd, since he was standing next to Czecka, who stuck out from the rest of the people in the lobby like an oak surrounded by plantain trees. Daniel stood at the other side, while Colonel Calderon observed everything from further away with some of his men—unmistakable because of their black outfits—rubbing his chin with one hand, pensively studying the new arrival.

The assembly quieted down as Cacho approached San Miguel, and then erupted into noisy applause again as both men shook their hands warmly.

"You are the man responsible for all this?" Cacho shouted through the din. San Miguel noticed for the first time that the Machetero was wearing a T-shirt and a gray overall with an insignia on its upper right hand side that showed several rolling waves and read, "Grand Laguna Hotel". Cacho caught his glance and smiled. "I had to shed my clothes," he said to his curious host. "Electronic bugs, you know?"

"Of course," San Miguel answered, laughing and shaking his head. "I should have thought about it." It was not true. San Miguel had considered the possibility that the ex-prisoner's clothes would carry some sort of tracking or transmitting device. He just didn't care, at that stage of the game.

"From what I can see, that's about the only thing that you have not thought about," Cacho joked, a smirk forming in his mouth.

San Miguel was about to answer, but saw that the Machetero's attention had already shifted to the gigantic man standing beside him. "If I may introduce you, this is my associate, Czecka. He is my...enforcer."

"What else?" Cacho said with utter amazement, extending his hand to the behemoth, wincing when he shook it.

"And this is my second in command, Daniel."

Cacho paused, and then took Daniel's hand with a thoughtful expression. *He was trying to read his face,* San Miguel thought with amusement. But he was trying to do it with the wrong man. Daniel's perennial insolent façade made most of his passing acquaintances discount him as a harmless flake or an irreverent jerk, a dangerous error of judgment to make in his case, and one which Daniel used to his full advantage.

"I have heard a great deal about you," Daniel said in a tone that could have been interpreted either as extreme flattery or mockery.

"Really?" Cacho answered, refusing to take the bait. "We'll have to sit down sometime and see how much of it is true."

"And this is Johnny Ray, the President of the FEPI," San Miguel hurried along, before the conversation between Daniel and Cacho could progress any further. "The FEPI has provided the volunteers to keep the order in the city and to act as our eyes. Their help has been invaluable."

"It is such an honor," Johnny blurted out awkwardly, genuinely moved by the Machetero leader's arrival. "You have always been my hero. This is Yajaira Velazquez, my vice-president."

Cacho kept a straight face, but San Miguel noticed a slight narrowing around the corners of his mouth and his eyes, the type that happens to someone who is trying not to laugh. Yajaira, looking very nervous, gave him the back of her hand, and Cacho kissed it unhesitatingly.

"Johnny, Yajaira, it is so good to be involved with patriots of your caliber," he stated charmingly. Yajaira opened her mouth to speak, but the Machetero moved on.

"And this man is Dionisio Calderon," San Miguel continued, pointing to the lean man dressed in black who had stood in the background, observing the freed Machetero. The Venezuelan colonel snapped his heels and nearly stood at attention, gripping Cacho's hand firmly. "His men are responsible for securing San Juan from anyone that tries to invade it. You may have noticed the wreck of the helicopter close to the hotel."

Cacho shook his head. "I'm sorry to say that I did not. I guess I was looking someplace else." His gaze traveled back to Yajaira. "There's so much to see."

"He also provided the heavy armament that helped to destroy the Puerta de Tierra police station."

Cacho's eyes gleamed with interest, a thousand questions running through his brain, but he limited his reaction to a formal nod. "Our nation will be eternally grateful for what you and your men have accomplished," he told Calderon.

"The honor is mine and of my men," the colonel replied proudly.

San Miguel spoke again, apparently to the Machetero leader, but in reality for the benefit of everyone present there.

"Two nights ago, when we met in our Calle de San Sebastian quarters, all of the people that you have just met, and Mr. Andrade as well," San Miguel directed an appreciative look towards El Alacran, who did not even bat an eyelid in acknowledgment, "I made a solemn vow. I said that I would be in command of this operation until such time as Adalberto Cacho was freed from his political imprisonment and delivered safely to us. It sounded like a wonderful fantasy at that time, did it not?" he said, beaming to those around him.

Johnny and Yajaira nodded emphatically, while Colonel Calderon thoughtfully chewed on a fingernail. Andrade lifted slightly his half-closed eyes to stare curiously at San Miguel.

"As my associates can attest, I never make promises that I don't intend to keep. Therefore, Mr. Cacho, I officially relinquish to you my command of this operation, and I humbly place my men and myself at your disposition."

San Miguel's announcement was followed by a tense moment of silence. Next to San Miguel, Czecka knotted his thin eyebrows into one, barely visible, V-shaped line, the massive muscles on his crossed forearms bulging with uneasiness. Daniel's face, on the other hand, could not hide the thin, linear smile that his pressed lips formed. Johnny and Yajaira stared at San Miguel with surprise and admiration, while Calderon lowered his gaze to the floor and continued to chew on his fingernail.

Several persons began to clap, and the applause rapidly grew in intensity and volume when Cacho embraced San Miguel. Then, grabbing San Miguel's left arm by the wrist, the freed Machetero leader raised it as signal of triumph and unity.

The clapping would have continued unabated for minutes, had Cacho not gestured with his other hand to the crowd to quiet down. Quickly, the noise in the room died out until only the distant sound of the waves breaking on the reefs beyond the Grand Laguna Hotel could be heard.

"I thank you all," he said, looking at the exuberant faces that surrounded him. "When I woke up this morning, the last thing in the world that I imagined was that I would be standing here now in front of all of you, receiving the command of this great enterprise." There was a ripple of laughter among the crowd. "Jail does terrible things to you. If you're not alert, it creeps into your spirit and stifles it into a sort of complacent despair. You know that you're not going anywhere, that you're not going to meet anyone or do anything of import. Your days become a continuous blur of non-eventful gaps. You just...exist."

He paused, and let the silence in the room fill the void left by his words.

"This morning, when I woke up, I just existed. Now, thanks to all of you, I am *alive*. It is time that we do the same for our country, which has been held captive for more than a hundred years."

Somebody in the crowd shouted "Amen!" causing Cacho to smile.

"There is a proverb that says: 'God squeezes but He does not choke.' Our struggle to make our country free has been 'squeezed' mightily during the last few years by those who would wish to make us a permanent fixture of the American Empire. Statehood and absorption have never seemed closer. But here we are, against all odds, given the opportunity to fight back!" Cacho raised his right fist into the air, provoking a spontaneous cheer. "To regain what is ours!" he shouted through the noise. "To tell our imperialist oppressors and their spineless lackeys that our lonely star is too big to fit in their flag, that we will never, *never* submit to them!"

San Miguel watched with a satisfied smile as those around him went berserk with emotion. Cacho waited for a moment, then raised his hands to continue.

"It took a foreigner to get us back on track," he said, directing a friendly glance at San Miguel, "and for that we will be forever grateful. But it is up to us to continue this revolution, until we have made our country free!"

He had no idea how correct he was, San Miguel thought. *Very soon, they would be fighting on their own.*

"I accept with great humility the command of the forces of liberation that presently occupy San Juan, although I will rely greatly on your good sense and counsel to continue this struggle to its conclusion," Cacho said directly to San Miguel, who nodded graciously. "It will be an honor to fight alongside all of you." More cheering followed, but Cacho motioned for it to stop. "But there is a lot still to do, and I have a lot of catching up to do, so I'm asking all of you not to let your guards down. Our fight is far from over. Our enemies are very powerful and they are still out there. I thank all of you from the bottom of my heart."

As the crowd began to dissolve, he turned to San Miguel. "Is there some place private where we can meet?"

"Of course," San Miguel replied. "We have a conference room where we can discuss—"

"Good!" Cacho did not let him finish. "Aristides!" he said to El Alacran, beckoning him with his hand to join him as he began to follow San Miguel to the conference room. Andrade moved next to him but said nothing. "I want you to go to La Fortaleza right now...You have the means to get there?" he asked his associate loudly enough for the others to hear him.

"Yes," El Alacran answered, almost as a hiss.

"When you get there, execute Governor Pietrantoni and...who else is there?"

Upon listening to the Machetero's instructions, San Miguel stopped abruptly and looked back in shock. "Isn't that a bit extreme?" he asked with undisguised concern. Further away, he saw Johnny and Yajaira grow pale. "This is your chief hostage! Are you going to throw him away for nothing?"

Cacho looked at San Miguel. Although he continued to smile, his amiable expression hardened into a cold, businesslike stare.

"Governor Pietrantoni is the biggest obstacle to Puerto Rico's independence at this time, and he is an enemy of our people" he explained patiently. "We will never trade him away, and I cannot afford the risk that he escapes or that he is rescued further down the road. There is nobody left in his Cabinet, in his party, who has the charisma or public support to win a plebiscite with any convincing percentage of the voters, only him. So we kill him now. Besides, we have plenty of other hostages with which we can negotiate." Cacho returned his attention to Andrade. "Who else is there?"

"The Secretary of State, Arizmendi. And the Governor's family, La Fortaleza staff, some of the security personnel—"

"Arizmendi? Really? The Governor's mastermind and puppeteer! Even better. Kill him as well, and the security personnel. Keep the others where they are."

Andrade nodded and began to move away.

"When the authorities find out, they may be more predisposed to launch another attack," San Miguel suggested in a diplomatic tone.

"The authorities will launch another attack regardless of what we do," Cacho answered dismissively. "I know that and so do you. Probably tonight. So let's make the best use of our assets while we still have them."

San Miguel remained silent, doing his utmost to hide his misgivings. If the Governor was executed, the rest of his plans could be jeopardized. He exchanged a covert glance with Daniel who, along with Czecka, was standing behind the Machetero leader. Daniel nodded imperceptively, and melted away into the crowd.

"So that's settled then," Cacho said happily. "Shall we convene in the conference room?"

San Miguel nodded curtly. "This way, please," he said, indicating a path to the hotel's business center.

"After you," Cacho responded, waiting not only for San Miguel to lead, but for the others to follow, directing a friendly smile at Yajaira as she passed him by. As he walked behind the group, he began to hum a tune that San Miguel did not recognize. It was the tune of "We're off to see the Wizard," from the "Wizard of Oz".

CHAPTER XLVIII

From the third floor of the hotel's parking building, Michelle could only see a fraction of the Grand Laguna Hotel's lobby, the southernmost portion of it, and even that view was significantly blocked by the roof over the carport. For the last fifteen minutes, she and Archie had been trying to observe the activity taking place in the hotel's reception area, while Negron kept a watch over the parking area where they were hiding. However, they had been unable to detect anything of import. A few moments before, they had heard some distant cheering and clapping, but whatever had caused it remained invisible to their eyes, cloaked by the white, bright, wave-shaped carport roof.

About five minutes into their watch, they had seen a sentry strolling through the front gardens of the hotel. Heading in their direction, he had ambled across the side street that separated the parking building from the hotel, and ominously disappeared from view. To their chagrin, they had been unable to see where the sentry had gone, since in order to do so, they would have been forced to stick their heads out through the open gap that existed between the ceiling and the cement wall that concealed them, and that would have exposed them to anyone looking in their direction. As it was, the sentry could have entered their building, or continued to walk down the sidewalk directly below them towards the lagoon.

It had made them nervous to lose track of the guard. They had warned Negron to be on the alert for any unusual sounds, and they had been very quiet, listening for approaching noises and hiding between one of the parked cars—a red Town & Country minivan—and the half concrete wall from where they watched the hotel. However, as the time passed without incident, their confidence had been gradually restored, until they had assumed that the sentry had moved on elsewhere.

"It's no use," Michelle said gloomily. "We can't see much from here."

Getting to the garage's third level had been surprisingly easy, although very tense. After consuming their sandwiches, they had abandoned El Palacio del Pavochon through its back exit, and walked down the narrow service alley that ended at one of the sides of the parking building. Covering the two-block distance had taken them less than two minutes, but advancing through the service road had taken a toll on their nerves. Except for a large trash bin about halfway through the walk, there had been no place to hide. Had any of the terrorists entered the alley or watched from any of the bordering buildings, the three friends would have been trapped within the enclosed passageway.

There had been no connection from the alleyway into the parking building. Fortunately, the garage's first floor was at ground level, and after peering into its neon-lit interior and ascertaining that no one was there, they had climbed over its exterior half wall and hid behind one of the vehicles parked inside. A quick inspection had revealed that they had wandered into what seemed to be the valet parking area. It was brimming with automobiles.

From there they had dashed towards the garage's internal stairwell, where Negron had caused such a racket pulling open the stairs' metal, partially rusted door that they had thought it would rouse the entire terrorist garrison in the hotel. Not waiting to find out, they had rushed up to the building's third level and taken cover behind an old minivan. They had waited what seemed to be an eternity for the telltale noises of pursuit, but none had followed. Instead, they were surprised to hear the growing staccato of an approaching helicopter. They could not see it from where they were hiding. But the noise continued to grow in intensity until it echoed from the walls of the surrounding buildings, so loudly that it seemed as if the helicopter was about to land on the rooftop above them. Then, for a brief spell, the chopper's din had diminished in pitch, only to rev up again. Gradually, the noise had begun to fade until it had dissipated entirely.

They had exchanged looks of curiosity.

"Do you think that they have dropped off someone for truce talks?" Negron had suggested in a hushed tone.

"No," Archie had replied. "They can discuss that over the phone, the same way that the terrorists made their demands."

"*If* they can communicate by phone," Negron had countered, refusing to concede to the logic of Archie's observation.

"If we can communicate, then they certainly can," Michelle had observed, trying to reason things out like her boss, Doel, had taught her to do, nipping at the bud the discussion between the two men. "I think the government just gave in to their demands," she had concluded correctly. "I think that that helicopter just delivered Adalberto Cacho to the terrorists."

"You know, maybe it's all part of the plan," Negron had said in a meditative tone.

"What is?" Archie had asked.

"Maybe the government is planning to lure all of the terrorists together into San Juan and then wipe them out..." Negron said absently, then considered his own proposition, and his face darkened. "Of course, it wouldn't make sense, wiping out our police station and all the other horrible stuff that has happened..."

Archie looked at him as if he were crazy. "Welcome back to earth, space cadet," he said in an ironic tone.

They had made their way to the westernmost corner of the garage, from where the main entrance to the Grand Laguna's lobby was partially visible. There, they had attempted to spy on the activities conducted by the terrorists. But they had not been very successful at viewing anything.

"Maybe if we stay here for a while longer..." Archie suggested.

"No! We need to get closer," Michelle stated flatly.

Archie rolled his eyes in despair. "You can't get much closer than this!"

"What? What's happening?" Negron asked from the opposite side of the minivan, as he listened to the sound of their voices without understanding what they were saying.

"Be quiet!" Archie hissed back, then turned to Michelle. "We can't get any closer without going into the hotel itself."

Michelle considered Archie's words in silence. "So we'll have to go into the hotel, then," she concluded with such conviction that she surprised herself.

Archie regarded her with disbelief. He began to respond, but stopped, struck by how beautiful she looked, even with her disheveled hair, her oversized clothes, her lack of makeup, and her swollen upper lip. *It was her green eyes,* he thought. *Witches' eyes.* They had taken possession of his soul, and he would do whatever she asked of him.

"It's not fair," he muttered, shaking his head resignedly.

"What is not fair?" she asked back, the faint outline of a smile forming on her lips.

He stared at her for several seconds, not saying a word. *My God*, he said to himself, *was he falling in love with her?*

"Life," he answered at last, saying the first thing that came to his mind. "Life is not fair."

Her eyes lit up with amusement, making him blush.

"What?" he asked in a mortified tone.

"You're funny, sometimes, you know?" she said simply, looking at him as if she was seeing him for the first time.

"It's not my intention to be funny," he answered, trying to stay serious but cracking a smile.

"I know!" she replied, grinning comically, her puffed up lip looking like a small, wide beak. "That's what makes it really funny!" Then, as she returned her attention to the hotel's main entrance, her body tensed. "Archie, look!"

A handful of men were exiting the hotel lobby from under the entrance's canopy and heading towards the building next to the main tower. Archie squinted his eyes, trying to get a better view, wishing he had a set of binoculars, but the group was too far away to make out any faces. He counted six persons, five men and a woman.

His attention was instantly drawn to the most prominent member of the small procession, a bald-headed giant of a man who stuck out not only because of his immense height—he made the others seem like children—but because of the raw power that his body exuded. *Were the terrorists recruiting trolls,* he pondered, and prayed that he would never meet with him.

The man's hugeness contrasted starkly with the smallest member of the group. Even at the considerable distance between them, Archie could tell by the curves of her body that she was a woman, and quite a sexy one at that. A male neck-turner, if he had ever seen one. He wondered what role she played in the hijacking.

It was the last person in the party, however, who ultimately captured Archie's attention. He was dressed entirely in black, either bald or with the hair cut so short that he looked bald, and even though he was among the shortest men in the group, he seemed extremely fit and athletic. He walked as straight as a board, with an air of unassuming authority that could have only been picked up in the military.

Archie recognized him instantly. It was the man that he had led to the roof of El Falansterio; the man he had confused for a Colombian drug cartel operative; the man who had overseen the destruction of the Puerta de Tierra police station and later machine-gunned the men trying to cross the Condado Lagoon. *Colonel Calderon.*

By purposely focusing his mind on the present mission, Archie had been able to isolate from his thoughts, for long stretches of time, the frightening images of that morning's massacre, of the dozens of police bodies strewn on the parking lot pavement, of the overpowering stench from the burning cars and the police building, of the screams from the wounded.

However, it had all come back with a vengeance earlier that day when he and the others had nearly run into the colonel and overheard him discuss with another man his plans to destroy the men attempting to rescue the Grand Laguna Hotel hostages. He had felt sick, listening to that killer's voice again. It had taken a tremendous act of willpower for Archie to control his massive feelings of guilt. Fortunately for him, there had been other urgent, life or death matters to pursue, and he had been able to once again push away the hideous mental pictures of the massacre, and to concentrate on the business at hand.

Like the throbbing pain of a deep wound, his guilty feelings had resurfaced at different moments in the following hours, unbidden, dreaded, unwanted; sudden, periodic pangs of conscience that soured his inner peace and caused him to taste his own bile in his mouth. Nevertheless, he had managed to deal with them, burying them time and again under his present concerns, until they had become a dull weight in his soul.

But now, the colonel had unexpectedly reappeared. And with him had returned that crushing sensation of helplessness and remorse, overwhelming his ability to think, and making him feel faint and nauseous. Archie had to hold on with one hand to the upper edge of the cement wall in order not to lose his balance.

It had all happened because of him, his head screamed. Because of his smug, stupid contempt for the local authorities, because of his greed for easy money, he had led the black-clad monster to the rooftop of El Falansterio. *He had been the instrument that the colonel had used to murder dozens of San Juan's policemen.* He could not escape the guilt or the blame.

"Are you okay?" he heard Michelle ask with alarm. "You look sick."

Archie nodded automatically and turned his head away. Just a moment before, he had been amazed to discover that he was falling in love with Michelle. Now he felt like a fraud. *How could he face her and keep from her what he had done? How could he engage Negron in a normal conversation—Negron, who had been trapped in a police car and forced to witness the slaughter of his comrades—knowing that it had been him who had led the killers to the roof of El Falansterio?*

"I'm okay," he managed to answer, unable to hide the anguish in his voice.

Michelle directed a sharp look at him, but returned her gaze to the band of men below. "That has to be the biggest man that I have ever seen," she mused with mixture of fear and revulsion in her voice. "He doesn't look like a Machetero." She kept darting quick looks at Archie, as if examining his face to see his reaction.

Archie breathed in deeply. "Yes," he agreed dully, wiping the sweat off his forehead with the back of his hand.

"Do you recognize any of those people?" she asked him. "Not the big one, I know you'd know if you'd ever seen that one before. But the others..." She stared directly at him. "Have you seen any of the others before?"

Archie groaned inwardly. *It was time.* He could not hide his secret forever. Not from her. Michelle continued to watch him closely, as if she suspected something.

"I..." he hesitated. He desperately wanted her to like him. If he told her the truth, she would despise him. *Or would she? Maybe she would appreciate his candor. Maybe she would understand that never in a million years he would have led those men to the rooftop of El Falansterio had he guessed what they were up to.* "I have to tell you something..."

He could see her expression tense, but she remained silent.

"When we were in the construction site and we overheard the two terrorists talking..." Archie vacillated. *Was her face showing traces of knowing suspicion, or was it his imagination?* "I had met one of the two men before..."

Michelle's countenance hardened. "Met? Not seen, but actually met? Which one, the taller one? San Miguel, I think he called himself. Is that the one?"

Archie shook his head. "No, the other one. The military type. The guy dressed in black."

"Go on," she urged him, her green eyes lost in thought, as if trying to recall the man.

He sighed. "I guided him to the roof of El Falansterio," he confessed at last, searching her face for a reaction. He did not like what he saw. She seemed shocked and dismayed, but to her credit, continued to listen. "I know it sounds bad...I mean, it is bad. But it's not like what it sounds," he added urgently, trying to explain himself. "I didn't know what they were going to do! I didn't even know who they were until it was too late! They just offered to pay me if I let them into the building and took them to roof."

The conversation was not going as he had hoped. Michelle was no longer looking at him, her visage a mask of pain and disappointment. "You didn't know what they were doing?" she asked incredulously. "What did you *think* they were doing? How...what is your connection to them? Should we be afraid of you?"

Archie felt his cheeks burn with the sting from her rebuke. Desperately, he tried to explain himself. "A stranger approached me, said someone had mentioned to him that I lived in El Falansterio, and offered to pay me two thousand dollars if I allowed some people from his organization—"

"What organization?" Michelle cut in.

"He never said, just his organization—"

"And that didn't sound fishy to you?"

Of course it had sounded fishy to him, Archie thought. *But the money had been good and he hadn't cared.* "I...I...It sounded strange, but..." He was at a loss for words. "I never imagined..."

Michelle closed her eyes. When she opened them, she stared at him as if he were a stranger. "You say you didn't know what they were doing until it was too late. You didn't see their weapons? Their machine guns and rifles?"

"They were carrying them in bags. I didn't see them until it was too late."

"You couldn't have warned the police?"

Archie had asked himself that question a thousand times. There had been a brief moment, when he had first noticed the machine guns, where he could have attempted to flee. But had he decided to run, rather than try to talk himself out of the roof, he doubted if he would have been alive at that moment. "I tried," he responded weakly. "I really did. I tried to leave to warn the others. But they tied me up until the shooting was over, and then they let me go."

"Just like that? They let you go just like that, instead of killing you?" she said with disbelief. "And in the process, they paid you the two thousand dollars."

"Yes," he replied. He was beginning to get angry, humiliated by her sarcastic tone. "That's exactly how it happened. I'm sorry if you don't believe me."

"It's not a matter of whether she believes you or not," Negron's voice suddenly materialized from behind him, startling him. He was leaning against the side of the minivan, his legs bent together in front of him, his arms wrapped around his knees. Apparently, he had been sitting there for some time, curious about what his companions were discussing. "It's a matter of trust," he said bitterly. "It's funny, here I've been all this time feeling guilty about running away from the station in the middle of the shootout and abandoning the others, while all the time I've been traveling with the man that helped set up the ambush."

"That's not fair!" Archie protested angrily. "I didn't help them set up the ambush! And I helped both of you, didn't I?" He looked at Michelle for support, but she turned her head away.

"That's the only reason why I'm not kicking your ass right now. You really thought you could lead a bunch of thugs to the roof of the building in front of the police station and that there wouldn't be any consequences?" Negron said with contempt. "Really? What did you think they were going to do? Fix some leaks?"

Archie raised his hands in frustration. "I don't know...what I thought they were going to do," he said. "I just didn't think."

"Yeah...Well, I don't think that I want you hanging around with us any more," Negron said, his voice shaking with emotion.

"That's stupid. You need all the help you can get," Archie replied.

"Not yours. I don't trust you any more." Negron looked away. "We'll manage without your help."

"Michelle..." Archie pleaded, not knowing what else to say. "He's just reacting viscerally! He doesn't know what he's doing and most of the time he doesn't really care! He just wants revenge, and he'll get you killed in the process!"

Negron exploded with rage, twisting his body with surprising speed, charging his unprepared companion. The two men rolled on the floor, pounding, kicking, and cursing each other, while Michelle tried to separate them. Unable to drag them apart, she grabbed Negron's hair and pulled it back, but tripped over the two struggling bodies and hit the door of the van with her head and her elbow. She fell back, half-stunned by the blow, and began to rub her elbow, tears rolling down her cheeks in frustration. As both men realized what had happened, they stopped fighting and rushed to her side.

"Are you okay?" Archie asked, still panting from the exertion of the brawl, not daring to touch her. One of his lips was bleeding, and his right cheek was scratched.

She shook her head, still crying. "Just go," she said to him.

Archie blinked, as if he had been slapped on the face. For a few seconds he did nothing. Then he pulled out the gun he had been carrying in his waist, and placed it at Michelle's feet.

"You will need this," he said softly. He turned to Negron. "I'm sorry if I've hurt any of you. That was never my intention."

Negron remained quiet, his sight diverted from his redheaded companion. Like Archie, he was disheveled and beaten up.

Archie slowly got up and walked away, not taking any precautions to avoid being seen. He did not care. He was heartbroken. He now realized that being with Michelle and Negron had made him forget how miserable his life had become, and given him a sense of purpose and redemption.

The metal door of the emergency stairs slammed behind him, making him feel as if a chapter of his life had closed behind it as well. He felt numb and distraught. He could only think of Michelle, how they had climbed those same stairs together less than a half-hour before, still friends. He cursed himself for attempting to be honest with her, but knew that anything less would have made their relationship—whatever it had been—seem fake and cheap. *It was his fault. He was bearing the fruits of his childish, irresponsible behavior. He deserved everything that happened to him.*

Archie descended to the first level of the parking building, and walked back to the half-wall bordering the service alley that they had used to sneak into the garage. Verifying that nobody was there, he slid out of the building and began to make his way back towards the alley's exit. For the first time since that morning, he noticed that his bad leg hurt him considerably and that he was limping. The weight of the dead police officers seemed literally to be driving him into the ground.

He wondered what he would do now. He could not return to his apartment in El Falansterio, not now, maybe never again. Not with the blackened ruins of the police station across the street serving as a grim reminder of his incredible stupidity. He would rather sleep in a Muñoz Rivera Park bench than spend another minute in his house. He did not know where to go, whom to seek, or what to do.

He began to slow down, and then stopped completely. Not caring whether he was seen or not, he sat down and leaned against the wall of one of the structures bordering the alley. *If he did not know where he was going, what was the use of walking in any direction? He should as well lie down and die.*

Archie held his head between his hands, unable to think, oblivious of the world, losing track of time. He would have stayed that way forever, but suddenly an angry series of explosions shook him out of his mental isolation. They were shots, a lot of them. And they were coming from the garage.

He stood up, and without thinking about it began to run back towards the building he had just abandoned. The shooting continued unabated, echoing from the concrete walls in the parking building and now mixed with the intermittent wails, honks, and whines of activated car alarms.

He ran as fast as he could, limping on his bad leg, and reached the first level in a matter of seconds. He began to climb into the building, but just then saw two men with AK-47s running towards the stairs, and he let himself fall back into the alley. As he heard the metal door of the stairwell screech open and then slam shut, he began to pull himself up again, and cleared the building's outer wall.

He hid behind a car and looked around. He saw no one at first, but before he could abandon his cover, he discovered another man slowly making his way through the car-filled parking area. Like the other two, he was carrying a semiautomatic rifle. He was a black man of average height and probably in his early twenties, whose main outstanding features were his long, light brown hair—which he had braided into scores of Jamaican-style beaded strands—his similarly braided goatee, and a knitted cap bearing the Puerto Rican colors.

Unlike the others who had rushed upstairs, the braided man was conducting a search of the valet parking, walking a few steps at a time, squatting to look under the parked vehicles, then moving a few more steps to repeat the operation. He was half a dozen yards away, gradually making his way towards Archie.

The redheaded fugitive acted instinctively, placing his knees on the bumper of a black luxury car, raising his legs off the floor, and crouching behind the car's hood as much as possible. But the movement created by the weight of his body activated the alarm of the automobile, causing its horn to blare continuously and the lights of the car to flicker on and off. Archie abandoned the black car immediately and, stooping, scurried to the next parked vehicle, hoping that the approaching armed man had not seen him. He dashed all the way to the right front wheel of the vehicle, concealing his feet behind it, and waited.

The braided man rushed towards the honking, flashing car, AK-47 in hand. As he got to it, he slowed down and cautiously started to walk through the narrow space between it and the vehicle behind which Archie was hiding.

All of Archie's frustrations, all his feelings of guilt and pent-up anger flared up in an eye's blink. Not pausing to think, he circled the vehicle that separated him from the terrorist and charged the armed man.

Deafened by the din of the car's alarm, the terrorist did not hear Archie approach him until the redhead was half a dozen steps away. Even so, it was not so much the noise as a reflection on the black car's window that alerted the braided man about the impending attack. The man turned immediately, trying to level his weapon to fire it at his aggressor, but got struck a split second before he could finish lowering his gun.

Archie's head smashed into the braided man's chin, his shoulder hitting the AK-47 and shoving it upwards as the man pressed the trigger. The rifle was set in its automatic firing mode, and it discharged the content of its clip wildly into the air. The bullets ricocheted off the walls and the roof, hitting the cars around them, causing several windows to explode in a shower of glass, and puncturing a PVC water pipe on the ceiling.

Archie carried such force with his tackle that he lifted the other man off his feet and drove him several steps backwards before both of them fell against the parking's wall. The braided man's head crashed into the concrete half-wall with a sickening thud, his body absorbing most of Archie's weight. Almost instantly, the redhead pulled himself up to his knees and punched the man's face twice before realizing that the terrorist was not moving. His neck had broken with the force of the fall.

Archie pried the rifle from the dead man's hands and set it on the floor. In a pouch slung over one of the terrorist's shoulders he found several clips of ammunition, and swiftly dislodged it off the corpse. He also pulled off from the dead man's left arm the "Libre como el Coqui" arm-band, and slipped it on, substituting it for the piece of black cloth that he had been wearing. Finally, he put on the braided man's knit cap with the Puerto Rican flag, hoping that by covering his red hair he would attract less attention.

Grabbing the AK-47 and the pouch, he did a fast survey of the parking lot. He saw no one. However, with the racket that the brief clash had produced and the water spewing from the roof, he doubted that that would be the case for very long.

He felt his heart pounding so hard that he thought it would burst. But he welcomed the fear, knowing it would keep him on his toes. As he sprinted towards the stairs, he realized that the shooting he had heard before had stopped. He pulled the metal door open and it repeated its horrendous clatter, making him cringe, but there was no other way about it. If he was going to rescue his two friends, he had to hurry.

He paused briefly, only long enough to attach a new ammunition clip to his rifle. Hearing nothing, he began to tiptoe his way up towards the third floor. When he reached it he stopped, and placed his ear on the door. Like in the valet parking area, he could hear the alarm of several cars blazing, probably set off by the shootout. *Good,* he thought, *it would help to mask any noises that he made. It may have even masked the noises of the shooting downstairs.*

Taking a deep breath, he placed his elbow on the door and nudged it gently. It opened with a slight squeak, soft enough—he hoped—to escape notice. But the powerful breeze coming from the sea suddenly caught hold of the opening door and thrust it open so violently that it would have crashed against the wall, had Archie not managed to grab its doorknob with his left hand and hold on for dear life. In the process, he fumbled his rifle, nearly losing its grip, clutching it by the barrel just before it hit the floor.

"Jesus!" he whispered between heavy breaths, carefully shutting the door behind him.

The exit from the stairs faced the opposite direction of the corner where he, Negron, and Michelle had previously hidden, which was for-tunate, because otherwise he could have barged into the middle of whatever was happening there. As he stepped out of the stairwell, he inadvertently kicked several spent cartridges strewn over the floor and sent some spinning under the parked cars. *Shit,* he thought, *I hope they didn't see this.*

Archie set his rifle in the semi-automatic mode—so that it would only discharge one shot when he squeezed the trigger—leaned against one of the stairwell's walls, and peeped around the corner. Any terrorists waiting for him there would have concealed themselves behind the parked vehicles.

Taking a long look, he ran towards a parrot-green colored Hummer located across the traffic lane, pointing his rifle towards the corner where he had abandoned Michelle and Negron. Nothing stirred except for the flashing lights of a few vehicles.

Sneaking a glance from behind the Hummer's front window, he saw that the minivan behind which they had hidden was riddled with bullets, its windows shattered and its rear tires flat. The minivan's horn was honking loudly and intermittently. Then he noticed a dark, shiny puddle on the floor and his heart sank.

He walked out from behind his cover and approached the destroyed vehicle slowly, ready to fire at the first sign of any suspicious movement, but nobody challenged him. When he reached the minivan, he knelt next to the puddle, swiped his index finger over it, and smelled it.

It was blood. He was used to its distinct stench. He had smelled it in Iraq dozens of times before, not only when he had helped staunch a wound of one of his fallen comrades under the stifling desert sun or helped them get evacuated to a hospital, but when the hot shrapnel of a bomb had shredded his right thigh and shattered his knee. It was a smell that he never forgot.

He searched for further clues around him to determine what had happened but there was very little to go on. Just a few spent brass cartridges from Michelle and Negron's guns. He looked under the minivan and at first saw nothing. However, as he began to raise his head from the floor, a glint of reflected sunshine caught his eye. It was a small object, lying next to one of the deflated tires. Extending his arm, he reached for the object, and knew, even before he had removed it from under the vehicle, that is was the satellite phone.

Michelle must have disposed of it when she knew that she could not escape, hoping that it would not be discovered. It would have been very bad if the terrorists examined the list of called numbers, and managed to trace one of them to the Police Superintendent. Or to WKPA for that matter.

The evidence that Michelle had kept her wits despite her desperate situation raised Archie's battered spirits. It gave him hope that she and Negron were still alive. The bloodstain had not spread over a large area, which probably meant that the wound was not life threatening. And it could have been blood from one of the terrorists. There was still hope for his friends.

With renewed energy, Archie scanned the area around the minivan. As he had hoped, it took him little time to find additional drops of blood on the floor. They were not many, but they pointed in the direction of the parking level's elevator. He began to follow them.

His friends were alive. And he was going to find them.

Daniel shut his satellite phone with disgust. The phones had seemed like a great idea during the planning stage, and they had served their purpose when the spike in calls had clogged all the local communications systems. But they had their disadvantages. He had tried to reach George, and after he had failed to reach him, had followed up with Hassam, but both phones had been unavailable. He made a third call, this time attempting to contact the man they called Faberge because of his exaggerated use of cologne. To his relief, Faberge answered on the second ring.

"Hello!" he said cheerfully.

"Faberge?" Daniel had no time to spend on pleasantries, and he let it know with the tone of his voice.

"Yes," Faberge's voice sobered up immediately.

"You know who's talking to you?" Daniel hated to use his code name, Roberto Clemente.

"Yes," Faberge repeated dutifully.

"Now listen carefully. You have to locate Marc Anthony—"

"Marc who?"

Daniel paused, not letting his temper show. "George," he said patiently.

"Oh...Oh, yes! Marc Anthony!"

"Tell him that he must remove the package immediately. That people are heading in his direction right now to destroy it. Do you understand?"

"Yes! I'll get Geo...Marc Anthony right away," Faberge answered dutifully, finally appreciating the gravity of the situation.

"Hurry. You have less than fifteen minutes before these people get there."

"I will get him right now."

Faberge stood up from the bench where he was sitting in the garden, and placing his hands on his lips, whistled to his other two companions guarding the outer walls of La Fortaleza. The two men, previously alerted by George, trotted wordlessly towards him. They conferred briefly, and then all three trotted towards the Executive Mansion.

The second fight for La Fortaleza was about to begin.

"Interim Governor Rovira is calling you," an aide announced to Superintendent Maldonado, handing him a portable phone. Maldonado took it reluctantly. During the last half hour, the government technicians had managed to establish a direct connection between the San Geronimo Plaza Hotel and the Electoral Commission Building, where the Interim Governor and his Cabinet were headquartered. Cellular phones and landlines had also begun to show signs of life, but the service was spotty and unreliable at best. The last thing that Maldonado wanted at that moment was to waste any time feuding with that asshole. *Hell. He'd rather be talking to the terrorists.* But he knew he had to take it.

"Maldonado here," he said tersely.

"I just happened to watch on TV Adalberto Cacho get off a helicopter and get released to the terrorists," the Interim Governor stated in a neutral voice that made the Superintendent smile. He knew that Rovira was in reality foaming at his mouth.

"Yes, sir. So did I."

"And I presume that you did not have anything to do with it!" the Interim Governor stated in a sarcastic tone.

"You presume correctly, sir," Maldonado stated with the sweet innocence of truth.

"You lie!" Rovira shouted angrily into the phone.

"How so, sir?" Maldonado asked pleasantly. "You know that I have no jurisdiction over federal prisoners. Talk to Franceschini." *So,* he thought, *the President had not managed or bothered to reach Rovira Melendez yet to explain the situation. Even better. It would be fun to see later the Interim Governor stick his tail between his legs.*

The Superintendent heard Rovira sputter with rage, and covered the mouthpiece of his telephone to avoid being overheard as he laughed.

"Franceschini, you, it's all the same thing!" Rovira replied in an accusatory tone. *"You know that Franceschini wouldn't have dared move his little pinky if you hadn't authorized him to do it!"*

"You have it all wrong, sir," Maldonado responded in an exaggeratedly concerned voice. "If you're going to be our next governor, you have to learn the difference between the local and federal governments. Franceschini is a federal employee. He does not respond to—"

"Are you mocking me?" Rovira cut in irately.

"I don't think there's any need to," Maldonado answered drily. "You seem to be doing fine by yourself."

Rovira lowered his voice to a soft growl. It was easy for the Superintendent to imagine his face, his mouth tightened into feral smirk, his eyes narrowed to two deep slits, as if ready to attack. *"Now listen to me, you piece of shit! I know for a fact that you knew ahead of time that Cacho was going to be released, and that you negotiated a cease-fire with him until tomorrow at noon, while you collect the money that they are demanding. In exchange, the Macheteros held off the execution of hostages. Don't deny it, Captain Ramirez told me about it. You knew that Cacho was going to be released, and you did not inform me about it!"*

"As I recall, I personally sent Captain Ramirez to you to discuss possible alternatives regarding the hostages in the Grand Laguna Hotel. I never heard back from you, so I supposed that you were not interested in what I was doing." It was a lame excuse to his gross insubordination, but Maldonado was past the point of caring.

"I will fire you for this!"

"No you won't. Not now, anyway. Who will you substitute me with, Montañez? He hates your guts more than I do, as does most of the police force, by the way. Captain Ramirez? I would love to see him try! He'd mess up things so fast and hard, that you'd probably have to surrender the rest of the island to the terrorists. That is, of course, if he accepts to take charge. I suspect that he'll shit in his pants first. So go ahead. You have the authorization to do it."

There was a pause, and then a disdainful chuckle. *"You misunderstand me,"* Rovira said in a calmer voice. *"I don't intend to fire you now. I'll make it clear to the press that I, under the extreme situation that we were facing, had no choice but to keep you in that position. And when you fail—as you have so miserably failed so far and inevitably will—then I'll fire you."*

It was a win-win situation for Rovira, Maldonado knew. If the Superintendent succeeded in taking back Old San Juan at an acceptable cost, Rovira could always claim that he had never lost faith in him and for that reason had opted to "circle the wagons and fight off the Indians", as he had made it a point to say in his last conference with the press. If Maldonado failed, then Rovira could claim that he had been forced to leave him in charge against his better judgment because the White House had forced his hands. A win-win situation, either way.

"Thank you for your vote of confidence, Mr. *Interim* Governor," Maldonado said, emphasizing the central word in Rovira's title. "For the good of Puerto Rico, I'll do my best to disappoint you."

"For the good of Puerto Rico, I hope you do," Rovira replied in an almost jovial tone. *"I'm glad that we've had this chat and cleared the air."*

Maldonado felt certain that the conversation was being recorded, and that the latter part of it would be edited and used by the Interim Governor when and how he deemed it most convenient.

"One more thing," Rovira said. *"You may not like it, but I am your Governor at least for the present. Therefore, I cannot be left uninformed about any important news that come your way or any decisions that you make. Not knowing ahead of time that the feds ordered the release of Adalberto Cacho was a breach of duty and common courtesy on your part that I will not tolerate again. Is that understood?"*

It was a speech strictly made for the benefit of the press, probably to be made public soon in order to explain Cacho's release, but Maldonado did not care. "Understood," Maldonado answered and hung up before Rovira could say anything else.

The Superintendent signaled his aide to approach him and handed back to her the phone. "Yomaris, I need you to get hold of Franceschini as quickly as possible," he said to her.

Something that Rovira had commented during their conversation had captured Maldonado's attention to the point that he had been anxious to finish the call. Now, he waited impatiently for the FBI man to get through.

"Mario!" he said jovially when Yomaris returned with the call. "I need to ask you a question."

"Shoot."

"I just had a conversation with Rovira Melendez—" Maldonado began to say.

"And what did that paragon of virtue want?" Franceschini interrupted humorously.

"Well, there was something that he said that made me curious..."

Something in the Superintendent's guarded manner of speaking made Franceschini adopt a more sober tone. *"Is this a safe line?"* he asked automatically.

"Yes."

"What did our friend say?"

"He accused me of knowing ahead of time that Cacho was going to be released..." Maldonado said, pausing slightly.

"Which is true...And?..."

"And that I had negotiated Cacho's release in exchange for stopping the hostages' executions until tomorrow at noon, while we obtained the money that they demanded."

Franceschini took several seconds to comment. Maldonado could sense the FBI man's wheels turning in his head.

"You haven't made public the terms of the truce, have you?" he asked after mulling it over.

"No," the Superintendent replied.

"So how did Rovira Melendez know the details of your conversation with San Miguel?"

"Rovira said that Ramirez told him," Maldonado answered, and waited for his friend's reaction.

"Ramirez? How did he find out?" Franceschini asked slowly, as if searching his mind for a possible answer and not being able to find one.

"Exactly," Maldonado said in a quiet voice.

For a long pause, neither man spoke.

"Can you get a search warrant and an order to tap his phones from a federal magistrate?" Maldonado inquired.

"Of his house and his other phones? Sure. It'll take me about an hour to get it."

"I'll have one of my men start searching his office in our Hato Rey headquarters," the Superintendent said. "And I'll ask him to come here, to the hotel. I'd rather have him away from Rovira."

"As if you didn't have enough on your plate already, huh?" Franceschini said in a sympathetic tone.

Maldonado grunted. "See you in an hour," he said, and hung up.

CHAPTER XLIX

If the Governor's office was the brain of La Fortaleza, El Salon de los Espejos—the Hall of Mirrors—was probably its heart. As its name suggested, its walls were covered with ten enormous mirrors imported from Spain in the nineteenth century, each separated by long, glass-paneled double doors decorated with golden curtains. Elaborately-carved gilded frames bordered each of the mirrors, complemented by small, delicate, equally ornate tables with marble tops holding beautiful statuettes, highly crafted bronze clocks, and decorative candelabra.

Genovese white and gray tiles covered the floor, and two enormous hand-painted porcelain urns flanked its corners at one end of the hall. A great glass chandelier, imported from the famed ceramic house of La Granja in Spain, imbued the hall with bright, airy light.

El Salon de los Espejos was by far the largest chamber in the Governor's mansion, and consequently was often used for important ceremonies, receptions, and the signing of laws. It was the traditional site where every year the Governor greeted all of the legislators, Supreme Court justices, Cabinet members, religious leaders, and other prominent citizens, and had seen black-tie galas for the likes of President Kennedy, Pablo Casals, and King Juan Carlos of Spain, as well as countless receptions for world renowned actors, writers, athletes, astronauts, beauty queens, military heroes and politicians. Most recently, it had hosted a short press conference for Secretary of State Francis McClellan, where he had announced that the next G-20 World Economic Summit would be held in Puerto Rico on May of that year.

It had therefore not been a surprise that the new masters of La Fortaleza had decided to gather all of their hostages there.

A total of nine prisoners had been captured alive during the nighttime raid. Several others had been killed and a few had managed to escape. Those captured had been forced to sit on the Persian rug in the middle of the hall. One of the hostages, a bodyguard of the Governor, had been shot in the left thigh, and his scalp gotten creased by a bullet. None of the injuries had been life threatening, although the leg's upper bone had been broken and the scalp had bled profusely, staining most of his shirt. The man, temporarily bandaged by Nereida—Pietrantoni's son's nanny—was in obvious pain.

Francisco and Alfredo sat huddled next to Nereida, each under one of her arms. The boys were still wearing pajamas, the raid occurring so swiftly that they had been unable to change. The frightening uncertainty of their situation, the disappearance of the Governor, and the violence she had witnessed had nearly overwhelmed her. Strangely enough, it had been the children, and her desire to keep them safe, that had given her the strength to go on.

Nereida had been dressing when she had heard two loud bangs, like the explosions of firecrackers, somewhere within the living quarters of the third floor. Ever the nanny, she had attributed the noise to one of the boys sneaking in some of the mini explosives into the mansion, and quickly buttoning her blouse, she had rushed to Francisco's room. There had been some voices coming from the direction where the Governor's suite was located, around the corridor's corner, but she had not bothered to listen—a prudent habit in La Fortaleza—and continued her brisk walk in the opposite direction. To her relief and surprise, she had found both children sleeping despite the commotion.

As she was about to exit the room, she had seen a stranger with a rifle hoofing his way through the corridor towards her, just as several more detonations shattered the morning's peace. Frightened, she had backed into Francisco's room and locked the door. She had tried to get to the children, who by that time had been awakened by the noise, but the door had been blasted open, its lock torn apart by bullets, and two men had burst into the room. Amidst shouts and threats, the intruders had forced Nereida and the two children to rush down to the Hall of Mirrors. It had been a terrifying moment, but Nereida's cool demeanor had helped Alfredo and Francisco to keep a brave face.

The two boys had stayed awake during most of the day, scowling at their captors with the open resentment that only young children can demonstrate, while following their movements with not an insignificant degree of curiosity. However, by mid afternoon, the strain of that morning had begun to take a toll. Despite a valiant effort, Francisco had succumbed to the creeping lethargy that constant fear inevitably provoked, finally falling asleep on Nereida's lap. Alfredo had nodded and righted himself several times, refusing to lose track of what was happening around him. However, he was fighting a losing battle.

Nereida gazed at Alfredo and could not suppress a smile. In the few hours that they had spent together, she had grown fond of the bright, somewhat awkward, headstrong boy. Francisco had told her about how Alfredo had stood by him when two large boys had bullied and harassed him, and she could see Alfredo in her mind doing just that. Francisco had inherited his father's height, and was taller than his friend. Even so, Alfredo had not hesitated to step in between the two bullies and, according to Francisco, had thoroughly "whipped"—that was the word that Francisco had used—one of them, and frightened the other away. The kid had spunk. She was glad that he was Francisco's friend, and that he could keep him company during those terrifying moments.

A few steps away from Nereida and the children sat Secretary of State Alberto Arizmendi. True to his "Double A" nickname, he had not stopped fidgeting since the moment that he had been brought down from the guestroom where he had spent the night and forced to sit on the carpet with the others. Unable to stay still for a long time, he had stretched his arms and legs on several occasions, squatted, stood up to stretch some more, crossed and uncrossed his legs, attempted unsuccessfully to engage his guardians in a conversation, inquired—as the shifts changed—about the status of the Governor, constantly glanced at his watch, hummed several songs, yawned repeatedly, and napped sporadically, snoring loudly. Always a smart dresser and a neatness freak, he looked particularly disheveled—uncombed, unshaved, and only partially clothed. He had been captured as he was putting his clothes on, and had been dragged from his room in an undershirt and the pants of his business suit.

He looked almost like a cartoon character, helpless, impatient, and out of place, Nereida thought. But his eyes, she noticed, had never ceased to covertly take in every word, action, or gesture produced by the terrorists. Like the pink bunny that constantly beat his drum on TV, Double A never ceased to stir. However, despite outward appearances, most of the activity happened in his brain.

Further away sat Patria, the head housekeeper of La Fortaleza, in a separate circle with two other maids; Maria, a young, rather pretty brunette who had started to work in the Executive Mansion just four months before, and Altagracia, a half-Dominican, half-Puerto Rican veteran who for seventeen years had run the kitchen with effortless efficiency. Four other domestic employees, including two of Altagracia's helpers in the kitchen, lived outside of the compound and had failed to report for work that morning.

La Fortaleza, however, was Patria's domain, a domain that she ruled with an iron fist. A short, dark-skinned, fairly rounded woman, she had survived seven changes of administration, a feat not matched by anyone else in the Executive Mansion.

No one, not even the strong-willed Governor Alarcon, had ever dared to interfere with her in the upkeep and handling of the day-to-day matters of the venerable house. Therefore, the assault on La Fortaleza had not merely constituted a tragedy, but a personal affront to her. Not only had the lives of her staff, of the Governor—whom she had come to value and admire as a great man—and of the Governor's dear family been placed in jeopardy, but the continued survival of the institution to which she had devoted her entire celibate life was now in doubt.

If looks could kill, as the old saying went, then the armed hijackers would have been stone-cold dead by now. Patria would glare at them, following them wherever they moved, wincing every time one of the hoodlums—as she called them—breezed past one of the porcelain vases, or draped a leg over an arm of one the elegant, Louis XIV chairs that graced the hall. It was akin to witnessing a sacrilege; the desecration of Puerto Rico's venerable past.

Closest to Nereida and Francisco sat Orlando Picon, Pietrantoni's personal bodyguard. Picon had been captured just as he had finished showering and was getting dressed after his morning jog with the Governor. While he was buttoning his shirt, he had heard two distant explosions that he immediately identified as bullet shots. He had grabbed his holster out from his locker, and was turning to run towards the Executive Mansion's living quarters when the butt of a rifle had smashed into the side of his face, knocking him out.

He had awakened on the locker room's floor, a deep gash across his left forehead, his hands tightly fastened behind his back by a heavy plastic fastener, his ankles bound as well. Later, his knees still wobbly from the blow, he had been untied and steered at gunpoint to the Hall of Mirrors to join the others. Along the way, he had trudged past the sprawled bodies of two of his men, one shot in the back of the neck and the other apparently wounded several times in the chest, both killed in the outer grounds of La Fortaleza. Both had been his close friends.

Of all the hostages gathered in the mirrored chamber, none felt as bitter or distressed as Picon. He had failed the Governor, his family, and his staff. He had been caught flatfooted, like the rankest of amateurs. Under his watch, La Fortaleza had fallen into the hands of terrorists, the Governor had been made a prisoner or worse, and most of his men had been captured or killed. He had failed miserably, and he wanted to redeem himself. So he watched, and waited.

Early in the morning, as the survivors of the assault had been rounded up, there had been an animated flow of armed men coming and going from the hall; quiet, dangerous men dressed entirely in black, and noisier, more boisterous men clad in civilian clothes, celebrating the capture of the principal resident of the mansion. At times, there had been almost as many captors as captives, but as the day progressed, the activity had settled into a routine involving three guards: one stationed by the curtains that divided the Hall of Mirrors from the neighboring Blue Room; one standing at the opposite end of the chamber, by the exit to the Piano Room; and a third blocking another access to the hall, one of two doors that connected to the Oriental Gallery.

Shortly before noon, Altagracia and Maria had been sequestered to the kitchen, to prepare sandwiches and refreshments for the hostages and the terrorists garrisoned in La Fortaleza. Then the food had been brought to the Hall of Mirrors, to be consumed by the prisoners, along with several pitchers of the ice-cold lemonade for which Maria was justifiably famous.

The captives were treated with a cool civility that bordered on veiled contempt, but were allowed to visit the nearby restrooms under armed escort, and regularly provided with water. They were not, however, allowed to speak to each other, a restriction that had been especially stressful to the scared children. By the late afternoon, the uncertainty of the wait had begun to wear thin on the frayed nerves of the prisoners.

Nereida's neck and back felt as stiff as a board. She tried to move as little as possible, in order not to disturb Francisco's sleep. She worried. Worried about the unknown designs of the men who had captured La Fortaleza. Worried about her personal safety and that of her precious children. But most of all, she worried about the safety of Governor Pietrantoni. There had been no news about his whereabouts or his health. When Secretary of State Arizmendi had raised the subject with the terrorists, they had ignored him and ordered him to be quiet. For all she knew, the Governor could have been wounded or even killed in that morning's shootout.

There had been no truth to the rumors—so pervasive that they had even reached her ears—that she was having an affair with Francisco's father. The Governor had taken great pains to treat her with exaggerated courtesy and correctness, the type of courtesy and correctness usually adopted by people who are conscious that they are constantly in the public eye. He had been cordial and proper, to the degree of avoiding prolonged eye contact or conversations unrelated to Francisco's interests. He had made it a point never to meet with her alone, using his son, his friends or his staff as a buffer.

And she had fallen in love with him.

His unknown fate frightened her to the point of distraction. She could not bear the thoughts that he had suffered any harm, or even worse, that she would never see him alive again. She felt as if she had fallen prey to a nightmare from which she could not awake.

And then, quite suddenly, everything changed. Glancing at a mirror, she stirred involuntarily, suppressing a shout of surprise and rousing Francisco from his sleep. Next to her, she saw Arizmendi raise his eyes and stare with a mixture of joy and disbelief, while Picon was already jumping to his feet.

She turned around, her heart pounding, as if to verify that the reflection she had seen was real or a trick of her imagination.

And there, staring directly at her, was the Governor of Puerto Rico.

They had trekked through the entire length of the empty corridor, past the exit that led to the grand staircase, where the red-shirted terrorist with the red beret still sat on the plush chair that he had dragged from the Blue Room, guarding the approach to the stairs. Lucas had walked past the open entrance first, in case the bored Machetero was looking in their direction. But the man was facing the stairs, his back turned halfway from Lucas, and in any event his attention was focused on some activity—a game, probably—that he followed in his portable phone. The Governor had breezed by the open access without being noticed.

The entrance to the Blue Room had been next. The two men had stopped at the edge of the room's open doors, and Lucas had ventured a peek inside. It was empty. The set of heavy curtains at its opposite end were drawn, blocking the view of what lay beyond. Lucas and the Governor had paused briefly to stare into the room.

"Be very careful," the Governor had whispered urgently. "The Hall of Mirrors...where you were told that the hostages are? It's there, behind those curtains."

Lucas nodded.

As its name implied, the Blue Room was decorated in blue. Delicate, light, celestial blue, imbuing the room with a serene atmosphere that belied what was happening just on the other side, behind its closed curtains. Two gilded mirrors on each side of the drapes added depth to the hall, while its center wall was dominated by a large painting of a regally dressed woman, also clad in blue.

"That's Isabella II, the last kingless Queen of Spain," Pietrantoni volunteered softly, when he saw Lucas take a quick glance at the work of art. "She looks nice in that portrait, but in reality she had the face of a frog."

Lucas examined Pietrantoni's face with curiosity, wondering what had prompted him to give him that perfectly useless piece of information at that critical moment. Nerves made people say the strangest things in the strangest situations. God knew he had been guilty of saying a lot of stupid things during the heat of battle in Somalia.

"Is there any other access to the Hall of Mirrors?" he asked softly, taking a last glimpse of the frog-faced queen.

"There is...There are..." The Governor did a mental count in his head. "Five more, I believe. Two in the Oriental Corridor, two from the side of my office, one from the Piano Room."

Lucas considered the information briefly.

"The best chance to rescue the people inside the Hall of Mirrors is to determine as quickly as we can the location and number of terrorists guarding the place. It will be dangerous to bust out through the curtains not knowing how many hostiles there are or where they are located..." he reflected, more for his own benefit than to inform the Governor. As he spoke, he took a look over his shoulder at the corridor behind him. Twice before, he had thought that he had heard the echo of stealthy footsteps following them, and both times he had failed to see anything. This time was no different. The hallway extended all the way back to the Governor's office and beyond, looking as bleak and deserted as an unused mineshaft. Nevertheless, he could not shake the feeling that something was not quite right.

"I need to take a peek inside," he determined at last, pointing at the shut curtains in the Blue Room. "Keep a watch on the corridor, will you? If anything happens, run back to your office."

The Governor grimaced. "What for? To get shot there?"

Lucas turned on him, waving a finger in front of his face. "Now look," he said with barely contained annoyance. "The people of Puerto Rico chose you to be their Governor, and that's fine with me, whenever you're doing stuff that pertains to the Governor of Puerto Rico. But you're not doing Governor of Puerto Rico related stuff now. You chose to come with me, and this is not an elected position. I am in command here. If you want to stay with me, you'll do exactly as I tell you to do. And if I tell you to run, you run, do you understand?"

Pietrantoni's face reddened. It was obvious that he was not used to being addressed that way. For a moment, his facial expression reflected his internal struggle to contain his visceral anger. Then he nodded reluctantly.

Lucas said nothing. Instead, he began to walk towards the opposite side of the Blue Room. He stopped at the blue silk curtains that covered the view to the Hall of Mirrors, and cast a glance at Pietrantoni. The Governor was standing inside the room by the other entrance, looking down the corridor.

The drapes hung all the way to the floor, overlapping each other. Lucas could perceive no voices coming from the other side. There was no way to look into the Hall of Mirrors except by pulling the long curtains apart sufficiently to create a gap through which he could take a peek. He knelt, hoping that whatever movement occurred would be less apparent near the floor level. Placing the muzzle of his gun between the two overlapping fabrics, he began to slide one of the blue silk drapes to his right.

Someone close by suddenly coughed, startling him so much that he nearly let the curtain go. He instantly stopped what he was doing and, looking up to detect any movement in the draperies, listened intently. The person on the other side of the curtains cleared his throat loudly, and then made no further noise. After a few seconds, Lucas continued to part the overlapping folds of the curtains, until a bright, thin, triangular spot appeared in the bottom between them.

Placing both hands flat on the floor, he lowered his head and peered through the small opening. He was surprised to see the legs of a man standing just a few inches from where he was laying his head on the cool tile floor. If at that moment the man had decided to walk out through the curtains, he would have probably tripped over Lucas' prostrate body.

His heart skipped a beat as he saw the hostages huddled on the carpet near the center of the hall beyond, then leapt with joy when he discovered Alfredo sitting next to a woman—Nereida, he presumed—and the Governor's son. In total, he counted nine hostages, mostly women, including a wounded man. He wondered, trying not to despair, how he would extract that group from the heavily guarded Fortaleza.

He took a few more seconds to count and note the position of the armed men inside the hall. There were two others, in addition to the one standing next to the curtains. One, a tall, burly man with a very long and bushy mustache, guarded the opposite extreme of the hall. The second, either a man just out of his teens or a teen about to attain his legal age, waited by one of the two open entrances located near the center of the room.

Not losing another moment, Lucas tiptoed back to where the Governor waited.

"The prisoners are there," he said excitedly. Noticing the apprehension in Pietrantoni's eyes, he added, "Your son is fine."

"You saw him?" the Governor asked anxiously, not daring yet to hope, searching his companion's face for reassurance.

"Yes."

"Thank God!" Pietrantoni said with breathless relief.

"But it's going to be tricky, and we have to work fast. That black guy, George, should be back any minute now."

The Governor nodded, urging his companion to go on.

"I saw an open door close to the center of the Hall of Mirrors. Is there a way to get there from here?" Lucas asked.

"That must be one of the doors in the Oriental Gallery," Pietrantoni informed him. "This corridor ends where the gallery begins."

"Lead the way," Lucas ordered, anxious to get out from the exposed spot where they were standing.

They continued their march down the main corridor, passing several secretarial stations to their left, as well as the access to the crystal-laden, tennis-court sized State Dining Hall, and that to the smaller but elegant Informal Dining Room, its table still set with the plates and cutlery that had not been used for that morning's breakfast. There, Lucas suddenly stopped and walked in.

"It's this way!" the Governor called after him, pointing in the opposite direction, then following him into the informal dining room. "It's that way," he repeated when he caught up with his companion.

"I know," Lucas acknowledged, "but we need to talk a little more."

The Governor directed him a puzzled stare.

"Most of the hostages I saw inside of the Hall of Mirrors were women," Lucas continued. "Even if we manage to free them, how do we get them out? Of La Fortaleza, I mean. Can we get out of La Fortaleza without getting into a gun battle with the terrorists?"

The Governor thought for a moment. "No," he answered after a long pause.

"Then what good is it to rescue the hostages if we have nowhere to go?"

"Wait!" Pietrantoni said suddenly, his face brightening. "There's the secret passage that leads from the kitchen to the Austral Tower..."

"The Austrian Tower?"

"The *Austral* Tower," Pietrantoni responded, correcting him. "One of the two round towers that used to protect La Fortaleza's west wall. We could hide there until we're rescued..."

"You actually know where this secret passage is?" Lucas asked doubtfully.

"I have been there myself several times," Pietrantoni confirmed. "The history of this place fascinates me. There are several secret passages between some of its rooms," he continued to explain, raising his voice enthusiastically and being shushed by Lucas. "For security reasons, few people know about the former connection between the tower and this level of La Fortaleza. But the passage exists. If we hide there, the terrorists will search the second floor, but they won't find us. I don't think so, anyway..."

It was better than nothing, Lucas thought.

"Who else knows about this passage?"

"Some of the staff. Why?"

In case the Governor got shot before he got to the kitchen, Lucas thought to himself, but said nothing. Instead, he looked out into the main corridor, and finding it clear, resumed his walk towards the Oriental Gallery. Pietrantoni promptly returned to his position in front of Lucas, holding his Magnum behind his back. In a few steps, they reached the end of the corridor, and there made a sharp turn to the right.

"The Oriental Gallery," Pietrantoni said, pointing with his arm, his voice tinged with more than a hint of proprietary pride,

Unlike the somber corridor through which they had just traveled, the Galeria Oriental was a wide, tiled, brightly illuminated passageway that was lined on the left side with shuttered windows facing La Fortaleza's interior courtyard. Interspersed between the windows were columns of square, multicolored glass panes that, illuminated with the rays of the afternoon sun, washed the floor and the corridor's other wall with the warm hues of precious stones. The gallery also contained a substantial amount of furniture: high backed, dark wooden chairs and low tables lined against the windowless wall that bordered the Hall of Mirrors, standing silently like stiff sentinels. From where they stood, the two men could see the outline of the two doors that led into the Hall of Mirrors, the furthest of which was open.

"There are three men..." Lucas began to say, and hesitated. He had serious misgivings about placing Pietrantoni in harm's way. There was a very real possibility that the Governor of Puerto Rico would be seriously hurt or even killed if he intervened in the rescue attempt. Lucas would be known for the rest of his life—which at the moment seemed precariously short—as the man who had gotten the Governor shot in a mindless attempt to escape. "This is going to be tricky," he repeated. "Shots may be fired. If you want to back out, I can understand..."

Pietrantoni shook his head emphatically. He looked very pale and scared, but more determined than ever. "No! We had an agreement. We do this together."

"Mr. Governor, there are three armed men in there, maybe more that I didn't see."

"The more reason to get in together," he answered dismissively, glancing nervously down the corridor, as if he had heard something. His eyes returned to Lucas, admitting no challenge. "Alfaro, we do this together, as we agreed when we left my office. If there are three terrorists guarding the hostages, I'll cover the one furthest to the right, you take care of the others. If there are four, then it's two and two."

Lucas still vacillated.

"Alfaro...Lucas...Listen to me," the Governor pleaded. "My *son* is in there. If I thought that by staying away I would increase his chances of survival, I would stay out here. But I can help you....Please let me do it!"

Lucas nodded, in spite of himself. He sympathized with the Governor. He felt the same way about Alfredo. Besides, leaving Pietrantoni behind would be almost as dangerous as taking him with him. Anyone could appear in any of the corridors at any moment. And Pietrantoni knew the way to the secret passage.

"All right," he whispered. "We walk in as we planned. But you have to be very alert. Don't do anything until I tell you to do it."

Pietrantoni assented eagerly.

Lucas prepared to march on, but the Governor stopped him. He extended his hand to Lucas, his face filled with emotion. "I just want you to know that...thank you. Regardless of what happens, I will never forget this." Pietrantoni took Lucas' hand and shook it warmly. "Thank you."

"We'll get out of this together," Lucas heard himself say reassuringly, against his better judgment.

The Governor nodded once, and stepped into the multi-colored gallery, immediately acquiring the blue, green and orange tinges of the windows. Lucas followed him, pointing his gun at his back. As he trailed Pietrantoni, he thought how improbable the entire situation was. Had anybody told him that morning, when he awoke, that that afternoon he would be trekking down a gallery of La Fortaleza, pointing a Magnum .357 at the back of the Governor of Puerto Rico, he would have called him delusional. But there he was, moving through a rainbow-colored hallway at a steady pace to engage three terrorists that were holding several hostages, including his godson.

And then, before he could dwell any more on his fate, he walked into the Hall of Mirrors.

CHAPTER L

The Governor entered so swiftly and quietly, that the teenaged guard at the entrance did not notice him until he had nearly walked past him. Even then, reassured by the "Libre como el Coqui" armband worn by Lucas, the guard barely reacted.

Not so the burly, mustached sentry standing by the curtained entrance next to the Piano Room. A hardened veteran of the Macheteros, he instantly jumped to his feet, and pointed his submachine gun at the incoming men.

Others in the group also reacted instinctively. Orlando Picon, Pietrantoni's personal bodyguard, immediately got up, while Nereida, her back turned towards the new arrivals, stared at the mirror in front of her with an expression of utter surprise, turning and awakening Francisco.

At the opposite end of the room, the third guard—the man whose feet Lucas had seen from behind the Blue Room curtains—observed the unfolding events with confusion and a growing sense of concern, swiping from his eyes with his hand one long, limp hair that cascaded from his forehead.

"Stop right there!" the man with the mustache shouted, leveling his submachine gun at the Governor.

Pietrantoni stopped, keeping his gaze apparently on the floor, but in reality looking towards the sentry on his right, gauging the shot that he would have to make. He was so concentrated on his target that he did not see his son struggle free from Nereida's grasp and begin to move rapidly towards him.

"I'm bringing the Governor here with the rest of the prisoners," Lucas started to explain at the same time, with the tired, bored tone of someone forced to state the obvious. "Didn't anyone tell you that we are transporting all of the prisoners to the Grand—" he continued saying to the young guard closest to him, but then realized, from the man's expression of alarm, that he had discovered the gun that Pietrantoni was holding behind his back.

"Shit!" he whispered in dismay, seeing the terrorist open his mouth to warn the others, and smashing the man's face twice with his gun before he could utter a word. At the same time, he grabbed Pietrantoni by the scruff of his shirt and pulled him hard, causing him to trip and fall backwards.

Half a dozen bullets struck the wall where the Governor had stood just a fraction of a second before, as the burly terrorist near the Piano Room discharged his Uzi submachine gun. Several of the women screamed in terror, ducking to hide from the shooting. Only Picon kept his presence of mind, tackling Francisco from behind and pinning him to the ground by covering him with his body.

Confusion filled the room. From the other side of the hall, the Machetero standing by the Blue Room curtains pressed the trigger of his AK-47 and cursed, as the rifle failed to go off and he realized that he had the weapon on "Lock". Pietrantoni lay on his back, struggling to get up after tripping over one of Lucas' legs. The younger terrorist, whose face had been bloodied by Lucas, staggered forward, holding his head between his hands, making it impossible for the mustached guard by the Piano Room to fire his submachine gun without hitting him.

Kneeling on one leg behind the young guard, Lucas, turned and fired a wild shot at the man holding the AK-47. He missed, his bullet puncturing the sky blue curtain of the Blue Room, but it made the terrorist cringe and seek cover in the other room.

Lucas immediately shifted his attention to the man with the Uzi and waited for the teenager to move out of his line of fire. He saw the burly guard move to his right, desperately trying to get a clear shot, shouting at his associate to get out of the way. Then the man leveled his Uzi at the blinded youth and fired, riddling the young Machetero's body with bullets.

Almost simultaneously, Lucas dived under the legs of the dying terrorist and discharged his Magnum three times. As the body of the youth crashed on top of him, he watched two of his shots strike his target, one in the stomach and the other in the groin. The wounded man produced a deep, guttural squeal and crumpled to the ground, spraying the roof of the Hall of Mirrors with the last bullets in his Uzi's ammunition clip.

Lucas heard two shots fired next to him, and fought to push off him the corpse of the younger guard. The shots were answered by a distinct burst of an AK-47 rifle, and followed by several slower detonations from a handgun. As he managed to untangle himself from the dead body, he saw Pietrantoni standing partially behind the doorframe of the Oriental Corridor, still aiming his Magnum at the curtains of the Blue Room.

"Get back!" Lucas shouted at the Governor as he saw the barrel of the AK-47 appear through the drapes, and he fired his last two shots at the hidden terrorist. The rifle disappeared behind the curtains. Lucas scrambled, crab-like, back to where Pietrantoni was standing.

"Are you all right?" he asked the Governor, as he began to reload his gun.

"I'm fine, thanks to you," Pietrantoni answered. Then seeing the bloodstains on Lucas' shirt, asked in alarm. "Are *you* all right?"

"I may have peed in my pants, but I'm fine otherwise. Here!" Lucas handed Pietrantoni several bullets from his holster. "Load your gun."

"Did you hit him?" the Governor asked as he flipped open his revolver's barrel, emptied the spent cartridges, and began to feed new cartridges into it.

"I don't know. I don't think so," Lucas responded. He saw one of the hostages stir and shouted, "Stay where you are! Don't move!" Then, lowering his voice, he said to Pietrantoni, "We have to act fast. The noise we've made is going to bring every other Machetero in this place in—"

"Hey!" a shaky voice from across the hall interrupted him. "You out there!"

Lucas and the Governor exchanged a look of dismay.

"What do you want?" Lucas shouted.

"You'd better give up! I'll shoot the hostages if you don't!"

"I don't think you will!" Lucas answered him. "If you so much as peek through those curtains I swear I'll blast you to Kingdom come!"

"Blast you till Kingdom come?" the Governor repeated quizzically.

Lucas shrugged. "It'll make him think. I'm going to circle around, go to the Blue Room and engage him from there. You keep talking to him."

The Governor nodded in response, then bellowed at the terrorist. "Why don't *you* give up?"

Lucas chuckled and began to move away. Just then, he heard a muffled scream, followed by a new voice that shouted, "Okay, don't shoot! We're coming out!"

Lucas returned to the edge of the entrance and Pietrantoni withdrew, allowing him to assume his position and to look out.

For a moment, nothing happened. Then the limp haired guard and another man holding an arm around the guard's waist slowly slipped out between the curtains. At first, Lucas could not understand what was happening. He aimed his gun at the emerging duo and began to shout, "Don't try anything funny or I'll shoot through the two of—"

But then he stopped, as blood started to stream out of the leading terrorist's mouth, and his knees began to buckle. One of the women screamed, after the arm holding on to the bleeding man let go and the terrorist stumbled forward a couple of steps and collapsed on the Persian carpet.

The second man remained standing, clasping a long, bloody dagger in his upraised right hand and grinning. It was George.

"Don't shoot me, boss," the black man said to Lucas. "I'm on your side!"

The curtain next to George parted and a smaller, wiry, Arab-looking man stepped out holding an AK-47 across his arms.

"Place your weapons on the floor," Lucas ordered the men, still pointing his Magnum from behind the doorframe.

The Arab hesitated, but George chuckled and whispered to him to do as he was told, giving the example by letting his dagger fall on the carpet. The Arab followed suit, placing his rifle carefully on the ground.

"Hands behind your necks," Lucas said, stepping out of his cover.

"We're your friends!" George repeated with an exasperated laugh, nodding at the corpse in front of him. "Haven't I proved it?"

Followed by the Governor, Lucas approached the two strangers and with his feet, kicked the discarded weapons away from them. With the corner of his eye, he saw the man who had protected Francisco stand up and pick up the Uzi from the motionless burly Machetero lying by the Piano Room, pointing it at George and the Arab. Francisco ran to his father and hugged him hard, nearly making him stumble. Arizmendi also approached the Governor, beaming at his friend but having enough sense to remain silent until the status of their unknown rescuers was resolved. A few steps behind him, Alfredo stood up and began to move towards Lucas, but Lucas signaled him with his hand to stay where he was. With a hurt look, the boy did as he was told, remaining at Nereida's side.

The silent exchange did not go unnoticed by George, whose eyes clouded momentarily in deep thought, and then regained their mischievous light as he finally understood why the man pointing the gun at him had infiltrated La Fortaleza.

"Well, I'll be..." he mumbled with a rich laugh, shaking his head. "Why, you're not a federal agent! You're that boy's dad!"

"Who are you?" Lucas asked George, ignoring his last statement. His question was followed by the distant burst of automatic rifle fire coming from outside La Fortaleza.

"That must be my men right now, taking care of the other guards," George said with a mischievous grin.

"Who *are* you?" Lucas insisted, more confused than ever.

"That don't matter at all, boss," George replied. "Just consider me a friend, gather your people and get out of here." He chortled. "Maestes. That your real name? You fight good, Maestes!"

Lucas was at a loss. Governor Pietrantoni approached the group, telling Francisco to return to Nereida, and stared at George.

"You never wanted Tino to take me to the Grand Laguna Hotel, did you?" he stated more as a fact than as a question.

George did not answer. The shooting outside continued.

"Are you CIA?" Lucas asked him.

"You ask too many questions!" George said pleasantly, with no hint of impatience. "Now listen to me. I've helped you as much as I can, but there's more people coming here right now, and only so much that my people can do. They are coming to kill you."

Pietrantoni opened his mouth to speak, but George continued.

"Don't ask me how I know this, Guv, I just know. And I won't be able to protect you from them. So you've got to call your people, like lickety-split *now*, and ask them to pick you up as quickly as they can. Understand?"

Lucas and Governor Pietrantoni exchanged a look of bewilderment. *Was this man for real*, they seemed to ask each other. Behind them, the hostages had begun to get up and chatter excitedly. Some of the women were crying, others were asking if anyone had been hurt. Miraculously, none of the stray shots seemed to have hurt any of the hostages.

"You can try the telephones," George continued to say. "Though they weren't working so good a few hours ago. But I've heard they're coming back. You may get lucky."

"There are no telephones in the Hall of Mirrors," the Governor said, "I'll have to go to one of the secretarial offices."

"Excuse me, sir," said Patria, who had been listening attentively to the conversation from a distance.

"Yes, Patria," Pietrantoni said patiently, anxious to get to a telephone. "Are you all right?" he asked courteously.

"I'm fine, sir, thank you," the short, robust head keeper of La Fortaleza answered with a smile. "And we're all so happy to see that you are in good health!"

"Thank you, Patria." Pietrantoni answered, and then, trying to cut the conversation short, asked her, "Can you tell me where the closest telephone would be?"

"Well, that would be here, sir," Patria answered, sticking her hand into her ample bosom. "Will this do?"

George guffawed as she handed a cell phone to her boss, saying, "You go, girl!" and earning a fierce look of reproof from her.

Patria motioned the Governor to lower his head to her level, and whispered into his ear, "Between you and me, sir, I wouldn't trust that man for anything in the world!"

Pietrantoni smiled and nodded. "Thank you, Patria, I don't know what I'd do without you." She withdrew, taking several steps backwards as if withdrawing from royalty, and then turned, regarding the rest of her staff with a proud, triumphant look.

The Governor considered whom to call under the watchful gaze of everyone around him. The Police switchboard would be buzzing and inaccessible, he decided, and anyway, if he got through, he would probably spend a lot of time trying to convince the operator that he was indeed the Governor of Puerto Rico and that it was not a crank call. And God knew how much time would be spent attempting to patch the call through to the Superintendent. But there was one private number that he had used successfully on countless prior occasions, and that maybe he could reach now, if the phone service was working.

Dialing the seven-digit number, he waited, and then, with great relief, heard the phone begin to ring.

The cell phone inside Superintendent Maldonado's jacket began to chime like London's Big Ben, interrupting him just as the formal introductions were taking place. Maldonado had just received the five officers that had flown in with five of the six platoons of the Navy SEAL's Team 2. The officers had landed half an hour before at the Isla Verde International Airport, flown out of Virginia in a C-17 Boeing transport, along with eighty of their men and their corresponding gear. As soon as they landed, they had left their men behind unloading their equipment, and been whisked under police escort, sirens blaring, all the way down to the San Geronimo Plaza. There, they had been ushered to a small business meeting room, where Maldonado and Montañez had met them.

"Excuse me," he said, raising one hand and taking his cell phone out of his jacket with the other. "I didn't realize these things were working," he mumbled in an irritated tone. Only his family would call him through the cell phone, and his wife knew better than to contact him during the present crisis.

He stared hard at the miniscule digits that appeared on the telephone screen—he refused to use anything but the most rudimentary type of cell phone, claiming that the rest of the features in the more advanced models were too distracting and beyond his technical expertise—and inwardly cursed the inability of his eyes to discern the small print without the aid of reading glasses. He did not recognize the few blurry numbers that he could make out, and felt tempted to ignore the call. But at the last moment, he flipped his phone open.

"Hello," he said in a guarded tone, ready to chew up anybody who had disturbed his meeting without any real justification.

"*Superintendent Maldonado?*" a familiar voice replied on the other side.

"Yes?"

"This is Governor Pietrantoni."

Maldonado jumped out of his seat and stood up. Montañez and the visiting officers stared at him with alarm, not knowing what was happening.

"It's the Governor!" Maldonado announced, momentarily covering his cell phone's mouthpiece, and provoking a hushed gasp among the others. "Are you all right, sir?"

"I am fine, but we have very little time to talk," Pietrantoni replied.

"Go ahead, sir."

"La Fortaleza, as you probably know, was captured this morning by terrorists. I was separated from the rest of the hostages and kept in my office. Due to the heroic help of a friend, I managed to escape from my office and we've just freed the rest of the hostages."

"He's escaped!" Maldonado whispered excitedly to the others.

"But listen to me, listen to me!"

"Yes, sir."

"We're still trapped inside of La Fortaleza, and we're surrounded by the Macheteros. We've had some help from some insiders—"

"Insiders?" Maldonado immediately felt uneasy, his instincts warning him that something was wrong. "What insiders?"

There was a pause, as the Governor apparently moved to a more private location. *"Some of the terrorists,"* he said in a more subdued tone.

"Mr. Governor, you must be very careful. You can't trust—"

"I don't have any choice," Pietrantoni interrupted Maldonado, who remained stubbornly silent. *"Are you still there?"*

"I'm here."

"Can you fill me in briefly on the present situation?"

"I don't know what you know, so I'll tell you the basic information." Maldonado stopped, as he heard several popping noises over the telephone. "Is that gunfire?"

"Yes, it is. The insiders that I told you about? They're fighting the Macheteros in La Fortaleza. I don't know how long they'll manage to keep them away, though."

"There's fighting in La Fortaleza," Maldonado repeated to the others in the room. "Mr. Governor, you must seek a safe place to hide until we can come to get you. The situation right now is that the terrorists have destroyed the bridges between San Juan and the rest of the island. They have captured the Grand Laguna Hotel and a cruise ship. They have surface-to-air missiles, and they shot down one of our helicopters, and they are also very heavily armed. They destroyed the police station in Puerta de Tierra."

"Destroyed? What do you mean destroyed?"

"Ambushed our men with heavy caliber machine guns and snipers, and burned the station to the ground." Maldonado watched the faces of the Navy SEALs around him as he spoke. They were listening attentively, but showing little emotion.

"My God!" the Governor said, truly shocked.

"A contingent from the Navy SEALs arrived less than an hour ago. I'm meeting with them right now. But we won't be able to get to you until tonight. Not with the surface-to-air missiles keeping our helicopters off the air."

There was silence at the other end of the line.

"Are you there, Mr. Governor?"

"Yes...yes, I'm here," Pietrantoni replied absently, as if trying to absorb the information. *"One of the insiders told us others are coming to kill me..."* he said, more to himself than to the Superintendent. *"Apparently, the Macheteros are sending more men to La Fortaleza to execute me..."*

Maldonado closed his eyes in despair. "When?"

"Right now."

There was not much that Maldonado could do at that moment. He could not risk having another helicopter full of rescue troops to be shot out of the sky. The entire "insider" affair could be a ruse, to draw in more of his men and then shoot them as they approached the Executive Mansion, just as the terrorists had done in the Condado Lagoon. And if he moved first to free the hostages in La Fortaleza, the lives of the countless hostages in the Grand Laguna Hotel and the *Mardi Gras* would be placed in jeopardy.

"Mr. Governor," he said reluctantly. "We don't have the resources to get to you now. Not until tonight, when we can conduct a coordinated assault on all three places. If we hit one first, the terrorists have threatened to kill many of the hostages in the other locations in retaliation."

"I understand..." Pietrantoni responded, attempting to keep his voice calm. Let no one ever doubt his Governor's courage, Maldonado thought. *"Who's in charge now?"* Pietrantoni asked, almost as an afterthought.

"The Interim Governor is Rovira Melendez right now," Maldonado answered in a neutral tone.

"Then it seems that for the good of the country, I must survive, doesn't it?"

Maldonado barked a short, heart-felt laugh, despite the gravity of the situation. "Yes, sir, it seems that way."

"The shooting has stopped," the Governor said. *"I have to go. We'll hide in La Fortaleza. You know this place is full of secret passages. I will call you back at seven, if everything is all right."*

"We will try to get you out of there as quickly as we can, sir," Maldonado promised.

"Thank you. Tell Rovira that I escaped, and that you have my authority to do whatever you need to do. That may help to keep him out of your hair for a while."

Maldonado was amazed at how fast and intuitively the Governor could grasp what was happening in his government. But then again, the Governor knew about the mutual abhorrence between his Police Superintendent and his Secretary of Justice.

"I will, Mr. Governor. May God be with you," he added, but Pietrantoni had already hung up.

The Superintendent looked at the group gathered about him. "Gentlemen," he said, "we have a lot of work to do."

While the Governor spoke on the cell phone, Lucas had asked Picon to keep a watch over George and his companion, and turning away from them, opened his arms to his godson. Alfredo had run to him and embraced him, squeezing him with all his strength, not saying a word. Lucas loved the boy. All of the intense stress, the terrible nightmare he had lived in the past few hours, dissolved with that hard hug.

"Are you okay?" Lucas asked, pulling him back and examining him with concern. "I'm so sorry I couldn't get to you before."

Alfredo nodded quietly, as was his habit, only his eyes revealing the excitement and happiness of seeing his uncle. "Nereida took care of me," he told Lucas, directing a loving look in her direction. *He couldn't fault his nephew's infatuation,* Lucas thought. *Francisco's nanny was every bit as beautiful as the media portrayed her, even without makeup. And very well endowed, as his sister Vanessa had noted.*

She smiled warmly at him, beaming at the boy. "Alfredo is so brave! You must be very proud of your son."

"Thank you, but no," Lucas answered, certain that she had caught him staring at her cleavage and blushing. "I mean, I am proud of him, but he is not my son. He's my nephew... my godson. I was supposed to pick him up this afternoon," he said, realizing that in his embarrassment he was over-explaining his relationship with Alfredo. To his relief, she continued to smile.

"I must agree with the black gentleman," she said. "You fight very well."

"Don't he now?" George interjected from where he continued to stand, following the conversation very attentively. "He should work for me!"

"I think I'd better get to the others...see how they're doing," Lucas said apologetically to Nereida.

"Of course," she replied.

Turning to Alfredo, he asked him, "Will you take care of Nereida?"

"Sure," Alfredo responded proudly, embracing his godfather one more time, and whispering in his ear, "I think she's a *statehooder*, but she's very nice."

"Okay," Lucas whispered back, used to his godson's non-sequiturs.

He stood and approached the security man who had been wounded. "Can you walk?" he asked him.

"I can manage, with the help of others. And I can fight too, if necessary," the man answered, flinching slightly from the pain in his thigh when he moved accidentally. He was a blond man with a very pale, almost milk-colored complexion—whether from the loss of blood or a permanent condition was hard to tell—a round face, and hazel eyes, who must have been in no more than his early twenties. Carefully, he extended his right hand to shake that of Lucas. "I'm Billy, Billy Hazard."

"I'm Lucas. Nice to meet you, Billy."

"Hey, Maestes!" George called out from further away. "I need to check out what's happening with my men!"

Lucas stood up and walked up to where George waited. The black man grinned. "Listen, boss, I can understand, hell, I even commend you for not trusting me. If I were you, I'd be nervous too, and I wouldn't trust me neither. But right now it seems to me you don't have much of a choice. I killed the man that was shooting at you, remember? That should account as something."

"The way I remember it, you were the one who blew my cover in the Governor's office less than an hour ago," Lucas reminded him.

"Yeah! That was smart of me, wasn't it, seeing through your cover?" George said with a rumbling chuckle. "I didn't know who you were. What you wanted with the Governor. I'm supposed to protect him! Couldn't leave you alone with him!" he said in a plaintive voice. "Remember I told Tino to wait for me. You remember that, don't you?"

Lucas did not respond.

"Yeah, you remember," George insisted, smiling knowingly.

"You would have used your knife to interrogate me," Lucas said.

George shrugged. "Sure, if you didn't talk." He stared slyly at the Puerto Rican. "But you solved that problem for me. I *mis-estimated* you. Never thought you would'ave beat the crap out of Tino and helped the Governor escape while I was away. Never occurred to me in a thousand years! That's when I realized that we were on the same side."

"Who are you?" Lucas heard the Governor ask from behind him, as he returned from his cell phone conversation with Maldonado. He had walked out of the Hall of Mirrors to the Oriental Gallery, from where he had called Maldonado in order not to be overheard.

"Governor! I was telling your friend Maestes here...Your name isn't Maestes, is it? No? I thought so! I was telling him that I need to check out on my men." As if to emphasize what he was saying, the shooting renewed outside with a long burst of rifle fire, followed by single, sporadic detonations. "See? I have three of them out there, holding back a dozen Macheteros. I don't know how much longer they will last on their own."

"Who are you?" Pietrantoni repeated, refusing to drop the subject.

The black man lowered his gaze for a moment, and then looked up and smiled with mischief in his eyes. "I'm George, Guv, and that's all you need to know. And that's all I'm going to say, so you might as well not ask anymore."

The Governor took a quick glance at Lucas. "Do you trust him?" he asked him.

"Trust him?" Lucas shook his head. "As much as a hungry alligator."

George's smile exploded into a toothy grin that made him look like a caricature of Louis Armstrong.

"But I think that for some strange reason, his interests right now coincide with ours."

"Picon?" the Governor addressed his bodyguard, standing next to him.

"I agree, sir," he answered without taking his eyes off the two prisoners.

"Well, God help us then, because I agree as well," Pietrantoni said, arching an eyebrow, speaking as if he were choosing between the lesser of two evils.

"Thank you!" George bent down to pick up his knife even before Picon had lowered his Uzi.

The Arab man standing next to George tried to retrieve his AK-47 but hesitated, as Picon blocked his way.

"It's fine, Hassam," George told him, "we'll take the rifle that this man carried," he said, pointing at the corpse of the terrorist that he had stabbed in the back.

The Arab nodded once and disappeared behind the Blue Room's curtains.

"I suppose that you were able to get through to the police, and that they've told you that they can't do squat until tonight." George scrutinized the Governor's expression and grunted with satisfaction, confirming, despite Pietrantoni's efforts to hide it, that his supposition was correct. "I thought so. Stick to politics, Guv, you'll never be a good poker player!" Then his light banter changed to a strictly-business tone. "I will try to hold and mislead the Macheteros as long as I can, but I don't know how much time that will be. If you know a way out of here, take it! If you don't, but you know of a place where you can hide, hide! Anyway..." George turned his back on the hostages and exited through the curtain, waving carelessly a hand over his head. "Goodbye!"

Picon, Lucas, and the Governor watched in silence with a mixture of dread and relief as the black man left. Outside, the battle raged on.

"Maldonado's not rescuing us now, is he?" Arizmendi, who had been watching the exchange from a distance, stated matter-of-factly as he furiously chewed on a fingernail.

The Governor shook his head. "Not until tonight."

"So what do we do?" Double A asked, seeking his marching orders—as he always did—exclusively from Pietrantoni, masking his mounting concern for the benefit of the others.

"As the black gentleman suggested, we hide," the Governor answered.

Rovira Melendez finished his telephone conversation and pondered wordlessly on the news that he had just received. If what Montañez had just informed him was right, then Governor Pietrantoni not only was alive, but he had somehow managed to escape. It seemed unimaginable. Of all the scenarios that he had thought of, he had never considered Governor Pietrantoni capable of escaping from the terrorists on his own. Not that he was out of it yet. According to Montañez, there was no way of snatching him out of San Juan until that night's concerted rescue attempt.

Montañez had also urged the Interim Governor not to reveal to the press, for security reasons, about Pietrantoni's present situation.

Rovira had asked to speak to the Superintendent, but had been informed that he was busy at the moment, meeting with the officers of the Navy SEALs who would participate in the overnight rescue. It was a lie, of course, an excuse by Maldonado to avoid him. Rovira prided himself for his political "sixth sense", which had helped him attain his present lofty position in the government, and which inevitably would lead him to La Fortaleza, and his sixth sense now warned him that something was not right. Montañez had been very reserved and guarded in the information that he had provided over the telephone. When Rovira had asked him for more details, the colonel had courteously begged off, saying that it would not be safe to discuss the matter over the phone. It all stank to high heaven.

"Governor Pietrantoni has managed to escape," Rovira told Captain Ramirez, whom he had brought with him to the Electoral Commission's communications room. "Maldonado doesn't want me to tell the public about it."

Ramirez stared at Rovira, uncertain as to how he should react. "He's out of La Fortaleza?" he ventured after a pregnant pause.

"What?" Rovira seemed to be lost in his own thoughts. "Oh! No, no! He's still there. La Fortaleza continues to be surrounded by the terrorists, and the police won't be able to get to him until tonight. It seems that some insiders helped him to get rid of the people who were guarding him, but that they can't get him out from La Fortaleza. Maldonado doesn't want us to let the press know that Pietrantoni is free. I think he's planning something."

"Maldonado?" Ramirez snorted derisively. "Most probably."

"I mean, it's not as if the Macheteros don't know that he's escaped."

"Right!"

"Something is wrong..." Rovira stood up from behind the desk where he sat and began to pace slowly over the office's plush, blue carpet.

"He's setting you up," Ramirez concluded after a long silence. "He burned you by not letting you know ahead of time about the unauthorized release of Adalberto Cacho, and now he's trying to burn you again."

Rovira raised his right eyebrow quizzically. "How so?" he asked his companion.

"His name right now is mud. He wants to be the one who leaks the news of Pietrantoni's escape to the press, and somehow make them think that he was behind the escape. He wants you to continue to look uninformed, and show to everyone that he's the one running the show." Ramirez waited for Rovira's reaction.

"Keeping quiet about the Governor's escape doesn't make much sense, does it?" Rovira mused to himself.

Ramirez shook his head. "They're taking advantage of your good faith to make you look bad in front of the country," he said.

"It doesn't make much sense..." Rovira repeated, lingering on his own words.

"Do you want me to call a press conference?" Ramirez asked.

Rovira hesitated.

"Yes. I'll just tell them that Pietrantoni has escaped, but that we can't give them any more details, for security reasons," the Interim Governor replied, and then added, "Wait! I'd like you to be the standing next to me."

"Me?" Ramirez was utterly surprised and alarmed.

"It's time that they start seeing the face that will take over the Department when Maldonado is dismissed. What time is it?" Rovira asked, not bothering to look at his watch.

"It's five-o-five PM," the captain responded.

"We have to do this fast. Tell my secretary to arrange an emergency press conference for five thirty. I'll stay here, getting ready."

Ramirez hurried out of the meeting, and then ran to where Rovira's secretary—Margarita—a bleached, heavyset blonde in her late fifties who was very aware of the power that her boss wielded and treated the rest of the staff accordingly—had set up her temporary station, three offices away from the communications room. As she saw the police captain approach, her face soured. She could not understand what the Secretary of Justice saw in him, except for his spineless servility. That day had not been the best of her days, being forced to act as a buffer between Rovira and the press, the politicians, and everybody else in the world who wanted to speak to the Interim Governor. She had no desire whatsoever to speak to the captain at that moment.

"What do you want?" she asked him before he could say anything.

"The Governor wants you to make arrangements for an urgent press conference at 5:30," he answered, ignoring her contemptuous attitude.

Margarita sighed, as if the press conference had been Ramirez's fault, and then started dialing from a list that she had on her desk. The captain began to move away at a hurried pace towards one of the rear doors of the building.

"Hey!" Margarita called after him. "Where are you going?"

"I need to smoke a cigarette," Ramirez responded, and exited the building before she could say anything else.

San Miguel's satellite phone began to buzz like an angry insect on Pepe Cojones' chest, rousing him from his slumber. Lying on a lounge chair by the private beach of the Grand Laguna Hotel, he had been lulled to sleep by the cool breeze and the gentle lapping sound of the waves. Automatically, he looked at his watch and saw—*could it be so late already*—that it was nearly twenty minutes after five in the afternoon.

"Pedro Martinez," he answered calmly.

"Pedro, this is Ramon," an electronically disguised voice on the other side stated. The caller's code name immediately drew Pepe out of his complacency. It corresponded to the mole inside the Police Department.

"Wait," he said hurriedly. "Felipe is not here right now. I'll go get him."

"There is no time for that now," Ramon hissed nervously. *"Just convey to him the following information: as you probably know, the Governor has escaped. I can confirm to you that he's managed to communicate from La Fortaleza with the police. Apparently he had some inside help, so you'd better check on that. His escape is going to be announced at 5:30 by Rovira."*

Contrary to what Ramon had just communicated to him, Pepe had no idea that the Governor had escaped. "I'll tell Felipe immediately," he replied, jumping out of his lounge chair.

"Listen to me," Ramon continued. *"This is the most important part. The Governor is still in La Fortaleza. The authorities will not attempt to pick up the*

Governor out of La Fortaleza until tonight. They're afraid to be massacred, like they were massacred in the Condado Lagoon. In the meantime, he'll hide in La Fortaleza because, as you know, he's still surrounded by your people. If you search enough, you will find him there."

"Right," Pepe said. "Is that all?" he asked, anxious to get going.

"Yes...No! Tell Martinez that he owes me extra for this!"

CHAPTER LI

Smiling at the press, the Interim Governor strutted towards the podium followed by Ramirez. Even as he walked, Rovira signaled everyone to sit down, quietly conveying the urgency of his message. The standing audience rattled back to its seats and waited patiently while Rovira adjusted the microphones in front of him.

"This announcement will be brief," he said, "but not less important because of its brevity." Rovira cleared his throat. "Around 4:30 in the afternoon, Governor Roberto Pietrantoni escaped—"

The noise from the surprised crowd drowned the rest of the words in the sentence. Rovira raised his two hands, and waited for the clamor to die down. "The Governor escaped from the hands of the terrorists who have kept him as a hostage," he stated after order returned to the room.

"Where is the Governor now?" someone shouted, causing another shower of competing questions.

"Is he hurt?"

"Who is in charge of the government?"

"Were any terrorists captured or killed?"

"What about the other hostages?"

Smiling, Rovira once again urged the mass of reporters to be silent.

"For security reasons, I cannot tell you more at this moment," he said, looking confidently at the sea of faces in front of him.

Several hands shot up into the air, and Rovira hesitated momentarily. His gut instincts warned him to end the conference and leave the podium then. He definitely did not want the meeting to turn into a question and answer affair. But he had not liked the initial reaction of the press. It seemed less concerned about what he had not said than about what he had just announced. *Just like the liberal media, trying to dig up the bad news while ignoring the information he had just given.* It almost made him look as if he was not really in control of the situation.

Among those raising their hands he saw the friendly face of Carlos Padilla Cintron, the political analyst from the Teledifusora Broadcasting Syndicate, and he decided to call on him.

Padilla stood up. "Thank you, sir. I assume that when you make the announcement that Governor Pietrantoni has escaped, it's because you have spoken with him."

Rovira nodded tentatively.

"And yet he is not here, which leads me to believe that he is still in San Juan, and therefore, still in danger."

Rovira Melendez shrugged. "As I said, for security reasons I cannot say more at this time."

"It seems to me," the television commentator said with a smug expression, "that if the Interim Governor is not giving any more details for, quote: 'security reasons' it's due to one of two motives. Either he doesn't know where Pietrantoni is, or giving more information would put Pietrantoni even more at risk. Can you at least tell us which of the two reasons it is?"

The entire assembly grew still, waiting for an answer. Rovira Melendez's face grew red with anger. He had hoped that Padilla would have asked some innocuous question that would have paved his way for a graceful exit from the present predicament. Instead, the self-important political analyst had used the opportunity to look bold at Rovira's expense.

"As I said before," he answered with one of his characteristic feral smiles, "I won't answer that question at this moment."

"Then one of my suppositions is correct?" Padilla hurriedly interjected, smelling blood.

"I have nothing else to say," Rovira responded dryly, and stepped away from the podium. His withdrawal was followed with more shouted inquiries, which he ignored.

"That asshole!" he said, fuming, into Ramirez's ear as he walked away from the podium. "He's going to pay for this!"

F.B.I. Special Agent Franceschini watched with amusement from a small portable TV set in his office as Rovira retreated from the press corps. He laughed softly, enjoying the spectacle. "That pompous ass!" he said to himself. "Serves him right."

An urgent tapping on his open door distracted him from the news conference and made him look up. One of his men was standing by the doorframe, waving excitedly a few sheets of paper.

"Hot off the presses!" the man said.

"What is it?"

"A telephone conversation that originated from Captain Francisco Ramirez's cell phone just a few minutes ago. You'd better take a look at it."

Franceschini took the papers from his subordinate's extended hand, and placed them on his desk, pushing his reading glasses over his nose. His eyes widened as he scanned the first few sentences. He raised his gaze briefly, as if to confirm from his man that the source was genuine, then returned his full attention to the document.

"This settles it," he said, rubbing his chin thoughtfully. "Get Superintendent Maldonado on the line."

The F.B.I. agent shook his head in amazement. *After so much time...How could Ramirez have been so careless?*

The trail of blood droplets led Archie to the elevators in the lower level of the parking building, about a hundred feet away from the valet parking spaces where he had fought and killed the terrorist with the braided hair. It had been a difficult trail to follow. The sporadic traces of blood scattered over the floor had been few and sparse, a good indication that the wound suffered by one of the participants of the fight in the parking's third level had not been very serious. But at the same time, the scant crimson droplets had proven to be harder to find than he had imagined. Fortunately, what he lacked in talent as a tracker he made up with his common sense, which allowed him to pick up the lost trail twice after he imagined where his captured friends were being taken.

He also had been forced to move with a great deal of caution, making certain that he would not be seen, shifting swiftly from one hiding place to another. He had not taken the elevator down to the building's first level, not knowing who would be waiting there, but instead had climbed down the stairs.

His caution, though, had proven unnecessary. There was no one in the elevator area or anywhere nearby, which was very surprising, since he could still hear the blare of a car alarm coming from one the valet parking spaces. He would have thought that the racket that occurred while he fought the braided Machetero would have roused half of the men garrisoned in the hotel, and that the first level would be crawling with terrorists.

However, that had not been the case—at least thus far. The Macheteros in the hotel must have been busy doing something else, or they may have thought that by capturing Michelle and Negron, they had gotten rid of whoever had intruded into the garage. Whatever the reason, there was no one to be seen. Quietly, Archie had moved past the elevator and hidden behind the first level's half wall that faced the Grand Laguna Hotel.

But now, as he gazed intently at the opposite side of the street, his pursuit faltered. It was not so much that he had lost the scant traces of blood spread over the ground. Even though the gray tar of the street that separated the parking building from the hotel effectively concealed the dark spots he had been following, he could make out plainly enough the route that the terrorists must have taken, since there was only one path—a stairway hidden behind an earth-colored stone wall—that allowed access into the hotel. What gave him pause was that he would have to walk into the open in order to cross the street between the garage and the Grand Laguna Hotel, and then rush into the stairway without knowing what lurked behind the stone wall that partially concealed it.

The long shadows of the approaching evening were beginning to slither out of their daytime resting places, adding extra dimension and weight to the objects exposed to the sun's dwindling spotlight. All Archie had to do was to wait for another hour or so, and then, he would be able to cross within the cover of darkness.

But he could not afford to waste any time. Negron and Michelle had been caught reconnoitering the hotel grounds. Negron had been wearing one of the armbands that identified the terrorists, and the Macheteros would want to know where he got it from. There could be no doubt that he and Michelle would be questioned, and that the questioning would be rough. Archie had to get them out of there *now*.

Still, he had taken the precaution to survey, for almost half an hour, the movement in the immediate area in front of him. Not a single person had disturbed the unnerving stillness of the street.

"It's time to go," he whispered, regressing to his old habit of talking to himself when he was about to undertake a difficult endeavor.

Standing up from behind the half wall of the parking building, he calmly made his way past the ticket booth at the garage's entrance and headed towards the hidden stairs. He tried to move as naturally as he could, knowing that his limp would attract attention. But if it did, nobody challenged him. Archie reached the earth-colored wall at the other side of the street in no time.

He climbed the steps hidden behind the wall at a fast clip until he reached the stairs' middle landing. From there, the stairway turned to his right and rose eight more steps. He had been there several times before—once for a jobs fair, once for a wedding reception, once for El Chino's—the *bolitero* chieftain he had reached by satellite phone earlier that day—fiftieth birthday party, and he knew the layout fairly well.

Once he cleared the remaining steps, there would be a row of offices to his left, as well as another set of stairs that continued up towards the other floors of the building. Then the corridor would open up into a wide lobby where several enormous ballrooms and meeting areas—each interconnected to the other—would also be located to his left. To his right would be a wall of glass that separated the hotel gardens—including several flamingoes and peacocks—from the air-conditioned lobby.

Another wide corridor, not visible from where Archie stood, ran perpendicularly from the glass wall fringing the gardens across the entire width of the building, ending in the area where the taxis dropped off the guests of the hotel. A second, parallel corridor also cut across the building beyond the meeting areas, connecting the gardens to the main lobby of the Grand Laguna Hotel.

Looking into the hotel from the stairs' middle landing, Archie scanned the marble-covered floors from a nearly eye-level perspective, and again could not perceive any activity ahead of him. He climbed the remaining steps and confirmed, to his great relief, that the corridor beyond was empty. However, his elation was quickly dashed when he failed to find traces of blood anywhere on the shiny white floor underneath him.

He decided to explore the meeting area, and headed towards the ballrooms, walking past four offices on his left and crossing the first of two corridors that extended across the building. It was a careless mistake. Halfway down the corridor he had just crossed were three armed men, loitering near the entrance to the hotel's main ballroom. As he went by, one of them stared at him with a bored expression, and then returned to his conversation with the other two men.

Archie's head throbbed wildly as he stepped out of the men's line of sight. He stopped for a moment to gather his wits, massaging his forehead with one hand. He could feel a massive headache coming. His hands were sweating. *What had he been thinking of,* he asked himself. *Did he really believe that he could saunter casually into the heart of the Grand Laguna Hotel and not be seen?* If he was going to survive, he would have to be a lot more careful and deliberate.

Wiping his hands on his pants, he continued to walk into the hotel, casually examining the long row of doors to the main ballroom that extended to his left. As he passed the first set of the shut doors, he thought he heard the faint murmur of voices inside, and tried to ease open one of the door handles, but it was locked. He tried again with the next set of doors, obtaining the same result.

Could the voices that he heard inside be those of the hostages? Could they be in there? He felt certain of it, even though there was no way for him to verify it. But it made sense. The doors of the ballroom had probably been locked to prevent the hostages from escaping. He knew, from prior visits to the hotel, that the walls separating the ballroom from other smaller halls and meeting rooms could be detached to create a larger space. That was probably what the terrorists had done; they had eliminated some of the partitions between the ballroom and some of the other smaller halls, to create a bigger area where all of the hostages could be kept together. The three armed men that he had seen in the corridor—and any other men that were stationed inside the hall—guarded the only entrance through which the trapped guests could get in or out.

Had Michelle and Negron been taken there? If that was the case, he thought, *there was very little that he could do to secure their release except wait for their rescue.*

Archie stopped at the corner where a second perpendicular corridor—this one extending from the gardens to the center of the hotel's main lobby—intersected the passageway he was traversing. He did not dare to step into the corridor and expose himself to whoever was there—he was certain that more men would be gathered there—and risk being discovered as an intruder.

He turned around and started to walk back, uncertain about what he would do next. At the very least, he would call the police, and let them know what he suspected about the location of the hostages. But to do that, he would need to find an open space from where he could use his satellite phone.

When he got to the corridor where he had spotted the three armed men, he decided to cross it at a normal pace, turning his head towards the opposite side, as if staring at the hotel's gardens through the glass wall. He walked across the corridor with great trepidation, expecting to hear at any moment a shouted challenge from one the sentries, but if they saw him, they paid to him as little heed as they had when he had walked across the first time.

He stopped again once he had passed the corridor's gap, where the others could not see him, and paused to examine the gardens more carefully. They provided the open space that he needed to make the call, but it would mean exposing himself in a place that, facing the Condado Lagoon, was probably being guarded. He spent more than a minute searching for movement, but if any men were patrolling the gardens, they were very well concealed.

It occurred to him that the terrorists would be tempting targets for the police snipers on the other side of the lagoon, and that therefore any Macheteros stationed in the gardens would try to avoid being seen. On that same token, there was no possible way that the police could tell him apart from the terrorists, so if he walked outside he would—at least in theory—be as exposed to their fire as to that of the terrorists. Using the open space of the gardens was turning out to be a very dicey proposition.

Suddenly, several shouted words interrupted his thoughts. They were being uttered from inside one of the business offices near him, and their muffled content could not be understood through the closed door. However, Archie recognized one of the voices immediately. It was Michelle, and from her tone he could tell that she was in serious distress.

For the first time, Archie noticed that one of the offices was lit up. Holding the AK-47 with his right hand, he approached the office's door and slowly turned its handle. It yielded easily. Through the crack of the door, he saw a man leaning against a desk with his back turned towards him. Then he heard someone grunt with pain, and Michelle's voice scream, "Leave him alone!"

A man's voice cursed and said, "Shut up, bitch!" It was followed by a loud slap.

Archie reacted viscerally, and rushed into the room, shutting the door behind him.

It was a long room with two desks, most of its walls decorated with posters showing scenery from Puerto Rico. A man on his feet was leaning forward, resting his hands on the desk closest to the door. Another man stood further away, hovering angrily over the sitting figure of Michelle, who seemed to be reeling from a blow. Like the terrorist closest to him, her face was turned away from him. He could not find Negron anywhere.

The two men turned their heads towards him as he entered, but did not react immediately, thinking Archie was one of them.

"We still haven't gotten anything from them," the terrorist standing over Michelle, a young, rugged looking man with a two-day beard and cruel eyes said. Then his mouth clamped shut, as he realized that Archie was pointing his rifle at him and his companion.

"Hands above your head," Archie said with a calm that surprised him, prodding with the tip of his AK-47 the back of the man leaning against the desk and making him jump forward.

The young Machetero closest to Michelle hesitated, as if considering reaching for the gun he had strapped to his belt. Archie smiled. "By all means go for it," he dared the terrorist. "Let's see who fires first."

The guard raised his hands slowly and locked them over his head. Archie advanced towards him, forcing the other man to back away.

"Archie?" Michelle said, looking back, but her arms were tied to the armrests of her seat, and she could not turn her head enough to see him. "Is it really you?"

"Who else...would have such an effeminate pitch?" a disembodied voice mumbled from the floor.

"Negron?" Archie moved forward, and for the first time saw his friend's body lying behind the second desk. Most of his face was swollen, his eyes nearly shut, his hands and feet bound by rope.

Archie's neck changed to a deep crimson color, as he realized how severely his friend had been beaten. "Turn around, both of you!" he shouted at the two terrorists. "Place your hands up and lean against the wall."

"I had nothing to do with this!" the man who had been closer to the office's entrance assured him fervently. He was medium-sized and very thin, with a large, aquiline nose that seemed even bigger in proportion to the rest of his body. "You can ask her!"

"Shut up!"

Archie approached the man with the cruel eyes and pulled his gun out of his belt. The man flinched and Archie punched him hard in his right kidney. The terrorist's knees buckled, and he crumbled to the ground with a groan.

Archie quickly surveyed the room. On the surface of one of the two desks, he found a regular cell phone connected to a chord. Pocketing the cell phone, he disconnected the chord and approached the large-nosed man. "What's your name?" he asked him.

"Gregorio Alvarez," the man replied nervously.

"Turn around, Gregorio."

Gregorio did as ordered, facing Archie with edgy anticipation. Archie tossed him the chord, making him cringe.

"Tie up your buddy's hands behind his back. Tie them as hard as you can, because I'm going to check them, and if you do a flimsy job, I'll beat you up."

The man nodded and knelt next to his companion, but when he tried to grab his hands, the other man resisted, flipping over and clasping his hands in front of him. Archie stomped on his groin and the man grunted in pain.

"Tie him up now," he repeated to Alvarez.

This time, the younger terrorist did not resist.

"Now lie down, belly against the floor," Archie said when Gregorio finished tying his companion. The large nosed man complied immediately.

Archie tied him up with masking tape, wrapping his wrists more than twenty times to ensure that the binding was strong enough. Then he repeated the procedure on both men's ankles. After that, he cut two strips of cloth from Gregorio's shirt with a pair of scissors he had retrieved from one of the desks' drawers, and bound them around the two men's mouths.

At last he was free to turn to his friends. He knelt first next to Negron, whose face was so battered that he was hardly recognizable.

"Untie Michelle first," he said, barely able to speak.

"You talk too much," Archie said to him, cutting his bonds with the scissors. Negron slowly stretched his legs, wincing when he tried to sit but managing to do it nonetheless.

In the meantime, Archie had cut Michelle free. Her cheek still bore the mark of the hand that had slapped her, but otherwise she seemed fine. She embraced Archie as soon as he slashed through the plastic bindings that kept her tied to the chair, sobbing on his shoulder.

"Hey, it's okay!" Archie said gently, feeling very awkward but delighted by her reaction. He spotted a box of Kleenex tissues on the desk next to them, and pulled out one, handing it to her. She blew her nose, smiling.

"I'm so glad to see you!" she said.

"We'd better see how Negron is doing," Archie managed to say, despite his desire to keep watching her. He thought that she looked beautiful.

Negron was already climbing back to his feet when Archie and Michelle got to him. Archie placed his arm behind Negron's back and helped hold him up, making him flinch involuntarily when he grazed his friend's bruised ribs.

"How do you feel?" Michelle asked, with an expression of deep concern. She turned her gaze to the terrorist who had tortured Negron. "That animal kicked him several times in the ribs, and even on the face."

"It hurts," the rookie policeman said, "but it must look worse than it really is...I may have cracked a couple of ribs. I'd kick that son of a bitch, but I'm afraid it'll hurt me more than it will hurt him."

"That's no problem," Archie replied, and turned, stomping on the man's groin again. The man squeaked through his gag, and curled into a fetal position. "I can kick him for you."

"Thank you..." Negron said with effort. "Just don't make me laugh, okay? Laughing hurts like hell."

"Can you walk?" Archie asked him, trying not to stare too much at Negron's swollen face, in order not to alarm him.

Negron nodded.

"What happened?"

Michelle shook her head in disgust. "We screwed up. That's what happened. We felt so bad right after you left—"

"She felt worse than I did," Negron interjected, grinning sheepishly. Archie thought that he looked like the classic Robert De Niro photo from Raging Bull, right after a fight.

"That's not true," Michelle said. "He wanted to come after you. So we ran to the stairs, and when we opened the door, we came face to face with three of the terrorists, including this guy who was torturing Negron."

"Face to face?"

"Almost as close as we are now," Michelle answered.

"I think we scared them as much...as they scared us," Negron said weakly, smiling. "One of them screamed like a little girl."

"That was me," Michelle said.

"Yea, well, anyway...They were as surprised as we were," Negron continued. "One of them began to draw his gun...from his holster...but I slammed the door of the stairs on their faces..." The rookie policeman seemed to struggle to keep his composure, but laughed. "Owww! That hurt...It was fun, though..."

Michelle raised one of her eyebrows in exasperated impatience. "They were right behind us, and began to shoot at us, so we hid behind the cars, in the corner where we had been before."

Archie nodded. "I know, I was there. You must have put up a hell of a fight, from all the damage suffered by the cars around you. By the way, I saw the blood. Which one of you was wounded?"

"Oh! That was not us," Michelle responded. "One of the terrorists tried to sneak behind us, from one of the cars parked next to us..."

"But I shot him..." Negron interrupted. "Winged him, actually, on his right arm...He started to cry, like a little kid. Was bleeding all over the place..."

"We ran out of ammunition. We had to surrender. I kept thinking how much I had screwed everything up, how unfair I had been to you."

Archie said nothing. He felt so good, just being with his two friends again, that nothing else mattered.

"They took us to this office, and tied us up, and that guy," Michelle motioned with her head to the man who had been kicked twice in the groin, "sent the other one, Gregorio, to inform their leaders that they had captured some 'spies', and asked what they should do with us. But even before Gregorio returned, the other one had started to beat up Negron. He kept asking him where he had obtained the 'Libre como el Coqui' armband."

"I...I sort of provoked him..." the rookie policeman admitted with a rueful smile. "I called him 'mojon de gato'—cat turd."

"Yes," Michelle said, looking away nervously and trying unsuccessfully to suppress a snicker.

Archie also tried not to chuckle, but his eyes began to water and he chortled. His two friends joined him and they laughed uncontrollably, Negron holding on to his ribs and whispering "Oww!" every few seconds.

"You called him a cat turd?" Archie repeated between laughs.

"It seemed like the right thing...to do at the time," Negron answered.

Archie smiled.

"The leaders of the terrorists apparently didn't give that much importance to us, since Gregorio, when he returned, just told the other guy that if they got any information out of us they should let the others know," Michelle said. "So this guy kept hitting Negron to get him to say something. I think he wanted to impress his bosses. That's when you showed up."

"Asshole!" Archie turned to the prostrate figure of Negron's tormentor. "You're really good hitting people who are tied up, aren't you? Let's see how you like it now!" Archie raised his foot as if to tramp on the man's groin again, but the young terrorist squealed and covered his genitals, turning away from him.

"Nobody else has shown up in the office since Gregorio returned," Michelle said, plainly enjoying the man's discomfort.

"Good," Archie responded. "That means that they're not expecting anything to happen soon and that we have time to get out of here."

"We need—" Michelle began to say, but Archie, stealing a glance at the two bound men and making certain that they were not watching him, placed a finger across his lips, indicating to his friends that they should not discuss their plans within their hearing range.

Archie began to push the desk closest to the entrance of the office towards the other desk until he joined the two of them together, dividing the room into two halves, and enclosing the two terrorists behind the barrier created by the desks.

"That way they won't be able to roll on the floor and start pounding on the door," Archie explained. "We need to go." He looked at Negron. "Are you up to it?"

"Do I have any choice?"

"Not really."

"Then off we go."

They grabbed the terrorists' weapons, two guns and an AK-47, as well as their ammunition, and after Archie peeked through the front door, they exited the office. As they did, Archie turned off the office lights and locked the door from the inside. If anyone came looking for Michelle and Negron or the two terrorists, they would think that they had moved to some other place.

Outside, the sun had hidden beyond the horizon, and the hotel's lush gardens had become illuminated by automatic spotlights spread throughout the grounds.

"Follow me," Archie instructed the others. He passed the other offices and walked into the set of stairs that connected a small, lower lobby to the upper floors of the building. There, the friends huddled to discuss their plans.

"I think I found where the hostages are," Archie said softly to the others, aware of the stairway's echo, but could not continue as Michelle kissed him fully on the lips. He stopped, shocked, while Negron looked at them with an unreadable expression.

"That's for coming back to save us," she said to him.

Archie tried to continue, but had lost his track of thinking. It took him several seconds to remember what he was saying. "Wow!" he managed to say with breathless wonder.

"I'm sorry that I doubted you," Michelle told him, looking directly into his eyes and making him blush.

"Anyway..." he tried to marshal his thoughts in the spinning universe into which the beautiful reporter had suddenly plunged him. "I was saying...Thank you, by the way," he said, interrupting himself, knowing he was acting like a fool but unable to do much about it. "I was saying that I think I know where the hostages are."

Archie slowly recounted what he had seen and heard a few moments before, while the others listened attentively.

"We have to call the Superintendent and let him know," Michelle said when he had finished.

"Yea, but in order to use the satellite phone, we need to get out to an open space," Negron reminded his friends. "That is going is to be dangerous."

"I would not advise going into the open anywhere close to here," Archie said, while he examined the cell phone he had grabbed from the office. "But maybe we don't have to go into the open. Maybe we can use this regular cell phone."

"What are you doing?" Michelle asked. "I thought they weren't working."

"Hold on a second," Archie said, raising a hand to prompt her to hold her words, and dialing the cell phone for information. After waiting briefly, he nodded. "It's as I thought! It's ringing!" he confirmed with muted excitement. As the operator answered, he said, "I want to make a call to a Radium satellite phone. Is there an access code I need to dial in order to make the call from this cellular phone?"

Archie listened attentively, and after a long pause, replied, "Yes, I'll wait while you get the information." Placing a hand over the speaker, he turned to Michelle. "It's as I thought," he said to her. "The cell phones weren't working a while ago, when the calls peaked, but they seem to be working now. We can—" he stopped talking as the operator returned to the line. "Yes, I'm still here," Archie answered, and then listened as he received the requested information. "Hold on, hold on, let me write that down. The last four digits end in 2500? And after that, I dial the satellite phone number?" Negron entered the numbers into his phone. "Thank you," he said into the phone, and ended the call.

Archie smiled at his two companions, plainly pleased with himself. "Negron, don't forget that access code, okay?"

The battered rookie policeman moved his head affirmatively.

"Now, let's call the Superintendent from this cell phone" Archie said to Michelle.

"But we don't have the satellite number that the Superintendent gave us!" Michelle replied. "I entered the number into the satellite phone, and we lost it in the garage! I tossed it—"

"Under the blue minivan, when you were being captured by the terrorists?" Archie said, producing the satellite phone with a flourish, as if he had conjured it out of the air. "I found it. You're as smart as you are beautiful."

Michelle searched the Superintendent's telephone number in the satellite phone's directory and, after Archie had entered the satellite phone access code, she dictated the telephone number to him. The cell phone began to ring, but then the call was lost. Archie cursed under his breath and tried gain. This time, after a breathless moment, it continued to ring.

"It's working!" Archie said triumphantly, and handed the telephone to Michelle, saying, "They know you, not me."

A moment later, a female voice answered.

"Is this Superintendent Maldonado's telephone."

"Yes!" the female answered enthusiastically. *"Is this Michelle?"*

"Yes," she replied cautiously.

"Hold on, we've been waiting for you. I'll get the Superintendent."

CHAPTER LII

As Rovira Melendez walked out of the television screen, every eye in the business center's conference room turned to Adalberto Cacho and Angel San Miguel. The news had confirmed the inside information that San Miguel had obtained from his source in the Police Department just a few minutes before. It also coincided with the report that Cacho had just received from one of his men outside of La Fortaleza.

Sitting two chairs away from both men, Johnny Ray had to admire their composure—*sang froid*, the French called it—in the face of the recent set of events. It was a leadership trait that he lacked and hoped to acquire. Cacho seemed to be somewhat peeved, as if slightly piqued by an offensive odor, or irked by a line in a crossword puzzle that he could not solve. San Miguel's face showed no kind of emotion, his stare distant and contemplative. Had he been a poker player, he could have been playing in the professional circuit. Only the light tapping of his right thumb on the conference table betrayed the busy activity occurring within his brain.

Colonel Calderon, always the warrior, sat straight as a board, looking like a panther ready to spring into action at the slightest provocation, both of his eyebrows raised in what seemed to be thoughtful dismay. In stark contrast, Czecka stood stoically behind San Miguel, his expression a classic study of boredom and disinterest. At the beginning of the meeting, Cacho had invited Czecka to sit at the table. The mountain-sized human had refused, stating curtly, "I stay here." To which San Miguel had simply added, as if it were the most logical of explanations, "He likes to stand." Cacho had not insisted.

Daniel, San Miguel's other lieutenant, was inexplicably absent from the meeting, probably attending to some matter of the hostages in the hotel, while Andrade—El Alacran—had left for La Fortaleza to execute the Governor, an errand that now seemed to be on the brink of failing.

It was Yajaira, though, who worried Johnny. He had seen her unravel as the day progressed, becoming increasingly nervous and agitated. It was obvious that what she had expected to be a glorious, popular uprising had turned into an unimaginable nightmare. Her hands shook periodically, and when she spoke, she hardly sounded coherent.

Just as they were walking into the conference room, Yajaira had pulled him aside and confessed to him that she wanted to quit, to leave San Juan and return to her home. Johnny had reminded her that there was no safe way of abandoning the island of San Juan, but she had been irrational, saying that she would swim to the other side if necessary. He had finally managed to quiet her down by promising that he would speak with San Miguel that night and arrange for her transfer, hoping that in the meantime she would settle down.

"If what Rovira Melendez said is right," Cacho said calmly, "then Pietrantoni is still trapped inside of La Fortaleza. Our men still surround it, so he and the other prisoners have no means of escape."

"Unless there is some secret passage out of there," Johnny volunteered helpfully, earning a look of derision from Cacho.

"Andrade will be there shortly with four more men," Cacho continued saying. "I have not been able to reach him, but once he's there, he'll catch up quickly." The Machetero leader directed a quizzical glance at San Miguel. "Whoever is shooting from inside La Fortaleza...They're hidden inside and cannot be seen...But whoever it is, they or he, they seem to know how to shoot. Pietrantoni...I don't think he's so good with weapons."

"He is a member of the National Guard..." Johnny prompted.

Cacho moved his head from one side to another, as if expressing doubt.

"Somehow, he doesn't strike me as a man of action."

"Some of his bodyguards may be involved," San Miguel reminded his Machetero counterpart.

"That may explain it," Cacho responded with a smile that promptly soured into a smirk. "Have you heard from your men?" he inquired casually, but it was evident to Johnny that he was paying a great deal of attention to San Miguel's response.

"No," San Miguel responded in a concerned tone. "I tried calling George a few minutes ago, after I got the news from our...source, but got no response."

"George?" Cacho repeated the name, unable to place him.

"Please forgive me, I forgot that you haven't met him. George is one of my principal problem solvers. He was sharing the custody of the Governor with your men."

Cacho seemed puzzled. "That makes Pietrantoni's escape even more strange, don't you think? How do you think he managed to do it?"

San Miguel stared at his two hands, clasped in front of him, and considered the question. "It has occurred to me," he said thoughtfully, "that he may have gotten some inside help."

Cacho nodded in agreement. "Any suspicions of who?"

"I don't know your men well enough," San Miguel answered, shifting the onus of the inquiry on the Macheteros.

A tense silence followed. Cacho seemed to smile inwardly, as if amused by his counterpart's answer. "Well," he said, looking at the others, "we'll know soon enough." He stood up and looked at San Miguel. "We still have that connection with the Police Superintendent, don't we?"

"Yes," San Miguel nodded. "It's in a smaller conference room."

"Take me there. I'd like you to introduce him to me. In private."

The day ended abruptly, as it usually did in the winter, the ensuing nightfall gently spreading its dark mantle accompanied by a crisp, cool wind. The pale outline of a small moon, shaped like a yellow, curved sliver, appeared and disappeared from behind low, ghostly clouds that moved noiselessly with a different agenda from that of the land under them. The day's blue roiling ocean was swallowed by the inky blackness of the night, with only the deep-throated roar of the crashing waves and the periodic bursts of silver spray betraying its mighty presence.

"It smells like rain," Sergeant Cordero said more to himself than to his two fellow SWAT officers, looking up at the gloomy sky.

"It's getting chilly too," Raymond Tavarez, the dirty blond-haired youngster muttered, rubbing his two hands.

"Having second thoughts about swimming in that water?" Cordero teased. "Want me to do it?"

"I will do it, thank you, sergeant, sir," Raymond responded nervously, looking at the water. He had taken off his shirt, but placed back on his life jacket.

"Now let's review our signals before you go," Captain Gomez said to the youngster. "When you get there, you will tell the Superintendent that we are ready to create a diversion and try to take out any lookouts along the shore, but that we need to know at what time they are coming."

Raymond nodded. "One flash means that you should move immediately. If not, the flashes will indicate the hour of the assault, minus two. If it's at eight, there will be ten flashes. If it's at ten, twelve flashes. Always two more flashes than the real hour of the assault, right?"

"Right. Any long flashes after the short ones will indicate quarter hours. One long flash will mean fifteen minutes after the hour, two long flashes thirty minutes after the hour, and three forty-five minutes. That will give us a better idea of the exact time when they're coming. And if they don't want us to do anything, two long flashes, two short flashes, two long flashes, understood?"

"Understood."

"And if we don't see any flashes—'

"It will probably mean that I drowned or that I'm swimming towards Humacao or Africa," Raymond cut in.

"In which case, we'll proceed on our own at seven fifteen, and try to reconnoiter the hotel grounds, look for the hostages, maybe find some targets of opportunity, and if possible, find the means to communicate with the Superintendent," Gomez said, ignoring Raymond.

"Right!" Raymond said enthusiastically.

Gomez stared at the young policeman. "You should get going," he said, slapping Raymond on the shoulder. "Good luck!"

"You sure you don't want me to go?" Cordero asked, this time in earnest. Despite his forty-something odd years, the grizzled veteran still looked fit and trim. Only his white stubble betrayed his age.

"Thanks, sarge," Raymond answered, grinning, "but this is my job."

Cordero and Raymond began to skirt the small rocky promontory that jutted into the lagoon, staying in waist-deep water so that they would not be seen. They found it difficult to move, clinging to the razor sharp rocks that protruded from the edge, and trying to find footholds in the murky water that swished back and forth as the waves broke on the opposite side of the tiny outcrop of land. The water was cold, and even before they had reached the outermost tip of the extended rocks, the two men could feel a strong current pushing them out of the lagoon towards the sea.

Finally, the SWAT men reached the gap that existed between the reefs of the island of San Juan and those of El Condado. The wind blew stronger here, unhindered by the outcrop of land that had partially shielded the men while they moved behind it, every so often showering the police officers with the spray from the breaking waves. From where they had stopped, they could see the opposite shore, lit up by the row of hotels and condominiums that lined the northern coast.

"Can you hold me by the waist while I take off my boots?" Raymond shouted over the roar of the sea.

Cordero leaned against the rocks behind him and grabbed the youngster by the belt. "Go ahead!" he said close to his ear. "When you take your boots off, stand on mine so you don't cut your feet with the rocks below."

Raymond removed his boots, sometimes placing his head underwater, the noises of the surface immediately dulled by the more sedate sounds of rushing water, and the surprisingly loud clicking of fish.

"I'll come back for these later," Raymond said to his sergeant, tossing both boots over his head onto the land outcrop. "They're good boots!"

Cordero smiled. "Are you ready?" he asked.

Raymond was about to say yes, but changed his mind. "No! Wait a minute!"

He began to undo the Velcro bindings of his flotation device.

"What are you doing?" Cordero asked him, somewhat alarmed.

"I'm taking it off!" Raymond answered. "The current is too strong! I don't want this to drag me out to sea!"

"It will keep you afloat!"

"Yea, but it will also be a drag when I'm swimming against the current.

"You shouldn't swim against the current. You should swim parallel to the shore until the current weakens!" Cordero argued, as every good swimmer knew.

"I don't have time to drift with the current. I may end up in Humacao or Fajardo. By the time I get to shore, it may be hours from now!" Raymond explained. "We don't have the time! I'm going to make a dash to the reefs on the other side! I'll be in the San Geronimo Plaza in no time!"

"That's too risky!"

"That's what we get paid for!"

Cordero kept quiet. The boy was right. The purpose of swimming to the other side was to get to the Superintendent before any rescue attempt started. If he got caught in the current, and waited for it to weaken, it would probably be too late.

"Okay. But remember, if you don't reach the reefs, don't panic. Don't fight the current. Wait 'till it weakens. Float on your back. Then swim to shore."

"Wish me luck!" Raymond said. "You don't think there's any sharks out there, do you?"

"Probably, so swim fast! Are you ready?"

Raymond crouched, hesitated for one second, and then dove head-first into the dark mouth of the lagoon. The cold water numbed him, galvanizing him into action. He was a fast, strong swimmer, but he felt the current of the outgoing tide push him out towards the sea. He paddled and kicked with all his strength, raising his head every four strokes to see if he was swimming in the right direction. The separation between the rocky outcrop next to the fort and the reefs of El Condado must have been no more than fifty yards, and yet the current inexorably drove him further out, until it seemed as if he would not reach the other side.

The waves became rougher as he floated into the more open sea. Already the current had dragged him a few yards past the Condado reefs. Straining every sinew in his body, he began to swim against the heavy flow of water rushing out of the lagoon, keeping an eye on the coastal lights. For an eternity, it seemed as if he remained stationary in the water, not getting pushed further out to sea, but not getting any closer to the line of rocks that stuck out like jagged teeth all the way to the Condado shore. Then, gradually, he began to close the gap.

By that time he was exhausted. Every muscle in his arms, shoulders, and legs burned from the terrible strain to which he was subjecting his body. It became more and more difficult to move his extremities. He gasped for air every time he took a stroke, not getting enough, choking with the water. He knew that if he did not make it he would drown, exhausted beyond the point of return.

And then, his right hand hit a rock underwater, and he held on to it with the tips of his fingers, pulling himself forward. For a moment, he entertained the wild hope that he would be able to make his way to the reef, just an arms length away, by clinging to its base. But the rock was covered with a slippery veneer of algae that made it nearly impossible hang on, and as the water receded, Raymond lost his grip.

In a moment, the tide had separated him a dozen feet from his safe haven. He tried to lift his arms and swim, but they felt like lumps of lead. His heart beat wildly in his chest, his throat felt raw from the salt water that he had swallowed. He was lost, and he knew it. The only thing left to do was to float, and hope that he could regain some of his strength to make it ashore somewhere. But he knew he was too tired even to do that.

Just then an enormous wave engulfed him, hitting him with incredible force and violence, one moment tossing him forward on its crest, the next moment slamming him on a wall of rock that cut into his body like dozens of sharp, tiny razor blades. Out of oxygen, he opened his mouth to breathe and choked on seawater before his head broke through the surface. As the wave began to withdraw, he desperately grabbed on to the rocks and held on for dear life, determined not to get sucked back into the sea. And quite suddenly, he was coughing and clinging to the reef, free to his waist from the swirling, foaming water that was flowing back into the darkness behind him.

His chest heaving from the effort, he tried to recover his breath, but the growing roar of a new, incoming wave scared him into action, and he scrambled like a crab onto the higher part of the rocks. The wave, even larger than the previous one, crashed onto the reefs below him a moment later, enveloping his legs up to his knees and nearly making him lose his footing. But he kept on climbing until he reached the top, and there he sat to get his bearings.

He had somehow emerged close to where the stone of the dog sat on its eternal vigil, about half of the distance from the reefs to the Condado shore. He was bleeding from several cuts on his body, some of them deep. His feet and hands had suffered the most, and he was certain that the soles of his feet would be shredded by the time that he reached firm land.

He turned his gaze towards the San Geronimo fort, but it was too dark and too far away to determine if Cordero was still waiting by the edge of the small promontory from which he had started his swim. Looking at his watch, he saw that it was not yet 6:40 PM; it had taken him approximately ten minutes to get to the other side.

He was shivering. While he was in the water, the clouds had thickened considerably, and the strength of the wind and the waves had picked up. Cordero had been right. It was going to rain.

He could not waste any more time. He would still have to negotiate over the rest of the reefs, and that would be difficult and painful. It was time to go.

Interim Governor Rovira Melendez walked to the window of the President of the Electoral Commission's office—the office that he had commandeered for the present crisis—and looked outside. The row of broadcasting mobile units, each supporting a tall, thin aluminum tower loaded with telecommunications gear and thick, curly wires, extended nearly all the way down to the Muñoz Rivera Avenue on both of its sides. Many of the news vehicles were artificially illuminated, attracting—like giant night bug zappers—hundreds of curious bystanders who had gradually gravitated to the Emergency Command Center.

The area had acquired a carnival-like atmosphere. Food vendors had quickly grasped the need to feed the droves of news enthusiasts who had peregrinated to the Electoral Commission Building to personally witness the unfolding news. The sidewalks were clogged with hot dog, taco, refreshment, and ice cream carts; *bacalaito fritos*—fried codfish pancakes—and *carne al pincho*—barbecued squares of nondescript meat pinched a la shish kabob—stands; and even a popcorn machine. Small bars that were usually closed on Sundays were selling cold beer up to three blocks away.

Puerto Ricans had never needed an excuse to gather and celebrate, and that night proved to be no exception. The only thing missing had been the music that usually blared from enormous loudspeakers, although Rovira Melendez had ordered that two huge television screens be placed at each end of the building, to broadcast the news as they occurred.

Being a consummate politician, the Interim Governor had been particularly careful to project to the viewing public the right mixture of concern and strong leadership expected in a terrible crisis, trying to follow the Rudy Giuliani 9/11 model. He had at various times ordered the heads of the various governmental agencies to give status updates on the activities and precautions that their personnel was presently undertaking. He had personally addressed the crowd in the street twice, reassuring those present—many of them his followers—that they should not be concerned about their personal safety, that all of the necessary measures to restore order were being enforced, and that he would lead Puerto Rico out of that terrible crisis. A crisis, he had subtly hinted on several occasions, which had not been of his making.

A few people on the street noticed that he was standing behind the window and waved. Rovira smiled and waved back. The overall public response had been good. He was fast becoming the new face of Puerto Rico before the world. He doubted that Governor Pietrantoni would come out of the present crisis alive. Not that he wished him any harm. But even though Pietrantoni had escaped, it seemed very difficult that he would be able to evade for long the terrorists surrounding La Fortaleza. And if that happened, Rovira—by law—would become the official governor of Puerto Rico.

Yet even if Pietrantoni somehow managed to survive, Rovira Melendez's reputation would be greatly enhanced by the way he had handled the greatest emergency ever faced in the island's modern history. Setting aside the last press conference, from which he was still smarting, Rovira had provided the strong, steady leadership that was required in that type of extreme situation. Pietrantoni would not stand a chance against him in the next general elections.

It was essential that he continued to give the impression that he was doing everything in his power to rescue the hostage governor and his family. The last press conference had been a clumsy attempt to foster that impression, he now acknowledged, but even so it would still help in the end. What he needed was to follow up with further reports, as the events of the night unfolded, either showing that he was on top of the rescue operations if they were successful, or distancing himself from them and blaming Maldonado and the federal government if they failed.

And if they failed, he would be at the head of the nation mourning those killed, and urging his fellow countrymen to honor the memory of those who had fallen by continuing the march towards statehood and a brighter future. *Under his leadership.*

Somebody knocked on the door, and then it opened before Rovira could answer. His secretary Margarita, wearing a bored expression and a dress too tight for her robust constitution, shuffled into the room.

"Colonel Montañez is here to see you," she announced.

"Who?" Rovira asked in a surprised tone.

"Colonel Montañez," she repeated.

Superintendent Maldonado's best friend, Rovira thought. That was a surprise. He had thought that Montañez would be in the San Geronimo Plaza war room, with his buddy. *Why would he be here?* He had expected to get an earful from the Superintendent after the press conference, but Maldonado had remained strangely silent. Maybe Montañez had been sent to personally convey to him Maldonado's displeasure.

Rovira smiled, anticipating the moment when he would send Maldonado and his deputy to hell.

"Send him in," he instructed his secretary.

"He's here with two of his men," Margarita said doubtfully.

Rovira shrugged. "Wait two minutes, and let them all in."

He walked to the desk and sat behind it, picking up a folder from the Elections Commission and pretending to read from it.

Montañez entered a moment later, followed by his two companions, and walked to the front of the desk. Rovira failed to acknowledge them, seemingly absorbed in his scrutiny of the Electoral Commission document. The three arrivals continued to stand, waiting in silence.

Finally, after a few minutes, Rovira looked up and gave Montañez a toothy, mirthless grin. "Sorry to keep you waiting, Colonel. I'm very busy right now."

As he spoke he flashed a glance at Montañez's two companions. Although dressed in civilian garb, he could tell that they were policemen. He was amazed by their size. Montañez was a big man, taller than Rovira, and more powerfully built. His men were bigger. Probably some of Montañez's so-called elite unit of the Untouchables. With his right hand, he motioned to his visitors to be seated, but they remained standing.

"To what do I owe this visit?" Rovira asked, dispensing with the small talk.

"Mr. Secretary, despite my previous request to you over the phone not to reveal to the press that the Governor had escaped, you went ahead and did it. The Superintendent gave you very confidential information at the urging of Governor Pietrantoni himself, and you betrayed his trust." Like Rovira, Montañez wasted no time on niceties.

So he had been right, thought the Interim Governor. Montañez had been sent by Maldonado to chastise and intimidate him. Rovira leaned back on his chair, and propping his chin on his right hand, stared with studied insolence at the three men standing before him. *If that fat country bumpkin of a Superintendent thought that he could scare him by sending three of his thugs with a personal message, he was dead wrong.*

"Please tell Maldonado that I really don't have time for this nonsense," he said with a measured sense of impatience bordering on righteous indignation. "I am the present Governor of Puerto Rico, and it corresponds to me to determine what I reveal and what I don't reveal to the people of Puerto Rico. I don't have to give any explanation of what I do to that fat, vulgar alcoholic, and much less to the flunkies that he sends. Go back to your master, Colonel, and tell him that. And tell him this as well, that his days as Superintendent are coming to an end, and that he's lucky that he will get a retirement pension, because after I'm through with him, nobody will hire him. Believe me, I'll make certain of that." Rovira picked up the Electoral Commission folder and pretended to renew his reading. "Now, unless you have anything else to say, please leave," he stated, not taking his eyes from the folder he was perusing.

Rovira tried not to smile. *Maldonado was so easy to deal with that is was embarrassing. Had he not despised the man so much, he would have felt sorry for him. Sending three men to scare him? Really? He should expose him for using government resources for his own benefit. Maybe he would. Maybe he'd add this as another reason for firing him when he announced his dismissal.*

Rovira looked up and was surprised to see Montañez and his two companions still standing before him. "You're still here, I see?" he inquired, arching one eyebrow to show his irritation. "Are you confused? Do you need me to repeat the message?"

"Actually, yes, I am confused," Montañez said earnestly. "You said that we should leave if we didn't have anything else to say—"

"Yes?" Rovira said impatiently.

"Well, I do have something else to say," the Colonel said, as if explaining the obvious.

Rovira stared at the man as if he were retarded. "So go ahead!" he prompted, starting to truly get angry.

"You're under arrest," Montañez stated simply.

Rovira chuckled, examining the faces of the three men, his face turning red as he realized they were in dead earnest.

"I have been instructed to do this as quietly as I can—" Montañez continued.

"You bet you have!" Rovira roared, standing up and moving towards the door of the office. But one of Montañez's men moved faster and blocked his way.

"I am the Governor of Puerto Rico!" he shouted. "Get out of my way! You have no authority to arrest me!"

Montañez shook his head slowly, as if it pained him to contradict the stunned politician.

"In the first place," the police colonel stated, raising his index finger and holding it with his other hand, as if counting, "you are *not* the Governor of Puerto Rico. He is alive and well and, as you yourself disclosed to the world, he is in direct communication with us. So as far as the police is concerned, we follow his commands, not yours. As to my authority to arrest you," Montañez raised his middle finger and showed it to Rovira before holding it with his other hand, "that is a matter to be determined by the courts later," Montañez took out a pair of handcuffs. Rovira stared at them in horror. "Now, Mr. Secretary of Justice, will you come with us peacefully, or do I have to 'cuff you?"

"Why?...What are the charges?" he asked, standing straight and trying to keep the last vestiges of dignity that he had. He was shaking noticeably, whether from fear or anger, Montañez could not tell.

"Participating in reckless conduct that has endangered the life of Governor Roberto Pietrantoni," Montañez replied with a straight face. Both of his men maintained blank expressions.

Rovira tried to laugh, but instead produced a half snort full of spit. His face had continued to darken, and by now was nearly purple.

"Those charges won't progress in a court of law, and I'll accuse all of you of illegal imprisonment and kidnapping!" he said contemptuously.

Montañez closed the distance between him and the Interim Governor until only a few inches separated the two men, forcing the other man to take an involuntary step back.

"Maybe," the policeman said quietly, gently grabbing Rovira's arm and turning him towards the door. "But for now, you won't be able to harm any other innocent people."

"Where are you taking me?" Rovira asked, now thoroughly scared, unwilling to move. "There are other policemen out there! Captain Ramirez is out there! I'll scream for help and they'll come to rescue me! I'll expose you in front of the world press! This is a *coup d'état!"*

Montañez, who had begun to edge the Interim Governor forward, suddenly stopped.

"That reminds me," he said casually to his prisoner. "You won't find Ramirez out there."

Rovira stared at the policeman with contemptuous disbelief, but realized that he was not bluffing.

"The F.B.I. arrested him just as we were coming here to get you. It seems that the man was a mole, a drug cartel contact. Also, he was warning the terrorists about what we were doing." Montañez sighed. "It's a dirty shame," he said wistfully. "I think he was your prime candidate for Police Superintendent, wasn't he? Wasn't he standing next to you during your last press conference? We're keeping it quiet for the moment. It's too embarrassing." Maldonado had also kept the press in the dark about Ramirez's arrest, hoping that he could use him against the terrorists, but Montañez kept that piece of information to himself.

The news stunned Rovira Melendez into silence. For a moment, his legs seemed about to fail him, prompting Montañez and another of his men to hold him up. His mouth hung half open, as if the air had been forced out of his lungs. He stared uncomprehendingly at the floor.

"So go ahead," Montañez continued. "Talk to the press. Tell them that you're being arrested. And we'll use the same press conference to let the press know about your friend's arrest, and about our suspicions that you were his accomplice."

"That is a lie! You are blackmailing me!" Rovira Melendez exploded, looking desperate and literally foaming at his mouth. Montañez watched him with curious interest. When Maldonado discussed with him Rovira's arrest, Montañez had been of the opinion that Interim Governor was indeed acting in concert with Ramirez and the terrorists. Maldonado had disagreed. *The man was a vain and arrogant peacock, and many other things as well,* the Superintendent had said. *An asshole for sure. But he was not a traitor.* Montañez had not been convinced then, but Rovira's present reaction had been genuine. Once more, the Superintendent's instincts had proven superior to his own.

"Blackmailing you? No, I'm just telling you what the consequences will be if you persist in your present course of action," the police colonel answered. "I'm really protecting you from doing something rash that you'll later regret. But it's really up to you…"

Rovira eyed Montañez with a mixture of fear and curiosity. *You had to admire the guy,* Montañez thought. *The man was a survivor. Had he been traveling on the Titanic, and everyone but one person drowned, that person would have been him.* Montañez could almost see the wheels in his brain spinning.

"What do you mean?" the Interim Governor asked.

"Well, as I was saying, there are two ways to go about this. Way number one, you come out screaming and kicking out of this place, we formalize our charges against you and reveal to the press the Captain Ramirez fiasco."

"What do you mean, *'formalize'* the charges against me?" Rovira inquired distrustfully.

So the man had caught his hint, Montañez thought, smiling inwardly. *Good.*

"I mean that if the Governor escapes with his life, we may not bring any criminal charges against you," he answered.

Rovira mulled over the policeman's response. "What is the second alternative?"

"You come with us quietly now. No handcuffs. A press person—one of our men—will inform the press that you are suffering from an incapacitating migraine, and that you are going home for the night to rest."

"How long will that excuse hold up?" Rovira asked doubtfully.

"As long as the crisis exists. We hope to end it tonight, but your headache may last longer," Montañez replied with a deadpan expression. He was really relishing the moment.

"And leave the government headless?" he inquired plaintively, seeking an opening. "The department heads need coordination in order to function adequately during the present crisis."

"Under the Law of Interim Succession, if the Secretary of Justice is incapacitated to act as Interim Governor, the Secretary of the Treasury will take his place. We have spoken with Rosa Gonzalez, and she has indicated that she is willing to assume the governorship while Governor Pietrantoni returns to us."

Rovira Melendez's face became distorted with a look of pure hatred. *So it had gotten to that point,* it seemed to say. Maldonado had actually dared to go behind his back, and secured an ally in the Cabinet. The Secretary of the Treasury was a staunch supporter of Pietrantoni and a well-regarded, indefatigable member of his Cabinet, responsible for reforming and streamlining Puerto Rico's Tax Code. It was obvious that she had been a very willing participant in what effectively was a *coup d'état* by the Police Department.

Montañez observed Rovira's discomfiture with mute pleasure. *Sometimes,* he reflected, *the extra perks of the job far outweighed the miserable salary that he received.*

"I will not forget this," Rovira promised, his voice dripping with concentrated venom.

"I hope not," Montañez replied.

CHAPTER LIII

"This is the Superintendent," Maldonado said into the telephone that served as the hotline between the terrorists in the Grand Laguna Hotel and the Command Center in the San Geronimo Plaza.

The demand to speak with Maldonado had come shortly after he had finished talking to Michelle on the cell phone. She had done better than he had imagined, infiltrating the hotel and discovering the area where the hostages were being held. How she had managed to do that he had no idea, but if the information proved to be correct, it would be invaluable to the rescue efforts.

Before ending the conversation, she had promised to call him again if she could find out anything about the number and location of the terrorists. He had given her his personal cell phone number, and warned her not to take any unnecessary risks, to which she had responded that he should not worry, because she was a shameless coward. The Superintendent had laughed. He wished he had more cowards like her.

He had relayed the information immediately to the head of SEAL Team 2, Navy Commander Jason McAllister, who had advised him that his men would be ready to mount the simultaneous rescue attempts by 9:00 PM, less than three hours from then. Given the desperate situation of the Governor in La Fortaleza, the time was much later than Maldonado had hoped for, but considering the difficulty of mounting three coordinated and complex operations at the same time, he knew that it could not be helped.

A few seconds after ending that conversation, San Miguel had summoned him to the phone. The call had struck him as odd and filled him with foreboding. There was no reason why the terrorist would need to call him now.

"Your voice sounds tired, my friend," San Miguel said amiably.

Maldonado bit his tongue, preferring not to provoke him. "Go ahead," he said.

"I am calling you on behalf of Adalberto Cacho. He has assumed full command of our struggle for liberation. He is here with me now," San Miguel informed him.

Had Maldonado detected a certain sense of hesitation in his counterpart's voice? His sense of alarm became more acute. He had met Cacho once, shortly after he had been arrested. He had found the Machetero leader to be a very dangerous, very intelligent psychopath who, in order to further his cause, valued human life as much as a person with a cold valued tissue paper.

"Superintendent Maldonado?" a different voice said. Maldonado recognized it instantly. *"Cacho here,"* the Machetero said curtly. *"I was watching the television just now, and I saw Rovira Melendez announce that the Governor had escaped. I don't understand it. Why would Rovira know that? Why would he make that public? He's just making life more difficult for you..."* Cacho paused, and then said, as if it just had occurred to him, *"Oh wait, is that it? Does he want to make life more difficult for you?"*

"Is there a point to this conversation?" Maldonado asked irritably, letting his temper get the better of him. He heard Cacho laugh mirthlessly.

"You're right. I'm just having a little fun. I'm contacting you to let you know that unless the Governor gives up within the next...one hour, I will start shooting five hostages every half hour, until his...safe return."

Maldonado leaned against the desk, too stunned to speak. "We had a deal that nobody else would be killed! *You* were released based on that promise! We're raising the money that you asked for!"

"Sorry, but 'we' does not include 'me'," Cacho answered, emphasizing both words. *"Your deal was with San Miguel,"* he indicated, carelessly disclosing his companion's name. *"I arrived later, remember? Besides, you broke your agreement when the Governor escaped. It's a whole new ballgame."*

"The Governor escaped without our aid. You can't hold us responsible for something that we can't control!"

"If he escaped without your aid, then he can return without it as well. That simplifies your job significantly, doesn't it? All you have to do is call him up and tell him what will happen if he doesn't give up. Being a bleeding heart politician, he'll give up for the good of his people."

"We can't get in contact with him!" Maldonado protested weakly, already anticipating his adversary's reply. It did not take any time for Cacho to express it.

"Do you take me for a fool? It's obvious that he communicated with you. How else would Rovira know that he had escaped? I mean, really, Mr. Superintendent, we're not that stupid."

Maldonado winced. It was as he had feared. By appearing on television to toot his own horn and let the world know that the Governor had escaped, Rovira Melendez had complicated everything a thousand fold.

"Look," he said desperately. "That was a fluke. The Governor got through to us through one of La Fortaleza's landlines. He's probably not even there any more! We need—"

"Then for the sake of the hostages, you'd better find him. You have one hour," Cacho interrupted.

"If you start killing hostages, we will be forced to go in," Maldonado warned him grimly. "We will find you, and we will kill you."

Cacho laughed.

"What you're telling us is that if we do nothing, you won't try to do anything tonight? Really? Do you seriously want me to believe that? That you won't try to come in tonight anyway? Don't you think we know what you're up to? We're waiting for you, so go ahead and try it. From what I heard, you didn't do such a good of a job this afternoon," he gloated. *"And if by any chance your men manage to break through, then all of the hostages will be shot before your men can get to them. It will be messy and bloody, to say the least. Not a nice image for the people who are watching worldwide."*

"I doubt very much that you'd do that, Cacho," Maldonado responded shrewdly. "It would hurt your cause beyond any kind of redemption."

This time the Machetero leader failed to respond immediately, and Maldonado smiled, knowing he had struck a nerve. It was true. The Macheteros had acquired a Robin Hood type of reputation by conducting quick, highly visible raids against the American government and its *capitalist* instruments. There had been some civilian casualties, but they had been few and accidental. Mass murder had never been their style, and it would tarnish the image that they had so carefully cultivated.

Cacho answered slowly and carefully, as if he wanted Maldonado to grasp his thinking process. *"You would be amazed how a year in jail alters your outlook on politics. No nation ever gained its independence by relying on a few daring displays of courage, no matter how impressive they are. They gained their independence in long, heavy struggles, usually long, heavy, bloody struggles, where you either destroy your oppressors or wear them down to a point that they throw up their hands in despair and give you what you want. It's time that the people of Puerto Rico take us seriously, and realize that our struggle is not just a passing fad, that our cause is for real. And if we have to massacre a hotel full of guests in order to be taken seriously, then so be it. Nobody will doubt us after that."*

Maldonado listened with growing dread. He was convinced that Cacho was speaking sincerely, although when the time came, *if* the time came to do the killing, he hoped that Cacho's resolve would falter.

"Do you give me your word that you will not hurt the Governor?" the Superintendent asked, trying to gauge what was at stake.

"No," Cacho responded flatly. *"It is 6:15 right now. I'll tell you what. I'll give you an extra half hour bonus. You have until 7:45 to find him. Do your best."*

Daniel walked into the conference room as Cacho strode out, each man nodding to the other. He stared questioningly at San Miguel, who continued to stand in contemplative silence close to the speakerphone that connected them to the Police Superintendent. Czecka stood mutely behind him like a giant guardian angel.

Their years of close association warned Daniel not to say anything. His boss would acknowledge his presence in due time. Daniel had lost all communications with George. None of the satellite phones carried by him or his men had responded to his latest calls. That could mean they were all indoors, or that they were dead. Only time would tell.

"Any word from George?" San Miguel asked him, after snapping out from his trancelike concentration.

Daniel shook his head. "I can't reach him."

San Miguel accepted his subordinate's statement without further questions. If Daniel assured him that he could not contact George, then there was no possible way that the man could be reached.

"We're leaving," San Miguel said. "Warn the others."

"And Calderon?"

"Calderon knows where and when our rendezvous point will be. He leaves when he leaves."

Daniel regarded his boss with amusement. The glorious day was coming to an abrupt end, and San Miguel was cutting lose all excess weight. Soon, the people's revolution would begin to unravel, and all of the useful fools who had joined it would be laid by the wayside.

Including Adalberto Cacho.

CHAPTER LIV

The Windjammer Café had been designed to cater to that sizable crowd in a cruise ship that either returns to the ship from the daily land excursions after the main dining rooms have closed, or that prefers a less structured, faster, more varied dining experience. Located on the twelfth deck, next to the main swimming pool and the spa, the café could accommodate up to six hundred hungry passengers at any given time, and provide an eclectic selection of dishes, including an Italian buffet, a Chinese-food-Japanese-sushi station, a hamburger-hot-dog-steak-French fries stand, the ever ubiquitous salad bar, and a fairly impressive array of desserts. Its wide entrance—as well as the rest of the facility's interior—had been decorated with dark polished wood, brass fittings and gold trimmings, imitating the appearance of a tall sailing ship, even containing in the middle of its main access an old ship's helm.

Directly opposite to the Windjammer were located the glass doors—now closed—of the Portofino Trattoria, one of the *Mardi Gras'* five elite specialty restaurants that required reservations and charged an extra fare for its food. During the last hour, its darkened interior had been the ideal spot from where John McFadden and Ernan had monitored the movements of the passengers who were periodically brought up in long, single lines to pick up food at the Windjammer Café. Both men had taken turns to spy from behind a long display table covered by a red tablecloth, from where they remained invisible to those on the other side of the glass doors.

The two fugitives had hoped to discover the gaunt figure of the Countess of Gilly in one of the hostage migrations, but so far they had had no luck. Either she had already visited the café before they had sneaked into the trattoria, or she had been kept apart from the other prisoners. She could also have been hurt or killed, but John preferred not to dwell on those possibilities, knowing that the guilt would drive him crazy.

It had not been easy getting there. After beating a hasty retreat from the Stardust Theater's back stage, they had hidden in a broom closet in the fifth deck to discuss where they could find an area open enough to use the satellite phone. Despite his extensive travels on cruise ships, and particularly in the *Mardi Gras*, John was amazed of how difficult it was to locate such a place in the enormous sea vessel. Three locations immediately had come to mind: the main pool, the jogging track on deck fourteen, and the bow of the ship, but chances were that all three places would be watched by the terrorists' sentries. For a brief spell, John had considered using again the small terrace adjacent to the crew's quarters, where the Countess of Gilly had been captured and from where John had plunged into the bay, but that site had proven to be too dangerous.

It had been Ernan who had come up with a solution.

"How about the balcony of the Condessa's cabin?" he had suggested, immediately earning an appreciative look from his companion. The Countess' suite faced San Juan Bay. From its balcony, they would have an unobstructed view of the horizon that would allow their phone to transmit to the hovering communication satellites. Best of all, the cabin was located nine decks above them, almost directly above their heads.

"But how do we get in?" John asked. All cabin doors locked automatically after they closed, and required the use of an electronic key to open.

"Leave that to me," the tiny Filipino had answered cryptically.

Using the nearest of the crew's stairways, the two men had made their way up, painfully conscious of the hollow echoes that their footsteps produced, constantly listening for other noises. They were panting by the time that they reached the fourteenth deck, fatigued not so much by the effort of climbing so many floors as from the constant fear of being discovered.

John had taken a peep into the corridor and found it deserted.

"It seems okay, but we have to be careful," he said to Ernan. "If the terrorists suspect that the Countess was involved in the disappearance of the woman we killed, they may have searched the room. I doubt that they'll still be there, but if anything happens, you run like hell, understood?"

"You don't have to tell me to run, Mr. McFadden," the short maitre had replied. "That comes very naturally to me."

"So how do we get in?"

"Follow me," the Filipino had answered, walking into the corridor. He had not traveled far, detouring just two doors away from the Countess' cabin to get into a large closet where two maintenance carts—laden with towels, sheets, and toiletries—were stored. On the wall next to the closet's entrance was a metallic container, very similar to a fuse box.

"There should be two master keys in here," Ernan said, searching one of the maintenance carts and extracting a screwdriver from a large plastic cup. "Unfortunately, the box is locked, you know, for security reasons. We need to pry it open." The Filipino had handed the screwdriver to his companion. "Here, you're stronger."

John crammed the tip of the screwdriver into the edge of the box, right under its tiny lock, and pulled hard. The lock gave way after the second attempt, and the top of the box swung open. As Ernan had promised, two electronic keys were hanging from two separate hooks.

Taking possession of both of them, they had continued to the Countess' suite and used one to open its door. They had slipped quietly into the suite and bolted the door behind them. Now, if anyone tried to enter, he would have to break down the door.

Ernan had become increasingly nervous as they had neared the cabin, unconsciously rubbing his wounded arm and muttering unintelligible phrases. By the time they had walked in, he was shaking noticeably.

"I feel the ghost of her presence," he had whispered to McFadden in a frightened voice, referring not to the Countess of Gilly, but to the nasty female terrorist that he had smothered with a pillow and hidden under the bed covers just a few hours before.

"Don't be silly!" John had snapped back at him. "Ghosts don't exist, and if they did, hers would be in hell by now."

But inwardly, he could not shake his own uneasy feelings. It almost felt if they were being watched. The room remained undisturbed, just like they had left it that morning. It was a good sign, as far the Countess was concerned. The hijackers did not seem to have tied the disappearance of their female comrade to her. Otherwise, they would have torn the room apart looking for the missing woman. It also showed that they had a very limited amount of people guarding the ship, and did not have the manpower to conduct an exhaustive search. That would change, John suspected, as more terrorists sought refuge on board.

The breakfast still lay on the dining room table, only partially consumed, and the white bedspread covering the Countess' bed remained crisp and untouched, hiding its macabre occupant under its pillows. The stench of death had not yet wafted through the sheets into the suite's air-conditioned atmosphere. *That,* John thought, *was due to change soon.*

The satellite had picked up their phone's signal in record time, and John had been talking to FBI Agent Moylan less than thirty seconds later. John briefed his contact about the location of the hostages and conveyed the reassuring news that the passengers were not being separated into different parts of the ship, except when they were herded in large groups to the Windjammer Café to eat. Moylan had been ecstatic about the news, speculating that if the hostages were not being divided, it probably meant there were not enough terrorists to keep an eye on more than one group. He ended the conversation by promising John that help was on the way, but that he did not want to disclose any details, in case he or Ernan were captured and interrogated. Moylan asked John to stay where he was, where he had satellite reception, in case the authorities needed to contact him.

Of course, there had been no way that John and Ernan would have remained in that suite. Its third, involuntary occupant could not be ignored, even when covered by pillows and a bedspread. Imagined or not, the mood in the cabin was oppressive and suffocating. They needed to get out.

Besides, John could not drive the Countess from his mind. Her name kept creeping into his conversation, distracting him and weighing on his soul. He needed to find out what had happened to her, and if possible, to see how he could help her. *But how?*

"Is there some way of you can get me into the Portofino Restaurant?" he had asked Ernan impulsively.

"The trattoria?" the Filipino's eyes wandered aimlessly as he tried to visualize a route. "Sure. I can get you there. We use the kitchen entrance. Why? Are you hungry for Italian food?"

"Isn't the Portofino in front of the Windjammer Café?"

Ernan had grasped his companion's unstated idea immediately. "We can watch the prisoners from there. Maybe catch sight of the Condessa..."

John had nodded.

"What about the FBI?" Ernan had asked, doubtfully. "They told us to stay here."

"Do you want to stay here?"

"No," Ernan had answered, involuntarily sneaking a glimpse towards the bedroom.

"Then screw the FBI. They don't need us any more. We have to see if we can help the Countess, don't you think?"

"I will take you there."

Even though the Portofino Trattoria had only been two decks below them, they had been forced to take a circuitous route, following several corridors normally accessible only to the crew, briefly entering a pizza and hamburger cafeteria on the jogging and tennis court deck, and then descending through a stairway at the back of the cafeteria that spiraled into the Portofino's kitchen. From there, they had entered the darkened restaurant and, keeping out of sight, almost immediately caught a glimpse of a group of hostages marching out of the Windjammer Café.

However they had not sighted the Countess of Gilly, their frustration mounting with each passing minute. By 7:00 PM, John had grown desperate.

"Where *is* she?" he muttered to himself, hitting the floor with the palm of his hand after the last group of hostages had filed past them. Ernan stared at him, not really knowing what to say. "There must be a way that we can find her."

"You must be patient, Mr. McFadden. In a few hours, help will come."

"You don't understand! She was captured because of my fault."

The Filipino shook his head. "No, Mr. McFadden. She was captured because she chose to follow you after you told her to stay with me."

"I should have stayed with her."

"They would have captured you too. Maybe, they would have shot you dead. And if they had captured you, I would have suffocated inside that washing machine," the small Filipino argued.

John kept a bitter silence. Ernan's reasoning was sound. There was really nothing he could have done, except fight the terrorists. And probably get captured, if not killed. But he could not erase from his mind the last look of the Countess, as he abandoned her to her fate. It had been a look of utter betrayal. No, worse, a look of disappointment, as if for the first time she had seen through his outward façade, and known him for the coward that he was.

"We will be safe here. All we have to do is wait," Ernan repeated, mistaking his friend's failure to respond for a grudging acceptance of their helpless situation.

Just then, a new group of hostages began to make their way into the Windjammer Café. Ernan instinctively lowered his head, and embraced his knees, not bothering to look at the new arrivals, already resigned to the idea that the Countess would not be there. John watched with intense concentration, examining each person, glimpsing at his watch every few seconds.

"Three minutes," he said, sitting next to Ernan.

"What?"

"It takes almost three minutes for the entire group to walk in or out of the cafe," John explained, staring again at his watch as if to confirm his observation. "Twenty minutes between each group to arrive, and ten to twelve more minutes for them to gather their food and leave. They are adhering very strictly to those time limits."

Ernan nodded vaguely, not knowing where his friend was going.

Sensing his confusion, John repeated, "Ten minutes for the hostages to gather whatever food they can and to get out of the café."

Ernan continued to nod. "But the Condessa, she was not there, was she?"

John did not answer immediately, lost in his own thoughts. "Eh? No, she was not there. But have you noticed how many guards walk up and down with the hostages?"

Ernan shook his head.

"Two," John responded to his own question. "Two guards. One at the beginning of the line, and one at the end. And it's a long line. That means that if anyone tried to escape, except maybe those at the beginning or the end of the line, they could do it easily."

"But..." Ernan tentatively wagged a finger, to remind the Australian, "but that man on the stage, he said to the hostages that each of them had a number, and that if anyone escaped, they would shoot the hostage with the number in front and the one with the number behind the person who had escaped."

It was a convoluted explanation, but John nodded in agreement. Each hostage had been assigned a specific number. The terrorists knew that they did not have the manpower to keep in sight every person moving up and down from the Stardust Theater to the Windjammer Café. However, it did not matter, since they had threatened to kill the person in front and behind anyone who escaped. Thus, the terrorists had placed the onus on each passenger to make certain that those in front and in the back of them would not escape, or they would forfeit their lives. Even unguarded, nobody would dare to escape.

"I have been watching the guards," John stated. "It's always the same two, that short-haired girl in short shorts and the man who came up to where we were hiding back stage."

"The fart man?" Ernan asked seriously, raising both eyebrows and forcing John to stifle a chuckle.

"The fart man," he confirmed. "Why not more? Because they don't have that many more, and some have to stay in the theater guarding those who remain, don't you think? And guarding the ship, of course."

"That would be the logical conclusion, yes."

"I don't think that there must be more than three of them down there, in the theater, if that many," John said. It was a bold but not an unreasonable assumption.

This time, both men nodded. A contemplative silence followed.

"And always, when the hostages get here, one of them, the woman usually goes into the café, and the other one waits by the door," John said as an afterthought. He continued to deliberate under Ernan's watchful gaze. "Have you seen them count?"

"What?" The last question took Ernan by surprise.

"Have you seen the terrorists count the hostages when they go in or out of the restaurant?"

The Filipino examined John's face with growing concern. For some reason, he did not like the turn that the conversation was taking. "I haven't noticed," he confessed.

"Well I have. You know how many times they have counted the number of hostages coming out of the Windjammer Cafe? Zero! I think that they are so confident that nobody will escape that they don't even bother to check if any of the hostages are missing."

"That is because they know that nobody will let the other hostages escape. It's too risky!"

"But what if instead of escaping, somebody joined them?"

"You mean, like somebody who wanted to eat dinner twice, and joined the line even though they did not call their number?"

"I mean like somebody who is hiding in the ship joins the line and gets into the theater..."

Ernan gazed at his friend uncomprehendingly and then his eyes widened. "Oh no, Mr. McFadden, that is crazy talk! Why would you do a thing like that?"

"To see if I can find her down there."

"It's madness! Maybe they don't count up here, but they count when the hostages return to the theater. You will be found out!"

"I don't think that they count down there either," John replied. "The interval between the time that each group comes up is too short. If they started counting the hostages, it would take them much longer."

"You don't know that for a certainty. What if you are wrong and they count downstairs?"

"If they do, they won't get very upset if they get two hundred and one instead of two hundred. If it was one hundred and ninety-nine, or anything less than two hundred, they would probably check again. But more than two hundred? They'll probably think that they miscounted. And that's if they count at all, which I don't think they will."

"But suppose you get into the theater, what will you do then?"

"I told you already. Search for the Countess, of course," John replied as if it were the most normal thing to do.

Ernan shook his head vigorously. He was beginning to feel very scared. "That is not what I mean, Mr. McFadden. What I meant is—"

"I know, I know. I'm being very obtuse," John answered before his friend could finish. "I don't know what I'll do once I'm there. I'll try to help the Countess any way that I can, even if it's just keeping her company until we're all rescued." He sighed, and slapped Ernan's shoulder. "Don't look so glum! Look, I know it's crazy. I'm a natural born coward, and I'd rather stay here. But it's..." he shook his head, lost for words. "She has to know that I didn't leave her behind. If something happens to her, and she never finds out that I cared enough for her to come back, I won't be able to live with myself. I may not be able to save her, but at least I can unbreak her heart."

"Mr. McFadden, if I may be so bold. But have you considered that maybe she doesn't care about you as much as you think she does?" Ernan suggested shrewdly, in a last desperate attempt to convince him to stay. "Maybe her heart is not broken because you left, and she will not appreciate as much as you think that you came back."

John winced, as if he had been doused with a bucket of cold water. *Could Ernan be right? Could he actually be fooling himself, by thinking that the Countess gave a hoot about what he did or did not do?* He doubted it. He had known the Countess forever, and counted her as a real and dear friend. They had never shared a bed, and she paid him generously for the time they spent together, but both enjoyed each other's company immensely, and had grown very fond of each other through the years. The hurt he had seen in her eyes as he jumped into the bay had been real. He ought to know. He made his living from reading others' expressions.

"I think she cares," he answered. "But you know what? Even if she didn't, this is something that I must do for myself." John took a peek from behind the table and saw that the entrance to the Windjammer Café was deserted. He stood up and walked quickly to the glass doors of the Portofino Trattoria, grabbing their handles and moving them to see if the doors were open. They were locked, but by turning a latch at the metal bottom frame of the right door, he managed to open it.

He examined his watch and saw that more than five minutes had passed since the last group had exited the café. Soon, the next batch of hostages would be coming up the stairs. Hurrying back to Ernan, he pulled out the satellite phone from his pocket.

"Here!" he said, handing the telephone to the Filipino, who took it with a terrified expression. "I'm going to go to the café, and join the next group." Ernan opened his mouth to protest, but John quieted him. "My mind is made up, and there's hardly any time left. Now listen. I want you to stay here until our rescuers come. You'll be safe here. If you feel the need to report anything to the FBI, use the phone. The number is marked under "FBI". You have the master key, you can use it to get into any of the suites. It doesn't have to be the Countess' cabin."

He extended his hand and Ernan shook it hesitantly. Then the Filipino embraced John.

"God bless you and be with you, Mr. McFadden," he said with tears in his eyes. "I will be praying for your and the Condessa's safe return."

"Thank you, my friend. I'll see you when this is over, okay?" he said, smiling more confidently that he felt. "Now close the door behind me. I don't want anyone getting in here."

John heard Ernan click the trattoria's glass door behind him, as he ambled across the corridor towards the café, and shuddered. *He was on his own now.*

His plan was simple. He would hide behind one of the buffet tables, and when the crowd began to move in, grab a plate and mingle with the others. When they left, he would leave with them. It should work, at least until he got to the theater.

But as he entered the Windjammer Café, he almost bumped into a man who appeared out of nowhere, startling him out of his wits. "Good God!" he muttered involuntarily.

The unexpected person, a curly blond man in his twenties, seemed as surprised as him. He was holding a steaming tray of hamburgers with two towels, and nearly spilled it on John.

A kitchen aide, the Australian realized too late. Further away, two other waiters looked at them with curiosity and then continued with their chores. *How could he have been so stupid,* he thought. *Somebody had to prepare the food for the hostages. The idea had completely slipped his mind. And he was going to outwit the terrorists?*

"Are you from the next group?" the waiter asked with a thick Eastern European accent, looking for the others.

John hesitated. He could try to brazen it out, and invent some story to distract him and drive him away, or tell him the truth and hope that as a fellow hostage, the waiter would help him. He opted for a variation of the latter alternative.

"I became separated from the rest of my group and I'm afraid that if they see me, they'll think that I was trying to escape and kill me," he said in a terrified voice, not faking his fear. "Please help me to hide until the next group comes in, so I can then join them and return to the theater."

The waiter stared at him with an expression of uncertainty, his blue eyes wavering between the risk he would undertake aiding a fugitive— the crew had obviously been threatened to death by the terrorists—and his natural sympathy for the lost passenger. Then he nodded once, curtly. "This way," he said, pointing to the stand holding the Italian pasta and pizzas. "Hide behind the table. A lot of people come here and you'll be able to mingle with them."

John thanked him and headed towards the table.

"Wait," the waiter called out after him.

John turned, his pulse racing.

"Take this," the man said, giving him an empty plate. "It will look more believable if it seems that you're taking some food."

The muted noise of feet coming up the carpeted metal stairway made both men turn their heads towards the entrance of the café.

"They are coming! Quick!" the food attendant said, pointing towards the buffet table. John scurried towards the indicated spot and hid behind the left end of the long, white cloth-covered food stand.

A few seconds later, the cafeteria became flooded with the noises of incoming people, followed by the busy sounds of plates and cutlery. Soon hushed voices began to approach the front and sides of the table, as the crowd inside the café expanded.

John took a deep breath and dropped his fork on the wooden floor. Then he stood and leaned to pick it up. Those people on the other side of the table did not notice him, but a portly female in her late fifties who had begun to circumnavigate the table while stuffing as much food as she could into her plate, stepped back with a startled gesture.

"My goodness!" she said in a very surprised, somewhat irritated voice. "Where did *you* come from?"

John flashed a smile, regarding her with his most charming expression. "I do apologize, miss," he said with a much more thicker Australian accent than the more neutral tone that he normally used, knowing that it would appeal to her. "I move so fast that sometimes I tend to startle people." He grabbed a spatula and scooped out of a hot tray a large piece of lasagna. "Would you like some? Before it disappears?" he asked her in a conspiratorial tone.

The hard-set lines around the woman's mouth melted into a pleasant grin, as she allowed him to accommodate the lasagna on her plate. "Well, thank you! With all of these hungry people, you have to move fast," she replied in a flirty voice. John groaned inwardly, but continued to smile.

For the next ten minutes, the throng of hungry hostages hovered over the dozen serving tables, grabbing as many provisions as they could, while a woman armed with an AK-47 rifle watched them with the half bored expression of someone who had already seen the show several times before. As the time expired, she placed a whistle hanging about her neck in her lips and blew it sharply three times.

"Time is over! Form the line!" she shouted with a harsh strength that belied her feminine, five-foot frame. She moved towards the furthest end of the café, close to the kitchen doors, passing very close to John and directing an appraising look at the handsome Australian.

John began to stride towards the center of the crowd, where the hostages were already beginning to assemble. The volume of noise rose significantly, as people compared their assigned numbers or looked for the same faces that had preceded or followed them when they had come up to the Windjammer Café. Faster than he expected, the throng began to congeal into a long, cramped file.

Holding on to his plate, John skirted the forming column, moving surreptitiously among the mass of people who were trying to find their places. He stopped close to the middle of the line, moving forward when a woman in front of him eyed him with suspicious fear and grabbed the arm of the man next to her—presumably her husband. John continued to skip along the line, as those ahead of him kept closing the gap that he created and forcing him to shift towards the front.

For a moment, John feared that nobody would allow him to slip in unnoticed, progressively getting displaced towards the head of the agglomerating hostages. There was a particularly harrowing moment when a short, fat man accused him of trying to sneak into his place and prompted others around him to stare at him uncomfortably. But two persons later, he came upon a tall, lanky man who never gave him a second glance, and he lingered there. A freckled, teen-aged girl standing behind him observed him hesitantly and opened her mouth to speak, but by then the column of prisoners had begun to move and she automatically followed John as he marched forward.

When he exited the café, he darted a quick look towards the door of the Portofino Trattoria, and thought he caught a glimpse of Ernan's scared eyes peering from behind a table. It was all in his imagination, he knew. There was no way that he could see into the darkened restaurant.

Few of the hostages spoke to each other, and those who did spoke in hushed whispers. They seemed to walk in a daze, keeping their eyes on the floor or on the backs of those ahead of them. John settled into the rhythm of the long, moving line, concentrating on each step he descended, listening to the footsteps that made the carpeted staircase vibrate, watching the hostages' hands sliding on the polished wood banisters.

He felt a mixture of utter terror and breathless excitement, anticipating the surprised look of the Countess when she saw him walk into the theater and realized the risk he had taken to find her. It would be a story that he would be able to relate in dinner conversations for the rest of his life. *If he survived.*

Just as he had guessed, there were no guards watching the line. The fear of the indiscriminate executions that the terrorists had instilled on their hostages had proven to be a very effective deterrent. Nobody dared to break away.

The armed woman leading the column of diners stopped at the main entrance to the Stardust Theater, and allowed her prisoners to walk in. John noticed that she was counting the hostages in an absent, uninterested fashion as they entered the theater. When he passed by her, he turned right immediately, into the lane between the last row of seats in the mezzanine and the slightly higher balcony accommodations behind it. He stopped after a dozen paces, ostensibly to eat out of his plate, watching the hijacker furtively.

As the last of the hostages came in, the armed woman's expression changed to one of confusion. She looked uncertainly around her, prompting John to shift his gaze away from her. He waited, slowly chewing on a hamburger that he could hardly swallow because his throat felt so dry, hoping that she would move on, too busy to do a recount.

Then a whistle blew behind him, and he almost dropped his plate. His heart beating so hard that he could hardly stop his hands from shaking, he heard the voice of the man who had been on the stage announce, "Numbers one thousand two hundred and one, to one thousand four hundred! Form a line!"

People from all over the theater began to stand up and head for the central aisle of the mezzanine, which led to the theater's main exit. The relatively noiseless hall hummed with the muted voices of passengers searching for their places in the line. John looked back at the female terrorist, and saw that she was busy overlooking the organization of the new column of diners. He sighed with relief.

Slowly, he made his way inside the main floor, looking for the Countess. It was not easy. The theater had been designed to hold over one thousand spectators. It occupied about a sixth of the fifth and sixth decks of the *Mardi Gras*, with a second floor of balconies. A gigantic, glass chandelier hung from its high ceiling, while the sides of its open stage were decorated with glittering curtains that showed images of scantily dressed chorus girls. The floor was covered by a plush, red carpet laced with a design of golden ropes and anchors, a motif that had been reproduced in gold bas-relief on the façade of the surrounding balconies.

Presently holding a crowd of almost two and one half times its number of seats, the passengers and crew had spilled onto the floor on the aisles, to the space in front of the stage, and into any other available area in the main floor. Some families huddled in close circles, sometimes sitting on the hand rests or the floor between the rows of seats.

John had not realized how difficult it would be to find the Countess. Standing near the back of the theater, with most of the heads turned away from him, it was nearly impossible to see her face. She could even be on the second floor. In order to conduct a thorough search, he would have to walk through the mezzanine, where most of the transit of the captives occurred when the lines to go to the Windjammer Café were formed or when the hostages lined up to go to the restrooms. If he started to wander indiscriminately through the hall, he would surely attract the attention of the bad guys.

He decided to move whenever a new line formed or disbanded and—like now—the crowd stirred. That way, he could meander through the theater unnoticed. The throng that had responded to the numbers announced over the public address system was already thinning, giving him a better view of the entire theater. Therefore, he opted to stay where he was and make his initial scan of the hostages from there.

And then he saw her.

She had been in plain view, all along. He just had skimmed over her, distracted by the flow of the people in front of her. And what he saw filled him with dread and uncontrollable anger.

Half a dozen, evenly spaced columns supported the second floor of the theater. The columns were hardly visible, except when you had the misfortune to sit behind one of them. But now, there were persons tied to some of the pillars. And one of those persons was the Countess.

She was sitting on the edge of the balcony area in the mezzanine, facing forward, her wrists bound behind the column closest to the right side of the stage. From where he stood, he could not tell if she was still alive. Her head was down, and a sign hung from a string around her neck announcing in black, magic marker letters: "I TRIED TO ESCAPE."

Not pausing to think, John strode towards his friend, stepping over and pushing his way through the scores of passengers blocking his way. Some of the people complained out loud or cursed him, but he did not hear them, his mind flooded with grief and rage. *How dare they,* he thought. *How could they treat her like that?*

The new line of hostages going to the Windjammer Café began to exit the theater, masking the stir that John had created as he moved towards the Countess. But somehow she sensed his arrival, raising her head a few seconds before he got there, and looking in his direction. There was a purple bruise on her left cheek, and her eyes were watery and bloodshot.

A thin, loving smile appeared on her dry, cracked lips. Her expression radiated unspoken pride.

"You're here, I see," she said in a tired voice, as he approached.

"I thought I'd surprise you, although you don't seem that surprised," he replied, his voice shaking with emotion as he silently examined her.

"I knew you would come back," she stated with a certainty that admitted no denial.

"Then you know me better than I know myself. I was running away, you know."

"Shhhhhh!" she hissed softly, directing a warning look towards the stage. "They will hear you."

The short, thin terrorist who seemed to be the leader of the group was sitting on the edge of the stage about two dozen yards away, trying to engage in a conversation with two attractive female passengers sitting in the front row who warily answered his questions. There was another armed man by the main entrance, but John could discover no others. He assumed that there would be at least one more guard—maybe more—on the second floor, but if so, he could not see them.

"I'm going to untie you," he whispered to her.

"No, *mon cher*," she pleaded under her breath. "This will get you nowhere. They will see you and hurt you, and I will still be tied up."

John shook his head. "No. They are not paying any attention. Now is the time to do it. When I release you, keep your arms behind your back until the next group to the Windjammer Café is called. Then, when everybody stands up, we move."

"Please! Don't do this foolish thing!" she begged him.

"Be still!" John squeezed between a middle-aged couple that was standing next to the Countess, and placed his right hand behind the column. The couple glanced at him nervously and edged away, but they said nothing.

While continuing to look at the man sitting on the stage, John located the Countess' tied hands and began to feel for the knot. The hands were bound by a silky type of rope that coiled tightly several times around each of her wrists.

The knot was located between her two hands, in a very difficult place to reach. Even worse, it had been tightened into a small, tangled lump that bit into the Countess' swollen flesh and made it almost impossible for John to untie it blindly. The Australian struggled for a couple of minutes, stopping whenever the thin terrorist cast a bored look in his general direction, his armpits quickly becoming drenched in sweat. Still, the knot remained as securely fastened as ever.

Suddenly, his hand was slapped away from the Countess' wrists. Nearly startled out of his wits, John looked back into the balcony section behind him, and was confronted by the bearded face of a huge, bear-like man sitting directly behind the column.

"Don't move," the man warned him in a deep, soft, Southern drawl. "I'll untie her. Just cover me, okay?"

John moved his head once in the affirmative, slowly removing his stiff arm from behind the column.

The bearded stranger began to untie the bound wrists of the Countess, but even using both of his hands, it took him several minutes to undo the knot.

"There you go," the man said, leaning forward to speak as close as he could to the Countess and John, as he finally freed her from her ties. The Countess winced as her sore arms moved after being constrained for such a long time, but she kept them behind her. "My wife and I are holding you and covering your hands," the bear-like man added. "Nobody can see that you're free."

"Thank you," John said, moved by the man's kindness. "Bless you for taking the risk to help us."

"It's our pleasure, believe me," the man responded. "I'm just sorry we didn't do it before. Now we're going to let go her hands, so be sure that you hold her, okay? Because she might lose her balance and fall."

John nodded, and placed an arm behind the Condessa, around her waist. It was an awkward pose, since the balcony on which the Countess sat was at about the height of John's shoulder, but nobody seemed to notice.

The large Southerner sat back, looking casually around him.

John and the Countess remained as they were until the last batch of hostages that had gone up to the Windjammer Café began to flow back into the theater a short time later. As before, the volume of the conversation rose when the incoming prisoners began to move back to their places, some finding them occupied by opportunistic neighbors.

The thin man sitting on the stage watched them enter and, saying something to the two women he had been flirting with, he stood up and walked to a stool on the center of the stage, where he had left his hand microphone. He picked it up and switched it on, tapping it to hear if it was working.

"Okay," he said in a pleasant, tour-guide sort of voice, "numbers from one thousand four hundred and one to one thousand six hundred, it's time to get your dinner."

A new rumble of the two hundred hostages who began to get up from their places to form a new column followed the announcement. In the momentary disorder that followed, John embraced the Countess and pulled her down from the edge of the balcony, tearing away with his hands the sign that had been hanging from her neck and letting it slip to the floor.

"Can you walk?" he asked her, and she nodded curtly. He turned his head towards the good Samaritan who had helped him, to warn him that for his own safety he should also go, but he and his wife had already left.

John grabbed the Countess' hand and gently pulled her after him, walking further down the semicircular aisle that existed between the main theater seats and the balconies.

"Follow me," he said, leading her to a short flight of carpeted steps that existed at the end of the balcony closest to the stage, and that connected to an enclosed corridor behind the balcony seats. He knew that if the thin terrorist looked in their direction he would see them climbing the stairs and heading in the opposite direction from where the line to the Windjammer Café was forming, but he hoped that the man would still be more interested in continuing his conversation with the two sexy women.

"This way," he told the Countess, taking her up the stairs, unwilling to look at the stage. An idea had begun to form in his mind. If it worked, they would be able to leave the theater now. But they would have to act fast. The Countess seemed exhausted, and even though she continued to follow him without complaining, they had a very hard time negotiating their way through the people strewn or standing on almost every square inch of the crowded steps.

When they reached the top of the stairs, the two friends turned to the right into the aisle behind the balcony seats. John sighed with relief as they lost sight of the man sitting on the stage.

It was darker there, and even more crowded than in the mezzanine, as many of the passengers and entire families tried to put as much distance between the terrorists and themselves as possible. It was flawed thinking on their part, John realized. Apart from the narrow stairway that he and the Countess had just used to get out of the main hall, the only other way to get out of the corridor was through an emergency exit to their left—which had been chained shut—or through the Stardust's main exit, further to their right. In the case of a panic, the packed hallway could turn into a deathtrap.

"We have to get out of here," John told the Countess, as he paused for a moment to let his companion catch her breath.

"But *mon cher*, we can only leave through the main exit, where the line is forming, the line to the cafeteria," the Countess countered, looking confusedly about her, trying to discover some other escape route that she was not aware of.

"Precisely," John answered, pulling her by the hand and renewing his march towards the main exit.

"But the door...It will be watched!"

"Maybe, maybe not." John stopped and stared into the Countess' eyes. "I have an idea. Do you trust me?"

The Countess stared at him and smiled. "With my life. I always have."

John embraced her and kissed her on the cheek. "Then follow me, and do exactly as I do."

As they continued to make their way towards the central exit through the dark, semicircular corridor, John reviewed his plan one last time in his mind. They could not remain in the theater indefinitely. Sooner or later, one of the terrorists was bound to discover that the Countess was missing from the column where she had been tied, and he would raise the alarm, so the less time they spent in the Stardust, the better their chances of survival.

There were only two ways to escape from the theater: using the backstage exit, which meant climbing onto the stage and somehow sneaking unobserved past the thin terrorist sitting there; or infiltrating the food line that was about to leave for the Windjammer Cafe. He had opted for the second alternative.

It would be risky, but it could be done. After all, he had done it in the opposite direction. His key concern was whether there would be somebody at the entrance counting the hostages as they passed by, or if, as when he had left the Windjammer Café, there would only be a guard leading and another one following the line. If the latter was the case, then the chances of slipping into the line, and then escaping before they reached the café, were not farfetched. They would have to deal with the overzealous hostages who would be afraid of reprisals. But he had thought of a solution for that as well.

However, he first had to reach and join the column of departing hostages before it made its way out of the theater. If not, he and the Countess would have to wait almost half an hour before the next batch of prisoners left for the cafe, and he was afraid that by that time, the Countess' disappearance would be noted, no matter how distracted the terrorists were.

To his relief, as he rounded the corridor, he was greeted by the view of the newly formed line. It was already moving out of the theater like a giant, uncoordinated centipede. Squeezing the Countess' hand, John pressed forward through the crowd until he reached the edge of the marching prisoners, and surreptitiously searched for guards at the entrance. There were none. As he had imagined, the short-haired woman with the whistle had left at the head of the column, while the second terrorist would follow at the rear, closing the theater's doors when the last of the hostages had exited.

The prisoners kept very close to each other, making certain that they did not lose their place in the line. As John approached them, they closed their ranks even more, staring at the two arriving strangers with suspicion. John looked to his left, and noticed that the beginning of the line had already disappeared upwards into the ship's main stairway, while in the opposite direction, the end of the line still extended all the way down to the stage.

He examined with intense interest the people filing past him, waiting for the right moment to step in. He had made his living by reading people's faces—mostly women's—and their body language, and by making instant decisions about their characters, priding himself on his powers of observation. Now, he would have to test them to stay alive.

For five interminable seconds he waited, scanning the crowd and marking its steady progress. Then, abruptly, he cut into the line, pulling the Countess with him. He stepped in front of a young looking man with a few scattered hairs growing over his lip, and a deep-red, sunburned complexion who, surprised by the unexpected intrusion, nearly tripped over his flip flops. John had seen him several times at the pool during the cruise, one of several college students taking a Caribbean vacation before returning to their frigid alma maters. He was wearing a light blue, short-sleeved T-shirt that identified him as a North Carolina Tarheel, and shredded denim shorts.

"Please forgive me but," John inquired in an anxious tone, walking along him as he spoke, "what is your number?"

"One thousand, four hundred and sixty-two," he replied, somewhat flustered.

"Oh dear," John said to the Countess, "we're way, way behind..."

"I'm one thousand, four hundred and sixty one," a middle-aged woman with a raspy voice and jet-black hair walking in front of them said zealously, casting at them a dark stare. John had also seen her before. She was one of the regulars at the Casino.

"We're numbers one thousand, four hundred twenty-four and twenty-five," he confessed in a hushed whisper to the two hostages. "She was in the restroom when the announcement for our group was made, and we nearly missed it."

"Well, you're way off your number," the lady said in a peevish, exasperated tone. "You've got to move up."

"I'm afraid that if we start moving up now they'll think we're escaping," John said, more to the sunburned college boy than to the obnoxious casino player. "Do you mind if we stay here until we get upstairs?" he asked timidly, just as they emerged from the theater. To his surprise, he discovered an armed man standing a few yards ahead of the line, reviewing the progress of the hostages.

The North Carolina student looked inquiringly at the black haired lady, who in turn stared at the terrorist and decided not to make a scene, huffing reproachfully and turning away from the other three.

"I guess there's no harm in that," the college boy answered.

John felt the Countess squeeze his hand hard twice, and saw her look away from the guard. Without exchanging words, he realized immediately what was happening: the terrorist standing by the exit had been one of the gunmen who had captured her. Instinctively, he stepped between the guard and the Countess, blocking the man's view of her face. He wondered if the hijacker had seen *him* before, when he had jumped off the ship, and if so, whether he would recognize him now. He tried to calm himself by thinking that the odds of the man associating him with the fugitive he had glimpsed for scarcely second, diving from the fourth level deck—or of believing that somehow John had returned to the ship— would be very slim indeed.

However, even as he was thinking that, the armed man fixed his eyes directly on him. He was in his mid-thirties, sporting a dark goatee, with a body frame bordering towards the heavyset former athlete who had let himself go. John did not remember him at all, but the man's deadpan expression changed to a curious stare, and he began to approach them with increasing speed. John's heart sank, and he braced himself to flee, holding on firmly to the Countess' hand.

"Hey, you!" the man shouted, and John turned to face him. But the man was addressing someone behind him, and when John looked back, he noticed that there was a wide gap in the line.

"Stay close together!" the terrorist ordered to an older man with a walrus mustache who had stopped walking, distracted by a conversation with another woman.

The harassed passenger mumbled an apology, and grabbing by the arm the portly woman to whom he had been talking, hurriedly dragged her forward while she glared at him and at the terrorist.

John and the Countess exchanged a quick look of relief, and continued to trek forward, staring straight ahead. They passed so closely by the armed man that they could smell the strong reek of alcohol in his breath. Apparently, he had helped himself to some of the ample stores of spirits in the theater's bar.

As they left the terrorist behind and reached the ship's main staircase, John relaxed his grip on the Countess, and they began to climb the stairs' wide, padded steps. The main exit of the Stardust Theater was located on the *Mardi Gras'* fifth level, near the bow. The hostages would have to walk up seven more decks before they got to the Windjammer Café. During the ship's voyage to San Juan, John and the Countess had avoided using the elevators and climbed up and down the stairs. The exercise had helped to keep them fit, and burned some of the enormous amount of calories that they were fed on a daily basis. But among the passengers, there were some that found even climbing from one deck to another a taxing experience. Now, those passengers slowed the progress of the line, stopping to take in deep breaths, leaning on the banisters.

As the file slowly snaked up the stairway, John planned his next move. He would make a dash for freedom halfway up to the café, when the two armed escorts would be separated from each other by hundreds of hostages and at least four levels of the ship.

"We're leaving the line soon," he whispered to the Countess. "Just follow me."

The Countess nodded slightly, without looking at him.

When they reached the Casino on the eighth level, John stepped out of the line and knelt on one knee, ostensibly to tie a lose shoelace. The

Countess stayed by his side, waiting patiently for him to finish. John looked around him, to ascertain that none of the guards were close, and then stood up. Grabbing the Countess' hand, he began to walk into the Casino.

However, he had taken only a couple of steps when a male voice shouted, "Hey! You can't leave! Get back here!"

John looked back and saw that the line had stopped moving, and that several of the hostages were staring at him and the Countess with horrified expressions. The beefy man with the walrus mustache had abandoned his portly female companion, and now approached him and seized him roughly by the arm.

"You can't leave!" he said indignantly. "You'll get the people in the front and back of you killed!"

Others in the stalled file voiced their disapproval. The man began to pull John back into the line.

"You don't understand!" John tried to explain over the shouts of hostages. "We don't have any assigned numbers. If she stays in the line," he said, pointing to the Countess, "they'll kill her!"

But the man would not release him, and as more people crammed into the stairs, the protests grew more numerous and louder.

Alarmed, John tried to pull away, but the animated walrus-mustached man's hand tightened harder around his arm. "You're not going anywhere!" he bellowed in an angry voice.

A few of the other passengers began to move towards them, apparently to help the mustached man drag the two strays back into the fold. With the corner of his eye John observed as in the stairs behind him, some of the hostages crowded there began to open up a way for someone from below to come through.

Realizing that their chances of escape were quickly evaporating, John crossed his right leg behind the man who had latched on to him, pulled him hard in his direction, and when the man resisted, reversed his thrust, pushing the walrus-mustached hostage over his leg. The man lost his balance and fell backwards, releasing John's arm and momentarily blocking the way of the others who were approaching him.

Almost at the same instant, the terrorist at the rear of the line cleared his head over the eighth deck's floor, and as he continued to climb, leveled his rifle at the small group gathered in the Casino.

"Stay where you are!" he shouted at the top of his lungs, over the scared voices of the hostages who were trying to explain to him what was happening.

John and the Countess ran into the Casino, seeking cover behind the curving rows of slot machines.

"Get out of the way!" they heard the gunman behind them shout at the hostages still in his way, and then several shots rang out, piercing the metal casings and shattering the glass of several of the gaming machines behind them.

But by that time, the fleeing couple had moved out of the terrorist's line of fire, and was making its way towards the center of the Casino. John abruptly turned right, and led the Countess to a glass door on a wall framed by two gray, Gothic-looking columns that were topped by carved images of goblins and a red neon sign that read "The Catacombs". McFadden pulled the door open, and they rushed inside without saying a word, stepping from the glittering, red-carpeted décor of the Casino into a gloomy, dungeon-like hall.

The Catacombs was a two-story nightclub decorated in a medieval-vampire-castle, architectural nightmare style, which could be accessed both from the Casino and from the seventh level promenade. The Countess and John knew it well, it being one of the haunts they frequented during the late hours of the night for a nightcap, when the usually quiet nightspot gathered the last of the day's revelers to continue partying until the wee hours of the morning. The two friends would sit in one of the red-velvet backed, darkened, circular booths close to the dance floor on the lower level and people-watch, occasionally dancing when the mood suited them.

The white Plexiglas floor of the upper level, usually illuminated at night, showed now as dull gray under their hurrying feet in the barely lit barroom. Trying to put some distance between them and their pursuer, the two friends rushed down a narrow spiral staircase that connected the nightclub's two floors, and walked across the dancing floor to behind the main bar.

"You hide here," John said to the Countess, helping her to crawl into a gloomy, small space under bar, between two metal kegs of beer. The darkness of the cramped space, supplemented by the lack of lights in the nightclub, made her invisible even when John looked under the bar's counter.

Footsteps on the upper level made John look up apprehensively and raise a warning finger over his lips. He began to search for a place to hide, starting to move from behind the bar, but just then he heard the terrorist running down the spiral stairs. Knowing he had no time to search for a better hiding place, he reversed his steps and slipped behind a satin, blood-red curtain decorating the wall at the back of the serving counter.

"I know you're here!" a male voice said a few seconds later. "I saw you come in. The more time you make me waste searching for you, the harder it will be for you and your lady friend when I find you."

The voice seemed to get closer with every word that the terrorist uttered, even though John could not place the man in relation with the rest of the floor.

Then the gunman stopped talking altogether. John strained his ears to detect his movements, but could hear nothing. For an excruciatingly long time he waited, afraid that the heavy sound of his breathing would give him away. His legs began to shake from the strain of standing on his toes.

Damn that man in the line, he thought to himself. *Damn him to hell a thousand times! He was supposed to be helping his fellow hostages, not the terrorists! How easily some people became instruments of their torturers! If he ever survived this ordeal,* he promised himself, *he would find the man with the walrus mustache and really let him know what he thought about him.*

But as the seconds became minutes, nothing happened. *It was just too quiet for anybody to still be out there,* John thought. *Maybe the man had exited through the lower level door of the nightclub.*

He decided to take a very careful peek outside. With two fingers, he grabbed the rim of the curtain and gingerly began to inch it to one side, while edging his head towards the resulting orifice.

He had no time to finish. The curtain suddenly flew open, exposing him to the same goateed terrorist that he had seen at the exit of the Stardust Theater. Before he could move, the man crashed the butt of his rifle into his stomach, driving the air out of his lungs and causing him to pitch forward. John desperately tried to grasp his aggressor by his shirt as his knees buckled, but the terrorist easily avoided him.

Gasping for air, John held on to the man's knees, his vision filled with thousands of small, multicolored stars. The gunman struck his face with his right knee, making John lose his grip and fall to the floor, where the terrorist began to pummel him with his iron-tipped construction boots. McFadden contracted his body into the fetal position, covering his head with his arms, but the terrorist's blows became stronger and more deliberate.

"I...hate...stupid...hostages...that...make...me...lose...my...time!"   the terrorist stated with evident satisfaction, punctuating every word with a kick.

One blow struck John on the top of his head and snapped it back, nearly making him lose consciousness. With a last, frantic effort, he grabbed on to one of the man's boots and hung on to it, nearly making him lose his balance. But the gunman stepped hard on his fingers with his free foot, forcing John to release him, and with even more vigor, renewed his kicks, cursing loudly as he did so.

Then his words slurred and turned into an unintelligible high-pitched scream—whether from rage or shock John could not tell—and the kicking stopped. John dazedly looked up in time to see the man turning away from him and holding a hand over his back, blood oozing through his fingers. Dropping his rifle, the terrorist groaned as a long, cutting knife sliced in and out of his stomach twice.

"Stop! Please!" the man yelled, trying to grab the knife and nearly losing four of his fingers as the knife's edge cut through them. Then his legs failed him and he crumpled onto the floor, landing next to John.

Barely conscious, the Australian pushed himself upwards with his right arm, his body pulsing with raw pain, and tried to sit up. He saw the terrorist lying fully stretched behind the bar, his eyes gazing confusedly at him. A crimson puddle of blood continued to expand on the floor from his lower back and his stomach, much like thick red ink spilling from a bottle.

John instinctively drew back as the expanding stain threatened to reach his pants, avoiding it, in his confused mind, as if the terrorist's blood carried lethal poison or some deadly infecting agent with it. He clumsily tried to get up, stumbling as he did so. But a strong hand—surprisingly strong for a seventy-year old woman—grasped his arm and steadied him back to his feet.

Below him, the dying man passively observed as the two friends embraced, the last few vestiges of comprehension in his eyes finally ebbing into a vacant stare.

The Countess smiled weakly, evidently shaken. Her hand, still holding the long cutting knife that she had thrust several times into the terrorist's body, was dyed in red almost up to her wrist. She examined John's face with concerned care, but seemed relieved by what she saw.

"We have to stop getting these kinds of beatings, *mon cher*," she said, widening her smile and tenderly touching a big bruise on John's forehead. He winced. "You have a nasty bump," she said. She turned to the bar and, grabbing a towel, slid open the lid of the icebox under the bar's counter, packing some ice into the towel. "Here, put this on your head."

John did as ordered, still trying to rearrange his jumbled thoughts. "We should go before they start looking for us," he said.

"*Oui*," the Countess responded. She knelt beside the body of the goateed terrorist and searched his jacket, retrieving three ammunition clips, plus a folded switchblade and a satellite phone that she pulled out of his right pants pocket. Then she grabbed the dead man's rifle, and handed it to John. "We may need all of this before the day is over," she told him. "Especially if this ship sails away with us in it."

"Then let's do everything possible to make sure that it doesn't sail," John responded.

Taking a black tablecloth from one of the round tables surrounding the dance floor, they covered the corpse, making it less visible in the dimly lit spot.

Then they left.

CHAPTER LV

El Alacran exited from the red Mercedes even before it had screeched to a halt, and strode towards the cluster of men talking excitedly in the open courtyard in front of La Fortaleza. Four more Macheteros, each carrying an AK-47 rifle, hurried after him.

Two bodies, part of the Machetero group that had guarded the Executive Mansion, lay sprawled on the pavement, both obviously dead. One of them was a very young looking man wearing what must have been a tight white T-shirt, now tarnished with a wide splotch of crimson in the area of the stomach, the second a man dressed in old style green Army fatigues and boots, with the left part of his head missing. Andrade knew them both, but if he felt any sense of loss for their demise, his cold, neutral expression betrayed none. He quietly took in what had happened as he walked towards the three men clustered in the courtyard, but his gaze never strayed from them.

He was still wearing the business suit he had worn that morning to capture the Municipal Police station, minus the jacket and the tie. Under his left arm he wore a holster carrying a silver Mamba Parabellum automatic pistol which in any other man of his slight build would have seemed ridiculously oversized, but that somehow looked right on him. With his present clean-cut garb, he had the appearance of a disgruntled accountant. However, his eyes carried the same deadly threat of a cobra's stare.

The group fell silent as he approached it, one of the men—a tall, very fat Machetero—wiping his nose with his sleeve, and seemingly trying to stifle what seemed to be sobs from heavy crying. Andrade recognized him as Alberto, a fairly new recruit from Adjuntas, a town in the central mountains of Puerto Rico. Beside him stood Ruben, stroking his white beard nervously, most probably dreading Andrade's reaction to the news that he was about to receive.

El Alacran's attention centered, however, on the third man, the black man with the perpetual grin who even San Miguel seemed to treat with guarded respect. *George.* They had brushed shoulders a couple of times during the preparatory stages of the operation, and he had been impressed by the man's buffoonish but quiet efficiency. A smart man, despite his constant efforts to appear as an uncouth bumpkin. And therefore, a dangerous man.

"Alacran," the man with the cropped, white beard nervously greeted Andrade, with the express purpose of giving his version of the facts first. "I'm glad you're here. I was at the guardhouse near the entrance gate. We heard some shooting inside La Fortaleza, so I sent Junito to find out what was happening, but as he neared the stairs, somebody shot him." The man pointed to the body of the young man who had been shot in the stomach.

"They killed him..." the fat Machetero sobbed, but Andrade ignored him.

"Tomasin ran to help him but they got him too. Shot him in the head. Then they started shooting at us and we took cover and shot back at them."

"*They...*" Andrade said quietly. "You keep saying '*they*'...Who is '*they*'?"

There was a confused pause, since none of the men there knew for certain who had shot at them.

"The Governor and the other hostages, I think," Ruben answered lamely.

"You *think*?" Andrade repeated Ruben's answer with what sounded like amused contempt, but was barely contained anger. "You haven't checked?"

Ruben's voice shook slightly. "The shooting has just stopped, Alacran," he explained. "I sent my men inside to see what happened."

"I see," Andrade said, with half-closed eyelids, part of his mind analyzing the information he had just received, the other part still taking in his surroundings. The signs of the firefight were evident. The walls of La Fortaleza were pocked with bullet holes, and several of its windows had been blown out. The guardhouse and its immediacies had also been riddled with bullets, even its bulletproof glass showing several impact marks. From the damage to the guardhouse he could tell that the shooting coming from La Fortaleza had been surprisingly accurate, contrary to the scattered shots taken by his men. Whoever had started the firefight from the inside of the Executive Mansion knew what he was doing.

After he had spoken with Governor Pietrantoni and left for the Grand Laguna Hotel, El Alacran had taken stock of the exact number of hostages in La Fortaleza. In addition to the Governor, nine other prisoners had been taken into custody: two male bodyguards, one of them wounded and not of much use for anything, two boys, the Secretary of State Arizmendi, and four women. He knew that Pietrantoni had some National Guard background, but Arizmendi would have been useless firing a weapon. That would leave the Governor and one of his bodyguards to keep his men—and San Miguel's professionals—at bay. A great feat of arms. More than that; the people inside of La Fortaleza had fought more effectively than those outside.

"Why did they stop shooting?" Andrade asked. "Did you hit anyone?"

"Maybe," Ruben shrugged helplessly, not knowing what else to say. "After a while, they stopped firing at us. George was the first one to come out of there," the nervous terrorist pointed towards the entrance to the mansion's main stairway.

Andrade's cold gaze became fixed upon the black man.

"The Governor's men were also shooting at us from the garden windows," George explained. "My men and I had to take cover and fire back." He chuckled, raising an eyebrow. "It was pretty hairy out there for a while. A lot of shooting back and forth."

Andrade nodded slowly. "Did any of your men get wounded?" he asked.

"Only a few scratches." George produced one hearty laugh. "One of my men got grazed in the ass, but not much more than that."

"A lot of shooting..." Andrade repeated, almost distractedly.

"A lot."

"But not much loss of blood."

George lowered his eyes to the floor, smiling amusedly. "Except for that shot in the ass."

El Alacran stared at him impassively. "How many men would you say were firing at you?" he asked matter-of-factly.

"Two, maybe three at most, taking pot shots at us from the upper windows," George responded, looking back up from the floor, his smile undimmed.

Andrade considered the answer, and then made as if to walk towards La Fortaleza. However, after taking two steps he stopped. "Tell me," he said, looking back at the black man. "How did you get inside of La Fortaleza?"

"Inside?" George asked with a puzzled tone.

"I thought Ruben said that he saw you walk out of the entrance to the stairs..." Andrade explained.

"Oh, I wasn't *all the way inside,* if you know what I mean..." he said, turning his answer into a sly, sexual innuendo, but when he failed to elicit any reaction from the Machetero, he continued. "I just went to the stairs, after they had stopped shooting for a while. So I ran inside, and when nobody tried to kill me, I went up the stairs. I saw one of your men there, in the stairs. He was dead, of course," he said wistfully. "Then I ran here, to ask Ruben to send some men inside. Which he did."

Ruben nodded in confirmation, trying to determine from El Alacran's unreadable expression if he had acted correctly.

"So you haven't been inside yourself?" Andrade insisted.

"Nah-ah," the black man confirmed, shaking his head.

"And your men?"

"Did any of them go inside, you mean? No. I kept them in the gardens, in case," a rumbling chuckle interrupted him. "In case the Governor decides to take a stroll."

"So you don't know where the Governor or the rest of the hostages are?" El Alacran inquired, already knowing the answer.

"They've got to be inside, boss," the black man suggested innocently, as Andrade watched him. "They couldn't sneak past your men and mine..."

Again, the Machetero leader took a long time to respond. A thin line, akin to an amused smirk, appeared on his lips. His eyes met those of George, and for a fleeting moment the faces of both men openly revealed the deep contempt in which they held each other. Then the moment passed, and the two men reassumed their detached conversation.

"You're right, of course," Andrade finally said, with little hesitation. He turned to the men who had come with him. "Let's go inside," he told them, and began to walk towards La Fortaleza, but stopped once again, after George failed to follow. "What, you're not coming?" he asked the black man with a hint of irony.

"I need to get back to the hotel," George replied apologetically. "I received a call from San Miguel asking me to meet him there, and when the boss calls—"

"You run?" Andrade completed the black man's statement with evident disdain.

"Yeah!" George flashed him a Satchmo grin. "Just like you and Chocho, Cocho, Caco—"

"Cacho," Andrade corrected with a venomous stare.

"Yeah! Just like you and Cacho."

"You should take the Mercedes back to the hotel," Andrade suggested with uncharacteristic generosity. "We'll take one of the Governor's limousines after we find him."

"That's okay, boss," George replied cheerfully, and he began to walk away. "I can get my own car."

"I insist," El Alacran said in a voice oozing with so much hostility that it made George stop and look back.

For one second the black man seemed to consider refusing Andrade's imperious offer with a witty remark, but then he shrugged and laughed. "If you insist, but I'm not a good driver. I'd hate to damage that pretty car of yours."

"I'm not that attracted to capitalist toys, so you can wreck it as you like, Mr. George," Andrade answered. "Fermin," he said to one of his companions, "do you have the keys?"

El Alacran extended his hand and got the keys from the Machetero driver. "Here!" he turned to the black man and tossed him the keys. "Enjoy it."

"Thank you, boss!" George missed the toss, and the keys fell to the ground. He picked them up gingerly, as if afraid of getting stung. As he began to walk away, Andrade pulled out his Mamba, and cocked it. The sound made the black man stop. "You gonna shoot me?" George asked pleasantly, his back still turned towards the Machetero leader, his hand slipping over his holster.

El Alacran pointed his gun at the black man, stunning the rest of the men present.

"If you're telling the truth," he said slowly, "your men should still be in the gardens making sure the Governor does not escape, right? Including the one that was shot in the ass. Should we check? I can get Fermin to bring them here."

George turned slowly, his lips extended into a feral, bitter smile. He said nothing.

"No? I thought so. They're not there, are they? They've already left, down the same rope that they used to climb the wall last night. Right? And you were going to leave us now as well. Walk out of here as if nothing had happened. So where is the Governor and the other hostages?"

The other Macheteros in the courtyard pointed their weapons at the black man.

"I don't know what you're talking about, boss," George said with a rumbling chuckle that sounded hollow. "We's on the same side, remember?"

"I seemed to think so, yes. But now it seems that *we's not* on the same side anymore. So where is the Governor? He couldn't have escaped with your men. There were women and children who could not climb down that rope. He would not leave them behind. Too...honorable. So where is he?"

"Like I told you, Mr. Alacran, he's gotta be inside," George insisted.

"What I don't understand is why you didn't climb down the rope with the rest of your men," Andrade continued saying, ignoring George. "Drawing the attention of my men away from yours while they escaped, I imagine. Maybe distracting some of my men here while the Governor hid, is that it? Or maybe you thought that you could just walk out of here later and brag about it to your men. How you fooled the stupid Macheteros." Andrade examined George's face, trying to read his expression. The black man had stopped talking, watching El Alacran with a fixed smile. "So where is he? I'll give you up to the count of three to tell me, and then I'll shoot you. One!"

George swallowed hard. "Boss, I don't know what you're talking about!"

"Two!"

George did not wait for three, drawing his gun out of his holster with dazzling speed, and managing to fire twice, hitting the man standing next to Andrade on the chest, and grazing Andrade's left ear. Then, a hail of bullets wracked his body.

Touching his ear and staring briefly at the blood on his fingers, El Alacran walked to where George had fallen, and knelt next to him. Despite all the shots fired, the black man had been struck only three times. But the wounds were fatal. One bullet had pierced his right lung, another his abdomen, and the third his right thigh, and he was bleeding to death.

Andrade observed him silently for a few seconds, and then asked, almost in a bored tone, "Why did you betray us?"

George grinned, his teeth stained with blood. "That's...for you...to find out," he whispered.

"I will," El Alacran promised, and stood up, not bothering to interrogate the fallen man any further. "Call Cacho," he told Ruben. "I need to talk to him."

"What about him?" Ruben asked, jerking his head at the dying man.

"What about him?" Andrade repeated, and walked away.

The room was small, pitch-black, hot, and humid, impregnated with the kind of dank, musty smell that could only accumulate through the passage of centuries. To make matters worse, there was hardly space to fit everyone into it. It had taken the group of escaped hostages less than five minutes to reach the kitchen from the Hall of Mirrors after George had left them. Headed by Governor Pietrantoni, they had made their way through the lavish Blue Room under the stern and regal gaze of Queen Isabella's deceptively beautiful painting, walked across the main corridor of the palace, and entered the luxurious State Dining Room. Picon, Pietrantoni's bodyguard, had preceded the Governor, armed with an Uzi, while Lucas guarded the rear with the captured AK-47.

The elongated table used for official state dinners was not yet set, although in preparation for the post State of the Island Address Dinner scheduled for that Tuesday, several silver candelabra and the gold silverware were already bunched at one end of the table, waiting to be cleaned or polished, as were an assortment of fine glass wine glasses, porcelain plates and other dinner accoutrements. Patria, the head housekeeper, looked mortified. She did not like anybody outside of her staff—not even the Governor or the First Governess—to see anything out of place, and had felt relieved that the small group of refugees had not lingered there, filing past the head of the table and turning right, into the Informal Dining Room.

The latter was an open, airy room, lined with a long row of windows that allowed the entry of light during the mornings and a cool breeze from the bay during the night. It looked more like a family room, where the residents of La Fortaleza could breakfast at a round dark oak dining table, or sip from a frothy latte ("*café con leche*") while sitting on one of the plush sofas or padded chairs that filled the rest of the room.

The Governor had continued moving towards the kitchen, really a conglomerate of three rooms equipped with several large ovens, grills and refrigerators, and stocked to the hilt with a huge pantry and other food storage areas, that allowed La Fortaleza to handle any type of social activity.

Altagracia, the mansion's main chef, had followed Pietrantoni into the kitchen with a half-puzzled expression, wondering what he intended to do there. Unless the escapees hid inside of the pantry—an obvious place for the terrorists to search—she had no idea how they would escape detection within her domain. Possibly, she thought, the Governor was using the kitchen's back exit to descend undetected into La Fortaleza's lower level.

However, Pietrantoni had stopped in the kitchen's central room, in front of a tall, ancient wooden cupboard, used mostly to show old cooking utensils and tableware from prior administrations. He had slid upwards a rectangular, decorative panel on the side of the cupboard and squeezed his arm through it. After moving it haphazardly up and down for a few seconds, his hand had latched onto something. Grunting, the Governor had pulled down with a great deal of effort until, with a loud crack, whatever was behind the food cabinet had given way, and the entire cabinet had swung open sideways—towards him—like a door.

Altagracia and her helper, Maria, had gasped, too stunned to say anything, but Patria had watched with quiet satisfaction, as if she had been aware all the time of what was there.

"Wow!" Alfredo had said, looking at his friend Francisco. "A secret passage! Did you know about this?"

Francisco had merely shaken his head, his surprised expression confirming his silent denial.

"We discovered it less than a year ago, while this part of the kitchen was being remodeled and the kitchen staff was on vacation," Pietrantoni had said with proprietary pride. "Only Patria, Nereida and I know about its existence...well, and the three carpenters who worked here...And now you people."

"You couldn't tell me? Your right hand man?" Arizmendi had whispered with mock indignation.

"And run the risk of having you crawling within the walls of my house, or worse, hiding somebody else to spy on me, just to gain a little political leverage? I'd have to be crazy!" Pietrantoni had shuddered.

Lucas had smiled, enjoying the friendly banter between the two friends.

"It's a secret connection between the kitchen and the Austral Tower. Not much of a secret passage, I'm afraid. It was probably just a short corridor that existed at one time between the tower and the main living quarters, before the tower fell into disuse and the passage was sealed, but we can hide here until we're rescued."

"And it leads to the...you said, the Austral...Tower?" Lucas had repeated.

"Austral," Pietrantoni had confirmed. "It means southern. I don't know if you've seen the two large towers that flank the western wall of La Fortaleza..."

Lucas nodded. "A long time ago."

"They were built during the times when San Juan was attacked by pirates and privateers, when La Fortaleza was not only the seat of the governor but an actual fortress. The Austral Tower was the last of the two towers to be built. It was used to garrison troops but never actually saw battle—"

"You will learn very quickly that the Governor is a very enthusiastic history buff," Arizmendi had cut Pietrantoni short, raising his eyes in despair. "If given the opportunity, he will give you spontaneous lectures on anything that he finds remotely entertaining, even when we're being followed by a bunch of terrorists that want to kill us and we should be hiding!"

The Governor had grinned sheepishly. "I do tend to get carried away sometimes, don't I? Okay, it's time to get in. You'll lead the way, Alberto?" he said to Arizmendi.

The Secretary of State had looked uncertainly into the dark space. "Are there any spiders in there?"

"Probably," the Governor had replied with a straight face. "That's why I'm sending you in first."

Reluctantly, Double A had complied, but as he walked into the chamber, a loud crash had startled the group. Maria, the youngest of the staff, had accidentally knocked down with her elbow a porcelain bowl filled with flour. The white powder had exploded into a white cloud, covering most of the floor and the surrounding furnishings with a pale film of pallid dust.

Maria had apologized profusely, but the Governor had comforted her, making little of the incident. However, Lucas had grasped the seriousness of mishap immediately. As the group moved into the chamber, it left behind a multitude of imprints and tracks on the spilled, powdery substance, clearly showing that a small crowd had recently trampled the floor space in front of the secret entrance.

Patria had noticed it as well, and had quietly approached Lucas.

"Mr. Lucas, I can get some brooms and trays and try to sweep this mess off the floor, sir, if that's okay with you," she suggested.

"That would be great, Patria, thank you," Lucas had said appreciatively. He had watched as the head housekeeper walked to a small closet opposite to the secret entrance and pulled out two brooms, giving one to Altagracia. The two women had begun to carefully brush away the thin white dust, trying to avoid, as much as possible, raising another cloud of flour.

The two other female hostages and the children had followed Arizmendi into the hidden room, so that only the Governor, Lucas, and the two bodyguards remained outside.

"Is there still an open connection from that hiding place to the Austral Tower?" Lucas had asked the Governor in a hushed tone, intended to be heard only by Pietrantoni.

"As far as I know, yes," the Governor had answered, looking questioningly at Lucas.

"We'd better check. We may need an exit strategy. This may be the best place to hide, but if we're found out," Lucas had taken a quick, involuntary look at where Altagracia and Patria were sweeping the flour and shards of broken porcelain, "we have to have a means of escape. If not..." Lucas had not elaborated further.

Pietrantoni had nodded. "Let's make sure the other exit works."

The two men had squeezed between the cluster of anxious refugees already waiting inside the chamber, and made their way to the opposite side of the small room. There, Lucas found the small outline of a long, flat lever—the length of a baseball bat—attached to the wall at about the height of his waist. When he had placed the palm of his hand on the wall, it had felt surprisingly smooth. Rapping it with his knuckles, he had discovered that it was made out of wood.

The Governor had grabbed the end of the lever with both of his hands and pulled it down, but the lever had not yielded. "Help me," he had asked Lucas.

Slowly, the two men had continued to pull it until with a loud "cra-a-a-ck", it had slid free from its hidden catch. The wall had given way with a modest push by Pietrantoni, hinging on its left side and opening away from where the two men stood.

It had revealed a medium sized, circular space. Soft light from the late afternoon sun filtered through a few, scattered, slit-like windows built mostly for defensive purposes. The room smelled dank and moldy, its only source of ventilation coming from the tower's narrow windows. It contained no furniture, except for the wooden, empty cabinet that must have held at one time lances or muskets or other utensils of war, and which now served to conceal the secret exit. There was a breach in its stone floor that allowed a brick-walled, spiral staircase to snake upwards from the tower's base and to continue upwards.

"This is one of the intermediate levels of the tower," Pietrantoni said.

"Where do the stairs go?" Lucas had asked the Governor in a whisper.

"Up, they go to another level, and then to the tower's turret," Pietrantoni had responded. "There's nothing up there but a sundial clock. Down, they lead to an exit outside of the western wall, close to the gardens."

"So the terrorists can gain access to the tower from that lower entrance..."

The Governor had shrugged. "The answer to that question...The answer is yes, but there's an iron gate there, and it's always locked. So they would have to break down the lock in order to get in."

"So if we have to get out of the tower, would we have to break that lock as well?"

As Pietrantoni was about to answer, a commotion originating at the opposite side of the secret chamber interrupted them.

"We hear voices!" Patria had said, making her way to the Governor. "Some men are coming."

"Quick! Get everybody inside and close the doors on both sides!" the Governor had ordered.

"But we haven't finished cleaning the floor!" Patria protested.

"There's no time," Pietrantoni had replied. "Get Altagracia inside."

But Lucas had already returned to the kitchen, and had gathered those who had stayed behind, herding them towards the secret chamber. A last look at the area where the women had been working revealed that much of the spilled flour had been swept away, as had most of the footprints of the escapees. However, he spotted at least half a dozen partial shoe imprints on parts of the floor that had escaped the broom, as well as a few shards of the destroyed porcelain bowl. Nevertheless, the compromised area was beyond the false cabinet entrance, so it would have to do, Lucas had decided, as the voices of the approaching searchers grew dangerously near.

Making certain that everyone was inside, he had pulled back the false kitchen cabinet until it clicked shut. There had been a collective groan as an almost absolute blackness—the Governor had also shut the exit to the Austral Tower, so that no light would filter through the kitchen's cupboard—engulfed the frightened refugees. One of the women—difficult to tell which in the darkness—had begun to mumble to herself something unintelligible, possibly a prayer, provoking several angry hisses. It had taken all of the Governor's considerable authority and powers of persuasion, as well as some gentle prodding by Nereida, to finally silence everyone. Arizmendi had contributed by briefly turning on a tiny keychain flashlight, and flashing it onto the roof. The narrow beam of dusty white light had settled the frayed nerves of the chamber's occupants, and even produced some faint smiles of relief on the faces of those illuminated by it. Anxiously, the group waited.

CHAPTER LVI

"Adalberto!" El Alacran said without any introductions, as he received the cell phone from one of his men.

"Aristides," Cacho acknowledged, addressing Andrade by his first name, as he always did. *"Did you find Pietrantoni?"*

"Not yet. But he's still inside of La Fortaleza. It's just a matter of time."

"We have to find him," Cacho urged. His voice showed no emotion, but Andrade knew him well enough to know, just by the abruptness of his inquiry, how much the Governor's disappearance mattered to him.

"Don't worry, Adalberto, I will find him," El Alacran assured him. "And I will kill him."

There was a pause on the other end of the line. *"But that's not the main reason why you're calling me, is it, Aristides?"* the Machetero leader stated, causing Andrade to press his lips into his *rigor mortis* smile. Cacho could read his voice as well as Andrade could read Cacho's.

"No, it isn't. We've been betrayed."

"By San Miguel?" Again, Cacho surprised Andrade by his keen insight of the situation, despite his relatively short time out of prison.

"By San Miguel," El Alacran confirmed. "Pietrantoni was freed by his men. I think they killed Tino and the others inside La Fortaleza, and then fired at our people outside to give Pietrantoni time to hide."

"How did you find out?"

"I suspected it from the beginning. The men inside La Fortaleza who fired at us were professionals, expert marksmen. They killed two of our men in the first minute of the fighting. I questioned their leader, a black man called George, about what had happened, and he said that two or three men from inside La Fortaleza had shot at his men, who were stationed in the gardens. I didn't believe him."

"Why not?"

"I knew the exact number of prisoners in La Fortaleza. There were two bodyguards. Two! And one of them was wounded. The other men were Pietrantoni and the Secretary of State, Arizmendi. Do you think that they could have managed to put up the strong resistance that kept our men away? Not even Superman could that. The black man was lying," El Alacran said spitefully.

"You don't like George, I gather?" Cacho said with a chortle.

"He didn't rub me one way or the other," Andrade replied truthfully.

"I knew that San Miguel's dribble about Puerto Rico's plight and the world movement to fight the imperialist oppression was just a lot of hot air," Cacho said matter-of-factly, with only a tinge of regret. *"The question is, what are they after? Who are they? Why go through all the trouble they have gone through to get me here and then betray us? Did you get any information out of this George character?"*

"No. He tried to shoot me. He succeeded in nicking off part of my left ear. I had to kill him."

"That's a pity," Cacho said drily.

"Killing him or having my ear nicked?"

"Killing him, killing him. I'm sure the nick on your ear will be an improvement," Cacho responded with the deadpan humor that characterized their relationship. *"Any ideas on why they betrayed us?"*

Andrade paused to think.

"A CIA plot?" he suggested without much conviction. "A way of getting the Macheteros and all the other...*subversives*—Andrade pronounced the word with scorn—together, to kill them all without having to go through the legal process?"

Cacho did not reply immediately, as if mulling over Andrade's suggestion. *"You know, the CIA has done a lot of crazy things in its time, but going so far just to kill a bunch of Macheteros, I think that is even beyond them."*

"I would do it."

"I know you would. Fortunately for the world, there's not that many like you out there, and we have you."

"What, then?"

"I don't know..." Cacho paused, then added darkly, *"But I intend to find out. What about the other men from San Miguel's group in La Fortaleza? What do they have to say?"*

"I will tell you when I find them...*If* I find them," Andrade corrected. "I suspect that the only thing we will find from them is the dust that they left behind as they ran away."

"I suspect the same thing here with San Miguel," Cacho said, after thinking it over.

"All jest aside, be careful, my brother," El Alacran said earnestly. "I never believed for a moment all of San Miguel's mumbo jumbo about sympathizing with our cause. No stranger mobilizes an army to fight for a cause that is not his. Not even the Archangel Saint Michael. That man has his own agenda, whatever it is. But it was worth participating in this enterprise, because I got the opportunity to free you, and wreck the *statehooders'* case to make Puerto Rico a state. At least, we've managed to do that. But I never thought that the foreigners would betray us so openly and so soon. So be careful, Adalberto. It's almost nighttime. Expect an attack on the Grand Laguna soon, and don't count on the help of San Miguel or his friends. You should consider withdrawing to the safe house that we spoke about when we were at the rooftop of the hotel."

"I will—"

"I mean right now," El Alacran interrupted. "The *Mardi Gras* is another of San Miguel's tricks, another distraction for the Americans and for us alike. Go to the place that I secured *now*, and stay there. Until this mess blows over. You will be safe there, and well-taken care of. And nobody will find you. Take our best men, and leave the others in the hotel, to distract the rescuers, but leave *now*. I will find the Governor and kill him and join you there."

Andrade paused to get Cacho's reaction. When the latter failed to say anything, he said, "Are you there?"

"I hear you," Cacho finally answered with a hesitation that mortified Andrade. El Alacran had been accused of being a cold-blooded killer, beholden to no one, unable to feel any kind of bond or affection to any other human being, and it was all true. Except for Cacho. The two men had been together most of their lives, and in the process become as close as any brothers. Andrade could have chosen to abandon Cacho and let him rot in jail. Instead, he had risked it all by joining an operation led by men he did not trust. The fact that Cacho hesitated to flee and seek the safety of the safe house he had secured vexed him.

"Go *now*, Adalberto," Andrade insisted. "The revolution needs you alive."

"I will, I will," Cacho stubbornly replied. *"I just have to find San Miguel first. I have to find out what is behind all of this."*

"Let it be. I suspect that we will find out soon enough."

"Don't worry about me. I'll go to the safe house, I swear. I'm releasing one of the hostages with my prison clothes, so that the federal authorities track him while I escape."

It was Andrade's turn to remain quiet.

"Are you there?" Cacho inquired.

"Don't waste your time, Adalberto. Go while you may. Goodbye." El Alacran hung up, and walked towards La Fortaleza.

Orlando Picon, the Governor's personal bodyguard, remained standing closest to the false door of the secret chamber, his ear pressed against the wall, trying to listen what was happening outside.

"Do you hear anything?" Pietrantoni asked him.

Picon shook his head. Then, uncertain that he had been seen by the Governor, whispered, "No, not yet."

The Governor turned to Lucas. "You were asking about the locked door at the base of the tower..."

"I was asking you if we would have to break the lock if we need to use that exit," Lucas whispered.

"What door would that be?" a female voice within the chamber inquired.

"Is that you, Patria?" the Governor asked before Lucas could answer.

"Yes, Mr. Governor. What door is Mr. Lucas referring to?"

"The lock to the door at the entrance of the Austral Tower. Do you have the key?"

"Yes."

"Here, with you now?"

"Yes. The young terrorist took all of my keys away after he brought me to the Hall of Mirrors, but I took them out of his pocket after...after he died."

"Patria carries the keys to all of the doors of La Fortaleza," Pietrantoni explained to Lucas. "Fortunately for her, many of the locks open with the same key. Otherwise, she would be leaning permanently to one side."

Picon stirred and raised one hand in warning. "They're here," he announced in a soft voice.

"We've searched everywhere," Ruben reported to El Alacran as he slowly climbed the stairs leading to the second floor of La Fortaleza. "No luck so far."

"You did not find any of the hostages?" Andrade asked calmly, as he observed the body of the sentry who had sat at the top landing on a plush chair. His throat had been slit, and blood had spilled over most of the luxurious chair he had occupied. A piece of chewed, pink bubblegum hung from his lower lip.

"None," Ruben answered nervously.

"Good," said Andrade, thoroughly confusing his colleague. As he continued to walk towards the Hall of Mirrors, he snickered. "You don't understand, do you?" he asked his subordinate, not looking back.

"Well..." Ruben hesitated. "I mean—"

"You mean you don't. It's simple. Some of the hostages were women and children. It would be very difficult for them to climb all the way down to the bay using a rope hanging from one of the walls, don't you think?"

Ruben nodded.

"So if they can't be found, the odds are that they're all hiding together."

"Couldn't the Governor have run away?" Ruben ventured.

El Alacran shook his head, as if despairing of his comrade's lack of imagination.

"Let's suppose that he had, even though he is not the kind of man who would abandon any of his staff. He's too full of himself to do that. But let's suppose, just for the sake of it, that he, and somehow his young son, and maybe even his live-in whore managed to climb down a rope several stories high, that would mean that others would have been left behind, right?"

"I suppose so..."

"So where are they? Where are the people who were left behind?"

"Hiding in some special hiding place..."

"Precisely. That's where they *all* are. Unless there is a tunnel from La Fortaleza to the city," Andrade added to himself, almost as an after-thought. "But if there is, we'll find it and follow them."

The two men entered the Hall of Mirrors, where El Alacran stopped to quietly examine the scene of the breakout. He immediately saw that there had been an intense firefight and yet, miraculously, none of the hostages had been killed. Even more miraculously, only one of the large mirrors in the hall had been struck by two stray bullets.

There was no doubt about it; whoever had killed his men had been a professional. George had definitely been involved.

"A pity," Andrade muttered, gazing at the bullet holes and the damage that the room had suffered. "Such a pretty room."

"As you can see, a lot of blood was spilled here," Ruben said, pointing at the corpse of the younger terrorist, which lay sprawled near one of the exits to the Oriental Gallery. "Some of the hostages stepped on the blood when they fled, and headed in this direction." Ruben pointed at the par-tial imprints of footsteps on the gallery floor that led away towards the dining room area. "They do not last long, unfortunately, but it seems that they went to the kitchen. One of the hostages knocked a bowl full of flour to the floor there."

El Alacran nodded once. "Show me."

The kitchen floor looked as if it had been partially swept and abandoned. The floor still contained bits and pieces of the porcelain bowl that had shattered. However, the tiles below the only counter where the bowl could have rested had been swept clear of most of the debris and the spilled flour. That was not the case a few feet further away, where an area of the kitchen had been left partially covered by the fine white powder, and where a set of tracks heading towards the kitchen's back exit was clearly evident. El Alacran stared at the tracks area with intense curiosity.

"We think that they went that way and fled to the lower level," Ruben continued saying. "I sent one of my men to follow them."

"Are those his footprints?" El Alacran asked, pointing at the tracks on the flour-covered tiles.

"Yes, I think so," the bearded Machetero replied.

"So where are the tracks of the hostages?" Andrade asked him.

Ruben regarded his superior with a blank stare.

"You really don't think that they levitated over that part of the floor, do you?" El Alacran stated sarcastically. "They're here! The prisoners are here! They're hidden somewhere in the kitchen! Search this room!"

Andrade examined the area around him. There were two opposing wooden cupboards, one containing modern cooking utensils, the other decorative artifacts from prior occupants of La Fortaleza. Dropping to one knee, he focused his attention on the lower corners of the latter of the two cupboards, and immediately found what he was looking for.

"See here," he pointed to a barely visible line of fine flour powder that curved away from the cabinet's right hand corner. "The flour here was swept away into a half-moon shape. This cupboard opens somehow towards us. They're hiding behind it. Give me your Uzi," he hissed. "Go get a couple of men." Ruben nodded and ran away.

Carefully, Andrade leaned forward and tried to move the cupboard, but it was firmly attached to the wall. Flicking off the sub machinegun's safety, he stood in front of the cabinet and fired at it at point-blank range. Some of the ornaments on the cabinet's shelves exploded into hundreds of fragments, and the wood splintered and shattered, partially exposing what seemed to be an empty void behind it.

Instinctively, he stepped aside, expecting return fire from the other side of the cabinet, but none came. Replacing the Uzi's ammunition clip, he placed its muzzle where the wood had splintered, and fired into the darkness. Several shots ricocheted off the unseen walls of the hidden space, but he heard no screams of fear or pain.

"There has to be some sort of lever or panel somewhere to open this thing," he muttered to himself, and began to rap on the splintered backboard, without any success. Again he examined the cupboard's exposed side, and tapped on its surface, obtaining the same results.

He heard the sound of approaching footsteps behind him and turned to see Ruben running into the kitchen with two other men.

"We're going to have to break a hole into this cabinet," Andrade said, returning his attention to the cupboard's side. Through the kitchen's windows, he noticed that it was growing dark outside. "And we'll need flashlights," he added. "Find some flashlights, hurry!"

The two men disappeared while Ruben, slipping his fingers through one of the wider cracks in the shattered backboard, pulled backwards with all his strength. A sharp shard of wood suddenly broke away, piercing his hand with a large splinter. With a harsh intake of breath, Ruben quickly withdrew his hand, and pulled the splinter out.

Just then one of the men returned carrying a heavy pedestal in the shape of a column that must have held a bust or a vase in one of the adjacent rooms. Raising it with the aid of Ruben, he began to crash it against the fractured back panel of the cupboard. Slowly, the wood began to give way, each strike shattering larger pieces of the cupboard's back panel.

"I have flashlights!" Alberto, the fat Machetero shouted, waiving two elongated silver cones in his hands. Two more men had come with him.

Andrade snatched one of the flashlights from Alberto and switched it on, grunting with satisfaction when it produced a beam of light. He walked to the front of the cabinet, where the men had lowered the heavy pedestal after opening a gap in the backboard big enough for a man to crawl through.

Cautiously, as if expecting a snake to spring from the hole, Andrade flashed his light into the chamber hidden beyond the cupboard and peered inside.

The space was empty. Some of the bullets he had fired had penetrated into the small room and struck what seemed to be another wooden surface on its opposite side. A vertical sliver of pale light gleamed in the darkness, outlining the edge of a barely open door.

"They've escaped through an exit on the other side!" El Alacran shouted angrily. Stepping away from the hole, he turned to Ruben. "Go! Follow them! Hurry!"

The bearded Machetero pointed his Uzi into the chamber and, placing one leg inside, ducked his head and moved inside. Two other Macheteros followed, until only Alberto and Andrade remained. The portly revolutionary hesitated, afraid he would not fit in the gap but not wanting to appear helpless before his superior.

"You're too fat!" El Alacran sneered, beginning to move through the opening. "Go and alert the others. See if there's a way out below."

Alberto mumbled what sounded like an apology, and shuffled out of the kitchen.

By the time Andrade entered the hidden chamber, his men had pushed open the room's other exit and were examining the circular hall beyond it with a flashlight, its beam slithering over the tower's bare stone walls and floor. The sun had set, and it was dark inside.

"There's a spiral stairway on the other side of the room that goes up through the roof and down through the floor," Ruben whispered to Andrade, as the latter exited the smaller chamber, pointing the flashlight at the staircase. "The question is which way did they go, up or—"

"Shhhhhh!" Andrade cautioned. "I think I heard something..."

The men waited, halting their conversation for several seconds. Then they tensed, as a few faint noises, like the muffled scraping of the sole of leather shoes on stone, echoed from above.

Ruben gestured with his hand to one of his men to approach the stairs. The man moved noiselessly to the edge of the stairwell and paused. A second Machetero followed. Halfway up, the rising steps disappeared behind a stone wall, creating a spiral corridor no wider than three feet.

The man popped his head into the circular passageway and withdrew it immediately. The stairs were faintly illuminated by the glow of outside lights that filtered through one of the tower's narrow windows. The steps were barely visible as the corridor spiraled upwards out of sight. The Machetero had seen no one.

Crouching, the man walked into the stairway and disappeared behind its inner wall. Five noiseless seconds passed, and then the stairwell erupted in thunderous gunfire, the multiple flashes from the discharged guns briefly lighting the inside of the tower like deafening, erratic strobe lights in a jam-packed discotheque. Just as suddenly, the gun blasts stopped, and the body of the Machetero rolled past the open landing of the stairs and continued to tumble onto the stairs below. The metallic 'clink' of several discharged shells and the harsher 'clack-clack-clack' of an AK-47 followed the dead man, as the discarded objects bounced downwards on the stone steps.

Inside the round tower's room, Ruben flattened himself against a wall, and looked back at his superior with a scared expression.

Andrade sighed. Almost casually, he walked to the edge of the stairway's landing and stopped at its edge.

"Mr. Governor! Please give yourself up! There is no way out!" he shouted, and then in a lower voice added, "At least, no way that I know of..." Raising his volume again, he said. "I will get you! If you give yourself up, though, I will spare the others! What do you say?"

Andrade waited, and was about to speak again when a disembodied voice shouted down derisively, "The Governor isn't here!"

El Alacran's dark eyes gleamed with malice. "Really? Where is he?"

"He had to go to a doctor's appointment," the voice answered. "He caught herpes from your mother."

El Alacran chuckled. "Yes," he said in an amused tone. "That's what happens when you deal with whores. How is Nereida, by the way?"

No one answered. Andrade signaled Ruben to approach him, and got hold of his Uzi when he got near. Without looking, he extended his hand into the rising corridor and fired the weapon until it ran out of ammunition, the discharged bullets ricocheting wildly off the spiraling walls. There was no reply fire.

"Are you still alive, asshole?" El Alacran shouted.

The insult was greeted by silence.

With a wave of his hand, Andrade beckoned Ruben and the other terrorist to approach him. "We're going to have to storm the stairs, firing with everything we've got."

Ruben stared at him as if he were insane. "Maybe we should wait. He may be dead, or dying," he suggested, hopefully. The second terrorist, a lean man in his late twenties with a crooked nose and a long chin that had earned him the nickname of "El Brujo" ("The Warlock") listened nervously.

"Then we don't have to worry, do we?" Andrade replied softly with a sour smile. He returned the sub machine gun to his companion. "You should load this. Brujo, lie down on the stairs. When I count to three, open fire with everything you've got. As soon as you're empty I will follow." El Alacran looked at Ruben. "Have you reloaded yet?" he asked him.

"I'll be finished in a second," the bearded terrorist answered. His hands were shaking so badly that he was having problems sliding the new clip of ammunition into the Uzi. Andrade snatched it away from him and slapped the clip in.

"Give me the rest of your ammunition," he said in a subdued, angry tone. "You reload as quickly as you can, and follow me, understand?" he said to El Brujo.

"Yes, Alacran," El Brujo whispered.

"You too," he said unpleasantly to Ruben, who nodded anxiously.

"If I fall, open fire and keep going, but don't shoot unless you're sure that I'm out of the way. I don't want to get shot in the back, okay?" El Alacran stared from one face to another, making certain they were listening to him, and eliciting visual confirmation from each of them. "Okay! Now take your positions."

Reluctantly, El Brujo moved past the other two men and, stooping, crawled slowly into the shadows covering the stairs' landing. With exaggerated care, he sat on a step and gingerly leaned forward on the rising steps, holding his assault rifle in front of him so it wouldn't rattle on the steps.

However, before he had finished, the "pop-pop-pop" sounds of distant automatic gunfire and the faint voices of shouting men disturbed the tower's silence. The noises originated from below, apparently from the gardens or La Fortaleza's central courtyard.

The disembodied voice at the top of the stairs rumbled with laughter. "Surprise, surprise! I told you the Governor wasn't here." A burst of automatic gunfire followed, making El Brujo crawl hurriedly out of the stairs.

Andrade stood up and roared angrily, while firing the Uzi into the stairwell. After he had spent all of his ammunition, he stood in silence, breathing heavily. "We've been duped," he told his two companions. "We've been kept here while the Governor tries to escape. Brujo!" he said to the large-chinned terrorist, still sprawled on the floor. "You stay here. Make sure that nobody comes down this way."

"Yes, Alacran," El Brujo responded with relief, as he began to pick himself up.

"Ruben, with me!" Andrade said to the bearded Machetero, already walking back to the kitchen's secret chamber. "We have work to do...And you up there!" he shouted back into the stairwell, "I'll be back for you!"

"I'll be here!" the man at the top of the stairs responded cheerfully.

CHAPTER LVII

They had been discovered.

For a moment, it had seemed as if the Macheteros had abandoned the gardens. Then out of the gloom, a male voice had shouted, "Stop right there!"

Picon, the Governor's bodyguard, discharged several bursts of fire from his Uzi into the dark shrubs ahead of him and began to back up. "Get back!" he shouted to the others.

"Back up!" Lucas repeated, also firing blindly in the direction of the gardens.

They had just exited from the gate in the western wall of La Fortaleza that connected the Executive Mansion's two towers, and were following the contours of the wall to get to the cover of the gardens, when one of the Macheteros had shouted the alarm. Now, the frightened fugitives withdrew and huddled behind the open gate, uncertain of where they should go.

In front of them, reflecting the faint, silvery glow of a half moon, lay San Juan Bay, perfectly visible over the upper ramparts of the massive city walls on which La Fortaleza was perched. However, there was no way to escape to the promenade below except by a five story vertical drop. With the Macheteros blocking their way through the gardens, and shots ringing out of the Austral Tower, the only other open route was through the central courtyard of La Fortaleza.

Several bullets whizzed past the gate as Picon, covering the rear, reached the rest of the group and took cover behind the left corner of the arched entrance.

"I've got two more clips and then I'm out," he told Lucas.

"We have to go, Mr. Governor," Lucas said to Pietrantoni, watching for movement in the courtyard. So far, none of the terrorists had gotten there, but it would only be a matter of time. And then, they would be completely surrounded and exposed to the enemy fire. "If you have a place to hide, I suggest you get us there now," he said, already convinced that their only real choice would be to go through the courtyard and fight their way through any terrorists guarding the front entrance of the Executive Mansion.

He had begun to plan his new route of escape even as they had withdrawn from the gardens. Three powerful halogen floodlights bathed the west wall's gate, the wall and the towers that flanked it in a white light brighter than daylight, making the group plainly visible to any attackers that came their way. If they were to survive the next few seconds, he had to put them out.

Taking Picon's Uzi, he aimed it at the spotlight closest to the gardens, and fired two short bursts, causing the lamp to explode and immediately dimming the brightness that surrounded them. Then, methodically, he destroyed the remaining floodlights, allowing the shadows of the night to envelop the walls of La Fortaleza. However, he knew that after their enemies' eyes adapted to the darkness, the group would be partially visible under the moon's sickly, pale glow. They had to move *now*.

Returning the weapon to Picon, he said to him, "We'll have to fight our way out of here, and go out through the front gate. I'll take the others through the courtyard, and you cover our rear. Don't fire unless you're fired upon. They can't see us now. Are you ready?"

Picon nodded and stood up.

"Wait!" The Governor grabbed Lucas' arm. "I know of a place where we can hide!" He turned his head and spoke in the direction of the others. "Alberto," he said to Arizmendi, "we're going to need your tiny flashlight."

There was a pause, then a voice said, "Don't lose it!"

"Everyone, listen up!" Pietrantoni said immediately. "I want all of you to grab the hand of somebody else, so no one is left behind. I'm going to lead you to the center of the courtyard. There's a tunnel there, and it's going to be very dark—"

Altagracia's voice interrupted him with a *"Santo Dios!"* but he continued.

"There is no reason to worry. I have been there twice myself, and we can hide until we're rescued. But we have to do it right now."

Lucas felt Alfredo grab his hand nervously. "Don't worry," he whispered to his godson, mustering as much confidence in his voice as he could, "the Governor knows what he's doing."

Pietrantoni did not wait any longer, striding into the courtyard, holding on to Francisco's hand. Francisco, in turn, grabbed Nereida. One by one the rest followed, staring warily at their surroundings as they followed the Governor.

The courtyard was enclosed by the enormous wall they had just abandoned, and the three buildings, connected to each other, that formed the main compound of La Fortaleza. A faint light filtered from some of Executive Mansion's upper windows, throwing elongated patches of yellow light on the cobblestoned floor. However, no one seemed to be looking out of the windows.

The site of the archeological dig had been cordoned off with yellow tape, a tall mound of dirt and stones accumulated on one side of the dig. The entrance to the tunnel gaped out of the ground like a small bomb crater. A ladder protruded from it.

The Governor removed the tape and turned on the flashlight, directing its beam into the hole. It revealed the tunnel's floor, some twelve to fifteen feet further down.

"Nereida, you go first," the Governor said. "When you get down, I'll pass the flashlight to you."

Grabbing hold of the ladder, the First Nanny began to descend while Pietrantoni illuminated the steps with his narrow beam of light. Next to him, Francisco watched with fascinated concern. It took her no time to get down.

"Francisco," the Governor whispered to his son, "you're next. When you're halfway down, I'll pass you the flashlight so you can give it to Nereida, right?"

"Don't worry, dad," Francisco replied, and hurried down the ladder.

One by one, the line of fugitives disappeared into the ground, until only the Governor, Picon, Altagracia and Lucas were left.

"You should be next, Mr. Governor," the bodyguard said.

"After Altagracia," Pietrantoni replied, but the cook shied away.

"I'll handle it, sir," Lucas said. "They're looking for you. Please hurry down."

Pietrantoni hesitated and then began to descend the ladder.

"Altagracia, please come," Lucas said gently, extending his hand, concerned about the look on the woman's face. It was one of raw fear, just the snap of a thread away from irrational panic.

"No!" she said, shaking her head and backing up. "We'll be buried alive in there."

"No we won't," Lucas replied calmly, taking a tentative step forward. "It will be all right, I promise."

"No!" she said more loudly.

Suddenly a shot rang out from a corner of the compound and a bullet thudded into the mound of dirt.

"Stop!" a voice that Lucas recognized as that of the fat Machetero shouted from the shadows.

Picon, standing up to his chest in the ladder, returned the fire. Lucas tried to take advantage of the confusion, and moved towards Altagracia, but she ran away screaming. Several shots hit the ground around her but none of them struck her, and then she disappeared into the shadows of La Fortaleza.

"Get them!" another, shriller voice shouted, and more shots ricocheted off the cobblestones where Lucas was standing. Not bothering to duck for cover, Lucas sprinted towards the entrance of the tunnel, shouting at Picon, "Get down, get down!"

The bodyguard stopped firing, and rushed down the ladder. Lucas tumbled down a second later, partially landing on one of Picon's shoulders, partially held by the Governor and Arizmendi.

"They're coming!" Lucas said breathlessly, "Let's get as much inside as we can. Pull the ladder away!"

Picon and Arizmendi pulled the ladder back, sliding it into the tunnel past its scared occupants, spraying lose soil over all of them as its top scratched the edges of the excavation. Lucas stared upwards apprehensively, the tunnel's entrance showing as an inky blue irregular circle surrounded by pitch-black darkness. The withdrawal of the ladder would not stop the terrorists permanently, but it would delay them.

"Grab hands!" Pietrantoni ordered, as he moved to the head of the line, followed by Lucas.

"Do you know where this tunnel leads to?" the latter asked, trying to hide his concern.

"Not exactly," the Governor answered truthfully, as he retrieved the flashlight from Nereida, and shone it on the others. "Okay," he shouted, "Everybody hold hands! Let's move on!" Grabbing Lucas' hand, he began to walk into the underground passageway. "The Institute of Culture," he continued saying in a lower voice to Lucas, "has only penetrated the tunnel to where it forks into two, about a quarter of a mile from here. They were going to bring a structural engineer to determine what are the risks of a cave-in before they moved in any further."

Lucas rolled his eyes. "Great!" he whispered.

Pietrantoni chortled. "It's not as bad as it sounds. I was here three days ago with a hardhat. Walked with the Institute of Culture people—"

"Maria Belen?" Lucas interrupted, not remembering her last name.

"Maria Belen Garcia," the Governor acknowledged enthusiastically. "You know her?"

"She's a friend of the family's," Lucas replied, not believing he was holding a social chat with the Governor of Puerto Rico as armed Macheteros pursued them to kill them.

"Brilliant person. She headed the tour, with two others. When we got to the fork in the tunnel, I wanted to go on, but she forbade it. Said it was too dangerous."

Arizmendi's tiny flashlight formed a ring of light in front of the Governor as he continued to move forward, illuminating the curved roof and the walls down to Pietrantoni's knees, rendering the rest of his legs invisible in the darkness. Lucas could see very little beyond that bright ring, and when he turned to look back, could not discern any shapes beyond those of Nereida and Francisco.

It was not a big passageway, its roof and walls made of old, red bricks. Lucas could touch the two sides of the corridor at the same time without having to fully extend his arms, and he noticed that the Governor had to lean forward in order to avoid hitting the ceiling.

Suddenly, the tunnel made a forty-five degree turn to the right.

"It makes turns like this several times before it gets to the fork," Pietrantoni explained. "I think this tunnel was designed to help the Governor move under the city unobserved, and also as an emergency escape route. Just like it is being used now, as a matter of fact. The Spaniards were great at building fortifications and defenses. They hardly ever designed straight tunnels, where their enemies could rush straight at them or fire into them as they retreated. These passages were designed to disorient and confuse their enemies, and to protect their soldiers."

"Somewhat like your politics," Double A muttered back in the line, producing several invisible snickers.

That was good, Lucas thought—both the angled tunnels and the humor—as he dodged a root sticking out from the ceiling. Both would help them in their escape. On the other hand, there was no cell phone reception where they were now. When the rescuers came, later that night, they would have no idea where the Governor was. Hopefully, they'd be able to follow the signs of the struggle. But for now, the small band of runaways was on its own.

So much had happened in the last half hour. They had escaped from the Austral Tower just in time. Picon, his ear pressed against the seam between the false cupboard and the wall, had breathlessly warned the others that the terrorists were in the kitchen.

"I think they've seen some of the footprints on the flour," the Governor's bodyguard had whispered, provoking several gasps and scared murmurs. The Governor had gently shushed them.

As quietly as possible, Pietrantoni and Lucas had pushed open the exit to the Austral Tower, and allowed everyone to file out of the secret chamber, closing the door behind them.

The Governor had retrieved from Patria the key that opened the lock of the iron gate at the base of the tower, and asked Arizmendi to lead the way down the stairs using his pocket flashlight. Lucas had stayed behind to cover their retreat, urging Alfredo to go down with Nereida, while Picon had followed the Secretary of State, in case they stumbled into any terrorists.

As the small procession of fugitives spiraled out of sight, Lucas and Billy Hazard—the wounded bodyguard—had waited in the circular hall, their guns ready. With the flashlight gone, their eyes had gradually adjusted to the ensuing darkness until, helped by the pale moonlight filtering through the tower's window slits, they had begun to distinguish between the different shades of black that surrounded them.

At about that same time, they had heard the sharp report of automatic fire coming from the kitchen. It had been followed by a series of strong thuds, which unmistakably confirmed the terrorists' attempts to break through the false cabinet that separated them from the secret chamber.

"We may have to fight them while the others get out, and then make a run for it," Lucas had told the bodyguard. Then seeing the sorry state of his companion, had added, "In fact, I think you'd better start going down now. You're in no shape to make a run for it."

"You're right," Hazard had answered. "I can't run for it. I can't even walk for it," he had added tiredly. Hazard was in bad shape. Even though Nereida had bandaged his injured left leg, fresh blood was oozing through his bandages, and he had to lean against the wall to stay upright.

"Then I'll help you get down," Lucas had replied.

"No," Hazard had said, slowly moving towards the stairs. "That won't save me, and it will kill you."

The banging on the kitchen cupboard had stopped suddenly, then been renewed with greater fury.

"Our best chance to survive...for both of us to survive...is for you to leave me behind," Hazard had concluded with chilling logic.

"They'll kill you. You can't stay behind," Lucas had protested.

Hazard had shaken his head. "It doesn't make sense for both of us to stay here or for both of us to run. I have an idea," he had said. "If you help me get up there," he pointed to the stairs climbing towards the floor above them, "I may be able to hold them indefinitely from the top of the stairs. I have these two guns," he said, showing to Lucas the two Glocks that they had captured from the dead terrorists, "and plenty of ammunition. I can make them believe that we are all up there, and shoot down at them as they try to get up the stairs."

Lucas had said nothing. What Hazard suggested made sense, but it probably would get him killed.

"Can you help me up, please?" the bodyguard had said, sensing Lucas' hesitation. Then, grabbing his arm, he added, "Please, there's no other way. I can't run. Help me do my job."

Reluctantly, Lucas had nodded, and placed the bodyguard's right arm over his shoulders. Together, they had climbed fifteen steps to the next landing of the tower.

"Here," Lucas had said handing his AK-47 to Hazard. "This may come in handy." Then, as he helped the wounded bodyguard to sit on the steps, he had added half-heartedly, "I can stay with you."

"Stop playing the hero," Hazard had answered more harshly than he intended, wincing from the pain on his left thigh. "Your kid needs you," he had said more gently. "And you're crucial for the Governor's survival. Go!"

They shook hands.

"Take these." Lucas had given him two curved clips of the AK-47's ammunition. "We'll come back for you," he promised.

"You'd better," the bodyguard had answered with a scared smile.

Lucas had hurried down the spiraling stairs, sometimes feeling his way through patches of nearly absolute darkness. About halfway through, he had heard voices above him, but kept descending. When he reached the bottom, he had found the Governor waiting by the already open gate.

"I was afraid you weren't coming," Pietrantoni had said. "Where's Hazard?"

"He stayed behind," Lucas had replied without any further explanation. "Where to now?"

The Governor had looked up, as if considering whether to pursue the subject, but then thought better of it. "Through the gardens, and then to the garages. It's our only way out."

But the Macheteros had blocked their escape, and now the small group of refugees was underground, traipsing through a long-forgotten passageway of doubtful structural integrity used by God knows who to get to God knows where. And if they were pursued—and there was no reason to think that they would not be pursued—and they reached a dead end—which was a distinct possibility—they would be in for the fight of their lives. If the Macheteros were smart, they would seal the tunnel in and let the hostages suffocate. But then, they wouldn't know if the Governor had escaped via another exit.

His thoughts turned to Jennie, and his heart sank. She would be going crazy, not knowing anything about him, trying to stick to her daily routine in order not to scare the children. His mother and aunts would also be in deep distress, as would his sister Vanessa--Alfredo's mother— who would be dying every second that she failed to hear from her son.

A metallic "clang" echoed through the tunnel from afar, and the fugitives automatically increased their pace, many of them staring backwards apprehensively towards the darkness that closed in behind them.

They had to hurry.

The terrorists were coming.

CHAPTER LVIII

"You're leaving!" Cacho said with the same disappointment of a schoolteacher confronting a student who failed to hand in his homework. He was flanked by two of his men, each armed with an automatic rifle.

San Miguel looked back with a start, one of his legs already inside the front passenger seat of a brand new Buick Regal. His startled expression, however, immediately softened as he recognized the Machetero leader. He stepped out of the automobile and stood up to his full height.

"Cacho! You move silently! You gave me a start," he said with an ingratiating smile.

"Leaving already?" Cacho repeated, smiling back. He watched as Daniel slid silently out from the Regal's driver seat.

"Well...yes. I decided to go and see for myself what was happening at La Fortaleza," San Miguel answered pleasantly. "You seem to have things here firmly under control."

Cacho's smile turned into an involuntary smirk. "Not exactly," he said cryptically.

San Miguel raised an eyebrow in genuine puzzlement. "Oh? How so?" he asked solicitously.

"I've been checking up on your men. Couldn't find any at their posts, except for the Venezuelans. But then, the Venezuelans aren't really your men, are they? You and your friend Daniel are about the last of your group here."

"That's strange," San Miguel expressed, casting a questioning glance at Daniel, who merely shrugged, leaning against the car. "There has to be some error. Are you sure about that?"

Cacho nodded slowly with a perplexed expression, as if sharing San Miguel's surprise. "It was strange to me too," he said. "I've been watching them leave for the last ten minutes, three carfuls of them. They were so busy getting away that they didn't see me watching them from behind those bushes." He pointed to some shrubs to his right, filled with white hibiscus lowers. "Pretty, aren't they?" he said, leveling his sub machinegun at San Miguel, while his men took aim at Daniel.

"Wait!" San Miguel slowly raised his arms, his empty hands facing Cacho, his friendly smile unchanged. "Calm down, please. You're making a mistake. I'm the person who got you out of jail, remember?"

A hint of amused curiosity crossed Cacho's face. It was as if San Miguel meant everything that he said. *A good actor. Almost as good as him.* With the corner of his eyes, he saw Daniel lowering his hands to his waist.

"Please keep your hands on top of the car's roof," he warned him, prompting his two men to focus their weapons on him. Daniel obeyed with cheerful promptness.

"Yes," Cacho continued, addressing San Miguel's last query. "I've wondered about that myself. Why *would* you go through all that trouble, move—as we say here in Puerto Rico—the heavens and the earth to get me free, and then betray me?"

"Yes! Exactly!" San Miguel replied, then added somewhat confusedly, "Betray? What do you mean by betray? We were going to La—"

"Why did you help the Governor escape after you captured him?" Cacho continued to muse out loud as if San Miguel had not spoken.

"Help the Governor escape?" San Miguel's smile disappeared. He seemed to at last be taking Cacho seriously. "You're blaming me for that too?" he asked with sober indignation, his eyes hardening.

From the car, Daniel observed the two terrorist leaders with quiet fascination.

"You had better watch what you're saying. You insult my honor," San Miguel said indignantly.

Definitely a good actor, Cacho thought to himself. *Maybe even a little bit better than me. It was time to shock him.*

"Your man George confessed..." he said, and when San Miguel opened his mouth to protest, he added, "just before we killed him."

For a second, Cacho watched San Miguel's façade crumble, and a trace of fear appear on his face. The man was a control freak, and Cacho had wrested the control away from him. Even when taking into consideration the ghostly neon light of the open-air valet parking, he looked pale and shaken. From behind the open front door of the Buick Regal, Daniel took an involuntary step backwards, and then realizing he was about to get shot, placed both of his hands back on the car's roof.

But San Miguel recovered quickly, his expression reflecting outrage and pain. "You killed George! Why?!"

Cacho sighed, shaking his head sadly. *He too could act.* "I told you already. He let the Governor escape." He shook his head sadly and stared at San Miguel. "Angel, Angel! Or whatever your real name is. The game is over! Your men have left." He stole a glance at Daniel, who seemed so affected by the news that he was leaning on the car in order not to fall down. "Well, most of your men anyway. So now, it's time for you to pay. You've come to *my* country, created the biggest crisis in its history, got me released—for which I will be forever grateful—*only to hand us back to the Yankees*?" he shouted incredulously, letting his rising anger get the best of him. "You and your friend are dead men!"

He sighed, trying to collect his wits.

"The question is *why*. *Why*, my friend?"

San Miguel's outraged demeanor changed to one of cold defiance. "Why should I tell you? You're going to kill me anyway."

Cacho's lips twisted into a weird grin. "I may have been carried away," he answered in a calmer voice. "I may let you live, depending on the truthfulness of your explanation." *It was a lie, but what was a lie to a professional liar?*

San Miguel stared sullenly at the ground, as if considering his options. "All right," he said at last, "but my story will take a few minutes to tell. And after I finish, you'll see that I was justified in doing what I did."

Cacho looked at his watch. He had pledged to the Superintendent that in about twenty-five minutes he would start executing hostages, until the Governor was returned to him, and at the time he had intended to follow through with his threat. But he did not have the stomach to do it. He had never enjoyed killing innocent civilians, and any executions now would be pointless, with the revolt about to collapse. He would listen to San Miguel's explanation, kill him, and withdraw to the El Alacran's safe house before the American rescuers attacked.

But his men were still under standing orders to start executing the hostages at fifteen minutes to eight, barely enough time to listen to San Miguel and rush back to the hotel to stop the killings.

"Give me the short, five minute version," he said.

A different San Miguel raised his eyes from the ground. His brooding, surly expression had changed. Normally pleasant and unemotional, his face radiated contempt. A mocking, derisory smile distorted his lips, almost as if he was enjoying the moment.

Cacho felt the giant's shadow before he saw him. He heard a sickening "smack", and the head of the Machetero standing to his right partially caved in, spattering him with blood. At the same time, Daniel drew his gun out of his holster with blinding speed, shooting several times through the open car door's window and striking the other Machetero on the chest and his right shoulder.

Cacho began to swing his weapon around, but Czecka easily swatted it out of his hand with a baseball-bat-sized piece of wood, almost simultaneously grabbing the Machetero leader by his neck. Effortlessly, the huge man raised Cacho into the air, and like a rag doll slammed him to the ground, pinning him down and squeezing his throat.

As Cacho struggled to breathe, San Miguel sauntered up to him, crouched, and looked into his face.

"Did you really believe that you were going to kill us? I've had Czecka trailing you for some time now. Surprising how inconspicuous he can be for such a big man, isn't it?" he said in a calm, almost sad voice. "You should have just let us go. It would have never come to this."

Cacho's face was beginning to turn purple, his hands uselessly trying to pry Czecka's vise-like grip from his throat.

"I would have liked to let you go. You would have been a constant thorn in the American's side, and that is good for me. But you killed George..." San Miguel's expression darkened. "I liked George, may he rest in peace."

Cacho's eyes were bulging, his tongue sticking out of his mouth, his cheeks and neck a deep purple.

"But I will answer your question, since you were curious enough to ask. All of this, the revolution, the killing of hostages, your liberation from jail, it was all a ruse, a trick to draw everyone's attention away from our real mission, which unfortunately involves the destruction of San Juan. Not now. But give it a few months' time. When it happens, San Juan's name will become synonymous with Armageddon."

Cacho began to convulse violently, his eyes staring wildly at his tormentor, and then he stopped moving abruptly.

"Is he dead?" San Miguel asked Czecka.

The huge man stared up at him with his blank face, his thin, almost continuous eyebrows knotted upwards at an almost ninety-degree angle. It was his way of saying, "Duh! It's obvious, isn't it?"

San Miguel nodded once, grudgingly. "A pity. I had better plans for him. May God receive his soul in Heaven, if he is worthy."

Daniel watched San Miguel and Czecka return to the car, and then sat back into the driver's seat and turned the car on. As always, he had enjoyed watching San Miguel perform.

But now, it was time to leave.

Correcaminos was not certain if he had been officially allowed to stay in the provisional police headquarters set up in the San Geronimo Plaza, or had just been forgotten in the aftermath of the Condado Lagoon massacre. Be that as it may, Superintendent Maldonado had not ordered him evicted, even after Michelle had managed to establish direct contact with the police chief. His presence had not been questioned by the policemen coming in on later shifts, who had probably assumed that he had the authority to be there. Just in case, however, he had taken great pains to keep out of everybody's way and witness in absolute silence the ongoing operations.

The hotel staff had continuously kept their police guests supplied with food, stacking a table next to the communications equipment with small sandwiches and *hors d'ouvres*, as well as with orange juice, coffee, and refreshments. Unlike the Superintendent—who during the last four hours had only drunk straight black coffee—the reporter had taken full advantage of the proffered food.

With Doel's express blessing, Correcaminos planned to remain embedded there indefinitely, until the emergency ended, even if it took another day, a week, or even a month. Not that he expected that the crisis—by the movement that he had observed recently—would last much longer, but if it did, he was ready to stay there.

He could not leave. Getting into the command center had almost gotten him arrested; he had challenged a policeman almost twice his size to a boxing match; had missed several newscasts; and even lost touch with Michelle. But it had all been worthwhile. What an incredible—and even better, exclusive—story had unfolded before his eyes!

Few reporters had ever been allowed to observe the handling of a crisis of such nature from the very seat of command. However, Maldonado had allowed him to do just that. In an almost careless fashion, the police chief had given him unrestricted access to the provisional command center, hiding nothing, letting him absorb the tension and the human emotions that such an impossible situation generated. He had seen the Superintendent and his top officers age before his eyes, rage at the terrorists, joke and laugh out loud, and celebrate the few good news that reached them too far and in between. It almost seemed as if Maldonado wanted an independent observer to keep a moment-by-moment record of the ongoing crisis.

But the constant tension had taken a toll. By 6:30 PM, he felt physically and mentally exhausted. He had sat on one of the dozens of generic hotel seats scattered about the cold, cavernous ballroom to rest his feet, moving the chair as closely as he could to the television monitors that showed the surroundings of the Grand Laguna Hotel, and promptly dozed off.

A strong hand on his shoulder shook him awake a half hour later, followed by a rough but not unfriendly voice that said, "The Superintendent wants to see you."

Startled, he searched for Maldonado in the large, semi dark room, but was unable to find him.

"He wants to talk to you in private," the burly policeman who had awakened him explained with a half smile, enjoying his just-out-of-his-sleep, confused expression.

Still only half conscious, Correcaminos sprang to his feet, and followed the police officer out of the command center to an office just outside of the ballroom, the same office from which he had escaped a few hours before. For an instant, he thought that he was about to be booted out of the provisional headquarters, as he should have been hours before. But if that was the case, he quickly reasoned, the Superintendent would not have asked to see him first. Maldonado would have just sent one of his flunkies to do the dirty deed.

His heart began to pound with excitement as a new thought dawned on him: for some reason, Maldonado wanted to meet with him. And whatever the reason was, it was bound to be exciting.

He did not know what to expect, but the scene into which he walked surprised him. He found the Superintendent leaning against the front of the office's main desk, his hands grasping its edge, engaged in an earnest conversation with a sandy-haired, disheveled man wrapped in a blanket. Correcaminos noticed that the man had several cuts on his hands and face. Montañez stood next to him, totally engrossed by the story the man was telling, his eyes occasionally flicking to a small television set on the room's second desk that showed—its volume turned off—the Grand Laguna Hotel.

They all stopped talking to look at the new arrival.

"Thank you, Ruiz," Maldonado said to the policeman who had awakened Correcaminos. "You may return to your post."

"Yes, sir," Ruiz answered immediately, his face showing his clear disappointment at not being allowed to stay. He took one last glance at the sandy-haired man and left.

"Mr. Frontera," Maldonado said to the reporter, addressing him by his real name, "this is Raymond Tavarez. He's a member of our SWAT team and—I'm happy to say—a survivor from this afternoon's disastrous foray."

"Hey!" the man in the blanket said cheerfully, flashing a toothy grin. Correcaminos noticed that he was very young, maybe even in his late teens. His hands were shaking. "You're the sportscaster from WKPA TV!" Raymond assumed a dramatic tone, imitating the new arrival's voice. "This is Correcaminos Frontera, reporting from el Choliseo!" He laughed a bit too loudly.

Correcaminos looked at the Superintendent quizzically.

"You must forgive officer Tavarez's enthusiasm. I think his adrenaline is still pumping at a hundred revolutions per second. He just swam across from the San Geronimo Fort and nearly got swept out to the sea."

"You were at the San Geronimo?" Correcaminos repeated uncertainly.

"Not exactly *in* the fort. We hid from the terrorists behind the outside wall, in a trench between the fort and the reefs," Raymond volunteered before his superiors could put in another word. "After...my boat was sunk, I was swept there along with Captain Gomez and Sergeant Abe Cordero."

"You were very lucky. The currents there can be quite strong," Correcaminos said.

"You're telling me!" Raymond laughed again, his hands still shaking.

"They're still there, the captain and Sergeant Cordero," Maldonado said. "They're sort of waiting for our instructions. That's why they sent Raymond. But we can't communicate with them by phone or radio, just signal the approximate time that we want them to move in. If we don't signal them to stop, they intend to start moving into the hotel on their own at 7:15 PM."

Correcaminos looked at his watch. That would mean that the men would be taking the initiative into their own hands in less than ten minutes.

An awkward pause followed, as Montañez looked at his boss, as if seeking his silent permission to speak. Maldonado nodded.

"The Navy SEALs will be conducting a raid tonight, but it is doubtful that they will be able to get to the Grand Laguna before nine o'clock at the earliest, and even that time is looking more and more difficult to make," Montañez said.

Correcaminos waited in breathless silence for the colonel to continue, trying to figure out why the Police Department's top brass was discussing its secret rescue plans with him, and where he fit into the scheme of things. So far, he could not think of a single reason why he was receiving the highly classified information. Obviously, they were not doing it to help him keep the public informed.

"There is," Montañez continued, "one additional bit of crucial information that affects our plans, and where we could use your help and input. Just a few minutes ago, Adalberto Cacho informed us that he will start killing five hostages, starting at seven forty-five tonight, every half hour until the Governor gives himself up to the terrorists." Montañez eyed Correcaminos with curiosity. "You do know that the Governor managed to escape the terrorists, and that he is hiding in La Fortaleza."

Correcaminos nodded, then shook his head. "I mean, I heard some gossip that he had escaped. I didn't know he was hiding in La Fortaleza. I hadn't heard about the hostages."

"The Governor is hiding in La Fortaleza," Maldonado confirmed. *Had the circles under his eyes grown even darker*, Correcaminos wondered? "I personally spoke to him a couple of hours ago."

"So we need to use whatever resources we have in place to try to stop the executions," Montañez said.

"Those resources being Captain Gomez and the sergeant, whatever his name is..." Correcaminos stated, thrilled with the information he had just received, but still uncertain about his role in the matter.

"And Michelle Alfaro and her two companions," Maldonado added, looking straight at the newscaster. "You don't know this, but I spoke directly with Miss Alfaro a short time ago. She's discovered where the hostages are being kept. She is hiding somewhere in the hotel. Our SWAT people stranded in San Geronimo don't have that information. We need her to meet Gomez and guide him to the hostages, so that they...remove the people who are doing the executions and defend the hostages until the SEALs can get into the act."

All of the faces in the room turned to him. Now Correcaminos understood why he had been summoned to that meeting.

"I can't paint you a rosy picture," Maldonado continued. "Meeting our SWAT officers will be very dangerous. Ms Alfaro and her companions will have to evade whatever sentries the Macheteros have posted on the shore, and even worse, since our men are not expecting them, they may mistake her for the enemy."

"And you want me to convince her to do it?" he asked, overwhelmed by the preposterous idea of having to convince his beloved friend to participate in what sounded like a suicidal mission.

The policemen hesitated, both looking very uncomfortable.

"We've been told that you are one of Michelle's closest friends," Maldonado insisted.

"And so, you want *me* to convince her to risk her life to get the SWAT officers to the hostages," he repeated in a peeved tone, more as a statement than as a question.

Maldonado crossed his arms. "Honestly, we're not sure if you can do anything...We don't know if you would want to do anything," he said helplessly. "But...we're at the end of the rope. If we don't get our SWAT team in there in time, many of the hostages will surely die, and the rest will remain at the mercy of the terrorists. We need to do everything that is in our power to do."

"Has it occurred to you that if we do nothing, and the SEALs rescue the bulk of the hostages, only a few of them will be killed, and that if Michelle stumbles into the terrorists, she and her friends, and most probably your men also, may be wiped out? You may end up losing more people trying to save the few tourists that are executed than if you do nothing!" Correcaminos expressed with angry dismay.

Maldonado made as if to speak, but Montañez intervened.

"Yes, we've taken that into consideration, although the 'few' tourists that may be executed before the SEALs arrive may add up to twenty or twenty-five, or more. That is far from being a few."

Correcaminos shook his head, unable to challenge the colonel's logic.

"Listen," Montañez said in a subdued tone. "We don't have any time left. I...we have great faith in Michelle. She has been able to penetrate the perimeter set up by the Macheteros in the Grand Laguna and is hiding inside the hotel right now. We need her help."

"She won't get to them in time," Correcaminos objected half-heartedly, looking directly at Maldonado.

The Superintendent sighed.

"We've tried everything else. Tried to buy more time, but they won't give it to us. Threatened them, but they've laughed at us. This is the only alternative that we've got left. That *they've* got left! Michelle and her friends are in the hotel now. They can decide for themselves, better than anyone, if what we're asking of them is impossible or too risky to do, or if it's worth a chance. If they decide not to do it, then that's it. We won't pressure them to do it, I promise you. But don't automatically condemn twenty or twenty-five innocent people to die because you don't know them and it won't hurt you as much if they die as if someone you know, like Michelle, dies. It's not fair to those people. You *know* that if Michelle was one of the persons that was chosen to be executed, and there was somebody else who could warn the SWAT team, you wouldn't hesitate a second to ask him to do it. Or would you?"

Correcaminos cast down his eyes, looking very mortified.

"Mr. Frontera," Maldonado said in sympathetic tone of voice. "I won't impose this task on you if you don't want to undertake it. I just thought she might...I don't know. I suppose I *did* hope secretly that you being in the conversation would have some influence on her decision, or something like that..." He looked at the digital clock on the desk and noted the time. "But we've already spent five minutes of the precious time that we have left to try to save those hostages. We have to call her *now*, before it's too late. Do you wish to participate in the conversation?"

Correcaminos barked a short laugh. "You don't know her very well, do you?" he said bitterly. "When you start telling her what you want, she'll volunteer before you finish! This is the kind of thing that she lives for. You don't need me. But yes, I'll talk to her."

"Thank you," Maldonado said gratefully.

"Oh, don't thank me. I'll try to dissuade her from doing it," he answered truthfully.

"I'll let you talk first," the Superintendent said. "Then let me talk to the policeman who's with her."

Michelle, Archie, and Negron silently observed Fort San Geronimo, trying to perceive any movement around the moonlit walls of the old fortification. They were lying on the floor of room 3220 of the Grand Laguna Hotel, which gave them a view of the Condado Lagoon area and eastern grounds of the hotel. Somehow, the lights of the Dos Hermanos Bridge were still working, illuminating the awful gap that existed between the main hotel strip and the bridge.

"Do you see anyone?" Michelle asked.

"You mean, anyone besides you guys?" Negron asked in a louder voice than he should, making Archie roll his eyes and provoking a shushing noise from Michelle. "No," he answered, lowering his voice, "but if they're as good as they're supposed to be, we will not see them."

They were in one of the empty rooms of the hotel. It had taken the rookie policeman ten harrowing minutes to figure out how to open the lock to the room, while Archie kept a lookout in the corridor close to the elevator doors, but finally, with a triumphant "Aha!", he had pushed the room's heavy wooden door open.

"I didn't know lock-picking was one of the courses taught in the Police Academy," Michelle had remarked as they invaded the empty room. Its bed was unmade, and various plastic cups, soda cans, and an open bottle of Bacardi, as well as several male and female articles of clothing, were scattered over the night tables, the bed, and the writing desk. They had kept the lights of the room off, not only to avoid detection by the terrorists, but afraid that a lit room could draw fire from the police snipers across the lagoon.

"They should teach lock-picking in the Police Academy," Negron answered with a crooked smile. "It's a very useful skill. I learned to open locks in San Sebastian, where I come from." San Sebastian del Pepino was a beautiful town nestled in the central mountain peaks of the island. Despite its small size, it had produced a significant number of Puerto Rico's most influential citizens. Proud of their origin, their residents called themselves the "Pepinianos". "I learned it from the son of our preacher, 'Houdini' Montalvo. Where he learned it from I have no idea, but he was quite good at it. We used to pick the locks of our high school and do all sorts of pranks."

"Oh, you were one of those punks who trash schools?" Archie had said, trying to bait him, but Negron had taken it in stride.

"Oh no, nothing like that. Just a lot of innocent jokes. Like once, we wrapped all of the school doors in newspaper, outside and inside. You should have seen the principal's face scratching his head and interrogating the janitor. Another time we sneaked a cow into the biology lab. You can imagine the shouts of Mrs. Alvarez that morning, especially after she stepped on a cow pie. Another time we placed an iguana inside this particularly nasty girl's locker. Stuff like that. It used to drive them crazy! We started the rumor that aliens were doing those things, and it caught like wildfire."

Archie shook his head. "Only in San Sebastian," he said.

"Once you learn how to pick a lock, you don't forget," Negron said in an almost wistful tone. "Houdini was a good teacher."

"Didn't people suspect Houdini?" Michelle asked.

"Why? He was the preacher's son."

"But his nickname. You know, Houdini, after the escape artist? Some people must have tied two and two together."

"Houdini was an escape artist?" Negron had asked, incredulously.

Archie had stared at his friend, to determine if he was pulling his leg, but from his guileless expression had determined that he was dead serious.

They had crawled on their bellies to the edge of the balcony, Negron with a great deal of care and discomfort, and looked through its railings, to survey the gardens below, as well as the low wall fringing the lagoon. At first, they had been unable to detect any of the lookouts posted in the perimeter of the hotel. But gradually, small movements and fleeting shadows—a leg lazily extended beyond the fringe of the shadows cast by the stone fence bordering the lagoon, the flicker of a cigarette light in the garden—began to expose their hidden positions.

By 7:10 PM, they had spotted three sentries, one hidden close to the gazebo in the gardens, another behind some shrubs, the third crouched behind the low fence separating the hotel grounds from the water.

One of them, the first they spotted because of his uneasy, almost constant movements, kept staring at his watch, as if impatiently waiting for someone to arrive. He was stationed behind some shrubs, at a spot where the grounds of the Grand Laguna Hotel tapered into the public sidewalk that edged the lagoon. Finally, his impatience seemed to have won, and he had crawled out of sight towards the hotel.

"Maybe he has to take a crap," Negron had suggested.

Michelle had crawled back into the room and prepared to call the Superintendent through her cell phone to inform him about the sentries, when it had begun to vibrate, nearly causing her to drop it from the surprise. With her heart pounding like a hammer inside her chest, she had answered and been surprised to be addressed by Correcaminos. She had listened quietly as her friend explained the police chief's request. After two minutes, she had said, "Tell him that we will do our best." Then she had passed the phone to Negron, whispering, "The Superintendent wants to talk to you," almost causing the young policeman to faint. It had been a brief conversation, during which Negron had answered "Yes, sir" four times, and then added, "It will be my honor, sir", and hung up.

The two friends had quickly informed Archie about the Superintendent's request. Like Negron, he had agreed without hesitation. They had crawled back to the balcony, to see if they could detect the movements of the two SWAT officers, but had been unable to see them.

"But if the time frame is right, those SWAT people by the fort should be reaching the shore at any moment. We have to hurry!" Archie added, looking at the time. "So...how do we go about it?"

"I have an idea," Michelle said.

CHAPTER LIX

Frankie Redondo lit his third cigarette in the last hour, cupping his hands to hide his Zippo's flame, his back turned towards the lagoon to make the light even less visible. The police was too far away anyway—separated by the lagoon—and after the drubbing that its supposedly elite SWAT team had been given that afternoon, he felt fairly certain that they would not dare to attempt a second raid. Not that same day, anyway.

Nevertheless, their unit commander, had spread the word that that an attack by the "American special forces", whoever they were, was likely that night. He did not believe it, but the Macheteros guarding the hotel had been placed on full alert. A few lookouts had been posted up front, behind the stone fence facing the lagoon, and in the gardens. They were sparse and few, a sort of tripwire alarm to alert the others in case of an invasion, while the Venezuelans kept watch to the north, in the pool and beach areas, and San Miguel's men in the gardens and surrounding the convention hall where the hostages were being held. And in the main lobby, over a dozen more well armed Macheteros and about thirty FEPIstas stood ready to beef up their lines, wherever they were needed.

If the Americans tried to penetrate their perimeter, they would be repelled with heavy loses. With the Venezuelans' superior firepower, and the Macheteros' fighting experience, they wouldn't stand a chance.

Frankie had been assigned to patrol the hotel's gardens. He kept himself behind the tall flower shrubs and the night's long shadows, to avoid becoming a target to one of the government's snipers, but he was not afraid. He did not fear the Americans. In fact, he hoped they came his way. That way he would be the one who would fire the first shot of the second lagoon massacre.

Frankie took a long pull from his cigarette and exhaled it into the garden, closing his eyes with deep satisfaction. He opened them as the smoke cloud began to dissipate, and to his great surprise saw the body of a woman, like a ghostly vision, materialize from within the mist.

He should have reacted immediately, but for a moment he stood mesmerized by the unexpected vision. There was something oddly different about her. Her face was bruised and discolored, her upper lip swollen, her clothes somewhat baggy and ill-fitting, and yet, she exuded an unmistakable sensuality, her green eyes gleaming in the moonlight, almost as if they possessed a source of light of their own, the sensual curves of her body overcoming the unflattering garments that covered her, her bruised mouth curved in an attractive, sensual smile.

He finally reacted when she was almost within arm's reach, straightening up abruptly from the pole of the gazebo on which he was leaning, and discarding his half-finished cigarette into the garden's pond. He pointed his automatic rifle at her, making her stop.

"Who are you?" he asked suspiciously, trying to better discern her features in the darkness. There was something vaguely familiar about her face.

The woman placed a finger under the black armband that she wore around her upper arm, showing the words "Libre Como el Coqui" to the bewildered sentry. "A friend, she replied with a slight lisp. "I'm sorry. I didn't mean to scare you."

"Scare me?" Frankie answered with a snort of derision. "Who said I'm scared? I just haven't seen you around before."

"I'm making the rounds to the sentries," the green-eyed woman explained. "To see if any of you need food. We don't want you starving out here." She sniffed the air. "Were you smoking?" she asked, and before he could deny it, she added, "I could use a good smoke."

"Sure." Frankie lowered his weapon, leaning it against the gazebo's railing, and fished in his pockets for a pack of cigarettes. As he did, she took a step closer to him, still smiling. He did not hear the faint footsteps behind him, distracted by the green-eyed lady's approach.

He stared at her, squinting to see her better in the shadows. "What happened to your—" he began to ask her, but a heavy object crashed against the back of his neck. He staggered forward, dazedly, but managed to stay on his feet. He heard someone mutter a curse and hurry after him, and then the heavy object struck him two more times, on the right side of his forehead and on his cheek. He only got to feel the first of the two blows, total blackness overwhelming his senses.

Michelle shuddered involuntarily, grabbing one leg of the fallen terrorist and letting Archie grab the other. Together, they dragged the man into the bushes.

"What time is it?" Felipe inquired nervously for the fifth time during the last half hour. "I think my watch stopped." Of the three Macheteros stationed at the entrance of the ballroom, he had initially seemed the most aloof and unemotional. His companions called him Albizu Junior behind his back, due to his proclivity to act and even dress like the 1940's revolutionary leader—from his openly superior demeanor to his trimmed mustache, his curly, wavy hair, and even his elegant, slightly outmoded manner of dress. But as the hour to kill the first of the hotel prisoners neared, his nerves began to unravel, and he became progressively fidgety and petulant, engaging in a series of stream-of-consciousness monologues, constantly asking about the time.

El Cano—literally meaning "the light-haired one" because of his thin, ash-blond hair—smiled and stretched his arms without removing the straw, touristy hat covering his face. He was lying on two chairs, and had already made it clear that he did not own a watch—never had and never would. Therefore, he felt no obligation to say anything. Besides, he despised Felipe. Albizu Jr. brought out the mean streak in him.

Pedro, the third guard, knew what the time was but squinted at his watch through his thick glasses. With full, black hair that he combed straight back and kept pasted to his head with a heavy, shiny pomade; a wide, short body with muscular, hairy arms; and a slight hunch accentuated by a long, angular nose, he looked like an oversized mole. "It's time," he just said.

None of the three men stirred for a moment.

"Well," Felipe stated with as much authority as he could muster, "then you two should go in and pick the five hostages."

El Cano took his hat off his face and sat up, his blue eyes alighting on the nervous Albizu Jr. He smiled pleasantly.

"Sure, I'll choose them, you kill them, okay?"

Felipe turned his head sharply, as if he had been stung by an angry bee. He stammered a few, incomprehensible sounds, then managed to organize his thoughts sufficiently to say, "I'm sorry, but I am the liaison with Cacho. I have to stay here."

El Cano laughed. He regarded Felipe with amusement. "*Liaison*, that's a fancy word. Somehow, I think of you more like a cross between a gofer and a messenger boy, a brown-nosing messenger boy, for that matter. I've seen how you operate. You don't want to dirty your hands. You just want to be taken out of here, don't you? Cuddle up with our commanders in a cushy place," he said, as if addressing a baby, "not having to face the risk that the rest of us are facing."

"That's a lie!" Felipe hissed back at him, his voice full of loathing. "Cacho personally told me how much he relies on my reports. You know how essential it is to keep him informed."

"Forgive me, Felipe, but the bullshit is overwhelming me, and I may gag," El Cano said dismissively, standing up and stretching again. He was not taller than his companion, but Albizu Jr's slighter frame made the latter look a lot smaller. "You don't want to get your hands dirty, that's all," the blond Machetero repeated.

"That's not true!" Felipe protested with indignation. "You don't know—"

"We're wasting a lot of time here," Pedro interrupted in a tired voice, talking to his two comrades with the same weariness of a parent trying to separate his children for the eleven hundredth time. "It's seven thirty-five already. We have another ten minutes to get this done. We'll decide who does what by strict chance."

Pedro grabbed a piece of hotel stationary and ripped three, roughly equal strips of paper from it, writing a name on each of them. Folding them, he dropped them into a plastic cup. He placed a hand over the cup's rim and shook the inside contents vigorously. "Whoever comes out first will kill the first five hostages. Whoever comes out second will shoot the second five hostages half an hour later, and so on and so forth, until we're told to stop the executions." He placed the cup on a chair, still covering it with his hand. "Whoever does the killing chooses his hostages. The first two names take the hostages to the gardens, the other stays here to guard the ballroom's entrance. Now, that sounds fair, doesn't it?"

"Whatever," El Cano responded impatiently. Despite his outward bluster, he felt just as nervous as Albizu Jr.

"I don't...I don't....I don't fully understand," the latter stammered.

"Just look away and pick out a name," Pedro told him.

Reluctantly, the nervous Machetero inserted two fingers into the cup, and with a pincer-like movement pulled out one of the folded paper strips. He opened it with dread, and all of his fears seemed to materialize, growing instantly pale and nearly swooning. He let the paper strip drop to the floor. El Cano picked it up and snickered.

"This is great!" he said, the corners of his mouth curling into a cruel grin. "There is Divine Justice after all."

Felipe turned angrily on Pedro. "This isn't fair! I shouldn't have been the first one to pick a name. Why does it have to be me? Cano enjoys doing the killings anyway! He's doing this to spite me!" he protested petulantly.

"It was all fair and square. You will take the first five hostages. Let's see who goes with you to the gardens to execute them." Pedro extended the cup to El Cano, who continued to smile gleefully. "Cano! Your turn."

El Cano's beefy fingers nearly didn't fit in the paper cup, but finally, after nearly knocking the cup from Pedro's hands, he managed to get hold of one of the remaining names.

"I hope it's me," El Cano said with sincere relish, as he unfolded the strip of paper. "I'd love to see how he's going to botch up the executions."

By his comrade's face of disappointment, Pedro immediately guessed that his name had come up. Resignedly, he stood up.

"Come on, Felipe," he said to his distraught companion. "Let's go find us five winners."

As the interminable hours of his captivity lingered into the night, Mark Sampson had begun to despair. At the beginning of the ordeal, he had braced himself for the rescue action that he thought would inevitably come, carefully examining the vast, hostage-filled ballroom and gradually moving towards a corner—away from the obnoxious, deaf, noisy old man who had nearly given his identity away—that he deemed would be the furthest from any fighting that took place. Indeed, sometime during the afternoon, he and the other hostages heard prolonged shooting and dozens of large explosions that he thought presaged his impending deliverance, but nothing had come of it. The shots had tapered off, and then ceased altogether. And no rescue had come.

During the subsequent hours, his nerves had unraveled. The conditions in the convention hall had steadily deteriorated. Although food had been served at lunchtime, no dinner had yet been provided, and the visits to the restrooms had been discontinued an hour before, after one of the terrorists had announced that the "the toilets had broken down", and that other alternatives were being considered. None, however, had been offered, and when an older man had indicated his urgent "need to go", he had been bluntly advised that he would have "to hold it or do it in his pants". The man had held for another half hour, and then peed on himself. Half a dozen others had since then followed his lead, and certain portions of the hall had begun to smell with the acrid stench of urine.

Shortly after the noise of the explosions, a woman had become hysterical and begun to scream that they were all going to be killed, like the ten guests who had been removed earlier from the ballroom and never returned. She had rapidly been carried out by two guards, and not seen again. Small children constantly cried, and older guests complained about their pain and the hardness of the floor. One doctor continuously made rounds around the ballroom, attending to the increasing number of health complaints, from migraines to chest palpitations to dizziness and nausea, all caused mostly by the unbearable tension they were all undergoing. Another doctor had been spirited away from the hall for undisclosed motives and to an undisclosed location—Mark surmised to treat some of the terrorists—and been returned an hour later. The man had kept to himself, speaking to no one, apparently instructed, under penalty of punishment, to remain silent.

There were no further news of April or any of the other dozen hostages who had been selected at random and marched out of the ballroom, just a few minutes before the explosions and the shooting had begun. He suspected that the two events were interconnected, and feared that they were all dead. Of course, he had no way of knowing it, but where would she and the others be otherwise? He felt broken-hearted for her, but there was really nothing that he could have done.

The situation was rapidly spinning out of control. He could not believe that his staff and the U. S. government had not taken the necessary actions to secure his release. He was a very valuable hostage. He was certain that if the authorities tried to exchange him for some jailed terrorist, he would have been freed by now. To be fair, there could be some concern that revealing his identity would place him in danger, as he himself had felt at the beginning of the ordeal. But the situation had changed.

He had become more and more convinced that if he was to walk out of that hellish hotel alive, he had to take matters into his own hands and act quickly. Already the essential services had been stopped. That could only mean one thing: that they were planning to get rid of the hostages soon. The prisoners seemed to sense it. The mood in the grand hall had changed from inconvenienced discomfort to tense expectation. He had to get out of there now.

He had counted three terrorists—two women and a man—inside the ballroom, in addition to those guarding the doors. All of them looked extremely young and almost as scared as the people that they were guarding. They had been in charge of moving the groups to the restrooms, distributing the food, and solving some of the minor problems that arose from such a massive assembly. They were armed with automatic rifles—AK-47's, if his knowledge of guns had not abandoned him—but by the way that they handled them, they seemed to be very unfamiliar with their weapons. Obviously, they were helpers of some sort, not the hardened terrorists who had blown up the bridges, taken over the hotel, and made all of the important decisions.

He had begun to form a plan in his mind. His initial strategy had been to melt into the crowd. But staying in the crowd was now the danger. He had to separate himself from the rest of the hostages. He had to let the terrorists know what an important person they had caught in their net.

He was certain that if he was allowed to speak to the leader of the terrorists, he could convince him of his usefulness to their cause, whatever that cause was. He suspected, by their looks, hair, and skin, that they were Muslims, and that gave him some pause, since he had publicly chastised the President for failing to protect his state from radical Islamists who could easily be profiled and identified when they entered the country. But he doubted very much that these men would be aware of that. Besides, sometimes hardliners made the best negotiators, like anti-communist Nixon and the establishment of diplomatic relations with Red China.

He could offer to negotiate in their behalf, helping them to secure some of their goals while avoiding further bloodshed. Maybe he would not be freed, but by becoming a player in the game, he'd be spared the fate of the other non-players.

He had decided to approach the younger male guard—he definitely wanted to stay as far away as possible from the fat female with the flip flops who seemed to hate everybody, including her other companions— when the door to the ballroom opened and two of the *real* terrorists walked in. They stopped just beyond the door and eyed the prisoners warily, pausing to whisper to each other. They quickly chose four hostages—all of them men in their twenties or thirties—and seemed to be searching the crowd for others. *The next group of hostages to be executed?* Mark wondered.

He had to act quickly. It was the perfect opportunity, and he took it. Climbing up to his feet, he started to walk towards them, provoking curious glances from the other guests through which he tried to navigate.

Mark waved at the two terrorists, and when they failed to notice him, he shouted, "Excuse me! Excuse me! Can I talk to you for a moment?"

The fat female guarding the ballroom saw him and shouted at him to return to his place. Already halfway to the entrance, Mark turned his head towards her and raised his hand, signaling her to wait, while pointing at the two men by the entrance. "I need to talk to these gentlemen," he explained to her in a friendly voice, continuing to walk towards them.

The sour-faced woman opened her mouth, amazed by the effrontery of the prisoner, and shouted at the top of her lungs, "Sit down this instant!" fumbling for her gun.

Mark continued to approach the other two terrorists, who had stopped talking and were watching him with interest. In fact, most of the prisoners in the ballroom were now aware of his progress, those farthest away craning their necks or crouching to find the source of the disruption. "It's all right!" Mark shouted at the woman, flashing his most charming smile. "I'm not trying to escape. I just need to talk to them for a moment."

"Sit down this instant, asshole! OR I WILL SHOOT YOU!" she screeched.

The woman was by now totally enraged, her face beet red either from her anger or her efforts to shout. She began to stride rapidly towards the rebellious prisoner, crashing through the sitting crowd, forcing those in her path to scurry or be trampled. For the first time, Mark hesitated. He looked at the two terrorists standing by the door and said, "Please!"

The shorter of the two, a man wearing thick glasses, nodded briefly and shouted at the approaching female, "It's okay. We'll handle this." But the woman continued to stamp her way through the scampering hostages, oblivious of the terrorist's instructions.

Rolling back his eyes in exasperation, the man with the eyeglasses placed two of his fingers on his lips and whistled shrilly. "You!" he said loudly, pointing at the angry guard. "I said *I* will handle this!"

The woman stopped abruptly, her face reflecting surprise and indignation. She glared at the disobedient prisoner, and finally began to withdraw. The man with the glasses motioned Mark with his hand to approach him.

"Thank you!" Mark said gratefully, as he reached them, beginning to extend his hand to shake that of the bespectacled terrorist, then stopping midway as he thought better of it. "Hi!" he said, flashing another of his "winning" smiles. "My name is Mark Sampson. You may know me from the newspapers..."

The two terrorists exchanged a vacant look, signaling to the Florida politician that they had no idea of who he was. *It did not matter,* Mark thought, *they would soon know*. He noticed that many of the nearby hostages were listening to the conversation, and lowered his voice.

"My name is Mark Sampson, Speaker of the House in Florida..." He waited, to see if they finally recognized him, but getting no reaction, continued, getting nearer to the two men and lowering his tone of voice. "You will find that I have a great deal of pull in the federal government, and that I could be very useful in any negotiations with them. If you will take me to your superiors, I will be glad to elaborate," he said in English, looking now at the second terrorist, a thin man with a trimmed mustache and a dignified expression who would not look him in the eyes. "Can we talk outside?" he asked, painfully aware that he was being overheard by some of the prisoners.

The terrorist glanced at his companion, who nodded and pointed to the door. Relieved, Mark strode towards the exit.

As he and the other four hostages moved, Pedro whispered to Felipe, "I think our fifth victim chose himself, don't you?"

Felipe nodded, managing a sickly smile.

"It's seven twenty-five," Cordero whispered, looking expectantly at his captain. "We haven't heard from Tavarez and we're already ten minutes overdue."

They had been straining their eyes towards the dim coast north of the San Geronimo Plaza Hotel during the last hour, hoping to catch even the faintest glimmer of a flashlight, but nothing had broken the landscape of the night. The wind had picked up and the sea increased its violence, its waves battering the rocks that surrounded the northern boundary of the small fort. The rain clouds had passed, and a half moon, unhindered by any clouds, cast a ghostly glow over the land and the sea below it, creating deep shadows where its rays failed to penetrate.

Gomez' body felt stiff as a board, his head still buzzing with a dull ache from the heavy blow he had received. They had taken stock of the equipment that they carried with them, and had confirmed that they possessed a very respectable inventory of weapons. It included the M16 left behind by Tavarez with eight ammunition clips, two MP-5K compact sub machineguns with a dozen ammunition clips, their two Glock .40 pistols with twenty four clips, six smoke canisters and another six flashbang grenades, in addition to a set of binoculars, the illegal silencer carried by Cordero, two small water canteens already depleted, and a first aid kit. *If they got into a firefight,* Gomez thought with satisfaction, *there would a hell of a shootout.*

He wondered if Raymond had made it to the other side. He fervently hoped so, since otherwise it meant that he had been swept out into the ocean and was still trying to swim ashore—if the sea had not swallowed him. He liked the kid a great deal. It tortured him to think that he had drowned.

Regardless of what had happened, they had not been ordered to stop. So now, they were faced with a choice. Despite what they had told Raymond, the two men had continued to debate after his departure what they should do if they received no instructions. A wrong decision on their part could have dire consequences in the rescue operation, not to mention their lives.

The worst-case scenario—the nightmare scenario, really—would be that by continuing with their planned incursion they somehow tipped the terrorists about the time and location of the real rescue operation; that as they tried to penetrate the enemy lines they would be discovered, and would draw the Macheteros to the actual spot where the special forces—whoever they were—intended to conduct their raid. After all, neither Gomez nor Cordero had any idea of when and where the main rescuers would strike.

However, the odds of that happening were slim. It was very doubtful that the rescue team would concentrate its attack on one particular spot, and that the chosen spot would happen to be the San Geronimo Fort. Not knowing where the hostages were, the special forces would cover a broader area, first securing the perimeter, then moving inside. Also, if the rescuers intended to conduct their raid any time soon, they would have probably reached the San Geronimo walls by now.

The two SWAT officers intended to eliminate as many of the enemy lookouts as they could without engaging in a firefight. If they were discovered, they would try to draw the fight away from the shore and into the parking building to the south of the Grand Laguna Hotel, where none of the hostages were bound to be. The real rescue party would have a much better time cutting through the token enemy forces that were left behind guarding the hotel.

They had also considered the possibility that they would be acting prematurely, that by trying to penetrate the enemy lines they would be stirring a hornets' nest hours before the main operation took place, that if they were captured or killed, the terrorists would try to retaliate against the hostages, killing several of them. After all, his SWAT team had only moved after the lives of some of the hostages had been placed in immediate, dire danger, and no other alternative had been left open to the government authorities. Afterwards, for reasons unknown to Gomez and Cordero, the execution of hostages had stopped, at least temporarily. But a failed incursion on their part could restart it.

Gomez knew that the Superintendent had always contemplated a night rescue attempt, and that if he had negotiated any truce with the terrorists, his main objective would have been to gain time until he could take advantage of the night's darkness. Gomez also knew that Maldonado would not wait long after the night fell. Every passing minute brought new risks and perils to the trapped guests, and allowed the Macheteros to prepare better for the attack that they knew would come sooner or later. After all, they were not stupid. Maldonado would strike, and do it soon.

So overall, the benefits of their plan outweighed its possible risks. But there was another reason for going in. *It was their job.* Their unit had been sent to rescue the hostages and been decimated in the process. They owed it to their men, to all who had fallen that day, to try. They could not sit and wait for the rescue to happen.

"It's time to go," Gomez confirmed, standing up and leaning against the old San Geronimo fort's wall.

Sergeant Cordero drew out of his satchel bag the elongated dark metal cone that he used to silence his Glock and screwed it onto the gun's barrel. He stretched out to an upright position and, not uttering another word, scampered over the sharp, dark rocks at the base of the old fort. Gomez followed.

Fort San Geronimo was shaped like a giant square, or if the bridge that connected it to San Juan was included, like a square banjo lying on its side.

The bridge, about fifty feet long, was flanked by high brick and mortar walls, and was wide enough to allow a carriage or a supply wagon to transit over it. It was designed to hem in any invaders who tried to storm the fort's main entrance, making them an easy target for the men defending the fort's west wall. Supported by a wide arch, the bridge spanned a shallow pool of calm water protected from the rolling waves of the sea by a string of reefs to the north, and a second set of reefs to its south.

In order to get to the Grand Laguna Hotel, the two SWAT officers would have to ford the chest-high waters of the pool and climb the rocks lining the shore of the hotel. They would have to cross the shallow pool as close to the bridge as possible, trying to blend with the gloom of its underbelly.

The two men came to a stop at the edge of the water, crouching below the rounded corner of the fort, where its southern wall ended and the pool began. There, they surveyed the shore, their gray and black uniforms blending nearly perfectly with the shadows of the wall cast by the moon.

"See anything?" Gomez asked his sergeant.

Cordero failed to respond for a breathless moment, then whispered, "There!" pointing to a spot about thirty yards down from the bridge's end. Gomez looked just in time to catch a glimpse of the faint outline of a head, behind the low stone wall. Then the head ducked out of sight. "A sentry, taking a peek," the grizzled veteran murmured with the same intensity of a doctor examining a wound. "Trying to catch sight of a Navy SEAL swimming in the lagoon. Amateur!"

"Those amateurs kicked our collective asses today," Gomez reminded his sergeant.

"Amateurs nevertheless, captain," Cordero replied. "And now it's *our* time to kick theirs. I'll go first, if you don't mind, sir."

Gomez was about to reply, but by then Cordero had already climbed down from the reef and dipped his legs up to his knees in the dark, still waters of the pool. Gomez turned his attention back to the spot where they had seen the Machetero's head pop up, ready to warn his sergeant of any movement, but all he could perceive were the palm fronds stirring a further distance away in the strong ocean breeze. When he returned his gaze to Cordero, the sergeant was chest-deep inside the pool about half the distance to the shore, his compact submachine gun in one hand above the water, moving as closely as possible to the bridge looming above him.

In less than a minute, Cordero reached the rocks on the other side, scurrying like a crab over them and sitting, his gun pointing upwards, against the outer face of the low stone wall.

Gomez came next, slipping feet first into the cold water. As he moved, he watched the tall buildings of the Grand Laguna Hotel tower over him, many of its rooms fully lit, probably left that way after their occupants had been taken away at gunpoint. He wondered how visible he would be to anyone looking down from them, but chose not to dwell on the thought, blessing his dark clothes and helmet.

Cordero had already begun to move behind the fence, quietly approaching the place where he had seen the outline of the sentry's head. By the time that Gomez reached the shore, the sergeant was crouching close to the spot where the terrorist was hiding.

Gomez reached the stone fence and the two SWAT officers exchanged a fleeting look. Somewhere on the other side sat at least one—maybe more—fully armed Machetero who could alert the rest of the men in the perimeter. Leaning against the wall, Gomez made two quick tugging motions with his right arm, the signal between both men to "pull the plug".

Cordero unsheathed his knife, turned around, and knelt, facing the fence. He scraped his knife twice on the wall's stones, producing two short, metallic rattles. Then he lobbed the dagger a few feet to his left and held his Glock with both hands. The dagger clattered briefly a few yards away, as it bounced over the rocks next to the wall, and became wedged in a large crack.

The outline of a head, followed by his torso, popped up from behind the stone barrier, about a yard from where Cordero had calculated it would appear. The sergeant coolly adjusted his aim and fired two rounds into the sentry's head, the "thud, thud" of his bullets masked by the distant roar of the waves. The man instantly sank behind the wall.

Cordero retrieved his dagger, and with surprising agility for a man in his forties, speedily jumped over the fence. He almost landed on the body of the terrorist he had just shot. The man had collapsed into a kneeling position, the left part of his face scraping against the rough side of the wall before it hit the ground. Had the terrorist's visage not been turned sideways and been lying in a vast puddle of blood, he would have appeared to be a devout Muslim praying towards Mecca.

The sergeant immediately sat next to the dead Machetero, hoping that anyone looking from the distance would confuse him with the dark bulk of the motionless sentry. Even so, he felt terribly exposed. He was sitting at the edge of a wide sidewalk that followed the contours of the lagoon and separated the Grand Laguna grounds from the shore. To his left, the sidewalk curved into the condominiums and buildings that rose behind the hotel, while to his right it snaked northward about a hundred yards before turning westward out of sight. He could not make any other lookouts hiding behind the wall, but knew that meant nothing.

The lush hotel gardens lined the opposite side of the sidewalk and flanked it all the way to the northern shore. Large-leaved "elephant ears", trimmed bushes of yellow, pink and red hibiscus flowers, clusters of small palm trees, and giant, fan-shaped traveler plants created hundreds of hidden nooks and dark spots where any number of persons could hide—or be hiding. Every second that Cordero stayed there increased exponentially his chances of being discovered.

From behind the fence, he heard the rough, scratchy sound of a knife scraping stone, and gratefully answered with two scrapes of his own. Gomez at once fell next to him, sitting at his side, his eyes wandering nervously from one side to another as he held on to his MP-5K sub machinegun.

"You okay?" the SWAT captain asked.

Cordero nodded.

"Let's go then."

Both men jumped to their feet and rushed straight across the sidewalk into the garden in front of them. There they paused, hiding under the ponderous canopy of a clutch of enormous elephant ears.

Without saying a word, Gomez signaled his sergeant to begin moving to the right, towards the main tower of the hotel. Cordero chose a path partially covered by tall ferns and hibiscus bushes that swayed softly in the wind and would help to camouflage their progress. Gomez followed at a five-second interval, sprinting from cover to cover, trying to discover any hidden enemies who attempted to surprise Cordero.

They had planned to move parallel to the sidewalk, hoping to take out any sentries that they discovered hiding in the perimeter of the stone wall, and in the process gather any information that they could about the hostages' whereabouts. However, they had marched only a few feet beyond the San Geronimo bridge when the sergeant stopped. He had reached a wide clearing where only grass grew for about thirty yards and which was apparently used for holding open-air affairs for the hotel.

Cordero scanned the area for movement from behind a group of small palm trees, detected none, and—making certain that his captain was well concealed—decided to make a run for it. However, as he sprang out of his cover and took his first two steps, a voice to his left called out of the vegetation in a hoarse whisper, "Gomez! Cordero! Wait!"

Cordero instantly dropped to the ground and searched for the source of the words, pointing his guns towards the plants flanking him, uncertain of where to aim.

"Gomez!" he heard someone call softly from somewhere slightly behind him, close to the part of the garden that he had just abandoned. Bewildered, he turned.

"Don't shoot!" the voice said urgently. "We're friends!"

With the corner of his eyes, Cordero saw Gomez inching his way towards the area where the voice seemed to originate from.

"If you are a friend, show yourself!" Cordero said. He had not finished speaking when he heard some rustling to his left, and to his great amazement, a woman emerged from some nearby shrubs with her arms upraised.

"My name is Michelle Alfaro," the woman whispered nervously. "Superintendent Maldonado sent me to guide you to the hostages. You're heading the wrong way," she said, and when Cordero hesitated she added urgently, "Quickly, please! We don't have any time to spare! The terrorists are going to execute some of the hostages!"

As if to verify her statement, a burst of automatic fire shattered the night's peace, making Michelle flinch and Gomez duck in the bushes behind her. It seemed to come from a short distance away. Several more shots followed, and then no more.

"My God!" Michelle said loudly to herself. "It's started!"

Gomez stood up and strode towards her, while Cordero ran back to where they were.

"Can you take us to the hostages now?" he asked her, not bothering to introduce himself or ask her what she was doing there.

"Yes, my friends are there now, trying to stop the killings."

"Then take us to them."

CHAPTER LX

"Don't kill me! Please, don't kill me!" the hostage pleaded, as he knelt on the ground, his hands raised in a gesture of utter helplessness. He screamed when Negron gently placed a hand on his shoulder, then began to sob loudly. Among some bushes, Archie watched in a daze. He had been shot in his right lung, and was barely able to move. He seemed to hear some shouts in the distance, faint voices that sounded more curious than alarmed, but he could not tell for certain. *After all,* he reasoned, *the Macheteros were supposed to execute five hostages, and some shooting had been expected. The other terrorists guarding the hotel should not be surprised by the sounds of gunfire. Except, maybe, by how much gunfire there had been.*

But it was all a matter of time. Soon, the place would be swarming with terrorists. However, in his fading world, that did not seem to matter any more.

He heard Negron at first quietly, then more sharply, urge the hostage to stand up and to come with him, and saw the kneeling man look up as if awaking from a nightmare, and stumble up to his feet. A short distance away, a Machetero writhed in agony on the ground, holding both hands over a bleeding belly, while four other men watched in apparent confusion.

Archie closed his eyes. Everything had spun out of control all too quickly. After he and Michelle had knocked out the sentry in the garden, they had decided to split up. Michelle had headed towards the San Geronimo fort to alert the SWAT people, while—it being the time for the executions to begin—he and Negron had rushed towards the entrance that connected the gardens to the hotel, assuming that the terrorists would carry out the killing of the hostages outside of the hotel facilities.

They had hidden behind some of the bushes that fringed the entrance to the convention area, and waited there in silence. Scarcely minute later, frantic, breathless shouts had announced the arrival of the Macheteros. A group of five hostages, led by two armed terrorists, had filed out of the hotel into the garden. It was the first man in the line of the five prisoners who was screaming. He was pleading for his life. Those behind him were staring sullenly at the floor, either too scared to say anything, resigned to their fate, or simply too embarrassed by the sorry spectacle of the hostage who preceded them.

"You're making a big mistake!" the man, garbed in jogging shorts, had screamed as he was half-dragged, half-pushed by the two armed men and thrown unceremoniously into the garden, tripping and sprawling on the ground.

"Get up on your knees..." the shorter but brawnier of the two terrorists had said as calmly as possible, pushing his glasses up the bridge of his nose. When the prisoner failed to obey, the man kicked him once in the ribs. "On your knees, or I'll shoot you where you are!" the Machetero said angrily.

The other four hostages watched from a few feet away, guarded by the second armed terrorist.

Sobbing, the man slowly got back on his knees and raised his hands. "I am an American representative!" he said, shaking uncontrollably. "I can be of great help to your cause! Pleeeease! Listen! Listen!" Spit mixed with his tears dribbled down his chin. "There's hundreds of others inside...these four others here..." he said, pointing at the other prisoners, "who...they're not as important as I am! Please!"

Archie had been so repulsed by the prisoner's pleas that he felt tempted not to do anything to save him. He knew that Negron would be feeling the same way or even worse, would be thinking of shooting him himself.

"You should be the one to do it," he had heard the other terrorist, a thin, nervous-looking man who was guarding the others, hiss in a petulant, almost feminine voice.

The shorter man shook his head emphatically. "Felipe, we've already been over this!" he shouted over the crying man's loud babble. Grabbing his companion by the arm, he pushed him towards the prisoner. "Now do your job or I'll shoot you as well, damn you!"

Felipe breathed in deeply and took a step forward, while his companion covered the other four men. He shouldered his AK-47 and took out his semi-automatic pistol, pulling back its slide and putting a bullet in its chamber. His hand had trembled so violently that he had to steady it with his other hand. Somehow, he managed to place his gun less than an inch away from the hostage's head and closed his eyes.

Archie had been about to order him to stop when Negron had shouted at the top of his lungs, "Step away from that man and raise your hands, or we will shoot!"

Surprised, the shorter of the two Macheteros had leveled his rifle at the general direction of Negron's voice and blindly opened fire. Negron and Archie had immediately fired back. Several bullets had whizzed past Archie's head, shredding the vegetation around it, and something hot had struck him on the chest. As he had fallen to his knees, he had seen various shots strike the spectacled terrorist, one of them hitting him on the head and splitting his eyeglasses into three large flying fragments.

The second Machetero had begun to back away, discharging his pistol wildly, but almost immediately had collapsed from Negron's return volley, doubling over his stomach and shouting, "You've killed me! You've killed me!"

"I'm hit!" Archie had gasped, dropping his gun and holding on to one of the bushes. He had heard Negron run towards him, but waved him away, saying, "Get the hostages first!"

The rookie policeman had hesitated, then run towards the cringing jogger. Archie lost his grip on the bush and pitched forward, placing his hands on the ground. But his arms slowly failed him, and he let himself fall. The grass felt wet and cool on his cheek, and in the background, he heard Negron's voice address the hostages, urging them to "Come on! Help me carry my friend out of here!"

Then he heard the crying man answer, "There's no time! We've got to get out of here!"

Funny, he thought, listening to what seemed to be the heavy footfalls of men coming through the shrubs behind him—Macheteros, most probably—*I have been to the Grand Laguna Hotel's gardens dozens of times, but I never thought that I would die here.* He tried to turn, to defend his friend from the approaching men, but couldn't find the strength, coughing up blood. He heard an irate Negron cursing the man they had just saved and was forced to smile by the originality of his friend's insults. A strange peace possessed him. *It was okay,* he thought, *they had done their best. There were worst ways to die.*

Suddenly there were voices all around him, and somebody placed an arm under his neck. There was a sharp intake of breath, and a female voice—Michelle's voice—said shakily, "Archie..." and nothing more. He felt Michelle hold on to his hand. Then other hands grabbed him and lifted him off the ground, and he felt himself floating forward.

They had stirred the hornets' nest. The terrorists would be there soon and in heavy numbers. They had a minute, if not less, to act. And so, they did the only thing that they could do. They attacked.

Negron led the way, angry beyond reason, abandoning the man he had just rescued when he failed to move. Gomez and Cordero followed him closely, and then Michelle and the four other hostages, three of them carrying Archie's limp body.

They charged through the corridor that led to the hotel's main ballroom, screaming like madmen, firing their weapons sporadically without taking aim. El Cano, who had just roused himself up from his chair by the ballroom's entrance and taken a few tentative steps towards the garden to find out what was happening, saw the men coming, stopped dead on his tracks, and ran away in the opposite direction towards the lobby, screaming, "They're coming! They're coming! The Americans are here!", and quickly disappearing from sight.

The improbable rescue team continued their furious race until they reached the entrance of the convention hall, and stormed into it, both Negron and Gomez screaming "Everybody down! Everybody down or we will shoot!"

There was instant bedlam inside as the hostages scrambled to the floor, many of them screaming in panic or urging others to move. Of the three FEPI guards inside, only the fat unpleasant woman with the flip-flops reacted, clumsily aiming her AK-47 at Gomez. But the SWAT captain fired first, cutting her down with a short burst of his sub machinegun. With a loud, husky "Ohhhhh!", the woman fell backwards into a curtained wall, and trying to grab the drapes, slowly slipped to the floor.

The male FEPI guard, standing on the stage, speedily dropped his weapon and placed his hands on his head, while the other female lay flat on the ground, abandoning her rifle and cradling her head between her arms.

"Everybody stay where you are!" Negron shouted as he walked among the hostages, searching for possible hidden terrorists. His beat up face made him look a lot tougher than he really was.

The men carrying Archie lay him gently on the floor a few yards away from the entrance, while Cordero stayed by the door, watching the corridor. A quick glance both ways showed him that the passageway was empty.

In the meantime, Michelle walked into the hall and looked around her anxiously. "Is there a doctor in the house?" she yelled.

"Please! We need a doctor!" Negron shouted.

Three hands shot up from among the hundreds of bodies huddled on the floor.

"Stand up and go with her," the rookie policeman ordered.

Two men, one of them in his seventies, the other very young, and the third a heavyset, wide-chinned woman in her thirties, rose from the floor and began making their way over the people who carpeted the ground.

"Any person who participated in the hotel takeover, stand up with your hands on your heads now! Those close to the people who held you up, point at them!"

A gaggle of hands formed a circle around the female guard, who began to get up warily with her hands raised above her head. Dozens of other hostages pointed at the stage, even though the FEPI student needed no prompting to stand up.

"You!" Negron shouted at the female FEPIsta, "get up on the stage where I can see you!"

Gomez continued to walk towards the center of the enormous hall. He saw, with approval, that Negron was recruiting some of the hostages to tie up the surviving terrorists and to gather their weapons.

From a cursory examination of the ballroom, he immediately grasped the helplessness of their situation. It would be nearly impossible to defend the great hall from a determined assault by the terrorists. In addition to the only open entrance, there were three more sets of wide doors spread at even intervals along the corridor wall, all of them locked, and two other sets of locked doors on the shorter wall of the ballroom, closest to the gardens. The walls were made of cinder block and the doors of solid oak, but they would not withstand for long heavy sustained fire or explosives.

It was the wall behind the stage, parallel to the long corridor wall, which gave him the most pause. It was basically a series of hollow partitions covered with a stiff, plastic-like material that could be easily pierced by bullets. Sooner or later, when the terrorists lost some men trying to recapture the hostages, they would seek other alternatives. It was just a matter of time before they started shooting through the partitions behind the stage. And when they did, the result would be catastrophic.

Cordero switched off most of the lights of the ballroom from the master switch by the entrance door, submerging the scared crowd in a dim, yellowish gloom and provoking a collective groan of dismay. One of the doctors attending Archie's wound protested loudly, saying he needed more light, but quieted down when Michelle asked the three men who had carried Archie to move him to another area with better visibility.

"Hostiles are coming!" Cordero suddenly shouted from the door at his captain. Gomez ran back to the entrance and crouched next to the sergeant. Cordero gestured to him to be silent, and pointed in the direction of the corridor that connected to the hotel's lobby. With his hand, he raised three fingers, indicating the number of men approaching.

Gomez leaned on the floor and took a quick peek out of the door. He saw three armed men warily approaching, crouching to make themselves as small a target as possible. Unslinging his MP-5K sub machinegun from his shoulder, he stepped out of the door and without taking aim emptied the ammunition that remained in his weapon, stepping back inside when he had finished. He heard screams of surprise and pain and the sound of something crashing on the floor, then the hurried noise of retreating footsteps. When he looked out, one of the men lay on the floor, while the other two had disappeared.

"They'll be back," Cordero said matter-of-factly, without bothering to look. "It's time for me to go."

Gomez hesitated, and then nodded. "I know," he replied. "Darken the corridor first."

Cordero aimed his sub machinegun at the three plastic-covered panels of neon lights closest to the entrance—each at a distance of ten feet from the other—and methodically destroyed them, one of the lamps falling and hanging from a wire. The lighting around the entrance dwindled into a grayish-blue gloom.

The two SWAT officers examined the darkened corridor and noted with satisfaction that it remained empty. Almost directly across from them was a small ornamental Japanese garden containing a small pond with lotus flowers and goldfish, and various small, un-Japanese flower shrubs and palm tress. Two cement benches, where conventioneers could sit to catch the sun's rays through an open roof, bordered the pond. With the corridor lights shot to pieces, the small garden was mostly shrouded by the night, only the frail luminescence of the moon filtering through the roof into its northern half.

"You have everything you need?" Gomez asked his companion.

"I'm good," Cordero answered, patting the satchel bag close to his knees. He slung it over his shoulder. The two men shook hands.

"Go," Gomez whispered, and Cordero scurried across the corridor and disappeared into the courtyard in front of them, hiding behind the shrubs. The SWAT captain turned his attention briefly into the hall, and found Negron overlooking the tying up of the captured guards. He waved at him, beckoning him to approach. The rookie policeman nodded, spoke briefly to his appointed deputies, and sauntered to the entrance.

"We haven't been introduced," Gomez said as he approached, extending his hand. "Captain Camilo Gomez—"

"From SWAT," Negron finished saying, shaking his hand vigorously. "I know. We watched—"

"The massacre in the lagoon." It was Gomez's turn to finish the other man's sentence.

"Edgardo Negron, at your service. Policeman. I was at the Puerto de Tierra Police Station massacre. Nice to meet you."

Gomez examined him with newfound admiration. "You've had a very rough day, today. Haven't you, Negron?"

Negron shrugged. "Yes, sir. We all have."

"I need you to stand guard here while I try to organize matters inside. If you see anyone coming, shout. My sergeant, the one who carried your friend, is out there, in that garden straight across from us. So if you see anyone dressed in a black SWAT uniform, don't shoot. I'll try to get you some more help in a few minutes."

"Yes, sir."

Gomez stared at the rookie policeman for a few more seconds. "You were very brave just now," he told him. "I'm very proud of you."

"Yes, sir," Negron answered awkwardly, but could not hide his pride. "Thank you, sir."

Gomez turned around without saying anything else, and walked back to the middle of the hall. A hundred stares from anxious, frightened guests followed his progress. Taking a deep breath, he spoke in a loud voice.

"If I could have your attention, please!" An expectant hush rapidly spread through the ballroom, quieting even some of the crying children. "We are police officers from SWAT. We're here to protect you from the...fanatics that have taken over this hotel, until the main rescue force can get you safely out of here." There was a smattering of heartfelt applause and cheers, but most of the crowd continued to listen apprehensively. "Now, the main rescue party can't get here for the next hour, and the people who kept you locked up here may try to come back." He let his words linger and sink in before continuing. "So we need you to follow instructions... If you do, everything will be all right."

He spoke with as much outward confidence as he could muster, but did not really feel it. He would be very surprised if they were able to withstand another attack without suffering serious casualties. Glancing at the stage, he noticed that the men that Negron had recruited to tie up the guards had gathered three semi-automatic rifles, at least four handguns, and what seemed to be scores of ammunition cartridges. It brought to mind the next subject of his speech.

"I'd like to know if there is anybody here who is familiar with guns or semi-automatic rifles?" Nearly a dozen men and even one woman raised their hands, mostly young and, by their appearance, army veterans or police officers. "I need your help. Take all of the weapons and ammunition on the stage and meet me by the entrance."

Gomez watched the volunteers stand up, some speaking briefly to their families or friends, others heading directly towards the stage. He was violating every rule of safety that had been drilled into him as a

SWAT officer by arming civilians and placing them in the path of danger, but he had no choice. If his instincts were right, they were in for the fight of their lives, all of them, and he would need all of the resources that he could muster.

He turned his attention back the crowd, where the faint noise of small chatter had begun. "The rest of you, listen up! I want you to move away from the walls. Leave a corridor between yourselves and them. If there is any fighting, the volunteers may need to be running from one place to another. I don't want them to be tripping over you. Also, those close to the entrance, move to another place in the hall. I don't want anybody *on* the stage, but if you want to sit on the floor next to it, it's okay. And when the shooting starts, I need you all to lay low. Not standing or sitting, but as low as you can get. It's an inconvenience, but think that soon, God willing, we'll all be out of here."

He paused, in case anybody noted an objection. To his chagrin, a man in his fifties raised his hand. Gomez nodded at him. "Yes?"

The man stood up. "Our daughter was taken away early this afternoon, just before the shooting started. She and nine others—" His voice broke, as the grief and anxiety that he felt overwhelmed him. He took several deep breaths to steady himself and, clearing his throat, tried to continue. "Please forgive me...Do you have any information about them?"

Others in the room echoed the question; wives, parents, and friends of the people who had been picked out to go to some unknown destination. An old man also mentioned a Florida politician in a jogger's suit.

"Sorry, but I don't have any information about them at this moment," he answered. "I do know that until the time that I left for this mission, we had not been informed of any hurt hostages." He watched the man who had inquired about his daughter slump back to the floor and embrace his wife, and his heart went out for him. "Don't despair," he said, trying to reassure him. "We *will* find them, have faith. Oh, and one more thing. We may have to turn off the rest of the lights in this hall, if the terrorists come back. So don't be alarmed if that happens. It's for our own good."

Again he paused, waiting for more questions. This time, the crowd remained silent.

"Okay," he said. "Let's get to work."

He got back to Negron's side just as the first of the volunteers began to arrive. The policeman eyed him skeptically and muttered, "You're arming the hostages? Really?"

Gomez shrugged, saying nothing, and waited for the others to join them.

For the last two hours, Johnny Ray and Yajaira had been sitting at the Grand Laguna's main bar, enjoying a spectacular Atlantic sunset from the room's panoramic windows, taking advantage of the hotel's free amenities, and discussing several FEPI pending matters. Lebron, their Secretary-General, had joined them at six-thirty, after spending all day on the roof of the Banco Cosmopolitano Building in Old San Juan transmitting Johnny's recorded message to the island of Puerto Rico.

Even though he had sat most of the day in the shade, Lebron had managed to acquire a lobster-red sunburn, which covered every hairless inch of his face and ended in large "V" that delineated his *guayabera's* neckline. Lacking a mirror, he had not realized how much of the sun's fire his exposed skin had absorbed until Yajaira had pointed it out in a gale of laughter. However, instead of feeling ashamed, he had quickly embraced his unanticipated condition as his badge of courage, his proof to the world of his active participation in the revolution, and had worn it proudly, even though everybody else mocked him or averted their eyes and smiled.

The bar, an enormous space separated from the pool area and the beach by massive glass panes that extended from the roof to the floor, was filled with FEPI members who were resting before their next shifts began—both the Grand Laguna Hotel and the *Mardi Gras* had been designated as official "food" and "sleep" areas for those who were off duty—and with the fifteen Macheteros who served as a reserve in case that the hotel was attacked. Hardly a chair or sofa in the establishment was empty, some of the men even spilling onto on its plush, carpeted floor, others taking a quiet drink, and a few playing dominoes and chess.

The three FEPIstas had been calling their various "cell leaders", making certain that the FEPI patrols were functioning efficiently, trying to resolve the problems that inevitably arose in an operation of that magnitude. So far, the news had been very reassuring.

Of the forty-four "cells" that patrolled San Juan in three different shifts, forty-one had reported no significant setbacks and were more or less sticking to their assigned schedules. The worst incident of the day had been the accidental death of one of *El Joyero de San Juan's* employees. Johnny had disbanded the cell involved in that unintended tragedy, getting medical help for the man whose wrist had been broken in a fight with another of *El Joyero's* employees, and reassigning the other two members of the group to another cell. He had asked Lebron, before coming to meet with Yajaira and him in the Grand Laguna, to go to the jewelry store and release the employees locked up in the cellar, but the Secretary-General had found the cellar empty. *Just as well,* Johnny thought. He would let matters be as they were, and conduct no further investigation of the incident. Tomorrow, he would send a detail to dispose of the body.

Apart from that, it had been mostly smooth sailing. The gun of one of the cell leaders had been lost, stolen while its bearer was having lunch and had left it on a park bench; one of their trucks had accidentally hit a pedestrian, fortunately with no serious consequences; one of the groups had been shot at by unknown assailants who had chanted "USA! USA!" and run away without anyone getting wounded; and there had been about a dozen angry exchanges with San Juan residents, but only one had come to blows.

What concerned Johnny the most was that there had been four desertions; four freedom fighters who had just walked away. Where they had gone to he could not fathom. After all, the island of San Juan was physically disconnected from the rest of the country. But it worried him, nonetheless. He hoped it did not become a bigger trend, he told to his two companions, as he sipped from his second glass of scotch on the rocks. He could not understand, with all of the spectacular successes of that day, why some of the revolution's faithful would abandon their cause. Maybe he could convince Cacho to address some of his people the next day and stiffen their resolve. He would have to talk to him about that.

Johnny felt good. The liquor had dulled the day's many concerns. He could not take his eyes away from Yajaira, who looked particularly fetching. He felt tired, but the good kind of tired, where after almost two nights without sleep, he could relax and let his guard down.

Lebron had never been so talkative or effusive. He spoke about the day's events in non-ending superlatives—the *incredible* defeat by the *heroic* forces of the revolution—and was already making plans to set up a central revolutionary government headed and co-chaired by three Puerto Ricans: Johnny, Cacho, and an "undetermined" third. It had to be three, he explained, in order to break any deadlock.

After a listless afternoon, Yajaira had also recovered most of her lost spirits, and if not entirely her bubbly self, was mellow and talkative. She suggested that as FEPI Vice President, she should commandeer one of the cars in the hotel's valet parking in the morning, and visit each of their cells to discuss their needs and raise their morale. Johnny thought it was a splendid idea. Lebron had maintained a neutral silence.

As the consumption of alcohol increased, the FEPI officers' plans had grown in scale and magnitude. Tomorrow they should start recruiting local supporters of the revolution. The FEPI ranks had not been inundated, as they had hoped, with volunteers from the city during the first day, but in hindsight, they had expected too much.

"The people didn't know what we stand for," Johnny had reasoned.

"But the radio broadcast precisely explained what we stand for and what we want," Lebron countered, with a half-puzzled, half-angry expression.

Johnny mulled over his Secretary-General's last statement, while Yajaira regarded the sweaty, *guayaberaed* man with hostility.

"It takes time," Johnny finally concluded. "Tomorrow, we open the supermarkets, to let those people who were surprised by the revolution replenish their food supplies. We need to show them that we are their friends, and that we are here... to free them from the oppression of the capitalists and their big corporations, not to tyrannize them."

Yajaira nodded emphatically.

"But how do we stop them from looting?" Lebron asked skeptically.

"No looting!" Johnny replied immediately, slamming his hand on the plush, orange-colored armrest of his overstuffed chair. "Nobody steals anything. They pay for the food."

"Our troops—it was the first time that Lebron referred to the FEPI volunteers as 'their troops'—will also need food, and they have no money..." Lebron intimated.

"Good point." Johnny realized that his mind was a little bit clouded by the alcohol, and tried to concentrate on the business at hand. However, the sight of Yajaira distracted him. Maybe he should have her make an inventory of the food available in Old San Juan. But no, it would take her forever to do it. She should stick to what she did best: raising the morale of their people. God knew she raised his.

"That sun that you absorbed today must have sharpened your wits," he told Lebron, who immediately beamed at him, while Yajaira raised an eyebrow in silent disgust. "Whoever controls the food in Old San Juan controls the city. It will be some time before we coerce the Commonwealth government to send food into the city. They will, eventually. It's a humanitarian concern. They wouldn't let the population of Old San Juan starve. But in the meantime, we must control and ration the food. So tomorrow, we need to take an inventory of the food resources that we have in Old San Juan, and make certain that our people...including those who join us, are supplied adequately."

"But that will take a *lot* of time," Lebron said doubtfully. "A week at least. Do you know how many food markets there are in San Juan? How difficult and time consuming it's going to be to inventory the food?"

"It may be easier than you think," Johnny replied, unfazed. "All of these markets have computerized inventories, don't they? It's just a matter of getting the information from them. I want you to be in charge of this, Felipe," he said to his Secretary-General, addressing him by his first name. "Take Cerebrito, with you. He's a computer whiz. He'll get the information easily. Start with the big supermarkets, then the smaller ones, then the bakeries and the restaurants. I'll try to get you some help from some of the cells. We'll need to patrol the streets to avoid looting. I'll take care of that tomorrow."

"Food might be just the right inducement for some of the people who are sitting on the fence to join us..." Lebron suggested with a wry smile.

"Napoleon, he said that an army travels on its stomach," Johnny agreed. "Maybe the promise of food is what we need to attract more converts to our cause."

Johnny sat back and took a long sip from his scotch. Then he noticed that Yajaira seemed as dismayed by Lebron's sudden rise in importance as the latter's ego was buoyed up by his newly assigned functions. He tried to cheer her up.

"Yajaira, I want you to become the face of our revolution. I want you to humanize our noble ideas, to give them a recognizable image. And it doesn't hurt that you are a beautiful woman."

Yajaira stared at Johnny with the newfound interest of a hungry cat that is offered food.

"Very early tomorrow morning, before Cerebrito leaves with Felipe to take the food inventory, I want you to go with him to the Banco Cosmopolitano roof and record a new message, an appeal for food. Tell the people of Puerto Rico that their compatriots in San Juan are short of food, and that the siege by the Americans will eventually, sooner than later, bring starvation to the residents here. Give it a humanitarian spin, with no political overtones, something that will plant in their heads the idea of the plight of our people here. It won't produce food immediately, but it will begin to create a consciousness about the problem." Johnny looked from one face to another, seeking questions or objections, but both of his followers seemed to be lost in their own thoughts. "Our campaign will make it easier to later exchange prisoners for food," he added as an afterthought.

The reference about the prisoners sobered the mood. Yajaira, especially, had been very affected by the events that had taken place in the hotel and the execution of the hostage from the rooftop. Lebron, who had been absent, asked for the details of what had taken place, exulting in the defeat of the police attack, listening somberly to the description of the killing of the tourist, but accepting it as a "necessary evil".

"Sometimes, a few must sacrifice for the sake of the many," the Secretary-General said sententiously. "How was the meeting with Cacho? You did get to meet him in person, didn't you?" he asked in a hero-worship voice.

"Of course we met him!" Yajaira answered enthusiastically before Johnny could speak, glad to be able to put one over Lebron. "The man oozes charisma..." She stopped talking as the distant firing of automatic weapons interrupted her. Johnny and Lebron stood up to listen, as did others in the bar.

"Did you hear that?" Johnny asked. "Were those shots?"

"It sounded like the backfire of a motorcycle to me," Lebron said dismissively, but his eyes were scared.

"Shhhhh! Listen!" They waited, but heard nothing else. However, as they were about to sit down, new explosions rang out, consecutive "pop-pop-pops" like those made by automatic weapons fire, or as Lebron suggested, the successive bursts of a noisy motorcycle. Then the noise stopped again.

By now, most of the people in the bar were listening, and many had stood up from their seats. When no more noises followed, someone at the other end of the bar made a loud, unintelligible comment that provoked the nervous laughter of those around him. Slowly, people began to sit back on their chairs, and gradually, the pleasant sound of subdued conversation began to fill the void that had been created by the distant discharges.

However, as Yajaira prepared to continue with her effusive description of Cacho, new noises—this time the shouts of a man—interrupted her and drew everyone's attention to the lobby. At first, Johnny failed to spot the person who was screaming, but then he spotted a man rushing into the other side of the bar, where the reserves for the Macheteros had set up camp. Several of the men there immediately clustered around him.

Like the FEPIstas, the Macheteros had been taking advantage of the free alcohol, and some of them would sporadically burst into loud laughter or shout insults at each other. A game of dominoes, in particular—a very serious activity in Puerto Rico for those who played it well—would provoke occasional shouting matches or exclamations of triumph or dismay, as the ivory-colored pieces of the game were slammed on the playing table.

But those noises changed now. The voices that originated from the group bunched around the new arrival denoted surprise, shock, and outrage. Johnny stood up and wandered closer to the agitated men, approaching one of them, a former FEPI student with fully tattooed arms that he knew from the University of Puerto Rico.

"What's the matter?" he asked his friend. Several of the Macheteros were grabbing their weapons as they listened to an agitated blond man speak.

"It's the American special forces! They've violated the truce and attacked us by surprise!" Johnny's acquaintance answered excitedly. "El Cano, that man over there..." he pointed to the blond man in the center of the assembled crowd, "he managed to shoot his way out of the ambush, but he thinks that his comrades are dead, and that the Americans captured the hostages. We're getting ready to counterattack."

The news made Johnny's stomach turn. Although there had been some talk at the meeting that afternoon about a possible night rescue attempt by American rescue forces—paratroopers or scuba divers, he imagined—San Miguel had assured everyone present that he would post his men, along with some of the Macheteros, all along the perimeter of the area where the hostages were being kept. Also, Calderon's Venezuelans had been shifted to the northern boundary of the hotel, to blunt any attack coming from the Atlantic or the north coast of San Juan. *Surely, even if the Americans managed to infiltrate the hotel undetected from the side of the lagoon and managed to eliminate some of the sentries, sooner or later they would have run up against the defensive barrier set up by San Miguel's men. And yet, the special forces had managed to capture the hostages without being detected until they had reached the guard at the entrance of the hall where they kept the prisoners? It didn't make any sense.*

Nervously, Johnny pushed his way through the crowd to get closer to the man that was speaking.

"Has anybody alerted Cacho or San Miguel?" he shouted, interrupting the excited chatter that encompassed El Cano.

"That's what I was meaning to do," El Cano answered sheepishly.

"But has anybody else alerted any of them?" Absolute silence gave him the answer that he sought. "We need to get to them immediately. To Colonel Calderon too."

Two of the men in the group volunteered to search for the absent leaders, running away in opposite directions.

"Is there anyone between the American special forces and us right now?" Johnny asked next. "If the special forces decide to move into the lobby, is there anyone to stop them?"

Most of the Macheteros considered the FEPIstas to be a group of rank amateurs that sometimes hindered the cause more than they helped it. Therefore, Johnny's question earned him several hostile stares.

One of the Macheteros, a balding man in his forties bearing a surprising resemblance—despite a swollen, bloodied nose—to Yankee baseball player Alex Rodriguez, looked appraisingly in the direction from where El Cano had come, and said, "We have men posted where the corridor to the convention hall connects to the lobby. If anyone tries to come here, we will know about it."

"Forgive me," Johnny objected, "but we also had sentries guarding the lagoon, and somehow the special forces managed to slip through them unnoticed."

The Machetero shot an angry glance at the FEPI upstart, and then turned his attention back to El Cano.

"How many men did you say that attacked you?" he asked.

The blond man shrugged. "I don't know for sure...I didn't see clearly."

"Ten? Twenty?"

El Cano shrugged again. "I don't know. Ten...Five, maybe. But there could have been others behind them...They were coming from the gardens of the hotel."

"If it was a big force, why didn't they follow you here, to engage the rest of us and catch us by surprise?" the Alex Rodriguez look-alike mused to himself. "Why didn't they get into a big firefight with San Miguel's men?" he added, repeating Johnny's question as if it had just occurred to him.

Johnny opened his mouth to speak, but the man ignored him.

"It seems to me that whoever attacked were few, five, like you said before. It's the only way they could have slipped through our sentries. Besides, if there were many, they would be attacking us now, before we recovered from their surprise."

There were several murmurs of agreement.

"Maybe San Miguel's men already have them surrounded," somebody else in the crowd said.

"Maybe," the Alex Rodriguez lookalike responded, "but we have to make certain that's the case. If those hostages get away..." The Machetero left the rest of his words lapse. Apparently, he was the person there who commanded the most respect, since nobody interrupted him. He considered the situation for a moment. "Well...we're supposed to be the reserves in case of an attack, and this sure as hell qualifies as one. Let nobody say that we stood here and let the revolution collapse around us." He pointed to the eight men standing to his left. "You men circle around the pool area to the gardens until you contact San Miguel's men, and help seal any gap that the hostages can use to escape. Be careful that the foreigners in the pool area don't confuse you for the enemy. That could turn nasty. The rest will come with me to the corridor that connects the lobby to the convention area, and block any attempt by the Americans to move into the hotel. We won't attack until I hear from Cacho, but I'll test their strength with a couple of men." He picked up his rifle, and slid a black beret over his head. "Let's go," he said, and began to walk away.

The crowd quickly dispersed, forming into two groups that headed into the opposite ends of the hotel, leaving behind Johnny, a few other FEPIsta onlookers that included Yajaira and Lebron, and El Cano. Still shaken by the experience, the latter let himself drop into a chair and closed his eyes. Johnny approached him, anxious to get more information, motioning Lebron and Yajaira to stay away.

"Do you know what happened to our people inside the hall?" he asked the blond Machetero.

El Cano opened his eyes and glanced at him as if he were a nuisance. He leaned forward, found a half finished drink on a small round table in front of him, and drank it.

"You mean your FEPI people inside the hall?" He shook his head. "Nah! I don't even know what happened to the other two people who were with me. I think they're probably dead, from all the shooting that I heard. Felipe and Pedro had just taken five of the hostages to the garden to execute them, when I heard the shots. There were more than I expected to hear, since they were supposed to shoot the hostages in the head, and one shot for each would have done the trick, and I thought—"

"Wait!" Johnny interrupted him. "What do you mean you were going to kill five hostages? Why were you going to kill five hostages?"

"Cacho's orders," El Cano responded. Then, watching Johnny grow pale, he smiled. "Cacho and San Miguel didn't say anything to you? I guess they thought it wasn't important for you to know, so let me put you up to date. Cacho ordered us to shoot five hostages every half hour, starting at seven forty-five until he ordered otherwise. Why seven forty-five and not eight or seven thirty is very strange, you know what I mean? But Cacho is Cacho. We were supposed to throw the bodies into an open...a well lit place, so that the bodies could be seen from the Condado buildings." He looked hard at Johnny. "You sure that he didn't tell you anything about this? No?"

Johnny Ray shook his head in bewilderment, too shocked to pretend he was in the know.

"I thought that he was bluffing to the police authorities. Cacho is not the type of person who likes to kill civilians. But the word to stop the executions never came."

Johnny felt too stunned to speak. Without realizing it, he had grabbed hold of the headrest of the chair behind which he was standing and was squeezing it so tightly that his fingers hurt. Behind him, Lebron and Yajaira—who had heard the exchange—watched him apprehensively, looking distraught. As in a daze, Johnny walked away from El Cano and headed towards them.

"Perhaps they meant to tell you, and couldn't find you," Yajaira suggested in a consoling tone. "Maybe Cacho got distracted..." she continued, but stopped, silenced by Johnny's wild stare.

"Distracted? He got so distracted that he forgot to tell me, one of his main partners in the revolution, that he was going to start killing five people every half hour? We've been sitting here since a little over six! Do you really believe that he didn't know where to find me? And how about San Miguel? Why didn't he tell me?" he said bitterly.

Lebron made as if to speak, but thought better of it and cast his eyes to the floor in contemplative silence.

"It's over," Johnny said so softly that neither of his companions understood him. "It's over," he repeated more loudly. "The revolution has gotten out of control. They've taken it away from us. We were supposed to start something new, to inspire our people to fight for their freedom. To lead by our example. Instead, we've resorted to killing innocent people! We've become terrorists, just what they accuse us of being. The revolution is dead. It's over. Let's just call it quits and go home before we lose some of our people."

"Don't say that!" Lebron pleaded, his eyes bulging, looking almost comically white in the midst of his cherry-red, sunburned face. ""There is still a role for us to play. We cannot give up our struggle against the imperial capitalists now, not when we are so close to victory! If we abandon this struggle now, we lose everything!"

Johnny regarded his dogmatic associate with the sad pity of a friend watching another make a fool of himself. "We never had anything to lose in the first place, Felipe," he answered. "They just used us. We are a tool, that's all. A useful tool, but a tool nevertheless. They're not going to share the power with us. They don't respect us. Soon, they won't need us, and they'll discard us or maybe absorb us, take the best of us into their ranks. But don't expect more than that. They're not going to treat us as equals. They're not treating us as equals. At least not Cacho. San Miguel seemed to be sincere...Maybe if he would have stayed in command...But now that Cacho is in command...He's taken over. Everything has changed...We've been betrayed...We've been betrayed. It's over."

Johnny saw Yajaira's eyes water as she wringed her hands in despair, while Lebron recoiled from his words as if he had been struck physically. However, Johnny could not take back his words because they were true. And as he uttered them, he had come to the sudden realization that he had been feeling that way for a long part of the day, ever since the decision to sacrifice the first of the hostages from the roof of the hotel had been conveyed to him by San Miguel. He had just been fooling himself, hoping that his uneasiness was just nerves, and that in the end everything would be all right. Now, as he faced the reality of their situation, he felt an odd sense of relief admitting it, as if a great weight had been lifted from his shoulders.

"They still need us, Johnny," Lebron said with as much conviction as he could muster, but it sounded more as a hollow plea than as a statement. "We are their eyes out there. We are policing the streets. There's still a role for us to play."

Yajaira assented, still wringing her hands, her eyes urging Johnny to relent in his decision to abandon the cause. He hesitated, clenching his jaw in stubborn silence. But then, more for her sake than for the revolution, he decided to make one final attempt at salvaging the FEPI's role in the operation, even though he knew it would end in failure. *Let no one say I did not try,* he thought, not relishing the idea of confronting the Machetero leader.

"I'll go talk to Cacho," he said resignedly. "I'll lay the whole matter before him. If the FEPI is to stay in this fight, then it has to be as an equal partner," he stated in a tone that admitted no contradictions. "And no more executions of hostages, either. When they kill a hostage, they are killing the revolution...Sullying our most precious of causes, the freedom of our people."

"And the liberation of the proletariat," Lebron added automatically.

Yajaira nodded thankfully, but still Lebron insisted.

"But even if we're not equal partners...What if we're offered an important role in the revolution?" he asked in a half hopeful, half guarded fashion.

"No," Johnny replied immediately, before mulling it over and softening his stance. "It would have to be a really significant role, not a vague promise to shut us up." Then he thought about it again and shook his head. "No, we can't accept a watered-down proposal. When we entered into this business, we agreed to risk our lives on the basis that we would be treated as equal partners. We will continue the same way or not at all. Are we in agreement?"

"Good luck!" El Cano, who had overheard the conversation with a great deal of amusement, said in an ironic tone from the bar, raising a glass in their direction.

"Are we in agreement?" Johnny repeated, ignoring the Machetero's taunting words.

"Yes!" Yajaira answered with newfound enthusiasm.

Lebron nodded reluctantly. "I will abide by your decision. But...don't decide anything rashly!"

Johnny allowed himself a weak smile. "I won't. Gather any of our people that are in the hotel. Tell them to wait for me here. I will meet with all of you here after I talk to Cacho."

New shots, sounding like a string of exploding firecrackers, briefly disturbed the silence of the night. The three FEPIstas exchanged a worried look.

"I'd better hurry," Johnny said, and as he left, shouted over his shoulder. "If for some reason the enemy breaks through, we will meet at the *Mardi Gras!*"

And with those words, he disappeared forever from their lives.

CHAPTER LXI

Since mid afternoon, Hangars 3 and 4 of the Isla Grande Airport had been commandeered by SEAL Team 2, to prepare for the simultaneous assaults on the Grand Laguna Hotel, the *Mardi Gras*, and La Fortaleza. Usually, an operation of that scope and complexity required months of intensive analysis, planning, and rehearsals. It involved the painstaking study of hundreds of aerial photographs, the review of hundreds of pages of reports from on-the-ground covert operatives, possibly the construction of mock duplicates of the places to be raided, and dozens of practice dry runs. In this case, however, SEAL Team 2 would have just a few hours to piece together their entire operation.

Initial preparations had started during the three and a half hour flight in their C-17 BOEING transport from their base in Little Creek, Virginia to Puerto Rico. Unfortunately, the SEALs had not been mobilized until close to 1100 hours, after the local authorities in Puerto Rico had come to grips with the nature and the extent of the attack that had been launched on their capital city. Five platoons of Navy SEALs—eighty men in total—had been dispatched within the hour while the balance, one platoon of sixteen men, had remained behind to supervise the loading of the heavier equipment and the ammunition not brought in the initial flight.

Before the C-17 BOEING transport had landed at Luis Muñoz Marin International Airport in Isla Verde, the three principal objectives had been identified, and the men divided accordingly: two platoons assigned to the Grand Laguna Hotel rescue mission, two to the *Mardi Gras*, and one to La Fortaleza. They had received the blueprints of the Governor's Mansion about half an hour into the flight via email. Copies had been printed and distributed to the men assigned to rescue the Governor, designated as "Group Able", to be studied and memorized. The blueprints the *Mardi Gras* and of the Grand Laguna Hotel's first two floors had followed a few minutes later, and given to Groups Bravo and Charlie accordingly.

Two tourist buses had whisked the men and their equipment to the two hangars in the Isla Grande Airport. The hangars were located almost within view of Old San Juan, less than a mile away from both the San Juan Yacht Club and Dock B, where the *Mardi Gras* was moored. At the same time, a black limousine had transported five of the SEAL team's officers to the San Geronimo Plaza Hotel to meet briefly with Superintendent Maldonado.

In the two hangars, members of the Army Corps of Engineers had traced on the floor, with masking tape, the life-size outlines of the lobby and of the corridors that led to the meeting halls of the Grand Laguna Hotel. Waist-high rope partitions with paper streamers hanging from them were added to make the blueprint outlines three-dimensional. Similar arrangements were made for the dining room areas of the *Mardi Gras*, the Stardust Theater, and the ship's lobby, and for the second floor of the southern wing of La Fortaleza. Photographs showing the actual appearance of the three objectives were amplified and placed along the outlined blueprints, to flesh out the bare bones schematics memorized by the men.

The three groups were briefed about the two major encounters between the police and the terrorists at the Puerta de Tierra Police Station and the Condado Lagoon, and shown the extensive video recordings of the latter engagement. The images of the failed SWAT water crossing were viewed in sober silence, and then reviewed a dozen more times, as the men gauged the damage done and tried to estimate the number of enemy combatants and the caliber and types of weapons utilized.

However, by mid afternoon the SEALs still lacked key information that could seriously affect or even doom their combined rescue operations. They had no intelligence about the exact location of the kidnapped civilians. Without it, they would be forced to act on educated guesses, and conduct lightning searches of the broad areas where they suspected the hostages to be hidden, wasting precious time and increasing the risks that the hostages would be killed before the SEALs could reach them. They also had no idea of the number of terrorists that guarded them, how they were armed, and if the locations where the civilians were kept were rigged with explosives, a not-too-remote possibility in light of the relative ease with which the bridges connecting San Juan to the rest of the island had been demolished.

Despite all of this, a generalized battle plan had been drawn for the three sites. For the Grand Laguna Hotel, it called for a sea landing to the west of the resort, and a subsequent approach by foot from the west—the side opposite to the lagoon—from where an attack would be least expected. The SEALs would scuba dive up to the northern coast of San Juan, then rendezvous by the abandoned Normandie Hotel, adjacent to the Grand Laguna.

From there, they would make their way through the western grounds of the hotel, which included the open-air valet parking area and a large decorative garden that even contained parts of a wall and a sentry box from an old Spanish fortification. Beyond that lay the reception area and the lobby of the hotel, where hopefully the hostages would be. If not, the rescue force would have to split up, one group searching the casino and the large nightclub on the second floor of the main tower, the second group branching south and sweeping the area of the convention facilities in the hotel annex.

If the mission for Group Charlie—the group assigned to recapture the Grand Laguna—seemed daunting, that assigned to Group Bravo appeared to be suicidal. The assault force on the *Mardi Gras* would have no choice but to slip into the ship from the water, since the surface-to-air missile threat precluded an approach by helicopter. Satellite photographs had revealed that the passengers were not being kept on the open decks, but had also shown at least two men making the rounds carrying semi-automatic weapons.

The greatest chance of success for Group Bravo hinged upon the SEALs being able to board the ship without being detected, a daunting proposition in itself. In order to do so, they would have to capture a boarding ramp, and kill any guards on it before they could raise the alarm. Once inside, the men would face a labyrinth of corridors, stairs and public areas, and scramble to half a dozen different locations that were large enough to hold the hostages, including the multi-story lobby, the casino, two separate dining rooms, and the theatre. The rescuers would split into three groups, and hit the lobby, the theatre and one of the dining rooms first.

The most likely scenario, however, involved getting discovered by the terrorists in the early going, and having to storm the ship. If in addition to that, the passengers had been separated into smaller, separate groups, the prospects of conducting an effective rescue without incurring in heavy casualties looked slim at best.

Group Able would cover the smallest of the three locations, but by far the most delicate. Placed atop a high bluff that was surrounded by impossibly high, vertical walls, La Fortaleza presented a formidable problem for the Navy SEALs. The terrorists had captured it when no attacks were expected: they had surprised the men who guarded it, men who had grown complacent in the safety that the once impregnable battlements of the Governor's palace offered, men who had never imagined that anyone would be crazy enough to breach those defenses.

It would be different now. The terrorists knew with a fair degree of certainty that the government authorities would attempt to rescue the Governor and his family soon. Even if a small group of men was garrisoned in La Fortaleza, it could cause havoc before the SEALs could fight their way there. They could kill the Governor, his family, and all his staff.

Matters were even more complicated by the real possibility that the objective was protected by surface-to-air missiles. It eliminated, as in the other two rescue areas, a direct approach by helicopter. Therefore, six of the sixteen men that formed Group Able had been assigned to scale the western wall of La Fortaleza, hopefully undetected, while the remaining ten men surrounded the compound from the adjacent buildings and tried to pick off with silenced rifles any terrorists that moved within their telescopic sights. If the wall climbers were discovered, then the land force would storm the Executive Mansion's main gate, and try to reach the hostages before they were killed. It went without saying that the odds of that happening were not good.

The gloomy prospects did not deter SEAL Team 2 from preparing to conduct full, all-out war on the terrorists. Navy Commander Jason McAllister, a veteran from the Iraq and Afghanistan wars and a participant in more than a dozen covert raids and rescue operations, headed the SEALs. A married man for twenty-five years and a father of five children—all of them girls—he had the physical appearance more of a tall and lanky intellectual, or of a corporation CEO, than of a warrior.

He had acquired his height—a little over six feet three inches—late in life, and because of his small, bony frame, had been the target of bullies during most of his high school years. Encouraged by his father, he had fought back, taking up boxing and beating kids both bigger and older than him. The experience had made him quietly tough and utterly fearless, qualities that would later become apparent in the field of combat.

Even more important, he had the knack of listening to what others had to say without sacrificing his ability to act quickly and decisively, a talent that many people in command situations surprisingly lacked. His style of leadership was quiet but firm. He would sit silently through his staff's briefings, his bright, intensely blue-green eyes boring into the usually self-conscious speaker, and at the end of the session ask a few terse questions in a low voice. Then he would either endorse the proposed course of action, or inject his own, curt modifications until the plan met his satisfaction.

He disliked scolding his subordinates in public, preferring to call them aside and explain the error of their ways. However, as some members of his staff had quickly discovered, he did not tolerate arrogance, complacency or bullying, and he would—without raising his voice and with unerring logic—publicly humiliate those who dared to exhibit those traits in front of him. At the same time, he was generous in praise for those who deserved it—even to the point of self-effacing his own role in some of his successful military operations in order to highlight the actions of his subordinates—and had earned a reputation for fairness and unselfishness that was reciprocated by the absolute loyalty of his men.

Needless to say, McAllister and Superintendent Maldonado had instantly liked each other. After their preliminary meeting in the San Geronimo Plaza Hotel headquarters, they had kept in close and constant contact, discussing the evolving plans of action, exchanging bits of intelligence, and integrating the local forces—both the police and the National Guard—into the rescue missions.

It would have been foolish not to do so. Puerto Rico had a force of 17,000 police officers, of which 3,000 had quietly gathered in Miramar, close to the border of the lagoon, as well as 2,600 National guardsmen. Even though they would not participate in the initial assaults to the three terrorist-held objectives, they would move in strength into San Juan once the hostages had been secured. The National Guard had transported, in three long flatbeds, three Bailey bridges, pre-fabricated steel and aluminum truss structures, each forty feet long, that were light enough to be carried by hand, and which would be used to span the gaps in the Miramar bridge closest to the San Juan Yacht Club.

The flatbeds with the bridges had been parked behind the Justice Department Building in Miramar, out of sight from the terrorists, covered by camouflage-colored canvas to keep them invisible from the prying eyes of any would-be Machetero sympathizers. Once the Bailey bridges were installed over the broken span of the road, a dozen National Guard Humvees armed with heavy machine guns would speed over them to secure a beachhead in front of the burned out yacht club. Five hundred policemen and guardsmen would follow, eliminating or arresting those terrorists still in the streets, and imposing martial law in the island of San Juan.

But before all of that could happen, the SEALs had to save nearly four thousand civilian hostages trapped in three different locations of the island, including the Governor of Puerto Rico and his family. It was a daunting proposition under any circumstances, and without any additional intelligence on the whereabouts of the hostages and the strength of the terrorists, it could turn into an unmitigated disaster.

The first break had come early in the afternoon, as Commander McAllister and Superintendent Maldonado were meeting in the San Geronimo Plaza. A call from no other than the Governor himself had come through to the Superintendent. With the help of another man, Pietrantoni had managed to escape, not from the La Fortaleza compound itself but from his captors inside it. The Governor had informed Maldonado that the terrorists still held the ground around the Executive Mansion, and that they were seeking to kill him. He had asked for immediate help, but after being advised by the Superintendent that a rescue would not be feasible until nighttime, had indicated that he would try to hide with the rest of the hostages in one of the secret chambers of the old palace. For security reasons, he had not said where.

The unexpected news had both elated and worried McAllister. Certainly, the freeing of the hostages would significantly simplify his men's mission. It leveled the playing field. Now, the SEALs could stage an open, all out assault on La Fortaleza and not worry about any retaliation by the terrorists against the Governor or his people.

On the other hand, there was no way that the time of the rescue could be moved up significantly. As Maldonado had explained to the Governor in their telephone conversation, La Fortaleza was just one of three operations that the SEALs would have to conduct simultaneously. To carry out one of the three assaults ahead of the others would allow the terrorists in the other two sites to exact retribution on their prisoners.

Besides, the SEALs needed the time to prepare. As he and his officers were being driven from the airport to the San Geronimo Plaza to meet with Superintendent Maldonado, McAllister had given himself until 2100 hours—9:00 PM civilian time—to get his men ready for the assaults. However, even that deadline had seemed overly optimistic and difficult to attain. As in a theatrical production, each SEAL team member was assigned a particular role, and had to perform it with split second exactitude or else, the lives of his comrades and the success of the operation would be seriously compromised. Also, a significant part of their equipment—including their scuba gear, their communications paraphernalia, and most of their weapons and explosives—was still being flown to Puerto Rico. When it got there, it would need to be assembled, checked, and sorted out between the three different task forces.

McAllister had preferred a dawn attack, knowing that the terrorists expected a night raid, and that they would be prone to let their guard down when the expected raid failed to materialize. Many of them would be asleep.

However, too many hostages were at risk, too much at stake to wait out the night. Every passing moment allowed the terrorists to become more entrenched in their captured strongholds. Every second increased the likelihood that the Governor's hiding place would be discovered, and that he, his family and his staff would be executed. McAllister had to act as quickly as possible.

Against his better judgment, and avoiding the stare of his subordinate officers, the SEAL Commander heard himself promise Maldonado that he would try to move up the rescue operations to 2000 hours. As they shook hands, the Superintendent assured him that his men would be ready.

More good news had greeted McAllister as his car rolled into the cavernous, empty bowels of Hangar 3 in the Isla Grande Airport. Maldonado had just called. He had gotten information from the FBI that the bulk of the hostages in the *Mardi Gras* were being kept in the ship's theater. Apparently, the FBI had spoken with some passengers hiding in the ship. They had also reported that in addition to the main gangway that connected the sixth deck to the dock, there was an open cargo bay close to the bow of the ship at dock level, that gave access to one of the *Mardi Gras'* storage areas. According to the FBI, its sources estimated the number of terrorists on board at a dozen, give or take two men, but that could vary at any moment.

McAllister had called Maldonado back.

"I was informed that you spoke with the FBI about some intelligence it obtained from the *Mardi Gras*."

"Yes, I did. Special Agent Franceschini, my liaison with the FBI, called me right after you and your men had left."

"That information...Do you know how it got to the FBI?"

"It's stranger than you think," Maldonado had answered honestly. *"Apparently some of the passengers contacted Washington directly, using a satellite phone."*

"A satellite phone?" McAllister repeated, clearly puzzled.

"You weren't here when this whole thing exploded," Maldonado explained. *"Right after the bridges were damaged, our communications systems got overloaded with thousands of calls. Nobody could get through. The Macheteros seem to have anticipated that, and used satellite phones, which are not dependent on our local communications systems. We know that because of that reporter I told you about in our meeting, Michelle Alfaro. She got hold of one of those phones too, and that's how she got through to us. Apparently, the people on the Mardi Gras figured it out too, and used a satellite phone to get through to Washington."*

"Not to sound like a prophet of doom, but do you know if the FBI considers the information trustworthy?"

"You mean, can we trust that the information was submitted by real passengers, and not by the Macheteros themselves?" Maldonado had asked.

"After all, you said that the terrorists were using satellite phones to communicate with each other. And those passengers who spoke to the FBI are directing us to enter the ship through a particular entrance. It could all be a trap," McAllister suggested cautiously.

"I see what you mean. I can tell you that the FBI seemed very certain that the call was genuine. The name of the caller appeared as a passenger in the ship's manifest," Maldonado had said, then added quickly. *"I know, the Macheteros could have gotten hold of the list of passengers and used the name of one of them to sound more authentic, but the FBI ran the conversation through a voice stress analysis, and it passed with flying colors."*

McAllister considered the information. Intelligence agencies had been using the voice stress analysis technology or VSA as a counterterrorism measure for some time now. The VSA used computers to measure the involuntary, micro-muscle tremors in the voice of an individual and determine that individual's stress levels. Although still not accepted as evidence of truthfulness by the courts, the results of the VSA analyses had proven to be extremely accurate and a useful weapon in the war against terror.

"Of course," Maldonado had said, as if reading his counterpart's mind, *"there's always a margin for error..."*

"Of course," McAllister had responded distractedly, his mind already considering the ramifications of the new information he had received. After that, the conversation had ended quickly. The SEAL commander had thanked Maldonado, and then called a meeting with his three group commanders.

The meeting had been short. He had conveyed to them the intelligence that he had just received, and canvassed their opinions. They had all favored trusting the report and acting on the basis of the information they had just received. One of them, an Alabaman named Jeb Stuart who headed Group Bravo, suggested that maybe the FBI should call back its contact in the *Mardi Gras* and tell him that no attack would be forthcoming until dawn, just to throw him off the track in the remote case that he was a terrorist or was captured and interrogated. However, McAllister rejected the idea, saying that the erroneous information could cause more problems than those that it could solve. Stuart had left immediately to meet with his staff and modify the plans for the raid of the *Mardi Gras*.

The next piece of valuable intelligence had reached McAllister as he and his men were gathering their gear to abandon Hangar 3, a few minutes after 6:00 PM.

"McAllister, this is Maldonado," the Superintendent had said, and continued without waiting for a response. *"I have some good information that will interest you."*

"Shoot," the Navy Commander had responded.

"We have on-the-ground confirmation about the...location of the hostages in the Grand Laguna Hotel. They are at the main ballroom area. Did you get that?"

McAllister had exchanged a quick look with his two officers, motioning them to approach. "This is reliable information, I take it?"

"As reliable as it gets," the Superintendent had said.

The news was huge. It would help the SEALs to concentrate their forces on the spot where the hostages were supposedly being held, instead of searching the entire grounds of the hotel. Despite this, Maldonado sounded shaken.

"Thank you. That should help us a lot. You should know that we are heading now for the boats. I'm told we should be there in about half an hour," he had told the police chief, hoping to raise his spirits.

"There is more," Maldonado had volunteered. Something about the Superintendent's voice confirmed that something was wrong.

"I just had a conversation with our friend, Adalberto Cacho, the leader of the Macheteros," the policeman explained. *"He blames us for the escape of the Governor. He will start executing five hostages in the Grand Laguna Hotel every thirty minutes, starting at seven forty-five tonight, unless we give him the Governor."*

"That makes our rescue mission too late for some of the hostages," the SEAL Commander had commented somberly. A long silence had followed. "I can try to accelerate my people, try to make up for as much time as I can." McAllister had prompted half-heartedly.

Maldonado had considered McAllister's suggestion for a few seconds.

"No," he had said at last. *"No. Whatever time it takes, it takes. It is absolutely essential that your men are fully prepared, or else the operation will fail."*

"Yes, sir," McAllister responded sympathetically. "I will do my best to speed up matters without jeopardizing the operation."

Any run-of-the-mill official, more concerned with his public image than with the actual safety of the hostages, would have insisted that the SEALs move in immediately, regardless of how ill-prepared they were. McAllister had known a few of them during his career. It took a very brave man to make a conscious decision not to move before a rescue operation had a real chance of success, knowing that any deaths resulting from the delay would be blamed on him. San Juan was very lucky to have a man like Maldonado at the helm of its police force.

McAllister's last communication with the Superintendent had come through the radio, as Group Charlie was boarding the three police launches that would transport them to the drop off area, one half mile off the northern coast of San Juan. The SEAL Commander was meeting with his two main officers, ensigns Watts and Aguirre, and the boat's captain, when the radio communication came in.

As in his prior conversation, the Superintendent had come right to the point. He had just received word that two of the SWAT officers who had participated in that afternoon's rescue attempt had somehow managed to reach Fort San Geronimo, the small fort next to the Grand Laguna Hotel, and that they were planning to create a diversion, in order to draw as many terrorists away from the western flank of the hotel as possible. Maldonado had paused briefly, as if gathering his courage to go on, and then added, *"However, they are at the right place at the right time, and I intend to use them to stop the execution of the hostages while you get there, unless you tell me otherwise."*

McAllister had held his breath for a few seconds, conscious of the shocked stares of the other men in the cabin of the boat. "What would you propose that they do?"

"It's a long shot, I know," Maldonado acknowledged, *"but the men would move into the hotel garden, where almost certainly the executions will take place, and try to stop the terrorists from carrying them out."*

"And if it comes to a shootout?"

"Then, at the very least, my men will have created the diversion that they intended to create in the first place," Maldonado answered. *"At least, we will have tried to do something to stop the killing."*

That was not a valid reason to act, McAllister almost replied, but bit his tongue. He could understand the tremendous stress that the Superintendent was under, and his need to "do something" to save the hostages. While the SEALs had been his only alternative, he had refrained from rushing them into a half-assed assault and let them move at their own speed. But now, unexpectedly, a new opportunity to stop the executions had dropped out of the sky, and he was desperate to take it.

It was a dangerous gamble. The intervention of SWAT—and that is all that it would be, a short-lived intervention—would almost certainly lure most of the terrorists in the hotel to the side of the lagoon and away from the approaching SEALs. However, the chances that the two SWAT men would stop the killing of the hostages—in fact, the chances that the SWAT men would survive—would be close to nil. Seeing it from a cold, unemotional point of view, a failed rescue attempt by the SWAT team would *not* be a bad thing for the men of Group Charlie. It would flush out most of the terrorists in the area from their hiding places, and lull them into a false sense of security, making them think that they had repulsed the government's last attempt of that day to save the trapped hotel guests.

"You realize that your men will probably get killed," McAllister said, feeling compelled to let the Superintendent know how he thought the matter would end, and trying to clear his conscience.

"I don't know..." Maldonado answered with much more optimism than the Navy SEAL expected. *"I have a gut feeling about them...They*

should have been long dead by now, and somehow they've survived, so don't underestimate them. But I need to get an answer from you this very moment, if we're going to do anything, because in less than fifteen minutes they will move into the hotel, unless we signal them to stop. If you tell me that what they do will endanger your operation, I will call it off."

McAllister took a deep breath. *May God help them and may God help us,* he thought, before committing himself. "As far as I am concerned, they have a green light from us."

"Thank you!" Maldonado said with evident delight and relief, and cut off communications.

Standing next to his commander, Ensign Aguirre stared at him quizzically, surprised by his decision. McAllister said nothing for a long while. Allowing the SWAT men to act on their own was unorthodox at best, and not within the planned-as-clockwork military maneuvers that normally characterized a Navy SEAL operation. But in combat, he had personally experienced how a hunch or a "gut feeling" sometimes proved more effective than all of the combined military strategy that he had been taught at officer school.

"Inform the men that two SWAT agents will be...moving into the hotel in a few minutes, from the Condado Lagoon side of the hotel."

Aguirre's questioning look intensified, as if asking, *"Is this a good thing?"* But he had enough sense to remain silent. Instead, he asked, "And our plans?"

"Remain the same," McAllister finished his ensign's sentence for him. "Just warn the men not to shoot anyone with a SWAT uniform."

"We're getting close to your drop off area," the captain of the boat announced.

McAllister looked to the shore and saw the faint outline of the streetlights that ran along the coast between the Grand Laguna Hotel all the way to the walls of Fort San Cristobal in Old San Juan. He had been so concentrated in his last conversation with Maldonado that he had not noticed when they had sailed past the Grand Laguna Hotel. Its main tower rose up in a partially illuminated spiral of glass and metal. The terrorists had not bothered to turn off its automatic lighting system, probably deciding that it would be to their advantage to let the surrounding grounds be as well lit as possible. Waves crashed on the piles of volcanic rock that surrounded hotel, rolling like dark, liquid hills, and exploding into boiling rivers of foam.

The SEALs would not land there, but a mile further to the west, where the road to Old San Juan rose and tall cliffs loomed over a narrow strip of beach. There they would gather, and approach the hotel on foot at a brisk speed.

It would be a long and dark swim to the tiny beach. And once they got there, it would take the SEALs at least another twenty minutes to get to the hotel grounds, barring any unforeseen events.

The small convoy of three police launches that had started from the Boca de Cangrejos Yacht Club, some ten miles to the east of the Grand Laguna Hotel, had run into problems almost immediately. One of the three identical aluminum-hulled Metal Shark boats provided by the police had unexpectedly stalled as it went out of the marina. Its crew had worked frantically to fix the problem, as the boat floated dead on the water, but it had been fifteen minutes before the ship's engines had roared back to life.

Finally under way, the launches—each of them thirty-six feet long— had navigated through the narrow confines of a passage between submerged reefs that ringed the yacht club, and then surged into the open ocean. There, they had encountered heavy swells, climbing up and sliding down the silver-black mounds of a foreboding, ever-shifting sea.

McAllister rode on the first of the three boats, holding on to a metal frame close to the captain's wheel to keep his balance. He shared the ship's small cabin—in addition to the captain—with his two ensigns and a crewman, while eight other SEALs and two other police crewmen sat on the deck of the open stern, quietly watching the two boats behind them.

The Navy SEAL Commander had kept looking impatiently at his watch, painfully aware of how late it was. It was 1935 hours, and the convoy still had a very long way to go.

McAllister discussed again with his officers the new information he had received, and fleshed out the details of the revised the plan of attack. Instead of dividing their forces and hitting both the lobby and ballroom areas simultaneously, the bulk of the men now would concentrate on the latter of the two, leaving a small force of six SEALs to keep at bay any terrorists in the lobby. Another six men would occupy the public parking building to the south of the Grand Laguna Hotel, to cut off any hostiles who tried to escape or move any of the hostages that way.

That still left eastern flank of the hotel, that is, the garden area and the side of the hotel facing the lagoon, in the hands of the terrorists. Originally, the plan had called for a swift strike into that area once the main attack began. It would have been a better strategy to capture the gardens before moving into the hotel, in order to envelop the ballroom area and trap the terrorists inside. But the SEALs had concluded that it would have been impossible to secure the lagoon side of the hotel without getting into a prolonged firefight. That, in turn, would take away the element of surprise the SEALs had in their favor, and increase the risk for the hostages. Therefore, McAllister had decided to move simultaneously into the ballroom and the gardens.

One serious concern for the SEALs were the heavily armed, well-trained men who had shredded to bits the SWAT rescue team that had tried to cross the lagoon earlier that afternoon. From the taped footage they had watched, it seemed that there had been at least three MAG machine guns firing at the advancing rafts, plus several snipers using high-powered rifles. If Group Charlie wandered into an ambush set up by those men, it could turn into a repeat of the SWAT debacle.

During the lagoon fighting, the heavily armed terrorists had occupied some of the buildings to the south of the Grand Laguna public parking area. By occupying the parking building, the SEALs hoped to cut off those heavily armed men from the rest of the fighting, and even surprise them if they tried to help their comrades in the hotel.

However, there was no guarantee that the terrorists were still in the same locations that they had occupied during the Condado Lagoon massacre. On the contrary, it would have been foolish of them to remain there, and as the terrorists had amply proved during that terrible day, they were not fools.

The three officers were still discussing their plans when the police captain slowed down his boat.

"We're here," he announced.

Thirty minutes later, Maldonado made another call to McAllister, to let him know that the SWAT men had driven away the Macheteros who were guarding the hostages, and were holding on to the ballroom where the prisoners were being kept. By that time, however, the three aluminum-hulled Metal Sharks were returning to their home base, and McAllister and his SEALs were submerged in the Atlantic Ocean heading towards the coast, unaware of the Superintendent's last message.

CHAPTER LXII

"Mario..." The Superintendent only uttered one word over the cell phone, but it alarmed the FBI agent. Maldonado's usually calm and deliberate voice sounded shaken and somber.

"Mr. Superintendent," Franceschini answered in as cheerful a voice as he could muster, trying to hide his concern. He did not ask Maldonado about the purpose of his call, knowing that the police chief would let him know when he was ready to do so, and never before.

"I wanted to tell you that based on that call that your people intercepted, Montañez has just arrested Captain Ramirez for corruption and consorting with the terrorists," the Superintendent informed him. Franceschini already knew that from his own sources, but waited for Maldonado to finish. *"They've taken him to our headquarters in Hato Rey."*

"Good," the FBI agent said tentatively, not acknowledging that he already knew. He sensed that more was to come, and waited with baited breath.

It took a while for the Superintendent to continue.

"After his arrest, Ramirez asked to talk with me," Maldonado continued. *"He had just heard that Montañez had placed Rovira under house arrest. He sounded very scared."*

"He must have smelled that we were unto him," Franceschini speculated.

"I'm sure that was part of the reason, yes," Maldonado confirmed. *"But...he sounded terrified. Not just the type of scared a person gets when he knows that he's going to get jail time, but the scared-for-his-life type of scared,"* the Superintendent said slowly, as if searching for the right words. *"You know what I mean?"*

He did. During the many years he had been in the law enforcement business, he had learned to recognize the voice of panic, that particular

793

moment when a person's sense for self-preservation overrode any other interests which that person could have.

"He wants to meet personally with me. In private. He says that he was just a go-between, a messenger for the real mole. He told me that even though he never met with the mole, he has a good idea of who he is. He is willing to give me his name, but only if I give him immediate police protection and place him under the witness protection program."

Maldonado stopped talking, to allow the FBI agent to absorb his words. Franceschini's head whirled with the news and the unspoken implications.

"Do you believe him?" he asked cautiously.

A short pause showed the Superintendent's distressed state of mind. *"Like I said, he sounded scared out of his wits, and I don't think it's because of the scandal or the jail time he will face. He sounded plain, old-fashioned panicked, as if he could be killed at any moment."*

"Did he give any hint about who the mole could be?"

"No, not a hint. He won't give away the information until he sees me. It's the only negotiating chip that he has left."

Franceschini considered the Superintendent's words. "I see," he said. "Are you going to see him at your headquarters?"

"In Hato Rey? No, I'm too busy. I'll meet him here, in the San Geronimo Plaza."

"Montañez is with him?" Franceschini asked, knowing he was treading on very sensitive ground.

"Yes..." Maldonado let his answer linger.

"He should be safe with him..." The FBI tossed his statement into the conversation as casually as he could, and listened intently.

Again, the Superintendent took a long time answering back. When he did, he could barely keep his voice from breaking. *"Mario, Montañez is the problem,"* he said with such intense anguish that he seemed to be wrenching his words involuntarily out of his soul. *"I could tell from Ramirez's tone. The man is terrified about being killed because he knows that the killer is there, in the police headquarters, with him. I'm afraid that if I ask Montañez to bring Ramirez here, Ramirez won't make it alive to the San Geronimo Plaza."*

"He wouldn't dare to harm him while he was in his care! All the evidence would point to him!"

"Montañez is a very intelligent, resourceful man. You know him. He'd make it look like an accident of some sort. An attempt by Ramirez to escape...Maybe he'd even disappear his body, and say that he escaped..."

Franceschini took a deep breath, trying to steady his voice. "You're certain about this?"

"I'm afraid so," Maldonado replied with a disconsolate voice. *"It all falls into place, doesn't it? All of the raids that came to nothing because somebody tipped the drug gangs ahead of time. All of key drug people that slipped away from us...Even the 'miraculous' arrests that Montañez and his...'Untouchables' managed to do, token, staged events to keep his credibility up. To build up his legend. I had been afraid of this for a long time, but refused to believe the obvious. Montañez is a close friend. More like a brother to me."*

"It could have been Ramirez acting alone," Franceschini suggested.

"Ramirez is an idiot. He's good at following instructions, but he doesn't have the intellectual capacity, or the balls for that matter, to establish the necessary contacts with the drug cartels, or to run such a successful covert operation for so long. No, Mario. Even if it breaks my heart to say it, I see Montañez's firm hand controlling all of this."

"But Montañez..." Franceschini searched for the right words to say, but his hesitation spoke more eloquently than any words he could utter. "I mean, I'll admit that I was one of the first to suggest that we should include him in our investigation, but it was just as a precautionary measure. He's...he's..."

"Our friend?" Maldonado said bitterly. *"So I thought."*

Both men stayed silent, as if hoping that the other would suddenly come up with some statement or idea that would clear Montañez from any blame.

"What do you want me to do?" Franceschini asked finally.

"I want you and your men to take over. I need you to protect Ramirez," Maldonado answered. *"I don't think that Montañez will dare to interfere with you."*

Franceschini sighed. "If that is what you want...I'll get to it right away. I will personally pick him up and bring him to the San Geronimo Plaza."

"Thank you, my friend," Maldonado said with sad relief. *"I owe you one."*

Franceschini hesitated. "What about Montañez?"

"I'll take care of him. I'll ask him to come back here, to the San Geronimo Plaza, to help me with the rescue mission. I'll tell him that the FBI is taking over."

"He'll be suspicious..."

"Maybe, but I'll blame you. I'll say you insisted in having first dibs, you know, drug trafficking, arms smuggling, all of that stuff that violates the Commerce Clause and the federal laws."

There were a slew of reasons that he could invoke to take over Ramirez, Franceschini agreed quietly.

"My men will be at the police headquarters in about half an hour, give or take. Is that okay with you?"

"Yes, thank you," Maldonado said again. *"And Mario?"*
"Yes?"
"Tell your men to be careful."

"I'm telling you, Mr. McFadden. You don't have anything to envy from Indiana Jones! You have saved me twice, you rescued the Condessa, and you escaped the pirates, all in a days work! You're sure that you are not a secret agent?" Ernan said enthusiastically.

John smiled in spite of himself. He was amused by the Filipino's wild praises, but it also made him think about the precariousness of their situation. For most of his adult life, he had avoided controversy, going into what he called the "social entertainment business", a harmless enterprise where he was able to interact with other people while keeping his emotions in check. All of that had changed that day.

Had anyone told him that morning that he'd still be on board of the *Mardi Gras* hiding inside one of its closed restaurants, he would have called that person delusional, and rightly so. He had never considered himself to be a man of action—still didn't—but for some reason beyond his comprehension he felt strangely fulfilled, as if a part of him that he had long thought discarded and forgotten, had suddenly reawakened from a recessed, dusty corner of his soul and stepped out into the open.

As a young man, John had backpacked through much of Australia, many times sleeping in the open or relying on the kindness of locals, owning only what he carried and earning his keep from any chores that he happened to stumble upon. There had been times when he had gone to sleep without a meal, and on more than one occasion he had spent more than a week without exchanging a word with another human being.

It had given him a sense of wonder and utter freedom, and infected him with the wanderlust that had guided his actions for the rest of his life. In those young, heady days he had seen himself as someday becoming a great writer of fiction, drawing upon his globe trotting experiences. He had carried with him a small notebook, jotting ideas, observations, events and even quaint expressions that he imagined, or happened to come about.

But somewhere, somehow along the way, the novelty had worn off. He wrote a journal of his travels in Australia, as well a several short stories, but he could not get them published. As he grew older, his high expectations of life crashed head on with reality. The promise of adventure that had served as his guiding star started to lose its luster. He began to trade the raw excitement of new discoveries for the safer, more comfortable life of a traveling companion, until he became resigned to the idea that he would spend the rest of his life—or most of it anyway—charming his way into the pockets of lonely, well-to-do ladies. He spent less and less time on his manuscripts, until he abandoned them altogether, stored in his computer in an untitled folder.

It was not a bad life. He got to see the world and sometimes more often than not met interesting people. It just was not what he visualized that he would end up doing. A tame, lusterless end to his dreams.

And then, out of the blue, this had happened. Like a shaken bottle of Coca Cola, all his long-dormant feelings had foamed up to the surface, filling him with a sense of exhilaration that he had not experienced since his young days in Australia. And despite the very real possibility that he would not survive to the end of that day—or maybe because of it—he felt more alive than he had felt since...since he could remember.

It had taken about twenty minutes for the Countess and him to make their way from the Catacombs nightclub back to the Trattoria. They had come through the kitchen, the same way that he and Ernan had used to originally get there. When the Filipino saw them, he had nearly given them away with a shout of pure joy, kissing the Countess twice on each cheek and nearly suffocating John with a tight embrace. Then he had noticed their battered faces, and his expression had darkened with anger and concern, asking who had done that to them and fussing over the Countess.

"Those savages!" he muttered furiously. "That they should strike a woman! And an old lady at that!" he expressed too loudly for John's comfort, and then, realizing what he had just said, he tried to fix it, adding, "Not that you are so old, *madame.* And you are still very pretty and look younger than your years!"

"But I am old, Ernan! Ancient, actually!" she said with a smile, regarding the embarrassed Filipino with affection.

"And hungry too, it seems," John added, looking around him. "Come on," he said, crouching towards the kitchen and slowly pushing its pivoting door to crawl through it. Ernan and the Countess followed. On a metal counter, they found some loaves of bread and a partially cut wheel of pecorino cheese. A further search in one of the three huge refrigerators of the kitchen uncovered some cold meats, and various desserts, which they ate ravenously, along with a bottle of wine that—to the amusement of his two companions—Ernan had uncorked by placing its bottom inside his shoe and banging it several time against a wall.

"Now for an after dinner," John said, mellowed by the wine and the food. Without saying anything else, he crawled out of the kitchen and got to the bar. Under the counter, he found a small refrigerator. He espied through its glass door several racks of bottles and, opening it, squatted to examine its content better. He discovered bottles of port, and chose a Sao Pedro 2000, which he slid out of its nook.

He was about to return to the kitchen, when he heard the noise of loud voices emanating from somewhere near the entrance of the Trattoria. The voices gave way to the jangling of glass and metal, as if a person was trying to shake open the restaurant's doors. Instinctively, John moved on his hands and knees from behind the bar to the table next to it, and then to the table beyond. He ducked, peeking under the table's cloth to the entrance of the Trattoria to get a better look.

There were two men outside, both in their low twenties. One was dressed completely in black, including a long sleeved shirt and what seemed to be black desert boots. His light brown hair was carefully coifed *a-la*-Elvis Presley, his eyes were hazel and—even from where John was hiding—they brimmed with insolent confidence. The second man was heavier than his companion, his blue polyester shirt revealing two layered sets of love handles. He had not shaved for several days, sporting the beginnings of an uneven beard, and was furiously sucking a lollipop that he constantly moved from one side of his mouth to the other as he shook the elongated metal handle of the Trattoria's door.

"Stand aside," the man in black ordered, and struck the door twice with the butt of his rifle, to no effect. Frustrated, he turned the rifle around and pointed it at the entrance.

The hijacker with the lollipop opened his mouth to say something but the man with the rifle fired a short burst, shattering the thick glass door into hundreds of nugget-sized fragments that scattered over the entrance's floor and under half a dozen tables. Several of the bullets whizzed all around John, knocking down chairs, breaking bottles and glasses, and making one of the tablecloths leap into the air like a scared ghost.

The lollipop man shouted and threw his hands into the air, backing away. "Holy shit!" he yelled. "You crazy bastard!"

The gunman laughed and walked into the restaurant, his booted feet crunching on the broken glass, his eyes scanning the Trattoria with indifferent calm while his companion continued to berate him.

"Those bullets could have bounced back and hit us!"

"*Bounced* back?" the man in black repeated with amusement. "Like if they were made of rubber? You really are an expert on guns, aren't you, gordo?" He continued examining his surroundings as he spoke. "Ah! There it is!" he exclaimed with relish, placing his rifle on a table and heading towards the Trattoria's bar. John backed up on all fours, ducking closer behind the table, grateful that the lights in the restaurant were turned off.

"And stop calling me gordo, okay?" the lollipop-sucking man said resentfully.

"It's just a term of endearment, my friend!" the rifleman responded, bringing down from the bar's upper shelf a 12 year old bottle of Bacardi Rum. "You know I mean nothing by it. And after all, you *are* a gordito," he added with a friendly smile.

The man with the lollipop looked back nervously at the destroyed door. "Are we supposed to be doing this?" he asked rhetorically, watching as the black-garbed man unscrewed the cap of the bottle of rum. "We're supposed to be looking for the couple that escaped, not destroying the ship...Or drinking."

The man with the Elvis hairdo leaned behind the bar and brought up two round-bottomed drinking glasses. He poured two generous servings into them from the 12 year old rum. "Here! This is just as good as a brandy. It should be drunk straight up. No ice, no coke—God forbid it! Just straight." He handed a glass to his companion, and raised his. "Salud!" he said, taking a long swallow. Then he glanced at his friend, who had not touched his rum. "Well, you're not going to drink, you ungrateful slob?"

"We're wasting our time here," the lollipop man said, fidgeting. "We're supposed to be looking for the people who escaped."

"I *am* looking," the black-garbed man responded, taking another swallow and lazily looking about him while leaning on the bar's counter. "I don't see you doing anything, though," he said at his companion.

The latter stared at his friend with speechless indignation. "What...It was... I..."

"Stop wasting our time and go look for the fugitives. Search the kitchen! Go, go, go!" The Elvis-coiffed man gestured with his free hand, as if scaring away a cat, and then turned his back on his companion. "Call me if somebody is hiding in there."

Directing a dark look at his friend, the lollipop man headed to the kitchen. John cursed himself for leaving his captured AK-47 behind him. Horrified, he watched the legs of the reluctant terrorist move towards the kitchen's swivel door, knowing that in a matter of seconds his friends would be discovered.

Then his eyes alighted on the butt of the automatic rifle that the black-garbed man had discarded, protruding slightly from the edge of a tabletop. McFadden was three tables away from it. To get to it, he would have to crawl in a semicircle and dash through the open spaces between the tables. It would be risky, but if discovered, he could still probably beat the rum-swilling terrorist to the rifle, even though he was not certain if he could fire the damned thing.

Holding his breath, he scampered on his hands and knees towards the first of the three tables, his right upper ribs—where he had been kicked—exploding with pain. He stopped and peeked from under it, afraid that his frantic crawling had produced too much noise. But the Elvis-coiffed man's legs never shifted, one of them resting on the bar's brass footrest, the other tapping on the floor. Taking advantage that the hijacker was turned away from him, John scurried across another open gap, towards the next table.

The rifle was now within his grasp, one open space away. McFadden readied himself for his last dash, adopting the position of a sprinter about to start a race, when he heard the terrorist softly say, "I see you...", and saw the man move a hand closer to his holster.

The Australian almost screamed in surprise. He started to rise from his hiding place, but stopped just in time as a voice some distance behind him defensively answered, "I was hungry!"

John crept under the table, moving with such haste that he hit one of the chairs and it made a scraping sound. Cursing himself for his clumsiness, he waited in near panic for a reaction by the terrorists, but if either of them heard the noise, they apparently thought it had been made by the other man.

"Stealing a salami from the refrigerator. Really?" the Elvis-coiffed terrorist said with exaggerated shock, scratching his groin. "And a loaf of bread under your arm! And then you complain when I call you gordito!"

"I was going to share it with you," the other terrorist said, offended.

"Were you now?" the other said, in a tone that implied that he did not believe him. "You know, pretty soon, hundreds of FEPIstas and Macheteros are going to board this ship to rest and eat, and here you are, stealing their food from the kitchen."

"I just took some salami and bread, what are you talking about? You should speak, destroying a part of the ship and stopping the search of the fugitives just to get drunk!"

"I'm not destroying the ship! Breaking through the glass door was a necessity, the only way we could get in!" the man dressed in black said with indignation. Then he smiled. "But I wouldn't mind getting drunk... I'll admit to that. So let's make a deal. I won't say anything about your salami, and you keep quiet about my drinking. Deal?"

"They'll smell it on your breath..." the lollipop man said in a more mollified tone.

"They'll smell your salami first. Deal?"

"Deal."

The two men shook hands, and the black-garbed man grabbed his rifle.

"I suppose you didn't see anyone in the kitchen, or were you too busy searching the refrigerators for food?" he asked with mischief in his voice, unable to stop a chuckle at the end of his question.

"You never give up, do you?" his companion said in a tired and indignant voice, becoming even more upset as he watched the gunman laugh at his own joke. "I searched and it was empty, okay? Like your brain!"

"Okay! Okay!" the Elvis-haired man said, drinking the last of his rum and starting to walk to the Trattoria's exit. "I was just kidding, geez! You're so sensitive!"

The portly terrorist followed him, pulling down his blue polo shirt and unconsciously emphasizing the love handles beneath it. He had been standing so close to John that the Australian could have stretched out his hand and touched the man's leg.

"Well, stop it," he said. "Your fat jokes are becoming very tiresome."

'Okay, gordo," the man dressed in black said, his voice receding as he walked out of the restaurant and down the stairs.

The last thing that John heard was an unintelligible outburst from the lollipop man, mingled with more laughter from his companion. He waited until the noise had abated, and then slowly crawled out from under the table.

He was shaking, still not recovered from the scare. It had been too close. For a moment he had thought that he would have to confront the black-clad Elvis-lookalike and point his own weapon at him. What would have happened after that was difficult to tell. He was glad that he had not been forced to find out.

Then he remembered the Countess and Ernan. Somehow, the portly terrorist had failed to see them. *How could that be?* Standing up, he quickly walked back into the kitchen. There was no one there.

"Countess? Ernan?" he called, sweeping with his eyes the rows of stainless steel cabinets, ovens, refrigerators, tables, and sundry equipment—scores of pot, pans, ladles, strainers, cutting knives, and generic containers—that lined every wall of the room. For a lingering moment nobody answered. Then he heard something stir next to him, and to his amazement, saw a bony hand break the surface of a large garbage pail filled with discarded vegetables. It was followed by the Countess' head and shoulders. She grinned at him.

"My God!" he muttered with disbelief, smiling back at her. Her hair was matted with strips of shredded lettuce, pickles, and strips of carrot and sauerkraut, her white blouse blotted with pale vegetable juices. "How did you get in there?"

"When we heard voices, we imagined that they would come searching for us in here. They did not sound like they had found you..."

"I hid under the a table."

"That is what I thought. So I helped hide Ernan, and then climbed to this table," she pointed to a tall table with several cutting boards and knives that stood next to the large plastic garbage tub where she had hidden, "and I shook myself into this can filled with vegetables until they covered me. I must stink like rotted salad, *n'est ce pas?*"

"I don't know, you look pretty tasty to me..." he said, cringing inwardly at his own lame joke, relief sweeping over him like a tidal wave. He flicked off some vegetables from her hair. "But where is Ernan?"

"Oh, Ernan!" the Countess exclaimed. "I completely forgot about him!"

"Where is he?"

"I placed him in the oven!" she answered as she ran to a huge stove and pulled its front door down, revealing the Filipino inside, bundled in the fetal position. Ernan extended a hand to John, and slowly swung his feet out from his cramped quarters.

"You're lucky that hungry terrorist decided not to cook something before he left," John said with a short laugh.

"That's it!" the small *maitre* mumbled as he tried to brush away the grease from his shirt, only managing to spread it more. "I'm not getting into another contraption for the rest of my life!" he said, provoking a grin from both of his friends. "I mean it!" He looked from one face to another with an earnest expression. "I'd rather die first!"

Suddenly, John's smile vanished and he raised a hand in warning, hushing his friend. "Quiet! They're coming back! I hear them!" he said urgently. "Everybody hide!"

Instinctively, Ernan re-entered the oven and pulled its door shut. John held on to the Countess' arm and placed his fingers across his lips, warning her to be silent. He began to snicker, and shook his head, indicating that he had fooled Ernan into re-entering the oven. She directed to him a reproachful stare, but could not help smiling.

John rapped softly on the oven's door. For several seconds, Ernan said nothing. Then they heard his voice say, "Shit! There is no one out there, is there?"

Slowly, he pushed open the hatch and cautiously stared out, seeing both of his friends shaking with laughter.

"You are terrible, *mon cher!*" the Countess chided, but could not stop giggling. "You scared poor Ernan to death!"

"Mr. McFadden, you are going to kill me from a heart attack!" Ernan protested, his eyebrows churned into a large "V". "Your sense of humor leaves a lot to be desired!"

"I'm so sorry!" John said, tears streaming from his eyes. "It's just...I couldn't resist the temptation! I'm so sorry!"

Ernan continued to stare darkly at him, but then cracked a sheepish smile. "That was an evil thing to do," he mumbled.

John extended his hand and the Filipino grabbed it, climbing out of the oven. "I'm really sorry, my friend. There's something wrong with me..." he said, drying his eyes with his shirt's sleeves, and beginning to sober up. "Anyway, did you guys hear what those two hijackers said while they were here?" he asked in a more serious tone to his two friends.

Ernan regarded him warily, not certain that the Australian was trying to fool him again or talking in earnest.

"More terrorists are starting to come into the ship. Many more. If the rescue team doesn't get here soon, it's going to become impossible to recapture the *Mardi Gras*. It will be crawling with terrorists."

"This is for real?" Ernan asked, still distrustful of his friend's motives.

"I wish it was not," John replied ruefully. "I don't know if you two heard from the kitchen what they were talking about..." The Countess and Ernan shook their heads. "But apparently there will be a lot more terrorists boarding the *Mardi Gras* soon...Any of you know what Macheteer...a Machetirios is? They mentioned that as some of the people who were coming."

The Filipino and the Countess stared back at him in silence, their expressions suddenly filled with foreboding.

"If they are coming," the Countess said, "we must stop them, then."

John nervously combed back his hair with his hands without realizing it. At any other moment, he would have disregarded her statement as frightfully naive and foolish, and tried to steer her away from the subject. But things had changed now. He had dared to enter the lion's den and had been able to walk out—if not unscathed, at least alive—acting on plans and schemes that just the day before he would have condemned as the ravings of a crazy man. In the past few hours, he had learned not to discard out of hand any suggestion put to him, no matter how unreal or impractical it sounded, without first thinking it through. So now, he considered carefully the Countess' statement.

"Stop them?" he repeated, looking at her. "How do we do that?"

"As long as the *Mardi Gras* is connected to the dock by the gangway, there is very little that we can do," Ernan blurted out in a tone that admitted no contradiction, and by which he meant that there was *no way* they could stop the "pirates" from climbing into the ship.

John mulled over the Filipino's off-hand conclusion, and realized that what he said made perfect sense.

"Do you know how we can disconnect the gangway*?" he asked Ernan.

The small *maitre* stared at him with utter horror and dismay, and emphatically shook his head.

The ramp connecting the *Mardi Gras* to the shore was a massive affair; an enormous, covered, steel-framed corridor enclosed in large, plastic sheets to protect the passengers from the wind and the rain. It rose diagonally from the dock to a height of fifty feet, twisting on itself like a large "Z", and then extended outwards and horizontally to connect with the *Mardi Gras*. It was controlled mechanically, like the ramps used to connect airplanes at the airport, the giant "Z" folding on itself or stretching until it reached the desired height.

John had no idea where the controls of the gangway were located. If he wanted to disconnect the ramp, he would first have to locate them, and figure out how they worked. It was not an attractive prospect, particularly since the ramp would be guarded.

"It shouldn't be too hard, though," John muttered to himself, lost in his own thoughts.

Ernan directed him a terrified stare. "What shouldn't be too hard? Disconnecting the ramp," he said suspiciously. "You're thinking of disconnecting the ramp, aren't you? With all due respect, Mr. McFadden, but are you *crazy*?"

John's attention returned to his friends, who watched him with expectant faces. He realized how much he had grown to care for them—the small Filipino with his white, filthy uniform and his wounded, bloody arm, who thought John was the re-incarnation of Indiana Jones; and the old, tough as nails woman who feared no one and who had shamed him into returning to the ship—and his heart went out to them.

"I'm sorry," he said, shaking his head as if awaking from a bad dream. "I was just talking to myself...thinking that if we found the controls to operate the gangway, it would not be very hard to operate them. To screw up the ramp, anyway."

"I would not want to contradict you, Mr. McFadden, but do you even know where the controls are and what they look like? There will probably be some sort of key to activate them. And even if we manage to do all that, wouldn't the pirates be able to move it back?" Ernan said, his tone reflecting the extreme difficulty of what he was proposing.

"I'm not saying that it will be easy..." John began to say, but stopped, astonished by his own statement. *My God*, he thought, *was that really him talking? Who was this new John McFadden that had taken over his body? He sounded just like White, the Australian who had urged his fellow crewmembers to take over the ship, and whom John had thought a madman. Now White was dead and he had taken his place. How the hell had that happened?*

And yet, if a hundred more terrorists boarded the ship, the results would be disastrous. The rescuers would be forced to fight their way through a small army, in very confined quarters crammed with hostages. It would be a bloodbath.

His old self would have asked "So what?" After all, he'd already done more than any reasonable man could expect. He was not responsible for the well being of the passengers and the crew. He, the Countess, and Ernan only had to hide and wait for the rescue, and they would be able to walk away from it all with only a few bruises and scars to brag about.

Of course, the terrorists could decide to sail away at any moment. Then where would they be?

"It's too difficult," Ernan repeated. "Those pirates will surely kill us when we try to find out how we can move the gangway."

"You're right..." John began to say slowly. Then he hesitated and fell into a long, contemplative silence. Ernan's worried countenance softened to one of hopeful relief. However, the Countess continued to observe him closely.

"I know a place where we can hide—" the Filipino began to say, but John interrupted him.

"There is, of course, another way..." John said softly, looking at the Countess. Her eyes brightened with gratification.

"I knew you would not give up so easily, *mon cher. Bravo!*" she said proudly, beaming at him even though she still had not heard his proposal.

John looked scared, as if he was starting something that could easily get out of control. "This is just a thought, but...Perhaps...perhaps we could burn the ramp. Make it unusable for the terrorists..."

Ernan made the sign of the cross, staring at John as if he were the devil. "But Mr. McFadden! That is pure madness! How do you intend to light the gangway on fire? With a lighter and some newspapers?"

John walked out of the kitchen, followed closely by his two friends. From the bar, he got hold of the bottle of rum from which the black-garbed man had been serving himself, and grabbing a glass, poured himself a drink.

"Salud!" he said, holding it up to his friends, and drank the rum in one gulp, gasping afterwards.

He lifted the bottle and showed it to his two friends.

"*This* is how we start the fire," he said.

CHAPTER LXIII

The stooped, thin man sat on a padded stool he had stolen from the Zanzi-bar Lounge in the *Mardi Gras*, at the mouth of the gangway on Deck 5. He had abandoned the stuffy, overcrowded Stardust Theater and sought the cool tranquility of the open bay. He still wore the same U.S. Customs uniform he had worn that morning when, as "Michael Rivera", he and Rodriguez, his gum-chewing companion, had boarded the ship demanding to see the captain.

He smiled, remembering how shocked the stuck-up Brit Ship Security Officer had been when they had informed him that the ship's Security Certificate had been forged. They had talked to him right there, where he was sitting now taking in the night's breeze. The ruse had worked surprisingly well. *What had been the name of the SSO? Bates?* He remembered, because he had been tempted to call him "Master-Bates" but had bitten his tongue at the last moment. *Well, Master-Bates was now a piece of cold meat in one of the ship's freezers. And soon, he would be "Bates" for the fishes.* He made a mental note to repeat his witty play on words to Rodriguez.

It had all been a lot of fun. He could still picture the captain's face when he had realized that they were hijacking the ship, and the sputtering, helpless rage of the Second Officer when Rodriguez had shot Bates. It had reminded him of Yosemite Sam, fuming helplessly at Bugs Bunny.

Rivera drew a pack of cigarettes from his pants front pocket, and tapped it to get one of the cigarettes out, pulling it out with his lips. He lit it with his Zippo lighter and took two short pulls from it, releasing the smoke into the night's air.

He felt content and at ease. Overall, the takeover of the *Mardi Gras* had unfolded with silky smoothness. There had been the murder of the Machetero who had been carrying the body of Bates out of the bridge, the escape of the two hostages, and the unexplained disappearance of some of their people, but those things were to be expected; some bumps in an otherwise smooth ride. He presumed that those from his group who had disappeared would eventually be found, tied up somewhere, or maybe even dead. *Either way, it served them right for being careless.*

Soon, the ship would be crawling with FEPIstas and a few more of the Macheteros, although most of the latter would be at La Fortaleza or in the Grand Laguna Hotel. The authorities—local or federal—would not dare to move into a ship crawling with hundreds of rebels. They had not dared to move on the *Achilles Lauro*, where only a handful of activists had held the ship hostage for days; much less would they dare to do it with the *Mardi Gras*, brimming with armed men. And if for any reason the rest of San Juan fell—an unlikely scenario at the moment—they would still be able to sail away, to the anger and consternation of the rest of the world.

Rivera took another pull from his cigarette, and puffed out a circle of smoke. He felt proud of his ability to make smoke rings. Not too many people could make them. Sometimes he couldn't do them at all. But tonight, the ring was perfect. *Just as everything else.* He watched with satisfaction as the circle of smoke expanded until it dissipated, then let his eyes wander over the empty deck.

It was a beautiful ship. He was certain that the ship's insurance company would pay a hefty ransom to get it back, once they had disembarked in Venezuela, or if they were able to stay in San Juan.

A sudden draft of frigid air made him look to his right, and he noticed that one of the automatic doors of the fifth deck had slid open, revealing for a moment the red-carpeted foyer that led inside. However, nobody had come out.

Curious, he thought, as the doors slid shut. The doors were controlled by an electric eye that sensed motion. They should not have opened by themselves.

Pulling his gun out of its holster, he slid off the stool and strode towards the door. It swished open as its electronic eye sensed his approach, revealing the insides of the ship and blasting him with another dose of icy air. He ambled into the foyer and looked about him.

To his left extended the mirrored, gold encrusted entrance to the Four Seasons Restaurant, an ornate—and now empty—hostess stand guarding its closed doors. To his right loomed the enormous ship's lobby, its hollow, multi-decked center framed by shiny, aluminum railings, spiraling stairs, and three oval-shaped, glass-walled elevators.

Normally the heart of the ship, nothing stirred within lobby, its empty elegance emphasizing the eerie loneliness that pervaded—except where the passengers were kept—throughout most of the great ship. Rivera walked into the main atrium and scanned the other decks above him. "Anybody here?" he shouted, but no one responded, only the pneumatic swish of the automatic door behind him altering the stillness of the space that surrounded him. *Strange*, he thought, turning back and walking out through the automatic doors.

"Drop the gun," a man's voice whispered behind him, startling him. Before he could turn to see who was speaking, he felt the hard muzzle of a gun pressed against his ribs. He complied, letting his pistol drop to the ground and raising his hands above his head.

He tried to glance over his shoulder at the faceless man addressing him, but a hand slapped him on the back of the head. "Keep looking to the front," the man behind him growled.

"What do you—" he began to say, but got slapped again.

"Walk," the disembodied voice said.

"Walk?" Rivera asked with a mixture of dread and contempt. "Walk where?"

"Opposite to the direction that this gun is pointing," the rogue passenger—it had to be one of the escaped passengers—responded, forcing him to move towards the stern of the ship, about a hundred yards away.

As he began to comply, Rivera heard more movement behind him. "Who are you?" he asked nervously. "What are you going to do with me?"

The faceless gunman did not respond. Rivera began to worry. There was nowhere where the rogue passenger could lock him up safely, without running the risk that the Machetero would raise the alarm. His thoughts inevitably raced back to the disappearance of some of his comrades earlier that day, and he shuddered involuntarily. His captor's reticence to speak did not bode well for him.

Suddenly, he heard the crashing of glass and the muffled "whumph" of an explosion, and the walls and deck chairs in front of him became bathed with a flickering, orange glow. Three more explosions followed, increasing the intensity of what could only be flames.

This time, Rivera looked back, and despite himself stopped to watch with dismay as the upper portion of the boarding ramp burned. At first, the conflagration seemed to be contained in the interior of the enclosed gangway, but in a matter of seconds, large orange flames started to shoot out from under the plastic panels that lined its walls and to consume them with voracious greed.

The growing blaze illuminated a wide area around the ramp, revealing the small figures of two armed men on the dock five decks below, who apparently had crept out of their hiding places to stare helplessly at the burning structure. Others on the pier began to arrive, pointing at the fire excitedly or merely stopping to watch, uncertain about what they should do.

"Keep walking," the man behind Rivera said, prodding his back with his gun. Rivera caught a quick glimpse of him, but the man's face was darkened by the shadows cast by the fire burning behind him.

"I don't know what you intend to gain by this," the Machetero told the rogue passenger, as they continued their way to the rear of the ship, "but you may have signed your own death warrant. This just makes it more difficult for us to free the other hostages."

The gunman said nothing until they got to the stern of the ship. Then he ordered Rivera to stop. By that time, the hijacker's hands were shaking. "If you think that by burning the ramp you will keep my comrades from boarding, you're sadly mistaken. There are other ways to get into this ship, you know?" the terrorist blurted out, trying to evince some reaction from the invisible gunman that would give him a clue about his fate.

"Then you will have to use one of them to get back aboard," the stranger answered. "Climb over the railing."

Rivera walked to the edge of the ship and placed his hands tentatively on the wooden handrail. He was so frightened that he could barely stand up. "You're not going to shoot me, are you?"

"I will, if you don't climb over the railing right now," the rogue passenger responded.

Clumsily, his legs trembling, Rivera clambered over the handrail and, holding on to it, stood on tiptoes on the edge of the deck, facing the gunman. For the first time, he got a good look of him, and felt very scared.

Physically, the man did not seem to be such a formidable foe. He must have been in his mid forties, and seemed ill at ease holding his gun. His clothes were filthy, his shirt stained with large splotches of dry blood, his pants grimy and ripped. Not the appearance that Rivera would have expected of the mysterious saboteur who had been roaming the ship and causing some of the other hijackers to disappear. On the contrary, the rogue passenger looked more like a shoddy, over-the-hill entertainer, or a stressed out psychoanalyst, or even a wedding planner, but definitely not like a killer. And he seemed exhausted.

However, something about his dead-set eyes left Rivera no doubt that he would shoot him without hesitation.

"What—" Rivera began to say, but the man cut him short.

"Jump."

"I can't swim," Rivera pleaded in a piteous voice. He was lying, but it was worth a try. Every second of delay increased the chances that somebody would see them.

"Jump now," the man said, not raising his voice, but pointing his gun straight at his face.

"Let me at least untie my shoes!" Rivera tentatively raised his right foot and placed it on one of the horizontal aluminum strips of the railing.

The blast of the gun caught him completely by surprise. The rogue passenger shifted his aim a fraction of a second before he fired, the bullet chipping off a chunk of the wood on the handrail, less that a foot away from Rivera's left hand. Instinctively, the fake customs officer released his hold of the railing, swinging outwards and losing his balance. The momentum of his body proved too strong for his other hand to keep its grip on the handrail, and with a yelp, he fell backwards, hitting the water below with a sharp splat.

John ran to the ship's edge and looked down, but he only saw the bubbling foam on the black water that marked the spot where the terrorist had fallen. He did not wait to find out if the man emerged. There was no time for that.

The hijacker had been right. There were other ways of getting on the *Mardi Gras* besides using the boarding ramp. He had used one of them, after stowing on board through the ship's cargo door close to the bow, the same door that he had told the FBI could be used by those trying to rescue them. That ramp, which was at the same level as the dock, was short and made entirely of metal; strong enough to support the weight of a forklift carrying crates and boxes into the ship's hold. It would be impossible to burn, and too heavy to dislodge and throw into the bay.

John suspected that the terrorists were not aware of it, having access to the ship through the main gangway. But now that the gangway was burning, it would only be a matter of time before they searched other means of getting on board, and noticed the smaller ramp. There was only one alternative: to shut it down.

That, however, would create another problem. The last time that they had communicated with the FBI, John had informed Agent Moylan that the rescue forces could use the open cargo hatch to infiltrate the ship. If they shut that door now to keep the terrorists out, they would also shut out the rescuers, and that seemed to be a problem without any solution.

"Maybe, after we burn down the gangway, we could move into the loading area and shoot anyone trying to get in that doesn't look like a policeman," the Countess had suggested. Ernan had directed towards her a terrified stare.

"No," John had answered, to the Filipino's intense relief. "We'd end up fighting the terrorists trying to get into the ship, and those already inside the *Mardi Gras*. We wouldn't last long."

"So there is nothing we can do," Ernan had countered before anybody else could say anything.

"Maybe if we threw a rope from the side..." the Countess had said.

John had considered that same idea himself. "Do you know where we can find a rope?" he had asked Ernan.

The Filipino had shaken his head. "I'm not sure. The maintenance shop, maybe. But that is on deck 2, and we'd have to walk to the other end of the ship," he indicated, extending his arm and moving it in an arc above his head to emphasize his point.

The three friends had thought about the alternative in silence. None of them relished the idea of walking across the enormous cruise ship to "maybe" find a rope. Besides, they would first have to let the FBI know about the change in their plans, if they could get hold of the FBI.

"I...have an idea," Ernan had said reluctantly, clearing his throat and breaking the long pause.

The Countess and John had regarded him with surprise. The little man seemed scared beyond his wits, and for good reason. He had seen several of his friends and work associates killed, been wounded, and been involved in the deaths of two of the ship's hijackers—or "pirates", as he referred to them. John had no doubt that it had been the worst day of his life. He was hungry, dirty almost beyond recognition, and exhausted, and it was no secret that he preferred to crawl into a corner and stay there until the entire ordeal was over. And yet, despite of it all, he was about to make a suggestion that—from his terrified expression—clearly involved taking a great risk.

"There is another door that the police can use to save us," he had announced. "Another cargo door, on the opposite side of the bow of the ship. It is also used to bring supplies into the *Mardi Gras.*"

"But if we open this other door," the Countess had said doubtfully, "won't the terrorists use it to get in as well?"

However, John had already understood where Ernan was heading. "The terrorists wouldn't have access to that door because it faces the water, right?"

Ernan nodded. "The *Mardi Gras* can take cargo from either of two its sides," he confirmed. "It is a necessity. There are some ports where it can only dock on its starboard side, or on its port side. So it has similar loading doors on each side."

"I don't fully understand..." the Countess said with a half puzzled expression. "Why wouldn't the terrorists be able to use the starboard door?"

"Because the other door faces the bay," John responded. "The FBI's people, if they're coming by boat or swimming, can use it to get in, but the terrorists would have to walk over the water. They wouldn't even realize that the door is open, since they can't see it from the ship or the dock! You're a genius, Ernan!" John had rubbed the Filipino's head, forcing him to grin.

"So we close the one that's open and we open the one that's closed, *n'est ce pas?*" the Countess said.

"We can even shine a light from the open door, to let the FBI know that the entrance is open, and the hijackers won't be able to see it."

"We should call the police and let them know what we plan to do, don't you think?" the Countess suggested.

They had tried. Risking being seen, John had sneaked out into the open air pool deck, and hiding behind a towel cart, had managed to obtain a satellite signal and contact the FBI in Washington. He had been patched up almost instantly with agents Tim Moylan and Maria Brown, who were still there and who had told him that Jose Medina, the third agent, was flying to Puerto Rico to meet with the police commissioner. John had whispered his plans to them, having to stop and repeat himself on several occasions. After he had finished, there had been a long pause.

"Hello? Are you still there?" he had asked with a certain degree of exasperation, looking over several bunched up towels to make certain that nobody was within hearing range.

"Your plan is very bold but very dangerous..." Moylan had responded. John had to press more his ear on the phone after the ambient noises from the FBI's side suddenly diminished. He thought for a moment that he had lost reception, but then realized that Moylan had probably placed his hand over his phone's speaker to discuss the matter further. Then Moylan had returned. *"Listen, John, we're told that the rescue operation is already under way. For security reasons, I can't tell you more about it, except that there is absolute radio silence between the rescue team and us. That means that we can't get through to them."*

"Not even in an emergency?"

"No, not even in an emergency."

John had said nothing, absorbing the news.

"So what should I do? If they're here soon, we can leave the door open and risk that other terrorists use it. What do we do?"

"We can't tell you when the rescue team will get there or how. For security reasons, they haven't even told us the details of what they're doing. We don't even know if they're using the door that you suggested they use."

"Can you at least tell me if they will be here soon?"

"Sorry, but I can't."

"Great! So what—" John had stopped, thinking he had heard a noise. A quick scan of the pool area revealed nothing. He had lowered his voice. "So what should I do?"

Moylan hesitated again. *"So far, you've done great. Better than anyone here expected,"* he had begun to say.

"So you've said several times," John answered in a peeved tone. "What I'm asking for is some guidance here. After all, you're the experts. Do we still go ahead with our plans? If we don't block the access to the ship soon, the terrorists will be here in droves."

"What I was going to say is that...it's very hard for us here to tell you what to do. Your gut instincts have gotten you this far, so...if you don't endanger your life too much, go ahead with your plans, and try to block their access," Moylan said. *"We will try to get through to the rescue team, but I can't guarantee anything."*

John had listened and hung up without saying goodbye. *Not endanger our lives too much...Really?* he had thought bitterly. He'd try to follow their instructions.

That conversation had taken place forty-five minutes ago. It was now well past 8:30, almost 8:45, and a massive fire was consuming the main ramp. They had shut down the main entry into the *Mardi Gras*, but they still had to close the loading ramp, and open the new access to the rescue team.

John took a last look at the burning gangway. Even from the stern, the flames looked huge. They had spread into the lower part of the ramp that ended at the dock, and were now threatening to consume the entire structure. Like giant fiery tears, the melting plastic panels of its windows rolled down from its sides, and helped to spread the blaze. Sooty, thick smoke, reeking of burnt rubber, billowed from the gangway's mouth and roof, and blanketed with a dark haze a large portion of the Promenade Deck.

Below, McFadden could see now dozens of persons on the dock, scurrying about like angry ants, trying to contain the fire. A few were holding on to a fire hose that they pointed at the gangway but that they had not managed to turn on. The smoke obscured his view of the portion of the dock where the cargo door lay open, but there seemed to be no movement in that direction. By that time, Ernan and the Countess would be well on their way to shutting the open gate, hopefully without running into any opposition.

It would take John at least fifteen minutes to get to where they were, since he was at the opposite end of the ship. For a moment, he debated whether he should walk down Deck 5 on the port side, since the smoke and the general confusion created by the fire would help to cover his progress and distract any hijackers that crossed his path. However, the gangway was burning so furiously that he doubted that he would be able to pass by it without getting burned. He decided instead to use the other side of the Promenade Deck.

In a hurry, he began to round the end of the ship, glancing at the spot where the captured terrorist had stood. Resisting the urge to take another look over the railing, he continued to jog towards the crew's stairway—barely fifty yards away—which he would use to get to the ship's lower decks. But just as he turned the corner, he collided with a man heading in the opposite direction. The man, who had been hurrying with two other companions to round the stern of the *Mardi Gras* and reach the fire, was as surprised as McFadden.

John fell heavily on top of the hijacker, driving the air out of him and hitting the man's forehead so hard with his mouth that he thought he had chipped one of his front teeth. In an instant he was up, trying to shake lose his right leg from the clutch of the fallen man's hands. He almost made it away, but then two sets of strong arms grasped him and shoved him back to the ground.

A storm of fists and kicks showered on him and kept him pinned to the ground. He heard grunts and curses and shouts, but could not understand anything that the men said. He managed to hold on to his gun, but a heavy boot crushed his hand, pressing the gun's handle against his fingers and making something crack. He tried to scream but could not manage even a whimper, the only noise coming out of him being the hollow sounds of his body as it was pounded into the floor.

Suddenly, everything stopped. His ears blared with a high-pitched squeal similar to that made by a television set after the station on its screen is no longer broadcasting. He felt someone pry off from his hand the gun that he could no longer release, and he instinctively took a deep breath as the pain of his broken fingers flooded his brain.

In the background, like the muted voice in a radio show, he heard a voice say, "We have to go. Shoot him."

"No," another, thicker voice countered. "I don't want to clean up the bloody mess that a shot to the head makes. He's almost dead, anyway. Let's just throw him overboard."

John felt several hands grip him by the arms and by his ankles, and this time he screamed, the white-hot pain of his multiple injuries almost causing him to faint. He heard laughter as one of his shoes slipped out of the grasp of one of his torturers, and then the same thick voice said, "On the count of three!"

His body began to swing back and forth, the pain on his arms and ribs excruciating, and on the third count, he was launched into the air. His right thigh struck something hard as his body cleared the railing, and then he began to fall very fast towards the still waters of the bay.

And all he could think, as he neared the water, was how cool and sweet the night air felt.

CHAPTER LXIV

The small circle of light surged ahead of the group as if it had a life of its own, crawling unevenly over every brick, crack, and protruding root in the walls and the roof of the tunnel. Having walked for close to half an hour, the line of refugees moved in a sullen, tired silence, each person holding on with one hand to the other's shoulder, everyone using as his guide the faint glow of Arizmendi's pocket flashlight. Patria, the head housekeeper, had volunteered to use the display window of her cell phone as a secondary light, but Lucas had decided to save it as a reserve, in case their tiny guiding light failed. Already, it had dimmed and flickered a couple of times. Those at the back of the line were barely able to see anything, basically relying on the guidance of the persons ahead of them.

A musty, dank smell, like that of damp earth mixed with the nastier odor of rot, grew steadily heavier as they traveled further into the bowels of the tunnel. *Sort of like a tomb would smell after a while,* Lucas thought to himself, instantly regretting the mental images that the thought conjured. He wondered how long it had been since another human being had roamed through those corridors, who he had been and who he had been with, what he had looked like, what his mission had been.

Three times they had stopped. The first time, Francisco had been walking behind Nereida, when he had stumbled and lost his grip on her shirt. He had broken his fall with hands, only suffering some minor scrapes, but Patria, who was following him, had tripped over his legs and pitched forward into the darkness. She had fallen hard, hitting her face on the invisible stone floor, and breaking her nose. It would have been worse, but Francisco had partially softened the impact of her body.

The old housekeeper had merely grunted, and said in a concerned voice, her nose already clogged up and bleeding, "Francisco! My child! Are you all right?"

They had stopped to help the fallen housekeeper and the boy get up. Knowing that she would not complain, the Governor had examined her with the small flashlight and promptly noticed the blood on her face. He had taken out his handkerchief and with Nereida's tender ministrations, they had managed to staunch the bleeding. Her right knee had swelled up, but she had assured everyone that she could walk, constantly apologizing for her clumsiness when she failed to keep up.

The second interruption to their underground progress had occurred less than five minutes later, when Maria, the youngest of the domestic employees, had felt something crawl over her shoulder. She had begun to scream, frantically sweeping her upper body with her hands and jumping up and down.

Once again, Governor Pietrantoni had rushed down the line to find out what had happened. His flashlight beam had revealed Secretary of State Arizmendi trying to console the distraught kitchen assistant, while she continued to sob and nervously brush her body. The Governor had managed to soothe the agitated woman, talking to her calmly while he examined her with his tiny key-chain light. A quick search over her head had revealed a thin root dangling from the tunnel's curved roof, and still sobbing softly, Maria had rejoined the line.

The last stop had occurred when the nine-person line had reached the point where the tunnel divided into two separate corridors like a giant "Y". Here, the Governor had stopped and briefly examined the two passageways and their surroundings with his flashlight. Both seemed to continue as far as the mini light beam could show. Hesitating, he had turned to Lucas.

"This is as far as I went the last time," he said. "I have no idea where either of them leads. They may both end up in blind alleys, for all I know. Any suggestions?"

"May I borrow the flashlight?" Lucas had asked Pietrantoni. With deliberate slowness, he examined the walls flanking each of the corridors, searching for telltale signs that could give him an indication of where the passages led. However, both pathways were indistinguishable from each other, made of long, red, uneven bricks held together by thick, gray mortar. The builders had not bothered to give any finish to the tunnels. The walls were rough and ugly, but after being entombed for centuries, they remained surprisingly intact, and free from moss or mildew.

With the exception of an intruding root here and there, or of some loose bricks, the low, arched roof seemed intact, if somewhat darker colored than the rest of the walls, the higher bricks stained gray or even black. Lucas nearly overlooked the variation in color, blaming the difference on the pitch-black gloom of the tunnel. But then he examined the ceiling more closely, and realized that the darker tones overhead were not caused by the tunnel's shadows but by soot, the soot created by the countless torches that had paraded through the ages inside the corridors. A second look showed him what he was seeking.

"The tunnel on the left was used a lot more than the one on the right," he told the Governor.

"How can you tell?" Pietrantoni asked.

Lucas pointed with the flashlight at the roof on the left entrance. "See the marks of the torches?" he said, slowly moving the light back and forth. "Now look at the right side. Hardly as dirty as the other one."

The Governor examined the curved ceiling and nodded. "You're right. Fascinating. So I guess that if we're hoping to find some way out at the end of one of these two ways, it's better that we use the more traveled route?"

Lucas shrugged, his gesture lost in the darkness. He handed the flashlight back to Pietrantoni. "It's the safer guess, but a guess, nevertheless. It may have been the main corridor once. It seems to head towards the end of the bay—"

"El Morro?" the Governor suggested, referring to the massive fortification that had guarded the mouth of San Juan Bay for centuries. "This could have been a way for transferring troops underground from La Fortaleza to El Morro or vice versa during the times of war."

"The movement of troops would account for the blackened ceiling. But there's no way of knowing if the tunnel has collapsed, or been filled up to sever its connection with La Fortaleza. The tunnel may lead to a dead end."

Alfredo, who was holding on to Lucas' hand, stepped forward and said, "Let's decide this the way Francisco and I do it." And before Lucas could stop him, began to recite, moving his hand with each word from one tunnel mouth to the other, "Juan, Pedro, Gratitud, el del peo fuiste tu! ('Someone farted, that is you!')," he concluded, his hand pointing to the left entrance.

"Alfredo!" Lucas whispered in a mortified voice, while behind them, Nereida and Francisco snickered.

Pietrantoni considered the choice for a brief moment. "I guess that settles it, right?" he said heartily. "The left tunnel it is. Let's go."

"Wait!" Lucas interjected, as the Governor took his first step forward. From one of his pants pockets, he fished out his car keys, and tossed them a few feet into the right tunnel. "I hate to do this, but if...when we get out of this, I'll come back and get them. Maybe the Macheteros will find them, and think we went that way. It's a long shot, but it may buy us some time."

"If it works, I'll buy you a car," the Governor assured him with deadpan seriousness.

The left tunnel initially extended for a long interval in an unwavering straight line, interrupted at irregular interludes by vertical niches in the walls, barely big enough to accommodate a man standing up. *Maybe ambush nooks for intruders who wandered inside, or places from where a rear guard could fire back on its pursuers,* Lucas thought, making a mental note of it. However, soon the tunnel angled slightly to the left and began to slope downwards.

"Interesting," the Governor whispered to himself. "We seem to be going down."

"Maybe we'll find the skeletons of some pirates down there," Alfredo said with breathless excitement. "Or trunks filled with gold doubloons and emeralds and diamonds!"

"Well, the administration could certainly use them!" Pietrantoni mused good-naturedly. "You have a great nephew, you know that?" he said to Lucas in a softer voice, as they walked on.

"I know," Lucas answered, smiling to himself, speaking very softly so that his godson would not hear him. "He's something else all right. He's like a little old man, very aware of world events and politics."

The Governor chuckled. "I know," he said. "He confessed to me that he is not a *statehooder,* was very apologetic about it."

Yes, Lucas thought with a grin, *that sounded like him.*

"He tried to fix things by saying that his father was a *statehooder.* Said you were not." Pietrantoni continued matter-of-factly.

Lucas felt his neck burn, even though he had no reason to feel embarrassed. But he was, after all, talking to the head of the Statehood Party. "I'm not very political..." he managed to say vaguely.

Pietrantoni laughed. "You don't have to apologize for it. Some of my best friends are *pop...*not *statehooders.*" As he said it, the Governor realized it was the second time in as many days that he had made that joke. He knew that if Arizmendi heard him he would roll his eyes in dismay. "And right now, believe me, you have a friend for life," he added gratefully. "I and my family owe you a great deal."

"We're all in this together," Lucas replied sincerely. During the time they had spent together, he had come to genuinely like and admire Pietrantoni. It was one thing to see the man in the news, and another to know him personally. Even though Lucas was not a *statehooder,* as Alfredo had gratuitously disclosed to the Governor, he felt tempted to tell him that he would vote for him in the next elections, but that would have sounded like fake flattery.

"I wish more people would feel like that," the Governor said in a wistful tone.

"Like what?" Lucas asked, wondering if Pietrantoni had read his mind.

"That we're all in it together," Pietrantoni answered. "There's so much more that could be accomplished if we all worked together."

Had Lucas heard that on TV the day before, he would have suspected that the Governor was trying to pander to the public's sympathies. But he knew now that the man truly meant it.

"Where did a jeweler from Old San Juan learn to fight like that, anyway?" Pietrantoni asked him.

"In the Army. I was a Ranger."

"Ah! That explains it," the Governor said, and kept quiet for a while. "And you're not a *statehooder*?" he added, almost as an afterthought. Most of the Puerto Ricans who volunteered to serve in the Army tended to favor statehood.

"It's complicated," Lucas said.

"I'm sorry. I didn't want to put you on the spot. Sometimes my mouth runs ahead of my prudence. Not good for a politician," Pietrantoni said apologetically. "It's just that...sometimes, my cause doesn't seem to attract the kind of people I would like to attract, and vice versa."

"Anyone in particular?...That you would rather not have attracted, I mean," Lucas asked, his curiosity getting the better of him.

"I see where your nephew gets his character from," the Governor said drily.

Lucas laughed. "No. He gets his character from his dad, believe me."

"An expressive guy, huh?"

"To put it mildly."

"And he's a *statehooder*, right?" Pietrantoni chuckled. "There might be hope for my party yet."

Without warning, the walls of the corridor suddenly vanished as the space around them expanded, and the footsteps of the advancing refugees echoed in the gloom ahead. Instinctively, they stopped. Pietrantoni glided the faint beam of light from his flashlight over the surrounding walls, and saw it travel in a wide curve, tripping over numerous, unknown dark shapes.

As the rest of the group continued to file in, they stopped, and followed the flashlight's glow with growing wonder.

"Awesome!" Alfredo exclaimed in a loud voice. "I was right!"

They had walked into a large, round hall, fifty to sixty feet across. And it was filled with objects: dozens of barrels, some stacked in two double rows, on top of each other; what seemed to be several oil lamps placed neatly over a plain, wooden plank supported by two of the barrels; long, rectangular, racks holding scores of lances, some of which ended in long, vicious-looking daggers, crossed at their bases by short, thin, metallic rods, while others were crowned with even nastier-looking spiked, double-edged axes; wooden frames storing double lines of broad, sharp-pointed swords, crossed in pairs like large "X"s; thick ropes, coiled like great snakes; dozens of tools, including various picks, shovels, hammers, and other unidentifiable objects; and interspersed between it all, several chests of various sizes, some made of plain wood, others decorated with elaborate, painted designs, and studded with large-headed nails.

Alfredo began to move towards the center of the hall, but Lucas stopped him, holding him gently by the shoulder. "Stay here," he told him. "You don't know if there are pits or holes in this place."

The young boy stared at his uncle with scared eyes, freezing where he stood. In the meantime, Pietrantoni continued to explore the hall with his flashlight, absorbed by what the light revealed.

"This is incredible! What do you suppose it was?" he said to Lucas.

"By the look of all the stuff in it, a storage place...or maybe an assembly hall of some sort," Lucas answered. He extended his hand to where the Governor held the flashlight. "May I?" he asked. Pietrantoni handed the tiny lantern to him without hesitation.

"Picon," said Lucas, addressing the Governor's personal bodyguard without looking in his direction. "I need you to go back into the corridor and keep watch from one of the niches we passed along the way. If you hear anything, you come back here to warn us, but don't engage them."

"Yes, sir," Picon answered, not questioning the ex-Ranger's authority, but hesitated as he turned to leave, saying, "I will need Patria's cell phone to find the way..."

"Patria, could you lend Picon your cell phone?" the Governor said to his housekeeper, knowing that unlike Picon, she would only take instructions from him.

"Of course, Mr. Governor," she answered from somewhere in the darkness, her voice sounding very congested as she spoke through her swollen nose. A moment later a greenish glow outlined the huddled bodies of the escaped hostages. A dark shape at the back of them extended an arm and retrieved the cell phone, momentarily illuminating the corridor through which they had just traveled. Rapidly, Picon and the light faded into the gloom beyond.

"If the screen goes out, press any of the numbers and it will turn back on!" Patria whispered hoarsely after the departing bodyguard.

Lucas began to walk towards the center of the room, first illuminating the floor ahead of him, then sweeping the walls. The Governor followed him, telling his son and Alfredo to remain with the others.

"If you're looking for a way out," Pietrantoni told him quietly, trying not to be overheard by the others, "I haven't found any. There's some large iron rings on the walls. Maybe we should try pulling them. See what happens."

Lucas had noticed them also, but doubted that they were the locks for any hidden door. The room seemed to be a dead end. And if that was the case, it was very bad news. It would leave them with two choices: either double back through the corridor which they had traveled, and hope that they could reach the entrance to the other tunnel before the terrorists got there, or barricade themselves in there until the promised rescue arrived. Neither of the alternatives seemed very palatable, and he was certain that some of his companions would panic when they found out they were trapped.

"It doesn't make sense…" he said thoughtfully.

"I know," the Governor agreed, somewhat defensively.

Lucas shifted his gaze to him. "Oh! I wasn't talking about what you said about the iron rings. It's worth a try. I was just wondering…Why would the Spaniards build this room as a dead end? Especially after such a long passage. It doesn't make sense."

"Sometimes," Pietrantoni suggested, "the Spaniards would build dead end rooms under some of their own fortifications and fill them up with powder. If the enemy captured the fortifications above, they would detonate the powder to destroy the captured defenses with the invaders in them. Maybe those barrels are powder," he said, pointing at where the bulk of the barrels had been piled up.

Lucas flashed the light in the direction of the barrels, and the two men walked towards them. The barrels were made of curved wooden planks held in place by metallic strips. One of them, placed on top of two other barrels, contained a wooden spigot close to its bottom. Pietrantoni tried to turn it, but its handle snapped. Lucas grabbed the entire spigot with his hand, and began to pull it, jiggling it up and down until it popped out. Nothing flowed out. He brought it to his nose, and winced.

"Phew! Smells like rancid oil," he said.

Lucas walked to one of the few barrels that did not have another one stacked on top and, placing the flashlight between his teeth, grabbed the barrel with both of his hands and moved it, at first tentatively, then harder. Something splashed inside it.

"The barrels aren't powder," he told the Governor. "Most likely some kind of oil for the lamps. Look!" he said, pointing the light beam at the long board on which several lamps rested. Next to it was an open barrel from which several sticks stuck out. He pulled one out and showed it to Pietrantoni. "Those are torches. The barrels provided fuel, some kind of oil, for the lamps and the torches. A supply of torches was kept here, which were probably soaked in the oil. So this was probably the place where the persons using the tunnels would get the torches or lamps to find their way in the darkness."

"So it doesn't make sense that they would place the source of their light in a dead end where they would have to travel through pitch black corridors just to get there!" the Governor concluded with certain relief, his mind already racing ahead.

"No," Lucas confirmed. "The soldiers who used this hall came from the outside, and then used the torches to move through to the tunnels. There has to be a way out of here."

"What if there once was an exit, but they closed it down to prevent people from using the tunnels?" Pietrantoni suggested. "After all, an open passage to La Fortaleza would constitute a security risk, wouldn't it?"

It was a possibility, Lucas thought. But if so, there would be a patch on the wall marking where the entrance had been sealed. Like the rest of the tunnels, the walls were made of exposed red brick and gray mortar. It would be easy to spot where an access had been blocked, even if the same material had been used to close it, which was not likely. At the very least, the arch of the roof of the blocked entrance would be visible on the wall.

"Some trapdoor on the floor, maybe?" Pietrantoni added when Lucas failed to answer.

Lucas shook his head. "We've been going down steadily for a while now. We're not much more above the sea level," he responded. "We're missing something."

Slowly and methodically, the two men walked once more around the room, examining the walls for the faint outline of cracks or joints, but found nothing unusual. On the contrary, the structure seemed impressively solid and compact, barely affected by the passing centuries.

The Governor tried to pull and turn each of the four metal rings embedded in the bricks, but if any of them held the secret to gain access to a hidden passageway, none of them yielded it. Next they moved the chests, to search for hidden trap doors below them. Some seemed empty, but three of them were substantially heavy, and one of them required the combined strength of the two men and of Arizmendi to budge them. Tempting though it was, they did not waste any time trying to open them. "I want to be here when Maria Belen opens these," Pietrantoni said, referring to the main archeologist of the Institute of Culture, and managing— for the sake of the others—to sound more optimistic than he felt.

They also searched behind the barrels and the racks of weapons, prompting Francisco to shout, "Take one of the swords, dad!" and forcing the Governor to shush him. Arizmendi used a large, double headed hammer to tap the walls and the floor, hoping to discover hollow areas, while Lucas and Pietrantoni rummaged through the discarded ancient artifacts in the round hall, searching for clues. It all came to no avail. After twenty minutes of frantic search, the room continued to seem as solid as a bomb shelter.

Frustrated and sweating profusely, the men paused to gather their wits. Time was running short. If they were going to try to reach the other branch of the tunnel, they would need to leave very soon, if it was not already too late.

"This is ridiculous," Arizmendi muttered to no one in particular. "No other way to get in or out, no reason to come here in the first place! No trap doors below, no doors on the walls...Maybe it was built by space aliens who dropped through the roof from the sky."

It took a few seconds for the Secretary of State's words to sink in, but when they did, both the Governor and Lucas reacted the same way. *The roof!* Both men looked up, as Lucas turned the beam of the flashlight onto the hall's ceiling and examined it eagerly.

It curved gently upwards from the upper edge of the room's circular walls to a height of between thirteen to fifteen feet, forming a shallow dome. Like the walls, it was made of brick and mortar, each rendered indistinguishable from the others by the pitch-black soot generated by the torches and the lamps that had accumulated there through the ages. However, even the uniformly dark film of filth could not hide the outline of several boards, maybe five feet in length by another five feet in width, that formed a flat, large rectangle at the highest point of the roof. Two wide beams, studded with large nails, extended across both ends of the boards, and from one of them protruded a thick, hand-sized metal ring. It was a trap door.

Lucas and Pietrantoni stared at each other and grinned.

"We were looking in the wrong direction," Lucas said. "Our exit is up there."

The ring was too high to reach, so the men pulled a trunk and rolled three of the barrels, placing one of them on top of the other two and forming a rough ladder.

Lucas climbed from the trunk to one of the barrels and then to the one on top of it, and gripped the ring. It was rusty and rough to the touch. He tried to pull it down, but the trapdoor did not budge. Next he attempted to push up the trapdoor, obtaining similar results. He then tried to turn the ring, first to the right and then to the left, with no effect. Frustrated, he pulled down again, increasing his efforts until he hung from the ring, his feet off the top of the barrel.

The ring moved slightly, and abruptly broke free from the wood. Lucas lost his footing and fell backwards, bouncing on one of the lower barrels and landing hard on the trunk. He heard Alfredo shout and felt his footsteps running towards him, followed by many others. In a moment, he was surrounded by several voices, asking anxiously if he was hurt, and helping him to get back on his feet.

"I'm okay, I'm okay," he assured them, briefly massaging his neck with his right hand, still holding on to the rusty iron ring with the other. He showed it to the Governor, shaking his head with annoyance. "That trapdoor won't budge," he said to him. "It's probably bolted from the other side. And the wood is partially rotted."

"Yes, I saw that," Pietrantoni replied, placing a friendly hand on his shoulder while Alfredo embraced his uncle. "You're sure you're all right."

"I'm fine. Really. Just my hurt pride," Lucas responded.

"Oh, is that what they call that part of the body now?" Arizmendi interjected, and everyone laughed.

"So what do we do now?" the Governor asked.

"We break through the wood," Lucas answered with as much confidence as he could muster. In reality, he felt sick to his stomach, knowing that it was already too late to turn back, and that if they did not succeed finding a way out, they would have to make a stand there and fight for their lives. "Maybe we can use some of the old tools."

"I have a hammer here!" Arizmendi volunteered.

"If we could find a chisel or an iron bar."

The Governor and Arizmendi quickly left to search among the instruments discarded on the ground, taking the only light source in the room with them, while the others huddled around the makeshift ladder. Lucas felt a small hand search for his and grabbed it, pressing it between his.

"Have you and Francisco been taking care of Nereida? Is she doing okay?" he asked the scared boy.

"They have been very brave!" Nereida responded. "I don't think I could have made it here without my two bodyguards."

"I thought as much. You guys are tough!"

"I think Alfredo is braver than me," Francisco confessed. "I'm very scared."

"Scared has nothing to do with it, dummy!" Alfredo answered. "My uncle says that everyone feels scared, that it's what you do even when you're scared what makes you brave, isn't that right, *padrino*?" he said to his godfather.

Wise beyond his age, Lucas thought. *What a great kid.*

"That's right," he answered. "And you've both acted very bravely today. I'm very proud of the two of you."

"You scraped your hands and knees and didn't cry," Alfredo reminded Francisco, forcing Lucas to smile in the darkness.

"How do you feel, Patria?" Nereida asked the old housekeeper.

"Well, it hurts when I touch it, Miss Nereida, but it's not so bad," she answered through her stuffed-up nose. "Of course, I don't have a mirror to see how I look, but at my age, I believe any change in the face is an improvement."

"Patria!" Nereida chided. "You're a very elegant woman!"

"If elegance is determined by the number of wrinkles, I would imagine that I am," the old housekeeper countered, making Maria chuckle.

The clinking of metal and the shuffle of approaching footsteps interrupted them, as the Governor and his Secretary of State returned from their foray.

"We didn't find a chisel," Pietrantoni said, "but we got all of these." He spread several tools over the chest's lid, including a small hatchet, an instrument that looked like a thick, sharp-edged spatula, and best of all, a short crow bar with a rounded, sharp point at one end and two bent teeth at the other.

Arizmendi dropped his heavy hammer on top of them, making all the other tools clang and shake. "I also brought you this, and just in case," he placed a sword diagonally over the rest of the instruments, *"this."* It was a plain sword, a straight, unadorned blade that ended in a hilt covered with rotting leather and a curved hand guard; the simple, mass-produced type of weapon commonly used by the troopers of the Spanish garrisons in the New World. However, it still incited unspoken awe from the group that surrounded it. It was a direct connection with the past occupants of that dark hall.

"The Institute of Culture will kill us when it sees how we've messed up this room," Pietrantoni said half in jest, half seriously.

Better them than the terrorists, Lucas thought, picking up Arizmendi's hammer and hefting on his left hand the crowbar. Instead, he said, "This will do."

Asking the Governor to aim his flashlight at the trapdoor hovering above them, he began to climb again the improvised ladder.

CHAPTER LXV

El Alacran hurried behind Ruben, the latter's body outlined by the bright glow of the flashlight that he carried. Behind him followed four more men; Luis, a tall, athletic man in his early thirties with premature gray hair and blue eyes; Andres, a stringy, taciturn man with crossed eyes and a bald pate; El Cubano, so nicknamed because he spoke with a Cuban-like accent and always carried a machete; and Pablo, a clean shaven, philosophy-major-turned-revolutionary whose main distinguishing feature was the absence of his middle and index fingers from his right hand as a result of an accident while in gun training.

It had taken them a long time, much longer than Andrade had desired, to get into the tunnel. The delay had been inevitable, of course, since the excavation that led into the underground passageway was much deeper than he had imagined, and the refugees had withdrawn the ladder at its entrance. They had used a rope to allow Andres to descend and recover the discarded ladder.

Andrade had also invested ten minutes interrogating the cook from La Fortaleza's staff who had refused to enter the tunnel. She had been captured by Alberto, who had brought her proudly to him as he had entered the courtyard. The fat Machetero had informed him that he had seen some shadowy figures sneaking into the hole in the center of the enclosed courtyard, and that he had exchanged fire with them. However, it had been too dark to verify if the Governor had been one of the escapees.

The maid, Altagracia, had confirmed it to Andrade. She had been hysterical and incoherent, but El Alacran had gotten her to focus on his questions after crouching next to where she sat on the floor, and smashing her pinky finger with his gun's handle. After threatening to continue breaking every other finger in her right hand, she had spoken freely.

She had informed him that the Governor had sneaked into the tunnel with the Secretary of State, a bodyguard, two children, the Governor's lover, and two other women. She had also mentioned a man who was not part of the staff and who had been responsible for the hostages' rescue. A very dangerous man, she had said, who had personally killed the men that guarded them in the Hall of Mirrors.

As he heard the frightened woman speak, Ruben—the white-bearded Machetero who had guarded La Fortaleza's gate, had remembered the Venezuelan soldier he had screened at the gate, and wondered out loud if there was any relationship between him and the stranger to which the captured woman referred. A few questions by Andrade had immediately made it apparent that the two men were one and the same.

El Alacran's eyes had narrowed as he heard the story. Aware of his leader's famous outbursts of temper, Ruben had gotten progressively nervous as he described how the intruder had gained access into La Fortaleza. However, Andrade had remained uncharacteristically quiet throughout the narrative.

"And you say he was carrying one of those surface-to-air bazooka weapons?"

"Yes, Alacran. With a briefcase with the missiles and everything," Ruben had elaborated anxiously. "And he wore one of the black armbands that identifies our allies. Later on, Tino discovered that he was a fake, an impostor, and captured him. The last I heard, Tino was interrogating him."

Alberto, who had been overhearing the conversation, confirmed his comrade's story with several nods. Andrade's expression remained unchanged.

"Why didn't you mention any of this before?" he asked icily.

The other two Macheteros had stared at him in raw panic.

"I...What can I say, I had forgotten about it with all of the fighting that followed."

El Alacran had sighed. "You are stupid beyond belief," he had said in a low, venomous hiss, devoid of all passion. Somehow, it had sounded more ominous than any curse he could have uttered. "You did not find him...or his body, when you searched for the hostages in La Fortaleza, did you?"

Ruben moved his head once in the negative, while Alberto continued to shake his vigorously. "No, Alacran," the former had confessed. "I didn't see him. But I was not looking for him, so I may have missed him..." he had started to say, but a withering look from Andrade had silenced him.

"You did *not* see him there, did you?" El Alacran had repeated with infinite patience.

"No," Ruben had admitted, sensing that to try to minimize his mistake would only increase the wrath of his leader. "No, I don't think so..."

"Well, this lady claims he's still alive," El Alacran had said, slowly tilting his head towards the sobbing kitchen cook. "Shall I break another of her fingers to see if she's telling the truth?" he had asked with a malicious glimmer in his eyes. Altagracia had screamed in terror, withdrawing her hands behind her back.

"No," Ruben had answered. "It's not necessary, Alacran. I believe her. I did not see that man anywhere."

"I believe her as well," Andrade had said in a flat, almost bored voice. He had briefly looked at the archeological dig, a few yards away, where Andres had just popped out of the hole and was signaling to him that he had recovered the ladder hidden by the hostages.

"So we now know how the Governor escaped from La Fortaleza, don't we?" he said, rubbing his chin, speaking to no one in particular. "That man...What was his name?"

"Maestes," Ruben prompted quickly.

"Maestes, if that is his real name...Maestes probably worked for the black guy, George. And for San Miguel. He killed Tino and freed the hostages, with the help of George..."

Ruben and Alberto had nodded in heartfelt agreement.

"And he's probably down there, in that hole, helping the Governor escape. So it's not going to be that easy to kill them. It's going to be dangerous down there. We're probably dealing with a professional..." he had assured the other two with a tinge of reproof, not raising his voice. "All because you failed to do your job properly. What shall we do?" he had asked mildly, and saying nothing more, had begun to move his right hand towards his gun. However, instead of drawing it, he had slipped his fingers under its leather holster and scratched his ribs.

His lips had drawn into a tight smirk as he saw all color drain from Ruben's face. "Relax," he had told him, "I'm not going to kill you...Although I should." He had glimpsed briefly at Alberto. "You too," he had said to him, almost causing the big man to faint. "But I need you both. Our cause is in desperate need of men, even of people like you. So be grateful for that."

Alberto had thanked him profusely; Ruben had lowered his head and stared at the ground repentantly. Andrade had questioned the distraught woman for a few more moments, trying to learn more about the weapons that the hostages carried—some guns and a few rifles, she had answered—and probing what she knew about the tunnel—almost nothing, except that it was an ongoing excavation, which pleased El Alacran—and then he had stood up and indolently stretched his arms over his head.

"Come," he had told Ruben. "We're going to find the Governor, and you're going first."

Ruben had accepted his fate with stoic resignation, knowing that to protest would not have been a wise thing to do. As they were leaving, El Alacran had approached Alberto and whispered to him, "Get rid of her." Uncertain of what he meant, the big Machetero had stared at him, prompting Andrade to lean forward and whisper, "Kill her. We don't have time to guard her." Then, raising his voice, he had added. "I don't think you will fit down there, so stay here and watch the hole, in case they try to slip by us while we're searching for them down there, understood?"

"Yes, Alacran," Alberto had answered, fear showing in his eyes.

The descent into the archeological dig had inexplicably made Andrade's hackles rise, making him feel as if he had stepped into a grave. It was a grave of sorts, one of the last undiscovered vestiges of a Spanish Empire that had kept the island under its thumb for four hundred years. In another era, Andrade would have been fighting the Spanish overlords for the freedom of Puerto Rico, and chasing down the tunnel some overblown aristocrat appointed by the king as the governor of Puerto Rico. It would have been the same thing as now, just different tools and different players.

The length and the good condition of the underground corridor had astonished him. He wondered how far it went, and where it stopped. The white, wide beam of the flashlight that Ruben carried illuminated the passageway for a long distance, but even so, the tunnel seemed to go on indefinitely. He was certain that it *would* stop; otherwise, somebody would have discovered it long ago, but for a long time there was nothing in sight.

Andrade prided himself for not letting anything scare him, but that place belonged to the ghosts. It smelled mostly like dirt—El Alacran had spent more than his share of time in trenches and caves, and knew the smell well—but it contained others odors as well; a tinge of the sweet fragrance of decaying vegetation, although no plants grew there; the pungent odor of Ruben's nervous sweat; a hint from the heavy, salty tang of the bay; but most of all, it smelled of death. People had died there at one time. He could still smell them. And soon there would be others.

Suddenly, the tunnel had taken an abrupt turn to the right. The Macheteros had approached it cautiously, sending Ruben ahead, knowing that it could be the perfect place for an ambush. But no one had been waiting for them. Twice more they had encountered sharp turns, both times the direction of the passageway shifting sharply to the left. Both times Ruben had turned the corner to find no one.

As he walked further into the tunnel, Andrade had begun to feel disoriented. Time became unreliable and uncertain in the inky darkness that stretched both ahead and behind them, encapsulating their small cocoon of light like a giant snake that slowly swallowed a mouse. He lost all sense of direction, not knowing where he was or where he was heading.

On a couple of isolated occasions he thought he had heard the faint echo of noises ahead, and with fierce whispers ordered his men to stop. But when he listened, he could sense nothing but the emptiness of the tons of earth tightly packed about them. *He should stop imagining things,* he told himself. *The hostages were there. They would not escape.*

He felt extremely curious about the mystery man who had appeared out of nowhere to kill his men. He thought he had known, during the preparation for the operation, the main players in San Miguel's camp. This one, however, did not fit the description of any of them. Daniel, maybe, but Daniel had been at the Grand Laguna Hotel with him while the Governor escaped. Besides, most of his men knew Daniel by sight.

Ruben stopped unexpectedly, nearly causing Andrade to bump into him. El Alacran focused his attention on the two new entrances that had appeared before them.

"Give me your flashlight," he instructed Ruben, who did so with cheerful promptness. Andrade examined first the left entrance, and then the one to the right, directing his beam into the entrails of both passageways. Both seemed the same, except...

"Look!" Andres, the quickest of the six men in the group, had exclaimed. "Turn back, turn back!" he had said to Andrade right after the latter had swept with his light the tunnel to the right.

"What is it?" El Alacran had begun to ask, bringing his flashlight back into the passageway. And then he had seen it. The faint glint of something silver on the floor. Before he could say anything else, Andres had run to it and picked up.

"Ha!" he said in an amused tone, and laughed. "Car keys! Do you think that the Spaniards drove their Toyotas down here?"

All of the other Macheteros laughed save for Andrade, who extended his left hand towards Andres and with his fingers gestured impatiently to his subordinate to hand him the keys. "Let me see."

"They must have fallen from the pocket of one of the hostages," the younger Machetero suggested, as Andrade briefly examined the keys, and then looked back into the tunnel. *An accidental loss, or a lure to throw them off the track?* His gut instincts inclined him to believe the latter, but his mind pushed him towards the opposite conclusion. After all, the keys had been found a fair distance away from the entrance to the corridor, and could have been missed altogether by the Macheteros. Had it not been for the sharp eyes of Andres, that could have been the case. If the hostages wanted to mislead them, they would have dropped them in a more obvious place, where they would be easily seen.

Was Maestes playing sophisticated mind games with him? El Alacran doubted it, he thought. He would not try to over-think the problem and find 'the fifth leg of the cat', as the Puerto Rican saying went. He would listen to his reason, and not his gut feelings.

"Good eyes, Andres, even if they're crossed. We'll go this way," he said, pointing at the right corridor. Then grabbing Ruben by the arm, he added, "But you stay here, in case Andres misled us. If you see or hear anything moving in there, fire. The only way that anyone can come out of here is over your dead body. Do you understand?"

"Yes, Alacran," Ruben answered in an abashed voice. "Nobody will get through here."

"Keep your flashlight. Andres, get Luis' flashlight and lead the way. We're getting close to them, so try not to make any noises. And you, Ruben, turn off your flashlight. Only turn it on if you hear noises."

Ruben assented, his gesture lost in the tunnel's gloom.

"Let's go!" El Alacran ordered.

In a moment they were gone, leaving the white-bearded Machetero alone in an impenetrable obscurity, listening to the muted thumps of his heart.

Lucas lifted the hammer and began to pound the iron crowbar at an angle, quickly inserting its round, sharp head under one of the two beams that crossed each end of the trapdoor. Once it was firmly embedded in the wood, he pulled the crowbar down with short, sharp tugs. The thick beam did not budge.

"I'm going to place all of my weight on the crowbar, to see if I can separate this board," he warned Pietrantoni, who was illuminating the area where Lucas was working.

"Wait a moment!" the Governor said, and gave the flashlight to Arizmendi. "Hold it," he told him. "I'm going to grab your legs. I'm not sure you can take another fall."

"Please be careful," Nereida begged the men from further away.

Pietrantoni climbed up to one of the lower barrels, stood behind Lucas, and wrapped his arms around his knees. "Okay," he said.

Lucas raised his feet, so that he was no longer standing on top of the upper barrel, and hung from the end of the crow bar. The crossbeam creaked, and some of the nails on one of its extremities slowly began to separate from the boards to which they were attached. Then, with a loud crash, the beam gave way. Lucas landed with his feet on the barrel, but lost his balance and began to lurch forward. However, the Governor held on to his legs and steadied him.

"Watch out!" Lucas warned, as the separated piece of wood momentarily hung from its last nail, and then fell noisily on the floor.

Lucas looked down at the Governor and smiled. "Thank you!" he said.

"That piece of wood made enough noise to raise the dead from their resting place," Pietrantoni said with some concern.

"Enough to let the Macheteros know where we are, if they're anywhere nearby," Lucas responded, turning his gaze back to the trapdoor. Several of the longer boards that had been secured by the crossbeam had slightly separated from the ceiling. However, he could not see what lurked behind them. Pietrantoni was right. The noise that he was making would soon give them away. He had to hurry.

Slipping his fingers behind one of the loose boards, he pulled it down, bending it until it came free. "Watch it!" he warned the Governor, holding on to the piece of wood as it dropped. This time, he managed to keep his grip on it, so that it did not crash onto the floor. Arizmendi hurried and grabbed it, momentarily diverting the light away from the trap door. After he had deposited the board on the ground, he returned the light beam to the ceiling.

Lucas grabbed another board and, aided by the crowbar, began to separate it from the others. The board bent and protested with a heavy cra-a-ack, and then it came lose. Each of the boards measured close to five feet in length by about six inches in width, so with two of them out, he had a good view of what lay above them. To his dismay, he saw that it was brick, a different kind of brick from that of the rest of the tunnel, a brighter red, smaller, with less mortar holding it, but brick nevertheless.

"Shit!" he whispered.

"What is it?" Pietrantoni asked anxiously.

"Brick! Somebody sealed the trapdoor with brick!"

The two men considered their situation for a moment without saying anything.

"Do you think you can use your hammer and crowbar to see what's beyond that brick?" Arizmendi asked. When nobody responded, he added, "Don't mind me. I'm just a useless lawyer that doesn't know anything about buildings..."

Lucas shrugged. "No, no, you're right. It's worth a try," he said. "But move away from under me. I don't want any of these bricks falling on any of you..."

He felt the Governor's arms release his knees, and heard him say, "Be careful." The oval beam of the flashlight wavered and grew fainter as Arizmendi drew away, but the Secretary of State did his best to keep the light on the trapdoor.

"This is going to make noise," Lucas warned.

Raising the crow bar, he began to hammer away at the mortar, at first bringing down dust and chips of the bonding material, then managing to shatter in half one of the bricks. It fell on the barrels and bounced off to the floor with a great deal of clatter, nearly hitting Lucas' right foot.

"Be careful!" Pietrantoni repeated.

Lucas grabbed the crow bar with his two hands, and turning it around, used its curved teeth to attack the broken brick. It fell off easily, as did the five bricks next to it, cascading in a noisy shower of dust and debris. He stopped to inspect his progress, but all he could see beyond the removed material were shadows. Cautiously, he extended his hand, hoping it would break into the surface beyond, but his fingers hit something solid.

"What did you find?" Pietrantoni asked impatiently.

"I don't know," Lucas responded. "There's a smooth, solid surface over the bricks."

There was a collective groan from the people below.

Lucas rapped on the surface with his knuckles. He thought it sounded hollow. "Wait, don't give up hope yet," he told the others. Raising his crow bar, he tapped its pointed end on the exposed surface. It produced a definitely hollow sound. Heartened by the response, he pounded the crow bar with his hammer. On the second try, it went through, meeting no resistance. Lucas extended his arm, and the iron tool disappeared completely through the hole up to his closed fist.

"There's empty space up there!" he exclaimed triumphantly, provoking a shout of joy from those below.

"Be quiet!" the Governor gently urged in a happy voice. "The Macheteros will hear us!"

The celebratory chatter quickly dwindled to excited murmurs and muffled exchanges.

"I'm going to work as quickly as I can, but this is going to make a lot of noise," Lucas whispered to the Governor. "It will take a while. Maybe we should start forming a barricade with the barrels at the entrance of the hall…Just in case the Macheteros come this way before I finish," he suggested.

Pietrantoni walked wordlessly to where the barrels were stored, almost disappearing in the gloom. "I could use some help here," he said, after he tried to move one of them.

"I'll help if somebody grabs my flashlight," Arizmendi offered.

"I will hold it," Nereida volunteered.

"You know," the Governor said with a grunt, after he and Double A managed to lay one of the barrels on its side and began to roll it towards the entrance, "this is the most cooperative I have ever found you to be since I was elected."

"That's because it's the most useful and intelligent thing you've done since you were elected," Arizmendi replied, without missing a beat.

"I wouldn't doubt it," Pietrantoni replied dryly. "Not with the advice I get from the people in my Cabinet."

Turning his attention away from them, Lucas seized another of the boards and began to pull it down. He winced when it snapped free, convinced that it was impossible for the terrorists not to hear the racket he was producing. He felt his stomach contract with fear, imagining what would happen if they were caught in the hall before they could escape, and tried to concentrate on the business at hand. But it was no use. The Macheteros were coming. He could feel them closing in. He had to hurry.

Time was running short.

It sounded at first like a product of his overactive imagination. A faint noise, no more than a gentle sigh. For several seconds he stopped breathing, looking into the darkness ahead of him, although it was so dark that there was nothing to see.

Then he heard it again; the short intake of air from someone approaching on the balls of his feet, desperately trying not to disturb the oppressive stillness of the ancient tunnel. The slight scraping of a shoe sole on the uneven floor followed it. Picon recognized the sound immediately; he had made several like it getting there, despite his great care not to reveal his presence.

For the first few minutes after abandoning the others, the Governor's bodyguard had used the glow of Patria's cell phone to find his way through the corridor. He had walked past three of the niches embedded in the corridor's walls, two to his right and one to his left, but considered them to be too close to the round hall to be of any use. He needed to get out further, closer to where the tunnel split into two, so that there would be enough time to warn the others when he heard the Macheteros coming.

After the first five minutes, he had turned off the cell phone, afraid that he would be seen, and had continued to trek slowly through pitch black corridor in complete blindness, keeping his way by tracing the rough contours of the brick wall with the tips of his fingers of his left hand, while holding on to his sub machinegun with the other. Periodically he would stop and listen. When the darkness ahead yielded no sounds, he would renew his march with snail-like care, every tiny noise that he produced expanded in his mind a hundred times.

It had taken every ounce of his willpower to bypass four more niches in the left wall and to continue to walk towards what he knew would be his inevitable clash with the oncoming terrorists. If by any chance they were moving rapidly—and there was no reason to believe that they were not—and they used a powerful enough flashlight, he could be caught flatfooted in the corridor and be forced into a shootout where his only cover would be provided by the small recesses in the walls that he had skirted. It would almost certainly be a fight to the death.

But his resolve to go on was strengthened by the feeling of shame that burned inside of him; the shame of letting himself be captured so easily by the Macheteros in La Fortaleza. He was the head of the Governor's bodyguards. On his shoulders had fallen the responsibility to keep the Governor and all of the other members of La Fortaleza safe, and he had failed miserably. All of his men were dead or missing, as well as many members of the Executive Mansion's staff. And the only reason why the Governor was still alive was thanks to the providential intervention of Lucas Alfaro.

But now, he had been given a second chance, and he would not waste it. He was not a deeply religious man, a token Catholic his mother had called him with a sad smile, but he honestly believed that he had been kept alive for a purpose, and he intended to live up to it, whatever his fate would be.

Still, the steady uphill walk into the unfathomable gloom unnerved him. As a child, he had always been intimidated by what he could not see. He had overcome his fears by training in the martial arts and forcing himself to confront those who tried to torment or bully him, and it had worked well, giving him a sense of confidence and security that eventually had gotten him to the police force, and later to La Fortaleza. But still, his childhood nightmares loomed in the back of his mind. It terrified him to think that he would die there, unseen, entombed, never to feel the heat or see the glow of the sun again.

He had finally stopped on the eighth niche, telling himself it was far enough, and waited there in silence. Deprived of his sight, he focused his attention on any suspicious sounds, but there was nothing to detect. He was in a void. No wind, no traffic, no birds, no rustling of the leaves, no dogs barking, no human chatter, not even the light splat of a rogue drop of water leaking from the roof. *Nothing.* It was as if his ears had been plugged with cotton, and the only sounds he could hear were his breath and his wild heartbeat.

Suddenly, unexpectedly, he had heard tapping noises coming from the direction of the Governor's party. Sharp noises, like the banging of metal. And then they had stopped, just as abruptly as they had started, enveloping him in the same deafening silence that had accompanied him through his lonely trek in the tunnel. A moment later, the banging had returned, slightly louder and more urgent than before. And then it had stopped again.

So it had continued for several intervals. Slight, sharp, repeated sounds, and then momentary silence. The noise both comforted him and made him nervous. It reminded him that his friends were just a few minutes away from him and that he was not as alone as the suffocating calm of the underground passageway made him feel. On the other hand, he worried that during those noisy intervals, he would not hear the terrorists approaching.

It was unnerving. He thought about his mother. He was not married, and visited her every week in Barceloneta, about an hour's drive from San Juan. She would be going out of her mind right now with the news about the assault on La Fortaleza. It had to be in the news by now. His heart ached for the families of his dead comrades. Some of them had small children. One had recently been married, just the month before.

He was not a very religious man...But in the silent gloom that enveloped him, he concentrated his thoughts on God, and found solace doing it. Until, during one of the intervals between the bouts of banging, he had heard the noise. First a sigh, then a faint footfall. There could be no doubt that someone was approaching, maybe more than one. He had expected to hear the terrorists approaching from a fair distance and to have time to run away to warn the others without being seen. But the hidden menace crawling towards him down the darkened corridor had surprised him. He could literally sense the person moving, just a couple of feet away now. If he tried to leave, he would expose himself and probably get shot in the back. He had to make his stand there.

He flattened himself against the wall of the niche, holding on to his sub machinegun, and held his breath. He could hear the Machetero now clearly, breathing heavily and pausing to clear his throat. He felt something breeze by his face—the man's upraised hand, probably—as it followed the contours of the wall just as Picon had followed them, not touching his nose but barely missing it.

There seemed to be just one person, but he could not risk it. He stayed completely still, and let the presence pass him, smelling his sweat as he went by. He began to count, deciding to move when he got to twenty, listening intently to detect any other noises behind the person who had just crept past him.

There were none.

Slipping his hand into his pocket, he pulled out Patria's cell phone and with exaggerated care stepped out from the niche. He raised his right hand to his shoulder and began to level his sub machinegun in the direction of the intruder, but his cell phone slipped from his grasp. For a heart stopping moment he fumbled with the two objects trying to keep them from falling and hitting the floor, but finally, he managed to grab both, pinning the rebellious phone against the body of his Uzi.

He waited, sweating profusely, trying not to breathe. Surely, the man ahead of him must have heard him. Yet as the moment expanded, his hopes began to grow. Maybe the man was deaf. Perhaps he had thought that he had made the noise. More carefully than ever, he began to shift the cell phone to his left hand while holding on to his sub machinegun with his right.

Suddenly, a bright, white light flooded the corridor, blinding him. Someone behind the light muttered something incomprehensible, and the beam wavered wildly, as the man went for his weapon.

Picon reacted immediately. He knew that the noise of shots would draw whatever other terrorists were searching the tunnels. So instead of shooting his sub machinegun, he charged towards the high-powered beam. He ran with his arms open, dropping the cell phone as his left arm and shoulder collided with the body behind the light. His momentum threw his opponent off balance, making him tumble backwards, but as both men fell, something struck him very hard on the left side of his face.

Stunned, Picon held on to his opponent's arm as it swung to strike him again with a long, metallic flashlight, the swiftly shifting light creating the impression that the corridor was oscillating around them. The bodyguard managed to blunt the force of the incoming blow by pushing himself against his opponent, so that the flashlight struck him ineffectually on the back. At the same time, he raised his right elbow and brought it down sharply, smashing it hard on his enemy's face.

Almost simultaneously, his groin seemed to explode in excruciating pain as a knee crushed into it. Both men fell backwards in opposite directions, losing the objects that they held in their hands. The light that had solidified their surroundings went off abruptly as the flashlight clattered on the ground, submerging the fighters in a numbing sea of blackness.

For an instant, both men lay dazed where they had fallen, trying to recover their wits, listening for each other's movements. Still hurting, Picon began to sit up while moving his hands about him, searching for his Uzi. Then he heard the other man scramble over the floor, also apparently trying to recover his lost weapon, and he reached out to stop him.

He managed to grab part of a shoe, but the terrorist easily shook it free and continued to crawl away. Picon followed him on all fours, still hurting from the numbing blow he had received in the groin. He heard the metallic scraping sound of something being dragged over the floor, and realized that the Machetero had stumbled onto one of the lost weapons. With a supreme effort, he sprang forward and careened into the terrorist. He fell on top the man as the latter was attempting to raise his rifle, slapping it aside and trapping it between his chest and that of the terrorist.

Picon gripped his adversary's wrist with his left hand and the barrel of the rifle with his right. The Machetero began to curse and scream, twisting and turning his body to slip out from under the weight of his enemy, trying to reach the trigger of his rifle with his free hand. But the Governor's bodyguard was bigger and stronger, and he managed to keep the Machetero pinned to the ground.

Picon could sense the terrorist tiring fast, but he knew that it would be only a matter of time before the terrible racket they were making attracted the attention of the others. He could not afford the luxury to wait any longer. He sat up suddenly, relaxing his pressure on the rifle, and snatched the weapon away.

In a wild, desperate effort, the Machetero attempted to uppercut Picon's jaw with the lower edge of his hand but missed in the darkness, grazing instead the bodyguard's cheek and ear. Picon punched him back, hitting him somewhere on the face and, holding on to the rifle, pulled away.

Then, with a wicked swing, he brought the butt of the rifle down to where the man's head had been. It struck the Machetero squarely on the face with a sickening, bone-crunching "smack", silencing his screams. The bodyguard followed up with another swing and struck again, but it had not been necessary. The body under him had gone limp with the first blow.

Scrambling back to his feet, Picon anxiously began to sweep with his hands on the floor around him, searching for his sub machinegun and the other discarded objects. He located the man's flashlight a few feet away, close to the wall, but could not make it work. To make matters worse, he could not find the Uzi or Patria's cell phone after another five minutes of search. The tunnel seemed to have swallowed them up.

He paused, trying to orient himself, and in the distance he noticed a dim light heading towards him, followed a couple of seconds later by the sound of urgent footsteps. Crouching, he turned and quietly hurried away.

CHAPTER LXVI

"Sir!" Sergeant Alfonsin gingerly shook Colonel Calderon's shoulder, loath to wake his superior officer. The Venezuelan Special Forces colonel had dozed off on one of the lounge chairs spread throughout the Grand Laguna's beach, lulled to sleep by the soft lapping of the waves and the cool breeze of the sea.

Calderon opened his eyes and, without moving, looked around him uncertainly before recognizing his surroundings. The two men were located behind a high wall that separated the upper pool deck from the hotel's artificially created beach, shielding them and rendering them invisible from the police snipers in the San Geronimo Plaza. Not that it was a necessary precaution; the distance between the San Geronimo Plaza and the Grand Laguna's beach was considerable, and the odds of a sniper finding its mark there were lower than nil. Nevertheless, if Calderon had learned anything in his long military career, it was that it paid to be cautious.

The rest of the Venezuelan contingent had melted into the shadowy backgrounds of the beach and the pool area, and formed a defensive perimeter around the north and northwestern boundaries of the hotel, the areas most likely to be hit by the government forces in any misguided rescue attempt.

"Sergeant Alfonsin," the colonel acknowledged, automatically looking at his wrist. "What time is it?" he asked, even though he could see it on his watch.

"It's 2048 hours, sir," Alfonsin answered. The thirty-year-old veteran looked as fresh as daylight, only a slight stubble on his face betraying the long day he had endured.

Colonel Calderon stretched his legs and stiffly swung them out of the lounge chair onto the sand below. Soon it would be time to leave. Without notifying anyone, he would gather his men and his weapons and abandon the hotel. He could not understand it, never would, but orders were orders, and he had been ordered to be in La Perla by 2300 hours, or 11:00 PM by civilian terms.

He had been to La Perla twice, to reconnoiter the area and locate the safe house to which he and his men would withdraw. He had insisted that all of his men do the same; that they personally learn the way to the safe house, in case any of them had to find it on his own—as would be the case with the Venezuelan surface-to-air missile operators scattered about Old San Juan.

He had found the place to be a self-contained community, leading a completely unconnected existence from the rest of Old San Juan. It was an anomaly. La Perla was located in a small pocket of land on the north-western shore of San Juan Island, and only separated from the rest of the city by the giant, twenty-foot wide wall that had encircled the ancient town and connected the San Cristobal and El Morro fortresses. But it was true; La Perla led a separate existence from the rest of Puerto Rico. The police hardly ventured into its narrow streets, and only a few cars—those of its residents—ever dared to cross the only, tunnel-like portal that connected it to the rest of the world.

Needless to say, as he wandered through its streets Calderon had stuck out like a flashing neon sign. But no one had attempted to interfere with his progress, perhaps because of his no-nonsense, tough-as-nails appearance, but most probably because he had been seen visiting El Gordo Purcell's big, pink house by the shore, and nobody dared to disturb any of El Gordo Purcell's acquaintances. As the local drug lord, Purcell lorded over parts of the community with the power of a benevolent dictator, dispensing money and favors to his followers whenever they were needed or requested, ruthlessly squashing anyone or anything that threatened to interfere with his business. Calderon wondered how San Miguel had established the contact, but was not surprised that he had gained access to the drug lord. Nothing about San Miguel surprised him any more.

To abandon the patriots who had taken over the island of San Juan to free it from Yankee imperialism made no sense to Calderon. He had not been given any explanation by his commanders in Caracas or later—as he had hoped—by San Miguel. He had just been ordered to be in Purcell's big pink residence by 2300 hours.

Aided by the Venezuelans, the revolutionaries had made tremendous strides towards attaining Puerto Rico's independence from the United States. They had shown how easily control could be wrested from the American forces and their local lackeys, and how difficult it would be for Washington to absorb the Puerto Rican nation into its soul quenching statehood status. They had smashed, in a matter of hours, the Commonwealth police forces representing the pro-American government in San Juan, and easily repulsed the counterattack by the best troops that the local authorities and the federal government could throw at them. They had even managed to gain the freedom of one of the main leaders in he island's struggle for self-rule.

And it had all been accomplished for what? To give it all up now? He was not accustomed to running away. It was a bitter pill to take.

And the way that they had been ordered to leave! Silently skulking away like a guilty lover after a night's tryst, exiting secretly and abruptly, and without warning! It almost amounted to a planned betrayal, as if it had been purposely designed to cause the collapse of everything that they had achieved. He could understand his government's interest in excising any signs or vestiges of the Venezuelans' participation in the present revolution. If it became known to the United States, the Americans would certainly use that information to claim that there had been no revolt by the local patriots, but an invasion by President Fanelli's socialist government.

But to leave this way...

"I'm sorry to disturb you," Alfonsin said quietly, "but the Macheteros are asking for our help."

Calderon stared at his sergeant with wordless curiosity.

"It seems that a small force of American commandos slipped into the hall where the hostages were being kept and expelled the Macheteros." Alfonsin had his boss's full attention now. "The commandos managed to throw the Macheteros out of the hall. The Macheteros have them surrounded, but their attempts to recapture the hall have not succeeded. I think I heard some of the shooting that happened maybe twenty minutes ago."

"You should have woken me up then," Calderon said testily.

"I'm sorry, sir," Alfonsin replied, not sounding sorry at all. The sergeant major jealously guarded his commander's health. "But you seemed exhausted, and the shooting tapered off very quickly. I did not want to wake you up unless it proved to be a real emergency. There has been a lot of celebratory shooting by the revolutionaries today. But this seems to be real. They are asking for our assistance."

"What about San Miguel's men? They were supposed to be guarding—in strength—the grounds around the hall," Calderon asked. He began to stand up, brushing his hands against his pants to remove the sand.

The sergeant shrugged. "They did not say, sir," he replied.

The colonel silently considered the Macheteros' request for help. The new, unsettling developments showed how much the revolutionaries still needed the Venezuelans' professional expertise. No matter how good they were, the American commandos would not have slipped through his out-fit's defensive perimeter. The Macheteros were brave and passionate fighters, but they lacked discipline. However, he had expected a lot more from San Miguel's men. He had seen them in action, and they had proven to be seasoned, fearless fighters. They should never have allowed the ene-my to infiltrate through their lines.

The capture of the hostages could only mean one thing: San Miguel and his men had already withdrawn and left the east flank open. That meant that unless the Venezuelans plugged the gap, the Puerto Rican patriots would be exposed to a larger attack from the side of the lagoon.

Calderon hesitated. He could follow San Miguel's lead and pull out his men now. His men had fought bravely and were exhausted. Withdrawing would be the safest and wisest thing to do, before things got worse.

Or he could wait a little longer—an hour, perhaps—and help the Macheteros recapture the hostages. He was certain that they could easily accomplish their goal in the allotted time, and still have enough time to get to La Perla.

The decision was obvious.

"Sergeant Alfonsin."

"Sir!"

"Alert the Macheteros that we are moving two thirds of our men into the garden area, and that we will help them recapture the hall where the hostages are located. Tell them not to fire from the lobby, so that they don't hit any of our men accidentally. Leave four men here to watch the pool area and the beach. Corporal Caraballo should be in charge of them. We'll teach those commandos how professional soldiers fight."

"Yes, sir!" Alfonsin saluted smartly, already anticipating the impend-ing skirmish.

"Don't look so excited, sergeant. We're just giving the rebels a little help, that's all."

"Yes, sir," the sergeant answered with a conspiratorial smile. Calderon smiled back at him.

Just one hour, the colonel thought. *That's all. And then we'll leave.*

Michelle waited in silence in the fringe of the medical team while Dr. Schaeffer, working under the glow of two flashlights, finished attending to Archie's wounds. In his early seventies, the man seemed more like a sunburned, white-haired, white-goateed ageing surfer than a retired sur-geon. However, assisted by a square-jawed nurse and a young, scared looking intern, he had undertaken with brisk efficiency the desperate task of keeping the wounded man alive.

Between the three of them, they had stripped their patient to his waist, uncovering a puncture-like hole on his upper, right chest through which air and blood bubbled in and out as Archie attempted to breathe. Dr. Schaeffer had asked the nurse to seal the wound with her fingers while he, taking one of the two flashlights that had illuminated his patient, searched the room for possible materials that he could use to staunch the flow of blood.

"Can I help you?" Michelle inquired solicitously, unconsciously wringing her hands while she watched the nurse press her fingers on Archie's wound.

"I need adhesive tape," Dr. Schaeffer replied, already searching with his eyes the immediacy of the stage where the terrorists had sat, and settling his gaze on a box. "And alcohol. Oh, and also... if can find any small bags..." he said as he walked towards the cardboard box.

Bags, Michelle had thought, turning on her own flashlight. "What kind of bags?" she said out loud.

"I have a bag," a man sitting on the floor close to her volunteered, raising his hand with what seemed to be a small shopping bag with the Walgreens logo. Several of the other hostages raised their hands with additional materials. Michelle gathered them all, hoping one of them would satisfy the old doctor's odd request. In the meantime, the retired surgeon had finished rummaging through the box on the stage, and was returning to Archie's side with a roll of silver duct tape and a pair of scissors. By the time that Michelle joined him, he was kneeling next to his patient, cleaning his wound with a cloth napkin doused in scotch, while he spoke pleasantly with those around him.

"Will any of these do?" she asked, showing to him the bags that she had collected.

The doctor finished cleaning the wound and looked at the materials that the reporter had produced. Moving his index finger over them, he selected a plastic sandwich bag with a grunt of satisfaction.

"Sterilize this for me, will you?" he said to the square-jawed nurse, while he began to pull and cut several strips of tape from the roll. Then with the scissors, he reduced the sandwich bag to a smaller square and placed it over the wound, taping three of its sides to Archie's chest. The fourth side he left open.

After that, the doctor observed Archie's breathing for more than a minute. It was irregular and ragged, making the taped plastic square stick to the puncture hole every time that Archie inhaled, and causing the plastic to rise and flutter slightly through its open end every time that he exhaled. The doctor nodded once with apparent satisfaction, and said to the intern. "Watch him. If his condition worsens, let me know." Then he stood up and addressed Michelle.

"Your friend...he is your friend, is he not?" he asked her.

Michelle nodded emphatically.

"He has what is called a 'sucking chest' wound," he told her. "The bullet punctured his chest and is allowing air to enter between the chest and his lung."

Michelle waited while the doctor cleared his throat. She tried not to show how distressed she felt, but it was difficult. Archie looked pale, his lips showing a light blue tinge. He was barely conscious, which was probably for the best, but coughed sporadically, and a couple of times had coughed up blood. Even with her very limited medical knowledge, it was apparent to her that he could not survive any prolonged siege by the terrorists. She saw Negron staring at her quizzically from the main entrance, half a hall away, and she extended the palm of her hand in his direction, signaling him to wait. She returned her full attention to the old surgeon.

"The air being sucked into his chest is causing his right lung to collapse," Dr. Schaeffer explained. "The more the air seeps in through the wound, the worst it gets. We have sealed the punctured aperture with the plastic cover. Now every time he breathes in, the plastic seals the wound. It does not allow any air to get in, even though it's open on one side to let any air that he expels from his chest to get out." He examined her face sternly, noticing her fear. Gently, he grabbed her left arm and moved further away from his patient. "I understand your concern, and I will not lie to you. Your friend is in a very serious condition. He needs to get to a hospital soon. But it could have been much worse. From the location of the wound, I don't think that any major blood vessels were damaged, and he did not sustain any injury to his spine, even though the bullet may have fractured some of his ribs."

He paused, and gazed briefly at Archie. The redhead continued to breathe very shallowly, but the dressing over the wound seemed to have lessened his cough and his eyes were half open. The nurse and the young doctor had propped up his back and head with several cushions, to ease his labored respiration.

"May I speak to him?" she asked.

"You may," the doctor responded, "as long as you are able to hide from him that face of utter panic that you have right now. It may not seem so to you, but he is very much aware of what is happening around him."

Michelle bit her lower lip, and took a shaky, deep breath. Composing herself, she walked back to Archie and knelt by his side. Gently, she grabbed his hand between both of hers and pressed it.

"So..." she said awkwardly. "The doctor says you can take the rest of the day off."

A thin smile appeared on Archie's lips, his chest continuing to rise and fall in abrupt, uneven, jerky spasms. He tried to say something but could only produce a soft sigh. Despite her determination not to cry, silent tears began to stream down her cheeks.

"I wanted...I wanted to ask you to forgive me for doubting you..." she whispered to him. "I was such a jerk..."

Archie's smile widened. He managed a weak nod, forcing Michelle to laugh.

"Okay, I deserved that!" she said, wiping away her tears. Freeing one of her hands, she caressed his red hair. "So listen," she said, "after all of this is over, how about if we go out on a date?"

Archie closed his eyes in an expression of pure bliss, but then he began to cough violently, flecking his chin with specks of blood. Michelle looked at the nurse kneeling beside her with alarm.

"He will be all right," the square-jawed woman reassured her, calmly wiping his patient's bloody chin and adjusting the cushions behind his back. Archie seemed to settle into an uneasy sleep, resuming his ragged breathing.

"Excuse me, Ms. Alfaro?" One of the hostages who had been armed by Captain Gomez—a tall, muscular, black man with a shaved head and a heavy Bostonian accent—approached her timidly. She looked up at him.

"I'm sorry to disturb you, but Captain Gomez asks if you have been able to contact the Puerto Rican Police Chief?"

"Maldonado?" Michelle answered dully.

"Captain Gomez has been informed by one of your friends," the man pointed at Negron, sitting on the floor behind the main entrance's doorframe, "that one over there, he told him that you can reach the Police Chief?"

Michelle cursed under her breath. *How could she have not thought of calling him immediately! She was not thinking straight. She was not doing her job as a reporter.* "Tell Captain Gomez that I will call him right now."

"Yes, ma'm," the black man answered courteously, obviously an ex-military man or a soldier on vacation. "The captain requests that you tell the Police Chief, Mal...do—"

"Maldonado." Michelle finished the name for him.

"That's the one!" The man flashed an apologetic smile. "I'm afraid I'm not very good with long Latin names. The Captain requests that you tell him what our situation is here, and that we are expecting a counterattack at any moment now, and that he should send any help he can as quickly as possible."

"Of course. Tell the Captain I'll call him right away."

The black man nodded and headed back to the main entrance.

Michelle began to search for the cellular phone she had taken away from the Machetero who had beat up Negron, but could not find it. For a panicky moment, she thought that she had lost it, but then she remembered that she had handed it back to Archie after she had finished her last conversation with the Superintendent. Tapping his front pants pockets gently, she found it and retrieved it. She hit the phone's automatic redial, and was surprised to hear the Superintendent himself answer on the second ring.

"*Ms. Alfaro,*" he said calmly.

"Mr. Superintendent," she replied, making a conscious effort to speak clearly, while covering her mouth and the phone's mouthpiece with her hand in order not to be overheard by the curious hostages that surrounded her. "This is our situation. We managed to intercept Captain Gomez and Sergeant..." she struggled to remembered the sergeant's name.

"*Cordero,*" Maldonado prompted for her.

"Yes, Cordero. With their help, we have captured the hall where the terrorists were holding the hostages. Not all of the hostages...There are about ten guests who were taken out of here in the afternoon and are unaccounted for, but we have most of them."

Michelle heard the Superintendent say to somebody else with him, "*Gomez and Cordero have secured the hostages!*" followed by loud cheers. "*Are you—*" Maldonado began to ask, but Michelle interrupted him.

"No, wait, please. There's more." Michelle lowered her voice even more. "We have one seriously wounded person, with a bullet in his chest, and we will have more wounded if we don't get help fast. We are surrounded, and Gomez expects that we will be counterattacked at any moment."

"*We're moving heaven and earth to get there as quickly as we can, Michelle,*" Maldonado responded, in an elated voice. "*Just hold on. We'll get there soon!*"

Michelle barely heard the Superintendent's last words, as the deafening sounds of heavy machine gun fire disrupted their conversation. To her horrified astonishment she saw some of the decorative tiles near the ballroom's main entrance splinter and disintegrate, spraying the defenders huddled near the doorframe with shards and chunks of broken porcelain. Other bullets thudded into the open wooden door, viciously chewing up its smooth, polished surface and filling it with holes.

People in the hall screamed and hugged the floor, while at the entrance, the defenders were forced to back off a few steps in order to avoid getting hit by ricocheting projectiles or pieces of debris. About ten men—the volunteers—stood nervously with their backs against the wall, some armed with AK-47s, others with handguns, waiting for the gunfire to abate, knowing that the assault would come then. Six others, all of them unarmed, stood by the other locked doors of the ballroom, ready to sound the alarm if any attackers tried to break through.

Michelle watched as the chaos unfolded before her, and realized that there was no way that the hostages could stop the tremendous firepower that had been unleashed upon them. *They were lost.* "Please!" she pleaded desperately over the phone. "We need your help now!"

Johnny Ray was at his wit's end. He had searched for Cacho and San Miguel, but they were nowhere to be found; not in the conference center, not in the pool area, or the restaurants, or the casino. They had simply vanished, along with Daniel and even the humongous Czecka.

He had hoped to find them directing the recapture of the freed hostages, but he had only stumbled at the last moment into Colonel Calderon, organizing his men near the garden area. The Venezuelan officer had been curt, simply stating to him that he had not seen the revolutionary leaders, and excusing himself to continue preparing for the assault on the convention hall. However, Johnny had noticed certain evasiveness in his eyes, as if the colonel had access to a lot more information than he was letting be known.

Shaken and concerned, he had begun to head back to the reception area when it occurred to him to search for the missing leaders in a small conference area that existed near the main elevators of the hotel. After Daniel had thrown down to his death a man from the hotel's rooftop, he had secluded the remaining nine hostages in the small conference room, to keep them isolated from the bulk of the other captured guests and the staff. There was no logical reason why San Miguel or Cacho would be there now, but nothing that night made sense to Johnny any more.

Despair overtook him. *Where were they?* He expected the heavy rattle of rifle and machinegun fire to erupt behind him at any moment. The attack on the hostages would begin soon, and he was certain that dozens of prisoners would be killed.

How had things gotten so out of hand? The additional killings would strip the revolution of its righteous aura and convert it into a brutal terrorist action. It would scare a lot of his fellow countrymen into statehood. He had to find Cacho and San Miguel to stop the madness.

Johnny stopped in front of the conference room and knocked on the door. At first, he heard no answer. Then an irritated voice shouted, "I said come in!"

As he stepped inside, Johnny immediately noted that the room was too small for the hostages. Located between the administrative offices and the elevators to the main tower, the space had originally been intended to stay closed, to be used eventually when the hotel needed to expand its administrative staff and offices. The Great Recession had taken care of that, however. Cost cutting measures had converted it into a very narrow conference room, which could barely accommodate the width of an eight-seat conference table, a photocopier, a small, waist high cabinet with a coffee maker, and a flat screen TV.

A man sat at the head of the room with the back of his chair leaning dangerously against the wall, a rifle resting just over his knees. He was wearing a Universal Studios cap that he had pulled all the way down to his eyebrows, but which was not enough to cover his heavily acne-filled face. A dark fuzz under his nose confirmed that he must still be in his teenager years, and a T-shirt bearing the image of Aragorn advancing with a drawn sword proclaimed him to be a fan of the Lord of the Rings saga. Like most of the other revolutionaries, he sported a pair of blue jeans and an undetermined brand of sneakers. Beyond him, around the conference table, were the hostages, occupying most of the space in the room.

Daniel, Johnny thought, could not have been accused of being partial to any ethnic, social, sex, or age category when selecting the hostages. It was as varied a group as he had ever seen.

A young man with a crew cut lay on top of the table, partially covered by a flowery bedspread somebody had snatched from one of the hotel's rooms, his head raised by two pillows, his right leg uncovered up to his thigh and dressed in bandages. A teen aged girl was sleeping on the floor, part of her body extended under the conference table, her head resting on the lap of a beautiful, sexy, blue-eyed brunette who could have graced the centerfold of any Playboy issue. An Irish-looking priest in his sixties sat next to the wounded man's head, while a middle-aged, butch-looking woman—Johnny had had a male gym instructor that looked like her—sat at the end of the table. The other seats were taken by a half-dressed man with a half-shaved face; a shifty-eyed, well-to-do-looking man who was either a politician, a lawyer, or both; and a blond, fit young man with an artificial tan. A tall, lanky man with a suntan that Johnny suspected went no further than the collar of his shirt and the fringe of his short sleeves sat on the floor at the opposite side of the Playboy model, exuding more authority than anyone else in the room. *A retired general, perhaps,* Johnny wondered.

All of them except the sleeping girl stared expectantly at the new arrival, their faces etched with a mixture of curiosity, fear, and hope. It was immediately evident that San Miguel, Cacho, or any of the other players who gravitated around them were not there.

The armed guard let the front legs of his chair drop back on the carpeted floor and stared wordlessly at Johnny.

"I'm looking for Cacho..." the FEPI leader began to say.

The Machetero shrugged, with insolent indifference. "I don't see him here..." he said in a mocking tone.

"I know that," Johnny replied impatiently. "I'm just asking if you have seen him recently. Or San Miguel, Daniel...No?"

"I haven't seen any of them for a while," the man responded in a hoarse, boyish voice, pushing his cap up and uncovering a forehead equally covered with acne, as well as thick, interconnected eyebrows.

"You have no idea where they might be?" Johnny insisted.

The young Machetero's forehead creased into an irritated frown. "I have not seen them for hours," he said. "But if I see them, I'll be sure send them your—" The "pop-pop-popping" of heavy, rapid fire interrupted his sarcastic reply.

Alarmed, Johnny turned to leave.

"Wait!" the Machetero said in a friendlier tone. "Do you know what's happening out there?"

"I don't know," the FEPI leader responded, "but if I find out, I'll be sure to let you know," he replied in the same sarcastic tone with which he had been addressed. He paused and listened anxiously as the shooting continued unabated, if anything increasing in volume and intensity.

The guard grinned sheepishly. "I'm sorry, man. I guess I had that one coming, eh?"

The intense noise of the firefight increased, forcing both men to stop their conversation for several minutes. Then three successive explosions made the floor shake, followed by more intense shooting. However, a short time later, most of the automatic gunfire began to die out, only the sound of a few more bursts filtering through the walls of the conference room like the last exploding kernels of a microwaved bag of popcorn.

"I heard that the Americans captured the ballroom where we kept the hostages," the acneed man said in an apprehensive tone to Johnny. "Is that true?"

The question produced an instant stir in the room, as most of the hostages whispered excitedly to each other. The Universal-capped guard turned to them. "Be quiet!" he shouted.

Johnny saw the double ponytails of the sleeping teenager stir on the brunette's lap, but the older woman hushed her back to sleep.

"Please," the guard insisted when Johnny failed to answer his inquiry. "They took my partner away almost half an hour ago. I'm stuck here with these prisoners. As long as I'm alone, I can't even go to the bathroom. I have to pee, you know. I won't be able to hold it forever."

Johnny regarded the young Machetero with wordless dismay. The man's sole concern about what was happening outside did not have anything to do with the revolution, but with his need to pee. Johnny opened the door, and motioned the guard to follow him, closing it partially when both had stepped outside.

"Yes, the rumors are true," he admitted to the acneed sentry. "The Americans have captured the hostages. But the rescuers were very few, and we will retake the ballroom soon, if we haven't already. That's what the shooting you just heard was all about."

The guard absorbed the news quietly, and then nodded. "Listen, man," he said to the FEPI leader, "I really do have to pee. Do you think you could keep a watch on these people while I go to the bathroom? I'll be right back."

Johnny hesitated momentarily but then relented with a shrug. "Okay, but please hurry. I have to find Cacho and San Miguel. It's urgent."

"Thank you! Here," the acneed man handed to Johnny his AK-47. "I won't be needing this where I'm going."

The FEPI leader accepted the weapon with evident lack of enthusiasm. Not saying another word, the guard departed in the direction of the lobby.

Johnny opened the door and walked back into the conference room, feeling painfully aware of the intense scrutiny to which the hostages were subjecting him. There was a palpable aura of hostility in the cramped quarters, and it was obviously directed towards him. He ventured a weak smile, but his captives consciously ignored it.

Although he had no reason to do so, he felt guilty. The hostages were living through a hellish nightmare, which only promised to get worse. None of it had been of his making. Not directly, anyway. It had not been his idea to threaten any of the hostages, and he certainly had tried to put a stop to the killings. But of course, they would not know that. To them, he was the face of the enemy, as guilty as the man who had thrown one of them off the roof of the hotel.

The unexplainable absence of Cacho and San Miguel grated on his already raw nerves. From the outset, San Miguel had micromanaged the entire operation with zealous and clockwork precision, leaving nothing to chance, personally directing every step of the revolution. It was true that he had transferred overall command to Cacho, but he would have never abandoned the Grand Laguna Hotel knowing that an attack by the Americans was imminent.

And Cacho! The Machetero had a reputation for courage and an iron will to resist. The fate of the revolution now rested on his shoulders. *How could he disappear at a crucial moment like this?*

No, something was definitely wrong. Except for Colonel Calderon—a well-intentioned foreigner, but a foreigner nevertheless—the entire leadership of the revolutionary forces was missing. If nobody assumed command, the revolution could collapse that same night, prematurely killed by a lack of direction.

But all of his concerns would be moot by now. The shooting had stopped. It probably meant that the Macheteros—most likely Calderon and his Venezuelans—had recaptured the ballroom. It would now all boil down now to counting the hostage casualties, and hoping that not too many people had been killed.

Johnny looked at his watch impatiently. *Only two minutes had elapsed since the guard had left for the bathroom! It had seemed like more.* Resignedly, he sat down to wait.

His eyes wandered to the man lying on the table. A medic from the Venezuelan group had tended to his wounds. He did not seem to be in any great physical pain, although a dark splotch of blood stained a portion of his bandages. However, his face was lined with worry and distress. For a second, the wounded man's gaze locked with Johnny's, and the FEPI leader instantly felt compelled to engage him in conversation.

"How do you feel?" he asked him. He saw the brunette raise her eyes with an expression of derision, and the priest look directly at him.

"My wife and my baby are in the ballroom," the wounded man answered, leaning on one elbow. "How do you think I feel?"

"I'm sure that they're all right," Johnny said, not feeling sure at all.

"No, you're not," the beautiful woman mumbled.

"I'm sorry? I didn't hear what you said," Johnny said uncertainly.

"I *said*, that you're not sure that his baby or his wife are okay!" the brunette replied in a loud, hostile voice, waking up the teenager.

Johnny felt the unfriendly glare of the other people in the room hit him like a solid beam of heat, and his face reddened. "I'm sorry for your present inconvenience," he said as calmly as he could. "I know it's been hard on all of you, but I have no power or control over the prisoners. Anyway, you'll soon be free. And it will be for a great cause, even if you don't know it."

"That is so much bullshit! You have control over us! You can set us free!" the beautiful woman observed crossly. Johnny's admiration for her had begun to wane considerably.

"In time," he answered, sorry that he had started the conversation.

"Yeah, right!" the contempt in the woman's voice felt like a slap on his face. He felt himself sweating profusely, but did not dare to wipe his face, fearing it would be taken as a sign of weakness. "Threatening women and children, placing the lives of babies at risk, killing innocent people! Great cause indeed!"

"No babies have been placed at risk!" Johnny snapped back at her angrily, then looking directly at the man on the table, he assured him in a softer voice. "Your baby is fine, believe me." He sighed and looked away, letting his attempt to establish a conversation drift into a tense silence.

CHAPTER LXVII

"Take cover!" Captain Gomez shouted into the ballroom, his voice barely audible over the roar of the automatic fire.

He saw the young black marine who had just spoken to Michelle fall, then fight his way back to his feet, saying, "I'm all right!" while trying to clear his eyes from splinters from a broken tile.

Gomez looked back at the men huddling against the wall behind him. "When the gunfire weakens, it means that they are coming for us. They have to advance through a narrow corridor, so maybe one or two of them will be firing their weapons, but not more. That's when we shoot back."

Some of the men nodded nervously, most merely listened.

"We will stop them *here!* At the entrance! If anyone falls, get his gun and continue to fight. *They will not go beyond this door!* Is that understood?"

"Yes, sir!" several of the men shouted, letting their pent up anger and frustration show through their voices.

"They have pushed us around long enough!" Negron shouted, caught in the emotion of the moment. *"Now we push them back!"*

"Yes, sir!" the men shouted with even more passion.

"Get ready!" Gomez ordered, beginning to move cautiously towards the doorframe as the machine gun fire began to wane.

Negron, along with three other men, followed him closely, while five others, all of them unarmed, stayed behind as reserves. Gomez, Negron, and one of the men braced their weapons against the edge of the wall, while the black marine and a short, wiry, Latin-looking man crouched on the floor and took aim at the open space in the entrance.

Then, suddenly, the shooting stopped. The lull barely lasted two seconds, but when the Macheteros renewed their fire, it came from the opposite direction directly towards the ballroom defenders. Dozens of bullets whizzed past the men standing by the doorframe, and crashed into an empty portion of the hall. The shots were of a lesser caliber than the heavy machine gun fire that had raked the opposite side of the entrance, but just as deadly. The Latin man crouching next to the black Marine screamed as he was hit twice on his left thigh, and rolled in agony over the floor. Two of the men waiting behind grabbed him by the shoulders and pulled him back, while another recovered his weapon, a Glock pistol, and took his place.

There was chaos inside the ballroom, as those closest to the shooting tried to scramble to a safer area, sometimes trampling those on the floor. Women, children and even some of the men cried and screamed in panic or pain, while others tried to restore some semblance of order or shout directions above the noise. Michelle, the nurse and the young doctor had to block a fat man who ran roughshod over several hostages and threatened to trample Archie, wrestling him to the ground.

At the entrance, Captain Gomez caught the faint flicker of movement in the darkness outside, and realized that the Macheteros were a lot closer than he had expected them to be, apparently having crawled towards the hostages while the heavy-caliber MAGs fired from the opposite side of the corridor. To his dismay, he saw the gray figures of two men appear at the entrance and aim their weapons at them.

"Shoot them!" he shouted.

In an ear-splitting second, both sides opened fired at point-blank range. Gomez discharged his MP-5K sub machinegun in short, deliberate bursts, aiming at the evasive shapes that crouched and fired wildly from the corridor into the hostage-filled ballroom. Each side fought with blind, fanatical fury, refusing to give ground, the multiple, pulsating flames of their guns blurring the outlines of the men who fired them, screams of anger and pain piercing through hellish din of the gunfire.

Time seemed to stretch to a slow crawl. Gomez saw Negron kneeling next to him, coolly firing round after round, adjusting his aim after every shot. In the corridor, he watched one Machetero fall backwards and another one spin sideways, grabbing his shoulder, only to be shot again in the back. But more attackers pressed on, stepping into the place where their comrades had fallen, blindly unloading their weapons into the ballroom's black void.

Then something slammed into his chest with the violence of a sledgehammer and he lost his balance, crashing on top of a man lying on the floor. He apologized loudly as he searched in the near pitch-black darkness for the telltale wetness of blood under his collarbone, but could find none, realizing with immense relief that his bulletproof vest had stopped the bullet that had struck him. *That is twice today that my body armor has saved my life,* he thought to himself, as he felt a pair of hands begin to pull him up from the floor. "*A la tercera va la vencida,*" ("The third time is the charm.") the Puerto Rican saying went, and he prayed that that third time would never come.

"Are you all right?" he heard Negron's concerned voice shout next to him.

"I'm okay!" he shouted back. "Keep fighting!" As he stumbled onto his knees, his left hand slipped on a puddle, and his arm slid forward until he managed to grab onto what he thought was the elbow of the man on top of whom he had fallen, but immediately realized that he was touching a bloody chin. The man under him did not move as Gomez hurriedly got back to his feet.

His fall and recovery had all happened in a matter of seconds, but by the time he was up he noticed that the intensity of the attack by the Macheteros was faltering. The rest of the defenders also seemed to sense it, fiercely holding their ground, fighting despite their wounds and their intense fear.

"We're going to win!" Gomez shouted, but just as he said so, somebody thrust the barrel of a submachine gun around the doorframe behind which he was standing and opened fire.

The discharge missed the SWAT officer's face by a tiny fraction of an inch, its flames singeing his right ear and rupturing his eardrum. Instinctively, he grabbed the weapon by its trigger guard and pushed it upwards as it continued to fire, while with his other hand he clutched the attacker by the throat. More men appeared behind him, and in a moment, the hall's entrance was clogged with men fighting hand to hand, as more of the defenders inside rushed to meet the attackers.

All around him men punched, shoved, kicked, cursed, and screamed, using their guns as clubs, firing at close range, falling as they were hurt or wounded. For a hopeful, breathless moment, Gomez thought that his men would hold, as their line refused to give ground and even pressed back on the terrorists. But the new attackers seemed to be of a different breed than those they had encountered before, ferocious fighters trained in hand-to-hand combat, and the desperate struggle began to turn their way.

Even the SWAT captain found himself hanging on for dear life, as the man he had grabbed easily freed himself from Gomez's grasp, nearly breaking his wrist in the process. Before the policeman could counter with a punch, the man crashed his elbow on his face, causing the dazed officer to tumble backwards and lose his grip on the sub machinegun. As he fell, Gomez saw his attacker point his weapon in his direction but managed to deflect it by kicking his arm just as the gun went off. Several bullets ricocheted off the wall, but none hit either of the two fighters.

The attacker cursed and re-aimed his sub machinegun, but by that time Gomez had unsheathed his dagger, and stabbed the terrorist on his leg. As the man instinctively leaned forward to grasp his leg, Gomez swept his knife in an upward arc and cut his neck open.

A torrent of blood soaked Gomez's hand and face as the dying man toppled over him. Even then, the SWAT captain saw another man advance towards him and furiously tried to push the dying man off him. Gomez began to draw his gun, but all of a sudden three explosions shook the foundations of the building, blotting out with dazzling incandescence everyone and everything in the immediate proximity.

The SWAT captain had tried to shut his eyes as soon as he heard the first of the explosions go off, but by then it was too late. He was blind and deaf to the world, at least for the next few seconds. It all depended now on Sergeant Abe Cordero.

Sergeant Abraham Cordero had settled behind the bushes of the small courtyard that faced the entrance to the Grand Laguna's main ballroom, and waited. His dark uniform blended perfectly with the murky light of the courtyard and made him invisible to the casual eye, so much so that at one moment, two men had silently slipped into the tiny garden and crouched, less than three feet away from where he hid, and discussed in hushed tones the best way to approach the hostages. Cordero had stayed perfectly still, gingerly wrapping his fingers around the hilt of his dagger but not daring to draw it out of its sheath to avoid making any noise. The men had lingered for about five minutes, and then returned to the hotel's garden, not really determining how they would conduct their attack.

About a quarter of an hour later, he had watched as eight men carrying assault rifles had begun to slowly crawl along the corridor's inner wall, coming from the direction of the hotel's lobby. They had hardly begun to move, when two MAG machine guns to his right opened fire, their heavy caliber bullets quickly turning into rubble the decorative tiles that graced the entrance to the ballroom, and shredding into bits and pieces portions of the open doors.

The men operating the machine guns were professionally trained soldiers, he had concluded almost instantly. Their fire was tight and precise, and they had positioned the two MAGs with such quiet efficiency that he had not noticed them until they began spitting out their deadly fare, even though they could not have been more than ten feet away from where he hid.

The men advancing from the lobby had stopped momentarily, afraid that a stray bullet could hit them. However, as they became accustomed to the precision of the fire coming from the opposite direction, they continued to move, crawling on the floor. When they were less than a yard away from the entrance, the machine gunners had stopped shooting. Then the attackers had stood up and begun their assault on the ballroom.

Cordero had been sorely tempted to intervene then, but knew that he had to wait. He was the hostages' last resort. He could not act prematurely. The moment that he stepped into the fight, he had to be able to create the greatest amount of damage in as little time as possible.

He had no illusions about what would happen to him. Gomez had warned him to make some noise, create some confusion, and withdraw into the ballroom. But from what he had seen, that would not be enough. The men conducting the attack were intent in breaking through at any cost. They had fought bravely and hard, and were not going to be intimidated by his surprise appearance. If the Macheteros recaptured the hostages, it would be very difficult for the Navy SEALs to conduct a rescue without heavy loss of life, both of their men and of the hostages. When he acted, his aim had to be to inflict as many casualties and to take down as many of their enemies as he could.

Surprisingly, he felt very calm, as if by accepting that he would probably not survive had rid him of all of his worries and misgivings. He was a widower, and his two children were grown. He had lived a fairly good and interesting life, a long enough life to become an old timer "farting dust", as his ex-Navy SEAL buddies would say, when referring to someone older.

Twice Cordero nearly intervened, but each time he held himself in check, as he watched the men in the ballroom beat back the terrorists' attacks. But then, half a dozen men began to rapidly approach the hostages from the opposite side of the corridor, and he prepared to act.

He had brought with him four M84 stun grenades—"flashbang" grenades, as they were generally called by the police—and a smoke canister and, except for the smoke canister—which he kept in his pocket—he carefully placed them around him. Now, as he saw the first of the newcomers raise his sub machinegun and fire it blindly around the entrance's doorframe, he grabbed one of the flashbang grenades, pulled out its circular pin, and lobbed it towards the hall's entrance. He quickly followed with two other grenades, throwing one towards the area where he thought the MAGs were located next to the courtyard, and the other at the advancing men.

Cordero barely had time to close his eyes and place his hands over his ears, before the awaited detonations went off. The blinding white light of 6 million candela and the ear shattering thuds of three, 180 decibel-high explosions flooded the entire area, overwhelming the attackers and defenders alike. Men stumbled dazedly in the corridor, covering their eyes, opening and closing their mouths to clear their ears.

Standing up, Cordero aimed his MP-5K submachine gun at the confused terrorists standing before him, and opened fire, cutting them down where they stood. Men screamed and cursed as they fell, while others threw themselves to the ground and covered their heads. He shot a dozen rounds at the Macheteros in the other end of the hall, but those men were already defeated and staggering back to the lobby, so he quickly turned and concentrated his fire on the MAGs stationed next to the courtyard.

From where he had been hiding, Cordero had been unable to make out where they were, concealed by the bushes that lined the edges of the courtyard. But now, as he walked towards them through the inner edge of the corridor, he saw the heavy machineguns and the men who operated them clearly.

He had lobbed his last flashbang grenade right in the midst of the two crews that operated the guns, causing havoc. Some were simply stunned, kneeling or sitting on the floor, shaking their heads or blinking repeatedly, as if trying to regain their sight. Others called their comrades' names or extended their hands, unable to see or hear them.

A couple of black uniformed men, however, those who apparently had been the furthest away from the explosions, seemed to have been less affected by the grenades, and were running towards the machine guns.

Cordero raised his weapon to stop them, but several shots rang out from his left, and a bullet struck him on the left arm, spinning him and causing him to fall. As he shifted his sight to the gunfire's source, he saw a man close to the garden with a sniper rifle, adjusting his aim to shoot him again. Desperately, the sergeant rolled on his back and fired his sub machinegun at the sniper. He missed, but caused the sniper's shot to go wide.

He continued to fire at the rifleman until his ammunition clip ran out, making his attacker run for cover. Then, putting his weapon aside, he extracted the smoke canister from his pocket, pulled out its fuse, and let it roll out a few feet between him and the MAG machine guns. With a loud fizz, purple smoke plumed out of the large, green can and began to fill the space in the corridor.

Cordero grabbed his MP-K5 sub machine gun and rolled several times on the floor, into the cloud of smoke and towards the two MAG machine guns. As he did so, three successive bullets struck the ground where he had laid, one of them hitting so close that it blew away the heel of his shoe. Almost simultaneously, he heard the characteristic "clak-clak" noise of one of the two MAGs' cocking levers.

Knowing that he was about to be shred to bits, Cordero pulled out his last clip of ammunition and shoved it into his sub machinegun, just as the MAG opened fire. He was concealed by the purple smoke, but even so the MAG's initial burst of fire almost killed him, two rounds singeing his hair and another striking him on the back, lodging itself between his left ribs and his bulletproof vest.

The pain was bone jarring, and nearly caused him to faint. But he swung his weapon over his head and fired blindly in the direction of the MAGs, sweeping his gun twice back and forth in a tight arc, continuing to shoot even after he heard screams and the MAG went abruptly silent.

His back hurt so much that for a moment he thought he would not be able to move. But then his legs responded, and he wobbled unsteadily towards the heavy machine guns under the cover of the purple smoke. As he moved, he drew his Glock out of his holster, and held it as steadily as he could with both of his hands, ready to shoot anyone that stepped in his way.

When he got to the MAGs, he found three dead men strewn about him, and two more wounded, one in the stomach and another in the leg. The one with the stomach wound hardly moved, merely producing periodic gasps, like a fish out of the water. The other man was trying to tie a tourniquet around his right thigh, and raised his hands as Cordero approached him. The sergeant quickly disarmed him of his gun, and allowed him to continue working on his wound.

The smoke was beginning to thin out as the SWAT sergeant turned his attention on the unmanned machinegun. He hoped that the sniper would not dare to shoot yet, unable to discern who was who through the purple haze, and hopefully unwilling to shoot one of his comrades by mistake. But the sergeant knew that the terrorists would be coming back soon.

His legs finally gave out on him as he got to one of the machineguns. Crawling behind it, he re-aimed it towards the garden area. The MAG was still loaded with the same belt of unfired rounds from where the bullet lodged in his back had probably come. He heard a noise behind him and turned, pointing his Glock at the soldier—why did he think of the man as a soldier, he wondered, but he did—who was crawling towards him.

"Don't shoot," the man shouted, raising his hands.

"Get away from here," Cordero growled. Grimacing from the pain, the "soldier" limped away from the area. He had not walked two paces when two shots rang out from the garden, and the wounded man dropped straight to the ground like a sack of potatoes.

Cordero's MAG came to life immediately, spitting out its deadly content and peppering the garden area with frightening violence. Glass shattered and the shadows of men scattered to seek refuge from the lethal shower of lead. But then some of the hidden terrorists began to fire back, their bullets buzzing past the wounded policeman, or ricocheting with loud "pings" on the marbled floor.

Undaunted, Cordero continued to discharge the heavy machine gun until it ran out of bullets. Then he began to crawl to the other MAG, but realized halfway there that it was out of ammunition. Grabbing his Glock, he sat back up and aimed it at where he thought one of the snipers had taken cover, firing it methodically.

As if waiting to empty his handgun, the terrorists held their fire. The smoke had begun to dissipate, and Cordero's body, sitting on the floor with its legs akimbo, became a more solid target with each passing second. Cordero continued to shoot with deliberate care, each brass cartridge ejected by his Glock distinctly clinking several times on the floor before he discharged his next round, until the slide of his gun stayed open when his ammunition clip emptied.

Slowly, barely able to hold on to his pistol, he began to search his pockets for another clip of ammunition, the corridor falling into an unnatural silence. Then the thunder of a single sniper's bullet shattered the newfound peace, and the sergeant reeled backwards and lay still on the floor.

Colonel Calderon surveyed the carnage with bitter incredulity, as the remainder of his men retook the two captured MAGs. Four men lay dead around the two machine guns—five, if you counted the dead policeman—and another was dying from a terrible stomach wound. Three more men had been killed and two others seriously wounded in the corridor trying to get into the ballroom. And Sergeant Alfonsin was missing, presumably killed or captured by the hostages inside the hall. His force had been decimated, reduced in less than fifteen minutes from fourteen men to six.

The Macheteros had also suffered heavy loses. From where he stood, Calderon counted six bodies in the corridor, and he was certain there would be more wounded and dead inside the ballroom.

How could this have happened? Up to that point, the opposition had been unable to endure the Venezuelans' withering fire, collapsing time and again like a house of cards. The ballroom was supposed to be held by less than a handful of the American Special Forces. His unit's weapons by far surpassed the hostages' limited firepower. Retaking the hostages should have been an easy operation with very little casualties.

The colonel looked at his watch, and saw that it was 2059 hours. Time was running short. In order to get to La Perla by 2400 hours, they would have to leave within the next couple of hours to be on the safe side. But there was still plenty of time to try again. *If he decided to try again...*

For a moment he debated whether he should just take his losses and leave. However, he discarded the idea almost as quickly as it had popped into his mind. To abandon the fight now, after the heavy casualties they had sustained, would be stupid and cowardly. It would also be dishonorable. Besides, he meant to avenge the death of his men.

"Ignacio," he said to the man standing beside him, who seemed stunned by the losses that they had sustained.

"Sir!"

"Go to the pool area. Gather the rest of the men and bring them here."

Ignacio stared at the colonel with surprise, but acknowledged the order and left.

"Load the machine guns, and get our men out of the corridor," he ordered quietly to the remaining members of his group. "As soon as the others come, we will attack."

As the men moved to carry out his orders, he grabbed one of them by the arm, the one who was carrying a Dragunov sniper rifle. "Stay here, Ricardo. I want you to keep a watch on the entrance to the ballroom. If anyone shows his head, blast it away."

The sniper moved into the courtyard where Cordero had hidden, and silently assumed a position from which he could cover the main entrance to the hall. From that distance, nearly across the corridor, it would be impossible to miss.

The colonel walked to the man with the stomach wound and knelt next to him. He grabbed his hand, but the soldier did not react. He had been filled with painkillers by their medic, and his shirt had been removed, but not much more. Their medic did not have sufficient training to treat him, and Calderon doubted that the man would survive another hour. His only hope was to recapture the hostages, and find a surgeon among them.

He knew each of his men's names; most had been under his command for a long time, some of them for years. This one was one of the new recruits, added to his unit at the last moment. Even so, it pained him more than he had ever imagined to see him dying.

He had failed his men, Calderon concluded bitterly. *He had been cocky and overconfident, and his soldiers had paid the price.*

"It will not happen again," he vowed to the dying man. He stared at one of the ballroom's several sets of closed doors, already knowing how he would conduct his next attack. "We have fought on the hostages' terms. Now we fight on ours."

CHAPTER LXVIII

"John...John!"

McFadden felt his lungs burning, as if they were going to explode. Then he realized that he was coughing desperately for air, and that it was not fire but excruciating pain coursing through his entire body that made him feel that way. He tried to stop coughing but couldn't, barely able to breathe as hardly any air flowed into his lungs.

"Here," an unknown male voice said, pushing a rubber mouthpiece into his mouth. "Try this. It's from my LARVUBA tank, but it's pure oxygen and it'll help you breathe better."

John tried to breathe through the mouthpiece, but choked.

"Easy...easy...Just pull on it softly," the stranger said. Slowly, McFadden began to breathe more easily. "There, that's a lot better," the man added.

John felt someone holding on to his hand, and tried to focus on the face behind it. Gradually, he managed to discern the features of the Countess of Gilly, looking down on him with a mixture of concern and relief.

"What..." he began to ask through the mouthpiece, but had to stop to gather strength. His throat felt as raw as if it had been trampled by a herd of buffaloes. He tried again. "What...happen..."

"You fell into the water," the stranger answered. "Fell almost right on top of one of our men. Don't you remember?"

John closed his eyes and tried to recollect how he had gotten there. He remembered the fire on the ramp, but not much more. *The water? He had fallen into the water? The bay? Again?*

"Were you forced to jump, *mon cher?*" the Countess asked him. "Were you escaping someone?"

McFadden racked his brain, trying reconstruct the events that had brought him there, but could not. He opened his mouth and let the mouthpiece slip out.

"I...I..." he began to say confusedly, but stopped, unable to continue.

"You splashed down just a few feet from where our group was swimming," the stranger said with a hint of amusement in his voice. "Almost got killed by one of our men before he realized that you were unconscious. We were heading towards the blinking lights in the open cargo hold," he explained.

John directed his eyes towards the Countess, who nodded. "Yes, John, they saw our lights! Who would have thought it? One moment we were flashing the flashlight with the S.O.S. Morse Code—"

"Oh, is that what it was?" the stranger said, smiling. John could make out only portions of his face under his wetsuit's hood; a broad chin, large brown eyes, a broad nose, the rest hidden by black camouflage paint.

"Short, short, short, long, long, long, short, short, short..." the Countess said, repeating the sequence that they had used to signal the approaching rescuers.

"Well, we just saw the lights you were flashing from the open cargo door. A bright light, by the way. A halogen light. Very white and very bright. Some of us saw it first shining over the water. A couple of us peeked, and saw where it was coming from."

"It was a very nice...eh...lamp. The type they use to search the water, Ernan told me," the Countess explained.

Ernan! John had forgotten about him. *Where was he?*

"Ernan tied a rope that went into the water. He and I were standing near the open entrance. We saw three of the divers appear right under the entrance, pointing their guns at us!" She raised her eyebrows and shook her head, smiling. "They gave us quite a scare! But I told them we were friends and they started to climb in. We were so happy! Then they carried you out of the water, and I was terrified! What were you doing there? You were supposed to be upstairs! How did you get there? You were pale and not breathing. It looked like you were dead!"

John tried to sit but a sharp jolt of pain forced him to desist from his attempt.

"Take it easy, buddy," the stranger said. "You're really beat up. Probably have a few ribs broken."

"Ernan..." John managed to say.

"He volunteered to be the guide for the navy men," the Countess explained.

Ernan had volunteered to guide the "navy men" to the hostages? Had the world changed while he was unconscious? Timid, scaredy-cat Ernan had volunteered to go back into the lion's den? John was amazed. But then, why should he? He himself, mister "don't-bother-me-it's-not-my-business" had ended up risking his life several times that day, and nearly getting pummeled out of existence. If he could have acted that way, why be astonished by Ernan's transformation?

"Just rest, okay?" the "navy man" said. "You're safe now." The stranger was sticking the needle of a syringe into a small flask and drawing out its liquid. "This will help you sleep until we get you into a hospital."

John felt a pinprick on his left arm, and almost immediately began to feel relief from his throbbing pain. He stared at the Countess' face and found it beautiful.

"You...you should give her..." he began to say, "some pain killers...also... She has been through a..."

But sleep overtook him.

Ensign Jeb Stuart knew that the ship's internal stairways would be narrow when he had reviewed the *Mardi Gras'* blueprints and practiced with the tape outlines in Hangar 3, but had never imagined it would be that cramped, and certainly not that noisy. The small Filipino steward had led him and eighteen of his men up the crew's bow staircase, a pipe-lined, paint-smelling internal passageway normally used by the staff to move about the enormous ship without being seen by the passengers. Hopefully, the SEALs would also be able to use it without being seen by the terrorists, but with the sporadic, echoing noises that the group was making on the metal stair steps, despite the men's best efforts to move silently, it all seemed like a dubious proposition at best.

Fortunately, they only had to travel up three decks, to Deck 5, where the Stardust Theater was located. Well, that and another to Deck 6, where there were two entrances to the second floor of the theatre. Stuart had split Group Bravo into two squads: the one which he led, and another eighteen man squad to take care of the terrorists on the dock and make certain that nobody else got on board.

In concept, their mission was pretty straightforward: to surround the theatre without being seen, sealing every exit, and to kill every terrorist inside. It was the execution that worried him. It would be very difficult to approach the Stardust Theatre without being seen. The Filipino, Ernan, had assured them that the terrorists were short-handed, and that there would not be more than three or four of them guarding the hostages. Even so, one unchecked gunman with a semiautomatic rifle or a sub machinegun could cause a tremendous loss of life, if he was not stopped in time.

Ernan had confirmed to the SEALs that there was a back entrance to the theatre on Deck 5. Stuart had seen it in the ship's blueprints, but the door had been marked differently from other doors on the deck, almost as an afterthought by the architect who had drawn up the plans. It was good to know that the entrance existed.

All of a sudden, the squad's point man in the stairs stopped and signaled those who followed to stop. Stuart grabbed the Filipino by the scruff of his neck, and gestured to him to be still. Ernan looked scared, but nodded, looking upwards fearfully.

Some decks above them a door swung open and somebody shouted, "Gordo! Are you there?" Instinctively, the men behind Stuart raised their weapons and pointed them towards the top landing in the stairs. Hernandez, the point man, quietly crawled up three steps and aimed his rifle at the steps beyond the landing.

"Damn!" the unknown voice said. "Where did that asshole go?" The sound of several footsteps followed, and then the noise of a door swung shut. For a long pause, the SEALs waited. Then the point man whispered, "Clear!" and they began to move again.

A large red number "5" was painted on the wall next to the door that exited to that deck. Here, the men stopped. The point man, Hernandez, slowly pushed open the door to the outside deck and peered through a crack, making sure that nobody was heading towards them from the stern of the ship. He could not look out in the opposite direction, where the shortest part of Deck 5 ended in the bow of the ship and the back door of the theater. To detect anyone approaching them from that side, they would have to rely on luck, and kill any terrorist they came upon before he sounded the alarm.

Although they had discussed extensively with Ernan the location of the Stardust's exits and doors before heading towards the theatre, Stuart reviewed the information one more time.

"How far to the door at the back of the theater did you say it was?" he asked the Filipino.

"About thirty yards from the exit of the stairs on Deck Five," Ernan responded in an exaggerated whisper. He kept glancing nervously from Stuart to the door where the point man kept his watch, afraid that somebody would open it unexpectedly and surprise them. "The door is right in the middle of the bow of the ship, so it's not visible from the rest of the deck. But the only way to get there is to get out to the Promenade Deck and run to the door, so we will be exposed until we round the corner. Also, you must be careful because you never know if there may be pirates coming from the opposite direction."

"How about upstairs? On Deck 6? Are there any other doors that lead to the Stardust from the deck?"

Ernan considered the question briefly and shook his head. "No, the only entrances to the theater are the main entrance on Deck 5 inside the ship, the two other entrances inside the ship to the theater's second floor on Deck 6, and the back outside entrance in the bow of the ship on Deck 5 that the crew uses to get in and out of the theater."

"Right. And you say that the back entrance leads to the dressing rooms, and then to the back of the stage?"

"Yes," Ernan replied. "When Mr. McFadden and I were there, we climbed up to the platform that the light and scenery technicians use, a platform above the stage. From there, you can see the stage and some of the seats in the theatre…where the passengers and the crew are sitting now."

"Good! Now how about the front entrances to the theater on Decks 5 and 6.? Is there anything we can use as cover to get near those doors?"

"There is an open space, like a small lobby, in front of the main entrance on Deck 5, with no place for anyone to hide. On Deck 6 there are two small entrances, one on each side of the theater," Ernan explained. "Above the entrance on Deck 5 there is no roof until Deck 11. It is all open space above it. The only exceptions are the two small bridges that connect Deck 6 to the upper floor of the theater. There are two stairs, each on each side of the main entrance, that go from the third deck all the way up to the top of the ship. The pirates use those stairs to bring hostages up to the Windjammer Café to eat, so you have to be careful that they are not using them when you are using them. On every landing from Deck 11 to Deck eh…5 there are balconies on each of the stairs where you can look down to the lobby in front of the main entrance of the Stardust Theater."

"So if I went to the sixth deck, I would be able to look down into the theater's main entrance?"

"You would be able to look down from the sixth, the seventh, the eighth…Any of them," Ernan confirmed, nodding.

"Okay. And you said that if we approach the main entrance in the fifth deck, there's nothing we can use as cover until we get to the theater doors?"

Again, Ernan considered the question a few seconds before answering. "No, I don't think so. I mean, there's a large sculpture of a few seagulls flying in the center of the lobby, but it's very…how can I describe it…"

"It's just a few seagulls flying, and nobody can hide behind it?" Stuart suggested.

"Right, right. It has too many large holes between the flying seagulls to hide."

"Gotcha." Stuart turned to the men crowded on the stairs behind him. They were all listening and waiting for his instructions. "You all know what you have to do. Johnson, you take your men and secure the Stardust's entrances on decks 5 and 6. I'll take the entrance in the back of the theatre. Now go to your positions. We move in 2105 hours. That's fifteen minutes from now. If anyone sees you, shoot them. Don't let them get inside the theater to warn the others. And remember to maintain radio silence." He looked around at the tense faces of his men, making certain there were no questions. "Okay. Let's move!"

Chief Petty Officer Paul Pinet looked out of the open cargo door. Until five minutes before, the door had been shut, closed by the Countess of Gilly and Ernan to prevent other terrorists from boarding the *Mardi Gras*. But now that the SEALs were on board, the cargo door had been reopened.

Wearing night vision goggles, Pinet stared straight out onto the dock. Almost as tall as McAllister but of a heftier build, he was cloaked by the shadows of the dark cargo hold, invisible to anyone looking from the outside. His infrared specs worked well, though. And as far as he could see, the portion of the dock stretching in front of him seemed devoid of any kind of activity.

Pinet walked to the open door, stealing a glance from its edge to his left. There, the scene was radically different. The four-story boarding ramp continued to burn unchecked about five hundred feet away. About half a dozen men were spraying it with a hose, but the water seemed to have little effect on the flames. Behind those fighting the conflagration, a crowd of maybe thirty or forty people watched in an unconcerned and almost festive mood. They seemed to be mostly young people, in their late teens or early twenties, and most were unarmed.

"Ready?" Pinet peered at his men. Nobody answered. "Move!" he said, and walked out onto the metal ramp that connected the ship to the wharf. Fifteen men followed, two staying behind to make certain that nobody from the outside sneaked past that door. Rather than running, the men strolled casually out of the ship and into the three-story passenger terminal, guessing correctly that the relative darkness in that part of the dock, and the blinding brightness of the fire would combine to hide them from any prying eyes, and that if any of the terrorists happened to see them, they would confuse the SEALs with some of their own people.

Their relaxed pace changed, however, once the men reached the open corridor under the building. There, some of the SEALs took positions behind the outside columns of the terminal, while a dozen continued to scurry under the outer arched passageway of the structure in the direction of the pier's gate. Every one hundred feet, one of the men would remain behind a column, and search for the armed men that roamed the dock.

By the time the squad reached the terminal's entrance, it had been reduced to eight men. Pinet raised four of his fingers, and pointed towards the interior of the building. Quickly, four of the men split from the group and scampered into the passenger terminal, rifles held in front of their faces, to sweep its three floors. Pinet and the other four SEALs ran to some wooden crates stored close to the dock's gate, and crouched behind them. Two kept watch, while their petty officer sat on the floor and examined his watch.

"Nearly twenty-one zero five hours," he said to himself. Ensign Stuart had ordered him to wait until 2120 hours before he engaged the terrorists on the dock. Stuart did not want to risk alerting the hijackers holding the passengers hostage inside the Stardust Theater with the noise of a prolonged firefight on the pier, even if the odds that the gunfire would be heard inside the distant, air-conditioned theater were slim to nil.

Just then, a man armed with an AK-47 rifle walked out from the guardhouse that controlled the vehicle access into the dock. The man, maybe thirty yards away, lit a flame and cupped his hands around a cigarette. Having lit it, he replaced his lighter in his shirt pocket, and began to stroll towards the entrance of the terminal building, trailing elongated clouds of smoke like a mini steam engine.

The SEAL on Pinet's left tapped him on the shoulder and raised one finger to signal that one man was approaching. Pinet got back to a crouching position and looked between two crates. The man was heading in their direction.

Pinet watched the sentry approach, hoping that he would turn around, debating whether he should intercept him if he walked into the terminal, or let his men inside do it. "Take him out," he whispered after a moment's hesitation to the man next to him, when it became apparent that the guard was heading into the building.

The SEAL keeping watch—a two-year veteran named Pat—aimed his M4A1 rifle at the center of the approaching man's chest and placed his index finger on the trigger. However, as he was about to shoot, a rowdy crowd of about a dozen men and women walked into the pier from the street, heading towards the ship. Pinet noticed that they all wore black bands on their arms, and realized they were some of youths that had been reported patrolling the streets of Old San Juan. They seemed both fascinated and surprised by the fire that they saw in the distance, pointing at the *Mardi Gras* and shouting and hooting incomprehensible remarks.

"Wait!" Pinet hissed to Pat. The SEAL nodded, without taking the armed terrorist out of his rifle sight.

The sentry stopped, distracted by the noise of the new arrivals, and stared at them. One of them asked him what was happening, and some of the others yelled a few wisecracks ("Hey! Did you notice the ship was on fire? Call Gandara—a famous former fire chief—to put the fire out! I'm hungry! How do we get in?"), earning a few choice, curse words from the guard as he examined their black armbands to make certain they were authorized to be there.

The group walked past the armed terrorist, taunting him and eliciting more insults from him, and then headed towards the large crowd already gathered by the fire. One of the new arrivals tossed an empty beer can over his shoulder that landed behind the crates where the SEALs were hiding. The can, colored in gold and bearing the name of "Medalla", bounced off the top of a box and fell close to Pinet. As the group continued its festive march towards the burning ramp, a female voice squealed with equal degrees of indignation and delight, eliciting several male laughs. The sentry took a long, satisfied pull from his cigarette, and watched the new arrivals walk away. Then he renewed his trek towards the terminal.

"Now," the SEAL petty officer said, as the rowdy bunch increased its distance from the wooden crates. "Take him out."

Muffled by a long sound depressor, the rifle spat out two bullets that thudded into the sentry's chest. The guard dropped to the ground instantly, his weapon clattering on the concrete floor. Had any of the revelers ahead of him turned their heads back, they would have clearly seen what had happened less than thirty feet away. However, they were all too preoccupied with the conflagration that was consuming the only apparent means that there was to get on board the ship.

"He's out," Pat reported evenly.

Two of the SEALs ran to the fallen gunman, grabbed him under the arms, and quickly dragged him behind the crates.

Pinet sat down again and looked at the time. *Damn*, he thought, *still ten minutes to 2120!*

Rodriguez was bored. After that morning's initial excitement, when he and Rivera had taken over the ship's bridge, the task of guarding the hostages had quickly turned into a dull and boring chore. Watching the frightened passengers from his seat on the Stardust Theatre's stage had been entertaining for a while. He had enjoyed fixing his eyes on some of the hostages and watching them react. Most squirmed or seemed to wilt under his gaze, terrified that he would pick them out of the crowd for some sinister purpose.

He particularly enjoyed looking at the beautiful women and seeing them blush, pretending that they were not aware of him or looking away in fear. One had been particularly brazen, and directed a saucy smile back at him. That had been her mistake. He had taken her to a cabin and "shown" her several new ways to enjoy sex. She had returned to the theater shaken and more than a little bruised and sore. But that was the price of good sex. *And it had been good.*

He smiled inwardly, remembering the shocked faces of the captain and his first mate when they had found out that Rivera and him were hijacking the *Mardi Gras.* At first, they had not been able to believe it. Then, after he had executed the security officer...*That pale man named Bates...*Their shocked, angry faces had been worth every second of the long year it had taken to prepare for the ship's takeover. He had thought that the first mate, that short, barrel-thick, bearded man that looked like a shrunken Viking, would literally burst from the rage, the veins on his thick neck bulging like stretched chords, his face acquiring a deep purple tinge.

It had been worth every second. To see the all-powerful captain swallow his pride and obey his every bidding...It had been the highlight of his life. Well, that and the time, five years before, when he had shot Fagundo, the police informer that had infiltrated their organization. He had shot off his kneecaps first, then broken his fingers one by one, then shot him in the groin. And before he bled to death, he had placed him in the trunk of a car and set it on fire. It had been a surprisingly gratifying experience. For him, anyway.

He would do the same with whomever had killed two of his men and Lucia. He had not found Lucia's body, but he was certain that she was dead. Otherwise, she would have reported back to him a long time ago. There had not been enough men to conduct a methodical, cabin-by-cabin search, which he was sure would yield the culprits and Lucia. But that would change soon, as more of the FEPIstas entered the ship. Who knows? Maybe Lucia would turn out to be alive. And when he caught the rebel passengers, he would conduct a repeat performance of Fagundo's execution, except he would do it in front of all of the passengers and crew. That would dispel from their minds any thoughts about rebellion or escape, if any such thoughts were still being considered.

Rodriguez's eyes wandered to where the first mate was sitting, right in the center of the first row of seats in the theater. He had forced the stubborn, angry officer to sit there in complete silence, regardless of his bodily needs. The utterance of a single word, or the least separation of his ass from that chair's cushion, he had warned, would mean instant death. He was perversely delighted to notice a dark stain on the man's crotch and the front part of the seat, and wondered how much longer he could go without a drink or food. It would not be long before the man started begging him for mercy. He made it a point to smile when the first officer was looking at him, and received a defiant glare in return. *The impudence of the man!*

An amusing notion, something to lighten his boredom, began to take form in his head. Standing up from his foldout chair, he walked to the edge of the stage and addressed the rebellious prisoner.

"You!" he said. "Folstad, right? I never forget a name. Folstad, come up here!" Rodriguez directed a sideways glance at Captain Clausen, who was sitting on another folding chair on the stage. The captain stirred uneasily.

Folstad crossed his thick arms and refused to move.

Rodriguez laughed once, and whipped out his Beretta from his holster, aiming it at the first officer. Those passengers sitting next to him abandoned their chairs, and the hushed chatter in the theater died out instantly. The two terrorists at the back of the hall and the one on the balcony floor stood up from their chairs and, holding on to their rifles, stared at the stage.

"I will do whatever it is that you want from him," Captain Clausen said, beginning to stand up from his seat.

"You will do nothing, captain, since I haven't asked you to do anything!" Rodriguez retorted in a peevish voice. "It is the services of this gentleman here that I require," he said, airily waiving his gun at Folstad. "Now, are you coming, or do I shoot you?"

For a seemingly eternal moment, the first officer failed to stir. Then ever so slowly, he got up from his seat. Deeply satisfied, Rodriguez turned to the rest of the hostages, and while Folstad ambled on his stiff legs to one of the stairs at the end of the stage, he said in a loud voice, "Ladies and gentlemen! Let's encourage our valiant first officer to get up here with a big round of applause!"

A mild flutter of lukewarm claps responded to the thin terrorist's demand, but Rodriguez began to stroll about the edge of the stage, waving both of his hands up and down, until the applause began to grow in volume and became a soulless ovation. By that time, Folstad had climbed to the stage and begun to approach his tormentor.

Rodriguez made it a point to stare at the first officer's soiled pants and to point and laugh at them as the unwilling applause faltered and died out completely.

"Turn around! Turn around!" he said to the stocky, mortified man, flicking his pistol back and forth in the direction of the crowd. Folstad's face turned deep red as he obeyed, folding his hands over his crotch.

"Ah, ah, ah! No hiding the peepee!" Rodriguez said with glee. "Hands behind your back!"

Humiliated, Folstad drew his hands back.

Rodriguez guffawed, and was joined by some of the sentries standing at the back of the hall. He turned his head briefly towards Clausen, shaking it sadly, and said, "Captain! This man has peed on his pants! Apparently, he has not been potty-trained! These are the people that you allow to handle your ship!"

Folstad stood quietly in front of the passengers, his head cast down.

"That's enough!" the captain said furiously, standing up again.

Rodriguez placed the barrel of his gun on Folstad's left temple. "Sit down, sir," he said with a cold smile. After Clausen obeyed, he turned back to the hostages. "Now ladies and gentlemen! There have been some passengers that have not followed our...safety rules. Right now we are in the process of finding them and they will be brought here in time for your entertainment. But before that, First Mate Folstad is going to give you a demonstration of how to cooperate. I tell him what to do, he cooperates."

Rodriguez cleared his throat and let a fat gob of spit fall onto his right shoe. "As you can see," he said, raising his leg, "my shoe is dirty! Mr. Folstad will now clean it...With his tongue."

Folstad clenched his jaw and the veins in his neck bulged, almost threatening to burst. His eyes filled with involuntary tears, and his arms shook. But he refused to move.

With a look of amusement, Rodriguez's smirk widened to a pleased grin. *Now this was entertainment!* The stubborn first mate had not disappointed him. Placing the gun under Folstad's chin, he leaned forward and said, "This gun will blow your brains out. It would be terrible to soil my shoes with the insides of your head."

"Dag!" Captain Clausen shouted. "For God's sake, do it!"

Folstad directed a fierce stare at his tormentor, and then closed his eyes. For a second, Rodriguez thought he would have to follow up on his threat. But then, the first mate's knees buckled, and he began to kneel.

Rodriguez moved the Beretta away from the prisoner's face, and opened his arms almost assuming a beatific pose, like Christ preparing to dispense a blessing. "You see?" he said in a triumphant voice, resting gently the barrel of his gun on his captive's left shoulder, as the first officer leaned his face to lick off the spit from his shoe. "*This* is coopera—!"

But his voice changed into a shrill squeal of pain, as Folstad suddenly grabbed his testicles with his massive right hand, and squeezed them with all his strength. Desperately, Rodriguez tried to step away from the first mate's iron grasp, firing his gun twice wildly to escape the intense agony to which he was being subjected. However, it only served to create more pressure, and Rodriguez fell on his knees.

One of the bullets missed and became embedded on one of the floor boards of the stage, just a few inches away from Folstad's right leg. The second struck the first mate's left shoulder blade, just as Folstad's left hand grabbed Rodriguez by his right wrist and swerved his gun away.

Despite his wound, Folstad managed to hold on to the terrorist's hand, and both men rolled on the floor. Folstad was up on his knees immediately, however, and releasing his enemy's groin, began to pummel Rodriguez's face with unchecked fury.

By this time, one of the terrorists at the back was hurrying towards the stage, screaming at the rogue hostage to stop or die, trying to make his way through the hosts of terrified passengers sitting on the floor. However, Folstad ignored him and continued to savage the fallen hijacker.

Then a second sentry advancing down another aisle stopped, aimed his rifle at the first mate's broad back, and after a moment's hesitation, fired.

CHAPTER LXIX

El Alacran squatted next to Ruben's limp body and examined it with his flashlight. The fallen man's right eye and cheekbone had been battered into a pulp, and blood was still oozing out from a deep gash on his right temple. There were no apparent gunshot wounds, but then, had there been any shooting, the Macheteros would have probably heard it. Ruben was still alive, but his breath was very shallow. His left eye was half open, but not reacting to the light that Andrade was flashing on it.

"Ruben," El Alacran asked softly, without much hope, just in case the hurt man was conscious, "who did this to you?" However, the downed terrorist did not react.

Andrade stood up and swept the beam of his flashlight around the body. He almost missed the Uzi sub machinegun, wedged under Ruben's back. Stepping over the body, he picked it up, and casually tossed it at Luis, who stood closest to him. "Here. Keep it. I have one already."

He shone his light further into the tunnel, where Andres had stationed himself in case any of the other hostages approached them, the latter's baldpate reflecting part of the glare.

They had followed the other tunnel for twenty minutes before they had come to a dead end, where the roof of the corridor had actually caved in, blocking any further progress. In a rare display of emotion, Andrade had kicked the mound of earth and bricks, shouting, "I should have listened to my instincts!" and run back towards the bifurcated entrance.

When they had gotten there, they had not found Ruben. Andrade had hesitated, wondering if his missing comrade had headed back to the exit of the tunnel, or if for some unexplained reason he had decided to explore on his own the other corridor. He concluded that it had to have been the latter. Ruben would not have dared to abandon his post. Something must have drawn him to enter into the other tunnel.

Just as El Alacran was about to act on his hunch, he had heard some distant shouts coming from the unexplored corridor. Not wasting another second, he had dashed into the left hand entrance, followed by the others. Along the way, the shouting died down, but periodically they listened to the distant sounds of banging, coming from up ahead. Five minutes later, they had stumbled upon the missing Machetero's body.

"He was ambushed," El Alacran stated with the same detached tone as if he had been referring to the state of the weather. "Those noises we've been hearing, they must have drawn Ruben here. Or maybe he was trying to be a hero, who knows. The thing is that somebody that he did not see ambushed him. Probably hid right there," he directed his flashlight's beam to a niche in the wall located very near to where the body lay. "It must have been this Maestes person. Which is not a bad thing," he reflected, almost as an afterthought. "If Maestes, or any of the other hostages were waiting here, it means that they have no way of getting out. If not, they would have beat the hell out of here a long time ago, don't you think so, Luis?" he asked his companion.

"It sounds logical," the tall Machetero answered. He was leaning forward, in order not to bump his head on the ceiling.

"Of course it does," El Alacran confirmed cheerfully. "So now it's our turn to find them and kill them."

The hole on the ceiling had grown to a width of five bricks, wide enough for the children and maybe some of the women to crawl through. With two more rows knocked out, there would be enough space for all of them to escape.

Lucas was drenched in sweat, his upraised arms and neck feeling like one continuous sore. Twice he had been forced to rest in order to catch his breath. Pietrantoni had tried to help him, but his progress had been too slow and erratic. After only knocking out five bricks in so many minutes, Lucas had taken over, claiming that he had developed a "knack" for it.

It was not an ill boast. In a bombardment of blows, the ex-Ranger tore fiercely into the bricked ceiling, sending pieces of debris flying all around him and forcing the others to stay at a safe distance. It had been very noisy and dusty, but there had been progress.

The others had built a barricade at the entrance of the circular hall, leaving a narrow space for Picon to squeeze through when he returned. It consisted of two stacks of barrels that only left uncovered the narrow arch of the tunnel's curved ceiling, near the hall's entrance. On the upper row, Pietrantoni and Arizmendi had left three small slits open through which, if the necessity arose, the hostages could shoot at the Macheteros.

Piling up the barrels had been a tough and arduous task for Arizmendi and Pietrantoni, which had sometimes required the help of the women. But at the end of their work, they had stood admiringly besides it, and Double A had dubbed their tiny barricade "Fort Olive Oil", in honor of the contents in the wooden casks.

It had been Patria who had alerted the rest about Picon's return. The bodyguard described to the others his unexpected encounter with the terrorist, and warned them about the Macheteros' impending approach, while La Fortaleza's housekeeper stood by one of the barricade's slits and kept an uneasy watch over the dark void beyond.

The huddled group had listened to Picon without interrupting, most of them too scared to say anything. Lucas had briefly stopped working and sat on top of the highest barrel, trying to catch his breath and listening, his feet dangling to one side. He had made a lot of progress opening a gap through the locked trapdoor, but he estimated that it would still require ten to fifteen more minutes before the hole became wide enough for the adults to fit through.

Also, more wooden casks would have to be added to increase the height of their makeshift ladder. Right now, the ceiling was separated from the top of the highest barrel by a height equivalent to Lucas' chin. The ex-Ranger could easily pull himself up into the chamber above them, but it would be very difficult for the women and children, and even the shorter Double A to do so.

"I lost my Uzi in the fight," Picon confessed guiltily. "I tried to look for it but couldn't find it, and then I saw the other Macheteros coming and had to leave. I lost Patria's phone too," he added, turning his head to where the housekeeper was keeping her watch.

"That's okay, Picon," the old lady said with maternal pleasantness. "I'll get another."

"I managed to take this, though," the bodyguard said, raising up the AK-47 rifle he had snatched from the terrorist. "But I only have the ammunition clip that's attached to it."

"We'll have to save our ammunition," Lucas said to him. "Do you know how to set the rifle for single action fire?"

The bodyguard looked at him uncertainly.

"Hand me the rifle." Lucas extended his arms and received the AK-47 from Picon. He detached the ammunition clip, and hunching down to catch the glow of the light held by Nereida, examined it. "The magazine seems to be full, which means you have about forty rounds to fire." He took the rifle in one of his hands and showed it to Picon. "See this here?" he asked, pointing at a lever slightly shorter than a finger. "This is the safety and fire selector. When it's up, it's locked. When it is centered, like it is right now...Jesus," he said with surprise, "the guy you fought had this set on the multi-fire mode! It's a miracle you both didn't get killed. Anyway, center is for multiple fire. When the lever is down, that's the single fire selector. The rifle will fire one round at a time. You'll want to keep it that way to save your ammo."

The bodyguard nodded as he received the rifle back from Lucas.

"You'll also want to have this," Lucas continued saying, unbuckling the cowboy-style gun belt he had captured from Tino, and handing it, with one of its ivory-handled revolvers, to Picon. "This is a 357 Magnum revolver. It's a five shooter. The gun belt holds about thirty bullets, enough for a decent gunfight. You know how to load it, right?"

"Yes," the bodyguard said.

"You can use it when your rifle runs out of ammo."

Picon accepted it and began to fasten the belt around his waist. "Thank you. I'd better get back to the barricade, although God help the Machetero that dares to tangle with Patria."

The housekeeper laughed gleefully.

"I have the other gun," Pietrantoni said, patting the handle of Tino's other revolver, which he had tucked under his belt.

"If you don't mind, Mr. Governor, I would rather have you and Mr. Arizmendi working on improving the way to get up here," Lucas said, pointing at the hole in the ceiling. "We're going to need more barrels for the ladies to climb up."

Pietrantoni did not hesitate. "Of course. Alberto," he said, addressing Double A by his first name, "will you help me?" He began to walk away before the Secretary of State could answer.

Arizmendi followed him obediently. "Okay," he grumbled in mock irritation, "but for this, you're going to have to start paying me overtime..."

During the conversation, Nereida had continued to illuminate the trapdoor with Arizmendi's pocket lantern—their only source of light—and the visibility in the large room was dim at best and nearly coal-black at the curved edges of the hall. To make matters worse, the glow of the flashlight was beginning to fade as its battery power, strained to the maximum, was running out. They all had to hurry, before they were forced to grope their way around on their hands and knees.

Lucas renewed his raucous hammering of the ceiling, replacing his fear of being overhead with the pressing need to create a new route of escape before the Macheteros got there. Below him, Pietrantoni and Arizmendi began to accumulate the wooden drums necessary to increase the height of the improvised ladder, rolling them on their sides, then pulling them upright next to where Lucas worked, all the time trying to duck the debris falling from the ceiling.

They had barely managed to bring in their third barrel, however, when a half dozen detonations erupted from the blocked corridor, briefly illuminating with bright, strobe-light like flashes the impenetrable murkiness that shrouded the tunnel. Several of the shots thudded into the thick-walled caskets that formed the barrier at the entrance of the hall, but one whizzed through the narrow, curved gap that existed between the piled-up barrels and the roof of the tunnel, ricocheting from the hall's ceiling and wall before striking the shaft of one of the ancient lances. Some of the women screamed, while Nereida knelt and embraced both of the children.

"Everybody down!" Lucas and Picon shouted almost simultaneously. The ex-Ranger jumped from the barrel that he was using as a platform and grabbed Nereida's small flashlight. He ran to the barricade, followed by the Governor and Arizmendi, the latter holding a sword. Had the moment not been so dangerous, he would have looked hilariously funny, a short, slightly pot-belied bureaucrat dressed in elegant business pants and a undershirt, holding on to the ancient blade, his face set with grim determination.

A gurgling, trickling noise coming from the barrels mixed with the echo of liquid splattering on the stone floor. Lucas felt his nostrils fill with an acrid, pungent smell and realized that some of the ancient oil stored in the wooden drums was spilling out through the newly created bullet holes.

"I counted four men from the gun flashes, but there may be more," Picon whispered. "Maybe fifty feet away. I think they may have seen the glow from the flashlight, maybe even the outline of the barricade, and decided to test us."

Lucas turned to the Governor. "The hole I was working on should be wide enough for us to squeeze through. If not, you'll have to finish the job. Get the women and children together and start getting them up. Picon and I will keep the Macheteros busy."

"Arizmendi can do that. I can help here."

"No!" Lucas answered, surprising himself by the vehemence of his response. "Look," he said in a more moderate tone, "you can help more by organizing the—"

He stopped in mid sentence, as a shout from the corridor interrupted him. It was a high-pitched voice, the voice of a small man. And yet, it carried easily over the hostages' barricade, conveying a tone of amusement and contempt.

"Hey, Pietrantoni, are you there?" it said.

The Governor directed a scared look at Lucas.

"El Alacran," he whispered.

"Go!" Lucas hissed at him. "We can't lose any more time."

"Pietrantoni! I know you're in there," the man in the corridor called out in a singsong voice. *"Come out, come out, wherever you are..."*

"Go!" Lucas insisted. "Please!"

"Roberto," Arizmendi said, addressing the Governor by his first name and pulling him by the arm, "Alfaro is right. Think of the women and the children, of Nereida and Francisco. They *need* us."

Reluctantly, Pietrantoni let himself be led towards the others.

"What was all that racket you were making in there anyway?" Andrade asked.

"Roaches!" Lucas answered. "We were killing roaches!"

"They must be very big roaches," the man in the tunnel commented, provoking the laughter of some of the other invisible men lurking in the dark passageway.

"What can I say? They were big."

"No, my friend, I think you were trying to dig your way out of there, weren't you?"

"If we were, it didn't work, did it? We're still here," Lucas responded in a tired voice.

"What did you expect? To find a magic exit after this had been buried for several centuries? Not likely."

Lucas stared through one of the barricade's slits into the corridor, trying to get a glimpse of the speaker. He could see nothing. "What do you want?" he shouted.

"What do I want? What do I want? What do you think I want?" the voice asked back, brimming with irony. *"I want the Governor to walk out and join us, is what I want!"*

"Why would he ever do that?" Lucas said, prompting a chuckle from Picon.

"Why indeed?" the man in the corridor answered, unfazed. *"I am trying to be reasonable, I guess. If you force us to go in, we kill everyone. If you give us the Governor, we'll let the rest of you go. How's that?"*

Lucas looked back towards the improvised ladder. Pietrantoni had placed Arizmendi's tiny pocket light on the edge of a barrel, pointing its decaying flicker of light in that direction. The weak beam revealed the outline of several bodies already starting to climb over the wooden casks, a taller figure—undoubtedly that of the Governor—helping a smaller body to get up. Thankfully, the Macheteros could not see what was happening.

"You'll have to give us fifteen minutes to discuss your proposal," Lucas shouted back at El Alacran.

"Fifteen minutes! What will you do with all that time? There's nothing to think about! I'll give you five and count yourself lucky. But first, I need to

verify that the Governor is there with you," the high-pitched voice said. *"I wouldn't want him to disappear while I'm talking to you."*

"I'm here," the Governor answered wearily from the center of the hall, where he had begun to climb the barrels.

"Is that you, Mr. Governor?" the Machetero shouted back.

"You should know my voice. I know yours," Pietrantoni answered.

"You do indeed, you do indeed," the man in the tunnel confirmed in a pleased tone. *"Okay, you have five minutes, and then we're coming for you."*

"Ten minutes!" Lucas pleaded. "It's not as if we're going anywhere." He and Picon exchanged a silent smile.

Andrade chortled. *"No, I believe you're stuck in there...Who is this anyway? Is that you, Maestes?"*

It took a moment for Lucas to register the name. "Yes..." he answered tentatively. "And you must be El Alacran."

A mirthless, rasping laughter confirmed Lucas' statement. The ex-Ranger felt his throat tighten with fear. It was Mogadishu, all over again. Somehow, he had managed to wander from his safe jewelry store job to the awful, terrifying nightmare that he thought he had escaped several years ago.

"Guilty as charged!" the voice in the corridor said with great gusto. *"So at last I get to meet you. You've caused us a great deal of trouble today!"*

"Yeah," Lucas replied candidly. "If it's any consolation, it wasn't my intention to do so."

El Alacran cackled with glee. *"Really! I'd hate to see what you can do when you set your mind to it!"* Andrade said, letting his skepticism creep into his voice. *"Come on! Who are you fooling? You know as well as I that San Miguel and you had all of this planned a long time ago."*

"San Mi-who?" It behooved Lucas to engage the Machetero leader in as long a conversation as he could. The more time they spent talking, the more time the others would have to escape. However, his curiosity was tweaked by the terrorist's comment.

"You're denying that you know San Miguel? The Archangel of Doom?" El Alacran tried to sound sarcastic, but his voice evinced a hint of incredulous interest.

Someone tapped Lucas hard on the shoulder. He was so concentrated in the conversation that he nearly jumped in surprise. He looked back and saw that it was Arizmendi, handing him something.

"Here!" Double A said. "I found this in one of my pockets! It's my lighter. You may need it if the flashlight goes off."

Lucas nodded absently, and watched the small, animated man scamper back to the ladder of barrels. "I don't know what you're talking about," he said to El Alacran.

"You sound like a good liar, Maestes...If that is your real name," the Machetero said with a certain degree of impatience. *"But we digress from our main topic of discussion. Is Pietrantoni coming out, or do we go in to find him?"*

"I thought we had five minutes to decide!" Lucas protested.

"That's before I found out that you were in there. Anyway, I can't see my watch."

"It is convenient for you to give us more time, so that we can talk things over. If you try to take this place by force, we'll shoot you down."

El Alacran cackled again.

"Maybe! It's possible that you'll kill some of us, but in the end, believe me, we'll get you!"

For a long moment nobody spoke, only the noise of the oil trickling out from some of the barrels disturbing peace in the long forgotten tunnel. Lucas was grateful for the liquid splatter; it helped to mask the hushed activity of the hostages behind the barricade. He looked at the object that Arizmendi had handed to him, and saw that is was a cylindrical, yellow butane lighter.

"Well?" Andrade asked impatiently.

Lucas thought desperately for a way to stall, but could think of nothing. Looking back, he thought he saw one of the women squeezing through the hole, but there were still at least four people still waiting below.

"Is that how much you value the lives of your men?" he blurted out impulsively. "They're not worth a wait of five more minutes?"

Lucas waited for an angry reply but got none. Apparently, he had struck a nerve.

"My men are more intelligent than that. They know when somebody is trying to play on their sympathies," El Alacran responded quietly, but Lucas sensed a certain hesitation in his voice.

"You would be better off with stupid men," Lucas replied. "Men who don't realize how little you care about them. Five minutes! That's all I'm asking to talk to the Governor and make a decision. Are they not worth that?" he shouted, his voice echoing in the long passageway.

Andrade snickered derisively. *"Who are you?"* he asked, not expecting an answer. Then he added, in a weary voice, *"Let no one say that El Alacran's men are not worth a five minutes' wait. Go talk to Pietrantoni! But Maestes, if I have to come in after him, I will personally cut your balls off."*

The "ladder" that rose to the trapdoor in the ceiling basically consisted of four "steps" or levels, the first step being the top of a wooden chest, the second step being the top of the first barrel, the third the top of two barrels—one piled over the other—and the final level being the top of three piled up barrels. To facilitate the steep scaling and give the climbers a wider base, they had made two parallel rows of steps, each next to the other, which could accommodate more than one person at a time.

The Governor had been the first to go up, stopping at the third level. Because of his height, he had been unable to stand completely upright, leaning forward, his neck and back grazing the curved ceiling. Ahead of him loomed the hole in the trapdoor that Lucas had hammered open, less than three feet above the top of the two uppermost barrels.

Pietrantoni extended his hand and helped Alfredo climb next to him. Others were moving up behind him. "Wait here," he said to the boy softly. "I'm going to take a look up there."

Alfredo had nodded nervously without saying a word. Turning, the Governor sat on one of the two uppermost wooden casks, his chest doubled over his knees. Then, ever so slowly, he twisted his body and slipped his torso past the torn boards, through the layer of bricks, and past the broken stone that had covered the bricks, until his head popped up on the other side.

He thought it was as dark as the hall below him—he could see nothing in front of him—until he looked over his shoulder and caught a fleeting glimpse of what seemed to be a distant, arched door, outlined by a very faint, silvery luminescence. He did not know what to make of it; so unreal and ethereal it appeared to be. For a moment he was confused, uncertain if what he was seeing was in fact a portal or a window, since it was located at a much higher level than the floor. Then, as his eyes grew accustomed to the room, he realized that the glow came from a gate located at the upper end of a rising incline or ramp, made partially visible by a pale, sickly glow that filtered from the outside.

The dank smell of seawater assailed his nostrils. As if to confirm his perception, he heard what seemed to be the muted noise of crashing waves a long, long distance away. *Or was that the remote echo of the wind, rushing through the lonely walls of their unknown refuge?* Either prospect excited him. It meant they had found a way out of their nightmarish escape route. With his heart pounding, he slipped back into the hole.

"All right, Alfredo," he whispered, guiding the boy to the third level. "Time to be brave. I'll help you crawl through. When you get to the other side, wait for the others there, okay?"

"Yes," the boy answered with grim determination. "What about my uncle?" he asked, looking down towards the barricade, unable to hide his anguish.

"Don't worry, he'll be fine. He knows what he's doing, and I'll make sure that he gets up here," Pietrantoni answered, gently slapping the boy's shoulder. "I promise you that we won't leave him behind."

Helped by the Governor, Alfredo stood up on the highest barrel, half of his body disappearing into the ceiling. Then one of his legs went up, and with a push from Pietrantoni, he went through.

Francisco came next. He stopped to embrace his father. "I love you, dad," he said, his voice breaking up with grief.

"I'll follow you soon," the Governor promised. "If I shout for you to run, you run as fast as you can with Nereida and Alfredo. You run towards the light, understand?"

The boy nodded, overcome with emotion, and embraced his father once more.

"Go. Go now," Pietrantoni said, gently leading him through the gap.

Maria, the cook's assistant, followed. Although Pietrantoni could hardly see her, he could feel her arms shaking. The Governor repeated his instructions to her, and then helped her up. She scrambled up with surprising agility, her ghostly outline quickly vanishing from sight.

Nereida came next. Even in the dim light, and after a day of unending terrors, she seemed calm and steady. For a moment, the Governor felt an irrational impulse to do what he had not dared to do for years, and tell her that he loved her, but his strict sense of correctness overruled his emotions.

"Are you all right?" he asked her with just the right degree of concern.

"Yes," she answered breathlessly, "but Patria is having trouble getting up here."

Pietrantoni glanced down and saw the older woman struggling to get to the second barrel, pushed from behind by a hassled Arizmendi, all semblance of modesty lost. Patria kept looking back at him, her expression a mixture of embarrassment and apologetic regret. The Governor barely suppressed a smile.

"There seems to be an exit in the chamber above," he said to Nereida. "Should anything happen, lead the others out."

"Nothing will happen," she assured him hurriedly, as if to dispel immediately any possibility that anything bad would happen, urgently searching and finding his hands.

"Nereida..." Pietrantoni began to say, but stopped.

"I know," she answered, "I love you too." Not saying another word, she stood up and squeezed through the hole.

Still stunned by her words, Pietrantoni saw one of Patria's hands catch the rim of the barrel where Nereida had been, and he heard Double A groan below her as he shoved her upwards by her behind. The Governor grabbed his housekeeper by the arm and helped her move up.

Panting, Patria rested when she reached the third barrel, sitting heavily on its lid. "Please forgive me, Mr. Governor," she said between breaths. "Old age is unrelenting. Twenty years ago, even ten, I might have climbed this on my own, but not any more. I'm afraid my time is running as short as my breath."

"Nonsense, Patria. You still have a few governors to serve."

The old housekeeper laughed. "I will settle for the time that you're there." She looked up at the hole in the ceiling and her expression changed. "I don't think that I can fit through there," she said in a worried tone.

Pietrantoni followed her gaze and then returned his eyes to her. She was right. It would be a very tight fit. Not only was Patria a heavyset woman, but a very buxom lady.

"Let's try it," he said.

Slowly, holding on to the Governor, she slid her head and upraised hands past the trapdoor but stopped a second later. "I can't," she said, still pushing upwards, and then with a panic in her voice said to someone above her, "Don't pull me!"

Pietrantoni heard Nereida's voice say from above, "Francisco, Alfredo, don't pull her arms."

"I'm stuck!" Patria said. "I can't move up or down!"

"It's okay," Pietrantoni whispered to her. "I'll help you." Turning to Arizmendi, he said. "Find the hammer and the crowbar. We've got to widen the hole."

The Secretary of State jumped down from the wooden cask where he was waiting and briefly searched the floor, coming up with the tools that his friend had requested. Pietrantoni took them and placed the pointy end of the crow bar under the grey mortar that held together the bricks.

"Take a deep breath," he said to Patria, and clenching his jaw, began to hammer away.

CHAPTER LXX

Twenty minutes, and the acneed guard had not returned. Five times Johnny had stood up, opened the conference room's door, and stared outside into the corridor. On every occasion, no one had been there.

He had been duped, he concluded furiously. That little, conniving, human zit had taken advantage of his good nature and left him there, stuck with the hostages. The whole revolution was on the point of collapse, hamstrung by the disappearance of its top brass, and he—the only remaining leader of the operation—had been effectively taken out of the action by that idiot guard!

He could not wait any longer. He would call Yajaira and ask her to come here and watch the hostages until he could send somebody else to take her place. And that brunette bitch hostage, who had humiliated him in front of the others, would see what a beautiful and sexy woman *really* looked like, he thought irrationally. He began to reach for his cell phone in his right pants pocket, but just then, the conference room's door opened abruptly.

"It's about time that you—" Johnny began to say angrily, but stopped when he noticed it was El Cano, the man who had warned the others in the lobby about the sneak assault by the American special forces. His attitude had changed, though. He seemed confused, and stared wildly about him, as if expecting for something to happen at any moment.

"What is it?" Johnny asked him, alarmed.

El Cano's eyes focused on the FEPI leader, and he finally spoke. "All of the prisoners must come with me at once!" he said in a loud voice, not so much to Johnny as to the others inside the room. As he spoke, he waved his automatic rifle in their direction in a threatening fashion. "Get up! All of you!" he shouted.

"What *is* it?" Johnny insisted. "What is happening out there?"

The man stared at him as if he were some sort of hindrance. He grabbed Johnny by the arm and pulled him out of the conference room. "I didn't want to say this in front of the others, but we were ambushed," he said in a grave tone.

"Ambushed! By whom?"

"The men in the ballroom!" he replied, as if his answer was clearly evident.

"How could they ambush you?" Johnny asked with incredulity. "They were inside of the hall! Did more soldiers come? Did they have more powerful weapons?"

El Cano did not reply, trying to make his way back into the room, but Johnny stepped in front of him, his face demanding some answers. The edgy Machetero glared at him, and shook his head.

"Listen," he said in an angry, and what Johnny sensed was a defensive tone, "we just lost a *lot* of men. I don't have time to give you a blow-by-blow account of what happened. I have to get back, and I have to bring back with me the people in the conference room."

"Why?" Johnny did not like where the conversation was heading.

"We're using these hostages to get to the others. We're going to use them as shields to get into the ballroom."

Johnny's face grew pale. It was the same nightmare, happening all over again.

"Is Calderon on board with this?" he asked El Cano.

"Calderon, the foreigner? He doesn't know. But he has nothing to say about this."

"How about Cacho...San Miguel?" Johnny was groping for some kind of support.

"We haven't found either of them. But you know both of them had no problems in using this tactic," El Cano answered impatiently, and edged his way around Johnny Ray to get inside.

"But what if they don't give up?" Johnny asked in a fierce whisper, loud enough to be overheard by the people inside the room.

El Cano looked at them briefly, counting them. Then he turned his attention back to Johnny. "We may have to kill one or two of them, but in the end, they will give in." He pointed his rifle at the hostages, and shouted, "Get up!"

The prisoners did not stir. They had heard the end of the conversation between the two terrorists and refused to obey.

"I said move!" El Cano yelled at them angrily. "Or I swear by God I'll shoot all of you here!"

"No," Johnny said without thinking.

"What?" El Cano asked with apparent confusion, casting him a sideways glance as he continued to watch the hostages.

"I said no." Johnny raised his AK-47 and aimed it at his counterpart, who stared at him with dumbfounded surprise. "This ends here."

"Are you crazy?" the young Machetero asked him.

"No more killings!" Johnny replied firmly, and when El Cano ignored him and took a step towards the hostages, he prodded the nervous terrorist in the back with the tip of his rifle. "Stay away from the prisoners," he warned him. "Just drop your weapon and leave."

El Cano seemed to hesitate, but then with a quick movement grabbed Johnny's rifle by its barrel and tried to wrestle it away. His attack took Johnny by surprise and made him stumble backwards. But he held on to his weapon, dragging El Cano with him. The two struggling men fell on top of the busty brunette and the teenaged girl, who screamed and tried to get out of the way. The gray haired man sitting on the floor crawled under the table to intervene, but a wild swing of the rifle caught him on the chin and he staggered back. However, it galvanized the other prisoners into action. Several hands reached out and grabbed El Cano by his arms, legs, and neck, pinning him to the ground. Johnny was able to snatch the rifle away, and he stood up, backing away to the room's door.

The Machetero began to scream for help, but the middle aged butch woman covered his mouth with her hand. Johnny watched without uttering a word. Nervously, all of the hostages looked at him.

For a long moment, no one exchanged a word. Then Johnny said, "Tie him up, cover his mouth. Hurry!"

A frantic search for something to bind El Cano yielded nothing until the gray haired man, his right cheek bearing a deep purple mark where the rifle had struck him, disconnected a floor lamp and ripped off its cord, doing the same with a decorative table light propped on the storage cabinet. He bound El Cano's hands and feet tightly, and then the priest wrapped some of the excess bandages that had been used to dress the crew-cut man's wound around his mouth.

All attention returned to Johnny, who had observed the entire process without moving.

"I'm going to let you go—" he began, but was interrupted by enthusiastic applause and cheers from his listeners. "Shhhhhh..." he said gently, smiling despite himself. He felt intense relief, as if a terrible cloud had been removed from his soul. "We must be very quiet, and you must do exactly as I say."

"My family...my wife and baby daughter...what about them?" the wounded man asked. As he did so, he tried to sit up on the edge of the table, and the half-shaven man and the shifty-eyed politician instantly moved to help steady him.

Johnny shook his head emphatically. "That is out of my hands," he responded. "But you will be helping them if the...armed people here can't use you to get to them."

Several of the hostages nodded or voiced their agreement, and even the wounded man kept a resigned silence.

"And I promise you," Johnny added, "that after get you out I will return to see if I can stop the shooting." He was surprised to realize that he truly meant it, and resolved that whatever happened, he would follow through on his promise. Maybe he could enlist the help of Yajaira and Lebron. "Can you walk?" he asked the wounded man.

In response, the man slid off the table and gingerly moved towards the door, taking short steps whenever he placed pressure on the injured leg.

"Good! Will you two help him?" he said to the two men who had aided him to get up. They obliged immediately, each placing one of the arms of the wounded man over their shoulders.

"Now fast, before someone else comes here," he said. As he spoke, he noticed that El Cano had his eyes turned towards him and was listening intently. "Plug his ears with some of those Kleenex tissues, please," he said to no one in particular, pointing to a box of soft tissue paper on the cabinet's top.

The elderly priest flicked off one tissue, tore it in half, and knelt next to prostrate man. "Forgive me, my son," the minister said gently, "as I forgive you." He twisted each half of the tissue into a compact ball and pushed one inside each ear.

Johnny gestured to the hostages to approach, and they huddled around him. "You will form up in a line and follow my directions. I will be walking next to you, pointing my rifle at you. If we are stopped, let me do the talking and just look as angry and miserable as you did when I walked in here a while ago. Understood?"

Several in the group smiled nervously. The gray haired man and the crew-cut hostage maintained a somber silence.

"Where are you going to take us?" the brunette asked Johnny, and he was intensely gratified to note that for the first time, she addressed him with more than a hint of sympathy. *She was truly beautiful,* he thought, feeling something stir within him. *A shame he would not be able to see her again.*

"We're going to avoid the lobby. There's too many people there," he replied. "Instead, we'll take the back way through the pool area. There may be some guards there, but I'll explain to them that Cach...that the head of the Macheteros ordered me to transfer you to Old San Juan, for a special operation. Most of them know me," he assured them, unable to avoid taking a swift look at the brunette, "so there shouldn't be any problem. I will take you down to the beach, and from there to the Normandie Hotel." He noticed the blank stare of the hostages. "You know, the hotel that's not in operation right now, outside of the grounds of the Grand Laguna. From there you're on your own. Stay out of sight. There are patrols roaming the streets, and there are no police. The entire area, from the lagoon to Old San Juan, is under our control."

"Lord in Heaven," the priest muttered.

"Try to make it to one of the residential buildings, the condominiums, or one of the houses you see along the way. You will find them across the park. Just be careful when you cross any of the avenues, and make sure there are no lookouts or patrols approaching. I think..." he admitted ruefully, more to himself than to the others, "that you will find many people willing to help you." He stared at the faces that surrounded him. He sensed their fear, and felt sorry for them. "Don't worry," he reassured them, "everything will be all right." He looked at the priest. "Father, I'm not a very religious person, but...it wouldn't hurt if you gave us your blessing?"

The old priest raised both of his hands and closed his eyes, while everybody else bowed their heads. "Lord," he whispered, "please protect these good people who have had to endure so much evil on this day, and bring them and their families safely out of this place. And especially bless this young man whom you have brought out of nowhere to deliver us, and let him be your instrument for good. In the name of the Father, the Son, and the Holy Spirit."

"Amen," the others responded in unison.

"Let's go," Johnny said, and the hostages shuffled into a crowded line.

Like the ripples of a rising black tide, Group Charlie spread with quiet efficiency over the eastern grounds of the Grand Laguna Hotel. Looking like strange beaked birds, the SEALs moved through the shadows holding their weapons—HK-417 assault rifles and HK-MP5 sub machineguns—in front of their faces, using as cover the low shrubs, trees, and fences fringing the entrance to the Grand Laguna Hotel's lobby.

Close to the lobby's entrance ramp stood the ruins of an old Spanish guard post, a relic from the old defenses that had ringed the city in ancient times, and which now formed part of the landscape around the hotel. Large bougainvilleas bursting with bright red flowers flanked each side of the guardhouse, and would have swallowed it had not the hotel's gardeners kept them at bay. It was here where Commander McAllister and three other SEALs stopped, taking advantage of the cover that the shrubs and the ruins provided. One of the men took a position inside the sentry post, sweeping with his infrared telescopic lens the area of the long carport that led to the lobby. The two other men set up a defensive perimeter around their leader.

It had been a long, dark swim to the beach where the SEALs had landed. Not much more than a narrow strip of yellow sand and rocks, the beach came to an abrupt end at the foot of the almost vertical cliffs that extended for several miles, from a short distance beyond the Grand Laguna Hotel to the walls of Old San Juan. As they closed the shore, the SEALs had been forced to negotiate very shallow underwater reefs, but except for a few scrapes and a deep cut of one of the men's thighs, the forty men had managed to do extremely well.

Under the long shadows of the cliffs, they had quickly discarded their flippers and their UBA's—large, pursed shaped underwater breathing apparatus that they wore strapped to their chests and which expelled no bubbles—and begun their eastward trek towards the hotel, following the contours of the beach. They had been apprehensive about being spotted from above by any unseen sentries, but the satellite intelligence photographs and the information that the police had gathered—showing no enemy surveillance except for the random roving trucks of armed men— had held up remarkably well. Except for the dark tufts of wild weeds and the fronds from the palm trees, they had perceived no movement or activity on top of the steep crags.

Sticking as close as possible to the bottom of the cliffs, the sand crunching under their boots, the men from Group Charlie had swiftly covered the length of the beach, and from there edged the abandoned tennis courts and structures of the old Navy Officers' Club. Here, the cliffs had begun to lose their height until they had become level with the beach, and the grounds of the abandoned club had given way to an enormous open parking area for the vehicles that visited the public beach beyond.

Preceded by a four-man reconnaissance squad, the SEALs had continued moving at a quick pace along the edge of the beach, which was partially separated from the parking lot by the bent trunks and wide leaves of sea grape plants and scores of coconut trees that grew along the shore. Afterwards, the men had been forced to cross the wide-open terrain of the Third Millennium Park, past an elevated walkway that led to nowhere, past giant, metallic light posts partially rusted by the salt of the sea, past a baseball field and a jogging track, but always protected by the watchful eyes of the recon patrol. To any sentry that came upon the advancing SEALs, the sudden appearance of forty dark, armed-to-the-teeth figures sprinting through the empty, open space would have been a daunting, frightening experience that would probably have caused him to hide, rather than shoot or raise the alarm. However, not once had the advancing men come across another human being, friend or foe.

Finally, Group Charlie had reached El Escambron, a small beach separated from the Grand Laguna's beach by a string of reefs and a low concrete wall. In the 1930s, 40s, and 50s—long before the Grand Laguna had been built—El Escambron Beach Club had been *the* meeting place for San Juan's social elite, where the toast of town met to listen and dance to the sound of romantic crooners and big band music under the stars. It had long since faded into oblivion, however, the clubhouse abandoned and later demolished as the big hotels of San Juan, with their lavish nightclubs and casinos, had lured away the new generations. Now only the beach remained, along with a modest stand that served hamburgers and hot dogs to the random visitors that wandered into that corner of the Third Millennium Park.

Here, the SEALs had stopped and reassembled. Ensign Aguirre and eleven other men had separated from the main group, and followed the coast, jumping over the concrete wall that separated El Escambron from the Grand Laguna's beach area. The rest had advanced through the side parking area of the closed Normandie Hotel, and penetrated the Grand Laguna's western grounds by breaching the fence that separated the hotel's tennis courts from the outside world.

McAllister had feared that the front gardens of the hotel would be crawling with terrorist sentries. However, no one had challenged the SEALs' progress. Group Charlie had moved unopposed into the hotel grounds, extending its line from the tennis courts to the road that led to the reception area. It was almost as if the terrorists had withdrawn from the hotel, as if they had grown tired of the whole affair and just left.

Of course, it could also be a trap…

The SEAL commander retrieved from a small watertight case a set of binoculars and inspected through the bushes the view before him. To his surprise, he only picked out one man, leaning with a bored expression against one of the receiving area's columns. However, he could not see into the lobby itself. He spoke into the thin mouthpiece protruding over his mouth.

"Platoons, report," he whispered.

"Platoon One approaching Red Lobster. Should be in position in two minutes," McAllister's earpiece crackled to life. He recognized the voice speaking as that of Ensign Aguirre, who had skirted the small Grand Laguna beach and was leading his squad of eleven men towards the pool grounds. Five areas in the hotel had been designated with code names, in case the SEALs were overheard or their transmissions intercepted. The

pool area was "Red Lobster", the lobby "Cantina", the convention area "Party City", the hotel's parking building "Gasoline Alley", and the entrance to the hotel "Grand Central".

"Platoon Two, in position," a high pitched voice reported, belonging to Petty Officer Chow. Born in Shanghai, Chow had only become a U.S. citizen the year before, but of all of McAllister's non-commissioned officers, he was the smartest and most promising recruit. *"We have acquired two targets at Grand Central."*

Two! The number surprised McAllister, who had only been able to detect one sentry. *Were the terrorists so thinly spread?* He looked again through his binoculars, as he continued to receive reports from his men. *"Platoon Four, we have moved into Gasoline Alley. One target acquired."* The deep voice of the man reporting was undeniably that of chief petty officer Mike Flanagan, a twelve year SEAL veteran. Only Platoon Three, being McAllister's own unit, had failed to report.

McAllister felt a tap on his shoulder, and looked at the man crouching next to him. The latter pointed ahead of them, to the left. The SEAL commander focused his binoculars on the area to which his subordinate had pointed, and after a few seconds spotted the object of his attention.

Damn, McAllister thought to himself as he glimpsed at the terrorist he had missed. He was hidden in the shadows, close to a large wire cage that held two large parrots. How could he have been so careless?

Aguirre came back on the radio. *"Platoon One is in position. Red Lobster seems to be clear."*

No sentries in the pool area either? It all made little sense. Why would the terrorists leave most of the surroundings of the hotel unguarded? Had the SWAT intervention really drew them out? "Platoon One, please proceed with caution. Start moving towards Party City."

"Aye, aye, sir," Aguirre responded.

Abruptly, the sharp report of distant gunfire interrupted their conversation. Although difficult to pinpoint, the shots seemed to be coming from convention center area.

"Platoon Two, take out your targets and secure Grand Central. The rest of the platoons, move into Party City now!"

"Aye, sir," the Chinese petty officer replied.

The rattle of automatic fire got increasingly heavier. McAllister saw the sentry by the birdcage slowly get to his feet and stare warily in the direction of the convention area. The SEAL commander turned his head to the men on his right, and said, "Let's go!"

Ignoring the sentries, he stood up to his full height and began to push his way across the bushes. The terrorist leaning on the column stared at him with disbelief, but then his head jerked violently back and he crumpled to the floor, as one of Platoon Two's snipers shot him twice, through the head and in the chest. The man by the birdcage managed to take one step before three bullets also struck him, dying shortly after he hit the floor.

The grounds bordering the entrance road immediately came alive as the SEALs surged forward. Six of them quietly advanced at double speed towards the lobby, while the rest headed towards the long corridor that led to Party City.

Johnny Ray could not believe his good fortune. The back passageway that led to the pool area was empty, apparently all of the sentries drawn away into the fight to recapture the bulk of the hostages in the convention area. His small group of prisoners had managed to walk unopposed through the hotel, and now they were on the verge of exiting through the glass doors that opened to pool grounds.

There had been a moment of tension when loud shooting had erupted behind them, but they had soon realized that the gunshots were not directed at them. Even so, the wounded crew-cut man had insisted that he be allowed to go back to the ballroom to search for his family, but had been convinced by the tall, gray haired man that to do that would be tantamount to suicide.

Johnny had walked next to the short ragged line, pointing his AK-47 at the group, making loud, threatening remarks whenever they reached a point where sentries could be posted, urging encouragement in a lower voice whenever he felt no one could overhear him.

Sensing their approach, the glass doors of the back corridor slid open and a strong gust of cool, humid wind wafted in, messing their hair, whistling through the doorframe, carrying the strong smell of the sea. The brunette, who headed the line, hesitated for a moment, intimidated by the darkness outside, but Johnny reassured her by stepping out first.

"Come on!" he said to her. "You're almost there!"

The brunette nodded and smiled shyly at him. She renewed her march, followed by the others.

Johnny felt an inexplicable sense of elation. He was allowing some of their most precious commodities—the hostages—to escape. Without them and the others still trapped in the ballroom, the small band of revolutionaries would be unable to withstand for long the power of the federal government and its local allies. But keeping them there would only expose them to crazy schemes like the one proposed by El Cano, and cause innocent blood to be shed. He could not allow that.

The line of prisoners began to edge the main swimming pool, a huge, irregularly shaped affair, fed from above by a waterfall and a winding water slide that descended from a fifty-foot high artificial hill. The hill, which could be climbed through a set of rock-hewn steps at the back, provided the perfect lookout spot for a sentry, and Johnny had expected to see someone there. But inexplicably, nobody had challenged him. In fact, nobody seemed to be watching the entire pool area.

Johnny could not understand it, but he did not dwell on it. The revolution, all of San Miguel's careful, methodical planning, was swiftly collapsing around him. He had not had a lot of expectations of holding on for long to the island of San Juan anyway, he thought, but then he had to recognize that in his heart, he had harbored the wild hope that the revolution would somehow succeed, that it would spark a rebellion in the rest of Puerto Rico, despite all odds. Even now, he was not willing to give it up so easily. He would not use the hostages as shields, but maybe, when they were rescued, they would be able to speak in his behalf, on behalf of what he was trying to achieve.

"I must apologize to all of you," he heard himself say, to his own surprise, but he continued. "This...these killings...That is not what the majority of us stand for...We are fighting for our freedom, for the independence of—"

Two bullets thudded into Johnny's chest, causing him to stagger and drop his rifle. He stared incredulously at his shirt, swaying as blood gushed from his wounds and his legs turned to jelly. *There had been no sound of gunfire*, he thought, *there had been no gunfire*. He heard the brunette scream as he felt himself fall, and listened to the scuffle of hurried steps as urgent men's voices said, "We're friends! We're friends! You're safe now! Come this way! Hurry..."

Then everything blurred, and he closed his eyes. The floor was hard and wet, and smelled of chlorine. He thought of trying to get up, but then thought better of it. And with a sigh, his last breath escaped from his body.

CHAPTER LXXI

Jeb Stuart moved at a steady clip up the winding metal steps that led to the theater's catwalk. He was followed by two of his men and Ernan. The three SEALs climbed the stairs with effortless, noiseless speed, as if their feet were cushioned by air, while Ernan lagged behind, painfully conscious of his creaky progress. They could not yet see what was happening in the theater below, where the hostages were held, but had heard shots and shouts of anger and surprise.

A near brush with a rebel patrol had delayed them. There had been four of them, most bearing rifles, roaming the starboard side of Deck 5. They had abruptly exited from the ship's lobby, and had they not been involved in an animated, boisterous conversation, they would probably have sighted the first three infiltrators, who had just stepped out of the crew's stairway. However, the four terrorists had walked directly towards the ship's railing and stared down into the bay, as if searching for something or someone in the dark waters below. *Probably the man the SEALs had found drowning on their way into the ship,* Stuart thought. He and his men had quickly retreated back into the stairs from which they had emerged, just a few steps away. The SEALs could have easily disposed of the terrorists. However, they could not run the risk of entering into a noisy firefight that would have alerted the Macheteros in the theater of their presence or, even worse, where one of the gunmen escaped and raised the alarm.

So they had waited. It had taken the rowdy group of armed men four minutes to desist from their search, but finally they had lumbered towards the stern of the ship, their noisy output decreasing in volume as they distanced themselves from the waiting SEALs.

With no time to lose, Stuart had renewed his trek towards the prow even before the four terrorists had disappeared from sight. As Ernan had assured them, the rear entrance to the theater was unlocked, and led to a corridor lined on both sides with doors to the various dressing rooms. An entrance at the end of the corridor had opened up to the back of the stage, into a gloomy, cold, high-ceilinged space, separated from the rest of the theatre by a huge, heavy, black curtain.

Ernan had turned left, and pointed to a spiraling metal staircase that disappeared into the murky heights of the theater.

"That is where Mr. McFadden and I climbed," he had whispered to Stuart. "From up there, you'll be able to see many of the hostages and the pirates, and they won't be able to see you."

Stuart had nodded and begun to climb the stairs. But as he did, he had been startled by the sudden noise of shots, and seen the back curtain billow inwards—towards the back of the stage—probably the result of bullets striking it. He had been tempted to use his communications gear to verify the position of the rest of his men, but he could not risk any interaction between his transmissions and all of the sound and electronic equipment in the theatre, as far fetched as such an interaction could be. He could only hope that Johnson's group had managed to reach its designated areas, and that it would be ready for their attack.

If all went well, Johnson, Reid, Simenkowsky, and Todd would have by now rappelled from the two side balconies on the stairs of the seventh deck, and be waiting on both sides of the Stardust's main entrance. McLain and Quintero would be standing guard from the balconies, each with two other men in the wings ready to rush into the Stardust's upper floor, while the balance of his squad would seal up the rest of the approaches to the theater.

The four men waiting by the main entrance would have the hardest job. They would have to storm into the mezzanine without any prior knowledge of where their enemies were, or even how many of them there were. When preparing for the rescue in the Isla Grande hangar, they had practiced with a fiber optic snake camera, the type used by police and SWAT to spy on armed criminals through windows and doors. However, in an unforgivable snafu, the camera had been left behind.

His men would have to pin their hopes on the element of surprise and their fighting skills. If they were lucky, their enemies would be plainly identifiable by their black armbands and the weapons they were carrying. However, if any of them wandered into the hostage crowd, things could get very, very dicey.

It was for that reason that Stuart had chosen his two best sharpshooters to climb up into the catwalk with him. If any of the terrorists got lose among the passengers, Stuart's two snipers could well be the hostages' last resort. From their high vantage point, they would hopefully have a clearer view of the gunmen, and be able to pick them off before they moved into the throng of gathered passengers. However, with scarcely four minutes left before the assault began, the time to sweep the area and locate the terrorists was growing dangerously short.

Stuart reached the top of the stairs and stepped on the catwalk. It consisted of a narrow platform, narrower than his extended arms, attached by several metal tubes to the ceiling. Parallel safety railings made of horizontal wires bordered each side. Rows of multicolored spotlights, various sets of raised curtains, and several large props—bushes of various sizes, the outline of some buildings at night, a ponderous half moon and a huge pig with wings, among others—also hung from the ceiling close to the catwalk, all of which Stuart took in with a glance as he continued to move towards the center of the hovering walkway.

He could feel people moving below him, but was unable to see them until he reached his final destination and, crouching, looked down at the stage. Like disembodied shadows, his two men took positions on each of his sides, and without looking into the large telescopic sights of their rifles, calmly began to scan the scene under their feet.

Ernan's description of what they would see had been right on target. From where they crouched, the SEALs had a clear view of maybe the first four rows of the lower floor of the theatre, which were packed with men, women and children. The seats were spread in a giant semicircle around the stage, separated into three equal sections by two sloping aisles. A few prisoners, their faces puffed up from beatings, were tied up to some of the visible columns that supported the balcony floor. The two aisles that divided the seats of the mezzanine were also clogged with hostages. Several of the passengers were now standing, trying to move away from the approaching terrorists or gaping at the stage.

Stuart's attention, however, was immediately drawn to the stage below him, where a short, thick, powerfully-built man was being pulled away by a harassed looking terrorist—with very little success—from another man lying under him. The stocky man's white shirt—a ship's officer shirt bearing the epaulets of first mate—was soaked in blood, but even so the man hung on fiercely to his opponent's neck, whose face had begun to turn purple. Frustrated, the terrorist trying to aid his fallen friend desisted from his useless attempt to pull the attacker away and instead took a few hurried steps to where his rifle was lying on the floor and retrieved it. Returning to the struggling men, he swung the rifle sideways, striking the angry officer on the left temple. The ship's officer swooned and relaxed his grip on the fallen man but still managed to hold on. Finally, the officer tumbled sideways to the floor as he was struck a second time.

By that time, a second armed terrorist had managed to climb on the stage, and together with his companion, began to pound the bloodied officer with their rifles. Meanwhile, the man who had been the object of the short man's wrath slowly sat up, rubbing his neck and watching the beating.

"Stop!" he ordered hoarsely. "Help me get up."

He was a gaunt man dressed in some sort of uniform. From the cat-walk, Stuart could not discern most of his features except for what seemed to be a narrow mustache. After being helped back to his feet, he limped towards the wounded officer, directing at him a look of pure venom.

He stopped next to the fallen man and drew out his gun. Without saying a word, he pointed it at the officer's left kneecap and shot it. Folstad groaned in agony, moving his hands to hold his demolished knee, blood flowing through his fingers and staining his white pants. Several in the crowd screamed, while others shielded their children's eyes or instinctively lowered their faces. Stuart saw another man on the stage—the captain, by his insignias—shout with angry indignation and stand up from the folding chair where he had been sitting. He took a few steps towards the others, but one of the armed terrorists intercepted him and drove his rifle into his stomach, making him double down on his knees.

"Now lick my shoes," the gaunt terrorist said in a spiteful voice, thrusting his right shoe under the wounded man's chin. The first mate looked at the shoe for a moment, breathing very heavily. He had been shot in the back, and his face was etched with the pain from his throbbing knee. But he directed a defiant stare at the man standing above him, and let a gob of bloody spit fall on the shoe. The gaunt terrorist moved his foot back with a disgusted grunt and placed his gun on the wounded man's temple.

"You've blown your last chance," he said in an annoyed tone. "Prepare to die."

Stuart's two snipers—a sandy haired, nineteen year old called Merryweather and a taciturn, olive-skinned Italian named Rinaldi—turned their heads towards their squad leader, silently begging him to give them permission to open fire. Stuart hesitated for a fraction of a second, knowing that acting now, before the designated time of the attack, could jeopardize the entire rescue operation. But he could not wait any longer. "Shoot them," he ordered, and then, standing up, he shouted down at the stage, "Hey shithead! Look up here!"

The gunman stopped talking and looked about him in apparent confusion. As he did, the SEALs calmly centered their sights on the terrorists standing on the stage.

"The two on the right," muttered Rinaldi.

"Left," confirmed Merryweather.

They did not wait any further orders from their superior officer, their muffled rifles spitting out several bullets so quickly that their noise sounded like one prolonged "thud".

Stuart produced a short grunt of satisfaction, as the fired projectiles found their marks. Rinaldi's first two shots landed less than two inches apart on the center of the chest of one of the terrorists who had climbed the stage, causing him to drop down instantly like a curtain weight. The second man only had time to turn his head slightly towards his companion before two bullets perforated his right lung and a third struck him on the right shoulder, spinning him around as his knees began to buckle.

Standing almost vertically over the gaunt terrorist, Merryweather had the most difficult shot. A missed bullet could hit the wounded man on the floor, and a non-incapacitating hit could give the terrorist the opportunity to finish off the bleeding officer. But the young SEAL's shot struck true to the mark.

Merryweather was the unit's top marksman, and his bullet—the only one he fired—shattered the terrorist's collarbone, ripped through his left lung, and became embedded in his spine. The gaunt man shuddered grotesquely and, devoid of all strength, fell forward, his face grazing the first officer's left thigh and then slamming hard onto the stage. Somehow, he did not lose consciousness, his eyes staring with surprised disbelief at his intended victim's pants while he slowly choked with his own blood.

The SEAL snipers were already searching for new targets, but could find none from their limited vantage point. There were screams coming from the theater's balcony, but the stage's upper curtains blocked Stuart's view to the second floor. With still more than a minute left before the coordinated attack was scheduled to start, any remaining terrorist in the theater could create havoc among the unarmed hostages. He had to act quickly.

"Merryweather, cover us. Ernan, stay here. Rinaldi, with me," he snapped out at the men surrounding him, and began to run towards the catwalk's spiraling stairs.

Like everyone else inside the theater, Eric Aguayo had witnessed with an equal mixture of horror and fascination the events that had unfolded right in front of him on the stage, like some unreal, macabre play. When the bearded, stocky officer had been shot, Ingrid—his newlywed wife— had cringed and covered her face with her hands. She had begun to shake uncontrollably, even after he had placed his left arm over her shoulders and assured her that everything would be all right, that they would not be harmed as long as they obeyed the terrorists' orders. His eyes, however, had remained riveted to the stage, his morbid curiosity prevailing over his sense of pity and revulsion.

But suddenly, in a startling turn of events, the armed men in the center of the stage had seemingly self-destructed, dropping like so many pins struck by a bowling ball. It had happened so abruptly that Captain Clausen, still reeling from the blow to his stomach, had mutely stared at the unmoving, fallen men for several seconds without registering any reaction, as if waiting for them to get up.

Eric heard a guard on the mezzanine shouting angrily at the hostages to let him through, and like many of the passengers in front of him stood up to get a better view of what was happening below. He saw a guard trying to make his way through the crowded right aisle, striking with his rifle at those who were not fast enough to step out of his way, looking uncertainly from left to right.

Then, without warning, two men in military garb sprang out at a fast trot from behind the right curtains of the stage. The guard saw them and not waiting for the panicked passengers in front of him to scatter, fired a wild burst of semiautomatic fire that completely missed the approaching soldiers but almost struck the captain at the other end of the stage, peppering with bullets the floor and the curtain behind him, and knocking down the chair where the captain had been sitting.

Unexpectedly, without any of the two military men firing a shot, part of the terrorist's forehead disappeared in a puff of red and the man fell straight backwards on the carpeted aisle.

"Oh my God!" Eric said out loud, as he realized that a portion of the hijacker's head had been shot off. "Did you see that?" he asked excitedly to nobody in particular.

From below, he heard one of the soldiers yell, "Down! Down! Everybody down!"

"Get down!" he whispered to Ingrid, and began to obey the shouted command but froze when he looked at his wife.

There was an arm wrapped around her neck, pulling her off her chair and into the aisle, while a large gun was pressed against her head.

"Do as I say, or I'll blow your head off," a gruff voice said behind her.

Ingrid began to cry, but then made a choking noise as the man tightened his grip around her neck.

"Be quiet! You're not letting me think!" the armed man warned her, as he began to pull her back into the back exit of the theater. Eric saw his wife's eyes bulge out as air failed to reach her lungs, then heard her breathe desperately as her captor relaxed his grip. "No more crying, you understand?" the gruff voice said, and she shook her chin weakly.

Eric could not see the gunman's face, but he recognized his voice instantly. It was the terrorist who had been guarding the upper left entrance of the Stardust Theater since that morning, the same terrorist who had escorted them in the early afternoon to the Windjammer Café. Despite the circumstances, Eric had not disliked the man. Short—no more than five foot seven or eight inches—fit, and clean shaven, wearing a red T-shirt and jeans, the guard had not abused any of the prisoners and treated them with curt, almost shy respect.

"Please," Eric pleaded. "Let her go."

"I will," man answered earnestly. "Once she...and you, help me to get out of here. Stand up and walk up to me," he ordered.

Numbly, Eric walked out to the aisle and stood up in front of the terrorist and his wife. With the corner of his eyes he saw blurry movement to his right, but kept his gaze fixed on the man holding his wife.

"If you follow my instructions to the letter, we will all walk out of here alive. If not, we all die, do you understand?" the armed man said.

Eric nodded emphatically.

"You will walk behind me to cover my back," the terrorist said. Despite the hardness of his voice, he sounded scared. "I know what you're thinking. What will keep you from hitting me from the back to save your girlfriend. Nothing. But you better make sure that you knock me out, because if not I will kill her. So think about it before you run the risk."

"I won't attack you," Eric assured him anxiously.

"Okay. We move now, and you place both of your arms on my shoulders and stay as close as possible, understood?"

"Yes...Understood."

The terrorist took a long step to his left, turning Ingrid towards the closest exit. Awkwardly, the small party began to head towards the door. They had not walked more than four paces when two soldiers carrying rifles stepped out from each side of the theater's exit and blocked the fugitives' way.

"Sorry, son, but we can't let you go," the tallest of the two men said in a Texan drawl.

The gunman hesitated and stopped walking. He hid his head behind that of the captive woman, looking at the two intruders through her hair.

"I'll kill her," he said with half-hearted bravado.

The tall soldier spat on the ground, while his companion aimed his rifle at the woman. "You can...Shoot her, I mean. But then we'll kill you, and I don't think you'd like that."

"I'm willing to die for my country."

"Then do so, but spare the girl. Don't go to the afterlife with that in your conscience. Hell, you may even get to Heaven. But if you decide to live, just drop your weapon and we won't kill you."

Eric peeked from behind the gunman's shoulder and silently gestured at the two soldiers with his face, as if asking them whether he should do something. The soldier with the Texan drawl silently shook his head.

"I *will* kill her!" the terrorist shouted.

"We've been there already," the tall soldier answered. "I don't think you will, because then you'll die, and I don't think you're ready for that. So it's up to you. But I'll tell you what. We can't stay the rest of the night arguing about the same thing. So I'm walking up to you and you're going to give me that gun. And then we're all going to walk out of here alive."

The Texan began to move casually towards the hostages and the gunman, who instantly recoiled, pulling the girl back with him and nearly tripping with Eric.

"I'm warning you!" the man said nervously, pressing his left arm harder around Ingrid's neck.

"Yeah, yeah, whatever," the soldier continued to walk and extended his hand towards the terrorist. "Hand it over."

The gunman closed his eyes, and he moved his gun closer to the center of his hostage's cranium, his hand shaking noticeably. The tall Texan continued to approach him, and without breaking stride, placed his hand on the gun's barrel, and slowly, almost gently, moved it up and away until it was pointing towards the ceiling. Then, with a short tug, he took it out of the terrorist's hand.

"Hands on you head," he said calmly to the disarmed man, who was staring at him with a terrified expression. "Just let her go and put your hands on your head. I promise you, we won't shoot you."

Taking in a deep, shaky breath, the defeated terrorist released Ingrid and placed his hands over his head. The frightened woman collapsed to the floor, her legs unable to support her any more, while Eric ran to her and embraced her.

Keeping his rifle aimed at the disarmed guard, the Texan nodded to his companion, who ran into the theater's second floor.

"You did real good, son," the tall SEAL said to the terrorist. "Now spread your arms and legs and lean against the wall while I search you, and then we can get this sordid business behind us."

Chief Petty Officer Paul Pinet observed the crowd gathered on the dock in front of the burning ramp, uncertain about what he would do next. A bullhorn could have been useful. There must have been at least fifty people milling around the flames, their bodies outlined in the flickering light, noisily talking, shouting instructions, or just passively sitting on the floor or on some of the crates scattered among the wharf.

The SEALs were not trained to deal with this type of situation. When the rescue had been planned, his squad's mission had been plain and simple: to neutralize any sentries guarding the boarding area and keep the dock secure from any other hostiles who could reinforce the terrorists inside the *Mardi Gras*.

But this...*What was he supposed to do?* He certainly could not kill all of the people gathered around the fire. Well, that was not exactly true. His squad could *kill* all of the rebels standing on the dock, but that would be a massacre. Only about one in every five carried any kind of visible weapon, and for the most part, they behaved like young college students having a blast in a rock concert.

"Turner," Pinet addressed the man crouching next to him. "Warn the others, tell them that at..." he looked at his watch. It was 2119 hours, 9:19 PM. "At 2125 hours we move. We will start by shooting anyone who has a weapon and is standing apart from the crowd, and then envelop the rest of the crowd and order them to surrender. If anyone goes for a weapon, we shoot them, got it?"

"Yes, sir!"

Pinet tapped Turner's helmet. "Go!"

Taking a quick look over the crates, Turner ran out and disappeared into the dark open corridor under the terminal building.

"Find your targets, gentlemen," Pinet said to the other two SEALs waiting with him.

"Way ahead of you, sir," Pat, the SEAL who had shot the sentry at the dock's entrance answered, already looking through his HK-417's telescopic sight, his rifle pointing at a man sitting on some crates by the edge of dock, about 150 feet away, with an AK47 resting on his legs.

Pinet scanned the area for more armed men, and spotted another standing much closer to them, with his back turned towards them and his weapon slung over his shoulder, his attention totally focused on the men holding the fire hose that was spraying a long stream of white water over the fire.

Amateurs, Paul thought to himself. *Either that or just too cock-sure about their impregnable position.* If he had been them, he would have anticipated just the kind of night raid that the SEALs were conducting. *Hell, the fire should have been a dead giveaway that something out of the ordinary what happening.* Pinet didn't know who had started it, but whoever did had done the SEALs a huge favor. Maybe the terrorists had captured him. Maybe that was the reason why they felt so secure.

He saw a couple of women dancing in front of the fire, their sexy, tightly clad bodies highlighted by the flames. *Those people were actually having a good time! Amateurs having fun. What had they hoped to accomplish, anyway? They had to know that they could not hold on to Old San Juan indefinitely. Not like this. What was their goal?*

"Get ready," the chief petty officer instructed his men. "On my count...five...four...three...two...one...Fire!"

The HK-417 rifles thudded several times and by the abrupt, jerky movement of the guards' bodies, Pinet immediately knew that his men had found their marks. The man standing with his back towards them fell unnoticed, while a curly-haired woman saw the sentry sitting on the crates slump forward, and moved closer to examine him.

Standing up, Pinet began to head towards the gathered crowd. "Pat, stay here. Watch our backs. Hank, cover me." He felt reassured as he saw most of his other men walking out from their hiding places.

By then, a few of the other people milling about in the dock had realized that something was happening and were looking about them nervously. Two other sentries standing together close to the burning structure had fallen to the ground, the first of the two desperately grabbing on to his companion as he slid downward, then the second man's legs buckling and ceasing to support both of them. Several of the spectators around them had initially stared with amusement, and then realized, as the two men failed to get up and blood puddled around their bodies, that they had been shot.

"Everybody place your hands over your heads!" Pinet shouted at the top of his lungs. Those in the crowd closest to him gaped at him in shock and began to raise their hands, while others tried to escape.

"Hands on your head!" Pinet kept shouting, but very soon his voice was drowned by screams of surprise and fear. He saw people running in every direction, some directly to his waiting men and others towards the loading ramp of the ship. A stringy fellow with a tight, striped T-shirt dove off the dock directly into the bay, while those trying to put out the fire abandoned the hose. The pressurized hose snaked out of control, spraying jets of water wildly on the fleeing mob and the hull of the *Mardi Gras* until it fell off the side of the dock.

Pinet fired a long burst of his HK-M15 submachine gun into the air, and he heard others in his squad fire as well. Most of the men and women froze on their tracks and raised their hands, signaling their surrender. Two managed to rush into the ship, right into the cargo hold where four SEALs were waiting. Another made a dash to get to one of the rifles from one of the fallen sentries but was cut down by a machine gun volley as he began to pick it up.

It was all over in less than five minutes. Pinet walked to where his men were lining up their prisoners, making them empty out their pockets and searching them for weapons. One of the sentries that was shot was still alive, apparently wounded on his right foot and left shoulder. The SEAL petty officer took off his belt and knelt next to him.

"Here," he said to the wounded man. "Let me tie this above your wound to stop the bleeding."

The terrorist—a thin, dark complexioned teenager with a sullen expression—allowed Pinet to wrap his belt around the bleeding leg. The SEAL threaded the belt through its metal buckle, and pulled it tightly, causing the teenager to gasp.

"I'll call a medic to help you, okay?"

The wounded teenager nodded.

"Hey Mike!" Pinet called to one the men closest to him. "Get Tuotti in he—"

Something hot and heavy tore through Pinet's throat with such viciousness that the chief petty officer never heard the noise of the rifle that fired it. He saw Mike scream at him and then look up towards the ship, but by then he was falling, a lot of blood gushing out of his neck. He never got to see the gunman who had fired the shot from the *Mardi Gras'* fifth deck, or how his men riddled his body and everything around him with a storm of bullets. The medic arrived a couple of minutes later. But by that time, Chief Petty Officer Paul Pinet had died.

"The *Mardi Gras* is yours, sir," Jeb Stuart informed Captain Clausen. The SEAL commander extended his hand to the haggard looking cruise ship officer.

Clausen, who had been kneeling by the side of his wounded first mate until the SEALs' medical personnel had taken him away, shook the proffered hand warmly. "Thank you, Commander," he said in an emotion-filled voice. "I cannot express how grateful I am to you and your men."

The two men were standing on the Stardust Theater's stage, and even though only a few of the hostages could actually overhear their words, the enormous audience viewing them burst into a thunderous, standing ovation, cheering them.

"Actually, my men can only take part of the credit," Stuart shouted in order to be heard through the tremendous noise. "You had a lot of help from a few brave people inside your ship who risked their lives to give us crucial intelligence." Stuart turned his head and waved his arm at Ernan—standing by the right wing of the theater—ordering him to approach.

The tiny Filipino *maitre* walked out shyly from behind the curtain looking very embarrassed. As he reached the other two men, he held out his left hand half-heartedly towards his captain, but Clausen grabbed it, pulled him roughly towards him, and embraced him, his tall frame towering over that of his minute crewman. Sensing that the small man had in some way been responsible for their deliverance, the crowd roared with approval, increasing even more the already deafening clamor inside the theater.

"It was all Mr. McFadden," Ernan protested. "It was Mr. McFadden and the Condessa!" he insisted, but his voice was drowned by the applause, even after Captain Clausen leaned forward to hear better.

Clausen gripped the Filipino's left hand and Stuart's right, and raised them, turning towards the passengers and prompting more applause. Stuart's face reddened, particularly when he saw the smiling, slightly mocking faces of Rinaldi and Merryweather clapping along with the rest of the audience, and after a few seconds he gently disengaged his hand from the captain's grip.

"It is still too dangerous to allow your passengers to disembark," he told Clausen, leaning close to his ear. "My men have done a preliminary search of the ship, but it's a big ship. There may still be a few diehards hiding. There's still fighting also going on in Old San Juan. So until the situation becomes more stable, it would be dangerous to let the passengers out."

Stuart was not exaggerating. It would take several hours for Bravo Group to mop up the enemy presence in the *Mardi Gras*. The SEALs were conducting a deck-by-deck search of the ship, hunting down or capturing the hijackers that still roamed through it, unaware of the rescue.

So far, resistance by the terrorists had been weak and disorganized. Of the more than two-dozen hijackers discovered aboard the cruise liner, most had surrendered when confronted by the threat of inevitable termination. Four of them, a rowdy bunch who seemed more intent on causing damage to the property and injury to anyone who crossed their path, actually dared to fire upon a group of three SEALs that was sweeping through the eighth deck. They paid dearly for their attack, three of the group getting killed on the spot, the fourth sustaining serious injuries to his stomach and jaw.

By ten PM, Ensign Stuart's group had counted a total of five passengers and crewmembers killed, not a considerable number of casualties, considering the number of hostages on board. The toll had been much higher for the terrorists. The headcount so far had added up to sixteen, including those shot at the dock, and would probably rise before the night's gloom gave way to the sun. One SEAL, Chief Petty Officer Paul Pinet, had died as a result of a sniper's bullet. No other rescuers were killed or wounded.

First Mate Folstad's condition remained critical after being shot three times. Ray Tuotti, the SEALs' medic that Pinet had been summoning when he had been killed, had rushed from the dock to the theater after verifying that there was nothing he could do for his fallen comrade, and worked hard to stabilize the health of the ship's stocky first mate. Then, with the help of two other men, Tuotti had removed Folstad to the first deck hospital.

Clausen `considered thoughtfully Stuart's information while the applause continued and began to die down. Smiling at Ernan, he let him go, saying to him, "Please meet me later." The Filipino nodded and promptly exited the stage, anxious to find out how his hero, McFadden, was doing.

The Captain then returned his attention to the SEAL commander. "Do you know if Isla Grande is also overrun with terrorists?" he asked.

"Isla Grande is held by us," Stuart responded.

"Good. There are two docks for large cruise ships there. Maybe we could move *Mardi Gras* to one of them, so that the passengers can disembark there? I know it takes months to reserve a dock, but these are unusual times..."

Stuart immediately grasped Clausen's suggestion, surprised by how easily their present predicament could be solved. One of the docks in Isla Grande would be the perfect place to drop off the passengers, and transport the wounded to the hospitals.

"I'll get right on it, sir."

"And do you think your men could make certain that decks 5 and 6 are safe? There are various restaurants where we can feed our passengers while we move the ship."

"I believe they are secure, sir, but if you will give me twenty more minutes, I'll have my men comb their way through them to make certain," Stuart replied. "Now, by your leave, I have things to do," he said, and with a curt nod, left the stage.

To the captain's amusement, the applause and cheers increased in volume as the Navy SEAL departed, almost as if the crowd was clamoring for a curtain call. Clausen walked to the microphone—lying on the floor next to the covered body of the man who had tortured his first mate—and picked it up, gesturing with his hands to the passengers to make silence.

"Ensign Stuart, of the Navy SEALs—"

"Yeah!" somebody shouted, and a smattering of applause followed. Again, Clausen pleaded for some silence.

"Ensign Stuart has informed me that it is still not safe to get off the *Mardi Gras*." The announcement was received with tense attention.

"Apparently, what happened here is only part of a larger terrorist attack, and the authorities are still trying to...er...stabilize the situation in Old San Juan. Therefore..." he continued before anyone could interrupt him, "we are making arrangements to move our ship to another dock located in Isla Grande, an area controlled by the authorities, very close to where we are right now. There you will be able to disembark, and I am certain that arrangements have been made to secure lodging for those of you who do not live here, until you choose to leave the island."

The theater became filled with the murmur of a thousand voices,

"Please! Please! I know you are all very tired and anxious, and have a lot to talk about, but please let me finish and then you can talk among yourselves to your heart's content."

The crowd quickly settled down. "If any of you require medical attention, you should go to the infirmary downstairs immediately. Crew, all available waiters, cooks, and bartenders, please report to the restaurants and bars on decks 5 and 6. We should be opening the restaurants in half an hour, and the bars in fifteen minutes. All drinks are on the house until you leave this ship."

A general cheer, punctuated by several hoots and shouts, went off throughout the theater.

"It is very important, however, that you stay for the moment in decks 5 and 6. Even though the SEALs have liberated us from our captors, there may still be some stragglers hiding in other parts of the ship. As the other decks are cleared, we will announce them over the PA."

The captain looked around him while he gathered his thoughts.

"Finally, I ask you to keep in your prayers all those that were wounded by these...terrible men, especially our brave First Mate, who demonstrated tremendous courage despite the torture and humiliation that you personally witnessed. I also ask you to pray for those that were killed today. May their souls rest in peace."

CHAPTER LXXII

The sixteen men that comprised Group Able had started their underwater journey under the dark waters of San Juan Bay with a half hour head start over the other two groups. Theirs had been the longest swim, more than a mile in dark, murky waters where sharks were not an uncommon sight. Using the diving equipment that produced no bubbles—odd-looking contraptions that were designated as LAR V UBAs and that they called 'Larubas'—they had started from the tip of Isla Grande that protruded into San Juan's bay, and followed the contours of the coast until they had reached the promenade that bordered the walls of the city.

There, two of the men had crawled out of the water and scampered over the rocks and the low concrete barrier that separated the wide walkway from the bay. Moving in opposite directions, the SEALs made certain that they were not being watched. Fourteen others followed, six heading towards the wall, the others traveling towards the Gate of San Juan.

The group of six ran to a spot where the city wall angled inward, forming a small rectangular courtyard before it angled outwards again. They were in a public garden, decorated with various ornamental plants, including several palm trees that grew almost all the way to the top of the battlements.

Two of the SEALs carried waterproof, black satchels, each measuring about five feet in length. As they got under the vegetation's cover, they began to unzip the bags while the others kept watch around them. The team leader, Petty Officer First Class Frank Gabriel—or 'Gabe', as he was called by his men—began to examine the wall in front of him to find the best spot to climb it.

He was amazed by its size. The walls were a lot bigger than he had ever imagined. They rose upwards into the sky and seemed to disappear into the night.

Gabe gazed at the massive defenses for a few seconds, and cursed softly under his breath.

"Shit, somebody's been here before us," he said, as he saw a knotted rope dangling down from the top of the wall.

Seaman Kevin Flanagan walked next to him, carrying a cylindrical, wide-mouthed gun with a metal grappling hook protruding from its front. An elongated cloth bag was attached to its barrel. It was a TAIL gun, TAIL standing for "Tactical Air Initiated Launch". The odd shaped TAIL, almost as long as Flanagan was tall, was a state of the art hand-held mini-cannon that could launch a grappling hook without creating a lot of noise. The gun used compressed air to shoot the hook upwards, a pneumatic valve regulating the trajectory and length of the shot. A Kevlar cable, stowed in the cloth container, was attached to the rear end of the hook.

"Damn!" Flanagan muttered quietly, gingerly touching the rope already dangling from the wall and looking at his companion, "Is that how they did it? I guess we won't be using this then, will we?" he said, pointing to his TAIL gun.

Gabe shook his head. "You guess correctly."

"Do you think they're still up there?" Flanagan asked.

"Doubtful," Gabriel replied. He was the oldest of the four, and the one with the most experience, having served both in Iraq and Afghanistan. He continued to look up at the wall for several seconds, only his long nose and his white eyes visible under the dark camouflage paint that covered his face, but he could perceive no movement. "They must have used this place as the staging point for their attack on the Governor's mansion, and then moved in."

A third SEAL, carrying another TAIL launcher, joined the other two.

"There's a rope hanging from the wall!" he exclaimed with surprise.

"A very shrewd observation, Styles," Flanagan said.

"So we're not—"

"No!" responded Gabriel and Flanagan almost simultaneously.

Gabe walked to the rope and gave it a sharp tug. It held firmly.

"I'm going up. Cover me. If everything's okay, you follow."

Cautiously at the beginning, making certain that the rope held his weight, the SEAL petty officer started to scale the wall. After a few seconds he began to move faster until his eyes surpassed the upper edge of the battlements, and he could gaze at the gardens beyond. Seeing no one, he pushed himself over the thick wall and dropped behind some bushes.

Someone had hidden there before. Part of the bushes had been trampled into the ground, and on the floor, just a few feet away from him, lay the dark shapes of two men, probably some of the Governor's body-guards shot by the intruders.

Gabriel tugged the rope three times and it immediately stretched taut. He made a quick dash from the bushes across a white gravel path, finding cover behind an enormous, ornamental vase. From there he had a better view of the bodies of the two men sprawled on the floor. One had been shot in the back. Neither seemed to be breathing.

Slipping from his helmet over his eyes his infrared lenses, he scanned his surroundings carefully. The gardens were large and well kept, sepa-rated into many sections and terraces where anyone could hide. He could not, however, detect any telltale heat signatures of other men's bodies in the cool darkness of the night.

A soft wind stirred the leaves around him and then died down. La Fortaleza loomed like a mute, pale giant at the southern end of the gar-dens, most of the windows in its three floors fully lit. No one, at least no one alive, seemed to be guarding the inside of the mansion.

Styles slid over the wall so silently that Gabe only heard a faint rustle of the bushes behind which he landed. Gabriel waved at him and pointed across the yard towards the easternmost corner of La Fortaleza, where a set of terracotta stairs rose all the way to the building's second floor. Styles nodded, and sprinted towards the indicated direction, disappearing tem-porarily from Gabriel's line of sight as he descended into a lower terrace of the garden, and reappearing a few seconds later as he crouched behind the stairs' banisters and began to climb the steps. Ziggy Sabria, a ruggedly handsome, Cuban born volunteer, followed Styles a minute later.

The next two climbers, Seamen Quijano and Effinger, were sent to the opposite corner of the Governor's mansion, the northernmost of the two large towers that flanked La Fortaleza's huge, crenellated western wall that faced the bay. As they did so, they stumbled onto another body, still clutching an AK-47 rifle, propped up and partially hidden by a thorny bush of red bougainvilleas into which it had fallen.

"Jesus!" Lou Effinger, the largest and most pleasant man in the squad whispered. "What a way to go!"

Quijano made the sign of the cross as he continued moving rapidly towards the open gate in the wall, then stopped as he reached its edge. Carefully, he took a peek into the open courtyard beyond.

Flanagan was the last to climb. As he topped the wall, Gabriel rose to his feet, and signaled him to join him. He pressed the PTT ("Press To Talk") switch in his throat microphone and in a subdued, clear voice muttered: "Able two, this is Able one. We are in position, over."

"Able two, it's about time!" a calm voice responded. *"We're growing cobwebs here, over."*

Gabe was forced to smile as he recognized the distinctive voice of Joe Crowfeather, or "Injun Joe," as all the others called him. A quiet, unassuming man with hair so dark that even after it had been shorn off by an electric shaver, his head still looked black, he was the unit's most well liked man, and one of its fiercest warriors. Standing at a scant five feet, eight inches tall, the Seminole from Florida moved with the stealth of a shadow, could outfight anyone in his unit, and was ranked as one of SEAL Team 2's top five marksmen. He refused to be called a "Native American", referring to himself as a Seminole or an Indian; hence his politically incorrect nickname.

Along with three others, Injun Joe had been assigned to penetrate La Fortaleza's perimeter through its secondary exit, a narrow cobblestoned road that sloped downwards from the Executive Mansion's main entrance, bordering the mansion's gardens. The exit was situated just a short walk beyond the Gate of San Juan. When not used—which was most of the time—its access was blocked by a set of wrought iron gates that were reinforced on its bottom with steel plates. The gates opened towards the outside, so that no vehicle—except maybe a tank—could crash through them. Normally, two policemen stood watch on that sleepy corner of La Fortaleza. However, none were visible now. Motion sensitive lights and video cameras connected to the main guardhouse enhanced the exit's security.

Injun Joe's group ("Able Two") had been surprised to find no enemy sentries anywhere near the area. Their main concern, therefore, had focused on the security cameras. There were two of them, one covering everything to the right of the exit, the other everything to the left, both overlapping the area where the cobblestoned street approached the gates. Staying out of the cameras' visual range, the Seminole sharpshooter had blasted the one on the left to pieces with two shots from his long-range M107 rifle. At a mere one hundred foot distance, it had been an easy target. He had left the second camera untouched, hoping that anyone watching would consider that one of the cameras had malfunctioned. Two cameras breaking down simultaneously would have been too much of a coincidence.

After that, it had all boiled down to a footrace. The SEALs had rushed through the blind spot and easily cleared the ten-foot high wrought iron fence. Then, using the various cars parked on the narrow cobbled throughway as cover, they had quietly made their way towards the main entrance of La Fortaleza. They had stopped two cars away from the guardhouse, where they had a partial view of the open courtyard in front of the Governor's Mansion. They could not see, however, the main gate or the guardhouse itself, since their view was blocked by a four-story government building to their left.

"I see dead people," Injun Joe told Gabe through his PTT. "Three bodies, lying on the courtyard's pavement, over."

"How about any live ones, over?" Gabriel asked him.

"Zero. No one visible. Not inside, not outside, over," the Seminole Indian reported in a neutral tone.

Strange, Gabriel thought. It almost seemed as if the place had been abandoned in a hurry.

"Able 3, report," Gabe called to the remaining group of four SEALs. Their job was to get to the roof of the government building that blocked Injun Joe's view of the guardhouse at the main entrance. They had splintered from Injun Joe's group after they had crossed under the San Juan Gate, giving wide berth to the cameras of La Fortaleza and heading for the four-story building that was adjacent to the Executive Mansion's secondary exit.

A balding, square-jawed man called Kramer led them. One of the men unzipped a TAIL gun out of its waterproof bag, and setting the height gauge to fifty feet, placed it on the ground and aimed it towards the top of the building. It was not an easy shot. There were tall, leafy trees covering most of the street—*a good place to set up an ambush when the Governor was exiting that way,* Kramer thought—and the grapple would have clear its way through an opening in the branches that was no more than three feet wide.

"Still on our way," Kramer reported.

The TAIL operator looked at Kramer, and Kramer nodded. With a heavy thud, the grapple flew upwards, trailed by a gray thread of Kevlar rope. As it rose, it clipped several leaves off one of the surrounding branches but continued to ascend unimpeded, angling its way towards the building until it had cleared its four stories and landed on its roof.

Carefully, the TAIL operator began to pull on the rope, dragging the grapple until it stopped. Giving it three hard tugs, he began to climb, while two of his companions aimed their rifles upward, ready to shoot at any figure that appeared over the edge. Like a giant spider, the man quickly scaled the smooth wall and clambered over its side. A few seconds later he reappeared, motioning with his arm for the others to follow.

Once up, the four-man team swept the entire rooftop to make certain that nobody else shared it with them. The last of the climbers pulled the rope up and carried the hook with him. Satisfied that they were alone, they crouched their way to the building's southwestern corner, and peeked over the edge of its low wall.

They were higher than La Fortaleza, so much so that they could see the bay beyond it, its still waters shimmering in the pale moonlight. It was, in fact, a stunningly peaceful, beautiful sight. The walls of the old city extended northwards as far as the eye could see, while to the south the lights of the town of Cataño glimmered across the bay. Closer to them, La Fortaleza looked like decorative porcelain house, all of its windows lit with bright, yellow light, its large garden partially illuminated by a few vivid patches of exterior floodlights, but mostly covered by the soft silvery gleam of the moon.

To the careless eye, the scene would have looked like a travel poster depicting an idealized image of a Caribbean island. But as Kramer gazed at the landscape below him, he could not help but see the evidence of the heavy fighting that had taken place there.

Three bodies lay on the courtyard with dark splotches—presumably blood—pooling around them. The front walls of La Fortaleza were pocked with bullet holes, and several of its windows had been shattered, broken pieces of glass strewn everywhere.

Kramer leaned over the south edge of the building's corner and stared straight down. The main gates to La Fortaleza were open, a red Mercedes Benz parked between them. Directly below, and next to the gates, was the guardhouse, bright light spilling from its interior. Looking over to the opposite side of the corner, he saw Injun Joe's men hiding behind the parked cars.

Kramer pressed the PTT on his throat. "This is Able three. We are in position. I see the three bodies. The main gates are open and a red vehicle is parked between them. I can see no movement anywhere, over."

"Roger that," Gabriel replied. *"It's a go, then. We'll follow your lead."*

Kramer stared at the man who had recovered the grapple and confirmed that he had secured it to a large communications antenna that rose two-dozen feet from the roof's tarmac top. The man nodded and let the rope attached to the grapple fall down towards the guardhouse. Without saying a word, the man grabbed the rope and swung over the edge, rappelling down the face of the building to just above the top of the guardhouse.

"Go!" Kramer said through his PTT, and two of his men dropped smoke grenades that thumped on the ground and began to spew a heavy, thick gray mist that quickly enveloped the sentry outpost.

The man hanging from the rope jumped on the guardhouse's roof, and from there to the ground. Standing up, he opened the guardhouse's door and discharged his sub machinegun into the small structure without pausing to look. The two men inside never had a chance. They had both been sitting with their backs turned away from the windows, apparently watching television. The unexpected burst of bullets raked through the back of the first sentry, nearly slicing him in half, while the second man got hit on the neck and right shoulder. He managed to turn only to lose his left eye and left ear from the SEALs' continued fire, dropping dead to the ground.

"Clear!" the man whispered into his PTT. By that time, two of his companions had joined him. Through the haze, he saw the vague outline of Crowfeather's men sprinting towards the main stairway of La Fortaleza. Not giving them another thought, he walked into the guardhouse to make certain that no enemies had survived.

"Go!" Gabriel heard Kramer say, and immediately his men surged forward. He saw Effinger and Quijano rush through the gate to the compound's central courtyard, while on the opposite side of the mansion he listened to Styles and Sabria blast open the side door of the terrace.

"Come on, Kevin," he said to Flanagan, and the two men ran towards the gate in the crenellated wall. Both Effinger and Quijano had already disappeared from sight, and Gabe heard shouts coming from the compound's central courtyard. As he turned the corner and sprinted through the gate, he found Effinger pointing his rifle at a fat man and an older woman. An AK-47 rifle lay at the fat man's feet, and he was raising his hands far above his head, shouting at the two SEALs not to shoot him, while the woman looked around her in dazed confusion, crying.

Quijano also shouted as he approached them, apparently urging the woman in Spanish to place her arms behind her head. Shaking noticeably, the woman did as she was told.

"See what information you can get out of them, Ernie," Gabriel said to the Spanish speaking Quijano. "Call me as soon as you get something. I'll be upstairs, checking on the others."

"Yes, sir."

Gabe examined the two prisoners for a brief moment, noticing that the woman was wearing some sort of domestic help uniform. *Part of the staff, or an inside accomplice, perhaps,* he wondered. For a fraction of a second he hesitated, feeling the temptation to personally interrogate her. But from the emotional state of the woman, he realized that it would be a long while before they got any rational response out of her. Besides, Quijano would probably do a better job interrogating her in Spanish than he would with his limited vocabulary.

Followed by Flanagan, he continued his trek towards La Fortaleza, climbing the main stairway. He found one of Injun Joe's men guarding it from the top landing.

"No sign of anyone yet, sir," the SEAL informed him before he could ask. "Injun Joe and Mack are searching the Governor's office," he added, pointing down a long corridor. "The rest are going through other parts of the buildings."

Saying nothing, Gabriel continued down the corridor toward the executive offices, followed by Flanagan. However, they were met by Injun Joe and his companion, who were already returning from their search.

"They're not in the office area," Crowfeather reported to his superior officer, shaking his head. "There's two bodies in the waiting area. Their hands were tied behind their backs and they were executed. One of them strangled, the other one his throat cut."

"Strangled?" Gabriel repeated with incredulity. "Were they some of the Governor's men?"

Injun Joe paused, as if to form a mental image of the dead men. "No," he answered. "They seemed to be terrorists. They were wearing the black armbands."

"Huh!" Gabe grunted with surprise, considering the information as he turned around and began to head back towards the stairs. *Who would have executed those men, he wondered? Could it have been the Governor's secret rescuer?*

The last they had heard from Governor Pietrantoni was that he had escaped and would be hiding in some secret passage until the SEALs were able to rescue him. He had not told them, however, where he would hide, presumably because if his call was intercepted, he would run the risk of disclosing his hiding place to his pursuers. It gave Gabriel the hope that the Governor would still be alive. But at the same time, the strange goings-on in La Fortaleza made him fear the worst. He doubted very much that the Governor would have tied and strangled one of the terrorists, or ordered their execution—although he was not certain any more about what to expect from politicians—but if the Governor did not do it, that meant that somebody else, someone very dangerous, had been roaming through La Fortaleza at the same time that the Governor had escaped. And there was a more than fifty-fifty chance that that killer would not be a close friend of the Governor.

A SEAL approached Gabe at a fast clip as he neared the upper landing of the stairs. He recognized him as Ziggy Sabria, the Cuban that had broken into the Executive Mansion with Seaman Styles through the terrace.

"Sir!" he said breathlessly.

Gabriel held up his hand, as another of his men called him through the radio. *"Sir, we've found something you should see."*

Gabriel pressed his PTT. "Where are you?" he asked.

"In the kitchen," the voice responded.

"I'll be right there." Gabe looked at the men surrounding him. "Follow me," he said, heading towards the end of the corridor. Like all of the other men in Group Able, he had memorized the layout of the entire Governor's compound. "Talk to me," he said to Sabria, as they walked towards the kitchen.

"Sir, there are three bodies in the Hall of Mirrors. They appear to be terrorists. No women or children. No sign of the Governor."

As he got to the Blue Room, Gabriel slowed down briefly. He saw Styles rummaging through a body that lay almost exactly in the middle of the space that connected the Blue Room to the Hall of Mirrors, and noticed another body sprawled on the floor further beyond him. Styles directed a short glance in his direction but continued his search without uttering a word.

The four SEALs reached the kitchen a few seconds later. There was no need to ask the Seaman waiting for them why he had called. The kitchen was a mess. Flour covered a portion of the floor, showing the imprint of several footsteps. A kitchen cabinet had been partially destroyed—shredded to bits by gunfire—and been pulled aside. Beyond it lay what in the darkness seemed to be a small hidden chamber. It had to be the secret space where the Governor said he and the other hostages would hide.

"Any sign of life?" Gabe asked.

"No, sir," Boyd, the Seaman who had called, answered.

Gabriel walked to the edge of the entrance and peeked in. He could barely see anything, except for a faint vertical line of blurry light coming from the opposite side of the chamber. From his belt, next to his dagger, he pulled out a small flashlight and illuminated the murky chamber.

There was a half-open door at the other end of the room that had been struck by several bullets. He walked inside, followed by the others. Flashing his light, he found half a dozen dark droplets on the floor. He knelt, and swiped his index finger over one of them, examining his finger under the light. It was blood, but not enough blood to confirm a serious injury—a miracle, since a group of ten or so hostages would have been so pressed together in the small space that any bullets fired from the kitchen would by necessity have struck some of them. Probably, the hostages had abandoned the chamber before the shots were fired.

Gabe pointed his flashlight at the half-open door, and signaled Flanagan to follow him and the rest to cover them. Flicking off the light, he squeezed through the open space and took several quick steps to his right, crouching and pointing his sub machinegun into the room.

Flanagan stepped out right behind him but traveled in the opposite direction.

They found themselves in a wide, circular hall, dimly illuminated by a few, slit-like windows that allowed part of the moonlight to filter through them. The room was empty, so much so that its walls reverberated with the muffled scrapes of the SEALs' boots. There was a coffin-sized, rectangular opening on the floor close to the narrow window that faced the bay, ending on a short landing. Right after the landing, a curved, inner wall created a narrow, internal corridor. *Stairs,* Gabriel realized, *leading to the top and bottom of the tower.*

The sound of hurried footsteps reverberated through the opening of the stairs leading to the lower part of the tower. Gabe activated his PTT. "Effinger, somebody is trying to escape from the southern tower. See if you can intercept him."

"Roger that," Effinger answered.

"So you're back!" a voice coming from the gloom suddenly said in Spanish, startling the Navy SEAL.

"Whomever this is, you better come out with your hands up," the Navy SEAL said in English, turning back on his flashlight and aiming its beam at the entrance of the curved walled corridor that spiraled towards the tower's top. Quietly, he placed his lantern on the floor and moved away from it, signaling Flanagan to move closer to the source of the voice.

"Americans?" the voice said in English with a hint of hope and surprise.

"Yes. Navy SEALs."

"Can it really be? This is not some cruel joke from you, is it, Alacran?"

"I don't rightly know who this Alacran character is," Gabe said, "but if you're one of the Governor's friends, you're our friend as well. Is the Governor with you?"

"No."

"Where is he?"

"He left...with the others. Hey! How do I know you're not one of the Macheteros trying to...to fool me?" The man's voice sounded weak and tired.

"Do I sound like a Machetero?" Gabe asked.

The man chuckled. "No. But there's people who speak perfect English and are part of the...you know, the Machetero movement."

"Tell you what. I'll walk up to you, and you can tell me if I look like a Navy SEAL. If I don't, you can shoot me"

"Okay, but no weapons....I'll shoot you if I see that you are carrying one, understood?"

"Understood."

Gabriel took his .45 Colt out of his holster and lay it down on the floor with his sub machinegun. Picking up his flashlight, he walked towards the spiral staircase. Flanagan followed him a few paces behind, pointing his rifle at the source of the voice.

"I'm coming up!" Gabe warned, placing the flashlight on the landing, so that it would illuminate the stairs but not blind the man hiding in it.

He began to climb slowly with his hands above his head. At first, he could see no one, but then the figure of a man outstretched on the steps of the stairs came into view. He was dressed in tan pants and a long-sleeved, un-tucked shirt, and holding on to an AK-47 rifle. His left thigh had been dressed with some improvised cloth bandages that were drenched in blood. Even in the dim light, he looked very pale and feeble.

"Well what do you know," he said with a tired smile. "It *is* the Navy SEALs after all."

His rifle slipped from his hands and slid several steps down. Gabriel knelt next to him and grabbed his hand. "Flanagan, get the medic up here!" he shouted to his companion.

"Yes, sir!" the Irishman answered.

"Who are you?" Gabriel asked the wounded man.

"My name is Billy Hazard," the man answered weakly. He cleared his throat. "I'm one of the Governor's bodyguards. We...we were taken by surprise. Me and Picon, that's my boss, we were the only ones that survived...as far as I know."

"Where are the others?"

"I was...I was going to ask you," Hazard replied. "You didn't find them? They went down...to the gardens. To try to escape through the garage. You didn't find them?" he repeated with apparent concern.

"They were not in the gardens," Gabe said, his mind wandering. "But that may not be a bad thing. They may have gotten away. You say they went down? These stairs, you mean?" he pointed at the stairway spiraling downward.

Hazard nodded. "I stayed behind as a diversion. They thought the Governor was here, until the shooting started down in the yard." The bodyguard's face darkened with concern. "You say that you found nobody in the gardens?"

"No."

"Then they must have escaped. They were led by two very brave men. My boss, Picon... and a man called Lucas. He must be one of yours, because he fought like a one-man army...They must have gotten away." Hazard grabbed Gabriel's arm, and tried to get up. "We must find them!"

"We will find them, don't you worry," the SEAL answered, "but you must stay here."

"I can walk!" Hazard protested.

"No you can't. He turned his head back to the room. "Styles!"

"Sir!"

"Stay with Mr. Hazard until the doc gets here. Now Billy," he said to the wounded man, "you stay here. You've been a very brave man, but you need medical attention. I'll find the Governor. I promise."

"Sir! You should come to the central courtyard right away," Quijano said through the radio. Gabriel was at the base of the tower, trying to figure out what had happened. The iron-barred gate at the end of the stairs was open, proof that the hostages had escaped through it, but where had they gone? There had been shooting outside, but they had only found terrorist corpses. The Governor and his group had either made a clean getaway, or been captured and taken somewhere else. Effinger had caught a terrorist trying to sneak out of the tower. He had given up without a fight, and was waiting to be interrogated.

And now, finally, Quijano was calling with some news. *Back to where I started,* Gabriel thought as he hurried to the courtyard.

He found the fat terrorist they had captured sitting on the ground, his hands bound by a plastic strip behind his back, looking very sullen and defeated. The older woman sat opposite to him, directing venomous looks at the prisoner.

"Sir," Quijano approached his superior officer, while Effinger watched the captives. "It took a while, but I finally got some sense out of her. She was hysterical, and kept saying that the other guy wanted to kill her—"

"It's not true!" the fat terrorist interrupted from a distance with indignation. "El Alacran ordered me to kill her. I disobeyed him."

"You speak English!" Gabe said with surprise.

"Of course! Most of us do. What do you take us for, ignorant Americans?" The terrorist lowered his head and stared gloomily at the ground.

"The woman's name is Altagracia," Quijano continued saying. "She is one of the Governor's cooks. She's been babbling for a while about not going underground—"

"Underground?"

Quijano pointed to a mound of earth surrounded by yellow plastic tape. "As far as I could understand, the hostages went into that hole over there."

Gabriel walked to the mound of earth and for the first time saw there was a hole next to it. He looked for his flashlight, and realized that he had left it in the tower.

"Do you have a flashlight?" he asked Quijano, who answered by giving him his. He directed its light beam towards the hole until he found its bottom. Moving the lantern, he saw that it continued underground.

"It looks like an old tunnel! Must be…what? Twelve, fifteen feet down?" He turned towards the fat terrorist. "Do you know where this leads to?" he asked him.

The prisoner turned his head away.

"He doesn't want to talk," Effinger stated, repeating the obvious.

"Get a pail of water," Gabriel said. "We'll dunk his head in water until he talks."

The fat terrorist looked at the SEAL in shock. "You can't torture me," he said, more as a question than as a statement.

"The terrorists broke one of this woman's—Altagracia—fingers while they were questioning her," Quijano informed the others. "Maybe we could use the same method to get information out of this guy."

"Great idea," Gabriel said. "A lot more efficient."

"You're bluffing," the fat man said without much conviction. "You wouldn't do that."

"No? Effinger. Grab his right hand. Start with his thumb."

"Yes, sir!"

Effinger walked to the back of the bound man's hands. The terrorist had clamped his hands into two fists, but it was very easy for the SEAL to pry away his right hand's thumb. Effinger pulled it back until it could not stretch any more.

"Don't worry," he said consolingly. "It's not as if I'm cutting off."

Effinger began to apply more pressure on the finger and the terrorist screamed.

"I don't know where the tunnel goes!" he protested desperately. "They ran in there, and El Alacran followed them!"

"This 'El Alacran' person keeps popping up everywhere I go. When did this happen?" Gabe asked.

"Forty minutes, an hour ago," the prisoner answered in a defeated tone.

"How many people went with El Alacran?"

"Five…No, six, I think." The fat terrorist seemed to be on the verge of crying. "El Alacran ordered me to kill the woman, but I couldn't do it. Please! I've told you everything I know. Don't break my finger!"

"And nobody has come out of the hole since?" Gabriel asked, ignoring his entreaties.

The captive shook his head in despair, looking at the ground. Effinger released his finger and walked to where petty officer was standing.

"We're going after them," Gabriel said to him and the other three SEALs around him.

"Would you have broken his finger?" Effinger asked his superior officer.

Gabe directed a stone-faced glance at him, and began to walk towards the hole.

CHAPTER LXXIII

The intense banging on the ceiling, caused by Pietrantoni as he tried to widen the hole for Patria to crawl through, shattered the frail truce that Lucas had managed to negotiate. One of the men in the tunnel shouted something, and several guns opened fire, engulfing the tunnel in an earsplitting racket.

Lucas and Picon let their bodies fall to the floor, holding on to their weapons. Scores of bullets thumped into the barrels that protected them, making the wooden drums shake, causing more of their liquid to spill, or where the barrels were already empty, splintering wood and sometimes penetrating into the opposite side.

Then the gunfire began to slacken in intensity, and the two men rose to their knees and assumed their positions behind the slits in the barricade. As the shooting abated, El Alacran's shouts became more evident over the thunderous din, as did the hammering in the hall.

"Stop firing! Stop firing!"

Lucas and Picon exchanged a curious look.

"Hey Maestes! Are you still alive?" the Machetero yelled.

"Yes, thank you for your concern!" Lucas responded.

"What is that noise? Are you killing roaches again?"

"There's a terrible infestation—" Lucas began to say, but Andrade cut him sharply.

"It seems to me from that noise that somebody is trying to knock a hole through the wall."

Lucas looked at the improvised steps in the middle of the hall, where bits and pieces of the ceiling were cascading down with each noisy blow delivered by Pietrantoni's hammer.

"Nobody's knocking a hole through a wall," he answered truthfully.

"That was the wrong answer," the Machetero stated ominously. Then, addressing his men, he said, *"Kill them."*

Half a dozen automatic weapons opened fire. Lucas and Picon again dropped to the floor, as hundreds of rounds crashed into the already weakened barricade, splintering and shredding the wood, some of the more wildly fired shots grazing or ricocheting from the walls of the tunnel. Two of the top barrels began to lean forward as their sides were torn up, and then thudded into the floor, rolling into the corridor.

"Get ready to fire back!" Lucas shouted to his companion, who nodded curtly. "Set your weapon in automatic. It's no use firing individual rounds now! This barricade won't last more than a few minutes! Fire in short bursts!"

The bodyguard nodded again and Lucas raised his gun. "Now!" he ordered.

The two men sat up and looked through the slits between the remaining barrels. The tunnel was continuously illuminated by multiple blinks of light, as the muzzles from the terrorists' AK-47 rifles and Uzi sub machineguns discharged their deadly ware. Taking quick peeks through the slit, Lucas counted between four or five different sources of gunfire.

Picon slipped the barrel of his rifle through an opening on his side of the barricade. He began to discharge the AK-47 in short, deliberate bursts, raking the floor of the tunnel. The Macheteros' fire wavered instantly, as one of the men screamed in pain and another one cursed, apparently frightened or struck by the bullets.

For a moment, the corridor darkened, the terrorists only returning sporadic shots, the hurried sound of footsteps revealing their hasty retreat. Lucas slowly fired his revolver, aiming at the fleeting glimpses of moving bodies, his Magnum .357 thundering in the confined space, while Picon continued to spray the tunnel with sporadic gunfire.

Then a sub machinegun rattled out of the gloom, spitting dozens of rounds into the bullet-riddled barricade.

"*Fight, goddammit!*" El Alacran shouted from the darkness.

Both Lucas and Picon returned the fire, but one bullet hit a piece of the barrel next to where the bodyguard was shooting, showering his right eye with splinters, while another struck his rifle and a third his right shoulder. Picon fell backwards, dropping his rifle, while Lucas fired the three last rounds of his revolver.

"*Advance and continue to fire!*" Andrade screamed, heartened by the sudden silence of the barricade's defenders. There were several shouts as the Macheteros slowly advanced towards the barricade.

"Picon!" Lucas called out, crawling on all fours towards him.

"The rifle's busted," the bodyguard muttered in obvious pain.

Lucas sat next to Picon. "You're wounded," he said.

"I got hit on the shoulder. I think my right arm is broken," Picon whispered.

"They're coming. I'm going to need your handgun," Lucas said. He saw the faint outline of the gun's ivory handle sticking out from the bodyguard's waist and pulled it out. Although the terrorists continued to shoot, the intensity of the fire had by necessity decreased significantly, since at the most only two persons could fit through the width of the corridor blocked by the barrels.

Kneeling, Lucas fired blindly through the battered slit in the barricade. He heard a yelp of pain and someone curse, and thought he saw a body double up and fall, but then a thunderous volley drowned all the noise, and the barricade shook and groaned by the impact of dozens of more bullets. Several shots thudded into the barrels in front of him, and one whizzed through the open slit so close to his face that he instinctively raised his right hand to cover his ear. More of the wooden casks, empty of the oily fluid they held, began to shatter and buckle forward.

"We have to get out of here now!" Lucas shouted over the tremendous din. "This barricade won't hold long!" The ex-Ranger placed his companion's left hand over his shoulder, and both men scrambled to the right end of the tunnel's arched entrance, where the curved wall of the circular hall began.

Lucas let his companion rest and, leaning against the stone wall, began to reload one of the guns, feeding bullets from his gun belt into the Magnum's rotating cylinder at a maddeningly slow pace. The gun only held five rounds at a time, so he would have to make every shot count. He doubted that he would have the opportunity to reload again.

Another portion of the barricade fell, and its collapse was acknowledged by a shout of triumph further down the tunnel. The Macheteros continued their withering fire, intent on demolishing whatever was left of the barrier.

Amazingly, Arizmendi's tiny flashlight, which Pietrantoni had placed on the rim of one of the barrels of the makeshift ladder, had continued to work, untouched by any bullets, washing with a failing, tenuous light the center of the hall. Lucas briefly glimpsed at the impromptu structure of wooden drums, and saw movement on the barrel steps, although he could not tell who or how many were still there. However, Pietrantoni had stopped the hammering that had provoked the shootout.

Fortunately for them, the terrorists did not have a direct view of the improvised staircase. The tunnel ended on the right side of the circular hall. The hall's center was not visible to anyone traveling through the dark passageway. That, however, was about to change, as the Macheteros approached the entrance.

It was the sight of Arizmendi's small pocket lantern that reminded Lucas about his last contact with the Secretary of State and planted a wild idea in his head. It was an irrational, desperate impulse, but there was very little else to do. Tapping his pants pockets, he located what he was looking for and pulled it out. He unbuckled his gun belt and gave it to Picon with the other unloaded gun.

"Here," he said to the wounded bodyguard, "try to load this while I do something, and get ready to run to the ladder, whatever happens next."

"What are you—" Picon began to ask, but before he could finish his question, Lucas had crawled back to the barricade.

The shooting had once more abated, as the Macheteros neared the remains of the barrier that had blocked the entrance. Of the second tier of barrels that had formed the barricade, all but two had collapsed, its remnants looking like lonely, ragged teeth in a giant, punched-out mouth. The oil they had contained puddled all around them, its rancid, acrid smell having grown even more unpleasant; a great part of it already thickening like a gooey resin.

Lucas heard El Alacran urging his men to get to the barricade, his voice sounding so close now that he thought that he would jump over the tattered barrels at any moment. Taking the yellow lighter that he had retrieved from his pocket, the Puerto Rican began to thumb it desperately to get a flame. He lit it on his third try. The lighter's glow drew the attention of the men walking towards him and some of them began to shoot in his direction.

Lucas ducked behind one of the two barrels that had not been knocked down, and touched its oil-drenched wood with the flame of his lighter. For a heart-stopping heartbeat, nothing happened, but then the fire caught. He retreated quickly as red flames greedily licked, and then engulfed the barrel, and with amazing speed spread to the others below. Like a river of fire it flowed over the soaked floor into the corridor, and onto the oil puddle in the circular hall. One of the bottom barrels, apparently still full with the volatile fluid, exploded, scattering burning pieces of wood in every direction.

The speed of the conflagration took Lucas by surprise. Before he realized it, a wall of red flame rose before him and rolled like a burning carpet under his feet. He began to run away, trying to escape from the singeing heat and losing his gun in the process. He heard shouts of fear and dismay behind him, and then a dull, heavy thud overtook him, its force sweeping him forward like a rag doll and knocking him unconscious.

Governor Pietrantoni had attacked the bricks blocking Patria's progress with manic energy, knowing that the racket he was creating would galvanize the awaiting terrorists into action. Even so, the violence of the Macheteros' attack had shocked him. Although the hostages did not stand in the direct line of fire, several stray bullets ricocheted from the hall's walls, zipping past the terrified refugees, three of them becoming embedded in the barrels that held them. One landed so close to Arizmendi's right foot that he backed up abruptly and lost his balance, falling from the second tier of barrels onto the barrel below, the sword he was holding clanging on the floor.

"God damn it!" the Secretary of State had cursed, rubbing his right thigh and jumping to the ground to retrieve his lost blade. "Working for you is too dangerous!" he said to the Governor.

Pietrantoni had not stopped his frantic hammering, if anything increasing the rhythm of his blows. In the pauses between them, he could listen to Patria, invoking the Holy Virgin and dozens of saints, moaning whenever a brick shifted against her ample bosom. Then, quite suddenly, a whole row of the red blocks had yielded to a vicious swing of the hammer, cascading onto the ground below.

With renewed enthusiasm, Pietrantoni began to knock down large chunks of the ceiling until Patria slid free from the hole's hold.

"Are you all right?" he asked her. "Did I hurt you?

The old housekeeper slowly shook her head while she tried to recover her breath. "I'm fine," she answered. "Thank you, Mr. Governor."

"We have to hurry. Do you think you can make it up there now?"

Patria nodded and knelt on top of the uppermost barrel. Then, aided by Pietrantoni, she clumsily stood up, and managed to squeeze through the ceiling, raising both legs at the same time as unseen hands in the chamber above pulled her up.

"It's your turn, Alberto," the Governor said to Arizmendi.

The Secretary of State began to climb over the barrels, but stopped. "No, Mr. Governor," he said. "You go next."

"No, my friend, I will not leave without you."

"Don't waste any more time!" Double A retorted with surprising vehemence. "You are the Governor of Puerto Rico! You have a duty to survive!"

"Duty to survive?" Pietrantoni repeated with incredulity, but stopped, as a red glow suddenly illuminated the hall, growing with astonishing speed and intensity. Both men looked towards the barricade at the entrance, and realized for the first time that the barrels and the floor that surrounded them were burning fiercely. They saw Lucas running, and a barrel burst into flames, and then a bigger explosion shook the room, making the entire hall shudder.

Without giving it any further thought, the two friends jumped down from the piled up wooden drums and ran to his fallen companion. A small flame flickered from the lower part of one of Lucas' pants' legs, and Arizmendi patted it with his hands until he managed to snuff it out.

The Governor sat by Lucas and raised his head. To their right, the barricade burned fiercely, producing thick, hazy smoke that was rapidly accumulating in the ceiling and escaping through the trapdoor. Bits and pieces of burning wood surrounded them. Screams of pain, mingled with shouts of anger, filtered through the curtain of flames from the bowels of the tunnel.

"Mr. Governor, we should go!" he heard Picon say behind him. He turned his head and for the first time noticed his bodyguard. He appeared to be wounded in the right arm, his shirt and hand soaked in blood.

Pietrantoni nodded. "Lucas is unconscious," he began to explain, but as he spoke he felt his friend stir. Lucas opened his eyes and looked around him in a dazed and confused stupor.

"We have to go," he said, repeating almost word for word Picon's last statement.

"That was quite a fire you've started there, Alfaro," Arizmendi said.

"Yeah," Lucas glanced at the entrance. "That lighter of yours really packs a punch." Holding on to Pietrantoni and Arizmendi's hands, he sat up, and then stood.

The four men limped together towards the makeshift ladder, while behind them the Macheteros continued to scream.

The fire had started out of nowhere, a torrent of red flames rolling over the floor and spreading into the tunnel so quickly and unexpectedly that the men had to retreat or be consumed by it. As it was, they had managed to pull Andres away, wounded by a bullet in the left foot, before the blaze reached him, but Luis, struck twice in the chest and much closer to the hall's entrance, had not been so fortunate. Agonizing on the floor and his clothes soaked in the evil smelling liquid that had spilled out of the barrels, he had lit up like a torch before the rest of the men could get to him. His screams of agony had terrorized the rest of the men, all except El Alacran, who had stepped up to the edge of the flames and discharged his Uzi on the writhing body of his burning companion until the man had stopped screaming.

El Cubano and Pablo had watched with horror from a safe distance, coughing periodically as the tunnel began to fill with smoke. Andres leaned against the wall, trying to tie a tourniquet around his ankle with his belt.

"Come on, Alacran!" El Cubano shouted, his Cuban accent more marked than ever. "We're going to suffocate in here!"

"Nobody is going anywhere," the Machetero leader said in a barely audible growl, directing a fierce stare at his men, while he detached the spent ammo clip from his Uzi and attached another.

"But the fire—"

"Is burning out. That substance on the ground won't last forever," he assured them. It was true. Already the intensity of the flames on the floor was diminishing, only the barrels of the barricade continuing to blaze as fiercely.

Aiming his sub machinegun at the burning barrier, he began to fire at it, concentrating on one drum on the barricade's right hand corner. The Uzi's unrelenting assault began to crumble the burning barrel, which shot off crimson sparks and chunks of smoking debris, until it disintegrated into a glowing mass of embers, creating a gap in the wall of flames.

Reloading again, Andrade stared back at his men. "Come on!" he said to them, and began to run towards the hall's entrance, some thirty feet away. Knee-high flames licked at his legs and some of the lit oil splattered over his black leather shoes, but the small, spindly man dressed as an accountant did not waver, opening fire midway through his dash to kill any enemies who stood in his way.

Then he was through the gap, clearing the flames and diving to the floor. He tried to find the hostages but the hall was hazy with smoke and silent except for the crackle of the fire as it consumed the barricade.

He saw several archeological artifacts; swords, lances, chests and other objects that he could not quite make out through the hazy air. And more barrels, some stacked close to the wall, others bunched up in the center of the room. But he could not see the hostages.

Just then, Pablo rushed through the narrow gap in the barricade and knelt next to El Alacran, looking nervously from one side to the other.

"Where is El Cubano?" Andrade asked him, standing up. He began to walk around the perimeter of the hall, looking for hidden openings in the walls.

"He left. He said he was going to help Andres get back to La Fortaleza," Pablo replied, his three-fingered hand nervously moving up and down the barrel of his AK-47.

El Alacran nodded, not showing any kind of emotion, although he swore to himself that he would make El Cubano regret his insubordination. Now, however, he could not afford to get distracted by such a trifling matter.

The hostages were not there. Somehow, they had managed to find a way out. *But how?* Until a few minutes ago, they had been there, trying to stop him from getting in, hammering away at something. Surely, they had not vanished into thin air.

El Alacran retraced his steps back to the barricade. It continued to blaze violently, producing a strange red flame and faint black smoke that rose to the curved ceiling and...

And then he saw it. How stupid he had been! The smoke was flowing through an opening on the roof located directly over the barrels piled up in the middle of the hall.

El Alacran walked to the center of the room, and for the first time noticed the rubble surrounding the mound of accumulated drums. He had assumed they were debris from the barricade, but now he realized that they were pieces of brick.

"Come on!" he shouted to Pablo, beginning to climb the ladder of barrels. "They escaped through the roof!"

Headed by Pietrantoni, the hostages walked up a steep ramp that led to what seemed to be an outside gate, and hopefully to their freedom.

It had been the Governor who had first recognized where they were. Dimly illuminated by the orange glow filtering through the hole in the floor, the chamber into which he had climbed had looked very familiar to him. They were inside an ancient Spanish fortification; that was plain to see. A large storage area, from the looks of it, with high ceilings and windowless, thick walls.

It was the dark object embedded about ten feet high into one of the walls that had finally revealed to Pietrantoni their exact location. It looked like the end of a small, burned out, wooden beam, protruding about one foot out of the wall's surface. In reality, it was a piece of shrapnel fired by an American battleship during the Spanish American War, which had penetrated through the ten-foot thick outer wall of El Morro. It had been left there as a reminder of the war, to be admired by the countless future generations of Puerto Ricans and tourists who visited the fort.

Pietrantoni had been there countless times, mostly as a boy, when he dreamed of fighting pirates and corsairs. Had anybody told him then that as a grown man he would have dug his way into that room from an underground chamber, fighting for his life, he would have laughed. But here he was, doing just that, except that he was not fighting pirates but much more dangerous men, whose only mission at the moment was to find him and kill him.

Lucas had been the last one up. There had been a brief moment when everyone had embraced and celebrated their improbable escape, and then Lucas had quieted them down as they listened to the sound of gunfire in the chamber below them.

"We have to leave," Lucas had whispered.

"Follow me!" the Governor said. "I know the way..."

Lucas and Arizmendi had exchanged a look of curiosity. "This I have to see," Double A had muttered, causing a few chuckles.

Grabbing Francisco's hand, Pietrantoni had begun to walk up the ramp that led to the outside. Nereida had followed, holding on to Alfredo, while Patria limped behind them, assisted by Maria and Arizmendi. Lucas brought up the rear, with Picon's left arm draped over his shoulders. The bodyguard seemed to be in great pain and had lost a lot of blood, but had insisted in being the last man out.

As the group reached the top of the ramp, the Governor groaned with dismay. Before them stretched a large courtyard, surrounded on all sides by large, arched rooms that had served for various purposes during the long history of El Morro. Here troops had once been quartered and drilled. The main kitchen, with huge, table-like ovens, had been located there, as had been the troop's mess hall, and the washing area. And in the nineteenth century, some of the rooms had been used as cells to hold as prisoners the Puerto Rican patriots who had fought for independence from Spain.

The pale glow of a half moon washed over the open space, inevitably evoking ghostly images from the past. A cool breeze, smelling of the sea, stirred past the arched columns that surrounded the square, and brought with it the roar of the Atlantic's perennial assault on the fort's rocky shore.

The courtyard was the hostages' way to freedom. Another steep ramp, not visible from where the hostages stood, led from the open square to higher fortifications that faced the sea and the entrance to the bay, where the main batteries of the fortress had been located. From there, a long set of stairs rose almost ten stories high, all the way to the upper levels of the enormous bastion, and to the fort's main entrance.

But the hostages could not leave the room into which they had climbed. An iron-barred gate blocked their way, secured by a heavy, double-padlocked chain, making it impossible to exit into the courtyard.

"Good Lord," the Governor whispered in utter frustration. "Will anything be easy tonight? Why would anyone lock up this place? There's nothing here to steal!"

Lucas examined the lock. There was no way that they could break the thick chain. They were trapped, with no way out.

"Can't we shoot the lock?" Arizmendi asked. "Picon has a gun, doesn't he?"

Lucas shook his head. "That's movie stuff," he said, grabbing the lock and showing it to the others. "This is a heavy, thick padlock. The only way to open it is with armor piercing bullets, and the person shooting will probably get hit by the shrapnel or the ricocheting bullet."

"But I've seen it—" Arizmendi began to protest weakly.

"On TV, right?"

The Secretary of State nodded. "And in the movies," he added weakly.

"So what do we do now?" the Governor asked. "Those men..." he began to say, but stopped when he looked at the scared faces of those surrounding him. "I don't think they will follow us through that fire, but we can't stay here forever."

Lucas examined the iron bars of the gate. They were not very thick; a modern contraption installed to keep people out, rather than in, and avoid possible vandalism, or stop anyone from sneaking in to do mischief when the fort was closed. Maybe they could be bent.

"I'd like to try to bend one or two of those bars," he said to the Governor, pointing at the gate. "Maybe we can manage to sneak through them..."

"Oh no!" mumbled Patria. "Not again."

"It's worth a try," Pietrantoni agreed. "How do you want to do this?"

"You, Arizmendi, and I can grab one of the bars at its center and pull, to see if it bends. Then we can pull the bar next to it in the opposite direction."

Pietrantoni nodded. "Okay," he said. "Alberto, come over here," he said to Arizmendi. When the latter failed to answer, he looked around for him. "Where *is* Alberto?"

There was a moment of confusion as nobody could find the Secretary of State. Several in the group called out to him, until a voice deep inside the chamber from which they had just emerged, shouted back, "I'm here!"

"What the hell are you doing back there?" Pietrantoni asked in a half angry, half concerned voice.

"I remembered that I left my sword close to the hole!" Double A answered. "I'm going to get it. Maybe we can use it some way to open the bars."

"Forget about the sword!" Pietrantoni said impatiently. "We need you here!"

"It will only be a second! I'm close to the hole already!"

"Is he always this way?" Lucas asked the Governor, smiling.

"You have no idea," Pietrantoni responded with resigned exasperation. "Let's try it without him."

El Alacran thought that he heard voices as he climbed towards the opening in the ceiling, and signaled Pablo with his finger across his lips to remain silent. There would be a moment when he would be exposed when he popped his head out of the hole, but that could not be avoided. The smoke coming out of the hole would partially conceal him. And his Uzi would take care of anyone who was near by.

Like a salamander, he crawled upwards, peering over the edge of the gap towards the source of the noise. He could hear the voices clearly now, if somewhat far away; a child or a young female urging someone to "pull", men grunting as if engaged in a struggle to lift or move something very heavy.

At first, it was difficult to see clearly through the rising haze and the chamber's relative gloom, but as his eyes got used to the dark, he detected the outline of several figures, maybe forty to fifty yards away. They were at the upper end of a ramp, clustered close to what seemed to be an arched door. Even though moonlight filtered through the ramp's exit, the hostages were not moving. Two of the larger shadows were engaged in some sort of arduous activity, while the rest watched around them.

They were stuck, Andrade thought exultantly. *Apparently trying to break through some sort of gate.* And they seemed pretty confident that they had not been followed, since nobody was looking in his direction. Not that they would have seen anything from there.

Not bothering to get out of the hole, El Alacran rose until his chest had cleared the floor, and aimed his Uzi sub machinegun at the group. He did not enjoy killing children, but there could be no other way about it. Leveling his weapon at the two men who were doing the work, he pressed the trigger. The Uzi failed to fire.

Andrade cursed softly, realizing that he had spent the last of his bullets opening the gap in the barricade. Angry at his own stupidity, he discarded the empty sub machinegun on the floor, and reaching to the holster under his left arm, drew out his Mamba Parabellum. As he slid off the gun's safety, he confirmed that it was already cocked and ready to be fired.

Gripping it with both hands, he rested his two elbows on the floor and took careful aim at what he thought was the tallest of the figures by the door. The hostages were so concentrated on their work that they had not even noticed the clatter of the Uzi as it hit the ground.

"This is as far as you go, Mr. Governor," he uttered with great relish.

He could not find the sword. Arizmendi was certain he had left it close to the hole, but it was so dark that he could not see it. At first, he had tried to locate it by dragging his foot over the floor in the hope that he would trip on it. When that had not worked, he had begun to grope on all fours, widening his area of search. It could not be *that* far away from the hole through which they had escaped.

He was so concentrated rummaging around that he failed to notice the figure of the man who silently emerged from the floor. It was not until he heard a sharp noise, similar to the clatter of a metallic object, that he realized that someone else was nearby.

He turned, and saw the head and chest of a man jutting out of the gap through which he and the other hostages had escaped from the chamber below. The unexpected sight nearly made him scream with fright, but he managed to choke down the cry in his throat as he realized that he was behind the man's back, and that the man was so concentrated on what was happening at the ramp that he had not noticed him.

Just then, the tips of his fingers came upon a cold, hard edge, which he recognized immediately as the blade of his lost sword. Not taking his eyes from interloper, he traced the blade back to its hilt and wrapped his fingers around it. As he did so, he saw the dwarfish figure in front of him look briefly down and bring up a silvery object that he carefully aimed at the unsuspecting group standing by the barred gate.

"Stop!" he screamed with all his strength, prompting all activity to cease at the ramp and the startled half man to twist with dazzling speed.

Grasping the sword with both hands, Arizmendi rose to his feet, and ran towards the hellish apparition that had risen from the ground. But as he moved forward, he stumbled, nearly falling head first, the tip of his blade shooting tiny sparks as it grazed the surface of the floor with a metallic rasp. He saw the apparition in the hole snarl and aim his gun at him, but by then the sword had plunged into the man's torso, a second before his gun went off. Arizmendi continued to fall forward holding on to the ancient weapon, so that that the blade carried the full weight of his body.

Unable to stop himself, the frightened Secretary of State gripped the hilt of the sword with all his strength, as the blade slid through the gunman's chest. The impaled terrorist opened his mouth in a soundless scream and tried to grab the blade with his left hand in a futile effort to stop its deadly progress, but the sword's sharp edges nearly severed most of his fingers. Then, abruptly, the sword stopped, as it ran completely through the surprisingly emaciated body, and its tip became embedded on the boards of the ceiling.

The sudden impact made Arizmendi lose his hold on the sword, and he would have pitched head first into the hole in the floor had he not been stopped by the skewered terrorist. Frantically backing away, the terrified Secretary of State looked at the man, who stared back at him in utter amazement. The Machetero opened his mouth as if to speak, but blood gushed out of it, spilling over his chin and chest. With a last, supreme effort, he raised his gun and aimed it at Arizmendi. But then, with a prolonged, gurgling hiss, he let his hand drop and stared blankly at his tormentor.

Arizmendi groaned and closed his eyes, sobbing. He felt someone place a hand on his shoulder, and looked up, surprised to see Lucas leaning over him. He was holding the terrorist's gun.

"Are you hurt?" he asked.

Arizmendi shook his head, but as an afterthought, patted his body to make certain. "I'm okay..." he said, his voice quaking.

Lucas helped him up to his feet. "Thank you," he said to the shaken Secretary of State. "You saved all our lives. You're a hero."

Double A nodded and fainted.

Pablo was waiting for El Alacran to move into the upper chamber when his leader's legs began to shake violently, and then separated completely from the top of the barrel, hanging limply like a ceiling appendage.

"Are you—" the Machetero began to ask, but stopped, as blood began to trickle from El Alacran's shirt and waist. Not saying another word, the terrorist jumped from the barrels and ran away in panic, trying to distance himself as quickly as possible from that hellish place.

The three men pulled at the metal bar and slowly it began to budge until it curved sideways. They rested for a second, catching their breaths, while the women and the children cheered. Then they moved to the second bar, pulling it in the opposite direction.

Further away, by the trapdoor, Picon stood watch over the limp figure of the dead terrorist, holding in his left hand the Mamba Parabellum. It was not his shooting hand, but if needs be, he could fire it point blank at anybody who attempted to enter from the chamber below.

However, nobody came.

CHAPTER LXXIV

FBI Special Agent Mario Franceschini escorted Captain Francisco Ramirez out of the General Police Headquarters in Hato Rey, followed by two of his men and Colonel Montañez. A black Lincoln Continental with another FBI agent standing by the open rear door waited for them, just outside the building's back exit.

The group of armed men moved quickly. Built like a fortress, the General Police Headquarters was a square, sprawling, ten-story building that towered over the National Guard armory, located to its right, and over the residential area to its left. No threat to the safety of the prisoner, protected by a bulletproof vest, could come from those areas. But to the west, close to the police parking lot, were several three-story buildings that belonged to the Nemesio Canales public housing project, and that posed a potential security risk for the prisoner.

Like many of the other public housing complexes in Puerto Rico, Nemesio Canales had at different times fallen under the influence of local drug lords who acted as the mini-rulers of the community. Difficult to control, sometimes bribing members of the police and the political establishment and buying the loyalty of many of the residents, the home-grown chieftains constituted a constant headache for the local authorities.

To counter the influence of the drug gangs, Superintendent Maldonado had established a series of programs in the communities that encouraged sports, cultural, and social activities, while at the same time conducting unannounced lightning strikes in those spots where drugs were sold or distributed. The programs had enjoyed a certain modicum of success, but by no means had eradicated all of the drug-related criminal activities. Every so often, rival gangs would clash in open shootouts or single gang members would be executed, and many innocent residents had been caught in the crossfire.

Nemesio Canales was not an exception. Placing a sniper with a long-range rifle on the rooftop of one of its buildings—to silence Ramirez before he could try to negotiate a deal with the authorities—would be a relatively easy thing to do for anyone who had the right connections. The police captain, therefore, had to board the waiting vehicle as quickly and as anonymously as possible.

Franceschini had been surprised when Montañez had shown up in the holding cells of the police building, as the FBI man was finishing the paperwork to transfer Ramirez to the federal facilities in Chardon Street, about two miles away. During their prior telephone conversation, Maldonado had assured Franceschini that he would call Montañez back to the interim command post in the San Geronimo Plaza, to keep him away from Ramirez while the transfer was being conducted. However, not only was Montañez there, but he had vehemently objected to the transfer of the prisoner to the federal authorities. Even after the FBI agent had claimed jurisdiction over the detained man and assured Montañez that the prisoner would be safe, the police colonel had questioned Franceschini's authority and refused to release the prisoner.

Only after the Superintendent had instructed his friend by telephone to hand over Ramirez to the FBI, had Montañez grudgingly relented, but then had demanded to ride with the prisoner to the Federal Building. For a moment, Franceschini had considered calling Maldonado again to order the colonel to stay in the police station, but after thinking it over he had agreed and allowed Montañez to come.

Captain Ramirez looked terrified. Rather than changing jails, he seemed to be walking to his execution. He kept glancing from side to side, as if expecting to be shot at any moment. When he got to the waiting car and Franceschini pushed his head down so that he would not hit the upper edge of the door, the captain rushed inside, closing his eyes with relief when Montañez slid next to him and slammed the car's door shut. Franceschini sat on the other side of the back seat, jamming Ramirez between him and Montañez. Two other agents sat up front, while a second black automobile, parked in front of the Lincoln, led the way.

The two FBI vehicles rolled out of the police parking lot with no lights flashing or sirens blaring, a precaution taken by Franceschini, who wanted the transfer to draw as little attention as possible. They waited for the red light to change, and then turned left into Roosevelt Avenue, driving past Plaza Las Americas—Puerto Rico's largest shopping mall—and the Hiram Bithorn Stadium. The small caravan continued towards the Hato Rey financial district, where it would turn left again to head east down Muñoz Rivera Avenue.

The night traffic was very light, as it usually was at that time of the night, when most of the activity in the restaurants was winding down, the stores in the area had closed, and people were preparing for the next workday. The two cars moved at a steady forty miles an hour, slowing down at red lights but continuing after verifying that there was no oncoming traffic. Even Ramirez had begun to relax as they passed the Telemundo Television Station and began to close in on the Muñoz Rivera Avenue intersection.

The crash happened quite suddenly and unexpectedly. A white van approaching the Lincoln on its right abruptly veered and nosedived into the rear of the FBI car, violently shaking the passengers inside. Ramirez screamed and Montañez's head partially hit the glass on the window, causing him to drop his shotgun.

"We're being attacked!" Franceschini shouted into a walkie-talkie. "Move! Move! Move!"

The black Lincoln accelerated, its right rear tire screeching and burning rubber as it rubbed the twisted metal where the van had struck. Franceschini saw the escort car also speed up, but then he was thrown sideways as the van hit the Lincoln a second time. There was a loud bang as the rear tire exploded, followed by the repeated thuds of the shredded rubber thumping on the car's undercarriage. Franceschini drew out his .45 Automatic and aimed it at Montañez, just as the latter recovered his shotgun.

"Don't move! Drop your shotgun or I'll shoot!" he yelled at the colonel, who stared back at him in surprise. "I mean it!"

The car was bouncing in the rear and noticeably slowing down. However, as the pursuing van approached it to ram it again, the Lincoln's driver slammed on the car's brakes and swerved his vehicle to the right. With no time to react, the van surged past the FBI car, narrowly missing it. The Lincoln continued changing lanes until it reached the last lane to its right.

"Turn into Hostos Avenue!" Franceschini instructed his driver. "It's a narrower street and the van will have less space to maneuver."

The damaged Lincoln made an abrupt turn to the right in the next street and entered Hostos Avenue, while the van and the lead FBI car continued down Roosevelt Avenue. Franceschini heard the screech of tires as their pursuer realized it had lost the Lincoln and presumably stopped to turn around and follow it. However, by that time, they had lost sight of the van.

"Hurry! Hide in the first alley you find and turn off the lights. Hopefully we'll lose them until reinforcements get to us," Franceschini said.

The driver sped up the car until he came upon a narrow alley to his right. Slowing down, he turned into it, and turned off the lights.

Ramirez looked deathly ill, his face bathed in perspiration. He was shaking uncontrollably, staring in panic at his companions.

"Don't kill me, please!" he sobbed.

"Why are you pointing your gun at me?" Montañez asked Franceschini angrily, ignoring the babbling prisoner. "Do you think I'm trying to kill Ramirez? Are you *crazy*?"

Lights flooded the inside of the car as the lead FBI vehicle rolled into the alley and parked behind the damaged Lincoln. Two agents immediately stepped off it bearing long arms, and walked towards the stopped car. Then the white van slowly came into view and parked perpendicularly to the alley's exit, blocking it.

"Get out of the car," Franceschini said to Montañez and Ramirez.

"Why?" Ramirez said, his fear mounting.

A thin smile appeared on Montañez's lips. "Don't you know? Franceschini is your partner. He's the main contact with the drug lords."

Ramirez stared incredulously at the FBI man, and understood at last. His bladder gave way and he peed in his pants. Franceschini sighed.

"I'm sorry it had to end this way, Alejo," he said to Montañez, leaning and grabbing the shotgun from the car's floor. "I like you. You've always been this...how can I describe it? This larger than life hero to me, fighting corruption and drug dealers. The leader of the Untouchables. But then Maldonado phoned me tonight and told me that Ramirez was talking to anyone who would listen. Claiming that he was not the main 'mole' in the police force, that he was just another pawn of the real mole, and that he could disclose his name in exchange for protection. Maybe even for some sort of immunity, eh Ramirez?"

"I never said anything to Maldonado!" Ramirez protested desperately, glancing nervously at the men approaching the car. "I never knew it was you! You always distorted your voice with one of those mechanical voice devices! Except for two times, we always spoke on the phone! And those two times that we met, you were in...in the shadows. I never saw you! How could I tell on you? How can I, even now? I never saw you!" he said frantically.

"No, you never did. And it's obvious you didn't know, or you wouldn't have told Maldonado that your contact was Montañez."

"Montañez? I never told Maldonado—"

"Please be quiet," Franceschini said to the terrified captain. "You talk too much." Then he looked at Montañez. "Maldonado called me," he explained casually, his gun pointed at Montañez's chest. "He told me that Ramirez wanted to talk to him. I was not overly concerned about that. Like this idiot said, I was ninety-nine point nine percent certain that there was no way that he could identify me. The fact that he had a telephone contact number didn't worry me. I was sure it could not be traced back to me. But there's always that tiny doubt that remains in the back of your mind. Had I somehow given myself away by some inadvertent mistake? Did he really know who the mole was? It was something that I was resigned to live with. So I decided that I would watch how matters developed, and if I saw the noose tightening, I...and my men, the six you see here, we'd get away."

Franceschini laughed. "But then, Maldonado called and asked me to take care of Ramirez! Can you believe that? And to make matters even better, he told me in strict confidence that he suspected that *you* were the mole. I agreed to take care of Ramirez with...how can I describe it? With great reluctance. To be fair, I protested your innocence, but your good friend Maldonado would not hear of it! It was you! He was certain of it. Incredible, isn't it?"

Ramirez groaned and began to sob loudly.

"But once Ramirez dies in your custody, you will become a prime suspect, don't you think?" Montañez said.

"Well...yes and no," Franceschini replied. "If you had not come, I would have told them that we were intercepted by some masked, armed men in a white van, and that they executed this...this fine specimen of a policeman."

"The white van was a nice touch," Montañez conceded sarcastically.

"Wasn't it, though? Of course, privately, I would have told Maldonado that one of the masked men sounded like you. One of my men would have confirmed my impression. The firearm that shot him would have appeared in the trunk of your car. I even instructed Ramirez—by telephone, before he was arrested—to plant in your desk in the police headquarters twenty thousand dollars in cash and the telephone he used to contact the terrorists. I would say there's more than enough evidence to convict you."

"I didn't know! I didn't know it would be used this way!" Ramirez protested between sobs.

"Yes you did, you slimy bastard," Franceschini sneered. "You thought you were framing him and that nothing would happen to you!" He returned his attention to Montañez. "I would have to be wounded to make it even more convincing, but that's part of the business. I was considering a shot here," he said, raising his left arm. "Nothing vital, of course."

Montañez considered the FBI agent's words in silence, while Ramirez continued to weep in the background. Franceschini looked at his watch.

"Anyway, we've already lost a lot of time. Anything else you'd like to know? Your insistence to come with us simplified matters even more. Now I can tell Maldonado that you hijacked us and forced our driver to lose our escort and bring us here. You shot Ramirez, but I managed to shoot you first before you were able to kill me. I'll still have to get some sort of wound—you're too good to have gone down without a fight—but somehow, miraculously, I managed to survive. I'll be distraught. How could a personal friend of mine act this way? How could he betray us, the Superintendent, me, the people he served, in such a cold-blooded fashion? I'll be grief-stricken."

Montañez shook his head sadly. "How could you do this to us? You're smart, talented, sure to make headway in the FBI. And you're our friend."

"And will be your friend until the moment you die," Franceschini responded with cold sincerity. "Friendship has nothing to do with this. A great career with the FBI? Don't make me laugh! How much higher do you think I'll go? Do you really think they'll promote a Puerto Rican to one of the top positions in the FBI? No, my friend, this is it. No matter how well I do, this is as far as I'll go. I'll retire some fifteen years from now with the thanks of people like you and Maldonado and a so-so pension, depending on how much costs the government is cutting at the time. Do you realize how much money I've made with the cartels? I can retire to a mansion in Europe tomorrow if I want to! Of course, I won't. I'll wait a couple of years, and then I'll do it, still lamenting your death."

Franceschini waited for Montañez to say something, but the colonel remained silent. "Is that it, then? No cursing or pleading for your life? Somehow, I imagined you'd do something else before you died. No?" He flicked his eyes towards the two men up front, returning them immediately to the police colonel. "Okay, then. Freddy, keep them covered while I slip on my gloves...."

Franceschini brought out a pair of gray linen gloves from the inside pocket of his jacket and began to put them on. "Fingerprints..." he explained. "I'll shoot Ramirez first with your shotgun. It will be messy, with all the blood and brains splashing around the car."

Ramirez screamed.

"I'll have to get out of the car and shoot him from your angle, just to be consistent when they examine the trajectory of the bullets...But we have to do it right, you know, for consistency." He finished putting on the gloves, grabbed the shotgun, and opened the car's door. "I'll be right with you," he said, but stopped, as he heard the sound of several police sirens approaching.

The two men standing next to the car turned their heads towards the end of the alley. The blue glare of police lights swept over the white van and flooded the street beyond. Franceschini saw the van accelerate and then crash into something out of sight, beyond the alley's corner. He heard several shouts, some gunshots, and then several plainclothes men and policemen began to pour into the alley. The two men flanking the car backed away, while those up front opened their doors and fled. However, there was nowhere to go in the enclosed alley.

Thinking fast, Franceschini tossed the shotgun inside the car and pulled out his FBI badge, flashing it at the oncoming policemen. "FBI! FBI!" he shouted just before he was tackled by two of the plainclothes men. "I'm Special Agent Mario Franceschini, dammit!" he shouted furiously, as the men flipped him on his belly and handcuffed his wrists behind his back. "I'm transferring a prisoner to our offices! You're making a mistake! The man in the back of the car, Colonel Montañez, he hijacked our vehicle and was trying to kill our prisoner! You're making a big mistake!"

The two men grabbed Franceschini by both of his arms and pulled him back to his feet. The FBI agent saw his driver and his companion walking towards the alley's exit with their arms raised above their heads. Then he watched Colonel Montañez step out of the rear of the Lincoln.

"He's the man you should arrest!" Franceschini shouted. "He was trying to execute Captain Ramirez!"

The two men stared uncertainly at the police colonel, and then at Captain Ramirez as he emerged from the other side of the car. The captain's pants were visibly wet.

"Are you all right, sir?" one of the men asked.

"Of course he's all right!" Franceschini said angrily. "He was trying to kill us, and I'm the one getting arrested! Don't let him get away!"

"I'm fine," Montañez answered calmly. "Sergeant Salgado, let me introduce you to Special Agent Franceschini of the FBI. Franceschini, this is Sergeant Claudio Salgado, or as you would call him, one of my 'Untouchables'."

"A pleasure, sir," Salgado said courteously.

"Read him his Miranda rights," Montañez said. "Then afterwards, ask him why he's wearing gloves."

"You have the right to remain silent..." Salgado began.

"You have no evidence!" Franceschini shouted, hoping the rest of his men would hear him and follow his lead. "It's your word against mine and that of my men!"

"He tried to kill me!" Ramirez cried, looking at the FBI agent, still so terrified that he had to hold on to the car's roof in order not to fall.

"There you go," Montañez said with a smile.

"Anything that you say can be used against you..." Salgado continued in a businesslike monotone.

"He's a liar! He's your partner! He wants to implicate me so that you can go free!" Franceschini protested angrily. He turned towards Salgado.

"Search his office! Go ahead, do it! I'm sure you'll find evidence there that—"

"You have the right to have an attorney present before and during the time you're being questioned..." Salgado stated.

"You have no evidence! Nobody will believe you or that...that...drug cartel mole", he said spitefully, nodding at Ramirez. "My men will back me up. It's your word against ours! Who do you think they'll believe?"

"If you can't afford an attorney, you have the right to have one appointed at public expense to represent you during the questioning," Salgado concluded.

"Oh! I almost forgot," Montañez said as an afterthought. "I also have this." He opened his jacket. Underneath, he was wearing a bulletproof vest. Taped to the vest was a small microphone. "We've been taping you since we left headquarters. I think your credibility is probably worth about as much as a wad of used toilet paper."

Franceschini took a step back, as if he had been physically struck. He heard a cell phone ring, and saw Montañez search his pants pockets and fish out an iPhone. He listened for several seconds, and then said, "Yes, sir," and ended the call. "That was Superintendent Maldonado. He's been listening with great interest to our conversation, live. He's asked me to tell you that he agrees with my assessment that your credibility is worth about as much as a wad of used toilet paper."

The FBI man slumped in the arms of his two custodians.

"Take him and his friends back to headquarters," Montañez said. Then noticing Ramirez, he added, "And find some new pants for this man."

CHAPTER LXXV

The concentrated fire of the two heavy-caliber MAG machine guns reverberated like deafening thunder, smashing into the two closed doors at the back of the ballroom. Like angry, mechanical wasps, the bullets slashed vicious holes into the wood and mangled the locked doorknobs, until the locks fell apart, leaving in their place a gaping hole about the size of a volleyball.

It was the moment that Colonel Calderon had been waiting for. Reinforced by the six men that he had left guarding the pool area, the Venezuelans stood ready to crash into the hall as soon as the MAGs finished dismembering the doors.

"They have forfeited their right to be treated with any kind of consideration. We shoot to kill anyone holding a gun," Calderon shouted to his men through the din of the gunfire. It was an unnecessary order; the men were in a killing mood, itching to avenge their fallen comrades.

The MAGs went suddenly still, as one of the doors began to swing inwards into the hall. The abrupt end of the shooting allowed the screams of terror from the hostages inside to be heard.

"Soldiers of Venezuela, this is our time!" Calderon shouted. "For our country and Puerto Rico!" he said, aiming his gun at the doors and marching forward.

Captain Gomez did not realize that they were being attacked from the rear until the crowd behind him began to scream and move away in panic from the back doors. He saw many people jumping and tripping over others, desperately pushing and shoving their way out of the line of fire, as some of the bullets began to penetrate the doors and hit the wall on the opposite side of the hall. The retreating hostages surged forward, swamping the narrow corridor along the outside wall and doors of the hall that he had managed to keep open up to that time, blocking his way to the back of the ballroom, and swallowing the lookouts that he had posted on the doors. Gomez found himself struggling to get through the crowd, followed by Negron and the ragged remnants of his recruits.

Suddenly, the doors flew open and three men entered, discharging their automatic weapons into the ceiling and shouting to the hostages to lie down on the floor. Raising his sub machinegun with both of his hands to eye level, Gomez took a deep breath and waited for the people blocking his way to drop down.

There was no way to get to the terrorists before they barged into the ballroom. So he would let them bring the fight to him.

The two advance men of Platoon One walked briskly from the pool area to the back corridor, their HK-417 semi automatic rifles ahead of them, staying as close as possible to the wall of the ballroom, stopping short of the corner that concealed the two MAGs firing at the hostages. The first man ventured a quick glimpse around the corner's edge and immediately pulled his head back, as he saw several armed men with their backs partially turned towards him, apparently waiting to move into the hall where the hostages were hiding. Then he ventured a second peek, counting the men in front of him.

He turned back to the man waiting a few yards behind him, and formed a zero with his hand by joining the tips of his thumb and middle fingers, indicating that there were ten men, and afterwards pumped his forearm up and down, signaling the others to hurry up. The second man relayed the signals, prompting Ensign Mark Aguirre and the rest of the squad to move forward until they had reached the advance men.

The lead SEAL backed up a couple of paces, and allowed his superior officer enough space to look out. Crouching, Aguirre watched the men for an instant, then stretched his left arm horizontally, ordering his men to form a line abreast. Three of the SEALs stood shoulder-to-shoulder and waited for the ensign's signal to attack, the rest forming behind them.

Just as they did so, the heavy machine guns stopped firing. The silence was instantly followed by the loud crash of a door, and the ragged firing of automatic weapons. Standing to his full height, Aguirre raised his sub machinegun and rushed forward.

"This is Platoon 1, engaging," he spoke into his PTT communications device, warning the other units.

Almost at the same time, McAllister's Platoon 3 surged forward, surrounding the Macheteros that were milling about the opposite end of the corridor. There were close to twenty of them, some arguing animatedly on the outer fringes of the group, most staring into the corridor that led to the main ballroom, watching the gun battle that unfolded at its opposite end.

None of them seemed to be aware of the SEALs' approach until an obese man stared distractedly towards the hotel's outside grounds and gaped at six of the Americans, not more than ten yards away, running in his direction. The obese man raised his weapon to fire at the same time that he shouted "The Americans!" but a barrage of bullets cut him down immediately.

Despite the shouted warning and the sound of gunshots, only a few of the other Macheteros stirred, either too concentrated on the fierce fighting taking place in the main ballroom area, or mistaking the gunfire for that of the Venezuelans. Two other men standing next to their fallen comrade looked about them confusedly, one of them crouching to examine the downed terrorist, the second realizing what was happening and raising his hands over his head.

"Throw your weapons down!" a voice shouted, as more of the Macheteros began to realize what was happening. Ten SEALs were now standing not more than a dozen feet away from them in a wide semicircle, aiming their semiautomatic rifles at the clustered terrorists. "Raise your hands over your heads!"

Most of the surrounded men obeyed without delay. One waved a gun ambiguously in front of his chest and was shot on the spot. That encouraged the rest of the men to speed their surrender. Guns clattered on the floor, as four of the SEALs shouldered the rifles and advanced to search and tie with self-locking plastic strips the wrists and ankles of the captured men.

"Platoon 2, secure the lobby," McAllister ordered, as he continued to watch the men who had just surrendered. "Capo," he shouted to the medic in his group, an enormous New Mexican—taller and more heavily built than McAllister—whom the men called "The Hulk". "Tend to the wounded."

Calmly, almost casually, he turned on his heels and began to walk towards the lobby.

Michelle saw the doors at the back of the ballroom break open and several men burst into the hall with their weapons blazing. Those around her instinctively shied away from the invaders in utter disorder, blinded by fear and trying to shove out of their way those who blocked them. A few tried to restore order but were ignored, either carried by the throng, or pushed down in the frenzy.

Afraid that Archie would be trampled to death, Michelle stood in front of him and tried to contain the advancing mass of people. However, the terrified hostages hit her like a tidal wave and knocked her off her feet.

She fell on top of two persons that were covering Archie's chest and head, trying to protect him with their bodies from the stampeding crowd. They were the young doctor and the nurse, she noticed, as she struggled to get back up. They were lying on their hands and knees, creating a space between them and the wounded redhead. Dr. Schaeffer was nowhere in sight, probably swept away by the fleeing mass of scared people.

Michelle crawled to them, spreading as much as she could over their backs to add to their protection, and prayed.

People were dropping to the floor or trying to run away, but still Captain Gomez did not have a clear shot at any of the men who had barged into the hall. He could see them clearly—four of them so far—but he could not shoot at them without risking hitting one of the hostages.

A bald, very fit man, possibly in his forties, was leading the attack. He was scanning the hall for his enemies, his fierce, hawk-like gaze sweeping over the fleeing hostages. Almost immediately, he spotted Gomez, and then flicked his eyes to the other hostages who were holding weapons. He spoke to one of his followers briefly, pointing at the SWAT captain, and then both men aimed their weapons in his direction.

Gomez realized that the two men were about to shoot him, regardless of the hostages that stood between them. Instantly, he raised his hands above his head and let his sub machinegun drop in an ostensive sign of surrender. He knew that the terrorists did not care about how many hostages died, and that to engage the armed men in a shootout would only lead to heavy loss of life.

"Don't shoot!" he shouted. "We surrender!"

Beside him, Negron turned his head livid with rage. "What are you doing?" he asked, looking at him as if he were insane. Across the hall, one of the terrorists prepared to fire but the bald man held his arm and said something to him.

"Do as I say!" Gomez ordered the rest of his men. "We can't fight through all of these people."

Negron shook his head in despair and dropped his AK-47, slowly raising his hands. The other men reluctantly followed his lead.

The rapid fire of several automatic weapons suddenly shook the corridor outside the hall. The bald man looked towards the shattered doors with surprise, and then, with a shocked expression, shouted at his companions to turn. But before the others could react, two of the terrorists were mowed down by gunfire.

Gomez hesitated, seeing his opportunity to act. But the man pointing the rifle at him must have read the SWAT officer's body language and fired, the first shot winging an unfortunate woman on the shoulder, the second and third shots hitting Gomez squarely on the chest.

As he fell, Gomez saw the back of the shooter's head explode, and then lost sight of him.

The SEALs opened fire just as the Venezuelans standing by the MAGs became aware of them. Almost at point-blank range, the concentrated blast of six automatic rifles riddled with bullets the five men standing closest to the MAG machineguns, scattering their bodies on the floor like discarded rag dolls. Another man, standing closer to the breached ballroom doors, saw what was happening and discharged wildly his AK-47 as he ran towards the heavy machineguns, but was killed a second later by the SEALs deadly fusillade.

Even before the man fell, Aguirre and two of his men had advanced towards the ballroom seeking new targets. They knew that they had to follow up immediately, to catch the terrorists off balance before they could cause any more damage. The scene inside was chaotic, with scores of hostages running and pushing to get out of harm's way.

There were four armed men inside, and two of them were in the process of turning to fire in their direction, while a third was aiming his rifle into the ballroom. Aguirre hesitated for a split second, afraid to miss and hit one of the civilians standing behind the terrorists, but then his training took over and he discharged a short burst from his sub machinegun, aiming it at the chest—the broadest part—of the man standing furthest to his right. At the same time, the two other SEALs fired.

Aguirre saw his target double over, as half a dozen bullets racked his lungs and stomach, one bullet striking the hand with which he held his rifle and sending two of his fingers spinning into the air. The second man grunted and fell down on his knees. For one second he held on to his rifle, trying to use it as a crutch, and then he pitched forward, slamming his face on the floor.

There was a scream of rage, and a hail of gunfire erupted from inside the hall. With the corner of his eye, Aguirre saw one of his men fall, and he ducked instinctively when a bullet grazed his helmet. When he looked back up, he was able to catch a glimpse of the man who had just fired at him, pointing his weapon into the ballroom, and running towards the hostages. He was following a bald man. He tried to aim his rifle at the fleeing terrorists, but by then they had pushed their way into the crowd.

"Sellers is down!" he heard the man next to him shout, but Aguirre was already running after the two armed men.

Calderon tried to clear a path along the press of terrified hostages, using the butt of his sub machinegun to open his way. He was followed closely by Corporal Caraballo, the last surviving member of his party.

The Venezuelan colonel ran towards the last set of doors at the back of the ballroom, praying that he could open them from the inside. He tried not to think about what had happened, knowing that he had to focus exclusively on what he was doing, or he would not leave the hotel alive. Even so, he could taste his own bile, the feeling of utter failure and despair choking and overwhelming him.

How could things have taken such a turn for the worse so quickly? he wondered despite his resolve not to dwell on their defeat, but he could not drive his doubts away. *It had been San Miguel,* he thought. *San Miguel had betrayed them. He had betrayed everyone by withdrawing too quickly from the field.* But he could find no solace from his determination. The decision to stay had been his and his alone. He could not lay the blame for the loss of his men on anyone but him.

As he got to the doors, he heard one of the Americans shout for everyone to lie down on the floor, and knew he only had a few seconds to make it out of the hall. People were scrambling to get out of his way, and dropping to the floor. Soon, he would have no cover. He felt Caraballo running just a few steps behind him, and he grieved for the loss of so many good men. *Damn the Americans! Where had they come from?*

He reached the doors and frantically shook their twin handles, but they were locked. He cursed, and walking back a few steps discharged the remainder of his ammunition clip at the door handles, but with little effect.

"Cover us!" he ordered Caraballo, while he knelt to reload his weapon.

The Venezuelan corporal turned, standing between the oncoming SEALs and his colonel. The throng of people they had used as cover had thinned out to one or two persons, the rest lying on the ground or moving away. Caraballo had no chance to fire, as he was hit several times by three of his advancing enemies. He fell backwards, landing just a foot away from his commanding officer.

"Hands in the air! Hands in the air!" several of the SEALs shouted as they approached Calderon.

The colonel stared at the dead face of his last soldier, and sighed. Grabbing his submachine gun, he stood up and shouted, "Viva Puerto Rico libre!"

A hail of bullets riddled his body and filled the door behind him with holes. He crashed backwards, slowly sliding to the ground, but one of the door handles snagged the belt of his pants, holding him up and causing his upper body to slump forward. Somehow, his corpse still managed to hold on to his automatic weapon, giving the impression that the dead colonel was trying to hand it down to his fallen companion. But then the belt gave way, and the body fell sideways and thudded on the ground.

"I don't think...I don't think Johnny has found Cacho or San Miguel," Yajaira told Lebron in a hushed, confidential tone.

The FEPI Secretary General stared at her with a mixture of disapproval and amusement. Yajaira had continued to drink heavily after Johnny had left, particularly when the shooting coming from the convention area had increased, and she was drunk. Not tipsy or talkatively drunk, but ten-times-over-the-legal-limit, difficult-to-stand-up drunk.

Unlike her, Lebron had kept his drinking under control, letting the ice water down his *Cuba libres,* eating snacks, and spacing his refills. It was essential to keep his wits on that most crucial of all nights, and he had caught himself falling asleep several times already, despite the intense fighting occurring just a few hundred yards from the club where they sat.

Yajaira's unceasing chatter had helped him to stay awake. He had never liked her; had thought her an airhead, not worthy of the exalted position that she held in the FEPI thanks—he suspected—to her voluptuous looks. But that night, he had welcomed her nervous babble. And he enjoyed, he had to admit to himself, looking at her. Even after two days of sleep deprivation, she looked fresh and sexy, from her glossy, perfectly painted red nails to her casual but well-groomed hair. *He could understand perfectly well what Johnny saw in her,* he reflected, and then banished the thought from his mind. *It was the alcohol doing the thinking for him. He had to focus on the important matters.*

"I don't think so either," Lebron responded just to say something.

"Because...Because..." she continued, ignoring his comment. "You know..."

He nodded, even though he didn't know.

It had been nearly a half hour since Johnny Ray had left, and Lebron was getting restless. From the intensity of the shooting, it was evident that the Macheteros and the Venezuelans had encountered very stiff opposition. He did not have a good feeling about what was happening. His instincts told him to leave. To abandon the hotel as fast as his legs could carry him.

"If Cacho agrees to our proposals, there will be a lot of work to do tomorrow," he said to Yajaira, who was looking intently at the armrest of his chair. She looked up surprised.

"Tomorrow! What about tomorrow?"

"You know, rationing the food in the supermarkets, restoring order in the streets—"

"That's *your* job! *I*," she said, raising her voice and pointing dramatically her index finger at him, "... *I* am the *face* of the revolution! That's what Johnny...that's what Johnny said, remember?"

Lebron opened his mouth to speak, but decided not to do so, opting to maintain a dignified silence. But at that moment, the subdued atmosphere of the bar was shattered by loud shouts and frightened screams.

Initially, Lebron thought that a fight had broken out between the Macheteros and some of the FEPI students waiting in bar, but then he saw several armed men dressed in helmets and dark uniforms overrunning the lounging area and instantly knew what was happening.

Taking a look at Yajaira—who seemed hopelessly unaware of the ongoing raid—he stood up and wordlessly walked to the front left corner of the bar. There, he opened a glass door that gave access to a long, narrow balcony facing the hotel's beach and pool area, and stepped out. He saw a uniformed man approaching him at a canter and, in a panic, climbed over the balcony's edge and dropped into some ornamental plants growing ten feet below.

The plants, wide-leafed beach grape shrubs, clawed at his arms, legs and face, and tore his *guayabera,* but cushioned his clumsy fall. He struggled to get up and move under the balcony's roof, fighting the branches that like a slow motion nightmare clutched at him, and expecting to be shot at any moment, but his pursuer never jumped after him.

Finally clearing the shrubs, he half-crawled, half-ran under the balcony until he reached the open beach. There he hesitated for several seconds, searching for possible hunters, and taking a deep breath, ran into the night.

The SEALs rounded up most of the people who had been waiting in the lobby and the lounge, except for two that jumped off from the bar's balcony. The terrorists, mostly young, university student types, had given up without a fight. Many had been drunk, others had been sleeping, all had been terrified of the armed men in dark uniforms that had materialized from nowhere and screamed at them to drop their weapons and raise their hands or die.

Yajaira had watched the commotion from her table, unable to break through her alcohol-induced stupor in time to realize what was happening. When she finally became aware that she was being arrested, she stood up and tried to slap the uniformed man—a burly, six foot two inches tall Tennessean—on the face. The SEAL gently held her by the wrist, and asked her to turn around.

"I will *not* turn around!" she answered in a sharp tone. "Why should I...why should I...*You* turn around!"

The SEAL tried to stifle a grin, but couldn't. Noticing the smile, Yajaira became furious.

"Do you know who you are dealing with?" she demanded indignantly. "Do you?"

"No, m'am, I don't," the Tennessean answered courteously. His eyes involuntarily wandered to her tight T-shirt.

"I am Yajaira Velazquez," she said, as if the name would provoke instant recognition. "I am the vice...I am the vice...I am the vice president of the Federacion de Estudiantes Puertorriquenos Independentistas. The FEPI! That's right. The FEPI! And these people are my...people! If you touch me again, I won't be responsible for...whatever they do to you... "

"I'm sorry, m'am, but I have to tie you up, so if you would be so kind as to turn around..."

For the second time, Yajaira tried to slap the tall soldier. This time, however, he leaned his head back, making her miss, and using her own impulse, spun her by the shoulders and tipped her unto the sofa behind her. Before she could get up, he grabbed her wrists and bound them with a plastic strip.

Yajaira cursed him, her cries partially muffled by one of the sofa's cushions, her legs flailing.

"You stupid asshole! Wait 'till Johnny and Cacho and San Miguel hear about this! I am the face of the revolution! Lebron! Lebron! Where the hell are you!"

Yajaira screamed for another five minutes, and then fell asleep.

Captain Gomez sat on the floor, his legs outstretched in front of him, tiredly rubbing his forehead. His ribs hurt with every breath, as if somebody had been hitting them with a hammer all day long. He was certain that his chest would look like one giant black and blue sore once he took off his bulletproof vest. Still, it could have been worse. Had he not been wearing his vest, the bullets that it had stopped would have been embedded in his body. "*A la tercera va la vencida.*" Not this time.

Negron, who had been hovering over the injured, returned with one of the SEALs and slowly, fighting through his own pain, knelt next to him.

"I counted four dead guests, about two dozen injured, but only two seriously, as far as I can tell. The rest are mostly bumps and bruises," he said. "It could have been a lot worse."

Gomez nodded and looked up at the uniformed soldier who had arrived with Negron.

"This is Commander Jason McAllister," Negron said. "He directed the rescue."

McAllister extended his hand, and Gomez shook it.

"You put up a hell of a fight," the SEAL commander said gently. There was no bluster or bravado in his voice, but rather a calm sadness. "We've captured most of the terrorists and scattered the rest. You saved a lot of lives today."

"My sergeant?" Gomez asked, already anticipating the answer.

"I'm sorry. He didn't survive." McAllister stared directly at the SWAT captain, and shook his head. He had seen men die several times in his military career, and knew that the best way to deliver bad news was to do it quickly.

Gomez's jaw tightened noticeably, and for a long moment he could not speak. Then, in an unsteady voice, he said, "He saved me today in the lagoon...I shouldn't have...shouldn't have sent him..." but could not continue speaking.

"He was a brave man, who did what he had to do," McAllister said curtly. "And so did you. Don't dwell on it any more. Celebrate his courage and his sacrifice."

Gomez nodded, tears streaming from his eyes.

"We have advised your Superintendent that the hostages in the hotel are safe. The National Guard and the police are placing Bailey bridges on two of the destroyed bridges and moving equipment and personnel into San Juan even as we speak." McAllister told Gomez and Negron, changing the subject.

"Can they send a helicopter to evacuate the wounded?" Negron asked him. Archie weighed heavily in his mind.

McAllister shook is head. "We are trying to secure the area, but there's no guaranty that there are no more terrorists hiding with surface-to-air missiles, and we can't risk having another helicopter getting shot down. But the Superintendent assured me that several ambulances are coming, and they should be here soon. While we wait, my medic is helping the wounded, although there's some fine doctors among the hostages as well."

Negron nodded, and stood up. "If you'll excuse me, sir, I want to see how my friend is doing," he said, walking away.

McAllister lingered, as if considering whether to say something or go. Yielding to his initial impulse, he crouched next the SWAT captain.

"Look around you," he said softly, nodding at the crowd about them. The hostages were being kept in the ballroom until the authorities made certain that the hotel and its surrounding grounds were secure. A fleet of buses was scheduled to cross into the island of San Juan once the Bailey bridges had been installed, and take the hostages to several of the big hotels in the Condado, the Convention Center, and the Isla Verde areas. For the first time, people were moving about the hall; loud, animated talk and even sporadic laughter resonating where wordless terror had been the norm.

"You, your sergeant, that kid Negron...you saved these people. You could have run away, but you didn't. You risked your lives to save them." McAllister took out a pack of bubble gum out of his shirt pocket and offered some to Gomez, who shook his head and thanked him. He unwrapped one piece of gum and began to chew it with great relish. "Bazookas," he smiled. "Greatest chewing gum ever made." His deep blue eyes examined the captain's face with sympathy. Gomez turned his gaze away, staring vacantly at the crowd. "I know how you feel. Your sergeant was your personal friend, and you feel responsible for placing him in harm's way. But that was his job, wasn't it? He was a SWAT officer. He knew the risks that came with his occupation... You knew them too."

Gomez nodded sullenly. McAllister placed his hand on the shaken man's shoulder.

"I know that's there's nothing I can say or do that will make you feel better. I know it. I've been there. It's the worse feeling in the world losing a friend. And when that friend dies following your orders, you start wondering...you know, if he'd be alive if you hadn't given them. Don't go there. Move on or you'll go crazy."

Gomez said nothing.

"I was told that your sergeant was surrounded by the bodies of six dead terrorists. Six!"

"He was an ex Navy SEAL," Gomez said in a low voice.

"Was he now?" McAllister said in a half surprised tone. "So he was the right man for the right job. He did a superb piece of fighting out there. Stopped the terrorists dead on their tracks. Your decision to use him in an ambush was successful beyond all measure."

"It should have been me," Gomez muttered bitterly, his gaze returning to the SEAL's face.

"Yeah," McAllister removed his black helmet and swept his hair back. "Well, I think that's pretty arrogant on your part."

Gomez said nothing, but his eyes reflected his surprise.

"What you're saying is that you could have done as well or better than your sergeant—"

"That's not what I said," Gomez replied angrily.

"Well would you or wouldn't you have done better than your sergeant?"

"Much worse, probably! What does that have to do—"

"Everything!" McAllister answered fiercely. "Everything! You were in command, and you decided to send the best man suited for the job. Had you done anything else, you would have been negligent in your duty. You would have increased the terrorists' chances of success." The Navy SEAL's expression hardened, his blue eyes boring directly into those of the SWAT officer. "I am sorry for your loss, but glad for your decision," he said in a tone that carried no sympathy. "You made an excellent decision, and your sergeant died in the process. That's life! There's a chain of command, and people must follow it. You made the decision, he executed it. Brilliantly, I may add. You would have preferred to have died instead of him? Maybe. But ask yourself this: had you not made your decision, would all the people you see walking about be here now?"

McAllister stood up, and offered his hand to the captain.

"There's a lot of work to do before we can get these people out of here. I sure could use your help."

Gomez smiled weakly and grabbed the SEAL's forearm with his hand, wincing with pain as he was pulled up to his feet. He turned to walk out through the hall's main exit, but McAllister stopped him and pointed towards the opposite end of the room.

"This way," he said, and began to find his way through the clusters of hostages sitting on the floor.

As Gomez followed, a woman shouted, "God bless you, captain!" and then, a male voice added, "Bravo!" Others extended their hands to touch him, or voiced their gratitude. Many began to clap, until the applause spread throughout the hall and the people began to stand, giving the rescuers a thunderous ovation.

McAllister smiled inwardly. He had calculated the hostages' reaction, and used it to distract Gomez out of his grief. However, other matters weighed in his mind. As he approached Ensign Aguirre, his mood changed. "Any news from Able and Bravo?" he asked.

"None, sir," Aguirre responded. "They must be busy."

McAllister nodded. "See what you can find out." While they had been securing the hotel, he had been too busy to think about the other teams. But now, the worst part of the night began.

Because now, he had to wait for the news.

CHAPTER LXXVI

"Clemente, Clemente, Clemente," the radio repeated in a loud, crisp voice. It was the pre-set code word confirming that the Grand Laguna Hotel had been captured. The dozen or so police officers and staff waiting in the cold, cavernous ballroom of the San Geronimo Plaza, burst into wild, spontaneous cheers, back slaps, and high-fives. Only the large, bear-like hunched figure of the Superintendent remained impassive, Correcaminos noticed, like a basketball coach whose team has established a lead, but still has a minute to play.

"Call Colonel Lamoutte," he instructed to one of his orderlies while he watched the television screens showing the Grand Laguna from a distance, as if hoping to catch a glimpse of what was happening there. Nothing was visible from that distance, though. "Tell him to get his National Guard boys to deploy the two Bailey bridges now and to move into San Juan."

"Yes, sir," the orderly, a young policeman who clearly idolized his boss began to move away but Maldonado held him by the arm. "Alert our people that we're moving in as soon as those bridges are in."

"Sir, yes, sir!"

Correcaminos watched with mounting fascination as the veteran policeman continued to orchestrate the rescue operations while keeping all of his emotions in check. He wondered how the man could maintain a calm façade, after all he had been through and everything that was at stake. In less than twenty-four hours, the Superintendent had seen the police building in Puerta de Tierra burned to the ground, with most of its occupants killed or wounded. He had witnessed the massacre of his SWAT team after being forced by the Interim Governor to order an attack that he had never wanted to conduct, and then been blamed for it.

Correcaminos knew how much the Superintendent personally cared about his men. During his tenancy as police chief, he had turned what had been a dispirited, bureaucratized, under-equipped, and partially corrupt organization into an efficient, effective, highly motivated crime-fighting force. He spoke of his men with the same pride with which a father spoke of his children. The killing of policemen, a frequent occurrence before he had assumed command, had dropped dramatically, from thirty-eight policemen the year when he had taken over to four last year. The reasons were clearly evident. Maldonado had integrated the police into the communities it protected; once distant figures of authority, many policemen had become recognizable human faces in the neighborhoods they patrolled. He had secured better and safer equipment for his men, and established procedures that dramatically lessened the life threatening risks that his men took on a daily basis. And most important of all, he had made it clear that anybody killing a cop would get caught.

All of that had changed in one day. Under Maldonado's watch, the police force had lost more men than at any other moment in its entire history, and it had all been displayed to the rest of the world on TV. His competency and even his honesty had been called into question, and he had been subjected to enormous political pressure. It was enough to break any man, or at least to make him crawl under a bed. During his long career, the police chief had been accused by his many detractors of being a closet alcoholic. If anything could drive a man to drink, it would have been the events of that day. And yet, Maldonado had somehow continued to fight on, rallying everyone around him, refusing to buckle under the intense stress to which he had been subjected.

"There is still a lot to be done, and a lot that we don't know, gentlemen," the Superintendent muttered somberly to those around him. "Don't drop the ball now. Everybody back to their posts."

As the elated mood subsided, Correcaminos decided to approach the Superintendent. He did so reluctantly, knowing that he had been allowed to remain in the police command center without any express authorization, and that if he was perceived as a nuisance he would be thrown out of there in less time than it took an enema-filled patient to fart. But he could not let the opportunity pass.

"Excuse me, sir," he said, nudging his way to the police chief.

Maldonado glanced at him briefly. "Yes?"

"I heard you say that you have no details of what has happened in the Grand Laguna beyond getting the confirmation that it has been secured."

Maldonado nodded, looking at him with curiosity. He was definitely not, Correcaminos noted, a handsome man. His nose was too big for his face, and the bags under his eyes, one of the features that newspaper caricaturists always loved to emphasize, had grown with the passage of the day. But his eyes were alive, reflecting an electric vitality that the rest of his body failed to convey.

"I can call Michelle Alfaro and find out what is the precise situation in the Grand Laguna."

"I know," he answered. "But you won't. I will." The Superintendent opened his beefy right hand and showed to the reporter his small cell phone. "I was about to make the call."

Correcaminos nodded resignedly. "Great minds think—" he began to say, but desisted from continuing after he received a withering look from the police chief. "By all means, sir."

Maldonado hit the menu button and then searched for "recent calls", his fingers looking too thick to effectively press the correct commands. But the screen flashed "Calling Michelle Alfaro", and the Superintendent pressed the phone to his ear.

He waited so long for an answer, that Correcaminos thought she had missed the call. Then the tough policeman's features softened, and he said in a purposefully non-committal tone, "Ms. Alfaro, this is Superintendent Maldonado."

Relieved almost to the point of tears, Correcaminos heard his protégé's familiar voice respond, but could not understand what she was saying. He felt tempted to tell Maldonado to put her on the speaker, but knew that would have been unwise, and instead moved closer to the Superintendent, hoping to catch some of her words.

"I hope that you are well," Maldonado said, after he had finished listening to her. Then, after a brief pause, he directed a quick look at the anxious reporter and nodded reassuringly. "I'm glad," he said. "Tell me about your present situation."

The Superintendent's brows knotted in intense concentration as he listened to Michelle's report. Every so often he would gently urge her to continue, saying, "Yes...yes..." while at other moments he would listen quietly for long spells, not wanting to interrupt. Once he pressed his eyes together and shook his head after apparently listening to very bad news.

Correcaminos only caught bits and pieces of the conversation: "fine... Archie...wounded...has been stabilized...heroic...Cordero...dead terrorists... hurry...God..."

"Don't worry, help will be arriving very soon," Maldonado assured her. "We are in the process of bridging some of the gaps on the bridges..." He paused, as Michelle told him something. "Yes, yes, you can tell the others that help will soon be there. What's that?" He paused again, and the shadow of a smile drew on his lips. "No, I can't authorize you to tell anything yet to your editor. Not yet, not while the rescue operations are still ongoing..." He paused and winked at Correcaminos, who smiled.

"What's that? Yes, the rescue operations are still going on in other parts of Old San Juan. But I promise you this: I won't allow any press to cross the bridges until you give your report first. Is that agreeable to you?...Good. Now here's somebody else who wants to say hi to you."

Maldonado extended the phone to Correcaminos. "Make it quick," he said, and walked away.

"Hey baby!" Correcaminos said, trying to sound casual and choking on his second word. He had to pause before he could continue.

"You're crying!" Michelle said gleefully, to his intense mortification. *"How sweet!"*

"I'm *not* crying!" he replied. "A fly flew into my mouth and I choked, that's all. I'm not crying."

"You are too! You're using your manly voice to cover it up! The voice that you use every time that you choke up. That's so sweet!"

"I swear to God, I don't know why I waste my time talking to you!"

"I'm okay," she said in response to his unspoken question.

"What?"

"I'm okay, I'm okay, don't worry about me, all right?"

"Who said I was worried about you? It's the scoop I'm worried about. You're sitting on the biggest story of the year. Heck, probably of the decade! That's what I'm concerned about!" Correcaminos heard a sob and stopped talking. "I'm sorry, honey," he said. "I was joking."

"It's tears of relief," she said, trying to regain her composure.

"I'm sorry," Correcaminos repeated, not knowing what else to say. "Are you really okay? You're not hurt, are you?"

"No," Michelle replied, then said in a calmer voice, *"No. Sorry about the display of emotions. I've seen too many people around me die and get hurt, I guess. I'm okay now."*

"Okay, so listen. I suspect that Maldonado will authorize us to broadcast our news soon. Things are moving very fast. So make a mental summary about what you have to say—"

"I have it already," Michelle said before he could finish.

"You think you have it, but may forget some of the stuff when the time comes. Make an outline of all of the important points that you want to make. Review them in your head, okay?"

"Okay, okay," she answered with a hint of impatience.

Correcaminos saw Maldonado signaling to hang up.

"Honey, I have to go now. Stay with the soldiers...the SEALs, okay? You never know who's still out there."

"Yes, dad," Michelle responded in a bratty voice.

"I'm not old enough to be your dad, so stop calling me that," Correcaminos said with fake indignation, smiling. Then he added, "I love you, you know? And I'm so proud of you..." He could not continue, his emotions getting the better of him.

"*I love you too,*" Michelle replied, sounding tired but happy.

"Just remember you owe all of your success to me," he added, hoping to provoke her.

"*Yes, dad,*" she repeated.

"Dammit! I'm not your dad!" Correcaminos said as he ended his conversation.

The second code word reached the command center twenty-six minutes later. "*Cepeda, Cepeda, Cepeda*" signaled that Group Bravo had rescued the hostages in the *Mardi Gras.* Apparently, the passengers had been rescued at an even earlier time than the hostages of the Grand Laguna Hotel, but Group Bravo's commander, Jeb Stuart, had delayed the announcement of the *Mardi Gras'* deliverance until he had been absolutely certain that the ship was secure. Stuart's first call was followed, fifteen minutes later, by a request from the *Mardi Gras* to prepare one of the docks in Isla Grande so that the hostages could disembark there.

Maldonado thought it a splendid idea. He called the Secretary of the Treasury and now Interim Governor, Rosa Gonzalez, to make the necessary arrangements.

"*How's our friend doing?*" the Secretary asked with a dry chuckle. She was a no-nonsense professional who had served on several administrations, and a former large law firm tax attorney who had earned the reputation of being the foremost authority on the local tax code. She had also developed along the years a strong bond with the Police Superintendent.

"Rovira? He's at his home, resting," Maldonado answered matter-of-factly. "Why, having seconds thoughts?"

"*Who, me? No, I'm thoroughly enjoying this. What's the worse that can happen? That we get fired? You think Pietrantoni would be so foolish as to fire the most qualified members of his cabinet? And if he does, he'd be doing both of us a favor, don't you think? Getting us out of the crappy jobs that we have? No, no regrets. I'll get that dock for you right away. In the meantime, do you have any news to give me?*"

"Forgive me, I should have called a long time ago," Maldonado answered in a mortified tone.

"*You keep forgetting I'm the Interim Governor now, do you?*" Gonzalez chortled. "*Well, I don't blame you. You have a lot in your plate. I'll forgive you this time. So what's the latest news?*" she asked.

"The SEALs have retaken the Grand Laguna Hotel and the *Mardi Gras.* I spoke with Michelle Alfaro a few minutes ago—"

"The reporter?"

"Yes. She is at the Grand Laguna. There were some limited casualties, five or six of the tourists. No official tally yet. But the rest are safe."

"Thank God!"

"We have no details on the *Mardi Gras* yet."

"And the Governor?" Gonzalez asked guardedly.

"No news on him yet," Maldonado answered.

"God help him and his family," the Treasury Secretary said fervently. *"We must pray for them, Roberto."*

"I haven't stopped praying since this morning. God must be getting pretty irritated with my whining by now."

"You never whine, Roberto. That's what I like about you. Keep me posted, will you? I don't want to look like a fool when the reporters start questioning me. I'll call you back in ten minutes to let you know which dock will be available."

"Thank you, Madame Governor," Maldonado said affectionately.

"Sounds good, doesn't it? If it wasn't that Pietrantoni was missing, I'd actually enjoy it."

The first of three National Guard M117 armored vehicles rolled noisily over the narrow Bailey bridge, its big wheels causing the metal plates of the bridge to clatter noisily as the transport tried to reach the island of San Juan. While it did, three random bullets clanked off its angled armored plates, causing the guardsman sitting in its turret to open fire with the vehicle's heavy, .50-caliber machine gun. The gunfire pocked the fire-blackened walls of the San Juan Yacht Club, and sent out a shower of red-hot embers from the yacht club's still smoldering ruins. The enemy snipers discharged a couple of more shots and disappeared into the night, chased by a hail of bullets from the approaching M117.

The temporary bridge over which the National Guard truck traveled consisted of four, equally sized, pre-constructed sections, each measuring ten feet in length, which were light enough to be carried by eight men. Each section was made of cris-crossed steel beam panels, connected on the bottom by several 19-foot wide transoms. The sections were attached to each other on rollers that rested on the bridgehead—the portion of the bridge that had not been destroyed by the explosives—and pushed forward as each section was completed. The four sections had been brought to Miramar on two flatbed trucks, which had lain hidden from sight behind the Department of Justice Building, across from the San Juan Yacht Club. After given the go ahead, the two flatbeds had backed up to the edge of the lagoon, where a National Guard engineering unit had unloaded them with the aid of the police.

It had taken less than an hour for the police and the National Guard to extend the provisional crossing structure over the gap in the destroyed Miramar bridge. It would have taken them much less—the National Guard team had assembled the bridges over a dozen times to extend them over roads washed away by heavy rains and storms—but they had come under sniper fire as they carried the ten-foot sections to the gap on the bridge.

Fortunately, the snipers had been poor shots. Either that, or they had just opened fire to scare away the engineers. Colonel Manfredo Lamoutte, the National Guard commanding officer in charge of the bridge crossings, had retaliated immediately, ordering all of the military vehicles parked near the three destroyed Miramar bridges to return fire. The guardsmen had fired back with relish, raking the burned out remains of the San Juan Yacht Club and its immediate area with hundreds of bullets, temporarily silencing the terrorist shooters.

As the second of the M117s crossed the bridge, a dozen guardsmen followed it, using it as cover. The two armored vehicles stopped in front of the club, the men on their turrets aiming their machine guns at the its walls while the guardsmen on foot searched the structure. It soon became apparent that the few terrorists that had taken pot shots at the engineers had vacated the premises.

With no further opposition, the main rescue force began to roll over the narrow bridge: more armored vehicles, dozens of Humvees filled with National Guardsmen, more than fifty police patrol cars and vans, and even several companies of guardsmen on foot to secure the opposite shore of the lagoon. When the second Bailey bridge was installed, the flow of personnel and vehicles increased even more, bringing into San Juan ambulances, and a fleet of shuttles narrow enough to fit through the temporary bridges. Fire trucks, more than a dozen of them, followed the armed convoys and stopped in front of the San Juan Yacht Club, where they began to douse the smoking remains of the marina. Other trucks waited for the police vehicles to make their way towards their burned station.

Like a flood, the police and National Guard slowly spread over Puerta de Tierra, heading west towards Old San Juan over the Muñoz Rivera, Constitution and Fernandez Juncos Avenues. In order to avoid any ambushes, they moved in small convoys, preceded by M117s or armed Humvees, and followed by police vehicles flashing their blue lights and sounding their sirens. More men followed on foot, branching in small squads into the smaller side streets and fanning over the open spaces like the Luis Muñoz Rivera and the Third Millennium parks. Despite warnings by the police through loudspeakers for the citizens to remain inside their houses until further notice, thousands of people flooded the streets to greet their oncoming liberators in a carnival-like atmosphere, slowing the convoys' westward progress to a crawl.

Sometimes, sporadic shootings from the rebels would break out, causing the crowds to disperse in panic. These were mostly isolated incidents, however: lone snipers firing one or two shots, melting away as soon as the advancing forces fired back. In the Fernandez Juncos Avenue, two pickup trucks had erupted noisily from a side street close to the Falansterio, and several youths crouching on its beds had shouted and waived their fists, discharging their rifles and handguns at the advance vehicles of the National Guard and speeding away towards the docks. They had been arrested shortly thereafter by the SEALs guarding the *Mardi Gras,* offering no resistance.

A more serious scuffle occurred in the Muñoz Rivera Avenue close to the abandoned Normandie Hotel and the Sixto Escobar Stadium. There, the rescuers came under heavy crossfire from at least eight to twelve terrorists armed with automatic weapons who hid on the high walls of the stadium and behind the thick pine trees lining the three-lane highway. The rebels had held their fire until the armored vehicles passed, and then hit the two police cars behind them. A heavy firefight ensued where one policeman was killed and three others wounded.

But the ambushers suffered heavy casualties as well. The .50 caliber bullets of the M117's machine gun shredded through the trunk of one the pines trees where one of the gunmen was hiding, blinding him with some of the flying splinters, and slicing through his left shoulder. As the blind man stumbled backwards, the upper trunk of the tree was torn apart by the incoming bullets and it crushed the unfortunate man. Another rebel, hiding a few trees further away, was struck by a random shot squarely in the middle of his forehead and killed instantly. A dozen guardsmen circled behind the stadium and opened fire on the snipers shooting at the road from the upper bleachers. Most of the terrorists escaped, but one was severely wounded, and left behind by his comrades. The fight lasted less than fifteen minutes, but it managed to stop the progress of the rescue caravan. By that time, it was close to midnight.

The *Mardi Gras,* protected by an impenetrable ring of Navy SEALs, finally slipped its moorings at 12:30 PM, and left Dock B, traveling less than a mile to the Pan American Pier in Isla Grande. There, it was received by scores of large tourist buses, taxis, and ambulances, and hundreds of reporters. The newspeople's efforts to interview the passengers were for naught, however, as the area was cordoned off by the police while bus upon bus picked up the liberated hostages and whisked them off to several of the major hotels in the metropolitan area. Dozens of reporters hopped into the cars and gave chase to the departing buses, hoping to have better luck in their final destinations.

And still, even while order was being restored to the island of San Juan, no word had come to Maldonado about the Governor's fate.

CHAPTER LXXVII

They heard the noise of men approaching long before they saw them. The SEALs doused their lights and backtracked, cramming into two of the niches that appeared in the walls periodically. They had to be very careful. If the terrorists had recaptured the hostages, they could not engage in a firefight. They would have to let them pass, and try to capture them by surprise.

By the sound of the voices, they could tell that someone was in great pain, and that another had lost his patience and was shouting to the complainer to shut up. There was a lot of shuffling and scraping, as if one of the men was being dragged by the others, as well as occasional curses, grunts, and heavy breathing.

The impenetrable blackness of the corridor grew lighter as the terrorists got nearer, until Gabriel and Quijano—hidden in the first of the two niches—were able to see the arched brick wall opposite to them. Then three men walked past them, two of them holding the third by his shoulders, so concentrated on their slow progress that they failed to see the two soldiers standing a mere arms length away. The two SEALs waited, to see if anyone else was following, but when the tunnel began to grow darker again and the noise fainter, they stepped out of their hiding places, and leveled their weapons at the retreating men.

"STOP!" Gabriel shouted at the top of his lungs.

One of the terrorists produced a terrified, high-pitched "Yaaaaaa!", apparently startled out of his wits by the unexpected disturbance behind him, and then more voices joined the ruckus, this time in English, as the other SEALs moved to block the way of the retreating men.

"Drop your weapons!" Gabriel heard several of his men scream, as the corridor became flooded with light. "Don't move!"

The men carrying the wounded man threw their rifles to the ground and raised their hands, letting their companion drop to the floor. Gabe saw Flanagan approach them at a fast clip and kick their weapons away. Then another SEAL pushed the two terrorists that remained standing against the wall and made them spread their arms and legs, while a third one searched the wounded man on the floor.

"Where is the Governor?" Quijano asked in Spanish to the prisoner closest to him, a young, clean-shaven man in his early twenties. The man was exhausted and unnerved, shaking so badly that he could hardly stand. Gabriel watched him closely. It was not the sudden appearance of the SEALs that had scared him so. He seemed to be in a state of shock, as if he had just walked out of hell.

"He escaped," the man answered simply.

"Are you El Alacran?" Quijano asked on impulse.

The man closed his eyes and shook his head. "El Alacran is dead. The others are dead. The Governor escaped."

"Which way did he go?"

"Follow the corridor to the left, always to your left. Eventually, you will find the others."

There was something very troubling about the way that the prisoner talked. It gave Gabe a very bad feeling.

"Flanagan, Quijano, come with me," he ordered. "The rest of you take the prisoners back. After you get rid of them get back here and follow the tunnel, always to your left."

By the time that the three SEALs got to point where the corridor divided in two, the heavy smell of burned wood mixed with rancid oil clung in the air, and the flashlights' narrow beams traveled in long, white lines, framed by a fine, misty haze. They had not walked for long when they found a man with a white, manicured beard whose head had been bashed in by a heavy blow.

"One of the Governor's people?" Gabriel said absently.

"Hard to tell," Flanagan replied, flashing his flashlight on the dead man's face as he walked by.

A few minutes later they saw the outline of what seemed to be the end of the tunnel, its arched exit highlighted by a flickering, reddish glow.

"Fire..." Gabe muttered to himself. The charred body of a man, still smoking and reeking of burned meat, lay about twenty feet away from the flames. The men gingerly stepped over the corpse and quietly scurried towards the end of the passageway.

There had been a great fire there. Scraps of wood and what seemed to be the remains of barrels still burned there, although at the height of the conflagration, the flames had reached and blackened part of the dome-like roof of the hall into which the SEALs now entered. The signs of an intense gun battle were everywhere; the brick walls were chipped with bullet holes, easily spotted by their color contrast with the duller-colored walls.

The SEALs examined the scene of the fighting in silent awe. There were barrels piled up like a small pyramid in the center of the room, and ancient Spanish garrison weapons—pikes, lances, and swords—stored in racks bordering most of the walls. There was also an array of tools lying on top of a long table, and dozens of more barrels stacked on one side.

During its time, the place must have been some kind of a hidden supply warehouse. But if so, what was its use? There were no doors, except for the arched entrance through which they had walked in. *Why would anyone store so many supplies in a blind alley? It made no sense. And with no other doors to exit, where had the hostages gone?*

It was Flanagan who first noticed the two legs dangling from the ceiling, above the piled up wooden drums. Nudging Gabriel with his elbow, he pointed towards the grotesque sight. "Weird chandelier, isn't it?" he said.

Gabriel missed the legs at the beginning, partially hidden in the hall's semidarkness. Then he flashed his lantern at the spot to which his companion was pointing, and was shocked by what he saw.

There was a small opening in the ceiling, maybe four or five feet in diameter, not more. Two legs in what seemed to be the pants of a business suit protruded from it, showing elegant silk stockings and what seemed to be expensive leather shoes. Blood was slowly dripping from the right foot and plopping on top of one of the drums.

Had the law of physics prevailed, the body suspended inside the hole should have fallen back to earth. Even if its torso had been lying on the level above, the blood would have accumulated in the legs and dragged the body down. However, that body refused to drop.

"I pray to God that's not the Governor," Gabe fervently said.

Already Quijano was climbing over the barrels, looking up with a mixture of curiosity and disgust. There was a strong smell of feces and blood.

"If not the Governor, surely one of his aides. Do you see the fancy clothes?"

Gabriel did not answer, observing Quijano as he reached the top. The climber paused, looked up at the body, and then gingerly pulled its left leg. The body swung slightly sideways but did not fall. Grabbing its swollen ankle, he pulled harder with no better results. More blood began to drip down the other leg.

"It's stuck!" Quijano shouted down.

"Can you dislodge it? Seems to me that's the way the others went," Gabriel replied.

Quijano illuminated the hole with his flashlight. It was not very wide, but there was no reason why the body would be stuck, being thinner than the hole through which it was sticking. Then something attracted his attention. There was something coming out of the dead man's belly. On a hunch, he directed his light to the body's back and saw a long object protruding from it.

"Ewww! Gross!" he whispered, realizing what had happened.

"What is it?" Flanagan asked.

"I'm not sure but..." Quijano grabbed both of the man's ankles and pulled them sideways, towards him. There was a rasping, metallic sound, and then the body pitched forward, making the SEAL lose his balance and almost fall. The dead man's face struck the upper edge of the hole and dropped through it, crashing on the barrels below.

Flanagan and Gabriel rushed to examine the dislodged body, while Quijano stood up on the highest of the barrels and squeezed his upper half through the open hole.

"Jesus H. Christ!" Flanagan whispered to himself. "Somebody skewered the poor guy like shish-kebab! Is it the Governor?"

Gabe examined the corpse with detached curiosity for several seconds. "No," he said at last. "Too short."

"The Secretary of State, maybe?"

Again, Gabe hesitated. "Maybe. He was shorter. But he doesn't look like the photos the Superintendent showed to us. No, a terrorist. Look at his armband," he concluded.

Both men turned their gaze upwards. Quijano had disappeared into the hole.

"Hey! Quijano!" Flanagan shouted. "Did you find anything?"

The vanished SEAL did not reply.

"Quijano!" Gabriel shouted. "Are you okay?" Then, activating his throat's PTT, he added, "Quijano, report!"

The two SEALs exchanged a look of concern when their companion failed to answer, and Flanagan began to hurriedly clamber over the barrels. Just then, Quijano's head stuck out of the opening, startling the Irishman and making him curse.

"The Governor's not here," he reported. "No one is. This is some sort of old castle. There's a big hall here, and a ramp that goes up to an outside exit, and I can hear the sea."

"You think the hostages left that way?" Gabe asked.

"I know they did," Quijano answered. "The exit is shut by an iron-barred door. Somebody twisted two of the bars to make a hole big enough to escape."

"So where are they?" Flanagan asked to no one in particular.

"I guess we're going to have to find out," Gabriel answered, slinging his sub machinegun over his shoulders and beginning to climb the drums. "Up we go."

"Your Grace...Your Grace!" Archbishop Pedro Garrido woke up at the urgent knocking on the door of his room and looked at the digital clock on his night table. The red luminous letters showed 1:17 PM.

He was exhausted and in great pain. It had been a very long day. He had been awake since five in the morning from the previous day, as was his normal Sunday routine, and held the six o'clock mass in his personal chapel along with fathers Felipe and Bernard—the two other priests who shared quarters with him in the parochial building next to the San Juan Cathedral—and his live-in housekeeper Lybia.

Afterwards, he had enjoyed one of the few luxuries that he allowed himself for the day: a two-scrambled egg and English muffin breakfast with a large cup of café latte, while he read the several newspapers of the day. The angry discourse of the country's politicians about contraception troubled him greatly. As the chief clergyman in Puerto Rico, the medium-sized, spare man was obligated to follow the dictates of Rome and reject contraception as a viable birth-control method. However, he had opted to remain silent on the subject. A relatively young man—only forty-two years old—educated in the University of Notre Dame with a law degree from Purdue, Archbishop Garrido was known for his progressive social views, his fearless outspokenness against class injustice and poverty, and his sharp, analytical mind. Therefore, his stubborn silence on contraception had been keenly noticed, and all sorts of rumors and speculations had begun to surface in the newspapers.

So far, he had refused to be drawn into the birth control debate, which had in the last year become a political issue. There were much more pressing matters—matters of real importance—that the Church needed to address: the prevention of drug abuse, the protection of abused women and children, the urgent medical, feeding, and housing needs of the poor: central issues that Jesus had tackled in his time and would have addressed today. But now an editorial on "El Nuevo Dia" had urged him to weigh on the matter, particularly since Governor Pietrantoni was being urged to drop from the local health plan the coverage of contraceptive devices. *Damn El Nuevo Dia*, he thought in a very un-priestly fashion. *Now everybody else would start pressing him for his opinion.*

That Sunday, as every other Sunday during the last three years that he had served as Archbishop of San Juan, Garrido had crammed the day with activities. He had been scheduled to give mass and celebrate the sacrament of confirmation in the Perpetuo Socorro parish in Miramar. Afterwards, he would visit the Stella Maris Church in El Condado, to ordain two new deacons. And that only covered the morning hours.

But around 8:30 AM, Father Felipe had called his attention to what was being reported on the radio. Turning on the television set, they had watched with mounting concern the reports indicating that the bridges connecting San Juan to the rest of the island had been blown up, and that the San Juan Yacht Club was burning. Subsequent attempts to communicate with the Miramar parish had failed. All telephone lines, in fact, sounded busy or were dead. The television reported shootouts throughout the city, and there were frightening news about the complete destruction of the main police station in Puerta de Tierra.

Around 9:00 in the morning, a pickup truck carrying several armed men had rolled down the steep cobblestoned Del Cristo Street, advising the residents of Old San Juan through a bullhorn that "the revolution" had begun, and urging them to avoid the streets in case of fighting. More frightening news had followed. "Unknown terrorists," suspected of being Macheteros, had captured la Fortaleza. Secretary of Justice Rovira—*God help the country*, thought Garrido—was running the government. The terrorists had also hijacked a cruise ship moored in the bay, and seized control of the Grand Laguna Hotel, its staff and its guests.

By mid-morning, the television stations were showing the destruction caused by the explosives planted on the bridges. In a televised press conference, Police Superintendent Maldonado revealed the demands of the terrorists. Hostages would begin to be thrown off the roof of the Grand Laguna if their demands were not met.

Denied of the basic means of communication, Archbishop Garrido had sent Father Felipe and Father Bernard to the other churches in Old San Juan and Puerta de Tierra, to order all parishes to maintain all of the churches, food kitchens, and help centers open for any persons who needed shelter, food or medical assistance. All masses were to be held as scheduled for that day, unless the mass celebrants or the faithful ran the risk of physical injury.

In the meantime, he had decided to personally visit the Grand Laguna Hotel to plead for the lives of the hostages. Father Bernard, just returning from his mission on foot to the other churches, had pleaded to him not to go. The roads were unsafe and filled with armed men with bad intentions, he asserted. He was too valuable for the Church and would be taken as a hostage himself. If anything, Father Bernard urged, he should let him go instead. Archbishop Garrido adamantly refused. He would not send anyone on a mission that he thought too risky for himself.

In the end, the two priests had driven out together in the parish's 2003 Prius and, brandishing a white flag—a white pillowcase, really—had headed to the Grand Laguna Hotel. Miraculously, they had encountered none of the groups of armed men that patrolled the streets of San Juan on pickup trucks or on foot. It had not been until they made their way into the hotel's main entrance that they had been stopped by a young armed sentry who had gawked at them as if they had dropped out of heaven. The guard had listened to the priests with astonishment as they pleasantly requested to talk to his leader. Despite several attempts by the young terrorist to send the Archbishop away, Garrido had courteously but firmly refused to go. Sweating profusely and after a great deal of hesitation, the sentry had escorted the unexpected arrivals to the lobby of the hotel.

There, Garrido had waited—surrounded by tired and suspicious armed men who were resting in the reception area—while the sentry tried to coordinate a meeting. They had waited less than five minutes when a man bearing what Archbishop Garrido thought was an uncanny resemblance to Yankee baseball player Alex Rodriguez had arrived, followed by the young, very chastised-looking sentry.

"You can't meet with any of our leaders now. They are too busy," the man had said without any preamble.

"This will not take more than fifteen minutes," the Archbishop had replied, smiling.

"Fifteen minutes or one minute, the answer is still the same. Now leave."

Archbishop had leveled his gaze on the man. They were about the same height and build, and if anything, the priest looked the stronger of the two.

"You never spoke to your leader, did you?" he had said to the young sentry.

The sentry's face had reddened. "I tried," he stammered, "but—"

"I didn't let him waste our leader's time," the Alex Rodriguez double had finished for his younger counterpart. "We don't need your pious hocus pocus here. Be happy that we don't take you as a hostage and toss you off the roof."

"That is precisely what I'm here for," the priest had answered dryly. "I would like to make a proposal to your leader in exchange for the safety of the prisoners." Garrido had taken a step forward, moving past the surprised look-alike and addressing his companion. "Please take me to whomever it is that is in command."

The older terrorist had grabbed the Archbishop by his left arm and violently jerked him around, throwing a hard punch to his face. However, Garrido had easily avoided it and landed a short, wicked jab on his nose, followed by another blow to his neck. Gagging and holding his face, the terrorist had landed on his knees.

The argument between the two men had drawn the attention of several of the other men in lobby, and seeing their comrade fall, four of them had attacked the priest, showering him with punches and striking him with their rifles. Covering his head with his arms and elbows, Garrido had been driven to the ground, where he had continued to be pummeled until the pounding had abruptly stopped.

Dazed, bleeding and breathless, his ears ringing, he had seen a man in his early thirties addressing his aggressors, his eyes darting from him to the Alex Rodriguez look-alike with cat-like curiosity, his lips half-smiling with amusement. Although unable to hear most of what the man said, it was clear that the new arrival commanded the respect of everyone around him. Then, together with Father Bernard, who was bleeding under his left eye, the man had grabbed one of Garrido's arms and helped him back to his feet, returning him to the Prius.

There, the man had helped the Archbishop into the front passenger seat, and gently closed the door after him. Garrido had attempted to speak, but the man had shaken his head.

"Please, father, desist from trying to meet with us. Believe me, there is nothing you can do. You tried. Now go."

Later on that day, as the distraught housekeeper dressed the Archbishop's wounds, Garrido had asked Father Bernard what had happened during the fight.

"I tried to pull away the men who were hitting you," the older priest, his left eye black and a large bandage over his left cheek, had explained, "when...by the way, Your Grace, where did you learn to fight like that?"

"I know some boxing. I also served in Iraq. Go on."

"This man...Daniel was his name...He appeared out of nowhere and immediately stopped the fight. He listened to what had happened, and told the men to let us go. He also said...you were a brave and foolish man, but that your bravery had saved your life."

By nighttime, the telephone service had been partially restored, and the Archbishop had refused to go to bed until he had finished hearing reports from each of the churches in the San Juan and Puerta de Tierra areas. Finally, close to ten-thirty, his staff had prevailed on him to rest. He had taken a Benadryl to help him sleep.

Now, scarcely an hour after midnight, Father Felipe was rousing him from his sleep.

"Please forgive me, Your Grace," the priest, a good-looking, black-haired Franciscan who had just come out of Seminary School, said in a contrite but excited voice. "It's the Governor!"

A chill ran down the Archbishop's spine. Governor Pietrantoni was his personal friend.

"What happened? Is he hurt?"

"He's here!" Father Felipe said joyfully. "He and his family and his staff! They have escaped and are seeking refuge with us!"

"Can it be true?" Garrido said excitedly. He tried to sit and winced with pain. "Thank you, Holy Father, for your boundless mercy!" He looked at his young aide. "You let them in, of course?"

"Of course! They are in the living room downstairs."

"That is not safe enough. Move them to the chapel...No! Wait! To my office. If the terrorists try to break in and search the house, the Governor and the others can get to the back terrace, and from there climb to the roofs of the buildings around us and hide there."

"Yes, Your Grace!"

"Tell them I'll be with them as soon as I put on my cassock. Offer them something to eat and drink. They must be hungry." Garrido smiled happily, placing his hand on Father Felipe's shoulder. "This is great news!"

Archbishop Garrido's office was the largest in the parochial building, but not large at all. Located on the upper, third floor, it had enough space to hold a desk, two brown, leather-bound chairs, and three floor-to-ceiling bookcases that were not enough to hold the hundreds of books that were piled atop each other. Many of the volumes, Lucas observed, dealt with complicated matters of the faith, but were not limited to the Catholic religion. There were books from other religions, ranging from such diverse topics as the teachings of the Dalai Lama (*"The Art of Happiness"*), to something called Jainism (*"How the Paths of Jainism Parallel Many of our Christian Doctrines"*, *"Jainism and the New Spirituality"*), to scores of Muslim texts (*"A Manual of Hadith"*, *"Muhammad, The Prophet"*). But apart from those, what tickled the most Lucas' fancy were the more than two dozen spy and war novels assigned a space of honor on the third and fourth shelves of the bookcase at the opposite end from where the desk was located, that displayed such names as Le Carre, Forsythe, Follet, and Clancy.

Behind the desk hung a poster-sized photograph of a younger, smiling Garrido with a fuller head of hair, surrounded by about two-dozen men and women of all ages, standing in front of what seemed to be the walls of Old Jerusalem. To the left of the desk hung a second, smaller framed photograph of Garrido and another man in a desert setting, both fully garbed in army battle uniforms, Garrido's helmet bearing a black cross, the other man showing two gold stars. Further to the right, a pair of French doors opened up to a large terrace that was almost level with the roof of the contiguous San Juan Cathedral.

Lucas had never met the Archbishop, but had admired him almost from the day that he had been transferred from Chicago to San Juan. He had found the man to be everything that he expected a true man of God to be; humble despite his exalted position, direct and sparing of words rather than bombastic and long-winded, unyielding in his beliefs but willing to dialogue, and—a spot close to Lucas' heart—a person with a great sense of humor. He was pleased to see, as he tiredly walked into the Archbishop's office, that its contents seemed to reinforce his personal perception of the man.

After the grueling ordeals of that day, several in the group had finally begun to show their extreme fatigue, as the adrenaline that had kept their bodies going petered out. Patria, the oldest of the escapees, could barely make it up to the third floor and had to be led to one of the leather-bound chairs, where she carefully rested with a long, blissful sigh. She had bruised her ribs while trying to slide her robust waist through the hole in the ceiling, and was breathing shallowly to avoid the pain.

Picon had been half carried, half led by Lucas and the Governor to the other chair, where Father Bernard had spread a towel. His right arm hung limply from his side, his shoulder broken from a bullet, but he seemed embarrassed about all the attention he was receiving, and had insisted that Nereida take the chair. The priest had brought alcohol and bandages from a cabinet next to the office, and had begun to gently pull the blood-clotted shirt off the bodyguard's wound.

Nereida was carrying Francisco, who had fallen asleep while they waited in the living room. She had managed to carry him up the three flights of stairs, and had settled into the Archbishop's chair after the Governor had pulled it out for her from behind the desk. Lucas was amazed by the beauty of the woman. Her clothes were dirty and stained from dirt and red brick dust, her hair disheveled, but she still looked incredibly sensual and attractive. No wonder rumors constantly surfaced about a secret romance between her and the Governor. Lucas and Nereida's eyes crossed, and he realized that he had been staring at her overly too much. Embarrassed, he diverted his gaze.

Maria, the youngest of the women in the group, had wandered into the office examining everything with the half-absent kind of curiosity of someone who has managed to escape from a hellish ordeal and seeks reassurance in her new surroundings. Young and fairly pretty, she looked extremely tired, a slim smile of relief etched on her lips, her eyes distant and lost in thought.

Arizmendi had also been infected by the same bug as the others. The usually effusive, uncontainable, outspoken Secretary of State maintained a dull silence, his normally direct and piercing eyes now downcast and contemplative. As he entered the Archbishop's office, he had walked straight to one of its corners and slumped inconspicuously on the carpet. Lucas could only imagine the thoughts crossing his mind. He had impaled another human being—granted, an evil human being—with a medieval sword, and seen him squirm until the life abandoned his body. It was not a thing that he would easily forget, and something about which he would have nightmares for the rest of his life.

He worried about Alfredo, but could not feel more proud of him. His eight-year old godson had experienced, in that day of his life, more tension, intense fear and outright terror than most persons would experience during their entire lives. Lucas, and even more than Lucas, Nereida, had tried to shield him and reassure him throughout the ordeal, but there had been no effective way of truly masking the grisly fighting and dying that had trailed them as they tried to escape. Lucas had heard in some television show that children were more resilient and tended to recover more easily from traumatic experiences than adults. He hoped it was true.

Already, his godson's best friend, Francisco, had begun to deal with the stress of the day by shutting down his body and falling asleep. Alfredo had refused to do so, holding on to his godfather's hand and silently watching everyone around him. When one of the priests and the parish house's caretaker had walked into the room carrying trays of coffee, pastries, and juice, Lucas had been relieved to see that Alfredo had been the first to attack them, grabbing two large Danish coffee cakes and consuming them greedily. *It was a good sign,* Lucas thought. *Maybe Alfredo would come through the nightmare relatively unscathed.*

Governor Pietrantoni had hovered from one person to another, trying to ascertain that they were all right. But unlike everyone else, he seemed to have become more invigorated as the night progressed. It was as if a great weight had been lifted off his shoulders. He spoke enthusiastically and maybe a bit too loudly, but who could blame him? His family, his best friend, and many close members of his staff had survived. There was reason to celebrate. Their loss would have been something too terrible to contemplate.

But there was also a deep sadness behind his eyes. The attack had cost the lives of many of his bodyguards, most of which had been his personal friends. His government had been sorely tested and, even to a political amateur like Lucas, it was evident that the Governor would come under heavy attack in the weeks to come. And yet, somehow, Lucas suspected that Pietrantoni would survive; more than survive, prevail and thrive. He had seen the Governor act under the most extreme of circumstances—circumstances that would have overwhelmed most men—and not break. Compared to those circumstances, the post-revolt period would be a walk in the park.

Lucas looked at his watch and saw it was past one thirty in the morning. It had taken them a long time to get to the Archbishop's house. After crawling out through the bent steel bars, the refugees had found themselves in the lower courtyard of El Morro Castle. Lucas had visited the place probably more than twenty times, not only as a young boy, but in school outings and as a tour guide for the many relatives and friends who visited the island and wanted to explore the massive fortress.

Not knowing if any terrorists were stationed there—after all, Lucas had stumbled upon a pair of ground-to-air operators on the roof of the Metropolitan Center—he had warned the others to be quiet. They had climbed the long, steep ramp that connected the lower half of the fort to its central level, nervously searching for movement in the dark shadows that surrounded them, and then rushed to the fort's main entrance.

The gate was blocked by a double set of heavy wooden doors, each about fifteen feet high by seven feet wide, reinforced by thick, criscrossing beams. In the days when El Morro belonged to Spain, the big doors would remain open during the day to allow the transit of horses and carts carrying supplies. At night, the gates would be closed. A smaller door, about the size of those used in modern houses, had been built into one of its two bigger counterparts to permit the entrance of unexpected visitors, and presently it was the only door used to enter and exit from the fort. The visiting hours long over, that door had been closed and locked from the outside.

The Governor and Lucas had tried to break the door open by hitting it simultaneously, but only managed to bruise their shoulders, and made so much noise that they feared any terrorists in the fort would be alerted to their presence. Another attempt, this time to open the door of the National Parks' rangers' office and search for keys, had met the same fate.

Lucas had then climbed to the wall over the gate, only to confirm that there was an approximate fifteen to a twenty-foot drop from it to an open grassy surface outside. He could have risked a jump, but he knew that most of the others would not be able to manage it.

He was about to give up when he came upon a spot, next to the gate itself, where the grass-covered ground rose to within some ten feet of the wall. Running back to the central courtyard, he began to search through the various storerooms, former living quarters, and prison cells that lined it, remembering that every time he had visited the old fortress he had always come across some sort of restoration work. He had struck gold just fifteen minutes into his search, finding an extendable aluminum ladder that was being used to plaster some of the walls in one of the fort's former powder rooms.

Recruiting the help of the Governor and Arizmendi, they had carried the ladder up to the wall above the gate, and carefully lowered it down. It was still three feet shorter than the wall, but there was a waist-high horizontal ridge on the outside of the wall, which the hostages could use as a first step before climbing down the ladder. The descent would not be easy, and they would be fully exposed to anyone watching the fortress from the outside, but Lucas doubted that the fort would be kept under surveillance by the terrorists.

It had been a slow and sometimes nerve wracking affair—Patria had nearly slipped off the wall's ridge before the Governor, standing on the ladder below her, had planted his right hand on her behind—but they had all made it safely to the ground. From there, they had scurried towards the old city wall that fringed San Juan Bay, and paused under its shadow to discuss where they could seek refuge.

Maria had offered her house, which she shared with her parents and three other sisters, but she lived in Puerta de Tierra, and getting there would involve a long, two-mile walk, too risky under the present uncertain conditions. As Lucas had explained to the others, there were roving gangs of armed vigilantes on the streets who would recognize and arrest the Governor on sight. Arizmendi lived in Miramar, and most of the others, including Patria, the Governor, and his family had just escaped from their place of residence. Picon's home, a second story flat on the Caleta de las Monjas, a side street close to La Fortaleza, was also discarded out of hand.

That left only the optometrist's apartment in the Metropolitan Center where Lucas had dropped off his mother and aunts that morning, or *El Joyero de San Juan*. Although the most viable of all alternatives, it still involved traveling through several of the narrow streets of the old city, and using the building's entrance that was located in front of City Hall and the Plaza de Armas, the same area that Lucas had been forced to avoid after it had been occupied by two dozen or more of the armed vigilantes.

Faced with no place to go, it had been Patria who had unwittingly suggested the best solution. "Don't worry, Mr. Governor," she had said reassuringly. "You are a good man, and God would not have gone through all the trouble He's gone through only to deliver us back into the hands of those evil men." And closing her eyes, she had begun to pray.

The Governor had watched her at first with a sad, grateful smile, and then his eyes had lit up. "God will help us!" he had said with newfound hope, instantly drawing everybody else's attention. "Well, God's representative in San Juan, anyway. We could try to hide in the Archbishop's residence."

"Next to the Cathedral?" Lucas had asked.

The Governor had nodded. "Archbishop Garrido is a good friend...And even if he wasn't, he would still help us!"

Lucas had mentally visualized the route that they would have to take to get there. They would still have to travel through several streets with very little cover except for the cars parked in them, but the Archbishop's house was significantly closer than the Metropolitan Center, and they would not have to risk going anywhere near the Plaza de Armas or La Fortaleza.

"It's worth a try," he had said. "But you must follow my instructions to the letter."

He had organized the hostages like a small army patrol, where he had taken the lead, moving more than twenty yards ahead of the rest, to make certain that there were no enemies in sight, Picon bringing up the rear. Somewhere along the way, they had heard a tremendous explosion coming from the sea, and for a few terrifying seconds they had stopped, waiting to see if anything else happened, before renewing their journey.

They had followed the inner contours of the old city wall, past the sprawling, domed building of the School of Plastic Arts and the Institute of Culture. There, they had waited while Lucas ran into Beneficencia Street. The street sloped upwards and angled slightly to the right, passing the magnificent Quincentennial Plaza and ending in San Jose Church, the oldest church in the Western Hemisphere. However, Lucas had only sprinted through a short portion of the street, turning right into the smaller Plaza de la Beneficencia, and hiding behind one of its several decorative concrete structures.

To his relief, the area had looked abandoned. Most of the windows in the surrounding houses were closed and shuttered, still battened up to keep out the bewildering array of men and weapons that had accosted the city since early that morning. He could smell the pungent smell of barbecued sausages and onions wafting in the night's breeze from one of the houses ahead of him, and despite the tremendous strain under which he was, his mouth had watered instantly. Muted voices from a television set escaped from another undetermined point—or maybe from the same house were the sausages were being barbecued, it was hard to tell— somehow making Lucas feel more reassured. Scampering back to the sidewalk, he had signaled the others to come.

They had crossed the Plaza de la Beneficencia and continued east for a short stint through San Sebastian Street. It seemed incredible that the street—the venue of the Fiestas de San Sebastian that had been packed with thousands of noisy revelers, food stands, and arts and crafts stalls just the day before—could now be so empty. Moving a short distance at a fast pace, they had reached the Callejon del Hospital, and descended a block to Sol Street. There, after moving past a couple of houses, they had turned right into the picturesque, stepped alley of the Escalinata de las Monjas (the "Stairway of the Nuns"), which spilled into the Las Monjas Street, the Children's Museum, and the Cathedral Plaza.

There was not quite another square like Cathedral Plaza. To Lucas, this was probably one of the most beautiful spots in Old San Juan. Separated by Cristo Street from the rising steps of the ponderous Cathedral, and dropping precipitously towards the bay, the square boasted a lush, green canopy of giant banyan trees. El Convento, an old nunnery restored into a luxury hotel, flanked its northern side, while the Children's Museum, another beautifully renovated eighteenth century building, guarded its western fringe. There was no activity in the hotel, its old wooden doors shut to the outside world. Lucas wondered if it too had been captured by the terrorists.

The hostages had hidden behind the massive trunk of one of the banyan trees, and waited for Lucas to call on the Archbishop. The parish house stood to the right of the cathedral, its windows dark, its entrance guarded by a locked iron gate. Lucas had easily climbed over the gate and pressed several times the doorbell without any apparent result. He had begun to bang loudly on the door, when it had opened a fraction, held back by a safety chain, and a young man had peeked through the opening.

"What do you want?" the man had asked suspiciously, looking down at Lucas' hands to see if he was carrying any weapons.

"I'm sorry to bother you at this time of the night, but we need your urgent help," Lucas had responded. "The Governor of Puerto Rico and his family need the Archbishop's help."

"The Governor?" the man had asked in a surprised voice, looking behind the night visitor and finding no one there. "He's a prisoner in La Fortaleza."

"He and his family have escaped and are hiding in the plaza across the street. The terrorists are looking for him. Please! We need your help!"

"Wait here a moment!" the man had answered. He had closed the door, taking the safety chain off its track, and reopened it, stepping outside. He was wearing a black cassock, and carried with him a small metal ring full of keys.

"Where are they?" he had asked urgently, unlocking the iron gate.

Lucas had briefly looked up and down Cristo Street, and then signaled to his awaiting companions to come.

"Quickly! Quickly!" the priest had urged them, as they hurried through the narrow alley guarded by the gate and entered the parish building. The priest had locked the gate, and closed the door to the parish house, securing it with various locks and chains. He had ushered them into the living room, while he got hold of the Archbishop, and returned a few minutes later, to lead them to the third floor.

That had happened barely twenty minutes before, and during that time, a semblance of normalcy and relief had returned to their lives, so much so that their desperate flight through the dark tunnels of La Fortaleza and their fearful journey through the still streets of the city now seemed more like an unreal part of a horror movie.

"How do you take your coffee?"

Lucas looked up and was surprised to see Governor Pietrantoni hovering with a cup of coffee in his hand. He immediately began to stand up despite the Governor's protests.

"Sir..." he began to say, accepting the proffered cup.

"Is that dark enough for you?" Pietrantoni asked, referring to the coffee. "See if the sugar is okay."

Lucas took a sip. It was a little low on sugar, but hot and creamy.

"It's fine, sir. Thank you."

"Please don't call me sir," the Governor smiled. "Not in private anyway."

"Thank you, Mr. Governor."

"Roberto. My personal friends call me Roberto."

Lucas smiled. "Roberto. The coffee is fine. Thank you."

Pietrantoni extended his hand, and Lucas had to shift the cup to his left hand to shake it.

"I owe you my life," the Governor said, letting for a second his emotions to show in his voice. He paused briefly, trying to regain his composure. "I owe my son's life...Nereida's life, to you. I will never forget it."

Lucas felt everyone else's eyes on him and blushed. "On the contrary, sir...Roberto. It has been my honor to be at your side today. Any lesser man than you would have cracked with the pressure. You provided the strength to keep us all together."

Pietrantoni beamed, flattered by Lucas' words. "Thank you, coming from a brave man like you, that is high praise indeed."

"I guess you'll vote for him next time, won't you, godfather?" Alfredo blurted, provoking a spontaneous burst of laughter.

Lucas began to respond, but at that moment, the Archbishop barged into the office.

"When Father Felipe told me you were here, I thought, he's drinking too much wine from the sacristy. But here you are! Here are all of you! God be praised!"

The Archbishop embraced the Governor, flinching slightly, as if in pain. Lucas was surprised that the Archbishop's face was bruised, as if he had been beaten up. The bridge of his nose was swollen, as was his left cheekbone and the lip below it. Watching him next to the Governor, he thought how very much alike the two men were. Pietrantoni was taller and leaner, and had a fuller head of hair than Garrido, while the latter had a stronger build, penetrating blue eyes to Pietrantoni's shrewd brown, and a thinner face with more prominent cheekbones. But both men exuded an aura of natural confidence, both were quick to laugh or smile, and both had the innate talent of listening to those around them and making them feel at ease.

"I was just telling this man that we owe our lives to him," the Governor said to Garrido, examining the priest's face but saying nothing about the bruises that he saw, while pointing with his hand at Lucas. "Archbishop Garrido, this is Lucas Alfaro. You may know him from *El Joyero de San Juan*, he's one of the owners. Lucas, this is my sometimes jogging partner, Archbishop Pedro Garrido. Beware of him. If he likes you, he will try to make you a priest."

"I would settle for a deacon. You're Fanny Pietri's son?" the Archbishop said before Lucas could respond. "Of course! I can see the resemblance. I don't know what you did, but bless you for it."

Fanny Pietri's son, Lucas thought to himself, smiling inwardly. *It seemed like everybody who was anybody knew his mother.* He made it a point to tell her.

"Thank you, Your Grace, but the Governor is being modest. He and Picon..." He pointed to the wounded bodyguard, who shook his head modestly, "and really the rest of the people here all played a major role in getting us here."

The Archbishop looked all around him, smiling broadly at everyone in the room. *He was a natural politician,* Lucas thought. *Fortunately for Pietrantoni, he had chosen God over politics.*

"Like I said, Archbishop Garrido is my jogging partner...sometimes. I pick him up in the mornings..." the Governor began to say, but then he stopped, unable to continue. Remembering that some of the bodyguards who jogged with him were dead, the events of the day had finally overwhelmed him.

Garrido watched him with concern, placing a hand on his arm. "It's hard, and I know that nothing I can say can be of consolation. But I'm glad that at least all of you are safe."

The Governor acknowledged his friend's words with a nod, and cleared his throat.

"Thank you, Pedro. But what happened to you?"

Garrido raised an eyebrow. "I had a close encounter with some of the terrorists. Nothing that can't be told some other time. I imagine that you're in need of news."

"Yes, I am. What have you heard?"

"I'm afraid that not much. When I went to bed, the situation was more or less the same, except that word was circulating that you had escaped. If you want to, we can turn on the TV."

"Do you have a telephone I can use? I could try to get through to the Superintendent."

The Archbishop turned to Father Felipe. "Father, please get the Governor a cell phone."

"Yes, Your Grace." The young priest darted out of the office before he had finished speaking.

CHAPTER LXXVIII

Police Superintendent Maldonado closed his eyes with newfound relief as his staff watched him expectantly. "Yes, Mr. Governor, this is Maldonado. It's so good to hear you!"

The dozen or so staffers burst into a spontaneous cheer, but immediately some of them began to hush the others, so they could listen to the conversation.

"And your family is all right?" the Superintendent was asking, pausing to listen for several seconds. "That is excellent, Mr. Governor. I will send the Navy SEALs and the police to secure the house of the Archbishop right away, sir!" Maldonado covered the mouthpiece of his cell phone and spoke rapidly to the female aide standing closest to him, while continuing to listen to Pietrantoni. "Get to it immediately. The SEALs are the closest to them. Tell them how to get there. And send two dozen policemen as well. Coordinate everything, so that they don't end up shooting at each other."

"Yes, sir," she responded and left.

"Yes," Maldonado said to the Governor, lifting the hand that had been covering the speaker. "Please stay where you are. Help is coming soon...What's that? Yes, sir, we have retaken the Grand Laguna Hotel and the *Mardi Gras*. Yes, yes, most of the hostages are safe. We are starting to evacuate the guests from the hotel now. But there are still some hostile elements roaming around the—" He paused, as Pietrantoni asked a question. "Yes, we've retaken San Juan, but there's still some hostile elements in the city that we're rounding up. That's why you should stay where you are until help gets there. I've kept a news blackout on what's happening in San Juan because I did not want to jeopardize your safety, but I will alert the news media soon and let them know what is happening."

Maldonado listened quietly for several minutes. Then he said, "Yes, sir, there are many matters that we need to discuss. However, I think you should rest first. Me?" The Superintendent laughed. "No, I don't think I'll sleep tonight." The Governor said something, and Maldonado shrugged his shoulders. "Well, if we're both going to be awake, let's meet at six...Five? Five in the morning will be fine. In the Archbishop's house. I'll be there. I will see you then..." Again he paused to listen to the Governor. "I understand. I'll send an ambulance right away, and two police cars to drive the others home." He looked at his watch. "So I will see you in...about three and a half hours then. Goodbye, sir. It's so good to hear your voice."

Michelle's cell phone buzzed three times before she was able to pick up the call. To her surprise, it was her news editor, Doel.

"So where are you?" he asked right off the bat.

"I'm in the back parking area of the Grand Laguna Hotel. They're picking up the wounded in ambulances, and taking out the guests to other hotels," she replied, surprised by her boss's casual attitude. After all, she had not spoken to him since that morning, when he had sounded terrified about her safety.

She felt very depressed. She had just walked with Archie and two paramedics as he was being wheeled to one of the ambulances, holding on to his hand, while Negron followed on the other side of the stretcher. The redhead's eyes were slightly open, but his breathing was very labored and shallow, and he was not reacting to her or Negron's nervous chatter. As the paramedics had prepared to push the stretcher into the back of the ambulance, she had lovingly combed with her hand the hair off his forehead and kissed him.

"I will be at the hospital soon," she had promised, even though she was not certain if he had heard or understood her.

Negron had gotten into the ambulance behind him, despite the protests of the medical personnel who wanted to examine the injured rookie policeman. "I'm family!" he had protested with such conviction that nobody had dared to question him.

As the ambulance had left—one of more than a dozen lined up to pick up the wounded and the dead—a group of four SWAT officers, two lined on each side—had passed by her carrying another stretcher with a covered body, followed by Captain Camilo Gomez. Several of the policemen near them had stopped what they were doing and saluted, standing at attention. She realized that the men were carrying the remains of Sergeant Abraham Cordero, word of his courage and fighting prowess—as evidenced by the terrorist bodies they had found around him—spreading like wildfire among the rescuers. Gomez had nodded curtly at her as he walked past her, and then climbed into an ambulance after his dead companion.

"So do you think you could do a report about what happened in the hotel?" Doel asked her over the telephone.

In the background, she heard Correcamino's voice saying, *"Let her be!"* and she had to smile despite the intense sadness that she felt.

"I'll be at WKPA as soon as I can," she answered.

"Don't go to WKPA. We'll come to you."

"When will you get here?"

"Now," a voice said so closely behind her that she jumped. When she turned around, she found Doel and Correcaminos standing behind her, both men grinning.

"Oh my God!" she said, and ran towards them, hugging Doel so hard that she nearly threw him to the ground. Then she began to cry, letting go all of the pent-up tension and grief she held back during that long, terrible day. Correcaminos observed her quietly for several seconds, and then began to clear his throat making exaggerated noises. "I think that's enough, dammit!"

Michelle looked at him over Doel's shoulder, and smiled, tears streaming down her cheeks. She released Doel and walked towards Correcamino's outstretched arms, embracing him. "That's better," he said. "Just watch out for the suit...don't stain it with your mascara."

Michelle laughed, still crying, and tried to wipe her tears away. For a change, the sportscaster looked like a wreck, his fine linen suit wrinkled, his tie—usually perfectly knotted and held by a tiepin—disheveled and half open, his normally coifed-to-perfection and shiny-with-pomade hair messy and uncombed. She wondered how she looked to them. Her upper lip was a lot less swollen, but her black eye must have been worse.

"Where have you been all day?" she asked them with an amused stare.

"Do you think you've been the only one working? This man here," Correcaminos said, directing a look of contempt at Doel, "has kept me locked up with the Superintendent all night long."

"Stop complaining so much, you cry baby. Because of my insistence you were able to witness—"

"Cry baby!" Correcaminos interrupted. "Listen, you effeminate version of a news editor, if Michelle didn't have to witness the violence, I'd beat you up..." But he stopped, noticing Michelle's sudden somber expression. "I'm sorry, that was so stupid of me. Of course you've witnessed a *lot* of violence today. I'm so sorry!"

"It's okay. I'm okay," she said, sniffling. Correcaminos removed a handkerchief from his breast pocket and handed it to her.

For the first time, she noticed the cameraman standing behind Doel, an old friend of hers everyone called "Fofo". He had been quietly filming their conversation.

"How...how did you guys get here?" she asked, still surprised by their sudden appearance.

"Compliments of my buddy, the Superintendent Maldonado," Correcaminos responded, beaming with pride. "You have the exclusive, before the rest of the press gets here."

"It's the least he could have done after you risked your life the way you did," Doel added.

Correcaminos snorted derisively. "*Now* he's concerned!"

Doel ignored him. "Are you up to it?" he asked her.

Michelle nodded.

"Good! No make up. This is your time to shine. The people will see you the way you came out of this ordeal. We're going to record it in the station, and then transmit it, so if you need to cut, just do it, okay?"

"She doesn't need any makeup," Correcaminos said to himself. "She's beautiful the way she is."

Fofo handed a microphone to the sportscaster, who gave it to Michelle. The cameraman spoke briefly through a mouthpiece he had attached to his neck, listened through his earphones, and nodded. "In five..." he said raising his open hand, and lowering one finger, "four..." He went silent, and continued the countdown with his fingers.

"I am standing on the outside grounds of the Grand Laguna Hotel," she began to say as Fofo's hand became a closed fist, "near the hotel's convention facilities. As you can see behind me, the police and the National Guard are evacuating the hundreds of guests who until about an hour ago were the object of the worst terrorist attack in the history of our country. Because of the incredible bravery of a few men, both policemen, Navy SEALs, and private citizens alike, most of the trapped guests are now able to walk away from their terrible ordeal."

She paused, trying to steady her hands, which were grasping the microphone too tightly. "But not everyone was so fortunate. Six guests lost their lives tonight, most of them defending their fellow hostages from the terrorists while help arrived. These people are true heroes, who did not hesitate to place themselves in the path of terror in order to save the lives of countless others, and our thoughts and prayers are with their families and friends, who have suffered such a terrible loss."

Michelle thought about Archie, and for a brief moment struggled to hold back her tears.

"About two-dozen other persons have been injured, three seriously. The wounded are being treated or transported to hospitals by a host of medical personnel that has arrived here during the past half hour. The toll seems high, but it is not. Considering the more than a thousand guests who were staying in this hotel, and the fierce fighting that happened here just a couple of hours ago, it is nothing short of a miracle that more people were not hurt or killed. The toll could have been, should have been, much, much higher."

Michelle briefly looked around her, staring at the procession of guests that were being led to the rescue vehicles.

"Right now we are located in front of the parking building area, where the freed hostages are being picked up by the shuttles that will transport them to different hotels in the Metropolitan area. Apart from the heavy volume of the traffic coming and going, and the strong security that surrounds us, the hotel grounds don't seem to have been affected by the terrorists' brief reign of terror. But if you walk just a little bit further into the hotel, into the convention facilities area, and especially to the Grand Laguna's main ballroom, you will find an entirely different picture. Much of it has been destroyed during the intense fighting that took place here, reduced to the kind of debris you only see in photos of war torn countries, and you wonder how anyone could have survived it."

She paused again, feeling her throat parched, gathering her thoughts.

"This morning, as I headed for work, my taxi was trapped in the crossfire between the terrorists and the police in the Puerta de Tierra Station. As I tried to escape, I had the incredible good fortune to run into two extraordinary men, one of them a resident of the area and the other a young policeman who survived the Puerta de Tierra shootout. They could have hidden or run away, but instead they saved my life and that of several others who were with me. Later that day, when we managed to contact Superintendent Maldonado, they agreed to infiltrate the Grand Laguna Hotel to find out where the terrorists kept the hostages and provide information to the police to help in the rescue operations. I went along with them."

Very aware of what must have been her frightful appearance, she swept some stray hairs off her forehead.

"Later that night, we were able to meet with two SWAT officers who had managed to swim to the San Geronimo Fort, and from there penetrate the grounds of the Grand Laguna Hotel. In what can only be described as an incredible feat of valor, my two companions and the two SWAT officers then captured the main ballroom where the hostages were being kept. However, one of my two companions was seriously wounded in the chest, and the ballroom was surrounded by dozens of terrorists who remained in the hotel. Twice, the terrorists attacked us, but due to the heroic efforts of my companions, the SWAT officers, and some of the guests, we were able to repulse them."

Again she paused, but this time she could not stop tears from filling her eyes, and she clumsily wiped them off with the back of one of her wrists. In the background, she saw Doel mouth silently the word "E-A-S-Y" and she nodded imperceptively.

"It is…very difficult for me to describe everything that I witnessed here today. It would take hours, if not days, to do so, and I will be trying to do that in the days to come. It is not an easy story to tell. There were plenty of moments when I thought I would not survive. During the last hour of the fighting, when it got the most intense, we were in the dark, and there was chaos all around us. The terrorists attacked us with machine guns and rifles, and at some moments the struggle got so fierce that it came down to hand-to-hand combat. But they never managed to break through. Somehow, we held, we held until the Navy SEALs got here and saved us. We held, at the terrible cost of the life of one of the SWAT officers, whose name I have been asked not to disclose yet, and of some very brave guests who volunteered to defend us. But we held them."

Michelle stopped, looking at Doel and Correcaminos, who were standing behind the cameraman. Both seemed to be completely absorbed by her words, so much so that neither moved.

"We never really knew who the terrorists were or what they wanted. We don't know where they came from. We have no idea if this was conducted by extreme elements from outside the island, or local extremists or a combination of both. All we can tell at this moment is that they were very well organized and extremely well armed. I have not had the opportunity to talk to the Navy SEALs, but I am informed that they captured about two-dozen persons, most of them apparently are university students, who were involved with the terrorist activities. Many of them are being transferred to police vans to be jailed in separate detention centers. Most of the more disciplined and trained hijackers—Macheteros, I have heard many claim—were killed either in their attempt to retake the hostages, or wiped out by the Navy SEALs. Time will tell who these people are, and what motivated them. I have also been informed that the group of hostages that were taken away from the ballroom and up to the rooftop, and who were used as human shields to throw one guest from the roof, were rescued by the SEALs, and that they are in good health."

Michelle seemed to gather strength as she continued to speak.

"There has been no word from Adalberto Cacho, the Machetero leader who was released earlier via helicopter from the Bayamon Federal Penitentiary as one of the demands of the terrorists. We also have no information if any of the other leaders of the revolt—whoever they are—have been captured or are still at large, or what Cacho's connection to these persons is. If what I have seen in the hotel is a reflection of what is happening in the rest of San Juan, hundreds of policemen, National Guardsmen, and other security forces are pouring over the provisional bridges connecting the island of San Juan to Miramar recently set up by the authorities. WKPA news will continue to report as the events unfold. We have been advised, however, that these temporary bridges are for the exclusive use of the authorities, at least for the moment, and that private citizens should stay clear of the area and allow the ongoing rescue to continue."

Michelle stared again at her two mentors and, for the first time, the corner of her lips curved into an impish smile.

"I will be reporting back to you live in tomorrow's 9:00 o'clock news, and further during the week, there will be a full hour program where I will expand on what I was able to personally witness today," she said without any kind of authorization from her news editor, and saw Doel raise an eyebrow and Correcaminos grin with pleasure. "Nevertheless, I would not like to leave you without these parting reflections. Today, I saw the very worst of what humanity can produce: the kidnapping of innocent victims, including women and children; the wanton destruction of property; the callous, heartless executions and killings of hostages. But I was also fortunate to witness humanity at its best. I saw total strangers willing to face the overwhelming might of the terrorists; I saw doctors and nurses working with what little materials they had to save the lives of the wounded; I saw mothers and fathers shielding their children with their bodies to save them from the stray bullets flying around them; I saw policemen and soldiers lay their lives on the line of duty to protect hundreds of total strangers; I saw dozens of random acts of kindness and personal sacrifice among what were basically trapped strangers, people helping others to safety, giving their places to those that were hurt or more vulnerable, sharing their food and water, trying to keep the morale of those who despaired even when the world threatened to collapse around them; and I witnessed the personal concern and dedication of Superintendent Maldonado and all of his people, as they never gave up and tried to extricate us from the terrible evil that was visited upon us. It is these, and many other images that reflect the intrinsic decency and kindness of our fellow human beings, that will stay with me for the rest of my life."

"I ask you that you pray for those who lost their lives or were wounded today here and in other parts of San Juan. Our hearts and love go to them and to their families. Mom, if you are by any chance watching, I'll be home soon." Michelle blew a kiss at the TV. "Reporting from the Grand Laguna Hotel, this is Michelle Alfaro, for WKPA news."

El Gordo Purcell's home in La Perla was a three-story, flamingo-pink-colored, reinforced concrete building that bordered the beach—if the narrow strip of sand between the sea and the tall rocks on which the building was perched could be called a "beach". Despite the strong, almost perennial breeze coming from the Atlantic, its aluminum Miami-style windows were always closed, the ventilation to all three floors provided by two massive air conditioning units installed on the roof. An industrial-sized generator on the side of the building, ringed by a chain link fence, guaranteed that Purcell's residence never lost power.

Contrary to what may have been expected, there were no armed guards in front of the pink building, although video cameras ringed its entire perimeter, and a guard armed with an Uzi sub machinegun sat on an aluminum chair in the back of the compound, facing the sea. The glass sliding doors that opened to the back terrace were bullet-proof, and three or four equally armed gunmen lounged in the entertainment center behind them. The red door at the building's entrance was made of three-inch steel, and it would have taken a tank to knock it down.

The extra precautions were unnecessary. El Gordo Purcell, who had not been "gordo"—or fat—for the last ten years after he had become a convert of Dr. Atkins' diet, ruled his surroundings with a benevolent iron fist, dispensing all kinds of favors and gifts to its residents, demanding absolute loyalty, and ruthlessly eliminating anyone who opposed him. Soft spoken, self-effacing, and barely standing at five foot four, the middle-aged drug lord had established a mini empire not only in La Perla, but beyond the massive ancient walls of the city, an empire that covered all of Old San Juan, into Puerta de Tierra. A small army of "employees" distributed crack, cocaine, marihuana, ecstasy, and other lesser known drugs at the best prices in town in small plastic packages—bearing such brand names as "Snow White", "Agueybana", "El Mago de Oz", and "Camarero"—that even included a printed certification about the "purity" of the product. No drugs were allowed to be sold within the radius of four blocks of the flamingo-colored residence.

Purcell had managed to keep out of the public eye with a combination of massive bribes, an extensive system of intelligence gathering, and extreme violence. His far reach extended to many of the island's best-known politicians, judges and—despite Maldonado's and Montañez's best efforts—dozens of law enforcement officers.

It was his harmless personal appearance, however, which provided him with his greatest cover. Clean-shaven, small, and plain-looking, refusing to wear any of the heavy gold chains and other attention-calling accoutrements of many of his contemporaries, he could have successfully doubled as a store clerk or the manager of a fast food restaurant. The looks, however, were deceiving. As a teenager, he had worked as a *"gatillero"* or "triggerman", in charge of defending the turf of Don Pedro, his former boss, earning a reputation as a fierce hit man, and later avenging his boss's murder and taking over his business. He had been fat then, weighing close to two hundred pounds despite his short height, until his brother, also fat, had died from a heart attack. On the day of the funeral, he had quit smoking and started a diet.

San Miguel had contacted him through the Ojeda-Santacruz family from the Medellin drug cartel, the same source that had given him access to the police mole simply known as "Ramon". Months before, he and Daniel had visited the pink residence in La Perla, where they had sat in a huge living room in the second floor—lavishly decorated with African animal prints, pelts, and the heads of several antelopes—and discussed business.

In essence, San Miguel had explained—after congratulating him for his exquisite furnishings—that he would be conducting an "operation" in San Juan.

"The operation will involve close to...sixty men," San Miguel had informed Purcell, as he picked up a delicate porcelain cup filled with potent espresso coffee from a tray that one of the drug lord's men had placed on a round glass table in front of him. The figures of three kneeling black slaves with their hands upraised held the transparent glass tabletop. Daniel had stifled a chuckle as he raised up his cup and took a sip of the coffee.

Purcell had leaned forward, not bothering to conceal his interest. "Is this a drug related operation?" he had asked.

"No. Nothing of the sort," San Miguel had replied courteously. "We would never dare to invade your turf."

Purcell had considered the answer and then nodded, tilting his head slightly. "Forgive my curiosity," he had said, "but the Ojeda brothers said that you wanted to use this house in particular. This, as you know, is my private residence. I take great pains in keeping my business away from everything that I do. Why this house in particular? And what do I stand to gain in this matter?"

San Miguel had smiled. "As to the gain, I am willing to pay you one hundred thousand dollars to let my men assemble here for a couple of hours. I would call that fair, wouldn't you?"

Purcell had shrugged. "Just for meeting here?" His eyes had flicked briefly to Daniel, looking for more clues.

"I would need you to store six inflatable rafts and the inflating equipment," San Miguel had replied.

"Ahhh!" Purcell's face had brightened, as he began to understand. "You need a place from where you can launch the rafts, like the beach behind my house."

"Exactly," San Miguel had taken a short swallow of the espresso and sighed appreciatively. "This is good coffee."

"The best in the world. "Oro Negro, from Adjuntas. Do you know that for many years the popes used to buy their coffee directly from Puerto Rico?"

San Miguel had shaken his head in silent wonder.

"It's true. One of the many things foreigners don't know about Puerto Rico." Purcell had finished his coffee and placed his cup over one of the kneeling slaves. "But back to business. One hundred thousand dollars is a hefty sum of money, don't get me wrong. But I am very worried that your people get into some sort of trouble with the law, not that it's any of my business, and that the authorities chase them to my house. That would be very bad."

"You have no reason to be concerned," San Miguel had assured him. "When this happens, the authorities will be very, very busy dealing with other matters, and I'll make certain we're not followed. After all, our safety depends on it."

"You say 'when this happens'... *When* does *this* happen?" Purcell had directed another look at Daniel, who had merely smiled.

"For safety reasons, I can't tell you until the day before," San Miguel had answered for his companion. "This must be kept a secret until the very end. But it will be sometime during January or February of next year,"

Purcell had nodded thoughtfully, as if arguing with himself. "Had you come in here referred by anybody else but the Ojeda brothers, I would have said no. But the Ojedas, as I call them, they are family, and they vouched for you. I will let you use my home. I will even inflate the rafts for you when the time comes, but for two hundred thousand dollars. Not that I distrust you, but I will post my own men to make certain that you're not followed. That costs money."

San Miguel had winced at the mention of the sum and placed his cup on the table. "Very well," he had conceded in a dull tone, even though he had been prepared to offer up to three hundred thousand dollars for the use of the house, "two hundred thousand it is."

He had extended his hand towards Purcell, who had shaken it.

That had happened six months before. When San Miguel had contacted El Gordo Purcell through the pre-arranged telephone number, the drug lord's only response had been, "Everything will be ready."

Three carloads of San Miguel's men had arrived to the flamingo-pink compound around 8:00 PM, disgorging sixteen passengers coming from the Grand Laguna Hotel. Two of Purcell's men had disposed of the vehicles, so that they would not be traced back to the building. Momentarily detained, San Miguel, Daniel, and Czecka had arrived fifteen minutes later.

A few of Colonel Calderon's men, basically those who had handled the surface-to-air missiles in Forts San Cristobal and El Morro, had arrived close to ten. Four more of the Venezuelans, the two stationed on the roof of the building located next to the Grand Laguna Hotel who had shot down the SWAT helicopter with one of their missiles, and two other men stranded from the rest of Calderon's group while guarding the approaches to the hotel's pool area, managed to reach Purcell's house half an hour later.

No more would be coming, one of the last Venezuelan stragglers had warned, barely able to contain his tears. He had been shot in his left calf as he and his partner barely escaped with their lives from the hotel. Calderon and the rest of his men were either dead, wounded or captured in a lightning, unexpected attack by U.S. special forces.

All of the men, as they arrived, had put on dark clothes, blackened their hands and faces, and begun to transfer their weapons and equipment onto the rafts lying on the small sand strip behind the pink building. Da'ud, one of San Miguel's men who had escorted the ten hostages to the roof of the Grand Laguna Hotel, had placed a square, car battery-sized radio on a table in the back terrace, and putting on headphones, had begun to monitor its transmissions. He was using a VLF band—very low frequency radio waves—waiting for a signal that confirmed the arrival of their transport.

San Miguel stood next to him, watching him distractedly, his thoughts elsewhere. It had all gone beyond his wildest expectations. He would miss George, who had proven his worth a thousand times over, and was sorry that Cacho had been killed. He would have preferred to unleash the Machetero leader on the American authorities, but some things could not be avoided. San Juan would show that any modern city in the world could be subject to a concerted terrorist attack. People would talk about what had happened in the last two days for decades to come, and never really feel safe. It would be discussed in the same breath as the destruction of the Twin Towers in New York and the bombings in London, and at the very least, provoke hundreds of millions of additional expenditures by the capitalist powers to beef up even more their ever vulnerable security.

And yet, everything that had happened would pale in comparison to what he had planned for the second stage of the operation. If that came to be—as it inevitably would—its repercussions would be felt around the world for decades to come. And the most significant thing was that the second stage had already been set into motion, and that it would come to fruition without the need of any further intervention. Although he had planned to return to San Juan later to make certain that everything was on track.

To do that, however, he needed to escape. He had been surprised by how quickly the authorities were recovering the control over the hijacked island. Already, there were scattered radio rumors that the police was bridging the gap of some of the destroyed bridges, and that vehicles and personnel would soon pour into San Juan. He hoped they would continue to be distracted in their attempts to recapture the Grand Laguna Hotel and the *Mardi Gras* and to try to find the Governor, and would not pay any attention to what was happening in La Perla.

Hopefully, the Governor had survived. That would make everything a lot simpler. If not, San Miguel had access to some publicists, both in Puerto Rico and stateside, who would be glad to argue that the Puerto Rican government and the rest of the world should not be intimidated by terrorist acts, and that life should by all means continue as planned. In fact, he had to a large extent pinned the success of the final stage of his plan on the sense of defiance that the people of Puerto Rico would express in the days to come, on the "they-had-been-bloodied-but-were-unbowed" kind of attitude that hopefully would soon sweep the island-nation.

Regardless of the turn of future events, San Juan was doomed. It was a terrible shame, since he had come to like the old city and its mostly happy-go-lucky residents, but a justifiable evil.

"God will understand," he had muttered to himself, earning a curious look from Daniel.

The signal had come at 11:42 PM, five prolonged beeps followed by five short ones. Da'ud had merely nodded at San Miguel and Daniel, who had walked to the others.

"Time to go!" Daniel shouted, rousing the men sitting on the floor or watching an Arnold Schwarzenegger movie in the giant television screen of the family room next to the glass sliding doors.

The men moved quickly, walking to the beach and pulling three of the rafts onto the water until they floated. Czecka held one of the barges in place while the rest of the passengers climbed or slid into it. Two other inflatable boats had been dragged into the water. Each raft only held from ten to twelve men, since barely thirty of the expected sixty men had managed to reach La Perla. El Gordo Purcell's beach was sheltered by a small cove that partially broke the waves coming from the sea. Even so, the men holding the other rafts—two per raft—were having trouble keeping them steady.

"You have more rafts than you need," Purcell said to San Miguel, as both men walked into the outside terrace. His eyes, however, were fixed on Czecka, who jutted out of the water like a large boulder.

San Miguel nodded. "We suffered more casualties than we expected."

Purcell glanced at him casually, "I will dispose of them," he said, adding, as he returned his attention to Czecka, "Damn! That's a big man! I could use someone like him."

San Miguel said nothing, smiling.

"You created quite a brouhaha out there today," Purcell continued saying. "Did you achieve what you wanted?"

"Yes," San Miguel had responded simply. He extended his hand to the drug lord. "It was a pleasure doing business with you."

Purcell shook the proffered hand lamely, apparently disappointed by his companion's reticence to disclose more information. "I hope your boat makes it," he said. "I don't see anything out there."

"Oh, it will be, it will be. Goodbye, my friend."

San Miguel began to walk towards the raft held by Czecka. Already the men in the other two inflatable boats had begun to row away, the raft carrying Daniel and Da'ud leading the way. As the two rubber crafts abandoned the safety of the cove, a large wave broke ahead them, raising their bows at a steep angle and drenching the men inside. Both rafts cleared the wave and righted themselves, while the men continued to paddle frantically to reach the relative safety of the deeper water.

San Miguel watched them for a moment, and then prepared for their turn. His raft easily negotiated the first swell that hit them, but then got caught in the drop between it and an enormous wave that followed it. It pushed the rubber boat up, almost vertically, and would have capsized if Czecka had not rushed to its prow and helped it to break through the wall of water. One of the men at the rear was swept overboard, but managed to hold on to the yellow rope attached to the side of the raft, and he was pulled back aboard safely.

A third wave broke over them, partially swamping the small craft with white foam. But by then they had cleared the area where the waves crashed against the shore, and they were able to ride the next swell before it broke. San Miguel saw Daniel several yards ahead, looking anxiously in his direction as his raft rose and disappeared between the undulating waves, before he returned his attention to the sea's dark horizon.

The men continued to row, now at a more settled rhythm, gradually expanding their distance from the shore. Soon, La Perla had dwindled into a collection of white and yellow lights.

Now for the rendezvous, San Miguel thought, unable to keep his excitement down, his heart pounding in his chest. It was just a matter of ten minutes more, and they would be safe. He could not see them yet, but he knew that they would be there. The VLF radio had confirmed it.

And then, out of nowhere, the bright oblong white circle of a spotlight appeared on the water, rushing over the waves towards them like a hungry shark. Shocked, San Miguel turned towards the source of the light, and saw the pale outline of a ship moving in their direction. The spotlight swept over one of the rafts ahead of them, stopped, and moved back until it captured the small craft within its blinding glare.

A shrill siren pierced through the sullen moaning of the sea, as the ship barreled towards the raft, cutting through the swells with surprising ease. It was a Coast Guard cutter, probably more than two hundred feet long, and it was closing in on the three rafts at great speed.

San Miguel saw the men in the raft under the spotlight go for their weapons, but the crew on the approaching ship must have seen them as well, because suddenly the water ahead of the raft erupted with a line of intermittent splashes, just as the noise of heavy machine gun fire reached his ears.

"Get your guns ready," San Miguel shouted to the people on his raft. Already, Czecka was holding an AK-47. "They haven't seen us, so we may be able to surprise them when they get close to the others," he said hopefully, but he knew it was a lost fight. At the most, they could gain some time, but they were no match for the heavy armament of the cutter.

"*This is the Coast Guard!*" a loudspeaker boomed from the ship, the boat's high turret now looming over the inflatable boats less than a hundred yards away, it's spotlight turning into bright daylight the area around the discovered raft. "*Put down your weapons and place your hands behind your heads or we will fire!*"

San Miguel saw some of the men do as they were told, but then others opened fire. The Coast Guard cutter retaliated immediately, it's first shots splashing between the raft under the spotlight and San Miguel's own boat, but then the subsequent fire honing in on the illuminated vessel. Two men were hit with devastating effect, one of them blasted overboard. It was all it took to snuff out any further resistance. The remaining men raised their hands in surrender.

"Hold your fire," San Miguel warned to the others on his raft. "Let it get closer."

The white cutter began to reduce its speed as it got nearer to its prey, the glare of its spotlight blinding the men on the rubber raft. Someone was shrieking in agony, probably wounded by the Coast Guard ship's heavy fire.

"*Throw your weapons over the side,*" the loudspeaker boomed.

"Get ready..." San Miguel began to say as the cutter drew near, but at that same moment a deafening explosion drowned his voice, the shock waves shaking the tiny inflatable boat.

To his astonishment, San Miguel saw an enormous tongue of flame and smoke jet upwards from the center of the Coast Guard vessel's hull. A ball of fire enveloped the ship and billowed into the sky, spreading a rain of burning debris hundreds of yards away, transforming the dark night into day.

In mute, astonished silence, the men on the rafts watched the prow of the ship disappear into the water in a matter of seconds and the ship break in two, as its other half, the larger of the two, continued to burn unchecked, with secondary explosions punctuating every few seconds its last death throes. A strong odor of diesel mixed with the stench of charred rubber and seared wood, and large, isolated patches of flame blistered the surface of the water around the sinking wreck.

Suddenly, an oblong, rectangular shape broke the surface of the water like the giant fin of a prehistoric shark, scarcely a few yards away from the rubber rafts. It quickly rose from the sea until it abruptly extended horizontally, revealing the smooth outline of a submarine. There were no markings or numbers anywhere on the vessel. If it had ever shown any, they had been painted over.

The men on the raft began to cheer wildly as two small figures appeared on top of the turret. One of them began to wave urgently at the inflatable boats, while the other examined his surroundings with a pair of binoculars.

"Hurry!" San Miguel urged to his men, picking up a paddle. "This fire is going to draw the attention of everybody for miles around."

To his great satisfaction, he noticed that the other two rafts were already making their way towards the awaiting war vessel. He had never seen a ship sunk by a torpedo before, had never imagined such destruction, much less coming from an outmoded, second-hand Venezuelan submarine. But then the torpedoes and their launching mechanism had probably been modernized, and that had made all the difference.

San Miguel's raft reached the submarine in less than five minutes, its soaked, tired men scrambling over a net hanging from the side, and running towards an open hatch on the wet deck. San Miguel and Czecka were the last to climb in, the sullen giant flinging a wounded man from one of the other rubber boats over his shoulder, and carrying him effortlessly like a rag doll.

When two police helicopters arrived a quarter of an hour later to investigate the explosion, only the three empty rafts and some patches of burning debris remained as mute witnesses of what had happened just a few minutes before. The submarine and its precious cargo had long vanished into the sea.

CHAPTER LXXIX

Lucas caught himself nodding as the police car rounded the underpass between Kennedy and Roosevelt Avenues, and he raised his wrist to look at the time without moving the rest of his arm in order not to awake Alfredo. He watched his godson with a mixture of amusement and relief, as he slept against his shoulder, noticing the faint fuzzy outline of a mustache on his upper lip. The kid was growing up. Soon he would turn into a full-blown teenager, and the charming innocence and casual wonder with which he saw the world—and which Lucas enjoyed so much—would change. Not that it would necessarily be a bad thing. In fact, it was a necessary part of life. And he was certain that Alfredo would grow into a wonderful human being. But he would miss the brave, outspoken, charming little boy that snuggled against his arm.

It was close to three o'clock in the morning and his neighborhood, usually brimming with traffic and pedestrians, was deserted except for a couple of cats rummaging through some boxes piled on top of a dumpster in the San Patricio Plaza shopping center. As the police car turned right into San Patricio Avenue, he noticed that the traffic lights had been turned off and were instead flashing an intermittent yellow. Ahead, the tall condominiums lining the street were dark except for half a dozen apartments. He tried to imagine who would be up at that ungodly hour—people who could not sleep, probably, or maybe someone trying to meet some work deadline or studying for a test, or a bloodshot mother feeding her new born baby, or maybe just people who had gone to sleep and forgotten to turn off their lights. It brought back to mind his last moments with Governor Pietrantoni, who had refused to rest despite the advice of Archbishop Garrido and Secretary of State Arizmendi, and who was probably dealing with the administrative nightmare that must necessarily follow an aborted coup.

The Governor had insisted in walking Lucas and Alfredo down to the police car. He had shaken the young boy's hand, who had looked solemn and shy. Pietrantoni had asked him, "Will you come visit Francisco and I to La Fortaleza soon?"

Alfredo had answered, tiredly but without hesitation, "Sure!"

Then the Governor had turned to Lucas and shook his hand again. "I would ask one more favor of you, if you don't mind," he had said. "Will you come to the legislature tomorrow night...you and Alfredo...to listen to my address about the state of the island?"

"You're not postponing your address?" Lucas had asked in a surprised tone, before he could stop himself. Then, before Pietrantoni could answer, he had said. "Of course we'll be there. It will be an honor."

"Thank you," the Governor had replied, and begun to walk back into the Archbishop's residence.

As Lucas was about to climb into the police car, however, he had stopped, ushered Alfredo inside, and told him to wait for him there. Then he had rushed back after the retreating Governor. "Governor Pietrantoni!" he had called out.

The Governor had turned and stared at him quizzically as he approached.

"The terrorists...they killed a man inside the jewelry store," he said in a low voice.

"In *El Joyero*?" Pietrantoni asked with surprise.

"Yes, his name was Antonio. He had been with us since as long as I can remember. He was like family to all of us. They shot him as he tried to defend my Aunt Maria." There was no need for Lucas to say who *they* were.

"I'm very sorry to hear that. My condolences," the Governor said.

"I broke one of the killer's wrists, but he is still out there somewhere." Pietrantoni suppressed a chuckle.

"I figured that if you were involved, the killer would not escape unscathed. I'll call Maldonado so that he keeps a lookout for anybody with a broken wrist," Pietrantoni said, anticipating his friend's request. "Is the body still in the jewelry store? Can the police gain access to the store?" he asked Lucas.

"Yes. We covered Antonio with a piece of cloth. The door to the *Joyero* is unlocked. I can wait for them there if they come to examine the scene of the murder."

The Governor shook his head. "No. Go home. You've been through enough for one day. I'll take care of it. Tomorrow, when you're rested, the police will contact you to take your statement. Did your mother and your aunts also witness the killing?"

"Yes."

"Are they all right?"

"Yes. I mean...I don't know emotionally..."

"But not physically harmed," Pietrantoni finished for Lucas. "They should rest as well. I'll have the body removed, so that they don't have to see it, and post a guard to keep watch over the jewelry store."

"Thank you, sir," Lucas said gratefully. He almost turned to return to the police car, but stopped again. "Oh," he said to Pietrantoni, shaking his head with mortification. "There is another thing I almost forgot!"

The Governor smiled. "Fire away."

"On the rooftop of the Metropolitan Center there are two terrorists," Lucas said almost apologetically. "One of them is dead. I shot him."

Pietrantoni raised an eyebrow but said nothing. Nothing about Lucas Alfaro surprised him any more.

"The other one may or may not be alive," Lucas continued. "I tied him up and placed him close to the exit to the stairs..."

"I'll see to it that the police take care of them." The Governor regarded Lucas for several seconds with affection. "Any other bodies I should warn the police about?"

"I think you saw all the others," Lucas had replied with an abashed grin.

"Good. After all of this is over, we'll have to sit down and talk for a long while. Just you and me...maybe Picon and Arizmendi. I may convince you to become my personal bodyguard, if you ever become tired of being a jeweler. But enough for today. Go back to your family. Goodnight, Lucas."

"Goodnight, Mr. Governor."

Pietrantoni had leaned forward and whispered. "I thought I had asked you to call me Roberto..."

"Only in private, sir," Lucas had answered just as softly, gesturing with his eyes at the policemen around them.

The Governor sighed. "Okay. Just remember... If you can be at the legislature tomorrow at seven in the evening, I will be very grateful to you. Just tell them who you are. They'll be waiting for you." He waved as Lucas walked back to the police car, and then added, "Oh! And please bring your wife, and Alfredo's parents along, okay?...Vanessa. That *is* your sister's name, right? And her husband. Tell them they're invited too." He snickered. "I'll need all of the supporters I can get."

As the car pulled away, Lucas had shaken his head in amazement. After all of the events of that day, the Governor still had remembered Vanessa's name! *What a politician! Wait until his sister heard about it!* There would be no standing her.

Leaning forward, he had said to the policeman driving the car, "We need to make a short stop at the Metropolitan Center if you don't mind. I need to pick up my aunt and my mother."

The driver had directed a look at him that seemed to say, "I'm tired and it's late and I'm not a taxi driver," but in the end he only had nodded.

The drive had been short—less than two minutes from the archbishop's home through the eerily empty streets of Old San Juan. The Plaza de Armas was quiet, long abandoned by the scores of young revelers who had occupied it earlier that day. The car pulled up to the large ornamental entrance of the residential portion of the building, and Lucas stepped out immediately. "I'll be right back," he promised to the policeman, who said nothing. "Come on, Alfredo," he said to his godson. "Let's give them a surprise."

Francesca, the optometrist who lived in the fifth floor, had closed the double, wrought iron gates that protected the doors to her apartment, placing two huge padlocks between them. No light could be seen filtering under the entrance doors, but both Alfredo and Lucas could listen to soft snoring coming from within.

Alfredo had directed a gleeful look at his godfather. "I'll hide!" he had said. "You knock on the door."

Fearing that his mother would die from a heart attack when she did not see the boy, Lucas had forbidden him to scare her, and rapped the door twice, sharply. Fannie had opened it, first looking through a crack, and then shouting with delight "They're here! They're here!" and running to the rooms at the back of the apartment to wake up the others.

Maria had been the first to come. "I told them you would be all right!" she had said delightedly. Then she had added in a whisper. "I was about to strangle Evelyn! She kept saying that maybe you should have brought with you some jewels from *El Joyero* to bribe the terrorists."

"Well," Evelyn said behind her, "that's better than what *you* wanted to do! She wanted to go to Fortaleza and search for you, as if those communists would just let her walk in!"

"She was driving me crazy!" Maria had responded. "I just wanted to get out of here!"

Lucas smiled. It was good to listen to his aunts' chatter again. It was the closest thing to normality that he had experienced since that morning.

Still waiting to get in, Alfredo had begun to tell them in a fast, excited torrent of words everything that had happened to him in La Fortaleza, further adding to the din. Finally, Fannie had arrived with Francesca, who carried with her a ring of keys.

"Move over, girls," the optometrist said to Maria and Evelyn, who were bombarding Lucas and Alfredo with questions while criticizing each other's inquiries.

Francesca opened the iron gates and Alfredo sprang forward, embracing Fannie by the waist. The other women enveloped him in a warm cocoon of arms, fussing over him and commenting on his torn, dirty clothes. Francesca watched from a safe distance, her eyes shining, beaming at Lucas.

"We feared the worst," the old optometrist had said in a low voice. "Maria wanted to take action, *any* action. She wasn't very rational about it, but she thought we had to do *something*. Evelyn wanted to offer as many jewels as the terrorists would take. She loves you a lot, considering that *El Joyero* is her life. Your mother just sat and watched TV, not saying anything, hoping to hear some news. She also managed to get through to the police, but as you can imagine, they knew nothing about nothing. They took her number and promised to call her if they found out anything. I gave each of them a Xanax, and got them to sleep at 11:00. I convinced them that it was better to sleep through the uncertainty than to stay awake imagining the worst."

"And you were right," Lucas had replied, watching with amusement how Alfredo held court among his aunts and his grandmother. Francesca and him listened for a while. "I don't know what we would have done without you," Lucas told her.

"Ah!" Francesca had waved her hand dismissively. "I always enjoy the company of the Pietri sisters. They're always very entertaining. I would have gone crazy here alone, unable to eat out or go shopping." She stopped talking, listening to Alfredo begin to describe their escape through the tunnel. "Is that true?" she had asked Lucas, after a while. "You escaped from the terrorists through a secret pirate tunnel?"

Lucas had raised his eyebrows and sighed. "The short answer is yes. But it's a very long story, and we have a police car waiting for us downstairs." He turned to the Pietri sisters and raised his voice over their excited chatter. "Excuse me...Maria, Evelyn, mom, Alfredo..." Gradually, he managed to quiet them down. "There is a car waiting for us to take us home, and I know for a fact that the driver is very impatient to get rid of us. If you want a ride to your homes in Miramar, you have to come with me now."

"We can get to Miramar?" Evelyn had asked in a surprised tone. "I thought the communists had destroyed the bridges."

"They're not communists, they're Macheteros," Maria said.

"Same thing!"

Maria had raised her eyes in exasperation. "Let's go. The faster we drop this woman at her house, the better."

Fannie had walked to Lucas and, her eyes filling with tears, embraced him, saying nothing for a long time, one of her hands rubbing his back as if to reassure herself that he was really there. Finally she had looked up at him. Her eyes were red and her cheeks wet, but she was smiling. "My son," she had said proudly.

"Let's go home, mom," he had said, kissing her.

They had left the Metropolitan Center ten minutes later. Several policemen were directing traffic at the provisional bridges, the one closest to the burned out ruins of El San Juan Yacht Club being used for outgoing traffic, and another Bailey bridge parallel to it for the incoming vehicles. Hundreds of cars, Humvees, police cars, buses and ambulances waited their turn to move into San Juan along the Baldorioty De Castro Avenue, which rimmed the Condado Lagoon. Their bright lights formed a river of white, red and blue that rippled on the black waters of the lagoon. A second stream of vehicles spilled out of Miramar along Ponce De Leon Avenue, adding to the general disorder.

Fortunately, traffic had been lighter coming out of San Juan. Even so, they had been forced to wait fifteen minutes while several other official vehicles, mostly ambulances, were allowed to cross. While the police car lingered by the entrance to the provisional bridge, they had watched in sullen silence the smoking remains of the San Juan Yacht Club, where three fire engines were still parked, while dozens of firefighters sprayed the smoldering embers with their hoses.

"Wow…" Maria had muttered glumly. "Poor San Juan Yacht Club. It'll be years before it recovers from this. I wonder what else they destroyed."

"Well, the Police Station, didn't you hear?" Evelyn had said with the impatience of someone who is stating the obvious.

Maria had opened her mouth to respond, but had opted to remain quiet.

Before the police car had dropped Evelyn at her house and Maria and Fannie at their apartment building, Lucas had warned them that the police would be contacting them the next day to take their statements about Antonio. Evelyn had for a few minutes insisted that they return to *El Joyero* early in the morning to reopen the store. They had already lost a lot of business, she said, and their special anniversary sale had been supposed to start on Monday. But she had finally been convinced to stay at home after Lucas had assured her that the rest of the businesses would be closed the next day, and that opening the jewelry store would only be a waste of electricity.

As she got out of the car, Fannie had made the sign of the cross on Lucas' forehead, and repeated the prayer she had mouthed every night, since the time he could remember: "May God guard and bless you." *God had*, Lucas thought to himself as he watched her and Maria make their way into their apartment building's lobby. *More than Fannie could ever imagine.*

Lucas' thoughts returned to the present as the police car turned left on the corner of the Chrissy Gonzalez Park, where Lucas jogged every morning. With no warning, the patrol car turned on its siren and its police lights, waking up Alfredo and prompting Lucas to take a glimpse through his window. He saw a crowd of twenty or more people standing in front of his house.

"What's happening out there?" he asked the driver, while Alfredo leaned over him to look outside.

"Courtesy of the Governor," the driver answered, finally cracking a smile. "He called ahead your wife and your sister to let them know that you and the boy were coming. I don't know who the other people are!"

They seemed to be friends and family, Lucas determined as they drew nearer. His sister Vanessa and his brother-in-law Michael were there, but so were many others; their next door neighbors, and those next door to them; a couple who lived nearby and carpooled with Vanessa to drive Alfredo and their son to school; two of his female cousins and their husbands; and others he did not recognize. The whole thing had his sister's hand written all over it. The Governor had tried to do the favor to call ahead his family to tell them that Alfredo and he were coming, and Vanessa had decided to receive them with a surprise welcoming party. He sighed. He had hoped to go straight to bed.

And then he saw Jeannie. She was standing at the edge of the crowd, staring anxiously at the oncoming vehicle. Even as the others burst into cheers and applause, she remained still, nervously wringing her hands, looking scared and concerned.

Alfredo burst out of the car before it had come to a full stop, pushing the door so hard that it almost closed back on him. He ran straight to his mother, who dropped on her knees to receive him with a relieved hug, while Michael wrapped his arms around both of them. They were immediately engulfed by the host of well-wishers about them, who fussed and cuddled Alfredo, while trying to listen to his non-stop, excited stories.

Jeannie continued to peer into the police car with apprehension, ignoring everybody else. When Lucas emerged, her eyes examined him carefully, as if to make certain that he was not hurt. Her taut, worried expression melted into relief, and she began to walk, then run towards him, crying. She jumped on him, wrapping her legs around him and kissing him breathlessly on the lips, making him stumble backwards and almost fall. He laughed even as she kissed him, kissing her back, feeling her warmth overwhelm him.

Several in the crowd also laughed and applauded, and his cousin Lily shouted, "Get a room!" Even the driver of the police car seemed to enjoy the moment, turning on the police siren while they continued to kiss.

"Oh God, I love you!" he whispered hoarsely to her, as she placed her feet back on the ground. She had lost one of her shoes, which somehow had landed on the street. "I told you I'd come back," he told her tenderly, wiping some of her tears away.

She looked up at him worriedly. "You're all beat up," she said, touching with the tip of her fingers a bruise on his cheek and making him wince.

"Yeah, and dirty and sweaty. I must really stink."

She nodded. "Yes, you do. But I don't care."

"Where are Gabriel and Sofia?" he asked, searching around him.

"They're sleeping. Cristina is taking care of them." Cristina was her niece. "They kept asking when you were coming home, and I told them you had to stay at work with Tutti—the name they called Fannie—until tomorrow. Gabriel kept asking all night if it was already 'tomorrow', until he went to sleep."

And if I had not come back, he had almost asked, but then Michael arrived and embraced him, lifting him off the ground and making him grunt with pain.

"I don't know how to thank you..." he said, his emotions choking the rest of his words. Vanessa, right behind him, held on to his arm, weeping as well.

"Thank you, brother..." she managed to say. "When we didn't hear from you or Alfredo—" She stopped, unable to continue.

For a long time, nobody spoke. *It was so good to be back home*, Lucas thought. He almost felt guilty, being surrounded by so many loved ones, feeling so happy and relieved, while so many others were in mourning that night. He would have to arrange for Antonio's funeral tomorrow. Antonio had lived alone.

"You had it worse," he said, meaning it. "We were so busy all of the time that we didn't have time to think. You had to wait all night long, not knowing what was happening. I would have gone crazy."

"Tell me about it!" Vanessa said, directing a stern look at Michael. "*He* was driving me crazy! Telling me all night long that he was going to San Juan!"

"I swear to you that if those sons-of-bitches harmed Alfredo or—"

"Did you hear about Michelle?" Vanessa interrupted quite suddenly. "She was in the Grand Laguna Hotel with the hostages!"

Lucas had already heard about it from his mother. At first he had been alarmed. But Fannie had assured him that Michelle was fine. Fannie had received a call from Michelle earlier in the night. That was when she had learned that she had not made it to work at WKPA, but had been trapped in the fighting in front of the police station, and had later infiltrated the Grand Laguna Hotel. He had listened to his mother's tale with disbelief, shaking his head in wonder. *Classical Michelle. Fearless Michelle.* "Yes," he said. "It's been quite a night for all of us." He directed a mischievous look at his sister Vanessa. "And the Governor invited you and Michael to his State of the Island address tomorrow."

"Yesss..." Vanessa's eyes gleamed with pleasure, her cheeks still wet with tears. "He told me over the phone, when he called to let us know that you were coming. He remembered my first name!"

Lucas laughed. "You're hard to forget, just like your son."

Jeannie clung to Lucas' arm, smiling happily. *She really must love me,* he thought, *because I really stink.*

It took another twenty minutes for Jeannie and Lucas to escape from the crowd, and ten more minutes to thank Cristina for babysitting their children. Lucas went into Sofia and Gabriel's rooms and watched them sleep, kissing each on the forehead. Gabriel didn't stir, but Sofia sat up abruptly and looked around her confusedly, smiling and throwing her arms around her father's neck.

"Daddy!" she said, still half asleep. Lucas hushed her and guided her back to her pillow, where she made several kissing sounds and promptly dozed off.

Afterwards, Jeannie sat on their bed and quietly observed him as he undressed, noting the welts and bruises all over his body.

"Are you sure you don't want to go to the hospital?" she asked after seeing a particularly large skin discoloration that covered Lucas' right ribcage.

Lucas stared at his injury with surprise. "I didn't even know it was there," he assured her. However, when he touched it with a finger he drew a sharp intake of breath. "Okay, it hurts a little. But I'm okay."

Jeannie said nothing, but continued watching him with a concerned expression.

"You're just lusting after my body," he said, trying to lighten the mood.

"You're such a pig!"

"But it's true," he added, leering at her.

She gasped with disbelief. "Here I am, worrying to death about you, and all you can think about is sex!"

"But it's *true,*" he insisted.

"Well...yes!" She stood up and slowly walked to him, and tenderly embraced him. "I was so afraid..." she said softly.

"So was I," he confessed "Not so much about dying, but of not seeing you and the children again."

He kissed her tenderly several times on the lips. It felt good.

"Thank you," he told her.

"For what?"

"For letting me go look for Alfredo."

Jeannie remained silent. Lucas felt her body tense up.

"I know your instincts were to tell me not to go, but you kept quiet. That took a lot of courage," he said. "It's just that...I kept seeing the face of Alfredo and I couldn't bear the thought of him being terrorized by the men who seized him."

"I know..." she responded. "That's why I let you go. But don't ever ask me to do this again. Because next time, I *will* lose it."

Lucas laughed half-heartedly. She separated from him and looked at him directly in the eyes. "I mean it, Lucas," she said sternly.

He stared at her back. "There won't be a next time," he said. "I promise."

John McFadden was discussing with Ernan and the Countess how to steal some food from the Windjammer Cafe without being discovered by the hijackers, mainly roast beef sandwiches from the deli section of the restaurant. However, Ernan insisted in getting a slice of the lemon meringue pie, which was located close to the female terrorist that they had killed in the Condessa's room. *Except they had not killed her, because she was standing there with a rifle, looking very angry.* Failing to heed his advice not to get the pie, Ernan had begun to crawl towards the food table when the door to the room opened and a nurse pushing a cart noisily walked in and approached his bed.

"You're awake," she said pleasantly, as she wrapped a blood pressure gauge around his right arm. She was a black, plump woman in her thirties, wearing purple nurse's scrubs with a flowery pattern. The medical gadget inflated rapidly, causing him to feel his own heartbeats as the blood coursed through his arm. "Just relax," she said, placing a thermometer in his mouth.

John looked around him and realized that he was in a hospital room. His lips were cracked and dry, and his left arm was connected to an IV, which looked like it was about to run out of fluid. He tried to move, but the sudden flash of pain in his ribs convinced him to stay still. The nurse pulled out a clipboard from her cart and wrote down his pressure. "A hundred and twenty-two over seventy-two. And your temperature is right on the dot. For a man that has been banged up as much as you, you're all right."

"Where am I?" he managed to ask in a raspy voice.

"Presbyterian Hospital, love. They brought you here last night. The old Frenchwoman refused to go to another room, even though she was all beat up and dehydrated too."

John looked around him, but could not find the Countess, only a reclining chair with some ruffled sheets and a pillow.

"She's not here now, sweetie," the nurse said when she saw him looking at the chair. "She went to have some breakfast at the cafeteria. She should be back soon. Now, how are you feeling?"

John closed his eyes. "Like a cruise ship ran over me."

"Did it?" The nurse stared at him with a look of half disbelief, one hundred percent curiosity. "There's all sort of rumors about what happened in the *Mardi Gras*. That the terrorists executed more than a hundred passengers. That they killed all of the crew. That they tried to sink the ship. That the government is hiding what really happened. Is there anything that you can tell me about it?"

John didn't want to tell her anything. He didn't want to talk. He just wanted her to leave, and let him rest. *Dead? Yes, he had seen several.* White, the Australian who wanted to fight the terrorists and retake the ship, and most of the group that followed him; Harshad, the fat Indian steward, who had resisted the terrorists in the corridor of the crew's quarters until he had been shot to death; the scary woman they had asphyxiated with a pillow in the Countess' room; the man that the Countess had stabbed in the Gothic bar; and countless others he didn't care to remember. There was plenty to talk about. But he didn't utter a word.

The nurse continued doing her work, ignoring his silence. She changed the IV bag, checked his catheter, and placed some pills on the table next to him, with a foam cup full of water. "The doctor prescribed some Acetaminophen tablets for the pain in your ribs. You have five broken ribs. The doctor will give the full details. He should be here by eleven. Do you want the tablets now?"

"I will give them to him," a familiar voice said behind her. Looking over her shoulder, he saw the Countess approaching his bed. Her left arm was in a blue sling, and her left cheek and eye were discolored, but she was grinning happily. As the nurse withdrew, the Countess rounded the bed and grabbed John's hand. "It's so good to see you awake, *mon cher*," she said, bringing his hand up and kissing it.

"I am so glad that... you made it safely from the *Mardi Gras*," he answered, the effort of talking hurting his ribs.

"You are in pain," she said, grabbing the cup and the pain tablets. "Here, this should help you."

John swallowed them, grunting when he had to lean forward to drink the water.

"And Ernan?" he asked. He had grown fond of the tiny Filipino maitre.

"I have not seen him since we left the ship. I left in the ambulance with you after the ship was moved to another dock," she responded.

"The ship...it was rescued, then?"

"Yes, *mon cher*. In great part thanks to you."

Much good that would do him, he thought. From the crappy way that he felt, it would probably take him months to mend. He would have to live off his emergency funds, probably exhaust them, before he could sail again.

"You have been in the news, although not by name," the Countess continued saying. "Apparently the FBI is giving credit for the rescue to a heroic passenger who risked his life to save the others by finding out where the hostages were and giving eh...information to the FBI that they passed on to the SEALs. They have not officially revealed your name, to...to...how do you say... protect your privacy, but I think the word has spread despite of it. There are reporters downstairs that are waiting to see you, but the hospital is not allowing them to come in. I think you deserve to be recognized, don't you?"

"You were the brave one..." he responded, grimacing as he tried to shift his body. "I ran away, remember?"

"But you came back! You came back even though you did not have weapons to defend yourself, even when you were scared! Against all odds, you came back, *mon cher!* I call that magnificent courage. You were braver than the SEALs. After all, they had guns, and they knew how to fight. You had to survive by your wits."

"You shamed me into coming back," he admitted to her. "I *was* scared. Terrified. It was that look of disappointment that you gave to me before I jumped. I couldn't bear the shame. If you survived, and I was certain that you would, my reputation as an escort would be ruined."

She tut-tutted, shaking her head. She was old, but he could still see in her the attractive, beautiful woman she had been in her younger days. "So it was a business decision, is what you are saying? Then you must be a poor businessman, because a dead escort is worse for business than an escort who has lost his reputation. Besides, you know most people would never find out about your...your jumping off into the bay. You knew I would not have said anything. No, my friend, you did it out of the noble goodness of your heart."

It was true. Even if she had talked, except for a few repeat clients, no-body would know who he was or what he had done. *More stupid of him to have risked his life.* But for some strange reason, her words comforted him. He felt extremely tired, so much so that even speaking a few words exhausted him. He must have dozed off, because when he was gently shaken awake by the Countess, several people were surrounding his bed.

He was startled by their presence. They were all smiling and looking at him, and for a chilling moment he thought that he had died. Then he saw that one of the people was Ernan. He was dressed in an immaculately white uniform, some sort of bandage protruding from his jacket's right sleeve. Beside him stood an immense man, so tall that Ernan barely seemed to reach his waist, clad also in a resplendent seaman's uniform and holding his cap under his right arm. His bushy eyebrows and a thick, blond beard should have given him instantly away, but it was his deep-set, fierce, blue eyes which finally allowed John, still very drowsy from his abrupt awakening and his medications, to identify him as Captain Clausen.

Two other visitors completed the group that ringed the bed. One was of a medium height, somewhere in his forties, with light brown hair and sporting a very deep tan, the type that must be constantly renewed to remain. He held in his hands some kind of wooden object, shaped like a shield. He was wearing a white, long-sleeved, tropical-style shirt that fell over khaki slacks and which showed, on one of its pockets, a pin with a red Viking ship, the logo of Scandinavian Cruise Lines. The second visitor stood at about the same height, except that she was a shapely, blond woman wearing a loose, light-blue, sleeveless dress and holding a professional looking camera with a large flash.

"Hello, Mr. McFadden!" Ernan said enthusiastically before anybody else could utter a word. "It is so great to see that you are recovering from your injuries!"

"Ernan..." John extended his hand to him, while the Countess pressed the lever on the side of the bed to sit him more upright. There were tears of happiness in the Filipino's eyes as he leaned forward to embrace his friend.

"Careful," the Countess warned Ernan. "Mr. McFadden has a few broken ribs."

The Filipino moved back as if pulled by a string. "I am so sorry! I did not know. Please forgive me!" He looked at the others, and overwhelmed by his emotions, said, "This man...he is the salt of the earth! He is the bravest man I have ever known, and I am forever in his debt." He raised John's hand to his lips and kissed it with emotion. The woman with the camera flashed a picture.

"We all are in your debt," Captain Clausen said, in a calmer voice. "As we are in yours, Ernan, and yours, Countess. Last night, we learned everything you did to help free the hostages and my ship. It is an extraordinary story."

"Indeed," the man with the deep tan confirmed enthusiastically. "You three helped to avert a real catastrophe, bad enough as it was."

Ernan nodded vigorously, and then realized that he was being included in the praises. "It was all Mr. McFadden...And the Condessa, of course. I was just there as a...as an extra wheel."

"Don't be so humble, Ernan," the captain said sternly. "This concerns you as much as the others. This is Mr. Roger Manning, vice-president of public relations for Scandinavian Cruise Lines." Clausen nodded at the man in the white shirt, who raised the wooden shield he was holding in his hands to show it to John. The shield was embossed with an engraved golden plaque.

"On behalf of Scandinavian Cruise Lines, we would like to recognize your extraordinary feats of valor yesterday on board our cruise ship, the *Mardi Gras*. The inscription in the plaque reads: 'To John McFadden, for his extraordinary feats of valor...' I'm sorry to repeat myself, but you deserve it... 'For his extraordinary feats of valor on board the *Mardi Gras*. As our Viking forebears said, *Cattle die, kinsmen die. All men are mortal. But words of praise will never perish, nor a noble name. We will never forget you*.'"

The tanned man made as if to hand the plaque to John, looking at the camera while the woman photographer flashed away. Peeved by his companion's display, the captain took over.

"Countess, you will also get a plaque, as will you, Ernan. By the way, you have been promoted to Food and Beverages Manager of the *Brazile Carnivale*, effective immediately. You are to report to New Orleans within the next two days for its next sailing. I have already spoken with its captain, and he anxiously awaits you."

Ernan looked dumbstruck. All blood seemed to drain from his face, and he appeared to be on the verge of fainting. "I don't know what to say..." he mumbled, new tears streaming from his eyes. "Thank you!"

"As for you, Mr. McFadden, and you, Countess, your money is no longer good with us. From this moment henceforth, you will be entitled to travel in any of our ships in the best accommodations available for the rest of your lives, at our expense." Captain Clausen allowed himself a satisfied smile as he watched the shocked faces of his two former passengers. He stared directly at the Australian. "It is a fact that the air of the sea does wonders to cure long term injuries," he said to him. "I would urge you not to waste the opportunity."

"I need a few more photos," the female with the camera said with a British accent. John recognized her as one of the photographers aboard the *Mardi Gras*.

For the next several minutes, the photographer took several pictures of the group, showing the plaque and shaking hands. Then the man with the deep tan excused himself and left, followed by the blond woman. The captain and Ernan remained.

"Please forgive the glitz and glitter," Clausen said when they were gone. "It's an integral part of Manning's job, and he does it well. I don't envy him, in fact. Now he has to face the reporters downstairs to give the official statement for Scandinavian."

"How is your First Officer doing?" John asked him.

"Folstad?" At the mention of his name, Clausen seemed suddenly tired. "I went to see him early this morning. He is in another hospital...the Doctors Hospital, I think, in the Metropolitan area. He is still in a critical condition, but I think he will pull through."

"And you?"

"Tired. Angry and tired. The *Mardi Gras* did not deserve the treatment it got. It will be withdrawn from circulation to be repaired...Or at least that will be the official explanation. Most probably it will be refitted, redecorated, and renamed. Nobody likes to travel in a ship where many of its crew were murdered. There will be a naval inquiry, and many civil suits, I am certain of that. But miraculously, there were no passenger deaths, and the crew behaved properly at all times. Remember, the ship was boarded by the terrorists after they overwhelmed the authorities on shore. We should come out of it... if not well, at least...the company will survive. If I'm lucky, I might get another ship eventually."

"I don't see why you shouldn't!" the Countess said indignantly. "How could anyone say anything to the contrary? You were very brave. An example to the rest of us."

"You are very kind, madam," the captain replied courteously. "But only time will tell, eh?" Clausen put on his hat, and extended his hand to John. "Mr. McFadden. It has been an honor. Maybe, if fortune smiles on us, I may have the pleasure of sharing my table with you and the Countess in some future voyage."

"I have no doubt about it," John answered, shaking the captain's hand warmly, and flinching from the pain that the handshake inflicted.

"*Au revoir, mon brave capitaine,*" the Countess said, as he kissed her on both cheeks.

"*Au revoir,* my dear Countess. It has been a pleasure to sail with you," he answered, bowing formally. He stared at Ernan. "Are you coming with me? I can give you a ride."

The former maitre looked miserably at his two friends, wondering if he would ever see them again. He walked to the Countess, and kissed her hand. "Condessa..." he said, but could not continue.

"My dear Ernan, don't cry," the Countess said, embracing him. "God guided you to my cabin yesterday morning for a purpose. Without your help and your knowledge of the ship we would not have survived. Our destinies were tied, never to be undone. So no goodbyes, please. We will soon meet again."

The Filipino held John's hand in both of his. "You are a good man, Mr. McFadden," he said, managing a smile. "A little crazy perhaps, but good. God bless you!"

John tried to keep his emotions in check but felt strangely moved by the departure of the little man standing by his bed. It was not true, as the Countess said, that Ernan's arrival to her cabin had been a blessing in disguise. On the contrary, the Filipino's presence had exposed the two of them to great danger, after the female terrorist they had snuffed to death with a pillow had followed him there. He was not a great believer of Divine Intervention, either. He doubted that God, if a God existed, had sent them Ernan to save them. And most of the time, the Filipino had proven to be much more of a pain and a hindrance than a help.

But it was an undeniable fact that during the last twenty-four hours, he had grown very fond of the little man. They had been through a lot together, and he would miss him.

"Goodbye, my friend. Congratulations on your promotion. You deserve it. Take good care of yourself...as you did of us," he said, adding the small lie at the end.

Ernan's eyes lit up with pride. "It was an honor risking my life with you."

"We know where you are, and we will visit you," John added as the Filipino followed Captain Clausen out of the room. Ernan waved and left, wiping his eyes.

For a long moment the Countess and John failed to say anything, each lost in his own thoughts. Then the Countess said: "Will we?"

"Will we what?" John asked, not understanding the question.

"You said to Ernan that *we* will visit him."

John considered her observation for a moment. "I did say *we*, didn't I?" He said at last with a tinge of amusement. "Well, I've been thinking...It will take me some time to recover before I return to my...escort services, right?"

The Countess nodded, uncertain about where the conversation was taking them.

"And the captain did tell us that we have a free pass to travel on board the Scandinavian Cruise Line whenever we want..."

"Yes..."

"You, know, I've always wanted to travel around the world. It would take months to do so, connecting from one ship to another, but it would be fun. The only thing is, I'd need someone to help me, me being a cripple and all that..."

The Countess directed him a serious glance, but then had to divert her face in order not to laugh. "So you need a sort of...assistant, is what you're saying."

John shrugged. "Assistant, nurse...fellow adventurer..."

"Fellow adventurer..." the Countess seemed to consider the idea. "The thought is quite appealing."

"Well, more nurse and assistant…"

The Countess slapped his arm with fake indignation, and he cringed.

"Okay!" he said, raising his hands in surrender and laughing. "Fellow adventurer! So will you come?"

"You will not jump off the ship?"

"I swear, on my mother's health."

"Your mother, she is alive?" the Countess asked with apparent disbelief.

"No," he answered, earning another light slap. "But it would be really great to have the pleasure of your company."

The Countess' eyes narrowed with delight. "Very well, then. Let's see the world together."

Lebron was awakened by the sound of men's voices, and he instinctively rolled off the park bench, dropping into the flowery bushes behind it. Nervously, he listened to the men approach, hoping they had not seen him.

"I'm telling you it had to be sabotage," a deep-voiced man, almost as deep-voiced as Popeye, was saying. "Coast Guard cutters just don't blow up by themselves."

"It was the terrorists," a second voice agreed. "But not through sabotage. The Macheteros couldn't just walk into the cutter and plant a bomb!"

"I wouldn't put anything beyond the reach of the Macheteros," a third, more nasal voice interjected. "Not after what they did here yesterday."

Three pairs of military boots, into which army camouflage pants were tucked, came into view. *National Guardsmen sweeping the area,* the FEPI Secretary General thought.

"I don't know," the second voice said. "The people we've been picking up sure don't look like Macheteros. More like young fire-eaters from the University of Puerto Rico. They don't seem so dangerous to me. Amateurs, if you ask me."

One of the men walking stopped in front of the bench, and Lebron's heart skipped a beat. "Wait a second, while I drink some water," the man with the nasal voice said. The other boots stopped. There was a pause, followed by the smattering of lips and a satisfied sigh. "Ahhh! This water is cold! From what I heard, the people captured in the Grand Laguna last night were a mixed batch. Some were armed Macheteros, some college students. Useful fools, I call them."

"So if not by sabotage," the deeper voice insisted, "what caused that Coast Guard boat to sink so fast? There wasn't a single survivor."

"So far. There might be some," the second voice said. "You want to know what I think sank that boat? Surface-to-air missiles! That's what I think sank that boat. The same missiles that shot out the helicopter over the lagoon yesterday."

There was a contemplative silence, and then the boots began to move again.

"Can those missiles hit ships at sea?" the man with the nasal voice asked as the men moved away.

"I don't see why not," the second man replied. Then, after another pause, he said almost out of hearing. "Did you hear they found Cacho dead in the Grand Laguna Hotel? Strangled, they say he was..."

"Those Navy SEALs don't fool around, do they?"

Lebron lay still on the ground until the voices dissipated, too shocked by the news to move. He saw a black ant carrying an unidentifiable crumb of something almost twice its size disappear into a crack under the concrete park bench, and wished that he could have done the same.

Cacho dead? Strangled by the SEALs? It seemed impossible! And yet, why should he be surprised? The imperialistic government of the United States had a long history of murdering its political antagonists ever since John Wilkes Booth had shot Lincoln. Maybe even before that. President Obama had ordered Osama Bin Laden killed. Lebron did not doubt that the same orders had been issued for Cacho. Don't bring him back alive. Better dead and permanently silenced. That's probably the reason that he had been released from the federal prison in the first place.

Lebron had warned everyone that the revolt would end disastrously, crushed by the powerful boot of the American military war machine like one of the tiny ants he had just seen. But Johnny Ray would not listen. *Even if they failed—as if there had been any doubt that they wouldn't—the revolt would derail Pietrantoni's bid for statehood,* Johnny had argued. *Well...maybe. But at what cost?*

Johnny had probably been arrested and would spend the rest of his life in a federal prison, if the American assassins did not kill him first. *So would Yajaira,* he reflected, not with a certain degree of perverse pleasure. The FEPI would also suffer significant losses, although eventually it would recover. The sacrifices made by those who had been killed or arrested might even draw in new recruits into the FEPI's ranks. And with the arrest of Johnny and Yajaira, he was left as the sole remaining leader of the organization.

It therefore devolved upon him to not to be caught. To reorganize the FEPI. To survive to tell to the world the story about their glorious, if short-lived struggle to gain the independence of their country. And he was the man best qualified to do it.

The previous night he had barely escaped from the Grand Laguna Hotel grounds. He had run, fled as fast as his legs could carry him, scrambling through bushes and dashing over open spaces, not bothering to hide from the American forces, just trying to put as much distance as he could between him and them. He had acted recklessly and carelessly; panicked, some might have said. By the time he had reached the relative safety of the Muñoz Rivera Park, his *guayabera* was tattered beyond repair, his pants ripped and dirty. He could barely breathe from the physical effort of running all the way to the park, and his mouth felt as dry as talcum powder.

But it had worked. Somehow, he had broken through the Navy SEALs' iron ring around the hotel and left them behind. He had quenched his thirst with the lukewarm water from a public water fountain and, exhausted, had searched for a place to hide and lie down. He had found the park bench in a remote, dark corner of the park, and lain there to rest.

The next thing he remembered was that morning's voices. Fortunately, he had reacted fast. It was obvious that the government authorities had recaptured San Juan—as he had correctly predicted from the beginning—and were searching for those freedom fighters that had managed to escape the initial assault.

But what was he to do? His bedraggled appearance would immediately identify him as a rebel, and he had no valid way of explaining it. He had no food and nowhere to go, except to his dormitory in the university, and to get there, he had to cross the bridges and catch the Tren Urbano back to Rio Piedras. He could not conceive that the provisional bridges or whatever other means the authorities had used to cross into San Juan would not be watched, and there was no other way of getting across, except swimming. He was not a very good swimmer.

He could hide in the park for a couple of days, and hope that by then the search would be called off and that he would be able to take some public transportation to cross the bridge. After all, the island of San Juan could not remain sealed off for long. Many of the principal government and business offices in Puerto Rico were located there. Many people who lived there had to cross the bridges to get to work, see their doctors, go to school, shop, and travel. Trying to search everyone who tried to cross the bridges would create massive traffic jams and interrupt normal life in the city.

So he just had to hide and hold on until matters cooled off.

Lebron walked to the water fountain and splashed water on his face, drinking some afterward. His stomach growled in protest, wanting some food. He had not eaten anything since the day before at noon, except for the drinks he, Yajaira, and Johnny had shared at the Grand Laguna's Bar. He felt weak, and his head throbbed from what he suspected was a massive hangover. He desperately needed food.

He searched his pockets, and found a twenty-dollar bill plus some loose change in them. He could buy food; he just didn't know where he could find some. His watch informed him that it was nine thirty in the morning, but the park looked deserted. The two or three food stands that normally would sell refreshments, ice cream, and snacks were not operating, and the odds that any food establishments in San Juan would open for business were slim. But as his stomach growled again, he decided to chance it and look for nourishment.

He had observed a couple of cafeteria-style restaurants that bordered the Muñoz Rivera Avenue, just before the entrance road to the Grand Laguna Hotel. One was a local food eatery, the other a bakery frequented for breakfast by the personnel of the Supreme Court of Puerto Rico and the staff and guests of the hotel who did not want to pay the higher fares of the resort. If any food establishment was open, that would be it.

He began to move in the direction of the Grand Laguna Hotel, staying in the more wooded part of the park, darting from one dense area to the other. However, when he got to the fence surrounding the Supreme Court, he was forced to stop. There were two ways to continue: he could take the sidewalk that bordered Muñoz Rivera Avenue along the northern boundary of the Court, or he could take the sidewalk on the other side, which bordered the Avenida de la Constitucion.

He opted for the latter. The Avenida de la Constitucion sidewalk was five times as wide as its counterpart, a grand, old-style walkway adorned with mosaics of birds and flowers and fringed with huge, ancient banyan trees. It would offer more cover if any police patrols came that way.

He noticed with a mixture of concern and relief that few cars were transiting through the streets, although not in the same volume of a regular workday. They were mostly curious civilians, the same people who drove out after a hurricane to see the destruction in the streets. He could see no police or National Guard vehicles, though. They would probably be at the bridges, the hotel, and Old San Juan, trying to restore their grip on the city.

If Lebron was a good judge of character—and he knew he was—the area close to the Grand Laguna Hotel would be swarming with hundreds of curiosity seekers, and that would be good cover for him; he would be able to get lost in their numbers.

Taking heart, he began to walk down the wide walkway, staying close to the large trees. As he covered the distance, his hopes began to rise. The handful of cars that drove past him seemed to pay him little heed, seeming more intent on reaching the area of the hotel. Maybe it did not occur to the people who saw him that he was a revolutionary, especially when he was walking in the open, in the direction of the Grand Laguna

Hotel. *It paid to be daring and do the unexpected,* he told himself. That was the way he would escape.

But suddenly, everything changed. An old, champagne colored Toyota Camry driving through the Avenida de la Constitucion switched lanes from the opposite side of the road, and slowed down next to him. Lebron tried to ignore it, trudging forward and trying to look casual. But the car continued to move next to him at his same speed.

Lebron refused to look, even after the car honked his horn once. However, as the driver broke into an insistent series of intermittent honks, he had to look, fearful that if not, the noise would attract the attention of everyone around him.

At first, he thought that the Camry was empty. Then he noticed the outline of half a head, staring at him through the window. Irritated and fearful, he approached the car. A very small woman, maybe in her late forties, peered at him as she lowered the glass in her door.

"You're one of them," she said.

"One of whom?" Lebron asked roughly, knowing what she meant and taken aback by her statement.

"One of the people who tried to take over San Juan," she answered, not in the least intimidated by his gruff manner. She reminded him of his mother; tinted blond-with-a-hint-of-orange hair mostly bunched up on top of her head, shiny skin from some moisturizing cream, no makeup.

"You're mistaken," he replied.

"You're heading in the wrong direction," she said, ignoring his response. "The area close to the hotel is crawling with policemen. You'll get arrested if you go there."

Lebron involuntarily glanced in the direction of the Grand Laguna Hotel, biting his lower lip.

"You'd better come with me," she said. "You can stay in my house until things cool off a little."

Lebron hesitated, uncertain about the woman's offer.

"Come on!" she said impatiently. "They're going to see you any moment now!" She looked directly at his eyes. "Listen, I'm an *independentista.* What you did here was very, very brave, but very, very stupid. I can help you. So hop in and let's go. But hurry, because I can't stay here much longer."

Lebron hesitantly looked around him, licked his lips, and ran around the front of the car to get into the front passenger seat.

"Thank you," he said when he was inside. The woman said nothing and sped away.

CHAPTER LXXX

Constitution and Muñoz Rivera Avenues were teeming with cars seeking parking spaces, with self-appointed "parking attendants"—basically unemployed men who laid claim to portions of the parking spots along the street and offered to "take care" of your car for a fee—waving at and directing the frustrated drivers to park in "their spaces". Already, the parking building for the legislature had been filled to capacity, only giving access to senators, representatives, mayors, and agency heads who had arrived late. The vehicles transiting in front of the capitol, and those that extended behind them for a mile in either direction, were moving at a snail's speed, the air filled with the protest of their horns and the exhaust of their engines.

Lucas had anticipated the mess and left home at 4:00 PM, patiently enduring Jeannie's accusation that he was being exaggerated and anal. They had carpooled with Vanessa, Michael, and Alfredo in their minivan. They had hit a massive bottleneck of cars just after abandoning Kennedy Avenue and entering the Muñoz Rivera Expressway to bypass Miramar. Even though two more Bailey bridges had been placed over the gap of the Dos Hermanos Bridge—allowing more traffic to flow to and from the Condado hotel area into San Juan—it had taken them an hour at what Alfredo called "turtle pace" to get to the provisional bridge over the Condado Lagoon, where five different lanes, coming from various directions, merged into one.

The confluence of lanes, thrusting hundreds of Puerto Ricans not noted for their driving discipline or patience into a single, narrow, unidirectional bridge, could have resulted in total chaos, fighting, and even the loss of life. But Maldonado had anticipated the situation and prepared well, posting scores of policemen, aided by the National Guard, along the roads to coordinate the crossing and to keep tempers down.

Many of the drivers were people from all over the island who had come to see and photograph the damage caused by the terrorists in San

Juan. They stopped to gawk at and photograph the burned buildings, and even parked their vehicles on the sidewalks. The *Mardi Gras*, still moored across the San Antonio channel on Isla Grande, was also a major attraction that prompted many onlookers to slow down and stare, as if looking for lonely hijackers that had somehow managed to escape the attention of the authorities.

Michael, Lucas' brother-in-law, could not believe the destruction that had occurred. The San Juan Yacht Club had been leveled almost to the ground, only a few charred walls remaining upright, even its docks gone, the hulls of a few of the largest yachts sticking out of the murky water like dead whales. "Sweet Jesus!" he had whispered. "Who *did* this?"

Jeannie had held on to Lucas' left hand, while Alfredo had acted very nonchalantly, saying, "Oh yeah! You should have seen the fire in the tunnel."

They had not bothered to look for parking close to the capitol, heading straight to Lucas' monthly space in the Doña Fela parking building. The police had closed transit in the Fernandez Juncos Avenue one block before and one block after the burned down station, and a dozen men dressed in white protective uniforms, wearing masks with filters, were sifting through the debris to locate the bodies of those who had perished inside.

The detour had caused them to lose another forty minutes before the minivan had finally managed to reach the Doña Fela parking building.

It was about a half-mile walk from there to the capitol, and they had moved at a faster pace than the cars on the street. About two dozen news vans, with their long, transmission towers extended, were parked in front of the building on the lane usually reserved for the transit of the buses of the Metropolitan Authority. There were also several police cars and armed national guardsmen guarding the perimeter of the capitol, along with a crowd of several hundred onlookers lined on the sidewalk across the street.

Lucas saw several elegantly dressed men and women crossing the avenue or walking to get into the marbled, domed edifice. Wooden barriers had been set up on the sidewalks surrounding the capitol, and anyone trying to get in was herded through two openings in the fences, each at each opposite end of the capitol building, where attendants with lists required identification and checked the names of the invitees. Those allowed through then had to go through a metal detector, and afterwards were given a plastic-encased nametag.

There were about forty guests ahead of them by the time Lucas and his family reached the barrier's western entrance. He recognized several of them, mostly from appearances on TV or photographs in the newspapers: "Willito" Alvarez, the mayor of Caguas—one of the *populares'* last bastion cities—accompanied by Fidelise Soto, a shapely, blond, *merengue* singer; Zelda Rodriguez, a former comedienne turned senator; Marcos Estevez, the Chamber of Commerce's flamboyant, outspoken president and owner of the biggest supermarket chain in Puerto Rico; Jose "Palillo" Torres, the tough center for the Puerto Rican national basketball team, towering a full foot above the other taller men in the crowd; and Pastor Oscar Toro, head minister of the powerful "Voice of God" Christian congregation, clad in immaculate white from the tip of his patent leather shoes to his neatly pressed raw silk jacket. There were several men in military uniforms, top ranking policemen, consular heads, and scores of other elegantly dressed men and women, many of them wearing pins of the Puerto Rican and American flags.

On the upper steps of the Capitol, brightly illuminated by several spotlights, Secretary of Justice Rovira Melendez was being interviewed by a man holding a microphone, flashing his trademark wolfish grin at the camera behind the reporter. Lucas instinctively disliked the man, and remembered why—despite Governor Pietrantoni—he disliked the Statehood Party.

A young, dark-haired woman wearing a navy blue business suit and carrying a clipboard, approached Lucas before he had reached the end of the line and smiled prettily at him.

"Are you Lucas Alfaro?" she asked him, extending her hand before he could answer, and shaking his vigorously. "Hi, I'm Maggie Guillermetti, the Governor's legislative liaison." She examined the others in the group, saying, "And this must be your beautiful wife, Jennifer, and your sister Vanessa."

Lucas suppressed a chuckle, as he saw Jeannie eye the pretty legislative assistant with a neutral expression, while Vanessa stood straight as a rail and thrust her arm forward, pumping Maggie's hand with effusive enthusiasm.

"I'm very happy to meet you," she said in her most charming voice.

Maggie bent down and addressed Alfredo. "And you are Francisco's best friend, the famous Alfredo, right?" she said to the boy, who was wearing a dark suit with a red tie full of golden, Mickey Mouse heads. Placing her right hand lightly on the boy's shoulder, the Governor's aide lightly kissed him on the cheek.

Alfredo stared back at her with a love-struck expression. His cheeks reddened and he nodded, trying to say something, but only managing to produce a strange word that sounded like "Unda!"

Michael took a step forward and shook her hand while she examined him with an uncertain smile. "I'm Alfredo's father," he explained, "Michael." He seemed as impressed with her as his son.

"I can see the resemblance," she said with an appreciative look. She turned back to Lucas. "Governor Pietrantoni asked me to fetch you and your people as soon as you got here," she explained as she began to push back one of the wooden barriers to make a space through which they could leave the line. Michael and one of the policemen keeping watch on the crowd helped her to move it. "Thank you, Arturo," she said to the policeman with breathless charm. The policeman tipped his hat. Apparently, she was very well known by the security detail, since no one seemed to question her authority or object to what she was doing.

"I'm sorry that we didn't have time to send a limo to pick you up," she told Lucas as the group began to move through the gap in the barrier. "It's been hectic here during the last few hours. Everyone had assumed that the Governor's speech would be cancelled because of...you know, everything that happened yesterday," she said, whirling the hand with which she held her clipboard about her, her reference to the events of the previous day sounding more like an inconvenient spell of nasty weather than to an aborted revolution. She placed a hand gently on Lucas' arm, earning a withering glance from Jeannie. "You can imagine how crazy it's been," she confided to him. "Letting everybody know that the speech is still on, lining up the key players—even though some of them were affected by yesterday's attack—setting up the security. There's been no time to print the speech or pass it on a clean draft for the teleprompter, the Governor's still working on it! But that's Governor Pietrantoni for you!" she said happily. "Always unpredictable! Always keeping you on your toes. He didn't want you to wait in line. You are his special guests today."

Lucas watched Vanessa and saw the excitement gleaming in her eyes. *God help us*, he thought with amusement. *We will be hearing about this moment for years.*

"How did you know who I was?" Lucas asked her as they walked past the line of waiting guests, many of whom eyed them with curiosity and resentment.

"Oh, believe me, your description by the Governor was very accurate and vivid. 'Look for a young, somewhat serious, handsome guy,' he said," taking a sideways glance at him and enjoying his embarrassment. "Besides, I saw a picture of you."

"A photo? Where did you get that from?"

"You'd be surprised at the secret, personal files and photos to which the government has access," she whispered in a naughty, conspiratorial tone. "Actually, I found it in Vanessa's Facebook page," she confessed with a laugh. "Besides, not too many of our guests are beaten up and appear like they've just come out of a brawl." She stared at him with admiration. "Quite a fight, from the little that I've heard."

Lucas blushed, while behind him Michael whispered in his ear, "I think she's got the hots for you." Michael gasped as Vanessa pinched his arm with a prolonged, vicious twist.

Lucas saw Jeannie glancing at him, and wondered what she was thinking. He had not spoken much about what had happened during the previous twenty-four hours, giving her only a bare bones outline, in part not to alarm her, in part because he did not want to relive the harrowing events of that day. He knew how peeved his wife felt that their sexy guide had more details about what he had done than *her*, the woman who shared his bed. But it couldn't be helped. To dwell on the death and suffering he and Alfredo had witnessed would have been too much. He returned Jeannie's glimpse and smiled as lovingly as he could, but his smile was met with cold indifference.

Maggie led them away from the crowd, and then turned right, to a small, discreet entrance on the western end of the capitol building. The two policemen guarding the entrance greeted her with the kind of familiar warmth—bordering on open flirting—reserved for longtime friends. A metal detector blocked her way, but she walked right through it, setting off the alarm.

"Come on," she urged the visitors as they stopped to clear their pockets. "The Governor is waiting for these people," she informed an enormous guard standing next to the metal scanner who seemed to have stepped off the front line of an NFL team.

"Any of you carrying any weapons?" the man asked, eyeing them suspiciously, directing a particularly fierce glare at Alfredo. Then he grinned, and waved them in. "Come on in, folks."

They followed the long, green-carpeted corridor beyond the detector, passing scores of doors with smoked glass windows that bore the names of the most senior representatives in gold, hand painted letters. A musty smell of dust, storage boxes, and old paper pervaded the air and complemented the gloomy yellow light provided by wall lamps scattered every two offices along the narrow passageway. In an eerie way, it reminded Lucas of the tunnels below La Fortaleza. Looking at Alfredo's taut expression, he suspected that the young boy felt the same way.

As the corridor ended, Maggie stopped in front of the last door to the right—where its window displayed, in large, bold, black letters, "SPEAKER OF THE HOUSE," and below that "MARISEL DELGADO"—and rapped sharply on its wooden frame.

"Enter!" a familiar voice answered from inside.

As the pretty liaison officer pushed the door open, Lucas saw the unmistakable figure of Secretary of State Arizmendi—Double A— hunched over the desk normally used by the Speaker's secretary, a pen in hand, poring over several pages of heavily annotated text.

"Ah!" he said with genuine pleasure. "Lucas! Welcome! Please forgive me for not standing up right now, but as you can see," he gestured with his left hand over a mess of paper strewn on the desk, "we're running late!" He fixed his attention on the rest of the newcomers, and despite what he had said before, he stood up. "You must be Lucas' beautiful family. Alfredo I already know. We're war buddies, he and I. Right Alfredo?" The boy's chest swelled up with pride. "I'm Alberto Arizmendi, Double A for those who read about me in the wrong places."

"Mr. Secretary..." Lucas began to say, to introduce the rest of his family, but the electric politician interrupted him.

"Alberto, please. When we risk our lives together, we earn the right to call each other by our first names, don't you think?" he said, looking at the others in the group. Then his round face frowned, and he leaned forward, making some annotation on a page about some idea that had just occurred to him, gesturing to some invisible audience as he did so. He wore a white shirt, perfectly starched and ironed, with ivory cufflinks, its right sleeve already stained with blue ink from the ballpoint pen that he was holding in his hand. A dark blue jacket with vertical stripes hung from the back of the chair on which he had been sitting. "No, that doesn't sound right," he said to himself after mentally reviewing what he had just written, unconsciously combing the few long strands of hair that covered his mostly bald pate, and scratching furiously over the sentence he had just written.

"Alberto, this is my wife Jeannie," Lucas said. Arizmendi gave her a quick but full appreciative glance as he shook her hand with a firm handshake.

"Jeannie," he said, "I am very happy to make your acquaintance. Now I know why this man fought so hard to get back home."

Jeannie smiled, charmed by the relentlessly intense little man. He was pudgy, balding, and pale, and yet there was something very definitely sexy behind his dark, intelligent eyes.

"Thank you," she responded. "Lucas said you were very brave yesterday, although," she directed an unfriendly stare in her husband's direction, "he failed to elaborate on what had happened."

"Did he really say that I was brave?" Arizmendi placed his pen on the desk for a moment and beamed at her. "Well, coming from him that is very high praise indeed."

"And this is my sister Vanessa and her husband Michael," Lucas continued, ignoring the dig by his wife.

Vanessa almost curtsied, and said, "It's a pleasure to meet you, Mr. Double A." Her smile remained frozen as she realized what she had just said, while Alfredo turned his eyes toward the ceiling with a mortified expression.

If Arizmendi registered her use of his nickname, he failed to acknowledge it, saying in a charming voice, "I can see the family resemblance, although you and your sister Michelle are much prettier."

Vanessa blushed, and directed a quick, embarrassed glance at her brother as Double A returned his attention to the pages strewn over the desk. "You must excuse me for not being more sociable at this moment, but I work for a very stubborn man who would not postpone his speech to our nation for even one day. That leaves us about..." He examined his watch, and shook his head in despair. "About one hour to put something coherent together."

He was not being entirely honest. Like his boss, he had wholeheartedly supported the decision not to postpone the State of the Island address even for one day. It felt in his bones like the right thing to do; a show of strength and defiance that would prove to the Puerto Rican citizens and the rest of the world that the duly elected government of Puerto Rico would not be intimidated by any terrorist actions, and signal that everyday life continued as usual. But it also provided the opportunity, Arizmendi had argued with Pietrantoni, to promote the cause of statehood for Puerto Rico before a worldwide audience. After all, all of the major news networks would be covering today's speech. Another opportunity like that would not arise in another half millennium.

However, to Double A's great mortification, Pietrantoni had balked at the idea. He would not convert his speech before the legislature into a political rally. Too many people, from every political persuasion, had given up their lives to save San Juan from the calamity that had befallen on it, he had argued. To use that moment to advance his personal ideas would be dishonest and disrespectful. Angrily, grudgingly, Arizmendi had given up on the issue. It had been a shame. A golden opportunity lost. After all, the dead would not be aware of how they were used.

"I think the Governor wanted to see them as soon as they got here," Arizmendi said to Maggie, pointing at the closed door that led to the office of the Speaker.

"Is he alone in there?" she asked cautiously.

"His Majesty is in there with him," Arizmendi answered in an amused tone, referring to the Speaker of the House. "So is our beloved Secretary of Justice. Who knows? They might convince him to say something in support of the plebiscite. I think the Governor will be grateful for the interruption, anyway."

Maggie reluctantly raised her hand over the Speaker's door, and then, making up her mind, knocked on it softly.

"Yes?" a strong female voice shouted from within.

Holding on to the doorknob, Maggie pushed the door slightly ajar and slipped her head inside the Speaker's office. After a short, incomprehensible exchange, she finished opening the door, and gestured with her right hand to the visitors to walk in. "I'll be waiting outside," she whispered.

Lucas was the first to step in, followed by the others. They entered into a large, rectangular room, cramped with three enormous, over-stuffed brown leather sofas and a small, glass-topped bamboo table that served as an antechamber to an aircraft carrier-sized desk at its opposite end. Even from where they stood, Lucas could plainly see a hefty, hand carved, wooden nameplate resting on top of the desk, which read, in telescoping, 3-D letters, "MARISEL". It belonged to the present tenant of the office, Marisel Delgado, the Speaker of the House.

Several framed photographs decorated the walls, showing the Speaker next to various presidents—Bush and Obama prominent among them—as well as artists and movie stars—Johnny Depp, Benicio Del Toro, and JayLo—and various past and present local politicians. An oversized photo of former Governor Alarcon and the Speaker had been accorded a place of honor on a narrow table behind the desk, along with several other people—some of them children—whom Lucas imagined to be Delgado's family.

Lucas had seen the Speaker hundreds of times before, mostly on TV and the newspapers, but even so he was struck by how big she was. She must have stood at close to six feet tall and weigh in excess of three hundred pounds. One popular joke told about a time she had supposedly been driving towards the town of Manati in Puerto Rico. When she had stopped at the expressway's tollbooth, she had asked the attendant for directions. "How much more to Manati?" she had asked him. The attendant had examined her and, sizing her up, answered, "About four or five more pounds." It was an unkind joke, but accurate. The Speaker's neck was not visible, embedded in a double chin, her forearms spilling out of the short sleeves of her white pantsuit, her thick legs solidly planted on the ground.

The other person meeting with the Governor was Secretary of Justice Walter Rovira Melendez. Lucas was surprised to find him there, since less than fifteen minutes before he had been standing on the steps of the capitol getting interviewed. *The man must have flown up and down the building's stairs,* Lucas thought with amazement.

He was wearing a charcoal grey suit with a blue striped tie perfectly tailored for his trim, elegant figure, an American flag pin fastened to his left lapel. He stood at the same height of the Governor, but with a more muscular build, and his gray—flecked with black—hair and mustache enhanced his already distinguished appearance, giving him the aristocratic look that drove so many of his female admirers wild. His eyes were dark and burned with a fierce intensity that when combined with his wolfish grin, served to charm his followers and intimidate his opponents.

When Lucas entered the room, Rovira examined him with an air of mild curiosity and impatience, such as that of an adult interrupted by a noisy child in the middle of an important conversation. But the Governor made him feel immediately welcome, his tense expression softening into a friendly smile.

Pietrantoni was wearing no jacket, which he had placed over the back of the Speaker's desk chair, displaying a set of red suspenders over his plain white shirt that matched his red tie. On his hands he held a sheet of paper—presumably the part of the speech on which he had been working when Rovira and Marisel Delgado had interrupted him in his work. He seemed tired but elated, his face reflecting genuine pleasure to see him there.

"Lucas! How good of you to come!" he said as a greeting, stepping out from between the Secretary of Justice and the Speaker and shaking his hand vigorously. "I hope Maggie found you before you had to wait a long time in line."

"Maggie was very efficient. We barely waited at all," Lucas replied, immediately infected by the Governor's exuberance. With the corner of his eye he saw Jeannie break a smile, and knew that she had instantly succumbed to the man's easy, effortless charm. "I suspect that you haven't had much sleep," Lucas said to him, surprising himself for daring to ask such a personal question.

The Governor shrugged. "There have been better nights. I took short naps here and there," he answered with a humorous glance, obviously lying. "There will be ample opportunity to rest later." He leaned forward towards Alfredo, who had walked up next to his godfather, and said to him in a confidential voice, "We never finished talking about politics. Maybe next week we can sit and talk some more."

"Yes," the eight year old solemnly replied, not at all intimidated by the Governor's attention. "I would like that very much. Will Francisco be there?"

Lucas heard Vanessa and Michael laugh nervously.

"Of course he'll be there!" Pietrantoni answered, addressing him as an adult. "You're his best friend, aren't you?"

Alfredo nodded.

"Good! So it's a date." The Governor straightened himself up and looked at Alfredo's parents. "You should be very proud of your son. He is very smart and brave."

"I am," Vanessa said, taking great care to say as little as possible and avoid embarrassing herself again. She could not entirely resist the temptation, however, of adding, "I hope that Nereida and Alfredo are well."

"They are indeed, thank you for asking. Francisco is...a little tired and stressed out, but nothing that rest won't solve, I hope. Nereida is a very strong woman. Besides, she's got the company of Patria, my housekeeper.

They'll take care of each other." Pietrantoni stated, his eyes shifting while he talked to the man standing next to her. "Please forgive me for being so rude. You're Michael, Alfredo's dad right?" extending his hand to Lucas' brother-in-law. "The sole *statehooder* in the family, according to Alfredo."

Michael laughed a little too loudly and cleared his throat. "Yes, I'm the only stable person in the family."

The Speaker of the House chortled, while Rovira Melendez watched the exchange with a forced smile.

"Well," Pietrantoni said, staring directly at Lucas, "I have to thank God for the rest of your family's instability." He turned his head and spoke to Rovira and the Speaker. "This is Lucas Alfaro, the man who saved my life, the life of my son, and of all the other people trapped in La Fortaleza. Lucas, this is House Speaker Marisel Delgado and Secretary of Justice Walter Rovira Melendez."

"So this is our Puerto Rican Rambo!" the fat leader of the House majority said in a sugary tone. Her grin had widened, making her look, Lucas thought, like a smaller version of Jabba the Hut. "There are all sort of stories floating around about you. Where did you learn to kill terrorists? Or is that a natural talent?"

Lucas felt an intense aversion for the woman. She had asked the question in a sweet, innocent voice, but the glee in her eyes revealed how much she was enjoying portraying Lucas as a killer in front of his family. From where he stood, she looked like a maleficent frog, staring at the fly she was about to swallow.

"Lucas was an Army Ranger," Pietrantoni answered for him, noting his friend's discomfort.

"A veteran!" the Speaker rejoined with feigned enthusiasm, clapping her fleshy hands. "Thank you for defending our country. And our Governor, of course."

Pietrantoni was about to say something, but Rovira Melendez walked to Lucas and shook his hand. "It is an honor to meet you," he said, scrutinizing his face as he did so, as if committing him to memory. "You did a great thing yesterday saving our Governor and his family," he stated with stiff enthusiasm, trying to inject as much gratitude in his voice as he could.

"I think you're all giving me more credit than I really deserve," Lucas replied with forced courtesy, hoping he was masking his instinctive dislike for the Governor's two political companions. "We survived because we were able to work together, with the Governor holding us together."

"And humble too!" the Speaker exclaimed with smug approval.

"A true hero, no doubt," Rovira said, releasing his hand and stepping back. "I would recommend that the House of Representatives gives him some sort of recognition, a medal of some sort, for his courage."

The Speaker nodded slowly, as if considering the idea and liking it more as she thought about it. It would play well in the press. "Yes, yes, of course. I will arrange for something immediately," she said, taking out her Iphone and scribbling something on it with her pudgy thumbs.

"This is Jennifer, my wife," Lucas interjected, realizing he had not introduced her, and knowing that she would kill him if he didn't.

The Governor leaned and kissed her on the cheek. "Thank you," he said.

Jeannie looked at him puzzled. "For what?' she asked.

"For lending me your husband yesterday."

She smiled. "Thank you for keeping him safe and returning him to me," she whispered back.

"Oho!" Rovira Melendez exclaimed with a chuckle. "We have a politician in our midst!"

She glanced at him briefly, and returned her attention to the Governor.

"I would love if you could all join us in La Fortaleza for dinner, sometime next week perhaps? Nereida would be delighted to have you all visit her," Pietrantoni said.

Lucas noticed the quick exchange of looks between the Speaker and Rovira when the Governor mentioned the name of his son's nanny, and made a mental note to warn Pietrantoni about it. How, he did not know yet.

"We would love that," Jeannie said delightedly.

"Then it's a date. I'll have Maggie arrange it. I have reserved seats for you in the hemicycle in the House of Representatives so you can listen to the speech, however disastrous it turns out to be..." he directed a pointed stare at his two companions, who automatically shook their heads.

"Oh, nonsense, Roberto!" the Speaker said dismissively, her fleshy jowls shaking as she moved her head from side to side. "You always say the same thing, and you always do well. He's the best orator of us all," she confided to the others.

"Marisel has more faith in me than I do," Pietrantoni said coolly. "In any event, I just wanted to thank you once more." For a moment he seemed at a loss of words. Lucas opened his mouth to speak, but the Governor raised his hand, signaling him not to say anything. "I know, I know, you're going to say again that we all had something to do with our miraculous deliverance, and that we should all take credit for it, and you're right. But Lucas, without you, we wouldn't have survived. I believe that God acts in mysterious ways, and that yesterday, He sent you to save all of us...It was not a coincidence that Alfredo was there, and even less of a coincidence that you are his godfather."

There was genuine emotion in the Governor's voice. Somewhat awkwardly, he stepped forward and embraced Lucas. "Thank you, *my friend.*"

The Speaker lowered her head and swiped away a tear from under her right eye, while Rovira Melendez observed the Governor's spontaneous show of affection with contemplative interest.

"I am very proud to be your friend," Lucas responded as they separated. He genuinely liked the man, and his instincts told him that the two other politicians in the room were not among the Governor's closest allies.

As if on cue, Maggie opened the office's door and popped her head in. "I'm sorry, Governor, but Secretary Arizmendi is demanding that you give him more pages of the speech, if you have any."

Pietrantoni shook his head slightly and grimaced. "Soon!" he shouted at Arizmendi through the door. "Soon!" He turned to his visitors. "You'll have to excuse me," he said to them, "but duty calls. Even worse than duty, the Secretary of State calls me. Maggie will take you to your seats. Thank you for coming. I'll see you all next week."

As the door closed behind him, Lucas took a last glimpse at the Governor. He saw the Speaker and the Secretary of Justice closing in on him like a pair of hungry wolves, and felt sorry for him.

CHAPTER LXXXI

"I have to work on my speech," Pietrantoni indicated to his two colleagues, after his visitors had left, "so let's make this brief."

"There's not much more to say, so I'll be blunt, since you seem to refuse to listen to reason," Rovira rejoined. He stood ramrod straight, looking directly at the Governor. His forced smile had vanished as soon as the door had closed behind the inopportune visitors. "You are the president of the Statehood Party. They selected you to promote the cause of statehood. This is not a luxury that you can...choose or not choose, depending on how you feel. It is your sacred, unavoidable duty to do so. If you fail to promote our cause today, as you informed us a few minutes ago it is your intention to do, you will betray us all, the people who voted for you, the people who let you run for Governor, the people who rely on you, your party."

"Think about it, Roberto!" the Speaker said in a less severe tone, appealing to his reason. "You have a golden opportunity to plead our case before a national...no, not even national, an international audience!" She placed a hand on his arm. "The whole world is watching us! You are the hero of the moment! The one who stood up to the terrorists! You can tell the people that there is no way that this can happen again if we permanently join the United States!" She softened her voice. "Don't waste this opportunity," she pleaded. Then, as he failed to respond, her expression hardened. "Don't turn the rest of the party against you. The party made you. The party can take you down."

Pietrantoni said nothing. He gently pushed aside the Speaker's wood-carved name, and leaned against the edge of her desk, crossing his arms. He stared at the floor in thoughtful contemplation. His two colleagues watched him in silence.

What a fine pair of political allies, he thought to himself. During the previous year's elections, Marisel had backed him, if not very enthusiastically, at least with no open reservations. He had not been under any illusions, however. Like Rovira Melendez, Marisel was a political animal that belonged to former Governor Alarcon, who still remained loyal to him. However, she had had enough political sense to realize that the only way she could have been re-elected had been by hitching a ride on Pietrantoni's coattails. So she had given him her unconditional support, and gained the top leadership position in the House of Representatives.

But that was then, and this is now. During the past year, she had consolidated her hold on the House, wielding considerable power. Enough power to make Pietrantoni's next three years pure hell if she had a falling out with him. Her enmity would not come at a worse time, either. Although his instincts told him that the speech would not be the right time to rally his followers to the cause of statehood, he still wanted to win the plebiscite. It would be very difficult, if not impossible, to do so with some of the most influential members of his own party trying to sabotage him.

Pietrantoni raised his head and looked at his two colleagues. "You say that I have a sacred...what is it, duty? A sacred duty to promote the cause of statehood," he said to Rovira. "And you're right. I *do* have a duty to promote statehood. I have always wanted it for Puerto Rico, I have always fought for it, considered it the right thing for my country. To become part of the greatest nation on earth, to secure equal representation in Congress and be able to vote for the president."

Marisel nodded slowly in complete agreement. Rovira observed him with suspicion, knowing him too well and waiting for him to deliver his punch line.

"But it is precisely...because I *respect* our cause so much that I cannot cheapen it before the rest of the world. To make our case for becoming a state today, while honoring the memory of those who have fallen, by trying to *scare* our people to vote for our permanent union with the States, even though God knows how many of those who died did not support our cause, will only weaken our arguments on behalf of statehood. It will seem like a political ploy, and be called that by the press. It will cheapen our cause. It is precisely because of my sacred duty to statehood, that I cannot agree to that."

"You have no choice," the Speaker said in a peeved tone. "You risk losing the support of the party if you choose to do nothing today. *Everybody* is expecting it. It would break my heart if that happened..." Marisel let the unspoken threat hang.

"So let me get this straight," Pietrantoni stated in a subdued tone. "If I don't turn today's speech into some sort of political rally in favor of statehood, you'll all turn against me? Is that it?"

Pietrantoni's direct question seemed to catch Marisel by surprise. She darted an uncomfortable glance at Rovira, and then answered, "I wouldn't put it so bluntly..." but Rovira interrupted her.

"Regardless of how we feel, the truth is that you *will* turn the party against you. They will question where your loyalties are, and some will brand you as a traitor to our cause," he stated with the conviction that the Speaker lacked.

"I see," Pietrantoni said in a sullen, resigned voice that made his two companions breathe easier. "Well, I guess I don't have a choice."

"It's for the best," Marisel concurred with relief, adopting a sympathetic expression, trying to conceal the intense satisfaction she was feeling.

"Yes," the Governor replied dryly. "It's better that we take care of this matter now."

The Speaker smiled beatifically. Rovira said nothing, waiting for the Governor's next words with cautious optimism.

"I really must get back to my speech," Pietrantoni said, placing a hand behind Marisel's left forearm and gently ushering her out of her own office.

"Of course," she said, somewhat confused. Rovira followed them. "I *know* you will do the right thing."

"A moment in private, before I leave," the Secretary of Justice said quietly, as the Speaker plodded out of the waiting room.

Pietrantoni nodded.

"There is one other matter," Rovira indicated gravely. "You may or may not be aware of it."

Pietrantoni said nothing, waiting for Rovira to continue.

"While you were in the hands of the terrorists, Superintendent Maldonado sent his thug, Montañez, to intimidate me and place me under house arrest," Rovira said. He waited for the Governor to react, but continued when Pietrantoni failed to do so. "This is tantamount to a *de facto coupe de etat*, a rebellion within the government by its police force against its chief executive, who at that time happened to be me. This is a very serious offense. I expect nothing less than for you to require his resignation, immediately."

Pietrantoni regarded Rovira calmly. From his desk, Arizmendi watched with amused concern. He could not listen to the conversation, but he could guess what they were talking about, and was anticipating Pietrantoni's reaction. It would be fun, even though he was certain that as always, he would end up being his boss's lightning rod in the ensuing political storm.

"Yes," the Governor said calmly, "Maldonado told me about it early this morning. His version of what happened varies somewhat. He says that he sent Montañez to warn you that Captain Ramirez—your protégé,

I believe he is, is he not?—that Ramirez was in the pay of the terrorists, passing on important information to them. According to him, you were so affected by the news that you decided to go home. Rosa Gonzalez assumed the position of Interim Governor when you couldn't go on."

Rovira's face blanched. He compressed his lips into a tight line, while the veins in his neck bulged noticeably. "That is a vile lie!" he hissed angrily. "Montañez was sent to blackmail me and force me to give up the interim governorship. He came into my office with two of his thugs. I actually feared for my safety!"

"As I understand it, you placed the life of my family and my staff in danger when you prematurely told the press—why, I have no idea—that I had managed to escape from my office," the Governor responded coldly.

"A careless omission on my part. A stupid indiscretion caused by too much enthusiasm at the good news of your escape."

"Indeed. I hope that it was your enthusiasm that overwhelmed your common sense, because if I find out there were ulterior motives behind your...indiscretion, and that you placed my family and my staff in danger on purpose, I swear to God I'll file criminal charges against you," the Governor stated without shifting his gaze from Rovira's eyes.

The Secretary of Justice's face reddened noticeably. "So, if I understand you correctly, you will do nothing about it?" Rovira asked with indignation.

"As I see it, you have two choices: if you insist in lodging a complaint against Maldonado, I will conduct a full fledged investigation of everything that happened. I don't think you will come out of it looking very well," Pietrantoni said earnestly.

"And the second choice?" Rovira asked coolly.

"You do nothing, and the matter stays as it is," the Governor replied. "Well, not exactly as it is. I expect to have your written resignation on my desk by tomorrow morning. If not, I'll fire you."

Rovira attempted to smile, but only managed to bare his teeth.

"You are making a very serious mistake," he stated, raising his voice so Arizmendi could hear him. "I will make your life hell from now on..."

"No doubt," Pietrantoni replied tartly. "But not from within my administration. Now please leave. I have work to do."

Rovira hesitated, as if considering saying something else, then turned on his heels and abandoned the office.

"Well!" Arizmendi said cheerfully after a long, awkward silence. "That went well!"

The two friends exchanged a humorous look and laughed.

"There is going to be so much shit floating around soon..." Double A said dejectedly, as he took a distracted glance at the page that the Governor handed to him.

"That's okay," Pietrantoni replied with a mischievous smile, while he walked back into the Speaker's office, "I'm sure you'll be able handle it."

It was no use. Rovira Melendez had affected his concentration. For the last five minutes, Pietrantoni had been staring at a blank page, unable to put any words on paper. His hands were shaking slightly, whether from physical exhaustion, anger, worry, or a combination of all three he couldn't rightly tell. He had declared war on Governor Alarcon's main protégé, and knew that soon he would be in the political fight of his life. A lot of the top people in the party would side with Rovira.

But damn if he would fire Maldonado, and damn if he would tolerate Rovira to continue being a member of his cabinet. He'd rather have sex with the Speaker of the House! Not that he would, though.

His thoughts went back to the Superintendent. Maldonado had been at the Archbishop's residence at least fifteen minutes before the appointed hour, long before the first rays of the sun had scattered the darkness over San Juan. The Archbishop himself had led him to his office, where the Governor had been communicating all night long with several of his cabinet members and agency heads. The rest of the group had already left, delivered to their homes by the police. Nereida and Francisco were sleeping in one of the building's many guest rooms, while La Fortaleza crawled with a small army of forensic investigators, policemen, district attorneys, security experts, medical personnel, and federal officials. It would take several days before the Executive Mansion was fit for occupancy again, and Archbishop Garrido had offered his hospitality until that happened.

Pietrantoni had been shocked by the Superintendent's haggard appearance. Maldonado had never been noted for looking particularly good. Even as a young police colonel, when he had assumed for the first time the command of the Police Department, newspaper caricatures had portrayed him as a tall, stooped, (then) thin man with a bulbous nose, and bloodshot eyes with dark bags under them, features that his enemies had used to accuse him of heavy drinking and disreputable behavior. But that morning he looked exhausted. His eyes seemed to have sunk into their sockets; his cheeks were puffy and distended; and a web of thin, purple lines highlighted the rounded end of his nose. It was plainly evident that during the past twenty-four hours he had gone through hell.

Archbishop Garrido had exchanged a few pleasantries with the Superintendent, had ordered Father Bernard to bring up some breakfast for the three of them—eggs, toast, and coffee—and then had tried to excuse himself so his two guests could talk. Pietrantoni had insisted that he stay, however, for no logical reason except that he wanted to see how an intelligent man would react to what they were about to discuss. Maldonado—a devout Catholic—had accepted the Archbishop's presence without hesitation, and begun to brief the Governor about all of the day's prior developments.

He had begun with what had weighed the most in his mind: the terrible casualties suffered by the police force; fifteen killed in Puerta de Tierra, another five in ambushes of police patrol cars in Old San Juan, eight more in the Condado Lagoon massacre. Four more men who had been working in the police station were unaccounted for, presumably consumed by the fire. A preliminary report from La Fortaleza indicated that five bodyguards had also died. That came to a total of thirty-seven law and order officers who had lost their lives during the prior day's revolt, not counting the dozens of men that had been wounded.

"We paid a terrible price yesterday," the Superintendent said hoarsely, unconsciously wringing his hands.

"And of the wounded?" Pietrantoni inquired.

"Three were critically injured but are in stable condition. The rest are expected to recover." Maldonado paused as he remembered something else. "There was one more notable casualty. Sergeant Abraham Cordero, a veteran SWAT team member. He was killed in action after he single-handedly stopped a Machetero counter-attack against the hostages in the Grand Laguna Hotel. I am told that several dead terrorists surrounded his body, and that if not for him, God knows what would have happened. I am recommending that he be awarded posthumously the Medal of Valor."

Pietrantoni had watched Archbishop Garrido while the police chief spoke. A veteran of the Iraqi War, the priest had maintained a contemplative silence, his eyes lost in thought, his jaw tightly clenched.

"Apart from the police force, the casualties also include an undetermined number of civilians in the ship and the hotel, and in the city itself. I should have a better idea later today," Maldonado added wearily. "Many of them are part of the terrorists that attacked us. Also, late at night, a Coast Guard cutter exploded close to El Morro."

This had been news for the Governor and the Archbishop, who had exchanged a look of horror.

"Good God! When did this happen?"

"Around midnight last night. The details are sketchy. Apparently there were no survivors."

"The terrorists did this?" Archbishop Garrido ventured to ask after a shocked silence.

"We can't prove or disprove it at this moment, but taking into account the one-day war that we went through yesterday, I would say probably yes," the Superintendent answered.

The "one-day war", Pietrantoni thought to himself. *That was probably the best way to describe what had happened in San Juan during the last twenty-four hours.*

"I will pray for them and their families," the Archbishop said.

"Is the FBI investigating?" Pietrantoni asked, and immediately sensed that his question had struck a nerve. From the policeman's tense body language, he could tell that Maldonado had other urgent and unexpected news to deliver. The Superintendent was sitting with his shoulders hunched forward, his elbows resting on his legs, his hands clasped tightly. *Not a good sign*, Pietrantoni thought.

As if reading his boss's thoughts, Maldonado looked at Pietrantoni, darting a covert glance at the Archbishop, seeking the former's permission to continue. Pietrantoni nodded curtly, signaling him to speak openly before the priest.

"Last night I arrested Mario Franceschini," he stated reluctantly.

"The FBI man?" Pietrantoni asked in a shocked voice.

"The same," Maldonado confirmed.

"This is a delicate subject," the Archbishop said. "I should leave."

"No, Your Grace, please," Pietrantoni requested. "Just keep it to yourself, like confession secrets."

Garrido raised an eyebrow with an amused expression. "Very well."

"Please proceed," the Governor said to Maldonado in a much calmer voice than how he actually felt. The arrest of the top FBI agent in Puerto Rico, just as they were ending the "one-day war", did not come at the best time.

"For nearly two years," the Superintendent began, giving some background information for the benefit of the Archbishop, "we have been aware of an insider, call the person a 'mole' if you will, operating within the high ranks of the police."

Pietrantoni assented, confirming his knowledge of the affair.

"At different times, when conducting raids on spots where we knew drugs were being sold, or when we received information—reliable information—that drugs were about to enter the island, we would find the places empty or abandoned. In some instances, the traffickers had just left, ditching some of the merchandise they could not carry with them. Other times there was nothing. You may think," the Superintendent said directly to the Archbishop, "that maybe it was bad intelligence, and at the beginning I considered that too. I even thought for a moment that maybe it was some low ranking corrupt cops warning some of the local drug lords, coupled with some cases of actual misinformation. But I soon had to accept that the information was coming from the top of our organization. There were operations of which only a handful of us knew about until less than an hour before it was scheduled, and still the traffickers had received prior knowledge about them, and anticipated every move that we made, making us look foolish and amateurish. Even worse, several of our sources of information, our 'moles', if you will, were systematically uncovered and killed. It was all coming from within our own organization, and we had to do something to stop it."

There was a soft knock on the door, and then Father Bernard walked in. He was a short, balding man in his forties with a bushy brown beard that had already begun to show streaks of gray, and vivid blue eyes, the left one surrounded by a black shiner.

"Excuse me, Your Grace," he said in a soft, calm voice that exuded peace. "The 6:00 o'clock mass is due to start in fifteen minutes. Will you be giving it?"

The Archbishop looked at his watch and nodded, as if surprised by the time. "Yes, of course, father," he said absently. "Could you get everything ready? I will join you shortly."

Father Bernard bowed slightly and left.

"Ramirez soon became my prime suspect," Maldonado continued, as the priest walked out of the office. "He had access to most of the operations directed to dismantle drug distribution centers or to intercept drug shipments. He also had the means and the opportunity to find out the names of the informers. And let's face it, he's also an asshole, a man disliked by most of his subordinates not because he was tough with them but because he is vain and self-absorbed and incompetent, a man who got promoted in the force because of his political connections."

A thin smile appeared on the Archbishop's lips. Pietrantoni wondered if the same thing happened within the Church, if assholes there sometimes got promoted because of their connections.

"The killing of our informers was the worst part. They were executed in grotesque ways, sometimes cut into pieces and scattered in different places. We would receive calls where we could find them. It got so bad that many informers refused to talk to us any more, afraid that they would be next. I had to flush the mole out of the force, and I had to do it as quickly as possible."

"Not an easy task," Pietrantoni said, more to himself.

"There was one problem. There were a handful of cases...more like a dozen of them, where Ramirez had had no kind of contact or connection whatsoever, but where the traffickers had clearly been forewarned. These exceptions puzzled me, but made me investigate Ramirez further. I contacted a district attorney who's a friend of mine—I won't tell you his name right now, since it's not relevant to this story—and got him to get me a court authorization to tap his phones." Maldonado stopped and thought for a moment. "That was about three months, three months and a half ago. I also got hold of all of his phone call logs for the last two years."

Pietrantoni listened carefully, wondering what all of this had to do with Franceschini. At the beginning of Maldonado's narrative, he had thought that Ramirez had been just a footnote to the FBI man's story, but the captain continued to play a prominent role. He searched his mind for the man's face, knowing that he had probably met him a couple of times in police social functions or ceremonies. All that he could conjure was a tall thin man with a nervous disposition who would usually gravitate to the Rovira crowd and divert his eyes whenever the Governor happened to look in his direction. He couldn't remember his face, though.

"Did you only secure a court authorization for him, or did you examine other people's records?" Pietrantoni asked with curiosity.

"I also got court authorization to tap Colonel Montañez, who also had access to most of the drug-busting operations."

"Proceed."

"I put together a team of investigators that had nothing to do with the drug busts. Actually, they had nothing to do with the police. I convinced Rosa Gonzalez, our Secretary of the Treasury, to lend me a couple of her people who investigate white-collar crime."

That was news to Pietrantoni. If Rovira got wind that Maldonado had used Treasury Department agents for a case having nothing to do with tax evasion, he would create a big stink about the misuse of government resources. Although, if Ramirez was found to be profiting from the sale of police information, and not reporting his illegal earnings as income, he could be prosecuted for tax evasion. It had worked for Elliot Ness with Al Capone, after all.

"The lists of calls yielded very little surprises," Maldonado expressed. "Mostly, they were the usual communications with friends and relatives. There were long conversations with politicians, most prominently with—"

"Rovira Melendez," Pietrantoni said before the other could finish.

"Yes, Rovira Melendez. There were also police related calls, of course, and a smattering of numbers corresponding to retail businesses and restaurants. Each was thoroughly checked, and most discarded."

"You say '*most*'. Were any of them *not* discarded?" Pietrantoni asked.

"Two phone numbers," the Superintendent replied. "There were two numbers that raised further questions. The first was a private phone number listed under the name of Ramonita Pantojas. Do you know who Ramonita Pantojas is?"

The Archbishop exchanged a look of puzzlement with the Governor, and both shook their heads.

"She is a madam, the owner of the largest brothel in Caguas. She owns a three story building in the mountains bordering the city. Most of the conversations between Ramirez and her were very lengthy, some lasting in excess of a half hour. However, those conversations that we managed to intercept had to do with her business." Maldonado leaned forward and lowered his voice. "I must tell you, she has a very prominent list of clients. A who's who of San Juan's social elite. Although she is very careful not to discuss the price of her services over the phone. Ramirez called her often, and visited her about once a week, but the text of the recorded conversations—please forgive my bluntness, father—only reflects the exchanges between a lustful, infatuated man and a calculating businesswoman."

Archbishop Garrido did not seem shocked or embarrassed by the police chief's disclosure. Then again, Pietrantoni thought, as a priest, he must have been privy to all sorts of sordid confessions that inured him to those kinds of disclosures. For a moment, Pietrantoni was tempted to ask if the police captain was married, but had enough sense to avoid the question.

"We will have to take action to close down the place," he said instead.

Maldonado nodded, but his expression seemed to say: *But not now. We have bigger fish to fry now.*

"I considered that maybe they could be speaking in some sort of code. I even searched for suspicious phrases or patterns in the transcripts of the conversations, but...if Ramirez is pretending to have an affair with the madam to pass on information, then he should be a regular in a soap opera. He would have to be a darned good actor, and I don't think he has it in him. Nevertheless, we kept an around-the-clock surveillance on Ms Pantojas and continued to listen to their telephone calls until two weeks ago," the Superintendent said cryptically.

"Until two weeks ago? What happened two weeks ago?" Pietrantoni asked.

"We concentrated all of our attention on the second suspicious telephone number," Maldonado responded. "The funny thing is that we nearly overlooked the number at the beginning. It was a cell phone number. From the telephone records that we investigated, it appears that during he last two years Ramirez has only made three calls to that number."

It didn't make any sense, Pietrantoni thought. *If Ramirez was involved in the information leaks, and called that number to give out the information, by necessity there would have to be a lot of more calls.*

"Were they made to Franceschini?" the Archbishop asked, glancing at his watch. The ten minutes to go to the cathedral to say mass were close to expiring, but he didn't want to leave.

"No," Maldonado responded. "The telephone number was registered under the name of a man called Carlos Ortiz."

"Like the boxer?" the Archbishop, a boxing fan, observed.

"His address was listed in Rio Piedras, in an apartment building close to the main campus of the University of Puerto Rico. I dispatched a team to the address for a routine check, and the building's landlord—it's an apartment rental business—confirmed that a middle aged man named Carlos Ortiz had indeed rented an apartment there for several months, but moved out almost a year ago. However, when we checked the telephone records with the telephone company, Ortiz was still listed as living in the building."

"Was the account still active?" Pietrantoni asked, wondering how Ortiz paid his monthly bills.

"Oh, yes," Maldonado confirmed.

"Then how—"

"...Did Ortiz pay the telephone invoices?" the Superintendent finished the Governor's question. "We found out that the telephone company sent paperless invoices to Ortiz via email. When we checked the email address, the account also listed the same old address we had investigated before. We also found out that the telephone company receives automatic monthly payments from a checking account in Banco Cosmopolitano."

"Don't tell me," the Governor interjected. "The bank account also lists Ortiz's address as the one of the building he used to rent."

"Correct. We looked at the bank records of the checking account. It was set up two years ago, with a deposit of $10,000. It still has a balance of over $7,000, and is only used to pay Carlos Ortiz's phone number, nothing else. There's enough money deposited in the account to keep paying for the cell phone for years to come."

Archbishop Garrido stood up. "I have to leave," he said with evident mortification, reluctant to abandon his two guests in the middle of the story.

"Tell Father Bernard to give the mass," Pietrantoni prompted.

The Archbishop smiled. "Stand behind me, Satan. You tempt me too much. No, it is important that I give this mass. We must show everyone that life is back to normal, despite yesterday's terrible distractions." He shook hands with Maldonado, and turned to the Governor. "But I will be back!" he said to him. "So listen well and tell me how the story ends!"

"Only if you agree to forgive all of my sins," the Governor countered, only half-jokingly.

"I will be glad to hear your confession," Garrido replied with a mildly inquisitive look, and left.

"So tell me," Pietrantoni said to his Superintendent.

Maldonado served himself some orange juice from a glass pitcher that had been brought in with the coffee, and took a long swallow. "The more we discovered, the more questions arose," he continued to explain. "The whole setup immediately raised a lot of red flags. Who was this guy Ortiz? Where had he gone? Why had he set up an account to just pay the telephone, and not bothered to change his records anywhere? I sent a team back to the apartment building and showed the landlord some photographs, not just of Ramirez but of Montañez and a few others in the police top brass. He couldn't recognize any of them. We were at a loss. But then, as we were waiting for a court order to check the Carlos Ortiz cell phone's log for the last two years, we had another break. When I correlated the three calls that Ramirez had made to Carlos Ortiz to the botched-up drug busting operations, I discovered that each of the calls had been made within an hour before three of the botched-up raids had been scheduled to go off."

Pietrantoni understood the significance of the information immediately. "Wow!" he said. "It almost seemed as if the calls had been made at the very last moment. And it's too much of a coincidence that each call corresponded to a busted drug raid."

"To me," Maldonado indicated, "it seemed as if the calls had been made on an emergency basis, as if Ramirez had called just in the nick of time to warn the drug traffickers. But the most amazing thing was that Ramirez had not been part of any of those three raids. He had not known about them ahead of time, not until they were about to take place."

The Superintendent paused after his last statement, letting the Governor consider its implications. Pietrantoni pondered about it for a moment, and then opened his eyes. "Of course! He called the traffickers at the last moment, because he didn't find out about the raids until the very last moment."

"That is what I concluded as well. Apparently, Ramirez contacted Carlos Ortiz from his own cell phone when he didn't have enough advance warning about a police raid, and could not reach Ortiz through other channels. I then looked at the log of the telephone calls that our mystery person, Carlos Ortiz, had received. Apart from the three Ramirez calls, the rest of the calls to this fictitious Carlos Ortiz person—all of them—had been made from one single telephone. That telephone—a cell phone—we traced back to a subscriber named Cesar Torregrosa."

"So Ramirez and this...Cesar Torregrosa were the only two persons who ever made any calls to Carlos Ortiz," Pietrantoni repeated pensively. "Nobody else?"

"Just those two persons," Maldonado confirmed. "And all of the calls that Ortiz made from his cell phone were made exclusively to Torregrosa. None were made to Ramirez or to any other number." It was evident that the Superintendent was enjoying leading his boss through the investigative maze that he had traveled before. And as a former district attorney, Pietrantoni was enjoying it as well.

"So how about the calls that this other man…Torregrosa made to Ortiz? How did they cross-check with the police raids that were busted?" the Governor asked, departing from the basis that Maldonado had cross-checked Torregrosa's calls to the busted drug raids.

The Superintendent flashed a grin of approval. "Excellent question," he said. "Nearly every call made from Torregrosa's cell phone to Ortiz was made one or two days *before* one of the busted police raids was scheduled to take place," Maldonado replied with satisfaction. "All except for five. There were five calls that had no relationship with any raid."

"So to summarize, Ramirez made three calls from his cell phone to Ortiz, each of them about an hour before three of the busted police raids, while Torregrosa made almost all of his calls to Ortiz one or two days before the other busted drug raids…" Pietrantoni hesitated, trying to piece the puzzle together. "And five of Torregrosa's calls were not made anywhere close to any of the raids?"

Maldonado nodded. "One more thing that you should know. Guess what was the address listed for Torregrosa's cell phone?"

"Don't tell me that it was the same address of Carlos Ortiz's phone!" Pietrantoni said jokingly.

"Precisely."

"You're kidding!

"And like Ortiz, Torregrosa is making automatic payments from a pre-set bank account, but this time in Banco Santander."

"And the address listed in the bank account?"

"The same as Ortiz."

"So they were living together at one time?" the Governor asked, hazarding a wild guess.

"It puzzled me," the Superintendent confessed. "For a moment I was even convinced that Torregrosa and Ortiz were the same person. Then I correlated another set of dates. I correlated the dates of the five calls from Torregrosa to Ortiz that didn't have anything to do with the busted police raids with the dates on which some of our informers had been executed by the drug lords."

"And?"

"Three of those calls were made by Torregrosa to Ortiz within a day before our informers were executed. The other two unaccounted calls were the most recent. They happened just a few days ago. They don't seem to correlate to anything. I haven't checked the phone logs for the last two days to see if Torregrosa made any more calls to Ortiz, with all the other things going on. But I suspect that he did."

"So this Torregrosa guy, he warned the drug cartels about some of the ongoing raids days before they happened, unlike our friend Ramirez, who called Ortiz from his own phone only an hour or so before a few of the busted raids," Pietrantoni said, trying to tie loose ends together.

"And Torregrosa was also behind the murders of our undercover agents."

The Governor continued to think. *Why would Ramirez only call to inform on raids where he did not participate, and Torregrosa call on the raids of which Ramirez had prior knowledge?* The answer came to him in a flash, as he compared the time of the advance warnings by the two callers.

"Of course!" he exclaimed, slapping his forehead. "I guess the lack of sleep is making me dull. Ramirez and Torregrosa are the same person!"

Maldonado beamed at him with satisfaction. "Torregrosa is the alter ego of Ramirez. Ramirez used the Torregrosa cell phone to warn ahead of time about the raids that he knew about."

"But sometimes, he found out about *other* raids, just as they were about to happen!" Pietrantoni concluded triumphantly.

"Apparently, Ramirez was careful enough not to carry the Torregrosa cell phone with him. He knew we suspected that there was a mole in our department, and it would have been too risky for him to get caught with a cell phone that supposedly belonged to another man. He probably had it hidden in his house—we're conducting a search of it right now—from where he would call at his leisure his contact, Carlos Ortiz, using the Torregrosa cell phone. He must have been paid some flat fee for every raid that he unveiled to his masters. So when he heard about other raids, other raids in which he had no participation, he was greedy enough to take a chance and call from work from his own cell phone. A risky move, certainly, but one that probably earned him a lot of money. He also must have gotten a bonus for each informer's name that he revealed, that son of a bitch," Maldonado added scornfully.

Pietrantoni regarded the police chief with newfound admiration. Then he frowned.

"That would explain Ramirez," he said. "But you still haven't explained to me how you got to Franceschini." *And he better have to have a good explanation when later that day he discussed this matter with the FBI in Washington,* he thought.

"Ah, Franceschini," Maldonado repeated with bitter regret. "That one came from left field. I had no idea. In fact, I had discussed the problem with him a couple of times."

"How had he reacted?"

"Mario listened quietly, as he does most of the time, and offered to help. Fortunately, I just told him that I would let him know." The Superintendent tiredly sat back further into his chair and folded his arms over his chest. "The Ortiz-Torregrosa connection had several loose ends. For one, the raids involved shipments into the island by different local drug lords. As a district attorney, you *know* that most of these drug lords hate each other and are in constant war with each other. And yet, Ramirez was making calls to a *single* phone number, and a local phone number at that. He wasn't calling the drug lords directly, he was calling a central contact here in Puerto Rico, one person that was in turn contacting the local drug lords, or even the big drug cartels in South America."

"But you didn't know who?" Pietrantoni said, more as a statement than as a question.

"No, I didn't," Maldonado admitted.

"You said just now that there were 'several loose ends'. What other loose ends were there?"

The Superintendent shrugged. "One wasn't a loose end *per se*. It was a gut feeling. But it was the most compelling reason I had to think that there was somebody else. It was this constant, nagging doubt that Ramirez had the intellectual capacity and the cold-blooded guts to establish such a risky venture. That he would participate in a scam, because of his greed, yes. But to be the driving force behind it, to be the brains of the operation, to come up with the system to warn the drug lords..." Maldonado hesitated, as if picturing Ramirez in his mind, and then shook his head with a hopeless gesture, "No way."

"From what little contact I have had with the man, I would have to agree," Pietrantoni observed. "Besides, his friendship, or whatever it is that he has with Rovira, shows that he's an ass."

"Also, there were other busted raids for which no calls had been made either by Ramirez or by Torregrosa to Carlos Ortiz. Granted, it could have meant that Ramirez—alias Torregrosa—had met personally with Ortiz to warn him about those other raids, which could account for the lack of telephone records, but that did not seem likely. To me, it meant that there had to be a second person—somebody else in the police force—that had access to confidential information and was passing it on to the drug dealers," Maldonado explained to the Governor. "And it had to be someone high up in the command structure. A few days ago, against my better instincts, I began to think that Montañez was involved after all, although his telephone records and tapped conversations showed that he was squeaky clean. But Montañez is not Ramirez. He would have been a lot more careful in his dealings with the underworld.

He also had the guts and the brains to set up the kind of operation we were dealing with. I was at a loss as to what exactly to do next."

He was right. If Montañez had joined the dark side—as Pietrantoni had called his antagonists while he was a district attorney, from unreliable politicians and bankers to any kind of criminals—then they were dealing with a formidable opponent. Maldonado paused to sip some orange juice while the Governor waited patiently.

"Then, the terrorists struck. I did not know if our mole—or moles— was in contact with them, but nevertheless I decided to test Ramirez further, to see if I got any reaction from him. I included him in some of our deliberations, and fed him some wrong information about our rescue attempt of the Grand Laguna. In a private conversation with him, I hinted that SWAT would attempt to reach the hotel from the Atlantic, not from the Condado Lagoon. I also gave him the wrong time: two hours later than the intended attack. Then I sent him away to meet with Rovira, before we got to discuss the real plans for the rescue. If Ramirez was in fact in conversations with the enemy—as I was convinced that he was—he would not pass up the opportunity to call his friends. It would give us the last piece of damning evidence, direct evidence that we could use to arrest him. At the same time, the false information that I gave him would draw the strongest forces of the terrorists to the north, to the pool area, away from where the real attack was intended to happen. He did not disappoint me."

Maldonado made a face of disgust. "As he was heading to meet with Rovira, he made the call, using his cell phone. We intercepted and recorded his message. I felt elated and vindicated. At last, I had recorded the son of a bitch."

"But...the terrorists still waited for SWAT in the Condado Lagoon, even after Ramirez conveyed to them the wrong information," the Governor protested.

Maldonado nodded sadly. "I thought I had all the bases covered. There were only three persons who knew the exact details of the Grand Laguna's real rescue attempt: Montañez, the SWAT captain, Camilo Gomez, who was leading the mission...and Franceschini."

"It could have been Montañez," Pietrantoni pointed out.

"Yes, it could have," Maldonado admitted. "Right after we discussed our plans for the rescue of the Grand Laguna Hotel, he went out of our temporary Command Center presumably to make preparations for the assault. So did Franceschini. Either of them could have made the call, after they left the Command Center, to warn the terrorists about the impending attack. And for a couple of hours after the debacle that followed, my suspicions leaned towards Montañez. But then, just as I was considering isolating Montañez from any further sensitive information about our rescue operations, Franceschini unwittingly gave himself away."

"But Franceschini…" Pietrantoni said in a doubtful tone. "He's always been such an upright, straight shooter…"

"I still cannot believe it myself. It was by accident that I uncovered his alter ego, and I still think it is impossible that it's him, that there has to be another explanation. But now, with the benefit of hindsight, it is easy to put two and two together… Only Franceschini had advance knowledge about all of the busted drug raids, through Ramirez when they were local, or personally when conducted jointly with the FBI. Ramirez only knew about some of them. It had to be Franceschini who warned the drug cartels about the raids that Ramirez knew nothing about. And you know what? I haven't had time to look yet, but I would bet you my head that all of the busted raids for which there was not a call from Ramirez or Torregrosa were joint FBI-state operations."

Of course, Pietrantoni thought as—like his Superintendent had said—he began to "put two and two together. "So you're saying…that Franceschini is Carlos Ortiz, the mastermind behind the whole scheme."

"Yes," Maldonado responded passionately. "He recruited Ramirez to get information on state-run drug raids where the feds would have little or no information. He set up the bogus telephone accounts, and he contacted the drug lords."

And that was why, when Ramirez had called "Carlos Ortiz" to give him the wrong details about the Grand Laguna rescue mission, the terrorists had ignored the information, the Governor finally realized. Franceschini had *known* what the correct plans were. He had disregarded the erroneous information and told the Macheteros where the real attack would take place.

"Apparently, Ramirez and Franceschini spoke several times, at least twice, during the last day's events. The first time Ramirez called Franceschini—or Carlos Ortiz—to transmit to him the wrong information I had given to him about the Grand Laguna rescue operation. Up to that moment, it could have been either Franceschini or Montañez who had revealed the real rescue plans to the terrorists. But then a second conversation took place, where Franceschini unwittingly showed his hand. It happened when Cacho was released. Apparently, after Ramirez saw on TV that Cacho was being flown by helicopter to the Grand Laguna Hotel, he called Franceschini—Carlos Ortiz—to find out what, if anything, he knew about Cacho's release," Maldonado explained.

"How do you know *that?*" Pietrantoni asked, with a tinge of skepticism. After all, Maldonado had told him that he had not seen the telephone logs of Ramirez or Torregrosa for the last couple of days. How could he know the content of the second conversation?

"Funny enough, it was Rovira Melendez who alerted me to that second conversation," Maldonado replied, smiling. "You see, shortly after Cacho was released, Rovira called me. He was outraged, accusing me of going behind his back and of releasing Cacho against his express orders, all of which by the way, was true."

Pietrantoni nodded, suppressing a grin as he pictured his irate Secretary of Justice discovering on TV that the Machetero leader had been released from the Bayamon Federal Penitentiary.

"But Rovira went further. He revealed to me the details of my negotiations with the terrorists, *something that only Franceschini and I knew about*. And he said that *Ramirez* had told him about the negotiations, even though Ramirez was not supposed to know anything about it!"

"So how had Ramirez found out?" Pietrantoni mused out loud, the implications of what Maldonado had told him setting his imagination into overdrive.

"He could have only found out from Franceschini," Maldonado confirmed, before the Governor could express what he was thinking. "Ramirez could only have found out from Franceschini, during one of their telephone conversations yesterday. There was no other way."

"That was careless of Franceschini," Pietrantoni observed.

"Sometimes, even the smartest people grow complacent when they begin to feel invincible. Franceschini had operated for years under our radar. I am convinced that even though he recruited Ramirez to obtain inside information from the Police Department, Ramirez didn't know that Franceschini was Carlos Ortiz. They probably never met face to face, but through an intermediary, or maybe under disguise."

Pietrantoni slowly shook his head in amazement. "But if he didn't know that Franceschini was Carlos Ortiz, why did Ramirez call his contact to find out why Cacho was being released?"

"Because Ramirez knew that Carlos Ortiz—whoever he was—had ties with the federal government. After all, some of the busted raids were joint state-federal operations about which Ramirez had no advance knowledge. He knew that the other source of information to the drug cartels had to originate from the federal side of the law and order establishment."

"Someone in the FBI or the DEA."

"Precisely," Maldonado confirmed. "Still, I gave Franceschini one last chance. After I spoke with Rovira, I called Franceschini and mentioned to him that Ramirez had somehow found out about our secret negotiations with the Macheteros. Had Franceschini been innocent, he could have admitted that he had inadvertently disclosed that information to

Ramirez in an official telephone conversation, but Franceschini claimed to be ignorant about everything. So I pretended not to suspect him, and asked Franceschini to search Ramirez's house and tap his phone, even though the state police had already been tapping all of Ramirez's phones for several months.."

Pietrantoni sighed. Difficult as it was to believe, Maldonado's reasoning was sound.

"To avoid any suspicions, Franceschini had Ramirez's cell phone tapped immediately, thinking that the good captain would not make any further calls through his personal phone. But Ramirez is not a very bright man. After he and Rovira found out that the Governor had escaped, Ramirez used his cell phone to contact Carlos Ortiz and warn him about it. However, Carlos Ortiz—Franceschini—never answered him, apparently too busy doing something else. So Ramirez, knowing he would get a bonus for the additional information that he transmitted, made one last, desperate move: he called the terrorists directly, to a number that Franceschini—Ortiz—had given to Ramirez to use as a measure of last resort. Unfortunately for Ramirez—and for Franceschini—his conversation was recorded by the FBI, and brought to the attention of Franceschini. Our FBI friend had no alternative but to report the conversation to me."

"Which led to Ramirez's arrest," Pietrantoni concluded. *And to Rovira Melendez's destitution as Interim Governor*, he noted to himself with grim satisfaction.

The Governor stood up and walked to the double doors that led to the balcony. He could see the dome of the Cathedral, where Archbishop Garrido was giving the mass. It was a beautiful January morning, with a completely blue sky and a gentle, cool winter breeze. San Juan was waking up. No one could have said that just a few hours before, that lovely, ancient city had been the object of so much terror.

Franceschini…How could he have betrayed his people that way?

"After that, the rest was trying to get more solid evidence," Maldonado continued. "I mean, I *knew* that Franceschini had called the Macheteros to tell them about the SWAT rescue plans, but there was no solid evidence to arrest him. The framework, the bone structure of our investigation, was there, but we needed to give it substance, to put some meat over the bones, so to say. So I decided to set some bait for our rat."

Pietrantoni looked at his Superintendent with a mixture of respect and admiration. *How could a man, whose world was crumbling about him with a full-fledged revolution, keep enough presence of mind to focus on the capture of an elusive infiltrator? It boggled the imagination.*

"I concocted a story. I called him, told him that Ramirez was claiming to be a pawn, a go-between of the real mole, and that he was trying to plea bargain in exchange for disclosing the identity of his contact. Franceschini tried to sound as natural as he could, but I could feel his intake of breath when I told him that. He asked me if Ramirez had told me who the mole was, and I said no, that Ramirez claimed to have never met his contact face to face, but that he had a good idea of who he was."

"Is that true? Did Ramirez say that to you?" Pietrantoni asked.

"No, Ramirez never told me anything. It was all a bluff on my part. But like I told you before, I was convinced, still am, that Ramirez never met 'Carlos Ortiz' face to face. From what Montañez told me later, Ramirez literally shit in his pants when he found out in the car that Franceschini was his unknown contact. Franceschini was too smart to disclose his identity to somebody like Ramirez. He would only contact him by telephone, and pay him by having him pick up the money at a designated place, or depositing the money in some foreign bank account out of this jurisdiction. We'll find out soon enough."

"What did Franceschini say when you told him that Ramirez wanted to confess?"

"He kept quiet. He was calculating his options. Knowing him, he probably came to the realization that at worst, he would have time to escape. It would not be very hard to start anew in some foreign country with all the money that he must have accumulated from the drug cartels. But in any event, I gave him an immediate way out. I told him that I suspected Montañez, and that I wanted Ramirez to be transferred to the FBI facilities, for his personal protection. Franceschini jumped at the suggestion."

The Superintendent combed back his hair with his right hand. Watching him, Pietrantoni felt a surge of affection for the bearlike man. His suit—which he had not changed or removed throughout the ordeal—looked more rumpled that the skin of an aged elephant; a few brown spots—spilled coffee probably—dotted his usually impeccable white shirt; and a gray stubble whitened his fleshy jaw. He had bitten his fingernails to the quick, one of them actually showing blood, and his eyes were bloodshot and yellow. Pietrantoni could only imagine the crushing pressure that Maldonado had been forced to endure. And yet, there he was, uncomplaining, making certain that his boss received all of the relevant information that he would need to cope with the day's coming events.

"I told Montañez about my plan. We placed a transmitter in Ramirez's bulletproof vest, to avoid the risk of losing him. The Untouchables were placed on alert, to follow and protect the prisoner and their beloved boss. And the rest is history. Franceschini could not resist the temptation to kill Ramirez. He quickly considered Montañez's insistence to accompany prisoner in the FBI car as an added blessing. He would kill both Ramirez and Montañez, and claim that Montañez had killed Ramirez. The men he brought with him were involved in the drug scams, and he knew he could rely on their testimony to back up his story. It was all perfect."

"Except that you were on to him," Pietrantoni interjected.

"Yes, except for that," Maldonado repeated dully, looking tired. There was no satisfaction in his words, only disappointment. "We caught him red-handed."

Pietrantoni quietly mulled over the information. *Franceschini, who would have thought it.* "Why would he do it?" he mused to himself. "He seemed such a dedicated, effective lawman."

"And he was," Maldonado stated. "He fought crime with admirable zeal and efficiency...except when he was paid not to do so."

"Have you talked to him?"

"No, not yet. I intend to, when I finish this meeting."

"It's a shame. I liked him. I liked him a lot. I worked with him when I was district attorney."

"He was my friend," Maldonado retorted, unable to conceal his bitterness any more. "He kept me fooled all of this time. I should have seen through his façade a long time ago."

"How *could* you?" the Governor objected in a gentle tone. He walked to the Superintendent and placed a hand on his shoulder. "Yesterday, Puerto Rico went through the greatest crisis it has faced in its modern history. Had it not been for your steady leadership, I don't think we would have weathered it. You have nothing to apologize for, my friend. And if anybody dares to say otherwise, they will have to deal with me."

A faint smile appeared on Maldonado's lips. "With all due respect, sir," he said, "you'll get a lot of grief if you keep me as the Superintendent."

"Will I?" Pietrantoni responded with a hint of amused impatience. "Does the criticism matter to you?"

"No, sir," Maldonado answered.

"Then why should it matter to me?"

They had parted ways a short time later, just a few minutes before the Archbishop had returned from mass. As promised, Pietrantoni had given the priest a shortened version of Maldonado's report, but had been interrupted several times by pointed questions from his host.

"He's right about the grief you're going to get for keeping him as Superintendent," the Archbishop had said at the end of the story, playing devil's advocate. "Maybe you should let somebody else take over the Superintendent's position. With all the other matters that you have on your plate, this is going to be a distraction."

Pietrantoni had regarded Garrido with a flash of anger. "There is no person more qualified to be at the helm of the Police Department than Roberto Maldonado. I'll be damned if I give him up. Besides, in the up-coming political fight, I will need every friend I can get."

The Archbishop had smiled. "You can count on my support," he had said with affection. "But speaking of damnation. I think you said you wanted to confess something to me before I went to mass."

The Governor raised an eyebrow, looking flustered. Garrido's question had caught him off balance.

"I may have spoken too hastily. It's not a true confession, in the strict sense of the word, but...I guess it is a sort of confession. I just wanted to run something by someone I can trust...before I take the plunge, so to say."

The Archbishop regarded him with interest and sympathy. "I thank you for deeming me trustworthy enough to take me into your confidence. But I think I may have an idea of what you're going to say."

Pietrantoni's face reddened. "Am I so transparent?" he inquired contritely.

"I think it's about time," the Archbishop said cryptically, staring at the floor, and then raising his eyes to meet those of the Governor. "We're talking about Nereida, aren't we?"

Pietrantoni nodded.

"You're in love with her," Garrido stated.

"I have loved her for a long time," Pietrantoni confessed quietly. "But...I've never..."

"Told her?"

"More than that. I've never even given her a hint about how I feel. I've felt...I've been afraid that if I express my feelings openly to her, my enemies will claim that all of the rumors that have circulated since I was Governor—even before that, since the campaign, about an affair be-tween us—were true. That they will mock and humiliate her. That they'll hurt her and Francisco...But last night, things got pretty dicey. I thought we were going to die. And one of the thoughts that kept scaring me out of my wits all night long was the possibility that she would never know how much I love her. I nearly told her as much last night."

The Archbishop opened his hands and shrugged. "Seems to me that the answer is fairly obvious, don't you think?"

Pietrantoni was forced to smile despite his embarrassment. "But—"

"Look," Garrido interrupted. "I can't tell you what to do. However, it seems to me that there will always be rumors, especially by those who wish to harm you through her. Like you said, there are rumors *now* about an ongoing affair. Nereida is a wonderful woman. She's taken care of Francisco for what now, three years?"

"Almost four years," the Governor responded.

"Almost four. Do you think that Nereida is not aware of the rumors that have dogged you during that time? She is a smart woman. She is also very strong. She can take it. She *has* taken it, and she hasn't quit. From the standpoint of the Church, there is no canonical law forbidding the leader of a country from marrying his son's governess," the Archbishop said with a straight face, then cracked a warm smile. "Ana Gloria was a wonderful woman, Roberto. But she's been dead for five years. For the past...four years, Nereida has stepped into the void that Ana Gloria left behind her. She has raised Francisco as her son. If you love her, if you truly love her, there's nothing wrong with proposing to her. And if anybody has any problem with that, well, that's his or her problem. Don't let any more time slip by."

Pietrantoni had directed a nervous glance at his friend. "I wouldn't know how to broach the subject. I haven't talked romantically to a woman for years...I'd be tongue-tied."

Garrido chortled. "Are you asking me, *a priest*, for advice on how to propose? You're the Governor of Puerto Rico, for Christ's sake! I'm sure if you sit down with her, and tell her more or less what you've said to me...Maybe a little more romantically, it will be fine."

"Once I propose to her, I will place her in the limelight. She will become the center of attention of every gossip organization in the island. It may all scare her away," Pietrantoni protested. His hands were sweating.

"I don't think there's much risk of that happening," the Archbishop opined. "I have seen how she looks at you. I think she is head over heels in love with you, and that she won't mind the attention she gets from the press. She's a pretty strong woman, don't you think? Anyway, that's my personal opinion, and I think I'm a pretty shrewd observer. There was a time when I dated girls, you know."

"You, Father?" Pietrantoni said in mock shock.

Garrido ignored him. "If you think she may quit if you propose to her, preface your conversation with her by telling her that if she prefers to keep her relationship with you as it is right now, you won't mention it again."

Pietrantoni considered his friend's suggestion in silence. *It made sense. It would cause a stir, but so what? Most of what he did or say created a stir. It came as part of the job.*

"All right," he had told the Archbishop. "I'll talk to her after today's speech to the Legislature."

"And you'll probably be more nervous than during your speech to the Legislature," Garrido had said in a pleased tone. "I will pray for you."

A gentle knock on the Speaker's door shook the Governor out of his reverie. Arizmendi poked his head in.

"Nothing else ready?"

Pietrantoni shook his head.

"Writer's block, eh? I figured as much when I saw the Speaker and Rovira walk into the office. So you're winging it, huh?"

"I guess so," the Governor answered sheepishly.

Arizmendi waved a hand dismissively. "I wouldn't worry about it. You'll do fine. Besides, they'll give you a standing ovation for just showing up."

Double A was right. He wasn't worried. It was the second speech, the one to Nereida, that terrified him.

CHAPTER LXXXII

The "Hemicycle"—the name given to the wide balcony that encompassed the sides of chamber used as the House of Representatives, was packed to capacity, its upper rows filled with television and video cameras from news agencies from all over the world. Lucas watched several reporters speaking softly into hand-held microphones, standing with their backs turned to the great hall. Further below, on the green-carpeted, main floor, rows of extra seats had been arranged behind the desks of the representatives in order to accommodate the visiting senators, Cabinet members, other notable bureaucrats of the Administration, consuls, and federal officials attending the event.

A waist-high, polished-wood barrier, open in its center, divided the area generally reserved for the House representatives from an elevated, mahogany platform where the assistants to the Speaker usually sat. As in the rest of the main floor, several chairs, occupied by solemn-looking officials, had been added to accommodate some of the more distinguished visiting guests.

Higher still, at the head of the chamber, sat the Speaker of the House. A large, round emblem—Puerto Rico's official coat of arms—floated over her head on a white marble background behind her, showing a lamb resting on a book over a green background, the words *"Joannes est nomen ejus"*—"John is his name"—appearing in white letters below it. Symbols representing the kingdoms of Castile and Aragon—the kingdoms of King Ferdinand and Queen Isabella—and the Cross of Jerusalem, representing St. John the Baptist, decorated the outer rim of the emblem. Two large flags, one of the United States and the other of Puerto Rico, hung from the walls to the Speaker's right and left sides.

From her dais, the Speaker was gazing distractedly at the crowd below, leaning on her desk with the same ponderous majesty of a beached walrus. Another seat had been placed next to hers, to accommodate her younger, leaner counterpart, President of the Senate Carlos Cortez. A darling of the press and a staunch—at least outwardly—supporter of the Governor, Cortez seemed nervous, moving his head from side to side, examining the faces of the waiting audience, making occasional comments to the Speaker beside him. He looked like a startled seagull, next to Marisel's portly sea mammal.

Lucas had watched several addresses on television before, but he had never been aware of the extended, convoluted protocol that preceded the Governor's actual appearance. It included the taking of the quorum of the members of the House and the Senate, the official welcoming of the mayor of San Juan—another Rovira stalwart—and of the Resident Commissioner of Puerto Rico in Washington, the greeting of former Governors of Puerto Rico, the selection of a joint committee of fourteen members of the two chambers to seek and escort into the House the visiting Supreme Court Justices, and the selection of yet another committee of fourteen to fetch the Governor of Puerto Rico.

During the preliminary ceremony, Lucas saw Arizmendi slip unobtrusively from a side door to one of the empty chairs in the left front corner of the room. Lucas suspected that the Secretary of State could have made an appearance similar to that of the mayor of San Juan, but that he opted for the simpler, more anonymous entrance. Not so Rovira Melendez, who unlike other Cabinet members made a grand entrance to the enthusiastic applause of many of those present, and was introduced by the Speaker as the "Secretary of Justice *and* former Interim Governor of Puerto Rico".

Finally, after all of the protocol had been exhausted, it was the Governor's turn. Even before the Speaker could speak, an excited buzz spread through the lower floor, as some of the crowd saw him approach through the back entrance. The Speaker struck her gavel several times to still the noise, and then, in a tone more apt for a political rally, began to introduce the new arrival. However, her last words were drowned in a thunderous ovation, as everyone in the chamber stood up to applaud and cheer.

Pietrantoni slowly made his way down the central aisle of the hall, shaking as many of the multitude of hands that extended in his direction as he could, pausing to exchange a few words with some of his most prominent supporters, followed by the committee of representatives and senators that had come to escort him from the Speaker's office. Even the members of the opposition parties, *populares* and *independentistas* alike, at best lukewarm participants in events such as those, had joined enthusiastically in the spontaneous celebration, which only grew in intensity as he approached the main stage.

From where he sat, Lucas had initially not been able to see Governor Pietrantoni walk into the room. The Governor had assigned to Lucas and his family the best places in the House, the first row of the second floor, facing the platform where the Speaker and the President of the Senate sat. Alfredo had stood up as soon as the clapping began and tried to lean over the railing, prompting a scream of alarm from his mother and a sharp tug by the collar from his dad. But soon, Pietrantoni's tall, gaunt figure had become visible, to the delight not just of Alfredo but of everyone else in the balcony.

Lucas smiled, caught by the excitement that swept over the waiting public like a tidal wave. The man deserved the applause. A lesser politician would have taken the week off after the prior day's terrifying ordeal, taking stock of what had happened, carefully calculating what he would say next to his constituents. Pietrantoni had, if anything, intensified his work, somehow managing to labor without sleep throughout the day to reassure his country about the continuity of its government.

As he walked down the green-carpeted aisle, he seemed to draw strength from his people's passionate support, almost engulfed by the humanity that surrounded him. At that moment, he was by far the most admired and beloved figure in the island, and had become an unstoppable force in local politics. He could do—or even *un*do—as he wanted: a dangerous power in the hands of any politician, an inner voice warned Lucas. But the Governor was not just *any* politician. *Pietrantoni will not betray us*, he assured himself uneasily. *Pietrantoni will not betray us.*

As the Governor reached the front stage, he stopped briefly to say a few inaudible words to the Chief Justice of the Supreme Court, who had been one of his professors in law school, and then walked to the corner where Arizmendi sat and whispered something in his ear. Double A laughed and nodded enthusiastically. Pietrantoni then climbed to the platform where the Speaker and the President of the Senate stood, kissing the Speaker on the cheek and shaking the Senate President's hand. Afterwards, he walked down a couple of steps to a podium surrounded in the front and on each side by the transparent glass sheets of a teleprompter and decorated by a smaller emblem depicting the outline of La Fortaleza and bearing the words "The Governor of Puerto Rico".

There he waited for the applause to subside, but instead it increased. Pietrantoni acknowledged it for a moment, but then he raised his hands for the crowd to quiet down. However, his efforts were ignored. The applause continued unabated as the public stayed on its feet, joined by shouts, cheers, and shrill whistles. The Governor muttered the words "Thank you" over the microphone about a dozen different times to no effect.

From his seat, Lucas watched with fascination the face of the Speaker. She was clapping as well, but her expression, even though masked by a strained smile, reflected guarded concern...or was it fear? It was the same expression he had noticed on her when they had met the Governor in the Speaker's office. It troubled him. It made him wonder what she was truly thinking. His eyes wandered impulsively to where he had seen Rovira Melendez sit, but he could barely make him out from the rest of the standing crowd, his back turned towards him. His smile, during the meeting in the Speaker's office, had also been cold and artificial.

As the ovation extended, the Speaker began to grow restless. Lucas saw her bark something to the President of the Senate, and then grab hold of a large—apparently like everything else that she owned—wooden gavel. She rapped sharply on her desk, calling to order, but when the audience failed to respond, began striking the sound block with increased violence. Gradually, the chamber fell silent.

"I am aware of your enthusiasm for our Governor," she said coolly, "but you must allow him to speak." She turned her head towards Pietrantoni, and graced him with a bullfrog smile. "You may proceed, Mr. Governor."

"Thank you, Madame Speaker," Pietrantoni said in an equally courteous tone. He paused, taking a deep breath and directing his attention to the packed audience in front of him.

"Madame Speaker, Mr. President of the Senate, Mr. Resident Commissioner, Honorable Justices of the Supreme Court, members of the House and Senate, friends and fellow citizens." Pietrantoni paused briefly, staring contemplatively at the edge of his podium, and taking a deep breath before he continued. "Very early yesterday morning, a large group of highly motivated, well-organized and very well armed individuals conducted a concerted attack on Old San Juan and Puerta de Tierra. Using high-powered explosives, they blew up the four bridges connecting the island of San Juan to the rest of Puerto Rico. In a thoroughly calculated move, they ambushed our police force in Puerta de Tierra and burned down the station, just a few blocks from where now stand. And even though the policemen and policewomen who were there fought back bravely, they were no match for the heavy caliber machine guns and the high-powered sniper rifles that fired upon them. More than a dozen of our finest men and women lost their lives, and many others were severely wounded. Several police cars were ambushed in the streets and their occupants killed, wounded or captured."

The crowd waited in absolute silence while the Governor cleared his throat. He was holding on to the lectern with both hands, and for a brief second the exhaustion of the last day seemed to overwhelm him. But then he straightened his body, and continued to speak.

"The San Juan Yacht Club, a familiar landmark in our city for more than eighty years, did not survive the explosion of the bridges, and succumbed to the flames. Armed bands of roving men captured the Grand Laguna Hotel, and the cruise ship *Mardi Gras,* terrorizing hundreds—thousands—of innocent tourists and employees, threatening to throw a hostage off the roof of the hotel every hour until we acceded to all of their demands. You all witnessed on television what happened when our SWAT team tried to stop the executions. Our men were outmatched, outgunned, and massacred in the Condado Lagoon. One of our rescue helicopters was shot down from the sky by a surface-to-air missile, a military, state-of-the-art weapon that even many countries find difficult to come by, and yet these people had them. And as you will learn in the coming days, the terrorists were aided by persons both entrenched *within* our own security forces, as well as by armed professionals from other countries."

There was a sharp, audible intake of breath, followed by the buzz of hushed whispers. The Speaker banged her gavel on her desk, and urged the people to quiet down.

Lucas searched for Arizmendi, who sat at the end of the curved first row and whose face he could partially discern. He was stroking his chin in deep thought, apparently wondering where the Governor was going with his speech. It was evident that he did not approve of the speech's somber beginning. Lucas could imagine Double A lecturing the Governor about it. *"The people know about the disasters we have gone through! Why remind them of their misery? And why bring up the matter of traitors within our own ranks? That bombshell will distract your public from the rest of your message! Where are you going with this?"*

And yet, there was no denying that the audience was hanging onto every word that the Governor uttered despite his list of bad news.

"As you know, the terrorists also captured La Fortaleza. They killed six of the bodyguards and police protecting the compound, most of them..." he paused slightly, "my personal friends. They terrorized my staff and my family, and threatened to harm them unless I publicly agreed to their demands... But what did the these people want?"

Pietrantoni lowered his voice, forcing everybody to listen more closely. He had the full attention of his audience. Lucas noticed that a few of the persons sitting close to him literally hung from the edge of their seats.

"Shortly after I was captured, I had the most interesting conversation with a gentleman called Aristides Andrade. For those of you who don't recognize his name, he also went by the nickname of 'El Alacran'."

Another murmur of surprise welled up from the crowd. Pietrantoni waited for it to die down.

"El Alacran had many interesting things to say to me," he remarked. "He informed me that the revolutionaries had established a new government, the Socialist Republic of Puerto Rico, and that our government 'was no more'. When I told him that the majority of our people would not recognize his so called 'socialist republic', he replied that the 'majority of the people' had *nothing* to do with it, that the majority of the people would not know what was good for them if...what were his exact words? Oh, yes! They would not know what was good for them 'if goodness bit them in the ass'."

Lucas smiled, as he watched the Speaker turn her head and direct a look of disapproval at the Governor for his use of the vulgar expression. Many in the audience laughed. A few booed.

"El Alacran told me that *the people in power* decided who the real majority was, and that *they*—his group—were in power, so *they* would decide what the real majority wanted."

More boos, angry boos, directed at El Alacran's statement, erupted from the crowd. Pietrantoni nodded.

"He meant it," Pietrantoni attested somberly when the catcalls had subsided. "He handed to me a scrap of paper where I was to resign as Governor of Puerto Rico, condemn the 'colonialist oppression' of the United States, and ask the rest of the world to support *his* newly constituted government. He gave me a couple of hours to sign the document, threatening to harm my son if I refused to do so. It was evident that he meant every word that he said."

The chamber had grown silent again. Every eye was on the Governor, wondering what he would say next. But instead of continuing his story, he switched to an entirely different subject.

"On March 3, 1952, the people of Puerto Rico overwhelmingly approved our present Constitution. In its Preamble, it expressly established that 'The democratic system is *fundamental* to the life of the Puerto Rican community'; that 'We understand that the democratic system of government is one in which *the will of the people is the source of public power, the political order is subordinate to the rights of man, and the free participation of the citizen in collective decisions is assured*'."

Pietrantoni looked around him, both of his hands placed flat on the surface of the podium. No one dared to make any noise.

"It took our country centuries to gain these fundamental rights. Those who were alive before the Constitution was ratified lived and fought not only to maintain these rights, but to give them real meaning. Eighty to ninety percent of all of qualified voters have, time after time, exercised their right to vote in *each* of our elections, a record equaled by no other democracy in the world! Those generations that followed in the footsteps of the authors of our Constitution have grown within these same traditions. Yes, we have disagreed! Yes, we have argued! Sometimes bitterly. Sometimes intolerantly, irrationally, or with great anger. But we have never, *never* accepted that the will of our people is to be imposed or dictated by a select few."

A wild cheer followed his words as the audience rose to its feet. The Speaker wiped away tears of emotion from her cheeks with her pudgy fingers, and then accepted gratefully a handkerchief handed to her by the President of the Senate. After a minute, Pietrantoni began to speak again, and the crowd quickly settled down.

"I suspect that if El Alacran had returned a few hours later with my son and threatened to hurt or kill him, I probably would have signed that piece of paper. But it would have been meaningless, not worth the value of the scrap of paper that he wanted me to sign, and I think that he knew it. *Because I can't give your sovereignty away! Only you can do that!*" There was more applause, but Pietrantoni kept talking. "What El Alacran and his friends couldn't understand, what they will *never* understand, is that...they may be *temporarily* successful in stifling, by terror and the force of arms, our people's right to direct its own destiny, but in the end they will not prevail. *We are Puerto Ricans!*" he shouted as the applause increased. "*We are a democratic people, born and raised under a democratic government, entitled to express our will by means of that most precious of all rights, the right to vote, and we will never tolerate that any self-appointed despot, no matter how enlightened he may claim to be, steals that right from us!*"

Pietrantoni was forced to pause, since the ovation drowned his last words. Lucas took a sideways glance at his godson, and was pleased to see him standing next to his mother, two of his fingers between his lips, whistling at the Governor. Pietrantoni could not have given Alfredo a greater gift than inviting him to the State of the Island address. Wiser and smarter beyond his years—and beyond those of many of the adults standing around him—the kid had a unique sense of history, and would know that he was witnessing history that day. It was a day that he would never forget, one that Lucas suspected would steer Alfredo, in his future years, into the political arena.

"Fortunately for me," Pietrantoni continued when the crowd returned to its seats, "I was never forced to choose between signing El Alacran's document or seeing my son hurt. Before that could happen, I was rescued by the bravest man I've ever known." He directed a mischievous smile at Lucas, who shook his head in extreme embarrassment, anticipating what the Governor was about to say. Lucas felt Jeannie press his hand.

"This man—you'll be hearing a lot more about him in the coming days—penetrated La Fortaleza, single handedly rescued me from my armed captors, and then located and also rescued my staff and my son. After that, with the heroic help of two of my bodyguards and my fearless Secretary of State," there were some sympathetic chuckles as Pietrantoni motioned with his hand towards Arizmendi, "he managed to lead us out of La Fortaleza and out of harm. I am convinced that I would not be alive today, and possibly many others from my staff, had it not been for him." Pietrantoni turned his head towards the Speaker and the President of the Senate. "I am recommending that that man be awarded Puerto Rico's Medal of Valor for his extraordinary courage." The Speaker and the Senate President both nodded energetically.

Several people in the audience began to look up at the hemicycle, trying to locate the man to whom the Governor was referring. Lucas braced himself for what was about to happen.

"That man is here with us today. I ask you to give a big round of applause to him, the man I am honored to call my friend, Lucas Alfaro."

The hall exploded in a thunderous ovation, which increased into a deafening roar as Lucas slowly stood up. Most of the crowd had no idea of who he was, but he was young and fairly handsome, and looked modestly shy, so he instantly became a favorite of the public. He heard Vanessa shouting at the top of her lungs, and saw that she, Jeannie, and even Michael were crying. Alfredo slid through the aisle and embraced him by the waist. Below, the Governor applauded and laughed, enjoying his friend's apparent discomfiture. Lucas waved briefly, and began to sit down, but Jeannie held him up by his elbow.

"No," she said to him. "You *earned* this moment!" And then she added, "And so did I!" forcing him to smile.

The applause continued for several minutes, until Lucas finally managed to sit down.

"That boy...that boy you saw hugging Lucas," the Governor began to say over the noise of the sitting crowd, "bears watching in the future. His name is Alfredo, my son's best friend, and he was with us last night. They don't come any braver or smarter than him. He also deserves an applause."

Again the hall erupted into cheers, then laughter, as the boy happily waved at everyone.

"There were many, many other heroes yesterday, and some of their stories are just starting to surface. Of Captain Camilo Gomez, and Sergeant Abraham Cordero, of SWAT. Captain Gomez was knocked out of his raft, unconscious, as he tried to lead the rescue on the Grand Laguna Hotel, and was saved from drowning by Sergeant Cordero. They both hid behind the outside walls of Fort San Geronimo until nightfall, and then helped capture the ballroom in the hotel where the terrorists held the hostages. When the Macheteros counterattacked them with heavy machine guns and superior numbers, Gomez and Cordero led the defense that managed to hold off the terrorists until the Navy SEALs arrived. In that action, Cordero made the ultimate sacrifice for his trapped brothers, almost single-handedly stopping one of the attacks, but losing his life in the process."

Pietrantoni shot another glance at Lucas.

"And as if one member of the family wasn't heroic enough, Michelle Alfaro, Lucas' sister—you may know her as a member of the WKPA news team and may have seen her masterful live newscast from the hotel last night—accompanied by two strangers she met on the street after yesterday's revolt started, managed to infiltrate the Grand Laguna Hotel, communicate with Superintendent Maldonado, and help coordinate the rescue of the hostages. One of her companions was seriously wounded during the rescue, and is presently fighting for his life in the Presbyterian Hospital. Our prayers are with him," he said somberly.

"And like them, there were many others. Hotel guests who volunteered to fight against the terrorists while help arrived; medical personnel, guests from the hotel, who attended the wounded and even shielded them when the fighting moved into the ballroom; Florida Senator Mark Sampson, who as you already know from today's news report, managed to escape from the ballroom and was on his way to get help for the other hostages. I am told of a man, one of the passengers in the *Mardi Gras,* who at great peril to his life secured a satellite phone, contacted the FBI, and supplied information that proved essential in the SEALs' rescue of the other passengers trapped there. He too was severely wounded, and is presently recovering from his wounds."

Pietrantoni leaned forward, and it seemed to Lucas, directly fixed his gaze on Rovira Melendez, who was sitting in the first row of the lower floor. "We were particularly fortunate to have been guided by the steady hand of our Police Superintendent, Roberto Maldonado."

The mention of the police chief drew solid applause, to which the Governor joined, after urging Maldonado with his hand, who was sitting about ten seats to Lucas' left, to stand up. The Superintendent waved perfunctorily at the public for a few seconds and then returned to his seat.

"The pressure that Maldonado had to withstand would have cracked the will of many strong men, but our police chief is made of a different stuff. Not only was he able to restore order in San Juan, but because of his incredible initiative and drive, he actually discovered and arrested the persons inside our security forces who were feeding information to the terrorists."

Several heads turned towards the Superintendent with surprise, while the hall became filled with whispers. The Speaker placed a vertical finger across her lips, and the noise quickly quieted down.

"And then, of course, there was the Navy SEALs. Yesterday morning, those men were in Virginia. They had no idea that by late afternoon they would be *here,* risking their lives in so many ways to save so many of our people and of the people who were visiting us. But that is the nature of their job. To stand in the way of those who would do us harm and stop them dead in their tracks...And *that's* exactly what they did."

Lucas saw the Speaker nodding solemnly behind the Governor while a new round of solid applause and cheers made him pause.

"In less than a day, this elite fighting unit devised three separate, highly complex rescue plans and carried them through without a hitch. One of their officers, Chief Petty Officer Paul Pinet, was killed by a sniper on the *Mardi Gras* after the fighting had stopped and he was helping one of the wounded terrorists. His ultimate sacrifice and heroism will never be forgotten." Pietrantoni stopped briefly, giving the fallen SEAL a moment of silence.

"I had the opportunity to meet with some of them this morning," he continued. "They had formed a ring of steel around the Archbishop of San Juan's house, where I, my family, and my staff found refuge after escaping from La Fortaleza." The fleeting reference to his escape made several people in the audience lean forward with interest. It was a story of which only scant details had been made public. "I went downstairs to meet them and personally thank them. They were, for the most part, young kids, superbly trained soldiers—make no mistake about it—but still, young kids. When I thanked them, they almost seemed embarrassed by it, as if I was complimenting them for conducting a normal chore that they had been expected to do. Some seemed more excited about visiting Puerto Rico than about what had happened the night before, and asked me about the beaches and the sights in the island."

There was some muted laughter in the audience.

"They have already left. They have done their job and returned to Virginia, where they will wait for the next crisis to arise, and put their lives on the line again. To these brave, anonymous men, Puerto Rico owes a personal debt of gratitude."

Another strong applause followed the Governor's words. Once again he stared briefly at Lucas, but this time he remained serious.

"You know, nowadays, we use the word 'hero' so much that it has lost part of its original luster. It has almost become a commonplace expression," he said as the crowd quieted down. "We talk about the 'hero of the game', of 'super or mythological heroes', of the 'hero of the story'. Usually, these heroes are endowed with super powers or great physical abilities. And we lose sight of what a *real* hero is. Yesterday, we were reminded of what true heroes are..." The hall burst into spontaneous applause, but the Governor continued to talk over the noise. "Not su-perhuman figures with extraordinary strength or other abilities, but ordinary men and women who were willing to risk their lives to keep other people from harm and to defend our freedom. They did it not be-cause they possessed any uncommon strengths or powers, but because they thought it was the *right* thing to do. *That* is true heroism, and yes-terday, it was evident everywhere."

Again, Pietrantoni waited for the ovation to die down before he con-tinued.

"We must not fool ourselves. We have suffered great and terrible los-es. Parts of the infrastructure of the island of San Juan have been seriously damaged or destroyed. It will be months, if not years before our bridges are permanently repaired, our police facilities rebuilt, the San Juan Yacht Club and La Fortaleza restored, and the countless acts of loot-ing and wanton destruction, of stores, hotels, vehicles, and property made whole again. Some loses, of course, are irreparable. There is no way to make up for those who died, except to assure their families, wives, children and friends that they are not alone, and that we will nev-er forget and forever honor their loved ones' ultimate sacrifice."

Pietrantoni looked at the people assembled before him. Again, for a moment, he seemed very tired, leaning against the podium. But then he gathered his strength and stood up straight.

"Our national psyche has been bloodied and shaken, as many wonder why this happened. In the coming months we will be trying to find out who was behind this, and take the necessary measures to make certain that something like this never happens again. We will also not rest until every-one who had something to do with the harming of any of our people and our visitors is brought to justice. We already know that Adalberto Cacho, released from jail as a result of one of the terrorists' demands, was killed last night, apparently by some of his own allies. Also, the Macheteros' se-cond in command, known as El Alacran, who apparently was one of the main movers in yesterday's events, also died in last night's fighting."

Lucas noticed with approval that Pietrantoni did not mention how the Machetero leader had met his end. Any lesser politician, like Rovira Melendez, would have given a lot more details about the terrorist's grisly end, in order to gain more points from his audience.

"In total, about three dozen terrorists were killed during yesterday's revolt, and scores more were captured. But this was a well-planned, ex-tensive operation. I am certain that there a still a few ringleaders out there who managed to hide or escape. To them I make this promise: there is nowhere where you can hide. Wherever you are, wherever you hide or crawl under, we *will* find you."

The crowd reacted emotionally, standing on their feet and applauding and cheering wildly. Pietrantoni did not react, his expression apparently lost in deep thought. Even when his audience quieted down, he maintained silence for several seconds.

"Yesterday..." he began to say in a hoarse whisper, and then he paused. "There is no way to logically explain what happened yesterday. Our citizens were subjected to a cruel, unprovoked, and irrational attack by a dangerous bunch of... of armed criminals bent on destroying our democratic institutions. Innocent people were threatened at gunpoint, our infrastructure heavily damaged, our police force overwhelmed and decimated. And yet, throughout this terrible ordeal, our people never gave up. For one moment, we all stood together—*populares, statehooders, independentistas*—it did not matter. We fought back, shoulder-to-shoulder, often hand-to-hand, to preserve our freedom and the right to direct our own destiny."

Pietrantoni smiled sadly.

"Believe me, I am under no illusion that from this moment hence we will live in eternal bliss and harmony. I may be an optimist and a dreamer...heck, some people accuse me of being an unrealistic fool. But it would be too much, even from an unrealistic fool like me, to expect that a new era of fraternal cooperation will suddenly become the new guiding light in our political system. The sun will continue to rise on the east and set in the west. We are Puerto Ricans, after all, and as such, we will harbor a multitude of opinions about any given subject, and never be afraid to voice them and argue passionately about them. And that is as it should be. It keeps our democracy alive—noisy at times, and cumbersome, and sometimes downright exasperating—but *alive*!"

The Governor grasped the edge of the podium with both of his hands and he leaned forward, his normally pleasant expression hardening with defiance, his body growing taut with anger. "But *we'll be damned* if anybody ever attempts to dictate to us what we can think or do!"

Pietrantoni tried to go on, but his words were drowned by the spontaneous roar of approval from the crowd, and he was forced to stop. It was nearly three minutes before he could speak again.

"And so, my fellow citizens, I am happy to announce that the state of our island is, after all, fine. That today we stand as strong, as united, and as proud as we have ever been, facing the future with cautious but unbridled optimism, boundless hope, and unquestioned courage, and placing, as our forebears have always done since the first day that they stepped onto our shores, our trust in Providence. Thank you, and may God bless Puerto Rico."

The crowd rose to its feet, flooding the hall with a deafening ovation. Lucas felt the floor of the hemicycle shake from the intensity of the noise. He sensed the glare of floodlights behind him, and when he turned, saw that several reporters on the upper rows of the floor were standing in front of their network cameras, shouting into their microphones in order to be heard. Still other cameras followed the figure of the tall, lanky Governor, as he slowly tried to make his way through a solid mass of admirers.

There, Lucas thought, *walked the bravest man he had ever met.* Lucas' life and death struggle had ended the night before. The Governor's, he suspected, was just beginning.

Correcaminos walked out of the locker room and climbed into the mangy boxing ring. He was wearing a faded, sleeveless T-shirt that read: "WKPA TV, 2010 5K Marathon", and shiny, red shorts with a vertical white stripe. It was one of his least fashionable apparels, looking even shoddier when contrasted with his heavily pomaded, neatly coiffed hair. He greeted the referee—a short, stout man in his sixties who owned the gym and who placed a protective mouthpiece in Correcaminos' mouth—with the familiarity that only years of intimate acquaintance could breed, and then nodded at his opponent, who stood at the ring's opposite diagonal corner.

If the newscaster was intimidated by the burly policeman's size—the man looked even bigger than when Correcaminos had challenged him to a fight in the San Geronimo Plaza, a week before—he showed no outward signs of concern. On the contrary, it was the policeman who seemed ill at ease, partially leaning on the ropes, and casting nervous glances around the gym.

When the bell rang, Correcaminos moved in swiftly and landed several body blows before his surprised opponent could react. The policeman responded with two heavy haymakers that missed their mark, as the sportscaster partially retreated and then countered with a vicious, overhead punch that made the larger man stagger. Correcaminos continued to bounce on the balls of his feet, sizing up his opponent, readying for his next foray.

Stunned, the policeman stared at short sportscaster with newfound respect. "You can fight!" he said in a surprised tone.

Correcaminos shrugged, still moving. "Honestly, I'd rather have a beer," he mumbled through his mouthpiece.

The big policeman hesitated, and then laughed. He raised his two gloves, bumping them lightly against Correcaminos'. "My treat, little man," he said, placing an arm over the newscaster's shoulders.

EPILOGUE

CHAPTER I

El Joyero de San Juan hummed with the excited chatter of shoppers—dozens of them—as they examined the store's glass cases, asked the harried store attendants about the price of some of the exhibited items, or simply stopped to take photographs of the establishment, particularly of the several blown up newspaper and magazine covers that had been recently hung on the newly painted walls of the commercial establishment.

Coming up from the cellar, Lucas became aware of the crowd and groaned inwardly. As of late, the increasingly more numerous clientele had become more of a curse than a blessing. Ever since that fateful date when Governor Pietrantoni had singled him out from among the attending public in the House of Representatives, a gaggle of friends, distant family, and newly-found fans had begun to trickle into the store in an ever-growing volume until, during the past few weeks, the situation had become nearly unmanageable.

Lucas had become the main center of attention. His unexpected fame had proven a boon to the cash-strapped *El Joyero*. Scores of people—both locals and tourists—would flock to the store to catch a glimpse of the hero. Women normally outnumbered men on a three-to-one ratio, with a majority of them being women over forty, and many would openly fawn over him, trying to catch his eye. He had been afraid that Jennie would disapprove, but she had actually found it amusing, and would sometimes visit the store in her spare time just to enjoy his embarrassment.

Many of the older, long-standing clients had also rediscovered *El Joyero,* usually buying some of the higher priced items in its inventory. It seemed almost as if it had become fashionable to sport a piece of jewelry from *El Joyero de San Juan,* something to show or boast about in social gatherings.

Some people, it seemed to Lucas, appeared to have adopted the store as a gathering place, showing up regularly at a certain hour, asking for new merchandise, and gossiping with the Pietri sisters about the latest political or social news. Others brought family or acquaintances, to show them the store with an almost proprietary pride. Even some tours from cruise ships or land-based sightseeing companies had begun to schedule stops in the jewelry store.

Evelyn, ever the businesswoman of the three sisters, had found new ways to profit from all of the casual visitors, producing small bracelet charms that showed the façade of the jewelry store, or a map of Puerto Rico, or a palm tree, or an old Spanish sentry post, or La Fortaleza, each with the words of "*El Joyero de San Juan*" engraved on it. The store also sold similarly decorated medals, paperweights, and even earrings, in various sizes and metals. The items had proven to be extremely popular with tourists and first-time visitors.

It had been Evelyn's idea to blow up and frame the covers of several publications—local, national, and international—that chronicled the deeds of Lucas and Michelle during the terrorist revolt, including one that displayed an "El Nuevo Dia" full page color photo of Lucas receiving from the Governor the Medal of Valor, while his sister Michelle, already wearing a similar medal around her neck, beamed at them. Evelyn had also printed maps of Puerto Rico, matchboxes, and postcards with the "*El Joyero*" logo, and had suggested giving away to purchasers of $100 of merchandise or more, T-shirts bearing a photo of the store and reading: "*El Joyero de San Juan, Home of Lucas Alfaro*". Fortunately, Lucas had managed to quash that idea before the first order of one thousand T-shirts had been placed.

Not all of the changes of *El Joyero's* fortune had been for the better. Antonio's death remained a vivid memory in everybody's mind. Every morning, when Lucas opened the jewelry store, he expected to hear his voice, and felt his ghost's lingering, palpable, physical presence. The entire Pietri clan had accompanied Lucas and Jeannie to Antonio's funeral in the small town of Vega Baja. To their surprise, the funeral parlor had been packed. Antonio had been a shy man with no family, but apparently his good humor and gentle character had made him many friends.

Lucas had brought with him the notebook where Antonio wrote his poems to Mercedes, the mystery woman that rode the *publico* to work with him every morning, and with whom he had intended to have dinner the afternoon that he got killed. But Lucas had no idea of what Mercedes looked like. He had read the poems in the notebook, written in a surprisingly neat handwriting—considering that he wrote them in a moving, public transportation vehicle crammed with passengers. There were one hundred and fifty of the poems, each dated and numbered, the first one bearing the date of August 28, 2012, some running for several pages, most just a few paragraphs long. All referred to Mercedes.

However, the poems contained very few clues about her physical appearance, their content alluding more to his feelings about her than to her looks. The prose was often simplistic and amateurish, his rhymes sometimes forced, but his emotions for his secret love had a way of breaking through Antonio's limited writing talents, and the deep feelings that the shy man expressed had often moved Lucas to tears. Lucas had been tempted to show the poems to Jeannie to see her reaction, but he had felt that that would violate Antonio's keen sense of privacy. The poems had been intended for Mercedes, and Lucas would give them to her.

But what did she look like? Lucas had started searching for the prototype of the woman that Antonio had typically dated: busty, curvy, somewhat brash and flashy women, the opposite of Antonio's shy, self-effacing personality. There had been a few in the funeral parlor—he thought he recognized one that had visited *El Joyero,* and who had stopped an animated conversation with a young man to make a flirty wave at Lucas—but none seemed to fit the mental image he had formed of Antonio's source of inspiration.

Then his eyes had alighted on a young woman sitting alone in the corner of the parlor, and he had instantly known it was her. She was wearing a black skirt and a white shirt, with black pumps, her brown hair pulled back straight and tied in a bun at the end of her head. Her hands were resting on her lap and she was staring at them, lost in thought. As he approached her, she seemed to sense him and looked up. Her eyes—red from crying—were a little too close, and her lips too thin, but there was a sweetness to her expression that made her pretty.

"Mercedes," Lucas had said.

She had nodded, staring curiously at him.

"My name is Lucas Alfaro." Her face had registered instant recognition at the mention of the name.

"Of course, from *El Joyero de San Juan,* where Antonio worked," she had answered, standing up and smiling at him. "You were his boss. He often spoke about you, and about your mother, your aunts. You were his family." Her eyes flicked to the notebook that Lucas was holding in his right hand. "Is that...the notebook...Antonio's notebook?"

"Yes," Lucas had replied. "Antonio told me that he was going to have dinner with you...that day, the day that he died."

She looked at him sharply, and tears began to stream from her eyes. "We were going to meet that afternoon," she said. "But when I got to San Juan, our *publico* got into this terrible traffic jam. We were stuck for two hours without moving. I tried to call Antonio to let him know I would be late, but there was no way of getting through to him. The cell phone was busy all the time. Finally, the *publico's* driver gave up and told us he was turning back. I got off at Kennedy Avenue and tried to walk to the Condado Lagoon, but the police stopped me in Miramar. They told me that it wasn't safe, that the bridges had been destroyed, that there were gunmen on the other side of the lagoon."

The number of people using the telephones had overwhelmed the system, Lucas remembered.

"I knew that Antonio would try to find me, so I didn't have lunch, just in case he had managed to make it to the other side. I sat on a bench in Ponce De Leon Avenue, and called every half hour, all night long. I kept hoping that the bridges would reopen, and that somehow I would be able to find him. Close to dawn, his phone began to ring instead of sounding busy, but he would not answer. Some time in the morning, I returned home."

"You waited all that time?" Lucas said with amazement.

"I wanted to know that he was all right," she replied dully. "But when he would not answer his cell phone, I began to grow uneasy. The owner of a cafeteria close to where I waited approached me after he said he had seen me sitting there for hours, and got me to eat some breakfast. There was a small group of locals assembled around the cafeteria's TV, watching what was happening in San Juan. That's when I learned that the police had managed to cross the lagoon and save the hostages. I knew that if he was okay he would try to find me. He was always such a correct gentleman. So I returned to Vega Baja, hoping he had somehow made it back there." She wiped her tears with a tissue. "It was later that night that the news about his death were broadcast on the radio. Even so, I did not believe it. It was probably a mistake. Why would anyone kill *him*?" she asked plaintively, and covered her face, overwhelmed by grief.

Lucas stood awkwardly by her side, not knowing exactly what to say or do. Finally, she stopped sobbing, swiped her eyes with exaggerated harshness with the remnant of her Kleenex, and sat upright, staring at him with an embarrassed smile. "Please forgive me," she said to Lucas, "I know this is hard for you too."

Lucas shook his head, and then, realizing what he had done, hastened to add, "I mean, it is hard for me. I miss him terribly, every day, every minute that I spend in *El Joyero*. But you should not apologize for crying. I know how hard this is for you."

He handed the notebook to her.

Mercedes stared at it, and for a moment hesitated, before taking it reverently with both hands.

"The morning before he died, Antonio spoke to me about you," Lucas said to her. "He was very certain that you were his...the love of his life. He couldn't wait to go out on his first date with you." He sighed and smiled sadly. "You know, I'm not sure that he would have told you how he felt in your first date."

"He was a very shy man," Mercedes acknowledged, her eyes wandering, focusing on the memory of Antonio's face. She looked, Lucas thought, very beautiful. Antonio would have been very happy with her.

"And brave," Lucas added. "He died trying to save us. I'm sure that he would have wanted me to give you the notebook. It's all about you, in Antonio's own words."

Mercedes brow furrowed and she sobbed, embracing the notebook with both of her arms. Lucas lingered by her side for several minutes, and made her promise that she would keep in touch with him periodically. But he had not heard from her in the months that followed.

Life just went on, Lucas thought with a pang of sorrow, leaving behind those who fell by the wayside, slowly filling the gaps they left with new people and new experiences, but never quite managing to soothe the pain caused by their departure. For him, Antonio's absence continued to be as physically palpable as a concrete wall, from the moment he entered *El Joyero* early in the morning until the moment he went home.

The Pietri sisters had recently hired a new person to act as a combination of guard and odds-and-ends man to fill in Antonio's former position. Fortunately "Papo"—as the new guard-errand boy was called—had proven to be a fresh breath air. Awkward, gangly, and rail-thin, with a pimply, boyish face that made him look no older than fifteen even though he was twenty, Papo had made his own personal imprint on the *El Joyero* culture, and showed significant promise of becoming a permanent asset in the jewelry store's wacky crew.

Three more permanent employees had been hired to handle the tremendous increase in the volume of business: two local young females, and an older, veteran jewelry salesman from Cuba. Evelyn was already making greater plans, considering hiring a fourth worker and talking about expanding into the failing pizzeria next door.

As Lucas emerged from the basement, several people looked his way.

"There he is," Evelyn exclaimed, prompting more curious looks and even some scattered cheers, "the hero from La Fortaleza!"

One man, a tourist with a flowery Hawaiian shirt, made his way through the crowd, towing his wife behind him. "Stand next to him, Shylene!" he said to her, thrusting her towards him. "You don't mind, do you?" he asked Lucas, not really expecting an answer and raising his camera.

Before the "hero from La Fortaleza" could answer, the woman placed her arm around his waist and semi-wrapped her left leg around his legs.

"Say cheese!" the tourist muttered through clenched teeth, as he squatted to catch a better angle. Lucas directed a look of pure venom towards Evelyn, who watched with a mixture of amusement and guilt.

"Done!" the tourist grunted with satisfaction, after his camera's flash went off and he examined briefly the digital image on the screen. "Let's go," he said to his wife, slipping a dollar bill in Lucas' hand.

Incensed, Lucas followed the man to return his money, but was intercepted by a host of other admirers. Resignedly, he shook their hands, signed a few autographs, and allowed himself to be photographed. With the corner of his eye he picked out the small frame of his mother, Fannie, engaged in an earnest conversation with Elena Diaz, the old dowager heiress to the multimillion-dollar telecommunications empire founded by her now deceased husband, Manolo Diaz. The widow visited *El Joyero* twice a year, and invariably bought thousands of dollars of the most expensive—and most beautiful—merchandise that the store could offer.

A counter away, Lucas espied feisty Maria, overlooking the flow of the clientele and watching with unabashed amusement those who had flocked to meet the arriving hero. She had warned Lucas that Evelyn had to be stopped in her brazen attempts to cash in on his and Michelle's newly found fame. "If she refuses," she had said with absolute conviction, "I would consider getting an injunctive order from the court to keep her away from you." Now, from the distance, her expression gleefully telegraphed the words *"I told you so."*

Lucas was forced to smile despite himself. For the sake of the Pietri sisters and *El Joyero*, he would endure the autograph sessions. Hopefully, with time, the novelty would wear off, even if for now, he had to grin and bear it.

Fortunately for him, his sister Michelle arrived a couple of minutes later. She was the reason that he had come up from his workshop. She had called him to tell him that she had just finished her interview with the President, and that she had a free hour for an early dinner.

"It has to be early!" she had warned him. "Four thirty or so. I have to be in WKPA for the newscast by 6:30."

They had agreed that she would pick him up in *El Joyero* and have a sandwich together somewhere. She had told him to take Fannie with him, but that would be impossible with the Widow Diaz there. The widow's visits tended to last for hours, and usually culminated with a dinner of the two ladies.

Michelle waved at him happily, catching Evelyn's ever-watchful eyes. The Pietri marketer instinctively opened her mouth to announce her arrival—

"the Heroine of the Grand Laguna Hotel"—but Michelle cut her off with the abrupt, somewhat threatening gesture of her hand sweeping across her throat. Evelyn caught the message and reluctantly bit her tongue.

It took Lucas a few more minutes to get to the jewelry store's exit—where a love-struck Papo was talking enthusiastically with Michelle—but he finally got there, kissing his sister's cheek and quickly leading her away from the store.

"Whew!" he said gratefully, wiping imaginary sweat from his brow. "Thank you for rescuing me. For a moment I thought I wouldn't make it alive from in there!"

Michelle smiled. "It must be rough being a part of Evelyn's business development plans."

"I'd rather face the Macheteros in La Fortaleza," he said. It wasn't true, of course. He still had nightmares about La Fortaleza, mostly of fighting invisible enemies in the clammy, musty, earth-smelling blackness of the underground tunnels. However, enough time had passed to occasionally joke about it. It actually made him feel better. "So where are you taking me for dinner?"

"I thought you were taking *me* out for dinner," she replied, at the same time acknowledging with a smile two passersby—a mother and her teenaged daughter—who recognized her and whispered excitedly to each other. Lucas was used to this type of public reaction when he walked with his famous sister. People on the street would react spontaneously when they saw her, and she would invariably nod, smile, or say a few words to them. It was something Michelle had learned from observing their father, another famous television personality. Michelle noticed his brother's grin, and said, "At least, I have more manageable fans."

"Have you heard about the new hot dog place in Luna Street?" he asked her.

"Hot dogs? Is that where you're taking me to eat? Hot dogs? Really?" Michelle protested in a dismayed tone. "After I just finished interviewing the President of the United States? Really?"

"These are different hot dogs," Lucas answered her unfazed. "Colombian hot dogs. They dress them up with all sorts of different goodies: they serve them with different kinds of cheeses, even blue cheese, bacon, chorizo, different kinds of fancy sauces, caramelized onions, avocado, even with sweet plantains, if you ask for them."

"What's the name of this wonderful place?" Michelle asked, partially appeased.

"El Hotdogazo."

"El Hotdogazo," Michelle repeated, casting at him a doubtful glance. "Honestly, Lucas, how good can a placed named 'El Hotdogazo' be?"

Lucas rolled his eyes in mock exasperation. "I keep forgetting just how high maintenance and difficult you are!"

Michelle made a sputtering sound. "Me! High maintenance! What about—"

"You're even worse than your sister," he added with a malicious grin.

Michelle gasped. "You go too far!" she said indignantly, while trying to suppress a smile. Ever since they were children, they had run a gag—usually in front of Vanessa—about how strange, difficult, or obnoxious their middle sister was. Vanessa took it all in stride, claiming that only she was their parents' true daughter, and that Michelle and Lucas had been adopted after being found floating in a shipwreck. "All right," Michelle conceded in a hurt tone, while nodding at another person walking by. "I will try your 'Hotdogazo'. I've lost my appetite anyway, after your comparing me to Vanessa. It better be good, is all I'm saying."

"And if it is, you pay," Lucas said, cutting her short before she could say anything else. "Just for doubting me."

They walked across the Plaza de Armas, where most of the tables around the food stalls would soon be filled with people having dinner, and continued up the steeply inclined San Jose Street, which rose towards San Juan's highest hill. They walked past a clutter of art galleries, boutique restaurants, private residences, and tourist shops, each painted in bright, different pastel colors—sky blue, flamingo pink, canary yellow, tomato red, their doors and window frames highlighted in white and complemented by wrought iron balconies and wooden, nail studded doors—that so characterized the architecture of the ancient city. Some of the businesses seemed to be closed, but others had open corridors that allowed local pedestrians to spy into the lush, interior gardens, where local artists displayed their wares.

To their left, shortly after entering San Jose Street, they passed by the back end of the San Juan Cathedral, it's walled-in open space packed with cars that used it as a monthly parking area. Back in the days when Lucas had been a child, his mother Fannie had used to park her car there during the day. One evening, after closing the store, she had headed towards the parking lot and to her great surprise had discovered her car, a sky-blue Toyota Corolla, slowly rolling down San Jose Street in her direction during the rush hour traffic jam. Without thinking about the consequences, she had yanked open the car's front passenger door and slipped into its seat. A huge man had stared at her in silence.

"My name is Fannie Pietri," she had said to him without blinking an eye, "and the car that you're stealing is mine. Now I know that you can harm me, but I'm very well known in this town, and if anything happens to me, the police won't rest until they find you. However, if you step out of the car now, I will let you go without shouting for help. Otherwise, I'll fight and scream until you get arrested."

The thief, easily twice her size, had considered her words for several seconds, and then stopped the car, placed it in park, opened the door, and walked away. Fannie had shaken so much that she had trouble pressing the brake as she continued to drive the car downhill to pick up Maria at the jewelry store.

Small but feisty, his dad had called her with grudging admiration, after he had found out about the incident and scolded her for taking such a terrible risk. She had apologized, promising not to do anything so stupid again. But even then—Lucas had been not older than ten or eleven—he had been able to tell that she did not mean it.

Michelle was made of that same stuff; *small and feisty. And fearless.*

When they reached Luna Street, they turned to the right, traveling east in the direction of Fort San Cristobal. In the 50's and 60's, Calle Luna had been a street of ill repute, where the sailors from the U.S. Navy and from the warships of other countries that then docked in the bay, had come to drink and find female companionship. It had been lined with small, dingy bars and brothels, and was the scene for countless of brawls, stabbings, and robberies. That had changed.

Most of the drinking holes had disappeared, giving way to more upscale bars, antique shops, and boutique businesses. Lured by the tax breaks that the government granted to those who restored properties in the old city, many residents had moved in. And lately, a few new restaurants—mostly modest establishments serving good food—had begun to stray from the usual dining quarters of La Fortaleza and San Sebastian streets, and to establish their businesses there.

Two National Guardsmen, armed in their full regalia—including helmets, armor vests and M-16 rifles—walked past Michelle and Lucas. Armed foot patrols such as them had become a commonplace sight in Old San Juan during the last week, as the city prepared for the meeting of the G-20, the nineteen countries with the biggest economies in the world, plus the European Union. As the host of the present conference, President Sam Powell had chosen San Juan as the site of the conference. Although criticized by his opponents, who pointed out that drawing attention to Puerto Rico would only serve to draw attention to its territorial status, that Puerto Rico lacked the facilities to host such a major conference—which was not true—and that it had all been a political maneuver to gain the Latin vote, the President had opted to hold the conference there. His choice of venue had not been based on a whim.

For decades, ever since the 1950's, Puerto Rico had been the unofficial cultural bridge between the United States and South America. President

Kennedy had realized the island's great potential by fostering a close relationship with then Governor Luis Muñoz Marin and helping Puerto Rico develop economically through Operation Bootstrap, to make it a shining example of what a successful, democratic Latin country could achieve. But Kennedy had been killed in the third year of his first term, and his focus on Puerto Rico had fallen by the wayside, victimized by other major issues such as the war in Vietnam and the Cold War.

President Powell was aware of Puerto Rico's potential, and meant to take full advantage of it. The first President ever to come out of New Mexico, where he had served two very successful terms as governor, Powell had very strong connections to the Latin population in the United States. His wife, a former Miss USA named Maria Luisa Contreras, came from a prominent family of Mexican descent. Powell, as well as his two small children and his wife, spoke Spanish fluently.

In the last year, the President had visited Mexico and Argentina, in both instances drawing hundreds of thousands of enthusiastic fans, and enhancing Powell's relationship with his southern neighbors. South America contained some of the largest economies in the world, mostly untapped by the U.S. market, and maintained a marginal-at-best political relationship with the American nation. Powell meant to change that. And Puerto Rico played a key factor in his plans.

More than four million American citizens, true Latinos, lived on the island. Its actors and entertainers were well known not only in the United States but throughout the Latin American world. Except for Brazil and Belize, they spoke the same language as the rest of the South American nations, and even with Brazil, they shared the same cultural background and its mainly Catholic religion. There could be no better, natural way to start bridging a connection between the United States and South America than through this mostly Latin island that for more than one hundred years had been the closest partner of the American nation.

It was true that the G-20 Conference would draw attention to Puerto Rico's uncertain status as a nation, but that did not bother the President too much. Puerto Rico had captured the attention of the world with the attempted coup that had taken place a few months before, so that argument was academic. Besides, its Governor was preparing to hold a plebiscite at the end of the year, to determine if the island wanted to join the Union as its 51st state. So the status issue, whether the G-20 Conference was held in San Juan or not, would be at the forefront of national and international news. And if his actions created more Latino political support—in addition to the considerable Latino support that he already had—so be it. He would not complain about it.

After the failed terrorist revolt, many politicians—both national and international—a few security experts, and scores of political pundits, had questioned the wisdom of holding the G-20 Conference in the Caribbean island. The terrorists had shown, these people claimed, how easily security could be breached in San Juan, and how difficult it would be to keep safe the attending heads of state. Had something like that happened while most of the leaders of the world's foremost countries were meeting, the results could have been disastrous.

But the doom-and-gloom prophets had been silenced by others who were quick to point out that moving the Conference to another site would look very bad in the eyes of the world—more like an abdication to the acts of the extremists—and that there would not be any guarantee that the new designated host would be any safer than San Juan. If anything, it would be easier to control protesters and keep a tighter rein on security in a small island like San Juan than in a larger, more open city. With the strong safety measures that would be jointly undertaken by local and federal authorities, as well as by the foreign protective services of the countries attending the Conference, there could be no question that the guest world leaders would be completely safe.

In the past two days, the delegations from Russia—recently reinstated into the G-20 after the Ukraine crisis had ended—France, England, China, and India had flown into San Juan, headed by their respective chairmen, presidents, and prime ministers. All of the arrivals had been broadcast on television. More than a dozen other delegations were slated to land on the island by that night, before the conference began the next day. Traffic, normally heavy in the Metropolitan Area, had been snarled to a pitiful crawl as roads were closed or their direction changed to accommodate the transfer of the foreign delegations.

No arrival, however, had been as anticipated as that of President Powell and his First Lady on Air Force One. The appearance of the world's most famous aircraft had been broadcast on all television stations and followed by the high-powered, long distance lenses of their cameras as the presidential jumbo jet had approached the Puerto Rican coast. Hundreds of motorists had parked alongside the roads to look up at the sky as the radio stations announced the sighting of the plane. Tens of thousands of people, waving American and Puerto Rican flags, had lined up the entire route from the Luis Muñoz Marin International Airport to Old San Juan, hoping to catch a glimpse of the President and his First Lady. A bulletproof, glass bubble topped limousine had transported the presidential party, as well as Governor Pietrantoni and his fiancée Nereida, from the airport to the Grand Laguna Hotel, where the President would be staying.

All of the other heads of state would either stay at the Grand Laguna Hotel or the El Convento Hotel. The latter was a former Carmelite Convent located in the heart of Old San Juan, founded in the mid fifteen hundreds. It had been converted into a four star resort while preserving its Spanish colonial architecture. The two hotels had been reserved exclusively for the visiting world leaders and their most important cabinet members and ministers, including U.S. Secretary of Commerce Veronica Harte and Secretary of State Francis McClellan. Lesser staff members of the various national delegations had been distributed among other close hotels in the area, among them the Sheraton Hotel near the docks and other hotels in the Condado area.

The grounds around the two main hotels had been closed to traffic and turned into armed camps. Cris-crossing cement barriers guaranteed that no vehicle filled with explosives could crash into them, and forced the official limousines and automobiles of visiting diplomats to slowly zigzag back and force, in order to reach the hotels. A massive police presence, supplemented by the National Guard, police dogs, U.S. marshals and the FBI, as well as by the security details that each head of state brought along with them, made the areas impossible to infiltrate.

Checkpoints with metal detectors were established to allow authorized visitors in and out of the restricted areas. Cameras were installed on lampposts and some of the surrounding buildings, to cover every square foot of the grounds around the hotels. Wooden barriers, enveloped in bales of barbed wire, and protected by armed guards, sealed the hotel's perimeter. Manholes in any nearby streets were welded shut.

No protesters had been allowed to demonstrate within the confines of the old city itself. The Luis Muñoz Rivera Park, in Puerta de Tierra, had been allotted for the protesters' activities. A wall of watchful policemen made certain that no organized group made its way beyond that point. Anybody intending to use the park had to first submit to a search for weapons or explosive materials. Similar safety measures had been instituted around La Fortaleza. Police snipers had been assigned to patrol the rooftops of the surrounding buildings. Not even a "subversive fly" would be able to get through to the visiting dignitaries or the President, one television security expert had boasted.

"So how was your interview with the President?" Lucas asked Michelle, casting a sideways glance at her as they continued their walk towards the restaurant. Michelle smiled excitedly. She was still wearing her interview dress, a sober, emerald-colored, two-piece suit that ended in a tapered, slit skirt and beige, high-heeled shoes. Despite the conservative attire, she could not conceal the natural curves of her body, drawing the eyes of every male within sight.

"I wasn't disappointed," she answered enthusiastically. "The man is for real."

"Really? For really real?" Lucas interrupted, knowing his remark would bait his sister.

"As real as you are childish," she answered without skipping a beat, directing him an irritated look.

"That would make him very real," Lucas agreed with a straight face. "But honestly, what do you mean by 'real'?"

"I mean...I've been dealing with politicians for too many years. I can tell when they're going through the motions, or putting up a façade, or falling back on political clichés...That's what I mean by 'real'."

"And he wasn't any of those?"

"No. He was very interested in what we were talking. In fact, for a moment there, it seemed as if he was interviewing me. He started the conversation by asking me about the January terrorist attack. The 'Machetero incident', he called it. He knew everything about what had happened in the Grand Laguna Hotel and congratulated me for my reporting of the incident. He said he was 'moved' by the broadcast I made from the hotel right after the rescue."

"Wow! You must have been in seventh heaven!"

Michelle shrugged reluctantly in acknowledgement.

"And the fact that he looks a lot like George Clooney must have also impressed you."

Again Michelle shrugged, this time with a smile. "He *is* very handsome. I think handsomer than George Clooney. Taller, and with blue eyes."

Lucas laughed. "So he *won* you over even before he began the interview?"

"Are you implying that he tried to win me over so that I would go easier with him in the interview?" Michelle asked, bristling.

"No...Well, I don't know," he confessed honestly. "Most politicians are a mystery to me, so don't get excited about my comments, little sister."

As he finished his sentence, Lucas' attention was suddenly drawn to two men walking in their direction, about half a block away. Both were wearing flip-flops, and tight jeans. The taller of the two sported an expensive looking, red Ralph Lauren "Polo" shirt that flowed over his waist, his face partially hidden by a neatly cropped beard and fashionable sunglasses. His shorter companion wore a light blue, sleeveless shirt that fit tightly over his torso, revealing the slim, chiseled physique of a professional trainer. He was blond and clean-shaven, except for a mustache that extended the exact length of his upper lip.

He was certain that he did not know them, but could not help staring at them. There was something familiar about them—the way they walked, maybe—that made him stare at them, perhaps too intensely, since the two men, who had been talking animatedly, quickly quieted down and lowered their gazes as they walked by. Michelle noticed her brother's sudden tension, but opted to say nothing.

Lucas remained quiet as the two men—clearly tourists—walked past him, and he maintained a contemplative silence for several seconds afterwards. Had he turned his head, he would have been surprised to see the two tourists staring at him instead than at his sister. However, by that time, he had reached his destination.

"Ah!" he said, trying to focus on the business at hand. "Here we are. El Hotdogazo."

CHAPTER II

They stopped at the entrance of "El Hotdogazo". The place was barely more than fifteen feet wide, accommodating only about a dozen small, round tables, each surrounded by two or three high wooden benches. The façade of the building was painted purple, the entrance to the narrow establishment—its only source of natural light—covered by a set of glass doors that kept the air conditioned cooled atmosphere in and the noise of the street out. About five people stood in line in front of a counter to order food, while another two-dozen sat at the tables eating. Next to the entrance, on the outside, a plastic, person-sized hot dog, with large eyes, a long nose, and a wide grin, pointed eagerly towards the inside of the restaurant.

"Classy," Michelle muttered softly.

Lucas opened the door and they walked in. The place still smelled like new. As they went to the end of the line, some of the customers ahead of them recognized Michelle, and she went through the motions of acknowledging every one of their greetings. Examining the overhead menu, Lucas settled for an "Agueybana"—a hot dog topped by shredded, crispy pork and yucca chips dipped in 'mojo criollo'—while Michelle ordered a "Jíbaro in Paris"—a hot dog with brie, caramelized onions, and a slightly hot mint jelly. They also shared an order of sweet potato fries and had two beers.

"Mmmmmm....Good!" Lucas said after his first bite. "How's yours?"

She merely nodded, while chewing.

"Was I right or was I wrong?" Lucas insisted.

She mumbled something unintelligible as she chewed.

Lucas cupped his ear. "What's that? Did you say something?"

"Okay! Okay! It's good! It's delicious! Satisfied now?"

Lucas took another bite and smiled at her, showing her part of the food in his mouth.

"You pig!" she said, snorting and nearly choking.

"So you were saying about the President..."

Michelle nodded as she chewed and swallowed. "Before we started the interview, we talked about the terrorist attack. He knew more details about it than I did."

"Really?" Lucas asked with genuine interest, but Michelle stared at him with suspicion, as if he was to mock her again.

When Lucas failed to make any subsequent smart remarks, she said, "He even asked about Archie." She knew immediately that she had made a mistake mentioning Archie's name, and tried to gloss over it by adding, "...and you."

Lucas suppressed a knowing smile. *Archie, her redheaded companion in the Grand Laguna adventure.* The redhead had recovered slowly from his wounds after the shootout. Michelle had made it a point to visit him at the hospital as often as she could, at first to follow up on his condition, later just to talk. When on the first week of February he had been discharged from the hospital, they had continued to see each other.

With the help of Superintendent Maldonado—and some said of the Governor—Archie had been given an administrative position in the Police Department, to act as liaison between the press and the police chief. At first, the work had been more of a clerical nature, but as time progressed, Archie had shown a natural talent for the job, establishing a great relationship with the news media, and more and more becoming the face of the police in press conferences. Finally, he had been promoted as the Police Department's spokesman to the press.

Rumors about a budding romance between Michelle and him had inevitably begun to circulate as the two began to see more of each other. Lucas had not discussed the matter with his sister, but he was not certain how he felt about it. After all, the redhead had been an illegal lottery ("la bolita") numbers runner; even the Pietri sisters had bought numbers from him.

On the other hand, he had been Antonio's friend, and Antonio had been an inherently decent man. Besides, during the terrorist revolt Archie had saved not only a young policeman's life, but rescued Michelle from two armed rapists and followed her into the Grand Laguna Hotel—the center of all of the terrorist activity—to save her again. It had taken a lot of guts to walk into the Machetero-infested area, where hostages were being thrown from the roof of the hotel. He had nearly gotten killed doing it.

Since February, Lucas had talked to Archie a couple of the times that the redhead had dropped by *El Joyero* to meet Michelle. Lucas had instinctively liked him. Like Lucas, Archie seemed to be on the shy and quiet side. He had a firm handshake, and when he spoke, he looked at people directly into their eyes. He also had taken to his new position as police spokesman like fish to water, excelling in a job where smarter and more educated men than him had failed.

Most importantly, he genuinely seemed to care about Michelle. Not in the love-struck, blind, dazed sort of fashion, but in a steady, understated yet passionate way. It was very evident to anyone who saw them together, that they enjoyed each other's company immensely.

And yet, he had been a "bolitero"...

"So how's Archie?" Lucas asked innocently.

Michelle stared at him uneasily. "He's well," she answered matter-of-factly, staring at her food.

"You're still going out with him?" Lucas said in a neutral tone.

Michelle bristled. "Yes, I'm still going out with him," she answered a little more sharply than she intended. "Is that a problem?"

Lucas shook his head. "I figure that you're old enough to know what you're doing."

"I'm glad you realize that," she answered defiantly. "Archie is going to start taking a Communications Major at the U.P.R."

"Good for him," Lucas answered awkwardly, then added after a long pause, "Really, I'm really glad for him." He took a bite out of his "Agueybana" and examined her face. "I like him, you know," he told her.

"Thank you," she said in a more mollified tone. "I like him too."

"Do you love him?"

Michelle glanced at him with exasperation. "Will you quit it? I thought we were talking about the President."

Lucas shrugged. "Just asking. I am your big brother, after all."

Michelle ignored his last remark. "Did Fannie put you up to this?" she asked suspiciously.

"Fannie?" Lucas said in a surprised voice.

"Yes, Fannie. Our mother. Fannie."

"No," he answered truthfully, although Fannie had asked him just that morning what he knew about Archie and Michelle. "Fannie likes Archie, if you want to know. She told me so."

Michelle silently considered his brother's statement while she chewed on her "Jibaro" hot dog and swallowed. "So the President," she said, signaling to Lucas that she would not talk any more about the previous subject and forcing him to smile, "we spoke about the upcoming plebiscite."

The plebiscite—in addition to the visit by the G-20 countries—had been the main topic of discussion in Puerto Rico during the past two months. Scheduled for November of that year, the vote to decide whether Puerto

Rico would choose to continue with its present Commonwealth status or opt for statehood or independence, had come under a fierce attack by many of the principal figures in the pro-statehood movement, including former Governor Alarcon, former Secretary of Justice Rovira Melendez, and the Speaker of the House, Marisel Delgado, among many others. Governor Pietrantoni had been accused of sabotaging the cause of statehood by including the Commonwealth status as one of the alternatives in the plebiscite vote, instead of limiting the options to statehood or independence. The present Commonwealth form of government, the dissident voices argued, was nothing more than a sham, an elaborate façade to keep Puerto Rico as a colony of the United States. The only true alternatives for Puerto Rico were either to turn it into a state or grant it its independence. Therefore, Pietrantoni's opponents were urging all pro statehood voters to boycott the plebiscite.

As in most political contests in the island, the issues had soon become saturated with personal accusations. By including the Commonwealth option, the rebellious statehood party leaders argued, Pietrantoni was pandering to the *commonwealthers* to get reelected as Governor. Rovira had also begun a rumor that Nereida, the Governor's fiancé, was a Commonwealth sympathizer and that Pietrantoni was trying to please her. A series of rumors filtered into the press—mostly through the local gossip tabloids— portraying Nereida as the "real power behind the throne", manipulating her love-struck Governor to demand Rovira's resignation as Secretary of Justice, inducing him to include the Commonwealth formula in the plebiscite vote, and convincing him to announce his marriage to her on December of that year. Many diehard followers of former Governor Alarcon had even started a campaign to mail condoms to La Fortaleza, together with the message to *"Keep sex and politics apart"* written on them.

The smear campaign had infuriated Lucas. In Somalia, he had learned that during moments of great crisis, people tended to drop their public pretenses, and dealt more openly with each other. On the night of their escape from La Fortaleza, Pietrantoni had led, while Nereida had stuck to her role of taking care of the children. Not once had Nereida stepped out of bounds, or exhibited any influence over the Governor. On the contrary, even when under pressure, they had treated each other with distant, professional courtesy.

The charges leveled against Pietrantoni were ridiculous. And yet, thousands of people seemed to believe them. Even Michael, his brother-in-law, had considered them plausible, asking Lucas if he had observed any "suspicious behavior" while they were fleeing from the Macheteros. Alfredo had exhibited more common sense than his father, answering, "Come on, Dad. Grow up!"

Lucas' train of thought was interrupted abruptly as the two men he had watched on the street unexpectedly walked into El Hotdogazo. Taking a bite from his hot dog, he eyed their progress, this time trying to be less obvious about his interest in them. He could not shake the feeling that he had seen them before. However, he could not say where.

"What did he say?" Lucas asked Michelle, trying to continue his conversation with her. He watched the two men—*probably a gay couple*, Lucas thought—wander to the ordering area and examine the overhead menu.

"The President is very enthusiastic about making Puerto Rico a state," Michelle responded, also briefly staring at the two men before returning her attention to her brother. "Do you know them?" she asked Lucas, gesturing with her eyes to the new arrivals.

Lucas looked once more at the two men. Both had their backs towards him, and were busy reading the menu. Then the shorter one glanced briefly at their table, and for the bare fraction of a second, his eyes seemed to flicker with something akin to friendly curiosity. However, just as quickly, his gaze returned to the list of hot dogs, while his hand affectionately grazed his companion's left arm.

"If I do, I can't place them," Lucas answered.

"Probably visited *El Joyero* today or yesterday," Michelle suggested offhandedly.

"Maybe," Lucas agreed with some hesitation.

"He says that it's time that the four million Puerto Ricans that live here can vote for the President and be represented in Congress," Michelle said, returning to her conversation with the President.

"Especially if most of those new voters and congressmen vote for his party."

"Oh, he was honest enough to acknowledge that that would happen if Puerto Rico became a state. But he went further. He said that if Puerto Rico became a state, it would permanently alter the balance in Congress and the Senate. That Puerto Rico would gain five or six representatives in Congress, and that those five or six representatives would probably be Democrats, for whom most of the population leans towards, at least right now. And in the Senate, two Democratic Senators would definitely tip the balance in that party's favor. So he said that Republicans, as a whole, will oppose making Puerto Rico the 51st state."

"He said all of that on television? Isn't he making it harder for Puerto Rico to become a state by acknowledging that Puerto Rico will bolster the Democratic Party?"

"You think like me," Michelle said with a smile. "I asked him the same question."

"And what did he say?"

"He said that the Republicans were smart enough to figure out for themselves what would happen if Puerto Rico became a state, and that he did not want to insult their intelligence by trying to make it seem different. He also pointed out, however, that if the Republicans rejected Puerto Rico's bid for statehood due to political, party-related issues, it would be a slap in the face not only to Puerto Ricans, but to most of the Latino community in the United States. They would lose whatever little support they have with most Latinos in the country."

"So it's damn if you do, damn if you don't for the Republicans, and a win-win for the Democrats," Lucas observed.

"So what *is* important is how many Puerto Ricans vote for statehood," Michelle added, finishing the President's thoughts. "If the statehood option gets less than sixty percent, some say less than seventy percent, it will be very hard to get statehood to pass through Congress."

"Pietrantoni will never get a seventy percent vote for statehood. Even sixty percent will be very hard," Lucas concluded. "Even if his party was not split, it would be very difficult to do so. With the hard core followers of Alarcon sabotaging his campaign...he's doomed..."

Lucas mumbled his last words almost as an afterthought, as his attention was drawn back to the new arrivals. The taller man was talking to the man behind the cashier. Lucas could not pick out what he was saying, but something in his voice seemed eerily familiar. Michelle noticed it immediately.

"Am I boring you?" she asked.

Lucas stared at her vacantly. "I'm sorry, what did you say?"

Michelle sighed impatiently. "I said, am I boring you?"

Lucas saw the two men pick up their food and head towards a table at the rear of the restaurant. Neither stared at him as they walked past his table, although the shorter of the two men cast an admiring leer at Michele.

"No, of course not," Lucas answered, willing himself to look back at his sister. Something about the two men felt wrong. He still could not place or remember them, but they made his skin crawl. "I'm sorry. Please continue," he said, placing his hand over Michelle's. "What else did you discuss."

"Well...he had high praise for Governor Pietrantoni. Said he was one of the most capable politicians he had ever met," Michelle said, still a little unsettled.

Lucas nodded, struggling to keep his focus on the conversation. "The President is a very perceptive man. Maybe he'll offer him a position in his cabinet."

Michelle looked at him with surprise. "I also asked him about that! You're not as slow-witted as you look."

The Secretary of Labor and the Secretary of the Interior cabinet positions had become vacant in the last two weeks, the first due to health reasons, the second because of a sex scandal. The Powell administration had spent the time before the G-20 meeting in a damage control mode. The names of several substitute candidates had been floated around, but no official word about who the two new secretaries would be had yet been given.

"What did he say?" The subject drew back Lucas' full attention.

"He answered with a question," Michelle responded. "He asked me if I thought that if he nominated him, Pietrantoni would accept."

"And what did *you* say?" Lucas inquired.

"I told him that while the plebiscite was pending, I did not think that Pietrantoni would consider any offer. Not even the Presidency of the United States."

"Did you really?" Lucas said in a pleased tone. "Good for you!"

"You seem happy. I thought you opposed statehood."

"Well...I'm not sure about anything any more," he replied honestly. All of his life, he had been a pro-Commonwealth advocate, but a lot of his aversion for the statehood alternative had stemmed from his dislike of the politicians who had controlled the pro-statehood party. That had changed with Pietrantoni. As of late, he had found himself rooting more and more for the man's success.

"Don't let the Pietri sisters hear you," Michelle warned him only half-jokingly. "You should know that the President also mentioned you during the interview."

"In the public interview?" Lucas asked, flattered, but at the same time thinking what Evelyn would do to get some mileage for *El Joyero* out of the Presidential mention. He could picture it in his mind: Evelyn announcing to her awaiting clients that the President's friend had just entered the store. *God save him.*

"Yes, big brother. He called you a true, real life hero. Said he'd like to meet you before he leaves for the States, although he didn't say when."

"And you didn't follow through," Lucas said with apparent mortification.

Michelle chuckled and shrugged.

"So, my only chance to meet the President of the United States, and you blow it!"

"I'm sure if he's really interested in meeting you, he'll arrange it," Michelle replied, her grin widening, enjoying her brother's exaggerated reaction, knowing it was mostly an act. Vanessa, on the other hand, would have genuinely flipped out.

"Yeah, right!"

"Well, that's life, anyway. Some people actually get to meet the President. Others don't."

Lucas was forced to laugh. From the table at the back of the restaurant, both men briefly stared at them, and then renewed their conversation. For no apparent reason, Lucas felt uneasy. This time, Michelle did not notice his discomfort, as she looked at her watch.

"Oh my God! Twenty past five! I gotta run!"

"You sure you don't want coffee before you leave?"

"No, I'm late as it is." Michelle leaned over the table and pecked Lucas' cheek.

"I'll walk you to your car."

"No, that's okay. Stay and have your espresso. I know you want it."

Lucas stood up and embraced his sister. "Okay, when is your interview airing?"

"Tomorrow night at eight. But I'm showing a short preview in tonight's news." She smiled wickedly. "The part where he mentions you. That will get Evelyn going."

"Don't you dare..." he began to warn his sister, but by that time, she had blown him a kiss and left.

Lucas approached the counter and ordered a double espresso. He tried not to look at the two men, feeling very self-conscious. It was not until he received the coffee and walked to the sugar station that he chanced another glance at the strangers. To his relief, they were not looking at him, but were engaged in an intense discussion. Lucas took the opportunity to sit closer to them, and tried to listen in.

Staring at the street, he began to slowly sip his coffee while attempting to make out what the strangers were saying, but most of the words were spoken in whispers and could not be understood. He picked out a few phrases: "not yet..." "the batteries..." "at the van..." and something that sounded like "the cruise ship". It all seemed like the conversation of two tourists traveling on a cruise ship, worried about the batteries of their cameras, maybe thinking about returning to their tour van. *He was being paranoid, that was all, suspecting everyone and everything around him.*

Lucas drank the rest of the coffee and prepared to go. Just at that moment, the two men at the back of the restaurant moved out their chairs and began to walk towards El Hotdogazo's exit. As they passed Lucas' table, he overheard the tall man say, "Don't get distracted. Do it quickly."

The words stunned Lucas. In a flash, he was back on the rooftop of the Metropolitan Center, his hands spread against the wall, the two armed men speaking on the radio, seeking instructions about what they should do with him. Then a voice had answered back, *"This is San Miguel, you can't get distracted. Kill him quickly."*

It was him! The man tall man who had walked into *El Joyero* after Antonio had been shot. The man on the radio who had ordered him killed. He had had looked different then, but it was him.

Lucas felt sick. *What was he doing here?* He had to warn the police. He frantically searched for his cell phone and cursed, as he realized that he had left it on his desk in his workroom, back at *El Joyero*. Impulsively, he stood up and rushed to the restaurant's door, hoping he could still see where the two men were heading. He barely caught sight of them as they rounded the corner of Luna Street, and headed down the steep incline of Calle Norzagaray.

Praying that they would not board a vehicle, he ran after them, stopping just short of the corner and carefully peering from behind it. The tall man and his companion were still walking down the street, about a block away, their backs turned towards him, engaged in a casual conversation. Taking a deep breath, Lucas followed them.

By that time, he had concluded that they were walking back to one of the cruise ships docked in the bay, about a half-mile beyond. There were three cruise ships visiting San Juan that day, all of them scheduled to leave at night. He would follow San Miguel and find out on which of the ships he was staying, and then seek the help of the police.

He kept wondering why the man was there, why he had returned. If he and his companion were planning another revolt, they had chosen the wrong time. *The city was an armed camp, with the G-20 Conference happening there.*

Then it dawned on him. *The G-20 conference! They were there because of the G-20 conference! To conduct some terrorist act? To assassinate one of the visiting world leaders?* Nothing had happened thus far, and the two men appeared to be scheduled to depart on one of the cruise ships that night, *so what were they planning?* Whatever it was, time was running short.

The two terrorists stopped at the corner of Norzagaray and San Francisco Streets and waited for a chance to cross. Lucas slowed down and, as he had seen in countless spy movies, looked into a courtyard of an adjacent building, feeling foolish and amateurish. When he dared to chance a glance, he saw the men moving again, too intent in avoiding the afternoon's traffic to notice him. However, to his great surprise, he saw that they were moving in the wrong direction. Instead of continuing their walk towards the docks, they had crossed Norzagaray Street and headed east, along the northern edge of San Francisco Street.

Where were they going? There were no hotels in that direction, except for the Grand Laguna, more than a mile away. *Was that their destination?* Like all of the Old San Juan G-20 locations, the hotel was heavily guarded. They could not possibly hope to retake it, at least not without the help of a massive army. *What else was on their way? Fort San Cristobal, the Capitol Building...and the Luis Muñoz Rivera Park, where the demonstrators were gathered! Was that it? Had a small army secretly gathered there?*

Lucas crossed Norzagaray Street and speeded up his pace. He stopped again when he reached the eastern intersection of Norzagaray and San Francisco streets, and poked his head out of the corner, expecting to see the two men walking in the direction of the Muñoz Rivera Park. But they were nowhere to be seen.

Where were they? Had they boarded a vehicle after all? Crossed San Francisco and headed towards Constitution Avenue? How could he lose them so easily?

Panicking, he dashed down San Francisco Street, in the hopes of finding them again. He nearly rushed past them before he realized that they had turned left, into the parking area of Fort San Cristobal's visitors center. They were some fifty feet away, heading towards the glass doors that marked the entrance to the admissions area.

Lucas continued to walk, in case one of the two men looked back, and when he saw them enter, doubled back and followed them. *What were they doing there,* he wondered. Sightseeing? Could it be that they had returned to Old San Juan just to gloat? *It didn't make any sense!*

For a moment he hesitated. He could go back and try to get some help from the police, but he did not think that their response would be quick. His claim that he had spotted some terrorists would be received, if not with outright disbelief, at least with some skepticism, and during the delay the two men could easily slip away. He had to determine what their final destination was, and then get help. He had no choice but to follow them.

As he got closer to the visitors' center, his eyes caught the outline of the tall man through the glass doors, leaning over a counter, apparently talking to someone on the other side. Probably one of the park guides, he thought. The tall man's companion was not visible. His pace faltered for a split second, as he wavered between continuing into the visitors' area, or turning around and leaving. But he was committed now. If he turned back, he would probably be noticed and alert the two terrorists. Taking a deep breath, he pushed one of the doors and entered the air-conditioned room.

The biggest man he had ever seen stood at the other side of the counter. It was not just his height—he towered a full head over the other tall man—but his bulk. The man's chest was as thick as a boulder, his heavily muscled arms—framed by light blue, short sleeves that seemed to be ready to burst—looked as if they had been chiseled out of stone. He was entirely bald—a dead ringer for Mr. Clean, Fannie would have said—with a nearly featureless face that was highlighted by small, cold blue eyes, thin, continuous eyebrows, and a coal black mustache.

When he saw Lucas he scowled, as if he had discovered a fly in his soup, prompting the man standing in front of him to look back. A brief glance at the stranger he had followed was enough to convince Lucas that it was the same man who had walked into *El Joyero* four months before. He had grown a short beard and dyed it and his hair blond. Even his eyes—he remembered them green—had changed to amber. But still, the pleasant, crooked grin that seemed to be permanently etched to the lower half of his face betrayed him.

By the amused look on the man's face, Lucas knew he had been recognized, and immediately turned to leave. But he found a gun leveled so closely to his face that he nearly bumped into it, and had to back up a couple of steps.

Automatically, even before he could make out the features of the gunman, he tried to snatch the gun away. However, his hand only grabbed air, as the man holding the gun moved it out of the way with blurring speed.

"Raise your hands and move away from the door," he warned Lucas in a calm voice. "I would hate to shoot you."

Reluctantly, Lucas did as he was bidden. The man with the handgun was the second person he had seen at the restaurant, and now that he was able to examine him at a closer distance, he recognized him as well. He had also been present at *El Joyero* the day that Antonio had been killed; he had been the man who had asked Lucas about his military background. Like his companion, the man had altered his appearance, plucking his eyebrows, growing a mustache, and also dyeing his hair to a dark shade of blond. A small metal ring pierced his left eyebrow. It all combined to give him an almost lackadaisical, effeminate appearance, except for the fierceness in his eyes.

The man also seemed to know Lucas, his lips pursed into a half interested, half regretful smile. "You were right," he said to his taller companion. "It *is* Alfaro, the man who saved the Governor! Good for you, man!" he said earnestly to Lucas. "But I've seen you before, haven't I? And you've seen us. Otherwise, you wouldn't have recognized us on the street."

"Of course he has," the taller man said pleasantly, approaching him, while the giant behind the counter continued to glare from a distance. "Think back."

The shorter man narrowed his eyes, as if concentrating on his captive's features, slowly shaking his head as he failed to place him. Then his face lit up in recognition. "Why...yeah! Sure! He's the guy in that store!"

The tall man nodded. "The jewelry store."

"Yeah, where one of the street punks killed an attendant!" the gunman said delightedly. "I remember now! You broke the punk's wrist, as I recall. Good job, man!" he repeated. He considered the information for a couple of seconds more, and then stared at his prisoner with newfound admiration. "And you were the same person who rescued the Governor?" He shook his head in genuine wonderment. "Even after they locked you up in the basement with the others in the store? Incredible! Who *are* you? Batman?"

"He was trying to save his nephew, I think I read in the newspapers," the other man stated casually. There was no animosity in his voice. "Ended up saving the Governor and his entire staff. Lucas, I think is your first name, is it not? Lucas Alfaro."

Lucas nodded, still looking at the gun on the other man's hand. "And you are San Miguel."

The tall man nearly succeeded in hiding his surprise, but could not avoid a sharp blink of shock. However, he recovered immediately.

"I have been called that, yes, in addition to many other names," he answered noncommittally. "How did you come by that name?"

"You identified yourself with that name when you spoke over the radio," Lucas answered. "Just before you ordered your men to kill me to avoid any distractions."

San Miguel's younger companion guffawed, while the humongous man continued to glare. "So," the gunman said, "the pope is not infallible after all."

San Miguel raised an eyebrow, mildly amused.

"And you still remembered it, after all this time," he said. "I knew you recognized us when you passed by us in Luna Street. You had that expression of puzzlement and surprise, especially when you looked at me. I told Daniel—my friend here—that you had recognized me, and he said it was impossible. We couldn't risk that you alerted the authorities, so we followed you to the hot dog restaurant, to see how you reacted. Even so, it was hard to tell. You were much more discrete while you were there."

"We figured that if you followed us after you left the restaurant, then you were onto us," Daniel stated. "And you did. After that, it was a matter of leading you here where Czecka had already used the keys to get in and was waiting for us."

"Except that Daniel hid behind one of the parked cars," San Miguel said, picking up the story where Daniel had left it. He did not add that if Lucas had then decided to seek or call for help, Daniel would have shot him in the parking area. "But I see now that not only did you recognize me, but you remembered the name that I used the last time I was here."

"It is not hard to remember the name of the man who ordered you killed."

The tall man nodded. "Of course. I hope you don't hold that against me. It was a necessary precaution that fortunately did not come to happen."

Lucas did not answer. *Hold that against you?* he thought. *Just give me the chance, and I'll show you.* Instead, he said, "So now that we know each other, I'll be on my way."

That provoked another burst of laughter from the shorter man.

"Alas, no," San Miguel responded. "I'm afraid you can't leave."

"What do you want me to do with him?" the gigantic man asked, with as gruff a voice as Lucas had imagined the man would have. "Should I kill him now?"

"No, please!" San Miguel answered in a shocked voice. "Just bring him along with us."

CHAPTER III

The colossal man with the sour disposition—'Czecka', San Miguel had called him—led the way through the tunnel, blocking most of the view beyond his massive girth. He was almost doubling over, the maximum height of the passageway not exceeding by much five feet, his wide shoulders barely fitting through the arched roof.

Lucas came next, followed by Daniel, the shorter of the three terrorists, then San Miguel, holding a flashlight. Even so, the visibility was poor. Twice, Lucas had bumped into Czecka's massive rear, as the man stopped to get his bearings, the last time prompting an angry kick that fortunately had only grazed his right arm. Czecka was carrying what seemed to be an ultraviolet light lamp, with which he would sweep the tunnel's mortared walls periodically, searching for fluorescent markings. On his left hand he hefted a box slightly bigger than the size of a car battery.

Their progress had been slow and tortuous. After Lucas had been captured, the terrorists had locked the visitors center's glass doors, and walked into the large, air-conditioned corridor that tourists used to gain access into the fort. The corridor ascended at a gradual slope, and then branched into two smaller passageways heading in different directions. The small party had turned to the right, and after a short walk, had stopped in front of a locked door.

San Miguel had produced a set of keys—the same he had used to lock the center's glass doors—and given them to Czecka. Daniel had remained behind, guarding Lucas. The tree-like man had opened the lock and stepped outside, onto a wide, grassy area surrounded by the fort's huge walls. The rest of the group had followed, San Miguel closing the door behind them.

"We don't want anyone noticing us," he had explained to Lucas.

They had quickly crossed the grassy area, heading towards another large wall east of the main fortifications. In the times of Spain, that wall had been part of the multiple defenses that ringed Fort San Cristobal. Now, it was a pleasant area where locals and tourists alike could come to catch the sun.

It had taken them about a minute to stop in front of a low, arched entrance at the bottom of the eastern wall. Straight metal bars, locked by a padlock, barred its access. Lucas had no doubt that Czecka could have easily bent the bars—even torn the door from its hinges, he suspected—but instead, the big man used another key to open it.

"We made copies of the keys during our last visit here," San Miguel said, answering Lucas' puzzled look. "We didn't want the National Park Service to notice our interest in these tunnels. That's why we waited today until the rangers closed the fort down and left for the day."

There was a box with construction helmets and flashlights inside. San Miguel handed one of the helmets to Lucas.

"Wear it," he said to his captive. "The park rangers use them to give special tours through some of these tunnels. Galleries, they call them, and with good reason. I don't want you to bump your head while we're walking through them."

Lucas had been surprised by the man's apparent concern. He had wondered why they had not killed him by then, rather than drag him along into whatever it was they were doing. Now, San Miguel was making certain that he did not bump his head.

He heard Daniel snicker behind him, doing his best to stifle a burst of laughter, and turned to see what was the cause of his amusement. Czecka was trying to fit a helmet on his baldpate, but it would not fit, sticking out of the top of his head like a blue derby. It surprised Lucas, since the unfriendly terrorist's head had seemed disproportionately small for the rest of his enormous body. Maybe it was, but it was still big enough not to fit a helmet. Running out of patience, the large man tossed it back into the box from which he had pulled it out.

"Let's go!" San Miguel had said impatiently.

Czecka grabbed one of the flashlights, and grunting, leaned forward and disappeared into the small entrance.

"You next," the terrorist leader had said to Lucas, pointing in the direction of Czecka.

Daniel had followed, then San Miguel.

Once they were inside, the tunnel widened slightly and rose to a couple of inches over five feet. It looked very similar to the one into which Lucas and the captives from La Fortaleza had escaped—exposed red brick smoothed randomly by patches of white mortar or black soot—but better maintained. Its floor, apparently made of packed earth, was smooth and even, and continuously dropped in a gentle slope.

They traveled in silence for a couple of hundred yards, only the occasional scrape of a helmet or a grunt from Czecka heralding their progress. The air felt artificially cool and carried a faint odor of decay, but it did not feel as stuffy as the corridor under La Fortaleza. Lucas figured that they were moving through the length of one of the fort's massive outer walls.

About five minutes into the tunnel they stopped, where the passageway branched into three different openings. Again, Czecka chose the one furthermost to the right.

"This is where we depart from the usual tourist route," San Miguel told him from behind.

Lucas had noticed that the new route sloped downwards more abruptly, and he wondered how deep they were going underground. However, just a few minutes later, he heard the muted roar of waves breaking on the shore, and realized that they were still inside the fort's wall, heading towards the sea.

Czecka stopped one more time, and Lucas listened to the metallic tinkle of keys and then the grating sound of a rusted door giving way. The grim giant moved through the exit and straightened up to his full height, sighing with relief. Lucas followed, not knowing what to expect. He found himself in what seemed to be an underground chamber of undetermined size. The noise of the sea echoed from its ceiling above.

"Fascinating, isn't it?" San Miguel said in an elated tone, sweeping his light around the confines of the chamber.

It was a large square room, at least forty feet wide by forty feet long. Part of its floor had been excavated, and many areas were highlighted by strings tied to metal stakes, containing small shovels, brushes, and boxes with screen bottoms to sift earth. *An ongoing archeological dig*, Lucas concluded.

As the beam of light flicked over the ceiling, he noticed the outline of a square metal hatch. It instantly brought him back images of the round hall under El Morro, where the escapees from La Fortaleza had made their stand against El Alacran. He shuddered involuntarily.

"This room lies directly under the outward defenses of San Cristobal. The small fort above is known as 'El Abanico', located near the coast, opposite to your capitol building. Did you ever hear of it?" San Miguel asked his prisoner with a proprietary air.

Lucas shook his head. Like most Puerto Ricans, he had very little knowledge about the archeological treasures that existed in his country.

"The fort of El Abanico" resembles what its Spanish name implies, "The Fan"." San Miguel gestured to the ceiling, sweeping outward both of his arms. "It is a small outpost outside of the walls of San Cristobal that opens up to the east like a fan. It was intended to slow down any invading army that approached San Juan and its main line of defenses by land. Its main structure, where the fighting was supposed to occur, is upstairs, of course. But what very few people knew—then or now—is that under it existed this secret room, to which you could only have access by raising that trap door on the ceiling and using a ladder to come down. Well, that or coming through the tunnel that we just used."

San Miguel pointed the beam of his flashlight towards the metallic square that Lucas had noticed on the roof.

"That's where the trap door used to be. It's not the real trapdoor; the real one rotted away ages ago. You see, the Spaniards were master fort builders. Their defenses were designed not only to stop the enemy, but to lead him astray, through a series of zigzagging walls that ended in blind alleys where the enemy could be ambushed, or led to places that had mines below them that could blow up. They also built a system of tunnels through which they could move their troops from one place to another, without exposing them to enemy fire."

San Miguel looked around him admiringly, giving Lucas time to examine the room.

"For more than a century, after the forts around San Juan ceased to be used, this chamber lay forgotten under El Abanico. It's wooden trapdoor rotted out, but the few transients who sought refuge in the structure above, never thought of jumping down here, into what seemed to be a dangerous, dark hole. They used it to dump garbage and to defecate into it. A built-in latrine, it became. The metal trap door that you see is modern, installed by your government to keep unwanted visitors out and avoid people from falling in. It was placed here recently, a few years ago, after the Institute of Culture decided to investigate this room."

San Miguel swept his flashlight over the archeological dig, and then directed its light beam to a small wooden door on the opposite side of the chamber. "The archeologists who explored this place came upon an unexpected treasure trove of discarded artifacts accumulated through the ages. But after clearing out much of the debris, they found *that* door, by far the most important discovery of all. Because *that* door is the only existing portal to the vast system of tunnels that exists under the city of Old San Juan."

So the rumors were true, Lucas thought. *The tunnels under the city really did exist. But what did the tunnels have to do with the terrorists? Were they hiding in them, ready to strike the G-20 leaders in a vulnerable moment?*

He could not see how. The armed forces patrolling the streets of the city possessed enough firepower to stop any number of men that the terrorists could throw at them. Besides, if they had wanted to disrupt the

G-20 Conference, why did they spoil the surprise element by conducting the January attack? It made no sense.

San Miguel studied Lucas' puzzled expression and smiled. He seemed to enjoy his prisoner's confusion, but said nothing. They renewed their trek, heading towards the small door in the chamber to which San Miguel had just alluded. Czecka unlocked it with another of his keys. After that, he handed them back to his boss.

Lucas watched as San Miguel placed them in one of his pants pockets, and the Puerto Rican impulsively muttered, "The keys..."

"The keys," San Miguel repeated with a smug look on his face. "What about the keys?"

"The keys are the *key* to what you're doing, aren't they? You went through a lot of trouble to make copies of them, to gain access into the tunnels without being noticed." He hesitated, then decided to continue. "In fact, you made those copies during the revolt, didn't you? After you had locked out the park rangers in one of the fort's cells, where they were found later, if I recall correctly. That way, they would never be able to see you, and never know that you copied the keys."

San Miguel regarded Lucas with renewed interest. "That is very perceptive of you. Any other observations?"

Yes, Lucas thought, but realized that the more he revealed to the terrorist leader, the more he increased the chances that he would not walk out alive from there, if in fact that chance existed at all. So he kept quiet.

It must have been quite an effort to obtain copies of the keys in the middle of the revolt. The terrorists would have been forced to carry with them a key-making machine, or visit a place—in the middle of the fighting—where keys were duplicated. Either proposition must have been cumbersome and involved a lot of risk and effort, so the keys had to be a very crucial part of their plan.

And if they had duplicated the keys, it meant that from the outset they had planned to return to Fort San Cristobal at some later date, to use them when nobody expected it. Otherwise, Lucas had little doubt that Czecka could have easily broken into the fort any time he chose to do so, without the use of keys. They had taken extraordinary measures to sneak into the San Cristobal fort without being detected. *The question was why.*

He had often wondered why, of all the cities in the world, the terrorists had chosen Old San Juan to conduct a terrorist operation in such a grand scale, an operation that they must have known was doomed to fail from the outset. He had never accepted the theory that the Macheteros had been exclusively behind the January attacks. He knew for a fact that many outsiders had participated in the thwarted revolt; he had fought some of them himself. True, the eyes of the world had been riveted on Puerto Rico for a few days, and many pundits who—it seemed endlessly—examined the why's and wherefore's of the operation had proposed the theory that by choosing San Juan, the terrorists had made the point that, no matter its lack of strategic importance, no American city would really be safe from a terrorist attack. That the revolt had been staged to make the rest of the American nation—of the world—feel unsafe about where the terrorists would strike next. But to use up so many resources just to make that point, without any other practical results? It just didn't make any sense.

Lucas caught San Miguel studying him with a quizzical look and lowered his eyes. *The keys were the key,* he repeated to himself. The keys that gave San Miguel and his men unrestricted and undetected access to the tunnels under the city just as the G-20 Conference was taking place.

"Let's move on," San Miguel said to Czecka, who sighed deeply and then leaned his mammoth frame to squeeze through the door he had just opened, which was even smaller than that of the first tunnel through which they had traveled, nearly not fitting into it. "You next," the terrorist leader said to Lucas.

Even before he had finished going through the door, Lucas caught a whiff of the passage into which he was penetrating and recoiled. It smelled of death. Not the pungent stench of the carcass of a dead dog or rat, but the more subtle, pernicious odor of lingering, simmering decay, trapped permanently within the narrow, dark confines that lay ahead. He saw Czecka's body ahead of him, outlined by the glow of the flashlight he was holding in front of him, blocking most of the view beyond like a thick tree trunk growing straight out of the ground. The unpleasant man did not bother to look back at Lucas, treating him with the same open contempt that he would treat a pest.

The corridor here was wider than the one they had traversed before, the ceiling higher. Lucas could still not stand entirely upright, but could assume a more comfortable, upright stance.

"Whew!" he heard Daniel mutter behind him. "It really stinks in here! Is that you, Czecka?"

"Keep quiet and stop wasting Czecka's time," San Miguel said at the back of the line, chiding Daniel as if he was addressing an unruly teenager.

The four men renewed their trek, at first just following the only passageway available, but later—as the path branched out in different directions—pausing while Czecka flashed his ultraviolet light to verify the infrared markings on the walls and make certain that they were following the correct route. Lucas tried to keep a mental map of where they were heading, counting the number of steps he took up to the moment that the small party switched to another corridor, knowing that without a flashlight, any escape would have to rely on his memory. But after half an hour, he had lost count of the steps, and instead focused on remembering each of the turns they made.

They changed directions four times, three times turning to the left, the last time taking the central of three corridors. He was astounded by the length and variety of the tunnels. At times, the floor had sloped downwards, going deep into the bowels of the old city, the air feeling damp and clammy, most of the sound muffled as if someone had stuffed cotton into his ears. Twice, they walked past parts of the walls that had given way to the earth's unrelenting pressure, spilling brick and dark, rich dirt into the passageways, puddling the floors with dark, slippery water. In those places, the air felt particularly moist and malodorous. *As if the devil was trying to sneak out of hell,* Daniel had muttered, earning another reprimand from San Miguel.

Sometimes the floor leveled and the corridor turned in a wide curve with no other exits. There would be periodic nooks in the walls, like those Lucas had seen in the tunnel under La Fortaleza, where not more than one person could hide, but which could easily be used to surprise unwary travelers. Lucas made a mental note of them.

There were some moments when the ground slanted upwards, taking them closer to the surface, so close, in fact, that sometimes Lucas thought that he could hear the rumbling of the ceiling as heavy vehicles rolled overhead. *Garbage trucks,* Lucas surmised by the hour of the day, although he had no way of confirming it. Once he thought he heard far away voices filtering through invisible cracks. The others heard them too, and stopped briefly to listen. But when no other voices materialized, the men renewed their journey.

Occasionally there would be roots dangling from the ceiling—especially in those places where they were closer to the surface—or a few, startled roaches would scurry away from the four newcomers. Sometimes, invisible cobwebs would cling to the travelers' hands and faces. However, for subterranean passageways that had been abandoned for more than a hundred years and that were entrenched in the entrails of the old city, the ancient galleries were surprisingly free of vermin or debris.

There were random signs of human activity; not old artifacts from the Spanish colonial era, but more modern stuff: a couple of discarded boxes of synthetic fruit punch, a silver candy wrapper, a glass bottle of Coke, some scraps of what seemed to be white paper, three small, plastic bags. Lucas remembered his conversation with Antonio—it seemed now like ages ago—about how some of the tunnels had been used by drug smugglers to store or move their wares. At the time, he had thought the story an unsubstantiated, far-fetched rumor. Now, it all seemed more plausible than his own, implausible situation.

About twenty minutes into the tunnel, the men walked past an opening to their right that reverberated with the echoes of their footsteps. Daniel stopped momentarily and flashed his flashlight's beam into the breach, revealing a vast, empty chamber. As he moved the light about the walls of the room, his eyes caught a dull reflection on the floor. When he checked it with his flashlight, he discovered that, except for a narrow rim bordering the hall, most of the room's bottom was covered by water.

Daniel whistled softly. "It's a...It's a pool of some sort," he said, noticing that the water was rippling as if something was swimming over it.

San Miguel popped his head from behind him and said casually, "A cistern. Keep going."

Further on, the group began to pass other smaller openings in the walls—both to their left and to their right—that seemed to lead into small rooms. After walking past the first dozen, Czecka began to flash his ultraviolet light lamp on the edges of the openings to his right. Finally, with a satisfied grunt, he stopped and, looking back past Lucas and Daniel, said to San Miguel, "This is the one."

CHAPTER IV

At first, Lucas didn't see it. The room, barely wide enough to fit more than six people, was engulfed by moving shadows, as the flashlight's beam slid about its walls. Then Czecka—who seemed to occupy half of the small chamber all by himself—pulled away a dark gray sheet from the back of the room, and revealed what at first impression seemed to be a short, rectangular filing cabinet made of aluminum with small rubber wheels. Except for a tiny gauge issuing a faint, greenish light, and what looked like three light switches—all of them flipped in the same direction—Lucas did not notice any other markings, gadgets or indicators on the device.

"It's still here," San Miguel said with evident satisfaction and relief.

The three terrorists gazed upon it for several seconds with a silence bordering on reverence. Kneeling next to the object, Czecka leaned forward and stared intently at the gauge, then looked at San Miguel and nodded.

"Good," the leader of the terrorists said. "And the power level of the battery?" he inquired as an afterthought.

"Still about a quarter of the power left," Czecka answered in a guttural, off-hand tone.

"That's more than enough to take it to tomorrow at noon," Daniel whispered. "The battery is doing its job, just like they said it would."

"Still, we should not risk it. We should make certain that the battery doesn't fail us. Connect the spare."

The big man opened the small leather satchel he had been carrying, and slipped it off what appeared to be a squat, white, plastic container with two small terminals at one of its ends. Placing his flashlight on the floor, he lay on the ground, flat on his back, and peeked under the cabinet-sized object. He grabbed the white plastic container and, somewhat clumsily, attempted to fit it under the device.

"Gently," San Miguel cautioned him. "We don't want to damage the mechanism."

Czecka grumbled something unintelligible that sounded like a curse, as he struggled with the spare.

Lucas felt a sickening fear well up in his stomach, as he began to understand what was happening. Desperately, he searched for a means of escape, knowing that the terrorists would never allow him to leave that room alive. He was on the verge of panicking, even though he knew that if he panicked, he would seal his fate, so he fought his growing terror, trying to regain his mind's focus by engaging San Miguel in conversation.

"I gather that that thing over there is a bomb," he said to the tall terrorist, nodding in the device's direction.

"Yes indeed," San Miguel answered without taking his eyes from the work that Czecka was conducting.

"Destined for the G-20 Conference."

"Right again," the terrorist leader replied. "Since we dragged you down here, the least I can do is answer your questions, so ask away."

Lucas stared at the device. He had no knowledge about bombs, but he imagined the type of bomb he was looking at. "It's some sort of nuclear device, isn't it? You're planning to set off a nuclear device below the city, when the leaders of the world are all gathered together."

"Well, not *all* the leaders of the world. Those that count, though," San Miguel said with a faint smile. "But to answer your question, yes, it is a nuclear device. It's a rudimentary atomic bomb. It contains a critical mass of plutonium into which a 'bullet' is discharged to set it off. Not a very powerful or efficient bomb, I'm afraid, but I'm assured that the explosion will yield a ten to twenty kiloton blast, somewhere around the strength of the Hiroshima or Nagasaki bombs. Enough to destroy most of Old San Juan in any event," he earnestly assured his captive.

Even though he had suspected it, Lucas was stunned into momentary silence.

"You're wondering how we got the bomb here," San Miguel stated, erroneously interpreting his prisoner's lack of words for unstated curiosity. "Your ports are woefully inadequate to stop this kind of threat," he continued saying in a purely professorial way, as if discussing a difficult but solvable scientific problem with a student. "They are like huge sieves, where tons of illegal merchandise gets through every day. Even so, we could not risk losing our only nuclear device to a...an accidental discovery."

"So you smuggled it in," Lucas said, trying to keep the conversation going while he frantically sought for a way out.

The terrorist leader tentatively shook his head from one side to another. "Well...yes and no," he replied. "We obviously smuggled it in. Obviously, but not in the usual way that things get smuggled. Besides, we couldn't trust such precious cargo to any run-of-the-mill smugglers. No. We used a submarine from a country friendly to our cause. Venezuela, if you must know. About a year ago, we fitted the bomb materials into a modified torpedo. We placed a tracing device, just in case the torpedo malfunctioned, although the events proved there was no need for it. But better safe than sorry, as your American friends are fond to say. The submarine fired the disarmed torpedo at the coast, to a beach near Arroyo, in your east coast. Our team was waiting for it, and recovered it without a hitch."

Lucas' fear slowly began to turn into anger. *Focus,* he said to himself, his heart beating so fast that he thought it would burst out of his chest, *don't let your emotions cloud your thinking.* Even so, he could not stop himself from saying, "So you're planning to kill thousands of people to wipe out a dozen or so of the world leaders. You must be very proud."

"Careful..." he heard Daniel warn behind him.

San Miguel shrugged. "That's okay, Daniel," he said to his companion. "Alfaro has the right to voice what he thinks." He looked directly at Lucas. "Despite what you may think, I do not enjoy killing people—"

"You have a strange way of showing it, you son of a bitch!"

San Miguel grimaced.

"I really don't," he assured him patiently, despite the insult. "Not any more than President Truman enjoyed it when he ordered the cities of Hiroshima and Nagasaki bombed. He did it to avoid a greater wrong, in his case, to avoid the millions of deaths that would have occurred if the United States had been forced to invade Japan. I did not hear any Americans complain about it."

Lucas said nothing.

"No words to defend your wonderful compatriots? I thought so. You see, for decades, the Americans and their allies have waged a genocidal war against our people, against the people of the Third World, selling weapons to our oppressors, depleting and polluting our lands, and stealing our natural treasures and resources. They promote their godless culture, and insult our true God. They support our enemies with billions of dollars and modern weapons. Hundreds of thousands of our people die each year because of your American arrogance and intolerance. I grew up in a Lebanese refugee camp, after the American's pet ally, the Israelis, destroyed my village. My mother died from a broken heart and lack of medical help; my father died in an Israeli jail. So don't talk to me about morality. Your leaders are all immoral killers. It is time to bring them to justice."

"And in the meantime, if a few thousand innocent people are killed in the process, that doesn't matter to you. That is your justice?" Lucas said contemptuously.

"Of course it matters to me!" San Miguel retorted angrily. "And I will have to live with that in my conscience for the rest of my life. But sometimes, a few must die for the good of the many. When this bomb goes off, it will decapitate the world's major governments. It will cause tremendous turmoil and panic, and possibly the collapse of the world markets. Nobody will feel safe. Nobody will *be* safe! Everybody will be looking over his shoulder, because they will be afraid about who will be next. The governments who have lorded over their weaker brothers will have to accede to our demands, because otherwise, our next target may be them. It will be the beginning of the end for our First World oppressors."

Czecka finished his work under the nuclear device, and sat on the floor. "It's done," he announced.

"And the power indicator?"

The huge terrorist peered into the illuminated gauge. "A hundred percent power," he confirmed.

"Good. Then it's time we wrap up things here." He looked at Lucas. "I will not insult your intelligence by giving you any false hopes. You understand that I cannot let you go," he said to him.

"Why drag me all the way here to kill me?"

"Because nobody will find your body here. We can't run the risk of you being discovered prematurely, before noon tomorrow."

"One more life for the common good," Lucas responded sarcastically, prompting a laugh from Daniel.

"Well said," the latter expressed. "I admire brave men like yourself. I hope when my time comes, I will die as well as you." He turned to San Miguel. "I would like him to die as cleanly and painlessly as he can," he told him. "A shot in the head will do the trick."

Without warning, Lucas swiveled on his right foot and grasped the front end of Daniel's gun, trying to twist it away from his grasp. However, the terrorist managed to snatch it back, while Czecka—still crouching on the floor—swiped his left arm and pulled both of Lucas' legs off the ground, making him fall hard on his back. With befuddling quickness, the hulking man turned on Lucas and, before the Puerto Rican could recover his breath, pinned him to the ground with his knee while grasping his hands.

The weight of the massive terrorist felt as if a concrete column had fallen on Lucas' chest. Lucas gasped, trying to regain his senses, seeing with the corner of his eye Daniel kneel beside him and press his gun's barrel to his head. Overhead, as if in a surreal film, he could see the outline of Czecka's barrel-like chest and his upraised jaw, as he waited further instructions from his boss.

"No," San Miguel said to Daniel. "No shooting. It will probably not be heard, but we can't risk it."

Lucas felt Daniel hesitate, and then heard him say with regret, "Sorry, my friend, I really wanted to do this as painlessly as possible." He stood up and walked away.

"I will leave now," San Miguel said to Czecka. "I have the extra ultra-violet light, so I'll be able to find my way back."

"I'll stay with Czecka," Daniel offered.

"No," San Miguel replied. "There are a few things I want to discuss with you while we head out. You can wait for Czecka in El Abanico."

"Very well..." Daniel said hesitantly.

"Kill him as quickly and painlessly as you can. Don't delay more than you have to," San Miguel instructed Czecka. He turned his attention back to Lucas. "I am sorry that it came to this, Mr. Alfaro," he said in a dismissive tone. "You should not have followed us. May God have mercy on your soul."

Lucas tried to curse the departing terrorist, but could only manage a choked grunt.

Czecka waited for his two companions to leave, while quietly watching Lucas' face. Then, when he could no longer hear their conversation, he released his captive's left arm, and in a workmanlike, almost careless fashion, clamped his hand in a viselike grip around Lucas' neck.

It felt as if a rod of burning iron had shut Lucas' windpipe. He choked, panicking and trying to strike his giant tormentor with his freed hand. But his reach fell short; Czecka held him with his arm outstretched, calmly squeezing the life out of his lungs. Lucas tried to wiggle free from under him, but his body failed to move under the monster man's suffocating weight, as if it had been cemented to the ground.

Frantically, Lucas moved his free hand and found the fingers digging into his neck, following their outline until he located the little finger. Using his remaining strength, he wrapped his hand around Czecka's pinkie and pulled it back until he heard it snap. He did not release the finger, however, continuing to push the limp appendage back even further, then turning it wildly in every direction.

The terrorist made a barely audible sound and instinctively moved his hand away, letting go off the neck. Lucas knew that he would only have a scant second before the surly giant renewed his attack, so he pushed himself upwards with his left arm, and with the bent knuckles of his right hand struck Czecka's neck repeatedly and viciously. Surprised, Czecka gagged and backed up, briefly lifting his weight from Lucas' body. It was enough for Lucas to skitter from under him.

Still on his back, Lucas tried to kick him with his right leg. But Czecka, still gasping for air, effortlessly blocked the kick with his left hand, and grabbed him by the foot. With a sudden tug, he pulled Lucas back towards him, but as he did so, Lucas kicked him on the nose with his right leg, and he let go. Again Lucas backed up, so quickly and desperately that he banged the back of his head against one of the chamber's walls.

Blood dripped from Czecka's nose and onto his dense mustache. He glared at Lucas, and wiped the blood away with the back of his right hand, his broken pinky twisted at an odd angle. Slowly, he got to his feet and blocked the room's exit. Forced to bend forward because of the low ceiling, he looked like a crouching grizzly, ready to attack.

Lucas also stood up, moving as far away from his hulking opponent as he could, adopting a boxer's stance. He would have to move fast, hitting him and stepping out of his way, he told himself, trying to shift positions until he could get to the door and run. Under no circumstances could he let himself get pinned down again, or that would be the end of him. He doubted that his bear-like opponent would let him escape again.

Taking the initiative, he jabbed Czecka with three rapid punches, trying to hit his bleeding nose, hoping it would be tender and make him retreat. The terrorist made a throaty, angry noise and took a step back. Elated, Lucas attacked him again with a flurry of punches to the face.

It had been what the huge man had been waiting for. Seemingly out of nowhere, he swung his left arm in a wide arc and struck Lucas on his right ear.

It was a brutal blow, delivered with the strength of a sledgehammer. Lucas' vision became blurred with stars and his knees buckled. Desperately, he tried to stay on his feet, but began to tumble backwards. He would have fallen, but Czecka grabbed him by the shirt. With terrifying ease, he lifted Lucas in the air and tossed him into a wall.

Lucas hit the wall awkwardly, feeling a sharp jolt of pain in his left leg and back, and bouncing hard onto the ground. His head still reeling from the vicious punch, he saw Czecka approach, and crawled towards the nuclear device. As he did, he discovered the flashlight, still lying on the floor. He grabbed it and, in a moment of inspiration, looked for the "on-off" switch. He managed to turn the light off just as he saw Czecka's trunk-like leg swinging towards him, and curled like a ball, bracing for the shock.

Had the kick struck him squarely in the back, it would have fractured several ribs, and maybe broken his spine; had it been delivered to the head, it would have killed him or at the very least rendered him unconscious. But—forced to lean forward because of the low ceiling and disoriented by the sudden darkness—the giant man only managed to kick Lucas between his ribs and right elbow, wrenching his arm upwards.

Instinctively, Lucas rolled towards his adversary, causing him to trip over him in the pitch-black room. Czecka crashed into the nuclear bomb with a loud clang, and for the first time the large man shouted with rage. Careful not to damage the device, he stood up and turned around, but by that time Lucas had run away.

Lucas heard Czecka's heavy footsteps behind him and took a glance over his shoulder. He could not see anything in the pitch-black gloom of the tunnel, but knew that the terrorist could not be very far away, following the glow of his flashlight. For such a huge person who barely fit in the underground corridor, the man was barreling through it at a surprising speed.

Lucas' elbow throbbed with excruciating pain, but he could still extend his arm, which was good. He knew that he would have to use it soon, if he wanted to get out of there alive. He was still in the last of the corridors that had led the terrorists to the bomb, but at any moment now the passageway would split, and if he made the wrong turn, he could easily get lost. Czecka knew, or should know, that there was no need to kill Lucas, only to keep him underground until the nuclear device exploded. If the terrorist got back to El Abanico before Lucas did, he could lock up the entrance to the tunnels and trap Lucas inside.

There was only one chance of finding the way back, and that was by getting hold of the ultraviolet light that Czecka was carrying. And that meant fighting and defeating Sasquatch-sized terrorist who was chasing him.

But there was no way that he could beat the angry giant in a fistfight. Not without a weapon. The man was just too big and powerful. Lucas searched his pockets as he ran, trying to find anything that he could use. There were only his keys and his wallet. Holding each key between each of his fingers, he closed his right fist, so that the keys stuck out like short, blunt spikes. It was the best he could do, but that would not help him much unless he got into a close-range fight, a prospect that he dreaded to think about.

Lucas reached a spot where the corridor branched out into three arched openings, and he stopped. His instincts told him to go to the right, but he knew that if he made the wrong choice he would be lost. He listened to Czecka's hurried progress behind him—*was it his imagination, or was he actually feeling the ground shake*—and he knew that his pursuer would be there in a matter of seconds. He would have to make his stand there, he thought. He had no other choice.

He turned off the flashlight, and went down on all fours, blocking the corridor. Shielding his head with his arms, he braced for the impact. He heard the giant man increase his pace as he failed to see the light he had been following, his heavy boots crunching the loose dirt on the floor. The ground *was* shaking, Lucas thought. Czecka's increasingly louder, belabored breathing announced his impending arrival. *Like the angry snorts of a bull*, it seemed to Lucas. *I wonder if Theseus felt the same way when he felt the Minotaur approach.*

Czecka ran into him with the power of a compact car. Fortunately for Lucas, the big man struck him with one of the shins of his legs and tried to avoid him by raising his other foot. He failed to clear Lucas' back, however, and tumbled straight forward like a toppling sequoia. The blow turned Lucas sideways and partially drove the air out of him, but he was alert enough to hear a muted crack and a loud thud, as Czecka crashed head onto the column of one the arched entrances beyond.

Lucas struggled back up and turned on his flashlight, hoping that Czecka had knocked himself out or broken his neck. He had no such luck. The huge man was still down, his baldpate showing a deep, bloody gash. But he was stirring himself to a kneeling position while directing a murderous look in the direction of the light.

For the first time, Lucas noticed the holster strapped to the terrorist's waist. He ran towards it, and tried to unsnap the strap that held the gun in place. However, Czecka immediately guessed his intentions and snatched his leg, trying to knock him to the ground. Lucas lost the flashlight and grabbed on to his enemy's neck from behind, placing him in a headlock and trying to choke him. He wrapped his arm around the bear-sized man's throat and squeezed it with all of his strength, but it felt as effective as trying to squeeze the air out of a stone column.

Czecka got back to his feet, stumbling drunkenly while Lucas clung to his back. Then, regaining his balance, he backed into a wall, slamming Lucas against it. The jolt nearly knocked Lucas off his back, but the smaller man held on, pressing harder against the giant's neck. Czecka tried to shake him off, making Lucas' legs swing wildly from side to side, but still the smaller man held on.

Then Czecka strode forward, trying to put as much distance between him and the wall as he could. Lucas guessed his intentions immediately; the hulking terrorist was going to slam him against the wall again, but this time he would run backwards to gain as much momentum as he could. The resulting blow would probably crush his bones.

Lucas felt the muscles in Czecka's massive back tense up, and knew that the terrorist was about to make his run. The huge man was taking short gulps of air, even though Lucas continued to squeeze his neck with every ounce of strength he had left in his body. Then Czecka made his move, and began to travel backwards towards the wall.

Despairing, Lucas relaxed his grip, and partially uncovered his enemy's neck. He placed his right, spiked hand over the exposed throat, and racked it viciously with the line of keys he held between his fingers.

Warm blood gushed out of the giant's shredded jugular, splashing Lucas' hand and face. Lucas jumped off the back, but not soon enough to escape completely. Czecka's crashing bulk momentarily pinned his left arm and shoulder, causing Lucas to scream in pain. Then both men collapsed on the ground, partially stunned by the force of the blow.

Lucas tried to roll away from the fallen terrorist, but before he managed to do it, Czecka grabbed him by the scruff of his shirt's neck and dragged him back towards him. In one fluid motion, the massive man got up on his knees and locked Lucas' head under his right arm. With the crushing strength of a boa constrictor, the terrorist's heavily muscled arm began to tighten around the Puerto Rican's neck.

Lucas felt the pressure build until he thought his head would explode. Czecka's blood continued to fall freely, soaking the man's arm and dripping over Lucas' hair and cheeks, but still the giant held on with no signs of weakening. Lucas tried to hit him in the kidneys and the groin, but his arms bounced harmlessly off the terrorist's flanks. As he began to black out, his hand came upon his enemy's holster, and fumbling frantically, he managed to unsnap the holster's safety strap.

Maybe because of his terrible wound to the neck, or maybe because of his intense rage, Czecka never noticed when Lucas pulled out the gun. Flipping the safety lock with his thumb, Lucas stuck the gun's barrel on the terrorist's ribcage and fired repeatedly.

Czecka's body shook, more from the surprise than from the shock of the bullets. Then his grip on Lucas' head began to relax until he could hold it no more.

As Lucas righted himself up and wheezed desperately for air, the mortally wounded giant knotted his thin eyebrows in a quizzical, fierce scowl, staring in incomprehension at his chest. He tried to speak, but only a gargle came out of his mouth. His eyes seemed to roll into his head, and then his thick trunk pitched forward and slammed to the ground.

Stumbling back a couple of steps, Lucas hovered over his enemy's dead body, afraid that the man would somehow come back to life and attack him again. Then, thoroughly exhausted, he cautiously approached him and knelt beside him, quickly searching the fallen man's body, taking his ammunition and the ultraviolet lamp.

CHAPTER V

Daniel sat atop a large, overturned, empty plastic container, the type used to hold several gallons of paint, which the archeological team in the digging site must have utilized to remove dirt. He was waiting for Czecka, who was long overdue. But he knew that the big man was a perfectionist, and that he would tarry at the site of the bomb, until he satisfied himself that nothing would interfere with their plans. For all his fearsome, hulking presence, Czecka was as finicky as a fifteen-year-old debutante.

It was very quiet, inside the secret chamber under the El Abanico fortifications, but contrary to many of his comrades and brothers-in-arms—who conjured ghosts or felt uncomfortable in old, abandoned ruins—he enjoyed it that way. He had never been a history buff, not really caring to dwell too much on the lives of those who had preceded him. He did not believe in ghosts, inasmuch he did not believe in an afterlife, or any religions for that matter. Religions were the collective superstitions of self-deluding fools who wished and convinced themselves that they would continue to exist after they died. He held no such illusions. He preferred to live for the moment, as intensely and as fully as he could.

It was one of those subjects—*the* main subject—where he and San Miguel differed. He respected San Miguel; considered him one of the most intelligent men and most effective leaders he had ever known. But San Miguel cloaked all of his actions with religious reasons. He was a *jihadist*. He justified his acts as part of a divine plan; his killings as necessary evils to promote God's will. He found the corrupting hand of Capitalism in everything, and believed it to be the root of most of the world's wrongs. He felt certain that by doing God's work, his crimes would be forgiven.

Daniel saw it the other way around. If there was a God, then he was the greatest criminal of them all; the tormentor of innocent children, the creator of horrible diseases and famine, the spectator who sat idly by while he witnessed all kinds of massacres, tortures, and abuses, the inventor of natural catastrophes. If any crimes had to be forgiven, it was those that God had committed against humanity.

So what motivated Daniel? Boredom. He had always hated institutions and lawgivers, whose sole mission in life seemed to be to bind humanity in an ever tightening straightjacket. He deplored the holier-than-thou attitude of those who ran the institutions, and instinctively rebelled against anyone who invoked their authority or represented them.

Becoming a terrorist—he preferred the term "freedom fighter"—had come naturally to him, first as a university rebel rouser, then as a radical activist, and finally as full fledged freedom fighter. His main goal in life was to subvert oppressive institutions, and he found that most institutions *were* oppressive. Anything he could do to unravel the constrictive bindings of society he would do, providing him with immense pride and pleasure. He derived a deep thrill of risking his life in highly dangerous missions. It provided him with the ultimate adrenaline rush, which made him enjoy life all the more. He was under no delusion that he would live for long. But when that moment came, when his life and consciousness ended forever, he would have no regrets. He would have lived his life fully.

Even so, there were times that he doubted or disliked what he did. Like now. He had personally liked Alfaro. Had it been for him, he would have let him live. He also had misgivings about the massive destruction of life and property that would happen in just a few hours. San Juan, that beautiful city that had existed for more than five hundred years, would be snuffed out in an instant, reduced to a radioactive pile of rubble that would not be habitable for decades; its population, including its women and children, incinerated or crushed. It would be, as San Miguel had assured everyone, a blow that would shake loose all of the oppressive systems in the world, and would change history forever. But still, it would be a terrible price to pay.

At least he did not have to salve his conscience by invoking God, and he did not have to fear going to hell. When he died, he died, and that was all.

San Miguel had left ahead of his two companions, saying he would walk to the ship. It wasn't that far away. Less than a mile, in fact. Before leaving, he had reminded Daniel to lock and leave everything as if no one had been there. It was essential that their visit to San Cristobal remained unnoticed until noon of the next day. By that time, they would all be gone; the cruise ship, the world leaders, and San Juan. Well, Czecka would still be in Puerto Rico—he was too big and noticeable to travel as a passenger in the cruise ship—but he would be far away from the explosion.

Speaking of which, where was the old sourpuss? Daniel should have insisted on staying, to hurry him up. He would have to talk to him about his timing. One day, it would get them all killed.

Daniel wondered how soon it would take for San Miguel and him to learn about the nuclear explosion. They had booked passage on the *Orion Star*, one of the three cruise ships presently moored in the docks of San Juan. It was one of the latest line of ships that was so big that it had a street running through it, from prow to stern. It was scheduled to leave that night at ten, stopping in St. Thomas, St. Martin, Dominica, Curacao, and Aruba, before returning to San Juan.

Of course, if everything happened as planned, there would be no San Juan to return to. However, regardless of what happened, they had no intention of completing the trip. They would abandon the *Orion* in Aruba, catch a flight to Bonaire, and from there they would be picked up by a large private fishing yacht and whisked to Venezuela.

He was actually looking forward to the trip. He had never traveled on a cruise ship that size before, and could use the rest and relaxation before the next phase of their operation. The world would be a very unstable place after tomorrow at noon, when a great portion of its leaders would be wiped out as it met for lunch in the El Convento Hotel. He was certain that San Miguel and his merry band of men would be very busy in the months that followed. He would make it a point to enjoy his free time to the fullest, while he could. There would be many sexy women on board—single and married—and he had no doubt that he would be able to attract the eyes of more than one of them before their first day at sea was over.

His idle rumination stopped abruptly, as something caught his attention. He was sitting with his back turned towards the entrance of the tunnel, but even so he sensed the stealthy entrance of the newcomer. He knew immediately it was not Czecka; even if the huge man's footsteps had not betrayed him, the bulk of his body would have altered the feeling in the room. Casually, he leaned forward as if to tie one of his shoestrings, and grabbed the handle of the .38 Special he had strapped to his right ankle, pulling back its hammer with his thumb.

"I wouldn't do that if I was you," he heard a voice say a few yards away from him. "Place both hands slowly on top of your head and stand up," the voice said.

It was Alfaro, he thought with incredulity. *How in the hell had he escaped from Czecka?* He cursed himself under his breath. He had been careless beyond belief, relying blindly on Czecka's indestructibility.

"I see that you managed to leave Czecka behind," he said in a pleasantly surprised tone. "How—"

"Just do as I said," Lucas replied, cutting him off.

Still holding on to his right ankle, Daniel sighed. "Okay, but—"

With numbing speed, Daniel drew his gun and turned, diving towards the floor and opening fire. He fired blindly, shooting before he caught sight of Lucas, guessing where he was standing by the prior sound of his voice. But his intended target had shifted to the right and was kneeling on one leg, returning the fire.

Even so, Daniel saw several of his shots strike the masonry wall very closely behind Lucas, making the Puerto Rican flinch and drop into one of the shallow archeological ditches in the chamber. Daniel stopped firing, and crawled behind a low mound of dirt.

That had been close, he told himself, trying to remember how many shots he had discharged, his heart beating wildly. *Too close. Had it been three or four bullets that he had fired?* He felt a dull pain in his stomach and slid a hand to his belly. A sharp stab of pain made him wince. When he brought his hand back, it was drenched in blood.

"Shit," he whispered. "There goes the cruise." Then, raising his voice, he shouted, "Hey, Alfaro! Did I hit you?"

Lucas took some time to answer. "I don't think so," he said eventually. "And you?"

"You nicked me, all right," Daniel admitted with a short laugh. He paused, to gather his thoughts. "Last time I saw you, Czecka was sort of...crushing you into the floor." He stopped again. His lips were dry and numb, and he felt tired. "How did you manage to get out?"

"I'm not sure," Lucas answered honestly.

Daniel chuckled. "Did you...kill him?"

"Yes."

Daniel tried to whistle, but his lips were too dry. "Man, you're good," he said panting. His strength was ebbing too fast. He must be bleeding very badly. "Never thought anyone could take him...hand-to-hand, that is...Except me, maybe..." He waited for Lucas to reply, but when he didn't he continued speaking. "Anyway, I'm glad that...I'm glad...that if anyone beat him...it was you...I like you...Alfaro..."

"Thanks," Lucas answered. "Are you all right?"

Daniel had to think hard before he answered. "Right? No!" he said finally. "You shot me good...You wouldn't...wouldn't...give me the courtesy...of raising your head...for a moment, you know...so I can shoot you..."

Lucas laughed. "I'll pass on that one for now."

"I..I suspected...as much..." Daniel said. He was gasping for air now.

"Where is San Miguel?" Lucas shouted.

"San...Miguel..." Daniel repeated, as if trying to remember the name of a long forsaken acquaintance. "San Miguel...he's not...here..." *He was dying*, he realized with surprising resignation. *How had that happened? Just a few minutes before, he had been anticipating his sojourn on the Orion.*

His gun felt too heavy for his hand. It slipped away from his fingers, despite his efforts to hold it. "You can come...out...now..." he said in a loud gasp. "I can't...shoot...you...any...more..."

Daniel closed his eyes for a moment, letting his head rest on the ground. When he opened them again, he was amazed by how clearly he could see the individual grains of sand clinging to the lower part of his forearm, each an amber, crystalline box containing timeless secrets. He wondered what would happen to them when the bomb went off. It all seemed so irrelevant now, as if he was stepping off a train, and watching everyone leave without him.

"Hold on," he heard Lucas say. Then a hand cradled the base of his neck and placed it on something soft. "Do you have a cell phone?" Lucas asked with inexplicable urgency. "I'll call 911."

911. The digits of the emergency number struck him as impossibly funny. Daniel smiled, or at least tried to. "Tell...San Miguel..." he hissed with his last breath.

Lucas let Daniel's head rest on the floor, and closed his eyes. Like Daniel, he had felt a grudging respect for his enemy. Not so for San Miguel, whom he intended to hunt down. He began to search the dead terrorist's body, darting periodic looks towards the entrance of the passageway that led from El Abanico's underground chamber to the inner walls of Fort San Cristobal, afraid that San Miguel would return.

In Daniel's left pants pocket, he discovered a plastic I.D. card showing a round circle of tiny stars and the name of *"Orion Star"* over it. The blurry black and white image of Daniel's face smiled back at him next to the name and logo of the cruise ship, the words "Carlos Ramirez de Orellana" and "Cabin 8137" written below it. In the right pants pocket he found the keys to the fort's various locks and—as he had hoped—a Cell phone.

Lucas dialed 911, but after a second's wait the words "NO LOCAL RECEPTION" appeared on the screen. They were still too deep underground to establish communications, he realized.

He could not waste any further time, he told himself. San Miguel had spoken as if the bomb was set to go off at noon of the next day which, he seemed to recollect, would be the time that the ministers and heads of state would celebrate the conference's welcoming banquet in El Convento, hosted by President Powell. *But what if he was wrong? What if he had misunderstood San Miguel and the device was set to go off much earlier? What if San Miguel's device malfunctioned, and went off unexpectedly?* He had to get help as fast as he could.

So he ran. He ran, following the passageway that had brought him and the others from the outer perimeter of San Cristobal to El Abanico, the beam of his flashlight bouncing over the curved walls and ceiling of the tunnel, encasing him in a bubble of light that opened up the impenetrable gloom ahead of him and rapidly closed it behind him. He had lost his hard hat somewhere, and banged his head twice as he made his way through—one of the times hard enough to make him blink and pause for a few seconds. But after traveling through the maze that lay beyond El Abanico, the going was relatively easy.

He emerged into the open space between the fort's two sets of walls about ten minutes later, and gratefully breathed in the cool air of the night. He felt like a swimmer, surfacing to fill his lungs after a long dive. It was just shy of twenty minutes to eight, he confirmed when he looked at his watch. It seemed impossible that only an hour before, he, San Miguel, Daniel, and Czecka had entered the visitors' center of the fort.

He had turned off his flashlight before he exited the tunnel, hoping he would be less visible to San Miguel if he was waiting outside. Somehow, he suspected that behind the pleasant, professorial façade of the terrorist leader hid a very dangerous man. His gut instincts told him that San Miguel would not be there, that he would have returned to the ship. Nevertheless, he continued to move through the open ground at a fast pace, finally seeking concealment under one of the thick shadows cast by the fort's inner walls.

He took out Daniel's cell phone to call 911, but on impulse, dialed Michelle's phone instead. This time, he heard the ringing tone that confirmed that the call was going through.

"Brother," Michelle said at the other end, recognizing his voice as soon as he said hello, her voice a blend of amusement and relief. *"Where have you been hiding? You were supposed to give a lift to Mom and Maria, remember? And what's this strange phone number you're calling from? Where's your phone? Mom has called me about half a dozen times already. You're in big trouble, young man!"*

"Michelle," Lucas interrupted, and something in his tone must have alerted her that something was wrong, because she stopped talking.

"What is it?" she asked anxiously.

"I'm in Fort San Cristobal—" he began to explain, but she cut him off.

"Fort San Cristobal! Isn't it closed? What are you—"

"Listen to me!" Lucas said urgently. Michelle did as he instructed. "There's a bomb here. A nuclear bomb—"

"A what?"

"Please, just listen! The terrorists planted it here, when they took over San Juan in January. They intend to blow up the city with the G20 leaders."

Lucas heard Michelle take a sharp intake of breath.

"But...how..."

"I can hear other people there with you. Are there other people with you?" Lucas asked, ignoring her question.

"Yes, yes, Doel, Correcaminos, a few people from the Six O'clock News. We're having dinner at Amadeus."

Lucas noticed that the volume of the voices near her had subsided. "Don't say anything to them about the bomb! Not yet. We don't want to start a panic, okay?"

"Yes," Michelle replied breathlessly. Then, trying to avoid questions from her dinner companions, she added in a steadier voice the first thing that came to her mind. *"Sorry about your sprained ankle."*

It took Lucas a couple of seconds to understand that she was talking for the benefit of the others. In the background, he heard a male voice ask, *"Is he all right?"* and Michelle answer, *"Yes, he just tripped over his own feet, it seems."*

"Okay," he said. "Good. Is Archie with you?"

"No. I mean, not yet. He's supposed to meet us here soon," she responded.

"Call him. Tell him to get hold of Superintendent Maldonado. If anybody can reach him, it's him. Tell him to send his people to the visitors' center in Fort San Cristobal. I'll be waiting there. I would call 911, but God knows what would happen, or when I'd be able to reach Maldonado. I killed two terrorists. Archie is our best bet."

"You what?" Michelle reacted with alarm before she could stop herself, then lowered her voice. *"Are you all right?...I mean, besides your ankle?"*

Lucas could hear no nearby voices now, which meant that everybody was listening to what Michelle was saying.

"I'm okay, believe me," he replied patiently. "Tell Maldonado that I'll be here, waiting. Tell him that. In case he should not find me, tell him that the bomb is in a tunnel under the city. The access to the tunnel's entrance in a chamber under El Abanico—"

"Wait...What? Wait a moment." Lucas heard Michelle's voice as she addressed the others. Then there was a long pause, and she finally spoke to him again. *"Lucas, can you hear me?"* she asked in a more subdued tone.

"Yes," he answered.

"I told them I was having problems hearing you and walked out of the restaurant. We can talk freely now. El Abanico. You were saying something about El Abanico. What's El Abanico?"

"It's a small fortification, outside of the walls of San Cristobal, close to the Capitol Building. There's an underground chamber, under El Abanico, with an entrance to the tunnels under the city," Lucas explained. "To get there, you have to take another tunnel that starts inside the walls of the San Cristobal fort and that connects to the secret chamber under El Abanico. The terrorists somehow discovered all of this, and used the tunnels to hide the nuclear bomb."

"This all sounds too complicated for me. You'd better be there to guide the police."

"I intend to," Lucas said earnestly. "But just in case, tell Maldonado to get hold of the fort's rangers. Oh! And if not, get Maria Belen." Maria Belen was the Institute of Culture's archeologist who had told them about the existence of the tunnels close to La Fortaleza. "She should know."

"Okay. But it's better if you show them, okay?" Michelle insisted.

"I will, I will," Lucas replied impatiently. "This is just in case something happens to me. There may be other terrorists around."

"So hide already!" she said as if stating the obvious.

"Don't worry about me, I'll be fine!" he repeated. "I can take care of myself. I heard the terrorists say that the bomb is supposed to go off at noon tomorrow. Noon, got it?"

"Yes, noon tomorrow."

"So there should be time to do something about it. Now here's the tricky part...It's like a maze down there, under the ground. There are passages going every which way, after you go into the tunnel under El Abanico. The terrorists found their way because they marked the walls with a spray that glows green when you illuminate it with ultraviolet light. If for any reason I'm not here, tell Maldonado that his men should use ultraviolet lamps to find the way. Got it?"

"Got it."

"One more thing that I wanted to tell you..." Lucas wracked his brain, trying to remember what he was just about to say. "Oh, yes! Tell Maldonado that the terrorists said this was a ten to twenty kiloton bomb. This should help him with whatever evacuation plans he decides to undertake, okay?"

"Ten to twenty kiloton bomb. Is that big?" Michelle asked, unable to hide her concern.

"About the size of the Hiroshima atomic explosion," Lucas responded.

"Oh my God!"

"Now make your calls. Don't let anybody stop you until you get through to Maldonado. And not a word to anybody else, understand?"

"You take care of yourself, do you hear?" she said in a fearful, threatening tone. But he had already hung up.

CHAPTER VI

Superintendent Maldonado slumped back into his seat, grateful that he had finished his talk. He normally hated public speaking events, feeling very self-conscious about his limited oratory skills. Fortunately for his listeners, his address had been short. As the main police official in Puerto Rico, he had welcomed the heads and delegates of the G20's top security organizations to the gala dinner being held in their honor. The dinner was the beginning of three days of intensive meetings that had been scheduled to discuss anti-terrorist tactics by the different world police forces, using as a frame of reference the January Machetero revolt.

Maldonado had only managed to take a long swallow from his glass of water when a police sergeant had approached him and whispered into his ear that Archie had been trying to reach him over the phone for several minutes, but that his cell phone seemed to be turned off. The sergeant informed him that Archie had sounded very upset, and had said it was a matter of life and death. Would he be able to call him? Archie was waiting.

More perplexed than alarmed, Maldonado had excused himself from the two men sitting by his side, Assistant Director of the Secret Service Mark Esposito and the new head of the FBI in Puerto Rico John Frontera, and walked out of the Crystal Ballroom in the San Geronimo Plaza. It was not the same hall from which Maldonado had directed the rescue operations during the terrorist attack—that hall was located across the corridor and was being used for a senior prom—but a smaller ballroom with windows to the sea, large enough to comfortably accommodate the one hundred-plus visitors attending the dinner.

Outside, he found the red-carpeted corridor infested with tuxedo clad and long-gowned teenagers spilling out of the main ballroom, as well a few businessmen and more informally dressed tourists making their way to and from the nearby conference rooms, bars, and restaurants.

"Stay by the door," Maldonado said to the police sergeant and the two other men guarding the entrance of the Crystal Ballroom, and began to walk down the corridor, looking for a place where he could speak in private. After a few steps, he saw a glass door that seemed to lead to an outside balcony, and trying its handle, found that it was unlocked.

The door was heavy, and he had to push it with his shoulder to get it open. It slammed shut after he managed to squeeze through it, and he was instantly engulfed by the strong, almost wet breeze coming from the sea. It mussed his perfectly coiffed hair, and made him feel sticky and overdressed. He noted with satisfaction that nobody else had decided to brave the elements, and walking to the fence at the edge of the balcony, he pulled out his cell phone and called Archie.

"Shoot," he said as soon as his press spokesman answered.

Archie lost no time transmitting Lucas' message. Maldonado listened intently, grunting every once in a while, gripping his phone with increasing tension and shifting it slightly to hear better. Otherwise, he did not move. When Archie finished his report, Maldonado asked him to repeat the location where Lucas was waiting for the police. Before he hung up, he said, "Thank Ms. Alfaro...Michelle, for the information. Tell her to keep the news to herself, as her brother asked her to do. That was good thinking on his part. That goes for you too."

Maldonado sensed Archie's hesitation even before his assistant answered. *"Please forgive me for stepping out of bounds,"* the redhead said, *"but shouldn't we be trying to evacuate the people of San Juan?"*

"We need to know with greater certainty what we're dealing with. An order to evacuate because of an impending nuclear explosion—and we *will* have to explain why we're ordering the evacuation or many people not bother to leave—will create a general panic in the entire Metropolitan area. There will be chaos in the streets, another snag in our communications, massive traffic jams, and people injured or even killed. It may yet come to an order of evacuation, but we need to see what are the alternatives that we have, as quickly we can, before we come to that. Can I count on your and Michelle's discretion?"

"Yes, sir," Archie answered. *"I'll talk to her as soon as we hang up."*

"Thank you."

Maldonado took a deep, shaky breath before he made his next call, this time to his friend Montañez. The police colonel answered on the second ring, as if he had been waiting for the call. He greeted Maldonado with a jovial remark, but quickly quieted down as he sensed his boss's alarm, letting him speak with no interruptions.

"I need you to go to San Cristobal as quickly as you can," Maldonado told Montañez after he had finished transmitting the information he had received from Archie. "Take as many men as you need, but only those you trust. Don't give them any details, just that we've discovered some terrorists hiding in the tunnels."

"*Right.*"

"Take the bomb squad with you. I don't intend for them to disarm the nuclear device, I'm not sure they know how to do it. Anyway, we can't risk their triggering the bomb by accident and wiping out the city." Maldonado was thinking as he was talking, still not coming to grips with what he needed to do. "But maybe they can see if the bomb is booby trapped to go off if we try to move it. I need your *eyes* there as soon as possible to assess the situation, Alejo. We have to act swiftly, whatever we do."

"*You can count on me,*" Montañez assured his boss gravely.

"I know I can," Maldonado replied, feeling more reassured now that his friend would be handling the situation in San Cristobal. "I'll send six police cars to San Cristobal after I finish talking to you, to make sure they secure the area and protect Alfaro. I don't want him getting killed, especially since he's the only person who knows where the bomb is." A new thought occurred to the Superintendent. "I hope there are no other terrorists left in the tunnel who will consider blowing up the bomb ahead of schedule when they realize that we know about it."

"*I'll make certain that the place is in a secured lockdown as soon as I get there.*" Montañez said, with new urgency in his voice.

"The patrol cars should be there when you get there, but remember that you're running the operation."

"*Understood, sir.*" Montañez paused, and then for the first time allowed himself to comment on the news. "*Alfaro again!*" he said with amazement. "*How do you think he came by this information?*"

Maldonado grasped the meaning of his friend's unspoken doubts immediately. It was very improbable—in fact, incredible—that Lucas Alfaro, the man who had infiltrated La Fortaleza and rescued the Governor, had now somehow discovered a terrorist plot to blow up San Juan. Could there be a connection between him and the terrorists?

"I have no idea," Maldonado answered. "But God bless him if he's right." *And God have pity on him if he had anything to do with what was happening,* he thought to himself.

After ending his conversation with Montañez, the Superintendent made a quick call to the provisional police station in Puerta de Tierra, and instructed Captain Luis Gonzalez, the officer in command, to send six patrol cars to the San Cristobal visitors' center, where he would find a man named Lucas Alfaro waiting. He advised Gonzalez that his men were to protect Alfaro at all costs, and to place him under their custody until Colonel Montañez arrived. His men were also to secure the area from suspected terrorists who had attempted to infiltrate the fort's tunnels. As soon as they contacted Alfaro, he was to call him, the Superintendent, without talking to anybody else except Montañez.

Maldonado also ordered the police captain to locate the fort's rangers, and to bring them to San Cristobal as quickly as possible, using any means required.

Gonzalez, a twenty-year veteran of the police force, had enough sense not to question any of the Superintendent's orders, despite their strange, unexplained nature. The captain curtly confirmed the instructions, and hung up.

Maldonado paused to gather his thoughts. He would need to warn the delegations attending the G20 Conference, even though it increased the chances that the news of the nuclear device would leak to the general public. He had no choice, though. He knew that keeping quiet about it would constitute a serious breach of protocol, and when the other countries eventually found out—as inevitably they would—it could trigger an international crisis. *Damn it,* he thought, *what have we done to deserve this?*

His final call before he went back to the dining room was to Governor Pietrantoni. Like the others, the Governor listened quietly to Maldonado's summary of the events, and then asked, *"Have you warned the other heads of state?"*

"I am about to. I am having dinner with their security directors right now."

"Oh, that's right! You had that dinner tonight with all of the security people. Well, that will save a lot of calls on our part."

There was a pause. Then Maldonado said, "I would suggest that you and your family leave Old San Juan until this matter is resolved, sir."

It took the Governor a few seconds to answer. *"No, you know that I can't run away from San Juan and leave the city unaware of what is happening."*

"Then at least send your family away."

"If and when an evacuation is ordered, I will do so. Not before," Pietrantoni said in a voice that allowed no further argument about the matter. *"I won't detain you any further. I will call the President and let him know what's happening. Please let me know how the disposal of the bomb progresses, Roberto. God go with you."*

By the time Maldonado returned to the Crystal Ballroom, his guests were starting their second course of either filet mignon—the overwhelming favorite of the law-and-order crowd, it seemed—or some kind of fish in an orange sauce. Maldonado's salad lay undisturbed next to a covered plate keeping his main course warm.

The Superintendent walked to his place, and without sitting down grabbed a spoon and clinked it several times on his water glass.

"Gentlemen," he said, prompting most of the diners to look at him. Some were smiling, but their smiles faded when they saw his face. The chatter in the room quickly dried up. "I have received a call that requires our immediate attention," he announced. "However, due to its very sensitive nature, I request that all but the highest ranking person in your delegation leave the room. Please forgive me for being so abrupt, but it is all for good reason. I urge you to do this as quickly as you can, please."

After a brief, hesitant pause, the ballroom became filled with the noise of moving chairs and the buzz of hastily exchanged whispers. Maldonado noticed Frontera, the new FBI man, direct him a puzzled look, but to his credit ask nothing and continue to calmly cut his meat. Esposito also kept quiet, although his right hand unconsciously moved under his jacket, to where he kept his gun. A young Chinese man approached Maldonado and apologetically informed him that his boss, the director of China's First Squadron of the Central Security Bureau, needed a translator, and asked permission to stay by his boss's side. Maldonado responded by saying out loud, "If anyone requires a translator, the translator can also stay, of course."

The young Chinese translator nodded courtly and withdrew. Two other persons who were standing behind him, a man and a woman, also returned to their places, presumably waiting to ask the same question.

As the last of the lesser-ranked staff members exited, Maldonado called after them, ""Please close the doors behind you and make certain nobody comes in."

A tense silence followed as Maldonado waited for the doors to shut. His eyes wandered over the assembled security chiefs, many of whom had moved to some of the closer unoccupied seats. He had met many of them already. To a man, they had impressed him with their experience, integrity and professionalism. They were all members of an exclusive club, entrusted with keeping the heads of their countries alive. Unlike many of the politicians and self-important persons that they guarded, they had not gotten to their present positions by luck, charisma, or connections. They were men who had earned their right to be there. Hard, no nonsense men, whose main purpose in life was to keep their bosses alive.

"A moment ago, I received a call that terrorists, the same terrorists who attacked San Juan last January, have placed a nuclear bomb under old San Juan."

Maldonado's announcement was greeted with shocked and disbelieving expressions. However, except for the quiet whisper of the three translators, nobody spoke. Maldonado had calculated that that would be their reaction. He had excluded the security directors' general staff not only to reduce the risk of the news spreading, but also to lessen the chance of idle chatter. He wanted to make the announcement as quickly as possible and get on with his business.

"It has been programmed to go off tomorrow at noon, when the G20 leaders are having lunch together in El Convento."

"Excuse me, Mr. Superintendent," a crusty voice with a heavy Russian accent said. "But when you speak of a nuclear device, do you know what kind of a device you are talking about?"

Maldonado recognized the speaker as Casimir Bashnakov, Director of the Russian FSO or Federal Protection Service, the equivalent of the American Secret Service. He was a short, clean-shaven man in his fifties with intensely blond hair, almost the color of ash. Maldonado had exchanged a few words with him just before the dinner had started.

"I am told it has the capacity of a ten to twenty kiloton bomb," the Superintendent answered.

"That would be the size of the Nagasaki, Hiroshima bombs," said the Japanese Director of the Security Police Division, Keiji Kawaguchi, in charge of protecting the prime minister and his retinue. He also was a short man, with closely cropped, hair-brush style hair, a more than normal wrinkled face, and massive hands with brown knuckles that seemed disproportionate to the rest of his body. Maldonado had not had the opportunity to meet him yet.

Several of the assembled men exchanged troubled looks or shifted uncomfortably in their seats. By their body language, Maldonado could tell that they were barely restraining their instincts to stand and bolt to warn their delegations. Everyone stayed in his place, however.

The only female in the room, a young, very attractive, black haired translator for the director of Brazil's security outfit, the Bethalhao da Guarda Presidencial, raised her hand after conferring with her boss. "Director Costa would like to know how...certain...eh...how trustworthy is the information that you have acquired."

Maldonado nodded, looking at the Brazilian head of security, a gaunt, silver haired, older man, with thin lips that seemed to be fixed in a permanent sneer. "I received the information from the man who saved Governor Pietrantoni's life in La Fortaleza, when the terrorists tried to kill him. I can assure you that this is a very serious, capable person. We are sending personnel right now to protect him and have him guide us to the bomb."

Director Costa raised his eyebrows and exchanged several words with his female translator.

"So your police have not yet come in contact with the bomb," she asked, prompting several of the others in the room to listen intently.

"No, not yet," Maldonado confessed. "As I said, we have just received this information."

"So nothing is certain yet!" the Russian Bashnakov asserted.

For the first time, the silence in the room was disturbed by several murmurs. Maldonado saw Paul Hastings—the plump, balding representative from Scotland Yard—raise his hand, and pointed at him.

"Assuming, as we all must," he said, looking around the hall at the others, "that this threat is true...Do we have anyone at hand who can disarm this...thing?"

Maldonado turned to his Secret Service and FBI counterparts, and both of them shook their heads. "Unless someone in any of your parties is an atomic bomb expert, the answer is no. In any event, it is not my intention to disarm the bomb where it is. I cannot risk having the bomb go off under the city."

"And we don't even know for certain if the bomb is set to explode tomorrow or earlier," the Russian insisted.

"No," Maldonado admitted.

The sound of the voices got louder, making Maldonado fear that the meeting was getting out of control. He urgently clinked his glass several times, and the others quieted down. "We have no time to lose. As you all know, there is an emergency contingency plan, where at the slightest hint of danger to any of the visiting leaders, they are to move to our underground facilities in Roosevelt Roads in Ceiba."

Located on the east coast of the island about forty miles from San Juan, Roosevelt Roads had at one time been one of the largest naval bases of the U.S., until abandoned by the Navy and ceded to the government of Puerto Rico in 2004. It contained a fully operational airport, and countless underground bunkers capable of withstanding a full-scale nuclear attack. Furthermore, any nuclear blast occurring in the area of San Juan would have to surmount the formidable natural shield created by the mountains that surrounded the El Yunque rain forest reserve.

"Is the President flying out to Roosevelt Roads?" Bashnakov, who seemed to have assumed the role of main inquisitor in the group, asked.

Again, Maldonado cast another glance at Esposito, of the Secret Service, who said, "I don't know if the President even knows yet. Does he?" he asked Maldonado.

The Superintendent nodded. "The President, like the rest of your bosses, is being informed about it right now by the Governor of Puerto Rico."

"Then I will urge him to go to Roosevelt Roads, at least until the emergency is over," Esposito said.

The Russian grunted. "It would be unseemly for the Premier to scamper to safety while your President remains here. Please ask the President to let us know what he plans to do."

Maldonado tried not to shake his head in wonderment. Could it be possible that the Russians suspected this was all just a ploy to make Premier Kozlov lose face? "It will be up to each of your leaders to make a final decision. Whatever their decision is, they must keep the information to themselves. This is essential. I cannot emphasize it enough. We are not notifying the general public about this until we have more information available. We do not want to create a panic in the island that will serve no purpose but to tangle traffic in the streets and snarl our communications systems."

Maldonado looked around, trying to gauge the faces of the assembled security men. Even though a few nodded, it was very hard to read their expressions. "So that you know, it is my intention to move the bomb out of the tunnel where it is deposited, place it in a helicopter, and fly it out of San Juan, to dump it into the Atlantic."

"Is that possible?" Hastings, from England, inquired.

"I sincerely hope so," Maldonado responded earnestly. "If not, may God help us."

CHAPTER VII

Montañez followed Lucas through the dark passageway astonished at what he was seeing. He had heard about tunnels under the city, but he had never suspected of the honeycomb of passages that seemed to spread in every direction under Old San Juan. *A person could get lost here, and never be found. How had the terrorists discovered this place?*

Lucas stopped and swept with his ultraviolet lamp over the upper corner of one of the three arched entrances into which the tunnel divided, nodding with satisfaction when the outlines of an "X" marked in phosphorescent green appeared on the wall. "This way," he said to the policeman that preceded him, pointing to the central entrance. Even though he had assured Montañez that no more terrorists were left in the tunnel, the colonel was taking no chances. A policeman in full combat gear headed the ten-man procession, making certain that nothing happened to Lucas. Eight other agents, mostly members of the "Untouchables" plus a two-man bomb squad, trailed behind Montañez, each holding a flashlight. From a distance, the gaggle of men looked like a centipede made out of lights.

The mood was quiet and somber. They had walked past the corpses of the two terrorists—Lucas had identified them as Daniel and Czecka—and had been surprised by the violence of their deaths. Czecka, in particular, lying in a pool of his own blood, had been a startling and gruesome sight, even though Lucas had warned them that he would be there. Montañez had seen many dead men in his time—executed drug dealers, robbery victims, bank robbers, murder-suicide killers. In death, people tended to look smaller than in real life, as if death shrank them. Not so Czecka. The corpse sprawled on the floor belonged to a terrifying giant. If he had shrunk, Montañez shuddered to think what he must have looked like when he was alive.

And Alfaro! When Montañez had first seen him, waiting for his arrival, sitting in the rangers' office drinking coffee, it had seemed as if he had been hurt badly, his shirt, trousers, arms and neck covered in blood. Then it turned out that most of the blood came from the men he had killed. His face was beat up, especially his left side, which was puffy and swollen, and he seemed to cradle his left arm, but otherwise, he looked okay.

The colonel had met Lucas once before, when the latter had been awarded a medal by the House of Representatives. He had seemed like a harmless, peaceful man; lean and fit, yes, but also pleasant and easygoing. He had wondered then how such a man had managed to rescue the Governor from such a dangerous group as the Macheteros. Now, after witnessing the damage he had inflicted on the giant terrorist that night, his disbelief had, if anything, increased. It would have taken a cannon to stop someone like Czecka. Lucas had done it with his bare hands. In the dark.

Incredible.

They had begun to stop more often now, every time they came upon one of the low, square openings that periodically appeared in the right wall. Some of the openings were just niches, barely larger than the body of a short man, where soldiers could have concealed themselves to ambush an advancing invader. One had led to what seemed to be a large cistern, still filled with water. A few provided access to small rooms that could have been used as temporary storage places. It was in one of these where Lucas finally stopped.

"This is it," he said, pointing into the dark opening. "This is where the bomb is."

Some of the men behind Montañez automatically began to move towards the entrance, but the colonel stopped them with his arm.

"Wait," he said to Lucas. "You're sure the place is not booby trapped?"

"I fought Czecka for the first time in there, and we rolled all over the floor and even crashed a couple of times into the device. The bomb may be booby trapped in some way, but the room isn't."

Montañez nodded, satisfied. "Godoy, Contreras," he called back to some of the men behind him. "Come with me. Manolito, Vitin, walk a little further down the tunnel and keep watch there. I don't want anybody approaching us from that side. Juan, Nacho, the same behind us. The rest of you, stay here." Not waiting for the bomb squad to make its way through the tunnel, Montañez leaned forward and entered the small chamber, searching for the bomb with his flashlight.

He found it immediately. As appearances went, it was the most unimpressive bomb he had ever seen. It looked to him like a low icemaker with wheels. It had three switches on one side, all of them flipped in the same direction, and a small, elongated crystal gauge that glowed with a faint greenish tinge. In the James Bond movies, the gauge was usually a clock that ticked off the seconds, producing tiny beeps, as the device neared the ultimate moment of destruction. This gauge, however, contained a series of poorly illuminated "1"s and "0"s that did not change with the passage of time and gave no indication of when the explosion was scheduled to take place.

The bomb squad made its way into the chamber, carrying several canvas bags with them. Godoy, a prematurely gray-haired man in his early forties with a handlebar mustache and a wide, wizened forehead, walked past Montañez and knelt beside the bomb. His companion Contreras, a mousy man with a few strands of hair and a large bulbous nose, stood behind him, and began to open one of the bags that he was carrying. He took out a large lamp and turned it on, flooding the chamber with intense, white light.

Godoy began to examine the bomb with a businesslike air, muttering to himself as he did so. He placed his face flat on the floor, inspecting each of the wheels with concentrated curiosity, flashing at them with additional light from a pocket flashlight. Afterwards, he directed his attention to the underside of the bomb, gently sweeping his hand over its smooth bottom.

In the meantime, Contreras had brought out a yellow, square box connected through a wire to a black cylinder. The box contained a large glass, calibrated meter with a needle. Contreras flicked on a switch on the side of the box, and the box began to emit a raspy, clicking sound.

"Woooh!" Godoy said, while still examining the underside of the bomb. "Sounds active alright! What's the reading?"

"Close to six hundred, over six hundred microSieverts," Contreras answered, a quiver in his thin voice betraying his excitement.

"Take a look, Flaco," Godoy said to his companion after he finished his initial inspection, standing up and letting Contreras take his place. Wiping his forehead with a handkerchief, he said to Montañez, "I've never seen anything like this. It's radioactive, that's for sure. The Geiger counter that El Flaco used showed about six hundred microSieverts an hour, so there is radioactive material in there. How much, or how well shielded, it's hard to tell..."

"Is it safe to be here?"

"Because of the radiation? If we don't stay too long, it's okay. But if the bomb detonates, it won't matter." Godoy answered, making a weak attempt at a joke.

Montañez ignored him. "Can we move it? Do you think it's booby trapped?"

"The wheels are not connected to anything, and it seems to have been wheeled here, so it's fairly safe to say that we can move it. I don't know if it's rigged to go off if we try to open it, though. Do you concur, Flaco?"

"I concur," Contreras said from below. He had shifted his attention to the back of the device, not visible from where the men were standing.

Montañez breathed in deeply. "Okay, so let's move this thing out of here." He walked out of the chamber to where the others were waiting. "We'll take it from here," he said to Lucas. "You look pretty beat up, although from what I've seen along the way, you should have been dead. Can you find your way back to the outside by yourself?"

"Yes," Lucas answered. "Can you?"

Montañez chuckled. "We have two extra ultraviolet lights. Go have your injuries checked. Tell one of the patrols that I said they should take you to the hospital. Tell Captain Gonzalez that we're coming out with the..." he hesitated, "the device. The captain doesn't know it's a nuclear bomb, and you should not make him aware of it. Tell him to tell the Superintendent that he should make the necessary preparations to get rid of it. I don't know what he has in mind, but he should have had enough time to consult and decide what he wants to do." He extended his hand to Lucas. "I cannot thank you enough for your help. If we dodge this bullet, it will all be due to you."

Lucas shook his hand, flinching when he moved his swollen elbow. He had taken quite a beating from Czecka, and as time passed and the adrenaline in his body dropped, he had begun to feel with increasing intensity the pain of his injuries.

"There is still time..." he said clumsily, not knowing what else to say, searching for signs of hope in Montañez's eyes.

"Don't worry," the colonel answered with a confidence he did not have. "We'll get rid of this thing."

Lucas turned his back on Montañez, and for the fourth time that day began to travel down the ancient Spanish tunnel. *There is still time*, he kept repeating to himself. He looked at his watch. It was fifteen minutes past nine. *There is still time.*

It took Lucas twenty minutes to reach Captain Gonzalez, and another five to transmit to him Montañez's instructions. However, he changed parts of the colonel's message. As he had wandered through the dark, haunted bowels of the city, his thoughts had turned back to San Miguel. The man had been the moving force behind everything that had happened in San Juan; the tourists in the Grand Laguna Hotel had died because of him, and so had scores of police officers; many parts of the city had been damaged, burned down, or destroyed; his nephew had been terrorized, his sister nearly raped, and Antonio murdered. He had ordered the execution of Lucas twice, once while on the rooftop of the Metropolitan Center, and the other scarcely an hour ago. He had callously decided to incinerate San Juan to further his personal agenda

To allow him to escape would not only be inconceivable, it would be immoral. They had to get him and bring him back to San Juan. Maybe, if his life was threatened, he would help disarm the bomb, although Lucas doubted it. San Miguel was a religious fanatic, in Lucas' eyes the worst kind of adversary that San Juan could face, a man capable of justifying his most terrible acts for the sake of his god, and a man capable of dying for him. Lucas could not let him go. If the city could not be saved, then San Miguel should perish with it.

And Lucas knew where he was.

"Colonel Montañez also authorized me to take three police patrol cars to search for the only terrorist that escaped," he said with a straight face to Gonzalez, after he had finished relaying the message that Montañez had sent to Maldonado.

The police captain stared at him with curiosity bordering on doubt. "You are in no condition to go anywhere except to the hospital. If you tell me where he is, I can send my men to get him."

Lucas was prepared for that answer. "I'm the only know who can identify him."

Gonzalez mulled over Lucas' response for a moment. "Very well," he finally answered. "I'll tell my men to follow you. I have to stay here, you understand..."

"Of course," Lucas answered immediately.

"Where is the terrorist hiding?"

Lucas considered showing to Gonzalez the plastic ID he had found in one of Daniel's pockets, but was afraid the captain would insist on keeping it as evidence. Instead, he said, "I overheard the terrorists say that they would escape on the *Orion Star,* one of the cruise ships docked in San Juan."

Gonzalez took his time to answer, as if weighing the pros and cons of letting Lucas hunt for the terrorist, and finally said, "Very well. I will send some men with you." Lucas opened his mouth to thank him, but the captain raised his hand. "You go on the condition that you allow my men to do the fighting, if there's any fighting to be done."

Lucas laughed. "Believe me, I'm finished with fighting for the rest of my life," he answered sincerely, but Gonzalez regarded him skeptically.

The captain walked to the rangers' office's door and leaned out. "Negron!" he called.

"Sir!" a high-pitched, almost adolescent voice answered from outside.

"I need you. Come in here."

"Yes, sir."

A tall, skinny young man with black, bushy hair and brown, mischievous eyes walked into the rangers' office.

"This is Sergeant Edgardo Negron," Gonzalez informed Lucas. "Sergeant, this is Lucas Alfaro."

The two men shook hands.

"Lucas Alfaro, I've heard a lot about you. It's an honor to meet you," Negron said, his lips broadening into an engaging smile.

"Nice to meet you too," Lucas answered back. There was something familiar about the sergeant's face.

"Negron, Mr. Alfaro believes he knows the whereabouts of one of the terrorists who was here tonight," Gonzalez informed him. The sergeant's gaze never left Lucas' face, his eyes filled with excitement.

"Just tell me what I have to do," he said to Lucas.

"I overheard the terrorists saying that they were leaving San Juan tonight on the *Orion Star*. That's a cruise ship docked at the bay right now."

"Yeah, yeah," Negron acknowledged. "I know which ship it is. It's a large boat."

"You will take Alfaro in your patrol car, and take two other cars with you," Gonzalez told him. The captain was busy, looking for the Superintendent's phone number in his cell phone.

"But we have to hurry," Lucas said. "The ship may leave at any moment."

Negron looked at the time. "It's nine forty-five right now. The ships usually start leaving by ten."

Gonzalez looked away from the phone. "I'll phone ahead to the port and let them know that you're coming. I'll ask them to alert the *Orion's* captain and delay the ship's departure," he volunteered. "Now go! Good luck!"

"You're related to Michelle Alfaro," Negron stated casually as they exited the visitors' center.

"I'm his brother," Lucas acknowledged warily, resigned to listen to the questions and comments about his sister that usually followed, like: *"How is she really like?"* or *"Do you also work on TV?"* or *"How do you feel being his brother?"*

Instead, Negron said, "I know her."

"Oh?" Lucas cast him a curious, sideways glance as they continued to hurry towards the police car.

"I'm *Negron*," he said simply, as if the name should have meant something to Lucas. When his companion continued to look lost, he added, "One of the two men who went to the Grand Laguna Hotel with your sister?"

Of course! Lucas thought, embarrassed. *How could he have been so obtuse?* He must have seen his photograph—as he stood next to Michelle—in a hundred different newspaper and internet articles. In addition to being awarded several medals and becoming the object of various public recognitions, Negron had been promoted to police sergeant. "You're Edgardo," he said apologetically, slapping his forehead, then shaking his hand again. "Michelle has told me a great deal about you! Please forgive me for not recognizing you before."

Negron's face brightened. "That's okay. After the kind of night you've had, I wouldn't be in a position to recognize anyone."

The two men stopped as they reached the area where more than a dozen police cars were parked. Four of the several policemen waiting there gathered around them. Negron opened the trunk of one of the cars and began to rummage through its surprisingly cluttered content. He pulled out a white, wrinkled *guayabera* and handed it to Lucas.

"What's this?" Lucas asked.

"For you. It's an extra shirt that I keep for...social emergencies," Negron answered. "If you're going to board the *Orion,* you'd better remove that shirt you're wearing."

Lucas examined his shirt, realizing for the first time that it was caked in dry blood.

"Yeah," Negron said, as if reading his companion's thoughts. "You look like a zombie. If you go on board looking like that, you'll create a panic. Your face and arms don't look any better. I have some wipies in the car. They'll help you clean up."

While Lucas changed, the sergeant beckoned with his hand one of the nearby policemen. "Gather the men," he ordered. "Tell...Arrivi and Moreno to follow us in their cars."

"Where are we going?" the policeman inquired. He looked even younger than Negron, with a close-cropped haircut and the solemn, official attitude usually adopted by rookies.

"To hunt for terrorists," Negron answered happily. "Tell the others I'll brief them on the radio. Now hurry!" He turned his attention back to his companion. "Did she really talk a lot about me?" he asked Lucas.

"Who?" Lucas asked, unable to follow the sergeant's *non sequitur.*

"Michelle. Did she really talk about me?"

Lucas smiled. "Yes," he answered. "She really did."

"I have a huge crush on your sister, you know."

No, Lucas thought, *he didn't know.* Although it didn't surprise him.

CHAPTER VIII

Angel San Miguel—now Francisco Cofresi—leaned on the uppermost deck of the *Orion,* fifteen decks above the pier. He took a long drag from his cigarette and exhaled. The strong, cool breeze flowing over the ship's jogging track carried the smoke almost in a straight line towards Old San Juan.

A pity, he thought, for the hundredth's time. *He really liked San Juan.*

The city looked beautiful and romantic and vibrant, its lights gleaming in the cloudless Caribbean night. It must have looked like that three hundred years ago, when Drake had attempted to conquer it. More lights now, maybe, and a few taller buildings, but just a few. The influx of tourists and locals into the city—drawn by its nightlife, clubs, and restaurants—was just beginning. Soon its streets would be flooded with revelers.

A pity, really.

For more than five hundred years the city had endured—thrived, more than endured—San Miguel, ever the history buff, thought. Founded by the seeker of eternal youth, Juan Ponce De Leon, it had weathered the assault of pirates and hurricanes, adapting even to the godless threat of modern technology while still managing to retain its charm. Ponce de Leon had failed in his impossible quest, but the city he had founded had not. San Juan had found eternal youth. *And now, it would die young*.

A couple walked past him on the ship's jogging track, chatting agreeably, enjoying the moment, and ignoring him. They had no idea how close they had come to share the sad destiny of the city. In the decades to come, they would tell their grandchildren how they had been in San Juan the day before it had been destroyed. Would they know by then that the instrument of the city's destruction had sailed away on the same cruise ship with them? Probably not.

He considered looking for Daniel—he had not seen him get on board—but desisted from the idea. He doubted that he would see him much during the next six days of the cruise. They had booked separate cabins on different decks, and would pretend not to know each other. Not that he would be so hard to avoid. Their notions of relaxation and entertainment were not the same. Daniel would probably use his free time to immerse himself in the more mundane and depraved activities of the ship, while San Miguel would devote it mostly to meditation. San Miguel had long ago lost hope for the salvation of his friend's soul.

Taking a last puff from his cigarette, he flicked it over the railing and watched it fall. For a moment, it seemed as if it would fall into the water between the dock and the ship, but at the final seconds it drifted towards the edge of the pier, bursting into orange cinders as it struck the concrete.

He was about to return to his cabin, when something caught his eye. He noticed, for the first time, that there was a police car parked by the passengers' boarding entrance. Its lights were off, and there were no policemen near it, but it still struck him as odd. It had not been there when he boarded the *Orion*.

Scanning the rest of the dock, he discovered another police patrol vehicle stationed at the end of the pier, close to the water. It also seemed at first deserted, but after a quick search, he spotted two policemen standing by the shadows of the customs building. They were armed with long guns. He was too high up to see their faces, but they seemed to be concentrating their attention on the ship.

He told himself that he was being too suspicious, but at that moment he caught the movement of two other policemen, jogging towards the opposite end of the ship. *Something was happening*, he realized, his pulse quickening.

Instinctively, he felt for the gun that he had smuggled on board, feeling reassured when he found it. It had been surprisingly simple to get it into the ship. All of the passengers were forced to go through a metal detector and to place any objects or bags that they carried through an X-ray machine. However, the boarding passengers were not required to remove their belts or shoes, and almost invariably, the metal detector's alarm went off. Some of the boarders who set off the alarm were swept in a fast and casual manner with a hand-held metal detector; others were allowed to go through by the harried crew without further examination.

San Miguel had waited for the line of passengers to thicken before he attempted to get on board. He wore a large, oval belt buckle depicting the crenellated walls and a guardhouse of El Morro castle. Behind it he had tucked a .25 Seacamp revolver, the tip of its barrel and the lower end of its handle tucked into his pants' waist. The Seacamp was six inches long, and held five bullets. The metal buckle in front of it covered it almost completely.

As the alarm of the metal detector went off, one of the crewmembers checking the passengers had waved a hand device over him. It had squealed as it was swiped over the belt buckle, and San Miguel had apologized profusely, making as if to take off his belt. The crewman had congratulated him on the original buckle and let him go through.

Having the gun reassured him. It was not the type of weapon that he could use to hijack the ship, but it would come in handy if he had to create a diversion to escape. Not that the police were necessarily there to arrest him. They could be looking for anyone, or just be there as a heightened security reason in light of the G20 conference.

Nevertheless, he could not take any chances. Taking out his cell phone, he called Daniel. He immediately got Daniel's pre-recorded message, advising the caller about his unavailability, and hung up. The fact that it had not rung meant the phone was either turned off, or that it had no reception. He knew that the ship could interfere with the cell phone's receptivity. Nevertheless, he decided to look for Daniel.

He used the stairs, avoiding the elevators. Daniel was staying in a more modest cabin on the eighth deck, while San Miguel had taken a suite on deck fourteen. About to depart, the *Orion* was crawling with its newly arrived occupants, many of whom were exploring the ship. As he breezed past some of them, he covertly examined their faces, trying not so much to see if he could find Daniel as to detect signs of alarm or surprise in their expressions. He observed nothing out of the ordinary; only the excited, careless anticipation of happy vacationers about to depart on a cruise.

Many suitcases lined the walls of the corridor of the eighth deck, as the crew brought the luggage up to the rooms. Two young children, followed by their harried parents, bolted past him, prompting him to smile automatically. A moment later he cheerfully greeted a cabin steward who stopped working to welcome him aboard.

When he reached Room 8137, he noticed that Daniel's brown suitcase was still outside. He rapped loudly on the door, but as he had expected, nobody answered.

Could it be? he wondered, half concerned, half amused. There was still a chance that Daniel was exploring the ship, and that the police outside were just a coincidence. But he had never believed in coincidences.

Somehow, the police had found out about him. Or Daniel. Or both. He was certain that Daniel would never betray him. So if the police knew about both of them, their knowledge could only have come from Alfaro, and that was impossible. He had seen Czecka pinning him to the ground, just before he had left. Nobody escaped Czecka. Even less when Czecka's knee was crushing your chest.

San Miguel walked to the outside promenade on deck eight, on the side of the bay, and dialed Czecka's number. Like Daniel's, the automatic message recorder kicked in immediately.

Something was definitely wrong. Czecka's phone should have at least rung, unless he had turned it off or he was still underground. Neither of those alternatives would have been according to plan.

San Miguel calmly gathered his thoughts. If the police had captured Daniel, they would have found the *Orion's* boarding card in his pocket. However, there was nothing that connected San Miguel to Daniel. The police would probably be there following the only lead that they had, but not knowing who they were searching for. Even if they had captured Czecka alive—a highly unlikely supposition—they would still be unable to connect him to San Miguel.

The deep, bass blast of the ship's horn interrupted his thoughts. *The Orion was leaving!* He looked at his watch and saw it was slightly beyond half past ten. Staring into the water, he saw no boats—either from the police, the Coast Guard, or customs—surrounding the ship. A second blast of the horn confirmed that the ship was signaling its departure.

Trying to look nonchalant, he sauntered on the promenade around the stern to the other side of the ship. There, to his relief, he discovered two workers on the dock withdrawing the boarding ramp. Further along the pier, he saw two policemen leading a handcuffed man away from the ship. Even though he could not see the arrested man's face, he could definitely tell it was not Daniel. *So that's what they were doing! They were searching for somebody else. Probably a drug smuggler, or a wanted fugitive.*

He felt the vibrations of the ship's engines under his feet, and watched the thick stern rope slacken until another worker on the pier below slipped it over the dock tie. Elated, he noticed that the prow of the Orion had already begun to separate from its berth. *They were under way!*

A wave of relief surged through his body. *It had been a false alarm.* Daniel was probably on board, already celebrating the success of their mission. He would have to talk to him after the explosion was confirmed in the news. In critical moments like this, he could not afford not to know where Daniel was at all times. For a few heart-stopping moments he had thought that the operation had been blown, and he had considered abandoning the ship. Now he knew that everything would be fine. Nothing could stop now the events that he had set in motion.

He should not be celebrating the success of their mission yet, San Miguel chided himself, as he allowed himself to relax. All of his work, his tireless, meticulous planning and sacrifice would not be a success until the nuclear device went off. To celebrate ahead of time was to tempt fate. A hundred different things could still go wrong.

"Your attention please!" a male voice said over the P.A. system. *"Maritime regulations require that the ship conduct its emergency drill as it departs port. All passengers should go to their designated evacuation areas with your life vests within the next fifteen minutes. Please refer to the instructions located behind the doors of your cabins to determine where you are required to go."*

The P.A. system repeated its announcement, and San Miguel, like most of the passengers near him, headed for his cabin.

Montañez found Superintendent Maldonado waiting for him on the open grassy area between the two concentric walls of the San Cristobal fort when he and his men had finally emerged from the cramped confines of the tunnel. They were sweaty, dirty, and tired, having to push, maneuver, and sometimes carry the heavy, rectangular nuclear device through the dark, often cluttered underground passages.

It had been an unnerving, nightmarish task. They had moved as quickly as they could while trying to avoid any sudden jolts or movements that could accidentally trigger the device. The uncertainty of what they were doing—handling an unpredictable nuclear explosive that could in theory go off at any moment and reduce to ashes not only them but the capital of Puerto Rico—had taken a toll on their nerves.

Montañez had tried to convince himself that if the bomb had not detonated after they had moved it, it probably would not detonate throughout the rest of their underground journey. But the going had been so rough and difficult, that by the time he had reached the end of the long passage, Montañez had felt exhausted, his arms and legs shaking from the exertion.

The police colonel took a moment to slowly stretch to his full height and recover his breath, and then approached the Superintendent. As he did so, he noticed for the first time a Bell 407 police helicopter parked about fifty yards away.

"I got your message," Maldonado said to his friend.

Montañez jerked his thumb towards the helicopter. "I gather you haven't found an expert on nuclear bombs."

Maldonado shook his head. "We're flying the bomb out of here and dumping it in the Atlantic." He saw Montañez's face and read what he was thinking. "I know, I know. It's not the most environmentally friendly thing to do, but consider the alternative. We'll let it sink in the ocean, five hundred miles from here. If we're lucky, it won't even go off."

"The environmentalists will crucify you."

"The environmentalists will hopefully never find out," Maldonado responded, not really believing what he was saying.

Both men turned to look at the helicopter. A group of men had exited from it, and was helping Montañez's men to carry the bomb to the aircraft. The chopper's engine had begun to whirr, its rotor blades slowly coming back to life.

"How about the G20 VIP's?"

"They were informed about the bomb. As of fifteen minutes ago, most of them had opted to evacuate."

"Evacuate where?"

"Roosevelt Roads. There's a huge underground bunker there that can accommodate all of them."

Montañez looked at the Superintendent. "Who stayed?"

Maldonado smiled. "From what I last heard, the President of the United States, Premier Kozlov of Russia, the Japanese Prime Minister, Yamagata, and the French President, Lalande."

"Pretty gutsy call on their part," Montañez said with admiration.

"If the bomb doesn't kill them," Maldonado responded grudgingly. "Very irresponsible if they don't survive."

The two friends watched in silence as their men finished securing the bomb inside the Bell's cargo space behind the pilot's seat.

"Can that helicopter get it far enough away?" Montañez inquired.

"It's only flying the bomb to the Aguadilla Airport. It will fly fifty miles off the coast, just in case. The feds have secured a C-17 Globemaster, which is waiting in Aguadilla. The transport will fly it out five hundred miles into the Atlantic and dump the bomb by parachute. The bomb will be weighted with five hundred more pounds, so that it sinks as deep into the ocean as it can. The sea there is about fifteen thousand feet deep..."

Maldonado stopped as the helicopter's door shut and its engine roared to its full capacity. A cloud of dust and bits of grass swept over the knots of men gathered in the walled-in field, prompting them to shield their eyes. Gradually, almost tentatively, the aircraft separated from the ground and began to gain altitude. Then, with newly found strength, it whizzed out towards the sea.

"Does the pilot and the crew know what they're carrying?"

"They know that they are carrying a bomb. They don't know it's an atomic bomb."

"God help them," Montañez whispered sympathetically.

The lights of the helicopter became fainter as it moved towards the west and away from the coast.

"God help them,' Maldonado repeated.

CHAPTER IX

"Now you stay with me," Negron warned Lucas. "My men will take care of this."

They had climbed to the fourteenth deck, after Garrett, the ship's main security officer, had assured them that San Miguel had just walked into his room. Two of the six policemen who had boarded the *Orion* had begun to approach cabin 1413 from one end of the corridor, two from the other, their guns drawn. A few surprised passengers coming out of their rooms had been quickly hustled out of the area by security personnel following the policemen.

Lucas and Negron stayed about a third of the length of the corridor away from the advancing policemen, ready to approach and—hopefully—positively identify the arrested man.

They had gotten to the ship ten minutes before it was scheduled to depart. One of the three patrol cars had driven to the outer edge of the dock, to make certain nobody fitting the description that Lucas had given them over the radio got off the ship: a tall—maybe six feet, two or three inches—thin, bearded man with light brown hair, brown eyes, wearing flip flops, tight jeans, and a red polo shirt, although he could have changed. The other two police vehicles had parked at the opposite end of the dock, trying not to draw unnecessary attention.

Lucas and Negron had boarded the ship first, where Kevin Garrett, the ship's security officer, was already waiting for them. Garrett was a forty year old, ex Royal Marine who looked as formidable as if he had just stepped out of the British Armed Forces. He stood at a considerable height of six and a half feet, and was ripped with muscles that bulged through his immaculately pressed white ensign's uniform. His most prominent feature were his dark, intelligent eyes, which peered over a walrus-like, handlebar mustache.

He greeted the two Puerto Ricans with a formidable handshake, and was familiar not only with Lucas and Negron's participation in the January revolt—*"An honor to know both of you gentlemen"*—but had carefully studied the events that had taken place on the *Mardi Gras*, to avoid anything like that from happening aboard his ship. His face had darkened, as his two visitors had informed him about their suspicions that a terrorist had boarded the *Orion*.

"That is indeed bad news," he had told them in a thick Scottish accent. "Do you know who this gentleman is?" They were meeting in the security control office, next to the general counter in the ship's luxurious lobby. Two other crewmembers, a young man and an even younger woman, were scanning about three dozen small television screens that showed the activity in the ship's several corridors and public areas. Both were overhearing the conversation, while shuffling their eyes from the screens to the two new arrivals.

Lucas produced the boarding card that he had taken out of Daniel's pocket, earning a surprised look from Negron. "I don't know the alias that he is presently using, but I can identify him if I see him." He handed the card to the security officer. "This was his companion. They may be sharing the same cabin."

Garrett took the card, briefly examined its content, and handed it to his male assistant. "Paul, find out if..." he stared again at the name of the card, "Mr. Carlos Ramirez de Orellana has a roommate, and whether the roommate is on board."

"Yes, sir." The young security man, a light-skinned Jamaican with freckles and reddish, crinkly hair, rolled his chair to an onboard computer and swiped the card on a track on the keyboard. A larger photo of Daniel, followed by several lines of text, appeared on the screen. "No, sir, it's a single booking, and Mr. Orellana is not on board."

Negron cursed softly.

"You said this man *was* the companion of the one you're looking for. Am I to assume that Mr. Orellana has been detained?" Garrett asked.

"Permanently," Negron answered before Lucas could say anything.

"I see."

"His accomplice may be staying in another cabin," Lucas suggested.

"If he was not sharing a cabin with Mr. Orellana, would he be traveling alone?" Garrett asked.

"That was the impression I got," Lucas responded.

"Let us hope so," said Garrett. He looked at his assistant. "Paul?"

But Paul was already typing furiously on his keyboard. A list of names and room numbers appeared on the screen. "There are forty-two passengers traveling alone." He did a rapid count. "Thirty...four of them are males."

"Can you show their photos on the screen?" Lucas asked. "If I see him I will recognize him."

Paul raised his eyebrows and looked at his superior officer for authorization. Maintaining the privacy of the passengers was a sacred norm of the cruising industry.

Garrett did not hesitate, however. "Do it," he ordered his assistant. Lucas leaned next to him, followed by Negron, and stared at the screen.

The photos of the passengers began to appear on the screen, one by one.

"Too old...Too fat..." Lucas said, a new face appearing every time he discarded a name. "No...No..." He examined a man with a beard for a couple of seconds, and shook his head. "No, his features are too coarse...No... Definitely not...Bald..."

A phone by the screens rang, and the young woman answered it. "It's for you," she said to Garrett, and as he was going to tell her to take a message, she added, "It's the captain."

Garrett grabbed the phone and walked to the end of the room, engaging in a muted conversation.

Lucas found San Miguel on the twenty-seventh try. His features were somewhat blurred, as if he had moved the head when the photo was taken, but even so, his face was unmistakable. "That's him!" Lucas exclaimed excitedly.

Garrett stopped speaking and moved closer to the other men, looking over their shoulders. "Francisco Cofre...Cofresi," he read with a deplorable accent.

"Cofre*si*," Negron corrected, "with the accent at the end of the word, and the final '*i*' pronounced like a double 'e'. It's the name of a famous Puerto Rican pirate."

"Cofre*si*," Garrett repeated into the telephone. "Cabin 1413."

"He's on board," Paul confirmed. "Boarded at 7:58 PM."

Lucas began to speak, but Garrett motioned with his hand to wait, and listened to the phone.

"The captain wants to know what we should do. It is already ten minutes beyond our departure time. He is very concerned about the safety of the passengers," Garrett said after he had finished listening. "He is suggesting that we evacuate the ship."

"No," Lucas interjected urgently. "San...Cofresi is a very smart and dangerous man. If he senses that anything is wrong, God knows what he might do."

A nervous pause followed. "So what do you suggest?"

"Do you have surveillance cameras on the floor where he's staying?" Lucas asked.

Garrett exchanged a glance with Paul. "Cabin number 1413. That's corridor 14B, isn't it?" he said.

"This one here," the woman said, pointing at a screen. All of the men gathered around her.

Except for an attendant standing next to a cart full of towels and toilet paper, the corridor was empty. Several bags randomly lined the walls, next to some of the cabin doors.

"Which one is it?" Garrett asked, more to himself than to anybody else.

"It's difficult to tell," the young woman responded. A plastic oval tag on her shirt identified her as "Millie". "It's one of the cabins closer to the middle of the passageway."

"Keep an eye on that monitor, won't you Millie?" Garrett said. "If you see anyone coming in or out of any of the cabins, let me know immediately."

"We need to isolate him from the other passengers," Lucas told the others. "The ideal situation would be if he is in his room. Is there any way of finding out if he's there?"

"Other than knocking on the door? No," Garrett responded. "Excuse me for a moment," he said. He spoke briefly into the phone, listened for a few seconds, and hung up. "Captain Harrelson has agreed not to depart until this problem is resolved."

"Holding up the ship will only make Cofresi suspicious," Lucas observed.

"You're not suggesting that we leave, are you?" Garrett snapped back, a little more testily than he intended. Things were getting more complicated by the second.

"No," Lucas replied, ignoring Garrett's tone. "But by making him believe that the ship is leaving, we may be able to isolate him in his room. If he suspects something is wrong, we will lose him. He'll probably try to find protection by threatening the passengers."

"So what are you suggesting?"

"I seem to recall, when I took a cruise ship a few years ago, that the ship must schedule an evacuation drill where the passengers have to get a life preserver from their room and go to the lifeboat to which they have been assigned."

Garrett nodded slowly, trying to get the drift of where Lucas was heading. "We've scheduled one for eleven tonight," he confirmed. "Taking a life preserver is no longer required, but yes, we still have to conduct the drill."

"So suppose the ship ties off from the dock and very slowly makes its way towards the bay..."

"Making this Cofresi guy think that everything is okay," Negron prompted.

"Right. And then you announce the drill," Lucas continued. "But you would have to require that everyone gets a life preserver jacket from his room. Cofresi would have to go to his room to get one."

"If he's not there already," Negron warned.

"And that's where we isolate him!" Garrett finished Lucas' thought. "Brilliant!"

"We have to move fast. If he's in his room now and leaves before we can stop him, we'll lose a precious opportunity," Lucas cautioned the others.

"My men must be on board by now. I can have them seal the corridor from both ends," Negron said. In order to be as inconspicuous as possible, Negron had arranged to have six of his men board the ship at different intervals and wait quietly by the boarding ramp. That way, if San Miguel was watching the dock from any of the ship's decks, the police presence would be less noticeable. Of course, there was always the risk that he would be by the boarding ramp and see the policemen gather there.

"That will only work if Cofresi is in his cabin," Garrett pointed out. "If he's out and is heading for his cabin, he will notice the policemen when he gets to the corridor and know for sure that something is wrong. I have a better idea." The large, walrus-mustached security officer spoke to his male assistant. "Paul. Gather our people. Have them linger casually at the two ends of corridor 14B. If we see through our cameras our suspect coming into corridor 14B, or if we see him coming out of his room, we'll warn them so that they seal the corridor and stop him before he leaves."

"He may be armed," Lucas advised.

"Right. Tell our people to get their guns, but to conceal them. They may have to use them," Garrett said to Paul. As his assistant left, he addressed Millie. "No suspects yet?"

"No sir," she answered, not taking her eyes from the screen.

"You know," Garrett said to Lucas and Negron, "if this guy's as smart as you say he is, he may have noticed you or your men getting on board."

"Is there some way that I can get my men to the fourteenth floor without their being seen…You know, so that when the moment comes, they can help?" Negron asked.

"Yes, we can take them up through the crew's stairs and have them wait out of sight until the right moment. I'll have someone from the crew take them there shortly."

"But if he's already seen the police cars stationed on the dock, he may already be suspicious," Lucas warned.

"What if…" Negron said with a hint of hesitation, as if deliberating out loud. "What if we do something to make him think that the police is here to arrest somebody else? Like...if we openly 'arrest' somebody from your crew, and take him out of the ship in plain view of everyone? If he's watching, he'll think that we were not there for him. That we were there for another reason."

Lucas stared at the gangly police sergeant with newfound admiration. "It's worth a try."

"I'll get on all of this right away!" Garrett said, sounding almost cheerful now that they had a plan of action.

It had been Negron, glancing at the ship's various monitors with Lucas, who had first spotted San Miguel ten minutes later.

"Is that him?" he had asked Lucas, pulling him by the arm and pointing at the screen.

Lucas focused on the tall, bearded man appearing on the black and white monitor, and his heart skipped a beat. "That's him!" he confirmed excitedly, looking at the label under the screen. It read: "Corridor 8A". *Of course! He was looking for Daniel! How could he have been so stupid not to think about that?* "He knows something is wrong," he said to Garrett, who had rushed to his side. "He's looking for his companion."

The three men watched with horrified fascination as the terrorist knocked on the door of his associate's cabin, waited for a few seconds, and then began to stroll away.

"Damn!" Negron cried. "We need to get our men there right now!"

"They won't get there in time," Garrett responded weakly. "He'll be out in the public areas before we get to him."

Lucas watched him intently as he walked past the overhead camera, trying to detect anything in his body language that showed his real state of mind. However, the image on the screen was not very clear, and San Miguel's casual walk did not betray any nervousness on his part. On the contrary, he gave the impression of being mildly amused.

"We have to reassure him," he said to the others. "Are your men ready?" he asked Garrett and Negron. Garrett had arranged for one of his security men to be handcuffed and escorted off the ship by one of Negron's policemen. Both men were waiting in one of the crew's stairways to exit into the ship's lobby and walk out to a police car on the pier.

"Paul, tell them to walk out," Garrett said to his assistant, who had returned to the room a few minutes before. Paul hurried away. "That should reassure Mr. Cofresi."

"Tell them to take their time and walk out as slowly as they can. I want San Miguel to see them," Lucas added.

"Cofresi is moving out to the promenade on deck 8," Millie said, following him from one screen to another.

"On the side of the bay or the side of the pier?" Lucas asked.

"The bay."

"He won't see the arrest from there." Lucas turned to Garrett. "Tell the captain to cast off as soon as the policeman walks off with the arrested man. Tell him to do it as quickly as possible."

Garrett picked up the phone and called the bridge. Two minutes later, the *Orion* sounded its mighty horn.

"He's...He's moving again," Millie announced. The men crowded around her. It was dark outside and the camera did not cover the entire promenade, but they could see him moving towards the back of the ship.

"He's taken the bait!" Garrett said triumphantly. "He's going to the port side of the deck, to see what's happening."

San Miguel walked out of the camera's range, and Garrett and Millie automatically shifted their gaze to another monitor, showing a portion of the other side of the deck. Tensely, they waited for the tall terrorist to reappear.

"Maybe we should send my men to arrest him now," Negron suggested as he strained his eyes to find his quarry.

"Too many people near him," Lucas responded. Several of the passengers were leaning on the railing, watching the activity on the dock below. Suddenly, the floor vibrated slightly under his feet.

"We're moving," Garrett confirmed.

"There he is!" Negron said excitedly. San Miguel was walking in the direction of camera, looking with a fascinated expression towards the pier.

"Do you think he saw your men?" Garrett asked.

"From the way he's fixed his eyes on the dock, I'd say it's a fair possibility," Negron answered proudly.

"We'll find out soon enough," said Lucas, trying to hide his excitement.

"And now for the announcement," Garrett said, walking to the microphone connected to the Orion's PA system, and after cautioning the others with his finger to be quiet, pressing the switch to address the passengers. "Your attention, please! Maritime regulations require that the ship conduct its emergency drill as it departs port. All passengers should go to their designated evacuation areas with your life vests within the next fifteen minutes. Please refer to the instructions located behind the doors of your cabins to determine where you are required to go."

There was absolute silence as Garrett flicked off the microphone. Then Millie said, "He's moving!"

"Advise the others. As soon as he enters his room, we seal the corridor," Garrett said.

"My men will do that," Negron stated in a voice that admitted no contradiction.

"Very well," Garrett responded. "Paul, let us know the moment he enters the room," he raised his hand, showing to Paul the walkie-talkie he had just picked up from a cabinet next to the PA system. "The rest of you, come with me. We don't have much time."

By the time they got to the two policemen waiting in the stairway closest to the northern end of the corridor, Paul had called to warn that "Cofresi" had wandered into his room.

"Let's go!" Negron said, allowing his men to enter the corridor first. "Now you stay with me," he warned Lucas. "My men will take care of this."

The two policemen approaching from the opposite side of the hallway reached cabin 1413 first and stood by the door, their guns drawn and ready. The other two arrived a moment later, followed by Negron and Lucas.

Nobody spoke. They did not knock on the door, preferring for the terrorist to come out unaware that they were there. A minute passed, and then two, but still, nothing stirred. The waiting men concentrated their eyes on the elongated door handle under the electronic key opener, knowing it would move when Cofresi exited his cabin. The corridor remained deathly still, sealed by Garrett's men.

Lucas had begun to wonder if somehow San Miguel had gotten wind of their presence, when he heard the metallic rattle of a safety lock. The men around him tensed, and huddled closer to the entrance of the cabin.

Suddenly, the door of the room opposite to them flew open, and a very fat man, wearing one of the ship's orange life jackets like a large bib over his extended stomach, stepped out, urging loudly to someone behind him to hurry up. Then, as he turned his head and discovered the armed lawmen, his jaw dropped open and he shouted, "Oh my God, Edna, don't come out! There's a bunch of cops out here!"

To which a shrill female voice answered from inside, "What?!"

At that moment, the door of cabin 1413 swung partially open, but immediately slammed shut, just before the closest of the policemen rammed it with his shoulder. A sharp "click" followed, as the room's occupant slid the door's deadbolt.

Pandemonium ensued.

Lucas yelled to the gaping fat man to get back into his room and shut himself in it, while two of the policemen started to ram the locked door with their bodies. Then a shot rang out from inside the cabin, and one of the men dropped to the floor, grabbing his left shoulder.

"He's got a gun! Take cover!" Negron cried, grabbing the wounded man under the armpits and dragging him away from the cabin's entrance. Then he moved closer to the door's frame, and shouted, "This is the police! You cannot escape! Drop your gun and come out with your hands over your head!"

The man inside responded with another shot that went through the cabin's door and hit the door of the fat man's room.

Lucas looked for Garrett, and found him standing with two men a few yards away. He ran to him, and asked him urgently, "Do these rooms have balconies?"

Garrett nodded. "Yes, of course."

"Can Cofresi move from one balcony to another?"

Garrett nodded again. "Easily! The balconies are divided by thin walls. He can move from one balcony to another by holding on to the railings. You think he may try it?"

"What would you do in his place?" Lucas replied, as if stating the obvious. "Can you gain access to any of the nearby rooms?"

Garrett answered by pulling out of his pocket a white plastic card, unmarked except for a small black arrow on one of its ends. "I have a master key," he said. He looked at the two men standing next to him, and moved to the door of a cabin two doors removed from the one around which the policemen were standing. "We're going in," he told them, and inserted the key, arrow first, into the electronic lock. He turned the handle and the door opened.

"Negron!" Lucas hissed, prompting the policeman to look at him. Without saying anything else, Lucas pointed towards the open door, through which Garrett had already entered.

Negron nodded, and shouted again, "Cofresi! Don't make things hard on you! Give up now peacefully."

There was no answer of any kind.

Lucas walked into the newly opened cabin. It was a surprisingly large room, a lot more spacious than the interior cabin where he had traveled a few years before. A narrow corridor with an entrance to a small bathroom led to a queen-sized bed decorated in a flowery blue and green print. The bed lay opposite to a long cabinet topped by a large mirror, and on the wall next to it were two folded bunk beds, the upper one holding extra pillows and blankets. There were two open bags on the bed, presumably belonging to the occupants of that cabin.

Garrett had already walked to the balcony, and was leaning out of it to stare in the direction of Cofresi's cabin, his two companions waiting fretfully behind him.

"Do you see him?" Lucas asked as he got near him. He saw that the ship was inching its way through the middle of San Juan Bay.

"No," Garrett replied, still looking. He climbed over the railing, and began to move towards the next balcony. "Roger, follow me," he said to one of his companions. Eddie, tell the police what we're doing, and warn the others to keep the corridors sealed." Garrett crossed the dividing wall, and then climbed into the next balcony. Roger went next, and then Lucas.

They had entered another cabin similar to the one they had just been in, except that the order of the furniture was inverted. The occupants in this one had not yet opened their luggage, which was nowhere to be seen.

"Cofresi!" they heard Negron shout from the corridor. "This is your last chance! We're coming in!"

"Roger, search this room, in case Cofresi has already moved here from his cabin," he instructed his assistant.

"Yes, sir."

Garrett walked to the end of the balcony and drew his gun from his holster. The next room was cabin 1413. Holding his breath, he took a quick peek around the balcony's dividing wall and then withdrew his head. He turned to Lucas.

"The doors between the cabin and the balcony are open, but I can't see anyone inside the cabin," he said. "I'm going in."

"Wait. I'll warn the police that you're going in. I don't want you to get shot by mistake," Lucas replied. He walked to the exit of the room they had just entered and carefully opened the door, whispering something to the men standing in the corridor. Then he looked back to Garrett and nodded.

"Nobody is in this room," Roger reported as he finished his search.

The chief security officer took another look around the dividing wall, clambered over the balcony's railing, and disappeared from view.

CHAPTER X

Lucas waited next to Negron and three other police officers by the door of cabin 1413. The men did not exchange a word, hoping to hear what was happening inside. They could hear nothing, however.

Then a voice with a thick Scottish accent shouted, "I'm opening the door!" and the cabin's elongated handle rotated diagonally, allowing the door to swing open inwardly. One of the men stood in front of the entrance, and pointed his shotgun into the room.

"It's me," Garrett said in an irritated tone. "Our bird has flown the coop."

"Did you see where he went?" Lucas asked.

The security officer shook his head. "He must have stepped into another of the cabins through the balcony, on the opposite side from where I came from."

"Or jumped," Negron suggested, with a hint of hopeful malice in his voice.

"From fourteen decks up? It's possible, if he's desperate enough, but he'd probably break his neck..." said Garrett.

Lucas looked around the room. The main closet door was half open, several of San Miguel's pants and jackets already hanging inside, some of his shoes spilling out from the bottom. One of two suitcases lay open on the bed, half empty of its contents, while the second had been placed under the bed, as well as a handbag. A discarded, orange lifejacket lay on the floor. He crouched to have a better view of the space below the mattress, knowing that the cruise ships normally used it for storage area. However, except for the luggage and a large, plastic bag, there was nothing.

He stood up with a little bit of effort, his body feeling progressively sore from the beating it had received from Czecka. "Could he have climbed down to another deck, rather than going sideways to another cabin?" he asked.

Garrett considered the question briefly and cursed loudly. "We have balconies all the way down to the seventh deck! Of course he could have climbed down to another level, how could I have been so dense! It would be risky, but an able bodied person could swing down to the balcony below, and so on to any other deck with balconies, no problem."

"So if he moves fast enough, he could have gone to another deck, gotten into one of its cabins, and exited from there to...nearly anywhere in the rest of the ship," Lucas concluded, hoping that Garrett would for some unknown reason correct him.

"Yes," the Scotsman said. "Regrettably, that is so."

"The man is like a cockroach!" Negron exclaimed bitterly. "He disappears into any crack he can find!"

"It may be that he's still hiding in one of the cabins on this deck or those below," Garrett said, not really convinced of what he was saying. "I'll get my men and some of the crew to seal all of the corridors on this side of the ship down to deck 7." He walked out of the room without waiting for a response.

Negron followed him. "I think he's going to need the help of my men," he called back to Lucas before disappearing.

"Negron, wait!" Lucas shouted, forcing the young sergeant to poke his head through the room's open exit. "Tell Garrett to ask the captain to return to port. That way we can evacuate the passengers and get more police on board."

Negron nodded once and left without uttering a word.

Slowly, immersed in his own thoughts, Lucas walked to the balcony. He leaned over the railing and gazed down at the dark waters below. Garrett was right; it *was* too long of a drop. So where had San Miguel gone?

The *Orion* had stopped in the middle of the bay. From where he stood, Lucas could see the bright lights of Cataño, the small town that lay on the other side of the bay. Further south, the looming dark masses of the Cordillera Central—Puerto Rico's central mountain range—were dotted with the glow of thousands of homes and communities, shining brighter than the stars above.

It would be a terrible thing if someone like San Miguel, the driving force behind all of the awful events that had afflicted the island during the past few months, escaped. The man scared him. Lucas had met many dangerous men in his life, more than he'd care to count. Some had been crazy fanatics, like the armed thugs he had fought in Mogadishu, others had been human monsters of unspeakable power, like Czecka, and a few had been consummate professionals, like Daniel. But of all of the men he had met, he feared San Miguel the most.

Something about the man repelled him; made his skin crawl. Lucas knew that most people would not agree with his personal impression of San Miguel. He was—at least at a first glance—a personable, friendly, good-looking man who exuded confidence and who handled himself with wit and charm. But most people had not witnessed his darker side. A violent, dangerous criminal hid behind his calm façade. He was a psychopath, a man incapable of any kind of remorse, driven by uncompromising ideals—whatever they were—and endowed with the intelligence and the will to attain them.

They *had* to catch him. Otherwise, he suspected—he *knew*—that San Miguel would not leave them alone.

Lucas leaned further over the railing and saw the edge of the balcony on Deck 13. It would not be hard at all to swing into it from the floor above it. San Miguel could certainly do it.

He heard the cabin door close behind him, and turned to hear the latest news. Instinctively, he drew back in shock, as he saw the man that they were searching standing by the room's entrance. He was pointing a gun at him.

"So it *is* you!" San Miguel said to Lucas with genuine surprise.

San Miguel examined his adversary with open incredulity. *It could not be. By all accounts, Alfaro should have been dead.* Even after he had heard his voice from his hiding place, San Miguel could not believe it, had told himself that it had been a mistake, that he had confused Alfaro's voice with that of one of the policemen or the security personnel that were searching for him. *But there he was, standing in front of him, somewhat bruised but alive nevertheless.*

His only consolation was that Alfaro seemed as shocked to see him as he was to see Alfaro. His Puerto Rican adversary had probably imagined him far away, hiding in another cabin or roaming another part of the ship. The astonishment and anger on his face almost made up for all of the problems that he had caused. *Almost. But not quite.*

"Hands on your head," San Miguel said to him, motioning upwards with the barrel of his gun. Alfaro complied, wincing as he did so, apparently from the pain caused by some of his injuries.

"You almost caught me," San Miguel said, as he examined his adversary for weapons. "If it hadn't been for the screams in the corridor, and those klutzy policemen, I would have been in deep trouble."

"You speak as if you can still escape," Alfaro countered defiantly.

San Miguel could tell that his prisoner was upset with himself, for allowing himself to be captured so easily. He let him speak, knowing it was to his advantage to listen to anything that his adversary said.

"There's no way you can get out of here. If you jump, you'll probably die or be so hurt by the fall that you'll drown. If not, the police will find you in the water. And the ship is crawling with security personnel. Your best bet is to give up while you have the chance."

San Miguel regarded him with the same patient disdain of an elder listening to an ignorant youngster. "And yet, I just managed to fool the entire security force that was following me, including you, by the way, whom I consider to be the smarter of the lot."

That quieted Alfaro. His eyes surreptitiously wandered around the cabin, trying to determine where San Miguel had hidden, and making San Miguel chuckle inwardly.

It had been so easy to fool all of his pursuers.

From a very young age, when he smuggled arms into the West Bank under the Israeli soldiers' noses, he had learned never to underestimate the power of suggestion. Time and time again, the concept had proven crucial in his crusade as a freedom fighter: when properly motivated, people usually see what they expect to see, and act accordingly.

When he had boarded the *Orion*, he had spent the first twenty minutes examining his cabin, considering the possible alternatives of escape in the case of an emergency. The balcony had seemed like the most obvious route of escape. But for that same reason, he had discarded it immediately. The police were not stupid. If they didn't find him in his cabin, they would figure out that he had left it via the only other accessible exit in the room, and search the nearby rooms. Besides, climbing out of the balcony would be too risky, he would be exposed to anyone looking out, and be an easy target for a police sniper.

But if the balcony was not going to be his route of escape, it would certainly play an important role in it. From one of his two suitcases, San Miguel had unpacked a transparent, plastic bag. He had pulled out of it a black blanket, and extended it to its full length. Then, he had walked to the cabin's main closet and squeezed into it, noting with satisfaction that his head fit easily behind the metal rack on the top, with space to spare. Raising the black blanket up to his chin, he had looked into the mirror opposite to the closet. Additionally shrouded by the natural darkness of the small enclosure, his covered body had been invisible to the casual eye.

After that, he had carefully hung from the closet rack several of his suits and pants, and placed his shoes on the bottom. Then, he had entered the closet again, and slid his body behind the hung clothes, to see if he would still fit. It had been very tight, and he had been forced to move diagonally some of the hangers holding the clothes, but in the end the added props had enhanced his invisibility.

He had known that if his pursuers conducted a thorough search, they *would* find him. But if he misled them, made them think that he had left the room, the ruse would work. And if not, he still had his gun. Besides, he had thought at the time, he was being ultra cautious. He would never have to hide in the closet.

How wrong he had been! Less than an hour later, the police had almost caught him as he was about to exit his cabin. Only the fortuitous intervention of the passengers on the other side of the corridor, and his lightning fast reflexes, had allowed him to shut and lock the door before the police could rush in.

His instincts had taken over instantly. As he took off his lifejacket, he had fired one shot through the door, to keep the policemen at bay, and then rushed to the balcony, sliding its doors open, making certain not to pull back entirely the curtains behind the doors, so that they would be pulled outwards by the outside breeze, pointing to his route of escape. There had been more shouting outside, and to gain additional time he had fired a second shot. Grabbing the black blanket, he had rushed into the closet and hidden behind the hanging clothes, covering himself with the blanket. He had left the closet door half open on purpose, so that no one would make it a point to search it.

Then, gun in hand, he had waited.

It had taken several minutes, much longer than he had expected, for the authorities to enter the room. He had listened to his pursuers' conversation with breathless fascination, becoming more confident, as every second passed, that his ruse had worked. One voice had sounded very familiar, startling him when he realized that it was that of Alfaro. He had tried to convince himself that it was not him. Nevertheless, something in the back of his mind told him otherwise. *If not, how had they found him? And if so, did it mean that his whole operation was compromised?*

San Miguel had waited a few minutes after all the talk had ceased, and then eased himself slowly out of the closet. There was only one man left in the cabin. His face was turned away from him, but he had recognized the straggler immediately. Closing the cabin's door and locking it, he had aimed his gun at Alfaro.

"And Daniel and Czecka?" he asked, already knowing the answer.

"Dead," Alfaro confirmed.

"A shame," San Miguel said flatly, trying to show no emotion. However, he felt devastated. It was not so much the personal loss of his two companions, who would be very difficult to replace, as the confirmation that all of his plans were at risk. "And the authorities have been alerted about the bomb," he asserted, more as a statement than as a question. When Lucas delayed in responding, San Miguel concluded, "Of course they have, silly of me to ask! Otherwise, the police would not be here with you. No matter. There isn't much that they can do." He pointed at the room's queen-sized bed with the muzzle of his gun. "Sit, please," he said almost gently.

His prisoner complied, sitting at the foot of the bed.

"Sit at the corner closest to the balcony, please," San Miguel ordered him. "I want a good nine or ten feet of distance between us."

Slowly, Lucas slid to the farthest corner of the bed.

San Miguel leaned against the vanity opposite to the bed. For a long time he said nothing, considering what to do next. "I should kill you," he said finally, with some hesitation. "I, mean, I should have killed you a long time ago, and made certain that you did not endanger my plans. Who would have said that you'd escape Czecka? But now..." he sighed, resigned with what he had to do. "Now you're the person who is going to help me to get out of here. So I will keep you alive, despite what my gut instincts urge me to do. Still, I won't insult your intelligence by telling you that I will not kill you afterwards, unless I can find a safe way of escaping while leaving you behind, and that seems a very unlikely proposition at this moment. And since you're probably going to die anyway, you could choose to scream for help now, and get shot in the process. Or you could keep quiet, and hope for a chance to escape." He aimed his gun at Lucas' head. "So what will it be?"

San Miguel stopped talking and waited to see how his prisoner reacted. He felt equal parts of relief and disappointment when Alfaro did not respond; relief because Alfaro did not attempt to raise the alarm; disappointment because in the back of his mind, he wanted to kill him.

"Nothing?" San Miguel asked in a mild tone. "So I figured you out correctly. You'd rather stay alive for a few more minutes—a few more minutes could make all the difference, couldn't they? They could provide you with the opportunity to escape—better than sealing your fate right now and here. After all, that's what happened with Czecka and Daniel, didn't it? The opportunity to escape came up unexpectedly, and you took it. Tell me, I am curious. Tell me how you managed to kill my two best men."

"Drop your gun, and I will demonstrate it to you personally," Alfaro answered insolently.

He's trying to provoke me, San Miguel thought. *Trying to make me lose my patience so I don't concentrate on what I'm doing. It's the only way he will escape.*

"You don't like me very much, do you?" he said, with a tinge of resignation in voice. "Why?"

Alfaro stared at him with incredulity. "You're joking, right?"

"I am dead serious. Is it because I tried to kill you? Because I may kill you still? Believe me, I don't enjoy killing any more than you do. Maybe less. I am a peaceful man in principle, doing only what is strictly required of me, in order to free the world from its oppressive rulers. Sometimes, I'm forced to make tough choices for the benefit of the greater whole. But I hold no personal grudge against you. Do you know that it was my men who helped you escape from La Fortaleza, when the Macheteros attacked you?" San Miguel did not add at that the time, he had needed to keep the Governor alive in order to make certain that the G20 Conference was not changed to another venue, but that detail was of no consequence to their present discussion. "If I could," he offered, trying to sound as sincere as he could, "I would spare you."

"I guess that I should be grateful to you, then," his captive replied, trying to sound sarcastic. But San Miguel could tell that something else was running in his mind. Even as he spoke, the Puerto Rican's eyes darted surreptitiously from one place in the room to another, apparently searching for a means of escape.

"You're perhaps wondering why I'm wasting my time talking to you, instead of trying to leave this ship," San Miguel suggested.

"Honestly? No," Alfaro responded.

"Good. That spares me the effort of giving you any details," San Miguel said with the same patient voice of a parent addressing an unruly, wayward child. He walked to the cabin's door and unlocked it. Then he returned to the vanity, opposite to the bed. He enjoyed the look of puzzlement on Alfaro's face.

"And now we wait for someone to come in," he said. "So that we understand each other, if you attempt to do anything when our next visitor walks into this room, I will kill him before you can reach me. If you so much as move when our next visitor comes in, I *will* kill him. And then you. Is that understood?"

Alfaro nodded.

San Miguel looked at his watch. It was nearly 11:30 PM. For a while now, the ship had been shifting. He could feel it under his feet and in his body. It was returning to port.

Soon, one of Alfaro's police companions would miss him and start looking for him. Hopefully, that person would return to cabin 1413. San Miguel would capture him, force him to take off his uniform, and then kill him. Wearing the dead policeman's uniform, he would walk out of the *Orion* with Alfaro. If, as he hoped, the authorities in San Juan failed to disarm the bomb, there would still be enough time to escape to the main island and avoid the impact of the explosion. If he did not have enough time to escape...Well, he had always been prepared to die for his cause. It would be a quick, painless death, well worth his ultimate sacrifice.

Of course, if more than one policeman came looking for Alfaro, his plan would have to change. He could still handle two. Three plus Alfaro would be too much. If that was the case, he would point his gun at Alfaro's head, and try to force his way out of the ship. And then, he would improvise.

It was a desperate ploy, he knew, a radical departure from the meticulous, long considered planning that always preceded his actions. But he had no other alternative. As his bungling adversary had told him, jumping from the balcony would probably kill or injure him, and if he survived, the police boats circling the cruise ship would probably capture him. His best option was the one he was pursuing.

And in the end, either way, win or lose, he would kill Alfaro.

But he was anticipating himself. There was no reason to think that a whole detachment of policemen would come to the cabin to look for Alfaro. He just had to keep his thoughts clear and his nerves under control. And be patient.

God, he was certain, *would not let him down.*

CHAPTER XI

Lucas bided his time, trying to maintain a neutral façade while desperately searching for a way to disarm San Miguel before someone entered the room. But the terrorist did not shift his eyes away from him even for one second, leaning against the cabin's mirrored desk, some ten feet away.

At that moment, if he made a dash towards San Miguel, he would get shot. Whether the shot would stop him was another matter. It all depended on where he was injured, and how far his momentum would carry him. The odds that San Miguel would hit him on the head or the heart—thus killing him instantly—were low. He would be a moving target, and if he timed it right, he could probably disarm the terrorist before he fired a second shot.

His chances would be enhanced if at the time of the attack, San Miguel was distracted with something else. Lucas had quietly examined the objects that surrounded him, seeing how he could use them.

Next to him, and partially behind him he saw San Miguel's blue open suitcase, the type used nowadays by nearly everyone. It was partially empty, still containing some neatly folded shirts, a plastic, transparent bag holding a pair of brown shoes, some socks and undergarments, and a rolled brown belt.

He could make a quick grab for the suitcase, grasping it by the handle and swinging it at the terrorist. But he discarded that option almost immediately, knowing that—if anything—the effort would hinder his forward progress, and achieve very little else.

For the same reason, he discounted the idea of reaching for the belt and snapping it at San Miguel's face. It was too uncertain, and the likelihood of success slim at best.

It being a cruise ship, most of the objects in the cabin were fastened to the walls and the floor. There were no table lamps, clocks or unattached decorations; no cameras, fanny packs, souvenirs, or water bottles lying on the bed that he could grab and toss, as he sped toward the gunman, to divert his aim.

There was, however, on the vanity, a small metal tray holding an aluminum ice bucket, a pair of ice tongues, and two glasses. It was located midway between him and San Miguel, under the television set. He was certain that he could reach it as he moved towards San Miguel before the latter could fire, and flip its contents towards him. At best, it would create a distraction that could affect San Miguel's aim. At worst, it would make noise, increasing the chances that someone outside would hear it, and alert the shipboard authorities.

It was a very risky plan, with too many possible outcomes, but it was his only alternative. So the tray it was.

Lucas glanced casually at San Miguel and gauged once again the distance between them. Ten feet. Not less than nine feet at best.

San Miguel was still looking directly at him, his gun cocked and his finger on the trigger. He seemed amused, as if reading his mind and mocking him for his ridiculous plans. If Lucas moved now he would surely get shot. But he could not risk waiting much longer. Every passing second moved the two men closer to the moment when somebody else would enter the room, and then matters would get a lot more complicated.

But why not wait, a voice in the back of his mind insisted. San Miguel had threatened to shoot the incomer if Lucas so much as moved, but Lucas' chances of success would increase significantly if San Miguel had to struggle with two people at the same time. *Besides,* the tiny voice in the back of his head insisted, *he had already risked his life several times that night. Wasn't it fair that somebody else took the risk, even if unwittingly?*

Lucas was still debating with himself what to do when the cabin's door suddenly flew open and Negron breathlessly stepped in, talking loudly and excitedly even before he had spotted his friend, arching one of his eyebrows quizzically as he discovered Lucas sitting on the edge of the bed. "We still haven't found him, but he can't go very far. We are going floor to floor," he was saying.

Because of the angle of the open door, San Miguel stayed partially concealed behind it. Then Negron's expression began to change to one of shock and surprise, as he noticed the third person in the room.

But the policeman's abrupt entrance had also caught San Miguel completely unaware. The terrorist had apparently expected a knock, or even the jiggling sound of the door handle before anyone barged into the cabin. However, the young policeman had burst into the room, moving like a whirlwind towards Lucas, and San Miguel's attention had wavered for the fraction of a second, as the terrorist hesitated whether to aim his gun at the newcomer or at Lucas.

"Don't move," he began to say to the policeman, but by that time, Lucas had lunged forward, grabbing the edge of the metal tray with his right hand and flinging its contents towards the gunman.

As if in slow motion, Lucas saw the ice spill from the spinning bucket, the two glasses whirling, flashing and hitting the sprayed ice cubes, the tray wobbling like a failing frisbee. He saw Negron wince, trying to avoid the unexpected explosion of metal and ice, and San Miguel begin to turn his gun towards him. But he knew that he was a step ahead of the terrorist, and that he would reach him before he could steady his aim.

And then he tripped.

He tripped on his own feet, clumsily, awkwardly, inexplicably. And he felt himself fall towards San Miguel, forward, but not far enough to reach him. As he tumbled, he heard the gun discharge with a loud, sharp bang—akin to the detonation of a large firecracker. He saw a short, yellow flame spurt out from the tip of the gun's barrel, and felt something scrape, as if with fire, the top of his head.

He fell hard on the carpeted floor, just a few inches from the feet of the terrorist, so close that he could see with great detail the blue rubber flip flops that the man was wearing. He heard the tray crash against the vanity, and felt freezing bits of ice and water splash on his back and his neck. He knew that he only had a moment before San Miguel fired again, and blindly swung his arm upwards, trying to strike his enemy and deflect his aim.

But then, San Miguel's two feet flew upwards and backwards, barely missing Lucas' face, and his body and that of Negron crashed heavily into the mirror behind them, cracking it. The two struggling men fell in a tangle of arms and legs on top of Lucas and rolled away, grunting and flailing at each other with their fists. Lucas began to stand up, and then saw Negron righting himself and sitting over the prostrate figure of San Miguel. The rookie policeman held on with his left hand to the armed terrorist's wrist, and began to pummel his face repeatedly with his right fist.

"This...is...for...my...brother...policemen..." he shouted, punctuating each word with a punch. "You...son...of a...bitch!"

Lucas got up and snatched the gun from San Miguel's limp right hand and tucked it inside his belt. Then he grabbed Negron from behind by both of his arms and pulled him away from the terrorist's listless body.

San Miguel seemed dazed, bleeding from his mouth and nose. He made a feeble attempt to raise his head, but desisted immediately, letting his head fall back on the carpet and closing his eyes. Lucas helped Negron back to his feet, and panting, the police sergeant drew his gun. Holding it at arms' length, he pointed it at his fallen foe's forehead. Lucas gently pulled him away, so that San Miguel would not have the chance to reach for the gun and take it away.

"How did you find him?" Negron asked Lucas, still breathing heavily, taking sporadic glances at his friend.

"He found me," Lucas confessed. "He was hiding here all of the time."

Negron shook his head in wonderment. "I'm telling you, the man is like a cockroach." He continued to take short looks at Lucas, regarding him with increasing amazement. "You have a crease right through the middle of the top of your head, you know that?" he said.

Lucas instinctively raised his hand to his hair, and felt a burning pain on his scalp. With his index finger, he carefully traced a thin crease of raw skin that ran in a straight line about an inch away from his hairline to the top of his skull, nearly parting his hair in two halves. When he brought down his hand, the tips of his fingers were damp with blood.

Negron allowed himself a smile. "Neat hairdo," he said with a half chuckle.

"Yeah," Lucas nodded. "My wife is going to love this."

San Miguel stirred, and this time managed to lean on one of his elbows. Negron regarded him sternly, the smile on his face disappearing.

"Kneel," he said. "Hands over your head."

Ever so slowly, San Miguel did as he was ordered.

"Lucas," Negron said. "Would you mind searching him for hidden weapons?"

"I carry no other weapons," San Miguel interjected.

Lucas walked behind the kneeling terrorist and patted him with his hands from behind. Then he searched his legs, his ankles, and his crotch.

"He's clean," Lucas informed Negron.

The policeman nodded. Waiving his gun, he said to his prisoner, "Sit on the bed."

Lucas watched quietly as San Miguel shakily picked himself off from the floor and sat on the bed, just where Lucas had sat just a few moments before. He tried to read the terrorist's face, to somehow gauge what he was thinking.

All of San Miguel's carefully laid out plans were unraveling, and the prospect of spending the rest of his life inside a maximum-security prison was quickly turning into a reality. His life, as he had known it, was over. And yet, he seemed unnaturally calm, his face revealing no fear or defeat, only silent defiance.

"You have the right to remain silent," Negron began to recite. "Anything that you say or do may be used in a court of law against you."

"You did well to wait and not scream for help when I gave you the option to do it," San Miguel said almost in a whisper, ignoring the policeman and addressing Lucas directly. He wiped the blood trickling from his chin with the back of his hand. His shirt was stained with drops of blood and partially ripped, his hair disheveled.

Negron stopped momentarily, and then continued. "You have the right to speak to an attorney and to have an attorney present during questioning."

"You must feel really proud about what you did today," San Miguel muttered with just a hint of soured sarcasm. "After all, you have single-handedly deprived the oppressed people of the world from their greatest opportunity to free themselves from their corrupt overlords. I congratulate you."

Lucas turned his gaze away from the sitting man, telling himself it was not worth to engage him. Ever since his soldier days, he had trained himself to avoid entering into bitter arguments that usually led to angry, pointless exchanges. He knew that, no matter what he said, he would never convince a fanatic like San Miguel about the error of his ways.

But this time, his anger overwhelmed him. He had been kidnapped, beaten, and nearly executed, all because of the man sitting before him, and there he was, actually chiding him for spoiling his plans, and accusing him of helping to oppress humanity. *The gall of the man!* Before he could stop himself, he turned back to San Miguel and engaged him.

"You know, at some terrible times in my life, my path has crossed with some very warped, dangerous people. There have been a few that I would avoid stepping on, because they were so slimy. But you, my friend, you really take the cake. You are the worst kind of evil that I have had the misfortune to come across," Lucas said, knowing he should have stayed quiet, prompting a thin, satisfied smile from Negron. "You are so full of shit! You speak about...about *humanity,* as if you were God's emissary on earth, while in reality, all you're doing is feeding your massive ego. Humanity! What the hell do you know about humanity, trying to wipe out an entire city with a nuclear device!"

"God wiped out Sodom and Gomorrah to save the just from the evil," San Miguel retorted with serene indignation. "He wiped out almost the entire earth's population with a universal flood. He understands what I'm doing, even if unbelievers like you don't!"

For a moment, Lucas was tempted to dismiss the terrorist's arguments with an obscene gesture. But then, he was struck by the import of San Miguel's words. "Wow!" he said with horrified wonderment, shaking his head, "I get it now. How could I have been so obtuse?"

From the corner of the bed where he sat, San Miguel regarded him with silent, intense hostility.

"The flood, Sodom and Gomorrah, and now Old San Juan. You really think you're God's emissary, his prophet, don't you? Destroying the sinners to save the just. So what's next? The parting of the Red Sea? No, no, that's too small for you. The Apocalypse, maybe?" Lucas stared at him with contempt. "You're just a proud and arrogant man who wants to play God. Be careful, because your pride will lead you straight to hell."

He immediately sensed that he had struck a nerve, feeling perversely pleased about it. San Miguel clenched his jaw momentarily, as if he had been struck physically, and then snorted with derision.

"I seem to have underestimated you," he said with a composed, blood-stained smile. "I thought you were just a failed jeweler and an army has been, but I see you're smart enough, or you think you're smart enough, to try to plant doubts about the righteousness and sincerity of my motives. Get away from me, devil. God can see my soul. He will judge me justly."

Negron had listened with utter fascination to the exchange between the other two men, and now he renewed his recital of the warnings. "If you cannot afford an attorney," he stated, "one will be provided for you at the government's expense. Do you understand?"

"But since you have tried to get into my head," San Miguel continued as if Negron was not there, "let me reciprocate, and consider this: by interfering with my plans, you have sealed your own doom, and that of your family. Neither you, your son, your daughter or your wife will survive me." His bloody smile widened, as he saw that it was now he who had struck a nerve. Lucas stiffened, his hands grasping the edge of the table against which he was leaning. "You thought we didn't know about you and your family? Surely you are not that naïve. I've been following your heroic accounts in the press ever since I left San Juan on January. Your family is as good as dead. So are you. Once I give the word, my people will avenge me."

Negron laughed nervously. "I doubt very much that your people will ever hear from you again, after Uncle Sam places you in the dark hole where you're going to be buried for the rest of your life." The rookie policeman looked at Lucas for reaffirmation of what he had just said, but by the bleak expression on his friend's face, knew that his world had just shattered.

San Miguel stared mockingly at Lucas. *He was right,* Lucas knew. *No matter where his foe was imprisoned, he would always be able to get the word out to his followers, to his associates. He would remain connected to the outside world by his attorneys, his doctors, even by some of his guards. Sooner or later, San Miguel's friends would come for him and his family.*

"You may have a few months' reprieve before something happens. A year, at most," San Miguel taunted. "Then, who knows? A bomb in the jewelry store? One of your children disappears from school? Your wife burns inside your car? One of your sisters raped and killed? Who knows?"

"You miserable son of a bitch!" Lucas shouted, jumping on him and punching him several times on the face before Negron could pull him back. "And you call yourself a man of God?" Lucas continued to shout as San Miguel, rubbing his jaw and grinning, slowly sat back up. "If you want your revenge, come after me! Don't wage your war on women and children, you piece of shit!"

San Miguel paused, as he tried to recover his breath and composure. "What happens to you and your family..." he muttered with venomous anger, "is nothing in the scale of things, compared to the harm you have caused by your clumsy interference."

Lucas felt overwhelmed by despair. His thoughts raced desperately, already thinking about how he would protect his family. *Move away? Seek protection from the government? But what about his mother, his sisters, the whole family couldn't move away. He would ask the authorities to keep San Miguel completely isolated.* And yet, he knew that it was not possible.

Maybe if they let him go, he would forego his threats. It was worth a try. Surely Negron would sympathize with his position. San Miguel would be grateful. But he knew, even as he considered such a desperate alternative, that it was not possible. San Miguel was a monster. If Lucas let him go, he would come back, to cause further and greater damage. Lucas had foiled his plot to set off a nuclear device in San Juan. He had made him a lifelong enemy. For all of his religious pieties, San Miguel would never forgive him or his family.

Sitting on the bed, San Miguel watched Lucas' internal struggle with evident pleasure. He could read him like a book, and was enjoying every second of his agony.

Lucas felt Negron's hand fall on his shoulder. "Don't worry," the policeman said to him in his high-pitched voice. "This guy will never be able to reach anybody," he assured his friend with grim determination.

You don't understand, Lucas wanted to scream. *There's no way of isolating him completely from the rest of the world.* But something in Negron's eyes stopped him from saying anything.

San Miguel must have seen it too, because his smug expression suddenly changed to one of extreme concern, and he raised his right arm towards the policeman, motioning him to stop.

Negron's first bullet went through San Miguel's hand and struck him on the right shoulder. It would have been enough by itself to throw him back into the bed, but two other bullets that struck him on the chest speeded his backward fall.

The wounded terrorist gasped as blood began to spurt from his wounds, and stared with disbelief as the policeman walked next to him and aimed his gun at his forehead.

"Now let's see how you send word to your friends, you son of a bitch," Negron said, and fired.

CHAPTER XII

"It's been a tough night for you, I know," Governor Pietrantoni said to Lucas. It was three o'clock in the morning, and the Governor showed the faint stubble of an unshaved beard. But he seemed fully awake, and fresh, and full of enthusiasm. He was wearing a tan *guayabera* and blue jeans—the most informal attire in which Lucas had ever seen him, even when they were escaping through the tunnels under La Fortaleza—and he looked more like tall, thin college student than the chief executive of the island's government. "I apologize for not taking you straight to your home. But the President is waiting to see you. I promise that it will not take long, and then I'll return you to your family. I've already taken the liberty of calling Jennie, to tell her that I am in desperate need of your services, and let her know that you'll be coming home late."

Lucas nodded. "Thank you, Mr. Governor," he said with a certain degree of uncertainty.

"Roberto," Pietrantoni reminded him.

"Roberto," Lucas repeated. "It's nice of you to keep me company."

Pietrantoni chuckled. "Oh, believe me, I wouldn't miss this for anything in the world."

Both men were standing in a small waiting room, part of the Presidential Suite of the Grand Laguna Hotel. They were flanked by two Secret Service men, each as tall as Pietrantoni, who unlike the two Puerto Ricans, were fully dressed in jackets and ties. The two agents kept their eyes fixed on the set of double doors in front of the waiting group, showing no reaction—if they spoke Spanish—to the conversation of the Governor and his companion.

Waiting in the sanitized, air-conditioned atmosphere of the luxury suite, Lucas for the first time became conscious of his woefully bedraggled and shoddy appearance. After the *Orion* had docked, he had been interviewed by several FBI men who had boarded the ship.

Negron and him had had less than a couple of minutes to concoct a story about the death of the terrorist, wiping Lucas' fingerprints from San Miguel's gun and placing it in the terrorist's left hand—his right having been shot by one of Negron's bullets.

They had swiftly agreed to stick as much as possible to the actual facts, in order not to get tripped during the ensuing interrogation. They would say that Lucas had been surprised by San Miguel—as it had actually happened—and been forced to wait at gunpoint in the room. When Negron had entered the cabin, Lucas had attacked San Miguel and a struggle had ensued.

However—this is where the story changed—San Miguel had managed to push Lucas away and attempted to shoot him with his gun. Negron had pulled out his pistol and shot him on the shoulder and chest. As Negron got near him to take away his gun, San Miguel had tried to raise it, and been shot one last time on the face. They had pressed the terrorist's fingers and palm several times on his small gun, to get his prints on it.

Additional members of the police, as well as the ship's Security Officer Garrett, had burst into the room a few moments later. Negron had asked them to search for hidden explosives, knowing that it would help to muddle the scene of the crime. By the time the *Orion* had been secured back to the dock, the cabin had been turned upside down.

The FBI men quickly made everyone leave the cabin. Lucas was brought down to the security office, where he was interrogated by two agents. He felt very uneasy about how flimsy Negron's and his cover story was, and suspected that any decent interrogator could tear holes into it, but the agents seemed more interested in finding out what San Miguel had told Lucas, than on how San Miguel—Cofresi to the agents—had met his end.

Lucas was asked if San Miguel had referred to any other explosives or associates. Lucas replied that the terrorist seemed to be very upset because the bomb plot had failed, which tended to confirm that the device they had found was the only one planted. He told them that San Miguel seemed to be acting as part of a terrorist organization—making a vague reference about some his "associates" and how they would avenge his interference with the bomb plot—but that he had not identified any specific group or organization. He also confirmed that he had not seen any other persons—except for those killed in Fort San Cristobal—interact with him.

His interrogation had lasted more than two hours. Lucas believed that he would still be there, had not what he took to be another FBI agent entered the room and whispered something to the main interrogator. The FBI man had looked peeved, but nodded and said to Lucas, "You are wanted by the President." As he left, the agent had said, "I need you to come to our offices in Hato Rey tomorrow after lunch, to discuss further details." Lucas had nodded.

As he left the *Orion,* he had crossed paths with Negron. He had shaken his hand and whispered, "Stick to our story."

Negron had winked and smiled. "Say hi to your sister for me," he had whispered back.

A black, Lincoln limousine was waiting for him at the edge of the gangway. From the solid way it sat on its suspension, Lucas could tell that it was armored. A man in a *guayabera* opened the door, and the Governor's head popped out.

"Lucas!" he said in a happy, light tone. "Hop in!"

The Governor had quickly summarized to him what he had learned from Maldonado so far: that Lucas had followed a group of terrorists to the San Cristobal Fort *("How did you ever find them?"* he had asked in a humorous but truly curious voice.); that he had discovered that they were planting a nuclear bomb *("Thank God you chose to have hot dogs in that place, eh?"* he had said, glancing sideways at his companion with an expression that suggested that he did not really believe it had been a co-incidence.); that one of the terrorists had slipped into the *Orion ("That was a relief of sorts. It told me that he wasn't planning to set off the bomb until he was far away. It gave us some time to dispose of the thing.");* and that the terrorist had been killed by the police *("I know that the intelligence service of the United States will consider this a big loss of opportunity, you know, to gather more intelligence on these people, but personally, I say good riddance!").*

He had then asked Lucas for details, listening—as was his habit—without any interruptions, asking a few pointed questions at the end of his story. Lucas had stuck to the version he had given to the FBI, but something in the Governor's eyes had told him that Pietrantoni had caught some gaps in his testimony.

In the meantime, the limousine had made its way to the Grand Laguna Hotel, driving into one of the downward sloping ramps of the convention facilities and stopping next to an elevator in an underground parking lot.

Lucas had noticed three men, all wearing suits and ties, spread along the perimeter, and nobody else. The man with the *guayabera* had stepped out of the limousine and opened the door, allowing Lucas and the Governor to get off. The two men had stepped into an elevator that stopped in a small lobby, and from there been led through what seemed to be a service corridor to another elevator in the hotel's main tower. Like the parking lot, the surrounding area had been cleared of all onlookers except for the security people. There, another elevator had whisked them straight up to the three-story Presidential Suite, in the penthouse area.

The set of double doors in the waiting area opened from the inside, and a man that looked more like a butler than a security agent waved Pietrantoni and Lucas inside.

They walked into a lobby-sized room with polished floors. It contained several plush, large sofas and seats covered in very light-colored, almost white fabric, which were arranged in two distinct seating areas. A high ceiling was illuminated by several modern, abstract light fixtures, and at least a dozen large paintings, showing semi-modernistic images of tropical trees and forests—El Yunque rain forest, Lucas assumed—provided the otherwise pale surroundings with deep green, blue, and yellow hues. Enormous, at least twelve-foot glass panels rose at a sloping angle from the floor to the top of the room all along the extended, outer edge of the living room. They must have provided a spectacular view of the Atlantic and El Condado, Lucas imagined, but at the moment they were covered by heavy curtains.

The man that looked like a butler stepped outside of the room, and closed the set of double doors behind him.

President Powell stood by a small bar opposite to the doors, holding a glass with ice and what seemed to be scotch. Otherwise, the vast room was empty. As his visitors entered, he walked towards them, extending a friendly hand.

"Governor Pietrantoni," he said, greeting the Governor first. "I cannot congratulate you enough on the way your people have handled this whole thing. They are top professionals, every one of them. Please give my personal thanks to Superintendent Maldonado."

"Thank you, Mr. President. I'll make it a point of telling him," Pietrantoni answered. "I know he'll be pleased."

Lucas watched in silence, sizing up the man he had seen in so many photographs and news broadcasts before. Michelle had been right. He had a certain resemblance with George Clooney. His face might have been a little thinner, more oval, his hair grayer—pointedly more so than when he was running for office. He also seemed taller, maybe six two, six three. But he definitely handled himself with the actor's same easy charm and appeal. And his eyes—a clear, almost transparent blue—seemed to take in a lot more than his face revealed.

"Mr. Alfaro," he said, turning to Lucas. "I'm so glad to finally meet you." He shook the Puerto Rican's hand warmly, while holding on to the glass of scotch with his other hand. For a few seconds, he seemed to stare intently at his face—Lucas wondered how beat up he looked—and then he nodded several times. "Yes, I can see the resemblance to your sister. It's in the eyes, mostly."

Lucas found himself at a loss of words. "We take after my mother, I guess," he said clumsily.

"Do you? She must be an extraordinary woman. Here." The President handed the glass to him. It was brimming with ice and scotch. "I think you've earned it. You do drink, I hope."

"Yes I do. Thank you." Lucas took the proffered tumbler and sipped from it. It tasted like Heaven.

"Would you like some, Pietrantoni?" the President asked the Governor.

"Don't mind if I do," Pietrantoni answered with a tired grin.

"Yeah." The President paused, as if running several thoughts simultaneously through his head. "Yeah. I think we all deserve it. Please sit while I get them ready."

Lucas sat on the nearest sofa, sinking on its soft cushions, while Pietrantoni rested on a broad armchair. The President followed a few moments later, handing a glass to the Governor, and settling on another sofa, opposite to both of his visitors. He smiled and raised his glass.

"Cheers!" he said to his two companions, who raised their glasses in acknowledgement. The President sighed. "Premier Kozlov has been driving me crazy, calling me every fifteen minutes to find out what is the situation with the bomb, asking me if I'm going to the bomb shelter in the Ceiba base. He's refused to leave until I do. I guess it's some *macho* thing, trying not to look any less scared than me."

"So he's still in San Juan?" Pietrantoni asked.

President Powell sipped from his glass and nodded. "As far as I know. He and his entire Russian contingent. They all try to out-brazen each other, it seems. The Chinese left. They're the smartest of the lot. So did the Italians, the British, and most others. The French stayed for a while, and then left a few of their delegation, mostly security people." The President looked at his watch. "Anyway, Puerto Rico is officially out of the danger zone," he added, directing a look at the Governor. "I got word that the Globemaster transport dropped a parachute with the bomb over the Atlantic fifteen minutes ago. About two hundred miles beyond the Puerto Rico Trench, we don't want to be accused of causing the tectonic plates to shift."

Lucas understood the reference to the Puerto Rico Trench immediately, as did the Governor. It was the second deepest point in the world and the deepest in the Atlantic, dropping more than five miles into the sea. It had been created by the clash of two tectonic plates, the Caribbean Plate and the North American Plate. It lay just seventy-five miles north of Puerto Rico, and could produce massive earthquakes that could expose the northern coast of Puerto Rico to deadly tsunamis. It was therefore wise not to disturb the geologically sensitive area by dropping a nuclear device into it.

"If the bomb explodes when it's due to explode—if it goes off at all—it should have reached the bottom of the sea, at about three thousand feet. We're making sure no ships are even remotely nearby."

Lucas' thoughts flashed back to San Miguel, and he shuddered involuntarily, wondering if the terrorist would come back from his grave to avenge him. He caught the President looking at him again.

"I'm sorry if I stare too much," Powell said apologetically, as if reading his thoughts. "It's a flaw in my character, I guess. You know, one of the first things I did when I got to the Grand Laguna Hotel was to go down to the convention meeting facilities, and try to re-create in my mind the fighting that took place here. The hotel did a good job hiding the signs of the fighting, although I did find a couple of bullet holes high on one of the walls. And I thought, how did a handful of civilian hostages and a couple of policemen manage to hold off the onslaught of the heavily armed terrorists." He raised his eyebrows as he imagined the fighting that had taken place. "Those people fought against all odds. They should have lost; the Macheteros should have routed them, should have shredded them to bits. And yet, somehow, they held on."

The President exchanged glances with Pietrantoni. "You did the same thing in La Fortaleza," the Governor said to Powell. "You made me show you how we had escaped."

Powell assented. "Although the Secret Service did not allow me to go into the tunnels below La Fortaleza," he said in a regretful voice. "The point is, that in my position, I tend to meet many brave men who have laid their lives on the line for their country. And I keep wondering *what is it exactly* that makes then tick. I'm still trying to find a common trait in their characters, some common denominator that binds them all together. It must be there, somewhere, but it's not outwardly noticeable." He paused, and took another swallow. "It would be great if we could just tell at a glance..." he said cryptically. "What do you think, Lucas?"

Lucas thought about the President's query. His body was going into an adrenaline shutdown mode. The scotch was taking effect a lot faster than he expected. And Powell seemed like the kind of person who seemed to appreciate honest answers. "I don't think that there's a uniformly brave person in the world," he replied. "There's just circumstances where people decide to act, people who at other moments in their lives would run away and hide, or get paralyzed with fear."

"So the same person may be a hero one day and a coward the next?" the President asked.

"Something like that."

Powell considered the thought. "Maybe for most of us, yes, but I'm convinced that that's not the case for a few special people. Like you."

Lucas shrugged, and chuckled. "Luck helps a lot," he suggested.

"Yes," the President replied. "Except I know a lot of lucky people who are craven cowards, through and through."

"You never know," Lucas countered, amazed by his own boldness to contradict the President of the United States, "some of those people may surprise you one day."

The President laughed and slapped his knee. "By God, I would love for that to happen!" He leaned forward, and was about to say something when there was a soft knock on the double doors. The man who looked like a butler briefly opened them and said in a soft voice, "They're all back, Mr. President."

Powell acknowledged the news with a nod. "Thank you, Lewis. Let them all know that tomorrow's schedule remains unchanged."

"Yes, sir." Lewis gently pulled shut the two doors.

Powell looked at his watch. "It's past three thirty. I have a six o'clock breakfast in El Convento, but I'm willing to spend a little more time listening to your story, if you don't mind," he said to Lucas. He stood up and retrieved the tumblers from his two visitors, replenishing the glasses with new ice and scotch.

They spoke until nearly a quarter to five in the morning, both government executives keeping, for the most part, a fascinated silence. Encouraged by the alcohol, Lucas added more details to the story he had told to Pietrantoni, but he still kept enough presence of mind not to dwell on San Miguel's death.

The President took several minutes to speak after Lucas had finished, so much so that Lucas thought he had fallen asleep. Then his clear blue eyes turned thoughtfully towards the Puerto Rican.

"Your story is fascinating, and your actions nothing short of incredible. At the risk of sounding like a worn out cliché, our countries—both the United States and Puerto Rico—are very fortunate to have had you at their hour of need, and owe you our eternal gratitude. Your deeds, young man, are the stuff from which legends are made of. But having said all that," Powell paused and grimaced, "unfortunately, nobody must ever fully learn what you saved us from."

Powell stood up, and his two visitors rose after him.

"If it ever became known to the public that terrorists got hold of a nuclear bomb, and that they nearly set it off under an American city, it will create widespread panic and a national paranoia against any person looking remotely foreign." He looked directly at Lucas. "You can take credit for discovering the terrorists and following them into Fort San Cristobal, but there must be no mention of the nuclear bomb. We will tell the press that the terrorists were trying to plant a conventional bomb in El Convento, to kill as many of the visiting leaders as they could. There will be many loose ends, rumors that something bigger really happened, I'm certain, and we will have to talk to some of the other people involved in tonight's operation who may know or suspect about the nuclear device…"

"Like my sister," Lucas prompted.

"Like your sister," Powell repeated. "I'm hoping that we can appeal to their better instincts, and convince them, for the good of national security, not to talk about what they saw. But you will be key in this. Can I count on your discretion?"

Lucas saw Pietrantoni stare at him tensely, and nodded. "Yes, Mr. President. In fact," he blurted out, almost as an afterthought, swallowing hard, "I would prefer not to be mentioned at all."

"Oh?" Powell said with newfound curiosity. "I know you're a modest guy, but—"

"It has nothing to do with modesty, sir," Lucas countered impulsively, interrupting Powell. "It's just that…before he died, San Miguel…Cofresi… threatened to send word out to his associates that it was me who interfered with his plans. He promised to turn my life into a nightmare. He swore that his colleagues would avenge him by kidnapping and killing my family."

"He told you this before…Sergeant Negron shot him…" Powell asserted, stretching his words in mid-sentence as he considered the new information. Then his eyes lit up with hidden amusement, a faint smile appearing on his lips. "I see…" He nodded curtly. "That son of a bitch. He deserved to die," he said in a reflective tone, shooting a quick glance at Lucas. "Very well. It will be as you ask, then. Even though it pains me to keep your story secret."

Lucas sighed with relief. "Thank you, sir."

The President gripped Lucas' hand and shook it forcefully. "It has been a pleasure to meet you. May I at least host a private dinner for you and your family at the White House, a few weeks from now, maybe, when all of this is over? I'll include your mother and your sisters."

Lucas smiled. "It would be an honor, Mr. President."

"On the contrary, your visit will honor my house," the President responded.

The two Puerto Ricans left a few minutes later. Powell watched them go, finishing his drink.

Lewis walked in and waited for instructions. The President stretched his arms tiredly.

"Lewis!" he said happily. "What time is it?"

"Ten past five," the man who looked like a butler replied.

"No use going back to sleep now," the President concluded.

"No, sir."

"I'm hungry. Get me some breakfast."

"The usual, sir?"

"As long as it has eggs and bacon in it."

"Yes, sir."

"And Lewis..."

"Sir?"

"Get me the FBI Director on line."

"Now, sir?"

"Yes, now."

"Yes, sir," Lewis replied, and disappeared from the room.

Powell rubbed his eyes. He was tired, and did not look forward to the multiple conferences and appointments of the day. But he felt good.

Lucas was a good man and a fearsome warrior, but not, Powell feared, a very good liar. His version about the way that San Miguel had died had been devoid of details. It had sounded hollow and unconvincing, and raised a lot more questions than it answered. His explanation of why he wanted to remain anonymous had answered a lot of the questions. Either Lucas or Negron had executed San Miguel after he had threatened Lucas' family. Powell suspected it had been Negron, not because he knew the police sergeant, but because Lucas was an extremely honorable man who would not kill an unarmed person, regardless of the circumstances. He *was,* despite of what he had said to the contrary, the real thing. *A true hero.*

Any interrogator worth his salt would pick up quickly on the flimsy version of San Miguel's last moments and pounce on it relentlessly.

Powell would not let that happen.

His call to the FBI Director lasted less than ten minutes. Afterwards, the agents in charge of the investigation on board the *Orion* were instructed to focus their attention on finding the terrorist links, and to forget about how the terrorist died.

The next morning Lucas received a welcome surprise from the FBI. He did not have to come to their offices after lunch. If they needed him again, they would let him know.

At 12:07 in the afternoon of that same day, the United States Geological Survey reported an earthquake measuring 4.1 in the Richter Scale, originating in the bottom of the Atlantic Ocean, some three hundred miles northeast of the island of Puerto Rico. The seismic event was duly noted and recorded, and quickly buried in a slew of additional data from around the world. Other seismic monitoring agencies confirmed the event, giving it little importance.

Several technicians noted that the pattern of the quake showed a uniform wave expansion from the epicenter, and that the abruptness and duration of the occurrence were more consistent with those of a nuclear explosion than with those of a typical earthquake. However, the reports were later corrected to reflect that the seismic activity was indeed generated by an earthquake in the Atlantic's floor. The residents of San Juan never heard about the earthquake, their attention fixed on the aborted terrorist attack that had apparently been directed at the world leaders meeting in their city.

The G20 Conference concluded two days later on an optimistic agreement of mutual cooperation, an agreement that was quickly shelved and forgotten, subordinated to more pressing and important national issues.

ACKNOWLEDGEMENTS

It was nearly thirty years ago that—while waiting in a traffic jam to get into San Juan, my brother-in-law Paul Pinet expressed out loud, "You know, it would make a great novel if somebody blew up the bridges that connect San Juan to the rest of Puerto Rico." We discussed the premise briefly, and then I shelved it in some remote corner of my mind.

It revived four years ago, after I had retired from the practice of law. As I began writing the book, I was surprised by my wife Cira's enthusiastic reaction. She actually liked the story, and asked for more. It took me longer to finish than I expected, partly because I traveled a lot, but mostly because the book's characters took a life of their own that forced me, literally, to follow their exploits and report them as best I could. It was great fun, and I enjoyed it more than I ever imagined. However, it would have taken me much longer had Cira not—gently but firmly—urged me to keep going.

When I finished, our friend Anita Morales selflessly volunteered to proofread the manuscript, as did subsequently my brother-in-law Paul, my son-in-law Jason McAllister—you will recognize both Paul's and Jason's names when you read in the story about the exploits of the Navy SEALs—and—for a second time—Cira. Their observations, suggestions, and corrections were invaluable to me. Paul also acted as my technical advisor on the use of weapons, a subject about which I know very little.

As I stumbled along with the preparation of the manuscript and its proofreading, I was genuinely surprised and moved by the number of people who went out of their way to help me with the book, including Ines Barros and Noemi Martinez, who got me in contact with published authors who were willing to give me advice on how to get published; Guillermo Baralt and Luis Gonzalez Argueso, two of those authors, who did not hesitate to spend some of their precious time with a total stranger and share their experiences in the book-publishing business; to Arlene Richards—wife of IP Book's Editor-in-Chief—who gave me some very valuable pointers regarding some of the story's characters; to Dennis Martinez, Pinky Cuevas, Maricel Renta, my mom Nelly, my son-in-law Rafael Lopez de Azua, and my son Mario Alberto, all of whom provided me with information, newspaper clippings, and internet references on such subjects as the tunnels of Old San Juan, and how to get published.

A particular note of gratitude goes to our dear friends Art Lynch and Lourdes Rigual, who put me in contact with IP Books and set the whole thing in motion, and who have been, throughout the process, the book's unofficial patrons and most enthusiastic cheerleaders. I don't know what I would have done without their help.

Special thanks to—again—my son-in-law Rafa and my son Mario, who developed the idea for the cover, and to Jaime Valles—my nephew—who took their idea, tweaked it further, and did the incredible art that graces the front of the book. Also, a big thanks to my two former law partners and personal friends, Irwin Flashman, who provided the photograph for the back cover, and Carla Garcia, who has acted as my unofficial legal advisor.

Finally, I want to thank the entire crew at IP Books, who patiently guided me through the book publishing process, about which I know nothing, and most particularly Tamar Schwartz, IP's indefatigable Administrator, who put the whole thing together, and its Editor-in-Chief Arnie Richards, whose boundless enthusiasm, constant calls, and emails, convinced me that the book would actually be published.

To all of them, and to many that I'm sure I've overlooked (but never forgotten), thanks. You have made my dream come true.